IT

The terror, which would not end for another twenty-eight years – if it ever did end – began, so far as I know or can tell, with a boat made from a sheet of newspaper floating down a gutter swollen with rain.

PRAISE FOR STEPHEN KING

'King's imagination is vast. He knows how to engage the deepest sympathies of his readers . . . one of the great storytellers of our time' – *Guardian*

'Stephen King is one of America's finest writers' – *Scotsman*

'Stephen King is one of those natural storytellers . . . getting hooked is easy' – Frances Fyfield, *Daily Express*

'Mr. King's gift of storytelling is unrivaled. His ferocious imagination is unlimited' – George Pelecanos

ABOUT THE AUTHOR

STEPHEN KING. Photograph © Shane Leonard

There is a reason why Stephen King is one of the bestselling writers in the world, *ever*. Described by John Connolly as 'utterly compelling' and by the *Daily Express* as an author who can 'create an entire world and make the reader live in it', Stephen King writes stories which draw you in and are *impossible to put down*.

Stephen King is the author of more than fifty books, all of them worldwide bestsellers, including *Firestarter*, *The Stand* and recently *The Outsider*. Many of King's books have been turned into celebrated films and television series including *Misery*, *Pet Sematary* and *The Shawshank Redemption*. *IT* is the basis of two major films: *IT* (2017) and *IT CHAPTER TWO*, due for release in 2019.

King was the recipient of both America's prestigious 2014 National Medal of Arts and the 2003 National Book Foundation Medal for distinguished contribution to American Letters. In 2007 he also won the Grand Master Award from the Mystery Writers of America. He lives with his wife Tabitha King in Maine.

HAVE YOU READ . . . ?

CELL

Anyone using their mobile cellphones at the time of The Pulse is infected. Artist Clayton Riddell embarks on a terrifying journey though the 'crazies' to reach his son before the young boy switches on his phone. And time is running out . . .

DESPERATION

A group of unsuspecting travellers is stopped in the middle of the Nevada desert and lured to the abandoned mining town of Desperation where a terrifying transformation is taking place.

DREAMCATCHER

Four lifelong friends gather in the woods of western Maine for their annual hunting trip. Before long, the friends are plunged into a terrifying confrontation. Their only hope of survival is locked in their shared past . . .

INSOMNIA

Since his wife died, Ralph Roberts has been having trouble sleeping and he's started to observe some strange things going on in Derry, Maine. Before long, Ralph becomes enmeshed in events of cosmic significance.

NEEDFUL THINGS

There is a new shop in Castle Rock called Needful Things, run by a stranger. There's something here for everyone. At a price you can just about afford. But there is another price. There always is when your heart's most secret desire is for sale . . .

THE STAND

One man escapes from a biological weapons facility after an accident, carrying with him a rapidly mutating flu that wipes out most of the world's population. In the aftermath, survivors must choose between two factions and prepare for a confrontation between the forces of good and evil.

UNDER THE DOME

The small town of Chester's Mill, Maine, is sealed off from the rest of the world by an invisible force field. War veteran Dale Barbara must discover the source of the Dome before it's too late . . .

By Stephen King and published by
Hodder & Stoughton

NOVELS:

Carrie
'Salem's Lot
The Shining
The Stand
The Dead Zone
Firestarter
Cujo
Cycle of the Werewolf
Christine
Pet Sematary
IT
The Eyes of the Dragon
Misery
The Tommyknockers
The Dark Half
Needful Things
Gerald's Game
Dolores Claiborne
Insomnia
Rose Madder
Desperation
Bag of Bones
The Girl Who Loved Tom Gordon
Dreamcatcher
From a Buick 8
Cell
Lisey's Story
Duma Key
Under the Dome
11.22.63
Doctor Sleep
Mr Mercedes
Revival
Finders Keepers
End of Watch
Sleeping Beauties (co-written with Owen King)
The Outsider
Elevation

The Dark Tower I: The Gunslinger
The Dark Tower II:
The Drawing of the Three
The Dark Tower III: The Waste Lands
The Dark Tower IV: Wizard and Glass
The Dark Tower V: Wolves of the Calla
The Dark Tower VI: Song of Susannah
The Dark Tower VII: The Dark Tower
The Wind through the Keyhole:
A Dark Tower Novel

As Richard Bachman

Thinner
The Running Man
The Bachman Books
The Regulators
Blaze

STORY COLLECTIONS:

Night Shift
Different Seasons
Skeleton Crew
Nightmares and Dreamscapes
Hearts in Atlantis
Everything's Eventual
Just after Sunset
Stephen King Goes to the Movies
Full Dark, No Stars
The Bazaar of Bad Dreams

NON-FICTION:

Danse Macabre
On Writing (A Memoir of the Craft)

STEPHEN KING
IT

HODDER

Copyright © 1986 by Stephen King

First published in Great Britain in 1986 by Hodder and Stoughton
A division of Hodder Headline

This paperback edition published in 2019

The right of Stephen King to be identified as the Author of
the Work has been asserted by him in accordance with the
Copyright, Design and Patents Act 1988.

A Hodder paperback

21

British Library Cataloguing in Publication Data

King Stephen 1947—
It
I. Title
813'.54[F] PS3661.1483

ISBN 978 1 473 66694 8

Typeset in Bembo by Palimpsest Book Production Limited,
Falkirk, Stirlingshire
Printed and bound in Great Britain by
Clays Ltd, Elcograf S.p.A.

Hodder & Stoughton Ltd
Carmelite House
50 Victoria Embankment
London EC4Y 0DZ

This book is gratefully dedicated to my children. My mother and my wife taught me how to be a man. My children taught me how to be free.

NAOMI RACHEL KING, at fourteen;
JOSEPH HILLSTROM KING, at twelve;
OWEN PHILIP KING, at seven.

Kids, fiction is the truth inside the lie, and the truth of this fiction is simple enough: *the magic exists*.

S.K.

'This old town been home long as I remember
This town gonna be here long after I'm gone.
East side west side take a close look 'round her
You been down but you're still in my bones.'

– The Michael Stanley Band

'Old friend, what are you looking for?
After those many years abroad you come
With images you tended
Under foreign skies
Far away from your own land.'

– George Seferis

'Out of the blue and into the black.'

– Neil Young

CONTENTS

PART 1

THE SHADOW BEFORE

'They begin!
The perfections are sharpened
The flower spreads its colored petals
         wide in the sun
But the tongue of the bee
         misses them
They sink back into the loam
         crying out
– you may call it a cry
that creeps over them, a shiver
as they wilt and disappear . . .'
                    – William Carlos Williams,
                                      Paterson

'Born down in a dead man's town'
                    – Bruce Springsteen

CHAPTER ONE
AFTER THE FLOOD (1957)

1

The terror, which would not end for another twenty-eight years – if it ever did end – began, so far as I know or can tell, with a boat made from a sheet of newspaper floating down a gutter swollen with rain.

The boat bobbed, listed, righted itself again, dived bravely through treacherous whirlpools, and continued on its way down Witcham Street toward the traffic light which marked the intersection of Witcham and Jackson. The three vertical lenses on all sides of the traffic light were dark this afternoon in the fall of 1957, and the houses were all dark, too. There had been steady rain for a week now, and two days ago the winds had come as well. Most sections of Derry had lost their power then, and it was not back on yet.

A small boy in a yellow slicker and red galoshes ran cheerfully along beside the newspaper boat. The rain had not stopped, but it was finally slackening. It tapped on the yellow hood of the boy's slicker, sounding to his ears like rain on a shed roof . . . a comfortable, almost cozy sound. The boy in the yellow slicker was George Denbrough. He was six. His brother, William, known to most of the kids at Derry Elementary School (and even to the teachers, who would never have used the nickname to his face) as Stuttering Bill, was at home, hacking out the last of a nasty case of influenza. In that autumn of 1957, eight months before the real horrors began and twenty-eight years before the final showdown, Stuttering Bill was ten years old.

Bill had made the boat beside which George now ran. He had made it sitting up in bed, his back propped against a pile of pillows, while their mother played *Für Elise* on the piano in the parlor and rain swept restlessly against his bedroom window.

About three-quarters of the way down the block as one headed toward the intersection and the dead traffic light, Witcham Street was blocked to motor traffic by smudgepots and four orange sawhorses. Stencilled across each of the horses was DERRY DEPT. OF PUBLIC WORKS.

3

Beyond them, the rain had spilled out of gutters clogged with branches and rocks and big sticky piles of autumn leaves. The water had first pried fingerholds in the paving and then snatched whole greedy handfuls – all of this by the third day of the rains. By noon of the fourth day, big chunks of the street's surface were boating through the intersection of Jackson and Witcham like miniature white-water rafts. By that time, many people in Derry had begun to make nervous jokes about arks. The Public Works Department had managed to keep Jackson Street open, but Witcham was impassable from the sawhorses all the way to the center of town.

But, everyone agreed, the worst was over. The Kenduskeag Stream had crested just below its banks in the Barrens and bare inches below the concrete sides of the Canal which channelled it tightly as it passed through downtown. Right now a gang of men – Zack Denbrough, George's and Bill's father, among them – were removing the sandbags they had thrown up the day before with such panicky haste. Yesterday overflow and expensive flood damage had seemed almost inevitable. God knew it had happened before – the flooding in 1931 had been a disaster which had cost millions of dollars and almost two dozen lives. That was a long time ago, but there were still enough people around who remembered it to scare the rest. One of the flood victims had been found twenty-five miles east, in Bucksport. The fish had eaten this unfortunate gentleman's eyes, three of his fingers, his penis, and most of his left foot. Clutched in what remained of his hands had been a Ford steering wheel.

Now, though, the river was receding, and when the new Bangor Hydro dam went in upstream, the river would cease to be a threat. Or so said Zack Denbrough, who worked for Bangor Hydroelectric. As for the rest – well, future floods could take care of themselves. The thing was to get through this one, to get the power back on, and then to forget it. In Derry such forgetting of tragedy and disaster was almost an art, as Bill Denbrough would come to discover in the course of time.

George paused just beyond the sawhorses at the edge of a deep ravine that had been cut through the tar surface of Witcham Street. This ravine ran on an almost exact diagonal. It ended on the far side of the street, roughly forty feet farther down the hill from where he now stood, on the right. He laughed aloud – the sound of solitary, childish glee a bright runner in that gray afternoon – as a vagary of the flowing water took his paper boat into a scale-model rapids which had been formed by the break in the tar. The urgent water had cut a channel which ran along the diagonal, and so his boat travelled from one side of Witcham Street to the other, the current carrying it so fast that George had to sprint to keep up with it. Water sprayed out from beneath his galoshes in muddy sheets. Their buckles made a jolly jingling as George Denbrough ran toward his strange death. And the feeling which filled him at that moment was clear and simple love for his brother Bill . . . love and a touch of regret that Bill couldn't be here to see this and be a part of it. Of course he would try to describe it to Bill when he got home, but he knew he wouldn't be able to make Bill *see* it, the way Bill would have been able to make *him* see it if their positions had been reversed. Bill was good at reading and writing, but even at *his* age George was wise enough to know that wasn't the only reason why Bill got all A's on his report cards, or why his teachers liked his compositions so well. *Telling* was only part of it. Bill was good at *seeing*.

The boat nearly whistled along the diagonal channel, just a page torn from the Classified section of the Derry *News*, but now George imagined it as a PT boat in a war movie, like the ones he sometimes saw down at the Derry Theater with Bill at Saturday matinees. A war picture with John Wayne fighting the Japs. The prow of the newspaper boat threw sprays of water to either side as it rushed along, and then it reached the gutter on the left side of Witcham Street. A fresh streamlet rushed over the break in the tar at this point, creating a fairly large whirlpool, and it seemed to him that the boat must be swamped and capsize. It leaned alarmingly, and then George cheered as it righted itself, turned, and went racing on down toward the intersection. George sprinted to catch up. Over his head, a grim gust of October wind rattled the trees, now almost completely unburdened of their freight of colored leaves by the storm, which had been this year a reaper of the most ruthless sort.

2

Sitting up in bed, his cheeks still flushed with heat (but his fever, like the Kenduskeag, finally receding), Bill had finished the boat – but when George reached for it, Bill held it out of reach. 'N-Now get me the p-p-paraffin.'

'What's that? Where is it?'

'It's on the cellar shuh-shuh-shelf as you go d-downstairs,' Bill said. 'In a box that says Guh-Guh-hulf . . . *Gulf*. Bring that to me, and a knife, and a b-bowl. And a puh-pack of muh-muh-matches.'

George had gone obediently to get these things. He could hear his mother playing the piano, not *Für Elise* now but something else he didn't like so well – something that sounded dry and fussy; he could hear rain flicking steadily against the kitchen windows. These were comfortable sounds, but the thought of the cellar was not a bit comfortable. He did not like the cellar, and he did not like going down the cellar stairs, because he always imagined there was something down there in the dark. That was silly, of course, his father said so and his mother said so and, even more important, *Bill* said so, but still –

He did not even like opening the door to flick on the light because he always had the idea – this was so exquisitely stupid he didn't dare tell anyone – that while he was feeling for the light switch, some horrible clawed paw would settle lightly over his wrist . . . and then jerk him down into the darkness that smelled of dirt and wet and dim rotted vegetables.

Stupid! There were no things with claws, all hairy and full of killing spite. Every now and then someone went crazy and killed a lot of people – sometimes Chet Huntley told about such things on the evening news – and of course there were Commies, but there was no weirdo monster living down in their cellar. Still, this idea lingered. In those interminable moments while he was groping for the switch with his right hand (his left arm curled around the doorjamb in a deathgrip), that cellar smell seemed to intensify until it filled the world. Smells of dirt and wet and long-gone vegetables would merge into one unmistakable ineluctable smell, the smell of the monster, the apotheosis of all monsters. It was the smell of something for which he had no name: the smell of It, crouched and lurking and ready to spring. A creature which would eat anything but which was especially hungry for boymeat.

He had opened the door that morning and had groped interminably for the switch, holding the jamb in his usual deathgrip, his eyes squinched shut, the tip of his tongue poked from the corner of his mouth like an agonized rootlet searching for water in a place of drought. Funny? Sure! You betcha! *Lookit you, Georgie! Georgie's scared of the dark! What a baby!* The sound of the piano came from what his father called the living room and what his mother called the parlor. It sounded like music from another world, far away, the way talk and laughter on a summer-crowded beach must sound to an exhausted swimmer who struggles with the undertow.

His fingers found the switch! Ah!

They snapped it –

– and nothing. No light.

Oh, cripes! The power!

George snatched his arm back as if from a basket filled with snakes. He stepped back from the open cellar door, his heart hurrying in his chest. The power was out, of course – he had forgotten the power was out. Jeezly-crow! What now? Go back and tell Bill he couldn't get the box of paraffin because the power was out and he was afraid that something might get him as he stood on the cellar stairs, something that wasn't a Commie or a mass murderer but a creature much worse than either? That it would simply slither part of its rotted self up between the stair risers and grab his ankle? That would go over big, wouldn't it? Others might laugh at such a fancy, but Bill wouldn't laugh. Bill would be mad. Bill would say, 'Grow up, Georgie . . . do you want this boat or not?'

As if this thought were his cue, Bill called from his bedroom: 'Did you d-d-die out there, Juh-Georgie?'

'No, I'm gettin it, Bill,' George called back at once. He rubbed at his arms, trying to make the guilty gooseflesh disappear and be smooth skin again. 'I just stopped to get a drink of water.'

'Well, h-hurry up!'

So he walked down the four steps to the cellar shelf, his heart a warm, beating hammer in his throat, the hair on the nape of his neck standing at attention, his eyes hot, his hands cold, sure that at any moment the cellar door would swing shut on its own, closing off the white light falling through the kitchen windows, and then he would hear It, something worse than all the Commies and murderers in the world, worse than the Japs, worse than Attila the Hun, worse than the somethings in a hundred horror movies. It, growling deeply – he would hear the growl in those lunatic seconds before it pounced on him and unzipped his guts.

The cellar-smell was worse than ever today, because of the flood. Their house was high on Witcham Street, near the crest of the hill, and they had escaped the worst of it, but there was still standing water down there that had seeped in through the old rock foundations. The smell was low and unpleasant, making you want to take only the shallowest breaths.

George sifted through the junk on the shelf as fast as he could – old cans of Kiwi shoepolish and shoepolish rags, a broken kerosene lamp, two mostly empty bottles of Windex, an old flat can of Turtle wax. For some reason this can struck him, and he spent nearly thirty seconds looking at the turtle on the lid with a kind of hypnotic wonder. Then he tossed it back . . . and here it was at last, a square box with the word GULF on it.

George snatched it and ran up the stairs as fast as he could, suddenly aware that his shirttail was out and suddenly sure that his shirttail would be his undoing: the thing in the cellar would allow him to get almost all the way out, and then it would grab the tail of his shirt and snatch him back and –

He reached the kitchen and swept the door shut behind him. It banged gustily. He leaned back against it with his eyes closed, sweat popped out on his arms and forehead, the box of paraffin gripped tightly in one hand.

The piano had come to a stop, and his mom's voice floated to him: 'Georgie, can't you slam that door a little harder next time? Maybe you could break some of the plates in the Welsh dresser, if you really tried.'

'Sorry, Mom,' he called back.

'Georgie, you waste,' Bill said from his bedroom. He pitched his voice low so their mother would not hear.

George snickered a little. His fear was already gone; it had slipped away from him as easily as a nightmare slips away from a man who awakes, cold-skinned and gasping, from its grip; who feels his body and stares at his surroundings to make sure that none of it ever happened and who then begins at once to forget it. Half is gone by the time his feet hit the floor; three-quarters of it by the time he emerges from the shower and begins to towel off; all of it by the time he finishes his breakfast. All gone . . . until the next time, when, in the grip of the nightmare, all fears will be remembered.

That turtle, George thought, going to the counter drawer where the matches were kept. *Where did I see a turtle like that before?*

But no answer came, and he dismissed the question.

He got a pack of matches from the drawer, a knife from the rack (holding the sharp edge studiously away from his body, as his dad had taught him), and a small bowl from the Welsh dresser in the dining room. Then he went back into Bill's room.

'W-What an a-hole you are, Juh-Georgie,' Bill said, amiably enough, and pushed back some of the sick-stuff on his nighttable: an empty glass, a pitcher of water, Kleenex, books, a bottle of Vicks VapoRub – the smell of which Bill would associate all his life with thick, phlegmy chests and snotty noses. The old Philco radio was there, too, playing not Chopin or Bach but a Little Richard tune . . . very softly, however, so softly that Little Richard was robbed of all his raw and elemental power. Their mother, who had studied classical piano at Juilliard, hated rock and roll. She did not merely dislike it; she abominated it.

8

'I'm no a-hole,' George said, sitting on the edge of Bill's bed and putting the things he had gathered on the nighttable.

'Yes you are,' Bill said. 'Nothing but a great big brown a-hole, that's you.'

George tried to imagine a kid who was nothing but a great big a-hole on legs and began to giggle.

'Your a-hole is bigger than *Augusta*,' Bill said, beginning to giggle, too.

'*Your* a-hole is bigger than the whole *state*,' George replied. This broke both boys up for nearly two minutes.

There followed a whispered conversation of the sort which means very little to anyone save small boys: accusations of who was the biggest a-hole, who *had* the biggest a-hole, which a-hole was the brownest, and so on. Finally Bill said one of the forbidden words – he accused George of being a big brown *shitty* a-hole – and they both got laughing hard. Bill's laughter turned into a coughing fit. As it finally began to taper off (by then Bill's face had gone a plummy shade which George regarded with some alarm), the piano stopped again. They both looked in the direction of the parlor, listening for the piano-bench to scrape back, listening for their mother's impatient footsteps. Bill buried his mouth in the crook of his elbow, stifling the last of the coughs, pointing at the pitcher at the same time. George poured him a glass of water, which he drank off.

The piano began once more – *Für Elise* again. Stuttering Bill never forgot that piece, and even many years later it never failed to bring gooseflesh to his arms and back; his heart would drop and he would remember: *My mother was playing that the day Georgie died.*

'You gonna cough anymore, Bill?'

'No.'

Bill pulled a Kleenex from the box, made a rumbling sound in his chest, spat phlegm into the tissue, screwed it up, and tossed it into the wastebasket by his bed, which was filled with similar twists of tissue. Then he opened the box of paraffin and dropped a waxy cube of the stuff into his palm. George watched him closely, but without speaking or questioning. Bill didn't like George talking to him while he did stuff, but George had learned that if he just kept his mouth shut, Bill would usually explain what he was doing.

Bill used the knife to cut off a small piece of the paraffin cube. He put the piece in the bowl, then struck a match and put it on top of the paraffin. The two boys watched the small yellow flame as the dying wind drove rain against the window in occasional spatters.

'Got to waterproof the boat or it'll just get wet and sink,' Bill said. When he was with George, his stutter was light – sometimes he didn't stutter at all. In school, however, it could become so bad that talking became impossible for him. Communication would cease and Bill's school-mates would look somewhere else while Bill clutched the sides of his desk, his face growing almost as red as his hair, his eyes squeezed into slits as he tried to winch some word out of his stubborn throat. Sometimes – most times – the word would come. Other times it simply refused. He had been hit by a car when he was three and knocked into the side of a building; he had remained unconscious for seven hours. Mom said it was that accident which had caused the stutter. George sometimes got the feeling that his dad – and Bill himself – was not so sure.

The piece of paraffin in the bowl was almost entirely melted.

The match-flame guttered lower, growing blue as it hugged the cardboard stick, and then it went out. Bill dipped his finger into the liquid, jerked it out with a faint hiss. He smiled apologetically at George. 'Hot,' he said. After a few seconds he dipped his finger in again and began to smear the wax along the sides of the boat, where it quickly dried to a milky haze.

'Can I do some?' George asked.

'Okay. Just don't get any on the blankets or Mom'll kill you.'

George dipped his finger into the paraffin, which was now very warm but no longer hot, and began to spread it along the other side of the boat.

'Don't put on so much, you a-hole!' Bill said. 'You want to sink it on its m-maiden cruise?'

'I'm sorry.'

'That's all right. Just g-go easy.'

George finished the other side, then held the boat in his hands. It felt a little heavier, but not much. 'Too cool,' he said. 'I'm gonna go out and sail it.'

'Yeah, you do that,' Bill said. He suddenly looked tired – tired and still not very well.

'I wish you could come,' George said. He really did. Bill some-times got bossy after awhile, but he always had the coolest ideas and he hardly ever hit. 'It's your boat, really.'

'*She*,' Bill said. 'You call boats *sh-she*.'

'She, then.'

'I wish I could come, too,' Bill said glumly.

'Well . . .' George shifted from one foot to the other, the boat in his hands.

'You put on your rain-stuff,' Bill said, 'or you'll wind up with the fluh-hu like me. Probably catch it anyway, from my juh-germs.'

'Thanks, Bill. It's a neat boat.' And he did something he hadn't done for a long time, something Bill never forgot: he leaned over and kissed his brother's cheek.

'You'll catch it for sure now, you a-hole,' Bill said, but he seemed cheered up all the same. He smiled at George. 'Put all this stuff back, too. Or Mom'll have a b-bird.'

'Sure.' He gathered up the waterproofing equipment and crossed the room, the boat perched precariously on top of the paraffin box, which was sitting askew in the little bowl.

'Juh juh-Georgie?'

George turned back to look at his brother.

'Be c-careful.'

'Sure.' His brow creased a little. That was something your mom said, not your big brother. It was as strange as him giving Bill a kiss. 'Sure I will.'

He went out. Bill never saw him again.

3

Now here he was, chasing his boat down the left side of Witcham Street. He was running fast but the water was running faster and his boat was pulling ahead. He heard a deepening roar and saw that fifty yards farther down the hill the water in the gutter was cascading into a stormdrain that was still open. It was a long dark semicircle cut into the curbing, and as George watched, a stripped branch, its bark as dark and glistening as sealskin, shot into the stormdrain's maw. It hung up there for a moment and then slipped down inside. That was where his boat was headed.

'Oh shit and Shinola!' he yelled, dismayed.

He put on speed, and for a moment he thought he would catch the boat. Then one of his feet slipped and he went sprawling, skinning one knee and crying out in pain. From his new pavement-level perspective he watched his boat swing around twice, momentarily caught in another whirlpool, and then disappear.

'Shit and *Shinola*!' he yelled again, and slammed his fist down on the pavement. That hurt too, and he began to cry a little. What a stupid way to lose the boat!

He got up and walked over to the stormdrain. He dropped to his knees and peered in. The water made a dank hollow sound as it fell into the darkness. It was a spooky sound. It reminded him of –

'Huh!' The sound was jerked out of him as if on a string, and he recoiled.

There were yellow eyes in there: the sort of eyes he had always imagined but never actually seen down in the basement. *It's an animal,* he thought incoherently, *that's all it is, some animal, maybe a housecat that got stuck down in there –*

Still, he was ready to run – *would* run in a second or two, when his mental switchboard had dealt with the shock those two shiny yellow eyes had given him. He felt the rough surface of the macadam under his fingers, and the thin sheet of cold water flowing around them. He saw himself getting up and backing away, and that was when a voice – a perfectly reasonable and rather pleasant voice – spoke to him from inside the stormdrain.

'Hi, Georgie,' it said.

George blinked and looked again. He could barely credit what he saw; it was like something from a made-up story, or a movie where you know the animals will talk and dance. If he had been ten years older, he would not have believed what he was seeing, but he was not sixteen. He was six.

There was a clown in the stormdrain. The light in there was far from good, but it was good enough so that George Denbrough was sure of what he was seeing. It was a clown, like in the circus or on TV. In fact he looked like a cross between Bozo and Clarabell, who talked by honking his (or was it her? – George was never really sure of the gender) horn on *Howdy Doody* Saturday mornings – Buffalo Bob was just about the only one who could understand Clarabell, and that always cracked George up. The face of the clown in the stormdrain was white, there were funny tufts of red hair on either side of his bald head, and there was a big clown-smile painted over his mouth. If George had been inhabiting a later year, he would have surely thought of Ronald McDonald before Bozo or Clarabell.

The clown held a bunch of balloons, all colors, like gorgeous ripe fruit in one hand.

In the other he held George's newspaper boat.

'Want your boat, Georgie?' The clown smiled.

George smiled back. He couldn't help it; it was the kind of smile you just had to answer. 'I sure do,' he said.

The clown laughed. ' "I sure do." That's *good*! That's *very* good! And how about a balloon?'

'Well . . . sure!' He reached forward . . . and then drew his hand reluctantly back. 'I'm not supposed to take stuff from strangers. My dad said so.'

'Very wise of your dad,' the clown in the stormdrain said, smiling. *How*, George wondered, *could I have thought his eyes were yellow?* They were a bright, dancing blue, the color of his mom's eyes, and Bill's. 'Very wise indeed. Therefore I will introduce myself. I, Georgie, am Mr Bob Gray, also known as Pennywise the Dancing Clown. Pennywise, meet George Denbrough. George, meet Pennywise. And now we know each other. I'm not a stranger to you, and you're not a stranger to me. Kee-rect?'

George giggled. 'I guess so.' He reached forward again . . . and drew his hand back again. 'How did you get down there?'

'Storm just bleeeew me away,' Pennywise the Dancing Clown said. 'It blew the whole circus away. Can you smell the circus, Georgie?'

George leaned forward. Suddenly he could smell peanuts! Hot roasted peanuts! And vinegar! The white kind you put on your french fries through a hole in the cap! He could smell cotton candy and frying doughboys and the faint but thunderous odor of wild-animal shit. He could smell the cheery aroma of midway sawdust. And yet . . .

And yet under it all was the smell of flood and decomposing leaves and dark stormdrain shadows. That smell was wet and rotten. The cellar-smell.

But the other smells were stronger.

'You bet I can smell it,' he said.

'Want your boat, Georgie?' Pennywise asked. 'I only repeat myself because you really do not seem that eager.' He held it up, smiling. He was wearing a baggy silk suit with great big orange buttons. A bright tie, electric-blue, flopped down his front, and on his hands were big white gloves, like the kind Mickey Mouse and Donald Duck always wore.

'Yes, sure,' George said, looking into the stormdrain.

'And a balloon? I've got red and green and yellow and blue . . .'

'Do they float?'

'Float?' The clown's grin widened. 'Oh yes, indeed they do. They float! And there's cotton candy . . .'

George reached.

The clown seized his arm.

And George saw the clown's face change.

What he saw then was terrible enough to make his worst

imaginings of the thing in the cellar look like sweet dreams; what he saw destroyed his sanity in one clawing stroke.

'They *float*,' the thing in the drain crooned in a clotted, chuckling voice. It held George's arm in its thick and wormy grip, it pulled George toward that terrible darkness where the water rushed and roared and bellowed as it bore its cargo of storm debris toward the sea. George craned his neck away from that final blackness and began to scream into the rain, to scream mindlessly into the white autumn sky which curved above Derry on that day in the fall of 1957. His screams were shrill and piercing, and all up and down Witcham Street people came to their windows or bolted out onto their porches.

'They *float*,' it growled, 'they *float*, Georgie, and when you're down here with me, you'll float, too –'

George's shoulder socked against the cement of the curb and Dave Gardener, who had stayed home from his job at The Shoeboat that day because of the flood, saw only a small boy in a yellow rain-slicker, a small boy who was screaming and writhing in the gutter with muddy water surfing over his face and making his screams sound bubbly.

'Everything down here *floats*,' that chuckling, rotten voice whispered, and suddenly there was a ripping noise and a flaring sheet of agony, and George Denbrough knew no more.

Dave Gardener was the first to get there, and although he arrived only forty-five seconds after the first scream, George Denbrough was already dead. Gardener grabbed him by the back of the slicker, pulled him into the street . . . and began to scream himself as George's body turned over in his hands. The left side of George's slicker was now bright red. Blood flowed into the stormdrain from the tattered hole where the left arm had been. A knob of bone, horribly bright, peeked through the torn cloth.

The boy's eyes stared up into the white sky, and as Dave staggered away toward the others already running pell-mell down the street, they began to fill up with rain.

4

Somewhere below, in the stormdrain that was already filled nearly to capacity with runoff (there could have been no one down there, the County Sheriff would later exclaim to a Derry *News* reporter with a frustrated fury so great it was almost agony; Hercules himself would have been swept away in that driving current), George's newspaper boat shot onward through nighted chambers and long concrete hallways that roared and chimed with water. For awhile it ran neck-and-neck with a dead chicken that floated with its yellowy, reptilian toes pointed at the dripping ceiling; then, at some junction east of town, the chicken was swept off to the left while George's boat went straight.

An hour later, while George's mother was being sedated in the Emergency Room at Derry Home Hospital and while Stuttering Bill sat stunned and white and silent in his bed, listening to his father sob hoarsely in the parlor where his mother had been playing *Für Elise* when George went out, the boat shot out through a concrete loophole like a bullet exiting the muzzle of a gun and ran at speed down a sluiceway and into an unnamed stream. When it joined the boiling, swollen Penobscot River twenty minutes later, the first rifts of blue had begun to show in the sky overhead. The storm was over.

The boat dipped and swayed and sometimes took on water, but it did not sink; the two brothers had waterproofed it well. I do not know where it finally fetched up, if ever it did; perhaps it reached the sea and sails there forever, like a magic boat in a fairytale. All I know is that it was still afloat and still running on the breast of the flood when it passed the incorporated town limits of Derry, Maine, and there it passes out of this tale forever.

CHAPTER TWO
AFTER THE FESTIVAL (1984)

1

The reason Adrian was wearing the hat, his sobbing boyfriend would later tell the police, was because he had won it at the Pitch Til U Win stall on the Bassey Park fairgrounds just six days before his death. He was proud of it.

'He was wearing it because he *loved* this shitty little town!' the boyfriend, Don Hagarty, screamed at the cops.

'Now, now – there's no need for that sort of language,' Officer Harold Gardener told Hagarty. Harold Gardener was one of Dave Gardener's four sons. On the day his father had discovered the lifeless, one-armed body of George Denbrough, Harold Gardener had been five. On this day, almost twenty-seven years later, he was thirty-two and balding. Harold Gardener recognized the reality of Don Hagarty's grief and pain, and at the same time found it impossible to take seriously. This man – if you want to call him a man – was wearing lipstick and satin pants so tight you could almost read the wrinkles in his cock. Grief or no grief, pain or no pain, he was, after all, just a queer. Like his friend, the late Adrian Mellon.

'Let's go through it again,' Harold's partner, Jeffrey Reeves, said. 'The two of you came out of the Falcon and turned toward the Canal. Then what?'

'How many times do I have to tell you idiots?' Hagarty was still screaming. 'They killed him! They pushed him over the side! Just another day in Macho City for them!' Don Hagarty began to cry.

'One more time,' Reeves repeated patiently. 'You came out of the Falcon. Then what?'

2

In an interrogation room just down the hall, two Derry cops were speaking with Steve Dubay, seventeen; in the Clerk of Probate's office upstairs, two more were questioning John 'Webby' Garton, eighteen; and in the Chief of Police's office on the fifth floor, Chief Andrew Rademacher and Assistant District Attorney Tom Boutillier were questioning fifteen-year-old Christopher Unwin. Unwin, who wore faded jeans, a grease-smeared tee-shirt, and blocky engineer boots, was weeping. Rademacher and Boutillier had taken him because they had quite accurately assessed him as the weak link in the chain.

'Let's go through it again,' Boutillier said in this office just as Jeffrey Reeves was saying the same thing two floors down.

'We didn't mean to kill him,' Unwin blubbered. 'It was the hat. We couldn't believe he was still wearing the hat after, you know, after what Webby said the first time. And I guess we wanted to scare him.'

'For what he said,' Chief Rademacher interjected.

'Yes.'

'To John Garton, on the afternoon of the 17th.'

'Yes, to Webby.' Unwin burst into fresh tears. 'But we tried to save him when we saw he was in trouble . . . at least me and Stevie Dubay did . . . we didn't mean to *kill* him!'

'Come on, Chris, don't shit us,' Boutillier said. 'You threw the little queer into the Canal.'

'Yes, but –'

'And the three of you came in to make a clean breast of things. Chief Rademacher and I appreciate that, don't we, Andy?'

'You bet. It takes a man to own up to what he did, Chris.'

'So don't fuck yourself up by lying now. You meant to throw him over the minute you saw him and his fag buddy coming out of the Falcon, didn't you?'

'No!' Chris Unwin protested vehemently.

Boutillier took a pack of Marlboros from his shirt pocket and stuck one in his mouth. He offered the pack to Unwin. 'Cigarette?'

Unwin took one. Boutillier had to chase the tip with a match in order to give him a light because of the way Unwin's mouth was trembling.

'But when you saw he was wearing the hat?' Rademacher asked.

Unwin dragged deep, lowered his head so that his greasy hair fell in his eyes, and jetted smoke from his nose, which was littered with blackheads.

'Yeah,' he said, almost too softly to be heard.

Boutillier leaned forward, brown eyes gleaming. His face was predatory but his voice was gentle. 'What, Chris?'

'I said yes. I guess so. To throw him in. But not to kill him.' He looked up at them, face frantic and miserable and still unable to comprehend the stupendous changes which had taken place in his life since he left the house to take in the last night of Derry's Canal Days Festival with two of his buddies at seven-thirty the previous evening. 'Not to kill him!' he repeated. 'And that guy under the bridge . . . I *still* don't know who *he* was.'

'What guy was that?' Rademacher asked, but without much interest. They had heard this part before as well, and neither of them believed it – sooner or later men accused of murder almost always drag out that mysterious other guy. Boutillier even had a name for it: he called it the 'One-Armed Man Syndrome,' after that old TV series *The Fugitive*.

'The guy in the clown suit,' Chris Unwin said, and shivered. 'The guy with the balloons.'

3

The Canal Days Festival, which ran from July 15th to July 21st, had been a rousing success, most Derry residents agreed: a great thing for the city's morale, image . . . and pocketbook. The weeklong festival was pegged to mark the centenary of the opening of the Canal which ran through the middle of downtown. It had been the Canal which had fully opened Derry to the lumber trade in the years 1884 to 1910; it had been the Canal which had birthed Derry's boom years.

The town was spruced up from east to west and north to south. Potholes which some residents swore hadn't been patched for ten years or more were neatly filled with hottop and rolled smooth. The town buildings were refurbished on the inside, repainted on the outside. The worst of the graffiti in Bassey Park – much of it coolly logical anti-gay statements such as KILL ALL QUEERS and AIDS FROM GOD YOU HELLBOUND HOMOS!! – was sanded off the benches and wooden walls of the little covered walkway over the Canal known as the Kissing Bridge.

A Canal Days Museum was installed in three empty store-fronts downtown, and filled with exhibits by Michael Hanlon, a local librarian and amateur historian. The town's oldest families loaned freely of their almost priceless treasures, and during the week of the festival nearly forty thousand visitors paid a quarter each to look at eating-house menus from the 1890s, loggers' bitts, axes, and peaveys from the 1880s, children's toys from the 1920s, and over two thousand photographs and nine reels of movie film of life as it had been in Derry over the last hundred years.

The museum was sponsored by the Derry Ladies' Society, which vetoed some of Hanlon's proposed exhibits (such as the notorious tramp-chair from the 1930s) and photographs (such as those of the Bradley Gang after the notorious shoot-out). But all agreed it was a great success, and no one really wanted to see those gory old things anyway. It was so much better to accentuate the positive and eliminate the negative, as the old song said.

There was a huge striped refreshment tent in Derry Park, and band concerts there every night. In Bassey Park there was a carnival with rides by Smokey's Greater Shows and games run by local town-folk. A special tram-car circled the historic sections of the town every hour on the hour and ended up at this gaudy and amiable money-machine.

It was here that Adrian Mellon won the hat which would get him killed, the paper top-hat with the flower and the band which said I ♥ DERRY!

4

'I'm tired,' John 'Webby' Garton said. Like his two friends, he was dressed in unconscious imitation of Bruce Springsteen, although if asked he would probably call Springsteen a wimp or a fagola and would instead profess admiration for such 'bitchin' heavy-metal groups as Def Leppard, Twisted Sister, or Judas Priest. The sleeves of his plain blue tee-shirt were torn off, showing his heavily muscled arms. His thick brown hair fell over one eye – this touch was more John Cougar Mellencamp than Springsteen. There were blue tattoos on his arms – arcane symbols which looked as if they had been drawn by a child. 'I don't want to talk no more.'

'Just tell us about Tuesday afternoon at the fair,' Paul Hughes said. Hughes was tired and shocked and dismayed by this whole sordid business. He thought again and again that it was as if Derry Canal Days ended with one final event which everyone had somehow known about but which no one had quite dared to put down on the Daily Program of Events. If they had, it would have looked like this:

Saturday, 9:00 P.M.: Final band concert featuring the Derry High School Band and the Barber Shop Mello-Men.
Saturday, 10:00 P.M.: Giant fireworks show.
Saturday, 10:35 P.M.: Ritual sacrifice of Adrian Mellon officially ends Canal Days.

'Fuck the fair,' Webby replied.

'Just what you said to Mellon and what he said to you.'

'Oh Christ.' Webby rolled his eyes.

'Come on, Webby,' Hughes's partner said.

Webby Garton rolled his eyes and began again.

5

Garton saw the two of them, Mellon and Hagarty, mincing along with their arms about each other's waists and giggling like a couple of girls. At first he actually thought they *were* a couple of girls. Then he recognized Mellon, who had been pointed out to him before. As he looked, he saw Mellon turn to Hagarty . . . and they kissed briefly.

'Oh, man, I'm gonna barf!' Webby cried, disgusted.

Chris Unwin and Steve Dubay were with him. When Webby pointed out Mellon, Steve Dubay said he thought the other fag was named Don somebody, and that he'd picked up a kid from Derry High hitching and then tried to put a few moves on him.

Mellon and Hagarty began to move toward the three boys again, walking away from the Pitch Til U Win and toward the carny's exit. Webby Garton would later tell Officers Hughes and Conley that his 'civic pride' had been wounded by seeing a fucking faggot wearing a hat which said I ♥ DERRY. It was a silly thing, that hat – a paper imitation of a top hat with a great big flower sticking up from the top and nodding about in every direction. The silliness of the hat apparently wounded Webby's civic pride even more.

As Mellon and Hagarty passed, each with his arm linked about the other's waist, Webby Garton yelled out: 'I ought to make you *eat* that hat, you fucking ass-bandit!'

Mellon turned toward Garton, fluttered his eyes flirtatiously, and said: 'If you want something to eat, hon, I can find something *much* tastier than my hat.'

At this point Webby Garton decided he was going to rearrange the faggot's face. In the geography of Mellon's face, mountains would rise and continents would drift. *Nobody* suggested he sucked the root. *Nobody*.

He started toward Mellon. Mellon's friend Hagarty, alarmed, attempted to pull Mellon away, but Mellon stood his ground, smiling. Garton would later tell Officers Hughes and Conley that he was pretty sure Mellon was high on something. So he was, Hagarty would agree when this idea was passed on to him by Officers Gardener and Reeves.

He was high on two fried doughboys smeared with honey, on the carnival, on the whole day. He had been consequently unable to recognize the real menace which Webby Garton represented.

'But that was Adrian,' Don said, using a tissue to wipe his eyes and smearing the spangled eyeshadow he was wearing. 'He didn't have much in the way of protective coloration. He was one of those fools who think things really are going to turn out all right.'

He might have been badly hurt there and then if Garton hadn't felt something tap his elbow. It was a nightstick. He turned his head to see Officer Frank Machen, another member of Derry's Finest.

'Never mind, little buddy,' Machen told Garton. 'Mind your business and leave those little gay boyos alone. Have some fun.'

'Did you hear what he called me?' Garton asked hotly. He was now joined by Unwin and Dubay – the two of them, smelling trouble, tried to urge Garton on up the midway, but Garton shrugged them away, would have turned on them with his fists if they had persisted. His masculinity had borne an insult which he felt must be avenged. *Nobody* suggested he sucked the root. *Nobody*.

'I don't believe he *called* you anything,' Machen replied. 'And you spoke to him first, I believe. Now move on, sonny. I don't want to have to tell you again.'

'He called me a queer!'

'Are you worried you might be, then?' Machen asked, seeming to be honestly interested, and Garton flushed a deep ugly red.

During this exchange, Hagarty was trying with increasing desperation to pull Adrian Mellon away from the scene. Now, at last, Mellon was going.

'Ta-ta, love!' Adrian called cheekily over his shoulder.

'Shut up, candy-ass,' Machen said. 'Get out of here.'

Garton made a lunge at Mellon, and Machen grabbed him.

'I can run you in, my friend,' Machen said, 'and the way you're acting, it might not be such a bad idea.'

'*Next time I see you I'm gonna hurt you!*' Garton bellowed after the departing pair, and heads turned to stare at him. '*And if you're wearing that hat, I'm gonna kill you! This town don't need no faggots like you!*'

Without turning, Mellon waggled the fingers of his left hand – the nails were painted cerise – and put an extra little wiggle in his walk. Garton lunged again.

'One more word or one more move and in you go,' Machen said mildly. 'Trust me, my boy, for I mean exactly what I say.'

'Come on, Webby,' Chris Unwin said uneasily. 'Mellow out.'

'You like guys like that?' Webby asked Machen, ignoring Chris and Steve completely. 'Huh?'

'About the bum-punchers I'm neutral,' Machen said. 'What I'm really in favor of is peace and quiet, and you are upsetting what I like, pizza face. Now do you want to go around with me or what?'

'Come on, Webby,' Steve Dubay said quietly. 'Let's go get some hot dogs.'

Webby went, straightening his shirt with exaggerated moves and brushing the hair out of his eyes. Machen, who also gave a statement on the morning following Adrian Mellon's death, said: '*The last thing I heard him say as him and his buddies walked off was, "Next time I see him he's going to be in serious hurt."* '

6

'Please, I got to talk to my mother,' Steve Dubay said for the third time. 'I've got to get her to mellow out my stepfather, or there is going to be one hell of a punching-match when I get home.'

'In a little while,' Officer Charles Avarino told him. Both Avarino and his partner, Barney Morrison, knew that Steve Dubay would not be going home tonight and maybe not for many nights to come. The boy did not seem to realize just how heavy this particular bust was, and Avarino would not be surprised when he learned, later on, that Dubay had left school at age sixteen. At that time he had still been in Water Street Junior High. His IQ was 68, according to the Wechsler he had taken during one of his three trips through the seventh grade.

'Tell us what happened when you saw Mellon coming out of the Falcon,' Morrison invited.

'No, man, I better not.'

'Well, why not?' Avarino asked.

'I already talked too much, maybe.'

'You came in to talk,' Avarino said. 'Isn't that right?'

'Well . . . yeah . . . but . . .'

'Listen,' Morrison said warmly, sitting down next to Dubay and shooting him a cigarette. 'You think me and Chick here like fags?'

'I don't know —'

'Do we *look* like we like fags?'

'No, but . . .'

'We're your friends, Steve-o,' Morrison said solemnly. 'And believe me, you and Chris and Webby need all the friends you can get just about now. Because tomorrow every bleeding heart in this town is going to be screaming for you guys's blood.'

Steve Dubay looked dimly alarmed. Avarino, who could almost read this hairbag's pussy little mind, suspected he was thinking about his stepfather again. And although Avarino had no liking for Derry's small gay community – like every other cop on the force, he would enjoy seeing the Falcon shut up forever – he would have been delighted to drive Dubay home himself. He would, in fact, have been delighted to hold Dubay's arms while Dubay's stepfather beat the creep to oatmeal. Avarino did not like gays, but this did not mean he believed they should be tortured and murdered. Mellon had been savaged. When they brought him up from under the Canal bridge, his eyes had been open, bulging with terror. And this guy here had absolutely no idea of what he had helped do.

'We didn't mean to hurt 'im,' Steve repeated. This was his fall-back position when he became even slightly confused.

'That's why you want to get out front with us,' Avarino said earnestly. 'Get the true facts of the matter out in front, and this maybe won't amount to a pisshole in the snow. Isn't that right, Barney?'

'As rain,' Morrison agreed.

'One more time, what do you say?' Avarino coaxed.

'Well . . .' Steve said, and then, slowly, began to talk.

7

When the Falcon was opened in 1973, Elmer Curtie thought his clientele would consist mostly of bus-riders – the terminal next door serviced three different lines: Trailways, Greyhound, and Aroostook County. What he failed to realize was how many of the passengers who ride buses are women or families with small children in tow. Many of the others kept their bottles in brown bags and never got off the bus at all. Those who did were usually soldiers or sailors who wanted no more than a quick beer or two – you couldn't very well go on a bender during a ten-minute rest-stop.

Curtie had begun to realize some of these home truths by 1977, but by then it was too late: he was up to his tits in bills and there was no way that he could see out of the red ink. The idea of burning the place down for the insurance occurred to him, but unless he hired a professional to torch it, he supposed he would be caught . . . and he had no idea where professional arsonists hung out, anyway.

He decided in February of that year that he would give it until

July 4th; if things didn't look as if they were turning around by then, he would simply walk next door, get on a 'hound, and see how things looked down in Florida.

But in the next five months, an amazing quiet sort of prosperity came to the bar, which was painted black and gold inside and decorated with stuffed birds (Elmer Curtie's brother had been an amateur taxidermist who specialized in birds, and Elmer had inherited the stuff when he died). Suddenly, instead of drawing sixty beers and pouring maybe twenty drinks a night, Elmer was drawing eighty beers and pouring a hundred drinks . . . a hundred and twenty . . . sometimes a hundred and sixty.

His clientele was young, polite, almost exclusively male. Many of them dressed outrageously, but those were years when outrageous dress was still almost the norm, and Elmer Curtie did not realize that his patrons were just about almost exclusively gay until 1981 or so. If Derry residents had heard him say this, they would have laughed and said that Elmer Curtie must think they had all been born yesterday – but his claim was perfectly true. Like the man with the cheating wife, he was practically the last to know . . . and by the time he did, he didn't care. The bar was making money, and while there were four other bars in Derry which turned a profit, the Falcon was the only one where rambunctious patrons did not regularly demolish the whole place. There were no women to fight over, for one thing, and these men, fags or not, seemed to have learned a secret of getting along with each other which their heterosexual counterparts did not know.

Once he became aware of the sexual preference of his regulars, he seemed to hear lurid stories about the Falcon everywhere – these stories had been circulating for years, but until '81 Curtie simply hadn't heard them. The most enthusiastic tellers of these tales, he came to realize, were men who wouldn't be dragged into the Falcon with a chainfall for fear all the muscles would go out of their wrists, or something. Yet they seemed privy to all sorts of information.

According to the stories, you could go in there any night and see men close-dancing, rubbing their cocks together right out on the dancefloor; men french-kissing at the bar; men getting blow jobs in the bathrooms. There was supposedly a room out back where you went if you wanted to spend a little time on the Tower of Power – there was a big old fellow in a Nazi uniform back there who kept his arm greased most of the way to the shoulder and who would be happy to take care of you.

In fact, none of these things was true. When folks with a thirst did come in from the bus station for a beer or a highball, they sensed nothing out of the ordinary in the Falcon at all – there were a lot of guys, sure, but that was no different from thousands of workingmen's bars all across the country. The clientele was gay, but gay was not a synonym for stupid. If they wanted a little outrageousness, they went to Portland. If they wanted a lot of outrageousness – Ramrod-style outrageousness or Peck's Big Boy style outrageousness – they went down to New York or Boston. Derry was small, Derry was provincial, and Derry's small gay community understood the shadow under which it existed quite well.

Don Hagarty had been coming into the Falcon for two or three years on the night in March of 1984 when he first showed up with Adrian Mellon. Before then, Hagarty had been the sort who plays the field, rarely showing up with the same escort half a dozen times. But by late April it had become obvious even to Elmer Curtie, who cared very little about such things, that Hagarty and Mellon had a steady thing going.

Hagarty was a draftsman with an engineering firm in Bangor. Adrian Mellon was a freelance writer who published anywhere and everywhere he could – airline magazines, confession magazines, regional magazines, Sunday supplements, sex-letter magazines. He had been working on a novel, but maybe that wasn't serious – he had been working on it since his third year of college, and that had been twelve years ago.

He had come to Derry to write a piece about the Canal – he was on assignment from *New England Byways*, a glossy bi-monthly that was published in Concord. Adrian Mellon had taken the assignment because he could squeeze *Byways* for three weeks' worth of expense money, including a nice room at the Derry Town House, and gather all the material he needed for the piece in maybe five days. During the other two weeks he could gather enough material for maybe four other regional pieces.

But during that three-week period he met Don Hagarty, and instead of going back to Portland when his three weeks on the cuff were over, he found himself a small apartment on Kossuth Lane. He lived there for only six weeks. Then he moved in with Don Hagarty.

8

That summer, Hagarty told Harold Gardener and Jeff Reeves, was the happiest summer of his life – he should have been on the lookout, he said; he should have known that God only puts a rug under guys like him in order to jerk it out from under their feet.

The only shadow, he said, was Adrian's extravagantly partisan reaction to Derry. He had a tee-shirt which said MAINE AIN'T BAD BUT DERRY'S GREAT! He had a Derry Tigers high-school jacket. And of course there was the hat. He claimed to find the atmosphere vital and creatively invigorating. Perhaps there was something to this: he had taken his languishing novel out of the trunk for the first time in nearly a year.

'Was he really working on it, then?' Gardener asked Hagarty, not really caring but wanting to keep Hagarty primed.

'Yes – he was busting pages. He said it might be a terrible novel, but it was no longer going to be a terrible unfinished novel. He expected to finish it by his birthday, in October. Of course, he didn't know what Derry was really like. He thought he did, but he hadn't been here long enough to get a whiff of the real Derry. I kept trying to tell him, but he wouldn't listen.'

'And what's Derry really like, Don?' Reeves asked.

'It's a lot like a dead strumpet with maggots squirming out of her cooze,' Don Hagarty said.

The two cops stared in silent amazement.

'It's a *bad* place,' Hagarty said. 'It's a sewer. You mean you two guys don't *know* that? You two guys have lived here all of your lives and you don't *know* that?'

Neither of them answered. After a little while, Hagarty went on.

9

Until Adrian Mellon entered his life, Don had been planning to leave Derry. He had been there for three years, mostly because he had agreed to a long-term lease on an apartment with the world's most fantastic river-view, but now the lease was almost up and Don was glad. No more long commute back and forth to Bangor. No more weird vibes – in Derry, he once told Adrian, it always felt like thirteen o'clock. Adrian might think Derry was a great place, but it scared Don. It was not just the town's tightly homophobic attitude, an attitude as clearly expressed by the town's preachers as by the graffiti in Bassey Park, but that was one thing he had been able to put his finger on. Adrian had laughed.

'Don, every town in America has a contingent that hates the gayfolk,' he said. 'Don't tell me you don't know that. This is, after all, the era of Ronnie Moron and Phyllis Housefly.'

'Come down to Bassey Park with me,' Don had replied, after

seeing that Adrian really meant what he was saying – and what he was really saying was that Derry was no worse than any other fair-sized town in the hinterlands. 'I want to show you something, my love.'

They drove to Bassey Park – this had been in mid-June, about a month before Adrian's murder, Hagarty told the cops. He took Adrian into the dark, vaguely unpleasant-smelling shadows of the Kissing Bridge. He pointed out one of the graffiti. Adrian had to strike a match and hold it below the writing in order to read it.

SHOW ME YOUR COCK QUEER AND I'LL CUT IT OFF YOU.

'I know how people feel about gays,' Don said quietly. 'I got beaten up at a truck-stop in Dayton when I was a teenager; some fellows in Portland set my shoes on fire outside of a sandwich shop while this fat-assed old cop sat inside his cruiser and laughed. I've seen a lot . . . but I've never seen anything quite like this. Look over here. Check it out.'

Another match revealed STICK NAILS IN EYES OF ALL FAGOTS (FOR GOD)!

'Whoever writes these little homilies has got a case of the deep-down crazies. I'd feel better if I thought it was just one person, one isolated sickie, but . . .' Don swept his arm vaguely down the length of the Kissing Bridge. 'There's a lot of this stuff . . . and I just don't think one person did it all. That's why I want to leave Derry, Ade. Too many places and too many people seem to have the deep-down crazies.'

'Well, wait until I finish my novel, okay? Please? October, I promise, no later. The air's better here.'

'He didn't know it was the water he was going to have to watch out for,' Don Hagarty said bitterly.

10

Tom Boutillier and Chief Rademacher leaned forward, neither of them speaking. Chris Unwin sat with his head down, talking monotonously to the floor. This was the part they wanted to hear; this was the part that was going to send at least two of these assholes to Thomaston.

'The fair wasn't no good,' Unwin said. 'They was already takin down all the bitchin rides, you know, like the Devil Dish and the Parachute Drop. They already had a sign on the Bumper Cars that said "closed." Wasn't nothing open but baby rides. So we went down by the games and Webby saw the Pitch Til U Win and he paid fifty cents and he seen that hat the queer was wearing and he pitched at that, but he kept missing it, and every time he missed he got more in a bad mood, you know? And Steve – he's the guy who usually goes around saying mellow out, like mellow out this and mellow out that and why don't you fuckin mellow out, you know? Only he was in a real piss-up-a-rope mood because he took this pill, you know? I don't know what kind of a pill. A red pill. Maybe it was even legal. But he keeps after Webby until I thought Webby was gonna hit him, you know? He goes, You can't even win that queer's hat. You must be really wasted if you can't even win that queer's hat. So finally the lady gives in a prize even though the ring wasn't over it, cause I think she wanted to get rid of us. I don't know. Maybe she didn't. But I think she did. It was this noise-maker thing, you know? You blow it and it puffs up and unrolls and makes a noise like a fart, you know? I used to have one of those. I got it for Halloween or New Year's or some fuckin holiday, I thought it was pretty good, only I lost it. Or maybe somebody hawked it out of my pocket in the fuckin playyard at school, you know? So then the fair's closin and we're walkin out and Steve's still on Webby about not bein able to win that queer's hat, you know, and Webby ain't sayin much, and I know that's a bad sign but I was pretty 'faced, you know? So I knew I ought to like change the subject only I couldn't think of no subject, you know? So when we get into the parkin lot Steve says, Where you want to go? Home? And Webby goes, Let's cruise by the Falcon first and see if that queer's around.'

Boutillier and Rademacher exchanged a glance. Boutillier raised a single finger and tapped it against his cheek: although this doofus in the engineer boots didn't know it, he was now talking about first-degree murder.

'So I goes no, I gotta get home, and Webby goes, You scared to go by that queer-bar? And I go, Fuck no! And Steve's still high or something, and he says, Let's go grease some queermeat! Let's go grease some queermeat! Let's go grease . . .'

11

The timing was just right enough so that things worked out wrong for everyone. Adrian Mellon and Don Hagarty came out of the Falcon after two beers, walked up past the bus station, and then linked hands. Neither of them thought about it; it was just something they did. It was ten-twenty. They reached the corner and turned left.

The Kissing Bridge was almost half a mile upriver from here; they meant to cross Main Street Bridge, which was much less picturesque.

The Kenduskeag was summer-low, no more than four feet of water sliding listlessly around the concrete pilings.

When the Duster drew abreast of them (Steve Dubay had spotted the two of them coming out of the Falcon and gleefully pointed them out), they were on the edge of the span.

'Cut in! Cut in!' Webby Garton screamed. The two men had just passed under a streetlight and he had spotted the fact that they were holding hands. This infuriated him . . . but not as much as the hat infuriated him. The big paper flower was nodding crazily this way and that. 'Cut in, goddammit!'

And Steve did.

Chris Unwin would deny active participation in what followed, but Don Hagarty told a different story. He said that Garton was out of the car almost before it stopped, and that the other two quickly followed. There was talk. Not good talk. There was no attempt at flippancy or false coquetry on Adrian's part this night; he recognized that they were in a lot of trouble.

'Give me that hat,' Garton said. 'Give it to me, queer.'

'If I do, will you leave us alone?' Adrian was wheezing with fright, almost crying, looking from Unwin to Dubay to Garton with terrified eyes.

'Just give me the fucker!'

Adrian handed it over. Garton produced a switchknife from the left front pocket of his jeans and cut it into two pieces. He rubbed the pieces against the seat of his jeans. Then he dropped them to his feet and stomped them.

Don Hagarty backed away a little while their attention was divided between Adrian and the hat – he was looking, he said, for a cop.

'Now will you let us al –' Adrian Mellon began, and that was when Garton punched him in the face, driving him back against the waist-high pedestrian railing of the bridge. Adrian screamed, clapping his hands to his mouth. Blood poured through his fingers.

'*Ade!*' Hagarty cried, and ran forward again. Dubay tripped him. Garton booted him in the stomach, knocking him off the sidewalk and into the roadway. A car passed. Hagarty rose to his knees and screamed at it. It didn't slow. The driver, he told Gardener and Reeves, never even looked around.

'Shut up, queer!' Dubay said, and kicked him in the side of the face. Hagarty fell on his side in the gutter, semiconscious.

A few moments later he heard a voice – Chris Unwin's – telling him to get away before he got what his friend was getting. In his own statement Unwin verified giving this warning.

Hagarty could hear thudding blows and the sound of his lover screaming. Adrian sounded like a rabbit in a snare, he told the police. Hagarty crawled back toward the intersection and the bright lights of the bus station, and when he was a distance away he turned back to look.

Adrian Mellon, who stood about five-five and might have weighed a hundred and thirty-five pounds soaking wet, was being pushed from Garton to Dubay to Unwin in a kind of triple play. His body jittered and flopped like the body of a rag doll. They were punching him, pummelling him, ripping at his clothes. As he watched, he said, Garton punched Adrian in the crotch. Adrian's hair hung in his face. Blood poured out of his mouth and soaked his shirt. Webby Garton wore two heavy rings on his right hand: one was a Derry High School ring, the other one he had made in shop class – an intertwined brass DB stood out three inches from this latter. The letters stood for the Dead Bugs, a metal band he particularly admired. The rings had torn Adrian's upper lip open and shattered three of his upper teeth at the gum line.

'*Help!*' Hagarty shrieked. '*Help! Help! They're killing him! Help!*'

The buildings of Main Street loomed dark and secret. No one came to help – not even from the one white island of light which marked the bus station, and Hagarty did not see how that could be: there were people in there. He had seen them when he and Ade walked past. Would none of them come to help? None at all?

'*HELP! HELP! THEY'RE KILLING HIM, HELP, PLEASE, FOR GOD'S SAKE!*'

'Help,' a very small voice whispered from Don Hagarty's left . . . and then there was a giggle.

'*Bum's rush!*' Garton was yelling now . . . yelling and laughing. All three of them, Hagarty told Gardener and Reeves, had been laughing while they beat Adrian up. '*Bum's rush! Over the side!*'

'*Bum's rush! Bum's rush! Bum's rush!*' Dubay chanted, laughing.

'Help,' the small voice said again, and although the voice was grave, that little giggle followed again – it was like the voice of a child who cannot help itself.

Hagarty looked down and saw the clown – and it was at this point that Gardener and Reeves began to discount everything that Hagarty said, because the rest was the raving of a lunatic. Later, however, Harold Gardener found himself wondering. Later, when he found that the Unwin boy had also seen a clown – or said he had – he began to have second thoughts. His partner either never had them or would never admit to them.

The clown, Hagarty said, looked like a cross between Ronald McDonald and that old TV clown, Bozo – or so he thought at first. It was the wild tufts of orange hair that brought such comparisons to mind. But later consideration had caused him to think the clown really looked like neither. The smile painted over the white pancake was red, not orange, and the eyes were a weird shiny silver. Contact lenses, perhaps . . . but a part of him thought then and continued to think that maybe that silver had been the real color of those eyes. He wore a baggy suit with big orange-pompom buttons; on his hands were cartoon gloves.

'If you need help, Don,' the clown said, 'help yourself to a balloon.'

And it offered the bunch it held in one hand.

'They float,' the clown said. 'Down here we all float; pretty soon your friend will float, too.'

12

'This clown called you by name,' Jeff Reeves said in a totally expressionless voice. He looked over Hagarty's bent head at Harold Gardener, and one eye drew down in a wink.

'Yes,' Hagarty said, not looking up. 'I know how it sounds.'

13

'So then you threw him over,' Boutillier said. 'Bum's rush.'

'Not me!' Unwin said, looking up. He flicked the hair out of his eyes with one hand and stared at them urgently. 'When I saw they really meant to do it, I tried to pull Steve away, because I knew the guy might get banged up . . . It was like ten feet to the water . . .'

It was twenty-three. One of Chief Rademacher's patrolmen had already measured.

'But it was like he was crazy. The two of them kept yelling "Bum's rush! Bum's rush!" and they picked him up. Webby had him under the arms and Steve had him by the seat of the pants, and . . . and . . .'

14

When Hagarty saw what they were doing, he rushed back toward them, screaming '*No! No! No!*' at the top of his voice.

Chris Unwin pushed him backward and Hagarty landed in a teeth-rattling heap on the sidewalk. 'Do you want to go over, too?' he whispered. 'You *run*, baby!'

They threw Adrian Mellon over the bridge and into the water then. Hagarty heard the splash.

'Let's get out of here,' Steve Dubay said. He and Webby were backing toward the car.

Chris Unwin went to the railing and looked over. He saw Hagarty first, sliding and clawing his way down the weedy, trash-littered embankment to the water. Then he saw the clown. The clown was dragging Adrian out on the far side with one arm; its balloons were in its other hand. Adrian was dripping wet, choking, moaning. The clown twisted its head and grinned up at Chris. Chris said he saw its shining silver eyes and its bared teeth – great big teeth, he said.

'Like the lion in the circus, man,' he said. 'I mean, they were that big.'

Then, he said, he saw the clown shove one of Adrian Mellon's arms back so it lay over his head.

'Then what, Chris?' Boutillier said. He was bored with this part. Fairy tales had bored him since the age of eight on.

'I dunno,' Chris said. 'That was when Steve grabbed me and hauled me into the car. But . . . I think it bit into his armpit.' He looked up at them again, uncertain now. 'I think that's what it did. Bit into his armpit.

'Like it wanted to eat him, man. Like it wanted to eat his heart.'

15

No, Hagarty said when he was presented with Chris Unwin's story in the form of questions. The clown did not drag Ade up on the far bank, at least not that he saw – and he would grant that he had been something less than a disinterested observer by that point; by that point he had been out of his fucking mind.

The clown, he said, was standing near the far bank with Adrian's dripping body clutched in its arms. Ade's right arm was stuck stiffly out behind the clown's head, and the clown's face was indeed in Ade's right armpit, but it was not biting: it was smiling. Hagarty could see it looking out from beneath Ade's arm and smiling.

The clown's arms tightened, and Hagarty heard ribs splinter.

Ade shrieked.

'Float with us, Don,' the clown said out of its grinning red mouth, and then pointed with one of its white-gloved hands under the bridge.

Balloons floated against the underside of the bridge – not a dozen or a dozen dozens but thousands, red and blue and green and yellow, and printed on the side of each was I ♥ DERRY!

16

'Well now, that surely does sound like a lot of balloons,' Reeves said, and tipped Harold Gardener another wink.

'I know how it sounds,' Hagarty reiterated in the same dreary voice.

'You *saw* those balloons,' Gardener said.

Don Hagarty slowly held his hands up in front of his face. 'I saw them as clearly as I can see my own fingers at this moment. Thousands of them. You couldn't even see the underside of the bridge – there were too many of them. They were rippling a little, and sort of bouncing up and down. There was a sound. A funny low squealing noise. That was their sides rubbing together. And strings. There was a forest of white strings hanging down. They looked like white strands of spiderweb. The clown took Ade under there. I could see its suit brushing through those strings. Ade was making awful choking sounds. I started after him . . . and the clown looked back. I saw its eyes, and all at once I understood who it was.'

'Who was it, Don?' Harold Gardener asked softly.

'It was Derry,' Don Hagarty said. 'It was this town.'

'And what did you do then?' It was Reeves.

'I ran, you dumb shit,' Hagarty said, and burst into tears.

17

Harold Gardener kept his peace until November 13th, the day before John Garton and Steven Dubay were to go on trial in Derry District Court for the murder of Adrian Mellon. Then he went to see Tom Boutillier. He wanted to talk about the clown. Boutillier didn't – but when he saw Gardener might do something stupid without a little guidance, he did.

'There was no clown, Harold. The only clowns out that night were those three kids. You know that as well as I do.'

'We have two witnesses –'

'Oh, that's crap. Unwin decided to bring on the One-Armed Man, as in "We didn't kill the poor little faggot, it was the one-armed man," as soon as he understood he'd really gotten his buns into some hot water this time. Hagarty was hysterical. He stood by and watched those kids murder his best friend. It wouldn't have surprised me if he'd seen flying saucers.'

But Boutillier knew better. Gardener could see it in his eyes, and the Assistant DA's ducking and dodging irritated him.

'Come on,' he said. 'We're talking about independent witnesses here. Don't bullshit me.'

'Oh, you want to talk bullshit? Are you telling me you believe there was a vampire clown under the Main Street Bridge? Because that's *my* idea of bullshit.'

'No, not exactly, but –'

'Or that Hagarty saw a billion balloons under there, each imprinted with exactly the same thing as what was written on his lover's hat? Because that is *also* my idea of bullshit.'

'No, but –'

'Then why are you bothering with this?'

'*Stop cross-examining me!*' Gardener roared. 'They both described it the same and neither knew what the other one was saying!'

Boutillier had been sitting at his desk, playing with a pencil. Now he put the pencil down, got up, and walked over to Harold Gardener. Boutillier was five inches shorter, but Gardener retreated a step before the man's anger.

'Do you want us to lose this case, Harold?'

'No. Of course n –'

'Do you want those running sores to walk free?'

'No!'

'Okay. Good. Since we both agree on the basics, I'll tell you exactly what I think. Yes, there was probably a man under the bridge that night. Maybe he was even wearing a clown suit, although I've dealt with enough witnesses to guess maybe it was just a stewbum or a transient wearing a bunch of cast-off clothes. I think he was probably down there scrounging for dropped change or roadmeat – half a burger someone chucked over the side, or maybe the crumbs from the bottom of a Frito bag. Their *eyes* did the rest, Harold. Now is that possible?'

'I don't know,' Harold said. He wanted to be convinced, but given the exact tally of the two descriptions . . . no. He didn't think it was possible.

'Here's the bottom line. I don't care if it was Kinko the Klown or a guy in an Uncle Sam suit on stilts or Hubert the Happy Homo. If we introduce this fellow into the case, their lawyer is going to be on it before you can say "Jack Robinson". He's going to say those two little innocent lambs out there with their fresh haircuts and new suits didn't do anything but toss that gay fellow Mellon over the side of the bridge for a joke. He'll point out that Mellon was still alive after he took the fall; they have Hagarty's testimony as well as Unwin's for that.

'*His* clients didn't commit murder, oh no! It was a psycho in a clown suit. If we introduce this, that's going to happen and you know it.'

'Unwin's going to tell that story anyhow.'

'But Hagarty isn't,' Boutillier said. 'Because *he* understands. Without Hagarty, who's going to believe Unwin?'

'Well, there's us,' Harold Gardener said with a bitterness that surprised even himself, 'but I guess *we're* not telling.'

'*Oh, give me a break!*' Boutillier roared, throwing up his hands. '*They killed him!* They didn't just throw him over the side – Garton had a switchblade. Mellon was stabbed seven times, including once in the left lung and twice in the testicles. The wounds match the blade. Four of his ribs were broken – Dubay did that, bear-hugging him. He was bitten, all right. There were bites on his arms, his left cheek, his neck. I think that was Unwin and Garton, although we've only got one clear match, and that one's probably not clear enough to stand up in court. And so all right, there was a big chunk of meat gone from his right armpit, so what? One of them really liked to bite. Probably even got himself a pretty good bone-on while he was doing it. I'm betting Garton, although we'll never prove it. And Mellon's earlobe was gone.'

Boutillier stopped, glaring at Harold.

'If we let in this clown story we'll *never* bring it home to them. Do you want that?'

'No, I told you.'

'The guy was a fruit, but he wasn't hurting anyone,' Boutillier said. 'So hi-ho-the-dairy-o, along come these three pusholes in their engineer boots and they steal his life. I'm going to put them in the slam, my friend, and if I hear they got their puckery little assholes cored down there at Thomaston, I'm gonna send them cards saying I hope whoever did it had AIDS.'

Very fiery, Gardener thought. *And the convictions will also look very good on your record when you run for the top spot in two years.*

But he left without saying more, because he also wanted to see them put away.

18

John Webber Garton was convicted of first-degree manslaughter and sentenced to ten to twenty years in Thomaston State Prison.

Steven Bishoff Dubay was convicted of first-degree manslaughter and sentenced to fifteen years in Shawshank State Prison.

Christopher Philip Unwin was tried separately as a juvenile and convicted of second-degree manslaughter. He was sentenced to six months at the South Windham Boys' Training Facility, sentence suspended.

At the time of this writing, all three sentences are under appeal; Garton and Dubay may be seen on any given day girl-watching or playing Penny Pitch in Bassey Park, not far from where Mellon's torn body was found floating against one of the pilings of the Main Street Bridge.

Don Hagarty and Chris Unwin have left town.

At the major trial – that of Garton and Dubay – no one mentioned a clown.

CHAPTER THREE
SIX PHONE CALLS (1985)

1

Stanley Uris Takes a Bath

Patricia Uris later told her mother she should have known something was wrong. She should have known it, she said, because Stanley *never* took baths in the early evening. He showered early each morning and sometimes soaked late at night (with a magazine in one hand and a cold beer in the other), but baths at 7:00 P.M. were not his style.

And then there was the thing about the books. It should have delighted him; instead, in some obscure way she did not understand, it seemed to have upset and depressed him. About three months before that terrible night, Stanley had discovered that a childhood friend of his had turned out to be a writer — not a *real* writer, Patricia told her mother, but a novelist. The name on the books was William Denbrough, but Stanley had sometimes called him Stuttering Bill. He had worked his way through almost all of the man's books; had, in fact, been reading the last on the night of the bath — the night of May 28th, 1985. Patty herself had picked up one of the earlier ones, out of curiosity. She had put it down after just three chapters.

It had not just been a novel, she told her mother later; it had been a horrorbook. She said it just that way, all one word, the way she would have said sexbook. Patty was a sweet, kind woman, but not terribly articulate — she had wanted to tell her mother how much that book had frightened her and why it had upset her, but had not been able. 'It was full of monsters,' she said. 'Full of monsters chasing after little children. There were killings, and . . . I don't know . . . bad feelings and hurt. Stuff like that.' It had, in fact, struck her as almost pornographic; that was the word which kept eluding her, probably because she had never in her life spoken it, although she knew what it meant. 'But Stan felt as if he'd rediscovered one of his childhood chums . . . He talked about writing to him, but I knew

37

he wouldn't . . . I knew those stories made *him* feel bad, too . . . and . . . and . . .'

And then Patty Uris began to cry.

That night, lacking roughly six months of being twenty-eight years from the day in 1957 when George Denbrough had met Pennywise the Clown, Stanley and Patty had been sitting in the den of their home in a suburb of Atlanta. The TV was on. Patty was sitting in the love-seat in front of it, dividing her attention between a pile of sewing and her favorite game-show, *Family Feud*. She simply *adored* Richard Dawson and thought the watch-chain he always wore was terribly sexy, although wild horses would not have drawn this admission out of her. She also liked the show because she almost always got the most popular answers (there were no *right* answers on *Family Feud*, exactly; only the most popular ones). She had once asked Stan why the questions that seemed so easy to her usually seemed so hard to the families on the show. 'It's probably a lot tougher when you're up there under those lights,' Stanley had replied, and it seemed to her that a shadow had drifted over his face. 'Everything's a lot tougher when it's for real. That's when you choke. When it's for real.'

That was probably very true, she decided. Stanley had really fine insights into human nature sometimes. Much finer, she considered, than his old *friend* William Denbrough, who had gotten rich writing a bunch of horrorbooks which appealed to people's baser natures.

Not that the Urises were doing so badly themselves! The suburb where they lived was a fine one, and the home which they had purchased for $87,000 in 1979 would probably now sell quickly and painlessly for $165,000 – not that she wanted to sell, but such things were good to know. She sometimes drove back from the Fox Run Mall in her Volvo (Stanley drove a Mercedes diesel – teasing him, she called it Sedanley) and saw her house, set tastefully back behind low yew hedges, and thought: *Who lives there? Why, I do! Mrs Stanley Uris does!* This was not an entirely happy thought; mixed with it was a pride so fierce that it sometimes made her feel a bit ill. Once upon a time, you see, there had been a lonely eighteen-year-old girl named Patricia Blum who had been refused entry to the after-prom party that was held at the country club in the upstate town of Glointon, New York. She had been refused admission, of course, because her last name rhymed with *plum*. That was her, just a skinny little kike plum, 1967 that had been, and such discrimination was against the law, of course, har-de-har-har-har, and besides, it was all over now. Except that for part of her it was *never* going to be over. Part of her would always be walking back to the car with Michael Rosenblatt, listening to the crushed gravel under her pumps and his rented formal shoes, back to his father's car, which Michael had borrowed for the evening, and which he had spent the afternoon waxing. Part of her would always be walking next to Michael in his rented white dinner jacket – how it had glimmered in the soft spring night! She had been in a pale green evening gown which her mother declared made her look like a mermaid, and the idea of a kike mermaid was pretty funny, har-de-har-har-har. They had walked with their heads up and she had not wept – not then – but she had understood they weren't *walking* back, no, not really; what they had been doing was *slinking* back, *slinking*, rhymes with *stinking*, both of them feeling more Jewish than they had ever felt in their lives, feeling like pawnbrokers, feeling like cattle-car riders, feeling oily, long-nosed, sallow-skinned; feeling like mockies sheenies kikes; wanting to feel angry and not being able to feel angry, the anger came only later, when it didn't matter. At that moment she had only been able to feel ashamed, had only been able to ache. And then someone had laughed. A high shrill tittering laugh like a fast run of notes on a piano, and in the car she had been able to weep, oh you bet, here is the kike mermaid whose name rhymes with *plum* just weeping away like crazy. Mike Rosenblatt had put a clumsy, comforting hand on the back of her neck and she had twisted away from it, feeling ashamed, feeling dirty, feeling *Jewish*.

The house set so tastefully back behind the yew hedges made that better . . . but not *all* better. The hurt and shame were still there, and not even being accepted in this quiet, sleekly well-to-do neighborhood could quite make that endless walk with the sound of grating stones beneath their shoes stop happening. Not even being members of *this* country club, where the *maître d'* always greeted them with a quietly respectful 'Good evening, Mr and Mrs Uris.' She would come home, cradled in her 1984 Volvo, and she would look at her house sitting on its expanse of green lawn, and she would often – all too often, she supposed – think of that shrill titter. And she would hope that the girl who had tittered was living in a shitty tract house with a *goy* husband who beat her, that she had been pregnant three times and had miscarried each time, that her husband cheated on her with diseased women, that she had slipped discs and fallen arches and cysts on her dirty tittering tongue.

She would hate herself for these thoughts, these uncharitable thoughts, and promise to do better – to stop drinking these bitter gall-and-wormwood cocktails. Months would go by when she did not think such thoughts. She would think: *Maybe all of that is finally past me. I am not that girl of eighteen anymore. I am a woman of thirty-six; the girl who heard the endless click and grate of those driveway stones, the girl who twisted away from Mike Rosenblatt's hand when he tried to comfort her because it was a Jewish hand, was half a life ago. That silly little mermaid is dead. I can forget her now and just be myself.* Okay. Good. Great. But then she would be somewhere – at the supermarket, maybe – and she would hear sudden tittering laughter from the next aisle and her back would prickle, her nipples would go hard and hurtful, her hands would tighten on the bar of the shopping cart or just on each other, and she would think: *Someone just told someone else that I'm Jewish, that I'm nothing but a bignose mockie kike, that Stanley's nothing but a bignose mockie kike, he's an accountant, sure, Jews are good with numbers, we let them into the country club, we had to, back in 1981 when that bignose mockie gynecologist won his suit, but we laugh at them, we laugh and laugh and laugh.* Or she would simply hear the phantom click and grate of stones and think *Mermaid! Mermaid!*

Then the hate and shame would come flooding back like a migraine headache and she would despair not only for herself but for the whole human race. Werewolves. The book by Denbrough – the one she had tried to read and then put aside – was about werewolves. Werewolves, shit. What did a man like that know about werewolves?

Most of the time, however, she felt better than that – felt she *was* better than that. She loved her man, she loved her house, and she was usually able to love her life and herself. Things were good. They had not always been that way, of course – were things ever? When she accepted Stanley's engagement ring, her parents had been both angry and unhappy. She had met him at a sorority party. He had come over to her school from New York State University, where he was a scholarship student. They had been introduced by a mutual friend, and by the time the evening was over, she suspected that she loved him. By the mid-term break, she was sure. When spring came around and Stanley offered her a small diamond ring with a daisy pushed through it, she had accepted it.

In the end, in spite of their qualms, her parents had accepted it as well. There was little else they could do, although Stanley Uris would soon be sallying forth into a job-market glutted with young accountants – and when he went into that jungle, he would do so with no family finances to backstop him, and with their only daughter as his hostage to fortune. But Patty was twenty-two, a woman now, and would herself soon graduate with a BA.

'I'll be supporting that four-eyed son of a bitch for the rest of my life,' Patty had heard her father say one night. Her mother and father had gone out for dinner, and her father had drunk a little too much.

'Shh, she'll hear you,' Ruth Blum said.

Patty had lain awake that night until long after midnight, dry-eyed, alternately hot and cold, hating them both. She had spent the next two years trying to get rid of that hate; there was too much hate inside her already. Sometimes when she looked into the mirror she could see the things it was doing to her face, the fine lines it was drawing there. That was a battle she won. Stanley had helped her.

His own parents had been equally concerned about the marriage. They did not, of course, believe their Stanley was destined for a life of squalor and poverty, but they thought 'the kids were being hasty.' Donald Uris and Andrea Bertoly had themselves married in their early twenties, but they seemed to have forgotten the fact.

Only Stanley had seemed sure of himself, confident of the future, unconcerned with the pitfalls their parents saw strewn all about 'the kids.' And in the end it was his confidence rather than their fears which had been justified. In July of 1972, with the ink barely dry on her diploma, Patty had landed a job teaching shorthand and business English in Traynor, a small town forty miles south of Atlanta. When she thought of how she had come by that job, it always struck her as a little – well, eerie. She had made a list of forty possibles from the ads in the teachers' journals, then had written forty letters over five nights – eight each evening – requesting further information on the job, and an application for each. Twenty-two replies indicated that the positions had been filled. In other cases, a more detailed explanation of the skills needed made it clear she wasn't in the running; applying would only be a waste of her time and theirs. She had finished with a dozen possibles. Each looked as likely as any other. Stanley had come in while she was puzzling over them and wondering if she could possibly manage to fill out a dozen teaching applications without going totally bonkers. He looked at the strew of papers on the table and then tapped the letter from the Traynor Superintendent of Schools, a letter which to her looked no more or less encouraging than any of the others.

'There,' he said.

She looked up at him, startled by the simple certainty in his voice. 'Do you know something about Georgia that I don't?'

'Nope. Only time I was ever there was at the movies.'

She looked at him, an eyebrow cocked.

'*Gone with the Wind*. Vivien Leigh. Clark Gable. "I will think about it tomorrow, for tomorrow is anothah day." Do I sound like I come from the South, Patty?'

'Yes. South Bronx. If you don't know anything about Georgia and you've never been there, then why –'

'Because it's right.'

'You can't *know* that, Stanley.'

'Sure I can,' he said simply. 'I *do*.' Looking at him, she had seen he wasn't joking: he really meant it. She had felt a ripple of unease go up her back.

'*How* do you know?'

He had been smiling a little. Now the smile faltered, and for a moment he had seemed puzzled. His eyes had darkened, as if he looked inward, consulting some interior device which ticked and whirred correctly but which, ultimately, he understood no more than the average man understands the workings of the watch on his wrist.

'The turtle couldn't help us,' he said suddenly. He said that quite clearly. She heard it. That inward look – that look of surprised musing – was still on his face, and it was starting to scare her.

'Stanley? What are you talking about? *Stanley?*'

He jerked. She had been eating peaches as she went over the applications, and his hand struck the dish. It fell on the floor and broke. His eyes seemed to clear.

'Oh, shit! I'm sorry.'

'It's all right. Stanley – what were you talking about?'

'I forget,' he said. 'But I think we ought to think Georgia, baby-love.'

'But –'

'Trust me,' he said, so she did.

Her interview had gone smashingly. She had known she had the job when she got on the train back to New York. The head of the Business Department had taken an instant liking to Patty, and she to him; she had almost heard the click. The confirming letter had come a week later. The Traynor Consolidated School Department could offer her $9,200 and a probationary contract.

'You are going to starve,' Herbert Blum said when his daughter told him she intended to take the job. 'And you will be *hot* while you starve.'

'Fiddle-dee-dee, Scarlett,' Stanley said when she told him what her father had said. She had been furious, near tears, but now she began to giggle, and Stanley swept her into his arms.

Hot they had been; starved they had not. They were married on August 19th, 1972. Patty Uris had gone to her marriage bed a virgin. She had slipped naked between cool sheets at a resort hotel in the Poconos, her mood turbulent and stormy – lightning-flares of wanting and delicious lust, dark clouds of fright. When Stanley slid into bed beside her, ropy with muscle, his penis an exclamation point rising from gingery pubic hair, she had whispered: 'Don't hurt me, dear.'

'I will never hurt you,' he said as he took her in his arms, and it was a promise he had kept faithfully until May 27th, 1985 – the night of the bath.

Her teaching had gone well. Stanley got a job driving a bakery truck for one hundred dollars a week. In November of that year, when the Traynor Flats Shopping Center opened, he got a job with the H & R Block office out there for a hundred and fifty. Their combined income was then $17,000 a year – this seemed a king's ransom to them, in those days when gas sold for thirty-five cents a gallon and a loaf of white bread could be had for a nickel less than that. In March 1973, with no fuss and no fanfare, Patty Uris had thrown away her birth-control pills.

In 1975 Stanley quit H & R Block and opened his own business. All four in-laws agreed that this was a foolhardy move. Not that Stanley should not have his own business – God forbid he should not have his own business! But it was too early, all of them agreed, and it put too much of the financial burden on Patty. ('At least until the *pisher* knocks her up,' Herbert Blum told his brother morosely after a night of drinking in the kitchen, 'and then *I'll* be expected to carry them.') The consensus of in-law opinion on the matter was that a man should not even *think* about going into business for himself until he had reached a more serene and mature age – seventy-eight, say.

Again, Stanley seemed almost preternaturally confident. He was young, personable, bright, apt. He had made contacts working for Block. All of these things were givens. But he could not have known that Corridor Video, a pioneer in the nascent videotape business, was about to settle on a huge patch of farmed-out land less than ten miles from the suburb to which the Urises had eventually moved in 1979, nor could he have known that Corridor would be in the market for an independent marketing survey less than a year after its move to Traynor. Even if Stan had been privy to some of this information, he surely could not have believed they would give the job to a young, bespectacled Jew who also happened to be a damnyankee – a Jew with an easy grin, a hipshot way of walking, a taste for bell-bottomed jeans on his days off, and the last ghosts of his adolescent acne still on his face. Yet they had. They had. And it seemed that Stan had known it all along.

His work for CV led to an offer of a full-time position with the company – starting salary, $30,000 a year.

'And that really is only the start,' Stanley told Patty in bed that night. 'They are going to grow like corn in August, my dear. If no one blows up the world in the next ten years or so, they are going to be right up there on the big board along with Kodak and Sony and RCA.'

'So what are you going to do?' she asked, already knowing.

'I am going to tell them what a pleasure it was to do business with them,' he said, and laughed, and drew her close, and kissed her. Moments later he mounted her, and there were climaxes – one, two, and three, like bright rockets going off in a night sky . . . but there was no baby.

His work with Corridor Video had brought him into contact with some of Atlanta's richest and most powerful men – and they were both astonished to find that these men were mostly okay. In them they found a degree of acceptance and broad-minded kindliness that was almost unknown in the North. Patty remembered Stanley once writing home to his mother and father: *The best rich men in America live in Atlanta, Georgia. I am going to help make some of them richer, and they are going to make* me *richer, and no one is going to own me except my wife, Patricia, and since I already own her, I guess that is safe enough.*

By the time they moved from Traynor, Stanley was incorporated and employed six people. In 1983 their income had entered unknown territory – territory of which Patty had heard only the dimmest rumors. This was the fabled land of SIX FIGURES. And it had all happened with the casual ease of slipping into a pair of sneakers on Saturday morning. This sometimes frightened her. Once she had made an uneasy joke about deals with the devil. Stanley had laughed until he almost choked, but to her it hadn't seemed that funny, and she supposed it never would.

The turtle couldn't help us.

Sometimes, for no reason at all, she would wake up with this thought in her mind like the last fragment of an otherwise forgotten dream, and she would turn to Stanley, needing to touch him, needing to make sure he was still there.

It was a good life – there was no wild drinking, no outside sex, no drugs, no boredom, no bitter arguments about what to do next. There was only a single cloud. It was her mother who first mentioned the presence of this cloud. That her mother would be the one to finally do so seemed, in retrospect, preordained. It finally came out as a question in one of Ruth Blum's letters. She wrote Patty once a week, and that particular letter had arrived in the early fall of 1979. It came forwarded from the old Traynor address and Patty read it in a living room filled with cardboard liquor-store cartons from which spilled their possessions, looking forlorn and uprooted and dispossessed.

In most ways it was the usual Ruth Blum Letter from Home: four closely written blue pages, each one headed JUST A NOTE FROM RUTH. Her scrawl was nearly illegible, and Stanley had once complained he could not read a single word his mother-in-law wrote. 'Why would you want to?' Patty had responded.

This one was full of Mom's usual brand of news; for Ruth Blum recollection was a broad delta, spreading out from the moving point of the now in an ever-widening fan of interlocking relationships. Many of the people of whom her mother wrote were beginning to fade in Patty's memory like photographs in an old album, but to Ruth all of them remained fresh. Her concerns for their health and her curiosity about their various doings never seemed to wane, and her prognoses were unfailingly dire. Her father was still having too many stomach-aches. *He* was sure it was just dyspepsia; the idea that he might have an ulcer, she wrote, would not cross his mind until he actually began coughing up blood and probably not even then. *You know your father, dear – he works like a mule, and he also thinks like one sometimes, God should forgive me for saying so.* Randi Harlengen had gotten her tubes tied, they took cysts as big as golf-balls out of her ovaries, no malignancy, thank God, but twenty-seven ovarian cysts, could you *die*? It was the water in New York City, she was quite sure of that – the city air was dirty, too, but she was convinced it was the water that really got to you after awhile. It built up deposits inside a person. She doubted if Patty knew how often she had thanked God that 'you kids' were out in the country, where both air and water – but particularly the water – were healthier (to Ruth all of the South, including Atlanta and Birmingham, was the country). Aunt Margaret was feuding with the power company again. Stella Flanagan had gotten married again, some people never learned. Richie Huber had been fired again.

And in the middle of this chatty – and often catty – outpouring, in the middle of a paragraph, *à propos* of nothing which had gone before or which came after, Ruth Blum had casually asked the Dreaded

Question: 'So when are you and Stan going to make us grandparents? We're all ready to start spoiling him (or her) rotten. And in case you hadn't noticed, Patsy, we're not getting any younger.' And then on to the Bruckner girl from down the block who had been sent home from school because she was wearing no bra and a blouse that you could see right through.

Feeling low and homesick for their old place in Traynor, feeling unsure and more than a little afraid of what might be ahead, Patty had gone into what was to become their bedroom and had lain down upon the mattress (the box spring was still out in the garage, and the mattress, lying all by itself on the big carpetless floor, looked like an artifact cast up on a strange yellow beach). She put her head in her arms and lay there weeping for nearly twenty minutes. She supposed that cry had been coming anyway. Her mother's letter had just brought it on sooner, the way dust hurries the tickle in your nose into a sneeze.

Stanley wanted kids. *She* wanted kids. They were as compatible on that subject as they were on their enjoyment of Woody Allen's films, their more or less regular attendance at synagogue, their political leanings, their dislike of marijuana, a hundred other things both great and small. There had been an extra room in the Traynor house, which they had split evenly down the middle. On the left he had a desk for working and a chair for reading; on the right she had a sewing machine and a cardtable where she did jigsaw puzzles. There had been an agreement between them about that room so strong they rarely spoke of it – it was simply there, like their noses or the wedding rings on their left hands. Someday that room would belong to Andy or to Jenny. But where was that child? The sewing machine and the baskets of fabric and the cardtable and the desk and the La-Z-Boy all kept their places, seeming each month to solidify their holds on their respective positions in the room and to further establish their legitimacy. So she thought, although she never could quite crystallize the thought; like the word *pornographic*, it was a concept that danced just beyond her ability to quantify. But she did remember one time when she got her period, sliding open the cupboard under the bathroom sink to get a sanitary napkin; she remembered looking at the box of Stayfree pads and thinking that the box looked almost smug, seemed almost to be saying: *Hello, Patty! We are your children. We are the only children you will ever have, and we are hungry. Nurse us. Nurse us on blood.*

In 1976, three years after she had thrown away the last cycle of Ovral tablets, they saw a doctor named Harkavay in Atlanta. 'We want to know if there is something wrong,' Stanley said, 'and we want to know if we can do anything about it if there is.'

They took the tests. They showed that Stanley's sperm was perky, that Patty's eggs were fertile, that all the channels that were *supposed* to be open *were* open.

Harkavay, who wore no wedding ring and who had the open, pleasant, ruddy face of a college grad student just back from a midterm skiing vacation in Colorado, told them that maybe it was just nerves. He told them that such a problem was by no means uncommon. He told them that there seemed to be a psychological correlative in such cases that was in some ways similar to sexual impotency – the more you wanted to, the less you could. They would have to relax. They ought, if they could, to forget all about procreation when they had sex.

Stan was grumpy on the way home. Patty asked him why.

'I *never* do,' he said.

'Do what?'

'Think of procreation *during*.'

She began to giggle, even though she was by then feeling a bit lonesome and frightened. And that night, lying in bed, long after she believed that Stanley must be asleep, *he* had frightened her by speaking out of the dark. His voice was flat but nevertheless choked with tears. 'It's me,' he said. 'It's my fault.'

She rolled toward him, groped for him, held him.

'Don't be a stupid,' she said. But her heart was beating fast – much too fast. It wasn't just that he had startled her; it was as if he had looked into her mind and read a secret conviction she held there but of which she had not known until this minute. With no rhyme, no reason, she felt – knew – that he was right. There was something wrong, and it wasn't her. It was him. Something in him.

'Don't be such a klutz,' she whispered fiercely against his shoulder. He was sweating lightly and she became suddenly aware that he was afraid. The fear was coming off him in cold waves; lying naked with him was suddenly like lying naked in front of an open refrigerator.

'I'm not a klutz and I'm not being stupid,' he said in that same voice, which was simultaneously flat and choked with emotion, 'and you know it. It's me. But I don't know *why*.'

'You can't know any such thing.' Her voice was harsh, scolding – her mother's voice when her mother was afraid. And even as she scolded him a shudder ran through her body, twisting it like a whip. Stanley felt it and his arms tightened around her.

'Sometimes,' he said, 'sometimes I think I know why. Sometimes

I have a dream, a bad dream, and I wake up and I think, "I know now. I know what's wrong." Not just you not catching pregnant – everything. Everything that's wrong with my life.'

'Stanley, *nothing's* wrong with your life!'

'I don't mean from inside,' he said. 'From inside is fine. I'm talking about *outside*. Something that should be over and isn't. I wake up from these dreams and think, "My whole pleasant life has been nothing but the eye of some storm I don't understand." I'm afraid. But then it just . . . fades. The way dreams do.'

She knew that he sometimes dreamed uneasily. On half a dozen occasions he had awakened her, thrashing and moaning. Probably there had been other times when she had slept through his dark interludes. Whenever she reached for him, asked him, he said the same thing: *I can't remember.* Then he would reach for his cigarettes and smoke sitting up in bed, waiting for the residue of the dream to pass through his pores like bad sweat.

No kids. On the night of May 28th, 1985 – the night of the bath – their assorted in-laws were still waiting to be grandparents. The extra room was still an extra room; the Stayfree Maxis and Stayfree Minis still occupied their accustomed places in the cupboard under the bathroom sink; the cardinal still paid its monthly visit. Her mother, who was much occupied with her own affairs but not entirely oblivious to her daughter's pain, had stopped asking in her letters and when Stanley and Patty made their twice-yearly trips back to New York there were no more humorous remarks about whether or not they were taking their vitamin E. Stanley had also stopped mentioning babies, but sometimes, when she didn't know she was looking, she saw a shadow on his face. Some shadow. As if he were trying desperately to remember something.

Other than that one cloud, their lives were pleasant enough until the phone rang during the middle of *Family Feud* on the night of May 28th. Patty had six of Stan's shirts, two of her blouses, her sewing kit, and her odd-button box; Stan had the new William Denbrough novel, not even out in paperback yet, in his hands. There was a snarling beast on the front of this book. On the back was a bald man wearing glasses.

Stan was sitting nearer the phone. He picked it up and said, 'Hello – Uris residence.'

He listened, and a frown line delved between his eyebrows. '*Who* did you say?'

Patty felt an instant of fright. Later, shame would cause her to lie and tell her parents that she had known something was wrong from the instant the telephone had rung, but in reality there had only been that one instant, that one quick look up from her sewing. But maybe that was all right. Maybe they had both suspected that something was coming long before that phone call, something that didn't fit with the nice house set tastefully back behind the low yew hedges, something so much a given that it really didn't need much of an acknowledgment . . . that one sharp instant of fright, like the stab of a quickly withdrawn icepick, was enough.

Is it Mom? she mouthed at him in that instant, thinking that perhaps her father, twenty pounds overweight and prone to what he called 'the bellyache' since his early forties, had had a heart attack.

Stan shook his head at her, and then smiled a bit at something the voice on the phone was saying. 'You . . . *you*! Well, I'll be goddamned! Mike! How did y –'

He fell silent again, listening. As his smile faded she recognized – or thought she did – his analytic expression, the one which said someone was unfolding a problem or explaining a sudden change in an ongoing situation or telling him something strange and interesting. This last was probably the case, she gathered. A new client? An old friend? Perhaps. She turned her attention back to the TV, where a woman was flinging her arms around Richard Dawson and kissing him madly. She thought that Richard Dawson must get kissed even more than the Blarney stone. She *also* thought she wouldn't mind kissing him herself.

As she began searching for a black button to match the ones on Stanley's blue denim shirt, Patty was vaguely aware that the conversation was settling into a smoother groove – Stanley grunted occasionally, and once he asked: 'Are you sure, Mike?' Finally, after a very long pause, he said, 'All right, I understand. Yes, I . . . Yes. Yes, everything. I have the picture. I . . . what? . . . No, I can't absolutely *promise* that, but I'll consider it carefully. You know that . . . oh? . . . He did? . . . Well, you bet! Of course I do. Yes . . . sure . . . thank you . . . yes. Bye-bye.' He hung up.

Patty glanced at him and saw him staring blankly into space over the TV set. On her show, the audience was applauding the Ryan family, which had just scored two hundred and eighty points, most of them by guessing that the audience survey would answer 'math' in response to the question 'What class will people say Junior hates most in school?' The Ryans were jumping up and down and screaming joyfully. Stanley, however, was frowning. She would later tell her parents she thought Stanley's face had looked a little off-color, and so she did, but she neglected to tell them she had dismissed it at the time as only a trick of the table-lamp, with its green glass shade.

'Who was that, Stan?'

'Hmmmm?' He looked around at her. She thought the look on his face was one of gentle abstraction, perhaps mixed with minor annoyance. It was only later, replaying the scene in her mind again and again, that she began to believe it was the expression of a man who was methodically unplugging himself from reality, one cord at a time. The face of a man who was heading out of the blue and into the black.

'Who was that on the *phone?*'

'No one,' he said. 'No one, really. I think I'll take a bath.' He stood up.

'What, at seven o'clock?'

He didn't answer, only left the room. She might have asked him if something was wrong, might even have gone after him and asked him if he was sick to his stomach – he was sexually uninhibited, but he could be oddly prim about other things, and it wouldn't be at all unlike him to say he was going to take a bath when what he really had to do was whoops something which hadn't agreed with him. But now a new family, the Piscapos, were being introduced, and Patty just *knew* Richard Dawson would find something funny to say about that name, and besides, she was having the devil's own time finding a black button, although she knew there were loads of them in the button box. They hid, of course; that was the only explanation . . .

So she let him go and did not think of him again until the credit-crawl, when she looked up and saw his empty chair. She had heard the water running into the tub upstairs and had heard it stop five or ten minutes later . . . but now she realized she had never heard the fridge door open and close, and that meant he was up there without a can of beer. Someone had called him up and dropped a big fat problem in his lap, and had she offered him a single word of commiseration? No. Tried to draw him out a little about it? No. Even noticed that something was wrong? For the third time, no. All because of that stupid TV show – she couldn't even really blame the buttons; they were only an excuse.

Okay – she'd take him up a can of Dixie, and sit beside him on the edge of the tub, scrub his back, play Geisha and wash his hair if he wanted her to, and find out just what the problem was . . . or *who* it was.

She got a can of beer out of the fridge and went upstairs with it. The first real disquiet stirred in her when she saw that the bathroom door was shut. Not just part-way closed but shut tight. Stanley *never* closed the door when he was taking a bath. It was something of a joke between them – the closed door meant he was doing something his mother had taught him, the open door meant he would not be averse to doing something the teaching of which his mother had quite properly left to others.

Patty tapped on the door with her nails, suddenly aware, too aware, of the reptilian clicking sound they made on the wood. And surely tapping on the bathroom door, knocking like a guest, was something she had never done before in her married life – not here, not on any other door in the house.

The disquiet suddenly grew strong in her, and she thought of Carson Lake, where she had gone swimming often as a girl. By the first of August the lake was as warm as a tub . . . but then you'd hit a cold pocket that would shiver you with surprise and delight. One minute you were warm; the next moment it felt as if the temperature had plummeted twenty degrees below your hips. Minus the delight, that was how she felt now – as if she had just struck a cold pocket. Only this cold pocket was not below her hips, chilling her long teen-ager's legs in the black depths of Carson Lake.

This one was around her heart.

'Stanley? Stan?'

This time she did more than tap with her nails. She rapped on the door. When there was still no answer, she hammered on it.

'*Stanley?*'

Her heart. Her heart wasn't in her chest anymore. It was beating in her throat, making it hard to breathe.

'*Stanley!*'

In the silence following her shout (and just the sound of herself shouting up here, less than thirty feet from the place where she laid her head down and went to sleep each night, frightened her even more), she heard a sound which brought panic up from the belowstairs part of her mind like an unwelcome guest. Such a small sound, really. It was only the sound of dripping water. *Plink* . . . pause. *Plink* . . . pause. *Plink* . . . pause. *Plink* . . .

She could see the drops forming on the snout of the faucet, growing heavy and fat there, growing *pregnant* there, and then falling off: *plink*.

Just that sound. No other. And she was suddenly, terribly sure that it had been Stanley, not her father, who had been stricken with a heart attack tonight.

With a moan, she gripped the cut-glass doorknob and turned it. Yet still the door would not move: it was locked. And suddenly three *nevers* occurred to Patty Uris in rapid succession: Stanley never took a bath in the early evening, Stanley never closed the door unless he was using the toilet, and Stanley had never locked the door against her at all.

Was it possible, she wondered crazily, to *prepare* for a heart attack?

Patty ran her tongue over her lips – it produced a sound in her head like fine sandpaper sliding along a board – and called his name again. There was still no answer except the steady, deliberate drip of the faucet. She looked down and saw she still held the can of Dixie beer in one hand. She gazed at it stupidly, her heart running like a rabbit in her throat; she gazed at it as if she had never seen a can of beer in her whole life before this minute. And indeed it seemed she never had, or at least never one like this, because when she blinked her eyes it turned into a telephone handset, as black and as threatening as a snake.

'May I help you, ma'am? Do you have a problem?' the snake spat at her. Patty slammed it down in its cradle and stepped away, rubbing the hand which had held it. She looked around and saw she was back in the TV room and understood that the panic which had come into the front of her mind like a prowler walking quietly up a flight of stairs had had its way with her. Now she could remember dropping the beer can outside the bathroom door and pelting head-long back down the stairs, thinking vaguely: *This is all a mistake of some kind and we'll laugh about it later. He filled up the tub and then remembered he didn't have cigarettes and went out to get them before he took his clothes off* –

Yes. Only he had already locked the bathroom door from the inside and because it was too much of a bother to unlock it again he had simply opened the window over the tub and gone down the side of the house like a fly crawling down a wall. Sure, of course, sure –

Panic was rising in her mind again – it was like bitter black coffee threatening to overflow the rim of a cup. She closed her eyes and fought against it. She stood there, perfectly still, a pale statue with a pulse beating in its throat.

Now she could remember running back down here, feet stuttering on the stair-levels, running for the phone, oh yes, oh sure, but who had she meant to call?

Crazily, she thought: *I would call the turtle, but the turtle couldn't help us.*

It didn't matter anyway. She had gotten as far as zero and she must have said something not quite standard, because the operator had asked if she had a problem. She had one, all right, but how did you tell that faceless voice that Stanley had locked himself in the bathroom and didn't answer her, that the steady sound of the water dripping into the tub was killing her heart? *Someone* had to help her. Someone –

She put the back of her hand into her mouth and deliberately bit down on it. She tried to think, tried to *force* herself to think.

The spare keys. The spare keys in the kitchen cupboard.

She got going, and one slippered foot kicked the bag of buttons resting beside her chair. Some of the buttons spilled out, glittering like glazed eyes in the lamplight. She saw at least half a dozen black ones.

Mounted inside the door of the cupboard over the double-basin sink was a large varnished board in the shape of a key – one of Stan's clients had made it in his workshop and given it to him two Christmases ago. The key-board was studded with small hooks, and swinging on these were all the keys the house took, two duplicates of each to a hook. Beneath each hook was a strip of Mystik tape, each strip lettered in Stan's small, neat printing: GARAGE, ATTIC, D'STAIRS BATH, UPSTAIRS BATH, FRONT DOOR, BACK DOOR. Off to one side were ignition-key dupes labelled M–B and VOLVO.

Patty snatched the key marked UPSTAIRS BATH, began to run for the stairs, and then made herself walk. Running made the panic want to come back, and the panic was too close to the surface as it was. Also, if she just walked, maybe nothing would be wrong. Or, if there *was* something wrong, God could look down, see she was just walking, and think: *Oh, good – I pulled a hell of a boner, but I've got time to take it all back.*

Walking as sedately as a woman on her way to a Ladies' Book Circle meeting, she went up the stairs and down to the closed bathroom door.

'Stanley?' she called, trying the door again at the same time, suddenly more afraid than ever, not wanting to use the key because having to use the key was somehow too final. If God hadn't taken it back by the time she used the key, then He never would. The age of miracles, after all, was past.

But the door was still locked; the deliberate *plink* . . . pause of dripping water was her only answer.

Her hand was shaking, and the key chattered all the way around the plate before finding its way into the keyhole and socking itself home. She turned it and heard the lock snap back. She fumbled for the cut-glass knob. It tried to slide through her hand again – not because the door was locked this time but because her palm was wet with sweat. She firmed her grip and made it turn. She pushed the door open.

'Stanley? Stanley? St –'

She looked at the tub with its blue shower curtain bunched at the far end of the stainless steel rod and forgot how to finish her husband's name. She simply stared at the tub, her face as solemn as the face of a child on her first day at school. In a moment she would begin to scream, and Anita MacKenzie next door would hear her, and it would be Anita MacKenzie who would call the police, convinced that someone had broken into the Uris house and that people were being killed over there.

But for now, this one moment, Patty Uris simply stood silent with her hands clasped in front of her against her dark cotton skirt, her face solemn, her eyes huge. And now the look of almost holy solemnity began to transform itself into something else. The huge eyes began to bulge. Her mouth pulled back into a dreadful grin of horror. She wanted to scream and couldn't. The screams were too big to come out.

The bathroom was lit by fluorescent tubes. It was very bright. There were no shadows. You could see everything, whether you wanted to or not. The water in the tub was bright pink. Stanley lay with his back propped against the rear of the tub. His head had rolled so far back on his neck that strands of his short black hair brushed the skin between his shoulder-blades. If his staring eyes had still been capable of seeing, she would have looked upside down to him. His mouth hung open like a sprung door. His expression was one of abysmal, frozen horror. A package of Gillette Platinum Plus razor blades lay on the rim of the tub. He had slit his inner forearms open from wrist to the crook of the elbow, and then had crossed each of these cuts just below the Bracelets of Fortune, making a pair of bloody capital T's. The gashes glared red-purple in the harsh white light. She thought the exposed tendons and ligaments looked like cuts of cheap beef.

A drop of water gathered at the lip of the shiny chromium faucet. It grew fat. Grew *pregnant*, you might say. It sparkled. It dropped. *Plink*.

He had dipped his right forefinger in his own blood and had written a single word on the blue tiles above the tub, written it in two huge, staggering letters. A zig-zagging bloody fingermark fell away from the second letter of this word – his finger had made that mark, she saw, as his hand fell into the tub, where it now floated. She thought

Stanley must have made that mark – his final impression on the world
– as he lost consciousness. It seemed to cry out at her:

Another drop fell into the tub.
Plink.
That did it. Patty Uris at last found her voice. Staring into her
husband's dead and sparkling eyes, she began to scream.

2

Richard Tozier Takes a Powder

Rich felt like he was doing pretty good until the vomiting started.

He had listened to everything Mike Hanlon told him, said all the
right things, answered Mike's questions, even asked a few of his own.
He was vaguely aware that he was doing one of his Voices – not a
strange and outrageous one, like those he sometimes did on the radio
(Kinky Briefcase, Sexual Accountant was his own personal favorite, at
least for the time being, and positive listener response on Kinky was
almost as high as for his listeners' all-time favorite, Colonel Buford
Kissdrivel), but a warm, rich, confident Voice. An I'm-All-Right Voice.
It sounded great, but it was a lie. Just like all the other Voices were lies.

'How much do you remember, Rich?' Mike asked him.

'Very little,' Rich said, and then paused. 'Enough, I suppose.'

'Will you come?'

'I'll come,' Rich said, and hung up.

He sat in his study for a moment, leaning back in the chair
behind his desk, looking out at the Pacific Ocean. A couple of kids
were down on the left, horsing around on their surfboards, not really
riding them. There wasn't much surf to ride.

The clock on the desk – an expensive LED quartz that had
been a gift from a record company rep – said that it was 5:09 P.M.

on May 28th, 1985. It would, of course, be three hours later where Mike was calling from. Dark already. He felt a prickle of gooseflesh at that and he began to move, to do things. First, of course, he put on a record – not hunting, just grabbing blindly among the thousands racked on the shelves. Rock and roll was almost as much a part of his life as the Voices, and it was hard for him to do anything without music playing – and the louder the better. The record he grabbed turned out to be a Motown retrospective. Marvin Gaye, one of the newer members of what Rich sometimes called The All-Dead Band, came on singing 'I Heard It Through the Grapevine.'

 'Oooh-hoo, I bet your wond'rin how I knew . . .'

'Not bad,' Rich said. He even smiled a little. This *was* bad, and it had admittedly knocked him for a loop, but he felt that he was going to be able to handle it. No sweat.

He began getting ready to go back home. And at some point during the next hour it occurred to him that it was as if he had died and had yet been allowed to make all of his own final business dispositions . . . not to mention his own funeral arrangements. And he felt as if he was doing pretty good. He tried the travel agent he used, thinking she would probably be on the freeway and headed home by now but taking a shot on the off-chance. For a wonder, he caught her in. He told her what he needed and she asked him for fifteen minutes.

'I owe you one, Carol,' he said. They had progressed from Mr Tozier and Ms Feeny to Rich and Carol over the last three years – pretty chummy, considering they had never met face to face.

'All right, pay off,' she said. 'Can you do Kinky Briefcase for me?'

Without even pausing – if you had to pause to find your Voice, there was usually no Voice there to be found – Rich said: 'Kinky Briefcase, Sexual Accountant, here – I had a fellow come in the other day who wanted to know what the worst thing was about getting AIDS.' His voice had dropped slightly; at the same time its rhythm had speeded up and become jaunty – it was clearly an American voice and yet it somehow conjured up images of a wealthy British colonial chappie who was as charming, in his muddled way, as he was addled. Rich hadn't the slightest idea who Kinky Briefcase really was, but he was sure he always wore white suits, read *Esquire*, and drank things which came in tall glasses and smelled like coconut-scented shampoo. 'I told him right away – trying to explain to your mother how you picked it up from a Haitian girl. Until next time, this is Kinky Briefcase, Sexual Accountant, saying "You need my card if you can't get hard." '

Carol Feeny screamed with laughter. 'That's perfect! *Perfect*! My boyfriend says he doesn't believe you can just *do* those voices, he says it's got to be a voice-filter gadget or something –'

'Just talent, my dear,' Rich said. Kinky Briefcase was gone. W. C. Fields, top hat, red nose, golf-bags and all, was here. 'I'm so stuffed with talent I have to plug up all my bodily orifices to keep it from just running out like . . . well, just running out.'

She went off into another screamy gale of laughter, and Rich closed his eyes. He could feel the beginnings of a headache.

'Be a dear and see what you can do, would you?' he asked, still being W. C. Fields, and hung up on her laughter.

Now he had to go back to being himself, and that was hard – it got harder to do that every year. It was easier to be brave when you were someone else.

He was trying to pick out a pair of good loafers and had about decided to stick with sneakers when the phone rang again. It was Carol Feeny, back in record time. He felt an instant urge to fall into the Buford Kissdrivel Voice and fought it off. She had been able to get him a first-class seat on the American Airlines red-eye nonstop from LAX to Boston. He would leave LA at 9:03 P.M. and arrive at Logan about five o'clock tomorrow morning. Delta would fly him out of Boston at 7:30 A.M. and into Bangor, Maine, at 8:20. She had gotten him a full-sized sedan from Avis, and it was only twenty-six miles from the Avis counter at Bangor International Airport to the Derry town line.

Only twenty-six miles? Rich thought. *Is that all, Carol? Well, maybe it is – in miles, anyway. But you don't have the slightest idea how far it really is to Derry, and I don't, either. But oh God, oh dear God, I am going to find out.*

'I didn't try for a room because you didn't tell me how long you'd be there,' she said. 'Do you –'

'No – let me take care of that,' Rich said, and then Buford Kissdrivel took over. 'You've been a peach, my deah. A *Jawja* peach, a cawse.'

He hung up gently on her – always leave em laughing – and then dialed 207–555–1212 for State of Maine Directory Assistance. He wanted a number for the Derry Town House. God, *there* was a name from the past. He hadn't thought of the Derry Town House in – what? – ten years? twenty? twenty-five years, even? Crazy as it seemed, he guessed it *had* been at least twenty-five years, and if Mike hadn't called, he supposed he might never have thought of it again in his life. And yet there had been a time in his life when he had walked past that great red brick pile every day – and on more than one occasion he had *run* past it, with Henry Bowers and Belch Huggins and that other big boy, Victor Somebody-or-Other, in hot pursuit, all of them yelling little pleasantries like *We're gonna getcha, fuckface! Gonna getcha, you little smartass! Gonna getcha, you foureyed faggot!* Had *they ever gotten him?*

Before Rich could remember, an operator was asking him what city, please.

'In Derry, operator –'

Derry! God! Even the word *felt strange and forgotten in his mouth; saying it was like kissing an antique.*

'– do you have a number for the Derry Town House?'

'One moment, sir.'

No way. It'll be gone. Razed in an urban-renewal program. Changed into an Elks' Hall or a Bowl-a-Drome or an Electric Dreamscape Video Arcade. Or maybe burned down one night when the odds finally ran out on some drunk shoe salesman smoking in bed. All gone, Richie – just like the glasses Henry Bowers always used to rag you about. What's that Springsteen song say? Glory days . . . gone in the wink of a young girl's eye. What young girl? Why, Bev, of course. Bev . . .

Changed the Town House might be, but gone it apparently was not, because a blank, robotic voice now came on the line and said: 'The . . . number . . . is . . . 9 . . . 4 . . . 1 . . . 8 . . . 2 . . . 8 . . . 2. Repeat: . . . the . . . number . . . is . . .'

But Rich had gotten it the first time. It was a pleasure to hang up on that droning voice – it was too easy to imagine some great globular Directory Assistance monster buried somewhere in the earth, sweating rivets and holding thousands of telephones in thousands of jointed chromium tentacles – the Ma Bell version of Spidey's nemesis, Dr Octopus. Each year the world Rich lived in felt more and more like a huge electronic haunted house in which digital ghosts and frightened human beings lived in uneasy coexistence.

Still standing. To paraphrase Paul Simon, still standing after all these years.

He dialed the hotel he had last seen through the horn-rimmed spectacles of his childhood. Dialing that number, 1–207–941–8282, was fatally easy. He held the telephone to his ear, looking out his study's wide picture window. The surfers were gone; a couple were walking slowly up the beach, hand in hand, where they had been. The couple could have been a poster on the wall of the travel agency where Carol Feeny worked, that was how perfect they were. Except, that was, for the fact they were both wearing glasses.

Gonna getcha, fuckface! Gonna break your glasses!

Criss, his mind sent up abruptly. *His last name was Criss. Victor Criss.*

Oh Christ, that was nothing he wanted to know, not at this late date, but it didn't seem to matter in the slightest. Something was happening down there in the vaults, down there where Rich Tozier kept his own personal collection of Golden Oldies. Doors were opening.

Only they're not records down there, are they? Down there you're not Rich 'Records' Tozier, hot-shot KLAD deejay and the Man of a Thousand Voices, are you? And those things that are opening . . . they aren't exactly doors, are they?

He tried to shake these thoughts off.

Thing to remember is that I'm okay. I'm okay, you're okay, Rich Tozier's okay. Could use a cigarette, is all.

He had quit four years ago but he could use one now, all right.

They're not records but dead bodies. You buried them deep but now there's some kind of crazy earthquake going on and the ground is spitting them up to the surface. You're not Rich 'Records' Tozier down there; down there you're just Richie 'Four-Eyes' Tozier and you're with your buddies and you're so scared it feels like your balls are turning into Welch's grape jelly. Those aren't doors, and they're not opening. Those are crypts, Richie. They're cracking open and the vampires you thought were dead are all flying out again.

A cigarette, just one. Even a Carlton would do, for Christ's sweet sake.

Gonna getcha, four-eyes! Gonna make you EAT that fuckin bookbag!

'Town House,' a male voice with a Yankee tang said; it had travelled all the way across New England, the Midwest, and under the casinos of Las Vegas to reach his ear.

Rich asked the voice if he could reserve a suite of rooms at the Town House, beginning tomorrow. The voice told him he could, and then asked him for how long.

'I can't say. I've got –' He paused briefly, minutely.

What *did* he have, exactly? In his mind's eye he saw a boy with a tartan bookbag running from the tough guys; he saw a boy who wore glasses, a thin boy with a pale face that had somehow seemed to scream *Hit me! Go on and hit me!* in some mysterious way to every passing bully. *Here's my lips! Mash them back against my teeth! Here's my nose! Bloody it for sure and break it if you can! Box an ear so it swells up like a cauliflower! Split an eyebrow! Here's my chin, go for the knockout button! Here are my eyes, so blue and so magnified behind these hateful, hateful glasses, these horn-rimmed specs one bow of which is held on with adhesive tape. Break the specs! Drive a shard of glass into one of these eyes and close it forever! What the hell!*

He closed his eyes and said: 'I've got business in Derry, you see. I don't know how long the transaction will take. How about three days, with an option to renew?'

'An option to renew?' the desk-clerk asked doubtfully, and Rich waited patiently for the fellow to work it over in his mind. 'Oh, I get you! That's very good!'

'Thank you, and I ... ah ... hope you can vote for us in Novembah,' John F. Kennedy said. 'Jackie wants to ... ah ... do ovuh the ah ... Oval Office, and I've got a job all lined up for my ... ah ... brothah Bobby.'

'Mr Tozier?'

'Yes.'

'Okay ... somebody else got on the line there for a few seconds.'

Just an old pol from the DOP, Rich thought. *That's Dead Old Party, in case you should wonder. Don't worry about it.* A shudder worked through him, and he told himself again, almost desperately: *You're okay, Rich.*

'I heard it, too,' Rich said. 'Must have been a line cross-over. How we looking on that room?'

'Oh, there's no problem with that,' the clerk said. 'We do business here in Derry, but it really never booms.'

'Is that so?'

'Oh, ayuh,' the clerk agreed, and Rich shuddered again. He had forgotten that, too – that simple northern New England-ism for yes. *Oh, ayuh.*

Gonna getcha, creep! the ghostly voice of Henry Bowers screamed, and he felt more crypts cracking open inside of him; the stench he smelled was not decayed bodies but decayed memories, and that was somehow worse.

He gave the Town House clerk his American Express number and hung up. Then he called Steve Covall, the KLAD program director.

'What's up, Rich?' Steve asked. The last Arbitron ratings had shown KLAD at the top of the cannibalistic Los Angeles FM-rock market, and ever since then Steve had been in an excellent mood – thank God for small favors.

'Well, you might be sorry you asked,' he told Steve. 'I'm taking a powder.'

'Taking –' He could hear the frown in Steve's voice. 'I don't think I get you, Rich.'

'I have to put on my boogie shoes. I'm going away.'

'What do you mean, going away? According to the log I have right here in front of me, you're on the air tomorrow from two in the afternoon until six P.M., just like always. In fact, you're interviewing Clarence Clemons in the studio at four. You know Clarence Clemons, Rich? As in "Come on and *blow*, Big Man?" '

'Clemons can talk to Mike O'Hara as well as he can to me.'

'Clarence doesn't *want* to talk to Mike, Rich. Clarence doesn't want to talk to Bobby Russell. He doesn't want to talk to *me*. Clarence is a big fan of Buford Kissdrivel and Wyatt the Homicidal Bag-Boy. He wants to talk to *you*, my friend. And I have no interest in having a pissed-off two-hundred-and-fifty-pound saxophone player who was once almost drafted by a pro football team running amok in my studio.'

'I don't think he has a history of running amok,' Rich said. 'I mean, we're talking Clarence Clemons here, not Keith Moon.'

There was silence on the line. Rich waited patiently.

'You're not serious, are you?' Steve finally asked. He sounded plaintive: 'I mean, unless your mother just died or you've got to have a brain tumor out or something, this is called crapping out.'

'I have to go, Steve.'

'*Is* your mother sick? Did she God-forbid die?'

'She died ten years ago.'

'Have you got a brain tumor?'

'Not even a rectal polyp.'

'This is not funny, Rich.'

'No.'

'You're being a fucking busher, and I don't like it.'

'I don't like it either, but I have to go.'

'Where? Why? What is this? *Talk* to me, Rich!'

'Someone called me. Someone I used to know a long time ago. In another place. Back then something happened. I made a promise. We all promised that we would go back if the something started happening again. And I guess it has.'

'What something are we talking about, Rich?'

'I'd just as soon not say.' *Also, you'll think I'm crazy if I tell you the truth: I don't remember.*

'When did you make this famous promise?'

'A long time ago. In the summer of 1958.'

There was another long pause, and he knew Steve Covall was trying to decide if Rich 'Records' Tozier, aka Buford Kissdrivel, aka Wyatt the Homicidal Bag-Boy, etc., etc., was having him on or was having some kind of mental breakdown.

'You would have been just a kid,' Steve said flatly.

'Eleven. Going on twelve.'

Another long pause. Rich waited patiently.

'All right,' Steve said. 'I'll shift the rotation – put Mike in for you. I can call Chuck Foster to pull a few shifts, I guess, if I can find what Chinese restaurant he's currently holed up in. I'll do it because we go back a long way together. But I'm never going to forget you bushed out on me, Rich.'

'Oh, get down off it,' Rich said, but the headache was getting worse. He knew what he was doing; did Steve really think he didn't? 'I need a few days off, is all. You're acting like I took a shit on our FCC charter.'

'A few days off for what? The reunion of your Cub Scout pack in Shithouse Falls, North Dakota, or Pussyhump City, West Virginia?'

'Actually I think Shithouse Falls in Arkansas, bo,' Buford Kissdrivel said in his big hollow-barrel Voice, but Steve was not to be diverted.

'Because you made a promise when you were eleven? Kids don't make serious promises when they're eleven, for Christ's sake! And it's not even that, Rich, and you know it. This is not an insurance company; this is not a law office. This is *show-business*, be it ever so humble, and you fucking well know it. If you had given me a week's notice, I wouldn't be holding this phone in one hand and a bottle of Mylanta in the other. You are putting my balls to the wall, and you know it, so don't you insult my intelligence!'

Steve was nearly screaming now, and Rich closed his eyes. *I'm never going to forget it*, Steve had said, and Rich supposed he never would. But Steve had also said kids didn't make serious promises when they were eleven, and that wasn't true at all. Rich couldn't remember what the promise had been – wasn't sure he *wanted* to remember – but it had been plenty serious.

'Steve, I have to.'

'Yeah. And I told you I could handle it. So go ahead. Go ahead, you busher.'

'Steve, this is rid –'

But Steve had already hung up. Rich put the phone down. He had barely started away from it when it began to ring again, and he knew without picking it up that it was Steve again, madder than ever. Talking to him at this point would do no good; things would just get uglier. He slid the switch on the side of the phone to the right, cutting it off in mid-ring.

He went upstairs, pulled two suitcases out of the closet, and filled them with a barely glanced-at conglomeration of clothes – jeans, shirts, underwear, socks. It would not occur to him until later that he had taken nothing but kid-clothes. He carried the suitcases back downstairs.

On the den wall was a black-and-white Ansel Adams photograph of Big Sur. Rich swung it back on hidden hinges, exposing a barrel safe. He opened it, pawed his way past the paperwork – the house here, poised cozily between the fault-line and the brush-fire zone, twenty acres of timberland in Idaho, a bunch of stocks. He had bought the stocks seemingly at random – when his broker saw Rich coming, he immediately clutched his head – but the stocks had all risen steadily over the years. He was sometimes surprised by the thought that he was almost – not quite, but almost – a rich man. All courtesy of rock-and-roll music . . . and the Voices, of course.

House, acres, stocks, insurance policy, even a copy of his last will and testament. *The strings that bind you tight to the map of your life*, he thought.

There was a sudden wild impulse to whip out his Zippo and light it up, the whole whore's combine of wherefores and know-ye-all-men-by-these-present's and the-bearer-of-this-certificate-is-entitled's. And he could do it, too. The papers in his safe had suddenly ceased to signify anything.

The first real terror struck him then, and there was nothing at all supernatural about it. It was only a realization of how easy it was to trash your life. That was what was so scary. You just dragged the fan up to everything you had spent the years raking together and turned the mother-fucker on. Easy. Burn it up or blow it away, then just take a powder.

Behind the papers, which were only currency's second cousins, was the real stuff. The cash. Four thousand dollars in tens, twenties, and fifties.

Taking it now, stuffing it into the pocket of his jeans, he wondered if he hadn't somehow known what he was doing when he put the money in here – fifty bucks one month, a hundred and twenty the next, maybe only ten the month after that. Rathole money. Taking-a-powder money.

'Man, that's scary,' he said, barely aware he had spoken. He was looking blankly out the big window at the beach. It was deserted now, the surfers gone, the honeymooners (if that was what they had been) gone, too.

Ah, yes, doc — it all comes back to me now. Remember Stanley Uris, for instance? Bet your fur I do . . . Remember how we used to say that, and think it was so cool? Stanley Urine, the big kids called him. 'Hey, Urine! Hey, you fuckin Christ-killer! Where ya goin? One of ya fag friends gonna give you a bee jay?'

He slammed the safe door shut and swung the picture back into place. When had he last thought of Stan Uris? Five years ago? Ten? Twenty? Rich and his family had moved away from Derry in the spring of 1960, and how fast all of their faces faded, his gang, that pitiful bunch of losers with their little clubhouse in what had been known then as the Barrens — funny name for an area as lush with growth as that place had been. Kidding themselves that they were jungle explorers, or Seabees carving out a landing strip on a Pacific atoll while they held off the Japs, kidding themselves that they were dam-builders, cowboys, spacemen on a jungle world, you name it, but whatever you name it, don't let's forget what it really was: it was hiding. Hiding from the big kids. Hiding from Henry Bowers and Victor Criss and Belch Huggins and the rest of them. What a bunch of losers they had been — Stan Uris with his big Jew-boy nose, Bill Denbrough who could say nothing but '*Hi-yo, Silver!*' without stuttering so badly that it drove you almost dogshit, Beverly Marsh with her bruises and her cigarettes rolled into the sleeve of her blouse, Ben Hanscom who had been so big he looked like a human version of Moby Dick, and Richie Tozier with his thick glasses and his A averages and his wise mouth and his face which just begged to be pounded into new and exciting shapes. Was there a word for what they had been? Oh yes. There always was. *Le mot juste.* In this case *le mot juste* was *wimps.*

How it came back, how all of it came back . . . and now he stood here in his den shivering as helplessly as a homeless mutt caught in a thunderstorm, shivering because the guys he had run with weren't all he remembered. There were other things, things he hadn't thought of in years, trembling just below the surface.

Bloody things.

A darkness. Some darkness.

The house on Neibolt Street, and Bill screaming: *You k-killed my brother, you fuh-fuh-fucker!*

Did he remember? Just enough not to want to remember any more, and you could bet your fur on *that.*

A smell of garbage, a smell of shit, and a smell of something else. Something worse than either. It was the stink of the beast, the stink of It, down there in the darkness under Derry where the machines thundered on and on. He remembered George –

But that was too much and he ran for the bathroom, blundering into his Eames chair on his way and almost falling. He made it . . . barely. He slid across the slick tiles to the toilet on his knees like some weird break-dancer, gripped the edges, and vomited everything in his guts. Even then it wouldn't stop; suddenly he could see Georgie Denbrough as if he had last seen him yesterday, Georgie who had been the start of it all, Georgie who had been murdered in the fall of 1957. Georgie had died right after the flood, one of his arms had been ripped from its socket, and Rich had blocked all of that out of his memory. But sometimes those things come back, oh yes indeedy, they come back, sometimes they come back.

The spasm passed and Rich groped blindly for the flush. Water roared. His early supper, regurgitated in hot chunks, vanished tastefully down the drain.

Into the sewers.

Into the pound and stink and darkness of the sewers.

He closed the lid, laid his forehead against it, and began to cry. It was the first time he had cried since his mother died in 1975. Without even thinking of what he was doing, he cupped his hands under his eyes, and the contact lenses he wore slipped out and lay glistening in his palms.

Forty minutes later, feeling husked-out and somehow cleansed, he threw his suitcases into the trunk of his MG and backed it out of the garage. The light was fading. He looked at his house with the new plantings, he looked at the beach, at the water, which had taken on the cast of pale emeralds broken by a narrow track of beaten gold. And a conviction stole over him that he would never see any of this again, that he was a dead man walking.

'Going home now,' Rich Tozier whispered to himself. 'Going home, God help me, going home.'

He put the car in gear and went, feeling again how easy it had been to slip through an unsuspected fissure in what he had considered a solid life – how easy it was to get over onto the dark side, to sail out of the blue and into the black.

Out of the blue and into the black, yes, that was it. Where anything might be waiting.

3

Ben Hanscom Takes a Drink

If, on that night of May 28th, 1985, you had wanted to find the man *Time* magazine had called 'perhaps the most promising young architect in America' ('Urban Energy Conservation and the Young Turks,' *Time*, October 15, 1984), you would have had to drive west out of Omaha on Interstate 80 to do it. You'd have taken the Swedholm exit and then Highway 81 to downtown Swedholm (of which there isn't much). There you'd turn off on Highway 92 at Bucky's Hi-Hat Eat-Em-Up ('Chicken Fried Steak Our Specialty') and once out in the country again you'd hang a right on Highway 63, which runs straight as a string through the deserted little town of Gatlin and finally into Hemingford Home. Downtown Hemingford Home made downtown Swedholm look like New York City; the business district consisted of eight buildings, five on one side and three on the other. There was the Kleen Kut barber shop (propped in the window a yellowing hand-lettered sign fully fifteen years old read IF YOUR A 'HIPPY' GET YOUR HAIR CUT SOMEWHERES ELSE), the second-run movie house, the five-and-dime. There was a branch of the Nebraska Homeowners' Bank, a 76 gas station, a Rexall Drug, and the National Farmstead & Hardware Supply – which was the only business in town which looked halfway prosperous.

And, near the end of the main drag, set off a little way from the other buildings like a pariah and resting on the edge of the big empty, you had your basic roadhouse – the Red Wheel. If you had gotten that far, you would have seen in the potholed dirt parking lot an aging 1968 Cadillac convertible with double CB antennas on the back. The vanity plate on the front read simply: BEN'S CADDY. And inside, walking toward the bar, you would have found your man – lanky, sunburned, dressed in a chambray shirt, faded jeans, and a pair of scuffed engineer boots. There were faint squint-lines around the corners of his eyes, but nowhere else. He looked perhaps ten years younger than his actual age, which was thirty-eight.

'Hello, Mr Hanscom,' Ricky Lee said, putting a paper napkin on the bar as Ben sat down. Ricky Lee sounded a trifle surprised, and he was. He had never seen Hanscom in the Wheel on a week-night before. He came in regularly every Friday night for two beers, and every Saturday night for four or five: he always asked after Ricky Lee's three boys; he always left the same five-dollar tip under his beer stein when he took off. In terms of both professional conversation and personal regard, he was far and away Ricky Lee's favorite customer. The ten dollars a week (and the fifty left under the stein at each Christmas-time over the last five years) was fine enough, but the man's company was worth far more. Worthwhile company was always a rarity, but in a honkytonk like this, where talk always came cheap, it was scarcer than hen's teeth.

Although Hanscom's roots were in New England and he had gone to college in California, there was more than a touch of the extravagant Texan about him. Ricky Lee counted on Ben Hanscom's Friday-Saturday-night stops, because he had learned over the years that he *could* count on them. Mr Hanscom might be building a skyscraper in New York (where he already had three of the most talked-about buildings in the city), a new art gallery in Redondo Beach, or a business building in Salt Lake City, but come Friday night the door leading to the parking lot would open sometime between eight o'clock and nine-thirty and in he would stroll, as if he lived no farther than the other side of town and had decided to drop in because there was nothing good on TV. He had his own Learjet and a private landing strip on his farm in Junkins.

Two years ago he had been in London, first designing and then overseeing the construction of the new BBC communications center – a building that was still hotly debated pro and con in the British press (the *Guardian*: 'Perhaps the most beautiful building to be constructed in London over the last twenty years'; the *Mirror*: 'Other than the face of my mother-in-law after a pub-crawl, the ugliest thing I have ever seen'). When Mr Hanscom took that job, Ricky Lee had thought, *Well, I'll see him again sometime. Or maybe he'll just forget all about us.* And indeed, the Friday night after Ben Hanscom left for England had come and gone with no sign of him, although Ricky Lee found himself looking up quickly every time the door opened between eight and nine-thirty. *Well, I'll see him again sometime. Maybe.* Sometime turned out to be the next night. The door had opened at quarter past nine and in he had ambled, wearing jeans and a GO 'BAMA tee-shirt and his old engineer boots, looking like he'd come from no farther away than cross-town. And when Ricky Lee cried almost joyfully 'Hey, Mr Hanscom! Christ! What are *you* doin here?,' Mr Hanscom had looked mildly surprised, as if there was nothing in the least unusual about his being here. Nor had that been a one-shot; he had showed up every Saturday during the two-year course of his active involvement in the BBC job. He left London each Saturday morning at 11:00 A.M.

on the Concorde, he told a fascinated Ricky Lee, and arrived at Kennedy in New York at 10:15 A.M. – forty-five minutes *before* he left London, at least by the clock ('God, it's like time travel, ain't it?' an impressed Ricky Lee had said). A limousine was standing by to take him over to Teterboro Airport in New Jersey, a trip which usually took no more than an hour on Saturday morning. He could be in the cockpit of his Lear before noon with no trouble at all, and touching down in Junkins by two-thirty. If you head west fast enough, he told Ricky, the day just seems to go on forever. He would take a two-hour nap, spend an hour with his foreman and half an hour with his secretary. He would eat supper and then come on over to the Red Wheel for an hour and a half or so. He always came in alone, he always sat at the bar, and he always left the way he had come in, although God knew there were plenty of women in this part of Nebraska who would have been happy to screw the socks off him. Back at the farm he would catch six hours of sleep and then the whole process would reverse itself. Ricky had never had a customer who failed to be impressed with this story. Maybe he's gay, a woman had told him once. Ricky Lee glanced at her briefly, taking in the carefully styled hair, the carefully tailored clothes which undoubtedly had designer labels, the diamond chips at her ears, the look in her eyes, and knew she was from somewhere back east, probably New York, out here on a brief duty visit to a relative or maybe an old school chum, and couldn't wait to get out again. No, he had replied. Mr Hanscom ain't no sissy. She had taken a pack of Doral cigarettes from her purse and held one between her red, glistening lips until he lit it for her. How do you know? she had asked, smiling a little. I just do, he said. And he did. He thought of saying to her: I think he's the most God-awful lonely man I ever met in my life. But he wasn't going to say any such thing to this New York woman who was looking at him like he was some new and amusing type of life.

Tonight Mr Hanscom looked a little pale, a little distracted.

'Hello, Ricky Lee,' he said, sitting down, and then fell to studying his hands.

Ricky Lee knew he was slated to spend the next six or eight months in Colorado Springs, overseeing the start of the Mountain States Cultural Center, a sprawling six-building complex which would be cut into the side of a mountain. *When it's done people are going to say it looks like a giant-kid left his toy blocks all over a flight of stairs,* Ben had told Ricky Lee. *Some will, anyway, and they'll be at least half-right. But I think it's going to work. It's the biggest thing I've ever tried and putting it up is going to be scary as hell, but I think it's going to work.*

Ricky Lee supposed it was possible that Mr Hanscom had a little touch of stage fright. Nothing surprising about that, and nothing wrong about it, either. When you got big enough to be noticed, you got big enough to come gunning for. Or maybe he just had a touch of the bug. There was a hell of a lively one going around.

Ricky Lee got a beer stein from the backbar and reached for the Olympia tap.

'Don't do that, Ricky Lee.'

Ricky Lee turned back, surprised – and when Ben Hanscom looked up from his hands, he was suddenly frightened. Because Mr Hanscom didn't look like he had stage fright, or the virus that was going around, or anything like that. He looked like he had just taken a terrible blow and was still trying to understand whatever it was that had hit him.

Someone died. He ain't married but every man's got a fambly, and someone in his just bit the dust. That's what happened, just as sure as shit rolls downhill from a privy.

Someone dropped a quarter into the juke-box, and Barbara Mandrell started to sing about a drunk man and a lonely woman.

'You okay, Mr Hanscom?'

Ben Hanscom looked at Ricky Lee out of eyes that suddenly looked ten – no, twenty – years older than the rest of his face, and Ricky Lee was astonished to observe that Mr Hanscom's hair was graying. He had never noticed any gray in his hair before.

Hanscom smiled. The smile was ghastly, horrible. It was like watching a corpse smile.

'I don't think I am, Ricky Lee. No sir. Not tonight. Not at all.'

Ricky Lee set the stein down and walked back over to where Hanscom sat. The bar was as empty as a Monday-night bar far outside of football season can get. There were fewer than twenty paying customers in the place. Annie was sitting by the door into the kitchen, playing cribbage with the short-order cook.

'Bad news, Mr Hanscom?'

'Bad news, that's right. Bad news from home.' He looked at Ricky Lee. He looked through Ricky Lee.

'I'm sorry to hear that, Mr Hanscom.'

'Thank you, Ricky Lee.'

He fell silent and Ricky Lee was about to ask him if there was anything he could do when Hanscom said:

'What's your bar whiskey, Ricky Lee?'

'For everyone else in this dump it's Four Roses,' Ricky Lee said. 'But for you I think it's Wild Turkey.'

Hanscom smiled a little at that. 'That's good of you, Ricky Lee. I think you better grab that stein after all. What you do is fill it up with Wild Turkey.'

'*Fill* it?' Ricky Lee asked, frankly astonished. 'Christ, I'll have to roll you out of here!' *Or call an ambulance*, he thought.

'Not tonight,' Hanscom said. 'I don't think so.'

Ricky Lee looked carefully into Mr Hanscom's eyes to see if he could possibly be joking, and it took less than a second to see that he wasn't. So he got the stein from the backbar and the bottle of Wild Turkey from one of the shelves below. The neck of the bottle chattered against the rim of the stein as he began to pour. He watched the whiskey gurgle out, fascinated in spite of himself. Ricky Lee decided it was more than just a touch of the Texan that Mr Hanscom had in him: this had to be the biggest goddamned shot of whiskey he ever had poured or ever would pour in his life.

Call an ambulance, my ass. He drinks this baby and I'll be calling Parker and Waters in Swedholm for their funeral hack.

Nevertheless he brought it back and set it down in front of Hanscom; Ricky Lee's father had once told him that if a man was in his right mind, you brought him what he paid for, be it piss or poison. Ricky Lee didn't know if that was good advice or bad, but he knew that if you tended bar for a living, it went a fair piece toward saving you from being chomped into gator-bait by your own conscience.

Hanscom looked at the monster drink thoughtfully for a moment and then asked, 'What do I owe you for a shot like that, Ricky Lee?'

Ricky Lee shook his head slowly, eyes still on the steinful of whiskey, not wanting to look up and meet those socketed, staring eyes. 'No,' he said. 'This one is on the house.'

Hanscom smiled again, this time more naturally. 'Why, I thank you, Ricky Lee. Now I am going to show you something I learned about in Peru, in 1978. I was working with a guy named Frank Billings – understudying with him, I guess you'd say. Frank Billings was the best damned architect in the world, I think. He caught a fever and the doctors injected about a billion different antibiotics into him and not a single one of them touched it. He burned for two weeks and then he died. What I'm going to show you I learned from the Indians who worked on the project. The local popskull is pretty potent. You take a slug and you think it's going down pretty mellow, no problem, and then all at once it's like someone lit a blowtorch in your mouth and aimed it down your throat. But the Indians drink it like Coca-Cola, and I rarely saw one drunk, and I *never* saw one with a hangover. Never had the sack to try it their way myself. But I think I'll give it a go tonight. Bring me some of those lemon wedges there.'

Ricky Lee brought him four and laid them out neatly on a fresh napkin next to the stein of whiskey. Hanscom picked one of them up, tilted his head back like a man about to administer eyedrops to himself, and then began to squeeze raw lemon-juice into his right nostril.

'Holy Jesus!' Ricky Lee cried, horrified.

Hanscom's throat worked. His face flushed . . . and then Ricky Lee saw tears running down the flat planes of his face toward his ears. Now the Spinners were on the juke, singing about the rubberband-man. 'Oh Lord, I just don't know how much of this I can stand,' the Spinners sang.

Hanscom groped blindly on the bar, found another slice of lemon, and squeezed the juice into his other nostril.

'You're gonna fucking kill yourself,' Ricky Lee whispered.

Hanscom tossed both of the wrung-out lemon wedges onto the bar. His eyes were fiery red and he was breathing in hitching, wincing gasps. Clear lemon-juice dripped from both of his nostrils and trickled down to the corners of his mouth. He groped for the stein, raised it, and drank a third of it. Frozen, Ricky Lee watched his adam's apple go up and down.

Hanscom set the stein aside, shuddered twice, then nodded. He looked at Ricky Lee and smiled a little. His eyes were no longer red.

'Works about like they said it did. You are so fucking concerned about your nose that you never feel what's going down your throat at all.'

'You're crazy, Mr Hanscom,' Ricky Lee said.

'You bet your fur,' Mr Hanscom said. 'You remember that one, Ricky Lee? We used to say that when we were kids "You bet your fur." Did I ever tell you I used to be fat?'

'No sir, you never did,' Ricky Lee whispered. He was now convinced that Mr Hanscom had received some intelligence so dreadful that the man really *had* gone crazy . . . or at least taken temporary leave of his senses.

'I was a regular butterball. Never played baseball or basketball, always got caught first when we played tag, couldn't keep out of my own way. I was fat, all right. And there were these fellows in my home town who used to take after me pretty regularly. There was a fellow named Reginald Huggins, only everyone called him Belch. A kid named Victor Criss. A few other guys. But the real brains of the combination was a fellow named Henry Bowers. If there has ever been a genuinely evil kid strutting across the skin of the world, Ricky Lee, Henry Bowers was that kid. I wasn't the only kid he used to take after; my problem was, I couldn't run as fast as some of the others.'

Hanscom unbuttoned his shirt and opened it. Leaning forward, Ricky Lee saw a funny, twisted scar on Mr Hanscom's stomach, just above his navel. Puckered, white, and old. It was a letter, he saw. Someone had carved the letter 'H' into the man's stomach, probably long before Mr Hanscom had *been* a man.

'Henry Bowers did that to me. About a thousand years ago. I'm lucky I'm not wearing his whole damned name down there.'

'Mr Hanscom —'

Hanscom took the other two lemon-slices, one in each hand, tilted his head back, and took them like nose-drops. He shuddered wrackingly, put them aside, and took two big swallows from the stein. He shuddered again, took another gulp, and then groped for the padded edge of the bar with his eyes closed. For a moment he held on like a man on a sailboat clinging to the rail for support in a heavy sea. Then he opened his eyes again and smiled at Ricky Lee.

'I could ride this bull all night,' he said.

'Mr Hanscom, I wish you wouldn't do that anymore,' Ricky Lee said nervously.

Annie came over to the waitresses' stand with her tray and called for a couple of Millers. Ricky Lee drew them and took them down to her. His legs felt rubbery.

'Is Mr Hanscom all right, Ricky Lee?' Annie asked. She was looking past Ricky Lee and he turned to follow her gaze. Mr Hanscom was leaning over the bar, carefully picking lemon-slices out of the caddy where Ricky Lee kept the drink garnishes.

'I don't know,' he said. 'I don't think so.'

'Well get your thumb out of your ass and do something about it.' Annie was, like most other women, partial to Ben Hanscom.

'I dunno. My daddy always said that if a man's in his right mind —'

'Your daddy didn't have the brains God gave a gopher,' Annie said. 'Never mind your daddy. You got to put a stop to that, Ricky Lee. He's going to kill himself.'

Thus given his marching orders, Ricky Lee went back down

to where Ben Hanscom sat. 'Mr Hanscom, I really think you've had en –'

Hanscom tilted his head back. Squeezed. Actually *sniffed* the lemon-juice back this time, as if it were cocaine. He gulped whiskey as if it were water. He looked at Ricky Lee solemnly. 'Bing-bang, I saw the whole gang, dancing on my living-room rug,' he said, and then laughed. There was maybe two inches of whiskey left in the stein.

'That *is* enough,' Ricky Lee said, and reached for the stein.

Hanscom moved it gently out of his reach. 'Damage has been done, Ricky Lee,' he said. 'The damage has been done, boy.'

'Mr Hanscom, please –'

'I've got something for your kids, Ricky Lee. Damn if I didn't almost forget!'

He was wearing a faded denim vest, and now he reached something out of one of its pockets. Ricky Lee heard a muted clink.

'My dad died when I was four,' Hanscom said. There was no slur at all in his voice. 'Left us a bunch of debts and these. I want your kiddos to have them, Ricky Lee.' He put three cartwheel silver dollars on the bar, where they gleamed under the soft lights. Ricky Lee caught his breath.

'Mr Hanscom, that's very kind, but I couldn't –'

'There used to be four, but I gave one of them to Stuttering Bill and the others. Bill Denbrough, that was his real name. Stuttering Bill's just what we used to call him . . . just a thing we used to say, like "You bet your fur." He was one of the best friends I ever had – I did have a few, you know, even a fat kid like me had a few. Stuttering Bill's a writer now.'

Ricky Lee barely heard him. He was looking at the cartwheels, fascinated. 1921, 1923, and 1924. God knew what they were worth now, just in terms of the pure silver they contained.

'I couldn't,' he said again.

'But I insist.' Mr Hanscom took hold of the stein and drained it. He should have been flat on his keister, but his eyes never left Ricky Lee's. Those eyes were watery, and very bloodshot, but Ricky Lee would have sworn on a stack of Bibles that they were also the eyes of a sober man.

'You're scaring me a little, Mr Hanscom,' Ricky Lee said. Two years ago Gresham Arnold, a rumdum of some local repute, had come into the Red Wheel with a roll of quarters in his hand and a twenty dollar bill stuck into the band of his hat. He handed the roll to Annie with instructions to feed the quarters into the juke-box by fours. He put the twenty on the bar and instructed Ricky Lee to set up drinks for the house. This rumdum, this Gresham Arnold, had long ago been a star basketball player for the Hemingford Rams, leading them to their first (and most likely last) high-school team championship. In 1961 that had been. An almost unlimited future seemed to lie ahead of the young man. But he had flunked out of LSU his first semester, a victim of drink, drugs, and all-night parties. He came home, cracked up the yellow convertible his folks had given him as a graduation present, and got a job as head salesman in his daddy's John Deere dealership. Five years passed. His father could not bear to fire him, and so he finally sold the dealership and retired to Arizona, a man haunted and made old before his time by the inexplicable and apparently irreversible degeneration of his son. While the dealership still belonged to his daddy and he was at least pretending to work, Arnold had made some effort to keep the booze at arm's length; afterward, it got him completely. He could get mean, but he had been just as sweet as horehound candy the night he brought in the quarters and set up drinks for the house, and everyone had thanked him kindly, and Annie kept playing Moe Bandy songs because Gresham Arnold liked ole Moe Bandy. He sat there at the bar – on the very stool where Mr Hanscom was sitting now, Ricky Lee realized with steadily deepening unease – and drank three or four bourbon-and-bitters, and sang along with the juke, and caused no trouble, and went home when Ricky Lee closed the Wheel up, and hanged himself with his belt in an upstairs closet. Gresham Arnold's eyes that night had looked a little bit like Ben Hanscom's eyes looked right now.

'Scaring you a bit, am I?' Hanscom asked, his eyes never leaving Ricky Lee's. He pushed the stein away and then folded his hands neatly in front of those three silver cartwheels. 'I probably am. But you're not as scared as I am, Ricky Lee. Pray to Jesus you never are.'

'Well, what's the matter?' Ricky Lee asked. 'Maybe –' He wet his lips. 'Maybe I can give you a help.'

'The matter?' Ben Hanscom laughed. 'Why, not too much. I had a call from an old friend tonight. Guy named Mike Hanlon. I'd forgotten all about him, Ricky Lee, but that didn't scare me much. After all, I was just a kid when I knew him, and kids forget things, don't they? Sure they do. You bet your fur. What scared me was getting about halfway over here and realizing that it wasn't just Mike I'd forgotten about – I'd forgotten *everything* about being a kid.'

Ricky Lee only looked at him. He had no idea what Mr Hanscom

74

was talking about – but the man was scared, all right. No question about that. It sat funny on Ben Hanscom, but it was real.

'I mean I'd forgotten *all about it*,' he said, and rapped his knuckles lightly on the bar for emphasis. 'Did you ever hear, Ricky Lee, of having an amnesia so complete you didn't even know you *had* amnesia?'

Ricky Lee shook his head.

'Me either. But there I was, tooling along in the Caddy tonight, and all of a sudden it hit me. I remembered Mike Hanlon, but only because he called me on the phone. I remembered Derry, but only because that was where he was calling from.'

'Derry?'

'But that was *all*. It hit me that I hadn't even *thought* about being a kid since . . . since I don't even know when. And then, just like that, it all started to flood back in. Like what we did with the fourth silver dollar.'

'What *did* you do with it, Mr Hanscom?'

Hanscom looked at his watch, and suddenly slipped down from his stool. He staggered a bit – the slightest bit. That was all. 'Can't let the time get away from me,' he said. 'I'm flying tonight.'

Ricky Lee looked instantly alarmed, and Hanscom laughed.

'Flying but not driving the plane. Not this time. United Airlines, Ricky Lee.'

'Oh.' He supposed his relief showed on his face, but he didn't care. 'Where are you going?'

Hanscom's shirt was still open. He looked thoughtfully down at the puckered white lines of the old scar on his belly and then began to button the shirt over it.

'Thought I told you that, Ricky Lee. Home. I'm going home. Give those cartwheels to your kids.' He started toward the door, and something about the way he walked, even the way he hitched at the sides of his pants, terrified Ricky Lee. The resemblance to the late and mostly unlamented Gresham Arnold was suddenly so acute it was nearly like seeing a ghost.

'Mr Hanscom!' he cried in alarm.

Hanscom turned back, and Ricky Lee stepped quickly backward. His ass hit the backbar and glassware gossiped briefly as the bottles knocked together. He stepped back because he was suddenly convinced that Ben Hanscom was dead. Yes, Ben Hanscom was lying dead some-place, in a ditch or an attic or possibly in a closet with a belt noosed around his neck and the toes of his four-hundred-dollar cowboy boots dangling an inch or two above the floor, and this thing standing near the juke and staring back at him was a ghost. For a moment – just a moment, but it was plenty long enough to cover his working heart with a rime of ice – he was convinced he could see tables and chairs right through the man.

'What is it, Ricky Lee?'

'Nuh-n-nuh. Nothin.'

Ben Hanscom looked out at Ricky Lee from eyes which had dark-purple crescents beneath them. His cheeks burned with liquor; his nose looked red and sore.

'Nothin,' Ricky Lee whispered again, but he couldn't take his eyes from that face, the face of a man who has died deep in sin and now stands hard by hell's smoking side door.

'I was fat and we were poor,' Ben Hanscom said. 'I remember that now. And I remember that either a girl named Beverly or Stuttering Bill saved my life with a silver dollar. I'm scared almost insane by whatever else I may remember before tonight's over, but how scared I am doesn't matter, because it's going to come anyway. It's all there, like a great big bubble that's growing in my mind. But I'm going, because all I've ever gotten and all I have now is somehow due to what we did then, and you pay for what you get in this world. Maybe that's why God made us kids first and built us close to the ground, because He knows you got to fall down a lot and bleed a lot before you learn that one simple lesson. You pay for what you get, you own what you pay for . . . and sooner or later whatever you own comes back home to you.'

'You gonna be back this weekend, though, ain't you?' Ricky Lee asked through numbed lips. In his increasing distress this was all he could find to hold on to. 'You gonna be back this weekend just like always, ain't you?'

'I don't know,' Mr Hanscom said, and smiled a terrible smile. 'I'm going a lot farther than London this time, Ricky Lee.'

'Mr Hanscom –!'

'You give those cartwheels to your kids,' he repeated, and slipped out into the night.

'What the blue *hell*?' Annie asked, but Ricky Lee ignored her. He flipped up the bar's partition and ran over to one of the windows which looked out on the parking lot. He saw the headlights of Mr Hanscom's Caddy come on, heard the engine rev. It pulled out of the dirt lot, kicking up a rooster-tail of dust behind it. The taillights dwindled away to red points down Highway 63, and the Nebraska nightwind began to pull the hanging dust apart.

'He took on a boxcar full of booze and you let him get in that big car of his and drive away,' Annie said. 'Way to go, Ricky Lee.'

'Never mind.'

'He's going to kill himself.'

And although this had been Ricky Lee's own thought less than five minutes ago, he turned to her when the taillights winked out of sight and shook his head.

'I don't think so,' he said. 'Although the way he looked tonight, it might be better for him if he did.'

'What did he say to you?'

He shook his head. It was all confused in his mind, and the sum total of it seemed to mean nothing. 'It doesn't matter. But I don't think we're ever going to see that old boy again.'

4

Eddie Kaspbrak Takes His Medicine

If you would know all there is to know about an American man or woman of the middle class as the millennium nears its end, you would need only to look in his or her medicine cabinet – or so it has been said. But dear Lord, get a look into this one as Eddie Kaspbrak slides it open, mercifully sliding aside his white face and wide, staring eyes.

On the top shelf there's Anacin, Excedrin, Excedrin PM, Contac, Gelusil, Tylenol, and a large blue jar of Vicks, looking like a bit of brooding deep twilight under glass. There is a bottle of Vivarin, a bottle of Serutan (*That's 'Nature's' spelled backwards*, the ads on Lawrence Welk used to say when Eddie Kaspbrak was but a wee slip of a lad), and two bottles of Phillips Milk of Magnesia – the regular, which tastes like liquid chalk, and the new mint flavor, which tastes like mint-flavored liquid chalk. Here is a large bottle of Rolaids standing chummily close to a large bottle of Tums. The Tums are standing next to a large bottle of orange-flavored Di-Gel tablets. The three of them look like a trio of strange piggy-banks, stuffed with pills instead of dimes.

Second shelf, and dig the vites: you got your E, your C, your C with roseships. You got B-simple and B-complex and B-12. There's L-Lysine, which is supposed to do something about those embarrassing skin problems, and lecithin, which is supposed to do something about that embarrassing cholesterol build-up in and around the Big Pump. There's iron, calcium, and cod liver oil. There's One-A-Day multiples,

Myadec multiples, Centrum multiples. And sitting up on top of the cabinet itself is a gigantic bottle of Geritol, just for good measure.

Moving right along to Eddie's third shelf, we find the utility infielders of the patent-medicine world. Ex-Lax. Carter's Little Pills. Those two keep Eddie Kaspbrak moving the mail. Here, nearby, is Kaopectate, Pepto-Bismol, and Preparation H in case the mail moves too fast or too painfully. Also some Tucks in a screw-top jar just to keep everything tidy after the mail has gone through, be it just an advertising circular or two addressed to OCCUPANT or a big old special-delivery package. Here is Formula 44 for coughs, Nyquil and Dristan for colds, and a big bottle of castor oil. There's a tin of Sucrets in case Eddie's throat gets sore, and there's a quartet of mouthwashes: Chloraseptic, Cēpacol, Cēpestat in the spray bottle, and of course good old Listerine, often imitated but never duplicated. Visine and Murine for the eyes. Cortaid and Neosporin ointment for the skin (the second line of defense if the L-Lysine doesn't live up to expectations), a tube of Oxy-5 and a plastic bottle of Oxy-Wash (because Eddie would definitely rather have a few less cents than a few more zits), and some tetracyline pills.

And off to one side, clustered like bitter conspirators, are three bottles of coal-tar shampoo.

The bottom shelf is almost deserted, but the stuff which *is* here means serious business – you could cruise on this stuff, okay. On this stuff you could fly higher than Ben Hanscom's jet and crash harder than Thurman Munson's. There's Valium, Percodan, Elavil, and Darvon Complex. There is also another Sucrets box on this low shelf, but there are no Sucrets in it. If you opened that one you would find six Quaaludes.

Eddie Kaspbrak believed in the Boy Scout motto.

He was swinging a blue tote-bag as he came into the bathroom. He set it on the sink, unzipped it, and then, with trembling hands, he began to spill bottles and jars and tubes and squeeze-bottles and spray-bottles into it. Under other circumstances he would have taken them out handful by careful handful, but there was no time for such niceties now. The choice, as Eddie saw it, was as simple as it was brutal: get moving and keep moving or stand in one place long enough to start thinking about what all of this meant and simply die of fright.

'Eddie?' Myra called up from downstairs. 'Eddie, what are you *dooooing?*'

Eddie dropped the Sucrets box containing the 'ludes into the bag. The medicine cabinet was now entirely empty except for Myra's Midol and a small, almost used-up tube of Blistex. He paused for a moment and then grabbed the Blistex. He started to zip the bag closed, debated, and then threw in the Midol as well. She could always buy more.

'Eddie?' from halfway up the stairs now.

Eddie zipped the bag the rest of the way closed and then left the bathroom, swinging it by his side. He was a short man with a timid, rabbity sort of face. Much of his hair was gone; what was left grew in listless, piebald patches. The weight of the bag pulled him noticeably to one side.

An extremely large woman was climbing slowly to the second floor. Eddie could hear the stairs creak protestingly under her.

'What are you *DOOOOOOOOING?*'

Eddie did not need a shrink to tell him that he had, in a sense, married his mother. Myra Kaspbrak was huge. She had only been big when Eddie married her five years ago, but he sometimes thought his subconscious had seen the potential for hugeness in her; God knew his own mother had been a whopper. And she looked somehow more huge than ever as she reached the second-floor landing. She was wearing a white nightgown which swelled, comberlike, at bosom and hip. Her face, devoid of make-up, was white and shiny. She looked badly frightened.

'I have to go away for awhile,' Eddie said.

'What do you mean, you have to go away? What was that telephone call?'

'Nothing,' he said, fleeing abruptly down the hallway to their walk-in closet. He put the tote-bag down, opened the closet's fold-back door, and raked aside the half-dozen identical black suits which hung there, as conspicuous as a thundercloud among the other, more brightly colored, clothes. He always wore one of the black suits when he was working. He bent into the closet, smelling mothballs and wool, and pulled out one of the suitcases from the back. He opened it and began throwing clothes in.

Her shadow fell over him.

'What's this about, Eddie? Where are you going? You tell me!'

'I can't tell you.'

She stood there, watching him, trying to decide what to say next, or what to do. The thought of simply bundling him into the closet and then standing with her back against the door until this madness had passed crossed her mind, but she was unable to bring herself to do it, although she certainly could have; she was three inches taller than Eddie and outweighed him by a hundred pounds. She couldn't think of what to do or say, because this was so utterly unlike him. She could not have been any more dismayed and frightened if she had walked into the television room and found their new big-screen TV floating in the air.

'You can't go,' she heard herself saying. 'You promised you'd get me Al Pacino's autograph.' It was an absurdity – God knew it was – but at this point even an absurdity was better than nothing.

'You'll still get it,' Eddie said. 'You'll have to drive him yourself.'

Oh, here was a new terror to join those already circling in her poor dazzled head. She uttered a small scream. 'I can't – I never –'

'You'll have to,' he said. He was examining his shoes now. 'There's no one else.'

'Neither of my uniforms fit anymore! They're too tight in the tits!'

'Have Delores let one of them out,' he said implacably. He threw two pairs of shoes back, found an empty shoebox, and popped a third pair into it. Good black shoes, plenty of use left in them still, but looking just a bit too worn to wear on the job. When you drove rich people around New York for a living, many of them *famous* rich people, everything had to look just right. These shoes no longer looked just right . . . but he supposed they would do for where he was going. And for whatever he might have to do when he got there. Maybe Richie Tozier would –

But then the blackness threatened and he felt his throat beginning to close up. Eddie realized with real panic that he had packed the whole damned drugstore and had left the most important thing of all – his aspirator – downstairs on top of the stereo cabinet.

He banged the suitcase closed and latched it. He looked around at Myra, who was standing there in the hallway with her hand pressed against the short thick column of her neck as if she were the one with the asthma. She was staring at him, her face full of perplexity and terror, and he might have felt sorry for her if his heart had not already been so filled with terror for himself.

'What's happened, Eddie? Who was that on the telephone? Are you in trouble? You are, aren't you? What kind of trouble are you in?'

He walked toward her, zipper-bag in one hand and suitcase in the other, standing more or less straight now that he was more evenly weighted. She moved in front of him, blocking off the stairway, and at first he thought she would not give way. Then, when his face was about to crash into the soft roadblock of her breasts, she did give way . . . fearfully. As he walked past, never slowing, she burst into miserable tears.

'*I can't drive Al Pacino!*' she bawled. '*I'll smash into a stop-sign or something, I know I will! Eddie I'm scaaarrred!*'

He looked at the Seth Thomas clock on the table by the stairs. Twenty past nine. The canned-sounding Delta clerk had told him he had already missed the last flight north to Maine – that one had left La Guardia at eight-twenty-five. He had called Amtrak and discovered there was a late train to Boston departing Penn Station at eleven-thirty. It would drop him off at South Station, where he could take a cab to the offices of Cape Cod Limousine on Arlington Street. Cape Cod and Eddie's company, Royal Crest, had worked out a useful and friendly reciprocal arrangement over the years. A quick call to Butch Carrington in Boston had taken care of his transportation north – Butch said he would have a Cadillac limo gassed and ready for him. So he would go in style, and with no pain-in-the-ass client sitting in the back seat, stinking the air up with a big cigar and asking if Eddie knew where he could score a broad or a few grams of coke or both.

Going in style, all right, he thought. *Only way you could go in more style would be if you were going in a hearse. But don't worry, Eddie – that's probably how you'll come back. If there's enough of you left to pick up, that is.*

'Eddie?'

Nine-twenty. Plenty of time to talk to her, plenty of time to be kind. Ah, but it would have been so much better if this had been her whist night, if he could have just slipped out, leaving a note under one of the magnets on the refrigerator door (the refrigerator door was where he left all his notes for Myra, because there she never missed them). Leaving that way – like a fugitive – would not have been good, but this was even worse. This was like having to leave home all over again, and that had been so hard he'd had to do it three times.

Sometimes home is where the heart is, Eddie thought randomly. *I believe that. Old Bobby Frost said home's the place where, when you have to go there, they have to take you in. Unfortunately, it's also the place where, once you're in there, they don't ever want to let you out.*

He stood at the head of the stairs, forward motion temporarily spent, filled with fear, breath wheezing noisily in and out of the pinhole his throat had become, and regarded his weeping wife.

81

'Come on downstairs with me and I'll tell you what I can,' he said.

Eddie put his two bags – clothes in one, medicine in the other – by the door in the front hall. He remembered something else then . . . or rather the ghost of his mother, who had been dead many years but who still spoke frequently in his mind, remembered for him.

You know when your feet get wet you always get a cold, Eddie – you're not like other people, you have a very weak system, you have to be careful. That's why you must always wear your rubbers when it rains.

It rained a lot in Derry.

Eddie opened the front-hall closet, got his rubbers off the hook where they hung neatly in a plastic bag, and put them in his clothes suitcase.

That's a good boy, Eddie.

He and Myra had been watching TV when the shit hit the fan. Eddie went into the television room and pushed the button which lowered the screen of the Mural Vision TV – its screen was so big that it made Freeman McNeil look like a visitor from Brobdingnag on Sunday afternoons. He picked up the telephone and called a taxi. The dispatcher told him it would probably be fifteen minutes. Eddie said that was no problem.

He hung up and grabbed his aspirator off the top of their expensive Sony compact-disc player. *I spent fifteen hundred bucks on a state-of-the-art sound system so that Myra wouldn't miss a single golden note on her Barry Manilow records and her 'Supremes Greatest Hits,'* he thought, and then felt a flush of guilt. That wasn't fair, and he damn well knew it. Myra would have been just as happy with her old scratchy records as she was with the new 45-rpm-sized laser discs, just as she would have been happy to keep on living in the little four-room house in Queens until they were both old and gray (and, if the truth were told, there was a little snow on Eddie Kaspbrak's mountain already). He had bought the luxury sound system for the same reasons that he had bought this low fieldstone house on Long Island, where the two of them often rattled around like the last two peas in a can: because he had been able to, and because they were ways of appeasing the soft, frightened, often bewildered, always implacable voice of his mother; they were ways of saying: *I made it, Ma! Look at all this! I made it! Now will you please for Christ's sake shut up awhile?*

Eddie stuffed the aspirator into his mouth and, like a man miming suicide, pulled the trigger. A cloud of awful licorice taste roiled and boiled its way down his throat, and Eddie breathed deeply. He could feel breathing passages which had almost closed start to open up again. The tightness in his chest started to ease, and suddenly he heard voices in his mind, ghost-voices.

Didn't you get the note I sent you?

I got it, Mrs Kaspbrak, but —

Well, in case you can't read, Coach Black, let me tell you in person. Are you ready? Mrs Kaspbrak —

Good. Here it comes, from my lips to your ears. Ready? My Eddie cannot take physical education. I repeat: he canNOT take phys ed. Eddie is very delicate, and if he runs . . . or jumps . . .

Mrs Kaspbrak, I have the results of Eddie's last physical on file in my office — that's a state requirement. It says that Eddie is a little small for his age, but otherwise he's absolutely normal. So I called your family physician just to be sure and he confirmed —

Are you saying I'm a liar, Coach Black? Is that it? Well, here he is! Here's Eddie, standing right beside me! Can you hear the way he's breathing? CAN you?

Mom . . . please . . . I'm all right . . .

Eddie, you know better than that. I taught you better than that. Don't interrupt your elders.

I hear him, Mrs Kaspbrak, but —

Do you? Good! I thought maybe you were deaf! He sounds like a truck going uphill in low gear, doesn't he? And if that isn't asthma —

Mom, I'll be —

Be quiet, Eddie, don't interrupt me again. If that isn't asthma, Coach Black, then I'm Queen Elizabeth!

Mrs Kaspbrak, Eddie often seems very well and happy in his physical-education classes. He loves to play games, and he runs quite fast. In my conversation with Dr Baynes, the word 'psychosomatic' came up. I wonder if you've considered the possibility that —

— that my son is crazy? Is that what you're trying to say? ARE YOU TRYING TO SAY THAT MY SON IS CRAZY????

No, but —

He's delicate.

Mrs Kaspbrak —

My son is very delicate.

Mrs Kaspbrak, Dr Baynes confirmed that he could find nothing at all —

'— physically wrong,' Eddie finished. The memory of that humiliating encounter, his mother screaming at Coach Black in the Derry

Elementary School gymnasium while he gasped and cringed at her side and the other kids huddled around one of the baskets and watched, had recurred to him tonight for the first time in years. Nor was that the only memory which Mike Hanlon's call was going to bring back, he knew. He could feel many others, as bad or even worse, crowding and jostling like sale-mad shoppers bottlenecked in a department-store doorway. But soon the bottleneck would break and they would be along. He was quite sure of that. And what would they find on sale? His sanity? Could be. Half-Price. Smoke and Water Damage. Everything Must Go.

'Nothing physically wrong,' he repeated, took a deep shuddery breath, and stuffed the aspirator into his pocket.

'Eddie,' Myra said. '*Please* tell me what all of this is about!'

Tear-tracks shone on her chubby cheeks. Her hands twisted restlessly together like a pair of pink and hairless animals at play. Once, shortly before actually proposing marriage, he had taken a picture of Myra which she had given him and had put it next to one of his mother, who had died of congestive heart-failure at the age of sixty-four. At the time of her death Eddie's mother had topped the scales at over four hundred pounds – four hundred and six, to be exact. She had become something nearly monstrous by then – her body had seemed nothing more than boobs and butt and belly, all overtopped by her pasty, perpetually dismayed face. But the picture of her which he put next to Myra's picture had been taken in 1944, two years before he had been born (*You were a very sickly baby*, the ghost-mom now whispered in his ear. *Many times we despaired of your life . . .*). In 1944 his mother had been a relatively svelte one hundred and eighty pounds.

He had made that comparison, he supposed, in a last-ditch effort to stop himself from committing psychological incest. He looked from Mother to Myra and back again to Mother.

They could have been sisters. The resemblance was that close.

Eddie looked at the two nearly identical pictures and promised himself he would not do this crazy thing. He knew that the boys at work were already making jokes about Jack Sprat and his wife, but they didn't know the half of it. The jokes and snide remarks he could take, but did he really want to be a clown in such a Freudian circus as this? No. He did not. He would break it off with Myra. He would let her down gently because she was really very sweet and had had even less experience with men than he'd had with women. And then, after she had finally sailed over the horizon of his life, he could maybe take those tennis lessons he'd been thinking of for such a long time

84

(Eddie often seems very well and happy in his physical-education classes)

or there were the pool memberships they were selling at the UN Plaza Hotel

(Eddie loves to play games)

not to mention that health club which had opened up on Third Avenue across from the garage . . .

(Eddie runs quite fast he runs quite fast when you're not here runs quite fast when there's nobody around to remind him of how delicate he is and I see in his face Mrs Kaspbrak that he knows even now at the age of nine he knows that the biggest favor in the world he could do himself would be to run fast in any direction you're not going let him go Mrs Kaspbrak let him RUN)

But in the end he had married Myra anyway. In the end the old ways and the old habits had simply been too strong. Home was the place where, when you have to go there, they have to chain you up. Oh, he might have beaten his mother's ghost. It would have been hard but he was quite sure he could have done that much, if that had been all which needed doing. It was Myra herself who had ended up tipping the scales away from independence. Myra had condemned him with solicitude, had nailed him with concern, had chained him with sweetness. Myra, like his mother, had reached the final, fatal insight into his character: Eddie was all the more delicate because he sometimes suspected he was not delicate at all; Eddie needed to be protected from his own dim intimations of possible bravery.

On rainy days Myra always took his rubbers out of the plastic bag in the closet and put them by the coat-rack next to the door. Beside his plate of unbuttered wheat toast each morning was a dish of what might have been taken at a casual glance for a multi-colored pre-sweetened children's cereal, but which a closer look would have revealed to be a whole spectrum of vitamins (most of which Eddie had in his medicine-bag right now). Myra, like Mother, understood, and there had really been no chance for him. As a young unmarried man he had left his mother three times and returned home to her three times. Then, four years after his mother had died in the front hall of her Queens apartment, blocking the front door so completely with her bulk that the Medcu guys (called by the people downstairs when they heard the monstrous thud of Mrs Kaspbrak going down for the final count) had had to break in through the locked door between the apartment's kitchen and the service stairwell, he had returned home for a fourth and final time. At least he had believed then it was for the final time – *home again, home again, jiggety-jog; home again, home again, with Myra the hog.* A hog she was, but she was a sweet hog, and he loved her, and there had really been no chance for him at all. She had drawn him to her with the fatal, hypnotizing snake's eye of understanding.

Home again forever, he had thought then.

But maybe I was wrong, he thought. *Maybe this isn't home, nor ever was − maybe home is where I have to go tonight. Home is the place where when you go there, you have to finally face the thing in the dark.*

He shuddered helplessly, as if he had gone outside without his rubbers and caught a terrible chill.

'Eddie, *please!*'

She was beginning to weep again. Tears were her final defense, just as they had always been his mother's: the soft weapon which paralyzes, which turns kindness and tenderness into fatal chinks in one's armor.

Not that he'd ever worn much armor anyway − suits of armor did not seem to fit him very well.

Tears had been more than a defense for his mother; they had been a weapon. Myra had rarely used her own tears so cynically . . . but, cynically or not, he realized she was trying to use them that way now . . . and she was succeeding.

He couldn't let her. It would be too easy to think of how lonely it was going to be, sitting in a seat on that train as it barrelled north toward Boston through the darkness, his suitcase overhead and his tote-bag full of nostrums between his feet, the fear sitting on his chest like a rancid Vicks-pack. Too easy to let Myra take him upstairs and make love to him with aspirins and an alcohol-rub. And put him to bed, where they might or might not make a franker sort of love.

But he had promised. *Promised.*

'Myra, listen to me,' he said, making his voice purposely dry, purposely matter-of-fact.

She looked at him with her wet, naked, terrified eyes.

He thought he would try now to explain − as best he could; he would tell her about how Mike Hanlon had called and told him that it had started again, and yes, he thought most of the others were coming.

But what came out of his mouth was much saner stuff.

'Go down to the office first thing in the morning. Talk to Phil. Tell him I had to take off and that you'll drive Pacino −'

'Eddie I just *can't!*' she wailed. 'He's a big star! If I get lost he'll shout at me, I know he will, he'll *shout*, they all do when the driver gets lost . . . and . . . and I'll cry . . . there could be an accident . . . there probably *will* be an accident . . . Eddie . . . Eddie you have to stay home . . .'

'For God's sake! *Stop it!*'

She recoiled from his voice, hurt; although Eddie gripped his aspirator, he would not use it. She would see that as a weakness, one she could use against him. *Dear God, if You are there, please believe me when I say I don't want to hurt Myra. I don't want to cut her, don't even want to bruise her. But I promised, we all promised, we swore in blood, please help me God because I have to do this . . .*

'I hate it when you shout at me, Eddie,' she whispered.

'Myra, I hate it when I have to,' he said, and she winced. *There you go, Eddie — you hurt her again. Why don't you just punch her around the room a few times? That would probably be kinder. And quicker.*

Suddenly — probably it was the thought of punching someone around the room which caused the image to come — he saw the face of Henry Bowers. It was the first time he had thought of Bowers in years, and it did nothing for his peace of mind. Nothing at all.

He closed his eyes briefly, then opened them and said: 'You won't get lost, and he won't shout at you. Mr Pacino is very nice, very understanding.' He had never driven Pacino before in his life, but contented himself with knowing that at least the law of averages was on the side of this lie — according to popular myth most celebrities were shitheels, but Eddie had driven enough of them to know it usually wasn't true.

There were, of course, exceptions to the rule — and in most cases the exceptions were real monstrosities. He hoped fervently for Myra's sake that Pacino wasn't one of these.

'Is he?' she asked timidly.

'Yes. He is.'

'How do you know?'

'Demetrios drove him two or three times when he worked at Manhattan Limousine,' Eddie said glibly. 'He said Mr Pacino always tipped at least fifty dollars.'

'I wouldn't care if he only tipped me fifty cents, as long as he didn't *shout* at me.'

'Myra, it's all as easy as one-two-three. One, you make the pickup at the Saint Regis tomorrow at seven P.M. and take him over to the ABC Building. They're retaping the last act of this play Pacino's in – *American Buffalo*, I think it's called. Two, you take him back to the Saint Regis around eleven. Three, you go back to the garage, turn in the car, and sign the greensheet.'

'That's all?'

'That's all. You can do it standing on your head, Marty.'

She usually giggled at this pet name, but now she only looked at him with a painful childlike solemnity.

'What if he wants to go out to dinner instead of back to the hotel? Or for drinks? Or for dancing?'

'I don't think he will, but if he does, you take him. If it looks like he's going to party all night, you can call Phil Thomas on the radio-phone after midnight. By then he'll have a driver free to relieve you. I'd never stick you with something like this in the first place if I had a driver who was free, but I got two guys out sick, Demetrios on vacation, and everyone else booked up solid. You'll be snug in your own bed by one in the morning, Marty – one in the morning at the very, very latest. I apple-solutely guarantee it.'

She didn't laugh at apple-solutely, either.

He cleared his throat and leaned forward, elbows on his knees. Instantly the ghost-mom whispered: *Don't sit that way, Eddie. It's bad for your posture, and it cramps your lungs. You have very delicate lungs.*

He sat up straight again, hardly aware he was doing it.

'This better be the only time I have to drive,' she nearly moaned. 'I've turned into such a *horse* in the last two years, and my uniforms look so *bad* now.'

'It's the only time, I swear.'

'Who called you, Eddie?'

As if on cue, lights swept across the wall; a horn honked once as the cab turned into the driveway. He felt a surge of relief. They had spent the fifteen minutes talking about Pacino instead of Derry and Mike Hanlon and Henry Bowers, and that was good. Good for Myra, and good for him as well. He did not want to spend any time thinking or talking about those things until he had to.

Eddie stood up. 'It's my cab.'

She got up so fast she tripped over the hem of her own night-gown and fell forward. Eddie caught her, but for a moment the issue was in grave doubt: she outweighed him by a hundred pounds.

And she was beginning to blubber again.

'Eddie, you *have* to tell me!'

'I can't. There's no time.'

'You never kept anything from me before, Eddie,' she wept.

'And I'm not now. Not really. I don't remember it all. At least, not yet. The man who called was – is – an old friend. He –'

'You'll get sick,' she said desperately, following him as he walked toward the front hall again. 'I know you will. Let me come, Eddie, please, I'll take care of you, Pacino can get a cab or something, it won't kill him, what do you say, okay?' Her voice was rising, becoming frantic, and to Eddie's horror she began to look more and more like his mother, his mother as she had looked in the last months before she died: old and fat and crazy. 'I'll rub your back and see that you get your pills . . . I . . . I'll help you . . . I won't talk if you don't want me to but you can tell me everything . . . Eddie . . . *Eddie, please don't go! Eddie, please! Pleeeeeease!*'

He was striding down the hall to the front door now, walking blind, head down, moving as a man moves against a high wind. He was wheezing again. When he picked up the bags each of them seemed to weigh a hundred pounds. He could feel her plump pink hands on him, touching, exploring, pulling with helpless desire but no real strength, trying to seduce him with her sweet tears of concern, trying to draw him back.

I'm not going to make it! he thought desperately. The asthma was worse now, worse than it had been since he was a kid. He reached for the doorknob but it seemed to be receding from him, receding into the blackness of outer space.

'If you stay I'll make you a sour-cream coffee-cake,' she babbled. 'We'll have popcorn . . . I'll make your favorite turkey dinner . . . I'll make it for breakfast tomorrow morning if you want . . . I'll start right now . . . and giblet gravy . . . *Eddie please I'm scared you're scaring me so bad!*'

She grabbed his collar and pulled him backward, like a beefy cop putting the grab on a suspicious fellow who is trying to flee. With a final fading effort, Eddie kept going . . . and when he was at the absolute end of his strength and ability to resist, he felt her grip trail away.

She gave one final wail.

His fingers closed around the doorknob – how blessedly cool it was! He pulled the door open and saw a Checker cab sitting out there, an ambassador from the land of sanity. The night was clear. The stars were bright and lucid.

He turned back to Myra, whistling and wheezing. 'You need to understand that this isn't something I *want* to do,' he said. 'If I had a choice – any choice at all – I wouldn't go. Please understand that, Marty. I'm going but I'll be coming back.'

Oh but that felt like a lie.

'When? How long?'

'A week. Or maybe ten days. Surely no longer than that.'

'A week!' she screamed, clutching at her bosom like a diva in a bad opera. 'A week! Ten days! Please, Eddie! *Pleeeeeee –*'

'Marty, stop. Okay? Just stop.'

For a wonder, she did: stopped and stood looking at him with her wet, bruised eyes, not angry at him, only terrified for him and, coincidentally, for herself. And for perhaps the first time in all the years he had known her, he felt that he could love her safely. Was that part of the going away? He supposed it was. No . . . you could flush the *supposed*. He *knew* it was. Already he felt like something living in the wrong end of a telescope.

But it was maybe all right. Was that what he meant? That he had finally decided it was all right to love her? That it was all right even though she looked like his mother when his mother had been younger and even though she ate brownies in bed while watching *Hardcastle and McCormick* or *Falcon Crest* and the crumbs always got on his side and even though she wasn't all that bright and even though she understood and condoned his remedies in the medicine cabinet because she kept her own in the refrigerator?

Or was it . . .

Could it be that . . .

These other ideas were all things he had considered in one way or another, at one time or another, during his oddly entwined lives as a son and a lover and a husband; now, on the point of leaving home for what felt like the absolutely last time, a new possibility came to him, and startled wonder brushed him like the wing of some large bird.

Could it be that Myra was even *more* frightened than he was?

Could it be that his mother had been?

Another Derry memory came shooting up from his subconscious like a balefully fizzing firework. There had been a shoe store downtown on Center Street. The Shoeboat. His mother had taken him there one day – he thought he could have been no more than five or six – and told him to sit still and be good while she got a pair of white pumps for a wedding. So he sat still and was good while his mother talked with Mr Gardener, who was one of the shoe-clerks, but he was only five (or maybe six), and after his mother had rejected the third pair of white pumps Mr Gardener showed her, Eddie got bored and walked over to the far corner to look at something he had spotted there. At first he thought it was just a big crate standing on end. When he got closer he decided it was some kind of desk. But it sure was the kookiest desk he had ever seen. It was so narrow! It was made of bright polished wood with lots of curvy inlaid lines and carved doojiggers in it. Also, there was a little flight of three stairs leading up to it, and he had never seen a desk with *stairs*. When he got right up to it, he saw that there was a slot at the bottom of the desk-thing, a button on one side, and on top of it – entrancing! – was something that looked exactly like Captain Video's Spacescope.

Eddie walked around to the other side and there was a sign. He must have been at least six, because he had been able to read it, softly whispering each word aloud:

DO YOUR SHOES FIT RIGHT? CHECK AND SEE!

He went back around, climbed the three steps to the little platform, and then stuck his foot into the slot at the bottom of the shoe-checker. *Did* his shoes *fit right*? Eddie didn't know, but he was wild to *check and see*. He socked his face into the rubber faceguard and thumbed the button. Green light flooded his eyes. Eddie gasped. He could see a foot floating inside a shoe filled with green smoke. He wiggled his toes, and the toes he was looking at wiggled right back – they were his, all right, just as he had suspected. And then he realized it was not just his toes he could see; he could see his *bones*, too! The bones in his *foot*! He crossed his great toe over his second toe (as if sneakily warding off the consequences of telling a lie) and the eldritch bones in the scope made an X that was not white but goblin-green. He could see –

Then his mother shrieked, a rising sound of panic that cut through the quiet shoe store like a runaway reaper-blade, like a firebell, like doom on horseback. He jerked his startled, dismayed face out of the viewer and saw her pelting toward him across the store in her stocking feet, her dress flying out behind her. She knocked a chair over and one of those shoe-measuring things that always tickled his feet went flying. Her bosom heaved. Her mouth was a scarlet O of horror. Faces turned to follow her progress.

'*Eddie get off there!*' she screamed. '*Get off there! Those machines give you cancer! Get off there! Eddie! Eddieeeeeee –*'

He backed away as if the machine had suddenly grown red-hot.

In his startled panic he forgot the little flight of stairs behind him. His heels dropped over the top one and he stood there, slowly falling backward, his arms pinwheeling wildly in a losing battle to retain his departing balance. And hadn't he thought with a kind of mad joy *I'm going to fall! I'm going to find out what it feels like to fall and bump my head! Goody for me!* . . .? Hadn't he thought that? Or was it only the man imposing his own self-serving adult ideas over whatever his child's mind, always roaring with confused surmises and half-perceived images (images which lost their sense in their very brightness), had thought . . . or tried to think?

Either way, it was a moot question. He had not fallen. His mother had gotten there in time. His mother had caught him. He had burst into tears, but he had not fallen.

Everyone had been looking at them. He remembered that. He remembered Mr Gardener picking up the shoe-measuring thing and checking the little sliding gadgets on it to make sure they were still okay while another clerk righted the fallen chair and then flapped his arms once, in amused disgust, before putting on his pleasantly neutral salesman's face again. Mostly he remembered his mother's wet cheek and her hot, sour breath. He remembered her whispering over and over in his ear, 'Don't you *ever* do that again, don't you *ever* do that again, don't you *ever*.' It was what his mother chanted to ward off trouble. She had chanted the same thing a year earlier when she discovered the baby-sitter had taken Eddie to the public pool in Derry Park one stiflingly hot summer day – this had been when the polio scare of the early fifties was just beginning to wind down. She had dragged him out of the pool, telling him he must *never* do that, *never, never*, and all the kids had looked as all the clerks and customers were looking now, and her breath had had that same sour tang.

She dragged him out of The Shoeboat, shouting at the clerks that she would see them all in court if there was anything wrong with her boy. Eddie's terrified tears had continued off and on for the rest of the morning, and his asthma had been particularly bad all day. That night he had lain awake for hours past the time he was usually asleep, wondering exactly what cancer was, if it was worse than polio, if it killed you, how long it took if it did, and how bad it hurt before you died. He also wondered if he would go to hell afterward.

The threat had been serious, he knew that much.

She had been so scared. That was how he knew.

So terrified.

'Marty,' he said across this gulf of years, 'would you give me a kiss?'

She kissed him and hugged him so tightly while she was doing it that the bones in his back groaned. *If we were in water,* he thought, *she'd drown us both.*

'Don't be afraid,' he whispered in her ear.

'*I can't help it!*' she wailed.

'I know,' he said, and realized that, even though she was hugging him with rib-breaking tightness, his asthma had eased. That whistling note in his breathing was gone. 'I know, Marty.'

The taxi-driver honked again.

'Will you call?' she asked him tremulously.

'If I can.'

'Eddie, can't you please tell me what it is?'

And suppose he did? How far would it go toward setting her mind at rest?

Marty, I got a call from Mike Hanlon tonight, and we talked for awhile, but everything we said boiled down to two things. 'It's started again,' Mike said; 'Will you come?' Mike said. And now I've got a fever, Marty, only it's a fever you can't damp down with aspirin, and I've got a shortness of breath the goddamned aspirator won't touch, because that shortness of breath isn't in my throat or my lungs – it is around my heart. I'll come back to you if I can, Marty, but I feel like a man standing at the mouth of an old mine-shaft that is full of cave-ins waiting to happen, standing there and saying goodbye to the daylight.

Yes – my, yes! That would surely set her mind at rest!

'No,' he said. 'I guess I can't tell you what it is.'

And before she could say more, before she could begin again (*Eddie, get out of that taxi! They give you cancer!*), he was striding away from her, faster and faster. By the time he got to the cab he was almost running.

She was still standing in the doorway when the cab backed into the street, still standing there when they started for the city – a big black woman-shadow cut out of the light spilling from their house. He waved, and thought she raised her hand in return.

'Where we headed tonight, my friend?' the cabbie asked.

'Penn Station,' Eddie said, and his hand relaxed on the aspirator. His asthma had gone to wherever it went to brood between its assaults on his bronchial tubes. He felt . . . almost well.

But he needed the aspirator worse than ever four hours later, coming out of a light doze all in a single spasmodic jerk that caused the fellow in the business suit across the way to lower his paper and look at him with faintly apprehensive curiosity.

I'm back, Eddie! the asthma yelled gleefully. *I'm back and oh, I dunno, this time I just might killya! Why not? Gotta do it sometime, you know! Can't fuck around with you forever!*

Eddie's chest surged and pulled. He groped for the aspirator, found it, pointed it down his throat, and pulled the trigger. Then he sat back in the tall Amtrak seat, shivering, waiting for relief, thinking of the dream from which he had just awakened. Dream? Christ, if that was all. He was afraid it was more memory than dream. In it there had been a green light like the light inside a shoe-store X-ray machine, and a rotting leper had pursued a screaming boy named Eddie Kaspbrak through tunnels under the earth. He ran and ran

(he runs quite fast *Coach Black had told his mother and he ran plenty fast with that rotting thing after him oh yes you better believe it you bet your fur*)

in this dream where he was eleven years old, and then he had smelled something like the death of time, and someone lit a match and he had looked down and seen the decomposing face of a boy named Patrick Hockstetter, a boy who had disappeared in July of 1958, and there were worms crawling in and out of Patrick Hockstetter's cheeks, and that gassy, awful smell was coming from *inside* of Patrick Hockstetter, and in that dream that was more memory than dream he had looked to one side and had seen two schoolbooks that were fat with moisture and overgrown with green mold: *Roads to Everywhere*, and *Understanding Our America*. They were in their current condition because it was a foul wetness down here ('How I Spent My Summer Vacation,' a theme by Patrick Hockstetter – 'I spent it dead in a tunnel! Moss grew on my books and they swelled up to the size of Sears catalogues!'). Eddie opened his mouth to scream and that was when the scabrous fingers of the leper clittered around his cheek and plunged themselves into his mouth and that was when he woke up with that back-snapping jerk to find himself not in the sewers under Derry, Maine, but in an Amtrak club-car near the head of a train speeding across Rhode Island under a big white moon.

The man across the aisle hesitated, almost thought better of speaking, and then did. 'Are you all right, sir?'

'Oh yes,' Eddie said. 'I fell asleep and had a bad dream. It got my asthma going.'

'I see.' The paper went up again. Eddie saw it was the paper his mother had sometimes referred to as *The Jew York Times*.

Eddie looked out the window at a sleeping landscape litten only by the fairy moon. Here and there were houses, or sometimes clusters of them, most dark, a few showing lights. But the lights seemed little, and falsely mocking, compared to the moon's ghost-glow.

He thought the moon talked to him, he thought suddenly. *Henry Bowers. God, he was so crazy.* He wondered where Henry Bowers was now. Dead? In prison? Drifting across empty plains somewhere in the middle of the country like an incurable virus, sticking up Seven-Elevens in the deep slumbrous hours between one and four in the morning or maybe killing some of the people stupid enough to slow down for his cocked thumb in order to transfer the dollars in their wallets to his own?

Possible, possible.

In a state asylum somewhere? Looking up at this moon, which was approaching the full? Talking to it, listening to answers which only he could hear?

Eddie considered this somehow even more possible. He shivered. *I am remembering my boyhood at last*, he thought. *I am remembering how I spent my own summer vacation in that dim dead year of 1958.* He sensed that now he could fix upon almost any scene from that summer he wanted to, but he did not want to. *Oh God if I could only forget it all again.*

He leaned his forehead against the dirty glass of the window, his aspirator clasped loosely in one hand like a religious artifact, watching as the night flew apart around the train.

Going north, he thought, but that was wrong.

Not going north. Because it's not a train; it's a time machine. Not north; back. Back in time.

He thought he heard the moon mutter.

Eddie Kaspbrak held his aspirator tightly and closed his eyes against sudden vertigo.

5

Beverly Rogan Takes a Whuppin

Tom was nearly asleep when the phone rang. He struggled halfway up, leaning toward it, and then felt one of Beverly's breasts press against his shoulder as she reached over him to get it. He flopped back on his pillow, wondering dully who was calling on their unlisted home phone number at this hour of the night. He heard Beverly say hello, and then he drifted off again. He had put away nearly three sixpacks during the baseball game, and he was shagged.

Then Beverly's voice, sharp and curious – 'Whaaat?' – drilled into his ear like an ice-pick and he opened his eyes again. He tried to sit up and the phone cord dug into his thick neck.

'Get that fucking thing off me, Beverly,' he said, and she got up quickly and walked around the bed, holding the phone cord up with tented fingers. Her hair was a deep red, and it flowed over her night-gown in natural waves almost to her waist. Whore's hair. Her eyes did not stutter to his face to read the emotional weather there, and Tom Rogan didn't like that. He sat up. His head was starting to ache. Shit, it had probably already been aching, but when you were asleep you didn't know it.

He went into the bathroom, urinated for what felt like three hours, and then decided that as long as he was up he ought to get another beer and try to take the curse off the impending hangover.

Passing back through the bedroom on his way to the stairs, a man in white boxer shorts that flapped like sails below his considerable belly, his arms like slabs (he looked more like a dock-walloper than the president and general manager of Beverly Fashions, Inc.), he looked over his shoulder and yelled crossly: 'If it's that bull dyke Lesley, tell her to go eat out some model and let us sleep!'

Beverly glanced up briefly, shook her head to indicate it wasn't Lesley, and then looked back at the phone. Tom felt the muscles at the back of his neck tighten up. It felt like a dismissal. Dismissed by Milady. Mifuckinlady. This was starting to look like it might turn into a situation. It might be that Beverly needed a short refresher course on who was in charge around here. It was possible. Sometimes she did. She was a slow learner.

He went downstairs and padded along the hall to the kitchen, absently picking the seat of his shorts out of the crack of his ass, and opened the refrigerator. His reaching hand closed on nothing more alcoholic than a blue Tupperware dish of leftover noodles Romanoff. All the beer was gone. Even the can he kept way in the back (much as he kept a twenty-dollar bill folded up behind his driver's license for emergencies) was gone. The game had gone fourteen innings, and all for nothing. The White Sox had lost. Bunch of candy-asses this year.

His eyes drifted to the bottles of hard stuff on the glassed-in shelf over the kitchen bar and for a moment he saw himself pouring a splash of Beam over a single ice-cube. Then he walked back toward the stairs, knowing that was asking for even more trouble than his head was currently in. He glanced at the face of the antique pendulum clock at the foot of the stairs and saw it was past midnight. This intelligence did nothing to improve his temper, which was never very good even at the best of times.

He climbed the stairs with slow deliberation, aware – too aware – of how hard his heart was working. Ka-boom, ka-thud. Ka-boom, ka-thud. Ka-boom, ka-thud. It made him nervous when he could feel his heart beating in his ears and wrists as well as in his chest. Sometimes when that happened he would imagine it not as a squeezing and loosening organ but as a big dial on the left side of his chest with the needle edging ominously into the red zone. He did not like that shit; he did not need that shit. What he needed was a good night's sleep.

But the numb cunt he was married to was still on the phone.

'I understand that, Mike . . . yes . . . yes, I *am* . . . I know . . . but . . .'

A longer pause.

'Bill *Denbrough*?' she exclaimed, and that ice-pick drilled into his ear again.

He stood outside the bedroom door until he got his breath back. Now it was ka-thud, ka-thud, ka-thud again: the booming had stopped. He briefly imagined the needle edging out of the red and then willed the picture away. He was a man, for Christ's sake, and a damned good one, not a furnace with a bad thermostat. He was in great shape. He was iron. And if she needed to relearn that, he would be happy to teach her.

He started in, then thought better of it and stood where he was a moment longer, listening to her, not particularly caring about who she was talking to or what she said, only listening to the rising-falling tones of her voice. And what he felt was the old familiar dull rage.

He had met her in a downtown Chicago singles bar four years ago. Conversation had been easy enough, because they both worked in the Standard Brands Building, and knew a few of the same people. Tom worked for King & Landry, Public Relations, on forty-two. Beverly Marsh – so she had been then – was an assistant designer at Delia Fashions, on twelve. Delia, which would later enjoy a modest vogue in the Midwest, catered to young people – Delia skirts and blouses and shawls and slacks were sold largely to what Delia Castleman called 'youth-stores' and what Tom called 'headshops.' Tom Rogan knew two things about Beverly Marsh almost at once: she was desirable and she was vulnerable. In less than a month he knew a third as well: she was talented. *Very* talented. In her drawings of casual dresses and blouses he saw a money-machine of almost scary potential.

Not in the head-shops, though, he thought, but did not say (at least not then). *No more bad lighting, no more knock-down prices, no more shitty displays somewhere in the back of the store between the dope paraphernalia and the rock-group tee-shirts. Leave that shit for the small-timers.*

He had known a great deal about her before she knew he had any real interest in her, and that was just the way Tom wanted it. He had been looking for someone like Beverly Marsh all his life, and he moved in with the speed of a lion making a run at a slow antelope. Not that her vulnerability showed on the surface – you looked and saw a gorgeous woman, slim but abundantly stacked. Hips weren't so great, maybe, but she had a great ass and the best set of tits he had ever seen. Tom Rogan was a tit-man, always had been, and tall girls almost always had disappointing tits. They wore thin shirts and their nipples drove you crazy, but when you got those thin shirts off you discovered that nipples were really all they had. The tits themselves looked like the pull-knobs on a bureau drawer. 'More than a handful's wasted,' his college roommate had been fond of saying, but as far as Tom was concerned his college roommate had been so full of shit he squeaked going into a turn.

Oh, she had been some kind of fine-looking, all right, with that dynamite body and that gorgeous fall of red wavy hair. But she was weak . . . weak somehow. It was as if she was sending out radio signals which only he could receive. You could point to certain things – how much she smoked (but he had almost cured her of that), the restless way her eyes moved, never quite meeting the eyes of whoever was talking to her, only touching them from time to time and then leaping nimbly away; her habit of lightly rubbing her elbows when she was nervous; the look of her fingernails, which were kept neat but brutally short. Tom noticed this latter the first time he met her. She picked up her glass of white wine, he saw her nails, and thought: *She keeps them short like that because she bites them.*

Lions may not think, at least not the way people think . . . but they see. And when antelopes start away from a waterhole; alerted by that dusty-rug scent of approaching death, the cats can observe which one falls to the rear of the pack, maybe because it has a lame leg, maybe because it is just naturally slower . . . or maybe because its sense of danger is less developed. And it might even be possible that some antelopes – and some women – *want* to be brought down.

Suddenly he heard a sound that jerked him rudely out of these memories – the snap of her cigarette lighter.

The dull rage came again. His stomach filled with a heat which was not entirely unpleasant. Smoking. She was smoking. They had had a few of Tom Rogan's Special Seminars on the subject. And here she was, doing it again. She was a slow learner, all right, but a good teacher is at his best with slow learners.

'Yes,' she said now. 'Uh-huh. All right. Yes . . .' She listened, then uttered a strange, jagged laugh he had never heard before. 'Two things, since you ask – reserve me a room and say me a prayer. Yes, okay . . . uh-huh . . . me too. Goodnight.'

She was hanging up as he came in. He meant to come in hard, yelling at her to put it out, put it out *now*, *RIGHT NOW!*, but when he saw her the words died in his throat. He had seen her like this before, but only two or three times. Once before their first big show, once before the first private preview showing for national buyers, and once when they had gone to New York for the International Design Awards.

She was moving across the bedroom in long strides, the white lace nightgown molded to her body, the cigarette clamped between her front teeth (God he hated the way she looked with a butt in her mouth) sending back a little white riband over her left shoulder like smoke from a locomotive's stack.

But it was her face that really gave him pause, that caused the planned shout to die in his throat. His heart lurched – *ka-BAMP!* – and he winced, telling himself that what he felt was not fear but only surprise at finding her this way.

She was a woman who really came alive all the way only when the rhythm of her work spiked toward a climax. Each of those remembered occasions had of course been career-related. At those times he had seen a different woman from the one he knew so well – a woman who fucked up his sensitive fear-radar with wild bursts of static. The woman who came out in times of stress was strong but high-strung, fearless but unpredictable.

There was lots of color in her cheeks now, a natural blush high on her cheekbones. Her eyes were wide and sparkly, not a trace of sleep left in them. Her hair flowed and streamed. And . . . oh, looky here, friends and neighbors! Oh you just looky right *here*! Is she taking a suitcase out of the closet? A *suitcase*? By God, she is!

Reserve me a room . . . say me a prayer.

Well, she wasn't going to need a room in any hotel, not in the foreseeable future, because little Beverly Rogan was going to be staying right here at home, thank you very much, and taking her meals standing up for the next three or four days.

But she very well might need a prayer or two before he was through with her.

She tossed the suitcase on the foot of the bed and then went to her bureau. She opened the top drawer and pulled out two pairs of jeans and a pair of cords. Tossed them into the suitcase. Back to the bureau, cigarette streaming smoke over her shoulder. She grabbed a sweater, a couple of tee-shirts, one of the old Ship 'n Shore blouses that she looked so stupid in but refused to give up. Whoever had called her sure hadn't been a jet-setter. This was dull stuff, strictly Jackie-Kennedy-Hyannisport-weekend stuff.

Not that he cared about who had called her or where she thought she was going, since she wasn't going anywhere. Those were not the things which pecked steadily at his mind, dull and achy from too much beer and not enough sleep.

It was that cigarette.

Supposedly she had thrown them all out. But she had held out on him − the proof was clamped between her teeth right now. And because she still had not noticed him standing in the doorway, he allowed himself the pleasure of remembering the two nights which had assured him of his complete control over her.

I don't want you to smoke around me anymore, he told her as they headed home from a party in Lake Forest. October, that had been. *I have to choke that shit down at parties and at the office, but I don't have to choke it down when I'm with you. You know what it's like? I'm going to tell you the truth − it's unpleasant but it's the truth. It's like having to eat someone else's snot.*

He thought this would bring some faint spark of protest, but she had only looked at him in her shy, wanting-to-please way. Her voice had been low and meek and obedient. *All right, Tom.*

Pitch it then.

She pitched it. Tom had been in a good humor for the rest of that night.

A few weeks later, coming out of a movie, she unthinkingly lit a cigarette in the lobby and puffed it as they walked across the parking lot to the car. It had been a bitter November night, the wind chopping like a maniac at any exposed square inch of flesh it could find. Tom remembered he had been able to smell the lake, as you sometimes could on cold nights − a flat smell that was both fishy and somehow empty. He let her smoke the cigarette. He even opened her door for her when they got to the car. He got in behind the wheel, closed his own door, and then said: *Bev?*

She took the cigarette out of her mouth, turned toward him, inquiring, and he unloaded on her pretty good, his hard open hand stroking across her cheek hard enough to make his palm tingle, hard enough to rock her head back against the headrest. Her eyes widened with surprise and pain . . . and something else as well. Her own hand flew to her cheek to investigate the warmth and tingling numbness there. She cried out *Owww! Tom!*

He looked at her, eyes narrowed, mouth smiling casually, completely alive, ready to see what would come next, how she would react. His cock was stiffening in his pants, but he barely noticed. That was for later. For now, school was in session. He replayed what had just happened. Her face. What had that third expression been, there for a bare instant and then gone? First the surprise. Then the pain. Then the

(*nostalgia*)

look of a memory . . . of some memory. It had only been for a moment. He didn't think she even knew it had been there, on her face or in her mind.

Now: now. It would all be in the first thing she didn't say. He knew that as well as his own name.

It wasn't *You son of a bitch!*

It wasn't *See you later, Macho City.*

It wasn't *We're through, Tom.*

She only looked at him with her wounded, brimming hazel eyes and said: *Why did you do that?* Then she tried to say something else and burst into tears instead.

Throw it out.

What? What, Tom? Her make-up was running down her face in muddy tracks. He didn't mind that. He kind of liked seeing her that way. It was messy, but there was something sexy about it, too. Slutty. Kind of exciting.

The cigarette. Throw it out.

Realization dawning. And with it, guilt.

I just forgot! she cried. *That's all!*

Throw it out, Bev, or you're going to get another shot.

She rolled the window down and pitched the cigarette. Then she turned back to him, her face pale and scared and somehow serene.

You can't . . . you aren't supposed to hit me. That's a bad basis for a . . . a . . . a lasting relationship. She was trying to find a tone, an adult rhythm of speech, and failing. He had regressed her. He was in this car with a child. Voluptuous and sexy as hell, but a child.

101

Can't and aren't are two different things, keed, he said. He kept his voice calm but inside he was jittering and jiving. *And I'll be the one to decide what constitutes a lasting relationship and what doesn't. If you can live with that, fine. If you can't, you can take a walk. I won't stop you. I might kick you once in the ass as a going-away present, but I won't stop you. It's a free country. What more can I say?*

Maybe you've already said enough, she whispered, and he hit her again, harder than the first time, because no broad was *ever* going to smart off to Tom Rogan. He would pop the Queen of England if she cracked smart to him.

Her cheek banged the padded dashboard. Her hand groped for the doorhandle and then fell away. She only crouched in the corner like a rabbit, one hand over her mouth, her eyes large and wet and frightened. Tom looked at her for a moment and then he got out and walked around the back of the car. He opened her door. His breath was smoke in the black, windy November air and the smell of the lake was very clear.

You want to get out, Bev? I saw you reaching for the doorhandle, so I guess you must want to get out. Okay. That's all right. I asked you to do something and you said you would. Then you didn't. So you want to get out? Come on. Get out. What the fuck, right? Get out. You want to get out?

No, she whispered.

What? I can't hear you.

No, I don't want to get out, she said a little louder.

What — those cigarettes giving you emphysema? If you can't talk, I'll get you a fucking megaphone. This is your last chance, Beverly. You speak up so I can hear you: do you want to get out of this car or do you want to come back with me?

Want to come back with you, she said, and clasped her hands on her skirt like a little girl. She wouldn't look at him. Tears slipped down her cheeks.

All right, he said. *Fine. But first you say this for me, Bev. You say, 'I forgot about smoking in front of you, Tom.'*

Now she looked at him, her eyes wounded, pleading, inarticulate. You can make me do this, her eyes said, but please don't. Don't, I love you, can't it be over?

No — it could not. Because that was not the bottom of her wanting, and both of them knew it.

Say it.

I forgot about smoking in front of you, Tom.

Good. Now say 'I'm sorry.'

I'm sorry, she repeated dully.

The cigarette lay smoking on the pavement like a cut piece of fuse. People leaving the theater glanced over at them, the man standing by the open passenger door of a late-model, fade-into-the-woodwork Vega, the woman sitting inside, her hands clasped primly in her lap, her head down, the domelight outlining the soft fall of her hair in gold.

He crushed the cigarette out. He smeared it against the black-top.

Now say: 'I'll never do it again without your permission.'

I'll never . . .

Her voice began to hitch.

. . . never . . . n-n-n —

Say it, Bev.

. . . never d-do it again. Without your p-permission.

So he had slammed the door and gone back around to the driver's seat. He got behind the wheel and drove them back to his downtown apartment. Neither of them said a word. Half the relationship had been set in the parking lot; the second half was set forty minutes later, in Tom's bed.

She didn't want to make love, she said. He saw a different truth in her eyes and the strutty cock of her legs, however, and when he got her blouse off her nipples had been rock hard. She moaned when he brushed them, and cried out softly when he suckled first one and then the other, kneading them restlessly as he did so. She grabbed his hand and thrust it between her legs.

I thought you didn't want to, he said, and she had turned her face away . . . but she did not let go of his hand, and the rocking motion of her hips actually speeded up.

He pushed her back on the bed . . . and now he was gentle, not ripping her underwear but removing it with a careful consideration that was almost prissy.

Sliding into her was like sliding into some exquisite oil.

He moved with her, using her but letting her use him as well, and she came the first time almost at once, crying out and digging her nails into his back. Then they rocked together in long, slow strokes and somewhere in there he thought she came again. Tom would get close, and then he would think of White Sox batting averages or who was trying to undercut him for the Chesley account at work and he would be okay again. Then she began to speed up, her rhythm finally dissolving into an excited bucking. He looked at her face, the raccoon ringlets of mascara, the smeared lipstick, and he felt himself suddenly shooting deliriously toward the edge.

She jerked her hips up harder and harder – there had been no beergut between them in those days and their bellies clapped hands in a quickening beat.

Near the end she screamed and then bit his shoulder with her small, even teeth.

How many times did you come? he asked her after they had showered.

She turned her face away, and when she spoke her voice was so low he almost couldn't hear her. *That isn't something you're supposed to ask.*

No? Who told you that? Misterogers?

He took her face in one hand, thumb pressing deep into one cheek, fingers pressing into the other, palm cupping her chin in between.

You talk to Tom, he said. *You hear me, Bev? Talk to Papa.*

Three, she said reluctantly.

Good, he said. *You can have a cigarette.*

She looked at him distrustfully, her red hair spread over the pillows, wearing nothing but a pair of hip-hugger panties. Just looking at her that way got his motor turning over again. He nodded.

Go on, he said. *That's all right.*

They had been married in a civil ceremony three months later. Two of his friends had come; the only friend of hers to attend had been Kay McCall, whom Tom called 'that titsy women's-lib bitch.'

All of these memories went through Tom's mind in a space of seconds, like a speeded-up piece of film, as he stood in the doorway watching her. She had gone on to the bottom drawer of what she sometimes called her 'weekend bureau,' and now she was tossing underwear into the suitcase – not the sort of stuff he liked, the slippery satins and smooth silks; this was cotton stuff, little-girl stuff, most of it faded and with little puffs of popped elastic on the waistbands. A cotton nightie that looked like something out of *Little House on the Prairie*. She poked in the back of this bottom drawer to see what else might be lurking in there.

Tom Rogan, meanwhile, moved across the shag rug toward his wardrobe. His feet were bare and his passage noiseless as a puff of breeze. It was the cigarette. That was what had really gotten him mad. It had been a long time since she had forgotten that first lesson. There had been other lessons to learn since, a great many, and there had been hot days when she had worn long-sleeved blouses or even cardigan sweaters buttoned all the way to the neck. Gray days when she had worn sunglasses. But that first lesson had been so sudden and fundamental –

He had forgotten the telephone call that had wakened him out of his deepening sleep. It was the cigarette. If she was smoking now, then she had forgotten Tom Rogan. Temporarily, of course, only temporarily, but even temporarily was too damned long. What might have caused her to forget didn't matter. Such things were not to happen in his house for *any* reason.

There was a wide black strip of leather hanging from a hook inside the closet door. There was no buckle on it; he had removed that long ago. It was doubled over at one end where a buckle would have gone, and this doubled-over section formed a loop into which Tom Rogan now slipped his hand.

Tom, you been bad! his mother had sometimes said – well, 'sometimes' was maybe not such a good word; maybe 'often' would have been a better one. *You come here, Tommy! I got to give you a whuppin.* His life as a child had been punctuated by whuppins. He had finally escaped to Wichita State College, but apparently there was no such thing as a complete escape, because he continued to hear her voice in dreams: *Come here, Tommy. I got to give you a whuppin. Whuppin . . .*

He had been the eldest of four. Three months after the youngest had been born, Ralph Rogan had died – well, 'died' was maybe not such a good word; maybe 'committed suicide' would have been a better way to put it, since he had poured a generous quantity of lye into a tumbler of gin and quaffed this devil's brew while sitting on the bathroom hopper. Mrs Rogan had found work at the Ford plant. Tom, although only eleven, became the man of the family. And if he screwed up – if the baby shat her didies after the sitter went home and the mess was still in them when Mom got home . . . if he forgot to cross Megan on the Broad Street corner after her nursery school got out and that nosy Mrs Gant saw . . . if he happened to be watching American Bandstand while Joey made a mess in the kitchen . . . if any of those things or a thousand others happened . . . then, after the smaller children were in bed, the spanking stick would come out and she would call the invocation: *Come here, Tommy. I got to give you a whuppin.*

Better to be the whupper than the whupped.

If he had learned nothing else on the great toll-road of life, he had learned that.

So he flipped the loose end of the belt over once and pulled the loop snug. Then he closed his fist over it. It felt good. It made him feel like a grownup. The strip of leather hung from his clenched fist like a dead blacksnake. His headache was gone.

She had found that one last thing in the back of the drawer: an old white cotton bra with gunshell cups. The thought that this early-morning call might have been from a lover surfaced briefly in his mind and then sank again. That was ridiculous. A woman going away to meet her lover did not pack her faded Ship 'n Shore blouses and her cotton K-Mart undies with the pops and snarls in the elastic. Also, she wouldn't dare.

'Beverly,' he said softly, and she turned at once, startled, her eyes wide, her long hair swinging.

The belt hesitated . . . dropped a little. He stared at her, feeling that little bloom of uneasiness again. Yes, she had looked this way before the big shows, and then he hadn't gotten in her way, under-standing that she was so filled with a mixture of fear and competitive aggressiveness that it was as if her head was full of illuminating gas: a single spark and she would explode. She had seen the shows not as a chance to split off from Delia Fashions, to make a living – or even a fortune – on her own. If that had been all, she would have been fine. But if that were all, she also would not have been so ungodly talented. She had seen those shows as a kind of super-exam on which she would be graded by fierce teachers. What she saw on those occasions was some creature without a face. It had no face, but it did have a name – *Authority*.

All of that wide-eyed nerviness was on her face now. But not just there; it was all around her, an aura that seemed almost visible, a high-tension charge which made her suddenly both more alluring and more dangerous than she had seemed to him in years. He was afraid because she was here, all here, the essential *she* as apart from the she Tom Rogan wanted her to be, the she he had made.

Beverly looked shocked and frightened. She also looked almost madly exhilarated. Her cheeks glowed with hectic color, yet there were stark white patches below her lower lids which looked almost like a second pair of eyes. Her forehead glowed with a creamy resonance.

And the cigarette was still jutting out of her mouth, now at a slight up-angle, as if she thought she was goddam Franklin Delano Roosevelt. The cigarette! Just looking at it caused dull fury to wash over him again in a green wave. Faintly, far back in his mind, he remembered her saying something to him one night out of the dark, speaking in a dull and listless voice: *Someday you're going to kill me, Tom. Do you know that? Someday you're just going to go too far and that will be the end. You'll snap.*

He had answered: *You do it my way, Bev, and that day will never come.*

Now, before the rage blotted out everything, he wondered if that day hadn't come after all.

The cigarette. Never mind the call, the packing, the weird look on her face. They would deal with the cigarette. Then he would fuck her. Then they could discuss the rest. By then it might even seem important.

'Tom,' she said. 'Tom, I have to –'

'You're smoking,' he said. His voice seemed to come from a distance, as if over a pretty good radio. 'Looks like you forgot, babe. Where you been hiding them?'

'Look, I'll put it out,' she said, and went to the bathroom door. She flipped the cigarette – even from here he could see the teeth-marks driven deep into the filter – into the bowl of the john. *Fsssss.* She came back out. 'Tom, that was an old friend. An old *old* friend. I have to –'

'Shut up, that's what you have to do!' he shouted at her. 'Just shut up!' But the fear he wanted to see – the fear of him – was not on her face. There was fear, but it had come out of the telephone, and fear was not supposed to come to Beverly from that direction. It was almost as if she didn't see the belt, didn't see *him*, and Tom felt a trickle of unease. *Was* he here? It was a stupid question, but *was* he?

This question was so terrible and so elemental that for a moment he felt in danger of coming completely unwrapped from the root of himself and just floating off like a tumbleweed in a high breeze. Then he caught hold of himself. He was here, all right, and that was quite enough fucking psycho-babble for one night. He was here, he was Tom Rogan, *Tom by-God Rogan*, and if this dippy cunt didn't straighten up and fly right in the next thirty seconds or so, she was going to look like she got pushed out of a fast-moving boxcar by a mean railroad dick.

'Got to give you a whuppin,' he said. 'Sorry about that, babe.'

He had seen that mixture of fear and aggressiveness before, yes. Now for the first time ever it flashed out at him.

'Put that thing down,' she said. 'I have to get out to O'Hare as fast as I can.'

Are you here, Tom? Are you?

He pushed the thought away. The strip of leather which had once been a belt swung slowly before him like a pendulum. His eyes flickered and then held fast to her face.

'Listen to me, Tom. There's been some trouble back in my home town. Very bad trouble. I had a friend in those days. I guess he would have been my boyfriend, except we weren't quite old enough for that. He was only an eleven-year-old kid with a bad stutter back then. He's a novelist now. You even read one of his books, I think . . . *The Black Rapids*?'

She searched his face but his face gave no sign. There was only the belt penduluming back and forth, back and forth. He stood with his head lowered and his stocky legs slightly apart. Then she ran her hand restlessly through her hair – distractedly – as if she had many important things to think of and hadn't seen the belt at all, and that haunting, awful question resurfaced in his head again: *Are you there? Are you sure?*

'That book laid around here for weeks and I never made the connection. Maybe I should have, but we're all older and I haven't even thought about Derry in a long, long time. Anyway, Bill had a brother, George, and George was killed before I really knew Bill. He was murdered. And then, the next summer –'

But Tom had listened to enough craziness from within and from without. He moved in on her fast, cocking his right arm back over his shoulder like a man about to throw a javelin. The belt hissed a path through the air. Beverly saw it coming and tried to duck away, but her right shoulder struck the bathroom doorway and there was a meaty *whap*! as the belt struck her left forearm, leaving a red weal.

'Gonna whup you,' Tom repeated. His voice was sane, even regretful, but his teeth showed in a white and frozen smile. He wanted to see that look in her eyes, that look of fear and terror and shame, that look that said *Yes you're right I deserved it*, that look that said *Yes you're there all right, I feel your presence*. Then love could come back, and that was right and good, because he *did* love her. They could even have a discussion, if she wanted it, of exactly who had called and what all this was about. But that must come later. For now, school was in session. The old one-two. First the whuppin, then the fuckin.

'Sorry, babe.'

'Tom, don't do th –'

He swung the belt sidearm and saw it lick around her hip. There was a satisfying snap as it finished on her buttock. And . . .

And Jesus, she was grabbing at it! She was grabbing at the belt!

For a moment Tom Rogan was so astounded by this unexpected act of insubordination that he almost lost his punisher, *would* have lost it except for the loop, which was tucked securely into his fist.

He jerked it back.

'Don't you *ever* try to grab something away from me,' he said hoarsely. 'You hear me? You ever do that again and you'll spend a month pissing raspberry juice.'

'Tom, stop it,' she said, and her very *tone* infuriated him – she sounded like a playground monitor talking down to a tantrumy six-year-old. 'I *have* to go. This is no joke. People are dead, and I made a promise a long time ago –'

Tom heard little of this. He bellowed and ran at her with his head down, the belt swinging blindly. He hit her with it, driving her away from the doorway and along the bedroom wall. He cocked his arm back, hit her, cocked his arm back, hit her, cocked his arm back, hit her. Later that morning he would not be able to raise the arm above eye level until he had swallowed three codeine tablets, but for now he was aware of nothing but the fact that she was *defying* him. She had not only been smoking, *she had tried to grab the belt away from him*, and oh folks, oh friends and neighbors, she had asked for it, and he would testify before the throne of God Almighty that she was going to get it.

He drove her along the wall, swinging the belt, raining blows on her. Her hands were up to protect her face, but he had a clear shot at the rest of her. The belt made thick bullwhip cracks in the quiet room. But she did not scream, as she sometimes did, and she did not beg him to stop, as she usually did. Worst of all, she did not cry, as she *always* did. The only sounds were the belt and their breathing, his heavy and hoarse, hers quick and light.

She broke for the bed and the vanity table on her side of it. Her shoulders were red from the belt's blows. Her hair streamed fire. He lumbered after her, slower but big, very big – he had played squash until he had popped an Achilles tendon two years ago, and since then his weight had gotten out of hand a little bit (or maybe 'a lot' would have been a better way to put it), but the muscle was still there, firm cordage sheathed in the fat. Still, he was a little alarmed at how out of breath he was.

She reached the vanity and he thought she would crouch there, or maybe try to crawl under it. Instead she groped . . . turned . . . and suddenly the air was full of flying missiles. She was throwing cosmetics at him. A bottle of Chantilly struck him squarely between the nipples, fell to his feet, shattered. He was suddenly enveloped in the gagging scent of flowers.

'Quit it!' he roared. '*Quit it, you bitch!*'

Instead of quitting it, her hands flew along the vanity's littered glass top, grabbing whatever they found, throwing it. He groped at his

109

chest where the bottle of Chantilly had struck him, unable to believe she had hit him with something, even as other objects flew around him. The bottle's glass stopper had cut him. It was not much of a cut, little more than a triangular scratch, but was there a certain red-haired lady who was going to see the sun come up from a hospital bed? Oh yes, there was. A certain lady who –

A jar of cream struck him above the right eyebrow with sudden, cracking force. He heard a dull thud seemingly *inside* his head. White light exploded over that eye's field of vision and he fell back a step, mouth dropping open. Now a tube of Nivea cream struck his belly with a small slapping sound and she was – *was* she? was it *possible*? – yes! She was *yelling* at him!

'I'm going to the airport, you son of a bitch! Do you hear me? I have business and I'm going! You want to get out of my way because I'M GOING!'

Blood ran into his right eye, stinging and hot. He knuckled it away.

He stood there for a moment, staring at her as if he had never seen her before. In a way he never had. Her breasts heaved rapidly. Her face, all flush and livid pallor, blazed. Her lips were drawn back from her teeth in a snarl. She had, however, denuded the top of the vanity table. The missile silo was empty. He could still read the fear in her eyes . . . but it was still not fear of him.

'You put those clothes back,' he said, struggling not to pant as he spoke. That would not sound good. That would sound weak. 'Then you put the suitcase back and get into bed. And if you do those things, maybe I won't beat you up too bad. Maybe you'll be able to go out of the house in two days instead of two weeks.'

'Tom, listen to me.' She spoke slowly. Her gaze was very clear. 'If you come near me again, I'll kill you. Do you understand that, you tub of guts? I'll kill you.'

And suddenly – maybe it was because of the utter loathing on her face, the contempt, maybe because she had called him a tub of guts, or maybe only because of the rebellious way her breasts rose and fell – the fear was suffocating him. It was not a bud or a bloom but a whole goddam *garden*, the fear, the horrible fear that he was not *here*.

Tom Rogan rushed at his wife, not bellowing this time. He came as silently as a torpedo cutting through the water. His intent now was probably not merely to beat and subjugate but to do to her what she had so rashly said she would do to him.

He thought she would run. Probably for the bathroom. Maybe for the stairs. Instead, she stood her ground. Her hip whacked the wall as she threw her weight against the vanity table, pushing it up and toward him, ripping two fingernails down to the quick when the sweat on her palms caused her hands to slip.

For a moment the table tottered on an angle and then she shoved herself forward again. The vanity waltzed on one leg, mirror catching the light and reflecting a brief swimmy aquarium shadow across the ceiling, and then it tilted forward and outward. Its leading edge slammed into Tom's upper thighs and knocked him over. There was a musical jingle as bottles tipped over and shattered inside. He saw the mirror strike the floor on his left and threw an arm up to shield his eyes, losing the belt. Glass coughed across the floor, silver on the back. He felt some of it sting him, drawing blood.

Now she was crying, her breath coming in high, screamy sobs. Time after time she had seen herself leaving him, leaving Tom's tyranny as she had left that of her father, stealing away in the night, bags piled in the trunk of her Cutlass. She was not a stupid woman, certainly not stupid enough even now, standing on the rim of this incredible shambles, to believe that she had not loved Tom and did not in some way love him still. But that did not preclude her fear of him . . . her hate of him . . . and her contempt of herself for choosing him for dim reasons buried in the times that should be over. Her heart was not breaking; it seemed rather to be broiling in her chest, melting. She was afraid the heat from her heart might soon destroy her sanity in fire.

But above all this, yammering steadily in the back of her mind, she could hear Mike Hanlon's dry, steady voice: *It's come back, Beverly . . . it's come back . . . and you promised . . .*

The vanity heaved up and down. Once. Twice. A third time. It looked as if it were breathing.

Moving with careful agility, her mouth turned down at the corners and jerking as if in prelude to some sort of convulsion, she skirted the vanity, toe-stepping through the broken glass, and grabbed the belt just as Tom heaved the vanity off to one side. Then she backed up, sliding her hand into the loop. She shook her hair out of her eyes and watched to see what he would do.

Tom got up. Some of the mirror-glass had cut one of his cheeks. A diagonal cut traced a line as fine as thread across his brow. He squinted at her as he rose slowly to his feet, and she saw drops of blood on his boxer shorts.

'You just give me that belt,' he said.

Instead she took two turns of it around her hand and looked at him defiantly.

'Quit it, Bev. Right now.'

'If you come for me, I'm going to strap the shit out of you.' The words were coming out of her mouth but she couldn't believe it was her saying them. And just who was this caveman in the bloody undershorts, anyway? Her husband? Her father? The lover she had taken in college who had broken her nose one night, apparently on a whim? *Oh God help me*, she thought. *God help me now*. And still her mouth went on. 'I can do it, too. You're fat and slow, Tom. I'm going, and I think maybe I'll stay gone. I think maybe it's over.'

'Who's this guy Denbrough?'

'Forget it. I was —'

She realized almost too late that the question had been a distraction. He was coming for her before the last word was out of his mouth. She whickered the belt through the air in an arc and the sound it made when it smashed across his mouth was the sound of a stubborn cork coming out of a bottle.

He squealed and clapped his hands to his mouth, his eyes huge, hurt and shocked. Blood began to pour between his fingers and over the backs of his hands.

'You broke my mouth, you bitch!' he screamed, muffled. 'Ah God you broke my *mouth!*'

He came at her again, hands reaching, his mouth a wet red smear. His lips appeared to have burst in two places. The crown had been knocked from one of his front teeth. As she watched, he spit it to one side. Part of her was backing away from this scene, sick and moaning, wanting to shut her eyes. But that other Beverly felt the exultation of a death-row convict freed in a freak earthquake. That Beverly liked all of this just fine. *I wish you'd swallowed it!* that one thought. *Wish you'd choked on it!*

It was this latter Beverly who swung the belt for the last time — the belt he had used on her buttocks, her legs, her breasts. The belt he had used on her times without number over the last four years. How many strokes you got depended on how badly you'd screwed up. Tom comes home and dinner is cold? Two with the belt. Bev's working late at the studio and forgets to call home? Three with the belt. Oh hey, look at this — Beverly got another parking ticket. One with the belt . . . across the breasts. He was good. He rarely bruised. It didn't even hurt that much. Except for the humiliation. *That* hurt.

And what hurt worse was knowing that part of her craved the hurt. Craved the humiliation.

Last time pays for all, she thought, and swung.

She brought the belt in low, brought it in sidearm, and it whacked across his balls with a brisk yet heavy sound, the sound of a woman striking a rug with a carpet-beater. That was all it took. All the fight promptly went out of Tom Rogan.

He uttered a thin, strengthless shriek and fell on his knees as if to pray. His hands were between his legs. His head was thrown back. Cords stood out on his neck. His mouth was a tragedy-grimace of pain. His left knee came down squarely on a heavy, pointed hook of shattered perfume bottle and he rolled silently over on one side like a whale. One hand left his balls to grab his squirting knee.

The blood, she thought. *Dear Lord, he's bleeding everywhere.*

He'll live, this new Beverly – the Beverly who seemed to have surfaced at Mike Hanlon's phone call – replied coldly. *Guys like him always live. You just get the hell out of here before he decides he wants to tango some more. Or before he decides to go down cellar and get his Winchester.*

She backed away and felt pain stab her foot as she stepped on a chunk of glass from the broken vanity mirror. She bent down to grab the handle of her suitcase. She never took her eyes off him. She backed out the door and she backed down the hall. She was holding the suitcase in front of her in both hands and it banged her shins as she backed. Her cut foot printed bloody heel-prints. When she reached the stairs she turned around and went down quickly, not letting herself think. She suspected she had no coherent thoughts left inside anyway, at least for the time being.

She felt a light pawing against her leg and screamed.

She looked down and saw it was the end of the belt. It was still wrapped around her hand. In this dim light it looked more like a dead snake than ever. She threw it over the bannister, her face a wince of disgust, and saw it land in an S on the rug of the downstairs hallway.

At the foot of the stairs she grasped the hem of her white lace nightgown cross-handed and pulled it over her head. It was bloody, and she would not wear it one second longer, no matter what. She tossed it aside and it billowed onto the rubber-plant by the doorway to the living room like a lacy parachute. She bent, naked, to the suit-case. Her nipples were cold, hard as bullets.

'BEVERLY YOU GET YOUR ASS UPSTAIRS!'

She gasped, jerked, then bent back to the suitcase. If he was strong enough to scream that loud, her time was a good deal shorter than she had thought. She opened the case and pawed out panties, a blouse, an old pair of Levi's. She jerked these on standing by the door, her eyes never leaving the stairs. But Tom did not appear at the top of them. He bawled her name twice more, and each time she flinched away from that sound, her eyes hunted, her lips pulling back from her teeth in an unconscious snarl.

She jabbed the buttons of the blouse through the holes as fast as she could. The top two buttons were gone (it was ironic how little of her own sewing ever got done) and she supposed she looked quite a bit like a part-time hooker looking for one last quickie before calling it a night – but it would have to do.

'I'LL KILL YOU, YOU BITCH! YOU FUCKING BITCH!'

She slammed the suitcase closed and latched it. The arm of a blouse poked out like a tongue. She looked around once, quickly, suspecting that she would never see this house again.

She discovered only relief in the idea, and so opened the door and let herself out.

She was three blocks away, walking with no clear sense of where she was going, when she realized her feet were still bare. The one she had cut – the left – throbbed dully. She had to get something on her feet, and it was nearly two o'clock in the morning. Her wallet and credit-cards were at home. She felt in the pockets of the jeans and came up with nothing but a few puffs of lint. She didn't have a dime; not so much as a red penny. She looked around at the residential neighborhood she was in – nice homes, manicured lawns and plantings, dark windows.

And suddenly she began to laugh.

Beverly Rogan sat on a low stone wall, her suitcase between her dirty feet, and laughed. The stars were out, and how bright they were! She tilted her head back and laughed at them, that wild exhilaration washing through her again like a tidal wave that lifted and carried and cleansed, a force so powerful that any conscious thought was lost; only her blood thought and its one powerful voice spoke to her in some inarticulate way of desire, although what it was it desired she neither knew nor cared. It was enough to feel that warmth filling her up with its insistence. *Desire*, she thought, and inside her that tidal wave of exhilaration seemed to gather speed, rushing her onward toward some inevitable crash.

She laughed at the stars, frightened but free, her terror as sharp as pain and as sweet as a ripe October apple, and when a light came on in an upstairs bedroom of the house this stone wall belonged to, she grabbed the handle of her suitcase and fled off into the night, still laughing.

6

Bill Denbrough Takes Time Out

'*Leave?*' Audra repeated. She looked at him, puzzled, a bit afraid, and then tucked her bare feet up and under her. The floor was cold. The whole *cottage* was cold, come to that. The south of England had been experiencing an exceptionally dank spring, and more than once, on his regular morning and evening walks, Bill Denbrough had found himself thinking of Maine . . . thinking in a surprised vague way of Derry.

The cottage was supposed to have central heating – the ad had said so, and there certainly was a furnace down there in the tidy little basement, tucked away in what had once been a coal-bin – but he and Audra had discovered early on in the shoot that the British idea of central heating was not at all the same as the American one. It seemed the Brits believed you had central heating as long as you didn't have to piss away a scrim of ice in the toilet bowl when you got up in the morning. It was morning now – just quarter of eight. Bill had hung the phone up five minutes ago.

'Bill, you can't just *leave*. You *know* that.'

'I have to,' he said. There was a hutch on the far side of the room. He went to it, took a bottle of Glenfiddich from the top shelf and poured himself a drink. Some of it slopped over the side of the glass. 'Fuck,' he muttered.

'Who was that on the telephone? What are you scared of, Bill?'

'I'm not scared.'

'Oh? Your hands always shake like that? You always have your first drink before breakfast?'

He came back to his chair, robe flapping around his ankles, and sat down. He tried to smile, but it was a poor effort and he gave it up.

On the telly the BBC announcer was wrapping up this morning's batch of bad news before going on to last evening's football scores. When they had arrived in the small suburban village of Fleet a month before the shoot was scheduled to begin, they had both marvelled over the technical quality of British television – on a good Pye color set, it

115

really did look as though you could climb right inside. *More lines or something*, Bill had said. *I don't know what it is, but it's great*, Audra had replied. That was before they discovered that much of the programming consisted of American shows such as *Dallas* and endless British sports events ranging from the arcane and boring (champion darts-throwing in which all the participants looked like hypertensive sumo wrestlers) to the simply boring (British football was bad; cricket was even worse).

'I've been thinking about home a lot lately,' Bill said, and sipped his drink.

'Home?' she said, and looked so honestly puzzled that he laughed.

'Poor Audra! Married almost eleven years to the guy and you don't know doodley-squat about him. What do you know about that?' He laughed again and swallowed the rest of his drink. His laughter had a quality she cared for as little as seeing him with a glass of Scotch in his hand at this hour of the morning. The laugh sounded like something that really wanted to be a howl of pain. 'I wonder if any of the others have got husbands and wives who are just finding out how little they know. I suppose they must.'

'Billy, I know that I love you,' she said. 'For eleven years that's been enough.'

'I know.' He smiled at her – the smile was sweet, tired, and scared.

'Please. Please tell me what this is about.'

She looked at him with her lovely gray eyes, sitting there in a tatty leased-house chair with her feet curled beneath the hem of her nightgown, a woman he had loved, married, and still loved. He tried to see through her eyes, to see what she knew. He tried to see it as a story. He could, but he knew it would never sell.

Here is a poor boy from the state of Maine who goes to the University on a scholarship. All his life he has wanted to be a writer, but when he enrolls in the writing courses he finds himself lost without a compass in a strange and frightening land. There's one guy who wants to be Updike. There's another one who wants to be a New England version of Faulkner – only he wants to write novels about the grim lives of the poor in blank verse. There's a girl who admires Joyce Carol Oates but feels that because Oates was nurtured in a sexist society she is 'radioactive in a literary sense.' Oates is unable to be clean, this girl says. She will be cleaner. There's the short fat grad student who can't or won't speak above a mutter. This guy has written a play in which there are nine characters. Each of them says only a single word. Little by little the playgoers realize that when you put the single words together you come out with 'War is the tool of the sexist death merchants.' This fellow's play receives an A from the man who teaches Eh-141 (Creative Writing Honors Seminar). This instructor has published four books of poetry and his master's thesis, all with the University Press. He smokes pot and wears a peace medallion. The fat mutterer's play is produced by a guerrilla theater group during the strike to end the war which shuts down the campus in May of 1970. The instructor plays one of the characters.

Bill Denbrough, meanwhile, has written one locked-room mystery tale, three science-fiction stories, and several horror tales which owe a great deal to Edgar Allan Poe, H. P. Lovecraft, and Richard Matheson – in later years he will say those stories resembled a mid-1800s funeral hack equipped with a supercharger and painted Day-Glo red.

One of the sf tales earns him a B.

'*This is better*,' the instructor writes on the title page. '*In the alien counterstrike we see the vicious circle in which violence begets violence; I particularly liked the "needle-nosed" spacecraft as a symbol of socio-sexual incursion. While this remains a slightly confused undertone throughout, it is interesting.*'

All the others do no better than a C.

Finally he stands up in class one day, after the discussion of a sallow young woman's vignette about a cow's examination of a discarded engine block in a deserted field (this may or may not be after a nuclear war) has gone on for seventy minutes or so. The sallow girl, who smokes one Winston after another and picks occasionally at the pimples which nestle in the hollows of her temples, insists that the vignette is a socio-political statement in the manner of the early Orwell. Most of the class – and the instructor – agree, but still the discussion drones on.

When Bill stands up, the class looks at him. He is tall, and has a certain presence.

Speaking carefully, not stuttering (he has not stuttered in better than five years), he says: 'I don't understand this at all. I don't understand *any* of this. Why does a story have to be socio-anything? Politics . . . culture . . . history . . . aren't those natural ingredients in any story, if it's told well? I mean . . .' He looks around, sees hostile eyes, and realizes dimly that they see this as some sort of attack. Maybe it even is. They are thinking, he realizes, that maybe there is a sexist death merchant in their midst. 'I mean . . . can't you guys just let a story be a *story*?'

No one replies. Silence spins out. He stands there looking from one cool set of eyes to the next. The sallow girl chuffs out smoke and stubs her cigarette in an ashtray she has brought along in her backpack.

Finally the instructor says softly, as if to a child having an inexplicable tantrum, 'Do you believe William Faulkner was just telling *stories*? Do you believe Shakespeare was just interested in *making a buck*? Come now, Bill. Tell us what you think.'

'I think that's pretty close to the truth,' Bill says after a long moment in which he honestly considers the question, and in their eyes he reads a kind of damnation.

'I suggest,' the instructor says, toying with his pen and smiling at Bill with half-lidded eyes, 'that you have a *great deal* to learn.'

The applause starts somewhere in the back of the room.

Bill leaves . . . but returns the next week, determined to stick with it. In the time between he has written a story called 'The Dark,' a tale about a small boy who discovers a monster in the cellar of his house. The little boy faces it, battles it, finally kills it. He feels a kind of holy exaltation as he goes about the business of writing this story; he even feels that he is not so much *telling* the story as he is allowing the story to *flow through* him. At one point he puts his pen down and takes his hot and aching hand out into ten-degree December cold where it nearly smokes from the temperature change. He walks around, green cut-off boots squeaking in the snow like tiny shutter-hinges which need oil, and his head seems to *bulge* with the story; it is a little scary, the way it needs to get out. He feels that if it cannot escape by way of his racing hand that it will pop his eyes out in its urgency to escape and be concrete. 'Going to knock the *shit* out of it,' he confides to the blowing winter dark, and laughs a little – a shaky laugh. He is aware that he has finally discovered how to do just that – after ten years of trying he has suddenly found the starter button on the vast dead bulldozer taking up so much space inside his head. It has started up. It is revving, revving. It is nothing pretty, this big machine. It was not made for taking pretty girls to proms. It is not a status symbol. It means business. It can knock things down. If he isn't careful, it will knock *him* down.

He rushes inside and finishes 'The Dark' at white heat, writing until four o'clock in the morning and finally falling asleep over his ring-binder. If someone had suggested to him that he was really writing about his brother, George, he would have been surprised. He has not thought about George in years – or so he honestly believes.

The story comes back from the instructor with an F slashed into the title page. Two words are scrawled beneath, in capital letters. PULP, screams one. CRAP, screams the other.

Bill takes the fifteen-page sheaf of manuscript over to the wood-stove and opens the door. He is within a bare inch of tossing it in when the absurdity of what he is doing strikes him. He sits down in his rocking chair, looks at a Grateful Dead poster, and starts to laugh. Pulp? Fine! Let it be pulp! The woods were full of it!

'Let them fucking trees fall!' Bill exclaims, and laughs until tears spurt from his eyes and roll down his face.

He retypes the title page, the one with the instructor's judgment on it, and sends it off to a men's magazine named *White Tie* (although from what Bill can see, it really should be titled *Naked Girls Who Look Like Drug Users*). Yet his battered *Writer's Market* says they buy horror stories, and the two issues he has bought down at the local mom-and-pop store have indeed contained four horror stories sandwiched between the naked girls and the ads for dirty movies and potency pills. One of them, by a man named Dennis Etchison, is actually quite good.

He sends 'The Dark' off with no real hopes – he has submitted a good many stories to magazines before with nothing to show for it but rejection slips – and is flabbergasted and delighted when the fiction editor of *White Tie* buys it for two hundred dollars, payment on publication. The assistant editor adds a short note which calls it 'the best damned horror story since Ray Bradbury's "The Jar."' He adds, 'Too bad only about seventy people coast to coast will read it,' but Bill Denbrough does not care. Two hundred dollars!

He goes to his advisor with a drop card for Eh-141. His advisor initials it. Bill Denbrough staples the drop card to the assistant fiction editor's congratulatory note and tacks both to the bulletin board on the creative-writing instructor's door. In the corner of the bulletin board he sees an anti-war cartoon. And suddenly, as if moving of its own accord, his fingers pluck his pen from his breast pocket and across the cartoon he writes this: *If fiction and politics ever really do become interchangeable, I'm going to kill myself, because I won't know what else to do. You see, politics always change. Stories never do.* He pauses, and then, feeling a bit small (but unable to help himself), he adds: *I suggest you have a lot to learn.*

His drop card comes back to him in the campus mail three days later. The instructor has initialed it. On the space marked GRADE AT TIME OF DROP, the instructor has not given him an incomplete or the low C to which his run of grades at that time would have entitled him; instead, another F is slashed angrily across the grade line. Below it the instructor has written: *Do you think money proves anything about anything, Denbrough?*

'Well, actually, yes,' Bill Denbrough says to his empty apartment, and once more begins to laugh crazily.

In his senior year of college he dares to write a novel because he has no idea what he's getting into. He escapes the experience scratched and frightened . . . but alive, and with a manuscript nearly five hundred pages long. He sends it out to The Viking Press, knowing that it will be the first of many stops for his book, which is about ghosts . . . but he likes Viking's ship logo, and that makes it as good a place to start as any. As it turns out, the first stop is also the last stop. Viking purchases the book . . . and for Bill Denbrough the fairytale begins. The man who was once known as Stuttering Bill has become a success at the age of twenty-three. Three years later and three thousand miles from northern New England, he attains a queer kind of celebrity by marrying a woman who is a movie-star and five years his senior at Hollywood's Church in the Pines.

The gossip columnists give it seven months. The only bet, they say, is whether the end will come in a divorce or an annulment. Friends (and enemies) on both sides of the match feel about the same. The age difference apart, the disparities are startling. He is tall, already balding, already inclining a bit toward fat. He speaks slowly in company, and at times seems nearly inarticulate. Audra, on the other hand, is auburn-haired, statuesque, and gorgeous – she is less like an earthly woman than a creature from some semi-divine superrace.

He has been hired to do the screenplay of his second novel, *The Black Rapids* (mostly because the right to do at least the first draft of the screenplay was an immutable condition of sale, in spite of his agent's moans that he was insane), and his draft has actually turned out pretty well. He has been invited out to Universal City for further rewrites and production meetings.

His agent is a small woman named Susan Browne. She is exactly five feet tall. She is violently energetic and even more violently emphatic. 'Don't do it, Billy,' she tells him. 'Kiss it off. They've got a lot of money tied up in it and they'll get someone good to do the screenplay. Maybe even Goldman.'

'Who?'

'William Goldman. The only good writer who ever went out there and did both.'

'What are you talking about, Suze?'

'He stayed there and he stayed good,' she said. 'The odds on both are like the odds on beating lung cancer – it can be done, but who wants to try? You'll burn out on sex and booze. Or some of the nifty new drugs.' Susan's crazily fascinating brown eyes sparkle vehemently up at him. 'And if it turns out to be some meatball who gets the assignment instead of someone like Goldman, so what? The book's on the shelf there. They can't change a word.'

'Susan –'

'Listen to me, Billy! Take the money and run. You're young and strong. That's what they like. You go out there and they will first separate you from your self-respect and then from your ability to write a straight line from point A to point B. Last but not least, they will take your testes. You write like a grownup, but you're just a kid with a very high forehead.'

'I have to go.'

'Did someone just fart in here?' she returns. 'Must have, because something sure stinks.'

'But I do. I *have* to.'

'Jesus!'

'I have to get away from New England.' He is afraid to say what comes next – it's like mouthing a curse – but he owes it to her. 'I have to get away from Maine.'

'*Why*, for God's sake?'

'I don't know. I just do.'

'Are you telling me something real, Billy, or just talking like a writer?'

'It's real.'

They are in bed together during this conversation. Her breasts are small like peaches, sweet like peaches. He loves her a lot, although not the way they both know would be a really good way to love. She sits up with a pool of sheet in her lap and lights a cigarette. She's crying, but he doubts if she knows he knows. It's just this shine in her eyes. It would be tactful not to mention it, so he doesn't. He doesn't love her in that really good way, but he cares a mountain for her.

'Go on then,' she says in a dry businesslike voice as she turns back to him. 'Give me a call when you're ready, and if you still have the strength. I'll come and pick up the pieces. If there are any left.'

The film version of *The Black Rapids* is called *Pit of the Black Demon*, and Audra Phillips is cast as the lead. The title is horrible, but the movie turns out to be quite good. And the only part of him he loses in Hollywood is his heart.

'Bill,' Audra said again, bringing him out of these memories. He

121

saw she had snapped off the TV. He glanced out the window and saw fog nuzzling against the panes.

'I'll explain as much as I can,' he said. 'You deserve that. But first do two things for me.'

'All right.'

'Fix yourself another cup of tea and tell me what you know about me. Or what you think you know.'

She looked at him, puzzled, and then went to the highboy.

'I know you're from Maine,' she said, making herself tea from the breakfast pot. She was not British, but just a touch of clipped British had crept into her voice – a holdover from the part she played in *Attic Room*, the movie they had come over here to do. It was Bill's first original screenplay. He had been offered the directorial shot as well. Thank God he had declined that; his leaving now would have completed the job of bitching things up. He knew what they would all say, the whole crew. Billy Denbrough finally shows his true colors. Just another fucking writer, crazier than a shithouse rat.

God knew he felt crazy right about now.

'I know you had a brother and that you loved him very much and that he died,' Audra went on. 'I know that you grew up in a town called Derry, moved to Bangor about two years after your brother died, and moved to Portland when you were fourteen. I know your dad died of lung cancer when you were seventeen. And you wrote a best-seller while you were still in college, paying your way with a scholarship and a part-time job in a textile mill. That must have seemed very strange to you . . . the change in income. In prospects.'

She returned to his side of the room and he saw it in her face then: the realization of the hidden spaces between them.

'I know that you wrote *The Black Rapids* a year later, and came out to Hollywood. And the week before shooting started on the movie, you met a very mixed-up woman named Audra Phillips who knew a little bit about what you must have been through – the crazy decompression – because she had been plain old Audrey Philpott five years before. And this woman was drowning –'

'Audra, don't.'

Her eyes were steady, holding his. 'Oh, why not? Let us tell the truth and shame the devil. I was drowning. I discovered poppers two years before I met you, and then a year later I discovered coke and that was even better. A popper in the morning, coke in the afternoon, wine at night, a Valium at bedtime. Audra's vitamins. Too many important interviews, too many good parts. I was so much like a character in a Jacqueline Susann novel it was hilarious. Do you know how I think about that time now, Bill?'

'No.'

She sipped her tea, her eyes never leaving his, and grinned. 'It was like running on the walkway at LA International. You get it?'

'Not exactly, no.'

'It's a moving belt,' she said. 'About a quarter of a mile long.'

'I know the walkway,' he said, 'but I don't see what you're –'

'You just stand there and it carries you all the way to the baggage-claim area. But if you want, you don't have to just stand there. You can walk on it. Or run. And it seems like you're just doing your normal walk or your normal jog or your normal run or your normal all-out sprint – whatever – because your body forgets that what you're *really* doing is topping the speed the walkway's already making. That's why they have those signs that say SLOW DOWN, MOVING RAMPWAY near the end. When I met you I felt as if I'd run right off the end of that thing onto a floor that didn't move anymore. There I was, my body nine miles ahead of my feet. You can't keep your balance. Sooner or later you fall right on your face. Except I didn't. Because you caught me.'

She put her tea aside and lit a cigarette, her eyes never leaving him. He could only see that her hands were shaking in the minute jitter of the lighter-flame, which darted first to the right of the cigarette-end and then to the left before finding it.

She drew deep, blew out a fast jet of smoke.

'What do I know about you? I know you seemed to have it all under control. I know that. You never seemed to be in a hurry to get to the next drink or the next meeting or the next party. You seemed confident that all those things would be there . . . if you wanted them. You talked slow. Part of it was the Maine drawl, I guess, but most of it was just you. You were the first man I ever met out there who dared to talk slow. I had to slow down to listen. I looked at you, Bill, and I saw someone who never ran on the walkway, because he knew it would get him there. You seemed utterly untouched by the hype and hysteria. You didn't lease a Rolls so you could drive down Rodeo Drive on Saturday afternoon with your own vanity plates on some glitzy rental company's car. You didn't have a press agent to plant items in *Variety* or *The Hollywood Reporter*. You'd never done the Carson show.'

'Writers can't unless they also do card-tricks or bend spoons,' he said, smiling. 'It's like a national law.'

He thought she would smile, but she didn't. 'I know you were there when I needed you. When I came flying off the end of the walkway like O. J. Simpson in that old Hertz ad. Maybe you saved me from eating the wrong pill on top of too much booze. Or maybe I would have made it out the other side on my own and it's all a big dramatization on my part. But . . . it doesn't feel like that. Not inside, where I am.'

She snuffed the cigarette, only two puffs gone.

'I know you've been there ever since. And I've been there for you. We're good in bed. That used to seem like a big deal to me. But we're also good out of it, and now that seems like a bigger deal. I feel as if I could grow old with you and still be brave. I know you drink too much beer and don't get enough exercise; I know that some nights you dream badly –'

He was startled. Nastily startled. Almost frightened.

'I never dream.'

She smiled. 'So you tell the interviewers when they ask where you get your ideas. But it's not true. Unless it's just indigestion when you start groaning in the night. And I don't believe that, Billy.'

'Do I talk?' he asked cautiously. He could remember no dreams. No dreams at all, good *or* bad.

Audra nodded. 'Sometimes. But I can never make out what it is you say. And on a couple of occasions, you have wept.'

He looked at her blankly. There was a bad taste in his mouth; it trailed back along his tongue and down his throat like the taste of melted aspirin. *So now you know how fear tastes,* he thought. *Time you found out, considering all you've written on the subject.* He supposed it was a taste he would get used to. If he lived long enough.

Memories were suddenly trying to crowd in. It was as if a black sac in his mind were bulging, threatening to spew noxious

(*dreams*)

images up from his subconscious and into the mental field of vision commanded by his rational waking mind – and if that happened all at once, it would drive him mad. He tried to push them back, and succeeded, but not before he heard a voice – it was as if someone buried alive had cried out from the ground. It was Eddie Kaspbrak's voice.

You saved my life, Bill. Those big boys, they drive me bugshit. Sometimes I think they really want to kill me –

'Your arms,' Audra said.

Bill looked down at them. The flesh there had humped into

124

gooseflesh. Not little bumps but huge white knobs like insect eggs. They both stared, saying nothing, as if looking at an interesting museum exhibit. The goosebumps slowly melted away.

In the silence that followed Audra said: 'And I know one other thing. Someone called you this morning from the States and said you have to leave me.'

He got up, looked briefly at the liquor bottles, then went into the kitchen and came back with a glass of orange juice. He said: 'You know I had a brother, and you know he died, but you don't know he was murdered.'

Audra took in a quick snatch of breath.

'Murdered! Oh, Bill, why didn't you ever –'

'Tell you?' He laughed, that barking sound again. 'I don't know.'

'What happened?'

'We were living in Derry then. There had been a flood, but it was mostly over, and George was bored. I was sick in bed with the flu. He wanted me to make him a boat out of a sheet of newspaper. I knew how from daycamp the year before. He said he was going to sail it down the gutters on Witcham Street and Jackson Street, because they were still full of water. So I made him the boat and he thanked me and he went out and that was the last time I ever saw my brother George alive. If I hadn't had the flu, maybe I could have saved him.'

He paused, right palm rubbing at his left cheek, as if testing for beard-stubble. His eyes, magnified by the lenses of his glasses, looked thoughtful . . . but he was not looking at her.

'It happened right there on Witcham Street, not too far from the intersection with Jackson. Whoever killed him pulled his left arm off the way a second-grader would pull a wing off a fly. Medical examiner said he either died of shock or blood-loss. Far as I could ever see, it didn't make a dime's worth of difference which it was.'

'*Christ*, Bill!'

'I imagine you wonder why I never told you. The truth is I wonder myself. Here we've been married eleven years and until today you never knew what happened to Georgie. I know about your whole family – even your aunts and uncles. I know your grandfather died in his garage in Iowa City frigging around with his chainsaw while he was drunk. I know those things because married people, no matter how busy they are, get to know almost everything after awhile. And if they get really bored and stop listening, they pick it up anyway – by osmosis. Or do you think I'm wrong?'

'No,' she said faintly. 'You're not wrong, Bill.'

'And we've always been able to talk to each other, haven't we? I mean, neither of us got so bored it ever had to be osmosis, right?'

'Well,' she said, 'until today I always thought so.'

'Come on, Audra. You know everything that's happened to me over the last eleven years of my life. Every deal, every idea, every cold, every friend, every guy that ever did me wrong or tried to. You know I slept with Susan Browne. You know that sometimes I get maudlin when I drink and play the records too loud.'

'Especially the Grateful Dead,' she said, and he laughed. This time she smiled back.

'You know the most important stuff, too – the things I hope for.'

'Yes. I think so. But this . . .' She paused, shook her head, thought for a moment. 'How much does this call have to do with your brother, Bill?'

'Let me get to it in my own way. Don't try to rush me into the center of it or you'll have me committed. It's so big . . . and so . . . so quaintly awful . . . that I'm trying to sort of creep up on it. You see . . . it never occurred to me to tell you about Georgie.'

She looked at him, frowned, shook her head faintly – *I don't understand.*

'What I'm trying to tell you, Audra, is that I haven't even *thought* of George in twenty years or more.'

'But you told me you had a brother named –'

'I repeated a *fact*,' he said. 'That was all. His name was a word. It cast no shadow at all in my mind.'

'But I think maybe it cast a shadow over your dreams,' Audra said. Her voice was very quiet.

'The groaning? The crying?'

She nodded.

'I suppose you could be right,' he said. 'In fact, you're almost surely right. But dreams you don't remember don't really count, do they?'

'Are you really telling me you never thought of him at *all*?'

'Yes. I am.'

She shook her head, frankly disbelieving. 'Not even the horrible way he died?'

'Not until today, Audra.'

She looked at him and shook her head again.

'You asked me before we were married if I had any brothers or sisters, and I said I had a brother who died when I was a kid. You knew my parents were gone, and you've got so much family that it took up your entire field of attention. But that's not *all*.'

'What do you mean?'

'It isn't just George that's been in that black hole. I haven't thought of *Derry itself* in twenty years. Not the people I chummed with – Eddie Kaspbrak and Richie the Mouth, Stan Uris, Bev Marsh . . .' He ran his hands through his hair and laughed shakily. 'It's like having a case of amnesia so bad you don't know you've got it. And when Mike Hanlon called –'

'Who's Mike Hanlon?'

'Another kid that we chummed with – that I chummed with after Georgie died. Of course he's no kid anymore. None of us are. That was Mike on the phone, transatlantic cable. He said, "Hello – have I reached the Denbrough residence?" and I said yes, and he said, "Bill? Is that you?" and I said yes, and he said, "This is Mike Hanlon." It meant nothing to me, Audra. He might as well have been selling encyclopedias or Burl Ives records. Then he said, "From Derry." And when he said that it was like a door opened inside me and some horrible light shined out, and I remembered who he was. I remembered Georgie. I remembered all the others. All this happened –'

Bill snapped his fingers.

'Like that. And I knew he was going to ask me to come.'

'Come back to Derry.'

'Yeah.' He took his glasses off, rubbed his eyes, looked at her. Never in her life had she seen a man who looked so frightened. 'Back to Derry. Because we promised, he said, and we did. We *did*. All of us. Us kids. We stood in the creek that ran through the Barrens, and we held hands in a circle, and we had cut our palms with a piece of glass so it was like a bunch of kids playing blood brothers, only it was real.'

He held his palms out to her, and in the center of each she could see a close-set ladder of white lines that could have been scar-tissue. She had held his hand – *both* his hands – countless times, but she had never noticed these scars across his palms before. They were faint, yes, but she would have believed –

And the party! That party!

Not the one where they had met, although this second one formed a perfect book-end to that first one, because it had been the wrap party at the end of the *Pit of the Black Demon* shoot. It had been loud and drunk, every inch the Topanga Canyon 'do.' Perhaps a little less bitchy than some of the other LA parties she had been to, because the shoot had gone better than they had any right to expect, and they all knew it. For Audra Phillips it had gone even better, because she had fallen in love with William Denbrough.

What was the name of the self-proclaimed palmist? She couldn't remember now, only that she had been one of the makeup man's two assistants. She remembered the girl whipping off her blouse at some point in the party (revealing a *very* filmy bra beneath) and tying it over her head like a gypsy's scarf. High on pot and wine, she had read palms for the rest of the evening . . . or at least until she had passed out.

Audra could not remember now if the girl's readings had been good or bad, witty or stupid: she had been pretty high herself that night. What she *did* remember was that at one point the girl had grabbed Bill's palm and her own and had declared them perfectly matched. They were life-twins, she said. She could remember watching, more than a little jealous, as the girl traced the lines on his palm with her exquisitely lacquered fingernail – how stupid that was, in the weird LA film subculture where men patted women's fannies as routinely as New York men pecked their cheeks! But there had been something intimate and lingering about that tracery.

There had been no little white scars on Bill's palms then.

She had been watching the charade with a jealous lover's eye, and she was sure of the memory. Sure of the *fact*.

She said so to Bill now.

He nodded. 'You're right. They weren't there then. And although I can't absolutely swear to it, I don't think they were there last night, down at the Plow and Barrow. Ralph and I were hand-wrestling for beers again and I think I would have noticed.'

He grinned at her. The grin was dry, humorless, and scared.

'I think they came back when Mike Hanlon called. That's what I think.'

'Bill, that isn't possible.' But she reached for her cigarettes.

Bill was looking at his hands. 'Stan did it,' he said. 'Cut our palms with a sliver of Coke bottle. I can remember it so clearly now.' He looked up at Audra and behind his glasses his eyes were hurt and puzzled. 'I remember how that piece of glass flashed in the sun. It was one of the new clear ones. Before that Coke bottles used to be green, you remember that?' She shook her head but he didn't see her. He was still studying his palms. 'I can remember Stan doing his own hands last, pretending he was going to slash his wrists instead of just cut his palms a little. I guess it was just some goof, but I almost made a move on him . . . to stop him. Because for a second or two there he looked serious.'

'Bill, don't,' she said in a low voice. This time she had to steady the lighter in her right hand by grasping its wrist in her left, like a policeman holding a gun on a shooting range. 'Scars can't come back. They either are or aren't.'

'You saw them before, huh? Is that what you're telling me?'

'They're very faint,' Audra said, more sharply than she had intended.

'We were all bleeding,' he said. 'We were standing in the water not far from where Eddie Kaspbrak and Ben Hanscom and I built the dam that time –'

'You don't mean the architect, do you?'

'Is there one by that name?'

'God, Bill, he built the new BBC communications center! They're still arguing whether it's a dream or an abortion!'

'Well, I don't know if it's the same guy or not. It doesn't seem likely, but I guess it could be. The Ben I knew was great at building stuff. We all stood there, and I was holding Bev Marsh's left hand in my right and Richie Tozier's right hand in my left. We stood out there in the water like something out of a Southern baptism after a tent meeting, and I remember I could see the Derry Standpipe on the horizon. It looked as white as you imagine the robes of the archangels must be, and we promised, we *swore*, that if it wasn't over, that if it ever started to happen again . . . we'd go back. And we'd do it again. And stop it. Forever.'

'Stop *what*?' she cried, suddenly furious with him. 'Stop *what*? What the fuck are you *talking* about?'

'I wish you wouldn't a-a-ask –' Bill began, and then stopped. She saw an expression of bemused horror spread over his face like a stain. 'Give me a cigarette.'

She passed him the pack. He lit one. She had never seen him smoke a cigarette.

'I used to stutter, too.'

'You stuttered?'

'Yes. Back then. You said I was the only man in LA you ever knew who dared to speak slowly. The truth is, I didn't dare talk fast. It wasn't reflection. It wasn't deliberation. It wasn't wisdom. All reformed stutterers speak very slowly. It's one of the tricks you learn, like thinking of your middle name just before you introduce yourself, because stutterers have more trouble with nouns than with any other words, and the one word in all the world that gives them the most trouble is their own first name.'

'Stuttered.' She smiled a small smile, as if he had told a joke and she had missed the point.

'Until Georgie died, I stuttered moderately,' Bill said, and already he had begun to hear words double in his mind, as if they were infinitesimally separated in time; the words came out smoothly, in his ordinary slow and cadenced way, but in his mind he heard words like Georgie and *moderately* overlap, becoming *Juh-Juh-Georgie* and *m-moder-ately*. 'I mean, I had some really bad moments – usually when I was called on in class, and especially if I really knew the answer and wanted to give it – but mostly I got by. After George died, it got a lot worse. Then, around the age of fourteen or fifteen, things started to get better again. I went to Chevrus High in Portland, and there was a speech therapist there, Mrs Thomas, who was really great. She taught me some good tricks. Like thinking of my middle name just before I said "Hi, I'm Bill Denbrough" out loud. I was taking French I and she taught me to switch to French if I got badly stuck on a word. So if you're standing there feeling like the world's grandest asshole, saying "th-th-this buh-buh-buh-buh" over and over like a broken record, you switched over to French and "*ce livre*" would come flowing off your tongue. Worked every time. And as soon as you said it in French you could come back to English and say "this book" with no problem at all. If you got stuck on an s-word like ship or skate or slum, you could lisp it: thip, thkate, thlum. No stutter.

'All of that helped, but mostly it was just forgetting Derry and everything that happened there. Because that's when the forgetting happened. When we were living in Portland and I was going to Chevrus. I didn't forget everything at once, but looking back now I'd have to say it happened over a remarkably short period of time. Maybe no more than four months. My stutter and my memories faded out together. Someone washed the blackboard and all the old equations went away.'

He drank what was left of his juice. 'When I stuttered on "ask" a few seconds ago, that was the first time in maybe twenty-one years.'

He looked at her.

'First the scars, then the stuh-hutter. Do you h-hear it?'

'You're doing that on purpose!' she said, badly frightened.

'No. I guess there's no way to convince a person of that, but it's true. Stuttering's funny, Audra. Spooky. On one level you're not even aware it's happening. But . . . it's also something you can hear in your mind. It's like part of your head is working an instant ahead of the rest. Or one of those reverb systems kids used to put in their jalopies back in the fifties, when the sound in the rear speaker would come just a split second a-after the sound in the front s-speaker.'

He got up and walked restlessly around the room. He looked tired, and she thought with some unease of how hard he had worked over the last thirteen years or so, as if it might be possible to justify the moderateness of his talent by working furiously, almost non-stop. She found herself having a very uneasy thought and tried to push it away, but it wouldn't go. Suppose Bill's call had really been from Ralph Foster, inviting him down to the Plow and Barrow for an hour of arm-wrestling or backgammon, or maybe from Freddie Firestone, the producer of *Attic Room*, on some problem or other? Perhaps even a 'wrong-ring,' as the veddy British doctor's wife down the lane put it?

What did such thoughts lead to?

Why, to the idea that all this Derry-Mike Hanlon business was nothing but a hallucination. A hallucination brought on by an incipient nervous breakdown.

But the scars, Audra — how do you explain the scars? He's right. They weren't there . . . and now they are. That's the truth, and you know it.

'Tell me the rest,' she said. 'Who killed your brother George? What did you and these other children do? What did you promise?'

He went to her, knelt before her like an oldfashioned suitor about to propose marriage, and took her hands.

'I think I could tell you,' he said softly. 'I think that if I really wanted to, I could. Most of it I don't remember even now, but once I started talking it would come. I can sense those memories . . . waiting to be born. They're like clouds filled with rain. Only this rain would be very dirty. The plants that grew after a rain like that would be monsters. Maybe I can face that with the others –'

'Do they know?'

'Mike said he called them all. He thinks they'll all come . . . except maybe for Stan. He said Stan sounded strange.'

'It *all* sounds strange to me. You're frightening me very badly, Bill.'

'I'm sorry,' he said, and kissed her. It was like getting a kiss from an utter stranger. She found herself hating this man Mike Hanlon. 'I thought I ought to explain as much as I could; I thought that would be better than just creeping off into the night. I suppose some of them may do just that. But I have to go. And I think Stan will be there, no matter how strange he sounded. Or maybe that's just because I can't imagine not going myself.'

'Because of your brother?'

Bill shook his head slowly. 'I could tell you that, but it would be a lie. I loved him. I know how strange that must sound after telling you I haven't thought of him in twenty years or so, but I loved the *hell* out of that kid.' He smiled a little. 'He was a spasmoid, but I loved him. You know?'

Audra, who had a younger sister, nodded. 'I know.'

'But it isn't George. I can't explain what it is. I . . .'

He looked out the window at the morning fog.

'I feel like a bird must feel when fall comes and it knows . . . somehow it just knows it has to fly home. It's instinct, babe . . . and I guess I believe instinct's the iron skeleton under all our ideas of free will. Unless you're willing to take the pipe or eat the gun or take a long walk off a short dock, you can't say no to some things. You can't refuse to pick up your option because there *is* no option. You can't stop it from happening any more than you could stand at home plate with a bat in your hand and let a fastball hit you. I have to go. That promise . . . it's in my mind like a fuh-fishhook.'

She stood up and walked herself carefully to him; she felt very fragile, as if she might break. She put a hand on his shoulder and turned him to her.

'Take me with you, then.'

The expression of horror that dawned on his face then – not horror *of* her but *for* her – was so naked that she stepped back, really afraid for the first time.

'No,' he said. 'Don't think of that, Audra. Don't you *ever* think of that. You're not going within three thousand miles of Derry. I think Derry's going to be a very bad place to be during the next couple of weeks. You're going to stay here and carry on and make all the excuses for me you have to. Now promise me that!'

'Should I promise?' she asked, her eyes never leaving his. 'Should I, Bill?'

'Audra –'

'Should I? You made a promise, and look what it's got you into. And me as well, since I'm your wife and I love you.'

His big hands tightened painfully on her shoulders. 'Promise me! Promise! P-Puh-Puh-Pruh-huh –'

And she could not stand that, that broken word caught in his mouth like a gaffed and wriggling fish.

'I promise, okay? I promise!' She burst into tears. 'Are you happy now? Jesus! You're crazy, the whole thing is crazy, but I promise!'

He put an arm around her and led her to the couch. Brought her a brandy. She sipped at it, getting herself under control a little at a time.

'When do you go, then?'

'Today,' he said. 'Concorde. I can just make it if I drive to Heathrow instead of taking the train. Freddie wanted me on-set after lunch. You go on ahead at nine, and you don't know anything, you see?'

She nodded reluctantly.

'I'll be in New York before anything shows up funny. And in Derry before sundown, with the right c-c-connections.'

'And when do I see you again?' she asked softly.

He put an arm around her and held her tightly, but he never answered her question.

DERRY:

THE FIRST INTERLUDE

'How many human eyes . . . had snatched glimpses
of their secret anatomies, down the passage of years?'
– Clive Barker,
Books of Blood

The segment below and all other Interlude *segments are drawn from 'Derry: An Unauthorized Town History,' by Michael Hanlon. This is an unpublished set of notes and accompanying fragments of manuscript (which read almost like diary entries) found in the Derry Public Library vault. The title given is the one written on the cover of the looseleaf binder in which these notes were kept prior to their appearance here. The author, however, refers to the work several times within his own notes as 'Derry: A Look Through Hell's Back Door.'*

One supposes the thought of popular publication had done more than cross Mr Hanlon's mind.

January 2nd, 1985

Can an *entire city* be haunted?

Haunted as some houses are supposed to be haunted?

Not just a single building in that city, or the corner of a single street, or a single basketball court in a single pocket-park, the netless basket jutting out at sunset like some obscure and bloody instrument of torture, not just one area – but *everything*. The whole works.

Can that be?

Listen:

Haunted: 'Often visited by ghosts or spirits.' Funk and Wagnalls.

Haunting: 'Persistently recurring to the mind; difficult to forget.' Ditto Funk and Friend.

To haunt: 'To appear or recur often, especially as a ghost.' *But* – and listen! – *'A place often visited: resort, den, hangout . . .'* Italics are of course mine.

And one more. This one, like the last, is a definition of *haunt* as a noun, and it's the one that really scares me: '*A feeding place for animals.*'

Like the animals that beat up Adrian Mellon and then threw him over the bridge?

Like the animal that was waiting underneath the bridge?

A feeding place for animals.

What's feeding in Derry? What's feeding *on* Derry?

You know, it's sort of interesting – I didn't know it was possible

137

for a man to become as frightened as I have become since the Adrian Mellon business and still live, let alone function. It's as if I've fallen into a story, and everyone knows you're not supposed to feel this afraid until the *end* of the story, when the haunter of the dark finally comes out of the woodwork to feed . . . on you, of course.

On *you*.

But if this is a story, it's not one of those classic screamers by Lovecraft or Bradbury or Poe. I know, you see – not everything, but a lot. I didn't just start when I opened the Derry *News* one day last September, read the transcript of the Unwin boy's preliminary hearing, and realized that the clown who killed George Denbrough might well be back again. I actually started around 1980 – I think that is when some part of me which had been asleep woke up . . . knowing that Its time might be coming round again.

What part? The watchman part, I suppose.

Or maybe it was the voice of the Turtle. Yes . . . I rather think it was that. I know it's what Bill Denbrough would believe.

I discovered news of old horrors in old books; read intelligence of old atrocities in old periodicals; always in the back of my mind, every day a bit louder, I heard the seashell drone of some growing, coalescing force; I seemed to smell the bitter ozone aroma of light-nings-to-come. I began making notes for a book I will almost certainly not live to write. And at the same time I went on with my life. On one level of my mind I was and am living with the most grotesque, capering horrors; on another I have continued to live the mundane life of a small-city librarian. I shelve books; I make out library cards for new patrons; I turn off the microfilm readers careless users some-times leave on; I joke with Carole Danner about how much I would like to go to bed with her, and she jokes back about how much she'd like to go to bed with me, and both of us know that she's really joking and I'm really not, just as both of us know that she won't stay in a little place like Derry for long and I will be here until I die, taping torn pages in *Business Week*, sitting down at monthly acquisition meetings with my pipe in one hand and a stack of *Library Journals* in the other . . . and waking in the middle of the night with my fists jammed against my mouth to keep in the screams.

The gothic conventions are all wrong. My hair has not turned white. I do not sleepwalk. I have not begun to make cryptic comments or to carry a planchette around in my sportcoat pocket. I think I laugh a little more, that's all, and sometimes it must seem a little shrill and strange, because sometimes people look at me oddly when I laugh.

Part of me – the part Bill would call the voice of the Turtle – says I should call them all, tonight. But am I, even now, completely sure? Do I *want* to be completely sure? No – of course not. But God, what happened to Adrian Mellon is so much like what happened to Stuttering Bill's brother, George, in the fall of 1957.

If it *has* started again, I *will* call them. I'll have to. But not yet. It's too early anyway. Last time it began slowly and didn't really get going until the summer of 1958. So . . . I wait. And fill up the waiting with words in this notebook and long moments of looking into the mirror to see the stranger the boy became.

The boy's face was bookish and timid; the man's face is the face of a bank teller in a Western movie, the fellow who never has any lines, the one who just gets to put his hands up and look scared when the robbers come in. And if the script calls for anyone to get shot by the bad guys, he's the one.

Same old Mike. A little starey in the eyes, maybe, and a little punchy from broken sleep, but not so's you'd notice without a good close look . . . like kissing-distance close, and I haven't been that close to anyone in a very long time. If you took a casual glance at me you might think *He's been reading too many books*, but that's all. I doubt you'd guess how hard the man with the mild bank-teller's face is now struggling just to hold on, to hold on to his own mind . . .

If I have to make those calls, it may kill some of them.

That's one of the things I've had to face on the long nights when sleep won't come, nights when I lie there in bed wearing my conservative blue pajamas, my spectacles neatly folded up and lying on the nighttable next to the glass of water I always put there in case I wake up thirsty in the night. I lie there in the dark and I take small sips of the water and I wonder how much – or how little – they remember. I am somehow convinced that they don't remember *any* of it, because they don't *need* to remember. I'm the only one that hears the voice of the Turtle, the only one who remembers, because I'm the only one who stayed here in Derry. And because they're scattered to the four winds, they have no way of knowing the identical patterns their lives have taken. To bring them back, to show them that pattern . . . yes, it might kill some of them. It might kill *all* of them.

So I go over it and over it in my mind; I go over *them*, trying to re-create them as they were and as they might now be, trying to decide which of them is the most vulnerable. Richie 'Trashmouth' Tozier, I think sometimes – he was the one Criss, Huggins, and Bowers seemed to catch up with the most often, in spite of the fact that Ben was so fat. Bowers was the one Richie was the most scared of – the one we were all the most scared of – but the others used to really put the fear of God into him, too. If I call him out there in California would he see it as some horrible Return of the Big Bullies, two from the grave and one from the madhouse in Juniper Hill where he raves to this day? Sometimes I think Eddie was the weakest, Eddie with his domineering tank of a mother and his terrible case of asthma. Beverly? She always tried to talk so tough, but she was as scared as the rest of us. Stuttering Bill, faced with a horror that won't go away when he puts the cover on his typewriter? Stan Uris?

There's a guillotine blade hanging over their lives, razor-sharp, but the more I think about it the more I think they don't know that blade is there. I'm the one with my hand on the lever. I can pull it just by opening my telephone notebook and calling them, one after the other.

Maybe I won't have to do it. I hold on to the waning hope that I've mistaken the rabbity cries of my own timid mind for the deeper, truer voice of the Turtle. After all, what do I have? Mellon in July. A child found dead on Neibolt Street last October, another found in Memorial Park in early December, just before the first snowfall. Maybe it was a tramp, as the papers say. Or a crazy who's since left Derry or killed himself out of remorse and self-disgust, as some of the books say the real Jack the Ripper may have done.

Maybe.

But the Albrecht girl was found directly across the street from that damned old house on Neibolt Street . . . and she was killed on the same day as George Denbrough was, twenty-seven years before. And then the Johnson boy, found in Memorial Park with one of his legs missing below the knee. Memorial Park is, of course, the home of the Derry Standpipe, and the boy was found almost at its foot. The Standpipe is within a shout of the Barrens; the Standpipe is also where Stan Uris saw those boys.

Those dead boys.

Still, it could all be nothing but smoke and mirages. *Could* be. Or coincidence. Or perhaps something between the two – a kind of malefic echo. Could that be? I sense that it could be. Here in Derry, *anything* could be.

I think what was here before is still here – the thing that was here in 1957 and 1958; the thing that was here in 1929 and in 1930 when the Black Spot was burned down by the Maine Legion of White Decency; the thing that was here in 1904 and 1905 and early 1906

– at least until the Kitchener Ironworks exploded; the thing that was here in 1876 and 1877, the thing that has shown up every twenty-seven years or so. Sometimes it comes a little sooner, sometimes a little later . . . but it always comes. As one goes back the wrong notes are harder and harder to find because the records grow poorer and the moth-holes in the narrative history of the area grow bigger. But knowing where to look – and when to look – goes a long way toward solving the problem. It always comes back, you see.

It.

So – yes: I think I'll have to make those calls. I think it was meant to be us. Somehow, for some reason, we're the ones who have been elected to stop it forever. Blind fate? Blind luck? Or is it that damned Turtle again? Does it perhaps command as well as speak? I don't know. And I doubt if it matters. All those years ago Bill said *The Turtle can't help us*, and if it was true then it must be true now.

I think of us standing in the water, hands clasped, making that promise to come back if it ever started again – standing there almost like Druids in a ring, our hands bleeding their own promise, palm to palm. A ritual that is perhaps as old as mankind itself, an unknowing tap driven into the tree of all power – the one that grows on the borderline between the land of all we know and that of all we suspect.

Because the similarities –

But I'm doing my own Bill Denbrough here, stuttering over the same ground again and again, reciting a few facts and a lot of unpleasant (and rather gaseous) suppositions, growing more and more obsessive with every paragraph. No good. Useless. Dangerous, even. But it is so very hard to wait on events.

This notebook is supposed to be an effort to get beyond that obsession by widening the focus of my attention – after all, there is more to this story than six boys and one girl, none of them happy, none of them accepted by their peers, who stumbled into a nightmare during one hot summer when Eisenhower was still President. It is an attempt to pull the camera back a little, if you will – to see the whole city, a place where nearly thirty-five thousand people work and eat and sleep and copulate and shop and drive around and walk and go to school and go to jail and sometimes disappear into the dark.

To know what a place *is*, I really do believe one has to know what it *was*. And if I had to name a day when all of this really started again for me, it would be the day in the early spring of 1980 when I went to see Albert Carson, who died last summer – at ninety-one, he was full of years as well as honors. He was head librarian here from

1914 to 1960, an incredible span (but he was an incredible man), and I felt that if anyone would know which history of this area was the best one to start with, Albert Carson would. I asked him my question as we sat on his porch and he gave me my answer, speaking in a croak – he was already fighting the throat-cancer which would eventually kill him.

'Not one of them is worth a shit. As you damn well know.'

'Then where should I start?'

'Start what, for Christ's sake?'

'Researching the history of the area. Of Derry Township.'

'Oh. Well. Start with the Fricke and the Michaud. They're supposed to be the best.'

'And after I read those –'

'*Read* them? Christ, no! Throw em in the wastebasket! That's your first step. Then read Buddinger. Branson Buddinger was a damned sloppy researcher and afflicted with a terminal boner, if half of what I heard when I was a kid was true, but when it came to Derry his heart was in the right place. He got most of the facts wrong, but he got them wrong with *feeling*, Hanlon.'

I laughed a little and Carson grinned with his leathery lips – an expression of good humor that was actually a little frightening. In that instant he looked like a vulture happily guarding a freshly killed animal, waiting for it to reach exactly the right stage of tasty decomposition before beginning to dine.

'When you finish with Buddinger, read Ives. Make notes on all the people he talked to. Sandy Ives is still at the University of Maine. Folklorist. After you read him, go see him. Buy him a dinner. I'd take him to the Orinoka, because dinner at the Orinoka seems to *never* end. Pump him. Fill up a notebook with names and addresses. Talk to the old-timers he's talked to – those that are still left; there are a few of us, ah-hah-hah-hah! – and get some more names from them. By then you'll have all the place to stand you'll need, if you're half as bright as I think you are. If you chase down enough people, you'll find out a few things that aren't in the histories. And you may find they disturb your sleep.'

'Derry . . .'

'What about it?'

'Derry's not right, is it?'

'Right?' he asked in that whispery croak. 'What's right? What does that word mean? Is "right" pretty pictures of the Kenduskeag at sunset, Kodachrome by so-and-so, f-stop such-and-such? If so, then

Derry is right, because there are pretty pictures of it by the score. Is right a damned committee of dry-boxed old virgins to save the Governor's Mansion or to put a commemorative plaque in front of the Standpipe? If *that's* right, then Derry's right as rain, because we've got more than our share of old kitty-cats minding everybody's business. Is right that ugly plastic statue of Paul Bunyan in front of City Center? Oh, if I had a truckful of napalm and my old Zippo lighter I'd take care of *that* fucking thing, I assure you ... but if one's aesthetic is broad enough to include plastic statues, then Derry is right. The question is, what does right mean to you, Hanlon? Eh? More to the point, what does right *not* mean?'

I could only shake my head. He either knew or he didn't. He would either tell or he wouldn't.

'Do you mean the unpleasant stories you may hear, or the ones you already know? There are *always* unpleasant stories. A town's history is like a rambling old mansion filled with rooms and cubbyholes and laundry-chutes and garrets and all sorts of eccentric little hiding places ... not to mention an occasional secret passage or two. If you go exploring Mansion Derry, you'll find all sorts of things. Yes. You may be sorry later, but you'll find them, and once a thing is found it can't be unfound, can it? Some of the rooms are locked, but there are keys ... there are keys.'

His eyes glinted at me with an old man's shrewdness.

'You may come to think you've stumbled on the worst of Derry's secrets ... but there is always one more. And one more. And one more.'

'Do you —'

'I think I shall have to ask you to excuse me just now. My throat is very bad today. It's time for my medicine and my nap.'

In other words, here is a knife and a fork, my friend; go see what you can cut with them.

I started with the Fricke history and the Michaud history. I followed Carson's advice and threw them in the wastebasket, but I read them first. They were as bad as he had suggested. I read the Buddinger history, copied out the footnotes, and chased them down. That was more satisfactory, but footnotes are peculiar things, you know — like footpaths twisting through a wild and anarchic country. They split, then they split again; at any point you may take a wrong turn which leads you either to a bramble-choked dead end or into swampy quickmud. 'If you find a footnote,' a library-science prof once told a class of which I was a part, 'step on its head and kill it before it can breed.'

They *do* breed, and sometimes the breeding is a good thing, but I think that more often it is not. Those in Buddinger's stiffly written *A History of Old Derry* (Orono: University of Maine Press, 1950) wander through one hundred years' worth of forgotten books and dusty master's dissertations in the fields of history and folklore, through articles in defunct magazines, and amid brain-numbing stacks of town reports and ledgers.

My conversations with Sandy Ives were more interesting. His sources crossed Buddinger's from time to time, but a crossing was all it ever was. Ives had spent a good part of his lifetime setting down oral histories – yarns, in other words – almost verbatim, a practice Branson Buddinger would undoubtedly have seen as taking the low road.

Ives had written a cycle of articles on Derry during the years 1963–66. Most of the old-timers he talked to then were dead by the time I started my own investigations, but they had sons, daughters, nephews, cousins. And, of course, one of the great true facts of the world is this: for every old-timer who dies, there's a new old-timer coming along. And a good story never dies; it is always passed down. I sat on a lot of porches and back stoops, drank a lot of tea, Black Label beer, homemade beer, homemade rootbeer, tapwater, springwater. I did a lot of listening, and the wheels of my tape-player turned.

Both Buddinger and Ives agreed completely on one point: the original party of white settlers numbered about three hundred. They were English. They had a charter and were formally known as the Derrie Company. The land granted them covered what is today Derry, most of Newport, and little slices of the surrounding towns. And in the year 1741 everyone in Derry Township just disappeared. They were there in June of that year – a community which at that time numbered about three hundred and forty souls – but come October they were gone. The little village of wooden homes stood utterly deserted. One of them, which once stood roughly at the place where Witcham and Jackson Streets intersect today, was burned to the ground. The Michaud history states firmly that all of the villagers were slaughtered by Indians, but there is no basis – save the one burned house – for that idea. More likely, someone's stove just got too hot and the house went up in flames.

Indian massacre? Doubtful. No bones, no bodies. Flood? Not that year. Disease? No word of it in the surrounding towns.

They just disappeared. All of them. All three hundred and forty of them. Without a trace.

So far as I know, the only case remotely like it in American history is the disappearance of the colonists on Roanoke Island, Virginia. Every school-child in the country knows about that one, but who knows about the Derry disappearance? Not even the people who live here, apparently. I quizzed several junior-high students who are taking the required Maine-history course, and none of them knew a thing about it. Then I checked the text, *Maine Then and Now*. There are better than forty index entries for Derry, most of them concerning the boom years of the lumber industry. Nothing about the disappearance of the original colonists . . . and yet that – what shall I call it? – that *quiet* fits the pattern, too.

There is a kind of curtain of quiet which cloaks much of what has happened here . . . and yet people *do* talk. I guess nothing can stop people from talking. But you have to listen hard, and that is a rare skill. I flatter myself that I've developed it over the last four years. If I haven't, then my aptitude for the job must be poor indeed, because I've had enough practice. An old man told me about how his wife had heard voices speaking to her from the drain of her kitchen sink in the three weeks before their daughter died – that was in the early winter of 1957–58. The girl he spoke of was one of the early victims in the murder-spree which began with George Denbrough and did not end until the following summer.

'A whole slew of voices, all of em babblin together,' he told me. He owned a Gulf station on Kansas Street and talked in between slow, limping trips out to the pumps, where he filled gas-tanks, checked oil-levels, and wiped windshields. 'Said she spoke back once, even though she was ascairt. Leaned right over the drain, she did, and hollered down into it. "Who the hell are you?" she calls. "What's your name?" And all these voices answered back, she said – grunts and babbles and howls and yips, screams and laughin, don't you know. And she said they were sayin what the possessed man said to Jesus: "Our name is Legion," they said. She wouldn't go near that sink for two years. For them two years I'd spend twelve hours a day down here, bustin my hump, then have to go home and warsh all the damn dishes.'

He was drinking a can of Pepsi from the machine outside the office door, a man of seventy-two or -three in faded gray work fatigues, rivers of wrinkles flowing down from the corners of his eyes and mouth.

'By now you prob'ly think I'm as crazy as a bedbug,' he said, 'but I'll tell you sumpin else, if you'll turn off y' whirligig, there.'

I turned off my tape-recorder and smiled at him. 'Considering some of the things I've heard over the last couple of years, you'd have to go a fair country distance to convince me you're crazy,' I said.

He smiled back, but there was no humor in it. 'I was doin the dishes one night, same as usual – this was in the fall of '58, after things had settled down again. My wife was upstair, sleepin. Betty was the only kid God ever saw fit to give us, and after she was killed my wife spent a lot of her time sleepin. Anyway, I pulled the plug and the water started runnin out of the sink. You know the sound real soapy water makes when it goes down the drain? Kind of a suckin sound, it is. It was makin that noise, but I wasn't thinkin about it, only about goin out and choppin some kindlin in the shed, and just as that sound started to die off, I heard my daughter down in there. I heard Betty somewhere down in those friggin pipes. Laughin. She was somewheres down there in the dark, laughin. Only it sounded more like she was screamin, once you listened a bit. Or both. Screamin and laughin down there in the pipes. That's the only time I ever heard anything like that. Maybe I just imagined it. But . . . I don't think so.'

He looked at me and I looked at him. The light falling through the dirty plate-glass windows onto his face filled him up with years, made him look as ancient as Methuselah. I remember how cold I felt at that moment; how cold.

'You think I'm storying you along?' the old man asked me, the old man who would have been just about forty-five in 1957, the old man to whom God had given a single daughter, Betty Ripsom by name. Betty had been found on Outer Jackson Street just after Christmas of that year, frozen, her remains ripped wide open.

'No,' I said. 'I don't think you're just storying me along, Mr Ripsom.'

'And you're tellin the truth, too,' he said with a kind of wonder. 'I can see it on y'face.'

I think he meant to tell me something more then, but the bell behind us dinged sharply as a car rolled over the hose on the tarmac and pulled up to the pumps. When the bell rang, both of us jumped and I uttered a thin little cry. Ripsom got to his feet and limped out to the car, wiping his hands on a ball of waste. When he came back in, he looked at me as though I were a rather unsavory stranger who had just happened to wander in off the street. I made my goodbyes and left.

Buddinger and Ives agree on something else: things really are not right here in Derry; things in Derry have *never* been right.

I saw Albert Carson for the last time a scant month before he died. His throat had gotten much worse; all he could manage was a hissing little whisper. 'Still thinking about writing a history of Derry, Hanlon?'

'Still toying with the idea,' I said, but I had of course never planned to write a history of the township – not exactly – and I think he knew it.

'It would take you twenty years,' he whispered, 'and no one would read it. No one would *want* to read it. Let it go, Hanlon.'

He paused a moment and then added:

'Buddinger committed suicide, you know.'

Of course I had known that – but only because people always talk and I had learned to listen. The article in the *News* had called it a falling accident, and it was true that Branson Buddinger had taken a fall. What the *News* neglected to mention was that he fell from a stool in his closet and he had a noose around his neck at the time.

'You know about the cycle?'

I looked at him, startled.

'Oh yes,' Carson whispered. 'I know. Every twenty-six or twenty-seven years. Buddinger knew, too. A lot of the old-timers do, although that is one thing they won't talk about, even if you load them up with booze. Let it go, Hanlon.'

He reached out with one bird-claw hand. He closed it around my wrist and I could feel the hot cancer that was loose and raving through his body, eating anything and everything left that was still good to eat – not that there could have been much by that time; Albert Carson's cupboards were almost bare.

'Michael – this is nothing you want to mess into. There are things here in Derry that bite. Let it go. *Let it go.*'

'I can't.'

'Then beware,' he said. Suddenly the huge and frightened eyes of a child were looking out of his dying old-man's face. '*Beware.*'

Derry.

My home town. Named after the county of the same name in Ireland.

Derry.

I was born here, in Derry Home Hospital, attended Derry Elementary School; went to junior high at Ninth Street Middle School; to high school at Derry High. I went to the University of Maine – 'ain't in Derry, but it's just down the rud,' the old-timers say – and then I came right back here. To the Derry Public Library. I am a small-town man living a small-town life, one among millions.

But.

But:

In 1851 a crew of lumber jacks found the remains of another crew that had spent the winter snowed in at a camp on the Upper Kenduskeag – at the tip of what the kids still call the Barrens. There were nine of them in all, all nine hacked to pieces. Heads had rolled . . . not to mention arms . . . a foot or two . . . and a man's penis had been nailed to one wall of the cabin.

But:

In 1851 John Markson killed his entire family with poison and then, sitting in the middle of the circle he had made with their corpses, he gobbled an entire 'white-nightshade' mushroom. His death agonies must have been intense. The town constable who found him wrote in his report that at first he believed the corpse was grinning at him; he wrote of 'Markson's awful white smile.' The white smile was an entire mouthful of the killer mushroom; Markson had gone on eating even as the cramps and the excruciating muscle spasms must have been wracking his dying body.

But:

On Easter Sunday 1906 the owners of the Kitchener Ironworks, which stood where the brand-spanking-new Derry Mall now stands, held an Easter-egg hunt for 'all the good children of Derry.' The hunt took place in the huge Ironworks building. Dangerous areas were closed off, and employees volunteered their time to stand guard and make sure no adventurous boy or girl decided to duck under the barriers and explore. Five hundred chocolate Easter eggs wrapped in gay ribbons were hidden about the rest of the works. According to Buddinger, there was at least one child present for each of those eggs. They ran giggling and whooping and yelling through the Sunday-silent Ironworks, finding the eggs under the giant tipper-vats, inside the desk drawers of the foreman, balanced between the great rusty teeth of gearwheels, inside the molds on the third floor (in the old photographs these molds look like cupcake tins from some giant's kitchen). Three generations of Kitcheners were there to watch the gay riot and to award prizes at the end of the hunt, which was to come at four o'clock, whether all the eggs had been found or not. The end actually came forty-five minutes early, at quarter past three. That was when the Ironworks exploded. Seventy-two people were pulled dead from the wreckage before the sun went down. The final toll was a hundred and two. Eighty-eight of the dead were children. On the following Wednesday, while the city still lay in stunned silent contemplation of the tragedy, a woman found the head of nine-year-old Robert Dohay caught in the limbs of her back-yard apple tree. There was chocolate on the Dohay lad's teeth and blood in his hair. He was the last of the known dead. Eight children and one adult were never accounted for. It was the worst tragedy in Derry's history, even worse than the fire at the Black Spot in 1930, and it was never explained. All four of the Ironworks' boilers were shut down. Not just banked; shut down.

But:

The murder rate in Derry is six times the murder rate of any other town of comparable size in New England. I found my tentative conclusions in this matter so difficult to believe that I turned my figures over to one of the high-school hackers, who spends what time he doesn't spend in front of his Commodore here in the library. He went several steps further – scratch a hacker, find an overachiever – by adding another dozen small cities to what he called 'the stat-pool' and presenting me with a computer-generated bar graph where Derry sticks out like a sore thumb. 'People must have wicked short tempers here, Mr Hanlon,' was his only comment. I didn't reply. If I had, I might have told him that *something* in Derry has a wicked short temper, anyway.

Here in Derry children disappear unexplained and unfound at the rate of forty to sixty a year. Most are teenagers. They are assumed to be runaways. I suppose some of them even are.

And during what Albert Carson would undoubtedly have called the time of the cycle, the rate of disappearance shoots nearly out of sight. In the year 1930, for instance – the year the Black Spot burned – there were better than *one hundred and seventy* child disappearances in Derry – and you must remember that these are only the disappearances which were reported to the police and thus documented. *Nothing surprising about it*, the current Chief of Police told me when I showed him the statistic. *It was the Depression. Most of em probably got tired of eating potato soup or going flat hungry at home and went off riding the rods, looking for something better.*

During 1958, a hundred and twenty-seven children, ranging in age from three to nineteen, were reported missing in Derry. *Was there a Depression in 1958*? I asked Chief Rademacher. *No*, he said. *But people move around a lot, Hanlon. Kids in particular get itchy feet. Have a fight with the folks about coming in late after a date and boom, they're gone.*

I showed Chief Rademacher the picture of Chad Lowe which had appeared in the Derry *News* in April 1958. *You think this one ran away after a fight with his folks about coming in late, Chief Rademacher? He was three and a half when he dropped out of sight.*

Rademacher fixed me with a sour glance and told me it sure had been nice talking with me, but if there was nothing else, he was busy. I left.

Haunted, haunting, haunt.

Often visited by ghosts or spirits, as in the pipes under the sink; to appear or recur often, as every twenty-five, twenty-six, or twenty-seven years; a feeding place for animals, as in the cases of George Denbrough, Adrian Mellon, Betty Ripsom, the Albrecht girl, the Johnson boy.

A feeding place for animals. Yes, that's the one that haunts *me*.

If anything else happens – anything at all – I'll make the calls. I'll have to. In the meantime I have my suppositions, my broken rest, and my memories – my damned memories. Oh, and one other thing – I have this notebook, don't I? The wall I wail to. And here I sit, my hand shaking so badly I can hardly write in it, here I sit in the deserted library after closing, listening to faint sounds in the dark stacks, watching the shadows thrown by the dim yellow globes to make sure they don't move . . . don't change.

Here I sit next to the telephone.

I put my free hand on it . . . let it slide down . . . touch the holes in the dial that could put me in touch with all of them, my old pals.

We went deep together.

We went into the black together.

Would we come out of the black if we went in a second time? I don't think so.

Please God I don't have to call them.

Please God.

PART 2
JUNE OF 1958

'My surface is myself.
Under which
to witness, youth is
buried. Roots?

Everybody has roots.'
– William Carlos Williams,
Paterson

'Sometimes I wonder what I'm a-gonna do,
There ain't no cure for the summertime blues.'
– Eddie Cochran

CHAPTER FOUR

BEN HANSCOM TAKES
A FALL

1

Around 11:45 P.M., one of the stews serving first class on the Omaha-to-Chicago run – United Airlines's flight 41 – gets one hell of a shock. She thinks for a few moments that the man in 1-A has died.

When he boarded at Omaha she thought to herself: 'Oh boy, here comes trouble. He's just as drunk as a lord.' The stink of whiskey around his head reminded her fleetingly of the cloud of dust that always surrounds the dirty little boy in the Peanuts *strip – Pig Pen, his name is. She was nervous about First Service, which is the booze service. She was sure he would ask for a drink – and probably a double. Then she would have to decide whether or not to serve him. Also, just to add to the fun, there have been thunderstorms all along the route tonight, and she is quite sure that at some point the man, a lanky guy dressed in jeans and chambray, would begin upchucking.*

But when First Service came along, the tall man ordered nothing more than a glass of club soda, just as polite as you could want. His service light has not gone on, and the stew forgets all about him soon enough, because the flight is a busy one. The flight is, in fact, the kind you want to forget as soon as it's over, one of those during which you just might – if you had time – have a few questions about the possibility of your own survival.

United 41 slaloms between the ugly pockets of thunder and lightning like a good skier going downhill. The air is very rough. The passengers exclaim and make uneasy jokes about the lightning they can see flickering on and off in the thick pillars of cloud around the plane. 'Mommy, is God taking pictures of the angels?' a little boy asks, and his mother, who is looking rather green, laughs shakily. First Service turns out to be the only service on 41 that night. The seat-belt sign goes on twenty minutes into the flight and stays on. All the same the stewardesses stay in the aisles, answering the call-buttons which go off like strings of polite-society firecrackers.

'Ralph is busy tonight,' the head stew says to her as they pass in the

153

aisle; the head stew is going back to tourist with a fresh supply of airsick bags. It is half-code, half-joke. Ralph is always busy on bumpy flights. The plane lurches, someone cries out softly, the stewardess turns a bit and puts out a hand to catch her balance, and looks directly into the staring, sightless eyes of the man in I–A.

Oh my dear God he's dead, *she thinks.* The liquor before he got on . . . then the bumps . . . his heart . . . scared to death.

The lanky man's eyes are on hers, but they are not seeing her. They do not move. They are perfectly glazed. Surely they are the eyes of a dead man.

The stew turns away from that awful gaze, her own heart pumping away in her throat at a runaway rate, wondering what to do, how to proceed, and thanking God that at least the man has no seatmate to perhaps scream and start a panic. She decides she will have to notify first the head stew and then the male crew up front. Perhaps they can wrap a blanket around him and close his eyes. The pilot will keep the belt light on even if the air smooths out so no one can come forward to use the john, and when the other passengers deplane they'll think he's just asleep –

These thoughts go through her mind rapidly, and she turns back for a confirming look. The dead, sightless eyes fix upon hers . . . and then the corpse picks up his glass of club soda and sips from it.

Just then the plane staggers again, tilts, and the stew's little scream of surprise is lost in other, heartier, cries of fear. The man's eyes move then – not much, but enough so she understands that he is alive and seeing her. And she thinks: Why, I thought when he got on that he was in his mid-fifties, but he's nowhere *near* that old, in spite of the graying hair.

She goes to him, although she can hear the impatient chime of call-buttons behind her (Ralph is indeed busy tonight: after their perfectly safe landing at O'Hare thirty minutes from now, the stews will dispose of over seventy airsick bags).

'Everything okay, sir?' *she asks, smiling. The smile feels false, unreal.*

'Everything is fine and well,' *the lanky man says. She glances at the first-class stub tacked into the little slot on his seat-back and sees that his name is Hanscom.* 'Fine and well. But it's a bit bumpy tonight, isn't it? You've got your work cut out for you, I think. Don't bother with me. I'm –' *He offers her a ghastly smile, a smile that makes her think of scarecrows flapping in dead November fields.* 'I'm fine and well.'

'You looked'

(dead)

'a little under the weather.'

'I was thinking of the old days,' *he says.* 'I only realized earlier tonight that there were such things as old days, at least as far as I myself am concerned.'

More call-buttons chime. 'Pardon me, stewardess?' someone calls nervously.

'Well, if you're quite sure you're all right –'

'I was thinking about a dam I built with some friends of mine,' Ben Hanscom says. 'The first friends I ever had, I guess. They were building the dam when I –' He stops, looks startled, then laughs. It is an honest laugh, almost the carefree laugh of a boy, and it sounds very odd in this jouncing, bucking plane. '– when I dropped in on them. And that's almost literally what I did. Anyhow, they were making a helluva mess with that dam. I remember that.'

'Stewardess?'

'Excuse me, sir – I ought to get about my appointed rounds again.'

'Of course you should.'

She hurries away, glad to be rid of that gaze – that deadly, almost hypnotic gaze.

Ben Hanscom turns his head to the window and looks out. Lightning goes off inside huge thunderheads nine miles off the starboard wing. In the stutterflashes of light, the clouds look like huge transparent brains filled with bad thoughts.

He feels in the pocket of his vest, but the silver dollars are gone. Out of his pocket and into Ricky Lee's. Suddenly he wishes he had saved at least one of them. It might have come in handy. Of course you could go down to any bank – at least when you weren't bumping around at twenty-seven thousand feet you could – and get a handful of silver dollars, but you couldn't do anything with the lousy copper sandwiches the government was trying to pass off as real coins these days. And for werewolves and vampires and all manner of things that squirm by starlight, it was silver you wanted; honest silver. You needed silver to stop a monster. You needed –

He closed his eyes. The air around him was full of chimes. The plane rocked and rolled and bumped and the air was full of chimes. Chimes?

No . . . bells.

It was bells, it was the *bell, the bell of all bells, the one you waited for all year once the new wore off school again, and that always happened by the end of the first week. The* bell*, the one that signalled freedom again, the apotheosis of all school bells.*

Ben Hanscom sits in his first-class seat, suspended amid the thunders at twenty-seven thousand feet, his face turned to the window, and he feels the wall of time grow suddenly thin; some terrible/wonderful peristalsis has begun to take place. He thinks, My God, I am being digested by my own past.

The lightning plays fitfully across his face, and although he does not know it, the day has just turned. May 28th, 1985, has become May 29th

155

over the dark and stormy country that is western Illinois tonight; farmers back-sore with plantings sleep like the dead below and dream their quicksilver dreams and who knows what may move in their barns and their cellars and their fields as the lightning walks and the thunder talks? No one knows these things; they know only that power is loose in the night, and the air is crazy with the big volts of the storm.

But it's bells at twenty-seven thousand feet as the plane breaks into the clear again, as its motion steadies again; it is bells; it is the bell as Ben Hanscom sleeps; and as he sleeps the wall between past and present disappears completely and he tumbles backward through years like a man falling down a deep well — Wells's Time Traveller, perhaps, falling with a broken iron rung in one hand, down and down into the land of the Morlocks, where machines pound on and on in the tunnels of the night. It's 1981, 1977, 1969; and suddenly he is here, here in June of 1958; bright summerlight is everywhere and behind sleeping eyelids Ben Hanscom's pupils contract at the command of his dreaming brain, which sees not the darkness which lies over western Illinois but the bright sunlight of a June day in Derry, Maine, twenty-seven years ago.

Bells.

The bell.

School.

School is.

School is

2

out!

The sound of the bell went burring up and down the halls of Derry School, a big brick building which stood on Jackson Street, and at its sound the children in Ben Hanscom's fifth-grade classroom raised a spontaneous cheer — and Mrs Douglas, usually the strictest of teachers, made no effort to quell them. Perhaps she knew it would have been impossible.

'Children!' she called when the cheer died. 'May I have your attention for a final moment?'

Now a babble of excited chatter, mixed with a few groans, rose in the classroom. Mrs Douglas was holding their report cards in her hand.

'I sure hope I pass!' Sally Mueller said chirpily to Bev Marsh, who sat in the next row. Sally was bright, pretty, vivacious. Bev was also pretty, but there was nothing vivacious about her this afternoon, last day of school or not. She sat looking moodily down at her penny-loafers. There was a fading yellow bruise on one of her cheeks.

'I don't give a shit if I do or not,' Bev said.

Sally sniffed. Ladies don't use such language, the sniff said. Then she turned to Greta Bowie. It had probably only been the excitement of the bell signalling the end of another school-year that had caused Sally to slip and speak to Beverly anyhow, Ben thought. Sally Mueller and Greta Bowie both came from rich families with houses on West Broadway while Bev came to school from one of those slummy apartment buildings on Lower Main Street. Lower Main Street and West Broadway were only a mile and a half apart, but even a kid like Ben knew that the real distance was like the distance between Earth and the planet Pluto. All you had to do was look at Beverly Marsh's cheap sweater, her too-big skirt that probably came from the Salvation Army thrift-box, and her scuffed penny-loafers to know just how far one was from the other. But Ben still liked Beverly better – a *lot* better. Sally and Greta had nice clothes, and he guessed they probably had their hair permed or waved or something every month or so, but he didn't think that changed the basic facts at all. They could get their hair permed every *day* and they'd still be a couple of conceited snots.

He thought Beverly was nicer . . . and *much* prettier, although he never in a million years would have dared say such a thing to her. But still, sometimes, in the heart of winter when the light outside seemed yellow-sleepy, like a cat curled up on a sofa, when Mrs Douglas was droning on about mathematics (how to carry down in long division or how to find the common denominator of two fractions so you could add them) or reading the questions from *Shining Bridges* or talking about tin deposits in Paraguay, on those days when it seemed that school would never end and it didn't matter if it didn't because all the world outside was slush . . . on those days Ben would sometimes look sideways at Beverly, stealing her face, and his heart would both hurt desperately and somehow grow brighter at the same time. He supposed he had a crush on her, or was in love with her, and that was why it was always Beverly he thought of when the Penguins came on the radio singing 'Earth Angel' – 'my darling dear/ love you all the time . . .' Yeah, it was stupid, all right, sloppy as a used Kleenex, but it was all right, too, because he would never tell. He thought that fat boys were probably only allowed to love pretty girls inside. If he told anyone how he felt (not that he had anyone to tell), that person would probably laugh until he had a heart-attack. And if he ever told Beverly, she would either laugh herself (bad), or make retching noises of disgust (worse).

'Now please come up as soon as I call your name. Paul Anderson
... Carla Bordeaux ... Greta Bowie ... Calvin Clark ... Cissy
Clark ...'

As she called their names, Mrs Douglas's fifth-grade class came
forward one by one (except for the Clark twins, who came together as
always, hand in hand, indistinguishable except for the length of their
white-blonde hair and the fact that she wore a dress while he wore
jeans), took their buff-colored report cards with the American flag and
the Pledge of Allegiance on the front and the Lord's Prayer on the back,
walked sedately out of the classroom ... and then pounded down the
hall to where the big front doors had been chocked open. And then
they simply ran out into summer and were gone: some on bikes, some
skipping, some riding invisible horses and slapping their hands against
the sides of their thighs to manufacture hoofbeats, some with arms slung
about each other, singing 'Mine eyes have seen the glory of the burning
of the school' to the tune of 'The Battle Hymn of the Republic.'

'Marcia Fadden ... Frank Frick ... Ben Hanscom ...'

He rose, stealing his last glance at Beverly Marsh for the summer
(or so he thought then), and went forward to Mrs Douglas's desk, an
eleven-year-old kid with a can roughly the size of New Mexico – said
can packed into a pair of horrid new blue-jeans that shone little darts of
light from the copper rivets and went *whssht-whssht-whssht* as his big thighs
brushed together. His hips swung girlishly. His stomach slid from side to
side. He was wearing a baggy sweatshirt although the day was warm. He
almost always wore baggy sweatshirts because he was deeply ashamed of
his chest and had been since the first day of school after the Christmas
vacation, when he had worn one of the new Ivy League shirts his mother
had given him, and Belch Huggins, who was a sixthgrader, had cawed:
'Hey, you guys! Lookit what Santy Claus brought Ben Hanscom for
Christmas! A big set of titties!' Belch had nearly collapsed with the deli-
ciousness of his wit. Others had laughed as well – a few of them girls. If
a hole leading into the underworld had opened before him at that very
moment, Ben would have dropped into it without a sound ... or perhaps
with the faintest murmur of gratitude.

Since that day he wore sweatshirts. He had four of them – the
baggy brown, the baggy green, and two baggy blues. It was one of
the few things on which he had managed to stand up to his mother,
one of the few lines he had ever, in the course of his mostly complacent childhood, felt compelled to draw in the dust. If he had seen
Beverly Marsh giggling with the others that day, he supposed he would
have died.

'It's been a pleasure having you this year, Benjamin,' Mrs Douglas said as she handed him his report card.

'Thank you, Mrs Douglas.'

A mocking falsetto wavered from somewhere at the back of the room: 'Sank-ooo, Missus Dougwiss.'

It was Henry Bowers, of course. Henry was in Ben's fifth-grade class instead of in the sixth grade with his friends Belch Huggins and Victor Criss because he had been kept back the year before. Ben had an idea that Bowers was going to stay back again. His name had not been called when Mrs Douglas handed out the rank-cards, and that meant trouble. Ben was uneasy about this, because if Henry did stay back again, Ben himself would be partly responsible . . . and Henry knew it.

During the year's final tests the week before, Mrs Douglas had reseated them at random by drawing their names from a hat on her desk. Ben had ended up sitting next to Henry Bowers in the last row. As always, Ben curled his arm around his paper and then bent close to it, feeling the somehow comforting press of his gut against his desk, licking his Be-Bop pencil occasionally for inspiration.

About halfway through Tuesday's examination, which happened to be math, a whisper drifted across the aisle to Ben. It was as low and uncarrying and expert as the whisper of a veteran con passing a message in the prison exercise yard: 'Let me copy.'

Ben had looked to his left and directly into the black and furious eyes of Henry Bowers. Henry was a big boy even for twelve. His arms and legs were thick with farm-muscle. His father, who was reputed to be crazy, had a little spread out at the end of Kansas Street, near the Newport town line, and Henry put in at least thirty hours a week hoeing, weeding, planting, digging rocks, cutting wood, and reaping, if there was anything to reap.

Henry's hair was cut in an angry-looking flattop short enough for the white of his scalp to show through. He Butch-Waxed the front with a tube he always carried in the hip pocket of his jeans, and as a result the hair just above his forehead looked like the teeth of an oncoming power-mower. An odor of sweat and Juicy Fruit gum always hung about him. He wore a pink motorcycle jacket with an eagle on the back to school. Once a fourth-grader was unwise enough to laugh at that jacket. Henry had turned on the little squirt, limber as a weasel and quick as an adder, and double-pumped the squirt with one work-grimed fist. The squirt lost three front teeth. Henry got a two-week vacation from school. Ben had hoped, with the unfocused yet burning hope of the downtrodden and terrorized, that Henry would be expelled instead of suspended. No such luck. Bad pennies always turned up. His suspension over, Henry had swaggered back into the schoolyard, balefully resplendent in his pink motorcycle jacket, hair Butch-Waxed so heavily that it seemed to scream up from his skull. Both eyes bore the puffed, colorful traces of the beating his crazy father had administered for 'fighting in the playyard.' The traces of the beating eventually faded; for the kids who had to somehow coexist with Henry at Derry, the lesson did not. To the best of Ben's knowledge, no one had said anything about Henry's pink motorcycle jacket with the eagle on the back since then.

When he whispered grimly at Ben to let him copy, three thoughts had gone skyrocketing through Ben's mind – which was every bit as lean and quick as his body was obese – in a space of seconds. The first was that if Mrs Douglas caught Henry cheating answers off his paper, both of them would get zeros on their tests. The second was that if he didn't let Henry copy, Henry would almost surely catch him after school and administer the fabled double-pump to *him*, probably with Huggins holding one of his arms and Criss holding the other.

These were the thoughts of a child, and there was nothing surprising about that, because he *was* a child. The third and last thought, however, was more sophisticated – almost adult.

He might get me, all right. But maybe I can keep out of his way for the last week of school. I'm pretty sure I can, if I really try. And he'll forget over the summer, I think. Yeah. He's pretty stupid. If he flunks this test, maybe he'll stay back again. And if he stays back I'll get ahead of him. I won't be in the same room with him anymore . . . I'll get to junior high before he does. I . . . I might be free.

'Let me copy,' Henry whispered again. His black eyes were now blazing, demanding.

Ben shook his head and curled his arm more tightly around his paper.

'I'll get you, fatboy,' Henry whispered, a little louder now. His paper was so far an utter blank save for his name. He was desperate. If he flunked his exams and stayed back again, his father would beat his brains out. 'You let me copy or I'll get you bad.'

Ben shook his head again, his jowls quivering. He was scared, but he was also determined. He realized that for the first time in his life he had consciously committed himself to a course of action, and that also frightened him, although he didn't exactly know why – it would be long years before he would realize it was the cold-bloodedness of his calculations, the careful and pragmatic counting of the cost, with its intimations of onrushing adulthood, that had scared him even more than Henry had scared him. Henry he might be able to dodge. Adulthood, where he would probably think in such a way almost all the time, would get him in the end.

'Is someone talking back there?' Mrs Douglas had said then, very clearly. 'If so, I want it to stop *right now*.'

Silence had prevailed for the next ten minutes; young heads remained studiously bent over examination sheets which smelled of fragrant purple mimeograph ink, and then Henry's whisper had floated across the aisle again, thin, just audible, chilling in the calm assurance of its promise:

'You're dead, fatboy.'

3

Ben took his rank-card and escaped, grateful to whatever gods there are for eleven-year-old fatboys that Henry Bowers had not, by virtue of alphabetical order, been allowed to escape the classroom first so he could lay for Ben outside.

He did not run down the corridor like the other children. He *could* run, and quite fast for a kid his size, but he was acutely aware of how funny he looked when he did. He walked fast, though, and emerged from the cool book-smelling hall and into the bright June sunshine. He stood with his face turned up into that sunshine for a moment, grateful for its warmth and his freedom. September was a million years from today. The calendar might say something different, but what the calendar said was a lie. The summer would be much longer than the sum of its days, and it belonged to him. He felt as tall as the Standpipe and as wide as the whole town.

Someone bumped him – bumped him hard. Pleasant thoughts of the summer lying before him were driven from Ben's mind as he tottered wildly for balance on the edge of the stone steps. He grabbed the iron railing just in time to save himself from a nasty tumble.

'Get out of my way, you tub of guts.' It was Victor Criss, his hair combed back in an Elvis pompadour and gleaming with Brylcreem. He went down the steps and along the walk to the front gate, hands in the pockets of his jeans, shirt-collar turned up hood-style, cleats on his engineer boots dragging and tapping.

Ben, his heart still beating rapidly from his fright, saw that Belch Huggins was standing across the street, having a butt. He raised a hand to Victor and passed him the cigarette when Victor joined him. Victor took a drag, handed it back to Belch, then pointed to where Ben stood, now halfway down the steps. He said something and they both broke up. Ben's face flamed dully. They always got you. It was like fate or something.

'You like this place so well you're gonna stand here all day?' a voice said at his elbow.

Ben turned, and his face became hotter still. It was Beverly Marsh, her auburn hair a dazzling cloud around her head and upon her shoulders, her eyes a lovely gray-green. Her sweater, pushed to her elbows, was frayed around the neck and almost as baggy as Ben's sweatshirt. Too baggy, certainly, to tell if she was getting any chestworks yet, but Ben didn't care; when love comes before puberty, it can come in waves so clear and so powerful that no one can stand against its simple imperative, and Ben made no effort to do so now. He simply gave in. He felt both foolish and exalted, as miserably embarrassed as he had ever been in his life . . . and yet inarguably blessed. These hopeless emotions mixed in a heady brew that left him feeling both sick and joyful.

'No,' he croaked. 'Guess not.' A large grin spread across his face. He knew how idiotic it must look, but he could not seem to pull it back.

'Well, good. Cause school's out, you know. Thank God.'

'Have . . .' Another croak. He had to clear his throat, and his blush deepened. 'Have a nice summer, Beverly.'

'You too, Ben. See you next year.'

She went quickly down the steps and Ben saw everything with his lover's eye: the bright tartan of her skirt, the bounce of her red hair against the back of her sweater, her milky complexion, a small healing cut across the back of one calf, and (for some reason this last caused another wave of feeling to sweep him so powerfully he had to grope for the railing again; the feeling was huge, inarticulate, mercifully brief; perhaps a sexual pre-signal, meaningless to his body, where the endocrine glands still slept almost without dreaming, yet as bright as summer heat-lightning) a bright golden ankle-bracelet she wore just above her right loafer, winking back the sun in brilliant little flashes.

A sound – some sort of sound – escaped him. He went down the steps like a feeble old man and stood at the bottom, watching until she turned left and disappeared beyond the high hedge that separated the schoolyard from the sidewalk.

4

He only stood there for a moment, and then, while the kids were still streaming past in yelling, running groups, he remembered Henry Bowers and hurried around the building. He crossed the little-kids' playground, running his fingers across the swing-chains to make them jingle and stepping over the teeter-totter boards. He went out the much smaller gate which gave on Charter Street and headed off to the left, never looking back at the stone pile where he had spent most of his weekdays over the last nine months. He stuffed his rank-card in his back pocket and started to whistle. He was wearing a pair of Keds, but so far as he could tell, their soles never touched the sidewalk for eight blocks or so.

School had let out just past noon; his mother would not be home until at least six, because on Fridays she went right to the Shop 'n Save after work. The rest of the day was his.

He went down to McCarron Park for awhile and sat under a tree, not doing anything but occasionally whispering 'I love Beverly Marsh' under his breath, feeling more light-headed and romantic each time he said it. At one point, as a bunch of boys drifted into the park and began choosing up sides for a scratch baseball game, he whispered the words 'Beverly Hanscom' twice, and then had to put his face into the grass until it cooled his burning cheeks.

Shortly after that he got up and headed across the park toward Costello Avenue. A walk of five more blocks would take him to the Public Library, which, he supposed, had been his destination all along. He was almost out of the park when a sixth-grader named Peter Gordon saw him and yelled: 'Hey, tits! Wanna play? We need somebody to be right-field!' There was an explosion of laughter. Ben escaped it as fast as he could, hunching his neck down into his collar like a turtle drawing into its shell.

Still, he considered himself lucky, all in all; on another day the boys might have chased him, maybe just to rank him out, maybe to roll him in the dirt and see if he would cry. Today they were too absorbed in getting the game going – whether or not you could use fingers or get topsies when you threw the bat for first picks, which team would get their guaranteed last ups, all the rest. Ben happily left them to the arcana preceding the first ballgame of the summer and went on his way.

Three blocks down Costello he spied something interesting, perhaps even profitable, under someone's front hedge. Glass gleamed through the ripped side of an old paper bag. Ben hooked the bag out onto the sidewalk with his foot. It seemed his luck really was in. There were four beer bottles and four big soda bottles inside. The biggies were worth a nickel each, the Rheingolds two pennies. Twenty-eight cents under someone's hedge, just waiting for some kid to come along and scoff it up. Some *lucky* kid.

'That's me,' Ben said happily, having no idea what the rest of the day had in store. He got moving again, holding the bag by the bottom so it wouldn't break open. The Costello Avenue Market was a block farther down the street, and Ben turned in. He swapped the bottles for cash and most of the cash for candy.

He stood at the penny-candy window, pointing, delighted as always by the ratcheting sound the sliding door made when the storekeeper slid it along its track, which was lined with ball-bearings. He got five red licorice whips and five black, ten rootbeer barrels (two for a penny), a nickel strip of buttons (five to a row, five rows on a nickel strip, and you ate them right off the paper), a packet of Likem Ade, and a package of Pez for his Pez-Gun at home.

Ben walked out with a small brown paper sack of candy in his hand and four cents in the right front pocket of his new jeans. He looked at the brown bag with its load of sweetness and a thought suddenly tried to surface

(*you keep eating this way Beverly Marsh is never going to look at you*)

but it was an unpleasant thought and so he pushed it away. It went easily enough; this was a thought used to being banished.

If someone had asked him, 'Ben, are you lonely?,' he would have looked at that someone with real surprise. The question had never even occurred to him. He had no friends, but he had his books and his dreams; he had his Revell models; he had a gigantic set of Lincoln Logs and built all sorts of stuff with them. His mother had exclaimed more than once that Ben's Lincoln Logs houses looked better than some real ones that came from blueprints. He had a pretty good Erector Set, too. He was hoping for the Super Set when his birthday came around in October. With that one you could build a clock that really told time and a car with real gears in it. Lonely? he might have asked in return, honestly foozled. Huh? What?

A child blind from birth doesn't even know he's blind until someone tells him. Even then he has only the most academic idea of what blindness is; only the formerly sighted have a real grip on the thing. Ben Hanscom had no sense of being lonely because he had never been anything but. If the condition had been new, or more localized, he might have understood, but loneliness both encompassed his life and overreached it. It simply *was*, like his double-jointed thumb or the funny little jag inside one of his front teeth, the little jag his tongue began running over whenever he was nervous.

Beverly was a sweet dream; the candy was a sweet reality. The candy was his friend. So he told the alien thought to take a hike, and it went quietly, without causing any fuss whatsoever. And between the Costello Avenue Market and the library, he gobbled all of the candy in the sack. He honestly meant to save the Pez for watching TV that night – he liked to load them into the little plastic Pez-Gun's handgrip one by one, liked to hear the accepting click of the small spring inside, and liked most of all to shoot them into his mouth one by one, like a kid committing suicide by sugar. *Whirlybirds* was on tonight, with Kenneth Tobey as the fearless helicopter pilot, and *Dragnet*, where the cases were true but the names had been changed to protect the innocent, and his favorite cop show of all time. *Highway Patrol*, which starred Broderick Crawford as Highway Patrolman Dan Matthews. Broderick Crawford was Ben's personal hero. Broderick Crawford was *fast*, Broderick Crawford was *mean*, Broderick Crawford took absolutely no shit from nobody . . . and best of all, Broderick Crawford was fat.

He arrived at the corner of Costello and Kansas Street, where he crossed to the Public Library. It was really two buildings – the old stone structure in front, built with lumber-baron money in 1890, and the new low sandstone building behind, which housed the Children's Library. The adult library in front and the Children's Library behind were connected by a glass corridor.

This close to downtown, Kansas Street was one-way, so Ben only looked in one direction – right – before crossing. If he had looked left, he would have gotten a nasty shock. Standing in the shade of a big old oak tree on the lawn of the Derry Community House a block down were Belch Huggins, Victor Criss, and Henry Bowers.

5

'Let's get him, Hank.' Victor was almost panting.

Henry watched the fat little prick scutter across the street, his belly bouncing, the cowlick at the back of his head springing back and forth like a goddam Slinky, his ass wiggling like a girl's inside his new bluejeans. He estimated the distance between the three of them here on the Community House lawn and Hanscom, and between Hanscom and the safety of the library. He thought they could probably get him before he made it inside, but Hanscom might start screaming. He wouldn't put it past the little pansy. If he did, an adult might interfere, and Henry wanted no interference. The Douglas bitch had told Henry he had flunked both English and math. She was passing him, she said, but he would have to take four weeks of summer make-up. Henry would rather have stayed back. If he'd stayed back, his father would have beaten him up once. With Henry at school four hours a day for four weeks of the farm's busiest season, his father was apt to beat him up half a dozen times, maybe even more. He was reconciled to this grim future only because he intended to pass everything on to that fat little babyfag this afternoon.

With interest.

'Yeah, let's go,' Belch said.

'We'll wait for him to come out.'

They watched Ben open one of the big double doors and go inside, and then they sat down and smoked cigarettes and told travelling-salesman jokes and waited for him to come back out.

Eventually, Henry knew, he would. And when he did, Henry was going to make him sorry he was ever born.

6

Ben loved the library.

He loved the way it was always cool, even on the hottest day of a long hot summer; he loved its murmuring quiet, broken only by occasional whispers, the faint thud of a librarian stamping books and cards, or the riffle of pages being turned in the Periodicals Room, where the old men hung out, reading newspapers which had been threaded into long sticks. He loved the quality of the light, which slanted through the high narrow windows in the afternoons or glowed in lazy pools thrown by the chain-hung globes on winter evenings while the wind whined outside. He liked the smell of the books – a spicy smell, faintly fabulous. He would sometimes walk through the adult stacks, looking at the thousands of volumes and imagining a world of lives inside each one, the way he sometimes walked along his street in the burning smoke-hazed twilight of a late-October afternoon, the sun only a bitter orange line on the horizon, imagining the lives going on behind all the windows – people laughing or arguing or arranging flowers or feeding kids or pets or their own faces while they watched the boobtube. He liked the way the glass corridor connecting the old building with the Children's Library was always hot, even in the winter, unless there had been a couple of cloudy days; Mrs Starrett, the head children's librarian, told him that was caused by something called the greenhouse effect. Ben had been delighted with the idea. Years later he would build the hotly debated BBC communications center in London, and the arguments might rage for a thousand years and still no one would know (except for Ben himself) that the communications center was nothing but the glass corridor of the Derry Public Library stood on end.

He liked the Children's Library as well, although it had none of the shadowy charm he felt in the old library, with its globes and curving iron staircases too narrow for two people to pass upon them – one always had to back up. The Children's Library was bright and sunny, a little noisier in spite of the LET'S BE QUIET, SHALL WE? signs that were posted around. Most of the noise usually came from Pooh's Corner, where the little kids went to look at picturebooks. When Ben came in today, story hour had just begun there. Miss Davies, the pretty young librarian, was reading 'The Three Billy Goats Gruff.'

'Who is that trip-trapping upon my bridge?'

Miss Davies spoke in the low, growling tones of the troll in the story. Some of the little ones covered their mouths and giggled, but most only watched her solemnly, accepting the voice of the troll as they accepted the voices of their dreams, and their grave eyes reflected the eternal fascination of the fairytale: would the monster be bested . . . or would it feed?

Bright posters were tacked everywhere. Here was a good cartoon kid who had brushed his teeth until his mouth foamed like the muzzle of a mad dog; here was a bad cartoon kid who was smoking cigarettes (WHEN I GROW UP I WANT TO BE SICK A LOT, JUST LIKE MY DAD, it said underneath); here was a wonderful photograph of a billion tiny pinpoints of light flaring in darkness. The motto beneath said:

ONE IDEA LIGHTS A THOUSAND CANDLES.
– Ralph Waldo Emerson

There were invitations to JOIN THE SCOUTING EXPERIENCE. A poster advancing the idea that THE GIRLS' CLUBS OF TODAY BUILD THE WOMEN OF TOMORROW. There were softball sign-up sheets and Community House Children's Theater sign-up sheets. And, of course, one inviting kids to JOIN THE SUMMER READING PROGRAM. Ben was a big fan of the summer reading program. You got a map of the United States when you signed up. Then, for every book you read and made a report on, you got a state sticker to lick and put on your map. The sticker came complete with info like the state bird, the state flower, the year admitted to the Union, and what presidents, if any, had ever come from that state. When your got all forty-eight stuck on your map, you got a free book. Helluva good deal. Ben planned to do just as the poster suggested: 'Waste no time, sign up today.'

Conspicuous amid this bright and amiable riot of color was a simple stark poster taped to the checkout desk – no cartoons or fancy photographs here, just black print on white poster-paper reading:

> REMEMBER THE CURFEW.
> 7 P.M.
> DERRY POLICE DEPARTMENT

Just looking at it gave Ben a chill. In the excitement of getting his rank-card, worrying about Henry Bowers, talking with Beverly, and starting summer vacation, he had forgotten all about the curfew, and the murders.

People argued about how many there had been, but everyone agreed that there had been at least four since last winter – five if you counted George Denbrough (many held the opinion that the little Denbrough boy's death must have been some kind of bizarre freak accident). The first everyone was sure of was Betty Ripsom, who had been found the day after Christmas in the area of turnpike construction on Outer Jackson Street. The girl, who was thirteen, had been found mutilated and frozen into the muddy earth. This had not been in the paper, nor was it a thing any adult had spoken of to Ben. It was just something he had picked up around the corners of overheard conversations.

About three and a half months later, not long after the trout-fishing season had begun, a fisherman working the bank of a stream twenty miles east of Derry had hooked onto something he believed at first to be a stick. It had turned out to be the hand, wrist, and first four inches of a girl's forearm. His hook had snagged this awful trophy by the web of flesh between the thumb and first finger.

The State Police had found the rest of Cheryl Lamonica seventy yards farther downstream, caught in a tree that had fallen across the stream the previous winter. It was only luck that the body had not been washed into the Penobscot and then out to sea in the spring runoff.

The Lamonica girl had been sixteen. She was from Derry but

did not attend school; three years before she had given birth to a daughter, Andrea. She and her daughter lived at home with Cheryl's parents. 'Cheryl was a little wild sometimes but she was a good girl at heart,' her sobbing father had told police. 'Andi keeps asking "Where's my mommy?" and I don't know what to tell her.'

The girl had been reported missing five weeks before the body was found. The police investigation of Cheryl Lamonica's death began with a logical enough assumption: that she had been murdered by one of her boyfriends. She had lots of boyfriends. Many were from the air base up Bangor way. 'They were nice boys, most of them,' Cheryl's mother said. One of the 'nice boys' had been a forty-year-old Air Force colonel with a wife and three children in New Mexico. Another was currently serving time in Shawshank for armed robbery.

A boyfriend, the police thought. Or just possibly a stranger. A sexfiend.

If it was a sexfiend, he was apparently a fiend for boys as well. In late April a junior-high teacher on a nature walk with his eighth-grade class had spied a pair of red sneakers and a pair of blue corduroy rompers protruding from the mouth of a culvert on Merit Street. That end of Merit had been blocked off with saw-horses. The asphalt had been bulldozed up the previous fall. The turnpike extension would cross there as well on its way north to Bangor.

The body had been that of three-year-old Matthew Clements, reported missing by his parents only the day before (his picture had been on the front page of the Derry *News*, a dark-haired little kid grinning brashly into the camera, a Red Sox cap perched on his head). The Clements family lived on Kansas Street, all the way on the other side of town. His mother, so stunned by her grief that she seemed to exist in a glass ball of utter calm, told police that Matty had been riding his tricycle up and down the sidewalk beside the house, which stood on the corner of Kansas Street and Kossuth Lane. She went to put her washing in the drier, and when she next looked out the window to check on Matty, he was gone. There had only been his overturned trike on the grass between the sidewalk and the street. One of the back wheels was still spinning lazily. As she looked, it came to a stop.

That was enough for Chief Borton. He proposed the seven o'clock curfew at a special session of the City Council the following evening; it was adopted unanimously and went into effect the next day. Small children were to be watched by a 'qualified adult' at all times, according to the story which reported the curfew in the *News*. At Ben's school there had been a special assembly a month ago. The

Chief went on stage, hooked his thumbs into his gunbelt, and assured the children they had nothing at all to worry about as long as they followed a few simple rules: don't talk to strangers, don't accept rides with people unless you know them *well*, always remember that The Policeman Is Your Friend . . . and obey the curfew.

Two weeks ago a boy Ben knew only vaguely (he was in the other fifth-grade classroom at Derry Elementary) had looked into one of the stormdrains out by Neibolt Street and had seen what looked like a lot of hair floating around in there. This boy, whose name was either Frankie or Freddy Ross (or maybe Roth), had been out prospecting for goodies with a gadget of his own invention, which he called THE FABULOUS GUM-STICK. When he talked about it you could tell he thought about it like that, in capital letters (and maybe neon, as well). THE FABULOUS GUM-STICK was a birch branch with a big wad of bubble-gum stuck on the tip. In his spare time Freddy (or Frankie) walked around Derry with it, peering into sewers and drains. Sometimes he saw money – pennies mostly, but sometimes a dime or even a quarter (he referred to these latter, for some reason known only to him, as 'quay-monsters'). Once the money was spotted, Frankie-or-Freddy and THE FABULOUS GUM-STICK would swing into action. One downward poke through the grating and the coin was as good as in his pocket.

Ben had heard rumors of Frankie-or-Freddy and his gum stick long before the kid had vaulted into the limelight by discovering the body of Veronica Grogan. 'He's really gross,' a kid named Richie Tozier had confided to Ben one day during activity period. Tozier was a scrawny kid who wore glasses. Ben thought that without them Tozier probably saw every bit as well as Mr Magoo; his magnified eyes swam behind the thick lenses with an expression of perpetual surprise. He also had huge front teeth that had earned him the nickname Bucky Beaver. He was in the same fifth-grade class as Freddy-or-Frankie. 'Pokes that gum stick of his down sewerdrains all day long and then chews the gum from the end of it at night.'

'Oh gosh, that's bad!' Ben had exclaimed.

'Dat's wight, wabbit,' Tozier said, and walked away.

Frankie-or-Freddy had worked THE FABULOUS GUM-STICK back and forth through the grate of the stormdrain, believing he'd found a wig. He thought maybe he could dry it out and give it to his mother for her birthday, or something. After a few minutes of poking and prodding, just as he was about to give up, a face had floated out of the murky water in the plugged drain, a face with dead leaves plastered to its white cheeks and dirt in its staring eyes.

Freddy-or-Frankie ran home screaming.

Veronica Grogan had been in the fourth grade at the Neibolt Street Church School, which was run by people Ben's mother called 'the Christers.' She was buried on what would have been her tenth birthday.

After this most recent horror, Arlene Hanscom had taken Ben into the living room one evening and sat beside him on the couch. She picked up his hands and looked intently into his face. Ben looked back, feeling a little uneasy.

'Ben,' she said presently, 'are you a fool?'

'No, Mamma,' Ben said, feeling more uneasy than ever. He hadn't the slightest idea what this was about. He could not remember ever seeing his mamma look so grave.

'No,' she echoed. 'I don't believe you are.'

She fell silent for a long time then, not looking at Ben but pensively out the window. Ben wondered briefly if she had forgotten all about him. She was a young woman still – only thirty-two – but raising a boy by herself had put a mark on her. She worked forty hours a week in the spool-and-bale room at Stark's Mills in Newport, and after workdays when the dust and lint had been particularly bad, she sometimes coughed so long and hard that Ben would become frightened. On those nights he would lie awake for a long time, looking through the window beside his bed into the darkness, wondering what would become of him if she died. He would be an orphan then, he supposed. He might become a State Kid (he thought that meant you had to go live with farmers who made you work from sunup to sunset), or he might be sent to the Bangor Orphan Asylum. He tried to tell himself it was foolish to worry about such things, but the telling did absolutely no good. Nor was it just himself he was worried about; he worried for her as well. She was a hard woman, his mamma, and she insisted on having her own way about most things, but she was a good mamma. He loved her very much.

'You know about these murders,' she said, looking back at last.

He nodded.

'At first people thought they were . . .' She hesitated over the next word, never spoken in her son's presence before, but the circumstances were unusual and she forced herself. '. . . sex crimes. Maybe they were and maybe they weren't. Maybe they're over and maybe they're not. No one can be sure of anything anymore, except that some crazy man who preys on little children is out there. Do you understand me, Ben?'

He nodded.

'And you know what I mean when I say they may have been sex crimes?'

He didn't – at least not exactly – but he nodded again. If his mother felt she had to talk to him about the birds and bees as well as this other business, he thought he would die of embarrassment.

'I worry about you, Ben. I worry that I'm not doing right by you.'

Ben squirmed and said nothing.

'You're on your own a lot. Too much, I guess. You –'

'Mamma –'

'Hush while I'm talking to you,' she said, and Ben hushed. 'You have to be careful, Benny. Summer's coming and I don't want to spoil your vacation, but you have to be careful. I want you in by suppertime every day. What time do we eat supper?'

'Six o'clock.'

'Right with Eversharp! So hear what I'm saying: if I set the table and pour your milk and see that there's no Ben washing his hands at the sink, I'm going to go right away to the telephone and call the police and report you missing. Do you understand that?'

'Yes, Mamma.'

'And you believe I mean exactly what I say?'

'Yes.'

'It would probably turn out that I did it for nothing, if I ever had to do it at all. I'm not entirely ignorant about the ways of boys. I know they get wrapped up in their own games and projects during summer vacation – lining bees back to their hives or playing ball or kick-the-can or whatever. I have a pretty good idea what you and your friends are up to, you see.'

Ben nodded soberly, thinking that if she didn't know he had no friends, she probably didn't know anywhere near as much about his boyhood as she thought she did. But he would never have dreamed of saying such a thing to her, not in ten thousand years of dreaming.

She took something from the pocket of her housedress and handed it to him. It was a small plastic box. Ben opened it. When he saw what was inside, his mouth dropped open. '*Wow!*' he said, his admiration totally unaffected. '*Thanks!*'

It was a Timex watch with small silver numbers and an imitation-leather band. She had set it and wound it; he could hear it ticking.

'Jeez, it's the coolest!' He gave her an enthusiastic hug and a loud kiss on the cheek.

She smiled, pleased that he was pleased, and nodded. Then she grew grave again. 'Put it on, keep it on, wear it, wind it, mind it, don't lose it.'

'Okay.'

'Now that you have a watch you have no reason to be late home. Remember what I said: if you're not on time, the police will be looking for you on my behalf. At least until they catch the bastard who is killing children around here, don't you dare be a single minute late, or I'll be on that telephone.'

'Yes, Mamma.'

'One other thing. I don't want you going around alone. You know enough not to accept candy or rides from strangers – we both agree that you're no fool – and you're big for your age, but a grown man, particularly a crazy one, can overpower a child if he really wants to. When you go to the park or the library, go with one of your friends.'

'I will, Mamma.'

She looked out the window again and uttered a sigh that was full of trouble. 'Things have come to a pretty pass when a thing like this can go on. There's something ugly about this town, anyway. I've always thought so.' She looked back at him, brows drawn down. 'You're such a wanderer, Ben. You must know almost everyplace in Derry, don't you? The town part of it, at least.'

Ben didn't think he knew anywhere near all the places, but he did know a lot of them. And he was so thrilled by the unexpected gift of the Timex that he would have agreed with his mother that night if she had suggested John Wayne should play Adolf Hitler in a musical comedy about World War II. He nodded.

'*You've* never seen anything, have you?' she asked. 'Anything or anyone . . . well, suspicious? Anything out of the ordinary? Anything that scared you?'

And in his pleasure over the watch, his feeling of love for her, his small-boy gladness at her concern (which was at the same time a little frightening in its unhidden unabashed fierceness), he almost told her about the thing that had happened last January.

He opened his mouth and then something – some powerful intuition – closed it again.

What was that something, exactly? Intuition. No more than that . . . and no less. Even children may intuit love's more complex responsibilities from time to time, and to sense that in some cases it may be kinder to remain quiet. That was part of the reason Ben closed his mouth. But there was something else as well, something not so noble. She could be hard, his mamma. She could be a boss. She never called him 'fat,' she called him 'big' (sometimes amplified to 'big for his age'), and when there were leftovers from supper she would often bring them to him while he was watching TV or doing his homework, and he would eat them, although some dim part of him hated himself for doing so (but never his mamma for putting the food before him – Ben Hanscom would not have dared to hate his mamma; God would surely strike him dead for feeling such a brutish, ungrateful emotion even for a second). And perhaps some even dimmer part of him – the far-off Tibet of Ben's deeper thoughts – suspected her motives in this constant feeding. Was it just love? Could it be anything else? Surely not. But . . . he wondered. More to the point, she didn't know he had no friends. That lack of knowledge made him distrust her, made him unsure of what her reaction would be to his story of the thing which had happened to him in January. If *anything* had happened. Coming in at six and staying in was not so bad, maybe. He could read, watch TV,

(*eat*)

build stuff with his logs and Erector Set. But having to stay in all day as well would be *very* bad . . . and if he told her what he had seen – or thought he had seen – in January, she might make him do just that.

So, for a variety of reasons, Ben withheld the story.

'No, Mamma,' he said. 'Just Mr McKibbon rooting around in other people's garbage.'

That made her laugh – she didn't like Mr McKibbon, who was a Republican as well as a 'Christer' – and her laugh closed the subject. That night Ben had lain awake late, but no thoughts of being cast adrift and parentless in a hard world troubled him. He felt loved and safe as he lay in his bed looking at the moonlight which came in through the window and spilled across the bed onto the floor. He alternately put his watch to his ear so he could listen to it tick and held it close to his eyes so he could admire its ghostly radium dial.

He had finally fallen asleep and dreamed he was playing baseball with the other boys in the vacant lot behind Tracker Brothers' Truck Depot. He had just hit a bases-clearing home run, swinging from his heels and getting every inch of that little honey, and his cheering teammates met him in a mob at home plate. They pummelled him and clapped him on the back. They hoisted him onto their shoulders and carried him toward the place where their equipment was scattered. In the dream he was almost bursting with pride and happiness . . . and then he had looked out toward center field, where a chainlink fence marked the boundary between the cindery lot and the weedy ground beyond that sloped into the Barrens. A figure was standing in those tangled weeds and low bushes, almost out of sight. It held a clutch of balloons – red, yellow, blue, green – in one white-gloved hand. It beckoned with the other. He couldn't see the figure's face, but he could see the baggy suit with the big orange pompom-buttons down the front and the floppy yellow bow-tie.

It was a clown.

Dat's wight, wabbit, a phantom voice agreed.

When Ben awoke the next morning he had forgotten the dream but his pillow was damp to the touch . . . as if he had wept in the night.

7

He went up to the main desk in the Children's Library, shaking the train of thought the curfew sign had begun as easily as a dog shakes water after a swim.

'Hullo, Benny,' Mrs Starrett said. Like Mrs Douglas at school, she genuinely liked Ben. Grownups, especially those who sometimes needed to discipline children as part of their jobs, generally liked him, because he was polite, soft-spoken, thoughtful, sometimes even funny in a very quiet way. These were all the same reasons most kids thought he was a puke. 'You tired of summer vacation yet?'

Ben smiled. This was a standard witticism with Mrs Starrett. 'Not yet,' he said, 'since summer vacation's only been going on' – he looked at his watch – 'one hour and seventeen minutes. Give me another hour.'

Mrs Starrett laughed, covering her mouth so it wouldn't be too loud. She asked Ben if he wanted to sign up for the summer reading program, and Ben said he did. She gave him a map of the United States and Ben thanked her very much.

He wandered off into the stacks, pulling a book here and there, looking at it, putting it back. Choosing books was serious business. You had to be careful. If you were a grownup you could have as many as you wanted, but kids could only take out three at a time. If you picked a dud, you were stuck with it.

He finally picked out his three – *Bulldozer, The Black Stallion,* and one that was sort of a shot in the dark: a book called *Hot Rod,* by a man named Henry Gregor Felsen.

'You may not like this one,' Mrs Starrett remarked, stamping the book. 'It's extremely bloody. I urge it on the teenagers, especially the ones who have just got their driving licenses, because it gives them something to think about. I imagine it slows some of them down for a whole week.'

'Well, I'll give it a whirl,' Ben said, and took his books over to one of the tables away from Pooh's Corner, where Big Billy Goat Gruff was in the process of giving a double dose of dickens to the troll under the bridge.

He worked on *Hot Rod* for awhile, and it was not too shabby. Not too shabby at all. It was about a kid who was a really great driver, but there was this party-pooper cop who was always trying to slow him down. Ben found out there were no speed limits in Iowa, where the book was set. That was sort of cool.

He looked up after three chapters, and his eye was caught by a brand-new display. The poster on top (the library was gung-ho for posters, all right) showed a happy mailman delivering a letter to a happy kid. LIBRARIES ARE FOR WRITING, TOO, the poster said. WHY NOT WRITE A FRIEND TODAY? THE SMILES ARE GUARANTEED!

Beneath the poster were slots filled with pre-stamped postcards, pre-stamped envelopes, and stationery with a drawing of the Derry Public Library on top in blue ink. The pre-stamped envelopes were a nickel each, the postcards three cents. The paper was two sheets for a penny.

Ben felt in his pocket. The remaining four cents of his bottle money was still there. He marked his place in *Hot Rod* and went back to the desk. 'May I have one of those postcards, please?'

'Certainly, Ben.' As always, Mrs Starrett was charmed by his grave politeness and a little saddened by his size. Her mother would have said the boy was digging his grave with a knife and fork. She gave him the card and watched him go back to his seat. It was a table that could seat six, but Ben was the only one there. She had never seen Ben with any of the other boys. It was too bad, because she believed Ben Hanscom had treasures buried inside. He would yield them up to a kind and patient prospector . . . if one ever came along.

8

Ben took out his ballpoint pen, clicked the point down, and addressed the card simply enough: *Miss Beverly Marsh, Lower Main Street, Derry, Maine, Zone 2.* He did not know the exact number of her building, but his mamma had told him that most postmen had a pretty good idea of who their customers were once they'd been on their beats a little while. If the postman who had Lower Main Street could deliver this card, that would be great. If not, it would just go to the deadletter office and he would be out three cents. It would certainly never come back to him, because he had no intention of putting his name and address on it.

Carrying the card with the address turned inward (he was taking no chances, even though he didn't see anyone he recognized), he got a few square slips of paper from the wooden box by the card-file. He took these back to his seat and began to scribble, to cross out, and then to scribble again.

During the last week of school before exams, they had been reading and writing haiku in English class. Haiku was a Japanese form of poetry, brief, disciplined. A haiku, Mrs Douglas said, could be just seventeen syllables long – no more, no less. It usually concentrated on one clear image which was linked to one specific emotion: sadness, joy, nostalgia, happiness . . . love.

Ben had been utterly charmed by the concept. He enjoyed his English classes, although mild enjoyment was generally as far as it went. He could do the work, but as a rule there was nothing in it which gripped him. Yet there *was* something in the concept of haiku that fired his imagination. The idea made him feel happy, the way Mrs Starrett's explanation of the greenhouse effect had made him happy. Haiku was good poetry, Ben felt, because it was *structured* poetry. There were no secret rules. Seventeen syllables, one image linked to one emotion, and you were out. Bingo. It was clean, it was utilitarian, it was entirely contained within and dependent upon its own rules. He even liked the word itself, a slide of air broken as if along a dotted line by the 'k'-sound at the very back of your mouth: *haiku*.

Her hair, he thought, and saw her going down the school steps again with it bouncing on her shoulders. The sun did not so much glint on it as seem to burn within it.

Working carefully over a twenty-minute period (with one break to go back and get more work-slips), striking out words that were too long, changing, deleting, Ben came up with this:

> *Your hair is winter fire,*
> *January embers.*
> *My heart burns there, too.*

He wasn't crazy about it, but it was the best he could do. He was afraid that if he frigged around with it too long, worried it too much, he would end up getting the jitters and doing something much worse. Or not doing it at all. He didn't want that to happen. The moment she had taken to speak to him had been a striking moment for Ben. He wanted to mark it in his memory. Probably Beverly had a crush on some bigger boy – a sixth- or maybe even a seventh-grader, and she would think that maybe that boy had sent the haiku. That would make her happy, and so the day she got it would be marked in her memory. And although she would never know it had been Ben Hanscom who marked it for her, that was all right; *he* would know.

He copied his completed poem onto the back of the postcard (printing in block letters, as if copying out a ransom note rather than a love poem), clipped his pen back into his pocket, and stuck the card in the back of *Hot Rod*.

He got up then, and said goodbye to Mrs Starrett on his way out.

'Goodbye, Ben,' Mrs Starrett said. 'Enjoy your summer vacation, but don't forget about the curfew.'

'I won't.'

He strolled through the glassed-in passageway between the two buildings, enjoying the heat there (*greenhouse effect*, he thought smugly) followed by the cool of the adult library. An old man was reading the *News* in one of the ancient, comfortably overstuffed chairs in the Reading Room alcove. The headline just below the masthead blazed: DULLES PLEDGES US TROOPS TO HELP LEBANON IF NEEDED! There was also a photo of Ike, shaking hands with an Arab in the Rose Garden. Ben's mamma said that when the country elected Hubert Humphrey President in 1960, maybe things would get moving again. Ben was vaguely aware that there was something called a recession going on, and his mamma was afraid she might get laid off.

A smaller headline on the bottom half of page one read POLICE HUNT FOR PSYCHOPATH GOES ON.

Ben pushed open the library's big front door and stepped out.

There was a mailbox at the foot of the walk. Ben fished the postcard from the back of the book and mailed it. He felt his heartbeat speed up a little as it slipped out of his fingers. *What if she knows it's me, somehow?*

Don't be a stupe, he responded, a little alarmed at how exciting that idea seemed to him.

He walked off up Kansas Street, hardly aware of where he was

178

going and not caring at all. A fantasy had begun to form in his mind. In it, Beverly Marsh walked up to him, her gray-green eyes wide, her auburn hair tied back in a pony-tail. *I want to ask you a question, Ben*, this make-believe girl said in his mind, *and you've got to swear to tell the truth*. She held up the postcard. *Did you write this?*

This was a terrible fantasy. This was a wonderful fantasy. He wanted it to stop. He didn't want it to *ever* stop. His face was starting to burn again.

Ben walked and dreamed and shifted his library books from one arm to the other and began to whistle. *You'll probably think I'm horrible*, Beverly said, *but I think I want to kiss you*. Her lips parted slightly.

Ben's own lips were suddenly too dry to whistle.

'I think I want you to,' he whispered, and smiled a dopey, dizzy, and absolutely beautiful grin.

If he had looked down at the sidewalk just then, he would have seen that three other shadows had grown around his own; if he had been listening he would have heard the sound of Victor's cleats as he, Belch, and Henry closed in. But he neither heard nor saw. Ben was far away, feeling Beverly's lips slip softly against his mouth, raising his timid hands to touch the dim Irish fire of her hair.

9

Like many cities, small and large, Derry had not been planned – like Topsy, it just growed. City planners never would have located it where it was in the first place. Downtown Derry was in a valley formed by the Kenduskeag Stream, which ran through the business district on a diagonal from southwest to northeast. The rest of the town had swarmed up the sides of the surrounding hills.

The valley the township's original settlers came to had been swampy and heavily grown over. The stream and the Penobscot River into which the Kenduskeag emptied were great things for traders, bad ones for those who sowed crops or built their houses too close to them – the Kenduskeag in particular, because it flooded every three or four years. The city was still prone to flooding in spite of the vast amounts of money spent over the last fifty years to control the problem. If the floods had been caused only by the stream itself, a system of dams might have taken care of things. There were, however, other factors. The Kenduskeag's low banks were one. The entire area's logy drainage was another. Since the turn of the century there had been many serious floods in Derry and one disastrous one, in 1931. To make matters worse, the hills on which much of Derry was built were honeycombed with small streams — Torrault Stream, in which the body of Cheryl Lamonica had been found, was one of them. During periods of heavy rain, they were all apt to overflow their banks. 'If it rains two weeks the whole damn town gets a sinus infection,' Stuttering Bill's dad had said once.

The Kenduskeag was caged in a concrete canal two miles long as it passed through downtown. This canal dived under Main Street at the intersection of Main and Canal, becoming an underground river for half a mile or so before surfacing again at Bassey Park. Canal Street, where most of Derry's bars were ranked like felons in a police lineup, paralleled the Canal on its way out of town, and every few weeks or so the police would have to fish some drunk's car out of the water, which was polluted to drop-dead levels by sewage and mill wastes. Fish were caught from time to time in the Canal, but they were inedible mutants.

On the northeastern side of town — the Canal side — the river had been managed to at least some degree. A thriving commerce went on all along it in spite of the occasional flooding. People walked beside the Canal, sometimes hand in hand (if the wind was right, that was; if it was wrong, the stench took much of the romance out of such strolling), and at Bassey Park, which faced the high school across the Canal, there were sometimes Boy Scout campouts and Cub Scout wiener roasts. In 1969 the citizens would be shocked and sickened to discover that hippies (one of them had actually sewed an American flag on the seat of his pants, and *that* pinko-faggot was busted before you could say Gene McCarthy) were smoking dope and trading pills up there. By '69 Bassey Park had become a regular open-air pharmacy. *You just wait*, people said. *Somebody'll get killed before they put a stop to it*. And of course someone finally did — a seventeen-year-old boy had been found dead by the Canal, his veins full of almost pure heroin — what the kids called a tight white rail. After that the druggies began to drift away from Bassey Park, and there were even stories that the kid's ghost was haunting the area. The story was stupid, of course, but if it kept the speed-freaks and the nodders away, it was at least a *useful* stupid story.

On the southwestern side of town the river presented even more of a problem. Here the hills had been deeply cut open by the passing of the great glacier and further wounded by the endless water erosion of the Kenduskeag and its webwork of tributaries; the bedrock showed through in many places like the half-unearthed bones of dinosaurs. Veteran employees of the Derry Public Works Department knew that, following the fall's first hard frost, they could count on a good deal of sidewalk repair on the southwestern side of town. The concrete would contract and grow brittle and then the bedrock would suddenly shatter up through it, as if the earth meant to hatch something.

What grew best in the shallow soil which remained was plants with shallow root-systems and hardy natures – weeds and trash-plants, in other words: scruffy trees, thick low bushes, and virulent infestations of poison ivy and poison oak grew everywhere they were allowed a foothold. The southwest was where the land fell away steeply to the area that was known in Derry as the Barrens. The Barrens – which were anything *but* barren – were a messy tract of land about a mile and a half wide by three miles long. It was bounded by upper Kansas Street on one side and by Old Cape on the other. Old Cape was a low-income housing development, and the drainage was so bad over there that there were stories of toilets and sewer-pipes actually exploding.

The Kenduskeag ran through the center of the Barrens. The city had grown up to the northeast and on both sides of it, but the only vestiges of the city down there were Derry Pumphouse #3 (the municipal sewage-pumping station) and the City Dump. Seen from the air the Barrens looked like a big green dagger pointing at downtown.

To Ben all this geography mated with geology meant was a vague awareness that there were no more houses on his right side now; the land had dropped away. A rickety whitewashed railing, about waist-high, ran beside the sidewalk, a token gesture of protection. He could faintly hear running water; it was the sound-track to his continuing fantasy.

He paused and looked out over the Barrens, still imagining her eyes, the clean smell of her hair.

From here the Kenduskeag was only a series of twinkles seen through breaks in the thick foliage. Some kids said that there were mosquitoes as big as sparrows down there at this time of year; others said there was quicksand as you approached the river. Ben didn't believe it about the mosquitoes, but the idea of quicksand scared him.

Slightly to his left he could see a cloud of circling, diving seagulls: the dump. Their cries reached him faintly. Across the way he could see Derry Heights, and the low roofs of the Old Cape houses closest to the Barrens. To the right of Old Cape, pointing skyward like a squat white finger, was the Derry Standpipe. Directly below him a rusty culvert stuck out of the earth, spilling discolored water down the hill in a glimmering little stream which disappeared into the tangled trees and bushes.

Ben's pleasant fantasy of Beverly was suddenly broken by one far more grim: what if a dead hand flopped out of that culvert right now, right this second, while he was looking? And suppose that when he turned to find a phone and call the police, a clown was standing there? A funny clown wearing a baggy suit with big orange puffs for buttons? Suppose –

A hand fell on Ben's shoulder, and he screamed.

There was laughter. He whirled around, shrinking against the white fence separating the safe, sane sidewalk of Kansas Street from the wildly undisciplined Barrens (the railing creaked audibly), and saw Henry Bowers, Belch Huggins, and Victor Criss standing there.

'Hi, Tits,' Henry said.

'What do you want?' Ben asked, trying to sound brave.

'I want to beat you up,' Henry said. He seemed to contemplate this prospect soberly, even gravely. But oh, his black eyes sparkled. 'I got to teach you something, Tits. You won't mind. You like to learn new things, don'tcha?'

He reached for Ben. Ben ducked away.

'Hold him, you guys.'

Belch and Victor seized his arms. Ben squealed. It was a cowardly sound, rabbity and weak, but he couldn't help it. *Please God don't let them make me cry and don't let them break my watch*, Ben thought wildly. He didn't know if they would get around to breaking his watch or not, but he was pretty sure he would cry. He was pretty sure he would cry plenty before they were through with him.

'Jeezum, he sounds just like a pig,' Victor said. He twisted Ben's wrist. 'Don't he sound like a pig?'

'He sure do,' Belch giggled.

Ben lunged first one way and then the other. Belch and Victor went with him easily, letting him lunge, then yanking him back.

Henry grabbed the front of Ben's sweatshirt and yanked it upward, exposing his belly. It hung over his belt in a swollen droop.

'Lookit that gut!' Henry cried in amazed disgust. 'Jesus-please-us!'

Victor and Belch laughed some more. Ben looked around wildly for help. He could see no one. Behind him, down in the Barrens, crickets drowsed and seagulls screamed.

'You just better quit!' he said. He wasn't blubbering yet but was close to it. 'You just better!'

'Or what?' Henry asked as if he was honestly interested. 'Or what, Tits? Or what, huh?'

Ben suddenly found himself thinking of Broderick Crawford, who played Dan Matthews on *Highway Patrol* – that bastard was *tough*, that bastard was *mean*, that bastard took zero shit from anybody – and then he burst into tears. Dan Matthews would have belted these guys right through the fence, down the embankment, and into the puckerbrush. He would have done it with his belly.

'Oh boy, lookit the baby!' Victor chortled. Belch joined in. Henry smiled a little, but his face still held that grave, reflective cast – that look that was somehow almost sad. It frightened Ben. It suggested he might be in for more than just a beating.

As if to confirm this idea, Henry reached into his jeans pocket and brought out a Buck knife.

Ben's terror exploded. He had been whipsawing his body futilely to either side; now he suddenly lunged straight forward. There was an instant when he believed he was going to get away. He was sweating heavily, and the boys holding his arms had greasy grips at best. Belch managed to hold on to his right wrist, but just barely. He pulled entirely free of Victor. Another lunge –

Before he could make it, Henry stepped forward and gave him a shove. Ben flew backward. The railing creaked more loudly this time, and he felt it give a little under his weight. Belch and Victor grabbed him again.

'Now you hold him,' Henry said. 'You hear me?'

'Sure, Henry,' Belch said. He sounded a trifle uneasy. 'He ain't gonna get away. Don't worry.'

Henry stepped forward until his flat stomach almost touched Ben's belly. Ben stared at him, tears spilling helplessly out of his wide eyes. *Caught! I'm caught!* a part of his mind yammered. He tried to stop it – he couldn't think at all with that yammering going on – but it wouldn't stop. *Caught! Caught! Caught!*

Henry pulled out the blade, which was long and wide and engraved with his name. The tip glittered in the afternoon sunshine.

'I'm gonna test you now,' Henry said in that same reflective voice. 'It's exam time, Tits, and you better be ready.'

Ben wept. His heart thundered madly in his chest. Snot ran out of his nose and collected on his upper lip. His library books lay in a scatter at his feet. Henry stepped on *Bulldozer*, glanced down, and dealt it into the gutter with a sideswipe of one black engineer boot.

'Here's the first question on your exam, Tits. When somebody says "Let me copy" during finals, what are you going to say?'

'Yes!' Ben exclaimed immediately. 'I'm going to say yes! Sure! Okay! Copy all you want!'

The Buck's tip slid through two inches of air and pressed against Ben's stomach. It was as cold as an ice-cube tray just out of the Frigidaire. Ben gasped his belly away from it. For a moment the world went gray. Henry's mouth was moving but Ben couldn't tell what he was saying. Henry was like a TV with the sound turned off and the world was swimming . . . swimming . . .

Don't you dare faint! the panicky voice shrieked. *If you faint he may get mad enough to kill you!*

The world came back into some kind of focus. He saw that both Belch and Victor had stopped laughing. They looked nervous . . . almost scared. Seeing that had the effect of a head-clearing slap on Ben. *All of a sudden they don't know what he's going to do, or how far he might go. However bad you thought things were, that's how bad they really are . . . maybe even a little worse. You got to think. If you never did before or never do again, you better think now. Because his eyes say they're right to look nervous. His eyes say he's crazy as a bedbug.*

'That's the wrong answer, Tits,' Henry said. 'If just *anyone* says "Let me copy," I don't give a red fuck what you do. Got it?'

'Yes,' Ben said, his belly hitching with sobs. 'Yes, I got it.'

'Well, okay. That's one wrong, but the biggies are still coming up. You ready for the biggies?'

'I . . . I guess so.'

A car came slowly toward them. It was a dusty '51 Ford with an old man and woman propped up in the front seat like a pair of neglected department store mannequins. Ben saw the old man's head turn slowly toward him. Henry stepped closer to Ben, hiding the knife. Ben could feel its point dimpling his flesh just above his bellybutton. It was still cold. He didn't see how that could be, but it was.

'Go ahead, yell,' Henry said. 'You'll be pickin your fuckin guts off your sneakers.' They were close enough to kiss. Ben could smell the sweet smell of Juicy Fruit gum on Henry's breath.

The car passed and continued on down Kansas Street, as slow and serene as the pace car in the Tournament of Roses Parade.

'All right, Tits, here's the second question. If *I* say "Let me copy" during finals, what are *you* going to say?'

'Yes. I'll say yes. Right away.'

Henry smiled. 'That's good. You got that one right, Tits. Now here's the third question: how am I going to be sure you never forget that?'

'I . . . I don't know,' Ben whispered.

Henry smiled. His face lit up and was for a moment almost handsome. 'I know!' he said, as if he had discovered a great truth. 'I know, Tits! I'll carve my name on your big fat gut!'

Victor and Belch abruptly began laughing again. For a moment Ben felt a species of bewildered relief, thinking it had all been nothing but make-believe – a little shuck-and-jive the three of them had whomped up to scare the living hell out of him. But Henry Bowers wasn't laughing, and Ben suddenly understood that Victor and Belch were laughing because *they* were relieved. It was obvious to both of them that Henry couldn't be serious. Except Henry *was*.

The Buck knife slid upward, smooth as butter. Blood welled in a bright red line on Ben's pallid skin.

'Hey!' Victor cried. The word came out muffled, in a startled gulp.

'Hold him!' Henry snarled. 'You just hold him, hear me?' Now there was nothing grave and reflective on Henry's face; now it was the twisted face of a devil.

'*Jeezum-crow Henry don't really cut im!*' Belch screamed, and his voice was high, almost a girl's voice.

Everything happened fast then, but to Ben Hanscom it all seemed slow; it all seemed to happen in a series of shutterclicks, like action stills in a Life-magazine photo-essay. His panic was gone. He had discovered something inside him suddenly, and because it had no use for panic, that something just ate the panic whole.

In the first shutterclick, Henry had snatched his sweatshirt all the way up to his nipples. Blood was pouring from the shallow vertical cut above his bellybutton.

In the second shutterclick, Henry drew the knife down again, operating fast, like a lunatic battle-surgeon under an aerial bombardment. Fresh blood flowed.

Backward, Ben thought coldly as blood flowed down and pooled between the waistband of his jeans and his skin. *Got to go backward. That's the only direction I can get away in.* Belch and Victor weren't holding him anymore. In spite of Henry's command, they had drawn away. They had drawn away in horror. But if he ran, Bowers would catch him.

In the third shutterclick, Henry connected the two vertical slashes with a short horizontal line. Ben could feel blood running into his underpants now, and a sticky snail-trail was creeping down his left thigh.

Henry leaned back momentarily, frowning with the studied concentration of an artist painting a landscape. *After H comes E,* Ben thought, and that was all it took to get him moving. He pulled forward a little bit and Henry shoved him back again. Ben pushed with his legs, adding his own force to Henry's. He hit the white-washed railing between Kansas Street and the drop into the Barrens. As he did, he raised his right foot and planted it in Henry's belly. This was not a retaliatory act; Ben only wanted to increase his backward force. And yet when he saw the expression of utter surprise on Henry's face, he was filled with a clear savage joy — a feeling so intense that for a split second he thought the top of his head was going to come off.

Then there was a cracking, splintering sound from the railing. Ben saw Victor and Belch catch Henry before he could fall on his ass in the gutter next to the remains of *Bulldozer,* and then Ben was falling backward into space. He went with a scream that was half a laugh.

Ben hit the slope on his back and buttocks just below the culvert he had spotted earlier. It was a good thing he landed below it; if he had landed on it, he might well have broken his back. As it was, he landed on a thick cushion of weeds and bracken and barely felt the impact. He did a backward somersault, feet and legs snapping over his head. He landed sitting up and went sliding down the slope backward like a kid on a big green Chute-the-Chute, his sweatshirt pulled up around his neck, his hands grabbing for purchase and doing nothing but yanking out tuft after tuft of bracken and witch-grass.

He saw the top of the embankment (it seemed impossible that he had just been standing up there) receding with crazy cartoon speed. He saw Victor and Belch, their faces round white O's, staring down at him. He had time to mourn his library books. Then he fetched up against something with agonizing force and nearly bit his tongue in half.

It was a downed tree, and it checked Ben's fall by nearly breaking his left leg. He clawed his way back up the slope a little bit, pulling his leg free with a groan. The tree had stopped him about halfway down. Below, the bushes were thicker. Water falling from the culvert ran over his hands in thin streams.

There was a shriek from above him. Ben looked up again and saw Henry Bowers come flying over the drop, his knife clenched between his teeth. He landed on both feet, body thrown backward at a steep angle so he would not overbalance. He skidded to the end of a gigantic set of footprints and then began to run down the embankment in a series of gangling kangaroo leaps.

'*I'n goin oo kill ooo, Its!*' Henry was shrieking around the knife, and Ben didn't need a UN translator to tell him Henry was saying *I'm going to kill you, Tits.*

'*I'n goin oo huckin kill ooo!*'

Now, with that cold general's eye he had discovered up above on the sidewalk, Ben saw what he had to do. He managed to gain his feet just before Henry arrived, the knife now in his hand and held straight out in front of him like a bayonet. Ben was peripherally aware that the left leg of his jeans was shredded, and his leg was bleeding much more heavily than his stomach . . . but it was supporting him, and that meant it wasn't broken. At least he *hoped* that's what it meant.

Ben crouched slightly to maintain his precarious balance, and as Henry grabbed at him with one hand and swept the knife in a long flat arc with the other, Ben stepped aside. He lost his balance, but as he fell down he stuck out his shredded left leg. Henry's shins struck it, and his legs were booted out from under him with great efficiency. For a moment Ben gaped, his terror overcome with a mixture of awe and admiration. Henry Bowers appeared to be flying exactly like Superman over the fallen tree where Ben had stopped. His arms were straight out in front of him, the way George Reeves held his arms out on the TV show. Only George Reeves always looked like flying was as natural as taking a bath or eating lunch on the back porch. Henry looked like someone had shoved a hot poker up his ass. His mouth was opening and closing. A string of saliva was shooting back from one corner of it, and as Ben watched, it splatted against the lobe of Henry's ear.

Then Henry crashed back to earth. The knife flew out of his hand. He rolled over on one shoulder, landed on his back, and slid away into the bushes with his legs splayed into a V. There was a yell. A thud. And then silence.

Ben sat, dazed, looking at the matted place in the bushes where Henry had done his disappearing act. Suddenly rocks and pebbles began to bounce by him. He looked up again. Victor and Belch were now descending the embankment. They were moving more carefully than Henry, and hence more slowly, but they would reach him in thirty seconds or less if he didn't do something.

He moaned. Would this lunacy never end?

Keeping his eye on them, he clambered over the downed tree and began to scramble down the embankment, panting harshly. He had a stitch in his side. His tongue hurt like hell. The bushes were now almost as tall as Ben himself. The randy green smell of stuff growing out of control filled his nose. He could hear running water somewhere close, chuckling over stones and rilling between them.

His feet slipped and here he went again, rolling and sliding, smashing the back of his hand against a jutting rock, shooting through a patch of thorns that hooked blue-gray puffs of cotton from his sweatshirt and little divots of meat from his hands and cheeks.

He slammed to a jarring halt sitting up, with his feet in the water. Here was a little curving stream which wound its way into a thick stand of second-growth trees to his right; it looked as dark as a cave in there. He looked to his left and saw Henry Bowers lying on his back in the middle of the stream. His half-open eyes showed only whites. Blood trickled from one ear and ran toward Ben in delicate threads.

Oh my God I killed him! Oh my God I'm a murderer! Oh my God!

Forgetting that Belch and Victor were behind him (or perhaps understanding they would lose all interest in beating the shit out of him when they discovered their Fearless Leader was dead), Ben splashed twenty feet upstream to where Henry lay, his shirt in ribbons, his jeans soaked black, one shoe gone. Ben was vaguely aware that there was precious little left of his own clothes and that his body was one big rattletrap of aches and pains. His left ankle was the worst; it had already puffed tight against his soaking sneaker and he was favoring it so badly that he was really not walking but lurching like a sailor on shore for the first time after a long sea voyage.

He bent over Henry Bowers. Henry's eyes popped wide open. He grabbed Ben's calf with one scraped and bloody hand. His mouth worked, and although nothing but a series of whistling aspirations emerged, Ben could *still* make out what he was saying: *Kill you, you fat shit.*

Henry was trying to pull himself up, using Ben's leg as a pole. Ben pulled backward frantically. Henry's hand slipped down, then off. Ben flew backward, whirling his arms, and fell on his ass for a record-breaking third time in the last four minutes. He also bit his tongue again. Water splashed up around him. A rainbow glimmered for an instant in front of Ben's eyes. Ben didn't give a fuck about the rainbow. He didn't give a fuck about finding a pot of gold. He would settle for his miserable fat life.

Henry rolled over. Tried to stand. Fell back. Managed to get to his hands and knees. And finally tottered to his feet. He stared at Ben with those black eyes. The front of his flattop now leaned this way and that, like cornhusks after a high wind has passed through.

Ben was suddenly angry. No – this was more than being angry. He was *infuriated*. He had been walking with his library books under his arm, having an innocent little daydream about kissing Beverly Marsh, bothering nobody. And look at this. Just *look*. Pants shredded. Left ankle maybe broken, badly sprained for sure. Leg all cut up, tongue all cut up, Henry goddam Bowers's monogram on his stomach. How about all that happy crappy, sports fans? But it was probably the thought of his library books, for which he was liable, that drove him to charge Henry Bowers. His lost library books and his mental image of how reproachful Mrs Starrett's eyes would become when he told her. Whatever the reason – cuts, sprain, library books, or even the thought of the soggy and probably illegible rank-card in his back pocket – it was enough to get him moving. He lumbered forward, squashy Keds spatting in the shallow water, and kicked Henry squarely in the balls.

Henry uttered a horrid rusty scream that sent birds beating up from the trees. He stood spraddle-legged for a moment, hands clasping his crotch, staring unbelievingly at Ben. 'Ug,' he said in a small voice.

'Right,' Ben said.

'Ug,' Henry said, in an even smaller voice.

'Right,' Ben said again.

Henry sank slowly back to his knees, not so much falling as folding up. He was still looking at Ben with those unbelieving black eyes.

'Ug.'

'*Damn* right,' Ben said.

Henry fell on his side, still clutching his testicles, and began to roll slowly from side to side.

'Ug!' Henry moaned. 'My balls. Ug! Oh you broke my balls. Ug-ug!' He was now beginning to gain a little force, and Ben started to back away a step at a time. He was sickened by what he had done, but he was also filled with a kind of righteous, paralyzed fascination. '*Ug!* – my fuckin sack – *ug-UG!* – oh my fuckin *BALLS!*'

Ben might have remained in the area for an untold length of time – perhaps even until Henry recovered enough to come after him – but just then a rock struck him above the right ear with such a deep, drilling pain that, until he felt warm blood flowing again, Ben thought he had been stung by a wasp.

He turned and saw the other two striding up the middle of the stream toward him. They each had a handful of water-rounded rocks.

Victor pegged one and Ben heard it whistle past his ear. He ducked and another struck his right knee, making him yell with surprised hurt. A third bounced off his right cheekbone, and that eye filled with water.

He scrambled for the far bank and climbed it as fast as he could, grabbing onto protruding roots and hauling on handfuls of bushes. He made it to the top (one final stone struck his buttocks as he pulled himself up) and took a quick look back over his shoulder.

Belch was kneeling beside Henry while Victor stood half a dozen feet away, firing stones; one the size of a baseball clipped through the man-high bushes beside Ben. He had seen enough; in fact, he had seen much more than enough. Worst of all, Henry Bowers was getting up again. Like Ben's own Timex watch, Henry could take a licking and keep on ticking. Ben turned and smashed his way into the bushes, lumbering along in a direction he hoped was west. If he could cross to the Old Cape side of the Barrens, he could beg a dime off somebody and take the bus home. And when he got there he would lock the door behind him and bury these tattered bloody clothes in the trash and this crazy dream would finally be over. Ben thought of himself sitting in his chair in the living room, freshly tubbed, wearing his fuzzy red bathrobe, watching Daffy Duck cartoons on *The Mighty Ninety* and drinking milk through a strawberry Flav-R-Straw. *Hold that thought*, he told himself grimly, and kept lumbering along.

Bushes sprang into his face. Ben pushed them aside. Thorns reached and clawed. He tried to ignore them. He came to a flat area of ground that was black and mucky. A thick stand of bamboo-like growth spread across it and a fetid smell rose from the earth. An ominous thought

(*quicksand*)

slipped across the foreground of his mind like a shadow as he looked at the sheen of standing water deeper into the grove of bamboo-stuff. He didn't want to go in there. Even if it wasn't quicksand, the mud would suck his sneakers off. He turned right instead, running along the front of the bamboo-grove and finally into a patch of real woods.

The trees, mostly firs, were thick, growing everywhere, battling each other for a little space and sun, but there was less undergrowth and he could move faster. He was no longer sure what direction he was moving in, but still thought he was, on measure, a little ahead of the game. The Barrens were enclosed by Derry on three sides and bounded by the half-finished turnpike extension on the fourth. Sooner or later he would come out *somewhere*.

His stomach throbbed painfully, and he pulled up the remains of his sweatshirt for a look. He winced and drew a whistle of air in over his teeth. His belly looked like a grotesque Christmas-tree ball, all caked red blood and smeared green from his slide down the embankment. He pulled the sweatshirt down again. Looking at that mess made him feel like blowing lunch.

Now he heard a low humming noise from ahead – it was one steady note just above the low range of his hearing. An adult, intent only on getting the hell out of there (the mosquitoes had found Ben now, and while nowhere near as big as sparrows, they were pretty big), would have ignored it, or simply not heard it at all. But Ben was a boy, and he was already getting over his fright. He swerved to his left and pushed through some low laurel bushes. Beyond them, sticking out of the ground, were the top three feet of a cement cylinder about four feet wide. It was capped with a vented iron manhole cover. The cover was stamped with the words DERRY SEWER DEPT. The sound – this close it was more a drone than a hum – was coming from someplace deep inside.

Ben put one eye to a venthole but could see nothing. He could hear that drone, and water running down there someplace, but that was all. He took a breath, got a whiff of a sour smell that was both dank and shitty, and drew back with a wince. It was a sewer, that was all. Or maybe a combined sewer and drainage-tunnel – there were plenty of those in flood-conscious Derry. No big deal. But it had given him a funny sort of chill. Part of it was seeing the handiwork of man in all this overgrown jumble of wilderness, but he supposed part of it was the shape of the thing itself – that concrete cylinder jutting out of the ground. Ben had read H. G. Wells's *The Time Machine* the year before, first the Classics Comics version and then the whole book. This cylinder with its vented iron cap reminded him of the wells which lead down into the country of the slumped and horrible Morlocks.

He moved away from it quickly, trying to find west again. He got to a little clearing and turned until his shadow was as directly behind him as he could get it. Then he headed off in a straight line.

Five minutes later he heard more running water ahead, and voices. Kids' voices.

He stopped to listen, and that was when he heard snapping branches and other voices behind him. They were perfectly recognizable. They belonged to Victor, Belch, and the one and only Henry Bowers.

The nightmare was not over yet, it seemed.

Ben looked around for a place to go to earth.

10

He came out of his hiding place about two hours later, dirtier than ever, but a little refreshed. Incredible as it seemed to him, he had dozed off.

When he had heard the three of them behind him, coming after him still, Ben had come dangerously close to freezing up completely, like an animal caught in the headlamps of an oncoming truck. A paralytic drowsiness began to steal over him. The idea of simply lying down, curling up into a ball like a hedgehog, and letting them do whatever they felt they had to occurred to him. It was a crazy idea, but it also seemed like a strangely *good* idea.

But instead Ben began to move toward the sound of the running water and those other kids. He tried to untangle their voices and get the sense of what they were saying – anything to shake off that scary paralysis of the spirit. Some project. They were talking about some project. One or two of the voices were even a little familiar. There was a splash, followed by a burst of good-natured laughter. The laughter filled Ben with a kind of stupid longing, and made him more aware of his dangerous position than anything else had done.

If he was going to be caught, there was no need to let these kids in for a dose of his medicine. Ben turned right again. Like many large people, he was remarkably light-footed. He passed close enough to the boys to see their shadows moving back and forth between him and the bright water, but they neither saw him nor heard him. Gradually their voices began to fall behind.

He came to a narrow path which had been beaten down to the bare earth. Ben considered it for a moment, then shook his head a little. He crossed it and plunged into the undergrowth again. He moved more slowly now, pushing bushes aside rather than stampeding through them. He was still moving roughly parallel to the stream the other kids had been playing beside. Even through the intervening bushes and trees he could see it was much wider than the one into which he and Henry had fallen.

Here was another of those concrete cylinders, barely visible amid a snarl of blackberry creepers, humming quietly to itself. Beyond, an embankment dropped off to the stream, and here an old, gnarled elm tree leaned crookedly out over the water. Its roots, half-exposed by bank erosion, looked like a snarl of dirty hair.

Hoping there wouldn't be bugs or snakes but too tired and numbly frightened to really care, Ben had worked his way between the roots and into a shallow cave beneath. He leaned back. A root jabbed him like an angry finger. He shifted his position a little and it supported him quite nicely.

Here came Henry, Belch, and Victor. He had thought they might be fooled into following the path, but no such luck. They stood close by him for a moment – any closer and he could have reached out of his hiding place and touched them.

'Bet them little snotholes back there saw him,' Belch said.

'Well, let's go find out,' Henry replied, and they headed back the way they had come. A few moments later Ben heard him roar: 'What the fuck you kids doin here?'

There was some sort of reply, but Ben couldn't tell what it was: the kids were too far away, and this close the river – it was the Kenduskeag, of course – was too loud. But he thought the kid sounded scared. Ben could sympathize.

Then Victor Criss bellowed something Ben hadn't understood at all: 'What a fuckin baby dam!'

Baby *dam*? Baby *damn*? Or maybe Victor had said what a damn bunch of babies and Ben had misheard him.

'Let's break it!' Belch proposed.

There were yells of protest followed by a scream of pain. Someone began to cry. Yes, Ben could sympathize. They hadn't been able to catch him (or at least not yet), but here was another bunch of little kids for them to take out their mad on.

'Sure, break it,' Henry said.

Splashes. Yells. Big moronic gusts of laughter from Belch and Victor. An agonized infuriated cry from one of the little kids.

'Don't gimme any of your shit, you stuttering little freak,' Henry Bowers said. 'I ain't takin no more shit from nobody today.'

There was a splintering crack. The sound of running water downstream grew louder and roared briefly before quieting to its former placid chuckle. Ben suddenly understood. Baby dam, yes, that was what Victor had said. The kids – two or three of them it had sounded like when he passed by – had been building a dam. Henry and his friends had just kicked it apart. Ben even thought he knew who one of the kids was. The only 'stuttering little freak' he knew from Derry

School was Bill Denbrough, who was in the other fifth-grade classroom.

'You didn't have to do that!' a thin and fearful voice cried out, and Ben recognized that voice as well, although he could not immediately put a face with it. 'Why did you do that?'

'Because I *felt* like it, fucknuts!' Henry roared back. There was a meaty thud. It was followed by a scream of pain. The scream was followed by weeping.

'Shut up,' Victor said. 'Shut up that crying, kid, or I'll pull your ears down and tie em under your chin.'

The crying became a series of choked snuffles.

'We're going,' Henry said, 'but before we do, I want to know one thing. You seen a fat kid in the last ten minutes or so? Big fat kid all bloody and cut up?'

There was a reply too brief to be anything but no.

'You sure?' Belch asked. 'You better be, mushmouth.'

'I-I-I'm sh-sh-sure,' Bill Denbrough replied.

'Let's go,' Henry said. 'He probably waded acrost back that way.'

'Ta-ta, boys,' Victor Criss called. 'It was a real baby dam, believe me. You're better off without it.'

Splashing sounds. Belch's voice came again, but farther away now. Ben couldn't make out the words. In fact, he didn't *want* to make out the words. Closer by, the boy who had been crying now resumed. There were comforting noises from the other boy. Ben had decided there was just the two of them, Stuttering Bill and the weeper.

He half-sat, half-lay where he was, listening to the two boys by the river and the fading sounds of Henry and his dinosaur friends crashing toward the far side of the Barrens. Sunlight flicked at his eyes and made little coins of light on the tangled roots above and around him. It was dirty in here, but it was also cozy . . . safe. The sound of running water was soothing. Even the sound of the crying kid was sort of soothing. His aches and pains had faded to a dull throb, and the sound of the dinosaurs had faded out completely. He would wait awhile, just to be sure they weren't coming back, and then he would make tracks.

Ben could hear the throb of the drainage machinery coming through the earth – could even feel it: a low, steady vibration that went from the ground to the root he was leaning against and then into his back. He thought of the Morlocks again, of their naked flesh; he imagined it would smell like the dank and shitty air that had come up through the ventholes of that iron cap. He thought of their wells driven deep into the earth, wells with rusty ladders bolted to their sides. He dozed, and at some point his thoughts became a dream.

11

It wasn't Morlocks he dreamed of. He dreamed of the thing which had happened to him in January, the thing which he hadn't quite been able to tell his mother.

It had been the first day of school after the long Christmas break. Mrs Douglas had asked for a volunteer to stay after and help her count the books that had been turned in just before the vacation. Ben had raised his hand.

'Thank you, Ben,' Mrs Douglas had said, favoring him with a smile of such brilliance that it warmed him down to his toes.

'Suckass,' Henry Bowers remarked under his breath.

It had been the sort of Maine winter day that is both the best and the worst: cloudless, eye-wateringly bright, but so cold it was a little frightening. To make the ten-degree temperature worse, there was a strong wind to give the cold a bitter cutting edge.

Ben counted books and called out numbers; Mrs Douglas wrote them down (not bothering to double-check his work even on a random basis, he was proud to note), and then they both carried the books down to the storage room through halls where radiators clanked dreamily. At first the school had been full of sounds: slamming locker doors, the clackety-clack of Mrs Thomas's typewriter in the office, the slightly off-key choral renditions of the glee club upstairs, the nervous thud-thud-thud of basketballs from the gym and the scrooch and thud of sneakers as players drove toward the baskets or cut turns on the polished wood floor.

Little by little these sounds ceased, until, as the last set of books was totted up (one short, but it hardly mattered, Mrs Douglas sighed – they were all holding together on a wing and a prayer), the only sounds were the radiators, the faint *whissh-whissh* of Mr Fazio's broom as he pushed colored sawdust up the hall floor, and the howl of the wind outside.

Ben looked toward the book room's one narrow window and saw that the light was fading rapidly from the sky. It was four o'clock and dusk was at hand. Membranes of dry snow blew around the icy jungle gym and skirled between the teetertotters, which were frozen solidly into the ground. Only the thaws of April would break those bitter winter-welds. He saw no one at all on Jackson Street. He looked a moment longer, expecting a car to roll through the Jackson-Witcham intersection, but none did. Everyone in Derry save himself and Mrs Douglas might be dead or fled, at least from what he could see from here.

He looked toward her and saw, with a touch of real fright, that she was feeling almost exactly the same things he was feeling himself. He could tell by the look in her eyes. They were deep and thoughtful and far off, not the eyes of a schoolteacher in her forties but those of a child. Her hands were folded just below her breasts, as if in prayer.

I'm scared, Ben thought, *and she's scared, too. But what are we really scared of?*

He didn't know. Then she looked at him and uttered a short, almost embarrassed laugh. 'I've kept you too late,' she said. 'I'm sorry, Ben.'

'That's okay.' He looked down at his shoes. He loved her a little – not with the frank unquestioning love he had lavished on Miss Thibodeau, his first-grade teacher . . . but he *did* love her.

'If I drove, I'd give you a ride,' she said, 'but I don't. My husband's going to pick me up around quarter past five. If you'd care to wait, we could –'

'No thanks,' Ben said. 'I ought to get home before then.' This was not really the truth, but he felt a queer aversion to the idea of meeting Mrs Douglas's husband.

'Maybe your mother could –'

'She doesn't drive, either,' Ben said. 'I'll be all right. It's only a mile home.'

'A mile's not far when it's nice, but it can be a very long way in this weather. You'll go in somewhere if it gets too cold, won't you, Ben?'

'Aw, sure. I'll go into Costello's Market and stand by the stove a little while, or something. Mr Gedreau doesn't mind. And I got my snowpants. My new Christmas scarf, too.'

Mrs Douglas looked a little reassured . . . and then she glanced toward the window again. 'It just looks so cold out there,' she said. 'So . . . so inimical.'

He didn't know the word but he knew exactly what she meant. *Something just happened – what?*

He had seen her, he realized suddenly, as a person instead of just a teacher. That was what had happened. Suddenly he had seen her face in an entirely different way, and because he did, it became a new face – the face of a tired poet. He could see her going home with her husband, sitting beside him in the car with her hands folded as the heater hissed and he talked about his day. He could see her making them dinner. An odd thought crossed his mind and a cocktail-party question rose to his lips: *Do you have children, Mrs Douglas?*

'I often think at this time of the year that people really weren't meant to live this far north of the equator,' she said. 'At least not in this latitude.' Then she smiled and some of the strangeness either went out of her face or his eye – he was able to see her, at least partially, as he always had. *But you'll never see her that way again, not completely,* he thought, dismayed.

'I'll feel old until spring, and then I'll feel young again. It's that way every year. Are you sure you'll be all right, Ben?'

'I'll be fine.'

'Yes, I suppose you will. You're a good boy, Ben.'

He looked back at his toes, blushing, loving her more than ever.

In the hallway Mr Fazio said: 'Be careful of de fros'bite, boy,' without looking up from his red sawdust.

'I will.'

He reached his locker, opened it, and yanked on his snowpants. He had been painfully unhappy when his mother insisted he wear them again this winter on especially cold days, thinking of them as baby clothes, but he was glad to have them this afternoon. He walked slowly toward the door, zipping his coat, yanking the drawstrings of his hood tight, pulling on his mittens. He went out and stood on the snowpacked top step of the front stairs for a moment, listening as the door snicked closed – and locked – behind him.

Derry School brooded under a bruised skin of sky. The wind blew steadily. The snap-hooks on the flagpole rope rattled a lonesome tattoo against the steel pole itself. That wind cut into the warm and unprepared flesh of Ben's face at once, numbing his cheeks.

Be careful of de fros'bite, boy.

He quickly pulled his scarf up until he looked like a small, pudgy caricature of Red Ryder. That darkening sky had a fantastical sort of beauty, but Ben did not pause to admire it; it was too cold for that. He got going.

At first the wind was at his back and things didn't seem so bad; in fact, it actually seemed to be helping him along. At Canal Street, however, he had to turn right and almost fully into the wind. Now it seemed to be holding him back . . . as if it had business with him. His scarf helped a little, but not enough. His eyes throbbed and the moisture in his nose froze to a crack-glaze. His legs were going numb.

Several times he stuck his mittened hands into his armpits to warm them up. The wind whooped and screamed, sometimes sounding almost human.

Ben felt both frightened and exhilarated. Frightened because he could now understand stories he had read, such as Jack London's 'To Build a Fire,' where people actually froze to death. It would be all too possible to freeze to death on a night like this, a night when the temperature would drop to fifteen below.

The exhilaration was hard to explain. It was a lonely feeling – a somehow melancholy feeling. He was outside; he passed on the wings of the wind, and none of the people beyond the brightly lighted squares of their windows saw him. They were inside, inside where there was light and warmth. They didn't know he had passed them; only he knew. It was a secret thing.

The moving air burned like needles, but it was fresh and clean. White smoke jetted from his nose in neat little streams.

And as sundown came, the last of the day a cold yellowy-orange line on the western horizon, the first stars cruel diamond-chips glimmering in the sky overhead, he came to the Canal. He was only three blocks from home now, and eager to feel the heat on his face and legs, moving the blood again, making it tingle.

Still – he paused.

The Canal was frozen in its concrete sluice like a frozen river of rose-milk, its surface humped and cracked and cloudy. It was moveless yet completely alive in this harshly puritanical winterlight; it had its own unique and difficult beauty.

Ben turned the other way – southwest. Toward the Barrens. When he looked in this direction, the wind was at his back again. It made his snowpants ripple and flap. The Canal ran straight between its concrete walls for perhaps half a mile; then the concrete was gone and the river sprawled its way into the Barrens, at this time of the year a skeletal world of icy brambles and jutting naked branches.

A figure was standing on the ice down there.

Ben stared at it and thought: *There may be a man down there, but can he be wearing what it looks like he's wearing? It's impossible, isn't it?*

The figure was dressed in what appeared to be a white-silver clown suit. It rippled around him in the polar wind. There were oversized orange shoes on his feet. They matched the pompom buttons which ran down the front of his suit. One hand grasped a bundle of strings which rose to a bright bunch of balloons, and when Ben observed that the balloons were floating in his direction, he felt unreality wash over him more strongly. He closed his eyes, rubbed them, opened them. The balloons still appeared to be floating toward him.

He heard Mr Fazio's voice in his head. *Be careful of de fros' bite, boy.*

It had to be a hallucination or a mirage brought on by some weird trick of the weather. There could be a man down there on the ice; he supposed it was even technically possible he could be wearing a clown suit. But the balloons couldn't be floating toward Ben, into the wind. Yet that was just what they appeared to be doing.

Ben! the clown on the ice called. Ben thought that voice was only in his mind, although it seemed he heard it with his ears. *Want a balloon, Ben?*

There was something so evil in that voice, so awful, that Ben wanted to run away as fast as he could, but his feet seemed as welded to this sidewalk as the teetertotters in the schoolyard were welded to the ground.

They float, Ben! They all float! Try one and see!

The clown began walking along the ice toward the Canal bridge where Ben stood. Ben watched him come, not moving; he watched as a bird watches an approaching snake. The balloons should have burst in the intense cold, but they did not; they floated above and ahead of the clown when they should have been streaming out behind him, trying to escape back into the Barrens . . . where, some part of Ben's mind assured him, this creature had come from in the first place.

Now Ben noticed something else.

Although the last of the daylight had struck a rosy glow across the ice of the Canal, the clown cast no shadow. None at all.

You'll like it here, Ben, the clown said. Now it was close enough so Ben could hear the *clud-clud* sound its funny shoes made as they advanced over the uneven ice. *You'll like it here, I promise, all the boys and girls I meet like it here because it's like Pleasure Island in* Pinocchio *and Never-Never Land in* Peter Pan; *they never have to grow up and that's what all the kiddies want! So come on! See the sights, have a balloon, feed the elephants, ride the Chute-the-Chutes! Oh you'll like it and oh Ben how you'll float —*

And in spite of his fear, Ben found that part of him *did* want a balloon. Who in all the world owned a balloon which would float into the wind? Who had even *heard* of such a thing? Yes . . . he wanted a balloon, and he wanted to see the clown's face, which was bent down toward the ice, as if to keep it out of that killer wind.

What might have happened if the five o'clock whistle atop the

Derry Town Hall hadn't blown just then Ben didn't know . . . didn't *want* to know. The important thing was that it *did* blow, an ice-pick of sound drilling into the deep winter cold. The clown looked up, as if startled, and Ben saw its face.

The mummy! Oh my God it's the mummy! was his first thought, accompanied by a swoony horror that caused him to clamp his hands down viciously on the bridge's railing to keep from fainting. Of course it hadn't been the mummy, *couldn't* have been the mummy. Oh, there were Egyptian mummies, plenty of them, he knew that, but his first thought had been that it was *the* mummy – the dusty monster played by Boris Karloff in the old movie he had stayed up late to watch just last month on *Shock Theater*.

No, it wasn't *that* mummy, couldn't be, movie monsters weren't real, everyone knew that, even little kids. But –

It wasn't make-up the clown was wearing. Nor was the clown simply swaddled in a bunch of bandages. There *were* bandages, most of them around its neck and wrists, blowing back in the wind, but Ben could see the clown's face clearly. It was deeply lined, the skin a parchment map of wrinkles, tattered cheeks, and flesh. The skin of its forehead was split but bloodless. Dead lips grinned back from a maw in which teeth leaned like tombstones. Its gums were pitted and black. Ben could see no eyes, but *something* glittered far back in the charcoal pits of those puckered sockets, something like the cold jewels in the eyes of Egyptian scarab beetles. And although the wind was the wrong way, it seemed to him that he could smell cinnamon and spice, rotting cerements treated with weird drugs, sand, blood so old it had dried to flakes and grains of rust . . .

'We all float down here,' the mummy-clown croaked, and Ben realized with fresh horror that somehow it had reached the bridge, it was now just below him, reaching up with a dry and twisted hand from which flaps of skin rustled like pennons, a hand through which bone like yellow ivory showed.

One almost fleshless finger caressed the tip of his boot. Ben's paralysis broke. He pounded the rest of the way across the bridge with the five o'clock whistle still shrieking in his ears; it only ceased as he reached the far side. It had to be a mirage, *had* to be. The clown simply could not have come so far during the whistle's ten- or fifteen-second blast.

But his fear was not a mirage; neither were the hot tears which spurted from his eyes and froze on his cheeks a second after being shed. He ran, boots thudding on the sidewalk, and behind him he could hear the mummy in the clown suit climbing up from the Canal, ancient stony fingernails scraping across iron, old tendons creaking like dry hinges. He could hear the arid whistle of its breath pulling in and pushing out of nostrils as devoid of moisture as the tunnels under the Great Pyramid. He could smell its shroud of sandy spices and he knew that in a moment its hands, as fleshless as the geometrical constructions he made with his Erector Set, would descend upon his shoulders. They would turn him around and he would stare into that wrinkled, smiling face. The dead river of its breath would wash over him. Those black eyesockets with their deep glowing depths would bend over him. The toothless mouth would yawn, and he would have his balloon. Oh yes. All the balloons he wanted.

But when he reached the corner of his own street, sobbing and winded, his heart slamming crazed, leaping beats into his ears, when he at last looked back over his shoulder, the street was empty. The arched bridge with its low concrete sides and its oldfashioned cobblestone paving was also empty. He could not see the Canal itself, but he felt that if he could, he would see nothing there, either. No; if the mummy had not been a hallucination or a mirage, if it had been real, it would be waiting *under* the bridge – like the troll in the story of 'The Three Billy Goats Gruff.'

Under. Hiding under.

Ben hurried home, looking back every few steps until the door was safely shut and locked behind him. He explained to his mother – who was so tired from a particularly hard day at the mill that she had not, in truth, much missed him – that he had been helping Mrs Douglas count books. Then he sat down to a dinner of noodles and Sunday's leftover turkey. He stuffed three helpings into himself, and the mummy seemed more distant and dreamlike with each helping. It was not real, those things were never real, they came fully to life only between the commercials of the late-night TV movies or during the Saturday matinees, where if you were lucky you could get two monsters for a quarter – and if you had an extra quarter, you could buy all the popcorn you could eat.

No, they were not real. TV monsters and movie monsters and comic-book monsters were not real. Not until you went to bed and couldn't sleep; not until the last four pieces of candy, wrapped in tissues and kept under your pillow against the evils of the night, were gobbled up; not until the bed itself turned into a lake of rancid dreams and the wind screamed outside and you were afraid to look at the window because there might be a *face* there, an ancient grinning *face* that had not

201

rotted but simply dried like an old leaf, its eyes sunken diamonds pushed deep into dark sockets; not until you saw one ripped and clawlike hand holding out a bunch of balloons: *See the sights, have a balloon, feed the elephants, ride the Chute-the-Chutes! Ben, oh, Ben, how you'll* float –

12

Ben awoke with a gasp, the dream of the mummy still on him, panicked by the close, vibrating dark all around him. He jerked, and the root stopped supporting him and poked him in the back again, as if in exasperation.

He saw light and scrambled for it. He crawled out into afternoon sunlight and the babble of the stream, and everything fell into place again. It was summer, not winter. The mummy had not carried him away to its desert crypt; Ben had simply hidden from the big kids in a sandy hole under a half-uprooted tree. He was in the Barrens. Henry and his buddies had gone to town in a small way on a couple of kids playing downstream because they hadn't been able to find Ben and go to town on him in a big way. *Ta-ta, boys. It was a real baby dam, believe me. You're better off without it.*

Ben looked glumly down at his ruined clothes. His mother was going to give him sixteen different flavors of holy old hell.

He had slept just long enough to stiffen up. He slid down the embankment and then began to walk along the stream, wincing at every step. He was a medley of aches and pains; it felt like Spike Jones was playing a fast tune on broken glass inside most of his muscles. There seemed to be dried or drying blood on every inch of exposed skin. The dam-building kids would be gone anyway, he consoled himself. He wasn't sure how long he'd slept, but even if it had only been half an hour, the encounter with Henry and his friends would have convinced Denbrough and his pal that some other place – like Timbuktu, maybe – would be better for their health.

Ben plugged grimly along, knowing if the big kids came back now he would not stand a chance of outrunning them. He hardly cared.

He rounded an elbow-bend in the stream and just stood there for a moment, looking. The dam-builders were still there. One of them was indeed Stuttering Bill Denbrough. He was kneeling beside the other boy, who was propped against the stream-bank in a sitting position. This other kid's head was thrown so far back that his adam's apple stood out like a triangular plug. There was dried blood around his nose, on his chin, and painted along his neck in a couple of streams. He had something white clasped loosely in one hand.

Stuttering Bill looked around sharply and saw Ben standing there. Ben saw with dismay that something was very wrong with the boy propped up on the bank; Denbrough was obviously scared to death. He thought miserably: *Won't this day* ever *end?*

'I wonder if yuh-yuh-you could help m-m-me,' Bill Denbrough said. 'H-His ah-ah-ah-asp-p-irator is eh-hempty. I think he m-might be —'

His face froze, turned red. He dug at the word, stuttering like a machine-gun. Spittle flew from his lips, and it took almost thirty seconds' worth of 'd-d-d-d' before Ben realized Denbrough was trying to say the other kid might be dying.

CHAPTER FIVE
BILL DENBROUGH
BEATS THE DEVIL - I

1

Bill Denbrough thinks: I'm damned near space-travelling; I might as well be inside a bullet shot from a gun.

This thought, although perfectly true, is not one he finds especially comfortable. In fact, for the first hour following the Concorde's takeoff (or perhaps liftoff would be a better way to put it) from Heathrow, he has been coping with a mild case of claustrophobia. The airplane is narrow – unsettlingly so. The meal is just short of exquisite, but the flight attendants who serve it must twist and bend and squat to get the job done; they look like a troupe of gymnasts. Watching this strenuous service takes some of the pleasure out of the food for Bill, although his seatmate doesn't seem particularly bothered.

The seatmate is another drawback. He's fat and not particularly clean, it may be Ted Lapidus cologne on top of his skin, but beneath it Bill detects the unmistakable odors of dirt and sweat. He's not being very particular about his left elbow, either; every now and then it strikes Bill with a soft thud.

His eyes are drawn again and again to the digital readout at the front of the cabin. It shows how fast this British bullet is going. Now, as the Concorde reaches its cruising speed, it tops out at just over mach 2. Bill takes his pen from his shirt pocket and uses its tip to tap buttons on the computer watch Audra gave him last Christmas. If the machometer is right – and Bill has absolutely no reason to think it is not – then they are busting along at a speed of eighteen miles per minute. He is not sure this is anything he really wanted to know.

Outside his window, which is as small and thick as the window in one of the old Mercury space capsules, he can see a sky which is not blue but the twilight purple of dusk, although it is the middle of the day. At the point where the sea and the sky meet, he can see that the horizon-line is slightly bowed. I am sitting here, *Bill thinks*, a Bloody Mary in my hand and a dirty fat man's elbow poking into my bicep, observing the curvature of the earth.

He smiles a little, thinking that a man who can face something like that shouldn't be afraid of anything. But he is afraid, and not just of flying at eighteen miles a minute in this narrow fragile shell. He can almost feel Derry rushing at him. And that is exactly the right expression for it. Eighteen miles a minute or not, the sensation is of being perfectly still while Derry rushes at him like some big carnivore which has lain in wait for a long time and has finally broken from cover. Derry, ah, Derry! Shall we write an ode to Derry? The stink of its mills and its rivers? The dignified quiet of its tree-lined streets? The library? The Standpipe? Bassey Park? Derry Elementary School?

The Barrens?

Lights are going on in his head; big kliegs. It's like he's been sitting in a darkened theater for twenty-seven years, waiting for something to happen, and now it's finally begun. The set being revealed spot by spot and klieg by klieg is not, however, some. harmless comedy like Arsenic and Old Lace; *to Bill Denbrough it looks more like* The Cabinet of Dr Caligari.

All those stories I wrote, *he thinks with a stupid kind of amusement.* All those novels. Derry is where they all came from; Derry was the wellspring. They came from what happened that summer, and from what happened to George the autumn before. All the interviewers that ever asked me THAT QUESTION . . . I gave them the wrong answer.

The fat man's elbow digs into him again, and he spills some of his drink. Bill almost says something, then thinks better of it.

THAT QUESTION, *of course, was 'Where do you get your ideas?' It was a question Bill supposed all writers of fiction had to answer – or pretend to answer – at least twice a week, but a fellow like him, who made a living by writing of things which never were and never could be, had to answer it – or pretend to – much more often than that.*

'All writers have a pipeline which goes down into the subconscious,' he told them, neglecting to mention that he doubted more as each year passed if there even was such a thing as a subconscious. 'But the man or woman who writes horror stories has a pipeline that goes further, maybe . . . into the sub-subconscious, if you like.'

Elegant answer, that, but one he had never really believed. Subconscious? Well, there was something down there all right, but Bill thought people had made much too big a deal out of a function which was probably the mental equivalent of your eyes watering when dust got in them or breaking wind an hour or so after a big dinner. The second metaphor was probably the better of the two, but you couldn't very well tell interviewers that as far as you were concerned, such things as dreams and vague longings and sensations like déjà-vu really came down to nothing more than a bunch of mental farts. But they seemed to need something, all those reporters with their notebooks and their little Japanese tape-recorders, and Bill wanted to help them as much as he could. He knew that writing was a hard job, a damned hard job. There was no need to make theirs harder by telling them, 'My friend, you might as well ask me "Who cut the cheese?" and have done with it.'

He thought now: You always knew they were asking the wrong question, even before Mike called; now you also know what the right question was. Not *where* do you get your ideas but *why* do you get your ideas. There was a pipeline, all right, but it wasn't either the Freudian or Jungian version of the subconscious that it came out of; no interior drain-system of the mind, no subterranean cavern full of Morlocks waiting to happen. There was nothing at the other end of that pipe but Derry. Just Derry. And –

– and who's that, trip-trapping upon my bridge?

He sits bolt upright suddenly, and this time it's his elbow that goes wandering; it sinks deeply into his fat seatmate's side for a moment.

'Watch yourself buddy,' the fat man says. 'Close quarters, you know.'

'You stop whapping me with yours and I'll try to stop wuh-whapping you with m-mine.' The fat man gives him a sour, incredulous what-the-hell-you-talking-about look. Bill simply gazes at him until the fat man looks away, muttering.

Who's there?

Who's trip-trapping over my bridge?

He looks out the window again and thinks: We're beating the devil.

His arms and the nape of his neck prickle. He knocks back the rest of his drink in one swallow. Another of those big lights has gone on.

Silver. His bike. That was what he had called it, after the Lone Ranger's horse. A big Schwinn, twenty-eight inches tall. 'You'll kill yourself on that, Billy,' his father had said, but with no real concern in his tone. He had shown little concern for anything since George's death. Before, he had been tough. Fair, but tough. Since, you could get around him. He would make fatherly gestures, go through fatherly motions, but motions and gestures were all they were. It was like he was always listening for George to come back into the house.

Bill had seen it in the window of the Bike and Cycle Shoppe down on Center Street. It leaned gloomily on its kickstand, bigger than the biggest of the others on display, dull where they were shiny, straight in places where the others were curved, bent in places where the others were straight. Propped on its front tire had been a sign:

IT

Make an Offer

What actually happened was that Bill went in and the owner made him an offer, which Bill took – he wouldn't have known how to dicker with the Cycle Shoppe owner if his life depended on it, and the price – twenty-four dollars – the man quoted seemed very fair to Bill; generous, even. He paid for Silver with money he had saved up over the last seven or eight months – birthday money, Christmas money, lawn-mowing money. He had been noticing the bike in the window ever since Thanksgiving. He paid for it and wheeled it home as soon as the snow began to melt for good. It was funny, because he'd never thought much about owning a bike before last year. The idea seemed to come into his mind all at once, perhaps on one of those endless days after George died. Was murdered.

In the beginning, Bill almost did kill himself. The first ride on his new bike ended with Bill dumping it on purpose to keep from running smack into the board fence at the end of Kossuth Lane (he had not been so afraid of running into the fence as he had been of bashing right through it and falling sixty feet into the Barrens). He came away from that one with a five-inch gash running between the wrist and elbow of his left arm. Not even a week later he had found himself unable to brake soon enough and had shot through the intersection of Witcham and Jackson at perhaps thirty-five miles an hour, a little kid on a dusty gray mastodon of a bike (Silver was silver only by the most energetic reach of a willing imagination), playing cards machine-gunning the spokes of the front and back wheels in a steady roar, and if a car had been coming he would have been dead meat. Just like Georgie.

He got control of Silver little by little as the spring advanced. Neither of his parents noticed during that time that he was courting death by bicycle. He thought that, after the first few days, they had ceased to really see his bike at all – to them it was just a relic with chipped paint which leaned against the garage wall on rainy days.

Silver was a lot more than some dusty old relic, though. He didn't look like much, but he went like the wind. Bill's friend – his only real friend – was a kid named Eddie Kaspbrak, and Eddie was good with mechanical things. He had shown Bill how to get Silver in shape – which bolts to tighten and check regularly, where to oil the sprockets, how to tighten the chain, how to put on a bike patch so it would stay if you got a flat.

'You oughtta paint it,' he remembered Eddie saying one day, but Bill didn't want to paint Silver. For reasons he couldn't even explain to himself he wanted the Schwinn just the way it was. It looked like a real bow-wow, the sort of bike a careless kid regularly left out on his lawn in the rain, a bike

that would be all squeaks and shudders and slow friction. It looked like a bow-wow but it went like the wind. It would –

'It would beat the devil,' he says aloud, and laughs. His fat seatmate looks at him sharply; the laugh has that howling quality that gave Audra the creeps earlier.

Yes, it looked pretty shoddy, with its old paint and the oldfashioned package carrier mounted above the back wheel and the ancient oogah-horn with its black rubber bulb – that horn was permanently welded to the handlebars with a rusty bolt the size of a baby's fist. Pretty shoddy.

But could Silver go? Could he? Christ!

And it was a damned good thing he could, because Silver had saved Bill Denbrough's life in the fourth week of June 1958 – the week after he met Ben Hanscom for the first time, the week after he and Ben and Eddie built the dam, the week that Ben and Richie 'Trashmouth' Tozier and Beverly Marsh showed up in the Barrens after the Saturday matinee. Richie had been riding behind him, on Silver's package carrier, the day Silver had saved Bill's life . . . so he supposed Silver had saved Richie's, too. And he remembered the house they had been running from, all right. He remembered that just fine. That damned house on Neibolt Street.

He had raced to beat the devil that day, oh yeah, for sure, don't you just know it. Some devil with eyes as shiny as old deadly coins. Some hairy old devil with a mouthful of bloody teeth. But all that had come later. If Silver had saved Richie's life and his own that day, then perhaps he had saved Eddie Kaspbrak's on the day Bill and Eddie met Ben by the kicked-apart remains of their dam in the Barrens. Henry Bowers – who looked a little bit like someone had run him through a Disposall – had mashed Eddie's nose and then Eddie's asthma had come on strong and his aspirator turned up empty. So it had been Silver that day too, Silver to the rescue.

Bill Denbrough, who hasn't been on a bicycle in almost seventeen years, looks out the window of an airplane that would not have been credited – or even imagined, outside of a science-fiction magazine – in the year 1958. Hi-yo Silver, AWAYYY! he thinks, and has to close his eyes against the sudden needling sting of tears.

What happened to Silver? He can't remember. That part of the set is still dark; that klieg has yet to be turned on. Perhaps that is just as well. Perhaps that is a mercy.

Hi-yo.

Hi-yo Silver.

Hi-yo Silver.

2

'AWAYYY!' he shouted. The wind tore the words back over his shoulder like a fluttering crepe streamer. They came out big and strong, those words, in a triumphant roar. They were the only ones that ever did.

He pedaled down Kansas Street toward town, gaining speed slowly at first. Silver rolled once he got going, but getting going was a job and a half. Watching the gray bike pick up speed was a little like watching a big plane roll down the runway. At first you couldn't believe such a huge waddling gadget could *ever* actually leave the earth – the idea was absurd. But then you could see its shadow beneath it, and before you even had time to wonder if it was a mirage, the shadow was trailing out long behind it and the plane was up, cutting its way through the air, as sleek and graceful as a dream in a satisfied mind.

Silver was like that.

Bill got a little downhill stretch and began to pedal faster, his legs pumping up and down as he stood forward over the bike's fork. He had learned very quickly – after being bashed a couple of times by that fork in the worst place a boy can be bashed – to yank his underpants up as high as he could before mounting Silver. Later that summer, observing this process, Richie would say, *Bill does that because he thinks he might like to have some kids that live someday. It seems like a bad idea to me, but hey! they might always take after his wife, right?*

He and Eddie had lowered the seat as far as it would go, and it now bumped and scraped against the small of his back as he worked the pedals. A woman digging weeds in her flower-garden shaded her eyes to watch him pass. She smiled a little. The boy on the huge bike reminded her of a monkey she had once seen riding a unicycle in the Barnum & Bailey Circus. *He's apt to kill himself, though,* she thought, turning back to her garden. *That bike is too big for him.* It was none of her problem, though.

3

Bill had had more sense than to argue with the big boys when they broke out of the bushes, looking like ill-tempered hunters on the track of a beast which had already mauled one of them. Eddie, however, had rashly opened his mouth and Henry Bowers had unloaded on him.

Bill knew who they were, all right; Henry, Belch, and Victor were just about the worst kids in Derry School. They had beaten up on Richie Tozier, who Bill sometimes chummed with, a couple of times. The way Bill looked at it, this was partly Richie's own fault; he was not known as Trashmouth for nothing.

One day in April Richie had said something about their collars as the three of them passed by in the schoolyard. The collars had all been turned up, just like Vic Morrow's in *The Blackboard Jungle*. Bill, who had been sitting against the building nearby and listlessly shooting a few marbles, hadn't really caught all of it. Neither did Henry and his friends . . . but they heard enough to turn in Richie's direction. Bill supposed Richie had meant to say whatever he said in a low voice. The trouble was, Richie didn't really *have* a low voice.

'What'd you say, you little four-eyes geek?' Victor Criss enquired.

'I didn't say nothing,' Richie said, and that disclaimer – along with his face, which looked quite sensibly dismayed and scared – might have ended it. Except that Richie's mouth was like a half-tamed horse that has a way of bolting for absolutely no reason at all. Now it suddenly added: 'You ought to dig the wax out of your ears, big fella. Want some blasting powder?'

They stood looking at him incredulously for a moment, and then they took after him. Stuttering Bill had watched the unequal race from its start to its preordained conclusion from his place against the side of the building. No sense getting involved; those three galoots would be just as happy to beat up on two kids for the price of one.

Richie ran diagonally across the little-kids' playyard, leaping over the teetertotters and dodging among the swings, realizing he had run into a blind alley only when he struck the chainlink fence between the playyard and the park which abutted the school grounds. So he tried to go up the chainlink, all clutching fingers and pointing seeking sneaker-toes, and he was maybe two-thirds of the way to the top when Henry and Victor Criss hauled him back down again, Henry getting him by the back of the jacket and Victor grabbing the seat of his jeans. Richie was screaming when they peeled him off the fence. He hit the asphalt on his back. His glasses flew off. He reached for them and Belch Huggins kicked them away and that was why one of the bows was mended with adhesive tape this summer.

Bill had winced and walked around to the front of the building. He had observed Mrs Moran, one of the fourth-grade teachers, already hurrying over to break things up, but he knew they would get Richie hard before then, and by the time she actually arrived, Richie would be crying. Bawl-baby, bawl-baby, lookit-the-baby-bawl.

Bill had only had minor problems with them. They made fun

of his stutter, of course. An occasional random cruelty came with the jibes; one rainy day as they were going to lunch in the gym, Belch Huggins had knocked Bill's lunchbag out of his hand and had stomped it flat with one engineer boot, squishing everything inside.

'Oh, juh-juh-gee!' Belch cried in mock horror, raising his hands and fluttering them about his face. 'Suh-suh-sorry about your l-l-lunch, fuh-huh-huck-face!' And he had strolled off down the hall toward where Victor Criss was leaning against the drinking fountain outside the boys'-room door, just about laughing himself into a hernia. That hadn't been so bad, though; Bill had cadged half a PB & J off Eddie Kaspbrak, and Richie was happy to give him his devilled egg, one of which his mother packed in his lunch about every second day and which made him want to puke, he claimed.

But you had to stay out of their way, and if you couldn't do that you had to try and be invisible.

Eddie forgot the rules, so they creamed him.

He hadn't been too bad until the big boys went downstream and splashed across to the other side, even though his nose was bleeding like a fountain. When Eddie's snotrag was soaked through, Bill had given him his own and made him put a hand on the nape of his neck and lean his head back. Bill could remember his mother getting Georgie to do that, because Georgie sometimes got nosebleeds —

Oh but it hurt to think about George.

It wasn't until the sound of the big boys' buffalolike progress through the Barrens had died away completely, and Eddie's nose-bleed had actually stopped, that his asthma got bad. He started heaving for air, his hands opening and then snapping shut like weak traps, his respiration a fluting whistle in his throat.

'Shit!' Eddie gasped. 'Asthma! Cripes!'

He scrambled for his aspirator and finally got it out of his pocket. It looked almost like a bottle of Windex, the kind with the sprayer attachment on top. He jammed it into his mouth and punched the trigger.

'Better?' Bill asked anxiously.

'No. It's empty.' Eddie looked at Bill with panicked eyes that said *I'm caught, Bill! I'm caught!*

The empty aspirator rolled away from his hand. The stream chuckled on, not caring in the least that Eddie Kaspbrak could barely breathe. Bill thought randomly that the big boys had been right about one thing: it had been a real baby dam. But they had been having fun, dammit, and he felt a sudden dull fury that it should have come to this.

'Tuh-tuh-take it easy, Eh-Eddie,' he said.

For the next forty minutes or so Bill sat next to him, his expectation that Eddie's asthma attack would at any moment let up gradually fading into unease. By the time Ben Hanscom appeared, the unease had become real fear. It not only wasn't letting up; it was getting worse. And the Center Street Drug, where Eddie got his refills, was three miles away, almost. What if he went to get Eddie's stuff and came back to find Eddie unconscious? Unconscious or

(don't shit please don't think that)

or even dead, his mind insisted implacably.

(like Georgie dead like Georgie)

Don't be such an asshole! He's not going to die!

No, probably not. But what if he came back and found Eddie in a comber? Bill knew all about combers; he had even deduced they were named after those great big waves guys surfed on in Hawaii, and that seemed right enough – after all, what was a comber but a wave that drowned your brain? On doctor shows like *Ben Casey*, people were always going into combers, and sometimes they stayed there in spite of all Ben Casey's ill-tempered shouting.

So he sat there, knowing he ought to go, he couldn't do Eddie any good staying here, but not wanting to leave him alone. An irrational, superstitious part of him felt sure Eddie would slip into a comber the minute he, Bill, turned his back. Then he looked upstream and saw Ben Hanscom standing there. He knew who Ben was, of course; the fattest kid in any school has his or her own sort of unhappy notoriety. Ben was in the other fifth grade. Bill sometimes saw him at recess, standing by himself – usually in a corner – looking at a book and eating his lunch out of a bag about the size of a laundry sack.

Looking at Ben now, Bill thought he looked even worse than Henry Bowers. It was hard to believe, but true. Bill could not begin to imagine the cataclysmic fight these two must have been in. Ben's hair stood up in wild, dirt-clotted spikes. His sweater or sweatshirt – it was hard to tell which it had started the day as and it sure as shit didn't matter now – was a matted ruin, smeared with a sicko mixture of blood and grass. His pants were out at the knees.

He saw Bill looking at him and recoiled a bit, eyes going wary.

'Duh-duh-duh-hon't g-g-go!' Bill cried. He put his empty hands up in the air, palms out, to show he was harmless. 'W-W-We need some huh-huhhelp.'

Ben came closer, eyes still wary. He walked as if one or both of his legs was killing him. 'Are they gone? Bowers and those guys?'

'Yuh-Yes,' Bill said. 'Listen, cuh-han y-y-you stay with my fruhhend while I go get his muh-medicine? He's got a-a-a-a —'

'Asthma?'

Bill nodded.

Ben came all the way down to the remains of the dam and dropped painfully to one knee beside Eddie, who was lying back with his eyes mostly closed and his chest heaving.

'Which one hit him?' Ben asked finally. He looked up, and Bill saw the same frustrated anger he had been feeling himself on the fat kid's face. 'Was it Henry Bowers?'

Bill nodded.

'It figures. Sure, go on. I'll stay with him.'

'Thuh-thuh-hanks.'

'Oh, don't thank me,' Ben said. 'I'm the reason they landed on you in the first place. Go on. Hurry it up. I have to be home for supper.'

Bill went without saying anything else. It would have been good to tell Ben not to take it to heart — what had happened hadn't been Ben's fault any more than it had been Eddie's for stupidly opening his mouth. Guys like Henry and his buddies were an accident waiting to happen; the little kids' version of floods or tornadoes or gallstones. It would have been good to say that, but he was so tightly wound right now it would have taken him about twenty minutes or so, and by then Eddie might have slipped into a comber (that was another thing Bill had learned from Drs Casey and Kildare; you never *went* into a comber; you always *slipped* into one).

He trotted downstream, glancing back once. He saw Ben Hanscom grimly collecting rocks from the edge of the water. For a moment Bill couldn't figure out what he was doing, and then he understood. It was an ammo dump. Just in case they came back.

4

The Barrens were no mystery to Bill. He had played here a lot this spring, sometimes with Richie, more frequently with Eddie, sometimes all by himself. He had by no means explored the whole area, but he could find his way back to Kansas Street from the Kenduskeag with no trouble, and now did. He came out at a wooden bridge where Kansas Street crossed one of the little no-name streams that flowed out of the

Derry drainage system and into the Kenduskeag down below. Silver was stashed under this bridge, his handlebars tied to one of the bridge supports with a hank of rope to keep his wheels out of the water.

Bill untied the rope, stuck it in his shirt, and hauled Silver up to the sidewalk by main force, panting and sweating, losing his balance a couple of times and landing on his tail.

But at last it was up. Bill swung his leg over the high fork.

And as always, once he was on Silver he became someone else.

5

'Hi-yo Silver AWAYYY!'

The words came out deeper than his normal speaking voice – it was almost the voice of the man he would become. Silver gained speed slowly, the quickening clickety-clack of the Bicycle playing cards clothespinned to the spokes marking the increase. Bill stood on the pedals, his hands clamped on the bike-grips with the wrists turned up. He looked like a man trying to lift a stupendously heavy barbell. Cords stood out on his neck. Veins pulsed in his temples. His mouth was turned down in a trembling sneer of effort as he fought the familiar battle against weight and inertia, busting his brains to get Silver moving.

As always, it was worth the effort.

Silver began to roll along more briskly. Houses slid past smoothly instead of just poking by. On his left, where Kansas Street crossed Jackson, the unfettered Kenduskeag became the Canal. Past the intersection Kansas Street headed swiftly downhill toward Center and Main, Derry's business district.

Streets crossed frequently here but they were all stop-signed in Bill's favor, and the possibility that a driver might one day blow by one of those stop signs and flatten him to a bleeding shadow on the street had never crossed Bill's mind. It is unlikely he would have changed his ways even if it had. He might have done so either earlier or later in his life, but this spring and early summer had been a strange thundery time for him. Ben would have been astounded if someone were to ask him if he was lonely; Bill would have been likewise astounded if someone asked him if he was courting death. *Of cuh-cuh-course n-not!* he would have responded immediately (and indignantly), but that did not change the fact that his runs down Kansas Street to town had become more and more like *banzai* charges as the weather warmed.

This section of Kansas Street was known as Up-Mile Hill. Bill took it at full speed, bent over Silver's handlebars to cut down the wind resistance, one hand poised over the cracked rubber bulb of his oogah-horn to warn the unwary, his red hair blowing back from his head in a rippling wave. The click of the playing cards had mounted to a steady roar. The effortful sneer had become a big goofball grin. The residences on the right had given way to business buildings (warehouses and meat-packing plants, most of them) which blurred by in a scary but satisfying rush. To his left the Canal was a wink of fire in the corner of his eye.

'*HI-YO SILVER, AWAYYYY!*' he screamed triumphantly.

Silver flew over the first curbing, and as they almost always did at that point, his feet lost contact with the pedals. He was freewheeling, now wholly in the lap of whatever god has been appointed the job of protecting small boys. He swerved into the street, doing maybe fifteen miles an hour over the posted speed of twenty-five.

It was all behind him now: his stutter, his dad's blank hurt eyes as he puttered around his garage workshop, the terrible sight of the dust on the closed piano cover upstairs – dusty because his mother didn't play anymore. The last time had been at George's funeral, three Methodist hymns. George going out into the rain, wearing his yellow slicker, carrying the newspaper boat with its glaze of paraffin; Mr Gardener coming up the street twenty minutes later with his body wrapped in a bloodstained quilt; his mother's agonized shriek. All behind him. He was the Lone Ranger, he was John Wayne, he was Bo Diddley, he was anybody he wanted to be and nobody who cried and got scared and wanted his muh-muh-mother.

Silver flew and Stuttering Bill Denbrough flew with him; their gantry-like shadow fled behind them. They raced down Up-Mile Hill together; the playing cards roared. Bill's feet found the pedals again and he began to pump, wanting to go even faster, wanting to reach some hypothetical speed – not of sound but of memory – and crash through the pain barrier.

He raced on, bent over his handlebars; he raced to beat the devil.

The three-way intersection of Kansas, Center, and Main was coming up fast. It was a horror of one-way traffic and conflicting signs and stoplights which were supposed to be timed but really weren't. The result, a Derry *News* editorial had proclaimed the year before, was a traffic-rotary conceived in hell.

As always, Bill's eyes flicked right and left, fast, gauging the traffic flow, looking for the holes. If his judgment was mistaken – if he stuttered, you might say – he would be badly hurt or killed.

He arrowed into the slow-moving traffic which clogged the intersection, running a red light and fading to the right to avoid a lumbering portholed Buick. He shot a bullet of a glance back over his shoulder to make sure the middle lane was empty. He looked forward again and saw that in roughly five seconds he was going to crash into the rear end of a pick-up truck that had stopped squarely in the middle of the intersection while the Uncle Ike type behind the wheel craned his neck to read all the signs and make sure he hadn't taken a wrong turn and somehow ended up in Miami Beach.

The lane on Bill's right was full of a Derry-Bangor intercity bus. He slipped in that direction just the same and shot the gap between the stopped pick-up and the bus, still moving at forty miles an hour. At the last second he snapped his head hard to one side, like a soldier doing an over-enthusiastic eyes-right, to keep the mirror mounted on the passenger side of the pick-up from rearranging his teeth. Hot diesel from the bus laced his throat like a kick of strong liquor. He heard a thin gasping squeal as one of his bike-grips kissed a line up the coach's aluminum side. He got just a glimpse of the bus driver, his face paper-white under his peaked Hudson Bus Company cap. The driver was shaking his fist at Bill and shouting something. Bill doubted it was happy birthday.

Here was a trio of old ladies crossing Main Street from the New England Bank side to the Shoeboat side. They heard the harsh burr of the playing cards and looked up. Their mouths dropped open as a boy on a huge bike passed within half a foot of them like a mirage.

The worst – and the best – of the trip was behind him now. He had looked at the very real possibility of his own death again, and again had found himself able to look away. The bus had not crushed him; he had not killed himself and the three old ladies with their Freese's shopping bags and their Social Security checks; he had not been splattered across the tailgate of Uncle Ike's old Dodge pick-up. He was going uphill again now, speed bleeding away. Something – oh, call it desire, that was good enough, wasn't it? – was bleeding away with it. All the thoughts and memories were catching up – hi Bill, gee, we almost lost sight of you for awhile there, but here we are – rejoining him, climbing up his shirt and jumping into his ear and whooshing into his brain like little kids going down a slide. He could feel them settling into their accustomed places, their feverish bodies jostling each other. Gosh! Wow! Here we are inside Bill's head again! Let's think about George! Okay! Who wants to start?

You think too much, Bill.

No – that wasn't the problem. The problem was, he *imagined* too much.

He turned into Richard's Alley and came out on Center Street a few moments later, pedaling slowly, feeling the sweat on his back and in his hair. He dismounted Silver in front of the Center Street Drug Store and went inside.

6

Before George's death, Bill would have gotten the salient points across to Mr Keene by speaking to him. The druggist was not exactly kind – or at least Bill had an idea he was not – but he was patient enough, and he did not tease or make fun. But now Bill's stutter was much worse, and he really was afraid something bad might happen to Eddie if he didn't move fast.

So when Mr Keene said, 'Hello, Billy Denbrough, can I help you?,' Bill took a folder advertising vitamins, turned it over, and wrote on the back: *Eddie Kaspbrak and I were playing in the Barrens. He's got a bad assmar attack, I mean he can hardly breath. Can you give me a refill on his asspirador?*

He pushed this note across the glass-topped counter to Mr Keene, who read it, looked at Bill's anxious blue eyes, and said, 'Of course. Wait right here, and don't be handling anything you shouldn't.'

Bill shifted impatiently from one foot to the other while Mr Keene was behind the rear counter. Although he was back there less than five minutes, it seemed an age before he returned with one of Eddie's plastic squeeze-bottles. He handed it over to Bill, smiled, and said, 'This should take care of the problem.'

'Th-th-th-thanks,' Bill said. 'I don't h-have a-any m-m-muh-muh –'

'That's all right, son. Mrs Kaspbrak has an account here. I'll just add this on. I'm sure she'll want to thank you for your kindness.'

Bill, much relieved, thanked Mr Keene and left quickly. Mr Keene came around the counter to watch him go. He saw Bill toss the aspirator into his bike-basket and mount clumsily. *Can he actually ride a bike that big?* Mr Keene wondered. *I doubt it. I doubt it very much.* But the Denbrough kid somehow got it going without falling on his head, and pedaled slowly away. The bike, which looked to Mr Keene like somebody's idea of a joke, wobbled madly from side to side. The aspirator rolled back and forth in the basket.

Mr Keene grinned a little. If Bill had seen that grin, it might have gone a good way toward confirming his idea that Mr Keene was not exactly one of the world's champion nice guys. It was sour, the grin of a man who has found much to wonder about but almost nothing to uplift in the human condition. Yes – he would add Eddie's asthma medication to Sonia Kaspbrak's bill, and as always she would be surprised – and suspicious rather than grateful – at how cheap the medication was. Other drugs were so *dear*, she said. Mrs Kaspbrak, Mr Keene knew, was one of those people who believed nothing cheap could do a person much good. He could really have soaked her for her son's HydrOx Mist, and there had been times when he had been tempted . . . but why should he make himself a party to the woman's foolishness? It wasn't as though he were going to starve.

Cheap? Oh my, yes. HydrOx Mist (*Administer as needed* typed neatly on the gummed label he pasted on each aspirator bottle) was wonderfully cheap, but even Mrs Kaspbrak was willing to admit that it controlled her son's asthma quite well in spite of that fact. It was cheap because it was nothing but a combination of hydrogen and oxygen, with a dash of camphor added to give the mist a faint medicinal taste.

In other words, Eddie's asthma medicine was tapwater.

7

It took Bill longer to get back, because he was going uphill. In several places he had to dismount and push Silver. He simply didn't have the musclepower necessary to keep the bike going up more than mild slopes.

By the time he had stashed his bike and made his way back to the stream, it was ten past four. All sorts of black suppositions were crossing his mind. The Hanscom kid would have deserted, leaving Eddie to die. Or the bullies could have backtracked and beaten the shit out of both of them. Or . . . worst of all . . . the man whose business was murdering kids might have gotten one or both of them. As he had gotten George.

He knew there had been a great deal of gossip and speculation about that. Bill had a bad stutter, but he wasn't deaf – although people sometimes seemed to think he must be, since he spoke only when absolutely necessary. Some people felt that the murder of his brother wasn't related at all to the murders of Betty Ripsom, Cheryl Lamonica, Matthew Clements, and Veronica Grogan. Others claimed that George, Ripsom, and Lamonica had been killed by one man, and the other two were the work of a 'copy-cat killer.' A third school of thought held that the boys had been killed by one man, the girls by another.

Bill believed they had all been killed by the same person . . . if it *was* a person. He sometimes wondered about that. As he sometimes wondered about his feelings concerning Derry this summer. Was it still the aftermath of George's death, the way his parents seemed to ignore him now, so lost in their grief over their younger son that they couldn't see the simple fact that Bill was still alive, and might be hurting himself? Those things combined with the other murders? The voices that sometimes seemed to speak in his head now, whispering to him (and surely they were not variations of his own voice, for these voices did not stutter – they were quiet, but they were sure), advising him to do certain things but not others? Was it those things which made Derry seem somehow different now? Somehow threatening, with unexplored streets that did not invite but seemed instead to yawn in a kind of ominous silence? That made some faces look secret and frightened?

He didn't know, but he believed – as he believed all the murders were the work of a single agency – that Derry really *had* changed, and that his brother's death had signalled the beginning of that change. The black suppositions in his head came from the lurking idea that anything could happen in Derry now. *Anything.*

But when he came around the last bend, all looked cool. Ben Hanscom was still there, sitting beside Eddie. Eddie himself was sitting up now, his hands dangling in his lap, head bent, still wheezing. The sun had sunk low enough to project long green shadows across the stream.

'Boy, that was quick,' Ben said, standing up. 'I didn't expect you for another half an hour.'

'I got a f-f-fast b-bike,' Bill said with some pride. For a moment the two of them looked at each other cautiously, warily. Then Ben smiled tentatively, and Bill smiled back. The kid was fat, but he seemed okay. And he had stayed put. That must have taken some guts, with Henry and his j.d. friends maybe still wandering around out there someplace.

Bill winked at Eddie, who was looking at him with dumb gratitude. 'H–Here you g-go, E-E-E-Eddie.' He tossed him the aspirator. Eddie plunged it into his open mouth, triggered it, and gasped convulsively. Then he leaned back, eyes shut. Ben watched this with concern.

'Jeez! He's really got it bad, doesn't he?'

Bill nodded.

'I was scared there for awhile,' Ben said in a low voice. 'I was wonderin what to do if he had a convulsion, or something. I kept tryin to remember the stuff they told us in that Red Cross assembly we had in April. All I could come up with was put a stick in his mouth so he wouldn't bite his tongue off.'

'I think that's for eh-eh-hepileptics.'

'Oh. Yeah, I guess you're right.'

'He w-won't have a c-c-convulsion, anyway,' Bill said. 'That m-m-medicine will f-fix him right up. Luh-Luh-Look.'

Eddie's labored breathing had eased. He opened his eyes and looked up at them.

'Thanks, Bill,' he said. 'That one was a real pisswah.'

'I guess it started when they creamed your nose, huh?' Ben asked.

Eddie laughed ruefully, stood up, and stuck the aspirator in his back pocket. 'Wasn't even thinking about my nose. Was thinking about my mom.'

'Yeah? Really?' Ben sounded surprised, but his hand went to the rags of his sweatshirt and began fiddling there nervously.

'She's gonna take one look at the blood on my shirt and have me down to the Mergency Room at Derry Home in about five seconds.'

'Why?' Ben asked. 'It stopped, didn't it? Gee, I remember this kid I was in kindergarten with, Scooter Morgan, and he got a bloody nose when he fell off the monkey bars. They took *him* to the Mergency Room, but only because it kept bleeding.'

'Yeah?' Bill asked, interested. 'Did he d-d-die?'

'No, but he was out of school a week.'

'It doesn't matter if it stopped or not,' Eddie said gloomily. 'She'll take me anyway. She'll think it's broken and I got pieces of bone sticking in my brain, or something.'

'C-C-Can you get bones in your buh-buh-*brain*?' Bill asked. This was turning into the most interesting conversation he'd had in weeks.

'I don't know. If you listen to my mother, you can get anything.' Eddie turned to Ben again. 'She takes me down to the Mergency Room about once or twice a month. I hate that place. There was this orderly once? He told her they oughtta make her pay rent. She was really PO'd.'

'Wow,' Ben said. He thought Eddie's mother must be really weird. He was unconscious of the fact that now both of his hands were fiddling in the remains of his sweatshirt. 'Why don't you just say no? Say something like "Hey Ma, I feel all right, I just want to stay home and watch *Sea Hunt*." Like that.'

'Awww,' Eddie said uncomfortably, and said no more.

'You're Ben H-H-H-Hanscom, r-right?' Bill asked.

'Yeah. You're Bill Denbrough.'

'Yuh-Yes. And this is Eh-Eh-Eh-heh-Eh-Eh –'

'Eddie Kaspbrak,' Eddie said. 'I hate it when you stutter my name, Bill. You sound like Elmer Fudd.'

'Suh-horry.'

'Well, I'm pleased to meet you both,' Ben said. It came out sounding prissy and a little lame. A silence fell amid the three of them. It was not an entirely uncomfortable silence. In it they became friends.

'Why were those guys chasing you?' Eddie asked at last.

'They're a-a-always chuh-hasing s-someone,' Bill said. 'I h-hate those fuckers.'

Ben was silent a moment – mostly in admiration – before Bill's use of what Ben's mother sometimes called The Really Bad Word. Ben had never said The Really Bad Word out loud in his whole life, although he had written it (in extremely small letters) on a telephone pole the Halloween before last.

'Bowers ended up sitting next to me during the exams,' Ben said at last. 'He wanted to copy off my paper. I wouldn't let him.'

'You must want to die young, kid,' Eddie said admiringly.

Stuttering Bill burst out laughing. Ben looked at him sharply, decided he wasn't being laughed *at*, exactly (it was hard to say *how* he knew it, but he did), and grinned.

'I guess I must,' he said. 'Anyway, he's got to take summer-school, and he and those other two guys were laying for me, and that's what happened.'

'Y-You look like t-t-they kuh-hilled you,' Bill said.

'I fell down here from Kansas Street. Down the side of the hill.' He looked at Eddie. 'I'll probably see you in the Mergency Room, now that I think about it. When my mom gets a look at my clothes, she'll *put* me there.'

Both Bill and Eddie burst out laughing this time, and Ben joined them. It hurt his stomach to laugh but he laughed anyway, shrilly and a little hysterically. Finally he had to sit down on the bank, and the plopping sound his butt made when it hit the dirt got him going all over again. He liked the way his laughter sounded with theirs. It was a sound he had never heard before: not mingled laughter – he had heard that lots of times – but mingled laughter of which his own was a part.

He looked up at Bill Denbrough, their eyes met, and that was all it took to get both of them laughing again.

Bill hitched up his pants, flipped up the collar of his shirt, and began to slouch around in a kind of moody, hoody strut. His voice dropped down low and he said, 'I'm gonna killya, kid. Don't gimme no crap. I'm dumb but I'm big. I can crack walnuts with my forehead. I can piss vinegar and shit cement. My name's Honeybunch Bowers and I'm the boss prick round dese-yere Derry parts.'

Eddie had collapsed to the stream-bank now and was rolling around, clutching his stomach and howling. Ben was doubled up, head between his knees, tears spouting from his eyes, snot hanging from his nose in long white runners, laughing like a hyena.

Bill sat down with them, and little by little the three of them quieted.

'There's one really good thing about it,' Eddie said presently. 'If Bowers is in summer school, we won't see him much down here.'

'You play in the Barrens a lot?' Ben asked. It was an idea that never would have crossed his own mind in a thousand years – not with the reputation the Barrens had – but now that he was down here, it didn't seem bad at all. In fact, this stretch of the low bank was very pleasant as the afternoon made its slow way toward dusk.

'S-S-Sure. It's n-neat. M-Mostly n-nobody b-buh-bothers u-us down h-here. We guh-guh-hoof off a lot. B-B-Bowers and those uh-other g-guys don't come d-down here eh-eh-anyway.'

'You and Eddie?'

'Ruh-Ruh-Ruh –' Bill shook his head. His face knotted up like a wet dishrag when he stuttered, Ben noticed, and suddenly an odd thought occurred to him: Bill hadn't stuttered at all when he was mocking the way Henry Bowers talked. '*Richie!*' Bill exclaimed now, paused a moment, and then went on. 'Richie T-Tozier usually c-comes down, too. But h-him and his d-dad were going to clean out their ah-ah-ah –'

'Attic,' Eddie translated, and tossed a stone into the water. *Plonk*.

'Yeah, I know him,' Ben said. 'You guys come down here a lot, huh?' The idea fascinated him – and made him feel a stupid sort of longing as well.

'Puh-Puh-Pretty much,' Bill said. 'Wuh-Why d-don't you c-c-come back down tuh-huh-morrow? M-Me and E-E-Eddie were tuh-trying to make a duh-duh-ham.'

Ben could say nothing. He was astounded not only by the offer but by the simple and unstudied casualness with which it had come.

'Maybe we ought to do something else,' Eddie said. 'The dam wasn't working so hot anyway.'

Ben got up and walked down to the stream, brushing the dirt from his huge hams. There were still matted piles of small branches at either side of the stream, but anything else they'd put together had washed away.

'You ought to have some boards,' Ben said. 'Get boards and put em in a row . . . facing each other . . . like the bread of a sandwich.'

Bill and Eddie were looking at him, puzzled. Ben dropped to one knee. 'Look,' he said. 'Boards here and here. You stick em in the stream-bed facing each other. Okay? Then, before the water can wash them away, you fill up the space between them with rocks and sand –'

'Wuh-Wuh-We,' Bill said.

'Huh?'

'*Wuh-We* do it.'

'Oh,' Ben said, feeling (and looking, he was sure) extremely stupid. But he didn't care if he looked stupid, because he suddenly felt very happy. He couldn't even remember the last time he felt this happy. 'Yeah. *We*. Anyway, if you – *we* – fill up the space in between with rocks and stuff, it'll stay. The upstream board will lean back against the rocks and dirt as the water piles up. The second board would tilt back and wash away after awhile, I guess, but if we had a third board . . . well, look.'

He drew in the dirt with a stick. Bill and Eddie Kaspbrak leaned over and studied this little drawing with sober interest:

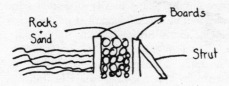

'You ever *built* a dam before?' Eddie asked. His tone was respectful, almost awed.

'Nope.'

'Then h-h-how do you know this'll w-w-work?'

Ben looked at Bill, puzzled. 'Sure it will,' he said. 'Why wouldn't it?'

'But h-how do you nuh-nuh-*know*?' Bill asked. Ben recognized the tone of the question as one not of sarcastic disbelief but honest interest. 'H-How can y-you *tell*?'

'I just know,' Ben said. He looked down at his drawing in the dirt again as if to confirm it to himself. He had never seen a cofferdam in his life, either in diagram or in fact, and had no idea that he had just drawn a pretty fair representation of one.

'O-Okay,' Bill said, and clapped Ben on the back. 'S-See you tuh-huh-morrow.'

'What time?'

'M-Me and Eh-Eddie'll g-get here by eh-eh-eight-th-thirty or so —'

'If me and my mom aren't still waiting at the Mergency Room,' Eddie said, and sighed.

'I'll bring some boards,' Ben said. 'This old guy on the next block's got a bunch of 'em. I'll hawk a few.'

'Bring some supplies, too,' Eddie said. 'Stuff to eat. You know, like sanwidges, Ring-Dings, stuff like that.'

'Okay.'

'You g-g-got any guh-guh-guns?'

'I got my Daisy air rifle,' Ben said. 'My mom gave it to me for Christmas, but she gets mad if I shoot it off in the house.'

'B-Bring it d-d-down,' Bill said. 'We'll play g-guns, maybe.'

'Okay,' Ben said happily. 'Listen, I got to split for home, you guys.'

'Uh-Us, too,' Bill said.

The three of them left the Barrens together. Ben helped Bill push Silver up the embankment. Eddie trailed behind them, wheezing again and looking unhappily at his blood-spotted shirt.

Bill said goodbye and then pedaled off, shouting 'Hi-yo Silver, *AWAYYY!*' at the top of his lungs.

'That's a *gigantic* bike,' Ben said.

'Bet your fur,' Eddie said. He had taken another gulp from his aspirator and was breathing normally again. 'He rides me double sometimes on the back. Goes so fast it just about scares the crap outta me. He's a good man, Bill is.' He said this last in an offhand way, but his eyes said something more emphatic. They were worshipful. 'You know about what happened to his brother, don't you?'

'No — what about him?'

'Got killed last fall. Some guy killed him. Pulled one of his arms right off, just like pulling a wing off'n a fly.'

'Jeezum-*crow!*'

'Bill, he used to only stutter a little. Now it's really bad. Did you notice that he stutters?'

'Well . . . a little.'

'But his *brains* don't stutter – get what I mean?'

'Yeah.'

'Anyway, I just told you because if you want Bill to be your friend, it's better not to talk to him about his little brother. Don't ask him questions or anythin. He's all frigged up about it.'

'Man, I would be, too,' Ben said. He remembered now, vaguely, about the little kid who had been killed the previous fall. He wondered if his mother had been thinking about George Denbrough when she gave him the watch he now wore, or only about the more recent killings. 'Did it happen right after the big flood?'

'Yeah.'

They had reached the corner of Kansas and Jackson, where they would have to split up. Kids ran here and there, playing tag and throwing baseballs. One dorky little kid in big blue shorts went trotting self-importantly past Ben and Eddie, wearing a Davy Crockett coonskin backward so that the tail hung down between his eyes. He was rolling a Hula Hoop and yelling 'Hoop-tag, you guys! Hoop-tag, wanna?'

The two bigger boys looked after him, amused, and then Eddie said: 'Well, I gotta go.'

'Wait a sec,' Ben said. 'I got an idea, if you really don't want to go to the Mergency Room.'

'Oh yeah?' Eddie looked at Ben, doubtful but wanting to hope.

'You got a nickel?'

'I got a dime. So what?'

Ben eyed the drying maroon splotches on Eddie's shirt. 'Stop at the store and get a chocolate milk. Pour about half of it on your shirt. Then when you get home tell your mama you spilled all of it.'

Eddie's eyes brightened. In the four years since his dad had died, his mother's eyesight had worsened considerably. For reasons of vanity (and because she didn't know how to drive a car), she refused to see an optometrist and get glasses. Dried bloodstains and chocolate milk stains looked about the same. Maybe . . .

'That might work,' he said.

'Just don't tell her it was my idea if she finds out.'

'I won't,' Eddie said. 'Seeya later, alligator.'

'Okay.'

'No,' Eddie said patiently. 'When I say that you're supposed to say, "After awhile, crocodile."'

'Oh. After awhile, crocodile.'

'You got it.' Eddie smiled.

'You know something?' Ben said. 'You guys are really cool.'

Eddie looked more than embarrassed; he looked almost nervous. 'Bill is,' he said, and started off.

Ben watched him go down Jackson Street, and then turned toward home. Three blocks up the street he saw three all-too-familiar figures standing at the bus stop on the corner of Jackson and Main. They were mostly turned away from Ben, which was damned lucky for him. He ducked behind a hedge, his heart beating hard. Five minutes later the Derry-Newport-Haven interurban bus pulled up. Henry and his friends pitched their butts into the street and swung aboard.

Ben waited until the bus was out of sight and then hurried home.

8

That night a terrible thing happened to Bill Denbrough. It happened for the second time.

His mom and dad were downstairs watching TV, not talking much, sitting at either end of the couch like bookends. There had been a time when the TV room opening off the kitchen would have been full of talk and laughter, sometimes so much of both you couldn't hear the TV at all. 'Shut up, Georgie!' Bill would roar. 'Stop hogging all the popcorn and I will,' George would return. 'Ma, make Bill give me the popcorn.' 'Bill, give him the popcorn. George, don't call me Ma. Ma's a sound a sheep makes.' Or his dad would tell a joke and they would all laugh, even Mom. George didn't always get the jokes, Bill knew, but he laughed because everyone else was laughing.

In those days his mom and dad had also been bookends on the couch, but he and George had been the books. Bill had tried to be a book between them while they were watching TV since George's death, but it was cold work. They sent the cold out from both directions and Bill's defroster was simply not big enough to cope with it. He had to leave because that kind of cold always froze his cheeks and made his eyes water.

'W-Want to h-hear a joke I heard today in s-s-school?' he had tried once, some months ago.

Silence from them. On television a criminal was begging his brother, who was a priest, to hide him.

Bill's dad glanced up from the *True* he was looking at and glanced at Bill with mild surprise. Then he looked back down at the magazine again. There was a picture of a hunter sprawled in a snowbank and staring up at a huge snarling polar bear. 'Mauled by the Killer from the White Wastes' was the name of the article. Bill had thought, *I know where there's some white wastes – right between my dad and mom on this couch.*

His mother had never looked up at all.

'It's about h-how many F-F-Frenchmen it takes to sc-c-herew in a luhhh-hightbulb,' Bill plunged ahead. He felt a fine mist of sweat spring out upon his forehead, as it sometimes did in school when he knew the teacher had ignored him as long as she safely could and must soon call on him. His voice was too loud, but he couldn't seem to lower it. The words echoed in his head like crazy chimes, echoing, jamming up, spilling out again.

'D-D-Do you know h-h-how muh-muh-many?'

'One to hold the bulb and four to turn the house,' Zack Denbrough said absently, and turned the page of his magazine.

'Did you say something, dear?' his mother asked, and on *Four Star Playhouse* the brother who was a priest told the brother who was a hoodlum to turn himself in and pray for forgiveness.

Bill sat there, sweating but cold – so cold. It was cold because he wasn't *really* the only book between those two ends; Georgie was still there, only now it was a Georgie he couldn't see, a Georgie who never demanded the popcorn or hollered that Bill was pinching. This new version of George never cut up dickens. It was a one-armed Georgie who was palely, thoughtfully silent in the Motorola's shadowy white-and-blue glow, and perhaps it was not from his parents but from George that the big chill was really coming; perhaps it was George who was the real killer from the white wastes. Finally Bill had fled from that cold, invisible brother and into his room, where he lay face down on his bed and cried into his pillow.

George's room was just as it had been on the day he died. Zack had put a bunch of George's toys into a carton one day about two weeks after he was buried, meaning them for the Goodwill or the Salvation Army or someplace like that, Bill supposed. Sharon Denbrough had spotted him coming out with the box in his arms and her hands had flown to her head like startled white birds and plunged themselves deep into her hair where they locked themselves into pulling fists. Bill had seen this and had fallen against the wall, the strength suddenly running out of his legs. His mother looked as mad as Elsa Lanchester in *The Bride of Frankenstein.*

'*Don't you DARE take his things!*' she had screeched.

Zack flinched and then took the box of toys back into George's room without a word. He even put them back in exactly the same

227

places from which he had taken them. Bill came in and saw his father kneeling by George's bed (which his mother still changed, although only once a week now instead of twice) with his head on his hairy muscular forearms. Bill saw his father was crying, and this increased his terror. A frightening possibility suddenly occurred to him: maybe sometimes things didn't just go wrong and then stop; maybe sometimes they just kept going wronger and wronger until everything was totally fucked up.

'D-Duh-Dad —'

'Go on, Bill,' his father said. His voice was muffled and shaking. His back went up and down. Bill badly wanted to touch his father's back, to see if perhaps his hand might be able to still that restless heaving. He did not quite dare. 'Go on, buzz off.'

He left and went creeping along the upstairs hall, hearing his mother doing her own crying down in the kitchen. The sound was shrill and helpless. Bill thought, *Why are they crying so far apart?* and then he shoved the thought away.

9

On the first night of summer vacation Bill went into Georgie's room. His heart was beating heavily in his chest, and his legs felt stiff and awkward with tension. He came to George's room often, but that didn't mean he liked it in here. The room was so full of George's presence that it felt haunted. He came in and couldn't help thinking that the closet door might creak open at any moment and there would be Georgie among the shirts and pants still neatly hung in there, a Georgie dressed in a rainslicker covered with red splotches and streaks, a rain-slicker with one dangling yellow arm. George's eyes would be blank and terrible, the eyes of a zombie in a horror movie. When he came out of the closet his galoshes would make squishy sounds as he walked across the room toward where Bill sat on his bed, a frozen block of terror —

If the power had gone out some evening while he sat here on George's bed, looking at the pictures on George's wall or the models on top of George's dresser, he felt sure a heart attack, probably fatal, would ensue in the next ten seconds or so. But he went anyway. Warring with his terror of George-the-ghost was a mute and grasping need — a hunger — to somehow get over George's death and find a decent way to go on. Not to forget George but somehow to find a way to make him not so fucking *gruesome*. He understood that his

228

parents were not succeeding very well with that, and if he was going to do it for himself, he would have to do it *by* himself.

Nor was it just for himself that he came; he came for Georgie as well. He had loved George, and for brothers they had gotten along pretty well. Oh, they had their pissy moments – Bill giving George a good old Indian rope-burn, George tattling on Bill when Bill snuck downstairs after lights-out and ate the rest of the lemon-cream frosting – but mostly they got along. Bad enough that George should be dead. For him to turn George into some kind of horror-monster . . . that was even worse.

He missed the little kid, that was the truth. Missed his voice, his laughter – missed the way George's eyes sometimes tipped confidently up to his own, sure that Bill would have whatever answers were required. And one surpassingly odd thing: there were times when he felt he loved George best in his fear, because even in his fear – his uneasy feelings that a zombie-George might be lurking in the closet or under the bed – he could remember loving George better in here, and George loving him. In his effort to reconcile these two emotions – his love and his terror – Bill felt that he was closest to finding where final acceptance lay.

These were not things of which he could have spoken; to his mind the ideas were nothing but an incoherent jumble. But his warm and desiring heart understood, and that was all that mattered.

Sometimes he looked through George's books, sometimes he sifted through George's toys.

He hadn't looked in George's photograph album since last December.

Now, on the night after meeting Ben Hanscom, Bill opened the door of George's closet (steeling himself as always to meet the sight of Georgie himself, standing in his bloody slicker amid the hanging clothes, expecting as always to see one pallid, fish-fingered hand come pistoning out of the dark to grip his arm) and took the album down from the top shelf.

MY PHOTOGRAPHS, the gold script on the front read. Below, Scotch-taped on (the tape was now slightly yellow and peeling), the carefully printed words GEORGE ELMER DENBROUGH, AGE 6. Bill took it back to the bed Georgie had slept in, his heart beating heavier than ever. He couldn't tell what had made him get the photograph album down again. After what had happened in December . . .

A second look, that's all. Just to convince yourself that it wasn't real the first time. That the first time was just your head playing a trick on itself.

Well, it was an idea, anyway.

It might even be true. But Bill suspected it was just the album itself. It held a certain mad fascination for him. What he had seen, or what he *thought* he had seen –

He opened the album now. It was filled with pictures George had gotten his mother, father, aunts, and uncles to give him. George didn't care if they were pictures of people and places he knew or not; it was the idea of photography itself which fascinated him. When he had been unsuccessful at pestering anyone into giving him new photos to mount he would sit cross-legged on his bed where Bill was sitting now and look at the old ones, turning the pages carefully, studying the black-and-white Kodaks. Here was their mother when she was young and impossibly gorgeous; here their father, no more than eighteen, one of a trio of smiling rifle-toting young men standing over the open-eyed corpse of a deer; Uncle Hoyt standing on some rocks and holding up a pickerel; Aunt Fortuna, at the Derry Agricultural Fair, kneeling proudly beside a basket of tomatoes she had raised; an old Buick automobile; a church; a house; a road that went from some-where to somewhere. All these pictures, snapped by lost somebodies for lost reasons, locked up here in a dead boy's album of photographs.

Here Bill saw himself at three, propped up in a hospital bed with a turban of bandages covering his hair. Bandages went down his cheeks and under his fractured jaw. He had been struck by a car in the parking lot of the A&P on Center Street. He remembered very little of his hospital stay, only that they had given him ice-cream milk shakes through a straw and his head had ached dreadfully for three days.

Here was the whole family on the lawn of the house, Bill standing by his mother and holding her hand, and George, only a baby, sleeping in Zack's arms. And here –

It wasn't the end of the book, but it was the last page that mattered, because the following ones were all blank. The final picture was George's school picture, taken in October of last year, less than ten days before he died. In it George was wearing a crew-neck shirt. His fly-away hair was slicked down with water. He was grinning, revealing two empty slots in which new teeth would never grow – *unless they keep on growing after you die*, Bill thought, and shuddered.

He looked at the picture fixedly for some time and was about to close the book when what had happened in December happened again.

George's eyes rolled in the picture. They turned up to meet Bill's own. George's artificial say-cheese smile turned into a horrid leer. His right eye drooped closed in a wink: *See you soon, Bill. In my closet. Maybe tonight.*

Bill threw the book across the room. He clapped his hands over his mouth.

The book struck the wall and fell to the floor, open. The pages turned, although there was no draft. The book opened itself to that awful picture again, the picture which said SCHOOL FRIENDS 1957–58 beneath it.

Blood began to flow from the picture.

Bill sat frozen, his tongue a swelling choking lump in his mouth, his skin crawling, his hair lifting. He wanted to scream but the tiny whimpering sounds crawling out of his throat seemed to be the best he could manage.

The blood flowed across the page and began to drip onto the floor.

Bill fled the room, slamming the door behind him.

CHAPTER SIX
ONE OF THE MISSING: A TALE FROM THE SUMMER OF '58

1

They weren't all found. No; they weren't all found. And from time to time wrong assumptions were made.

2

From the Derry *News*, June 21st, 1958 (page 1):

MISSING BOY PROMPTS NEW FEARS

Edward L. Corcoran, of 73 Charter Street, Derry, was reported missing last night by his mother, Monica Macklin, and his stepfather, Richard P. Macklin. The Corcoran boy is ten. His disappearance has prompted new fears that Derry's young people are being stalked by a killer.

Mrs Macklin said the boy had been missing since June 19th, when he failed to return home from school after the last day of classes before summer vacation.

When asked why they had delayed over twenty-four hours before reporting their son's absence, Mr and Mrs Macklin refused comment. Police Chief Richard Borton also declined comment, but a Police Department source told the *News* that the Corcoran boy's relationship with his stepfather was not a good one, and that he had spent nights out of the house before. The source speculated that the boy's final grades may have played a part in the boy's failure to turn up. Derry School Superintendent Harold Metcalf declined comment on the Corcoran boy's grades, pointing out they are not a matter of public record.

'I hope the disappearance of this boy will not cause unnecessary fears,' Chief Borton said last night. 'The mood of the community is understandably uneasy, but I want to emphasize that we log thirty to fifty missing-persons reports on minors each and every year. Most turn up alive and well within a week of the initial report. This will be the case with Edward Corcoran, God willing.'

Borton also reiterated his conviction that the murders of George Denbrough, Betty Ripsom, Cheryl Lamonica, Matthew Clements, and Veronica Grogan were not the work of one person. 'There are essential differences in each crime,' Borton said, but declined to elaborate. He said that local police, working in close co-operation with the Maine State Attorney General's office, are still following up a number of leads. Asked in a telephone interview last night how good these leads are, Chief Borton replied: 'Very good.' Asked if an arrest in any of the crimes was expected soon, Borton declined comment.

From the Derry *News*, June 22nd, 1958 (page 1):

COURT ORDERS SURPRISE EXHUMATION

In a bizarre new twist to the disappearance of Edward Corcoran, Derry District Court Judge Erhardt K. Moulton ordered the exhumation of Corcoran's younger brother, Dorsey, late yesterday. The court order followed a joint request from the County Attorney and the County Medical Examiner.

Dorsey Corcoran, who also lived with his mother and stepfather at 73 Charter Street, died of what were reported to be accidental causes in May of 1957. The boy was brought into the Derry Home Hospital suffering from multiple fractures, including a fractured skull. Richard P. Macklin, the boy's stepfather, was the admitting person. He stated that Dorsey Corcoran had been playing on a stepladder in the garage and had apparently fallen from the top. The boy died without recovering consciousness three days later.

Edward Corcoran, ten, was reported missing late Wednesday. Asked if either Mr or Mrs Macklin was under suspicion in either the younger boy's death or the older boy's disappearance, Chief Richard Borton declined comment.

From the Derry *News*, June 24th, 1958 (page 1):

MACKLIN ARRESTED IN BEATING DEATH
Under Suspicion in Unsolved Disappearance

Chief Richard Borton of the Derry Police called a news conference yesterday to announce that Richard P. Macklin, of 73 Charter Street, had been arrested and charged with the murder of his stepson, Dorsey Corcoran. The Corcoran boy died in Derry Home Hospital of reported 'accidental causes' on May 31st of last year.

'The medical examiner's report shows that the boy was badly beaten,' Borton said. Although Macklin claimed the boy had fallen from a stepladder while playing in the garage, Borton said the County Medical Examiner's report showed that Dorsey Corcoran was severely beaten with some blunt instrument. When asked what sort of instrument, Borton said: 'It might have been a hammer. Right now the important thing is the medical examiner's conclusion that this boy was struck repeated blows with some object hard enough to break his bones. The wounds, particularly those in the skull, are not at all consistent with those which might be incurred in a fall. Dorsey Corcoran was beaten within an inch of his life and then dumped off at the Home Hospital emergency room to die.'

Asked if the doctors who treated the Corcoran boy might have been derelict in their duty when it came to reporting either an incidence of child abuse or the actual cause of death, Borton said, 'They will have serious questions to answer when Mr Macklin comes to trial.'

Asked for an opinion on how these developments might bear on the recent disappearance of Dorsey Corcoran's older brother, Edward, reported missing by Richard and Monica Macklin four days ago, Chief Borton answered: 'I think it looks much more serious than we first supposed, don't you?'

From the Derry *News*, June 25th, 1958 (page 2):

TEACHER SAYS EDWARD CORCORAN 'OFTEN BRUISED'

Henrietta Dumont, who teaches fifth grade at Derry Elementary School on Jackson Street, said that Edward Corcoran, who has now been missing for nearly a week, often came to school 'covered with bruises.' Mrs Dumont, who has taught one of Derry's two fifth-grade classes since the end of World War II, said that the Corcoran boy came to school one day about three weeks before his disappearance 'with both eyes nearly closed shut. When I asked him what happened, he said his father had "taken him up" for not eating his supper.'

When asked why she had not reported a beating of such obvious severity, Mrs Dumont said, 'This isn't the first time I've seen such a thing as this in my career as a teacher. The first few times I had a student with a parent who was confusing beatings with discipline, I tried to do something about it. I was told by the assistant principal, Gwendolyn Rayburn in those days, to stay out of it. She told me that when school employees get involved in cases of suspected child abuse, it always comes back to haunt the School Department at tax appropriation time. I went to the principal and he told me to forget it or I would be reprimanded. I asked him if a reprimand in a matter like that would go on my record. He said a reprimand did not have to be on a teacher's record. I got the message.'

Asked if the attitude in the Derry school system remained the same now, Mrs Dumont said, 'Well, what does it look like, in light of this current situation? And I might add that I would not be speaking to you now if I hadn't retired at the end of this school year.'

Mrs Dumont went on, 'Since this thing came out I get down on my knees every night and pray that Eddie Corcoran just got fed up with that beast of a stepfather and ran away. I pray that when he reads in the paper or hears on the news that Macklin has been locked up, Eddie will come home.'

In a brief telephone interview Monica Macklin hotly refuted Mrs Dumont's charges. 'Rich never beat Dorsey, and he never beat Eddie, either,' she said. 'I'm telling you that right now, and when I die I'll stand at the Throne of Judgment and look God right in the eye and tell Him the same thing.'

From the Derry *News*, June 28th, 1958 (page 2):

'DADDY HAD TO TAKE ME UP 'CAUSE I'M BAD,' TOT TOLD NURSERY TEACHER BEFORE BEATING DEATH

A local nursery-school teacher who declined to be identified told a *News* reporter yesterday that young Dorsey Corcoran came to his twice-weekly nursery-school class with bad sprains of his right thumb and three fingers of his right hand less than a week before his death in a purported garage accident.

'It was hurting him enough so that the poor little guy couldn't color his Mr Do safety poster,' the teacher said. 'The fingers were swelled up like sausages. When I asked Dorsey what happened, he said that his father (stepfather Richard P. Macklin) had bent his fingers back because he had walked across a floor his mother had just washed and waxed. "Daddy had to take me up 'cause I'm bad" was the way he put it. I felt like crying, looking at his poor, dear fingers. He really wanted to color his poster like the other children, so I gave him some baby aspirin and let him color while the others were having Story Time. He loved to color the Mr Do posters – that was what he liked best – and now I'm so glad I was able to help him have a little happiness that day.

'When he died it never crossed my mind to think it was anything but an accident. I guess at first I thought he must have fallen because he couldn't grip very well with that hand. Now I think I just couldn't believe an adult could do such a thing to a little person. I know better now. I wish to God I didn't.'

Dorsey Corcoran's older brother, Edward, ten, is still missing. From his cell in Derry County Jail, Richard Macklin continues to deny any part in either the death of his younger stepson or the disappearance of the older boy.

From the Derry *News*, June 30th, 1958 (page 5):

MACKLIN QUESTIONED IN DEATHS OF GROGAN, CLEMENTS
Produces Unshakable Alibis, Source Claims

From the Derry *News*, July 6th, 1958 (page 1):

MACKLIN TO BE CHARGED ONLY WITH MURDER OF STEPSON DORSEY, BORTON SAYS
Edward Corcoran Still Missing

From the Derry *News*, July 24th, 1958 (page 1):

WEEPING STEPFATHER CONFESSES TO BLUDGEON DEATH OF STEPSON

In a dramatic development in the District Court trial of Richard Macklin for the murder of his stepson Dorsey Corcoran, Macklin broke down under the stern cross-examination of County Attorney Bradley Whitsun and admitted he had beaten the four-year-old boy to death with a recoilless hammer, which he then buried at the far end of his wife's vegetable garden before taking the boy to Derry Home Hospital's emergency room.

The courtroom was stunned and silent as the sobbing Macklin, who had previously admitted beating both of his stepsons 'occasionally, if they had it coming, for their own good,' poured out his story.

'I don't know what came over me. I saw he was climbing on the damn ladder again and I grabbed the hammer from the bench where it was laying and I just started to use it on him. I didn't mean to kill him. With God as my witness I never meant to kill him.'

'Did he say anything to you before he passed out?' Whitsun asked.

'He said, "Stop daddy, I'm sorry, I love you,"' Macklin replied.

'Did you stop?'

'Eventually,' Macklin said. He then began to weep in such a hysterical manner that Judge Erhardt Moulton declared the court in recess.

From the Derry *News*, September 18th, 1958 (page 16):

WHERE IS EDWARD CORCORAN?

His stepfather, sentenced to a term of two to ten years in Shawshank State Prison for the murder of his four-year-old brother, Dorsey, continues to claim he has no idea where Edward Corcoran is. His mother, who has instituted divorce proceedings against Richard P. Macklin, says she thinks her soon-to-be ex-husband is lying.

Is he?

'I, for one, really don't think so,' says Father Ashley O'Brian, who serves the Catholic prisoners at Shawshank. Macklin began taking instruction in the Catholic faith shortly after beginning his prison term, and Father O'Brian has spent a good deal of time with him. 'He is sincerely sorry for what he has done,' Father O'Brian goes on, adding that when he initially asked Macklin why he wanted to be a Catholic, Macklin replied, 'I hear they have an act of contrition and I need to do a lot of that or else I'll go to hell when I die.'

'He knows what he did to the younger boy,' Father O'Brian said. 'If he also did something to the older one, he doesn't remember it. As far as Edward goes, he believes his hands are clean.'

How clean Macklin's hands are in the matter of his stepson Edward is a question which continues to trouble Derry residents, but he has been convincingly cleared of the other childmurders which have taken place here. He was able to produce ironclad alibis for the first three, and he was in jail when seven others were committed in late June, July, and August.

All ten murders remain unsolved.

In an exclusive interview with the *News* last week Macklin again asserted that he knows nothing of Edward Corcoran's whereabouts. 'I beat them both,' he said in a painful monologue which was often halted by bouts of weeping. 'I loved them but I beat them. I don't know why, any more than I know why Monica let me, or why she covered up for me after Dorsey died. I guess I could have killed Eddie as easy as I did Dorsey, but I swear before God and Jesus and all the saints of heaven that I didn't. I know how it looks, but I didn't do it. I think he just ran away. If he did, that's one thing I've got to thank God for.'

Asked if he is aware of any gaps in his memory – if he could have killed Edward and then blocked it out of his mind – Macklin replied: 'I ain't aware of any gaps. I know only too well what I did. I've given my life to Christ, and I'm going to spend the rest of it trying to make up for it.'

From the Derry *News*, January 27th, 1960 (page 1):

BODY NOT THAT OF CORCORAN YOUTH, BORTON ANNOUNCES

Police Chief Richard Borton told reporters early today that the badly decomposed body of a boy about the age of Edward Corcoran, who disappeared from his Derry home in June of 1958, is definitely not that of the missing youth. The body was found in Aynesford, Massachusetts, buried in a gravel pit. Both Maine and Massachusetts State Police at first theorized that the body might be that of the Corcoran boy, believing that he might have been picked up by a child molester after running away from the

Charter Street home where his younger brother had been beaten and killed.

Dental charts showed conclusively that the body found in Aynesford was not that of the Corcoran youth, who has now been missing for nineteen months.

From the Portland *Press-Herald*, July 19th, 1967 (page 3):

CONVICTED MURDERER COMMITS SUICIDE IN FALMOUTH

Richard P. Macklin, who was convicted of the murder of his four-year-old stepson nine years ago, was found dead in his small third-floor Falmouth apartment late yesterday afternoon. The parolee, who had lived and worked quietly in Falmouth since his release from Shawshank State Prison in 1964, was an apparent suicide.

'The note he left indicates an extremely confused state of mind,' Assistant Falmouth Police Chief Brandon K. Roche said. He refused to divulge the note's contents, but a Police Department source said it consisted of two sentences: 'I saw Eddie last night. He was dead.'

The 'Eddie' referred to may well have been Macklin's stepson, brother of the boy Macklin was convicted of killing in 1958. It was the disappearance of Edward Corcoran which eventually led to Macklin's conviction for the beating death of Edward's younger brother, Dorsey. The elder boy has been missing for nine years. In a brief court proceeding in 1966 the boy's mother had her son declared legally dead so she could enter into possession of Edward Corcoran's savings account. The account contained a sum of sixteen dollars.

3

Eddie Corcoran was dead, all right.

He died on the night of June 19th, and his stepfather had nothing at all to do with it. He died as Ben Hanscom sat home watching TV with his mother, as Eddie Kaspbrak's mother anxiously felt Eddie's forehead for signs of her favorite ailment, 'phantom fever,' as Beverly Marsh's stepfather – a gent who bore, in temperament at least, a remarkable resemblance to Eddie and Dorsey Corcoran's stepfather – lifted a high-stepping kick into the girl's *derrière* and told her 'to get

out there and dry those goddam dishes like your mummer told you,'
as Mike Hanlon got yelled at by some high-school boys (one of whom
would some years later sire that fine upstanding young homophobe
John 'Webby' Garton) passing in an old Dodge while Mike pulled
weeds out of the garden beside the small Hanlon home out on Witcham
Road, not far from the farm owned by Henry Bowers's crazy father,
as Richie Tozier was sneaking a look at the half-undressed girls in a
copy of *Gem* he had found at the bottom of his father's socks-and-
underwear drawer and getting a regular good boner, and as Bill
Denbrough was throwing his dead brother's photograph album across
the room in horrified unbelief.

Although none of them would remember doing so later, all of
them looked up at the exact moment Eddie Corcoran died . . . as if
hearing some distant cry.

The *News* had been absolutely right about one thing: Eddie's
rank-card was just bad enough to make him afraid to go home and
face his stepdad. Also, his mother and the old man were fighting a lot
this month. That made things even worse. When they got going at it
hot and heavy, his mother shouted a lot of mostly incoherent accusations. His stepdad responded to these first with grunts, then yells to
shut up, and finally with the enraged bellows of a boar which has
gotten a quiver of porcupine needles in its snout. Eddie had never seen
the old man use his fists on her, though. Eddie didn't think he quite
dared. He had saved his fists for Eddie and Dorsey in the old days,
and now that Dorsey was dead, Eddie got his little brother's share as
well as his own.

These shouting matches came and went in cycles. They were
most common at the end of the month, when the bills came in. A
policeman, called by a neighbor, might drop by once or twice when
things were at their worst and tell them to tone it down. Usually that
ended it. His mother was apt to give the cop the finger and dare him
to take her in, but his stepdad rarely said boo.

His stepdad was afraid of the cops, Eddie thought.

He lay low during these periods of stress. It was wiser. If you
didn't think so, just look at what had happened to Dorsey. Eddie didn't
know the specifics and didn't want to, but he had an idea about Dorsey.
He thought that Dorsey had been in the wrong place at the wrong
time: the garage on the last day of the month. They told Eddie that
Dorsey fell off the stepladder in the garage – 'If I told him once to
stay off'n it I told him sixty times,' his stepdad had said – but his
mother wouldn't look at him except by accident . . . and when their

eyes did meet, Eddie had seen a frightened ratty little gleam in hers that he didn't like. The old man just sat there silently at the kitchen table with a quart of Rheingold, looking at nothing from beneath his heavy lowering eyebrows. Eddie kept out of his reach. When his stepfather was bellowing, he was usually – not always but usually – all right. It was when he stopped that you had to be careful.

Two nights ago he had thrown a chair at Eddie when Eddie got up to see what was on the other TV channel – just picked up one of the tubular aluminum kitchen chairs, swept it back over his head, and let fly. It hit Eddie in the butt and knocked him over. His butt still ached, but he knew it could have been worse: it could have been his head.

Then there had been the night when the old man had suddenly gotten up and rubbed a handful of mashed potatoes into Eddie's hair for no reason at all. One day last September, Eddie had come in from school and foolishly allowed the screen door to slam shut behind him while his stepdad was taking a nap. Macklin came out of the bedroom in his billowy boxer shorts, hair standing up in corkscrews, cheeks grizzled with two days of weekend beard, breath grizzled with two days of weekend beer. 'There now, Eddie,' he said, 'I got to take you up for slammin that fuckin door.' In Rich Macklin's lexicon, 'taking you up' was a euphemism for 'beating the shit out of you.' Which was what he then did to Eddie. Eddie had lost consciousness when the old man threw him into the front hall. His mother had mounted a pair of low coathooks out there, especially for him and Dorsey to hang their coats on. These hooks had rammed hard steel fingers into Eddie's lower back, and that was when he passed out. When he came to ten minutes later he heard his mother yelling that she was going to take Eddie to the hospital and he couldn't stop her.

'After what happened to Dorsey?' his stepdad had responded. 'You want to go to jail, woman?'

That was the end of her talk about the hospital. She helped Eddie into his room, where he lay shivering on his bed, his forehead beaded with sweat. The only time he left the room during the next three days was when they were both gone. Then he would hobble slowly into the kitchen, groaning softly, and get his stepdad's whiskey from under the sink. A few nips dulled the pain. The pain was mostly gone by the fifth day, but he had pissed blood for almost two weeks.

And the hammer wasn't in the garage anymore.

What about *that*? What about *that*, friends and neighbors?

Oh, the Craftsman hammer – the ordinary hammer – was still

there. It was the Scotti recoilless which was missing. His stepdad's special hammer, the one he and Dorsey had been forbidden to touch. 'If one of you touches that baby,' he had told them the day he bought it, 'you'll both be wearing your guts for earmuffs.' Dorsey had asked timidly if that hammer was very expensive. The old man told him he was damn tooting. He said it was filled with ball-bearings and you couldn't make it bounce back up no matter how hard you brought it down.

Now it was gone.

Eddie's grades weren't the best because he had missed a lot of school since his mother's remarriage, but he was not a stupid boy by any means. He thought he knew what had happened to the Scotti recoilless hammer. He thought maybe his stepfather had used it on Dorsey and then buried it in the garden or maybe thrown it in the Canal. It was the sort of thing that happened frequently in the horror comics Eddie read, the ones he kept on the top shelf of his closet.

He walked closer to the Canal, which rippled between its concrete sides like oiled silk. A swatch of moonlight glimmered across its dark surface in a boomerang shape. He sat down, swinging his sneakers idly against the concrete in an irregular tattoo. The last six weeks had been quite dry and the water flowed past perhaps nine feet below the worn soles of his sneakers. But if you looked closely at the Canal's sides, you could read the various levels to which it sometimes rose quite easily. The concrete was stained a dark brown just above the water's current level. This brown stain slowly faded to yellow, then to a color that was almost white at the level where the heels of Eddie's sneakers made contact when he swung them.

The water flowed smoothly and silently out of a concrete arch that was cobbled on the inside, past the place where Eddie sat, and then down to the covered wooden footbridge between Bassey Park and Derry High School. The bridge's sides and plank footing – even the beams under the roof – were covered with an intaglio of initials, phone numbers, and declarations. Declarations of love; declarations that So-and-so was willing to 'suck' or 'blow'; declarations that those discovered sucking or blowing would lose their foreskins or have their assholes plugged with hot tar; occasional eccentric declarations that defied definition. One that Eddie had puzzled over all this spring read SAVE RUSSIAN JEWS! COLLECT VALUABLE PRIZES!

What, exactly, did that mean? Anything? And did it matter?

Eddie didn't go into the Kissing Bridge tonight; he had no urge to cross over to the high-school side. He thought he would probably sleep in the park, maybe in the dead leaves under the bandstand, but for now it was fine just to sit here. He liked it in the park, and came often when he had to think. Sometimes there were people making out in the groves of trees which dotted the park, but Eddie left them alone and they left him alone. He had heard lurid stories in the playground at school about the queers that cruised in Bassey Park after sundown, and he accepted these stories without question, but he himself had never been bothered. The park was a peaceful place, and he thought the best part of it was right here where he was sitting. He liked it in the middle of summer, when the water was so low it chuckled over the stones and actually broke up into isolated streamlets that twisted and turned and sometimes came together again. He liked it in late March or early April, just after ice-out, when he would sometimes stand by the Canal (too cold to sit then; your ass would freeze) for an hour or more, the hood of his old parka, now two years too small for him, pulled up, his hands plunged into his pockets, unaware that his skinny body was shivering and shaking. The Canal had a terrible, irresistible power in the week or two after the ice went out. He was fascinated by the way the water boiled whitely out of the cobbled arch and roared past him, bearing sticks and branches and all manner of human trash along with it. More than once he had envisioned walking beside the Canal in March with his stepdad and giving the bastard a great big motherfucking push. He would scream and fall in, his arms pinwheeling for balance, and Eddie would stand on the concrete parapet and watch him carried off downstream, his head a black bobbing shape in the middle of the unruly whitecapped current. He would stand there, yes, and he would cup his hands around his mouth and scream: *THAT WAS FOR DORSEY, YOU ROTTEN COCKSUCKER! WHEN YOU GET DOWN TO HELL TELL THE DEVIL THE LAST THING YOU EVER HEARD WAS ME TELLING YOU TO PICK ON SOMEBODY YOUR OWN SIZE!* It would never happen, of course, but it was an absolutely grand fantasy. A grand dream to dream as you sat here by the Canal, a g –

A hand closed around Eddie's foot.

He had been looking across the Canal toward the school, smiling a sleepy and rather beautiful smile as he imagined his stepfather being carried off in the violent rip of the spring runoff, being carried out of his life forever. The soft yet strong grip startled him so much that he almost lost his balance and tumbled into the Canal.

It's one of the queers the big kids are always talking about, he thought, and then he looked down. His mouth dropped open. Urine spilled hotly down his legs and stained his jeans black in the moonlight. It wasn't a queer.

243

It was Dorsey.

It was Dorsey as he had been buried, Dorsey in his blue blazer and gray pants, only now the blazer was in muddy tatters, Dorsey's shirt was yellow rags, Dorsey's pants clung wetly to legs as thin as broomsticks. And Dorsey's head was horribly *slumped*, as if it had been caved in at the back and consequently pushed up in the front.

Dorsey was grinning.

'*Eddieeeee*,' his dead brother croaked, just like one of the dead people who were always coming back from the grave in the horror comics. Dorsey's grin widened. Yellow teeth gleamed, and somewhere way back in that darkness things seemed to be squirming.

'*Eddieeee . . . I came to see you Eddieeeeee . . .*'

Eddie tried to scream. Waves of gray shock rolled over him, and he had the curious sensation that he was floating. But it was not a dream; he was awake. The hand on his sneaker was as white as a trout's belly. His brother's bare feet clung somehow to the concrete. Something had bitten one of Dorsey's heels off.

'*Come on down Eddieeeee . . .*'

Eddie couldn't scream. His lungs didn't have enough air in them to manage a scream. He got out a curious reedy moaning sound. Anything louder seemed beyond him. That was all right. In a second or two his mind would snap and after that nothing would matter. Dorsey's hand was small but implacable. Eddie's buttocks were sliding over the concrete to the edge of the Canal

Still making that reedy moaning sound, he reached behind himself and grabbed the concrete edging and yanked himself backward. He felt the hand slide away momentarily, heard an angry hiss, and had time to think: *That's not Dorsey. I don't know what it is, but it's not Dorsey.* Then adrenaline flooded his body and he was crawling away, trying to run even before he was on his feet, his breath coming in short shrieky whistles.

White hands appeared on the concrete lip of the Canal. There was a wet slapping sound. Drops of water flew upward in the moonlight from dead pallid skin. Now Dorsey's face appeared over the edge. Dim red sparks gleamed in his sunken eyes. His wet hair was plastered to his skull. Mud streaked his cheeks like warpaint.

Eddie's chest finally unlocked. He hitched in breath and turned it into a scream. He got to his feet and ran. He ran looking back over his shoulder, needing to see where Dorsey was, and as a result he ran smack into a large elm tree.

It felt as if someone – his old man, for instance – had set off a dynamite charge in his left shoulder. Stars shot and corkscrewed through his head. He fell at the base of the tree as if poleaxed, blood trickling from his left temple. He swam in the waters of semiconsciousness for perhaps ninety seconds. Then he managed to gain his feet again. A groan escaped him as he tried to raise his left arm. It didn't want to come. Felt all numb and far away. So he raised his right and rubbed his fiercely aching head.

Then he remembered why he had happened to run full-tilt into the elm tree in the first place and looked around.

There was the edge of the Canal, white as bone and straight as string in the moonlight. No sign of the thing from the Canal . . . if there ever *had* been a thing. He continued turning, working his way slowly through a complete three hundred and sixty degrees. Bassey Park was silent and as still as a black-and-white photograph. Weeping willows draggled their thin tenebrous arms, and anything could be standing, slumped and insane, within their shelter.

Eddie began to walk, trying to look everywhere at once. His sprained shoulder throbbed in painful sync with his heartbeat.

Eddieeeee, the breeze moaned through the trees, *don't you want to see meeeee, Eddieeeee?* He felt flabby corpse-fingers caress the side of his neck. He whirled, his hands going up. As his feet tangled together and he fell, he saw that it had only been willow-fronds moving in the breeze.

He got up again. He wanted to run but when he tried another dynamite charge went off in his shoulder and he had to stop. He knew somehow that he should be getting over his fright by now, calling himself a stupid little baby who got spooked by a reflection or maybe fell asleep without knowing it and had a bad dream. That wasn't happening, though; quite the reverse, in fact. His heart was now beating so fast he could no longer distinguish the separate thuds, and he felt sure it would soon burst in terror. He couldn't run but when he got out of the willows he did manage a limping jogtrot.

He fixed his eyes on the streetlight that marked the park's main gate. He headed in that direction, managing a little more speed, thinking: *I'll make it to the light, and that's all right. I'll make it to the light, and that's all right. Bright light, no more fright, up all night, what a sight –*

Something was following him.

Eddie could hear it bludgeoning its way through the willow grove. If he turned he would see it. It was gaining. He could hear its feet, a kind of shuffling, squelching stride, but he would not look back, no, he would look ahead at the light, the light was all right, he would just continue his flight to the light, and he was almost there, almost –

The smell was what made him look back. The overwhelming smell, as if fish had been left to rot in a huge pile that had become carrion-slushy in the summer heat. It was the smell of a dead ocean.

It wasn't Dorsey after him now; it was the Creature from the Black Lagoon. The thing's snout was long and pleated. Green fluid dripped from black gashes like vertical mouths in its cheeks. Its eyes were white and jellylike. Its webbed fingers were tipped with claws like razors. Its respiration was bubbly and deep, the sound of a diver with a bad regulator. As it saw Eddie looking, its green-black lips wrinkled back from huge fangs in a dead and vacant smile.

It shambled after him, dripping, and Eddie suddenly understood. It meant to take him back to the Canal, to carry him down into the dank blackness of the Canal's underground passage. To eat him there.

Eddie put on a burst of speed. The arc-sodium light at the gate drew closer. He could see its halo of bugs and moths. A truck went by, headed for Route 2, the driver working his way up through the gears, and it crossed Eddie's desperate, terrified mind that he could be drinking coffee from a paper cup and listening to a Buddy Holly tune on the radio, completely unaware that less than two hundred yards away there was a boy who might be dead in another twenty seconds.

The stink. The overwhelming stink of it. Gaining. All around him.

It was a park bench he tripped over. Some kids had casually pushed it over earlier that evening, heading toward their homes at a run to beat the curfew. Its seat poked an inch or two out of the grass, one shade of green on another, almost invisible in the moon-driven dark. The edge of the seat smacked Eddie in the shins, causing a burst of glassy, exquisite pain. His legs flipped out behind him and he thumped into the grass.

He looked behind him and saw the Creature bearing down, its white poached-egg eyes glittering, its scales dripping slime the color of seaweed, the gills up and down its bulging neck and cheeks opening and closing.

'*Ag!*' Eddie croaked. It seemed to be the only noise he could make. '*Ag! Ag! Ag! Ag!*'

He crawled now, fingers hooking deep into the turf. His tongue hung out.

In the second before the Creature's fish-smelling horny hands closed around his throat, a comforting thought came to him: *This is a dream; it has to be. There's no real Creature, no real Black Lagoon, and even if there was, that was in South America or the Florida Everglades or someplace like that. This is only a dream and I'll wake up in my bed or maybe in the leaves under the bandstand and I –*

Then batrachian hands closed around his neck and Eddie's hoarse cries were choked off; as the Creature turned him over, the chitinous hooks which sprouted from those hands scrawled bleeding marks like calligraphy into his neck. He stared into its glowing white eyes. He felt the webs between its fingers pressing against his throat like constricting bands of living seaweed. His terror-sharpened gaze noted the fin, something like a rooster's comb and something like a hornpout's poisonous backfin, standing atop the Creature's hunched and plated head. As its hands clamped tight, shutting off his air, he was even able to see the way the white light from the arc-sodium lamp turned a smoky green as it passed through that membranous headfin.

'You're . . . not . . . real,' Eddie choked, but clouds of grayness were closing in now, and he realized faintly that it was real enough, this Creature. It was, after all, killing him.

And yet some rationality remained, even until the end: as the Creature hooked its claws into the soft meat of his neck, as his carotid artery let go in a warm and painless gout that splashed the thing's reptilian plating, Eddie's hands groped at the Creature's back, feeling for a zipper. They fell away only when the Creature tore his head from his shoulders with a low satisfied grunt.

And as Eddie's picture of what It was began to fade, It began promptly to change into something else.

4

Unable to sleep, plagued by bad dreams, a boy named Michael Hanlon rose soon after first light on the first full day of summer vacation. The light was pale, bundled up in a low, thick mist that would lift by eight o'clock, taking the wraps off a perfect summer day.

But that was for later. For now the world was all gray and rose, as silent as a cat walking on a carpet.

Mike, dressed in corduroys, a tee-shirt, and black high-topped Keds, came downstairs, ate a bowl of Wheaties (he didn't really like Wheaties but had wanted the free prize in the box – a Captain Midnight Magic Decoder Ring), then hopped on his bike and pedaled toward town, riding on the sidewalks because of the fog. The fog changed everything, made the most ordinary things like fire hydrants and stop-signs into objects of mystery – things both strange and a trifle sinister. You could hear cars but not see them, and because of the fog's odd acoustic quality, you could not tell if they were far or near until you actually saw them come rolling out of the fog with ghost-halos of moisture ringing their headlamps.

He turned right on Jackson Street, bypassing downtown, and then crossed to Main Street by way of Palmer Lane – and during his short ride down this little byway's one-block length he passed the house where he would live as an adult. He did not look at it; it was just a small two-story dwelling with a garage and a small lawn. It gave off no special vibration to the passing boy who would spend most of his adult life as its owner and only dweller.

At Main Street he turned right and rode up to Bassey Park, still wandering, simply riding and enjoying the stillness of the early day. Once inside the main gate he dismounted his bike, pushed down the kickstand, and walked toward the Canal. He was still, as far as he knew, impelled by nothing more than purest whim. Certainly it did not occur to him to think that his dreams of the night before had anything to do with his current course; he did not even remember exactly what his dreams had been – only that one had followed another until he had awakened at five o'clock, sweaty but shivering, and with the idea that he ought to eat a fast breakfast and then take a bike-ride into town.

Here in Bassey there was a smell in the fog he didn't like: a sea-smell, salty and old. He had smelled it before, of course. In the early-morning fogs you could often smell the ocean in Derry, although the coast was forty miles away. But the smell this morning seemed thicker, more vital. Almost dangerous.

Something caught his eye. He bent down and picked up a cheap two-blade pocket knife. Someone had scratched the initials EC on the side. Mike looked at it thoughtfully for a moment or two and then pocketed it. Finders keepers, losers weepers.

He glanced around. Here, near where he had found the knife, was an overturned park bench. He righted it, setting its iron footings back into the holes they had made over a period of months or years. Beyond the bench he saw a matted place in the grass . . . and leading away from it, two grooves. The grass was springing back up, but those grooves were still fairly clear. They went in the direction of the Canal.

And there was blood.

(*the bird remember the bird remember the*)

248

But he did not want to remember the bird and so he pushed the thought away. *Dogfight, that's all. One of 'em must have hurt the other one pretty bad.* It was a convincing thought by which he was somehow not convinced. Thoughts of the bird kept wanting to come back – the one he had seen out at the Kitchener Ironworks, one Stan Uris never would have found in his bird-book.

Stop it. Just get out of here.

But instead of getting out he followed the grooves. As he did he made up a little story in his mind. It was a murder story. Here's this kid, out late, see. Out past the curfew. The killer gets him. And how does he get rid of the body? Drags it to the Canal and dumps it in, of course! Just like an *Alfred Hitchcock Presents!*

The marks he was following *could* have been made by a dragging pair of shoes or sneakers, he supposed.

Mike shivered and looked around uncertainly. The story was somehow a little too real.

And suppose that it wasn't a man who did it but a monster. Like out of a horror comic or a horror book or a horror movie or

(a bad dream)

a fairytale or something.

He decided he didn't like the story. It was a stupid story. He tried to push it out of his mind but it wouldn't go. So what? Let it stay. It was dumb. Riding into town this morning had been dumb. Following these two matted grooves in the grass was dumb. His dad would have a lot of chores for him to do around the place today. He ought to get back and start in or when the hottest part of the afternoon rolled around he would be up the barn loft pitching hay. Yes, he ought to get back. And that's just what he was going to do.

Sure you are, he thought. *Want to bet?*

Instead of going back to his bike and getting on and riding home and starting his chores, he followed the grooves in the grass. There were more drops of drying blood here and there. Not much, though. Not as much as there had been in that matted place back there by the park bench he had set to rights.

Mike could hear the Canal now, running quiet. A moment later he saw the concrete edge materialize out of the fog.

Here was something else in the grass. *My goodness, it's certainly your day for finding things*, his mind said with dubious geniality, and then a gull screamed somewhere and Mike flinched, thinking again of the bird he had seen that day, that day just this spring.

Whatever that is in the grass, I don't even want to look at it. And that was oh so very true, but here he was, already bending over it, hands planted just above his knees, to see what it was.

A tattered bit of cloth with a drop of blood on it.

The seagull screamed again. Mike stared at the bloody scrap of cloth and remembered what had happened to him in the spring.

5

Each year during April and May the Hanlon farm woke up from its winter doze.

Mike would let himself know that spring had come again not when the first crocuses showed under his mom's kitchen windows or when kids started bringing immies and croakers to school or even when the Washington Senators kicked off the baseball season (usually getting themselves shellacked in the process), but only when his father hollered for Mike to help him push their mongrel truck out of the barn. The front half was an old Model-A Ford car, the back end a pick-up truck with a tailgate which was the remainder of the old henhouse door. If the winter hadn't been too cold, the two of them could often get it going by pushing it down the driveway. The truck's cab had no doors; likewise there was no windshield. The seat was half of an old sofa that Will Hanlon had scrounged from the Derry dump. The stick-shift ended in a glass doorknob.

They would push it down the driveway, one on each side, and when it got rolling good, Will would jump in, turn on the switch, retard the spark, step down on the clutch, punch the shift into first gear with his big hand clamped over the doorknob. Then he would holler: 'Put me over the hump!' He'd pop the clutch and the old Ford engine would cough, choke, chug, backfire . . . and sometimes actually start to run, rough at first, then smoothing out. Will would roar down the road toward Rhulin Farms, turn around in their driveway (if he had gone the other way, Henry Bowers's crazy father Butch probably would have blown his head off with a shotgun), and then roar back, the unmuffled engine blatting stridently while Mike jumped up and down with excitement, cheering, and his mom stood in the kitchen doorway, wiping her hands on a dishtowel and pretending a disgust she didn't really feel.

Other times the truck wouldn't roll-start and Mike would have to wait until his father came back from the barn, carrying the crank and muttering under his breath. Mike was quite sure that some of the words so muttered were swears, and he would be a little frightened of his daddy then. (It wasn't until much later, during one of those interminable visits to the hospital room where Will Hanlon lay dying, that he found out his father muttered because he was afraid of the crank: once it had kicked back viciously, flown out of its socket, and torn the side of his mouth open.)

'Stand back, Mikey,' he would say, slipping the crank into its socket at the base of the radiator. And when the A was finally running, he'd say that next year he was going to trade it for a Chevrolet, but he never did. That old A-Ford hybrid was still in back of the home place, up to its axles and henhouse tailgate in weeds.

When it was running, and Mike was sitting in the passenger seat, smelling hot oil and blue exhaust, excited by the keen breeze that washed in through the glassless hole where the windshield had once been, he would think: *Spring's here again. We're all waking up.* And in his soul he would raise a silent cheer that shook the walls of that mostly cheerful room. He felt love for everything around him, and most of all for his dad, who would grin over at him and holler: 'Hold on, Mikey! We gone wind this baby up! We gone make some birds run for cover!'

Then he would tear up the driveway, the A's rear wheels spitting back black dirt and gray clods of clay, both of them jouncing up and down on the sofa-seat inside the open cab, laughing like stark natural-born fools. Will would run the A through the high grass of the back field, which was kept for hay, toward either the south field (potatoes), the west field (corn and beans), or the east field (peas, squash, and pumpkins). As they went, birds would burst up out of the grass before the truck, squawking in terror. Once a partridge flew up, a magnificent bird as brown as late-autumn oaks, the explosive coughing whirr of its wings audible even over the pounding engine.

Those rides were Mike Hanlon's door into spring.

The year's work began with the rock harvest. Every day for a week they would take the A out and load the bed with rocks which might break a harrow-blade when the time came to turn the earth and plant. Sometimes the truck would get stuck in the mucky spring earth and Will would mutter darkly under his breath . . . more swears, Mike surmised. He knew some of the words and expressions; others, such as 'son of a whore,' puzzled him. He had come across the word in the Bible, and so far as he could tell, a whore was a woman who came from a place called Babylon. He had once set out to ask his father, but the A had been in mud up to her coil-springs, there had been thunderclouds on his father's brow, and he had decided to wait for a better time. He ended up asking Richie Tozier later that year and Richie told him *his* father had told him a whore was a woman who got paid for having sex with men. 'What's having sex?' Mike had asked, and Richie had wandered away holding his head.

On one occasion Mike had asked his father why, since they harvested rocks every April, there were always more of them the following April.

They had been standing at the dumping-off place near sunset on the last day of that year's rock harvest. A beaten dirt track, not quite serious enough to be called a road, led from the bottom of the west field to this gully near the bank of the Kenduskeag. The gully was a jumbled wasteland of rocks that had been dragged off Will's land through the years.

Looking down at this badlands, which he had made first alone and then with the help of his son (somewhere under the rocks, he knew, were the rotting remains of the stumps he had yanked out one at a time before any of the fields could be tilled), Will had lighted a cigarette and said, 'My daddy used to tell me that God loved rocks, houseflies, weeds, and poor people above all the rest of His creations, and that's why He made so many of them.'

'But every year it's like they come back.'

'Yeah, I think they do,' Will said. 'That's the only way I know to explain it.'

A loon cried from the far side of the Kenduskeag in a dusky sunset that had turned the water a deep orange-red. It was a lonely sound, so lonely that it made Mike's tired arms tighten with gooseflesh.

'I love you, Daddy,' he said suddenly, feeling his love so strongly that tears stung his eyes.

'Why, I love you too, Mikey,' his father said, and hugged him tight in his strong arms. Mike felt the rough fabric of his father's flannel shirt against his cheek. 'Now what do you say we go on back? We got just time to get a bath each before the good woman puts supper on the table.'

'Ayuh,' Mike said.

'Ayuh yourself,' Will Hanlon said, and they both laughed, feeling tired but feeling good, arms and legs worked but not overworked, their hands rock-roughened but not hurting too bad.

Spring's here, Mike thought that night, drowsing off in his room while his mother and father watched *The Honeymooners* in the other room. *Spring's here again, thank You God, thank You very much.* And turning to sleep, sinking down, he had heard the loon call again, the distance of its marshes blending into the desire of his dreams. Spring was a busy time, but it was a good time.

Following the rock harvest, Will would park the A in the high grass back of the house and drive the tractor out of the barn. There would be harrowing then, his father driving the tractor, Mike either riding behind and holding on to the iron seat or walking alongside, picking up any rocks they had missed and throwing them aside. Then came planting, and following the planting came summer's work: hoeing . . . hoeing . . . hoeing. His mother would refurbish Larry, Moe, and Curly, their three scarecrows, and Mike would help his father put mooseblowers on top of each straw-filled head. A mooseblower was a can with both ends cut off. You tied a length of heavily waxed and rosined string tightly across the middle of the can and when the wind blew through it a wonderfully spooky sound resulted – a kind of whining croak. Crop-eating birds decided soon enough that Larry, Moe, and Curly were no threats, but the mooseblowers always frightened them off.

Starting in July, there was picking as well as hoeing – peas and radishes first, then the lettuce and the tomatoes that had been started in the shed-boxes, then the corn and beans in August, more corn and beans in September, then the pumpkins and the squash. Somewhere in the midst of all that came the new potatoes, and then, as the days shortened and the air sharpened, he and his dad would take in the mooseblowers (and sometime during the winter they would disappear; it seemed they had to make new ones each spring). The day after, Will would call Norman Sadler (who was as dumb as his son Moose but infinitely more goodhearted), and Normie would come over with his potato-digger.

For the next three weeks all of them would work picking potatoes. In addition to the family, Will would hire three or four high-school boys to help pick, paying them a quarter a barrel. The A-Ford would cruise slowly up and down the rows of the south field, the biggest field, always in low gear, the tailgate down, the back filled with barrels, each marked with the name of the person picking into it, and at the end of the day Will would open his old creased wallet and pay each of the pickers cash money. Mike was paid, and so was his mother; that money was theirs, and Will Hanlon never once asked either of them what they did with it. Mike had been given a five-percent interest in the farm when he was five years old – old enough, Will had told him then, to hold a hoe and to tell the difference between witchgrass and pea-plants. Each year he had been given another one percent, and each year, on the day after Thanksgiving, Will would compute the farm's profits and deduct Mike's share . . . but Mike never saw any of *that* money. It went into his college account and was to be touched under absolutely no other circumstances.

At last the day would come when Normie Sadler drove his potato-digger back home; by then the air would have most likely turned gray and cold and there would be frost on the drift of orange pumpkins piled against the side of the barn. Mike would stand in the dooryard, his nose red, his dirty hands stuffed into his jeans pockets, and watch as his father drove first the tractor and then the A-Ford back into the barn. He would think: *We're getting ready to go to sleep again. Spring . . . vanished. Summer . . . gone. Harvest-time . . . done.* All that was left now was the butt end of autumn: leafless trees, frozen ground, a lacing of ice along the banks of the Kenduskeag. In the fields, crows would sometimes land on the shoulders of Moe, Larry, and Curly, and stay as long as they liked. The scarecrows were voiceless, threatless.

Mike would not exactly be dismayed by the thought of another year ending – at nine and ten he was still too young to make mortal metaphors – because there was plenty to look forward to: sledding in McCarron Park (or on Rhulin Hill out here in Derrytown if you were brave, although that was mostly for big kids), ice-skating, snowball fights, snowfort building. There was time to think about snowshoeing out for a Christmas tree with his daddy, and time to think about the Nordica downhill skis he might or might not get for Christmas. Winter was good . . . but watching his father drive the A back into the barn

(*spring vanished summer gone harvest-time done*)

always made him feel sad, the way the squadrons of birds heading south for the winter made him feel sad, or the way a certain slant of light could sometimes make him feel like crying for no good reason. *We're getting ready to go to sleep again . . .*

It was not all school and chores, chores and school; Will Hanlon had told his wife more than once that a boy needed time to go fishing, even if it wasn't fishing he was really doing. When Mike came home from school he first put his books on the TV in the parlor, second made himself some kind of snack (he was particularly partial to peanut-butter-and-onion sandwiches, a taste that made his mother raise her hands in helpless horror), and third studied the note his father had left him, telling Mike where he, Will, was and what Mike's chores were – certain rows to be weeded or picked, baskets to be carried, produce to be rotated, the barn to be swept, whatever. But on at least one schoolday a week – and sometimes two – there would be no note. And on these days Mike would go fishing, even if it wasn't really fishing he was doing. Those were great days . . . days when he had no particular place to go and consequently felt no urge to get there in a hurry.

Once in awhile his father left him another sort of note: 'No chores,' one might say. 'Go over to Old Cape & look at trolley tracks.' Mike would go over to the Old Cape area, find the streets with the tracks still embedded in them, and inspect them closely, marvelling to think of things like trains that had run right through the middle of the streets. That night he and his father might talk about them, and his dad would show him pictures from his Derry album of the trolleys actually running: a funny pole went from the roof of the trolley up to an electrical wire, and there were cigarette ads on the side. Another time he had sent Mike to Memorial Park, where the Standpipe was, to look at the birdbath, and once they had gone to the courthouse together to look at a terrible machine that Chief Borton had found in the attic. This gadget was called a tramp-chair. It was cast-iron, and there were manacles built into the arms and legs. Rounded knobs stuck out of the back and seat. It reminded Mike of a photograph he had seen in some book – a photograph of the electric chair at Sing Sing. Chief Borton let Mike sit in the tramp-chair and try on the manacles.

After the first ominous novelty of wearing the manacles wore off, Mike looked questioningly at his father and Chief Borton, not sure why this was supposed to be such a horrible punishment for the 'vags' (Borton's word for them) that had drifted into town in the twenties and thirties. The knobs made the chair a little uncomfortable to sit in, sure, and the manacles on your wrists and ankles made it hard to shift to a more comfortable position, but –

'Well, you're just a kid,' Chief Borton said, laughing. 'What do you weigh? Seventy, eighty pounds? Most of the vags Sheriff Sully posted into that chair in the old days would go twice that. They'd feel a bit oncomfortable after an hour or so, really oncomfortable after two or three, and right bad after four or five. After seven or eight hours they'd staat bellerin, and after sixteen or seventeen they'd staat cryin, mostly. And by the time their twenty-four-hour tour was up, they'd be willin to swear before God and man that the next time they came riding the rods up New England way they'd give Derry a wide berth. So far as I know, most of em did. Twenty-four hours in the tramp-chair was a helluva persuader.'

Suddenly there seemed to be more knobs in the chair, digging more deeply into his buttocks, spine, the small of his back, even the nape of his neck. 'Can I get out now, please?' he said politely, and Chief Borton laughed again. There was a moment, one panicked instant of time, when Mike thought the Chief would only dangle the key to the manacles in front of Mike's eyes and say, *Sure I'll let you out . . . when your twenty-four hours is up.*

'Why did you take me there, Daddy?' he asked on the way home.

'You'll know when you're older,' Will had replied.

'You don't like Chief Borton, do you?'

'No,' his father had replied in a voice so curt that Mike hadn't dared ask any more.

But Mike enjoyed most of the places in Derry his father sent or took him to, and by the time Mike was ten Will had succeeded in conveying his own interest in the layers of Derry's history to his son. Sometimes, as when he had been trailing his fingers over the slightly pebbled surface of the stand in which the Memorial Park birdbath was set, or when he had squatted down to look more closely at the trolley tracks which grooved Mont Street in the Old Cape, he would be struck by a profound sense of time . . . time as something real, as something that had unseen weight, the way sunlight was supposed to have weight (some of the kids in school had laughed when Mrs Greenguss told them that, but Mike had been too stunned by the concept to laugh; his first thought had been, *Light has* weight? *Oh my Lord, that's* terrible!) . . . time as something that would eventually bury him.

The first note his father left him in that spring of 1958 was scribbled on the back of an envelope and held down with a salt-shaker. The air was spring-warm, wonderfully sweet, and his mother had opened all the windows. *No chores,* the note read. *If you want to, ride your bike out to Pasture Road. You'll see a lot of tumbled masonry and old machinery out in the field on your left. Have a look around, bring back a souvenir. Don't go near the cellarhole! And be back before dark. You know why.*

Mike knew why, all right.

He told his mother where he was going and she frowned. 'Why don't you see if Randy Robinson wants to go with you?'

'Yeah, okay, I'll stop by and ask him,' Mike said.

He did, too, but Randy had gone up to Bangor with his father to buy seedling potatoes. So Mike rode his bike over to Pasture Road alone. It was a goodish ride – a little over four miles. Mike reckoned it was three o'clock by the time he leaned his bike against an old wooden slat-fence on the left side of Pasture Road and climbed into the field beyond. He would have maybe an hour to explore and then he would have to start home again. Ordinarily, his mother would not be upset with him as long as he was back by six, when she put dinner on the table, but one memorable episode had taught him that wasn't the case this year. On that one occasion when he had been late for dinner, she had been nearly hysterical. She took after him with a dishrag, whopping him with it as he stood open-mouthed in the kitchen entryway, his wicker creel with the rainbow trout in it at his feet.

'Don't you *ever* scare me like that!' she had screamed. 'Don't you *ever*! Don't you *ever*! *Ever-ever-ever!*'

Each *ever* had been punctuated by another dishrag swat. Mike had expected his father to step in and put a stop to it, but his father hadn't done so . . . Perhaps he knew that if he did she would turn her wildcat anger on him as well. Mike had learned the lesson; one whopping with the dishrag was all it took. Home before dark. Yes ma'am, right-o.

He walked across the field toward the titanic ruins standing in the center. This was, of course, the remains of the Kitchener Ironworks – he had ridden past it but had never thought to actually explore it, and he had never heard any kids saying that they had. Now, stooping to examine a few tumbled bricks that had formed a rough cairn, he thought he could understand why. The field was dazzlingly bright, washed by sun from the spring sky (occasionally, as a cloud passed before the sun, a great shutter of shadow would travel slowly across the field), but there was something spooky about it all the same – a brooding silence that was broken only by the wind. He felt like an explorer who has found the last remnants of some fabulous lost city.

Up ahead and to the right, he saw the rounded side of a massive tile cylinder rising out of the high field grass. He ran over to it. It was the Ironworks' main smokestack. He peered into its bore, and felt a fresh chill worm up his spine. It was big enough so he could have walked into it if he had wanted. But he didn't want to; God knew what strange guck there might be, clinging to the smoke-blackened inner tiles, or what nasty bugs or beasts might have taken up residence inside. The wind gusted. When it blew across the mouth of the fallen stack it made a sound eerily like the sound of the wind vibrating the waxed strings he and his dad put in the mooseblowers every spring. He stepped back nervously, suddenly thinking about the movie he and his father had watched last night on the *Early Show*. It had been called

Rodan, and watching it had seemed like great fun at the time, his father laughing and shouting 'Git that bird, Mikey!' every time Rodan made its appearance, Mike shooting with his finger until his mom popped her head in and told them to hush up before they gave her a headache with the noise.

It didn't seem so funny now. In the movie Rodan had been released from the bowels of the earth by these Japanese coal-miners who had been digging the world's deepest tunnel. And looking into the black bore of this pipe, it was all too easy to imagine that bird crouched at the far end, leathery batlike wings folded over its back, staring at the small, round boyface looking into the darkness, staring, staring with its gold-ringed eyes . . .

Shivering, Mike pulled back.

He walked aways down the smokestack, which had sunken into the earth to half of its circumference. The land rose slightly, and on impulse he scrambled his way up on top. The stack was a lot less scary on the outside, its tiled surface sunwarm. He got to his feet and strolled along, holding his arms out (the surface was really too wide for him to need to worry about falling off, but he was pretending he was a tightwire-walker in the circus), liking the way the wind blew through his hair.

At the far end he jumped down and began to examine stuff: more bricks, twisted molds, hunks of wood, pieces of rusty machinery. *Bring back a souvenir*, his father's note had said: he wanted a good one.

He wandered closer to the mill's yawning cellarhold, looking at the debris, being careful not to cut himself on the broken glass. There was a lot of it around.

Mike was not unmindful of the cellarhold and his father's warning to stay out of it; neither was he unmindful of the death that had been dealt out on this spot fifty-odd years before. He supposed that if there was a haunted place in Derry, this was it. But either in spite of that or because of it, he was determined to stay until he found something really good to take back and show his father.

He moved slowly and soberly toward the cellarhold, changing his course to parallel its ragged side, when a warning voice inside whispered that he was getting too close, that a bank weakened by the spring rains could crumble under his heels and pitch him into that hole, where God only knew how much sharp iron might be waiting to impale him like a bug, leaving him to die a rusty twitching death.

He picked up a window-sash and tossed it aside. Here was a dipper big enough for a giant's table, its handle rippled and warped by some unimaginable flash of heat. Here was a piston too big for him to even budge, let alone lift. He stepped over it. He stepped over it and –

What if I find a skull? he thought suddenly. *The skull of one of the kids who were killed here while they were hunting for chocolate Easter eggs back in nineteen-whenever-it-was?*

He looked around the sunwashed empty field, nastily shocked by the idea. The wind blew a low conch-note in his ears and another shadow cruised silently across the field, like the shadow of a giant bat . . . or bird. He became aware all over again of how quiet it was here, and how strange the field looked with its straggling piles of masonry and its beached iron hulks leaning this way and that. It was as if some horrid battle had been fought here long ago.

Don't be such a dip, he replied uneasily to himself. *They found everything there was to find fifty years ago. After it happened. And even if they didn't, some other kid – or grownup – would have found . . . the rest . . . since then. Or do you think you're the only person who ever came here hunting for souvenirs?*

No . . . no, I don't think that. But . . .

But what? that rational side of his mind demanded, and Mike thought it was talking just a little too loud, a little too fast. *Even if there was still something to find, it would have decayed long ago. So . . . what?*

Mike found a splintered desk drawer in the weeds. He glanced at it, tossed it aside, and moved a little closer to the cellarhold, where the stuff was thickest. Surely he would find something there.

But what if there are ghosts? That's but what. What if I see hands coming over the edge of that cellarhold, and what if they start to come up, kids in the remains of their Easter Sunday clothes, clothes that are all rotted and torn and marked with fifty years of spring mud and fall rain and caked winter snow? Kids with no heads (he had heard at school that, after the explosion, a woman had found the head of one of the victims in a tree in her back yard), *kids with no legs, kids flayed open like codfish, kids just like me who would maybe come down and play . . . down there where it's dark . . . under the leaning iron girders and the big old rusty cogs . . .*

Oh, stop it, for the Lord's sake!

But a shudder wrenched its way up his back and he decided it was time to take something – anything – and get the dickens out of here. He reached down, almost at random, and came up with a gear-toothed wheel about seven inches in diameter. He had a pencil in his pocket and he used it, quickly, to dig the dirt out of the teeth. Then he slipped his souvenir in his pocket. He would go now. He would go, yes –

But his feet moved slowly in the wrong direction, toward the cellarhold, and he realized with a dismal sort of horror that he needed to look down inside. He had to *see*.

He gripped a spongy support-beam leaning out of the earth and swayed forward, trying to see down and inside. He couldn't quite do it. He had come to within fifteen feet of the edge, but that was still a little too far to see the bottom of the cellarhold.

I don't care if I see the bottom or not. I'm going back now. I've got my souvenir. I don't need to look down into any crummy old hole. And Daddy's note said to stay away from it.

But the unhappy, almost feverish curiosity that had gripped him would not let go. He approached the cellarhold step by queasy step, aware that as soon as the wooden beam was out of his reach there would be no more grab-holds, also aware that the ground here was indeed squelchy and crumbly. In places along the edge he could see depressions, like graves that had fallen in, and knew that they were the sites of previous cave-ins.

Heart thudding in his chest like the hard measured strides of a soldier's boots, he reached the edge and looked down.

Nested in the cellarhold, the bird looked up.

Mike was not at first sure what he was seeing. All the nerves and pathways in his body seemed frozen, including those which conducted thoughts. It was not just the shock of seeing a monster bird, a bird whose breast was as orange as a robin's and whose feathers were the unremarkable fluffy gray of a sparrow's feathers; most of it was the shock of the utterly unexpected. He had expected monoliths of machinery half-submerged in stagnant puddles and black mud; instead he was looking down into a giant nest which filled the cellarhold from end to end and side to side. It had been made out of enough timothy grass to make a dozen bales of hay, but this grass was silvery and old. The bird sat in the middle of it, its brightly ringed eyes as black as fresh, warm tar, and for an insane moment before his paralysis broke, Mike could see himself reflected in each of them.

Then the ground suddenly began to shift and run out from beneath his feet. He heard the tearing sound of shallow roots giving way and realized he was sliding.

With a yell he threw himself backward, pinwheeling his arms for balance. He lost it and thumped heavily to the littered ground. Some hard, dull chunk of metal pressed painfully into his back, and he had time to think of the tramp-chair before he heard the whirring, explosive sound of the bird's wings.

He scrambled to his knees, crawled, looked back over his shoulder, and saw it rising out of the cellarhold. Its scaly talons were a dusky orange. Its beating wings, each more than ten feet across, blew the scraggy timothy grass this way and that, patternlessly, like the wind generated by helicopter rotors. It uttered a buzzing, chirruping scream. A few loose feathers slipped from its wings and spiraled back down into the cellarhold.

Mike gained his feet again and began to run.

He pounded across the field, not looking back now, afraid to look back. The bird did not *look* like Rodan, but he sensed it was the *spirit* of Rodan, risen from the cellarhold of the Kitchener Ironworks like a horrible bird-in-the-box. He stumbled, went to one knee, got up, and ran on.

That weird chirruping buzzing screech came again. A shadow covered him and when he looked up he saw the thing: it had passed less than five feet over his head. Its beak, dirty yellow, opened and closed, revealing a pink lining inside. It whirled back toward Mike. The wind it generated washed across his face, bringing a dry unpleasant smell with it: attic dust, dead antiques, rotting cushions.

He jigged to his left, and now he saw the fallen smokestack again. He sprinted for it, running all-out, his arms pumping in short jabbing strokes at his sides. The bird screamed, and he heard its fluttering wings. They sounded like sails. Something slammed into the back of his head. Warm fire traced its way up the nape of his neck. He felt it spread as blood began to trickle down the back of his shirt-collar.

The bird whirled around again, meaning to pick him up with its talons and carry him away like a hawk with a fieldmouse. Meaning to carry him back to its nest. Meaning to eat him.

As it flew at him, swooping down, its black, horribly *alive* eyes fixed on him, Mike cut sharply right. The bird missed him – barely. The dusty smell of its wings was overpowering, unbearable.

Now he was running parallel to the fallen smokestack, its tiles blurring by. He could see where it ended. If he could reach the end and buttonhook to the left, get inside, he might be safe. He thought the bird was too big to squeeze inside. He came very close to not making it. The bird flew at him again, pulling up as it closed in, its wings flapping and pushing air in a hurricane, its scaly talons now angled toward him and descending. It screamed again, and this time Mike thought he heard triumph in its voice.

He lowered his head, put his arm up, and rammed straight forward. The talons closed and for a moment the bird had him by the forearm. The grip was like the clutch of incredibly strong fingers tipped with tough nails. They bit like teeth. The bird's flapping wings were a thunder in his ears; he was dimly aware of feathers falling around him, some brushing past his cheeks like phantom kisses. The bird rose then, and for just a moment Mike felt himself pulled upward, first straight, then on tiptoe . . . and for one freezing second he felt the toes of his Keds lose contact with the earth.

'*Let me GO!*' he screamed at it, and twisted his arm. For a moment the talons held on, and then the sleeve of his shirt ripped. He thumped back down. The bird squalled. Mike ran again, brushing through the thing's tailfeathers, gagging at that dry smell. It was like running through a shower-curtain of feathers.

Still coughing, eyes stinging from both tears and whatever vile dust coated the bird's feathers, he stumbled into the fallen smoke-stack. There was no thought now of what might be lurking inside. He ran into the darkness, his gasping sobs taking on a flat echo. He went back perhaps twenty feet and then turned toward the bright circle of daylight. His chest was rising and falling in quick jerks. He was suddenly aware that, if he had misjudged either the size of the bird or the size of the smokestack's muzzle, he had killed himself as surely as if he had put his father's shotgun to his head and pulled the trigger. There was no way out. This wasn't just a pipe; it was a blind alley. The other end of the stack was buried in the earth.

The bird squalled again, and suddenly the light at the end of the smokestack was blotted out as it lighted on the ground outside. He could see its yellow scaly legs, each as thick as a man's calfs. Then it cocked its head down and looked inside. Mike found himself again staring into those hideously bright fresh-tar eyes with their gold wedding-rings of iris. The bird's beak opened and closed, opened and closed, and each time it snapped shut he heard an audible click, like the sound you hear in your own ears when you snap your teeth together hard. *Sharp*, he thought. *Its beak is sharp. I guess I knew birds had sharp beaks, but I never really thought about it until now.*

It squawked again. The sound was so loud in the tile throat of the stack that Mike clapped his hands to his ears.

The bird began to force itself into the mouth of the stack.

'No!' Mike cried. 'No, you can't!'

The light faded as more of the bird's body pressed its way into the stack's bore (*Oh my Lord, why didn't I remember it was mostly feathers? Why didn't I remember it could* squeeze?). The light faded . . . faded . . . was gone. Now there was only an inky blackness, the suffocating attic-smell of the bird, and the rustling sound of its feathers.

Mike fell on his knees and began to grope on the curved floor of the smokestack, his hands spread wide, feeling. He found a piece of broken tile, its sharp edges furred with what felt like moss. He cocked his arm back and pegged it. There was a thump. The bird uttered its buzzing, chirruping sound again.

'Get *out* of here!' Mike screamed.

There was silence . . . and then that crackly, rustling sound began again as the bird resumed forcing itself into the pipe. Mike felt along the floor, found other pieces of tile, and began to throw one after another. They thumped and thudded off the bird and then clinked to the tile sleeve of the smokestack.

Please, God, Mike thought incoherently. *Please God, please God, please God —*

It came to him that he ought to retreat down the smokestack's bore. He had run in through what had been the stack's base; it stood to reason that it would narrow as he backed up. He could retreat, yes, and listen to that low dusty rustle as the bird worked its way in after him. He could retreat, and if he was lucky he might get beyond the point where the bird could continue to advance.

But what if the bird got stuck?

If that happened, he and the bird would die in here together. They would die in here together and rot in here together. In the dark.

'*Please, God!*' he screamed, and was totally unaware that he had cried out aloud. He threw another piece of tile, and this time his throw was more powerful – he felt, he told the others much later, as if *someone* were behind him at that moment, and that *someone* had given his arm a tremendous push. This time there was no feathery thud; instead there was a splatting sound, the sound a kid's hand might make slapping into the surface of a bowl of half-solidified Jell-O. This time the bird screamed not in anger but in real pain. The tenebrous whirr of its wings filled the smokestack; stinking air streamed past Mike in a hurricane, flapping his clothes, making him cough and gag and retreat as dust and moss flew.

Light appeared again, gray and weak at first, then brightening and shifting as the bird retreated from the stack's muzzle. Mike burst into tears, fell to his knees again, and began grubbing madly for more pieces of tile. Without any conscious thought, he ran forward with both hands full of tiling (in this light he could see the pieces were splotched with blue-gray moss and lichen, like the surface of slate gravestones), until he was nearly at the mouth of the stack. He intended to keep the bird from coming back in if he could.

It bent down, cocking its head the way a trained bird on a perch will sometimes cock its head, and Mike saw where his last shot had struck home. The bird's right eye was nearly gone. Instead of that glittering bubble of fresh tar, there was a crater filled with blood. Whitish-gray goo dripped from the corner of the socket and trickled along the side of the bird's beak. Tiny parasites wriggled and squirmed in this pussy discharge.

It saw him and lunged forward. Mike began to throw chunks of tile at it. They struck its head and beak. It withdrew for a moment and then lunged again, beak opening, revealing that pink lining again, revealing something else that caused Mike to freeze for a moment, his own mouth dropping open. The bird's tongue was silver, its surface as crazy-cracked as the surface of a volcanic land which has first baked and then slagged off.

And on this tongue, like weird tumbleweeds that had taken temporary root there, were a number of orange puffs.

Mike threw the last of his tiles directly into that gaping maw and the bird withdrew again, screaming its frustration, rage, and pain. For a moment Mike could see its reptilian talons . . . Then its wings ruffled the air and it was gone.

A moment later he lifted his face — a face that was gray-brown under the dirt, dust, and bits of moss that the bird's wind-machine wings had blown at him — toward the clicking sound of its talons on the tile. The only clean places on Mike's face were the tracks that had been washed clean by his tears.

The bird walked back and forth overhead: *Tak-tak-tak-tak.*

Mike retreated a bit, gathered up more chunks of tile, and heaped them as close to the mouth of the stack as he dared. If the thing came back, he wanted to be able to fire at it from point-blank range. The light outside was still bright — now that it was May, it wouldn't get dark for a long time yet — but suppose the bird just decided to wait?

Mike swallowed, the dry sides of his throat rubbing together for a moment.

Overhead: *Tak-tak-tak.*

He had a fine pile of ammunition now. In the dim light, here beyond the place where the angle of the sun made a shadow-spiral inside the pipe, it looked like a pile of broken crockery swept together by a housewife. Mike rubbed the palms of his dirty hands along the sides of his jeans and waited to see what would happen next.

A space of time passed before something did – whether five minutes or twenty-five, he could not tell. He was only aware of the bird walking back and forth overhead like an insomniac pacing the floor at three in the morning.

Then its wings fluttered again. It landed in front of the smoke-stack's opening. Mike, on his knees just behind his pile of tiling, began to peg missiles at it before it could even bend its head down. One of them slammed into a plated yellow leg and drew a trickle of blood so dark it seemed almost as black as the bird's eyes. Mike screamed in triumph, the sound thin and almost lost under the bird's own enraged squawk.

'*Get out of here!*' Mike cried. '*I'm going to keep hitting you until you get out of here, I swear to God I will!*'

The bird flew up to the top of the smokestack and resumed its pacing.

Mike waited.

Finally its wings ruffled again as it took off. Mike waited, expecting the yellow feet, so like hen's feet, to appear again. They didn't. He waited longer, convinced it had to be some kind of a trick, realizing at last that that wasn't why he was waiting at all. He was waiting because he was scared to go out, scared to leave the safety of this bolthole.

Never mind! Never mind stuff like that! I'm not a rabbit!

He took as many chunks of tile as he could handle comfortably, then put some more inside his shirt. He stepped out of the smoke-stack, trying to look everywhere at once and wishing madly for eyes in the back of his head. He saw only the field stretching ahead and around him, littered with the exploded rusting remains of the Kitchener Ironworks. He wheeled around, sure he would see the bird perched on the lip of the stack like a vulture, a one-eyed vulture now, only wanting the boy to see him before it attacked for the final time, using that sharp beak to jab and rip and strip.

But the bird was not there.

It was really gone.

Mike's nerve snapped.

He uttered a breaking scream of fear and ran for the weather-beaten fence between the field and the road, dropping the last pieces of tile from his hands. Most of the others fell out of his shirt as the shirt pulled free of his belt. He vaulted over the fence one-handed, like Roy

Rogers showing off for Dale Evans on his way back from the corral with Pat Brady and the rest of the buckaroos. He grabbed the handlebars of his bike and ran beside it forty feet up the road before getting on. Then he pedaled madly, not daring to look back, not daring to slow down, until he reached the intersection of Pasture Road and Outer Main Street, where there were lots of cars passing back and forth.

When he got home, his father was changing the plugs on the tractor. Will observed that Mike looked powerful musty and dusty. Mike hesitated for just a split second and then told his father that he'd taken a tumble from his bike on the way home, swerving to avoid a pothole.

'Did you break anything, Mikey?' Will asked, observing his son a little more carefully.

'No, sir.'

'Sprains?'

'Huh-uh.'

'Sure?'

Mike nodded.

'Did you pick yourself up a souvenir?'

Mike reached into his pocket and found the gear-wheel. He showed it to his father, who looked at it briefly and then plucked a tiny crumb of tiling from the pad of flesh just below Mike's thumb. He seemed more interested in this.

'From that old smokestack?' Will asked.

Mike nodded.

'You go inside there?'

Mike nodded again.

'See anything in there?' Will asked, and then, as if to make a joke of the question (which hadn't sounded like a joke at all), he added: 'Buried treasure?'

Smiling a little, Mike shook his head.

'Well, don't tell your mother you was muckin about in there,' Will said. 'She'd shoot me first and you second.' He looked even more closely at his son. 'Mikey, *are* you all right?'

'Huh?'

'You look a little peaky around the eyes.'

'I guess I might be a little tired,' Mike said. 'It's eight or ten miles there and back again, don't forget. You want some help with the tractor, Daddy?'

'No, I'm about done screwing it up for this week. You go on in and wash up.'

266

Mike started away, and then his father called to him once more. Mike looked back.

'I don't want you going around that place again,' he said, 'at least not until all this trouble is cleared up and they catch the man who's doing it . . . you didn't see anybody out there, did you? No one chased you, or hollered you down?'

'I didn't see any people at all,' Mike said.

Will nodded and lit a cigarette. 'I think I was wrong to send you there. Old places like that . . . sometimes they can be dangerous.'

Their eyes locked briefly.

'Okay, Daddy,' Mike said. 'I don't want to go back anyway. It was a little spooky.'

Will nodded again. 'Less said the better, I reckon. You go and get cleaned up now. And tell her to put on three or four extra sausages.'

Mike did.

6

Never mind that now, Mike Hanlon thought, looking at the grooves which went up to the concrete edge of the Canal and stopped there. *Never mind that, it might just have been a dream anyhow*, and –

There were splotches of dried blood on the lip of the Canal.

Mike looked at these, and then he looked down into the Canal. Black water flowed smoothly past. Runners of dirty yellow foam clung to the Canal's sides, sometimes breaking free to flow downstream in lazy loops and curves. For a moment – just a moment – two clots of this foam came together and seemed to form a face, a kid's face, its eyes turned up in an avatar of terror and agony.

Mike's breath caught, as if on a thorn.

The foam broke apart, became meaningless again, and at that moment there was a loud splash on his right. Mike snapped his head around, shrinking back a little, and for a moment he believed he saw something in the shadows of the outflow tunnel where the Canal resurfaced after its course under downtown.

Then it was gone.

Suddenly, cold and shuddering, he dug in his pocket for the knife he had found in the grass. He threw it into the Canal. There was a small splash, a ripple that began as a circle and was then tugged into the shape of an arrowhead by the current . . . then nothing.

Nothing except the fear that was suddenly suffocating him and the deadly certainty that there was something near, something watching him, gauging its chances, biding its time.

He turned, meaning to walk back to his bike – to run would be to dignify those fears and undignify himself – and then that splashing sound came again. It was a lot louder this second time. So much for dignity. Suddenly he was running as fast as he could, beating his buns for the gate and his bike, jamming the kickstand up with one heel and pedaling for the street as fast as he could. That sea-smell was all at once too thick . . . *much* too thick. It was everywhere. And the water dripping from the wet branches of the trees seemed much too loud.

Something was coming. He heard dragging, lurching footsteps in the grass.

He stood on the pedals, giving it everything, and shot out onto Main Street without looking back. He headed for home as fast as he could, wondering what in hell had possessed him to come in the first place . . . what had drawn him.

And then he tried to think about the chores, the whole chores, and nothing but the chores. After awhile he actually succeeded.

And when he saw the headline in the paper the next day (MISSING BOY PROMPTS NEW FEARS), he thought about the pocket knife he had thrown into the Canal – the pocket knife with the initials EC scratched on the side. He thought about the blood he had seen on the grass.

And he thought about those grooves which stopped at the edge of the Canal.

CHAPTER SEVEN
THE DAM IN THE BARRENS

1

Seen from the expressway at quarter to five in the morning, Boston seems a city of the dead brooding over some tragedy in its past – a plague, perhaps, or a curse. The smell of salt, heavy and cloying, comes off the ocean. Runners of early-morning fog obscure much of what movement would be seen otherwise.

Driving north along Storrow Drive, sitting behind the wheel of the black '84 Cadillac he picked up from Butch Carrington at Cape Cod Limousine, Eddie Kaspbrak thinks you can feel this city's age; perhaps you can get that feeling of age nowhere else in America but here. Boston is a sprat compared with London, an infant compared with Rome, but by American standards at least it is old, old. It kept its place on these low hills three hundred years ago, when the Tea and Stamp Taxes were unthought of, Paul Revere and Patrick Henry unborn.

Its age, its silence, and the foggy smell of the sea – all of these things make Eddie nervous. When Eddie's nervous he reaches for his aspirator. He sticks it in his mouth and triggers a cloud of revivifying spray down his throat.

There are a few people in the streets he's passing, and a pedestrian or two on the walkways of the overpasses – they give lie to the impression that he has somehow wandered into a Lovecrafty tale of doomed cities, ancient evils, and monsters with unpronounceable names. Here, ganged around a bus stop with a sign reading KENMORE SQUARE CITY CENTER, *he sees waitresses, nurses, city employees, their faces naked and puffed with sleep.*

That's right, Eddie thinks, *now passing under a sign which reads* TOBIN BRIDGE. *That's right, stick to the buses. Forget the subways. The subways are a bad idea; I wouldn't go down there if I were you. Not down below. Not in the tunnels.*

This is a bad thought to have; if he doesn't get rid of it he will soon be using the aspirator again. He's glad for the heavier traffic on the Tobin

269

Bridge. He passes a monument works. Painted on the brick side is a slightly unsettling admonishment: SLOW DOWN! WE CAN WAIT!

Here is a green reflectorized sign which reads TO 95 MAINE, N.H., ALL NORTHERN NEW ENGLAND POINTS. He looks at it and suddenly a bone-deep shudder wracks his body. His hands momentarily weld themselves to the wheel of the Cadillac. He would like to believe it is the onset of some sickness, a virus or perhaps one of his mother's 'phantom fevers,' but he knows better. It is the city behind him, poised silently on the straight-edge that runs between day and night, and what that sign promises ahead of him. He's sick, all right, no doubt about that, but it's not a virus or a phantom fever. He has been poisoned by his own memories.

I'm scared, *Eddie thinks.* That was always what was at the bottom of it. Just being scared. That was everything. But in the end I think we turned that around somehow. We used it. But how?

He can't remember. He wonders if any of the others can. For all their sakes he certainly hopes so.

A truck drones by on his left. Eddie has still got his lights on and now he hits his brights momentarily as the truck draws safely ahead. He does this without thinking. It has become an automatic function, just part of driving for a living. The unseen driver in the truck flashes his running lights in return, quickly, twice, thanking Eddie for his courtesy. If only everything could be that simple and that clear, *he thinks.*

He follows the signs to 1-95. The northbound traffic is light, although he observes that the southbound lanes into the city are starting to fill up, even at this early hour. Eddie floats the big car along, pre-guessing most of the directional signs and getting into the correct lane long before he has to. It has been years — literally years — since he has guessed wrong enough to be swept past an exit he wanted. He makes his lane-choices as automatically as he flashed 'okay to cut back in' to the trucker, as automatically as he once found his way through the tangle of paths in the Derry Barrens. The fact that he has never before in his life driven out of downtown Boston, one of the most confusing cities in America to drive in, does not seem to matter much at all.

He suddenly remembers something else about that summer, something Bill said to him one day: 'Y-You've g-got a c-c-cuh-hompass in your head, E-E-Eddie.'

How that had pleased him! It pleases him again as the '84 'Dorado shoots back onto the turnpike. He slides the limo's speed up to a cop-safe fifty-seven miles an hour and finds some quiet music on the radio. He supposes he would have died for Bill back then, if that had been required; if Bill had asked him, Eddie would simply have responded: 'Sure, Big Bill . . . you got a time in mind yet?'

Eddie laughs at this – not much of a sound, just a snort, but the sound of it startles him into a real laugh. He laughs seldom these days, and he certainly did not expect to find many chucks (Richie's word, meaning chuckles, as in 'You had any good chucks today, Eds?') on this black pilgrimage. But, he supposes, if God is dirty-mean enough to curse the faithful with what they want most in life, He's maybe quirky enough to deal you a good chuck or two along the way.

'Had any good chucks lately, Eds?' he says out loud, and laughs again. Man, he had hated it when Richie called him Eds . . . but he had sort of liked it, too. The way he thought Ben Hanscom got to like Richie calling him Haystack. It was something . . . like a secret name. A secret identity. A way to be people that had nothing to do with their parents' fears, hopes, constant demands. Richie couldn't do his beloved Voices for shit, but maybe he did know how important it was for creeps like them to sometimes be different people.

Eddie glances at the change lined up neatly on the 'Dorado's dashboard – lining up the change is another of those automatic tricks of the trade. When the tollbooths come up, you never want to have to dig for your silver, never want to find that you've gotten in an automatic-toll lane with the wrong change.

Among the coins are two or three Susan B. Anthony silver dollars. They are coins, he reflects, that you probably only find in the pockets of chauffeurs and taxi-drivers from the New York area these days, just as the only place you are apt to see a lot of two-dollar bills is at a race-track payoff window. He always keeps a few on hand because the robot tolltaker baskets on the George Washington and the Triboro Bridges take them.

Another of those lights suddenly comes on in his head: silver dollars. Not these fake copper sandwiches but real silver dollars, with Lady Liberty dressed in her gauzy robes stamped upon them. Ben Hanscom's silver dollars. Yes, but wasn't it Bill who once used one of those silver cartwheels to save their lives? He is not quite sure of this, is, in fact, not quite sure of anything . . . or is it just that he doesn't want to remember?

It was dark in there, *he thinks suddenly.* I remember that much. It was dark in there.

Boston is well behind him now and the fog is starting to burn off. Ahead is MAINE, N.H., ALL NORTHERN NEW ENGLAND POINTS. *Derry is ahead, and there is something in Derry which should be twenty-seven years dead and yet is somehow not. Something with as many faces as Lon Chaney. But what is it really? Didn't they see it at the end as it really was, with all its masks cast aside?*

Ah, he can remember so much . . . but not enough.

He remembers that he loved Bill Denbrough; he remembers that well enough. Bill never made fun of his asthma. Bill never called him little sissy queerboy. He loved Bill like he would have loved a big brother . . . or a father. Bill knew stuff to do. Places to go. Things to see. Bill was never up against it. When you ran with Bill you ran to beat the devil and you laughed . . . but you hardly ever ran out of breath. And hardly ever running out of breath was great, so fucking great, Eddie would tell the world. When you ran with Big Bill, you got your chucks every day.

'Sure, kid, EV-ery day,' he says in a Richie Tozier Voice, and laughs again.

It had been Bill's idea to make the dam in the Barrens, and it was, in a way, the dam that had brought them all together. Ben Hanscom had been the one to show them how the dam could be built – and they had built it so well that they'd gotten in a lot of trouble with Mr Nell, the cop on the beat – but it had been Bill's idea. And although all of them except Richie had seen very odd things – frightening things – in Derry since the turn of the year, it had been Bill who had first found the courage to say something out loud.

That dam.

That damn dam.

He remembered Victor Criss: 'Ta-ta, boys. It was a real baby dam, believe me. You're better off without it.'

A day later, Ben Hanscom was grinning at them, saying:

'We could

'We could flood

'We could flood out the

2

whole Barrens, if we wanted to.'

Bill and Eddie looked at Ben doubtfully, and then at the stuff Ben had brought along with him: some boards (scrounged from Mr McKibbon's back yard, but that was okay, since Mr McKibbon had probably scavenged them from someone else's), a sledge hammer, a shovel.

'I dunno,' Eddie said, glancing at Bill. 'When we tried yesterday, it didn't work very good. The current kept washing our sticks away.'

'This'll work,' Ben said. He also looked to Bill for the final decision.

'Well, let's g-give it a t-t-try,' Bill said. 'I c-called R–R–R-Richie Tozier this m-morning. He's g-gonna be oh-over l-later, he s-said. Maybe him and Stuh-huh-hanley will want to h-help.'

'Stanley who?' Ben asked.

'Uris,' Eddie said. He was still looking cautiously at Bill, who seemed somehow different today – quieter, less enthusiastic about the idea of the dam. Bill looked pale today. Distant.

'Stanley Uris? I guess I don't know him. Does he go to Derry Elementary?'

'He's our age but he just finished the fourth grade,' Eddie said. 'He started school a year late because he was sick a lot when he was a little kid. You think *you* took chong yesterday, you just oughtta be glad you're not Stan. Someone's always rackin Stan to the dogs an back.'

'He's Juh-juh-hooish,' Bill said. 'Luh-lots of k-kids don't luh-hike him because h-he's Jewish.'

'Oh yeah?' Ben asked, impressed. 'Jewish, huh?' He paused and then said carefully: 'Is that like being Turkish, or is it more like, you know, Egyptian?'

'I g-guess it's more like Tur-hur-hurkish,' Bill said. He picked up one of the boards Ben had brought and looked at it. It was about six feet long and three feet wide. 'My d-d-dad says most J-Jews have big nuh-noses and lots of m-m-money, but Stuh-Stuh-Stuh –'

'But Stan's got a regular nose and he's always broke,' Eddie said.

'Yeah,' Bill said, and broke into a real grin for the first time that day.

Ben grinned.

Eddie grinned.

Bill tossed the board aside, got up and brushed off the seat of his jeans. He walked to the edge of the stream and the other two boys joined him. Bill shoved his hands in his back pockets and sighed deeply. Eddie was sure Bill was going to say something serious. He looked from Eddie to Ben and then back to Eddie again, not smiling now. Eddie was suddenly afraid.

But all Bill said then was, 'You got your ah-ah-aspirator, E-Eddie?'

Eddie slapped his pocket. 'I'm loaded for bear.'

'Say, how'd it work with the chocolate milk?' Ben asked.

Eddie laughed. 'Worked *great!*' he said. He and Ben broke up while Bill looked at them, smiling but puzzled. Eddie explained and Bill nodded, grinning again.

'E-E-Eddie's muh-hum is w-w-worried that h-he's g-gonna break and sh-she wuh-hon't be able to g-get a re-re-refund.'

Eddie snorted and made as if to push him into the stream.

'Watch it, fuckface,' Bill said, sounding uncannily like Henry Bowers. 'I'll twist your head so far around you'll be able to watch when you wipe yourself.'

Ben collapsed, shrieking with laughter. Bill glanced at him, still smiling, hands still in the back pockets of his jeans, smiling, yeah, but a little distant again, a little vague. He looked at Eddie and then cocked his head toward Ben.

'Kid's suh-suh-soft,' he said.

'Yeah,' Eddie agreed, but he felt somehow that they were only going through the motions of having a good time. Something was on Bill's mind. He supposed Bill would spill it when he was ready; the question was, did Eddie want to hear what it was? 'Kid's mentally retarded.'

'Retreaded,' Ben said, still giggling.

'Y-You g-g-gonna sh-show us how to b-build a dam or a-are you g-g-gonna si-hit there on your b-big c-c-can all d-day?'

Ben got to his feet again. He looked first at the stream, flowing past them at moderate speed. The Kenduskeag was not terribly wide this far up in the Barrens, but it had defeated them yesterday just the same. Neither Eddie nor Bill had been able to figure out how to get a foothold on the current. But Ben was smiling, the smile of one who contemplates doing something new . . . something that will be fun but not very hard. Eddie thought: *He knows how – I really think he does.*

'Okay,' he said. 'You guys want to take your shoes off, because you're gonna get your little footsies wet.'

The mind-mother in Eddie's head spoke up at once, her voice as stern and commanding as the voice of a traffic cop: *Don't you dare do it, Eddie! Don't you dare! Wet feet, that's one way – one of the thousands of ways – that colds start, and colds lead to pneumonia, so don't you do it!*

Bill and Ben were sitting on the bank, pulling off their sneakers and socks. Ben was fussily rolling up the legs of his jeans. Bill looked up at Eddie. His eyes were clear and warm, sympathetic. Eddie was suddenly sure Big Bill knew exactly what he had been thinking, and he was ashamed.

'Y-You c-c-comin?'

'Yeah, sure,' Eddie said. He sat down on the bank and undressed his feet while his mother ranted inside his head . . . but her voice was growing steadily more distant and echoey, he was relieved to note, as if someone had stuck a heavy fishhook through the back of her blouse and was now reeling her away from him down a very long corridor.

3

It was one of those perfect summer days which, in a world where everything was on track and on the beam, you would never forget. A moderate breeze kept the worst of the mosquitoes and blackflies away. The sky was a bright, crisp blue. Temperatures were in the low seventies. Birds sang and went about their birdy-business in the bushes and second-growth trees. Eddie had to use his aspirator once, and then his chest lightened and his throat seemed to widen magically to the size of a freeway. He spent the rest of the morning with it stuffed forgotten into his back pocket.

Ben Hanscom, who had seemed so timid and unsure the day before, became a confident general once he was fully involved in the actual construction of the dam. Every now and then he would climb the bank and stand there with his muddy hands on his hips, looking at the work in progress and muttering to himself. Sometimes he would run a hand through his hair, and by eleven o'clock it was standing up in crazy, comical spikes.

Eddie felt uncertainty at first, then a sense of glee, and finally an entirely new feeling – one that was at the same time weird, terrifying, and exhilarating. It was a feeling so alien to his usual state of being that he was not able to put a name to it until that night, lying in bed and looking at the ceiling and replaying the day. *Power.* That was what that feeling had been. Power. It was going to work, by God, and it was going to work better than he and Bill – maybe even Ben himself – had dreamed it could.

He could see Bill getting involved, too – only a little at first, still mulling over whatever it was he had on his mind, and then, bit by bit, committing himself fully. Once or twice he clapped Ben on one meaty shoulder and told him he was unbelievable. Ben flushed with pleasure each time.

Ben got Eddie and Bill to set one of the boards across the stream and hold it as he used the sledgehammer to seat it in the streambed. 'There – it's in, but you'll have to hold it or the current'll just pull it loose,' he told Eddie, so Eddie stood in the middle of the stream holding the board while water sluiced over its top and made his hands into wavering starfish shapes.

Ben and Bill located a second board two feet downstream of the first. Ben used the sledge again to seat it and Bill held it while Ben began to fill up the space between the two boards with sandy earth from the stream-bank. At first it only washed away around the ends of the boards in gritty clouds and Eddie didn't think it was going to work at all, but when Ben began adding rocks and muddy gook from the streambed, the clouds of escaping silt began to diminish. In less than twenty minutes he had created a heaped brown canal of earth and stones between the two boards in the middle of the stream. To Eddie it looked like an optical illusion.

'If we had real cement . . . instead of just . . . mud and rocks, they'd have to move the whole city . . . over to the Old Cape side by the middle of next week,' Ben said, slinging the shovel aside at last and sitting on the bank until he got his breath back. Bill and Eddie laughed, and Ben grinned at them. When he grinned, there was a ghost of the handsome man he would become in the lines of his face. Water had begun to pile up behind the upstream board now.

Eddie asked what they were going to do about the water escaping around the sides.

'Let it go. It doesn't matter.'

'It doesn't?'

'Nope.'

'Why not?'

'I can't explain exactly. You gotta let some out, though.'

'How do you know?'

Ben shrugged. *I just do*, the shrug said, and Eddie was silenced.

When he was rested, Ben got a third board – the thickest of the four or five he had carried laboriously across town to the Barrens – and placed it carefully against the downstream board, wedging one end firmly into the streambed and socking the other against the board Bill had been holding, creating the strut he had put in his little drawing the day before.

'Okay,' he said, standing back. He grinned at them. 'You guys should be able to let go now. The gook in between the two boards will take most of the water pressure. The strut will take the rest.'

'Won't the water wash it away?' Eddie asked.

'Nope. The water is just gonna push it in deeper.'

'And if you're ruh-ruh-wrong, we g-get to k-k-kill yuh-you,' Bill said.

'That's cool,' Ben said amiably.

Bill and Eddie stepped back. The two boards that formed the basis of the dam creaked a little, tilted a little . . . and that was all.

'Hot *shit*!' Eddie screamed, excited.

'It's g-g-great,' Bill said, grinning.

'Yeah,' Ben said. 'Let's eat.'

4

They sat on the bank and ate, not talking much, watching the water stack up behind the dam and sluice around the ends of the boards. They had already done something to the geography of the streambanks, Eddie saw: the diverted current was cutting scalloped hollows into them. As he watched, the new course of the stream undercut the bank enough on the far side to cause a small avalanche.

Upstream of the dam the water formed a roughly circular pool, and at one place it had actually overflowed the bank. Bright, reflecting rills ran off into the grass and the underbrush. Eddie slowly began to realize what Ben had known from the first: the dam was already built. The gaps between the boards and the banks were sluiceways. Ben had not been able to tell Eddie this because he did not know the word. Above the boards the Kenduskeag had taken on a swelled look. The chuckling sound of shallow water babbling its way over stones and gravel was now gone; all the stones upstream of the dam were underwater. Every now and then more sod and dirt, undercut by the widening stream, would fall into the water with a splash.

Downstream of the dam the watercourse was nearly empty; thin trickles ran restlessly down its center, but that was about all. Stones which had been underwater for God knew how long were drying in the sun. Eddie looked at these drying stones with mild wonder . . . and that weird other feeling. They had done this. *They*. He saw a frog hopping along and thought maybe old Mr Froggy was wondering just where the water had gone. Eddie laughed out loud.

Ben was neatly stowing his empty wrappers in the lunchbag he had brought. Both Eddie and Bill had been amazed by the size of the repast Ben had laid out with businesslike efficiency: two PB&J sandwiches, one baloney sandwich, a hardcooked egg (complete with a pinch of salt twisted up in a small piece of waxed paper), two fig-bars, three large chocolate chip cookies, and a RingDing.

'What did your ma say when she saw how bad you got racked?' Eddie asked him.

'Hmmmm?' Ben looked up from the spreading pool of water behind the dam and belched gently against the back of his hand. 'Oh! Well, I knew she'd be grocery-shopping yesterday afternoon, so I was able to beat her home. I took a bath and washed my hair. Then I threw away the jeans and the sweatshirt I was wearing. I don't know if she'll notice they're gone or not. Probably not the sweatshirt, I got lots of sweatshirts, but I guess I ought to buy myself a new pair of jeans before she gets nosing through my drawers.'

The thought of wasting his money on such a nonessential item cast momentary gloom across Ben's face.

'W-W-What about the way yuh-you w-were b-bruised up?'

'I told her I was so excited to be out of school that I ran out the door and fell down the steps,' Ben said, and looked both amazed and a little hurt when Eddie and Bill began laughing. Bill, who had been chowing up a piece of his mother's devil's food cake, blew out a brown jet of crumbs and then had a coughing fit. Eddie, still howling, clapped him on the back.

'Well, I almost did fall down the steps,' Ben said. 'Only it was because Victor Criss pushed me, not because I was running.'

'I'd be as h-hot as a tuh-tuh-tamale in a swuh-heatshirt like that,' Bill said, finishing the last bite of his cake.

Ben hesitated. For a moment it seemed he would say nothing. 'It's better when you're fat,' he said finally. 'Sweatshirts, I mean.'

'Because of your gut?' Eddie asked.

Bill snorted. 'Because of your tih-tih-tih —'

'Yeah, my tits. So what?'

'Yeah,' Bill said mildly. 'S-So what?'

There was a moment of awkward silence and then Eddie said, 'Look how dark the water's getting when it goes around that side of the dam.'

'Oh, cripes!' Ben shot to his feet. 'Current's pulling out the fill! Jeez, I wish we had cement!'

The damage was quickly repaired, but even Eddie could see what would happen without someone there to almost constantly shovel in fresh fill: erosion would eventually cause the upstream board to collapse against the downstream board, and then everything would fall over.

'We can shore up the sides,' Ben said. 'That won't stop the erosion, but it'll slow it down.'

'If we use sand and mud, won't it just go on washing away?' Eddie asked.

'We'll use chunks of sod.'

Bill nodded, smiled, and made an O with the thumb and forefinger of his right hand. 'Let's g-g-go. I'll d-dig em and y-you sh-show me where to p-put em ih-in, Big Ben.'

From behind them a stridently cheery voice called: 'My Gawd, someone put the Y-pool down in the Barrens, bellybutton lint and all!'

Eddie turned, noticing the way Ben tightened up at the sound of a strange voice, the way his lips thinned. Standing above them and aways upstream, on the path Ben had crossed the day before, were Richie Tozier and Stanley Uris.

Richie came bopping down to the stream, glanced at Ben with some interest, and then pinched Eddie's cheek.

'Don't *do* that! I hate it when you do that, Richie.'

'Ah, you love it, Eds,' Richie said, and beamed at him. 'So what do you say? You havin any good chucks, or what?'

5

The five of them knocked off around four o'clock. They sat much higher on the bank – the place where Bill, Ben, and Eddie had eaten lunch was now underwater – and stared down at their handiwork. Even Ben found it a little difficult to believe. He felt a sense of tired accomplishment which was mixed with uneasy fright. He found himself thinking of *Fantasia*, and how Mickey Mouse had known enough to get the brooms started . . . but not enough to make them stop.

'Fucking incredible,' Richie Tozier said softly, and pushed his glasses up on his nose.

Eddie glanced over at him, but Richie was not doing one of his numbers now; his face was thoughtful, almost solemn.

On the far side of the stream, where the land first rose and then tilted shallowly downhill, they had created a new piece of bogland. Bracken and holly bushes stood in a foot of water. Even as they sat here they could see the bog sending out fresh pseudopods, spreading steadily westward. Behind the dam the Kenduskeag, shallow and harmless just this morning, had become a still, swollen band of water.

By two o'clock the widening pool behind the dam had taken so much embankment that the spillways had grown almost to the size of rivers themselves. Everyone but Ben had gone on an emergency exped-ition to the dump in search of more materials. Ben stuck around, methodically sodding up leaks. The scavengers had returned not only with boards but with four bald tires, the rusty door of a 1949 Hudson Hornet, and a big piece of corrugated-steel siding. Under Ben's lead-ership they had built two wings on the original dam, blocking off the water's escape around the sides again – and, with the wings raked back at an angle against the current, the dam worked even better than before.

'Stopped that sucker cold,' Richie said. 'You're a genius, man.'

Ben smiled. 'It's not so much.'

'I got some Winstons,' Richie said. 'Who wants one?'

He produced the crumpled red-and-white pack from his pants pocket and passed it around. Eddie, thinking of the hell a cigarette would raise with his asthma, refused. Stan also refused. Bill took one, and, after a moment's thought, Ben took one, too. Richie produced a book of matches with the words ROI-TAN on the outside, and lit first Ben's cigarette, then Bill's. He was about to light his own when Bill blew out the match.

'Thanks a lot, Denbrough, you wet,' Richie said.

Bill smiled apologetically. 'The-The-Three on a muh-muh-hatch,' he said. 'B-Bad luh-luh-luck.'

'Bad luck for your folks when you were born,' Richie said, and lit his cigarette with another match. He lay down and crossed his arms beneath his head. The cigarette jutted upward between his teeth. 'Winston tastes good, like a cigarette should.' He turned his head slightly and winked at Eddie. 'Ain't that right, Eds?'

Ben, Eddie saw, was looking at Richie with a mixture of awe and wariness. Eddie could understand that. He had known Richie Tozier for four years, and he still didn't really understand what Richie was about. He knew that Richie got A's and B's in his schoolwork, but he also knew that Richie regularly got C's and D's in deportment. His father really racked him about it and his mother just about cried every time Richie brought home those poor conduct grades, and Richie would swear to do better, and maybe he even would . . . for a quarter or two. The trouble with Richie was that he couldn't keep still for more than a minute at a time and he couldn't keep his mouth shut at all. Down here in the Barrens that didn't get him in much trouble, but the Barrens weren't Never-Never Land and they couldn't be the Wild Boys for more than a few hours at a stretch (the idea of a Wild Boy with an aspirator in his back pocket made Eddie smile). The trouble with the Barrens was that you always had to leave. Out there in the wider world, Richie's bullshit was always getting him in trouble – with adults, which was bad, and with guys like Henry Bowers, which was even worse.

His entrance earlier today was a perfect example. Ben Hanscom had no more than started to say hi when Richie had fallen on his knees at Ben's feet. He then began a series of gigantic salaams, his arms outstretched, his hands *fwapping* against the muddy bank every time he bowed again. At the same time he had begun to speak in one of his Voices.

Richie had about a dozen different Voices. His ambition, he had told Eddie one rainy afternoon when they were in the little raftered room over the Kaspbrak garage reading Little Lulu comic books, was to become the world's greatest ventriloquist. He was going to be even greater than Edgar Bergen, he said, and he would be on *The Ed Sullivan Show* every week. Eddie admired this ambition but foresaw problems with it. First, all of Richie's Voices sounded pretty much like Richie Tozier. This was not to say Richie could not be very funny from time to time; he could be. When referring to verbal zingers and loud farts, Richie's terminology was the same: he called it Getting Off A Good One, and he got off Good Ones of both types frequently . . . usually in inappropriate company, however. Second, when Richie did ventriloquism, his lips moved. Not just a little, on the 'p'- and 'b'-sounds, but a lot, and on all the sounds. Third, when Richie said he was going to throw his voice, it usually didn't go very far. Most of his friends were too kind – or too bemused with Richie's sometimes enchanting, often exhausting charm – to mention these little failings to him.

Salaaming frantically in front of the startled and embarrassed Ben Hanscom, Richie was speaking in what he called his Nigger Jim Voice.

'Lawks-a-mussy, it's be Haystack Calhoun!' Richie screamed. 'Don't fall on me, Mistuh Haystack, suh! You'se gwineter cream me if you do! Lawks-a-mussy, lawks-a-mussy! Three hunnert pounds of swingin meat, eighty-eight inches from tit to tit, Haystack be smellin jest like a loader panther shit! I'se gwineter leadjer inter de raing, Mistuh Haystack, suh! I'se sho enuf gwineter leadjer! Jest don'tchoo be fallin on dis yere black boy!'

'D-Don't wuh-worry,' Bill said. 'It's j-j-just Ruh-Ruh-Richie. He's c-c-crazy.'

Richie bounced to his feet. 'I heard that, Denbrough. You better leave me alone or I'll sic Haystack here on you.'

'B-Best p-p-part of you r-ran down your fuh-fuh-hather's l-l-leg,' Bill said.

'True,' Richie said, 'but look how much good stuff was left. How ya doin, Haystack? Richie Tozier is my name, doing Voices is my game.' He popped his hand out. Thoroughly confused, Ben reached for it. Richie pulled his hand back. Ben blinked. Relenting, Richie shook.

'My name's Ben Hanscom, in case you're interested,' Ben said.

'Seen you around school,' Richie said. He swept a hand at the spreading pool of water. 'This must have been your idea. These wet ends couldn't light a firecracker with a flamethrower.'

'Speak for yourself, Richie,' Eddie said.

'Oh – you mean it was *your* idea, Eds? Jesus, I'm sorry.' He fell down in front of Eddie and began salaaming wildly again.

'Get up, stop it, you're splattering mud on me!' Eddie cried.

Richie jumped to his feet a second time and pinched Eddie's cheek. 'Cute, cute, *cute!*' Richie exclaimed.

'Stop it, I *hate* that!'

'Fess up, Eds – who built the dam?'

'B-B-Ben sh-showed us,' Bill said.

'Good deal.' Richie turned and discovered Stanley Uris standing behind him, hands in his pockets, watching quietly as Richie put on his show. 'This here's Stan the Man Uris,' Richie told Ben. 'Stan's a Jew. Also, he killed Christ. At least that's what Victor Criss told me one day. I been after Stan ever since. I figure if he's that old, he ought to be able to buy us some beer. Right, Stan?'

'I think that must have been my father,' Stan said in a low, pleasant voice, and that broke them all up, Ben included. Eddie laughed until he was wheezing and tears were running down his face.

'A Good One!' Richie cried, striding around with his arms thrown up over his head like a football referee signalling that the extra point was good. 'Stan the Man Gets Off A Good One! Great Moments in History! Yowza-Yowza-*YOW*za!'

'Hi,' Stan said to Ben, seeming to take no notice of Richie at all.

'Hello,' Ben replied. 'We were in the same class in second grade. You were the kid who –'

'– never said anything,' Stan finished, smiling a little.

'Right.'

'Stan wouldn't say shit if he had a mouthful,' Richie said. '*Which* he *FREE*-quently does – yowza-yowza-*YOW* –'

'Sh-Sh-Shut uh-up, Richie,' Bill said.

'Okay, but first I have to tell you one more thing, much as I hate to. I think you're losing your dam. Valley's gonna flood, pardners. Let's get the women and children out first.'

And without bothering to roll up his pants – or even to remove his sneakers – Richie jumped into the water and began to slam sods into place on the nearside wing of the dam, where the persistent current was pulling fill out in muddy streamers again. A piece of Red Cross adhesive tape was wrapped around one of the bows of his glasses, and the loose end flapped against his cheekbone as he worked. Bill caught Eddie's eye, smiled a little, and shrugged. It was just Richie. He could drive you bugshit . . . but it was still sort of nice to have him around.

They worked on the dam for the next hour or so. Richie took Ben's commands – which had become rather tentative again, with two more kids to general – with perfect willingness, and fulfilled them at a manic pace. When each mission was completed he reported back to Ben for further orders, executing a backhand British salute and snapping the soggy heels of his sneakers together. Every now and then he would begin to harangue the others in one of his Voices: the German Commandant, Toodles the English Butler, the Southern Senator (who sounded quite a bit like Foghorn Leghorn and who would, in the fullness of time, evolve into a character named Buford Kissdrivel), the MovieTone Newsreel Narrator.

The work did not just go forward; it *sprinted* forward. And now, shortly before five o'clock, as they sat resting on the bank, it seemed that what Richie had said was true: they had stopped the sucker cold. The car door, the piece of corrugated steel, and the old tires had become the second stage of the dam, and it was backstopped by a huge sloping hill of earth and stones. Bill, Ben, and Richie smoked; Stan was lying on his back. A stranger might have thought he was just looking at the sky, but Eddie knew better. Stan was looking into the trees on the other side of the stream, keeping an eye out for a bird or two he could write up in his bird notebook that night. Eddie himself just sat cross-legged, feeling pleasantly tired and rather mellow. At that moment the others seemed to him like the greatest bunch of guys to chum with a fellow could ever hope to have. They felt *right* together; they fitted neatly against each other's edges. He couldn't explain it to himself any better than that, and since it didn't really seem to need any explaining, he decided he ought to just let it be.

He looked over at Ben, who was holding his half-smoked cigarette clumsily and spitting frequently, as if he didn't like the taste of it much. As Eddie watched, Ben stubbed it out and covered the long butt with dirt.

Ben looked up, saw Eddie watching him, and looked away, embarrassed.

Eddie glanced at Bill and saw something on Bill's face that he didn't like. Bill was looking across the water and into the trees and bushes on the far side, his eyes gray and thoughtful. That brooding expression was back on his face. Eddie thought Bill looked almost haunted.

As if reading his thought, Bill looked around at him. Eddie smiled, but Bill didn't smile back. He put his cigarette out and looked around at the others. Even Richie had withdrawn into the silence of his own thoughts, an event which occurred about as seldom as a lunar eclipse.

Eddie knew that Bill rarely said anything important unless it was perfectly quiet, because it was so hard for him to speak. And he suddenly wished he had something to say, or that Richie would start in with one of his Voices. He was suddenly sure Bill was going to open his mouth and say something terrible, something which would change everything. Eddie reached automatically for his aspirator, pulled it out of his back pocket, and held it in his hand. He did this without even thinking about it.

'C-Can I tell you g-g-guys suh-homething?' Bill asked.

They all looked at him. *Crack a joke, Richie!* Eddie thought. *Crack a joke, say something really outrageous, embarrass him, I don't care, just shut him up. Whatever it is, I don't want to hear it, I don't want things to change, I don't want to be scared.*

In his mind a tenebrous, croaking voice whispered: *I'll do it for a dime.*

Eddie shuddered and tried to unthink that voice, and the sudden image it called up in his mind: the house on Neibolt Street, its front yard overgrown with weeds, gigantic sunflowers nodding in the untended garden off to one side.

'Sure, Big Bill,' Richie said. 'What's up?'

Bill opened his mouth (more anxiety on Eddie's part), closed it (blessed relief for Eddie), and then opened it again (renewed anxiety).

'I-I-If you guh-guh-guys I-l-laugh, I-I'll never h-hang around with you again,' Bill said. 'It's cuh-cuh-crazy, but I swear I'm not muh-haking it up. It r-r-really happened.'

'We won't laugh,' Ben said. He looked around at the others. 'Will we?'

Stan shook his head. So did Richie.

Eddie wanted to say, *Yes we will too, Billy, we'll laugh our heads off and say you're really stupid, so why don't you shut up right now?* But of course he could not say any such thing. This was, after all, Big Bill. He shook his head miserably. No, he wouldn't laugh. He had never felt less like laughing in his life.

They sat there above the dam Ben had showed them how to make, looking from Bill's face to the expanding pool and the likewise expanding bog beyond it and then back to Bill's face again, listening silently as he told them about what had happened when he opened George's photograph album – how Georgie's school photograph had turned its head and winked at him, how the book had bled when he threw it across the room. It was a long, painful recital, and by the time he finished Bill was red-faced and sweating. Eddie had never heard him stutter so badly.

At last, though, the tale was told. Bill looked around at them, both defiant and afraid. Eddie saw an identical expression on the faces of Ben, Richie, and Stan. It was solemn, awed fear. It was not in the slightest tinctured by disbelief. An urge came to him then, an urge to spring to his feet and shout: *What a crazy story! You don't believe that crazy story, do you, and even if you do, you don't believe we believe it, do you? School pictures can't wink! Books can't bleed! You're out of your mind, Big Bill!*

But he couldn't very well do so, because that expression of solemn fear was also on his own face. He couldn't see it but he could feel it.

Come back here, kid, the hoarse voice whispered. *I'll blow you for free. Come back here!*

No, Eddie moaned at it. *Please, go away, I don't want to think about that.*

Come back here, kid.

And now Eddie saw something else – not on Richie's face, at least he didn't think so, but on Stan's and Ben's for sure. He knew what that something else was; knew because that expression was on his own face, too.

Recognition.

I'll blow you for free.

The house at 29 Neibolt Street was just outside the Derry trainyards. It was old and boarded up, its porch gradually sinking back into the ground, its lawn an overgrown field. An old trike, rusting and overturned, hid in that long grass, one wheel sticking up at an angle.

But on the left side of the porch there was a huge bald patch in the lawn and you could see dirty cellar windows set into the house's crumbling brick foundation. It was in one of those windows that Eddie Kaspbrak first saw the face of the leper six weeks ago.

6

On Saturdays, when Eddie could find no one to play with, he often went down to the trainyards. No real reason; he just liked to go out there.

He would ride his bike out Witcham Street and then cut to the northwest along Route 2 where it crossed Witcham. The Neibolt

Street Church School stood on the corner of Route 2 and Neibolt Street a mile or so farther on. It was a shabby-neat wood-frame building with a large cross on top and the words SUFFER THE LITTLE CHILDREN TO COME UNTO ME written over the front door in gilt letters two feet high. Sometimes, on Saturdays, Eddie heard music and singing coming from inside. It was gospel music, but whoever was playing the piano sounded more like Jerry Lee Lewis than a regular church piano player. The singing didn't sound very religious to Eddie, either, although there was lots of stuff in it about 'beautiful Zion' and being 'washed in the blood of the lamb' and 'what a friend we have in Jesus.' The people singing seemed to be having much too good a time for it to really be sacred singing, in Eddie's opinion. But he liked the sound of it all the same – the way he liked to hear Jerry Lee hollering out 'Whole Lotta Shakin' Goin' On.' Sometimes he would stop for awhile across the street, leaning his bike against a tree and pretending to read on the grass, actually jiving along to the music.

Other Saturdays the Church School would be shut up and silent and he would ride out to the trainyard without stopping, out to where Neibolt Street ended in a parking lot with weeds growing up through the cracks in the asphalt. There he would lean his bike against the wooden fence and watch the trains go by. There were a lot of them on Saturdays. His mother told him that in the old days you could catch a GS&WM passenger train at what was then Neibolt Street Station, but the passenger trains had stopped running around the time the Korean War was starting up. 'If you got on the northbound train you went to Brownsville Station,' she said, 'and from Brownsville you could catch a train that would take you all the way across Canada if you wanted, all the way to the Pacific. The southbound train would take you to Portland and then on down to Boston, and from South Station the country was yours. But the passenger trains have gone the way of the trolley lines now, I guess. No one wants to ride a train when they can just jump in a Ford and go. You may never even ride one.'

But great long freights still came through Derry. They headed south loaded down with pulpwood, paper, and potatoes, and north with manufactured goods for those towns of what Maine people some-times called the Big Northern – Bangor, Millinocket, Machias, Presque Isle, Houlton. Eddie particularly liked to watch the northbound car-carriers with their loads of gleaming Fords and Chevies. *I'll have me a car like one of those someday*, he promised himself. *Like one of those or even better. Maybe even a Cadillac!*

There were six tracks in all, swooping into the station like strands of cobweb tending toward the center: Bangor and Great Northern Lines from the north, the Great Southern and Western Maine from the west, the Boston and Maine from the south, and Southern Seacoast from the east.

One day two years before, when Eddie had been standing near the latter line and watching a train go through, a drunken trainman had thrown a crate out of a slow-moving boxcar at him. Eddie ducked and flinched backward, although the crate landed in the cinders ten feet away. There were things inside it, live things that clicked and moved. 'Last run, boy!' the drunken trainman had shouted. He pulled a flat brown bottle from one of the pockets of his denim jacket, tipped it up, drank, then flipped it into the cinders, where it smashed. The trainman pointed at the crate. 'Take em home to yer mum! Compliments of the Southern-Fucking-Seacoast-Bound-for-Welfare Line!' He had reeled forward to shout these last words as the train pulled away, gathering speed now, and for one alarming moment Eddie thought he was going to tumble right out.

When the train was gone, Eddie went to the box and bent cautiously over it. He was afraid to get too close. The things inside were slithery and crawly. If the trainman had yelled that they were for him, Eddie would have left them right there. But he had said take em home to your Mom, and, like Ben, when someone said Mom, Eddie jumped.

He scrounged a hank of rope from one of the empty quonset warehouses and tied the crate onto the package carrier of his bike. His mother had peered inside the crate even more warily than Eddie himself, and then she screamed – but with delight rather than terror. There were four lobsters in the crate, big two-pounders with their claws pegged. She cooked them for supper and had been extremely grumpy with Eddie when he wouldn't eat any.

'What do you think the Rockefellers are eating this evening at their place in Bar Harbor?' she asked indignantly. 'What do you think the swells are eating at Twenty-one and Sardi's in New York City? Peanut butter and jelly sandwiches? They're eating *lobster*, Eddie, same as we are! Now come on – give it a try.'

But Eddie wouldn't – at least that was what his mother said. Maybe it was true, but inside it felt more to Eddie like couldn't than wouldn't. He kept thinking of the way they had slithered inside the crate, and the clicking sounds their claws had made. She kept telling him how delicious they were and what a treat he was missing until he started to gasp for breath and had to use his aspirator. Then she left him alone.

Eddie retreated to his bedroom and read. His mother called up her friend Eleanor Dunton. Eleanor came over and the two of them read old copies of *Photoplay* and *Screen Secrets* and giggled over the gossip columns and gorged themselves on cold lobster salad. When Eddie got up for school the next morning, his mother was still in bed, snoring away and letting frequent farts that sounded like long, mellow cornet notes (she was Getting Off Some Good Ones, Richie would have said). There was nothing left in the bowl where the lobster salad had been except a few tiny blots of mayonnaise.

That was the last Southern Seacoast train Eddie ever saw, and when he later saw Mr Braddock, the Derry trainmaster, he asked him hesitantly what had happened. 'Cump'ny went broke,' Mr Braddock said. 'That's all there was to it. Don't you read the papers? It's hap'nin all over the damn country. Now get out of here. This ain't no place for a kid.'

After that Eddie would sometimes walk along track 4, which had been the Southern Seacoast track, and listen as a mental conductor chanted names inside his head, reeling them off in a lovely Downeast monotone, those names, those magic names: Camden, Rockland, Bar Harbor (pronounced Baa Haabaa), Wiscasset, Bath, Portland, Ogunquit, the Berwicks; he would walk down track 4 heading east until he got tired, and the weeds growing up between the crossties made him feel sad. Once he had looked up and seen seagulls (probably just fat old dump-gulls who didn't give a shit if they ever saw the ocean, but that had not occurred to him then) wheeling and crying overhead, and the sound of their voices had made him cry a little, too.

There had once been a gate at the entrance to the trainyards, but it had blown over in a windstorm and no one had bothered to replace it. Eddie came and went pretty much as he liked, although Mr Braddock would kick him out if he saw him (or any other kid, for that matter). There were truck-drivers who would chase you sometimes (but not very far) because they thought you were hanging around just so you could hawk something – and sometimes kids did.

Mostly, though, the place was quiet. There was a guard-booth but it was empty, its glass windows broken by stones. There had been no full-time security service since 1950 or so. Mr Braddock shooed the kids away by day and a night-watchman drove through four or five times a night in an old Studebaker with a searchlight mounted outside the vent window and that was all.

There were tramps and hobos sometimes, though. If anything about the trainyards scared Eddie, they did – men with unshaven cheeks and cracked skin and blisters on their hands and coldsores on their lips. They rode the rails for awhile and then climbed down for awhile and spent some time in Derry and then got on another train and went somewhere else. Sometimes they had missing fingers. Usually they were drunk and wanted to know if you had a cigarette.

One of these fellows had crawled out from under the porch of the house at 29 Neibolt Street one day and had offered to give Eddie a blowjob for a quarter. Eddie had backed away, his skin like ice, his mouth as dry as lintballs. One of the hobo's nostrils had been eaten away. You could look right into the red, scabby channel.

'I don't have a quarter,' Eddie said, backing toward his bike.

'I'll do it for a dime,' the hobo croaked, coming toward him. He was wearing old green flannel pants. Yellow puke was stiffening across the lap. He unzipped his fly and reached inside. He was trying to grin. His nose was a red horror.

'I . . . I don't have a dime, either,' Eddie said, and suddenly thought: *Oh my God he's got leprosy! If he touches me I'll catch it too!* His control snapped and he ran. He heard the hobo break into a shuffling run behind him, his old string-tied shoes slapping and flapping across the riotous lawn of the empty saltbox house.

'Come back here, kid! I'll blow you for free. Come back here!'

Eddie had leaped on his bike, wheezing now, feeling his throat closing up to a pinhole. His chest had taken on weight. He hit the pedals and was just picking up speed when one of the hobo's hands struck the package carrier. The bike shimmied. Eddie looked over his shoulder and saw the hobo running along behind the rear wheel (*!!GAINING!!*), his lips drawn back from the black stumps of his teeth in an expression which might have been either desperation or fury.

In spite of the stones lying on his chest Eddie had pedaled even faster, expecting that one of the hobo's scab-crusted hands would close over his arm at any moment, pulling him from his Raleigh and dumping him in the ditch, where God knew what would happen to him. He hadn't dared look around until he had flashed past the Church School and through the Route 2 intersection. The 'bo was gone.

Eddie held this terrible story inside him for almost a week and then confided it to Richie Tozier and Bill Denbrough one day when they were reading comics over the garage.

'He didn't have leprosy, you dummy,' Richie said. 'He had the Syph.'

Eddie looked at Bill to see if Richie was ribbing him – he had never heard of a disease called the Sift before. It sounded like something Richie might have made up.

'Is there such a thing as the Sift, Bill?'

Bill nodded gravely. 'Only it's the Suh–Suh–*Syph*, not the Sift. It's s–short for syphilis.'

'What's that?'

'It's a disease you get from fucking,' Richie said. 'You know about fucking, don't you, Eds?'

'Sure,' Eddie said. He hoped he wasn't blushing. He knew that when you got older, stuff came out of your penis when it was hard. Vincent 'Boogers' Taliendo had filled him in on the rest one day at school. What you did when you fucked, according to Boogers, was you rubbed your cock against a girl's stomach until it got hard (your cock, not the girl's stomach). Then you rubbed some more until you started to 'get the feeling.' When Eddie asked what that meant, Boogers had only shaken his head in a mysterious way. Boogers said that you couldn't describe it, but you'd know it as soon as you got it. He said you could practice by lying in the bathtub and rubbing your cock with Ivory soap (Eddie had tried this, but the only feeling he got was the need to urinate after awhile). Anyway, Boogers went on, after you 'got the feeling,' this stuff came out of your penis. Most kids called it come, Boogers said, but his big brother had told him that the really scientific word for it was jizzum. And when you 'got the feeling,' you had to grab your cock and aim it real fast so you could shoot the jizzum into the girl's bellybutton as soon as it came out. It went down into her stomach and made a baby there.

Do girls like *that?* Eddie had asked Boogers Taliendo. He himself was sort of appalled.

I guess they must, Boogers had replied, looking mystified himself.

'Now listen up, Eds,' Richie said, 'because there may be questions later. Some women have got this disease. Some men, too, but mostly it's women. A guy can get it from a woman –'

'Or another g–g–guy if they're kwuh–kwuh–queer,' Bill added.

'Right. The important thing is you get the Syph from screwing someone who's already got it.'

'What does it do?' Eddie asked.

'Makes you rot,' Richie said simply.

Eddie stared at him, horrified.

'It's bad, I know, but it's true,' Richie said. 'Your nose is the first thing to go. Some guys with the Syph, their noses fall right off. Then their cocks.'

'Puh-Puh-Puh-leeze,' Bill said. 'I just a-a-ate.'

'Hey, man, this is science,' Richie said.

'So what's the difference between leprosy and the Syph?' Eddie asked.

'You don't get leprosy from fucking,' Richie said promptly, and then went off into a gale of laughter that left both Bill and Eddie mystified.

7

Following that day the house at 29 Neibolt Street had taken on a kind of glow in Eddie's imagination. Looking at its weedy yard and its slumped porch and the boards nailed across its windows, he would feel an unhealthy fascination take hold of him. And six weeks ago he had parked his bike on the gravelly verge of the street (the sidewalk ended four houses farther back) and walked across the lawn toward the porch of that house.

His heart had been beating hard in his chest, and his mouth had that dry taste again – listening to Bill's story of the dreadful picture, he knew that what he had felt when approaching that house was about the same as what Bill had felt going into George's room. He did not feel as if he was in control of himself. He felt *pushed*.

It did not seem as if his feet were moving; instead the house itself, brooding and silent, seemed to draw closer to where he stood.

Faintly, he could hear a diesel engine in the trainyard – that and the liquid-metallic slam of couplings being made. They were shunting some cars onto sidings, picking up others. Making a train.

His hand gripped his aspirator, but, oddly, his asthma had not closed down as it had on the day he fled from the hobo with the rotted nose. There was only that sense of standing still and watching the house slide stealthily toward him, as if on a hidden track.

Eddie looked under the porch. There was no one there. It was not really surprising. This was spring, and hobos showed up most frequently in Derry from late September to early November. During those six weeks or so a man could pick up day-work on one of the outlying farms if he looked even half-decent. There were potatoes and apples to pick, snowfence to string, barn and shed roofs which needed to be patched before December came along, whistling up winter.

No hobos under the porch, but plenty of sign they had been there. Empty beer cans, empty beer bottles, empty liquor bottles. A dirt-crusted blanket lay against the brick foundation like a dead dog.

There were drifts of crumpled newspapers and one old shoe and a smell like garbage. There were thick layers of old leaves under there.

Not wanting to do it but unable to help himself, Eddie had crawled under the porch. He could feel his heartbeat slamming in his head now, driving white spots of light across his field of vision.

The smell was worse underneath – booze and sweat and the dark brown perfume of decaying leaves. The old leaves didn't even crackle under his hands and knees. They and the old newspapers only sighed.

I'm a hobo, Eddie thought incoherently. *I'm a hobo and I ride the rods. That's what I do. Ain't got no money, ain't got no home, but I got me a bottle and a dollar and a place to sleep. I'll pick apples this week and potatoes the week after that and when the frost locks up the ground like money inside a bank vault, why, I'll hop a GS&WM box that smells of sugar-beets and I'll sit in the corner and pull some hay over me if there is some and I'll drink me a little drink and chew me a little chew and sooner or later I'll get to Portland or Beantown, and if I don't get busted by a railroad security dick I'll hop one of those 'Bama Star boxes and head down south and when I get there I'll pick lemons or limes or oranges. And if I get vagged I'll build roads for tourists to ride on. Hell, I done it before, ain't I? I'm just a lonesome old hobo, ain't got no money, ain't got no home, but I got me one thing; I got me a disease that's eating me up. My skin's cracking open, my teeth are falling out, and you know what? I can feel myself turning bad like an apple that's going soft, I can feel it happening, eating from the inside to the out, eating, eating, eating me.*

Eddie pulled the stiffening blanket aside, tweezing at it with his thumb and forefinger, grimacing at its matted feel. One of those low cellar windows was directly behind it, one pane broken, the other opaque with dirt. He leaned forward, now feeling almost hypnotized. He leaned closer to the window, closer to the cellar-darkness, breathing in that smell of age and must and dry-rot, closer and closer to the black, and surely the leper would have caught him if his asthma hadn't picked that exact moment to kick up. It cramped his lungs with a weight that was painless yet frightening; his breath at once took on the familiar hateful whistling sound.

He drew back, and that was when the face appeared. Its coming was so sudden, so startling (and yet at the same time so *expected*), that Eddie could not have screamed even if he hadn't been having an asthma attack. His eyes bulged. His mouth creaked open. It was not the hobo with the flayed nose, but there were resemblances. Terrible resemblances. And yet . . . this thing could not be human. Nothing could be so eaten up and remain alive.

The skin of its forehead was split open. White bone, coated with a membrane of yellow mucusy stuff, peered through like the lens of a bleary searchlight. The nose was a bridge of raw gristle above two red flaring channels. One eye was a gleeful blue. The other socket was filled with a mass of spongy brown-black tissue. The leper's lower lip sagged like liver. It had no upper lip at all; its teeth poked out in a sneering ring.

It shot one hand out through the broken pane. It shot the other through the dirty glass to the left, shattering it to fragments. Its questing, clutching hands crawled with sores. Beetles crawled and lumbered busily to and fro.

Mewling, gasping, Eddie hunched his way backward. He could hardly breathe. His heart was a runaway engine in his chest. The leper appeared to be wearing the ragged remains of some strange silvery suit. Things were crawling in the straggles of its brown hair.

'How bout a blowjob, Eddie?' the apparition croaked, grinning with its remains of a mouth. It lilted, 'Bobby does it for a dime, he will do it anytime, fifteen cents for overtime.' It winked. 'That's me, Eddie – Bob Gray. And now that we've been properly introduced . . .' One of its hands splatted against Eddie's right shoulder. Eddie screamed thinly.

'That's all right,' the leper said, and Eddie saw with dreamlike terror that it was crawling out of the window. The bony shield behind its peeling forehead snapped the thin wooden strip between the two panes. Its hands clawed through the leafy, mulchy earth. The silver shoulders of its suit . . . costume . . . whatever it was . . . began to push through the gap. That one glaring blue eye never left Eddie's face.

'Here I come, Eddie, that's all right,' it croaked. 'You'll like it down here with us. Some of your friends are down here.'

Its hand reached out again, and in some corner of his panic-maddened, screaming mind, Eddie was suddenly, coldly sure that if that thing touched his bare skin, he would begin to rot, too. The thought broke his paralysis. He skittered backward on his hands and knees, then turned and lunged for the far end of the porch. Sunlight, falling in narrow dusty beams through the cracks between the porch boards, striped his face from moment to moment. His head pushed through the dusty cobwebs that settled in his hair. He looked back over his shoulder and saw that the leper was halfway out.

'It won't do you any good to run, Eddie,' it called.

Eddie had reached the far end of the porch. There was a lattice-work skirt here. The sun shone through it, printing diamonds of light on his cheeks and forehead. He lowered his head and slammed into it with no hesitation at all, tearing the entire skirt free with a scream of rusted ha'penny nails. There was a tangle of rosebushes beyond and Eddie tore through these, stumbling to his feet as he did so, not feeling the thorns that scrawled shallow cuts along his arms and cheeks and neck.

He turned and backed away on buckling legs, pulling his aspirator out of his pocket, triggering it. Surely it hadn't really happened? He had been thinking about that hobo and his mind had . . . well, had just

(*put on a show*)

shown him a movie, a horror movie, like one of those Saturday-matinee pictures with Frankenstein and Wolfman that they had sometimes at the Bijou or the Gem or the Aladdin. Sure, that was all. He had scared himself! What an asshole!

There was even time to utter a shaky laugh at the unsuspected vividness of his imagination before the rotting hands shot out from under the porch, clawing at the rosebushes with mindless ferocity, pulling at them, stripping them, printing beads of blood on them.

Eddie shrieked.

The leper was crawling out. It was wearing a clown suit, he saw – a clown suit with big orange buttons down the front. It saw Eddie and grinned. Its half-mouth dropped open and its tongue lolled out. Eddie shrieked again, but no one could have heard one boy's breathless shriek under the pounding of the diesel engine in the trainyard. The leper's tongue had not just dropped from its mouth; it was at least three feet long and had unrolled like a party-favor. It came to an arrow-point which dragged in the dirt. Foam, thick-sticky and yellowish, coursed along it. Bugs crawled over it.

The rosebushes, which had been showing the first touches of spring green when Eddie broke through them, now turned a dead and lacy black.

'Blowjob,' the leper whispered, and tottered to its feet.

Eddie raced for his bike. It was the same race as before, only it now had the quality of a nightmare, where you can only move with the most agonizing slowness no matter how hard you try to go fast . . . and in those dreams didn't you always hear or feel something, some It, gaining on you? Didn't you always smell Its stinking breath, as Eddie was smelling it now?

For a moment he felt a wild hope: perhaps this really *was* a nightmare. Perhaps he would awake in his own bed, bathed in sweat, shaking, maybe even crying . . . but alive. *Safe*. Then he pushed the thought away. Its charm was deadly, its comfort fatal.

He did not try to mount his bike immediately; he ran with it instead, head down, pushing the handlebars. He felt as if he was drowning, not in water but inside his own chest.

'Blowjob,' the leper whispered again. 'Come back anytime, Eddie. Bring your friends.'

Its rotting fingers seemed to touch the back of his neck, but perhaps that was only a dangling strand of cobweb from under the porch, caught in his hair and brushing against his shrinking flesh. Eddie leaped onto his bike and pedaled away, not caring that his throat had closed up tight as Tillie again, not giving two sucks for his asthma, not looking back. He didn't look back until he was almost home, and of course there was nothing behind him when he finally did but two kids headed over to the park to play ball.

That night, lying straight as a poker in bed, one hand folded tightly around his aspirator, looking into the shadows, he heard the leper whisper: *It won't do you any good to run, Eddie.*

8

'Wow,' Richie said respectfully. It was the first thing any of them had said since Bill Denbrough finished his story.

'H-Have you g-g-got a-another suh-suh-higgarette, R-R-Richie?'

Richie gave him the last one in the pack he had hawked almost empty from his dad's desk drawer. He even lit it for Bill.

'You didn't dream it, Bill?' Stan asked suddenly.

Bill shook his head. 'N-N-No duh-dream.'

'Real,' Eddie said in a low voice.

Bill looked at him sharply. 'Wh-Wh-What?'

'Real, I said.' Eddie looked at him almost resentfully. 'It really happened. It was *real*.' And before he could stop himself — before he even knew he was going to do it — Eddie found himself telling the story of the leper that had come crawling out of the basement at 29 Neibolt Street. Halfway through the telling he began to gasp and had to use his aspirator. And at the end he burst into shrill tears, his thin body shaking.

They all looked at him uncomfortably, and then Stan put a hand on his back. Bill gave him an awkward hug while the others glanced away, embarrassed.

'That's a-all right, E-Eddie. It's o-o-okay.'

'I saw it too,' Ben Hanscom said suddenly. His voice was flat and harsh and scared.

Eddie looked up, his face still naked with tears, his eyes red and raw-looking. 'What?'

'I saw the clown,' Ben said. 'Only he wasn't like you said – at least not when I saw him. He wasn't all gooshy. He was . . . he was dry.' He paused, ducked his head, and looked at his hands, which lay palely on his elephantine thighs. 'I think he was the mummy.'

'Like in the movies?' Eddie asked.

'Like that but *not* like that,' Ben said slowly. 'In the movies he looks fake. It's scary, but you can tell it's a put-up job, you know? All those bandages, they look too neat, or something. But this guy . . . he looked the way a real mummy would look, I think. If you actually found one in a room under a pyramid, I mean. Except for the suit.'

'Wuh-wuh-wuh-hut suh-hoot?'

Ben looked at Eddie. 'A silver suit with big orange buttons down the front.'

Eddie's mouth dropped open. He shut it and said, 'If you're kidding, say so. I still . . . I still dream about that guy under the porch.'

'It's not a joke,' Ben said, and began to tell the story. He told it slowly, beginning with his volunteering to help Mrs Douglas count and store books and ending with his own bad dreams. He spoke slowly, not looking at the others. He spoke as if deeply ashamed of his own behavior. He didn't raise his head again until the story was over.

'You must have dreamed it,' Richie said finally. He saw Ben wince and hurried on: 'Now don't take it personal, Big Ben, but you got to see that balloons can't, like, float against the wind –'

'Pictures can't wink, either,' Ben said.

Richie looked from Ben to Bill, troubled. Accusing Ben of dreaming awake was one thing; accusing Bill was something else. Bill was their leader, the guy they all looked up to. No one said so out loud; no one needed to. But Bill was the idea man, the guy who could think of something to do on a boring day, the guy who remembered games the others had forgotten. And in some odd way they all sensed something comfortingly adult about Bill – perhaps it was a sense of accountability, a feeling that Bill would take the responsibility if responsibility needed to be taken. The truth was, Richie believed Bill's story, crazy as it was. And perhaps he didn't want to believe Ben's . . . or Eddie's, for that matter.

'Nothing like that ever happened to you, huh?' Eddie asked Richie.

Richie paused, began to say something, shook his head, paused again, then said: 'Scariest thing I've seen lately was Mark Prenderlist takin a leak in McCarron Park. Ugliest hogger you ever saw.'

Ben said, 'What about you, Stan?'

'No,' Stan said quickly, and looked somewhere else. His small face was pale, his lips pressed together so tightly they were white.

'W-W-Was there suh-homething, S-St-Stan?' Bill asked.

'No, I told you!' Stan got to his feet and walked to the embankment, hands in his pockets. He stood watching the water course over the top of the original dam and pile up behind the second watergate.

'Come on, now, Stanley!' Richie said in a shrill falsetto. This was another of his Voices: Granny Grunt. When speaking in his Granny Grunt Voice, Richie would hobble around with one fist against the small of his back, and cackle a lot. He still, however, sounded more like Richie Tozier than anyone else.

'Fess up, Stanley, tell your old Granny about the *baaaaad* clown and I'll give you a chocker-chip cookie. You just tell –'

'*Shut up!*' Stan yelled suddenly, whirling on Richie, who fell back a step or two, astonished. '*Just shut up!*'

'Yowza, boss,' Richie said, and sat down. He looked at Stan Uris mistrustfully. Bright spots of color flamed in Stan's cheeks, but he still looked more scared than mad.

'That's okay,' Eddie said quietly. 'Never mind, Stan.'

'It wasn't a clown,' Stanley said. His eyes flicked from one of them to the next to the next to the next. He seemed to struggle with himself.

'Y-Y-You can t-tell,' Bill said, also speaking quietly. 'W-We d-d-did.'

'It wasn't a clown. It was –'

Which was when the carrying, whiskey-roughened tones of Mr Nell interrupted, making them all jump as if they had been shot: '*Jay-sus Christ on a jumped-up chariot-driven crutch! Look at this mess! Jaysus Christ!*'

CHAPTER EIGHT
GEORGIE'S ROOM AND THE HOUSE ON NEIBOLT STREET

1

Richard Tozier turns off the radio, which has been blaring out Madonna's 'Like a Virgin' on WZON (a station which declares itself to be 'Bangor's AM stereo rocker!' with a kind of hysterical frequency), pulls over to the side of the road, shuts down the engine of the Mustang the Avis people rented him at Bangor International, and gets out. He hears the pull and release of his own breath in his ears. He has seen a sign which has caused the flesh of his back to break out in hard ridges of gooseflesh.

He walks to the front of the car and puts one hand on its hood. He hears the engine ticking softly to itself as it cools. He hears a jay scream briefly and then shut up. There are crickets. And as far as the soundtrack goes, that's it.

He has seen the sign, he passes it, and suddenly he is in Derry again. After twenty-five years Richie 'Trashmouth' Tozier has come home. He has —

Burning agony suddenly needles into his eyes, breaking his thought cleanly off. He utters a strangled little shout and his hands fly up to his face. The only time he felt anything even remotely like this burning pain was when he got an eyelash caught under one of his contacts in college — and that was only in one eye. This terrible pain is in both.

Before he can reach even halfway to his face, the pain is gone.

He lowers his hands again slowly, thoughtfully, and looks down Route 7. He left the turnpike at the Etna-Haven exit, wanting, for some reason he doesn't understand, not to come in by the turnpike, which was still under construction in the Derry area when he and his folks shook the dust of this weird little town from their heels and headed out for the Midwest. No — the turnpike would have been quicker, but it would have been wrong.

So he had driven along Route 9 through the sleeping nestle of buildings

298

that was Haven Village, then turned off on Route 7. And as he went the day grew steadily brighter.

Now this sign. It was the same sort of sign which marked the borders of more than six hundred Maine towns, but how this one had squeezed his heart!

Penobscot
County
D
E
R
R
Y
Maine

Beyond that an Elks sign; a Rotary Club sign; and completing the trinity, a sign proclaiming the fact that DERRY LIONS ROAR FOR THE UNITED FUND! *Past that one there is just Route 7 again, continuing on in a straight line between bulking banks of pine and spruce. In this silent light as the day steadies itself those trees look as dreamy as blue-gray cigarette smoke stacked on the moveless air of a sealed room.*

Derry, *he thinks.* Derry, God help me. Derry. Stone the crows.

Here he is on Route 7. Five miles up, if time or tornado has not carried it away in the intervening years, will be the Rhulin Farms, where his mother bought all of their eggs and most of their vegetables. Two miles beyond that Route 7 became Witcham Road and of course Witcham Road eventually became Witcham Street, can you gimme hallelujah world without end amen. And somewhere along there between the Rhulin Farms and town he would drive past the Bowers place and then the Hanlon place. A mile or so after Hanlon's he would see the first glitter of the Kenduskeag and the first spreading tangle of poison green. The lush lowlands that had been known for some reason as the Barrens.

I really don't know if I can face all of that, *Richie thinks.* I mean, let's tell the truth here, folks. I just don't know if I can.

The whole previous night has passed in a dream for him. As long as he continued travelling, moving forward, making miles, the dream went on. But now he has stopped — or rather the sign has stopped him — and he has awakened to a strange truth: the dream was the reality. Derry is the reality.

It seems he just cannot stop remembering, he thinks the memories will eventually drive him mad, and now he bites down on his lip and puts his hands together palm to palm, tight, as if to keep himself from flying apart. He feels that he will fly apart, and soon. There seems to be some mad part of him which actually looks forward to what may be coming, but most of him only wonders how he's going to get through the next few days. He –

And now his thoughts break off again.

A deer is walking out into the road. He can hear the light thud of its spring-soft hoofs on the tar.

Richie's breath stops in mid-exhale, then slowly starts again. He looks, dumbfounded, part of him thinking that he never saw anything like this on Rodeo Drive. No – he'd needed to come back home to see something like this.

It's a doe ('Doe, a deer, a female deer,' a Voice chants merrily in his head). She's come out of the woods on the right and pauses in the middle of Route 7, front legs on one side of the broken white line, rear legs on the other. Her dark eyes regard Rich Tozier mildly. He reads interest in those eyes but no fear.

He looks at her in wonder, thinking she's an omen or a portent or some sort of Madame Azonka shit like that. And then, quite unexpectedly, a memory of Mr Nell comes to him. What a start he had given them that day, busting in on them in the wake of Bill's story and Ben's story and Eddie's story! The whole bunch of them had damn near gone up to heaven.

Now, looking at the deer, Rich draws in a deep breath and finds himself speaking in one of his Voices . . . but for the first time in twenty-five years or more it is the Voice of the Irish Cop, one he had incorporated into his repertoire after that memorable day. It comes rolling out of the morning silence like a great big bowling ball – it is louder and bigger than Richie would ever have believed:

'Jay-sus Christ on a jumped-up chariot-driven crutch! What's a nice girrul like you doin out in this wilderness, deer? Jaysus Christ! You be gettin on home before I decide to tell Father O'Staggers on ye!'

Before the echoes have died away, before the first shocked jay can begin scolding him for his sacrilege, the doe flicks her tail at him like a truce flag and disappears into the smoky-looking firs on the left side of the road, leaving only a small pile of steaming pellets behind to show that, even at thirty-seven, Richie Tozier is still capable of Getting Off A Good One from time to time.

Richie begins to laugh. He is only chuckling at first, and then his own ludicrousness strikes him – standing here in the dawnlight of a Maine morning, thirty-four hundred miles from home, shouting at a deer in the accents of an Irish cop. The chuckles become a string of giggles, the giggles become guffaws, the guffaws become howls, and he is finally reduced to holding on to his car while tears roll down his face and he wonders dimly if he's going to wet his pants or what. Every time he starts to get control of himself his eyes fix on that little clump of pellets and he goes off into fresh gales.

Snorting and snickering, he is at last able to get back into the driver's seat and restart the Mustang's engine. An Orinco chemical-fertilizer truck snores by in a blast of wind. After it passes him, Rich pulls out and heads for Derry again. He feels better now, in control . . . or maybe it's just that he's moving again, making miles, and the dream has reasserted itself.

He starts thinking about Mr Nell again – Mr Nell and that day by the dam. Mr Nell had asked them who thought this little trick up. He can see the five of them looking uneasily at each other, and remembers how Ben finally stepped forward, cheeks pale and eyes downcast, face trembling all over as he fought grimly to keep from blubbering. Poor kid probably thought he was going to get five-to-ten in Shawshank for back-flooding the drains on Witcham Street, Rich thinks now, but he had owned up to it just the same. And by doing that he had forced the rest of them to come forward and back him up. It was either that or consider themselves bad guys. Cowards. All the things their TV heroes were not. And that had welded them together, for better or worse. Had apparently welded them together for the last twenty-seven years. Sometimes events are dominoes. The first knocks over the second, the second knocks over the third, and there you are.

When, Richie wonders, did it become too late to turn back? When he and Stan showed up and pitched in, helping to build the dam? When Bill told them how the school picture of his brother had turned its head and winked? Maybe . . . but to Rich Tozier it seems that the dominoes really began to fall when Ben Hanscom stepped forward and said 'I showed them

2

how to do it. It's my fault.'

Mr Nell simply stood there looking at him, lips pressed together, hands on his creaking black leather belt. He looked from Ben to the spreading pool behind the dam and then back to Ben again, his face that of a man who can't believe what he is seeing. He was a burly Irishman, his hair a premature white, combed back in neat waves beneath his peaked blue cap. His eyes were bright blue, his nose bright red. There were small nests of burst capillaries in his cheeks. He was a man of no more than medium height, but to the five boys arrayed before him he looked at least eight feet tall.

Mr Nell opened his mouth to speak, but before he could, Bill Denbrough had stepped up beside Ben.

'Ih-Ih-Ih-It w-wuh-wuh-was m-my i-i-i-i-idea,' he finally

managed to say. He heaved in a gigantic, gulping breath and as Mr Nell stood there regarding him impassively, the sun tossing back imperial flashes from his badge, Bill managed to stutter out the rest of what he needed to say: it wasn't Ben's fault; Ben just happened to come along and show them how to do better what they were already doing badly.

'Me too,' Eddie said abruptly, and stepped up on Ben's other side.

'What's this "me too"?' Mr Nell asked. 'Is that yer name or yer address, buckaroo?'

Eddie flushed brightly – the color went all the way up to the roots of his hair. 'I was with Bill before Ben even came,' he said. 'That was all I meant.'

Richie stepped up next to Eddie. The idea that a Voice or two might cheer Mr Nell up a little, get him thinking jolly thoughts, popped into his head. On second thought (and second thoughts were, for Richie, extremely rare and wonderful things), maybe a Voice or two might only make things worse. Mr Nell didn't look like he was in what Richie sometimes thought of as a chuckalicious mood. In fact, Mr Nell looked like maybe chucks were the last thing on his mind. So he just said, 'I was in on it too,' in a low voice, and then made his mouth shut up.

'And me,' Stan said, stepping next to Bill.

Now the five of them were standing before Mr Nell in a line. Ben looked from one side to the other, more than dazed – he was almost stupefied by their support. For a moment Richie thought ole Haystack was going to burst into tears of gratitude.

'Jaysus,' Mr Nell said again, and although he sounded deeply disgusted, his face suddenly looked as if it might like to laugh. 'A sorrier bunch of boyos I ain't nivver seen. If yer folks knew where you were, I guess there'd be some hot bottoms tonight. I ain't sure there won't be anyway.'

Richie could hold back no longer; his mouth simply fell open and then ran away like the gingerbread man, as it so often did.

'How's things back in the auld country, Mr Nell?' it bugled. 'Ah, yer a sight for sore eyes, sure an begorrah, yer a lovely man, a credit to the auld sod –'

'I'll be a credit to the seat of yer pants in about three seconds, my dear little friend,' Mr Nell said dryly.

Bill turned on him, snarled: 'For G-G-God's s-sake R-R-Richie shuh-shuh-hut *UP!*'

'Good advice, Master William Denbrough,' Mr Nell said. 'I'll bet Zack doesn't know you're down here in the Bar'ns playing amongst the floating turdies, does he?'

Bill dropped his eyes, shook his head. Wild roses burned in his cheeks.

Mr Nell looked at Ben. 'I don't recall your name, son.'

'Ben Hanscom, sir,' Ben whispered.

Mr Nell nodded and looked back at the dam again. 'This was your idea?'

'How to build it, yeah.' Ben's whisper was now nearly inaudible.

'Well, yer a hell of an engineer, big boy, but you don't know Jack Shit about these here Bar'ns or the Derry drainage system, do you?'

Ben shook his head.

Not unkindly, Mr Nell told him, 'There's two parts to the system. One part carries solid human waste – shit, if I'd not be offendin yer tender ears. The other part carries gray water – water flushed from toilets or run down the drains from sinks and washin-machines and showers; it's also the water that runs down the gutters into the city drains.

'Well, ye've caused no problems with the solid-waste removal, thank God – all of that gets pumped into the Kenduskeag a bit farther down. There's probably some almighty big patties down that way half a mile dryin in the sun thanks to what you done, but you can be pretty sure that there ain't shit stickin to anyone's ceiling because of it.

'But as for the gray water . . . well, there's no pumps for gray water. That all runs downhill in what the engineer boyos call gravity drains. And I'll bet you know where all them gravity drains end up, don't you, big boy?'

'Up there,' Ben said. He pointed to the area behind the dam, the area they had in large part submerged. He did this without looking up. Big tears were beginning to course slowly down his cheeks. Mr Nell pretended not to notice.

'That's right, my large young friend. All them gravity drains feed into streams that feed into the upper Barrens. In fact, a good many of them little streams that come tricklin down are gray water and gray water only, comin out of drains you can't even see, they're so deep-buried in the underbrush. The shit goes one way and everythin else goes the other, God praise the clever mind o man, and did it ever cross yer minds that you'd spent the whole live-long day paddlin around in Derry's pee an old wash-water?'

Eddie suddenly began to gasp and had to use his aspirator.

'What you did was back water up into about six o the eight central catch-basins that serve Witcham and Jackson and Kansas and four or five little streets that run between em.' Mr Nell fixed Bill Denbrough with a dry glance. 'One of em serves yer own hearth an home, young Master Denbrough. So there we are, with sinks that won't drain, washin-machines that won't drain, outflow pipes pourin merrily into cellars —'

Ben let out a dry barking sob. The others turned toward him and then looked away. Mr Nell put a large hand on the boy's shoulder. It was callused and hard, but at the moment it was also gentle.

'Now, now. No need to take on, big boy. Maybe it ain't that bad, at least not yet; could be I exaggerated just a mite to make sure you took my point. They sent me down to see if a tree blew down across the stream. That happens from time to time. There's no need for anyone but me and you five to know it wasn't just that. We've got more important things to worry about in town these days than a little backed-up water. I'll say on my report that I located the blow-down and some boys came along and helped me shift it out o the way o the water. Not that I'll mention ye by name. Ye'll not be gettin any citations for dam-building in the Bar'ns.'

He surveyed the five of them. Ben was furiously wiping his eyes with his handkerchief; Bill was looking thoughtfully at the dam; Eddie was holding his aspirator in one hand; Stan stood close by Richie with one hand on Richie's arm, ready to squeeze — hard — if Richie should show the slightest sign of having anything to say other than thank you very much.

'You boys got no business at all in a dirty place like this,' Mr Nell went on. 'There's probably sixty different kinds o disease breeding down here.' *Breeding* came out *braidin*, as in what a girl may do with her hair in the morning. 'Dump down one way, streams full of piss an gray water, muck an slop, bugs an brambles, quick-mud . . . you got no business at all in a dirty place like this. Four clean city parks for you boyos to be playin ball in all the day long and I catch you down here. Jaysus Christ!'

'Wuh-Wuh-We l-l-l-like it d-d-down h-here,' Bill said suddenly and defiantly. 'Wh-When w-w-we cuh-hum down h-here, nuh-ho-hobody gives us a-a-any stuh-stuh-hatic.'

'What'd he say?' Mr Nell asked Eddie.

'He said when we come down here nobody gives us any static,' Eddie said. His voice was thin and whistling, but it was also unmistakably

IT

firm. 'And he's right. When guys like us go to the park and say we want to play baseball, the other guys say sure, you want to be second base or third?'

Richie cackled. 'Eddie Gets Off A Good One! And . . . *You Are There!*'

Mr Nell swung his head to look at him.

Richie shrugged. 'Sorry. But he's right. And Bill's right, too. We like it down here.'

Richie thought Mr Nell would become angry again at that, but the white-haired cop surprised him – surprised them all – with a smile. 'Ayuh,' he said. 'I liked it down here meself as a boy, so I did. And I'll not forbid ye. But hark to what I'm tellin you now.' He leveled a finger at them and they all looked at him soberly. 'If ye come down here to play ye come in a gang like ye are now. Together. Do you understand me?'

They nodded.

'That means together *all the time*. No hide-an-seek games where yer split up one an one an one. You all know what's goin on in this town. All the same, I don't forbid you to come down here, mostly because ye'd be down here anyway. But for yer own good, here or anywhere around, gang together.' He looked at Bill. 'Do you disagree with me, young Master Bill Denbrough?'

'N-N-No, sir,' Bill said. 'W-We'll stay tuh-tuh-tuh –'

'That's good enough for me,' Mr Nell said. 'Yer hand on it.'

Bill stuck out his hand and Mr Nell shook it.

Richie shook off Stan and stepped forward.

'Sure an begorrah, Mr Nell, yer a prince among men, y'are! A foine man! A foine, foine man!' He stuck out his own hand, seized the Irishman's huge paw, and flagged it furiously, grinning all the time. To the bemused Mr Nell the boy looked like a hideous parody of Franklin D. Roosevelt.

'Thank you, boy,' Mr Nell said, retrieving his hand. 'Ye want to work on that a bit. As of now, ye sound about as Irish as Groucho Marx.'

The other boys laughed, mostly in relief. Even as he was laughing, Stan shot Richie a reproachful look: *Grow up, Richie!*

Mr Nell shook hands all around, gripping Ben's last of all.

'Ye've nothing to be ashamed of but bad judgment, big boy. As for that there . . . did you see how to do it in a book?'

Ben shook his head.

'Just figured it out?'

'Yes, sir.'

'Well if that don't beat Harry! Ye'll do great things someday, I've no doubt. But the Barrens isn't the place to do em.' He looked around thoughtfully. 'No great thing will ever be done here. Nasty place.' He sighed. 'Tear it down, dear boys. Tear it right down. I believe I'll just sit me down in the shade o this bush here and bide a wee as you do it.' He looked ironically at Richie as he said this last, as if inviting another manic outburst.

'Yes, sir,' Richie said humbly, and that was all. Mr Nell nodded, satisfied, and the boys fell to work, once again turning to Ben – this time to show them the quickest way to tear down what he had shown them how to build. Meanwhile, Mr Nell removed a brown bottle from inside his tunic and helped himself to a large gulp. He coughed, then blew out breath in an explosive sigh and regarded the boys with watery, benign eyes.

'And what might ye have in yer bottle, sor?' Richie asked from the place where he was standing knee-deep in the water.

'Richie, can't you ever shut up?' Eddie hissed.

'This?' Mr Nell regarded Richie with mild surprise and looked at the bottle again. It had no label of any kind on it. 'This is the cough medicine of the gods, my boy. Now let's see if you can bend yer back anywhere near as fast as you can wag yer tongue.'

3

Bill and Richie were walking up Witcham Street together later on. Bill was pushing Silver; after first building and then tearing down the dam, he simply did not have the energy it would have taken to get Silver up to cruising speed. Both boys were dirty, dishevelled, and pretty well used up.

Stan had asked them if they wanted to come over to his house and play Monopoly or Parcheesi or something, but none of them wanted to. It was getting late. Ben, sounding tired and depressed, said he was going to go home and see if anybody had returned his library books. He had some hope of this, since the Derry Library insisted on writing in the borrower's street address as well as his name on each book's pocket card. Eddie said he was going to watch *The Rock Show* on TV because Neil Sedaka was going to be on and he wanted to see if Neil Sedaka was a Negro. Stan told Eddie not to be so stupid, Neil Sedaka was white, you could tell he was white just listening to him. Eddie claimed you couldn't tell anything by listening to them; until last year he had been positive Chuck Berry was white, but when *he* was on *Bandstand* he turned out to be a Negro.

'My mother *still* thinks he's white, so that's one good thing,' Eddie said. 'If she finds out he's a Negro, she probably won't let me listen to his songs anymore.'

Stan bet Eddie four funnybooks that Neil Sedaka was white, and the two of them set off together for Eddie's house to settle the issue.

And here were Bill and Richie, headed in a direction which would bring them to Bill's house after awhile, neither of them talking much. Richie found himself thinking about Bill's story of the picture that had turned its head and winked. And in spite of his tiredness, an idea came to him. It was crazy . . . but it also held a certain attraction.

'Billy me boy,' he said. 'Let's stop for awhile. Take five. I'm dead.'

'No such I-I-luck,' Bill said, but he stopped, laid Silver carefully down on the edge of the green Theological Seminary lawn, and the two boys sat on the wide stone steps which led up to the rambling red Victorian structure.

'What a d-d-day,' Bill said glumly. There were dark purplish patches under his eyes. His face looked white and used. 'You better call your house when w-we get to muh-mine. So your f-folks don't go b-b-bananas.'

'Yeah. You bet. Listen, Bill –'

Richie paused for a moment, thinking about Ben's mummy, Eddie's leper, and whatever Stan had almost told them. For a moment something swam in his own mind, something about that Paul Bunyan statue out by the City Center. But that had only been a *dream*, for God's sake.

He pushed away such irrelevant thoughts and plunged.

'Let's go up to your house, what do you say? Take a look in Georgie's room. I want to see that picture.'

Bill looked at Richie, shocked. He tried to speak but could not; his stress was simply too great. He settled for shaking his head violently.

Richie said, 'You heard Eddie's story. And Ben's. Do you believe what they said?'

'I don't nuh-nuh-know. I th-hink they m-m-must have suh-seen suh-homething.'

'Yeah. Me too. All the kids that've been killed around here, I think all of *them* would have had stories to tell, too. The only difference between Ben and Eddie and those other kids is that Ben and Eddie didn't get caught.'

Bill raised his eyebrows but showed no great surprise. Richie had supposed Bill would have taken it that far himself. He couldn't talk so good, but he was no dummy.

'So now dig on this awhile, Big Bill,' Richie said. 'A guy could dress up in a clown suit and kill kids. I don't know why he'd want to, but nobody can tell why crazy people do things, right?'

'Ruh-Ruh-Ruh –'

'Right. It's not that much different than the Joker in a Batman funnybook.' Just hearing his ideas out loud excited Richie. He wondered briefly if he was actually trying to prove something or just throwing up a smokescreen of words so he could see that room, that picture. In the end it probably didn't matter. In the end maybe just seeing Bill's eyes light up with their own excitement was enough.

'B-B-But wh-wh-where does the pih-hicture fit i-i-in?'

'What do *you* think, Billy?'

In a low voice, not looking at Richie, Bill said he didn't think it had anything to do with the murders. 'I think it was Juh-Juh-Georgie's g-ghost.'

'A ghost in a *picture*?'

Bill nodded.

Richie thought about it. The idea of ghosts gave his child's mind no trouble at all. He was sure there were such things. His parents were Methodists, and Richie went to church every Sunday and to Thursday-night Methodist Youth Fellowship meetings as well. He knew a great deal of the Bible already, and he knew the Bible believed in all sorts of weird stuff. According to the Bible, God Himself was at least one-third Ghost, and that was just the beginning. You could tell the Bible believed in demons, because Jesus threw a bunch of them out of this guy. Real chuckalicious ones, too. When Jesus asked the guy who had them what his name was, the demons answered and told Him to go join the Foreign Legion. Or something like that. The Bible believed in witches, or else why would it say 'Thou shalt not suffer a witch to live'? Some of the stuff in the Bible was even better than the stuff in the horror comics. People getting boiled in oil or hanging themselves like Judas Iscariot; the story about how wicked King Ahaz fell off the tower and all the dogs came and licked up his blood; the mass baby-murders that had accompanied the births of both Moses and Jesus Christ; guys who came out of their graves or flew into the air; soldiers who witched down walls; prophets who saw the future and fought monsters. All of that was in the Bible and every word of it was true – so said Reverend Craig and so said Richie's folks and so said Richie.

He was perfectly willing to credit the possibility of Bill's explanation; it was the logic which troubled him.

'But you said you were scared. Why would George's ghost want to scare you, Bill?'

Bill put a hand to his mouth and wiped it. The hand was trembling slightly. 'H-He's probably muh-muh-mad at m-m-me. For g-getting him kih-hilled. It was my fuh-fuh-fault. I s-sent him out with the buh-buh-buh –' He was incapable of getting the word out, so he rocked his hand in the air instead. Richie nodded to show he understood what Bill meant . . . but not to indicate agreement.

'I don't think so,' he said. 'If you stabbed him in the back or shot him, that would be different. Or even if you, like, gave him a loaded gun that belonged to your dad to play with and he shot himself with it. But it wasn't a gun, it was just a boat. You didn't want to hurt him; in fact' – Richie raised one finger and waggled it at Bill in a lawyerly way – 'you just wanted the kid to have a little fun, right?'

Bill thought back – thought desperately hard. What Richie had just said had made him feel better about George's death for the first time in months, but there was a part of him which insisted with quiet firmness that he was not *supposed* to feel better. Of *course* it was your fault, that part of him insisted; not entirely, maybe, but at least partly.

If not, how come there's that cold place on the couch between your mother and father? If not, how come no one ever says anything at the supper table anymore? Now it's just knives and forks rattling until you can't take it anymore and ask if you can be eh-eh-eh-excused, please.

It was as if *he* were the ghost, a presence that spoke and moved but was not quite heard or seen, a thing vaguely sensed but still not accepted as real.

He did not like the thought that he was to blame, but the only alternative he could think of to explain their behavior was much worse: that all the love and attention his parents had given him before had somehow been the result of George's presence, and with George gone there was nothing for him . . . and all of that had happened at random, for no reason at all. And if you put your ear to *that* door, you could hear the winds of madness blowing outside.

So he went over what he had done and felt and said on the day Georgie had died, part of him hoping that what Richie had said was true, part of him hoping just as hard it was not. He hadn't been a saint of a big brother to George, that much was certain. They had had fights, plenty of them. Surely there had been one that day?

No. No fight. For one thing, Bill himself had still been feeling too punk to work up a really good quarrel with George. He had been sleeping, dreaming something, dreaming about some

(*turtle*)

funny little animal, he couldn't remember just what, and he had awakened to the sound of the diminishing rain outside and George muttering unhappily to himself in the dining room. He asked George what was wrong. George came in and said he was trying to make a paper boat from the directions in his *Best Book of Activities* but it kept coming out wrong. Bill told George to bring his book. And sitting next to Richie on the steps leading up to the seminary, he remembered how Georgie's eyes lit up when the paper boat came out right, and how good that look had made him feel, like Georgie thought he was a real hot shit, a straight shooter, the guy who could do it until it got done. Making him feel, in short, like a big brother.

The boat had killed George, but Richie was right – it hadn't been like handing George a loaded gun to play with. Bill hadn't known what was going to happen. No way he could.

He drew a deep, shuddering breath, feeling something like a rock – something he hadn't even known was there – go rolling off his chest. All at once he felt better, better about everything.

He opened his mouth to tell Richie this and burst into tears instead.

Alarmed, Richie put an arm around Bill's shoulders (after taking a quick glance around to make sure no one who might mistake them for a couple of fagolas was looking).

'You're okay,' he said. 'You're okay, Billy, right? Come on. Turn off the waterworks.'

'*I didn't wuh-wuh-want h-him t-to g-g-get kuh-hilled!*' Bill sobbed. '*TH-THAT WUH-WUH-WASN'T ON MY M-M-M-MIND AT UH-UH-ALL!*'

'Christ, Billy, I know it wasn't,' Richie said. 'If you'd wanted to scrub him, you woulda pushed him downstairs or something.' Richie patted Bill's shoulder clumsily and gave him a hard little hug before letting go. 'Come on, quit bawlin, okay? You sound like a baby.'

Little by little Bill stopped. He still hurt, but this hurt seemed cleaner, as if he had cut himself open and taken out something that was rotting inside him. And that feeling of relief was still there.

'I-I didn't w-want him to get kuh-kuh-killed,' Bill repeated, 'and ih-if y-y-you t-tell anybody I w-was c-c-cryin, I'll b-b-bust your n-n-nose.'

'I won't tell,' Richie said, 'don't worry. He was your brother, for gosh sake. If my brother got killed, I'd cry my fuckin head off.'

'Yuh-Yuh-You d-don't have a buh-brother.'

'Yeah, but if I did.'

'Y-You w-w-would?'

'Course.' Richie paused, fixing Bill with a wary eye, trying to decide if Bill was really over it. He was still wiping his red eyes with his snotrag, but Richie decided he probably was. 'All I meant was that I don't know why George would want to haunt you. So maybe the picture's got something to do with . . . well, with that other. The clown.'

'Muh-Muh-Maybe G-G-George d-d-doesn't nuh-nuh-know. Maybe h-he th-thinks —'

Richie understood what Bill was trying to say and waved it aside. 'After you croak you know everything people ever thought about you, Big Bill.' He spoke with the indulgent air of a great teacher correcting a country bumpkin's fatuous ideas. 'It's in the Bible. It says, "Yea, even though we can't see too much in the mirror right now, we will see through it like it was a window after we die." That's in First Thessalonians or Second Babylonians, I forget which. It means —'

'I suh-suh-see what it m-m-means,' Bill said.

'So what do you say?'

'Huh?'

'Let's go up to his room and take a look. Maybe we'll get a clue about who's killing all the kids.'

'I'm s-s-scared to.'

'I am too,' Richie said, thinking it was just more sand, something to say that would get Bill moving, and then something heavy turned over in his midsection and he discovered it was true: he was scared green.

4

The two boys slipped into the Denbrough house like ghosts.

Bill's father was still at work. Sharon Denbrough was in the kitchen, reading a paperback at the kitchen table. The smell of supper – codfish – drifted out into the front hall. Richie called home so his mom would know he wasn't dead, just at Bill's.

'Someone there?' Mrs Denbrough called as Richie put the phone down. They froze, eyeing each other guiltily. Then Bill called: 'M-Me, Mom. And R-R-R-R-R —'

'Richie Tozier, ma'am,' Richie yelled.

'Hello, Richie,' Mrs Denbrough called back, her voice disconnected, almost not there at all. 'Would you like to stay for supper?'

'Thanks, ma'am, but my mom's gonna pick me up in half an hour or so.'

'Tell her I said hello, won't you?'

'Yes ma'am, I sure will.'

'C-Come on,' Bill whispered. 'That's enough s-small talk.'

They went upstairs and down the hall to Bill's room. It was boy-neat, which meant it would have given the mother of the boy in question only a mild headache to look at. The shelves were stuffed with a helter-skelter collection of books and comics. There were more comics, plus a few models and toys and a stack of 45s, on the desk. There was also an old Underwood office model typewriter on it. His folks had given it to him for Christmas two years ago, and Bill sometimes wrote stories on it. He did this a bit more frequently since George's death. The pretending seemed to ease his mind.

There was a phonograph on the floor across from the bed with a pile of folded clothes stacked on the lid. Bill put the clothes in the drawers of his bureau and then took the records from the desk. He shuffled through them, picking half a dozen. He put them on the phonograph's fat spindle and turned the machine on. The Fleetwoods started singing 'Come Softly Darling.'

Richie held his nose.

Bill grinned in spite of his thumping heart. 'Th-They d-don't luh-luh-hike rock and r-roll,' he said. 'They g-gave me this wuh-one for my b-b-birthday. Also two P-Pat B-B-Boone records and Tuh-Tuh-Tommy Sands. I keep L-L-Little Ruh-Richard and Scuh-hreamin J-Jay Hawkins for when they're not h-here. But if she hears the m-m-music she'll th-think we're i-in m-my room. C-C-Come o-on.'

George's room was across the hall. The door was shut. Richie looked at it and licked his lips.

'They don't keep it locked?' he whispered to Bill. Suddenly he found himself hoping it *was* locked. Suddenly he was having trouble believing this had been his idea.

Bill, his face pale, shook his head and turned the knob. He stepped in and looked back at Richie. After a moment Richie followed. Bill shut the door behind them, muffling the Fleetwoods. Richie jumped a little at the soft snick of the latch.

He looked around, fearful and intensely curious at the same time. The first thing he noticed was the dry mustiness of the air – *No one's opened a window in here for a long time*, he thought. *Heck, no one's* breathed *in here for a long time. That's really what it feels like.* He shuddered a little at the thought and licked his lips again.

His eye fell on George's bed, and he thought of George sleeping now under a comforter of earth in Mount Hope Cemetery. Rotting there. His hands not folded because you needed two hands to do the old folding routine, and George had been buried with only one.

A little sound escaped Richie's throat. Bill turned and looked at him enquiringly.

'You're right,' Richie said huskily. 'It's spooky in here. I don't see how you could stand to come in alone.'

'H-He was my bruh-brother,' Bill said simply. 'Sometimes I w-w-want to, is a-all.'

There were posters on the walls – little-kid posters. One showed Tom Terrific, the cartoon character on Captain Kangaroo's program. Tom was springing over the head and clutching hands of Crabby Appleton, who was, of course, Rotten to the Core. Another showed Donald Duck's nephews, Huey, Louie, and Dewie, marching off into the wilderness in their Junior Woodchucks coonskin caps. A third, which George had colored himself, showed Mr Do holding up traffic so a bunch of little kids headed for school could cross the street. MR DO SAYS WAIT FOR THE CROSSING GUARD!, it said underneath.

Kid wasn't too cool about staying in the lines, Richie thought, and then shuddered. The kid was never going to get any better at it, either. Richie looked at the table by the window. Mrs Denbrough had stood up all of George's rank-cards there, half-open. Looking at them, knowing there would never be more, knowing that George had died before he could stay in the lines when he colored, knowing his life had ended irrevocably and eternally with only those few kindergarten and first-grade rank-cards, all the idiot truth of death crashed home to Richie for the first time. It was as if a large iron safe had fallen into his brain and buried itself there. *I could die!* his mind screamed at him suddenly in tones of betrayed horror. *Anybody could! Anybody could!*

'Boy oh boy,' he said in a shaky voice. He could manage no more.

'Yeah,' Bill said in a near-whisper. He sat down on George's bed. 'Look.'

Richie followed Bill's pointing finger and saw the photo album lying closed on the floor. MY PHOTOGRAPHS, Richie read. GEORGE ELMER DENBROUGH, AGE 6.

Age 6! his mind shrieked in those same tones of shrill betrayal. *Age 6 forever! Anybody could! Shit! Fucking anybody!*

'It was oh-oh-open,' Bill said. 'B-Before.'

'So it closed,' Richie said uneasily. He sat down on the bed beside Bill and looked at the photo album. 'Lots of books close on their own.'

'The *p-p-pages*, maybe, but n-not the *cuh-cuh-cover*. It c-closed itself.' He looked at Richie solemnly, his eyes very dark in his pale, tired face. 'B-But it wuh-wuh-wants y-you to oh-open it up again. That's what I th-think.'

Richie got up and walked slowly over to the photograph album. It lay at the base of a window screened with light curtains. Looking out, he could see the apple tree in the Denbrough back yard. A swing rocked slowly back and forth from one gnarled, black limb.

He looked down at George's book again.

A dried maroon stain colored the thickness of the pages in the middle of the book. It could have been old ketchup. Sure; it was easy enough to see George looking at his photo album while eating a hot dog or a big sloppy hamburger; he takes a big bite and some ketchup squirts out onto the book. Little kids were always doing spasmoid stuff like that. It could be ketchup. But Richie knew it was not.

He touched the album briefly and then drew his hand away. It felt cold. It had been lying in a place where the strong summer sunlight, only slightly filtered by those light curtains, would have been falling on it all day, but it felt cold.

Well, I'll just leave it alone, Richie thought. *I don't want to look in his stupid old album anyway, see a lot of people I don't know. I think maybe I'll tell Bill I changed my mind, and we can go to his room and read comic books for awhile and then I'll go home and eat supper and go to bed early because I'm pretty tired, and when I wake up tomorrow morning I'm sure I'll be sure that stuff was just ketchup. That's just what I'll do. Yowza.*

So he opened the album with hands that seemed a thousand miles away from him, at the end of long plastic arms, and he looked at the faces and places in George's album, the aunts, the uncles, the babies, the houses, the old Fords and Studebakers, the telephone lines, the mailboxes, the picket fences, the wheelruts with muddy water in them, the Ferris wheel at the Esty County Fair, the Standpipe, the ruins of the Kitchener Ironworks –

His fingers flipped faster and faster and suddenly the pages were blank. He turned back, not wanting to but unable to help himself.

Here was a picture of downtown Derry, Main Street and Canal Street from around 1930, and beyond it there was nothing.

'There's no school picture of George in here,' Richie said. He looked at Bill with a mixture of relief and exasperation. 'What kind of line were you handing me, Big Bill?'

'W-W-What?'

'This picture of downtown in the olden days is the last one in the book. All the rest of the pages are blank.'

Bill got off the bed and joined Richie. He looked at the picture of downtown Derry as it had been almost thirty years ago, old-fashioned cars and trucks, old-fashioned streetlights with clusters of globes like big white grapes, pedestrians by the Canal caught in mid-stride by the click of a shutter. He turned the page and, just as Richie had said, there was nothing.

No, wait — not *quite* nothing. There was one studio corner, the sort of item you use to mount photographs.

'It *w-w-was* here,' he said, and tapped the studio corner. 'L-Look.'

'Jeepers! What do you think happened to it?'

'I d-don't nuh-nuh-know.'

Bill had taken the album from Richie and was now holding it on his own lap. He turned back through the pages, looking for George's picture. He gave up after a minute, but the pages did not. They turned themselves, flipping slowly but steadily, with big deliberate riffling sounds. Bill and Richie looked at each other, wide-eyed, and then back down.

It arrived at that last picture again and the pages stopped turning. Here was downtown Derry in sepia tones, the city as it had been long before either Bill or Richie had been born.

'Say!' Richie said suddenly, and took the album back from Bill. There was no fear in his voice now, and his face was suddenly full of wonder. 'Holy shit!'

'W-What? What ih-ih-is it?'

'*Us!* That's what it is! Holy-jeezly-crow, *look!*'

Bill took one side of the book. Bent over it, sharing it, they looked like boys at choir practice. Bill drew in breath sharply, and Richie knew he had seen it too.

Caught under the shiny surface of this old black-and-white photograph two small boys were walking along Main Street toward the point where Main and Center intersected — the point where the Canal went underground for a mile and a half or so. The two boys showed up clearly against the low concrete wall at the edge of the

Canal. One was wearing knickers. The other was wearing something that looked almost like a sailor suit. A tweed cap was perched on his head. They were turned in three-quarter profile toward the camera, looking at something on the far side of the street. The boy in the knickers was Richie Tozier, beyond a doubt. And the boy in the sailor suit and the tweed cap was Stuttering Bill.

They stared at themselves in a picture almost three times as old as they were, hypnotized. The inside of Richie's mouth suddenly felt as dry as dust and as smooth as glass. A few steps ahead of the boys in the picture there was a man holding the brim of his fedora, his topcoat frozen forever as it flapped out behind him in a sudden gust of wind. There were Model-Ts on the street, a Pierce-Arrow, Chevrolets with running boards.

'I-I-I-I d-don't buh-buh-believe –' Bill began, and that was when the picture began to move.

The Model-T that should have remained eternally in the middle of the intersection (or at least until the chemicals in the old photo finally dissolved completely) passed through it, a haze of exhaust puffing out of its tailpipe. It went on toward Up-Mile Hill. A small white hand shot out of the driver's side window and signalled a left turn. It swung onto Court Street and passed beyond the photo's white border and so out of sight.

The Pierce-Arrow, the Chevrolets, the Packards – they all began to roll along, dodging their separate ways through the intersection. After twenty-eight years or so the skirt of the man's topcoat finally finished its flap. He settled his hat more firmly on his head and walked on.

The two boys completed their turn, coming full-face, and a moment later Richie saw what they had been looking at as a mangy dog came trotting across Center Street. The boy in the sailor suit – Bill – raised two fingers to the corners of his mouth and whistled. Stunned beyond any ability to move or think, Richie realized he could *hear* the whistle, could *hear* the cars' irregular sewing-machine engines. The sounds were faint, like sounds heard through thick glass, but they were *there*.

The dog glanced toward the two boys, then trotted on. The boys glanced at each other and laughed like chipmunks. They started to walk on, and then the Richie in knickers grabbed Bill's arm and pointed toward the Canal. They turned in that direction.

No, Richie thought, *don't do that, don't –*

They went to the low concrete wall and suddenly the clown

popped up over its edge like a horrible jack-in-the-box, a clown with Georgie Denbrough's face, his hair slicked back, his mouth a hideous grin full of bleeding greasepaint, his eyes black holes. One hand clutched three balloons on a string. With the other he reached for the boy in the sailor suit and seized his neck.

'*Nuh-Nuh-NO!*' Bill cried, and reached for the picture.

Reached *into* the picture.

'*Stop it, Bill!*' Richie shouted, and grabbed for him.

He was almost too late. He saw the tips of Bill's fingers go through the surface of the photograph and into that other world. He saw the fingertips go from the warm pink of living flesh to the mummified cream color that passed for white in old photos. At the same time they became small and disconnected. It was like the peculiar optical illusion one sees when one thrusts a hand into a glass bowl of water: the part of the hand underwater seems to be floating, disembodied, inches away from the part which is still out of the water.

A series of diagonal cuts slashed across Bill's fingers at the point where they ceased being his fingers and became photo-fingers; it was as if he had stuck his hand into the blades of a fan instead of into a picture.

Richie seized his forearm and gave a tremendous yank. They both fell over. George's album hit the floor and snapped itself shut with a dry clap. Bill stuck his fingers in his mouth. Tears of pain stood in his eyes. Richie could see blood running down his palm to his wrist in thin streams.

'Let me see,' he said.

'Hu-Hurts,' Bill said. He held his hand out to Richie, palm down. There were ladderlike slash-cuts running up his index, second, and third fingers. The pinky had barely touched the surface of the photograph (if it *had* a surface), and although that finger had not been cut, Bill told Richie later that the nail had been neatly clipped, as if with a pair of manicurist's scissors.

'Jesus, Bill,' Richie said. Band-Aids. That was all he could think of. God, they had been lucky – if he hadn't pulled Bill's arm when he did, his fingers might have been amputated instead of just badly cut. 'We got to fix those up. Your mother can –'

'Neh-neh-never m-mind m-my muh-huther,' Bill said. He grabbed the photo album again, spilling drops of blood on the floor.

'Don't open that again!' Richie cried, grabbing frantically at Bill's shoulder. 'Jesus Christ, Billy, you almost lost your *fingers!*'

Bill shook him off. He flipped through the pages, and there was a grim determination on his face that scared Richie more than anything else. Bill's eyes looked almost mad. His wounded fingers printed George's album with new blood – it didn't look like ketchup yet, but when it had a little time to dry it would. Of course it would.

And here was the downtown scene again.

The Model-T stood in the middle of the intersection. The other cars were frozen in the places where they had been before. The man walking toward the intersection held the brim of his fedora; his coat once more belled out in mid-flap.

The two boys were gone.

There were no boys in the picture anywhere. But –

'Look,' Richie whispered, and pointed. He was careful to keep the tip of his finger well away from the picture. An arc showed just over the low concrete wall at the edge of the Canal – the top of something round.

Something like a balloon.

5

They got out of George's room just in time. Bill's mother was a voice at the foot of the stairs and a shadow on the wall. 'Have you boys been wrestling?' she asked sharply. 'I heard a thud.'

'Just a lih-lih-little, M-Mom.' Bill threw a sharp glance at Richie. *Be quiet*, it said.

'Well, I want you to stop it. I thought the ceiling was going to come right down on my head.'

'W-W-We will.'

They heard her go back toward the front of the house. Bill had wrapped his handkerchief around his bleeding hand; it was turning red and in a moment would start to drip. The boys went down to the bathroom, where Bill held his hand under the faucet until the bleeding stopped. Cleaned, the cuts looked thin but cruelly deep. Looking at their white lips and the red meat just inside them made Richie feel sick to his stomach. He wrapped them with Band-Aids as fast as he could.

'H-H-Hurts like hell,' Bill said.

'Well, why'd you want to go and put your hand in there, you wet end?'

Bill looked solemnly at the rings of Band-Aids on his fingers, then up at Richie. 'I-I-It was the cluh-hown,' he said. 'It w-w-was the c-clown pretending to be Juh-Juh-George.'

'That's right,' Richie said. 'Like it was the clown pretending to be the mummy when Ben saw it. Like it was the clown pretending to be that sick bum Eddie saw.'

'The luh-luh-leper.'

'Right.'

'But ih-is it r-r-really a cluh-cluh-clown?'

'It's a monster,' Richie said flatly. 'Some kind of monster. Some kind of monster right here in Derry. And it's killing kids.'

6

On a Saturday, not long after the incident of the dam in the Barrens, Mr Nell, and the picture that moved, Richie, Ben, and Beverly Marsh came face to face with not one monster but two – and they paid to do it. Richie did, anyway. These monsters were scary but not really dangerous; they stalked their victims on the screen of the Aladdin Theater while Richie, Ben, and Bev watched from the balcony.

One of the monsters was a werewolf, played by Michael Landon, and he was cool because even when he was the werewolf he still had sort of a duck's ass haircut. The other was this smashed-up hotrodder, played by Gary Conway. He was brought back to life by a descendant of Victor Frankenstein, who fed all parts he didn't need to a bunch of alligators he kept in the basement. Also on the program: a MovieTone Newsreel that showed the latest Paris fashions and the latest Vanguard rocket explosions at Cape Canaveral, two Warner Brothers cartoons, one Popeye cartoon, and a Chilly Willy cartoon (for some reason the hat Chilly Willy wore always cracked Richie up), and PREVUES OF COMING ATTRACTIONS. The coming attractions included two pictures Richie immediately put on his gotta-see list: *I Married a Monster from Outer Space* and *The Blob.*

Ben was very quiet during the show. Ole Haystack had nearly been spotted by Henry, Belch, and Victor earlier, and Richie assumed that was all that was troubling him. Ben, however, had forgotten all about the creeps (they were sitting close to the screen down below, chucking popcorn boxes at each other and hooting). Beverly was the reason for his silence. Her nearness was so overwhelming that he was almost ill with it. His body would break out in goosebumps and then, if she should so much as shift in her seat, his skin would flash hot, as if with a tropical fever. When her hand brushed his reaching for the popcorn, he trembled with exaltation. He thought later that those three hours in the dark next to Beverly had been both the longest and shortest hours of his life.

Richie, unaware that Ben was in deep throes of calf-love, was feeling just as fine as paint. In his book the only thing any better than a couple of Francis the Talking Mule pictures was a couple of horror pictures in a theater filled with kids, all of them yelling and screaming at the gory parts. He certainly did not connect any of the goings-ons in the two low-budget American-International pictures they were watching with what was going on in town . . . not then, at least.

He had seen the Twin Shock Show Saturday Matinee ad in the *News* on Friday morning and had almost immediately forgotten how badly he had slept the night before – and how he had finally gotten up and turned on the light in his closet, a real baby trick for sure, but he hadn't been able to get a wink of sleep until he'd done it. But by the following morning things had seemed normal again . . . well, almost. He began to think that maybe he and Bill had just shared a hallucination. Of course the cuts on Bill's fingers weren't a hallucination, but maybe they'd just been paper-cuts from some of the sheets in Georgie's album. Pretty thick paper. Could of been. Maybe. Besides, there was no law saying he had to spend the next ten years thinking about it, was there? Nope.

And so, following an experience that might well have sent an adult running for the nearest headshrinker, Richie Tozier got up, ate a giant pancake breakfast, saw the ad for the two horror movies on the Amusements page of the paper, checked his funds, found them a little low (well . . . 'nonexistent' might actually have been a better word), and began to pester his father for chores.

His dad, who had come to the table already wearing his white dentist's tunic, put down the Sports pages and poured himself a second cup of coffee. He was a pleasant-looking man with a rather thin face. He wore steel-rimmed spectacles, was developing a bald spot at the back of his head, and would die of cancer of the larynx in 1973. He looked at the ad to which Richie was pointing.

'Horror movies,' Wentworth Tozier said.

'Yeah,' Richie said, grinning.

'Feel like you have to go,' Wentworth Tozier said.

'Yeah!'

'Feel like you'll probably die in convulsions of disappointment if you don't get to see those two trashy movies.'

'Yeah, yeah, I would! I know I would! *Graaaag!*' Richie fell out of his chair onto the floor, clutching his throat, his tongue sticking out. This was Richie's admittedly peculiar way of turning on the charm.

'Oh God, Richie, will you please stop it?' his mother asked him from the stove, where she was frying him a couple of eggs to top off the pancakes.

'Gee, Rich,' his father said as Richie got back into his chair. 'I guess I must have forgotten to pay you your allowance on Monday. That's the only reason I can think of for you needing more money on Friday.'

'Well . . .'

'Gone?'

'Well . . .'

'That's an extremely deep subject for a boy with such a shallow mind,' Wentworth Tozier said. He put his elbow on the table and then cupped his chin on the palm of his hand, regarding his only son with what appeared to be deep fascination. 'Where'd it go?'

Richie immediately fell into the Voice of Toodles the English Butler. 'Why, I spent it, didn't I, guv'nor? Pip-pip, cheerio, and all that rot! My part of the war effort. All got to do our bit to beat back the bloody Hun, don't we? Bit of a sticky wicket, ay-wot? Bit of a wet hedgehog, wot-wot? Bit of a –'

'Bit of a pile of bullshit,' Went said amiably, and reached for the strawberry preserves.

'Spare me the vulgarity at the breakfast table, if you please,' Maggie Tozier said to her husband as she brought Richie's eggs over to the table. And to Richie: 'I don't know why you want to fill your head up with such awful junk anyway.'

'Aw, Mom,' Richie said. He was outwardly crushed, inwardly jubilant. He could read both of his parents like books – well-worn and well-loved books – and he was pretty sure he was going to get what he wanted: chores and permission to go to the show Saturday afternoon.

Went leaned forward toward Richie and smiled widely. 'I think I have you right where I want you,' he said.

'Is that right, Dad?' Richie said, and smiled back . . . a trifle uneasily.

'Oh yes. You know our lawn, Richie? You are familiar with our lawn?'

'Indeed I am, guv'nor,' Richie said, becoming Toodles again – or trying to. 'Bit shaggy, ay-wot?'

'Wot-wot,' Went agreed. 'And you, Richie, will remedy that condition.'

'I will?'

'You will. Mow it, Richie.'

'Okay, Dad, sure,' Richie said, but a terrible suspicion had suddenly blossomed in his mind. Maybe his dad didn't mean just the front lawn.

Wentworth Tozier's smile widened to a predatory shark's grin. '*All* of it, O idiot child of my loins. Front. Back. Sides. And when you finish, I will cross your palm with two green pieces of paper with the likeness of George Washington on one side and a picture of a pyramid o'ertopped with the Ever-Watching Oculary on the other.'

'I don't get you, Dad,' Richie said, but he was afraid he did.

'Two bucks.'

'Two bucks for the *whole lawn*?' Richie cried, genuinely wounded. 'It's the biggest lawn on the *block*! Jeez, Dad!'

Went sighed and picked the paper up again. Richie could read the front page headline: MISSING BOY PROMPTS NEW FEARS. He thought briefly of George Denbrough's strange scrapbook – but that had surely been a hallucination . . . and even if it hadn't been, that was yesterday and this was today.

'Guess you didn't want to see those movies as bad as you thought,' Went said from behind the paper. A moment later his eyes appeared over the top, studying Richie. Studying him a trifle smugly, in truth. Studying him the way a man with four of a kind studies his poker opponent over the fan of his cards.

'When the Clark twins do it all, you give them two dollars *each*!'

'That's true,' Went admitted. 'But as far as I know, *they* don't want to go to the movies tomorrow. Or if they do, they must have funds sufficient to the occasion, because they haven't popped by to check the state of the herbiage surrounding our domicile lately. You, on the other hand, *do* want to go and find yourself lacking the funds to do so. That pressure you feel in your midsection may be the five pancakes and two eggs you ate for breakfast, Richie, or it may just be the barrel I have you over. Wot-wot?' Went's eyes submerged behind the paper again.

'He's blackmailing me,' Richie said to his mother, who was eating dry toast. She was trying to lose weight again. 'This is blackmail, I just hope you know that.'

'Yes, dear, I know that,' his mother said. 'There's egg on your chin.'

Richie wiped the egg off his chin. 'Three bucks if I have it all done when you get home tonight?' he asked the newspaper.

His father's eyes appeared again briefly. 'Two-fifty.'

'Oh, man,' Richie said. 'You and Jack Benny.'

'My idol,' Went said from behind the paper. 'Make up your mind, Richie. I want to read these box scores.'

'Deal,' Richie said, and sighed. When your folks had you by the balls, they really knew how to squeeze. It was pretty chuckalicious, when you thought it over.

As he mowed, he practiced his Voices.

7

He finished – front, back, and sides – by three o'clock Friday afternoon, and began Saturday with two dollars and fifty cents in his jeans. Pretty damn near a fortune. He called Bill up, but Bill told him glumly that he had to go up to Bangor and take some kind of speech-therapy test.

Richie sympathized and then added in his best Stuttering Bill Voice: 'G-G-Give em h-h-hell, Buh-Buh-Big Bih-Bill.'

'Your f-f-face and my buh-buh-butt, T-T-Tozier,' Bill said, and hung up.

He called Eddie Kaspbrak next, but Eddie sounded even more depressed than Bill – his mother had gotten them each a full-day bus-pass, he said, and they were going to visit Eddie's aunts in Haven and Bangor and Hampden. All three of them were fat, like Mrs Kaspbrak, and all three of them were single.

'They'll all pinch my cheek and tell me how much I've grown,' Eddie said.

'That's cause they know how cute you are, Eds – just like me. I saw what a cutie you were the first time I met you.'

'Sometimes you're really a turd, Richie.'

'It takes one to know one, Eds, and you know em all. You gonna be down in the Barrens next week?'

'I guess so, if you guys are. Want to play guns?'

'Maybe. But . . . I think me and Big Bill have got something to tell you.'

'What?'

'It's really Bill's story, I guess. I'll see you. Enjoy your aunts.'

'Very funny.'

His third call was to Stan the Man, but Stan was in dutch with his folks for breaking their picture window. He had been playing flying-saucer with a pie-plate and it took a bad bank. Kee-rash. He had to do chores all weekend, and probably next weekend, too. Richie commiserated and then asked Stan if he would be coming down to the Barrens next week. Stan said he guessed so, if his father didn't decide to ground him, or something.

'Jeez, Stan, it was just a window,' Richie said.

'Yeah, but a *big* one,' Stan said, and hung up.

Richie started to leave the living room, then thought of Ben Hanscom. He thumbed through the telephone book and found a listing for an Arlene Hanscom. Since she was the only lady Hanscom among the four listed, Richie figured it had to be Ben's number and called.

'I'd like to go, but I already spent my allowance,' Ben said. He sounded depressed and ashamed by the admission – he had, in fact, spent it all on candy, soda, chips, and beef-jerky strips.

Richie, who was rolling in dough (and who didn't like to go to the movies alone), said: 'I got plenty of money. You can gimme owesies.'

'Yeah? Really? You'd do that?'

'Sure,' Richie said, puzzled. 'Why not?'

'Okay!' Ben said happily. 'Okay, that'd be great! Two horror movies! Did you say one was a werewolf picture?'

'Yeah.'

'Man, I *love* werewolf pictures!'

'Jeez, Haystack, don't wet your pants.'

Ben laughed. 'I'll see you out in front of the Aladdin, okay?'

'Yeah, great.'

Richie hung up and looked at the phone thoughtfully. It suddenly occurred to him that Ben Hanscom was lonely. And that in turn made him feel rather heroic. He was whistling as he ran upstairs to get some comics to read before the show.

8

The day was sunny, breezy, and cool. Richie jived along Center Street toward the Aladdin, popping his fingers and singing 'Rockin' Robin' under his breath. He was feeling good. Going to the movies always made him feel good – he loved that magic world, those magic dreams. He felt sorry for anyone who had dull duties to discharge on such a day – Bill with his speech therapy, Eddie with his aunts, poor old Stan the Man who would be spending the afternoon scraping down the front-porch steps or sweeping the garage because the pie-plate he'd been throwing around swept right when it was supposed to sweep left.

Richie had his yo-yo tucked in his back pocket and now he took it out and tried again to get it to sleep. This was an ability Richie lusted to acquire, but so far, no soap. The crazy l'il fucker just wouldn't do it. Either it went down and popped right back up or it went down and dropped dead at the end of its string.

Halfway up Center Street Hill he saw a girl in a beige pleated skirt and a white sleeveless blouse sitting on a bench outside Shook's Drug Store. She was eating what looked like a pistachio ice-cream cone. Bright red-auburn hair, its highlights seeming coppery or some-times almost blonde, hung down to her shoulder-blades. Richie knew only one girl with hair of that particular shade. It was Beverly Marsh.

Richie liked Bev a lot. Well, he liked her, but not *that* way. He admired her looks (and knew he wasn't alone – girls like Sally Mueller and Greta Bowie hated Beverly like fire, still too young to understand how they could have everything else so easily ... and still have to compete in the matter of looks with a girl who lived in one of those slummy apartments on Lower Main Street), but mostly he liked her because she was tough and had a really good sense of humor. Also, she usually had cigarettes. He liked her, in short, because she was a good guy. Still, he had once or twice caught himself wondering what color underwear she was wearing under her small selection of rather faded skirts, and that was not the sort of thing you wondered about the other guys, was it?

And, Richie had to admit, she was one hell of a pretty guy.

Approaching the bench where she sat eating her ice cream, Richie belted an invisible topcoat around his middle, pulled down an invisible slouch hat, and pretended to be Humphrey Bogart. Adding the correct Voice, he *became* Humphrey Bogart – at least to himself. To others he would have sounded like Richie Tozier with a mild headcold.

'Hello, shweetheart,' he said, gliding up to the bench where she was sitting and looking out at the traffic. 'No sensh waitin for a bus here. The Nazish have cut off our retreat. The last plane leavesh at midnight. You be on it. He *needsh* you, shweetheart. So do I ... but I'll get along shomehow.'

'Hi, Richie,' Bev said, and when she turned toward him he saw a purple-blackish bruise on her right cheek, like the shadow of a crow's wing. He was again struck by her good looks ... only it occurred to him now that she might actually be beautiful. It had never really occurred to him until that moment that there might be beautiful girls outside of the movies, or that he himself might know one. Perhaps it was the bruise that allowed him to see the possibility of her beauty – an essential contrast, a particular flaw which first drew attention to itself and then somehow defined the rest: the gray-blue eyes, the naturally red lips, the creamy unblemished child's skin. There was a tiny spray of freckles across her nose.

'See anything green?' she asked, tossing her head pertly.

'You, shweetheart,' Richie said. 'You've turned green ash limberger cheese. But when we get you out of Cashablanca, you're going into the finesht hospital money can buy. We'll turn you white again. I shwear it on my mother'sh name.'

'You're an asshole, Richie. That doesn't sound like Humphrey Bogart at all.' But she smiled a little as she said it.

Richie sat down next to her. 'You going to the movies?'

'I don't have any money,' she said. 'Can I see your yo-yo?'

He handed it over. 'I oughtta take it back,' he told her. 'It's supposed to sleep but it doesn't. I got japped.'

She poked her finger through the loop of string and Richie pushed his glasses up on the bridge of his nose so he could watch what she was doing better. She turned her hand over, palm toward the sky, the Duncan yo-yo tucked neatly into the valley of flesh formed by her cupped hand. She rolled the yo-yo off her index finger. It went down to the end of its string and fell asleep. When she twitched her fingers in a come-on gesture it promptly woke up and climbed its string to her palm again.

'Oh bug-dung, look at that,' Richie said.

'That's kid stuff,' Bev said. 'Watch this.' She snapped the yo-yo down again. She let it sleep for a moment and then walked the dog with it in a smart series of snap jerks up the string to her hand again.

'Oh, stop it,' Richie said. 'I hate show-offs.'

'Or how about this?' Bev asked, smiling sweetly. She got the yo-yo going back and front, making the red wooden Duncan look like a Bo-Lo Bouncer Richie had had once. She finished with two Around the Worlds (almost hitting a shuffling old lady, who glared at them). The yo-yo ended up in her cupped palm, its string neatly rolled around its spindle. Bev handed it back to Richie and sat down on the bench again. Richie sat down next to her, his jaw hanging agape in perfectly unaffected admiration. Bev looked at him and giggled.

'Shut your mouth, you're drawing flies.'

Richie shut his mouth with a snap.

'Besides, that last part was just luck. First time in my life I did two Around the Worlds in a row without fizzing out.'

Kids were walking past them now, on their way to the show. Peter Gordon walked by with Marcia Fadden. They were supposed to be going together, but Richie figured it was just that they lived next door to each other on West Broadway and were such a couple of assholes that they needed each other's support and attention. Peter Gordon was already getting a pretty good crop of acne, although he was only twelve. He sometimes hung around with Bowers, Criss, and Huggins, but he wasn't quite brave enough to try anything on his own.

He glanced over at Richie and Bev sitting together on the bench and chanted, 'Richie and Beverly up in a tree! Kay-Eye-Ess-Ess-Eye-En-Gee! First comes love, then comes marriage −'

'− and here comes Richie with a baby carriage!' Marcia finished, cawing laughter.

'Sit on this, dear heart,' Bev said, and whipped the finger on them. Marcia looked away, disgusted, as if she could not believe anyone could be so uncouth. Gordon slipped an arm around her and called back over his shoulder to Richie, 'Maybe I'll see you later, four-eyes.'

'Maybe you'll see your mother's girdle,' Richie responded smartly (if a little senselessly). Beverly collapsed with laughter. She leaned against Richie's shoulder for a moment and Richie had just time to reflect that her touch, and the sensation of her lightly carried weight, was not exactly unpleasant. Then she sat up again.

'What a pair of jerks,' she said.

'Yeah, I think Marcia Fadden pees rosewater,' Richie said, and Beverly got the giggles again.

'Chanel Number Five,' she said, her voice muffled because her hands were over her mouth.

'You bet,' said Richie, although he hadn't the slightest idea what Chanel Number Five was. 'Bev?'

'What?'

'Can you show me how to make it sleep?'

'I guess so. I never tried to show anyone.'

'How did you learn? Who *showed* you?'

She gave him a disgusted look. 'No one *showed* me. I just figured it out. Like twirling a baton. I'm great at that −'

'No conceit in *your* family,' Richie said, rolling his eyes.

'Well, I *am*,' she said. 'But I didn't take classes, or anything.'

'You really can twirl?'

'Sure.'

'Probably be a cheerleader in junior high, huh?'

She smiled. It was a kind of smile Richie had never seen before. It was wise, cynical, and sad all at the same time. He recoiled a little from its unknowing power, as he had recoiled from the picture of downtown in Georgie's album when it had begun to move.

'That's for girls like Marcia Fadden,' she said. 'Her and Sally Mueller and Greta Bowie. Girls who pee rosewater. Their fathers help to buy the sports equipment and the uniforms. They got an in. I'll never be a cheerleader.'

'Jeez, Bev, that's no attitude to take –'

'Sure it is, if it's the truth.' She shrugged. 'I don't care. Who wants to do somersaults and show your underwear to a million people, anyway? Look, Richie. Watch this.'

For the next ten minutes she worked on showing Richie how to make his yo-yo sleep. Near the end, Richie actually began to get the hang of it, although he could usually only get it to come halfway up the string after waking it up.

'You're not jerking your fingers hard enough, that's all,' she said.

Richie looked at the clock on the Merrill Trust across the street and jumped up, stuffing his yo-yo into his back pocket. 'Jeepers, I gotta get goin, Bev. I'm supposed to meet ole Haystack. He'll think I changed my mind or somethin.'

'Who's Haystack?'

'Oh. Ben Hanscom. I call him Haystack, though. You know, like Haystack Calhoun, the wrestler.'

Bev frowned at him. 'That's not very nice. I like Ben.'

'Doan whup me, massa!' Richie screeched in his Pickaninny Voice, rolling his eyes and flapping his hands. 'Doan whup me, I'se gwineter be a good dahkie, ma'am, I'se –'

'Richie,' Bev said thinly.

Richie quit it. 'I like him, too,' he said. 'We all built a dam down in the Barrens a couple of days ago and –'

'You go down there? You and Ben play down there?'

'Sure. A bunch of us guys do. It's sorta cool down there.' Richie glanced at the clock again. 'I really gotta split for the scene. Ben'll be waiting.'

'Okay.'

He paused, thought, and said, 'If you're not doing anything, come on with me.'

'I told you. I don't have any money.'

'I'll pay your way. I got a couple of bucks.'

She tossed the remains of her ice-cream cone in a nearby litter barrel. Her eyes, that fine clear shade of blue-gray, turned up to his. They were coolly amused. She pretended to primp her hair and asked him, 'Oh dear, am I being asked out on a date?'

For a moment Richie was uncharacteristically flustered. He actually felt a blush rising in his cheeks. He had made the offer in a perfectly natural way, just as he had made it to Ben . . . except hadn't he said something to Ben about owesies? Yes. But he hadn't said anything about owesies to Beverly.

Richie suddenly felt a bit weird. He had dropped his eyes, retreating from her amused glance, and realized now that her skirt had ridden up a bit when she shifted forward to drop the ice-cream cone in the litter barrel, and he could see her knees. He raised his eyes but that was no help; now he was looking at the beginning swells of her bosoms.

Richie, as he usually did in such moments of confusion, took refuge in absurdity.

'Yes! A date!' he screamed, throwing himself on his knees before her and holding his clasped hands up. 'Please come! Please come! I shall ruddy kill meself if you say no, ay-wot? Wot-wot?'

'Oh, Richie, you're such a fuzzbrain,' she said, giggling again . . . but weren't her cheeks also a trifle flushed? If so, it made her look prettier than ever. 'Get up before you get arrested.'

He got up and plopped down beside her again. He felt as if his equilibrium had returned. A little foolishness always helped when you had a dizzy spell, he believed. 'You wanna go?'

'Sure,' she said. 'Thank you very much. Think of it! My first date. Just wait until I write it in my diary tonight.' She clasped her hands together between her budding breasts, fluttered her eyelashes rapidly, and then laughed.

'I wish you'd stop calling it that,' Richie said.

She sighed. 'You don't have much romance in your soul.'

'Damn right I don't.'

But he felt somehow delighted with himself. The world seemed suddenly very clear to him, and very friendly. He found himself glancing sideways at her from time to time. She was looking in the shop windows – at the dresses and nightgowns in Cornell-Hopley's, at the towels and pots in the window of the Discount Barn, and he stole glances at her hair, the line of her jaw. He observed the way her bare arms came out of the round holes of her blouse. He saw the edge of her slip strap. All of these things delighted him. He could not have said why, but what had happened in George Denbrough's bedroom had never seemed more distant to him than it did right then. It was time to go, time to meet Ben, but he would sit here just a moment longer while her eyes window-shopped, because it was good to look at her, and be with her.

9

Kids were ponying up their quarter admissions at the Aladdin's box-office window and going into the lobby. Looking through the bank of glass doors, Richie could see a crowd around the candy counter. The popcorn machine was in overdrive, spilling out drifts of the stuff, its greasy hinged lid jittering up and down. He didn't see Ben anywhere. He asked Beverly if she had spotted him. She shook her head.

'Maybe he already went in.'

'He said he didn't have any money. And the Daughter of Frankenstein there would never let him in without a ticket.' Richie cocked a thumb at Mrs Cole, who had been the ticket-taker at the Aladdin since a time well before the pictures had begun to talk. Her hair, dyed a bright red, was so thin you could see her scalp beneath. She had enormous hanging lips which she painted with plum-colored lipstick. Wild blotches of rouge covered her cheeks. Her eyebrows were drawn on in black pencil. Mrs Cole was a perfect democrat. She hated all kids equally.

'Boy, I don't wanna go in without him but the show's gonna start,' Richie said. 'Where in heck is he?'

'You can buy him a ticket and leave it at the box-office,' Bev said, reasonably enough. 'Then when he comes –'

But just then Ben came around the corner of Center and Macklin Streets. He was puffing, and his belly joggled beneath his sweatshirt. He saw Richie and raised one hand to wave. Then he saw Bev and his hand stopped in mid-flap. His eyes widened momentarily. He finished his wave and then walked slowly to where they stood under the Aladdin's marquee.

'Hi, Richie,' he said, and then looked at Bev briefly. It was as if he was afraid that an overlong look might result in a flash burn. 'Hi, Bev.'

'Hello, Ben,' she said, and a strange silence fell between the two of them – it was not precisely awkward; it was, Richie thought, almost *powerful*. And he felt a vague twinge of jealousy, because something had passed between them and whatever it had been, he had been excluded from it.

'Howdy, Haystack!' he said. 'Thought you went chicken on me. These movies goan scare ten pounds off your pudgy body. Ah say, Ah say, they goan turn your hair white, boy. When you come out of this theater, you goan need an usher to help you up the aisle, you goan be shakin so bad.'

Richie started for the box-office and Ben touched his arm. Ben started to speak, glanced at Bev, who was smiling at him, and had to start over again. 'I was here,' he said, 'but I went up the street and around the corner when those guys came along.'

'What guys?' Richie asked, but he thought he already knew.

'Henry Bowers. Victor Criss. Belch Huggins. Some other guys, too.'

Richie whistled. 'They must have already gone inside the theater. I don't see em buying candy.'

'Yeah. I guess so.'

'If I was them, I wouldn't bother paying to see a couple of horror movies,' Richie said. 'I'd just stay home and look in a mirror. Save some bread.'

Bev laughed merrily at that, but Ben only smiled a little. Henry Bowers had maybe only started out to hurt him that day last week, but he had ended up meaning to kill him. Ben was quite sure of that.

'Tell you what,' Richie said. 'We'll go up in the balcony. They'll all be sittin down in the second or third row with their feet up.'

'You positive?' Ben asked. He was not at all sure Richie understood what bad news those kids were . . . Henry, of course, being the worst news of all.

Richie, who had barely escaped what might have been a really bad beating at the hands of Henry and his spasmoid friends three months ago (he had managed to elude them in the toy department of Freese's Department Store, of all places), understood more about Henry and his merry crew than Ben thought he did.

'If I wasn't fairly positive, I wouldn't go in,' he said. 'I want to see those movies, Haystack, but I don't want to, like, *die* for em.'

'Besides, if they give us any trouble, we'll just tell Foxy to kick them out,' Bev said. Foxy was Mr Foxworth, the thin, sallow, glum-looking man who managed the Aladdin. He was now selling candy and popcorn, chanting his litany of 'Wait your turn, wait your turn, wait your turn.' In his threadbare tux and yellowing boiled shirt he looked like an undertaker who had fallen on hard times.

Ben looked doubtfully from Bev to Foxy to Richie.

'You can't let em run your life, man,' Richie said softly. 'Don't you know that?'

'I guess so,' Ben said, and sighed. Actually, he knew no such thing . . . but Beverly's being here had given the equation a crazy skew. If she hadn't come, he would have tried to persuade Richie to go to the movies another day. And if Richie had persisted, Ben might have bowed out. But Bev *was* here. He didn't want to look like a chicken in front of her. And the thought of being with her, in the balcony, in the dark (even if Richie was between them, as he probably would be), was a powerful attraction.

'We'll wait until the show starts before we go in,' Richie said. He grinned and punched Ben on the arm. 'Shit, Haystack, you wanna live forever?'

Ben's brows drew together, and then he snorted laughter. Richie also laughed. Looking at them, Beverly laughed, too.

Richie approached the ticket booth again. Liver Lips Cole looked at him sourly.

'Good ahfternyoon, deah lady,' Richie said in his best Baron Butthole Voice. 'I am in diah need of three tickey-tickies to youah deah old American flicktoons.'

'Cut the crap and tell me what you want, kid!' Liver Lips barked through the round hole cut in the glass, and something about the way her painted eyebrows were going up and down unsettled Richie so much that he simply pushed a rumpled dollar through the slot and muttered, 'Three, please.'

Three tickets popped out of the slot. Richie took them. Liver Lips rammed a quarter back at him. 'Don't be smart, don't throw popcorn boxes, don't holler, don't run in the lobby, don't run in the aisles.'

'No, ma'am,' Richie said, backing away to where Ben and Bev stood. He said to them, 'It always warms my heart to see an old fart like that who really likes kids.'

They stood outside awhile longer, waiting for the show to start. Liver Lips glared at them suspiciously from her glass cage. Richie regaled Bev with the story of the dam in the Barrens, trumpeting Mr Nell's lines in his new Irish Cop Voice. Beverly was giggling before long, laughing hard not long after that. Even Ben was grinning a little, although his eyes kept shifting either toward the Aladdin's glass doors or to Beverly's face.

10

The balcony was okay. During the first reel of *I Was a Teenage Frankenstein* Richie spotted Henry Bowers and his shitkicking friends. They were down in the second row, just as he had figured they would be. There were five or six of them in all – fifth-, sixth-, and seventh-graders, all of them with their motorhuckle boots cocked up on the seats in front of them. Foxy would come down and tell them to put their feet on the floor. They would. Foxy would leave. Up went the motorhuckle boots again as soon as he did. Five or ten minutes later Foxy would return and the entire charade would be acted out again. Foxy didn't quite have the guts to kick them out and they knew it.

The movies were great. The Teenage Frankenstein was suitably gross. The Teenage Werewolf was somehow scarier, though . . . perhaps because he also seemed a little sad. What had happened wasn't his own fault. There was this hypnotist who had fucked him up, but the only reason he'd been able to was that the kid who turned into the were-wolf was full of anger and bad feelings. Richie found himself wondering if there were many people in the world hiding bad feelings like that. Henry Bowers was just overflowing with bad feelings, but he sure didn't bother hiding them.

Beverly sat between the boys, ate popcorn from their boxes, screamed, covered her eyes, sometimes laughed. When the Werewolf was stalking the girl doing exercises in the gym after school, she pressed her face against Ben's arm, and Richie heard Ben's gasp of surprise even over the screams of the two hundred kids below them.

The Werewolf was finally killed. In the last scene one cop solemnly told another that this should teach people not to fiddle with things best left to God. The curtain came down and the lights came up. There was applause. Richie felt totally satisfied, if a little headachy. He'd probably have to go to the eye-doctor pretty soon and get his lenses changed again. He really would be wearing Coke bottles on his eyes by the time he got to high school, he thought glumly.

Ben twitched at his sleeve. 'They saw us, Richie,' he said in a dry, dismayed voice.

'Huh?'

'Bowers and Criss. They looked up here on their way out. They *saw* us!'

'Okay, okay,' Richie said. 'Calm down, Haystack. Just *caaalm* down. We'll go out the side door. Nothing to worry about.'

They went down the stairs, Richie in the lead, Beverly in the middle, Ben bringing up the rear and looking back over his shoulder every two steps or so.

'Have those guys really got it in for you, Ben?' Beverly asked.

'Yeah, I guess they do,' Ben said. 'I got in a fight with Henry Bowers on the last day of school.'

'Did he beat you up?'

'Not as much as he wanted to,' Ben said. 'That's why he's still mad, I guess.'

'Ole Hank the Tank also lost a fair amount of skin,' Richie murmured. 'Or so I heard. I don't think he was very pleased about that, either.' He pushed open the exit door and the three of them stepped out into the alley that ran between the Aladdin and Nan's Luncheonette. A cat which had been rooting in a garbage can hissed and ran past them down the alley, which was blocked at the far end by a board fence. The cat scrambled up and over. A trashcan lid clattered. Bev jumped, grabbed Richie's arm, and then laughed nervously. 'I guess I'm still scared from the movies,' she said.

'You won't –' Richie began.

'Hello, fuckface,' Henry Bowers said from behind them.

Startled, the three of them turned around. Henry, Victor, and Belch were standing at the mouth of the alley. There were two other guys behind them.

'Oh *shit*, I knew this was going to happen,' Ben moaned.

Richie turned quickly back toward the Aladdin, but the exit door had closed behind them and there was no way to open it from the outside.

'Say goodbye, fuckface,' Henry said, and suddenly ran at Ben.

The things that happened next seemed to Richie both then and later like something out of a movie – such things simply did not happen in real life. In real life the little kids took their beatings, picked up their teeth and went home.

It didn't happen that way this time.

Beverly stepped forward and to one side, almost as if she intended to meet Henry, perhaps shake his hand. Richie could hear the cleats on his boots rapping. Victor and Belch were coming after him; the other two boys stood at the mouth of the alley, guarding it.

'Leave him alone!' Beverly shouted. 'Pick on someone your own size!'

'He's as big as a fucking Mack truck, bitch,' Henry, no gentleman, snarled. 'Now get out of my –'

Richie stuck out his foot. He didn't think he meant to. His foot went out the same way wisecracks dangerous to his health sometimes emerged, all on their own, from his mouth. Henry ran into it and fell forward. The brick surface of the alley was slippery with spilled garbage from the overflowing cans on the luncheonette side. Henry went skidding like a shuffleboard weight.

He started to get up, his shirt blotched with coffee grounds, mud, and bits of lettuce. '*Oh you guys are gonna DIE!*' he screamed.

Until this moment Ben had been terrified. Now something in him snapped. He let out a roar and grabbed one of the garbage cans. For just a moment, holding it up, garbage spilling everywhere, he really *did* look like Haystack Calhoun. His face was pale and furious. He threw the garbage can. It struck Henry in the small of the back and knocked him flat again.

'Let's get out of here!' Richie screamed.

They ran toward the mouth of the alley. Victor Criss jumped in front of them. Bellowing, Ben lowered his head and rammed it into Victor's middle. '*Woof!*' Victor grunted, and sat down.

Belch grabbed a handful of Beverly's pony-tail and whipped her smartly against the Aladdin's brick wall. Beverly bounced off and ran down the alley, rubbing her arm. Richie ran after her, grabbing a garbage-can lid on the way. Belch Huggins swung a fist almost the size of a Daisy ham at him. Richie pistoned out the galvanized steel lid. Belch's fist met it. There was a loud *bonnngg!* – a sound that was almost mellow. Richie felt the shock travel all the way up his arm to the shoulder. Belch screamed and began to hop up and down, holding his swelling hand.

'Yondah lies da tent of my faddah,' Richie said confidentially, doing a very passable Tony Curtis Voice, and then ran after Ben and Beverly.

One of the boys at the mouth of the alley had caught Beverly. Ben was tussling with him. The other boy began to rabbit-punch Ben in the small of the back. Richie swung his foot. It connected with the rabbit-puncher's buttocks. The boy howled with pain. Richie grabbed Beverly's arm in one hand, Ben's in the other.

'*Run!*' he shouted.

The boy Ben had been tussling with let go of Beverly and looped a punch at Richie. His ear exploded with momentary pain, then went numb and became very warm. A high whistling sound began to whine in his head. It sounded like the noise you were supposed to listen for when the school nurse put the earphones on you to test your hearing.

They ran down Center Street. People turned to look at them. Ben's large stomach pogoed up and down. Beverly's pony-tail bounced. Richie let go of Ben and held his glasses against his forehead with his left thumb so he wouldn't lose them. His head was still ringing and he believed his ear was going to swell, but he felt wonderful. He started laughing. Beverly joined him. Soon Ben was laughing, too.

They cut up Court Street and collapsed on a bench in front of the police station: at that moment it seemed the only place in Derry where they might possibly be safe. Beverly looped an arm around Ben's neck and Richie's. She gave them a furious hug.

'That was great!' Her eyes sparkled. 'Did you see those guys? Did you *see* them?'

'I saw them, all right,' Ben gasped. 'And I never want to see them again.'

This sent them off into another storm of hysterical laughter. Richie kept expecting Henry's gang to come around the corner onto Court Street and take after them again, police station or not. Still, he could not stop laughing. Beverly was right. It had been great.

'The Losers' Club Gets Off A Good One!' Richie yelled exuberantly. 'Wacka-wacka-wacka!' He cupped his hands around his mouth and put on his Ben Bernie Voice: '*YOW-za YOW-za YOWZA, childrens!*'

A cop poked his head out of an open second-floor window and shouted: 'You kids get out of here! Right now! Take a walk!'

Richie opened his mouth to say something brilliant – quite possibly in his brand-new Irish Cop Voice – and Ben kicked his foot. 'Shut up, Richie,' he said, and promptly had trouble believing that he had said such a thing.

'Right, Richie,' Bev said, looking at him fondly. 'Beep-beep.'

'Okay,' Richie said. 'What do you guys want to do? Wanna go find Henry Bowers and ask him if he wants to work it out over a game of Monopoly?'

'Bite your tongue,' Bev said.

'Huh? What does that mean?'

'Never mind,' Bev said. 'Some guys are so *ignorant*.'

Hesitantly, blushing furiously, Ben asked: 'Did that guy hurt your hair, Beverly?'

She smiled at him gently, and in that moment she became sure of something she had only guessed at before – that it had been Ben Hanscom who had sent her the postcard with the beautiful little haiku on it. 'No, it wasn't bad,' she said.

'Let's go down in the Barrens,' Richie proposed.

And so that was where they went . . . or where they escaped. Richie would think later that it set a pattern for the rest of the summer. The Barrens had become their place. Beverly, like Ben on the day of his first encounter with the big boys, had never been down there before. She walked between Richie and Ben as the three of them moved single-file down the path. Her skirt twitched prettily, and looking at her, Ben was aware of waves of feeling, as powerful as stomach cramps. She was wearing her ankle bracelet. It flashed in the afternoon sun.

They crossed the arm of the Kenduskeag the boys had dammed up (the stream divided about seventy yards farther up along its course and became one again about two hundred yards farther on toward town), using stepping-stones downstream of the place where the dam had been, found another path, and eventually came out on the bank of the stream's eastern fork, which was much wider than the other. It sparkled in the afternoon light. To his left, Ben could see two of those concrete cylinders with the manhole covers on top. Below them, jutting out over the stream, were large concrete pipes. Thin streams of muddy water poured over the lips of these outflow pipes and into the Kenduskeag. *Someone takes a crap uptown and here's where it comes out*, Ben thought, remembering Mr Nell's explanation of Derry's drainage system. He felt a dull sort of helpless anger. Once there had probably been fish in this river. Now your chances of catching a trout wouldn't be so hot. Your chances of catching a used wad of toilet paper would be better.

'It's so beautiful here,' Bev sighed.

'Yeah, not bad,' Richie agreed. 'The blackflies are gone and there's enough of a breeze to keep the mosquitoes away.' He looked at her hopefully. 'Got any cigarettes?'

'No,' she said. 'I had a couple but I smoked them yesterday.'

'Too bad,' Richie said.

There was the blast of an air-horn and they all watched as a long freight rumbled across the embankment on the far side of the Barrens and toward the trainyards. Jeez, if it was a passenger train they'd have a great view, Richie thought. First the poor-folks' houses of the Old Cape, then the bamboo swamps on the other side of the Kenduskeag, and finally, before leaving the Barrens, the smoldering gravel-pit that was the town dump.

For just a moment he found himself thinking about Eddie's story again – the leper under the abandoned house on Neibolt Street. He pushed it out of his mind and turned to Ben.

'So what was your best part, Haystack?'

'Huh?' Ben turned to him guiltily. As Bev looked out across the Kenduskeag, lost in thoughts of her own, he had been looking at her profile . . . and at the bruise on her cheekbone.

'Of the *movies*, Dumbo. What was your best part?'

'I liked it when Dr Frankenstein started tossing the bodies to the crocodiles under his house,' Ben said. 'That was my best part.'

'That was gross,' Beverly said, and shivered. 'I hate things like that. Crocodiles and piranhas and sharks.'

'Yeah? What's piranhas?' Richie asked, immediately interested.

'Little tiny fish,' Beverly said. 'And they've got all these little tiny teeth, but they're wicked sharp. And if you go into a river where they are, they eat you right down to the bone.'

'Wow!'

'I saw this movie once and these natives wanted to cross a river but the footbridge was down,' she said. 'So they put a cow in the water on a rope, and crossed while the piranhas were eating the cow. When they pulled it out, the cow was nothing but a skeleton. I had nightmares for a week.'

'Man, I wish I had some of those fish,' Richie said happily. 'I'd put em in Henry Bowers' bathtub.'

Ben began to giggle. 'I don't think he takes baths.'

'I don't know about that, but I do know we better watch out for those guys,' Beverly said. Her fingers touched the bruise on her cheek. 'My dad went up the side of my head day before yesterday for breaking a pile of dishes. One a week is enough.'

There was a moment of silence that might have been awkward but was not. Richie broke it by saying his best part was when the Teenage Werewolf got the evil hypnotist. They talked about the movies – and other horror movies they had seen, and *Alfred Hitchcock Presents* on TV – for an hour or more. Bev spotted daisies growing on the riverbank and picked one. She held it first under Richie's chin and then under Ben's chin to see if they liked butter. She said they both did. As she held the flower under their chins, each was conscious of her light touch on their shoulders and the clean scent of her hair. Her face was close to Ben's only for a moment or two, but that night he dreamed of how her eyes had looked during that brief endless span of time.

Conversation was fading a little when they heard the crackling sounds of people approaching along the path. The three of them turned quickly toward the sound and Richie was suddenly, acutely aware that the river was at their backs. There was noplace to run.

The voices drew closer. They got to their feet, Richie and Ben moving a little in front of Beverly without even thinking about it.

The screen of bushes at the end of the path shook – and suddenly Bill Denbrough emerged. Another kid was with him, a fellow Richie knew a little bit. His name was Bradley something, and he had a terrible lisp. Probably went up to Bangor with Bill for that speech-therapy thing, Richie thought.

'Big Bill!' he said, and then in the Voice of Toodles: 'We are glad to see you, Mr Denbrough, mawster.'

Bill looked at them and grinned – and a peculiar certainty stole over Richie as Bill looked from him to Ben to Beverly and then back to Bradley Whatever-His-Name-Was. Beverly was a part of them. Bill's eyes said so. Bradley What's–His–Name was not. He might stay for awhile today, might even come down to the Barrens again – no one would tell him no, so sorry, the Losers' Club membership is full, we already have our speech-impediment member – but he was not part of it. He was not part of *them*.

This thought led to a sudden, irrational fear. For a moment he felt the way you did when you suddenly realized you had swum out too far and the water was over your head. There was an intuitive flash: *We're being drawn into something. Being picked and chosen. None of this is accidental. Are we all here yet?*

Then the intuition fell into a meaningless jumble of thought – like the smash of a glass pane on a stone floor. Besides, it didn't matter. Bill was here, and Bill would take care; Bill would not let things get out of control. He was the tallest of them, and surely the most handsome. Richie only had to look sideways at Bev's eyes, fixed on Bill, and then farther, to Ben's eyes, fixed knowingly and unhappily on Bev's face, to know that. Bill was also the strongest of them – and not just physically. There was a good deal more to it than that, but since Richie did not know either the word *charisma* or the full meaning of the word *magnetism*, he only felt that Bill's strength ran deep and might manifest itself in many ways, some of them probably unexpected. And Richie suspected if Beverly fell for him, or 'got a crush on him,' or whatever they called it, Ben would not be jealous (*like he would*, Richie thought, *if she got a crush on me*); he would accept it as nothing but natural. And there was something else: Bill was *good*. It was stupid to think such a thing (he did not, in fact, precisely think it; he *felt* it), but there it was. Goodness and strength seemed to radiate from Bill. He was like a knight in an old movie, a movie that was corny but still had the power to make you cry and cheer and clap at the end. Strong and good. And five years later, after his memories of what had happened in Derry both during and before that summer had begun to fade rapidly, it occurred to a Richie Tozier in his mid-teens that John Kennedy reminded him of Stuttering Bill.

Who? His mind would respond.

He would look up, faintly puzzled, and shake his head. *Some guy I used to know,* he would think, and would dismiss vague unease by pushing his glasses up on his nose and turning to his homework again. *Some guy I used to know a long time ago.*

Bill Denbrough put his hands on his hips, smiled sunnily, and said: 'Wuh-wuh-well, h-here we a-a-are . . . now wuh-wuh-wuh-what are w-we d-d-doing?'

'Got any cigarettes?' Richie asked hopefully.

11

Five days later, as June drew toward its end, Bill told Richie that he wanted to go down to Neibolt Street and investigate under the porch where Eddie had seen the leper.

They had just arrived back at Richie's house, and Bill was walking Silver. He had ridden Richie double most of the way home, an exhilarating speed-trip across Derry, but he had been careful to let Richie dismount a block away from his house. If Richie's mother saw Bill riding Richie double she'd have a bird.

Silver's wire basket was full of play six-shooters, two of them Bill's, three of them Richie's. They had been down in the Barrens for most of the afternoon, playing guns. Beverly Marsh had shown up around three o'clock, wearing faded jeans and toting a very old Daisy air rifle that had lost most of its pop – when you pulled its tape-wrapped trigger, it uttered a wheeze that sounded to Richie more like someone sitting on a very old Whoopee Cushion than a rifleshot. Her specialty was Japanese-sniper. She was very good at climbing trees and shooting the unwary as they passed below. The bruise on her cheekbone had faded to a faint yellow.

'What did you say?' Richie asked. He was shocked . . . but also a little intrigued.

'I w-w-want to take a l-look under that puh-puh-porch,' Bill said. His voice was stubborn but he wouldn't look at Richie. There was a hard spot of flush high on each of his cheekbones. They had arrived in front of Richie's house. Maggie Tozier was on the porch, reading a book. She waved to them and called, 'Hi, boys! Want some iced tea?'

'We'll be right there, Mom,' Richie said, and then to Bill: 'There isn't going to be anything there. He probably just saw a hobo and got all bent out of shape, for God's sake. You know Eddie.'

'Y-Yeah, I nuh-know E-E-Eddie. B-But ruh-remem-member the pi-pi-picture in the a-album?'

Richie shifted his feet, uncomfortable. Bill raised his right hand. The Band-Aids were gone now, but Richie could see circlets of healing scab on Bill's first three fingers.

'Yeah, but –'

'Luh-luh-histen to me-me,' Bill said. He began to speak very slowly, holding Richie's eyes with his own. Once more he related the similarities between Ben's story and Eddie's . . . and tied those to what they had seen in the picture that moved. He suggested again that the clown had murdered the boys and girls who had been found dead in Derry since the previous December. 'A-And muh-muh-haybe not just t-them,' Bill finished. 'W-What about a-a-all the o-ones who d-disappeared? W-What about E-E-Eddie Cuh-Cuh-Corcoran?'

'Shit, his stepfather scared him off,' Richie said. 'Don't you read the papers?'

'W-well, m-maybe he d-d-did, and m-maybe he d-d-didn't,' Bill said. 'I knew him a l-lih-little bit, t-too, and I nuh-nuh-know his d-dad b-b-beat him. And I a-also k-know he u-u-used to stay out n-nuh-hights s-sometimes to g-get aw-way from h-h-him.'

'So maybe the clown got him while he was staying away,' Richie said thoughtfully. 'Is that it?'

Bill nodded.

'What do you want, then? Its autograph?'

'If the cluh-cluh-cluh-hown killed the o-o-others, then h-he k-k-killed Juh-Georgie,' Bill said. His eyes caught Richie's. They were like slate – hard, uncompromising, unforgiving. 'I w-want to k-k-kill it.'

'Jesus Christ,' Richie said, frightened. 'How are you going to do that?'

'Muh-my d-dad's got a pih-pih-pistol,' Bill said. A little spittle flew from his lips but Richie barely noticed. 'H-He doesn't nuh-know I know, but I d-d-do. It's on the top sh-shelf in his cluh-cluh-hoset.'

'That's great if it's a man,' Richie said, 'and if we can find him sitting on a pile of kids' bones –'

'I poured the tea, boys!' Richie's mom called cheerily. 'Better come and get it!'

'Right there, Mom!' Richie called again, offering a big, false smile. It disappeared immediately as he turned back to Bill. 'Because I wouldn't shoot a guy just because he was wearing a clown suit, Billy.

341

You're my best friend, but I wouldn't do it and I wouldn't let *you* do it if I could stop you.'

'Wh-what i-if there r-really w-was a p-pile of buh-buh-bones?'

Richie licked his lips and said nothing for a moment. Then he asked Bill, 'What are you going to do if it's not a man, Billy? What if it really is some kind of monster? What if there really are such things? Ben Hanscom said it was the mummy and the balloons were floating against the wind and it didn't cast a shadow. The picture in Georgie's album . . . either we imagined that or it was magic, and I gotta tell you, man, I don't think we just imagined it. Your fingers sure didn't imagine it, did they?'

Bill shook his head.

'So what are we going to do if it's not a man, Billy?'

'Th-then wuh-wuh-we'll have to f-figure suh-homething e-else out.'

'Oh yeah,' Richie said. 'I can see it. After you shoot it four or five times and it keeps comin at us like the Teenage Werewolf in that movie me and Ben and Bev saw, you can try your Bullseye on it. And if the Bullseye doesn't work, I'll throw some of my sneezing powder at it. And if it keeps on coming after *that* we'll just call time and say, "Hey now, hold on. This ain't getting it, Mr Monster. Look, I got to read up on it at the library. I'll be back. Pawdon *me*." Is that what you're going to say, Big Bill?'

He looked at his friend, his head thudding rapidly. Part of him wanted Bill to press on with his idea to check under the porch of that old house, but another part wanted – *desperately* wanted – Bill to give the idea up. In some ways all of this was like having stepped into one of those Saturday-afternoon horror movies at the Aladdin, but in another way – a crucial way – it wasn't like that at all. Because this wasn't safe like a movie, where you knew everything would turn out all right and even if it didn't it was no skin off your ass. The picture in Georgie's room hadn't been like a movie. He had thought he was forgetting that, but apparently he had been fooling himself because now he could see those cuts whirling up Billy's fingers. If he hadn't pulled Bill back –

Incredibly, Bill was grinning. Actually *grinning*. 'Y-Y-You wuh-wanted m-me to take y-you to luh-luh-look at a p-picture,' he said. 'N-Now I w-want to t-take you to l-look at a h-house. Tit for t-tat.'

'You got no tits,' Richie said, and they both burst out laughing.

'T-Tomorrow muh-muh-morning,' Bill said, as if it had been resolved.

'And if it's a monster?' Richie asked, holding Bill's eyes. 'If your dad's gun doesn't stop it, Big Bill? If it just keeps coming?'

'Wuh-wuh-we'll thuh-thuh-think of suh-homething else,' Bill said again. 'We'll h-h-have to.' He threw back his head and laughed like a loon. After a moment Richie joined him. It was impossible not to.

They walked up the crazy-paving to Richie's porch together. Maggie had set out huge glasses of iced tea with mint-sprigs in them and a plate of vanilla wafers.

'Yuh-you w-w-want t-t-to?'

'Well, no,' Richie said. 'But I will.'

Bill clapped him on the back, hard, and that seemed to make the fear bearable – although Richie was suddenly sure (and he was not wrong) that sleep would be long coming that night.

'You boys looked like you were having a serious discussion out there,' Mrs Tozier said, sitting down with her book in one hand and a glass of iced tea in the other. She looked at the boys expectantly.

'Aw, Denbrough's got this crazy idea the Red Sox are going to finish in the first division,' Richie said.

'M-Me and my d-d-d-d-dad th-think t-they got a sh-shot at t-third,' Bill said, and sipped his iced tea. 'T-This is veh-veh-very go-good, Muh-Mrs Tozier.'

'Thank you, Bill.'

'The year the Sox finish in the first division will be the year you stop stuttering, mush mouth,' Richie said.

'*Richie!*' Mrs Tozier screamed, shocked. She nearly dropped her glass of iced tea. But both Richie and Bill Denbrough were laughing hysterically, totally cracked up. She looked from her son to Bill and back to her son again, touched by wonder that was mostly simple perplexity but partly a fear so thin and sharp that it found its way deep into her inner heart and vibrated there like a tuning-fork made of clear ice.

I don't understand either of them, she thought. *Where they go, what they do, what they want . . . or what will become of them. Sometimes, oh sometimes their eyes are wild, and sometimes I'm afraid for them and sometimes I'm afraid of them . . .*

She found herself thinking, not for the first time, that it would have been nice if she and Went could have had a girl as well, a pretty blonde

343

girl that she could have dressed in skirts and matching bows and black patent-leather shoes on Sundays. A pretty little girl who would ask to bake cupcakes after school and who would want dolls instead of books on ventriloquism and Revell models of cars that went fast.

A pretty little girl she could have understood.

12

'Did you get it?' Richie asked anxiously.

They were walking their bikes up Kansas Street beside the Barrens at ten o'clock the next morning. The sky was a dull gray. Rain had been forecast for that afternoon. Richie hadn't gotten to sleep until after midnight and he thought Denbrough looked as if he had spent a fairly restless night himself; ole Big Bill was toting a matched set of Samsonite bags, one under each eye.

'I g-got it,' Bill said. He patted the green duffel coat he was wearing.

'Lemme see,' Richie said, fascinated.

'Not now,' Bill said, and then grinned. 'Someone eh-eh-else might see, too. But l-l-look what else I bruh-brought.' He reached behind him, under the coat, and brought his Bullseye slingshot out of his back pocket.

'Oh shit, we're in trouble,' Richie said, beginning to laugh.

Bill pretended to be hurt. 'Ih-Ih-It was y-your idea, T-T-Tozier.'

Bill had gotten the custom aluminum slingshot for his birthday the year before. It had been Zack's compromise between the .22 Bill had wanted and his mother's adamant refusal to even consider giving a boy Bill's age a firearm. The instruction booklet said a slingshot could be a fine hunting weapon, once you learned to use it. 'In the right hands, your Bullseye Slingshot is as deadly and effective as a good ash bow or a high-powered firearm,' the booklet proclaimed. With such virtues dutifully extolled, the booklet went on to warn that a slingshot could be dangerous; the owner should no more aim one of the twenty ball-bearing slugs which came with it at a person than he would aim a loaded pistol at a person.

Bill wasn't very good at it yet (and guessed privately he probably never would be), but he thought the booklet's caution was merited – the slingshot's thick elastic had a hard pull, and when you hit a tin can with it, it made one hell of a hole.

'You doin any better with it, Big Bill?' Richie asked.

'A luh-luh-little,' Bill said. This was only partly true. After much study of the pictures in the booklet (which were labelled *figs*, as in fig 1, fig 2, and so on) and enough practice in Derry Park to lame his arm, he had gotten so he could hit the paper target which had *also* come with the slingshot maybe three times out of every ten tries. And once he had gotten a bullseye. Almost.

Richie pulled the sling back by the cup, twanged it, then handed it back. He said nothing but privately doubted if it would count for as much as Zack Denbrough's pistol when it came to killing monsters.

'Yeah?' he said. 'You brought your slingshot, okay, big deal. That's nothing. Look what *I* brought, Denbrough.' And from his own jacket he hauled out a packet with a cartoon picture on it of a bald man saying *Ah-CHOO!* as his cheeks puffed out like Dizzy Gillespie's. DR WACKY'S SNEEZING POWDER, the packet said. IT'S A LAFF RIOT!

The two of them stared at each other for a long moment and then broke up, screaming with laughter and pounding each other on the back.

'W-W-We're pruh-prepared for a-a-anything,' Bill said finally, still giggling and wiping his eyes with the sleeve of his jacket.

'Your face and my ass, Stuttering Bill,' Richie said.

'I th-th-thought it wuh-was the uh-uh-other way a-around,' Bill said. 'Now listen. W-We're g-gonna st-ha-hash y-your b-b-bike down in the B-Barrens. W-Where I puh-put Silver when we play. Y-You ride d-d-double b-behind me, in c-case w-we have to make a quih-hick g-g-getaway.'

Richie nodded, feeling no urge to argue. His twenty-two-inch Raleigh (he sometimes whammed his kneecaps on the handlebars when he was pedaling fast) looked like a pygmy bike next to the scrawny, gantrylike edifice that was Silver. He knew that Bill was stronger and Silver was faster.

They got to the little bridge and Bill helped Richie stow his bike underneath. Then they sat down, and, with the occasional rumble of traffic passing over their heads, Bill unzipped his duffel and took out his father's pistol.

'Y-You be goddam c-c-careful,' Bill said, handing it over after Richie had whistled his frank approval. 'Th-There's n-no s-s-safety on a pih-pihstol like that.'

'Is it loaded?' Richie asked, awed. The pistol, a PK-Walther that Zack Denbrough had picked up during the Occupation, seemed unbelievably heavy.

'N-Not y-yet,' Bill said. He patted his pocket. 'I g-g-got some buh-buh-buh-bullets in h-h-here. But my d-d-dad s-says s-sometimes you l-look a-and th-then, i-if the g-g-g-gun th-thinks y-you're not being c-c-careful, it l-loads ih-ih-itself. S-so it can sh-sh-shoot you.' His face uttered a strange smile which said that, while he didn't believe anything so silly, he believed it completely.

Richie understood. There was a caged deadliness in the thing that he had never sensed in his dad's .22, .30-.30, or even the shotgun (although there was something about the shotgun, wasn't there? – something about the way it leaned, mute and oily, in the corner of the garage closet; as if it might say *I could be mean if I wanted to; plenty mean, you bet* if it could speak). But this pistol, this Walther . . . it was as if it had been made for the express purpose of shooting people. With a chill Richie realized that *was* why it had been made. What else could you do with a pistol? Use it to light your cigarettes?

He turned the muzzle toward him, being careful to keep his hands far away from the trigger. One look into the Walther's black lidless eye made him understand Bill's peculiar smile perfectly. He remembered his father saying, *If you remember there is no such thing as an unloaded gun, you'll be okay with firearms all your life, Richie.* He handed the gun back to Bill, glad to be rid of it.

Bill stowed it in his duffel coat again. Suddenly the house on Neibolt Street seemed less frightening to Richie . . . but the possibility that blood might actually be spilled – that seemed much stronger.

He looked at Bill, perhaps meaning to appeal this idea again, but he saw Bill's face, read it, and only said, 'You ready?'

13

As always, when Bill finally pulled his second foot up from the ground, Richie felt sure that they would crash, splitting their silly skulls on unyielding cement. The big bike wavered crazily from side to side. The cards clothespinned to the fender-struts stopped firing single shots and started machine-gunning. The bike's drunken wavers became more pronounced. Richie closed his eyes and waited for the inevitable.

Then Bill bellowed, '*Hi-yo Silver, AWWAYYYYY!*'

The bike picked up more speed and finally stopped that seasick side-to-side wavering. Richie loosened his deathgrip on Bill's middle and held the front of the package carrier over the rear wheel instead. Bill crossed Kansas Street on a slant, raced down sidestreets at an ever-quickening pace, heading for Witcham as if racing down a set of geographical steps. They came bulleting out of Strapham Street and onto Witcham at an exorbitant rate of speed. Bill laid Silver damn near over on his side and bellowed '*Hi-yo Silver!*' again.

'Ride it, Big Bill!' Richie screamed, so scared he was nearly creaming his jeans but laughing wildly all the same. '*Stand* on this baby!'

Bill suited the action to the word, getting up and leaning over the handlebars and pumping the pedals at a lunatic rate. Looking at Bill's back, which was amazingly broad for a boy of eleven-going-on-twelve, watching it work under the duffel coat, the shoulders slanting first one way and then the other as he shifted his weight from one pedal to the other, Richie suddenly became sure that they were invulnerable . . . they would live forever and ever. Well . . . perhaps not *they*, but Bill would. Bill had no idea of how strong he was, how somehow sure and perfect.

They sped along, the houses thinning out a little now, the streets crossing Witcham at longer intervals.

'*Hi-yo Silver!*' Bill yelled, and Richie hollered in his Nigger Jim Voice, high and shrill, 'Hi-yo Silvuh, massa, thass raht! You is rahdin disyere bike fo *sho*! Lawks-a-mussy! Hi-yo Silvuh *AWWAYYY!*'

Now they were passing green fields that looked flat and depthless under the gray sky. Richie could see the old brick train station up ahead in the distance. To the right of it quonset warehouses marched off in a row. Silver bumped over one set of train tracks, then another.

And here was Neibolt Street, cutting off to the right. DERRY TRAINYARDS, a blue sign under the street-sign read. It was rusty and hung askew. Below this was a much bigger sign, yellow field, black letters. It was almost like a comment on the trainyards themselves: DEAD END, it read.

Bill turned onto Neibolt Street, coasted to the sidewalk, and put his foot back down. 'Let's w-w-walk from here.'

Richie slipped off the package carrier with mingled feelings of relief and regret. 'Okay.'

They walked along the sidewalk, which was cracked and weedy. Up ahead of them, in the trainyards, a diesel engine revved slowly up, faded off, and then began all over again. Once or twice they heard the metallic music of couplings being smashed together.

'You scared?' Richie asked Bill.

Bill, walking Silver by the handlebars, looked over at Richie briefly and then nodded. 'Y-Yeah. You?'

'I sure am,' Richie said.

Bill told Richie he had asked his father about Neibolt Street the night before. His father said that a lot of trainmen had lived out this way until the end of World War II – engineers, conductors, signalmen, yardworkers, baggage handlers. The street had declined with the trainyards, and as Bill and Richie moved farther along it, the houses became farther apart, seedier, dirtier. The last three or four on both sides were empty and boarded up, their yards overgrown. A FOR SALE sign flapped forlornly from the porch of one. To Richie the sign looked about a thousand years old. The sidewalk stopped, and now they were walking along a beaten track from which weeds grew half-heartedly.

Bill stopped and pointed. 'Th-there it i-i-is,' he said softly.

Twenty-nine Neibolt Street had once been a trim red Cape Cod. Maybe, Richie thought, an engineer used to live there, a bachelor with no pants but jeans and lots of those gloves with the big stiff cuffs and four or five pillowtick caps – a fellow who would come home once or twice a month for stretches of three or four days and listen to the radio while he pottered in the garden; a fellow who would eat mostly fried foods (and *no* vegetables, although he would grow them for his friends) and who would, on windy nights, think about the Girl He Left Behind.

Now the red paint had faded to a wishy-washy pink that was peeling away in ugly patches that looked like sores. The windows were blind eyes, boarded up. Most of the shingles were gone. Weeds grew rankly down both sides of the house and the lawn was covered with the season's first bumper crop of dandelions. To the left, a high board fence, perhaps once a neat white but now faded to a dull gray that almost matched the lowering sky, lurched drunkenly in and out of the dank shrubbery. About halfway down this fence Richie could see a monstrous grove of sunflowers – the tallest looked five feet tall or more. They had a bloated, nasty look he didn't like. A breeze rustled them and they seemed to nod together: *The boys are here, isn't that nice? More boys. Our boys.* Richie shivered.

While Bill leaned Silver carefully against an elm, Richie surveyed the house. He saw a wheel sticking out of the thick grass near the porch, and pointed it out to Bill. Bill nodded; it was the overturned trike Eddie had mentioned.

They looked up and down Neibolt Street. The chug of the diesel engine rose and fell off, then began again. The sound seemed to hang in the overcast like a charm. The street was utterly deserted. Richie could hear occasional cars passing on Route 2, but could not see them.

The diesel engine chugged and faded, chugged and faded.

The huge sunflowers nodded sagely together. *Fresh boys. Good boys. Our boys.*

'Y-Y-You r-ruh-ready?' Bill asked, and Richie jumped a little.

'You know, I was just thinking that maybe the last bunch of library books I took out are due today,' Richie said. 'Maybe I ought to –'

'Cuh-Cuh-Cut the c-crap, R-R-Richie. Are y-you ready or n-n-not?'

'I guess I am,' Richie said, knowing he was not ready at all – he was *never* going to be ready for this scene.

They crossed the overgrown lawn to the porch.

'Luh-look th-th-there,' Bill said.

At the far lefthand side, the porch's latticework skirt leaned out against a tangle of bushes. Both boys could see the rusty nails that had been pulled free. There were old rosebushes here, and while the roses both to the right and the left of the unanchored stretch of latticework were blooming in a lackadaisical way, those directly around and in front of it were skeletal and dead.

Bill and Richie looked at each other grimly. Everything Eddie said seemed true enough; seven weeks later, the evidence was still here.

'You don't really want to go under there, do you?' Richie asked. He was almost pleading.

'Nuh-nuh-no,' Bill said, 'b-but I'm g-gonna.'

And with a sinking heart, Richie saw that he absolutely meant it. That gray light was back in Billy's eyes, shining steadily. There was a stony eagerness in the lines of his face that made him look older. Richie thought, *I think he really does mean to kill it, if it's still there. Kill it and maybe cut off its head and take it to his father and say, 'Look, this is what killed Georgie, now will you talk to me again at night, maybe just tell me how your day was, or who lost when you guys were flipping to see who paid for the morning coffee?'*

'Bill –' he said, but Bill was no longer there. He was walking around to the righthand end of the porch, where Eddie must have crawled under. Richie had to chase after him, and he almost fell over the trike caught in the weeds and slowly rusting its way into the ground.

He caught up as Bill squatted, looking under the porch. There was no skirt at all on this end; someone – some hobo – had pried it off long ago to gain access to the shelter underneath, out of the January snow or the cold November rain or a summer thunder-shower.

Richie squatted beside him, his heart thudding like a drum. There

349

was nothing under the porch but drifts of moldering leaves, yellowing newspapers, and shadows. Too many shadows.

'Bill,' he repeated.

'Wh-wh-what?' Bill had produced his father's Walther again. He pulled the clip carefully from the grip, and then took four bullets from his pants pocket. He loaded them in one at a time. Richie watched this, fascinated, and then looked under the porch again. He saw something else this time. Broken glass. Faintly glinting shards of glass. His stomach cramped painfully. He was not a stupid boy, and he understood this came close to completely confirming Eddie's story. Splinters of glass on the moldering leaves under the porch meant that the window had been broken from inside. From the cellar.

'*Wh-what?*' Bill asked again, looking up at Richie. His face was grim and white. Looking at that set face, Richie mentally threw in the towel.

'Nothing,' he said.

'You cuh-cuhk-homing?'

'Yeah.'

They crawled under the porch.

They smell of decaying leaves was a smell Richie usually liked, but there was nothing pleasant about the smell under here. The leaves felt spongy under his hands and knees, and he had an impression that they might go down for two or three feet. He suddenly wondered what he would do if a hand or a claw sprang out of those leaves and seized him.

Bill was examining the broken window. Glass had sprayed everywhere. The wooden strip which had been between the panes lay in two splintered pieces under the porch steps. The top of the window frame jutted out like a broken bone.

'Something hit that fucker wicked hard,' Richie breathed. Bill, now peering inside – or trying to – nodded.

Richie elbowed him aside enough so he could look, too. The basement was a dim litter of crates and boxes. The floor was earth and, like the leaves, it gave off a damp and humid aroma. A furnace bulked to the left, thrusting round pipes at the low ceiling. Beyond it, at the end of the cellar, Richie could see a large stall with wooden sides. A horse stall was his first thought, but who kept horses in the jeezly cellar? Then he realized that in a house as old as this one, the furnace must have burned coal instead of oil. Nobody had bothered to convert the furnace because no one wanted the house. That thing with the sides was a coalbin. To the far right, Richie could make out a flight of stairs going up to ground level.

Now Bill was sitting down ... hunching himself forward ... and before Richie could actually believe what he was up to, his friend's legs were disappearing into the window.

'Bill!' he hissed. 'Chrissake, what are you *doing*? Get *outta* there!'

Bill didn't reply. He slithered through, scraping his duffel coat up from the small of his back, barely missing a chunk of glass that would have cut him a good one. A second later Richie heard his tennies smack down on the hard earth inside.

'Piss on this action,' Richie muttered frantically to himself, looking at the square of darkness into which his friend had disappeared. 'Bill, you gone out of your *mind*?'

Bill's voice floated up: 'Y-You c-c-can stay up th-there if you w-want, Ruh-Ruh-Richie. St-Stand g-g-guard.'

Instead he rolled over on his belly and shoved his legs through the cellar window before his nerve could go bad on him, hoping he wouldn't cut his hands or his stomach on the broken glass.

Something clutched his legs. Richie screamed.

'I-I-It's juh-juh-hust m-me,' Bill hissed, and a moment later Richie was standing beside him in the cellar, pulling down his shirt and his jacket. 'Wh-who d-did you th-think it w-was?'

'The boogeyman,' Richie said, and laughed shakily.

'Y-You g-go th-that w-way and I-I – I'll g-g-g-'

'Fuck that,' Richie said. He could actually hear his heartbeat in his voice, making it sound bumpy and uneven, first up and then down. 'I'm stickin with you, Big Bill.'

They moved toward the coalpit first, Bill slightly in the lead, the gun in his hand, Richie close behind him, trying to look everywhere at once. Bill stood beyond one of the coalpit's jutting wooden sides for a moment, and then suddenly darted around it, pointing the gun with both hands. Richie squinched his eyes shut, steeling himself for the explosion. It didn't come. He opened his eyes again cautiously.

'Nuh-nuh-nothin but c-c-coal,' Bill said, and giggled nervously.

Richie stepped up beside Bill and looked. There was still a drift of old coal in here, piled up almost to the ceiling at the back of the stall and trickling away to a lump or two by their feet. It was as black as a crow's wing.

'Let's –' Richie began, and then the door at the head of the cellar stairs crashed open against the wall with a violent bang, spilling thin white daylight down the stairs.

Both boys screamed.

Richie heard snarling sounds. They were very loud – the sounds a wild animal in a cage might make. He saw loafers descend the steps. Faded jeans on top of them – swinging hands –

But they weren't hands . . . they were paws. Huge, misshapen paws.

'*Cuh-cuh-climb the c-c-coal!*' Bill was screaming, but Richie stood frozen, suddenly knowing what was coming for them, what was going to kill them in this cellar that stank of damp earth and the cheap wine that had been spilled in the corners. Knowing but needing to see. '*There's a wuh-wuh-window at the t-top of the c-coal!*'

The paws were covered with dense brown hair that curled and coiled like wire; the fingers were tipped with jagged nails. Now Richie saw a silk jacket. It was black with orange piping – the Derry High School colors.

'*G-G-Go!*' Bill screamed, and gave Richie a gigantic shove. Richie went sprawling into the coal. Sharp jags and corners of it poked him painfully, breaking through his daze. More coal avalanched over his hands. That mad snarling went on and on.

Panic slipped its hood over Richie's mind.

Barely aware of what he was doing, he scrambled up the mountain of coal, gaining ground, sliding back, lunging upward again, screaming as he went. The window at the top was grimed black with coal-dust and let in next to no light at all. It was latched shut. Richie seized the latch, which was of the sort that turned, and threw all his weight against it. The latch moved not at all. The snarling was closer now.

The gun went off below him, the sound nearly deafening in the closed room. Gunsmoke, sharp and acrid, stung Richie's nose. It shocked him back to some sort of awareness and he realized that he had been trying to turn the thumb-latch the wrong way. He reversed the direction of the force he was applying, and the latch gave with a protracted rusty squeal. Coaldust sifted down on his hands like pepper.

The gun went off again with a second deafening bang. Bill Denbrough shouted, '*YOU KILLED MY BROTHER, YOU FUCKER!*'

For a moment the creature which had come down the stairs seemed to laugh, seemed to speak – it was as if a vicious dog had suddenly begun to bark out garbled words, and for a moment Richie thought the thing in the high-school jacket snarled back, *I'm going to kill you too.*

'*Richie!*' Bill screamed then, and Richie heard coal clattering and falling again as Bill scrambled up. The snarls and roars continued. Wood splintered. There were mingled barks and howls – sounds out of a cold nightmare.

Richie gave the window a tremendous shove, not caring if the glass broke and cut his hands to ribbons. He was beyond caring. It did not break; it swung outward on an old steel hinge flaked with rust. More coaldust sifted down, this time on Richie's face. He wriggled out into the side yard like an eel, smelling sweet fresh air, feeling the long grass whip at his face. He was dimly aware that it was raining. He could see the thick stalks of the giant sunflowers, green and hairy.

The Walther went off a third time, and the beast in the cellar screamed, a primitive sound of pure rage. Then Bill cried: '*It's g-got me, Richie! Help! It's g-g-got me!*'

Richie turned around on his hands and knees and saw the terrified circle of his friend's upturned face in the square of the oversized cellar window through which a winter's load of coal had once been funnelled each October.

Bill was lying spreadeagled on the coal. His hands waved and clutched fruitlessly for the window frame, which was just out of reach. His shirt and jacket were rucked up almost to his breastbone. And he was sliding backward . . . no, he was being *pulled* backward by something Richie could barely see. It was a moving, bulking shadow behind Bill. A shadow that snarled and gibbered and sounded almost human.

Richie didn't need to see it. He had seen it the previous Saturday, on the screen of the Aladdin Theater. It was mad, totally mad, but even so it never occurred to Richie to doubt either his own sanity or his conclusion.

The Teenage Werewolf had Bill Denbrough. Only it wasn't that guy Michael Landon with a lot of makeup on his face and a lot of fake fur. It was *real*.

As if to prove it, Bill screamed again.

Richie reached in and caught Bill's hands in his own. The Walther pistol was in one of them, and for the second time that day Richie looked into its black eye . . . only this time it was loaded.

They tussled for Bill – Richie gripping his hands, the Werewolf gripping his ankles.

'*G-G-Get out of h-here, Richie!*' Bill screamed. '*G-Get –*'

The face of the Werewolf suddenly swam out of the dark. Its forehead was low and prognathous, covered with scant hair. Its cheeks were hollow and furry. Its eyes were a dark brown, filled with horrible intelligence, horrible awareness. Its mouth dropped open and it began to snarl. White foam ran from the corners of its thick lower lip in twin streams that dripped from its chin. The hair on its head was swept back in a gruesome parody of a teenager's d.a. It threw its head back and roared, its eyes never leaving Richie's.

Bill scrambled up the coal. Richie seized his forearms and pulled. For a moment he thought he was actually going to win. Then the Werewolf laid hold of Bill's legs again and he was yanked backward toward the darkness once more. It was stronger. It had laid hold of Bill, and it meant to have him.

Then, with no thought at all about what he was doing or why he was doing it, Richie heard the Voice of the Irish Cop coming out of his mouth, Mr Nell's voice. But this was not Richie Tozier doing a bad imitation; it wasn't even precisely Mr Nell. It was the Voice of every Irish beat-cop that had ever lived and twirled a billy by its rawhide rope as he tried the doors of closed shops after midnight:

'Let go of him, boyo, or I'll crack yer thick head! I swear to Jaysus! Leave go of him now or I'll serve ye yer own arse on a platter!'

The creature in the cellar let out an ear-splitting roar of rage . . . but it seemed to Richie that there was another note in that bellow as well. Perhaps fear. Or pain.

He gave one more tremendous tug, and Bill flew out of the window and onto the grass. He stared up at Richie with dark horrified eyes. The front of his jacket was smeared black with coaldust.

'Kwuh-Kwuh-Quick!' Bill panted. He was nearly moaning. He grabbed at Richie's shirt. 'W-W-We guh-guh-hotta –'

Richie could hear coal tumbling and avalanching down again. A moment later the Werewolf's face filled the cellar window. It snarled at them. Its paws clutched at the listless grass.

Bill still had the Walther – he had held on to the gun through all of it. Now he held it out in both hands, his eyes squinched down to slits, and pulled the trigger. There was another deafening bang. Richie saw a chunk of the Werewolf's skull tear free and a torrent of blood spilled down the side of its face, matting the fur there and soaking the collar of the school jacket it wore.

Roaring, it began to climb out of the window.

Moving slowly, dreamily, Richie reached under his coat and into his back pocket. He brought out the envelope with the picture of the sneezing man on it. He tore it open as the bleeding, roaring creature pulled itself out of the window, forcing its way, claws digging deep furrows in the earth. Richie tore the packet open and squeezed it. *'Git back in yer place, boyo!'* he ordered in the Voice of the Irish Cop. A white cloud puffed into the Werewolf's face. Its roars suddenly stopped. It stared at Richie with almost comic surprise and made a choked wheezing sound. Its eyes, red and bleary, rolled toward Richie and seemed to mark him once and forever.

Then it began to sneeze.

It sneezed again and again and again. Ropy strings of saliva flew from its muzzle. Greenish-black clots of snot flew out of its nostrils. One of these splatted against Richie's skin and burned there, like acid. He wiped it away with a scream of hurt and disgust.

There was still anger in its face, but there was also pain – it was unmistakable. Bill might have hurt it with his dad's pistol, but Richie had hurt it more ... first with the Voice of the Irish Cop, and then with the sneezing powder.

Jesus, if I had some itching powder too and maybe a joy buzzer I might be able to kill it, Richie thought, and then Bill grabbed the collar of his jacket and jerked him backward.

It was well that he did. The Werewolf stopped sneezing as suddenly as it had started and lunged at Richie. It was quick, too – incredibly quick.

Richie might have only sat there with the empty envelope of Dr Wacky's sneezing powder in one hand, staring at the Werewolf with a kind of drugged wonder, thinking how brown its fur was, how red the blood was, how nothing was in black and white in real life, he might have sat there until its paws closed around his neck and its long nails pulled his throat out, but Bill grabbed him again and pulled him to his feet.

Richie stumbled after him. They ran around to the front of the house and Richie thought, *It won't dare chase us anymore, we're on the street now, it won't dare chase us, won't dare, won't dare –*

But it was coming. He could hear it just behind them, gibbering and snarling and slobbering.

There was Silver, still leaning against the tree. Bill jumped onto the seat and threw his father's pistol into the carrier basket where they had carried so many play guns. Richie chanced a glance behind him as he flung himself onto the package carrier and saw the Werewolf crossing the lawn toward them, less than twenty feet away now. Blood and slobber mixed on its high-school jacket. White bone gleamed through its pelt about the right temple. There were white smudges of sneezing powder on the sides of its nose. And Richie saw two other things which seemed to complete the horror. There was no zipper on the thing's jacket; instead there were big fluffy orange buttons, like pompoms. The other thing was worse. It was the other thing that made him feel as if he might faint, or just give up and let it kill him.

A name was stitched on the jacket in gold thread, the kind of thing you could get done down at Machen's for a buck if you wanted it.

Stitched on the bloody left breast of the Werewolf's jacket, stained but readable, were the words RICHIE TOZIER.

It lunged at them.

'*Go, Bill!*' Richie screamed.

Silver began to move, but slowly — much too slowly. It took Bill so long to get going —

The Werewolf crossed the rutted path just as Bill pedaled into the middle of Neibolt Street. Blood splattered its faded jeans, and looking back over his shoulder, filled with a kind of dreadful, unbreakable fascination that was akin to hypnosis, Richie saw that the seams of the jeans were giving way in places, and tufts of coarse brown fur had sprung through.

Silver wavered wildly back and forth. Bill was standing up, gripping the bike's handlebars from underneath, head turned up toward the cloudy sky, cords standing out on his neck. And still the playing cards were only firing single shots.

One paw groped for Richie. He screamed miserably and ducked away from it. The Werewolf snarled and grinned. It was close enough so Richie could see the yellowing corneas of its eyes, could smell sweet rotten meat on its breath. Its teeth were crooked fangs.

Richie screamed again as it swung a paw at him. He was sure it was going to take his head off — but the paw passed in front of him, missing by no more than an inch. The force of the swing blew Richie's sweaty hair back from his forehead.

'*Hi-yo Silver AWAYYY!*' Bill screamed at the top of his voice.

He had reached the top of a short, shallow hill. Not much, but enough to get Silver rolling. The playing cards picked up speed and began to burr along. Bill pumped the pedals madly. Silver stopped wavering and cut a straight course down Neibolt Street toward Route 2.

Thank God, thank God, thank God, Richie thought incoherently. *Thank —*

The Werewolf roared again — *oh my God it sounds like it's RIGHT BESIDE ME* — and Richie's wind was cut off as his shirt and jacket were jerked back against his windpipe. He made a gargling, choking sound and managed to grip Bill's middle just before he was pulled off the back of the bike. Bill tilted backward but held on to Silver's handlebar grips. For one moment Richie thought the big bike would simply do a wheelie and spill both of them off the back. Then his jacket, which had been just about ready for the rag-bag anyway, parted down the back with a loud ripping noise that sounded weirdly like a big fart. Richie could breathe again.

He looked around and stared directly into those muddy murderous eyes.

'*Bill!*' He tried to howl it, but the word had no force, no sound.

Bill seemed to hear him anyway. He pedaled even harder, harder than he ever had in his life. All his guts seemed to be rising, coming unanchored. He could taste thick coppery blood in the back of his throat. His eyeballs were starting from their sockets. His mouth hung open, scooping air. And a crazy, ineluctable sense of exhilaration filled him — something that was wild and free and all his own. A desire. He stood on the pedals; coaxed them; battered them.

Silver continued to pick up speed. He was beginning to feel the road now, beginning to fly. Bill could feel him go.

'*Hi-yo Silver!*' he screamed again. '*Hi-yo Silver, AWAYYY!*'

Richie could hear the fast rattle-thud of loafers on the macadam. He turned. The Werewolf's paw struck him above the eyes with stunning force, and for a moment Richie really did think the top of his head had come off. Things suddenly seemed dim, unimportant. Sounds faded in and out. The color washed out of the world. He turned back, clinging desperately to Bill. Warm blood ran into his right eye, stinging.

The paw swung again, striking the back fender this time. Richie felt the bike waver crazily, for a moment on the verge of tipping over, finally straightening out again. Bill yelled *Hi-yo Silver*, AWAY! again, but that was distant too, like an echo heard just before it dies out.

Richie closed his eyes and held on to Bill and waited for the end.

14

Bill had also heard the running steps and understood that the clown hadn't given up yet, but he didn't dare turn around and look. He would know if it caught up and knocked them flat. That was really all he needed to know.

Come on, boy, he thought. *Give me everything now! Everything you got! Go, Silver! GO!*

So once again Bill Denbrough found himself racing to beat the devil, only now the devil was a hideously grinning clown whose face sweated white greasepaint, whose mouth curved up in a leering red vampire smile, whose eyes were bright silver coins. A clown who was, for some lunatic reason, wearing a Derry High School jacket over its silvery suit with the orange ruff and the orange pompom buttons.

Go, boy, go – Silver, what do you say?

Neibolt Street blurred by him now. Silver was starting to hum good now. Had those running footfalls faded back a bit? He still didn't dare turn around to see. Richie had him in a death grip, he was pinching off his wind and Bill wanted to tell Richie to loosen up a little, but he didn't dare waste breath on that, either.

There, up ahead like a beautiful dream, was the stop-sign marking the intersection of Neibolt Street and Route 2. Cars were passing back and forth on Witcham. In his state of exhausted terror, this seemed somehow like a miracle to Bill.

Now, because he would have to put on his brakes in a moment (or do something *really* inventive), he risked a look back over his shoulder.

What he saw caused him to reverse Silver's pedals with a single snap-jerk. Silver skidded, laying rubber with its locked rear tire, and Richie's head smacked painfully into the hollow of Bill's right shoulder.

The street was completely empty.

But twenty-five yards or so behind them, by the first of the abandoned houses which formed a kind of funeral cortege leading up to the trainyards, there was a bright flick of orange. It lay close to a stormdrain cut into the curbing.

'Uhhhh . . .'

Almost too late, Bill realized that Richie was sliding off the back of Silver. Richie's eyes were turned up so Bill could only see the lower rims of the irises below his upper lids. The mended bow of his glasses hung askew. Blood was flowing slowly from his forehead.

Bill grabbed his arm, they both slipped to the right, and Silver overbalanced. They crashed to the street in a tangle of arms and legs. Bill barked his crazybone a good one and shouted with pain. Richie's eyes flickered at the sound.

'I am going to show you how to get to thees treasure, senhorr, but thees man Dobbs ees plenny dangerous,' Richie said in a snoring gasp. It was his Pancho Vanilla Voice, but its floating, unconnected quality scared Bill badly. He saw several coarse brown hairs clinging to the shallow head-wound on Richie's forehead. They were slightly kinky, like his father's pubic hair. They made him feel even more afraid, and he fetched Richie a strong smack upside the head.

'*Yowch!*' Richie cried. His eyes fluttered, then opened wide.

'What are you hittin me for, Big Bill? You'll break my glasses. They ain't in very good shape anyway, just in case you didn't notice.'

'I th-th-thought you w-w-were duh-duh-dying, or s-s-some-thing,' Bill said.

Richie sat up slowly in the street and put a hand to his head. He groaned. 'What hap –' And then he remembered. His eyes widened in sudden shock and terror and he scrambled around on his knees, gasping harshly.

'Duh-duh-don't,' Bill said. 'I-It's g-g-gone, R-R-Richie. It's gone.'

Richie saw the empty street where nothing moved and suddenly burst into tears. Bill looked at him for a moment and then put his arms around Richie and hugged him. Richie clutched at Bill's neck and hugged him back. He wanted to say something clever, something about how Bill should have tried the Bullseye on the Werewolf, but nothing would come out. Nothing except sobs.

'D-Don't, R-Richie,' Bill said, 'duh-duh-duh-h-h –' Then he burst into tears himself and they only hugged each other on their knees in the street beside Bill's spilled bike, and their tears made clean streaks down their cheeks, which were sooted with coaldust.

CHAPTER NINE
CLEANING UP

1

Somewhere high over New York State on the afternoon of May 29th, 1985, Beverly Rogan begins to laugh again. She stifles it in both hands, afraid someone will think she is crazy, but can't quite stop.

We laughed a lot back then, *she thinks. It is something else, another light on in the dark.* We were afraid all the time, but we couldn't stop laughing, *any more than I can stop now.*

The guy sitting next to her in the aisle seat is young, long-haired, good-looking. He has given her several appreciative glances since the plane took off in Milwaukee at half past two (almost two and a half hours ago now, with a stop in Cleveland and another one in Philly), but has respected her clear desire not to talk; after a couple of conversational gambits to which she has responded with politeness but no more, he opens his tote-bag and takes out a Robert Ludlum novel.

Now he closes it, holding his place with his finger, and says with some concern: 'Everything cool with you?'

She nods, trying to make her face serious, and then snorts more laughter. He smiles a little, puzzled, questioning.

'It's nothing,' *she says, once again trying to be serious, but it's no good; the more she tries to be serious the more her face wants to crack up. Just like the old days.* 'It's just that all at once I realized I didn't know what airline I was on. Only that there was a great big d-d-duck on the s-s-side —' *But the thought is too much. She goes off into gales of merry laughter. People look around at her, some frowning.*

'Republic,' *he says.*

'Pardon?'

'You are whizzing through the air at four hundred and seventy miles an hour courtesy of Republic Airlines. It's on the KYAG folder in the seat pocket.'

'KYAG?'

He pulls the folder (which does indeed have the Republic logo on the front) out of the pocket. It shows where the emergency exits are, where the flotation devices are, how to use the oxygen masks, how to assume the crash-landing position. 'The kiss-your-ass-goodbye folder,' he says, and this time they both burst out laughing.

He really is good-looking, she thinks suddenly – it is a fresh thought, somehow clear-eyed, the sort of thought you might expect to have upon waking, when your mind isn't all junked up. He's wearing a pullover sweater and faded jeans. His darkish blond hair is tied back with a piece of rawhide, and this makes her think of the ponytail she always wore her hair in when she was a kid. She thinks: I bet he's got a nice polite college-boy's cock. Long enough to jazz with, not thick enough to be really arrogant.

She starts to laugh again, totally unable to help it. She realizes she doesn't even have a handkerchief with which to wipe her streaming eyes, and this makes her laugh harder.

'You better get yourself under control or the stewardess will throw you off the plane,' he says solemnly, and she only shakes her head, laughing; her sides and her stomach hurt now.

He hands her a clean white handkerchief, and she uses it. Somehow this helps her to get it under control finally. She doesn't stop all at once, though. It just sort of tapers off into little hitchings and gaspings. Every now and then she thinks of the big duck on the side of the plane and belches out another little stream of giggles.

She passes his handkerchief back after a bit. 'Thank you.'

'Jesus, ma'am, what happened to your hand?' He holds it for a moment, concerned.

She looks down at it and sees the torn fingernails, the ones she ripped down to the quick tipping the vanity over on Tom. The memory of doing that hurts more than the fingernails themselves, and that stops the laughter for good. She takes her hand away from him, but gently.

'I slammed it in the car door at the airport,' she says, thinking of all the times she has lied about things Tom has done to her, and all the times she lied about the bruises her father put on her. Is this the last time, the last lie? How wonderful that would be . . . almost too wonderful to be believed. She thinks of a doctor coming in to see a terminal cancer patient and saying The X-rays show the tumor is shrinking. We don't have any idea why, but it's happening.

'It must hurt like hell,' he says.

'I took some aspirin.' She opens the in-flight magazine again, although he probably knows she's been through it twice already.

'Where are you headed?'

She closes the magazine, looks at him, smiles. 'You're very nice,' she says, 'but I don't want to talk. All right?'

'All right,' he says, smiling back. 'But if you want to drink to the big duck on the side of the plane when we get to Boston, I'm buying.'

'Thank you, but I have another plane to catch.'

'Boy, was my horoscope ever wrong this morning,' he says, and reopens his novel. 'But you sound great when you laugh. A guy could fall in love.'

She opens the magazine again, but finds herself looking at her jagged nails instead of the article on the pleasures of New Orleans. There are purple blood-blisters under two of them. In her mind she hears Tom screaming down the stairwell: 'I'll kill you, you bitch! You fucking bitch!' She shivers, cold. A bitch to Tom, a bitch to the seamstresses who goofed up before important shows and took a Beverly Rogan reaming for it, a bitch to her father long before either Tom or the hapless seamstresses became part of their lives.

A bitch.

You bitch.

You fucking bitch.

She closes her eyes momentarily.

Her foot, cut on a shard of perfume bottle as she fled their bedroom, throbs more than her fingers. Kay gave her a Band-Aid, a pair of shoes, and a check for a thousand dollars which Beverly cashed promptly at nine o'clock at the First Bank of Chicago in Watertower Square.

Over Kay's protests, Beverly wrote her own check for a thousand dollars on a plain sheet of typing paper. 'I read once that they have to take a check no matter what it's written on,' she told Kay. Her voice seemed to be coming from somewhere else. A radio in another room, maybe. 'Someone cashed a check once that was written on an artillery shell. I read that in The Book of Lists, I think.' She paused, then laughed uneasily. Kay looked at her soberly, even solemnly. 'But I'd cash it fast, before Tom thinks to freeze the accounts.'

Although she doesn't feel tired (she is aware, however, that by now she must be going purely on nerves and Kay's black coffee), the previous night seems like something she must have dreamed.

She can remember being followed by three teenaged boys who called and whistled but didn't quite dare come right up to her. She remembers the relief that washed over her when she saw the white fluorescent glow of a Seven-Eleven store spilling out onto the sidewalks at an intersection. She went in and let the pimply-faced counterman look down the front of her old blouse and talked him into loaning her forty cents for the pay phone. It wasn't hard, the view being what it was.

She called Kay McCall first, dialing from memory. The phone rang a dozen times and she began to fear that Kay was in New York. Kay's sleepy voice mumbled, 'It better be good, whoever you are' just as Beverly was about to hang up.

'It's Bev, Kay,' she said, hesitated, and then plunged. 'I need help.'

There was a moment of silence, and then Kay spoke again, sounding fully awake now. 'Where are you? What happened?'

'I'm at a Seven-Eleven on the corner of Streyland Avenue and some other street. I . . . Kay, I've left Tom.'

Kay, quick and emphatic and excited: 'Good! Finally! Hurray! I'll come and get you! That son of a bitch! That piece of shit! I'll come and get you in the fucking Mercedes! I'll hire a forty-piece band! I'll –'

'I'll take a cab,' Bev said, holding the other two dimes in one sweating palm. In the round mirror at the back of the store she could see the pimply clerk staring at her ass with deep and dreamy concentration. 'But you'll have to pay the tab when I get there. I don't have any money. Not a cent.'

'I'll tip the bastard five bucks,' Kay cried. 'This is the best fucking news since Nixon resigned! You get your buns over here, girl. And –' She paused and when she spoke again her voice was serious and so full of kindness and love that Beverly felt she might weep. 'Thank God you finally did it, Bev. I mean that. Thank God.'

Kay McCall is a former designer who married rich, divorced richer, and discovered feminist politics in 1972, about three years before Beverly first met her. At the time of her greatest popularity/controversy she was accused of having embraced feminism after using archaic, chauvinistic laws to take her manufacturer husband for every cent the law would allow her.

'Bullshit!' Kay had once exclaimed to Beverly. 'The people who say that stuff never had to go to bed with Sam Chacowicz. Two pumps a tickle and a squirt, that was ole Sammy's motto. The only time he could keep it up for longer than seventy seconds was when he was pulling off in the tub. I didn't cheat him; I just took my combat pay retroactively.'

She wrote three books – one on feminism and the working woman, one on feminism and the family, one on feminism and spirituality. The first two were quite popular. In the three years since her last, she had fallen out of fashion to a degree, and Beverly thought it was something of a relief to her. Her investments had done well ('Feminism and capitalism are not mutually exclusive, thank God,' she had once told Bev) and now she was a wealthy woman with a townhouse, a place in the country, and two or three lovers virile enough to go the distance with her in the sack but not quite virile enough to beat her at tennis. 'When they get that good, I drop them at once,' she said, and although Kay clearly thought this was a joke, Beverly wondered if it really was.

Beverly called a cab and when it came she piled into the back with her suitcase, glad to be away from the clerk's eyes, and gave the driver Kay's address.

She was waiting at the end of her driveway, wearing her mink coat over a flannel nightgown. Pink fuzzy mules with great big pompoms were on her feet. Not orange pompoms, thank God – that might have sent Beverly screaming into the night again. The ride over to Kay's had been weird: things were coming back to her, memories pouring in so fast and so clearly that it was frightening. She felt as if someone had started up a big bulldozer in her head and begun excavating a mental graveyard she hadn't even known was there. Only it was names instead of bodies that were turning up, names she hadn't thought of in years: Ben Hanscom, Richie Tozier, Greta Bowie, Henry Bowers, Eddie Kaspbrak . . . Bill Denbrough. Especially Bill – Stuttering Bill, they had called him with that openness of children that is sometimes called candor, sometimes cruelty. He had seemed so tall to her, so perfect (until he opened his mouth and started to talk, that was).

Names . . . places . . . things that had happened.

Alternately hot and cold, she had remembered the voices from the drain . . . and the blood. She had screamed and her father had popped her one. Her father – Tom –

Tears threatened . . . and then Kay was paying the cab-driver and tipping him big enough to make the startled cabbie exclaim, 'Thanks, lady! Wow!'

Kay took her into the house, got her into the shower, gave her a robe when she got out, made coffee, examined her injuries, Mercurochromed her cut foot, and put a Band-Aid on it. She poured a generous dollop of brandy into Bev's second cup of coffee and hectored her into drinking every drop. Then she cooked them each a rare strip steak and sautéed fresh mushrooms to go with them.

'All right,' she said. 'What happened? Do we call the cops or just send you to Reno to do your residency?'

'I can't tell you too much,' Beverly said. 'It would sound too crazy. But it was my fault, mostly –'

Kay slammed her hand down on the table. It made a sound on the polished mahogany like a small-caliber pistol shot. Bev jumped.

'Don't you say that,' Kay said. There was high color in her cheeks, and her brown eyes were blazing. 'How long have we been friends? Nine years? Ten? If I hear you say it was your fault one more time, I'm going to puke. You hear me? I'm just going to fucking puke. It wasn't your fault this time, or last time, or the time before, or any of the times. Don't you know most of your friends thought that sooner or later he'd put you in a body cast, or maybe even kill you?'

Beverly was looking at her wide-eyed.

'And that would have been your fault, at least to a degree, for staying *there and letting it happen. But now you're gone. Thank God for small favors. But don't you sit there with half of your fingernails ripped off and your foot cut open and belt-marks on your shoulders and tell me it was your fault.'*

'He didn't use his belt on me,' Bev said. The lie was automatic . . . and so was the deep shame which brought a miserable flush to her cheeks.

'If you're done with Tom, you ought to be done with the lies as well,' Kay said quietly, and she looked at Bev so long and so lovingly that Bev had to drop her eyes. She could taste salt tears in the back of her throat. 'Who did you think you were fooling?' Kay asked, still speaking quietly. She reached across the table and took Bev's hands. 'The dark glasses, the blouses with high necks and long sleeves . . . maybe you fooled a buyer or two. But you can't fool your friends, Bev. Not the people who love you.'

And then Beverly did cry, long and hard, and Kay held her, and later, just before going to bed, she told Kay what she could: That an old friend from Derry, Maine, where she had grown up, had called, and had reminded her of a promise she had made long ago. The time to fulfill the promise had arrived, he said. Would she come? She said she would. Then the trouble with Tom had started.

'What was this promise?' Kay asked.

Beverly shook her head slowly. 'I can't tell you that, Kay. Much as I'd like to.'

Kay chewed on this and then nodded. 'All right, fair enough. What are you going to do about Tom when you get back from Maine?'

And Bev, who had begun to feel more and more that she wouldn't be coming back from Derry, ever, said only: 'I'll come to you first, and we'll decide together. Okay?'

'Very much okay,' Kay said. 'Is that a promise, too?'

'As soon as I'm back,' Bev said steadily, 'you can count on it.' And she hugged Kay hard.

With Kay's check cashed and Kay's shoes on her feet, she had taken a Greyhound north to Milwaukee, afraid that Tom might have gone out to O'Hare to look for her. Kay, who had gone with her to the bank and the bus depot, tried to talk her out of it.

'O'Hare's lousy with security people, dear,' she said. 'You don't have to worry about him. If he comes near you, what you do is scream your fucking head off.'

Beverly shook her head. 'I want to avoid him altogether. This is the way to do it.'

Kay looked at her shrewdly. 'You're afraid he might talk you out of it, aren't you?'

Beverly thought of the seven of them standing in the stream, of Stanley and his piece of broken Coke bottle glinting greenly in the sun; she thought of the thin pain as he cut her palm lightly on a slant, she thought of them clasping hands in a children's circle, promising to come back if it ever started again . . . to come back and kill it for good.

'No,' she said. 'He couldn't talk me out of this. But he might hurt me, security guards or not. You didn't see him last night, Kay.'

'I've seen him enough on other occasions,' Kay said, her brows drawing together. 'The asshole that walks like a man.'

'He was crazy,' Bev said. 'Security guards might not stop him. This is better. Believe me.'

'All right,' Kay said reluctantly, and Bev thought with some amusement that Kay was disappointed that there was going to be no confrontation, no big blowoff.

'Cash the check quick,' Beverly told her again, 'before he can think to freeze the accounts. He will, you know.'

'Sure,' Kay said. 'If he does that, I'll go see the son of a bitch with a horsewhip and take it out in trade.'

'You stay away from him,' Beverly said sharply. 'He's dangerous, Kay. Believe me. He was like –' Like my father *was what trembled on her lips. Instead she said, 'He was like a wildman.'*

'Okay,' Kay said. 'Be easy in your mind, dear. Go keep your promise. And do some thinking about what comes after.'

'I will,' Bev said, but that was a lie. She had too many other things to think about: what had happened the summer she was eleven, for instance. Showing Richie Tozier how to make his yo-yo sleep, for instance. Voices from the drain, for instance. And something she had seen, something so horrible that even then, embracing Kay for the last time by the long silvery side of the grumbling Greyhound bus, her mind would not quite let her see it.

Now, as the plane with the duck on the side begins its long descent into the Boston area, her mind turns to that again . . . and to Stan Uris . . . and to an unsigned poem that came on a postcard . . . and the voices . . . and to those few seconds when she had been eye to eye with something that was perhaps infinite.

She looks out the window, looks down, and thinks that Tom's evil is a small and petty thing compared with the evil waiting for her in Derry. If there is a compensation, it is that Bill Denbrough will be there . . . and there was a time when an eleven-year-old girl named Beverly Marsh loved Bill Denbrough. She remembers the postcard with the lovely poem written on the back, and remembers that she once knew who wrote it. She doesn't remember anymore, any more than she remembers exactly what the poem said . . . but

*she thinks it might have been Bill. Yes, it might well have been Stuttering
Bill Denbrough.*

*She thinks suddenly of getting ready for bed the night after Richie and
Ben took her to see those two horror movies. After her first date. She had
cracked wise with Richie about it – in those days that had been her defense
when she was out on the street – but a part of her had been touched and
excited and a little scared. It really had been her first date, even though there
had been two boys instead of one. Richie had paid her way and everything,
just like a real date. Then, afterward, there had been those boys who chased
them . . . and they had spent the rest of the afternoon in the Barrens . . . and
Bill Denbrough had come down with another kid, she couldn't remember who,
but she remembered the way Bill's eyes had rested on hers for a moment, and
the electric shock she had felt . . . the shock and a flush that seemed to warm
her entire body.*

*She remembers thinking of all these things as she pulled on her nightgown
and went into the bathroom to wash her face and brush her teeth. She remembers thinking that it would take her a long time to get to sleep that night;
because there was so much to think about . . . and to think about in a good
way, because they seemed like good kids, like kids you could maybe goof with
and maybe even trust a little bit. That would be nice. That would be . . .
well, like heaven.*

*And thinking these things, she took her washcloth and leaned over the
basin to get some water and the voice*

2

came whispering out of the drain:
'Help me . . .'
Beverly drew back, startled, the dry washcloth dropping onto
the floor. She shook her head a little, as if to clear it, and then she
bent over the basin again and looked curiously at the drain. The bathroom was at the back of their four-room apartment. She could hear,
faintly, some Western program going on the TV. When it was over,
her father would probably switch over to a baseball game, or the fights,
and then go to sleep in his easy chair.

The wallpaper in here was a hideous pattern of frogs on lily pads.
It bulged and swayed over the lumpy plaster beneath. It was water-
marked in some places, actually peeling away in others. The tub was
rustmarked, the toilet seat cracked. One naked 40-watt bulb jutted
from a porcelain socket over the basin. Beverly could remember –
vaguely – that there had once been a light fixture, but it had been

broken some years ago and never replaced. The floor was covered with linoleum from which the pattern had faded, except for a small patch under the sink.

Not a very cheery room, but Beverly had used it so long that she no longer noticed what it looked like.

The wash-basin was also water-stained. The drain was a simple cross-hatched circle about two inches in diameter. There had once been a chrome facing, but that was also long gone. A rubber drain-plug on a chain was looped nonchalantly over the faucet marked C. The drain-hole was pipe-dark, and as she leaned over it, she noticed for the first time that there was a faint, unpleasant smell − a slightly fishy smell − coming from the drain. She wrinkled her nose a little in disgust.

'Help me −'

She gasped. It *was* a voice. She had thought perhaps a rattle in the pipes . . . or maybe just her imagination . . . some holdover from those movies . . .

'Help me, Beverly . . .'

Alternate waves of coldness and warmth swept her. She had taken the rubber band out of her hair, which lay spread across her shoulders in a bright cascade. She could feel the roots trying to stiffen.

Unaware that she meant to speak, she bent over the basin again and half-whispered, 'Hello? Is someone there?' The voice from the drain had been that of a very young child who had perhaps just learned to talk. And in spite of the gooseflesh on her arms, her mind searched for some rational explanation. It was an apartment house. The Marshes lived in the back apartment on the ground floor. There were four other apartments. Maybe there was a kid in the building amusing himself by calling into the drain. And some trick of sound . . .

'Is someone there?' she asked the drain in the bathroom, louder this time. It suddenly occurred to her that if her father happened to come in just now he would think her crazy.

There was no answer from the drain, but that unpleasant smell seemed stronger. It made her think of the bamboo patch in the Barrens, and the dump beyond it; it called up images of slow, bitter smokes and black mud that wanted to suck the shoes off your feet.

There were no really little kids in the building, that was the thing. The Tremonts had had a boy who was five, and girls who were three and six months, but Mr Tremont had lost his job at the shoe shop on Tracker Avenue, they got behind on the rent, and one day not long before school let out they had all just disappeared in Mr Tremont's rusty old Power-Flite Buick. There was Skipper

Bolton in the front apartment on the second floor, but Skipper was fourteen.

'*We all want to meet you, Beverly . . .*'

Her hand went to her mouth and her eyes widened in horror. For a moment . . . just for a moment . . . she believed she had seen something *moving* down there. She was suddenly aware that her hair was now hanging over her shoulders in two thick sheaves, and that they dangled close – very close – to that drainhole. Some clear instinct made her straighten up quick and get her hair away from there.

She looked around. The bathroom door was firmly closed. She could hear the TV faintly, Cheyenne Bodie warning the bad guy to put the gun down before someone got hurt. She was alone. Except, of course, for that voice.

'Who are you?' she called into the basin, pitching her voice low.

'Matthew Clements,' the voice whispered. 'The clown took me down here in the pipes and I died and pretty soon he'll come and take you, Beverly, and Ben Hanscom and Bill Denbrough and Eddie –'

Her hands flew to her cheeks and clutched them. Her eyes widened, widened, widened. She felt her body growing cold. Now the voice sounded choked and ancient . . . and still it crawled with corrupted glee.

'*You'll float down here with your friends, Beverly, we all float down here, tell Bill that Georgie says hello, tell Bill that Georgie misses him but he'll see him soon, tell him Georgie will be in the closet some night with a piece of piano wire to stick in his eye, tell him –*'

The voice broke up in a series of choking hiccups and suddenly a bright red bubble backed up the drain and popped, spraying beads of blood on the distained porcelain.

The choking voice spoke rapidly now, and as it spoke it changed: now it was the young voice of the child that she had first heard, now it was a teenaged girl's voice, now – horribly – it became the voice of a girl Beverly had known . . . Veronica Grogan. But Veronica was dead, she had been found dead in a sewer-drain –

'*I'm Matthew . . . I'm Betty . . . I'm Veronica . . . we're down here . . . down here with the clown . . . and the creature . . . and the mummy . . . and the werewolf . . . and you, Beverly, we're down here with you, and we float, we change . . .*'

A gout of blood suddenly belched from the drain, splattering the sink and the mirror and the wallpaper with its frogs-and-lily-pads pattern. Beverly screamed, suddenly and piercingly. She backed away from the sink, struck the door, rebounded, clawed it open, and ran for the living room, where her father was just getting to his feet.

'What the Sam Hill's wrong with *you*?' he asked, his brows drawing together. The two of them were here alone this evening; Bev's mom was working the three-to-eleven shift at Green's Farm, Derry's best restaurant.

'The bathroom!' she cried hysterically. 'The bathroom, Daddy, in the bathroom –'

'Was someone peekin at you, Beverly? Huh?' His arm shot out and his hand gripped her arm hard, sinking into the flesh. There was concern on his face but it was a predatory concern, somehow more frightening than comforting.

'No . . . the sink . . . in the sink . . . the . . . the . . .' She burst into hysterical tears before she could say anything more. Her heart was thundering so hard in her chest that she thought it would choke her.

Al Marsh thrust her aside with an 'O-Jesus-Christ-what-next' expression on his face and went into the bathroom. He was in there so long that Beverly became afraid again.

Then he bawled: '*Beverly! You come here, girl!*'

There was no question of not going. If the two of them had been standing on the edge of a high cliff and he had told her to step off – right *now*, girl – her instinctive obedience would almost certainly have carried her over the edge before her rational mind could have intervened.

The bathroom door was open. There her father stood, a big man who was now losing the red-auburn hair he had passed on to Beverly. He was still wearing his gray fatigue pants and his gray shirt (he was a janitor at the Derry Home Hospital), and he was looking hard at Beverly. He did not drink, he did not smoke, he did not chase after women. *I got all the women I need at home*, he said on occasion, and when he said it a peculiar secretive smile would cross his face – it did not brighten it but did quite the opposite. Watching that smile was like watching the shadow of a cloud travel rapidly across a rocky field. *They take care of me, and when they need it, I take care of them.*

'Now just what the Sam Hill is this foolishness all about?' he asked as she came in.

Beverly felt as if her throat had been lined with slate. Her heart raced in her chest. She thought that she might vomit soon. There was blood on the mirror, running in long drips. There were spots of blood on the light over the sink; she could *smell* it cooking onto the 40-watt bulb. Blood ran down the porcelain sides of the sink and plopped in fat drops on the linoleum floor.

'Daddy . . .' she whispered huskily.

He turned, disgusted with her (as he was so often), and began casually to wash his hands in the bloody sink. 'Good God, girl. Speak up. You scared hell out of me. Explain yourself, for Lord's sake.'

He was washing his hands in the basin, she could see blood staining the gray fabric of his pants where they rubbed against the lip of the sink, and if his forehead touched the mirror (it was close) it would be on his *skin*. She made a choked noise in her throat.

He turned off the water, grabbed a towel on which two fans of blood from the drain had splashed, and began to dry his hands. She watched, near swooning, as he grimed blood into his big knuckles and the lines of his palms. She could see blood under his fingernails like marks of guilt.

'Well? I'm waiting.' He tossed the bloody towel back over the rod.

There was blood . . . blood everywhere . . . *and her father didn't see it.*

'Daddy —' She had no idea what might have come next, but her father interrupted her.

'I worry about you,' Al Marsh said. 'I don't think you're ever going to grow up, Beverly. You go out running around, you don't do hardly any of the housework around here, you can't cook, you can't sew. Half the time you're off on a cloud someplace with your nose stuck in a book and the other half you've got vapors and megrims. I worry.'

His hand suddenly swung and spatted painfully against her buttocks. She uttered a cry, her eyes fixed on his. There was a tiny stipple of blood caught in his bushy right eyebrow. *If I look at that long enough I'll just go crazy and none of this will matter*, she thought dimly.

'I worry a *lot*,' he said, and hit her again, harder, on the arm above the elbow. That arm cried out and then seemed to go to sleep. She would have a spreading yellowish-purple bruise there the next day.

'An awful *lot*,' he said, and punched her in the stomach. He pulled the punch at the last second, and Beverly lost only half of her air. She doubled over, gasping, tears starting in her eyes. Her father looked at her impassively. He shoved his bloody hands in the pockets of his trousers.

'You got to grow up, Beverly,' he said, and now his voice was kind and forgiving. 'Isn't that so?'

She nodded. Her head throbbed. She cried, but silently. If she sobbed aloud – started what her father called 'that baby whining' – he might go to work on her in earnest. Al Marsh had lived his entire life in Derry and told people who asked (and sometimes those who did not) that he intended to be buried here – hopefully at the age of one hundred and ten. 'No reason why I shouldn't live forever,' he sometimes told Roger Aurlette, who cut his hair once each month. 'I have no vices.'

'Now explain yourself,' he said, 'and make it quick.'

'There was –' She swallowed and it hurt because there was no moisture in her throat, none at all. 'There was a spider. A big fat black spider. It . . . it crawled out of the drain and I . . . I guess it crawled back down.'

'*Oh!*' He smiled a little at her now, as if pleased by this explanation. 'Was *that* it? Damn! If you'd told me, Beverly, I never would have hit you. All girls are scared of spiders. Sam Hill! Why didn't you speak up?'

He bent over the drain and she had to bite her lip to keep from crying out a warning . . . and some other voice spoke deep inside her, some terrible voice which could not have been a part of her; surely it was the voice of the devil himself: *Let it get him, if it wants him. Let it pull him down. Good-fucking-riddance.*

She turned away from that voice in horror. To allow such a thought to stay for even a moment in her head would surely damn her to hell.

He peered into the eye of the drain. His hands squelched in the blood on the rim of the basin. Beverly fought grimly with her gorge. Her belly ached where her dad had hit her.

'Don't see a thing,' he said. 'All these buildings are old, Bev. Got drains the size of freeways, you know it? When I was janitorin down in the old high school, we used to get drowned rats in the toilet bowls once in awhile. It drove the girls crazy.' He laughed fondly at the thought of such female vapors and megrims. 'Mostly when the Kenduskeag was high. Less wildlife in the pipes since they put in the new drain system, though.'

He put an arm around her and hugged her.

'Look. You go to bed and don't think about it anymore. Okay?'

She felt her love for him. *I never hit you when you didn't deserve it, Beverly*, he told her once when she had cried out that some punishment had been unfair. And surely that had to be true, because he *was* capable of love. Sometimes he would spend a whole day with her, showing her how to do things or just telling her stuff or walking around town with her, and when he was kind like that she thought her heart would swell with happiness until it killed her. She loved him, and tried to understand that he had to correct her often because it was (as he said) his God-given job. *Daughters*, Al Marsh said, *need more correction than sons.* He had no sons, and she felt vaguely as if that might be partly her fault as well.

'Okay, Daddy,' she said. 'I won't.'

They walked into her small bedroom together. Her right arm now ached fiercely from the blow it had taken. She looked back over her shoulder and saw the bloody sink, bloody mirror, bloody wall, bloody floor. The bloody towel her father had used and then hung casually over the rod. She thought: *How can I ever go in there to wash up again? Please God, dear God, I'm sorry if I had a bad thought about my dad and You can punish me for it if You want, I deserve to be punished, make me fall down and hurt myself or make me have the flu like last winter when I coughed so hard once I threw up but please God make the blood be gone in the morning, pretty please, God, okay? Okay?*

Her father tucked her in as he always did, and kissed her forehead. Then he only stood there for a moment in what she would always think of as 'his' way of standing, perhaps of being: bent slightly forward, hands plunged deep − to above the wrist − in his pockets, the bright blue eyes in his mournful basset-hound's face looking down at her from above. In later years, long after she stopped thinking about Derry at all, she would see a man sitting on the bus or maybe standing on a corner with his dinnerbucket in his hand, shapes, oh shapes of men, sometimes seen as day closed down, sometimes seen across Watertower Square in the noonlight of a clear windy autumn day, shapes of men, rules of men, desires of men: or Tom, so like her father when he took off his shirt and stood slightly slumped in front of the bathroom mirror to shave. Shapes of men.

'Sometimes I worry about you, Bev,' he said, but there was no trouble or anger in his voice now. He touched her hair gently, smoothing it back from her forehead.

The bathroom is full of blood, Daddy! she almost screamed then. *Didn't you see it? It's everywhere! Cooking onto the light over the sink, even! Didn't you SEE it?*

But she kept her silence as he went out and closed the door behind him, filling her room with darkness. She was still awake, still staring into the darkness, when her mother came in at eleven-thirty and the TV went off. She heard her parents go into their room and she heard the bedsprings creaking steadily as they did their sex-act thing. Beverly had overheard Greta Bowie telling Sally Mueller that the sex-act thing hurt like fire and no nice girl ever wanted to do it ('At the end of it the man pees all over your bug,' Greta said, and Sally had cried: 'Oh yuck, I'd *never* let a boy do that to me!'). If it hurt as badly as Greta said, then Bev's mother kept the hurt to herself; Bev had heard her mom cry out once or twice in a low voice, but it hadn't sounded at all like a pain-cry.

The slow creak of the springs speeded up to a beat so rapid it was just short of frantic, and then stopped. There was a period of silence, then some low talk, then the sound of her mother's footsteps as she went into the bathroom. Beverly held her breath, waiting for her mother to scream or not.

There was no scream – only the sound of water running into the basin. That was followed by some low splashing. Then the water ran out of the basin with its familiar gurgling sound. Her mother was brushing her teeth now. Moments later the bedsprings in her parents' room creaked again as her mom got back into bed.

Five minutes or so after that her father began to snore.

A black fear stole over her heart and closed her throat. She found herself afraid to turn over on her right side – her favorite sleeping position – because she might see something looking in the window at her. So she just lay on her back, stiff as a poker, looking up at the pressed-tin ceiling. Some time later – minutes or hours, there was no way of telling – she fell into a thin troubled sleep.

3

Beverly always woke up when the alarm went off in her parents' bedroom. You had to be fast, because the alarm no more than got started before her father banged it off. She dressed quickly while her father used the bathroom. She paused (as she now almost always did) to look at her chest in the mirror, trying to decide if her breasts had gotten any bigger in the night. She had started getting them late last year. There had been some faint pain at first, but that was gone now. They were extremely small – not much more than spring apples, really – but they were *there*. It was true; childhood would end; she would be a woman.

She smiled at her reflection and put a hand behind her head, pushing her hair up and sticking her chest out. She giggled a little girl's unaffected giggle . . . and suddenly remembered the blood spewing out of the bathroom drain the night before. The giggles stopped abruptly.

She looked at her arm and saw the bruise that had formed there in the night – an ugly stain between her shoulder and elbow, a stain with many discolored fingers.

The toilet went with a bang and a flush.

Moving quickly, not wanting him to be mad with her this morning (not wanting him to even *notice* her this morning), Beverly pulled on a pair of jeans and her Derry High School sweatshirt. And then, because it could no longer be put off, she left her room for the bathroom. Her father passed her in the living room on his way back to his room to get dressed. His blue pyjama suit flapped loosely around him. He grunted something at her she didn't understand.

'Okay, Daddy,' she replied nevertheless.

She stood in front of the closed bathroom door for a moment, trying to get her mind ready for what she might see inside. *At least it's daytime*, she thought, and that brought some comfort. Not much, but some. She grasped the doorknob, turned it, and stepped inside.

4

That was a busy morning for Beverly. She got her father his breakfast – orange juice, scrambled eggs, Al Marsh's version of toast (the bread hot but not really toasted at all). He sat at the table, barricaded behind the *News*, and ate it all.

'Where's the bacon?'

'Gone, Daddy. We finished it yesterday.'

'Cook me a hamburger.'

'There's only a little bit of that left, t –'

The paper rustled, then dropped. His blue stare fell on her like weight.

'What did you say?' he asked softly.

'I said right away, Daddy.'

He looked at her a moment longer. Then the paper went back up and Beverly hurried to the refrigerator to get the meat.

She cooked him a hamburger, mashing the little bit of ground meat that was left in the icebox as hard as she could to make it look bigger. He ate it reading the Sports page and Beverly made his lunch – a couple of peanut-butter-and-jelly sandwiches, a big piece of cake her mother had brought back from Green's Farm last night, a Thermos of hot coffee heavily laced with sugar.

'You tell your mother I said to get this place cleaned up today,' he said, taking his dinnerbucket. 'It looks like a damn old pigsty. Sam Hill! I spend the whole day cleaning up messes over to the hospital. I don't need to come home to a pigsty. You mind me, Beverly.'

'Okay, Daddy. I will.'

He kissed her cheek, gave her a rough hug, and left. As she always did, Beverly went to the window of her room and watched him walk down the street. And as she always did, she felt a sneaking sense of relief when he turned the corner . . . and hated herself for it.

She did the dishes and then took the book she was reading out on the back steps for awhile. Lars Theramenius, his long blonde hair glowing with its own serene inner light, toddled over from the next building to show Beverly his new Tonka truck and the new scrapes on his knees. Beverly exclaimed over both. Then her mother was calling her.

They changed both beds, washed the floors and waxed the kitchen linoleum. Her mother did the bathroom floor, for which Beverly was profoundly grateful. Elfrida Marsh was a small woman with graying hair and a grim look. Her lined face told the world that she had been around for awhile and intended to stay around awhile longer . . . It also told the world that none of it had been easy and she did not look for an early change in that state of affairs.

'Will you do the living-room windows, Bevvie?' she asked, coming back into the kitchen. She had changed into her waitress uniform. 'I have to go up to Saint Joe's in Bangor to see Cheryl Tarrent. She broke her leg last night.'

'Yeah, I'll do them,' Beverly said. 'What happened to Mrs Tarrent? Did she fall down or something?' Cheryl Tarrent was a woman Elfrida worked with at the restaurant.

'She and that no-good she's married to were in a car wreck,' Beverly's mother said grimly. 'He was drinking. You want to thank God in your prayers every night that your father doesn't drink, Bevvie.'

'I do,' Beverly said. She did.

'She's going to lose her job, I guess, and he can't hold one.' Now tones of grim horror crept into Elfrida's voice. 'They'll have to go on the county, I guess.'

It was the worst thing Elfrida Marsh could think of. Losing a child or finding out you had cancer didn't hold a candle to it. You could be poor; you could spend your life doing what she called 'scratchin.' But at the bottom of everything, below even the gutter, was a time when you might have to go *on the county* and drink the worksweat from the brows of others as a gift. This, she knew, was the prospect that now faced Cheryl Tarrent.

'Once you got the windows washed and take the trash out, you can go and play awhile, if you want. It's your father's bowling night so you won't have to fix his supper, but I want you in before dark. You know why.'

'Okay, Mom.'

'My God, you're growing up fast,' Elfrida said. She looked for a moment at the nubs in Beverly's sweatshirt. Her glance was loving but pitiless. 'I don't know what I'm going to do around here once you're married and have a place of your own.'

'I'll be around for just about ever,' Beverly said, smiling.

Her mother hugged her briefly and kissed the corner of her mouth with her warm dry lips. 'I know better,' she said. 'But I love you, Bevvie.'

'I love you too, Momma.'

'You make sure there aren't any streaks on those windows when you're done,' she said, picking up her purse and going to the door. 'If there are, you'll catch the blue devil from your father.'

'I'll be careful.' As her mother opened the door to go out, Beverly asked in a tone she hoped was casual: 'Did you see anything funny in the bathroom, Mom?'

Elfrida looked back at her, frowning a little. 'Funny?'

'Well . . . I saw a spider in there last night. It crawled out of the drain. Didn't Daddy tell you?'

'Did you get your dad angry at you last night, Bevvie?'

'No! Huh-uh! I told him a spider crawled out of the drain and scared me and he said sometimes they used to find drowned rats in the toilets at the old high school. Because of the drains. He didn't tell you about the spider I saw?'

'No.'

'Oh. Well, it doesn't matter. I just wondered if you saw it.'

'I didn't see any spider. I wish we could afford a little new linoleum for that bathroom floor.' She glanced at the sky, which was blue and cloudless. 'They say if you kill a spider, it brings rain. You didn't kill it, did you?'

'No,' Beverly said. 'I didn't kill it.'

Her mother looked back at her, her lips pressed together so tightly they almost weren't there. 'You *sure* your dad wasn't angry with you last night?'

'*No!*'

'Bevvie, does he ever touch you?'

'What?' Beverly looked at her mother, totally perplexed. God, her father touched her every *day*. 'I don't get what you –'

'Never mind,' Elfrida said shortly. 'Don't forget the trash. And if those windows are streaked, you won't need your *father* to give you blue devil.'

'I won't

(*does he ever touch you*)

'forget.'

'And be in before dark.'

'I will.'

(*does he*)

(*worry an awful lot*)

Elfrida left. Beverly went into her room again and watched her around the corner and out of view, as she had her father. Then, when she was sure her mother was well on her way to the bus stop, Beverly got the floorbucket, the Windex, and some rags from under the sink. She went into the living room and began on the windows. The apartment seemed too quiet. Each time the floor creaked or a door slammed, she jumped a little. When the Boltons' toilet flushed above her, she uttered a gasp that was nearly a scream.

And she kept looking toward the closed bathroom door.

At last she walked down there and drew it open again and looked inside. Her mother had cleaned in here this morning, and most of the blood which had pooled under the sink was gone. So was the blood on the sink's rim. But there were still maroon streaks drying in the sink itself, spots and splashes of it on the mirror and on the wallpaper.

Beverly looked at her pale reflection and realized with sudden, superstitious dread that the blood on the mirror made it seem as if *her* face was bleeding. She thought again: *What am I going to do about this? Have I gone crazy? Am I imagining it?*

The drain suddenly gave a burping chuckle.

Beverly screamed and slammed the door and five minutes later her hands were still trembling so badly that she almost dropped the bottle of Windex as she washed the windows in the living room.

5

It was around three o'clock that afternoon, the apartment locked up and the extra key tucked snugly away in the pocket of her jeans, when Beverly Marsh happened to turn up Richard's Alley, a narrow walk-through which connected Main and Center Streets, and came upon Ben Hanscom, Eddie Kaspbrak, and a boy named Bradley Donovan pitching pennies.

'Hi, Bev!' Eddie said. 'You get any nightmares from those movies?'

'Nope,' Beverly said, squatting down to watch the game. 'How'd you know about that?'

'Haystack told me,' Eddie said, jerking a thumb at Ben, who was blushing wildly for no good reason Beverly could see.

'What movieth?' Bradley asked, and now Beverly recognized him: he had come down to the Barrens a week ago with Bill Denbrough. They had a speech class together in Bangor. Beverly more or less dismissed him from her mind. If asked, she might have said he seemed somehow less important than Ben and Eddie – less *there*.

'Couple of creature features,' she said to him, and duck-walked closer until she was between Ben and Eddie. 'You pitchin?'

'Yes,' Ben said. He looked at her quickly, then looked away.

'Who's winning?'

'Eddie,' Ben said. 'Eddie's real good.'

She looked at Eddie, who polished his nails solemnly on the front of his shirt and then giggled.

'Can I play?'

'Okay with me,' Eddie said. 'You got pence?'

She felt in her pocket and brought out three.

'Jeez, how do you dare to go out of the house with such a wad?' Eddie asked. 'I'd be scared.'

Ben and Bradley Donovan laughed.

'Girls can be brave, too,' Beverly said gravely, and a moment later they were all laughing.

Bradley pitched first, then Ben, then Beverly. Because he was winning, Eddie had lasties. They tossed the pennies toward the back wall of the Center Street Drug Store. Sometimes they landed short, sometimes they struck and bounced back. At the end of each round the shooter with the penny closest to the wall collected all four pennies. Five minutes later, Beverly had twenty-four cents. She had lost only a single round.

'Girlth cheat!' Bradley said, disgusted, and got up to go. His good humor was gone, and he looked at Beverly with both anger and humiliation. 'Girlth thouldn't be allowed to –'

Ben bounced to his feet. It was awesome to watch Ben Hanscom bounce. 'Take that back!'

Bradley looked at Ben, his mouth open. 'What?'

379

'Take it *back*! She didn't cheat!'

Bradley looked from Ben to Eddie to Beverly, who was still on her knees. Then he looked back at Ben again. 'You want a fat lip to math the reth of you, athhole?'

'Sure,' Ben said, and a grin suddenly crossed his face. Something in its quality caused Bradley to take a surprised, uneasy step backward. Perhaps what he saw in that grin was the simple fact that after tangling with Henry Bowers and coming out ahead not once but twice, Ben Hanscom was not about to be terrorized by skinny old Bradley Donovan (who had warts all over his hands as well as that cataclysmic lisp).

'Yeah, and then you all gang up on me,' Bradley said, taking another step backward. His voice had picked up an uncertain waver, and tears stood out in his eyes. 'All a bunth of *cheaterth*!'

'You just take back what you said about her,' Ben said.

'Never mind, Ben,' Beverly said. She held out a handful of coppers to Bradley. 'Take what's yours. I wasn't playing for keepsies anyway.'

Tears of humiliation spilled over Bradley's lower lashes. He struck the pennies from Beverly's hand and ran for the Center Street end of Richard's Alley. The others stood looking at him, open-mouthed. With safety within reach, Bradley turned around and shouted: 'You're jutht a little bith, that'th all! Cheater! Cheater! Your mother'th a *whore*!'

Beverly gasped. Ben ran up the alley toward Bradley and succeeded in doing no more than tripping over an empty crate and falling down. Bradley was gone, and Ben knew better than to believe he could ever catch him. He turned toward Beverly instead to see if she was all right. That word had shocked him as much as it had her.

She saw the concern in his face. She opened her mouth to say she was okay, not to worry, sticks-and-stones-will-break-my-bones-but-names-will-never-hurt-me . . . and that odd question her mother had asked

(*does he ever touch you*)

recurred. Odd question, yes – simple yet nonsensical, full of somehow ominous undertones, murky as old coffee. Instead of saying that names would never hurt her, she burst into tears.

Eddie looked at her uncomfortably, took his aspirator from his pants pocket, and sucked on it. Then he bent down and began picking up the scattered pennies. There was a fussy, careful expression on his face as he did this.

Ben moved toward her instinctively, wanting to hug and give

comfort, and then stopped. She was too pretty. In the face of that prettiness he felt helpless.

'Cheer up,' he said, knowing it must sound idiotic but unable to think of anything more useful. He touched her shoulders lightly (she had put her hands over her face to hide her wet eyes and blotchy cheeks) and then took them away as if she were too hot to touch. He was now blushing so hard he looked apoplectic. 'Cheer up, Beverly.'

She lowered her hands and cried out in a shrill, furious voice: 'My mother is not a whore! She . . . she's a *waitress*!'

This was greeted by absolute silence. Ben stared at her with his lower jaw sprung ajar. Eddie looked up at her from the cobbled surface of the alley, his hands full of pennies. And suddenly all three of them were laughing hysterically.

'*A waitress!*' Eddie cackled. He had only the faintest idea of what a whore was, but something about this comparison struck him as delicious just the same. 'Is *that* what she is!'

'Yes! Yes, she is!' Beverly gasped, laughing and crying at the same time.

Ben was laughing so hard he couldn't stand up. He sat heavily on a trashcan. His bulk drove the lid into the can and spilled him into the alley on his side. Eddie pointed at him and howled with laughter. Beverly helped him to his feet.

A window went up above them and a woman yelled, 'You kids get out of there! There's people that have to work the night shift, you know! Get lost!'

Without thinking, the three of them linked hands, Beverly in the middle, and ran for Center Street. They were still laughing.

6

They pooled their money and discovered they had forty cents, enough for two ice-cream frappes from the drugstore. Because old Mr Keene was a grouch and wouldn't let kids under twelve eat their stuff at the soda fountain (he claimed the pinball machines in the back room might corrupt them), they took the frappes in two huge waxed containers up to Bassey Park and sat on the grass to drink them. Ben had coffee, Eddie strawberry. Beverly sat between the two boys with a straw, sampling each in turn like a bee at flowers. She felt okay again for the first time since the drain had coughed up its gout of blood the night before – washed out and emotionally exhausted, but okay, at peace with herself. For the time being, anyway.

'I just don't get what was wrong with Bradley,' Eddie said at last – it had the tone of awkward apology. 'He never acted like that before.'

'You stood up for me,' Beverly said, and suddenly kissed Ben on one cheek. 'Thank you.'

Ben went scarlet again. 'You weren't cheating,' he mumbled, and abruptly gulped down half of his coffee frappe in three monster swallows. This was followed by a burp as loud as a shotgun blast.

'Get any on you, Daddy-o?' Eddie asked, and Beverly laughed helplessly, holding her stomach.

'No more,' she giggled. 'My stomach hurts. Please, no more.'

Ben was smiling. That night, before sleep, he would play the moment when she had kissed him over and over again in his mind.

'Are you really okay now?' he asked.

She nodded. 'It wasn't *him*. It really wasn't even what he said about my mother. It was something that happened last night.' She hesitated, looking from Ben to Eddie and back to Ben again. 'I . . . I have to tell somebody. Or show somebody. Or something. I guess I cried because I've been scared I'm going looneytunes.'

'What are you talking about, looneytunes?' a new voice asked.

It was Stanley Uris. As always he looked small, slim, and preternaturally neat – much too neat for a kid who was just barely eleven. In his white shirt, neatly tucked into his fresh jeans all the way around, his hair combed, the toes of his high-top Keds spotlessly clean, he looked instead like the world's smallest adult. Then he smiled, and the illusion was broken.

She won't say whatever she was going to say, Eddie thought, *because he wasn't there when Bradley called her mother that name.*

But after a moment's hesitation, Beverly did tell. Because somehow Stanley was different from Bradley – he was *there* in a way Bradley had not been.

Stanley's one of us, Beverly thought, and wondered why that should cause her arms to suddenly break out in bumps. *I'm not doing any of them any favors by telling*, she thought. *Not them, and not me, neither.*

But it was too late. She was already speaking. Stan sat down with them, his face still and grave. Eddie offered him the last of the strawberry frappe and Stan only shook his head, his eyes never leaving Beverly's face. None of the boys spoke.

She told them about the voices. About recognizing Ronnie Grogan's voice. She knew Ronnie was dead, but it was her voice all the same. She told them about the blood, and how her father had not seen it or felt it, and how her mother had not seen it this morning.

When she finished, she looked around at their faces, afraid of what she might see there . . . but she saw no disbelief. Terror, but no disbelief.

Finally Ben said, 'Let's go look.'

7

They went in by the back door, not just because that was the lock Bev's key fitted but because she said her father would kill her if Mrs Bolton saw her going into the apartment with three boys while her folks were gone.

'Why?' Eddie asked.

'You wouldn't understand, numbnuts,' Stan said. 'Just be quiet.'

Eddie started to reply, looked again at Stan's white, strained face and decided to keep his mouth shut.

The door gave on the kitchen, which was full of late-afternoon sun and summer silence. The breakfast dishes sparkled in the drainer. The four of them stood by the kitchen table, bunched up, and when a door slammed upstairs, they all jumped and then laughed nervously.

'Where is it?' Ben asked. He was whispering.

Her heart thudding in her temples, Beverly led them down the little hall with her parents' bedroom on one side and the closed bathroom door at the end. She pulled it open, stepped quickly inside, and pulled the chain over the sink. Then she stepped back between Ben and Eddie again. The blood had dried to maroon smears on the mirror and the basin and the wallpaper. She looked at the blood because it was suddenly easier to look at that than at them.

In a small voice she could hardly recognize as her own, she asked: 'Do you see it? Do *any* of you see it? Is it there?'

Ben stepped forward, and she was again struck by how delicately he moved for such a fat boy. He touched one of the smears of blood; then a second; then a long drip on the mirror. 'Here. Here. Here.' His voice was flat and authoritative.

'Jeepers! It looks like somebody killed a pig in here,' Stan said, softly awed.

'It all came out of the drain?' Eddie asked. The sight of the blood made him feel ill. His breath was shortening. He clutched at his aspirator.

Beverly had to struggle to keep from bursting into fresh tears.

She didn't want to do that; she was afraid if she did they would dismiss her as just another girl. But she had to clutch for the doorknob as relief washed through her in a wave of frightening strength. Until that moment she hadn't realized how sure she was that she was going crazy, having hallucinations, something.

'And your mom and dad never saw it,' Ben marvelled. He touched a splotch of blood which had dried on the basin and then pulled his hand away and wiped it on the tail of his shirt. 'Jeepers-creepers.'

'I don't know how I can ever come in here again,' Beverly said. 'Not to wash up or brush my teeth or . . . you know.'

'Well, why don't we clean the place up?' Stanley asked suddenly. Beverly looked at him. 'Clean it?'

'Sure. Maybe we couldn't get all of it off the wallpaper – it looks sorta, you know, on its last legs – but we could get the rest. Haven't you got some rags?'

'Under the kitchen sink,' Beverly said. 'But my mom'll wonder where they went if we use them.'

'I've got fifty cents,' Stan said quietly. His eyes never left the blood that had spattered the area of the bathroom around the wash-basin. 'We'll clean up as good as we can, then take the rags down to that coin-op laundry place back the way we came. We'll wash them and dry them and they'll all be back under the sink before your folks get home.'

'My mother says you can't get blood out of cloth,' Eddie objected. 'She says it sets in, or something.'

Ben uttered a hysterical little giggle. 'Doesn't matter if it comes out of the rags or not,' he said. '*They* can't see it.'

No one had to ask him who he meant by 'they.'

'All right,' Beverly said. 'Let's try it.'

8

For the next half hour, the four of them cleaned like grim elves, and as the blood disappeared from the walls and the mirror and the porcelain basin, Beverly felt her heart grow lighter and lighter. Ben and Eddie did the sink and mirror while she scrubbed the floor. Stan worked on the wallpaper with studious care, using a rag that was almost dry. In the end, they got almost all of it. Ben finished by removing the light-bulb over the sink and replacing it with one from the box of bulbs in the pantry. There were plenty: Elfrida Marsh had bought a two-year supply from the Derry Lions during their annual light-bulb sale the fall before.

They used Elfrida's floorbucket, her Ajax, and plenty of hot water. They dumped the water frequently because none of them liked to have their hands in it once it had turned pink.

At last Stanley backed away, looked at the bathroom with the critical eye of a boy in whom neatness and order are not simply ingrained but actually innate, and told them: 'It's the best we can do, I think.'

There were still faint traces of blood on the wallpaper to the left of the sink, where the paper was so thin and ragged that Stanley had dared do no more than blot it gently. Yet even here the blood had been sapped of its former ominous strength; it was little more than a meaningless pastel smear.

'Thank you,' Beverly said to all of them. She could not remember ever having meant thanks so deeply. 'Thank you all.'

'It's okay,' Ben mumbled. He was of course blushing again.

'Sure,' Eddie agreed.

'Let's get these rags done,' Stanley said. His face was set, almost stern. And later Beverly would think that perhaps only Stan realized that they had taken another step toward some unthinkable confrontation.

9

They measured out a cup of Mrs Marsh's Tide and put it in an empty mayonnaise jar. Bev found a paper shopping bag to put the bloody rags in, and the four of them went down to the Kleen-Kloze Washateria on the corner of Main and Cony Streets. Two blocks farther up they could see the Canal gleaming a bright blue in the afternoon sun.

The Kleen-Kloze was empty except for a woman in a white nurse's uniform who was waiting for her dryer to stop. She glanced at the four kids distrustfully and then went back to her paperback of *Peyton Place*.

'Cold water,' Ben said in a low voice. 'My mom says you gotta wash blood in cold water.'

They dumped the rags into the washer while Stan changed his two quarters for four dimes and two nickels. He came back and watched as Bev dumped the Tide over the rags and swung the washer's door closed. Then he plugged two dimes into the coin-op slot and twisted the start knob.

Beverly had chipped in most of the pennies she had won at pitch for the frappes, but she found four survivors deep down in the lefthand pocket of her jeans. She fished them out and offered them to Stan, who looked pained. 'Jeez,' he said, 'I take a girl on a laundry date and right away she wants to go Dutch.'

Beverly laughed a little. 'You sure?'

'I'm sure,' Stan said in his dry way. 'I mean, it's really breaking my heart to give up those four pence, Beverly, but I'm sure.'

The four of them went over to the line of plastic contour chairs against the Washateria's cinderblock wall and sat there, not talking. The Maytag with the rags in it chugged and sloshed. Fans of suds slobbered against the thick glass of its round porthole. At first the suds were reddish. Looking at them made Bev feel a little sick, but she found it was hard to look away. The bloody foam had a gruesome sort of fascination. The lady in the nurse's uniform glanced at them more and more often over the top of her book. She had perhaps been afraid they would be rowdy; now their very silence seemed to unnerve her. When her dryer stopped she took her clothes out, folded them, put them into a blue plastic laundry-bag and left, giving them one last puzzled look as she went out the door.

As soon as she was gone, Ben said abruptly, almost harshly: 'You're not alone.'

'What?' Beverly asked.

'You're not alone,' Ben repeated. 'You see –'

He stopped and looked at Eddie, who nodded. He looked at Stan, who looked unhappy . . . but who, after a moment, shrugged and also nodded.

'What in the world are you talking about?' Beverly asked. She was tired of people saying inexplicable things to her today. She gripped Ben's lower arm. 'If you know something about this, tell me!'

'Do you want to do it?' Ben asked Eddie.

Eddie shook his head. He took his aspirator out of his pocket and sucked in on it with a monstrous gasp.

Speaking slowly, picking his words, Ben told Beverly how he had happened to meet Bill Denbrough and Eddie Kaspbrak in the Barrens on the day school let out – that was almost a week ago, as hard as that was to believe. He told her about how they had built the dam in the Barrens the following day. He told Bill's story of how the school photograph of his dead brother had turned its head and winked. He told his own story of the mummy who had walked on the icy Canal in the dead heart of winter with balloons that floated against the wind. Beverly listened to all this with growing horror. She could feel her eyes widening, her hands and feet growing cold.

Ben stopped and looked at Eddie. Eddie took another wheezing pull on his aspirator and then told the story of the leper again, speaking as rapidly as Ben had slowly, his words tumbling over one another in their urgency to escape and be gone. He finished with a sucking little half-sob, but this time he didn't cry.

'And you?' she asked, looking at Stan Uris.

'I –'

There was sudden silence, making them all start the way a sudden explosion might have done.

'The wash is done,' Stan said.

They watched him get up – small, economical, graceful – and open the washer. He pulled out the rags, which were stuck together in a clump, and examined them.

'There's a little stain left,' he said, 'but it's not too bad. Looks like it could be cranberry juice.'

He showed them, and they all nodded gravely, as if over important documents. Beverly felt a relief that was similar to the relief she had felt when the bathroom was clean again. She could stand the faded pastel smear on the peeling wallpaper in there, and she could stand the faint reddish stain on her mother's cleaning rags. They had *done* something about it, that seemed to be the important thing. Maybe it hadn't worked completely, but she discovered it had worked well enough to give her heart peace, and brother, that was good enough for Al Marsh's daughter Beverly.

Stan tossed them into one of the barrel-shaped dryers and put in two nickels. The dryer started to turn, and Stan came back and took his seat between Eddie and Ben.

For a moment the four of them sat silent again, watching the rags turn and fall, turn and fall. The drone of the gas-fired dryer was soothing, almost soporific. A woman passed by the chocked-open door, wheeling a cart of groceries. She glanced in at them and passed on.

'I did see something,' Stan said suddenly. 'I didn't want to talk about it, because I wanted to think it was a dream or something. Maybe even a fit, like that Stavier kid has. Any you guys know that kid?'

Ben and Bev shook their heads. Eddie said, 'The kid who's got epilepsy?'

'Yeah, right. That's how bad it was. I would have rather thought I had something like that than that I saw something . . . really real.'

'What was it?' Bev asked, but she wasn't sure she really wanted

387

to know. This was not like listening to ghost-stories around a camp-fire while you ate wieners in toasted buns and cooked marshmallows over the flames until they were black and crinkly. Here they sat in this stifling laundromat and she could see great big dust kitties under the washing machines (ghost-turds, her father called them), she could see dust-motes dancing in the hot shafts of sunlight which fell through the laundromat's dirty plate-glass window, she could see old magazines with their covers torn off. These were all normal things. Nice and normal and boring. But she was scared. Terribly scared. Because, she sensed, none of these things were made-up stories, made-up monsters: Ben's mummy, Eddie's leper . . . either or both of them might be out tonight when the sun went down. Or Bill Denbrough's brother, one-armed and implacable, cruising through the black drains under the city with silver coins for eyes.

Yet, when Stan did not answer immediately, she asked again: 'What was it?'

Speaking carefully, Stan said: 'I was over in that little park where the Standpipe is –'

'Oh God, I don't like that place,' Eddie said dolefully. 'If there's a haunted house in Derry, that's it.'

'*What*?' Stan said sharply. 'What did you say?'

'Don't you *know* about that place?' Eddie asked. 'My mom wouldn't let me go near there even before the kids started getting killed. She . . . she takes real good care of me.' He offered them an uneasy grin and held his aspirator tighter in his lap. 'You see, some kids have been drowned in there. Three or four. They – Stan? Stan, are you all right?'

Stan Uris's face had gone a leaden gray. His mouth worked soundlessly. His eyes rolled up until the others could only see the bottommost curves of his irises. One hand clutched weakly at empty air and then fell against his thigh.

Eddie did the only thing he could think of. He leaned over, put one thin arm around Stan's slumping shoulders, jammed his aspirator into Stan's mouth, and triggered off a big blast.

Stan began to cough and choke and gag. He sat up straight, his eyes back in focus again. He coughed into his cupped hands. At last he uttered a huge, burping gasp and slumped back against his chair.

'What was that?' he managed at last.

'My asthma medicine,' Eddie said apologetically.

'God, it tastes like dead dogshit.'

They all laughed at this, but it was nervous laughter. The

others were looking nervously at Stan. Thin color now burned in his cheeks.

'It's pretty bad, all right,' Eddie said with some pride.

'Yeah, but is it kosher?' Stan said, and they all laughed again, although none of them (including Stan) really knew what 'kosher' meant.

Stan stopped laughing first and looked at Eddie intently. 'Tell me what you know about the Standpipe,' he said.

Eddie started, but both Ben and Beverly also contributed. The Derry Standpipe stood on Kansas Street, about a mile and a half west of downtown, near the southern edge of the Barrens. At one time, near the end of the previous century, it had supplied all of Derry's water, holding one and three-quarter million gallons. Because the circular open-air gallery just below the Standpipe's roof offered a spectacular view of the town and the surrounding countryside, it had been a popular place until 1930 or so. Families would come out to tiny Memorial Park on a Saturday or Sunday forenoon when the weather was fine, climb the one hundred and sixty stairs inside the Standpipe to the gallery, and take in the view. More often than not they spread and ate a picnic lunch while they did so.

The stairs were between the Standpipe's outside, which was shingled a blinding white, and its inner sleeve, a great stainless-steel cylinder standing a hundred and six feet high. These stairs wound to the top in a narrow spiral.

Just below the gallery level, a thick wooden door in the Standpipe's inner jacket gave on a platform over the water itself – a black, gently lapping tarn lit by naked magnesium bulbs screwed into reflective tin hoods. The water was exactly one hundred feet deep when the supply was all the way up.

'Where did the water come from?' Ben asked.

Bev, Eddie, and Stan looked at each other. None of them knew.

'Well, what about the kids that drowned, then?'

They were only a bit clearer on that. It seemed that in those days ('olden days,' Ben called them solemnly, as he took up this part of the tale) the door leading to the platform over the water had always been left unlocked. One night a couple of kids . . . or maybe just one . . . or as many as three . . . had found the ground-level door also unlocked. They had gone up on a dare. They found their way out onto the platform over the water instead of onto the gallery by mistake. In the darkness, they had fallen over the edge before they quite knew where they were.

'I heard it from this kid Vic Crumly who said he heard it from his dad,' Beverly said, 'so maybe it's true. Vic said his dad said that once they fell into the water they were as good as dead because there was nothing to hold onto. The platform was just out of reach. He said they paddled around in there, yelling for help, all night long, probably. Only no one heard them and they just got tireder and tireder until –'

She trailed off, feeling the horror of it sink into her. She could see those boys in her mind's eye, real or made-up, paddling around like drenched puppies. Going under, coming up sputtering. Splashing more and swimming less as panic set in. Soggy sneakers treading water. Fingers scrabbling uselessly for any kind of purchase on the smooth steel walls of the sleeve. She could taste the water they must have swallowed. She could hear the flat, echoing quality of their cries. How long? Fifteen minutes? Half an hour? How long before the cries had ceased and they had simply floated face-down, strange fish for the caretaker to find the next morning?

'God,' Stan said dryly.

'I heard there was a woman who lost her baby, too,' Eddie said suddenly. 'That was when they closed the place for good. At least, that's what I heard. They did use to let people go up, I know that. But then one time there was this lady and her baby. I don't know how old the baby was. But this platform, it's supposed to go right out over the water. And the lady went to the railing and she was, you know, holding the baby, and either she dropped it or maybe it just wriggled. I heard this guy tried to save it. Doing the hero bit, you know. He jumped right in, but the baby was gone. Maybe he was wearing a jacket or something. When your clothes get wet, they drag you down.'

Eddie abruptly put his hand into his pocket and brought out a small brown glass bottle. He opened it, took out two white pills, and swallowed them dry.

'What were those?' Beverly asked.

'Aspirin. I've got a headache.' He looked at her defensively, but Beverly said nothing more.

Ben finished. After the incident of the baby (he himself, he said, had heard that it was actually a kid, a little girl of about three), the Town Council had voted to lock the Standpipe, both downstairs and up, and stop the daytrips and picnics on the gallery. It had remained locked from then until now. Oh, the caretaker came and went, and the maintenance men once in awhile, and once every season there were guided tours. Interested citizens could follow a lady from the Historical Society up the spiral of stairs to the gallery at the top, where they could ooh and aah over the view and snap Kodaks to show their friends. But the door to the inner sleeve was always locked now.

'Is it still full of water?' Stan asked.

'I guess so,' Ben said. 'I've seen firetrucks filling up there during grassfire season. They hook a hose to the pipe at the bottom.'

Stanley was looking at the dryer again, watching the rags go around and around. The clump had broken up now, and some of them floated like parachutes.

'What did you see there?' Bev asked him gently.

For a moment it seemed he would not answer at all. Then he drew a deep, shuddering breath and said something that at first struck them all as being far from the point. 'They named it Memorial Park after the 23rd Maine in the Civil War. The Derry Blues, they were called. There used to be a statue, but it blew down during a storm in the forties. They didn't have money enough to fix the statue, so they put in a birdbath instead. A big stone birdbath.'

They were all looking at him. Stan swallowed. There was an audible click in his throat.

'I watch birds, you see. I have an album, a pair of Zeiss-Ikon binoculars, and everything.' He looked at Eddie. 'Do you have any more aspirins?'

Eddie handed him the bottle. Stan took two, hesitated, then took another. He gave the bottle back and swallowed the pills, one after another, grimacing. Then he went on with his story.

10

Stan's encounter had happened on a rainy April evening two months ago. He had donned his slicker, put his bird-book and his binoculars in a waterproof sack with a drawstring at the top, and set out for Memorial Park. He and his father usually went out together, but his father had had to 'work over' that night and had called specially at suppertime to talk to Stan.

One of his customers at the agency, another birdwatcher, had spotted what he believed to be a male cardinal – *Fringillidae Richmondena* – drinking from the birdbath in Memorial Park, he told Stan. They liked to eat, drink, and bathe right around dusk. It was very rare to spot a cardinal this far north of Massachusetts. Would Stan like to go down there and see if he could collect it? He knew the weather was pretty foul, but . . .

Stan had been agreeable. His mother made him promise to keep the hood of his slicker up, but Stan would have done that anyway. He was a fastidious boy. There were never any fights about getting him to wear his rubbers or his snowpants in the winter.

He walked the mile and a half to Memorial Park in a rain so fine and hesitant that it really wasn't even a drizzle; it was more like a constant hanging mist. The air was muted but somehow exciting just the same. In spite of the last dwindling piles of snow under bushes and in groves of trees (to Stan they looked like piles of dirty cast-off pillowcases), there was a smell of new growth in the air. Looking at the branches of elms and maples and oaks against the lead-white sky, Stan thought that their silhouettes looked mysteriously thicker. They would burst open in a week or two, unrolling leaves of a delicate, almost transparent green.

The air *smells green tonight*, he thought, and smiled a little.

He walked quickly because the light would be gone in an hour or even less. He was as fastidious about his sightings as he was about his dress and study habits, and unless there was enough light left for him to be absolutely sure, he would not allow himself to collect the cardinal even if he knew in his heart he had really seen it.

He cut across Memorial Park on a diagonal. The Standpipe was a white bulking shape to his left. Stan barely glanced at it. He had no interest whatsoever in the Standpipe.

Memorial Park was a rough rectangle which sloped downhill. The grass (white and dead at this time of year) was kept neatly cut in the summertime, and there were circular beds of flowers. There was no playground equipment, however. This was considered a grownups' park.

At the far end, the grade smoothed out before dropping abruptly down to Kansas Street and the Barrens beyond. The birdbath his father had mentioned stood on this flat area. It was a shallow stone dish set into a squat masonry pedestal that was really much too big for the humble function it fulfilled. Stan's father had told him that, before the money ran out, they had intended to put the statue of the soldier back up here again.

'I like the birdbath better, Daddy,' Stan said.

Mr Uris ruffled his hair. 'Me too, son,' he said. 'More baths and less bullets, that's my motto.'

At the top of this pedestal a motto had been carved in the stone. Stanley read it but did not understand it; the only Latin he understood was the genus classifications of the birds in his book.

IT

Apparebat eidolon senex.
— Pliny

the inscription read.

Stan sat down on a bench, took his bird-album out of the bag, and turned over to the picture of the cardinal one more time, going over it, familiarizing himself with the recognizable points. A male cardinal would be hard to mistake for something else – it was as red as a fire-engine, if not so large – but Stan was a creature of habit and convention; these things comforted him and reinforced his sense of place and belonging in the world. So he gave the picture a good three-minute study before closing the book (the moisture in the air was making the corners of the pages turn up) and putting it back into the bag. He uncased his binoculars and put them to his eyes. There was no need to adjust the field of focus, because the last time he had used the glasses he had been sitting on this same bench and looking at that same birdbath.

Fastidious boy, patient boy. He did not fidget. He did not get up and walk around or swing the binoculars here and there to see what else there might be to be seen. He sat still, field glasses trained on the birdbath, and the mist collected in fat drops on his yellow slicker.

He was not bored. He was looking down into the equivalent of an avian convention-site. Four brown sparrows sat there for awhile, dipping into the water with their beaks, flicking droplets casually back over their shoulders and onto their backs. Then a bluejay came hauling in like a cop breaking up a gaggle of loiterers. The jay was as big as a house in Stan's glasses, his quarrelsome cries absurdly thin by comparison (after you looked through the binoculars steadily for awhile the magnified birds you saw began to seem not odd but perfectly correct). The sparrows flew off. The jay, now in charge, strutted, bathed, grew bored, departed. The sparrows returned, then flew off again as a pair of robins cruised in to bathe and (perhaps) to discuss matters of importance to the hollow-boned set. Stan's father had laughed at Stan's hesitant suggestion that maybe birds talked, and he was sure his dad was right when he said birds weren't smart enough to talk – that their brain-pans were too small – but by gosh they sure *looked* like they were talking. A new bird joined them. It was red. Stan hastily adjusted the field of focus on the binoculars a bit. Was it . . . ? No. It was a scarlet tanager, a good bird but not the cardinal he was looking for. It was joined by a flicker that was a frequent visitor to the Memorial Park birdbath. Stan recognized him by the tattered right wing. As always, he speculated on how that might have happened – a close call with some cat seemed the most likely explanation. Other birds came and went. Stan saw a grackle, as clumsy and ugly as a flying boxcar, a bluebird, another flicker. He was finally rewarded by a new bird – not the cardinal but a cowbird that looked vast and stupid in the eyepieces of the binoculars. He dropped them against his chest and fumbled the bird-book out of the bag again, hoping that the cowbird wouldn't fly away before he could confirm the sighting. He would have *something* to take home to his father, at least. And it was time to go. The light was fading fast. He felt cold and damp. He checked the book, then looked through the glasses again. It was still there, not bathing but only standing on the rim of the birdbath looking dumb. It was almost surely a cowbird. With no distinctive markings – at least none he could pick up at this distance – and in the fading light it was hard to be one hundred percent sure, but maybe he had just enough time and light for one more check. He looked at the picture in the book, studying it with a fierce frown of concentration, and then picked up the glasses again. He had only fixed them on the birdbath when a hollow rolling *boom*! sent the cowbird – if it had been a cowbird – winging. Stan tried to follow it with the glasses, knowing how slim his chances were of picking it up again. He lost it and made a hissing sound of disgust between his teeth. Well, if it had come once it would perhaps come again. And it had only been a cowbird

(*probably a cowbird*)

after all, not a golden eagle or a great auk.

Stan recased his binoculars and put away his bird-album. Then he got up and looked around to see if he could tell what had been responsible for that sudden loud noise. It hadn't sounded like a gun or a car backfire. More like a door being thrown open in a spooky movie about castles and dungeons . . . complete with hokey echo effects.

He could see nothing.

He got up and started toward the slope down to Kansas Street. The Standpipe was now on his right, a chalky white cylinder, phantomlike in the mist and the growing darkness. It seemed almost to . . . to float.

That was an odd thought. He supposed it must have come from his own head – where else could a thought come from? – but it somehow did not seem like his own thought at all.

He looked at the Standpipe more closely, and then veered in that direction without even thinking about it. Windows circled the building at intervals, rising around it in a spiral that made Stan think of the barber pole in front of Mr Aurlette's shop, where he and his dad got their haircuts. The bone-white shingles bulged out over each of those dark windows like brows over eyes. *Wonder how they did that,* Stan thought – not with as much interest as Ben Hanscom would have felt, but with some – and that was when he saw there was a much larger space of darkness at the foot of the Standpipe – a clear oblong in the circular base.

He stopped, frowning, thinking that was a funny place for a window: it was completely out of symmetry with the others. Then he realized it wasn't a window. It was a door.

The noise I heard, he thought. *It was that door, blowing open.*

He looked around. Early, gloomy dusk. White sky now fading to a dull dusky purple, mist thickening a bit more toward the steady rain which would fall most of the night. Dusk and mist and no wind at all.

So . . . if it hadn't blown open, had someone pushed it open? Why? And it looked like an awfully heavy door to slam open hard enough to make a noise like that boom. He supposed a very big person . . . maybe . . .

Curious, Stan walked over for a closer look.

The door was bigger than he had first supposed – six feet high and two feet thick, the boards which composed it bound with brass strips. Stan swung it half-closed. It moved smoothly and easily on its hinges in spite of its size. It also moved silently – there was not a single squeak. He had moved it to see how much damage it had done to the shingles, blasting open like that. There was no damage at all; not so much as a single mark. Weirdsville, as Richie would say.

Well, it wasn't the door you heard, that's all, he thought. *Maybe a jet from Loring boomed over Derry, or something. Door was probably open all al –*

His foot struck something. Stan looked down and saw it was a padlock . . . correction. It was the *remains* of a padlock. It had been burst wide open. It looked, in fact, as if someone had rammed the lock's keyway full of gunpowder and then set a match to it. Flowers of metal, deadly sharp, stood out from the body of the lock in a stiff spray. Stan could see the layers of steel inside. The thick hasp hung askew by one bolt which had been yanked three-quarters of the way out of the wood. The other three hasp-bolts lay on the wet grass. They had been twisted like pretzels.

Frowning, Stan swung the door open again and peered inside.

Narrow stairs led upward, circling around and out of sight. The outer wall of the staircase was bare wood supported by giant cross-beams which had been pegged together rather than nailed. To Stan some of the pegs looked thicker than his own upper arm. The inner wall was steel from which gigantic rivets swelled like boils.

'Is anyone here?' Stan asked.

There was no answer.

He hesitated, then stepped inside so he could see up the narrow throat of the staircase a little better. Nothing. And it was Creep City in here. As Richie would *also* say. He turned to leave . . . and heard music.

It was faint, but still instantly recognizable.

Calliope music.

He cocked his head, listening, the frown on his face starting to dissolve a little. Calliope music, all right, the music of carnivals and county fairs. It conjured up trace memories which were as delightful as they were ephemeral: popcorn, cotton candy, doughboys frying in hot grease, the chain-driven clatter of rides like the Wild Mouse, the Whip, the Koaster-Kups.

Now the frown had become a tentative grin. Stan went up one step, then two more, head still cocked. He paused again. As if thinking about carnivals could actually create one; he could now actually *smell* the popcorn, the cotton candy, the doughboys . . . and more! Peppers, chili-dogs, cigarette smoke and sawdust. There was the sharp smell of white vinegar, the kind you could shake over your french fries through a hole in the tin cap. He could smell mustard, bright yellow and stinging hot, that you spread on your hotdog with a wooden paddle.

This was amazing . . . incredible . . . irresistible.

He took another step up and that was when he heard the rustling, eager footsteps above him, descending the stairs. He cocked his head again. The calliope music had gotten suddenly louder, as if to mask the sound of the footsteps. He could recognize the tune now – it was 'Camptown Races.'

Footsteps, yeah: but they weren't exactly *rustling* footsteps, were they? They actually sounded kind of . . . *squishy*, didn't they? The sound was like people walking in rubbers full of water.

> *Camptown ladies sing dis song, doodah doodah*
> *(Squish-squish)*
> *Camptown Racetrack nine miles long, doodah doodah*
> *(Squish-slosh – closer now)*
> *Ride around all night*
> *Ride around all day . . .*

Now there were shadows bobbing on the wall above him.

The terror leaped down Stan's throat all at once – it was like swallowing something hot and horrible, bad medicine that suddenly galvanized you like electricity. It was the shadows that did it.

He saw them only for a moment. He had just that small bit of time to observe that there were two of them, that they were slumped, and somehow unnatural. He had only that moment because the light in here was fading, fading too fast, and as he turned, the heavy Standpipe door swung ponderously shut behind him.

Stanley ran back down the stairs (somehow he had climbed more than a dozen, although he could only remember climbing two, three at most), very much afraid now. It was too dark in here to see anything. He could hear his own breathing, he could hear the calliope tooting away somewhere above him

(*what's a calliope doing up there in the dark? who's playing it?*)

and he could hear those wet footsteps. Approaching him now. Getting closer.

He hit the door with his hands splayed out in front of him, hit it hard enough to send sparkly tingles of pain all the way up to his elbows. It had swung so easily before . . . and now it would not move at all.

No . . . that was not quite true. At first it had moved just a bit, just enough for him to see a mocking strip of gray light running vertically down its left side. Then gone again. As if someone was on the other side of it, holding the door closed.

Panting, terrified, Stan pushed against the door with all of his strength. He could feel the brass bindings digging into his hands. Nothing.

He whirled around, now pressing his back and his splayed hands against the door. He could feel sweat, oily and hot, running down his forehead. The calliope music had gotten louder yet. It drifted and echoed down the spiral staircase. There was nothing cheery about it now. It had changed. It had become a dirge. It screamed like wind and water, and in his mind's eye Stan saw a county fair at the end of autumn, wind and rain blowing up a deserted midway, pennons flapping, tents bulging, falling over, wheeling away like canvas bats. He saw empty rides standing against the sky like scaffolds; the wind drummed and hooted in the weird angles of their struts. He suddenly understood that death was in this place with him, that death was coming for him out of the dark and he could not run.

A sudden rush of water spilled down the stairs. Now it was not popcorn and doughboys and cotton candy he smelled but wet decay, the stench of dead pork which has exploded in a fury of maggots in a place hidden away from the sun.

'*Who's here?*' he screamed in a high, trembling voice.

He was answered by a low, bubbling voice that seemed choked with mud and old water.

'The dead ones, Stanley. We're the dead ones. We sank, but now we float . . . and you'll float, too.'

He could feel water washing around his feet. He cringed back against the door in an agony of fear. They were very close now. He could feel their nearness. He could *smell* them. Something was digging into his hip as he struck the door again and again in a mindless, useless effort to get away.

'We're dead, but sometimes we clown around a little, Stanley. Sometimes we —'

It was his bird-book.

Without thinking, Stan grabbed for it. It was stuck in his slicker pocket and wouldn't come out. One of *them* was down now; he could hear it shuffling across the little stone areaway where he had come in. It would reach for him in a moment, and he would feel its cold flesh.

He gave one more tremendous yank, and the bird-book was in his hands. He held it in front of him like a puny shield, not thinking of what he was doing, but suddenly sure that this was *right*.

'Robins!' he screamed into the darkness, and for a moment the thing approaching (it was surely less than five steps away now) hesitated — he was almost sure it did. And for a moment hadn't he felt some give in the door against which he was now cringing?

But he *wasn't* cringing anymore. He was standing up straight in the darkness. When had that happened? No time to wonder. Stan licked his dry lips and began to chant: 'Robins! Gray egrets! Loons! Scarlet tanagers! Grackles! Hammerhead woodpeckers! Red-headed woodpeckers! Chickadees! Wrens! Peli —'

The door opened with a protesting scream and Stan took a giant step backward into thin misty air. He fell sprawling on the dead grass. He had bent the bird-book nearly in half, and later that night he would see the clear impressions of his fingers sunken into its cover, as if it had been bound in Play-Doh instead of hard pressboard.

He didn't try to get up but began to dig in with his heels instead, his butt grooving through the slick grass. His lips were pulled back over his teeth. Inside that dim oblong he could see two sets of legs below the diagonal shadowline thrown by the door, which now stood half-open. He could see jeans that had decayed to a purplish-black. Orange threads lay plastered limply against the seams, and water dripped from the cuffs to puddle around shoes that had mostly rotted away, revealing swelled, purple toes within.

Their hands lay limply at their sides, too long, too waxy-white. Depending from each finger was a small orange pompom.

Holding his bent bird-book in front of him, his face wet with drizzle, sweat, and tears, Stan whispered in a husky monotone: 'Chickenhawks ... grosbeaks ... hummingbirds ... albatrosses ... kiwis ...'

One of those hands turned over, showing a palm from which endless water had eroded all the lines, leaving something as idiot-smooth as the hand of a department-store dummy.

One finger unrolled ... then rolled up again. The pompom bounced and dangled, dangled and bounced.

It was beckoning him.

Stan Uris, who would die in a bathtub with crosses slashed into his forearms twenty-seven years later, got to his knees, then to his feet, then ran. He ran across Kansas Street without looking either way for traffic and paused, panting, on the far sidewalk, to look back.

From this angle he couldn't see the door in the base of the Standpipe; only the Standpipe itself, thick and yet somehow graceful, standing in the murk.

'They were dead,' Stan whispered to himself, shocked.

He wheeled suddenly and ran for home.

11

The dryer had stopped. So had Stan.

The three others only looked at him for a long moment. His skin was nearly as gray as the April evening of which he had just told them.

'Wow,' Ben said at last. He let out his breath in a ragged, whistling sigh.

'It's true,' Stan said in a low voice. 'I swear to God it is.'

'I believe you,' Beverly said. 'After what happened at my house, I'd believe *anything*.'

She got up suddenly, almost knocking over her chair, and went to the dryer. She began to pull out the rags one by one, folding them. Her back was turned, but Ben suspected she was crying. He wanted to go to her and lacked the courage.

'We gotta talk to Bill about this,' Eddie said. 'Bill will know what to do.'

'Do?' Stan said, turning to look at him. 'What do you mean, *do*?'

Eddie looked at him, uncomfortable. 'Well . . .'

'I don't want to *do* anything,' Stan said. He was looking at Eddie with such a hard, fierce stare that Eddie squirmed in his chair. 'I want to *forget* about it. That's all I want to *do*.'

'Not that easy,' Beverly said quietly, turning around. Ben had been right: the hot sunlight slanting in through the Washateria's dirty windows reflected off bright lines of tears on her cheeks. 'It's not just *us*. I heard Ronnie Grogan. And the little boy I heard first . . . I think maybe it was that little Clements kid. The one who disappeared off his trike.'

'So *what*?' Stan said defiantly.

'So what if it gets more?' she asked. 'What if it gets more kids?'

His eyes, a hot brown, locked with her blue ones, answering the question without speaking: *So what if it does?*

But Beverly did not look down or away and at last Stan dropped his own eyes . . . perhaps only because she was still crying, but perhaps because her concern somehow made her stronger.

'Eddie's right,' she said. 'We ought to talk to Bill. Then maybe to the Police Chief –'

'Right,' Stan said. If he was trying to sound contemptuous, it didn't work. His voice came out sounding only tired. 'Dead kids in the Standpipe. Blood that only kids can see, not grownups. Clowns walking on the Canal. Balloons that blow against the wind. Mummies. Lepers under porches. Chief Borton'll laugh his bum off . . . and then stick us in the loonybin.'

'If we all went to him,' Ben said, troubled. 'If we all went together . . .'

'Sure,' Stan said. 'Right. Tell me more, Haystack. Write me a book.' He got up and went to the window, hands in pockets, looking angry and upset and scared. He stared out for a moment, shoulders stiff and rejecting beneath his neat shirt. Without turning back to them he repeated: 'Write me a frigging *book*!'

'No,' Ben said quietly, 'Bill's going to write the books.'

Stan wheeled back, surprised, and the others looked at him. There was a shocked look on Ben Hanscom's face, as if he had suddenly and unexpectedly slapped himself.

Bev folded the last of the rags.

'Birds,' Eddie said.

'What?' Bev and Ben said together.

Eddie was looking at Stan. 'You got out by yelling birds' names at them?'

'Maybe,' Stan said reluctantly. 'Or maybe the door was just stuck and finally popped open.'

'Without you leaning on it?' Bev asked.

Stan shrugged. It was not a sullen shrug; it only said he didn't know.

'I think it was the birds you shouted at them,' Eddie said. 'But why? In the movies you hold up a cross . . .'

'. . . or say the Lord's Prayer . . .' Ben added.

'. . . or the Twenty-third Psalm,' Beverly put in.

'I know the Twenty-third Psalm,' Stan said angrily, 'but I wouldn't do so good with the old crucifix business. I'm Jewish, remember?'

They looked away from him, embarrassed, either for his having been born that way or for their having forgotten it.

'Birds,' Eddie said again. 'Jesus!' Then he glanced guiltily at Stan again, but Stan was looking moodily across the street at the Bangor Hydro office.

'Bill will know what to do,' Ben said suddenly, as if finally agreeing with Bev and Eddie. 'Betcha anything. Betcha any amount of money.'

'Look,' Stan said, looking at all of them earnestly. 'That's okay. We can talk to Bill about it if you want. But that's where things stop for me. You can call me a chicken, or yellow, I don't care. I'm not a chicken, I don't think. It's just that those things in the Standpipe . . .'

'If you weren't afraid of something like that, you'd have to be crazy, Stan,' Beverly said softly.

'Yeah, I was *scared*, but that's not the problem,' Stan said hotly. 'It's not even what I'm talking about. Don't you *see* –'

They were looking at him expectantly, their eyes both troubled and faintly hopeful, but Stan found he could not explain how he felt. The words had run out. There was a brick of feeling inside him, almost choking him, and he could not get it out of his throat. Neat as he was, sure as he was, he was still only an eleven-year-old boy who had that year finished the fourth grade.

He wanted to tell them that there were worse things than being frightened. You could be frightened by things like almost having a car hit you while you were riding your bike or, before the Salk vaccine, getting polio. You could be frightened of that crazyman Khrushchev or of drowning if you went out over your head. You could be frightened of all those things and still function.

But those things in the Standpipe . . .

He wanted to tell them that those dead boys who had lurched and shambled their way down the spiral staircase had done something worse than frighten him: they had *offended* him.

Offended, yes. It was the only word he could think of, and if he used it they would laugh – they liked him, he knew that, and they had accepted him as one of them, but they would still laugh. All the same, there were things that were not supposed to *be*. They offended any sane person's sense of order, they offended the central idea that God had given the earth a final tilt on its axis so that twilight would only last about twelve minutes at the equator and linger for an hour or more up where the Eskimos built their ice-cube houses, that He had done that and He then had said, in effect: 'Okay, if you can figure out the tilt, you can figure out any damn thing you choose. Because even light has weight, and when the note of a trainwhistle suddenly drops it's the Doppler effect and when an airplane breaks the sound barrier that bang isn't the applause of the angels or the flatulence of demons but only air collapsing back into place. I gave you the tilt and then I sat back about halfway up the auditorium to watch the show. I got nothing else to say, except that two and two makes four, the lights in the sky are stars, if there's blood grownups can see it as well as kids, and dead boys stay dead.' You can live with fear, I think, Stan would have said if he could. Maybe not forever, but for a long, long time. It's *offense* you maybe can't live with, because it opens up a crack inside your thinking, and if you look down into it you see there are live things down there, and they have little yellow eyes that don't blink, and there's a stink down in that dark, and after awhile you think maybe there's a whole other universe down there, a universe where a square moon rises in the sky, and the stars laugh in cold voices, and some of the triangles have four sides, and some have five, and some of them have five raised to the fifth power of sides. In this universe there might grow roses which sing. Everything leads to everything, he would have told them if he could. Go to your church and listen to your stories about Jesus walking on the water, but if I saw a guy doing that I'd scream and scream and scream. Because it wouldn't look like a miracle to me. It would look like an *offense*.

Because he could say none of these things, he just reiterated: 'Being scared isn't the problem. I just don't want to be involved in something that will land me in the nuthatch.'

'Will you at least go with us to talk to him?' Bev asked. 'Listen to what he says?'

'Sure,' Stan said, and then laughed. 'Maybe I ought to bring my bird-book.'

They all laughed then, and it was a little easier.

12

Beverly left them outside the Kleen-Kloze and took the rags back home by herself. The apartment was still empty. She put them under the kitchen sink and closed the cupboard. She stood up and looked down toward the bathroom.

I'm not going down there, she thought. *I'm going to watch* Bandstand *on TV. See if I can't learn how to do the Dog.*

So she went into the living room and turned on the TV and five minutes later she turned it off while Dick Clark was showing how much oil *just one* Stri-Dex medicated pad could take off the face of your average teenager ('If you think you can get clean with just soap and water,' Dick said, holding the dirty pad up to the glassy eye of the camera so that every teenager in America could get a good look, 'you ought to take a good look at this.').

She went back to the kitchen cupboard over the sink, where her father kept his tools. Among them was a pocket tape, the kind that runs out a long yellow tongue of inches. She folded this into one cold hand and went down to the bathroom.

It was sparkling clean, silent. Somewhere, far distant, it seemed, she could hear Mrs Doyon yelling for her boy Jim to get in out of the road, right *now*.

She went to the bathroom basin and looked down into the dark eye of the drain.

She stood there for some time, her legs as cold as marble inside her jeans, her nipples feeling sharp enough and hard enough to cut paper, her lips dead dry. She waited for the voices.

No voices came.

A little shuddery sigh came from her, and she began to feed the thin steel tape into the drain. It went down smoothly – like a sword into the gullet of a county fair sideshow performer. Six inches, eight inches, ten. It stopped, bound up in the elbow-bend under the sink, Beverly supposed. She wiggled it, pushing gently at the same time, and eventually the tape began to feed into the drain again. Sixteen inches now, then two feet, then three.

She watched the yellow tape slipping out of the chromed-steel case, which had been worn black on the sides by her father's big hand.

In her mind's eye she saw it sliding through the black bore of the pipe, picking up some muck, scraping away flakes of rust. Down there where the sun never shines and the night never stops, she thought.

She imagined the head of the tape, with its small steel buttplate no bigger than a fingernail, sliding farther and farther into the darkness, and part of her mind screamed *What are you doing?* She did not ignore that voice . . . but she seemed helpless to heed it. She saw the end of the tape going straight down now, descending into the cellar. She saw it striking the sewage pipe . . . and even as she saw it, the tape bound up again.

She wiggled it again, and the tape, thin enough to be limber, made a faint eerie sound that reminded her a little bit of the way a saw sounds when you bend it back and forth across your legs.

She could see its tip wiggling against the bottom of this wider pipe, which would have a baked ceramic surface. She could see it bending . . . and then she was able to push it forward again.

She ran out six feet. Seven. Nine –

And suddenly the tape began to run through her hands by itself, as if something down there was pulling the other end. Not just pulling it: *running* with it. She stared at the flowing tape, her eyes wide, her mouth a sagging O of fear – fear, yes, but no surprise. Hadn't she *known*? Hadn't she *known* something like this was going to happen?

The tape ran out to its final stop. Eighteen feet; an even six yards.

A soft chuckle came wafting out of the drain, followed by a low whisper that was almost reproachful: '*Beverly, Beverly, Beverly . . . you can't fight us . . . you'll die if you try . . . die if you try . . . die if you try . . . Beverly . . . Beverly . . . Beverly . . . ly-ly-ly . . .*'

Something clicked inside the tape-measure's housing, and it suddenly began to run rapidly back into its case, the numbers and hashmarks blurring by. Near the end – the last five or six feet – the yellow became a dark, dripping red and she screamed and dropped it on the floor as if the tape had suddenly turned into a live snake.

Fresh blood trickled over the clean white porcelain of the basin and back down into the drain's wide eye. She bent, sobbing now, her fear a freezing weight in her stomach, and picked the tape up. She tweezed it between the thumb and first finger of her right hand and, holding it in front of her, took it into the kitchen. As she walked, blood dripped from the tape onto the faded linoleum of the hall and the kitchen.

She steadied herself by thinking of what her father would say to her – what he would *do* to her – if he found that she had gotten his measuring tape all bloody. Of course, he wouldn't be able to see the blood, but it helped to think that.

She took one of the clean rags – still as warm as fresh bread from the dryer – and went back into the bathroom. Before she began to clean, she put the hard rubber plug in the drain, closing that eye. The blood was fresh, and it cleaned up easily. She went up her own trail, wiping away the dime-sized drops on the linoleum, then rinsing the rag, wringing it out, and putting it aside.

She got a second rag and used it to clean her father's measuring tape. The blood was thick, viscous. In two places there were clots of the stuff, black and spongy.

Although the blood only went back five or six feet, she cleaned the entire length of the tape, removing from it all traces of pipe-muck. That done, she put it back into the cupboard over the sink and took the two stained rags out in back of the apartment. Mrs Doyon was yelling at Jim again. Her voice was clear, almost bell-like in the still hot late afternoon.

In the back yard, which was mostly bare dirt, weeds, and clotheslines, there was a rusty incinerator. Beverly threw the rags into it, then sat down on the back steps. Tears came suddenly, with surprising violence, and this time she made no effort to hold them back.

She put her arms on her knees, her head in her arms, and wept while Mrs Doyon called for Jim to come out of that road, did he want to get hit by a car and be killed?

DERRY:

THE SECOND INTERLUDE

'Quaeque ipsa miserrima vidi,
Et quorum pars magna fui.'
– Virgil

'You don't fuck around with the infinite.'
– *Mean Streets*

Two more disappearances in the past week – both children. Just as I was beginning to relax. One of them a sixteen-year-old boy named Dennis Torrio, the other a girl of just five who was out sledding in back of her house on West Broadway. The hysterical mother found her sled, one of those blue plastic flying saucers, but nothing else. There had been a fresh fall of snow the night before – four inches or so. No tracks but hers, Chief Rademacher said when I called him. He is becoming extremely annoyed with me, I think. Not anything that's going to keep me awake nights; I have worse things to do than that, don't I?

Asked him if I could see the police photos. He refused.

Asked him if her tracks led away toward any sort of drain or sewer grating. This was followed by a long period of silence. Then Rademacher said, 'I'm beginning to wonder if maybe you shouldn't see a doctor, Hanlon. The head-peeper kind of doctor. The kid was snatched by her father. Don't you read the papers?'

'Was the Torrio boy snatched by his father?' I asked.

Another long pause.

'Give it a rest, Hanlon,' he said. 'Give *me* a rest.'

He hung up.

Of course I read the papers – don't I put them out in the Reading Room of the Public Library each morning myself? The little girl, Laurie Ann Winterbarger, had been in the custody of her mother following an acrimonious divorce proceeding in the spring of 1982. The police are operating on the theory that Horst Winterbarger, who is supposedly working as a machinery maintenance man somewhere in Florida, drove up to Maine to snatch his daughter. They further theorize that he parked his car beside the house and called to his daughter, who then joined him – hence the lack of any tracks other than the little girl's. They have less to say about the fact that the girl had not seen her father since she was two. Part of the deep bitterness

409

which accompanied the Winterbargers' divorce came from Mrs Winterbarger's allegations that on at least two occasions Horst Winterbarger had sexually molested the child. She asked the court to deny Winterbarger all visitation rights, a request the court granted in spite of Winterbarger's hot denials. Rademacher claims the court's decision, which had the effect of cutting Winterbarger off completely from his only child, may have pushed Winterbarger into taking his daughter. That at least has some dim plausibility, but ask yourself this: would little Laurie Ann have recognized him after three years and run to him when he called her? Rademacher says yes, even though she was two the last time she saw him. I don't think so. And her mother says Laurie Ann had been well trained about not approaching or talking to strangers, a lesson most Derry children learn early and well. Rademacher says he's got Florida State Police looking for Winterbarger and that his responsibility ends there.

'Matters of custody are more the province of the lawyers than that of the police,' this pompous, overweight asshole is quoted as saying in last Friday's Derry *News*.

But the Torrio boy . . . that's something else. Wonderful home life. Played football for the Derry Tigers. Honor Roll student. Had gone through the Outward Bound Survival School in the summer of '84 and passed with flying colors. No history of drug use. Had a girl-friend that he was apparently head-over-heels about. Had everything to live for. Everything to stay in Derry for, at least for the next couple of years.

All the same, he's gone.

What happened to him? A sudden attack of wanderlust? A drunk driver who maybe hit him, killed him, and buried him? Or is he maybe still in Derry, is he maybe on the nightside of Derry, keeping company with folks like Betty Ripsom and Patrick Hockstetter and Eddie Corcoran and all the rest? Is it

(later)

I'm doing it again. Going over and over the same ground, doing nothing constructive, only cranking myself up to the screaming point. I jump when the iron stairs leading up to the stacks creak. I jump at shadows. I find myself wondering how I'd react if I was shelving books up there in the stacks, pushing my little rubber-wheeled trolley in front of me, and a hand reached from between two leaning rows of books, a groping hand . . .

Had again a well-nigh insurmountable desire to begin calling them this afternoon. At one point I even got as far as dialing 404, the Atlanta area code, with Stanley Uris's number in front of me. Then I just held the phone against my ear, asking myself if I wanted to call them because I was really sure – one hundred percent *sure* – or simply because I'm now so badly spooked that I can't stand to be alone; that I have to talk to someone who knows (or *will* know) what it is I am spooked about.

For a moment I could hear Richie saying *Batches? BATCHES? We doan need no stinkin' batches, senhorr!* in his Pancho Vanilla Voice, as clearly as if he were standing beside me . . . and I hung up the phone. Because when you want to see someone as badly as I wanted to see Richie – or any of them – at that moment, you just can't trust your own motivations. We lie best when we lie to ourselves. The fact is, I'm still not one hundred percent sure. If another body should turn up, I will call . . . but for now I must suppose that even such a pompous ass as Rademacher may be right. She *could* have remembered her father; there may have been pictures of him. And I suppose a really persuasive adult could talk a kid into coming to his car, no matter what that child had been taught.

There's another fear that haunts me. Rademacher suggested that I might be going crazy. I don't believe that, but if I call them now, *they* may think I'm crazy. Worse than that, what if they should not remember me at all? *Mike Hanlon? Who? I don't remember any Mike Hanlon. I don't remember you at all. What promise?*

I feel that there will come a right time to call them . . . and when that time comes, I'll *know* that it's right. Their own circuits will open at the same time. It's as if there are two great wheels slowly coming into some sort of powerful convergence with each other, myself and the rest of Derry on one, and all my childhood friends on the other.

When the time comes, they will hear the voice of the Turtle.

So I'll wait, and sooner or later I'll know. I don't believe it's a question anymore of calling them or not calling them.

Only a question of *when*.

February 20th, 1985

The fire at the Black Spot.

'A perfect example of how the Chamber of Commerce will try to rewrite history, Mike,' old Albert Carson would have told me, probably cackling as he said it. 'They'll try, and sometimes they almost succeed . . . but the old people remember how things really went. They always remember. And sometimes they'll tell you, if you ask them right.'

There are people who have lived in Derry for twenty years and don't know that there was once a 'special' barracks for noncoms at the old Derry Army Air Corps Base, a barracks that was a good half a mile from the rest of the base – and in the middle of February, with the temperature standing right around zero and a forty-mile-an-hour wind howling across those flat runways and whopping the wind-chill factor down to something you could hardly believe, that extra half a mile became something that could give you frost-freeze or frostbite, or maybe even kill you.

The other seven barracks had oil heat, storm windows, and insulation. They were toasty and cozy. The 'special' barracks, which housed the twenty-seven men of Company E, was heated by a balky old wood furnace. Supplies of wood for it were catch-as-catch-can. The only insulation was the deep bank of pine and spruce boughs the men laid around the outside. One of the men promoted a complete set of storm windows for the place one day, but the twenty-seven inmates of the 'special' barracks were detailed up to Bangor that same day to help with some work at the base up there, and when they came back that night, tired and cold, all of those windows had been broken. Every one.

This was in 1930, when half of America's air force still consisted of biplanes. In Washington, Billy Mitchell had been courtmartialed and demoted to flying a desk because his gadfly insistence on trying to build a more modern air force had finally irritated his elders enough for them to slap him down hard. Not long after, he would resign.

So there was precious little flying that went on at the Derry base, in spite of its three runways (one of which was actually paved). Most of the soldiering that went on there was of the make-work variety.

One of the Company E soldiers who returned to Derry after his service tour came to an end in 1937 was my dad. He told me this story:

'One day in the spring of 1930 – this was about six months before the fire at the Black Spot – I was coming back with four of my buddies from a three-day pass we had spent down in Boston.

'When we come through the gate there was this big old boy standing just inside the checkpoint, leaning on a shovel and picking the seat of his suntans out of his ass. A sergeant from someplace down south. Carroty-red hair. Bad teeth. Pimples. Not much more than an ape without the body hair, if you know what I mean. There were a lot of them like that in the army during the Depression.

'So here we come, four young guys back from leave, all of us still feeling fine, and we could see in his eyes that he was just looking for something to bust us with. So we snapped him salutes as if he was General Black Jack Pershing himself. I guess we might have been all right, but it was one fine late-April day, sun shining down, and I had to shoot off my lip. "A good afternoon to you, Sergeant Wilson, sir," said I, and he landed on me with both feet.

'"Did I give you any permission to speak to me?" he asks.

'"Nawsir," I say.

'He looks around at the rest of them – Trevor Dawson, Carl Roone, and Henry Whitsun, who was killed in the fire that fall – and he says to them, "This here smart nigger is in hack with me. If the rest of you jigaboos don't want to join him in one hardworking dirty bitch of an afternoon, you get over to your barracks, stow your gear, and get your asses over to the OD. You understand?"

'Well, they got going, and Wilson hollers, "Doubletime, you fuckers! Lemme see the soles of your eighty-fucking-nines!"

'So they doubletimed off, and Wilson took me over to one of the equipment sheds and he got me a spade. He took me out into the big field that used to be just about where the Northeast Airlines Airbus terminal stands today. And he looks at me, kind of grinning, and he points at the ground and he says, "You see that hole there, nigger?"

'There was no hole there, but I figured it was best for me to agree with whatever he said, so I looked down at the ground where he was pointing and said I sure did see it. So then he busted me one in the nose and knocked me over and there I was on the ground with blood running down over the last fresh shirt I had.

'"You don't see it because some bigmouth jig bastard filled it up!" he shouted at me, and he had two big blotches of color on his cheeks. But he was grinning, too, and you could tell he was enjoying himself. 'So what you do, Mr A Good Afternoon To You, what you do is you get the dirt out of my hole. Doubletime!"

'So I dug for most two hours, and pretty soon I was in that hole up to my chin. The last couple of feet was clay, and by the time I finished I was standing in water up to my ankles and my shoes were soaked right through.

'"Get out of there, Hanlon," Sergeant Wilson said. He was sitting there on the grass, smoking a cigarette. He didn't offer me any help.

I was dirt and muck from top to bottom, not to mention the blood drying on the blouse of my suntans. He stood up and walked over. He pointed at the hole.

'"What do you see there, nigger?" he asked me.

'"Your hole, Sergeant Wilson," says I

'"Yeah, well, I decided I don't want it," he says. "I don't want no hole dug by a nigger. Put my dirt back in, Private Hanlon."

'So I filled it back in and by the time I was done the sun was going down and it was getting cold. He comes over and looks at it after I finished patting down the last of the dirt with the flat of the spade.

'"Now what do you see there, nigger?" he asks.

'"Bunch of dirt, sir," I said, and he hit me again. My God, Mikey, I came this close to just bouncing up off'n the ground and splitting his head open with the edge of that shovel. But if I'd done that, I never would have looked at the sky again, except through a set of bars. Still, there were times when I almost think it would have been worth it. I managed to hold my peace somehow, though.

'"That ain't a bunch of dirt, you stupid coontail night-fighter!" he screams at me, the spit flying off'n his lips. "That's *MY HOLE*, and you best get the dirt out of it right now! Doubletime!"

'So I dug the dirt out of his hole and then I filled it in again, and then he asks me why I went and filled in his hole just when he was getting ready to take a crap in it. So I dug it out again and he drops his pants and hangs his skinny-shanks cracker redneck ass over the hole and he grins up at me while he's doing his business and says, "How you doin, Hanlon?"

'"I am doing just fine, sir," I says right back, because I had decided I wasn't going to give up until I fell unconscious or dropped dead. I had my dander up.

'"Well, I aim to fix that," he says. "To start with, you better just fill that hole in, Private Hanlon. And I want to see some life. You're slowin down."

'So I got her filled in again and I could see by the way he was grinning that he was only warming up. But just then this friend of his came humping across the field with a gas lantern and told him there'd been a surprise inspection and Wilson was in hack for having missed it. My friends covered for me and I was okay, but Wilson's friends – if that's what he called them – couldn't be bothered.

'He let me go then, and I waited to see if his name would go up on the Punishment Roster the next day, but it never did. I guess he must have just told the Loot he missed the inspection because he was teaching a smartmouth nigger who it was owned all the holes at the Derry army base – those that had already been dug and those that hadn't been. They probably gave him a medal instead of potatoes to peel. And that's how things were for Company E here in Derry.'

It was right around 1958 that my father told me the story, and I guess he was pushing fifty, although my mother was only forty or so. I asked him if that was the way Derry was, why had he come back?

'Well, I was only sixteen when I joined the army, Mikey,' he said. 'Lied about my age to get in. Wasn't my idea, either. My mother told me to do it. I was big, and that's the only reason the lie stuck, I guess. I was born and grew up in Burgaw, North Carolina, and the only time we saw meat was right after the tobacco was in, or sometimes in the winter if my father shot a coon or a possum. The only good thing I remember about Burgaw is possum pie with hoecakes spread around her just as pretty as you could want.

'So when my dad died in an accident with some farm machinery, my ma said she was going to take Philly Loubird up to Corinth, where she had people. Philly Loubird was the baby of the family.'

'You mean my Uncle Phil?' I asked, smiling to think of anybody calling him Philly Loubird. He was a lawyer in Tucson, Arizona, and had been on the City Council there for six years. When I was a kid, I thought Uncle Phil was rich. For a black man in 1958, I suppose he was. He made twenty thousand dollars a year.

'That's who I mean,' my dad said. 'But in those days he was just a twelve-year-old kid who wore a ricepaper sailor hat and mended biballs and had no shoes. He was the youngest, I was the second youngest. All the others were gone – two dead, two married, one in jail. That was Howard. He never was any good.

'"You are goan join the army," your gramma Shirley told me. "I dunno if they start paying you right away or not, but once they do, you're goan send me a lotment every month. I hate to send you away, son, but if you don't take care of me and Philly, I don't know what's going to become of us." She gave me my birth certificate to show the recruiter and I seen she fixed the year on it somehow to make me eighteen.

'So I went to the courthouse where the army recruiter was and asked about joining up. He showed me the papers and the line where I could make my mark. "I kin write my name," I said, and he laughed like he didn't believe me.

'"Well then, you go on and write it, black boy," he says.

415

'"Hang on a minute," I says back. "I want to ast you a couple of questions."

'"Fire away then," he says. "I can answer anything you can ask."

'"Do they have meat twice a week in the army?" I asked. "My mamma says they do, but she is powerful set on me joining up."

'"No, they don't have it twice a week," he says.

'"Well, that's about what I thought," I says, thinking that the man surely does seem like a booger but at least he's an *honest* booger.

'Then he says, "They got it ever night," making me wonder how I ever could have thought he was honest.

'"You must think I'm a pure-d fool," I says.

'"You got that right, nigger," he says.

'"Well, if I join up, I got to do something for my mamma and Philly Loubird," I says. "Mamma says it's a lotment."

'"That's this here," he says, and taps the allotment form. "Now what else is on your mind?"

'"Well," says I, "what about trainin to be an officer?"

'He threw his head back when I said that and laughed until I thought he was gonna choke on his own spit. Then he says, "Son, the day they got nigger officers in this man's army will be the day you see the bleedin Jesus Christ doing the Charleston at Birdland. Now you sign or you don't sign. I'm out of patience. Also, you're stinkin the place up."

'So I signed, and watched him staple the allotment form to my muster-sheet, and then he give me the oath, and then I was a soldier. I was thinking that they'd send me up to New Jersey, where the army was building bridges on account of there being no wars to fight. Instead, I got Derry, Maine, and Company E.'

He sighed and shifted in his chair, a big man with white hair that curled close to his skull. At that time we had one of the bigger farms in Derry, and probably the best roadside produce stand south of Bangor. The three of us worked hard, and my father had to hire on extra help during harvesting time, and we made out.

He said: 'I came back because I'd seen the South and I'd seen the North, and there was the same hate in both places. It wasn't Sergeant Wilson that convinced me of that. He was nothing but a Georgia cracker, and he took the South with him wherever he went. He didn't have to be south of the Mason-Dixon line to hate niggers. He just *did*. No, it was the fire at the Black Spot that convinced me of that. You know, Mikey, in a way . . .'

He glanced over at my mother, who was knitting. She hadn't

looked up, but I knew she was listening closely, and my father knew
it too, I think.

'In a way it was the fire made me a man. There was sixty people
killed in that fire, eighteen of them from Company E. There really
wasn't any company left when that fire was over. Henry Whitsun . . .
Stork Anson . . . Alan Snopes . . . Everett McCaslin . . . Horton Sartoris
. . . all my friends, all dead in that fire. And that fire wasn't set by old
Sarge Wilson and his grits-and-cornpone friends. It was set by the
Derry branch of the Maine Legion of White Decency. Some of the
kids you go to school with, son, their fathers struck the matches that
lit the Black Spot on fire. And I'm not talking about the poor kids,
neither.'

'Why, Daddy? Why did they?'

'Well, part of it was just Derry,' my father said, frowning. He
lit his pipe slowly and shook out the wooden match. 'I don't know
why it happened here; I can't explain it, but at the same time I ain't
surprised by it.

'The Legion of White Decency was the Northerners' version
of the Ku Klux Klan, you see. They marched in the same white
sheets, they burned the same crosses, they wrote the same hate-notes
to black folks they felt were getting above their station or taking jobs
that were meant for white men. In churches where the preachers
talked about black equality, they sometimes planted charges of dynamite. Most of the history books talk more about the KKK than they
do about the Legion of White Decency, and a lot of people don't
even know there was such a thing. I think it might be because most
of the histories have been written by Northerners and they're ashamed.

'It was most pop'lar in the big cities and the manufacturin areas.
New York, New Jersey, Detroit, Baltimore, Boston, Portsmouth – they
all had their chapters. They tried to organize in Maine, but Derry was
the only place they had any real success. Oh, for awhile there was a
pretty good chapter in Lewiston – this was around the same time as
the fire at the Black Spot – but they weren't worried about niggers
raping white women or taking jobs that should have belonged to white
men, because there weren't any niggers to speak of up here. In Lewiston
they were worried about tramps and hobos and that something called
"the bonus army" would join up with something they called "the
Communist riffraff army," by which they meant any man who was
out of work. The Legion of Decency used to send these fellows out
of town just as fast as they came in. Sometimes they stuffed poison ivy
down the backs of their pants. Sometimes they set their shirts on fire.

'Well, the Legion was pretty much done up here after the fire at the Black Spot. Things got out of hand, you see. The way things seem to do in this town, sometimes.'

He paused, puffing.

'It's like the Legion of White Decency was just another seed, Mikey, and it found some earth that nourished it well here. It was a regular rich-man's club. And after the fire, they all just laid away their sheets and lied each other up and it was papered over.' Now there was a kind of vicious contempt in his voice that made my mother look up, frowning. 'After all, who got killed? Eighteen army niggers, fourteen or fifteen town niggers, four members of a nigger jazz-band . . . and a bunch of nigger-lovers. What did it matter?'

'Will,' my mother said softly. 'That's enough.'

'No,' I said. 'I want to hear!'

'It's getting to be your bedtime, Mikey,' he said, ruffling my hair with his big, hard hand. 'I just want to tell you one thing more, and I don't think you'll understand it, because I'm not sure I understand it myself. What happened that night at the Black Spot, bad as it was . . . I don't really think it happened because we was black. Not even because the Spot was close behind West Broadway, where the rich whites in Derry lived then and still live today. I don't think that the Legion of White Decency happened to get along so well here because they hated black people and bums more in Derry than they did in Portland or Lewiston or Brunswick. It's because of that soil. It seems that bad things, hurtful things, do right well in the soil of this town. I've thought so again and again over the years. I don't know why it should be . . . but it is.

'But there are good folks here too, and there were good folks here then. When the funerals were held afterward, thousands of people turned out, and they turned out for the blacks as well as the whites. Businesses closed up for most of a week. The hospitals treated the hurt ones free of charge. There were food baskets and letters of condolence that were honestly meant. And there were helping hands held out. I met my friend Dewey Conroy during that time, and you know he's just as white as vanilla ice cream, but I feel like he's my brother. I'd die for Dewey if he asked me to, and although no man really knows another man's heart, I think he'd die for me if it came to that.

'Anyway, the army sent away those of us that were left after that fire, like they were ashamed . . . and I guess they were. I ended up down at Fort Hood, and I stayed there for six years. I met your mother there, and we were married in Galveston, at her folks' house. But all through the years between, Derry never escaped my mind. And after the war, I brought your mom back here. And we had you. And here we are, not three miles from where the Black Spot stood in 1930. And I think it's your bedtime, Mr Man.'

'I want to hear about the fire!' I yelled. 'Tell me about it, Daddy!'

And he looked at me in that frowning way that always shut me up . . . maybe because he didn't look that way often. Mostly he was a smiling man. 'That's no story for a boy,' he said. 'Another time, Mikey. When we've both walked around a few more years.'

As it turned out, we both walked around another four years before I heard the story of what happened at the Black Spot that night, and by then my father's walking days were all done. He told me from the hospital bed where he lay, full of dope, dozing in and out of reality as the cancer worked away inside of his intestines, eating him up.

February 26th, 1985

I got reading over what I had written last in this notebook and surprised myself by bursting into tears over my father, who has now been dead for twenty-three years. I can remember my grief for him – it lasted for almost two years. Then when I graduated from high school in 1965 and my mother looked at me and said, 'How proud your father would have been!,' we cried in each other's arms and I thought that was the end, that we had finished the job of burying him with those late tears. But who knows how long a grief may last? Isn't it possible that, even thirty or forty years after the death of a child or a brother or a sister, one may half-waken, thinking of that person with that same lost empti-ness, that feeling of places which may never be filled . . . perhaps not even in death?

He left the army in 1937 with a disability pension. By that year, my father's army had become a good deal more warlike; anyone with half an eye, he told me once, could see by then that soon all the guns would be coming out of storage again. He had risen to the rank of sergeant in the interim, and he had lost most of his left foot when a new recruit who was so scared he was almost shitting peach-pits pulled the pin on a hand grenade and then dropped it instead of throwing it. It rolled over to my father and exploded with a sound that was, he said, like a cough in the middle of the night.

A lot of the ordnance those long-ago soldiers had to train with was either defective or had sat so long in almost forgotten supply depots that it was impotent. They had bullets that wouldn't fire and rifles that

419

sometimes exploded in their hands when the bullets did fire. The navy had torpedoes that usually didn't go where they were aimed and didn't explode when they did. The Army Air Corps and the Navy Air Arm had planes whose wings fell off if they landed hard, and at Pensacola in 1939, I have read, a supply officer discovered a whole fleet of government trucks that wouldn't run because cockroaches had eaten the rubber hoses and the fanbelts.

So my father's life was saved (including, of course, the part of him that became Your Ob'dt Servant Michael Hanlon) by a combination of bureaucratic porkbarrelling folderol and defective equipment. The grenade only half-exploded and he just lost part of one foot instead of everything from the breastbone on down.

Because of the disability money he was able to marry my mother a year earlier than he had planned. They didn't come to Derry at once; they moved to Houston, where they did war work until 1945. My father was a foreman in a factory that made bomb-casings. My mother was a Rosie the Riveter. But as he told me that night when I was eleven, the thought of Derry 'never escaped his mind.' And now I wonder if that blind thing might not have been at work even then, drawing him back so I could take my place in that circle in the Barrens that August evening. If the wheels of the universe are in true, then good always compensates for evil – but good can be awful as well.

My father had a subscription to the Derry News. He kept his eye on the ads announcing land for sale. They had saved up a good bit of money. At last he saw a farm for sale that looked like a good proposition . . . on paper, at least. The two of them rode up from Texas on a Trailways bus, looked at it, and bought it the same day. The First Merchants of Penobscot County issued my father a ten-year mortgage, and they settled down.

'We had some problems at first,' my father said another time. 'There were people who didn't want Negroes in the neighborhood. We knew it was going to be that way – I hadn't forgotten about the Black Spot – and we just hunkered down to wait it out. Kids would go by and throw rocks or beer cans. I must have replaced twenty windows that first year. And some of them weren't just kids, either. One day when we got up, there was a swastika painted on the side of the chickenhouse and all the chickens were dead. Someone had poisoned their feed. Those were the last chickens I ever tried to keep.

'But the County Sheriff – there wasn't any police chief in those days, Derry wasn't quite big enough for such a thing – got to work on the matter and he worked hard. That's what I mean, Mikey, when I say there is good here as well as bad. It didn't make any difference to that man Sullivan that my skin was brown and my hair was kinky. He come out half a dozen times, he talked to people, and finally he found out who done it. And who do you think it was? I'll give you three guesses, and the first two don't count!'

'I don't know,' I said.

My father laughed until tears spouted out of his eyes. He took a big white handkerchief out of his pocket and wiped them away. 'Why, it was Butch Bowers, that's who! The father of the kid you say is the biggest bully at your school. The father's a turd and the son's a little fart.'

'There are kids at school who say Henry's father is crazy,' I told him. I think I was in the fourth grade at that time — far enough along to have had my can righteously kicked by Henry Bowers more than once, anyway . . . and now that I think about it, most of the pejorative terms for 'black' or 'Negro' I've ever heard, I heard first from the lips of Henry Bowers, between grades one and four.

'Well, I'll tell you,' he said, 'the idea that Butch Bowers is crazy might not be far wrong. People said he was never right after he come back from the Pacific. He was in the Marines over there. Anyway, the Sheriff took him into custody and Butch was hollering that it was a put-up job and they were all just a bunch of nigger-lovers. Oh, he was gonna sue everybody. I guess he had a list that would have stretched from here to Witcham Street. I doubt if he had a single pair of underdrawers that was whole in the seat, but he was going to sue me, Sheriff Sullivan, the Town of Derry, the County of Penobscot, and God alone knows who else.

'As to what happened next . . . well, I can't swear it's true, but this is how I heard it from Dewey Conroy. Dewey said the Sheriff went in to see Butch at the jail up in Bangor. And Sheriff Sullivan says, "It's time for you to shut your mouth and do some listening, Butch. That black guy, he don't want to press charges. He don't want to send you to Shawshank, he just wants the worth of his chickens. He figures two hundred dollars would do her."

'Butch tells the Sheriff he can put his two hundred dollars where the sun don't shine, and Sheriff Sullivan, he tells Butch: "They got a lime pit down at the Shank, Butch, and they tell me after you've been workin there about two years, your tongue goes as green as a lime Popsicle. Now you pick. Two years peelin lime or two hundred dollars. What do you think?"

'"No jury in Maine will convict me," Butch says, "not for killing a nigger's chickens."

'"I know that," Sullivan says.

'"Then what the Christ are we chinnin about?" Butch asts him.

'"You better wake up, Butch. They won't put you away for the chickens, but they *will* put you away for the swastiker you painted on the door after you killed em."

'Well, Dewey said Butch's mouth just kind of dropped open, and Sullivan went away to let him think about it. About three days later Butch told his brother, the one that froze to death couple of years after while out hunting drunk, to sell his new Mercury, which Butch had bought with his muster-out pay and was mighty sweet on. So I got my two hundred dollars and Butch swore he was going to burn me out. He went around telling all his friends that. So I caught up with him one afternoon. He'd bought an old pre-war Ford to replace the Merc, and I had my pick-up. I cut him off out on Witcham Street by the trainyards and got out with my Winchester rifle.

'"Any fires out my way and you got one bad black man gunning for you, old hoss," I told him.

'"You can't talk to me that way, nigger," he said, and he was damn near to blubbering between being mad and being scared. "You can't talk to no white man that way, not a jig like you."

'Well, I'd had enough of the whole thing, Mikey. And I knew if I didn't scare him off for good right then I'd never be shed of him. There wasn't nobody around. I reached in that Ford with one hand and caught him by the hair of the head. I put the stock of my rifle against the buckle of my belt and got the muzzle right up under his chin. I said, "The next time you call me a nigger or a jig, your brains are going to be dripping off the domelight of your car. And you believe me, Butch: any fires out my way and I'm gunning for you. I may come gunning for your wife and your brat and your no-count brother as well. I have had enough."

'Then he *did* start to cry, and I never saw an uglier sight in my life. "Look what things has come to here," he says, "when a nih . . . when a jih . . . when a feller can put a gun to a workingman's head in broad daylight by the side of the road."

'"Yeah, the world must be going to a camp-meeting hell when something like that can happen," I agreed. "But that don't matter now. All that matters now is, do we have an understanding here or do you want to see if you can learn how to breathe through your forehead?"

'He allowed as how we had an understanding, and that was the last bit of trouble I ever had with Butch Bowers, except for maybe when your dog Mr Chips died, and I've got no proof that was Bowers's doing. Chippy might have just got a poison bait or something.

'Since that day we've been pretty much left alone to make our way, and when I look back on it, there ain't much I regret. We've had a good life here, and if there are nights when I dream about that fire, well, there isn't nobody that can live a natural life without having a few bad dreams.'

February 28th, 1985

It's been days since I sat down to write the story of the fire at the Black Spot as my father told it to me, and I haven't gotten to it yet. It's in *The Lord of the Rings*, I think, where one of the characters says that 'way leads on to way'; that you could start at a path leading nowhere more fantastic than from your own front steps to the sidewalk, and from there you could go . . . well, anywhere at all. It's the same way with stories. One leads to the next, to the next, and to the next; maybe they go in the direction you wanted to go, but maybe they don't. Maybe in the end it's the voice that tells the stories more than the stories themselves that matters.

It's his voice that I remember, certainly: my father's voice, low and slow, how he would chuckle sometimes or laugh outright. The pauses to light his pipe or to blow his nose or to go and get a can of Narragansett (Nasty Gansett, he called it) from the icebox. That voice, which is for me somehow the voice of all voices, the voice of all years, the ultimate voice of this place – one that's in none of the Ives interviews nor in any of the poor histories of this place . . . nor on any of my own tapes.

My father's voice.

Now it's ten o'clock, the library closed an hour ago, and a proper old jeezer is starting to crank up outside. I can hear tiny spicules of sleet striking the windows in here and in the glassed-in corridor which leads to the Children's Library. I can hear other sounds, too – stealthy creaks and bumps outside the circle of light where I sit, writing on the lined yellow pages of a legal pad. Just the sounds of an old building settling, I tell myself . . . but I wonder. As I wonder if somewhere out in this storm there is a clown selling balloons tonight.

Well . . . never mind. I think I've finally found my way to my father's final story. I heard it in his hospital room no more than six weeks before he died.

423

I went to see him with my mother every afternoon after school, and alone every evening. My mother had to stay home and do the chores then, but she insisted that I go. I rode my bike. She wouldn't let me hook rides, not even four years after the murders had ended.

That was a hard six weeks for a boy who was only fifteen. I loved my father, but I came to hate those evening visits – watching him shrink and shrivel, watching the pain-lines spread and deepen on his face. Sometimes he would cry, although he tried not to. And going home it would be getting dark and I would think back to the summer of '58, and I'd be afraid to look behind me because the clown might be there ... or the werewolf ... or Ben's mummy ... or my bird. But I was mostly afraid that no matter what shape It took, It would have my father's cancer-raddled face. So I would pedal as fast as I could no matter how hard my heart thundered in my chest and come in flushed and sweaty-haired and out of breath and my mother would say, 'Why do you want to ride so fast, Mikey? You'll make yourself sick' And I'd say, 'I wanted to get back in time to help you with the chores,' and she'd give me a hug and a kiss and tell me I was a good boy.

As time went on, it got so I could hardly think of things to talk about with him anymore. Riding into town, I'd rack my brain for subjects of conversation, dreading the moment when both of us would run out of things to say. His dying scared me and enraged me, but it *embarrassed* me, too; it seemed to me then and it seems to me now that when a man or woman goes it should be a quick thing. The cancer was doing more than killing him. It was degrading him, demeaning him.

We never spoke of the cancer, and in some of those silences I thought that we *must* speak of it, that there would be nothing else and we would be stuck with it like kids caught without a place to sit in a game of musical chairs when the piano stops, and I would become almost frantic, trying to think of something – anything! – to say so that we would not have to acknowledge the thing which was now destroying my daddy, who had once taken Butch Bowers by the hair and jammed his rifle into the shelf of his chin and demanded of Butch to be left alone. We would be forced to speak of it, and if we were I would cry. I wouldn't be able to help it. And at fifteen, I think the thought of crying in front of my father scared and distressed me more than anything else.

It was during one of those interminable, scary pauses that I asked him again about the fire at the Black Spot. They'd filled him full of dope that evening because the pain was very bad, and he had

424

been drifting in and out of consciousness, sometimes speaking clearly, sometimes speaking in that exotic language I think of as Sleepmud. Sometimes I knew he was talking to me, but at other times he seemed to have me confused with his brother Phil. I asked him about the Black Spot for no real reason; it had just jumped into my mind and I seized on it.

His eyes sharpened and he smiled a little. 'You ain't never forgot that, have you, Mikey?'

'No, sir,' I said, and although I hadn't thought about it in three years or better, I added what he sometimes said: 'It hasn't ever escaped my mind.'

'Well, I'll tell you now,' he said. 'Fifteen is old enough, I guess, and your mother ain't here to stop me. Besides, you ought to know. I think something like it could only have happened in Derry, and you need to know that, too. So you can beware. The conditions for such things have always seemed right here. You're careful, aren't you, Mikey?'

'Yes, sir,' I said.

'Good,' he said, and his head dropped back on his pillow. 'That's good.' I thought he was going to drift off again – his eyes had slipped closed – but instead he began to talk.

'When I was at the army base here in '29 and '30,' he said, 'there was an NCO Club up there on the hill, where Derry Community College is now. It was right behind the PX, where you used to be able to get a pack of Lucky Strike Greens for seven cents. The NCO Club was only a big old quonset hut, but they had fixed it up nice inside – carpet on the floor, booths along the walls, a jukebox – and you could get soft drinks on the weekend . . . if you were white, that was. They would have bands in most Saturday nights, and it was quite a place to go. It was just pop over the bar, it being Prohibition, but we heard you could get stronger stuff if you wanted it . . . and if you had a little green star on your army card. That was like a secret sign they had. Home-brew beer mostly, but on weekends you could sometimes get stronger stuff. If you were white.

'Us Company E boys weren't allowed any place near it, of course. So we went on the town if we had a pass in the evening. In those days Derry was still something of a logging town and there were eight or ten bars, most of em down in a part of town they called Hell's Half-Acre. They wasn't speakeasies; that was too grand a name for em. Wasn't anybody in em spoke very easy, anyhow. They was what folks called "blind pigs," and that was about right, because most of the customers

425

acted like pigs when they were in there and they was about blind when they turned em out. The Sheriff knew and the cops knew, but those places roared all night long, same as they'd done since the logging days in the 1890s. I suppose palms got greased, but maybe not as many or with so much as you might think; in Derry people have a way of looking the other way. Some served hard stuff as well as beer, and by all accounts I ever heard, the stuff you could get in town was ten times as good as the rotgut whiskey and bathtub gin you could get at the white boys' NCO on Friday and Saturday nights. The downtown hooch came over the border from Canada in pulp trucks, and most of them bottles had what the labels said. The good stuff was expensive, but there was plenty of furnace-oil too, and it might hang you over but it didn't kill you, and if you *did* go blind, it didn't last. On any given night you'd have to duck your head when the bottles came flying by. There was Nan's, the Paradise, Wally's Spa, the Silver Dollar, and one bar, the Powderhorn, where you could sometimes get a whore. Oh, you could pick up a woman at any pig, you didn't even have to work at it that hard – there was a lot of them wanted to find out if a slice off'n the rye loaf was any different – but to kids like me and Trevor Dawson and Carl Roone, my friends in those days, the thought of buying a whore – a *white* whore – that was something you had to sit down and consider.'

As I've told you, he was heavily doped that night. I don't believe he would have said any of that stuff – not to his fifteen-year-old son – if he had not been.

· 'Well, it wasn't very long before a representative of the Town Council showed up, wanting to see Major Fuller. He said he wanted to talk about "some problems between the townspeople and the enlisted men" and "concerns of the electorate" and "questions of propriety," but what he really wanted Fuller to know was as clear as a window-pane. They didn't want no army niggers in their pigs, botherin white women and drinkin illegal hooch at a bar where only white men was supposed to be standin and drinkin illegal hooch.

'All of which was a laugh, all right. The flower of white woman-hood they were so worried about was mostly a bunch of barbags, and as far as getting in the way of the men ... ! Well, all I can say is that I never saw a member of the Derry Town Council down in the Silver Dollar, or in the Powderhorn. The men who drank in those dives were pulp-cutters in those big red-and-black-checked lumberman's jackets, scars and scabs all over their hands, some of em missing eyes or fingers, all of em missing most of their teeth, all of em smellin like woodchips and sawdust and sap. They wore green flannel pants and green gumrubber boots and tracked snow across the floor until it was black with it. They smelled big, Mikey, and they walked big, and they talked big. They *were* big. I was in Wally's Spa one night when I saw a fella split his shirt right down one arm while he was armrassling this other fella. It didn't just *rip* – you probably think that's what I mean, but it ain't. Arm of that man's shirt damn near exploded – sort of *blew* off his arm, in rags. And everybody cheered and applauded and somebody slapped me on the back and said, "That's what you call an armrassler's fart, blackface."

'What I'm telling you is that if the men who used those blind pigs on Friday and Saturday nights when they come out of the woods to drink whiskey and fuck women instead of knotholes greased up with lard, if those men hadn't wanted us there, they would have thrown us out on our asses. But the fact of it was, Mikey, they didn't seem to give much of a toot one way or the other.

'One of em took me aside one night – he was six foot, which was damn big for those days, and he was dead drunk, and he smelled as high as a basket of month-old peaches. If he'd stepped out of his clothes, I think they would have stood up alone. He looks at me and says, "Mister, I gonna ast you sumpin, me. Are you be a Negro?"

'"That's right," I says.

'"*Commen' ça va!*" he says in the Saint John Valley French that sounds almost like Cajun talk, and grins so big I saw all four of his teeth. "I knew you was, me! Hey! I seen one in a book once! Had the same –" and he couldn't think how to say what was on his mind, so he reaches out and flaps at my mouth.

'"Big lips," I says.

'"Yeah, yeah!" he says, laughin like a kid. "Beeg leeps! *Épais lèvres!* Beeg leeps! Gonna buy you a beer, me!"

'"Buy away," I says, not wanting to get on his bad side.

'He laughed at that too and clapped me on the back – almost knocking me on my face – and pushed his way up to the plankwood bar where there must have been seventy men and maybe fifteen women lined up. "I need two beers fore I tear this dump apart!" he yells at the bartender, who was a big lug with a broken nose named Romeo Dupree. "One for me and one *pour l'homme avec les épais lèvres!*" And they all laughed like hell at that, but not in a mean way, Mikey.

'So he gets the beers and gives me mine and he says, "What's your name? I don't want to call you Beeg Leeps, me. Don't sound good."

'"William Hanlon," I says.

427

'"Well, here's to you, Weelyum Anlon," he says.

'"No, here's to you," I says. "You're the first white man who ever bought me a drink." Which was true.

'So we drank those beers down and then we had two more and he says, "You sure you're a Negro? Except for them *épais* leeps, you look just like a white man with brown skin to me."'

My father got to laughing at this, and so did I. He laughed so hard his stomach started to hurt him, and he held it, grimacing, his eyes turned up, his upper plate biting down on his lower lip.

'You want me to ring for the nurse, Daddy?' I asked, alarmed.

'No . . . no. I'm goan be okay. The worst thing of this, Mikey, is that you can't even laugh anymore when you feel like it. Which is damn seldom.'

He fell silent for a few moments, and I realize now that that was the only time we came close to talking about what was killing him. Maybe it would have been better − better for both of us − if we had done more.

He took a sip of water and then went on.

'Anyway, it wasn't the few women who travelled the pigs, and it wasn't the lumberjacks that made up their main custom who wanted us out. It was those five old men on the Town Council who were really offended, them and the dozen or so men that stood behind them − Derry's old line, you know. None of them had ever stepped a foot inside of the Paradise or Wally's Spa, they did their boozing at the country club which then stood over on Derry Heights, but they wanted to make sure that none of those barbags or peavey-swingers got polluted by the blacks of Company E.

'So Major Fuller says, "I never wanted them here in the first place. I keep thinking it's an oversight and they'll get sent back down south or maybe to New Jersey."

'"That's not my problem," this old fart tells him. Mueller, I think his name was −'

'*Sally* Mueller's father?' I asked, startled. Sally Mueller was in the same high-school class with me.

My father grinned a sour, crooked little grin. 'No, this would have been her uncle. Sally Mueller's dad was off in college somewhere then. But if he'd been in Derry, he would have been there, I guess, standing with his brother. And in case you're wondering how true this part of the story is, all I can tell you is that the conversation was repeated to me by Trevor Dawson, who was swabbing the floors over there in officers' country that day and heard it all.

'"Where the government sends the black boys is your problem, not mine," Mueller tells Major Fuller. "My problem is where you're letting them go on Friday and Saturday nights. If they go on whooping it up downtown, there's going to be trouble. We've got the Legion in this town, you know."

'"Well, but I am in a bit of a tight here, Mr Mueller," he says. "I can't let them drink over at the NCO Club. Not only is it against the regulations for the Negroes to drink with the whites, they couldn't anyway. It's an NCO club, don't you see? Every one of those black boys is a bucky-tail private."

'"That's not my problem either. I simply trust you will take care of the matter. Responsibility accompanies rank." And off he goes.

'Well, Fuller solved the problem. The Derry Army Base was a damn big patch of land in those days, although there wasn't a hell of a lot on it. Better than a hundred acres, all told. Going north, it ended right behind West Broadway, where a sort of greenbelt was planted. Where Memorial Park is now, that was where the Black Spot stood.

'It was just an old requisition shed in early 1930, when all of this happened, but Major Fuller mustered in Company E and told us it was going to be "our" club. Acted like he was Daddy Warbucks or something, and maybe he even felt that way, giving a bunch of black privates their own place, even if it was nothing but a shed. Then he added, like it was nothing, that the pigs downtown were off-limits to us.

'There was a lot of bitterness about it, but what could we do? We had no real power. It was this young fellow, a Pfc. named Dick Hallorann who was a mess-cook, who suggested that maybe we could fix it up pretty nice if we really tried.

'So we did. We really tried. And we made out pretty well, all things considered. The first time a bunch of us went in there to look it over, we were pretty depressed. It was dark and smelly, full of old tools and boxes of papers that had gone moldy. There was only two little windows and no lectricity. The floor was dirt. Carl Roone laughed in a kind of bitter way, I remember that, and said, "The ole Maje, he a real prince, ain't he? Give us our own club. *Sho!*"

'And George Brannock, who was also killed in the fire that fall, he said: "Yeah, it's a hell of a black spot, all right." And the name just stuck.

'Hallorann got us going, though . . . Hallorann and Carl and me. I guess God will forgive us for what we did, though – cause He knows we had no idea how it would turn out.

429

'After awhile the rest of the fellows pitched in. With most of Derry off-limits, there wasn't much else we could do. We hammered and nailed and cleaned. Trev Dawson was a pretty good jackleg carpenter, and he showed us how to cut some more windows along the side, and damned if Alan Snopes didn't come up with panes of glass for them that were different colors – sort of a cross between carnival glass and the sort you see in church windows.

'"Where'd you get this?" I asked him. Alan was the oldest of us; he was about forty-two, old enough so that most of us called him Pop Snopes.

'He stuck a Camel in his mouth and tipped me a wink. "Midnight Requisitions," he says, and would say no more.

'So the place come along pretty good, and by the middle of the summer we was using it. Trev Dawson and some of the others had partitioned off the back quarter of the building and got a little kitchen set up in there, not much more than a grill and a couple of deep-fryers, so that you could get a hamburg and some french fries, if you wanted. There was a bar down one side, but it was just meant for sodas and drinks like Virgin Marys – shit, we knew our place. Hadn't we been taught it? If we wanted to drink hard, we'd do it in the dark.

'The floor was still dirt, but we kept it oiled down nice. Trev and Pop Snopes ran in a lectric line – more Midnight Requisitions, I imagine. By July, you could go in there any Saturday night and sit down and have a cola and a hamburger – or a slaw-dog. It was nice. It never really got finished – we was still working on it when the fire burned it down. It got to be a kind of hobby . . . or a way of thumbing our noses at Fuller and Mueller and the Town Council. But I guess we knew it was ours when Ev McCaslin and I put up a sign one Friday night that said THE BLACK SPOT, and just below that, COMPANY E AND GUESTS. Like we were exclusive, you know!

'It got looking nice enough that the white boys started to grumble about it, and next thing you know, the white boys' NCO was looking finer than ever. They was adding on a special lounge and a little cafeteria. It was like they wanted to race. But that was one race that we didn't want to run.'

My dad smiled at me from his hospital bed.

'We were young, except for Snopesy, but we weren't entirely foolish. We knew that the white boys let you race against them, but if it starts to look like you are getting ahead, why, somebody just breaks your legs so you can't run as fast. We had what we wanted, and that was enough. But then . . . something happened.' He fell silent, frowning.

'What was that, Daddy?'

'We found out that we had a pretty decent jazz-band among us,' he said slowly. 'Martin Devereaux, who was a corporal, played drums. Ace Stevenson played cornet. Pop Snopes played a pretty decent barrelhouse piano. He wasn't great, but he wasn't no slouch, either. There was another fellow who played clarinet, and George Brannock played the saxophone. There were others of us who sat in from time to time, playing guitar or harmonica or juiceharp or even just a comb with waxed paper over it.

'This didn't all happen at once, you understand, but by the end of that August, there was a pretty hot little Dixieland combo playing Friday and Saturday nights at the Black Spot. They got better and better as the fall drew on, and while they were never great – I don't want to give you that idea – they played in a way that was different . . . hotter somehow . . . it . . .' He waved his skinny hand above the bedclothes.

'They played bodacious,' I suggested, grinning.

'That's right!' he exclaimed, grinning back. 'You got it! They played bodacious Dixieland. And the next thing you know, people from town started to show up at *our* club. Even some of the white soldiers from the base. It got so the place was getting crowded a right smart every weekend. That didn't happen all at once, either. At first those white faces looked like sprinkles of salt in a pepper-pot, but more and more of them turned up as time went on.

'When those white people showed up, that's when we forgot to be careful. They were bringin in their own booze in brown bags, most of it the finest high-tension stuff there is – made the stuff you could get in the pigs downtown look like soda pop. Country-club booze is what I mean, Mikey. Rich people's booze. Chivas. Glenfiddich. The kind of champagne they served to first-class passengers on ocean liners. "Champers," some of em called it, same as we used to call ugly-minded mules back home. We should have found a way to stop it, but we didn't know how. They was *town*! Hell, they was *white*!

'And, like I said, we were young and proud of what we'd done. And we underestimated how bad things might get. We all knew that Mueller and his friends must have known what was going on, but I don't think any of us realized that it was drivin em crazy – and I mean what I say: *crazy*. There they were in their grand old Victorian houses on West Broadway not a quarter of a mile away from where *we* were, listening to things like "Aunt Hagar's Blues" and "Diggin My Potatoes." That was bad. Knowing that their young people were there too, whooping it up right cheek by jowl with the blacks, that must have been ever so much worse. Because it wasn't just the lumberjacks and the barbags that were turning up as September came into October. It got to be kind of a thing in town. Young folks would come to drink and to dance to that no-name jazz-band until one in the morning came and shut us down. They didn't just come from Derry, either. They come from Bangor and Newport and Haven and Cleaves Mills and Old Town and all the little burgs around these parts. You could see fraternity boys from the University of Maine at Orono cutting capers with their sorority girlfriends, and when the band learned how to play a ragtime version of "The Maine Stein Song," they just about ripped the roof off. Of course, it was an enlisted-men's club – technically, at least – and off-limits to civilians who didn't have an invitation. But in fact, Mikey, we just opened the door at seven and let her stand open until one. By the middle of October it got so that any time you went out on the dancefloor you were standing hip to hip with six other people. There wasn't no room to dance, so you had to just sort of stand there and wiggle . . . but if anyone minded, I never heard him let on. By midnight it was like an empty freight-car rocking and reeling on an express run.'

He paused, took another drink of water, and then went on. His eyes were bright now.

'Well, well. Fuller would have put an end to it sooner or later. If it had been sooner, a lot less people would have died. All you had to do was send in MPs and have them confiscate all the bottles of liquor that people had brought in with them. That would have been good enough – just what he wanted, in fact. It would have shut us down good and proper. There would have been courtmartials and the stockade in Rye for some of us and transfers for all the rest. But Fuller was slow. I think he was afraid of the same thing some of us was afraid of – that some of the townies would be mad. Mueller hadn't been back to see him, and I think Major Fuller must have been scared to go downtown and see Mueller. He talked big, Fuller did, but he had all the spine of a jellyfish.

'So instead of the thing ending in some put-up way that would have at least left all those that burned up that night still alive, the Legion of Decency ended it. They came in their white sheets early that November and cooked themselves a barbecue.'

He fell silent again, not sipping at his water this time, only looking moodily into the far corner of his room while outside a bell dinged softly somewhere and a nurse passed the open doorway, the soles of her shoes squeaking on the linoleum. I could hear a TV someplace, a radio someplace else. I remember that I could hear the wind blowing outside, snuffling up the side of the building. And although it was August, the wind made a cold sound. It knew nothing of *Cain's Hundred* on the television, or the Four Seasons singing 'Walk Like a Man' on the radio.

'Some of them came through that greenbelt between the base and West Broadway,' he resumed at last. 'They must have met at someone's house over there, maybe in the basement, to get their sheets on and to make the torches that they used.

'I've heard that others came right onto the base by Ridgeline Road, which was the main way onto the base back then. I heard – I won't say where – that they came in a brand-new Packard automobile, dressed in their white sheets with their white goblinhats on their laps and torches on the floor. The torches were Louisville Sluggers with big hunks of burlap snugged down over the fat parts with red rubber gaskets, the kind ladies use when they put up preserves. There was a booth where Ridgeline Road branched off Witcham Road and came onto the base, and the OD passed that Packard right along.

'It was Saturday night and the joint was jumping, going round and round. There might have been two hundred people there, maybe three. And here came these white men, six or eight in their bottle-green Packard, and more coming through the trees between the base and the fancy houses on West Broadway. They wasn't young, not many of them, and sometimes I wonder how many cases of angina and bleeding ulcers there were the next day. I hope there was a lot. Those dirty sneaking murdering bastards.

'The Packard parked on the hill and flashed its lights twice. About four men got out of it and joined the rest. Some had those two-gallon tins of gasoline that you could buy at service stations back in those days. All of them had torches. One of em stayed behind the wheel of that Packard. Mueller had a Packard, you know. Yes he did. A green one.

'They got together at the back of the Black Spot and doused their torches with gas. Maybe they only meant to scare us. I've heard it the other way, but I've heard it that way, too. I'd rather believe that's how they meant it, because I ain't got feeling mean enough even yet to want to believe the worst.

'It could have been that the gas dripped down to the handles of some of those torches and when they lit them, why, those holding them panicked and threw them any whichway just to get rid of them.

Whatever, that black November night was suddenly blazing with torches. Some was holding em up and waving em around, little flaming pieces of burlap falling off'n the tops of em. Some of them were laughing. But like I say, some of the others up and threw em through the back windows, into what was our kitchen. The place was burning merry hell in a minute and a half.

'The men outside, they were all wearing their peaky white hoods by then. Some of them were chanting "Come out, niggers! Come out, niggers! Come out, niggers!" Maybe some of them were chanting to scare us, but I like to believe most of em were trying to warn us – same way as I like to believe that maybe those torches going into the kitchen the way they did was an accident.

'Either way, it didn't much matter. The band was playing louder'n a factory whistle. Everybody was whooping it up and having a good time. Nobody inside knew anything was wrong until Gerry McCrew, who was playing assistant cook that night, opened the door to the kitchen and damn near got blowtorched. Flames shot out ten feet and burned his messjacket right off. Burned most of his hair off as well.

'I was sitting about halfway down the east wall with Trev Dawson and Dick Hallorann when it happened, and at first I had an idea the gas stove had exploded. I'd no more than got on my feet when I was knocked down by people headed for the door. About two dozen of em went marchin right up my back, an I guess that was the only time during the whole thing when I really felt scared. I could hear people screamin and tellin each other they had to get out, the place was on fire. But every time I tried to get up, someone footed me right back down again. Someone landed his big shoe square on the back of my head and I saw stars. My nose mashed on that oiled floor and I snuffled up dirt and began to cough and sneeze at the same time. Someone else stepped on the small of my back. I felt a lady's high heel slam down between the cheeks of my butt, and son, I never want another half-ass enema like that one. If the seat of my khakis had ripped, I believe I'd be bleedin down there to this day.

'It sounds funny now, but I damn near died in that stampede. I was whopped, whapped, stomped, walked on, and kicked in so many places I couldn't walk 'tall the next day. I was screaming and none of those people topside heard me or paid any mind.

'It was Trev saved me. I seen this big brown hand in front of me and I grabbed it like a drownin man grabs a life preserver. I grabbed and he hauled and up I came. Someone's foot got me in the side of my neck right here –'

He massaged that area where the jaw turns up toward the ear, and I nodded.

'– and it hurt so bad that I guess I blacked out for a minute. But I never let go of Trev's hand, and he never let go of mine. I got to my feet, finally, just as the wall we'd put up between the kitchen and the hall fell over. It made a noise like – *floomp* – the noise a puddle of gasoline makes when you light it. I saw it go over in a big bundle of sparks, and I saw the people running to get out of its way as it fell. Some of em made it. Some didn't. One of our fellas – I think it might have been Hort Sartoris – was buried under it, and for just one second I seen his hand underneath all those blazing coals, openin and closin. There was a white girl, surely no more than twenty, and the back of her dress went up. She was with a college boy and I heard her screamin at him, beggin him to help her. He took just about two swipes at it and then ran away with the others. She stood there screamin as her dress went up on her.

It was like hell out where the kitchen had been. The flames was so bright you couldn't look at them. The heat was bakin hot, Mikey, roastin hot. You could feel your skin going shiny. You could feel the hairs in your nose gettin crispy.

'"We gotta break outta here!" Trev yells, and starts to drag me along the wall. "Come on!"

'Then Dick Hallorann catches hold of him. He couldn't have been no more than nineteen, and his eyes was as big as bil'ard balls, but he kept his head better than we did. He saved our lives. "Not that way!" he yells. "*This* way!" And he pointed back toward the bandstand . . . toward the fire, you know.

'"You're crazy!" Trevor screamed back. He had a big bull voice, but you could barely hear him over the thunder of the fire and the screaming people. "Die if you want to, but me and Willy are gettin' out!"

'He still had me by the hand and he started to haul me toward the door again, although there were so many people around it by then you couldn't see it at all. I would have gone with him. I was so shell-shocked I didn't know what end was up. All I knew was that I didn't want to be baked like a human turkey.

'Dick grabbed Trev by the hair of the head just as hard as he could, and when Trev turned back, Dick slapped his face. I remember seeing Trev's head bounce off the wall and thinking Dick had gone crazy. Then he was hollerin in Trev's face, "You go that way and you goan die! They jammed up against that door, nigger!"

'"You don't know that!" Trev screamed back at him, and then there was this loud *BANG*! like a firecracker, only what it was, it was the heat exploding Marty Devereaux's bass drum. The fire was runnin along the beams overhead and the oil on the floor was catchin.

'"I know it!" Dick screams back. "I know it!"

'He grabbed my other hand, and for a minute there I felt like the rope in a tug-o-war game. Then Trev took a good look at the door and went Dick's way. Dick got us down to a window and grabbed a chair to bust it out, but before he could swing it, the heat blew it out for him. Then he grabbed Trev Dawson by the back of his pants and hauled him up. "Climb!" he shouts. "*Climb*, motherfucker!" And Trev went, head up and tail over the dashboard.

'He boosted me next, and I went up. I grabbed the sides of the window and hauled. I had a good crop of blisters all over my palms the next day: that wood was already smokin. I come out headfirst, and if Trev hadn't grabbed me I mighta broke my neck.

'We turned back around, and it was like something from the worst nightmare you ever had, Mikey. That window was just a yellow, blazin square of light. Flames was shootin up through that tin roof in a dozen places. We could hear people screamin inside.

'I saw two brown hands waving around in front of the fire – Dick's hands. Trev Dawson made me a step with his own hands and I reached through that window and grabbed Dick. When I took his weight my gut went against the side of the building, and it was like having your belly against a stove that's just starting to get real good and hot. Dick's face came up and for a few seconds I didn't think we was going to be able to get him. He'd taken a right smart of smoke, and he was close to passing out. His lips had cracked open. The back of his shirt was smoldering.

'And then I damn near let go, because I could smell the people burning inside. I've heard people say that smell is like barbecuing pork ribs, but it ain't like that. It's more like what happens sometimes after they geld hosses. They build a big fire and throw all that shit into it and when the fire gets hot enough you can hear them hossballs poppin like chestnuts, and that's what people smell like when they start to cook right inside their clo'es. I could smell that and I knew I couldn't take it for long so I gave one more great big yank, and out came Dick. He lost one of his shoes.

'I tumbled off Trev's hands and went down. Dick come down on top of me, and I'm here to tell you that nigger's head was *hard*. I lost most of my breath and just laid there on the dirt for a few seconds, rolling around and holding my bellyguts.

'Presently I was able to get to my knees, then to my feet. And I seen these shapes running off toward the greenbelt. At first I thought they were ghosts, and then I seen shoes. By then it was so bright around the Black Spot it was like daylight. I seen shoes and understood it was men wearin sheets. One of them had fallen a little bit behind the others and I saw . . .'

He trailed off, licking his lips.

'What did you see, Daddy?' I asked.

'Never you mind,' he said. 'Give me my water, Mikey.'

I did. He drank most of it and then got coughing. A passing nurse looked in and said: 'Do you need anything, Mr Hanlon?'

'New set of 'testines,' my dad said. 'You got any handy, Rhoda?'

She smiled a nervous, doubtful smile and passed on. My dad handed the glass to me and I put it back on his table. 'It's longer tellin than it is rememberin,' he said. 'You goan fill that glass up for me before you leave?'

'Sure, Daddy.'

'This story goan give you nightmares, Mikey?'

I opened my mouth to lie, and then thought better of it. And I think now that if I had lied, he would have stopped right there. He was far gone by then, but maybe not that far gone.

'I guess so,' I said.

'That's not such a bad thing,' he said to me. 'In nightmares we can think the worst. That's what they're for, I guess.'

He reached out his hand and I took it and we held hands while he finished.

'I looked around just in time to see Trev and Dick goin around the front of the building, and I chased after them, still trying to catch m'wind. There was maybe forty or fifty people out there, some of them cryin, some of them pukin, some of them screamin, some of them doing all three things at once, it seemed like. Others were layin on the grass, fainted dead away with the smoke. The door was shut, and we heard people screamin on the other side, screamin to let them out, out for the love of Jesus, they were burning up.

'It was the only door, except for the one that went out through the kitchen to where the garbage cans and things were, you see. To go in you pushed the door open. To go out you had to pull it.

'Some people had gotten out, and then they started to jam up at that door and push. The door got slammed shut. The ones in the back kept pushin forward to get away from the fire, and everybody got jammed up. The ones right up front were squashed. Wasn't no way they could get that door open against the weight of all those behind. So there they were, trapped, and the fire raged.

'It was Trev Dawson that made it so it was only eighty or so that died instead of a hundred or maybe two hundred, and what he got for his pains wasn't a medal but two years in the Rye stockade. See, right about then this big old cargo truck pulled up, and who should be behind the wheel but my old friend Sergeant Wilson, the fella who owned all the holes there on the base.

'He gets out and starts shoutin orders that didn't make much sense and which people couldn't hear anyway. Trev grabbed my arm and we run over to him. I'd lost all track of Dick Halloran by then and didn't even see him until the next day.

"Sergeant, I have to use your truck!" Trev yells in his face.

'"Get out of my way, nigger," Wilson says, and pushes him down. Then he starts yelling all that confused shit again. Wasn't nobody paying any attention to him, and he didn't go on for long anyway, because Trevor Dawson popped up like a jack-in-the-box and decked him.

'Trev could hit damned hard, and almost any other man would have stayed down, but that cracker had a hard head. He got up, blood pouring out of his mouth and nose, and he said, "I'm goan kill you for that." Well, Trev hit him in the belly just as hard as he could, and when he doubled over I put my hands together and pounded the back of his neck just as hard as *I* could. It was a cowardly thing to do, hitting a man from behind like that, but desperate times call for desperate measures. And I would be lyin, Mikey, if I didn't tell you that hitting that poormouth sonofabitch didn't give me a bit of pleasure.

'Down he went, just like a steer hit with a poleaxe. Trev run to the truck, fired it up, and drove it around so it was facin the front of the Black Spot, but to the left of the door. He th'owed it into first, popped the clutch on that cocksucker, and here he come!

'"*Look out there!*" I shouted at that crowd of people standing around. "Ware that truck!"

'They scattered like quail, and for a wonder Trev didn't hit none of em. He hit the side of the building going maybe thirty, and cracked his face a good one on the steerin wheel of the truck. I seen the blood fly from his nose when he shook his head to clear it. He punched out reverse, backed up fifty yards, and come down on her again. *WHAM!*

The Black Spot wasn't nothing but corrugated tin, and that second hit did her. The whole side of that oven fell in and the flames come roarin out. How *anything* could have still been alive in there I don't know, but there was. People are a lot tougher than you'd believe, Mikey, and if you don't believe it, just take a look at me, slidin off the skin of the world by my fingernails. That place was like a smelting furnace, it was a hell of flames and smoke, but people came running out in a regular torrent. There were so many that Trev didn't even dare back the truck up again for fear he would run over some of them. So he got out and ran back to me, leaving it where it was.

'We stood there, watching it end. It hadn't been five minutes all told, but it felt like forever. The last dozen or so that made it out were on fire. People grabbed em and started to roll em around on the ground, trying to put em out. Looking in, we could see other people trying to come, and we knew they wasn't never going to make it.

'Trev grabbed my hand and I grabbed him back twice as hard. We stood there holding hands just like you and me are doing now, Mikey, him with his nose broke and blood running down his face and his eyes puffing shut, and we watched them people. *They* were the real ghosts we saw that night, nothing but shimmers shaped like men and women in that fire, walking toward the opening Trev had bashed with Sergeant Wilson's truck. Some of em had their arms held out, like they expected someone to save them. The others just walked, but they didn't seem to get nowhere. Their clo'es were blazin. Their faces were runnin. And one after another they just toppled over and you didn't see them no more.

'The last one was a woman. Her dress had burned off her and there she was in her slip. She was burnin like a candle. She seemed to look right at me at the end, and I seen her eyelids was on fire.

'When she fell down it was over. The whole place went up in a pillar of fire. By the time the base firetrucks and two more from the Main Street fire station got there, it was already burning itself out. That was the fire at the Black Spot, Mikey.'

He drank the last of his water and handed me the glass to fill at the drinking fountain in the hall. 'Goan piss the bed tonight I guess, Mikey.'

I kissed his cheek and then went out into the hall to fill his glass. When I returned, he was drifting away again, his eyes glassy and contemplative. When I put the glass on the nighttable, he mumbled a thank-you I could barely understand. I looked at the Westclox on his table and saw it was almost eight. Time for me to go home.

I leaned over to kiss him goodbye . . . and instead heard myself whisper, 'What did you see?'

His eyes, which were now slipping shut, barely turned toward the sound of my voice. He might have known it was me, or he might have believed he was hearing the voice of his own thoughts. 'Hunk?'

'The thing you saw,' I whispered. I didn't want to hear, but I *had* to hear. I was both hot and cold, my eyes burning, my hands freezing. But I had to hear. As I suppose Lot's wife had to turn back and look at the destruction of Sodom.

''Twas a bird,' he said. 'Right over the last of those runnin men. A hawk, maybe. What they call a kestrel. But it was big. Never told no one. Would have been locked up. That bird was maybe sixty feet from wingtip to wingtip. It was the size of a Japanese Zero. But I seen . . . seen its eyes . . . and I think . . . it seen me . . .'

His head slipped over to the side, toward the window, where the dark was coming.

'It swooped down and grabbed that last man up. Got him right by the sheet, it did . . . and I heard that bird's wings . . . The sound was like fire . . . and it hovered . . . and I thought, Birds can't hover . . . but this one could, because . . . because . . .'

He fell silent.

'Why, Daddy?' I whispered. 'Why could it hover?'

'It didn't hover,' he said.

I sat there in silence, thinking he had gone to sleep for sure this time. I had never been so afraid in my life . . . because four years before, I had seen that bird. Somehow, in some unimaginable way, I had nearly forgotten that nightmare. It was my father who brought it back.

'It didn't hover,' he said. 'It floated. It floated. There were big bunches of balloons tied to each wing, and it floated.'

My father went to sleep.

March 1st, 1985

It's come again. I know that now. I'll wait, but in my heart I know it. I'm not sure I can stand it. As a kid I was able to deal with it, but it's different with kids. In some fundamental way it's different.

I wrote all of that last night in a kind of frenzy – not that I could have gone home anyway. Derry has been blanketed in a thick glaze of ice, and although the sun is out this morning, nothing is moving.

I wrote until long after three this morning, pushing the pen faster and faster, trying to get it all out. I had forgotten about seeing the giant bird when I was eleven. It was my father's story that brought it back . . . and I never forgot it again. Not any of it. In a way, I suppose it was his final gift to me. A terrible gift, you would say, but wonderful in its way.

I slept right where I was, my head in my arms, my notebook and pen on the table in front of me. I woke up this morning with a numb ass and an aching back, but feeling free, somehow . . . purged of that old story.

And then I saw that I had had company in the night, as I slept.

The tracks, drying to faint muddy impressions, led from the front door of the library (which I locked; I always lock it) to the desk where I slept.

There were no tracks leading away.

Whatever it was, it came to me in the night, left its talisman . . . and then simply disappeared.

Tied to my reading lamp was a single balloon. Filled with helium, it floated in a morning sunray which slanted in through one of the high windows.

On it was a picture of my face, the eyes gone, blood running down from the ragged sockets, a scream distorting the mouth on the balloon's thin and bulging rubber skin.

I looked at it and I screamed. The scream echoed through the library, echoing back, vibrating from the circular iron staircase leading to the stacks.

The balloon burst with a bang.

PART 3

GROWNUPS

'The descent
made up of despairs
and without accomplishment
realizes a new awakening:
which is a reversal
of despair.

For what we cannot accomplish, what
is denied to love,
what we have lost in the anticipation –
a descent follows,
endless and indestructible.'
                    – William Carlos Williams,
                              Paterson

'Don't it make you wanta go home, now?
Don't it make you wanta go home?
All God's children get weary when they roam,
Don't it make you wanta go home?'
                              – Joe South

CHAPTER TEN
THE REUNION

1

Bill Denbrough Gets a Cab

The telephone was ringing, bringing him up and out of a sleep too deep for dreams. He groped for it without opening his eyes, without coming more than halfway awake. If it had stopped ringing just then he would have slipped back down into sleep without a hitch; he would have done it as simply and easily as he had once slipped down the snow-covered hills in McCarron Park on his Flexible Flyer. You ran with the sled, threw yourself onto it, and down you went – seemingly at the speed of sound. You couldn't do that as a grownup; it racked the hell out of your balls.

His fingers walked over the telephone's dial, slipped off, climbed it again. He had a dim premonition that it would be Mike Hanlon, Mike Hanlon calling from Derry, telling him he had to come back, telling him he had to remember, telling him they had made a promise, Stan Uris had cut their palms with a sliver of Coke bottle and they had made a promise –

Except all of that had already happened.

He had gotten in late yesterday afternoon – just before 6 P.M., actually. He supposed that, if he had been the last call on Mike's list, all of them must have gotten in at varying times; some might even have spent most of the day here. He himself had seen none of them, felt no urge to see any of them. He had simply checked in, gone up to his room, ordered a meal from room service which he found he could not eat once it was laid out before him, and then had tumbled into bed and slept dreamlessly until now.

Bill cracked one eye open and fumbled for the telephone's handset. It fell off onto the table and he groped for it, opening his other eye. He felt totally blank inside his head, totally unplugged, running on batteries.

He finally managed to scoop up the phone. He got up on one elbow and put it against his ear. 'Hello?'

'Bill?' It *was* Mike Hanlon's voice – he'd had at least that much right. Last week he didn't remember Mike at all, and now a single word was enough to identify him. It was rather marvellous . . . but in an ominous way.

'Yeah, Mike.'

'Woke you up, huh?'

'Yeah, you did. That's okay.' On the wall above the TV was an abysmal painting of lobstermen in yellow slickers and rainhats pulling lobster traps. Looking at it, Bill remembered where he was: the Derry Town House on Upper Main Street. Half a mile farther up and across the street was Bassey Park . . . the Kissing Bridge . . . the Canal. 'What time is it, Mike?'

'Quarter of ten.'

'What day?'

'The 30th.' Mike sounded a little amused.

'Yeah. 'Kay.'

'I've arranged a little reunion,' Mike said. He sounded diffident now.

'Yeah?' Bill swung his legs out of bed. 'They all came?'

'All but Stan Uris,' Mike said. Now there was something in his voice that Bill couldn't read. 'Bev was the last one. She got in late last evening.'

'Why do you say the last one, Mike? Stan might show up today.'

'Bill, Stan's dead.'

'What? How? Did his plane –'

'Nothing like that,' Mike said. 'Look, if it's all the same to you, I think it ought to wait until we get together. It would be better if I could tell all of you at the same time.'

'It has to do with this?'

'Yes, I think so.' Mike paused briefly. 'I'm sure it does.'

Bill felt the familiar weight of dread settle around his heart again – was it something you could get used to so quickly, then? Or had it been something he had carried all along, simply unfelt and unthought-of, like the inevitable fact of his own death?

He reached for his cigarettes, lit one, and blew out the match with the first drag.

'None of them got together, yesterday?'

'No – I don't believe so.'

'And you haven't seen any of us yet?'

'No – just talked to you on the phone.'

'Okay,' he said. 'Where's the reunion?'

'You remember where the old Ironworks used to be?'

'Pasture Road, sure.'

'You're behind the times, old chum. That's Mall Road these days. We've got the third-biggest shopping mall in the state out there. Forty-eight Different Merchants Under One Roof for Your Shopping Convenience.'

'Sounds really A-A-American, all right.'

'Bill?'

'What?'

'You all right?'

'Yes.' But his heart was beating too fast, the tip of his cigarette jittering a tiny bit. He had stuttered. Mike had heard it.

There was a moment of silence and then Mike said, 'Just out past the mall, there's a restaurant called Jade of the Orient. They have private rooms for parties. I arranged for one of them yesterday. We can have it the whole afternoon, if we want it.'

'You think this might take that long?'

'I just don't know.'

'A cab will know how to get there?'

'Sure.'

'All right,' Bill said. He wrote the name of the restaurant down on the pad by the phone. 'Why there?'

'Because it's new, I guess,' Mike said slowly. 'It seemed like . . . I don't know . . .'

'Neutral ground?' Bill suggested.

'Yes. I guess that's it.'

'Food any good?'

'I don't know,' Mike said. 'How's your appetite?'

Bill chuffed out smoke and half-laughed, half-coughed. 'It ain't so good, ole pal.'

'Yeah,' Mike said. 'I hear you.'

'Noon?'

'More like one, I guess. We'll let Beverly catch a few more z's.'

Bill snuffed the cigarette. 'She married?'

Mike hesitated again. 'We'll catch up on everything,' he said.

'Just like when you go back to your high-school reunion ten years later, huh?' Bill said. 'You get to see who got fat, who got bald, who got k-kids.'

'I wish it was like that,' Mike said.

'Yeah. Me too, Mikey. Me too.'

He hung up the phone, took a long shower, and ordered a breakfast that he didn't want and which he only picked at. No; his appetite was really not much good at all.

Bill dialed the Big Yellow Cab Company and asked to be picked up at quarter of one, thinking that fifteen minutes would be plenty of time to get him out to Pasture Road (he found himself totally unable to think of it as Mall Road, even when he actually saw the mall), but he had underestimated the lunch-hour traffic-flow . . . and how much Derry had grown.

In 1958 it had been a big town, not much more. There were maybe thirty thousand people inside the Derry incorporated city limits and maybe another seven thousand beyond that in the surrounding burgs.

Now it had become a city – a very small city by London or New York standards, but doing just fine by Maine standards, where Portland, the state's largest, could boast barely three hundred thousand.

As the cab moved slowly down Main Street (*we're over the Canal now*, Bill thought; *can't see it, but it's down there, running in the dark*) and then turned up Center, his first thought was predictable enough: how much had changed. But the predictable thought was accompanied by a deep dismay that he never would have expected. He remembered his childhood here as a fearful, nervous time . . . not only because of the summer of '58, when the seven of them had faced the terror, but because of George's death, the deep dream his parents seemed to have fallen into following that death, the constant ragging about his stutter, Bowers and Huggins and Criss constantly on the prod for them after the rockfight in the Barrens

(*Bowers and Huggins and Criss, oh my! Bowers and Huggins and Criss, oh my!*)

and just a feeling that Derry was cold, that Derry was hard, that Derry didn't much give a shit if any of them lived or died, and certainly not if they triumphed over Pennywise the Clown. Derryfolk had lived with Pennywise in all his guises for a long time . . . and maybe, in some mad way, they had even come to understand him. To like him, need him. *Love* him? Maybe. Yes, maybe that too.

So why this dismay?

Perhaps only because it seemed such *dull* change, somehow. Or perhaps because Derry seemed to have lost its essential face for him.

The Bijou Theater was gone, replaced with a parking lot (BY

PERMIT ONLY, the sign over the ramp announced; VIOLATORS SUBJECT TO TOW). The Shoeboat and Bailley's Lunch, which had stood next to it, were also gone. They had been replaced by a branch of the Northern National Bank. A digital readout jutted from the front of the bland cinderblock structure, showing the time and the temperature – the latter in both degrees Fahrenheit and degrees Celsius. The Center Street Drug, lair of Mr Keene and the place where Bill had gotten Eddie his asthma medicine that day, was also gone. Richard's Alley had become some strange hybrid called a 'mini-mall.' Looking inside as the cab idled at a stoplight, Bill could see a record shop, a natural-foods store, and a toys-and-games shop which was featuring a clearance sale on ALL DUNGEONS AND DRAGONS SUPPLIES.

The cab pulled forward with a jerk. 'Gonna take awhile,' the driver said. 'I wish all these goddam banks would stagger their lunch-hours. Pardon my French if you're a religious man.'

'That's all right,' Bill said. It was overcast outside, and now a few splatters of rain hit the cab's windshield. The radio muttered about an escaped mental patient from somewhere who was supposed to be very dangerous, and then began muttering about the Red Sox who weren't. Showers early, then clearing. When Barry Manilow began moaning about Mandy, who came and who gave without taking, the cabbie snapped the radio off. Bill asked, 'When did they go up?'

'What? The banks?'

'Uh-huh.'

'Oh, late sixties, early seb'nies, most of em,' the cabbie said. He was a big man with a thick neck. He wore a red-and-black-checked hunter's jacket. A fluorescent-orange cap was jammed down squarely on his head. It was smudged with engine-oil. 'They got this urban-renewal money. Reb 'nue Sharin, they call it. So how they shared it was rip down everythin. And the banks come in. I guess that was all that could afford to come in. Hell of a note, ain't it? Urban renewal, says they. Shit for dinner, says I. Pardon my French if you're a religious man. There was a lot of talk about how they was gonna revitalize the downtown. Ayup, they revitalized it just fine. Tore down most the old stores and put up a lot of banks and parking lots. And you know you still can't find a fucking slot to park your car in. Ought to string the whole City Council up by their cocks. Except for that Polock woman that's on it. String her up by her tits. On second thought, it don't seem like she's got any. Flat as a fuckin board. Pardon my French if you're a religious man.'

'I am,' Bill said, grinning.

'Then get outta my cab and go to fucking church,' the cabbie said, and they both burst out laughing.

'You lived here long?' Bill asked.

'My whole life. Born in Derry Home Hospital, and they'll bury my fuckin remains out in Mount Hope Cemetery.'

'Good deal,' Bill said.

'Yeah, right,' the cabbie said. He hawked, rolled down his window, and spat an extremely large yellow-green lunger into the rainy air. His attitude, contradictory but somehow attractive – almost piquant – was one of glum good cheer. 'Guy who catches that won't have to buy no fuckin chewing gum for a week. Pardon my French if you're a religious man.'

'It hasn't all changed,' Bill said. The depressing promenade of banks and parking lots was slipping behind them as they climbed Center Street. Over the hill and past the First National, they began to pick up some speed. 'The Aladdin's still there.'

'Yeah,' the cabbie conceded. 'But just barely. Suckers tried to tear that down, too.'

'For another bank?' Bill asked, a part of him amused to find that another part of him stood aghast at the idea. He couldn't believe that anyone in his right mind would want to tear down that stately pleasure dome with its glittering glass chandelier, its sweeping right-and-left staircases which spiraled up to the balcony, and its mammoth curtain, which did not simply pull apart when the show started but which instead rose in magical folds and tucks and gathers, all underlit in fabulous shades of red and blue and yellow and green while pulleys off stage ratcheted and groaned. *Not the Aladdin*, that shocked part of him cried out. *How could they ever even think of tearing down the Aladdin for a BANK?*

'Oh, ayup, a bank,' the cabbie said. 'You're fucking-A, pardon my French if you're a religious man. It was the First Merchants of Penobscot County had its eye on the 'laddin. Wanted to pull it down and put up what they called a "complete banking mall." Got all the papers from the City Council, and the Aladdin was condemned. Then a bunch of folks formed a committee – folks that had lived here a long time – and they petitioned, and they marched, and they hollered, and finally they had a public City Council meeting about it, and Hanlon blew those suckers out.' The cabbie sounded extremely satisfied.

'Hanlon?' Bill asked, startled. '*Mike* Hanlon?'

'Ayup,' the cabbie said. He twisted around briefly to look at Bill, revealing a round, chapped face and horn-rimmed glasses with old specks of white paint on the bows. 'Librarian. Black fella. You know him?'

'I did,' Bill said, remembering how he had met Mike, back in July 1958. It had been Bowers and Huggins and Criss again . . . of course. Bowers and Huggins and Criss

(*oh my*)

at every turn, playing their own part, unwitting visegrips driving the seven of them together – tight, tighter, tightest. 'We played together when we were kids. Before I moved away.'

'Well, there you go,' the cabbie said. 'It's a small fucking world, pardon my –'

'– French if you're a religious man,' Bill finished with him.

'There you go,' the cabbie repeated comfortably, and they rode in silence for awhile before he said, 'It's changed a lot, Derry has, but yeah, a lot of it's still here. The Town House, where I picked you up. The Standpipe in Memorial Park. You remember that place, mister? When we were kids, we used to think that place was haunted.'

'I remember it,' Bill said.

'Look, there's the hospital. You recognize it?'

They were passing the Derry Home Hospital on the right now. Behind it, the Penobscot flowed toward its meeting-place with the Kenduskeag. Under the rainy spring sky, the river was dull pewter. The hospital that Bill remembered – a white woodframe building with two wings, three stories high – was still there, but now it was surrounded, dwarfed, by a whole complex of buildings, maybe a dozen in all. He could see a parking-lot off to the left, and what looked like better than five hundred cars parked there.

'My God, that's not a hospital, that's a fucking college campus!' Bill exclaimed.

The cab-driver cackled. 'Not bein a religious man, I'll pardon your French. Yeah, it's almost as big as the Eastern Maine up in Bangor now. They got radiation labs and a therapy center and six hundred rooms and their own laundry and God knows what else. The old hospital's still there, but it's all administration now.'

Bill felt a queer doubling sensation in his mind, the sort of sensation he remembered getting the first time he watched a 3–D movie. Trying to bring together two images that didn't quite jibe. You could fool your eyes and your brain into doing that trick, he remembered, but you were apt to end up with a whopper of a headache . . . and he could feel his own headache coming on now. New Derry, fine. But the old Derry was still here, like the wooden Home Hospital

451

building. The old Derry was mostly buried under all the new construction ... but your eye was somehow dragged helplessly back to look at it ... to look *for* it.

'The trainyard's probably gone, isn't it?' Bill asked.

The cabbie laughed again, delighted. 'For someone who moved away when he was just a kid, you got a good memory, mister.' Bill thought: *You should have met me last week, my French-speaking friend.* 'It's all still out there, but it's nothing but ruins and rusty tracks now. The freights don't even stop no more. Fella wanted to buy the land and put up a whole roadside entertainment thing – pitch 'n putt, batting cages, driving ranges, mini golf, go-karts, little shack fulla video games, I don't know whatall – but there's some kind of big mixup about who owns the land now. I guess he'll get it eventually – he's a persistent fella – but right now it's in the courts.'

'And the Canal,' Bill murmured as they turned off Outer Center Street and onto Pasture Road – which, as Mike had said, was now marked with a green roadsign reading MALL ROAD. 'The Canal's still here.'

'Ayup,' the cabbie said. 'That'll always be here, I guess.'

Now the Derry Mall was on Bill's left, and as they rolled past it, he felt that queer doubling sensation again. When they had been kids all of this had been a great long field full of rank grasses and gigantic nodding sunflowers which marked the northeastern end of the Barrens. Behind it, to the west, was the Old Cape low-income housing development. He could remember them exploring this field, being careful not to fall into the gaping cellarhold of the Kitchener Ironworks, which had exploded on Easter Sunday in the year 1906. The field had been full of relics and they had unearthed them with all the solemn interest of archaeologists exploring Egyptian ruins: bricks, dippers, chunks of iron with rusty bolts hanging from them, panes of glass, bottles full of unnamable gunk that smelled like the worst poison in the world. Something bad had happened near here, too, in the gravel-pit close to the dump, but he could not remember it yet. He could only remember a name, Patrick Humboldt, and that it had something to do with a refrigerator. And something about a bird that had chased Mike Hanlon. What ... ?

He shook his head. Fragments. Straws in the wind. That was all.

The field was gone now, as were the remains of the Ironworks. Bill remembered the great chimney of the Ironworks suddenly. Faced with tile, caked black with soot for the final ten feet of its length, it had lain in the high grass like a gigantic pipe. They had scrambled up somehow and had walked along it, arms held out like tightwire walkers, laughing – He shook his head, as if to dismiss the mirage of the mall, an ugly collection of buildings with signs that said SEARS and J. C. PENNEY and WOOLWORTH'S and CVS and YORK'S STEAK HOUSE and WALDENBOOKS and dozens of others. Roads wove in and out of parking lots. The mall did not go away, because it was no mirage. The Kitchener Ironworks was gone, and the field that had grown up around its ruins was likewise gone. The mall was the reality, not the memories.

But somehow he didn't believe that.

'Here you go, mister,' the cabbie said. He pulled into the parking-lot of a building that looked like a large plastic pagoda. 'A little late, but better late than never, am I right?'

'Indeed you are,' Bill said. He gave the cab-driver a five. 'Keep the change.'

'Good fucking deal!' the cabbie exclaimed. 'You need someone to drive you, call Big Yellow and ask for Dave. Ask for me by name.'

'I'll just ask for the religious fella,' Bill said, grinning. 'The one who's got his plot all picked out in Mount Hope.'

'You got it,' Dave said, laughing. 'Have a good one, mister.'

'You too, Dave.'

He stood in the light rain for a moment, watching the cab draw away. He realized that he had meant to ask the driver one more question, and had forgotten – perhaps on purpose.

He had meant to ask Dave if he *liked* living in Derry.

Abruptly, Bill Denbrough turned and walked into the Jade of the Orient. Mike Hanlon was in the lobby, sitting in a wicker chair with a huge flaring back. He got to his feet, and Bill felt deep unreality wash over him – *through* him. That sensation of doubling was back, but now it was much, much worse.

He remembered a boy who had been about five feet three, trim, and agile. Before him was a man who stood about five-seven. He was skinny. His clothes seemed to hang on him. And the lines in his face said that he was on the darker side of forty instead of only thirty-eight or so.

Bill's shock must have shown on his face, because Mike said quietly: 'I know how I look.'

Bill flushed and said, 'It's not that bad, Mike, it's just that I remember you as a kid. That's all it is.'

'Is it?'

'You look a little tired.'

'I *am* a little tired,' Mike said, 'but I'll make it. I guess.' He

453

smiled then, and the smile lit his face. In it Bill saw the boy he had known twenty-seven years ago. As the old woodframe Home Hospital had been overwhelmed with modern glass and cinderblock, so had the boy that Bill had known been overwhelmed with the inevitable accessories of adulthood. There were wrinkles on his forehead, lines had grooved themselves from the corners of his mouth nearly to his chin, and his hair was graying on both sides above the ears. But as the old hospital, although overwhelmed, was still there, still visible, so was the boy Bill had known.

Mike stuck out his hand and said, 'Welcome back to Derry, Big Bill.'

Bill ignored the hand and embraced Mike. Mike hugged him back fiercely, and Bill could feel his hair, stiff and kinky, against his own shoulder and the side of his neck.

'Whatever's wrong, Mike, we'll take care of it,' Bill said. He heard the rough sound of tears in his throat and didn't care. 'We beat it once, and we can b-beat it a-a-again.'

Mike pulled away from him, held him at arm's length; although he was still smiling, there was too much sparkle in his eyes. He took out his handkerchief and wiped them. 'Sure, Bill,' he said. 'You bet.'

'Would you gentlemen like to follow me?' the hostess asked. She was a smiling Oriental woman in a delicate pink kimono upon which a dragon cavorted and curled its plated tail. Her dark hair was piled high on her head and held with ivory combs.

'I know the way, Rose,' Mike said.

'Very good, Mr Hanlon.' She smiled at both of them. 'You are well met in friendship, I think.'

'I think we are,' Mike said. 'This way, Bill.'

He led him down a dim corridor, past the main dining room and toward a door where a beaded curtain hung.

'The others –?' Bill began.

'All here now,' Mike said. 'All that could come.'

Bill hesitated for a moment outside the door, suddenly frightened. It was not the unknown that scared him, not the supernatural; it was the simple knowledge that he was fifteen inches taller than he had been in 1958 and minus most of his hair. He was suddenly uneasy – almost terrified – at the thought of seeing them all again, their children's faces almost worn away, almost buried under change as the old hospital had been buried. Banks erected inside their heads where once magic picture-palaces had stood.

We grew up, he thought. *We didn't think it would happen, not then, not to us. But it did, and if I go in there it will be real: we're all grownups now.*

He looked at Mike, suddenly bewildered and timid. 'How do they look?' he heard himself asking in a faltering voice. 'Mike . . . how do they look?'

'Come in and find out,' Mike said, kindly enough, and led Bill into the small private room.

2

Bill Denbrough Gets a Look

Perhaps it was simply the dimness of the room that caused the illusion, which lasted for only the briefest moment, but Bill wondered later if it wasn't some sort of message meant strictly for him: that fate could also be kind.

In that brief moment it seemed to him that *none* of them had grown up, that his friends had somehow done a Peter Pan act and were all still children.

Richie Tozier was rocked back in his chair so that he was leaning against the wall, caught in the act of saying something to Beverly Marsh, who had a hand cupped over her mouth to hide a giggle; Richie had a wise-ass grin on his face that was perfectly familiar. There was Eddie Kaspbrak, sitting on Beverly's left, and in front of him on the table, next to his water-glass, was a plastic squeeze-bottle with a pistol-grip handle curving down from its top. The trimmings were a little more state-of-the-art, but the purpose was obviously the same: it was an aspirator. Sitting at one end of the table, watching this trio with an expression of mixed anxiety, amusement, and concentration, was Ben Hanscom.

Bill found his hand wanting to go to his head and realized with a sorry kind of amusement that in that second he had almost rubbed his pate to see if his hair had magically come back – that red, fine hair that he had begun to lose when he was only a college sophomore.

That broke the bubble. Richie was not wearing glasses, he saw, and thought: *He probably has contacts now – he would. He hated those glasses.* The tee-shirts and cord pants he'd habitually worn had been replaced by a suit that hadn't been purchased off any rack – Bill estimated that he was looking at nine hundred dollars' worth of tailor-made on the hoof.

Beverly Marsh (if her name still *was* Marsh) had become a

stunningly beautiful woman. Instead of the casual pony-tail, her hair – which was almost exactly the same shade his own had been – spilled over the shoulders of her plain white Ship 'n Shore blouse in a torrent of subdued color. In this dim light it merely glowed like a well-banked bed of embers. In daylight, even the light of such a subdued day as this one, Bill imagined it would flame. And he found himself wondering what it would feel like to plunge his hands into that hair. *The world's oldest story*, he thought wryly. *I love my wife but oh you kid.*

Eddie – it was weird but true – had grown up to look quite a little bit like Anthony Perkins. His face was prematurely lined (although in his movements he seemed somehow younger than either Richie or Ben) and made older still by the rimless spectacles he wore – spectacles you would imagine a British barrister wearing as he approached the bench or leafed through a legal brief. His hair was short, worn in an out-of-date style that had been known as Ivy League in the late fifties and early sixties. He was wearing a loud checked sportcoat that looked like something grabbed from the Distress Sale rack of a men's clothing store that would shortly be out of business . . . but the watch on one wrist was a Patek Philippe, and the ring on the little finger of his right hand was a ruby. The stone was too hugely vulgar and too ostentatious to be anything but real.

Ben was the one who had really changed, and, looking at him again, Bill felt unreality wash easily over him. His face was the same, and his hair, although graying and longer, was combed in the same unusual right-side part. But Ben had gotten thin. He sat easily enough in his chair, his unadorned leather vest open to show the blue chambray work-shirt beneath. He wore Levi's with straight legs, cowboy boots, and a wide belt with a beaten-silver buckle. These clothes clung easily to a body which was slim and narrow-hipped. He wore a bracelet with heavy links on one wrist – not gold links but copper ones. *He got thin*, Bill thought. *He's a shadow of his former self so to speak . . . Ole Ben got thin. Wonders never cease.*

There was a moment of silence among the six of them that was beyond description. It was one of the strangest moments Bill Denbrough ever passed in his life. Stan was not here, but a seventh had come, nonetheless. Here in this private restaurant dining room Bill felt its presence so fully that it was almost personified – but not as an old man in a white robe with a scythe on his shoulder. It was the white spot on the map which lay between 1958 and 1985, an area an explorer might have called the Great Don't Know. Bill wondered what exactly was there.

Beverly Marsh in a short skirt which showed most of her long, coltish legs, a Beverly Marsh in white go-go boots, her hair parted in the middle and ironed? Richie Tozier carrying a sign which said STOP THE WAR on one side and GET ROTC OFF CAMPUS on the other? Ben Hanscom in a yellow hard-hat with a flag decal on the front, running a bulldozer under a canvas parasol, his shirt off, showing a stomach which protruded less and less over the waistband of his pants? Was this seventh creature black? No relation to either H. Rap Brown or Grandmaster Flash, not this fellow, this fellow wore plain white shirts and fade-into-the-woodwork J. C. Penney slacks, and he sat in a library carrell at the University of Maine, writing papers on the origin of footnotes and the possible advantages of ISBN numbers in book cataloguing while the marchers marched outside and Phil Ochs sang 'Richard Nixon find yourself another country to be part of' and men died with their stomachs blown out for villages whose names they could not pronounce; he sat there studiously bent over his work (Bill *saw* him), which lay in a slant of crisp white winterlight, his face sober and absorbed, knowing that to be a librarian was to come as close as any human being can to sitting in the peak-seat of eternity's engine. Was he the seventh? Or was it a young man standing before his mirror, looking at the way his forehead was growing, looking at a combful of pulled-out red hairs, looking at a pile of university notebooks on the desk reflected in the mirror, notebooks which held the completed, messy first draft of a novel entitled *Joanna*, which would be published a year later?

Some of the above, all of the above, none of the above.

It didn't matter, really. The seventh was there, and in that one moment they all felt it . . . and perhaps understood best the dreadful power of the thing that had brought them back. *It lives*, Bill thought, cold inside his clothes. *Eye of newt, tail of dragon, Hand of Glory . . . whatever It was, It's here again, in Derry. It.*

And he felt suddenly that *It* was the seventh; that It and time were somehow interchangeable, that It wore all their faces as well as the thousand others with which It had terrified and killed . . . and the idea that *It* might be *them* was somehow the most frightening idea of all. *How much of us was left behind here?* he thought with sudden rising terror. *How much of us never left the drains and the sewers where It lived . . . and where It fed? Is that why we forgot? Because part of each of us never had any future, never grew, never left Derry? Is that why?*

He saw no answers on their faces . . . only his own questions reflected back at him.

Thoughts form and pass in a matter of seconds or milliseconds, and create their own time-frames, and all of this passed through Bill Denbrough's mind in a space of no more than five seconds.

Then Richie Tozier, leaning back against the wall, grinned again and said: 'Oh my, look at this – Bill Denbrough went for the chrome dome look. How long you been Turtle Waxing your head, Big Bill?'

And Bill, with no idea at all of what might come out, opened his mouth and heard himself say: 'Fuck you and the horse you rode in on, Trashmouth.'

There was a moment of silence – and then the room exploded with laughter. Bill crossed to them and began to shake hands, and while there was something horrible in what he now felt, there was also something comforting about it: this sensation of having come home for good.

3

Ben Hanscom Gets Skinny

Mike Hanlon ordered drinks, and as if to make up for the prior silence, everyone began to talk at once. Beverly Marsh was now Beverly Rogan, it turned out. She said she was married to a wonderful man in Chicago who had turned her whole life around and who had, by some benign magic, been able to transform his wife's simple talent for sewing into a successful dress business. Eddie Kaspbrak owned a limousine company in New York. 'For all I know, my wife could be in bed with Al Pacino right now,' he said, smiling mildly, and the room broke up.

They all knew what Bill and Ben had been up to, but Bill had a peculiar sense that there had been no personal association of their names – Ben as an architect, himself as a writer – with people they had known as children until very, very recently. Beverly had paperback copies of *Joanna* and *The Black Rapids* in her purse, and asked him if he would sign them. Bill did so, noticing as he did that both books were in mint condition – as if they had been purchased in the airport newsstand as she got off the plane.

In like fashion, Richie told Ben how much he had admired the BBC communications center in London . . . but there was a puzzled sort of light in his eyes, as if he could not quite reconcile that building with this man . . . or with the fat earnest boy who had showed them how to flood out half the Barrens with scrounged boards and a rusty car door.

Richie was a disc jockey in California. He told them he was

known as the Man of a Thousand Voices and Bill groaned. 'God, Richie, your Voices were always so *terrible*.'

'Flattery will get you nowhere, mawster,' Richie replied loftily.

When Beverly asked him if he wore contacts now, Richie said in a low voice, 'Come a little closer, bay-bee. Look in my eyes.' Beverly did, and exclaimed delightedly as Richie tilted his head a little so she could see the lower rims of the Hydromist soft lenses he wore.

'Is the library still the same?' Ben asked Mike Hanlon.

Mike took out his wallet and produced a snap of the library, taken from above. He did it with the proud air of a man producing snapshots of his kids when asked about his family. 'Guy in a light plane took this,' he said, as the picture went from hand to hand. 'I've been trying to get either the City Council or some well-heeled private donor to supply enough cash to get it blown up to mural size for the Children's Library. So far, no soap. But it's a good picture, huh?'

They all agreed that it was. Ben held it longest, looking at it fixedly. Finally he tapped the glass corridor which connected the two buildings. 'Do you recognize this from anywhere else, Mike?'

Mike smiled. 'It's your communications center,' he said, and all six of them burst out laughing.

The drinks came. They sat down.

That silence, sudden, awkward, and perplexing, fell again. They looked at each other.

'Well?' Beverly asked in her sweet, slightly husky voice. 'What do we drink to?'

'To us,' Richie said suddenly. And now he wasn't smiling. His eyes caught Bill's and with a force so great he could barely deal with it, Bill remembered himself and Richie in the middle of Neibolt Street, after the thing which might have been a clown or which might have been a werewolf had disappeared, embracing each other and weeping. When he picked up his glass, his hand was trembling, and some of his drink spilled on the napery.

Richie rose slowly to his feet, and one by one the others followed suit: Bill first, then Ben and Eddie, Beverly, and finally Mike Hanlon. 'To us,' Richie said, and like Bill's hand, his voice trembled a little. 'To the Losers' Club of 1958.'

'The Losers,' Beverly said, slightly amused.

'The Losers,' Eddie said. His face was pale and old behind his rimless glasses.

'The Losers,' Ben agreed. A faint and painful smile ghosted at the corners of his mouth.

'The Losers,' Mike Hanlon said softly.

'The Losers,' Bill finished.

Their glasses touched. They drank.

That silence fell again, and this time Richie did not break it. This time the silence seemed necessary.

They sat back down and Bill said, 'So spill it, Mike. Tell us what's been happening here, and what we can do.'

'Eat first,' Mike said. 'We'll talk afterward.'

So they ate . . . and they ate long and well. Like that old joke about the condemned man, Bill thought, but his own appetite was better than it had been in ages . . . since he was a kid, he was tempted to think. The food was not stunningly good, but it was far from bad, and there was a lot of it. The six of them began trading stuff back and forth – spareribs, *moo goo gaipan*, chicken wings that had been delicately braised, egg rolls, water chestnuts wrapped in bacon, strips of beef that had been threaded onto wooden skewers.

They began with *pu-pu* platters, and Richie made a childish but amusing business of broiling a little bit of everything over the flaming pot in the center of the platter he was sharing with Beverly – including half an egg roll and a few red kidney beans. '*Flambé* at my table, I love it,' he told Ben. 'I'd eat shit on a shingle if it was *flambé* at my table.'

'And probably has,' Bill remarked. Beverly laughed so hard at this she had to spit a mouthful of food into her napkin.

'Oh God, I think I'm gonna ralph,' Richie said in an eerily exact imitation of Don Pardo, and Beverly laughed harder, blushing a bright red.

'Stop it, Richie,' she said. 'I'm warning you.'

'The warning is taken,' Richie said. 'Eat well, dear.'

Rose herself brought them their dessert – a great mound of baked Alaska which she ignited at the head of the table, where Mike sat.

'More *flambé* at my table,' Richie said in the voice of a man who has died and gone to heaven. 'This may be the best meal I've ever eaten in my life.'

'But of course,' Rose said demurely.

'If I blow that out, do I get my wish?' he asked her.

'At Jade of the Orient, all wishes are granted, sir.'

Richie's smile faltered suddenly. 'I applaud the sentiment,' he said, 'but you know, I really doubt the veracity.'

They almost demolished the baked Alaska. As Bill sat back, his belly straining the waistband of his pants, he happened to notice the glasses on the table. There seemed to be hundreds of them. He grinned a little, realizing that he himself had sunk two martinis before the meal and God knew how many bottles of Kirin beer with it. The others had done about as well. In their state, fried chunks of bowling pin would probably have tasted okay. And yet he didn't feel drunk.

'I haven't eaten like that since I was a kid,' Ben said. They looked at him and a faint flush of color tinged his cheeks. 'I mean it literally. That may be the biggest meal I've eaten since I was a sophomore in high school.'

'You went on a diet?' Eddie asked.

'Yeah,' Ben said. 'I did. The Ben Hanscom Freedom Diet.'

'What got you going?' Richie asked.

'You don't want to hear all that ancient history . . .' Ben shifted uncomfortably.

'I don't know about the rest of them,' Bill said, 'but I do. Come on, Ben. Give. What turned Haystack Calhoun into the magazine model we see before us today?'

Richie snorted a little. 'Haystack, right. I'd forgotten that.'

'It's not much of a story,' Ben said. 'No story at all, really. After that summer – after 1958 – we stayed in Derry another two years. Then my mom lost her job and we ended up moving to Nebraska, because she had a sister there who offered to take us in until my mother got on her feet again. It wasn't so great. Her sister, my Aunt Jean, was a miserly bitch who had to keep telling you what your place in the great scheme of things was, how lucky we were that my mom had a sister who could give us charity, how lucky we were not to be on welfare, all that sort of thing. I was so fat I disgusted her. She couldn't leave it alone. "Ben, you ought to get more exercise. Ben, you'll have a heart attack before you're forty if you don't lose weight. Ben, with little children starving in the world, you ought to be ashamed of yourself."' He paused for a moment and sipped some water.

'The thing was, she *also* trotted the starving children out if I didn't clean my plate.'

Richie laughed and nodded.

'Anyway, the country was just pulling out of a recession and my mother was almost a year finding steady work. By the time we moved out of Aunt Jean's place in La Vista and got our own in Omaha, I'd put on about ninety pounds over when you guys knew me. I think I put on most of it just to spite my Aunt Jean.'

Eddie whistled. 'That would have put you at about –'

'At about two hundred and ten,' Ben said gravely. 'Anyway, I was going to East Side High School in Omaha, and the phys. ed.

461

periods were . . . well, pretty bad. The other kids called me Jugs. That ought to give you the idea.

'The ragging went on for about seven months, and then one day, while we were getting dressed in the locker room after the period, two or three of the guys started to . . . to kind of slap my gut. They called it "fat-paddling." Pretty soon two or three others got in on it. Then four or five more. Pretty soon it was all of them, chasing me around the locker room and up the hall, whacking my gut, my butt, my back, my legs. I got scared and started to scream. That made the rest of them laugh like crazy.

'You know,' he said, looking down and carefully rearranging his silverware, 'that's the last time I can remember thinking of Henry Bowers until Mike called me two days ago. The kid who started it was a farmboy with these big old hands, and while they were chasing after me I remember thinking that Henry had come back. I think – no, I *know* – that's when I panicked.

'They chased me up the hall past the lockers where the guys who played sports kept their stuff. I was naked and red as a lobster. I'd lost any sense of dignity or . . . or of myself, I guess you'd say. Where myself was. I was screaming for help. And here they came after me, screaming "*Fat-paddling! Fat-paddling! Fat-paddling!*" There was a bench –'

'Ben, you don't have to put yourself through this,' Beverly said suddenly. Her face had gone ashy-pale. She toyed with her water-glass, and almost spilled it.

'Let him finish,' Bill said.

Ben looked at him for a moment and then nodded. 'There was a bench at the end of the corridor. I fell over it and hit my head. They were all around me in another minute or two, and then this voice said: "Okay. That's enough. You guys go change up."

'It was Coach, standing there in the doorway, wearing his blue sweatpants with the white stripe up the sides and his white tee-shirt. There was no way of telling how long he'd been standing there. They all looked at him, some of them grinning, some of them guilty, some of them just looking sort of vacant. They went away. And I burst into tears.

'Coach just stood there in the doorway leading back to the gym, watching me, watching this naked fat boy with his skin all red from the fat-paddling, watching this fat kid crying on the floor.

'And finally he said, "Benny, why don't you just fucking shut up?"

'It shocked me so much to hear a teacher use that word that I did. I looked up at him, and he came over and sat down on the bench I'd fallen over. He leaned over me, and the whistle around his neck swung out and bonked me on the forehead. For a second I thought he was going to kiss me or something, and I shrank back from him, but what he did was grab one of my tits in each hand and squeeze. Then he took his hands away and rubbed them on his pants like he'd touched something dirty.

'"You think I'm going to comfort you?" he asked me. "I'm not. You disgust them and you disgust me as well. We got different reasons, but that's because they're kids and I'm not. They don't know why you disgust them. I do know. It's because I see you burying the good body God gave you in a great big mess of fat. It's a lot of stupid self-indulgence, and it makes me want to puke. Now listen to me, Benny, because this is the only time I'm going to say it to you. I got a foot-ball team to coach, and basketball, and track, and somewhere in between I've got swimming team. So I'll just say it once. You're fat up here." And he tapped my forehead right where his damned whistle had bonked me. "That's where everybody's fat. You put what's between your ears on a diet and you're going to lose weight. But guys like you never do."'

'What a *bastard*!' Beverly said indignantly.

'Yeah,' Ben said, grinning. 'But he didn't *know* he was a bastard, that's how dumb he was. He'd probably seen Jack Webb in that movie *The D.I.* about sixty times, and he actually thought he was doing me a favor. And as it turned out, he was. Because I thought of something right then. I thought . . .'

He looked away, frowning – and Bill had the strangest feeling that he knew what Ben was going to say before he said it.

'I told you that the last time I can remember thinking of Henry Bowers was when the other boys were chasing after me and fat-paddling. Well, when the Coach was getting up to go, that was the last time I really thought of what we'd done in the summer of '58. I thought –'

He hesitated again, looking at each of them in turn, seeming to search their faces. He went on carefully.

'I thought of how *good* we were together. I thought of what we did and how we did it, and all at once it hit me that if Coach had to face anything like that, his hair would probably have turned white all at once and his heart would have stopped dead in his chest like an old watch. It wasn't fair, of course, but he hadn't been fair to me. What happened was simple enough –'

463

'You got mad,' Bill said.

Ben smiled. 'Yeah, that's right,' he said. 'I called, "Coach!"'

'He turned around and looked at me. "You say you coach track?" I asked him.

'"That's right," he said. "Not that it's anything to you."

'"You listen to me, you stupid stone-brained son of a bitch," I said, and his mouth dropped open and his eyes bugged out. "I'll be out there for the track team in March. What do you think about that?"

'"I think you better shut your mouth before it gets you into big trouble," he said.

'"I'm going to run down everyone you get out," I said. "I'm going to run down your best. And then I want a fucking apology from you."

'His fists clenched, and for a minute I thought he was going to come back in there and let me have it. Then they unclenched again. "You just keep talking, fatboy," he said softly. "You got the motor-mouth. But the day you can outrun my best will be the day I quit this place and go back to picking corn on the circuit." And he left.'

'You lost the weight?' Richie asked.

'Well, I did,' Ben said. 'But Coach was wrong. It didn't start in my head. It started with my mother. I went home that night and told her I wanted to lose some weight. We ended up having a hell of a fight, both of us crying. She started out with that same old song and dance: I wasn't really *fat*, I just had *big bones*, and a big boy who was going to be a big man had to eat big just to stay even. It was a . . . a kind of security thing with her, I think. It was scary for her, trying to raise a boy on her own. She had no education and no real skills, just a willingness to work hard. And when she could give me a second helping . . . or when she could look across the table at me and see that I was looking solid . . .'

'She felt like she was winning the battle,' Mike said.

'Uh-huh.' Ben drank off the last of his beer and wiped a small mustache of foam off his upper lip with the heel of his hand. 'So the biggest fight wasn't with my head; it was with her. She just wouldn't accept it, not for months. She wouldn't take in my clothes and she wouldn't buy me new ones. I was running by then, I ran everywhere, and sometimes my heart pounded so hard I felt like I was going to pass out. The first of my mile runs I finished by puking and then fainting. Then for awhile I just puked. And after awhile I was holding up my pants while I ran.

'I got a paper-route and I ran with the bag around my neck,

bouncing against my chest, while I held up my pants. My shirts started to look like sails. And nights when I went home and would only eat half the stuff on my plate my mother would burst into tears and say that I was starving myself, killing myself, that I didn't love her anymore, that I didn't care about how hard she had worked for me.'

'Christ,' Richie muttered, lighting a cigarette. 'I don't know how you handled it, Ben.'

'I just kept the Coach's face in front of me,' Ben said. 'I just kept remembering the way he looked after he grabbed my tits in the hallway to the boys' locker room that time. That's how I did it. I got myself some new jeans and stuff with the paper-route money, and the old guy in the first-floor apartment used his awl to punch some new holes in my belt – about five of them, as I remember. I think that I might have remembered the other time I had to buy a pair of new jeans – that was when Henry pushed me into the Barrens that day and they just about got torn off my body.'

'Yeah,' Eddie said, grinning. 'And you told me about the chocolate milk. Remember that?'

Ben nodded. 'If I did remember,' he went on, 'it was just for a second – there and gone. About that same time I started taking Health and Nutrition at school, and I found out you could eat just about all the raw green stuff you wanted and not gain weight. So one night my mother put on a salad with lettuce and raw spinach in it, chunks of apple and maybe a little leftover ham. Now I've never liked rabbit-food that much, but I had three helpings and just raved on and on to my mother about how good it was.

'That went a long way toward solving the problem. She didn't care so much *what* I ate as long as I ate a *lot* of it. She buried me in salads. I ate them for the next three years. There were times when I had to look in the mirror to make sure my nose wasn't wriggling.'

'So what happened about the Coach?' Eddie asked. 'Did you go out for track?' He touched his aspirator, as if the thought of running had reminded him of it.

'Oh yeah, I went out,' Ben said. 'The two-twenty and the four-forty. By then I'd lost seventy pounds and I'd sprung up two inches so that what was left was better distributed. On the first day of trials I won the two-twenty by six lengths and the four-forty by eight. Then I went over to Coach, who looked mad enough to chew nails and spit out staples, and I said: "Looks like it's time you got out on the circuit and started picking corn. When are you heading down Kansas way?"

'He didn't say a thing at first – just swung a roundhouse and knocked me flat on my back. Then he told me to get off the field. Said he didn't want a smartmouth bastard like me on his track team.

'"I wouldn't be on it if President Kennedy appointed me to it," I said, wiping blood out of the corner of my mouth. "And since you got me going I won't hold you to it . . . but the next time you sit down to a big plate of corn on the cob, spare me a thought."

'He told me if I didn't get out right then he was going to beat the living crap out of me.' Ben was smiling a little . . . but there was nothing very pleasant about that smile, certainly nothing nostalgic. 'Those were his exact words. Everyone was watching us, including the kids I'd beaten. They looked pretty embarrassed. So I just said, "I'll tell you what, Coach. You get one free, on account of you're a sore loser but too old to learn any better now. But you put one more on me and I'll try to see to it that you lose your job. I'm not sure I can do it, but I can make a good try. I lost the weight so I could have a little dignity and a little peace. Those are things worth fighting for."'

Bill said, 'All of that sounds wonderful, Ben . . . but the writer in me wonders if any kid ever really talked like that.'

Ben nodded, still smiling that peculiar smile. 'I doubt if any kid who hadn't been through the things we went through ever did,' he said. 'But I said them . . . and I meant them.'

Bill thought about this and then nodded. 'All right.'

'The Coach stood back with his hands on the hips of his sweatpants,' Ben said. 'He opened his mouth and then he closed it again. Nobody said anything. I walked off, and that was the last I had to do with Coach Woodleigh. When my home-room teacher handed me my course sheet for my junior year, someone had typed the word *excused* next to phys. ed. and he'd initialed it.'

'You beat him!' Richie exclaimed, and shook his clenched hands over his head. 'Way to go, Ben!'

Ben shrugged. 'I think what I did was beat part of myself. Coach got me going, I guess . . . but it was thinking of you guys that made me really believe that I could do it. And I did do it.'

Ben shrugged charmingly, but Bill believed he could see fine drops of sweat at his hairline. 'End of True Confessions. Except I sure could use another beer. Talking's thirsty work.'

Mike signalled the waitress.

All six of them ended up ordering another round, and they talked of light matters until the drinks came. Bill looked into his beer, watching

466

the way the bubbles crawled up the sides of the glass. He was both amused and appalled to realize he was hoping someone else would begin to story about the years between – that Beverly would tell them about the wonderful man she had married (even if he was boring, as most wonderful men were), or that Richie Tozier would begin to expound on Funny Incidents in the Broadcasting Studio, or that Eddie Kaspbrak would tell them what Teddy Kennedy was really like, how much Robert Redford tipped . . . or maybe offer some insights into why Ben had been able to give up the extra pounds while he had needed to hang onto his aspirator.

The fact is, Bill thought, *Mike is going to start talking any minute now, and I'm not sure I want to hear what he has to say. The fact is, my heart is beating just a little too fast and my hands are just a little too cold. The fact is, I'm just about twenty-five years too old to be this scared. We all are. So say something, someone. Let's talk of careers and spouses and what it's like to look at your old playmates and realize that you've taken a few really good shots in the nose from time itself. Let's talk about sex, baseball, the price of gas, the future of the Warsaw Pact nations. Anything but what we came here to talk about. So say something, somebody.*

Someone did. Eddie Kaspbrak did. But it was not what Teddy Kennedy was really like or how much Redford tipped or even why he had found it necessary to keep what Richie had sometimes called 'Eddie's lung-sucker' in the old days. He asked Mike when Stan Uris had died.

'The night before last. When I made the calls.'

'Did it have to do with . . . with why we're here?'

'I could beg the question and say that, since he didn't leave a note, no one can know for sure,' Mike answered, 'but since it happened almost immediately after I called him, I think the assumption is safe enough.'

'He killed himself, didn't he?' Beverly said dully. 'Oh God – poor Stan.'

The others were looking at Mike, who finished his drink and said: 'He committed suicide, yes. Apparently went up to the bathroom shortly after I called him, drew a bath, got into it, and cut his wrists.'

Bill looked down the table, which seemed suddenly lined with shocked, pale faces – no bodies, only those faces, like white circles. Like white balloons, moon balloons, tethered here by an old promise that should have long since lapsed.

'How did you find out?' Richie asked. 'Was it carried in the papers up here?'

'No. For some time now I've subscribed to the newspapers of those towns closest to all of you. I have kept tabs over the years.'

'I Spy.' Richie's face was sour. 'Thanks, Mike.'

'It was my job,' Mike said simply.

'Poor Stan,' Beverly repeated. She seemed stunned, unable to cope with the news. 'But he was so brave back then. So . . . determined.'

'People change,' Eddie said.

'Do they?' Bill asked. 'Stan was –' He moved his hands on the tablecloth, trying to catch the right words. 'He was an ordered person. The kind of person who has to have his books divided up into fiction and nonfiction on his shelves . . . and then wants to have each section in alphabetical order. I can remember something he said once – I don't remember where we were or what we were doing, at least not yet, but I think it was toward the end of things. He said he could stand to be scared, but he hated being dirty. That seemed to me the essence of Stan. Maybe it was just too much, when Mike called. He saw his choices as being only two: stay alive and get dirty or die clean. Maybe people really don't change as much as we think. Maybe they just . . . maybe they just stiffen up.'

There was a moment of silence and then Richie said, 'All right, Mike. What's happening in Derry? Tell us.'

'I can tell you some,' Mike said. 'I can tell you, for instance, what's happening now – and I can tell you some things about yourselves. But I can't tell you everything that happened back in the summer of 1958, and I don't believe I'll ever have to. Eventually you'll remember it for yourselves. And I think if I told you too much before your minds were ready to remember, what happened to Stan –'

'Might happen to us?' Ben asked quietly.

Mike nodded. 'Yes. That's exactly what I'm afraid of.'

Bill said: 'Then tell us what you can, Mike.'

'All right,' he said. 'I will.'

4

The Losers Get the Scoop

'The murders have started again,' Mike said flatly.

He looked up and down the table, and then his eyes fixed on Bill's.

'The first of the "new murders" – if you'll allow me that rather grisly conceit – began on the Main Street Bridge and ended underneath it. The victim was a gay and rather childlike man named Adrian Mellon. He had a bad case of asthma.'

Eddie's hand stole out and touched the side of his aspirator.

'It happened last summer on July 21st, the last night of the Canal Days Festival, which was a kind of celebration, a . . . a . . .'

'A Derry ritual,' Bill said in a low voice. His long fingers were slowly massaging his temples, and it was not hard to guess he was thinking about his brother George . . . George, who had almost certainly opened the way the last time this had happened.

'A ritual,' Mike said quietly. 'Yes.'

He told them the story of what had happened to Adrian Mellon quickly, watching with no pleasure as their eyes got bigger and bigger. He told them what the *News* had reported and what it had not . . . the latter including the testimony of Don Hagarty and Christopher Unwin about a certain clown which had been under the bridge like the troll in the fabled story of yore, a clown which had looked like a cross between Ronald McDonald and Bozo, according to Hagarty.

'It was him,' Ben said in a sick hoarse voice. 'It was that fucker Pennywise.'

'There's one other thing,' Mike said, looking at Bill. 'One of the investigating officers – the one who actually pulled Adrian Mellon out of the Canal – was a town cop named Harold Gardener.'

'Oh Jesus Christ,' Bill said in a weak teary voice.

'Bill?' Beverly looked at him, then put a hand on his arm. Her voice was full of startled concern. 'Bill, what's wrong?'

'Harold would have been about five then,' Bill said. His stunned eyes searched Mike's face for confirmation.

'Yes.'

'What is it, Bill?' Richie asked.

'H-H-Harold Gardener was the s-son of Dave Gardener,' Bill said. 'Dave lived down the street from us back then, when George was k-killed. He was the one who got to Juh juh . . . to my brother first and brought him up to the house, wrapped in a piece of qu-quilt.'

They sat silently, saying nothing. Beverly put a hand briefly over her eyes.

'It all fits rather too well, doesn't it?' Mike said finally.

'Yes,' Bill said in a low voice. 'It fits, all right.'

'I'd kept tabs on the six of you over the years, as I said,' Mike went on, 'but it wasn't until then that I began to understand just why

I had been doing it, that it had a real and concrete purpose. Still, I held off, waiting to see how things would develop. You see, I felt that I had to be absolutely sure before I . . . disturbed your lives. Not ninety percent, not even ninety-five percent. One hundred was all that would do it.

'In December of last year, an eight-year-old boy named Steven Johnson was found dead in Memorial Park. Like Adrian Mellon, he had been badly mutilated just before or just after his death, but he looked as if he could have died of just plain fright.'

'Sexually assaulted?' Eddie asked.

'No. Just plain mutilated.'

'How many in all?' Eddie asked, not looking as if he really wanted to know.

'It's bad,' Mike said.

'How many?' Bill repeated.

'Nine. So far.'

'It can't be!' Beverly cried. 'I would have read about it in the paper . . . seen it on the news! When that crazy cop killed all those women in Castle Rock, Maine . . . and those children that were murdered in Atlanta . . .'

'Yes, that,' Mike said. 'I've thought about that a lot. It's really the closest correlative to what's going on here, and Bev's right: that really was coast-to-coast news. In some ways, the Atlanta comparison is the thing about all of this that frightens me the most. The murder of nine children . . . we should have TV news correspondents here, and phony psychics, and reporters from *The Atlantic Monthly* and *Rolling Stone* . . . the whole media circus, in short.'

'But it hasn't happened,' Bill said.

'No,' Mike answered, 'it hasn't. Oh, there was a Sunday-supplement piece about it in the Portland Sunday *Telegram*, and another one in the Boston *Globe* after the last two. A Boston-based television program called *Good Day*! did a segment this February on unsolved murders, and one of the experts mentioned the Derry murders, but only passingly . . . and he certainly gave no indication of knowing there had been a similar batch of murders in 1957–58, and another in 1929–30.

'There are some ostensible reasons, of course. Atlanta, New York, Chicago, Detroit . . . those are big media towns, and in big media towns when something happens it makes a bang. There isn't a single TV or radio station in Derry, unless you count the little FM the English and Speech Department runs up at the high school. Bangor's got the corner on the market when it comes to the media.'

'Except for the Derry *News*,' Eddie said, and they all laughed.

'But we all know that doesn't really cut it with the way the world is today. The communication web is there, and at some point the story should have broken nationally. But it didn't. And I think the reason is just this: It doesn't want it to.'

'It,' Bill mused, almost to himself.

'It,' Mike agreed. 'If we have to call It something, it might as well be what we used to call It. I've begun to think, you see, that It has been here so long . . . whatever It really is . . . that It's become a part of Derry, something as much a part of the town as the Standpipe, or the Canal, or Bassey Park, or the library. Only It's not a matter of outward geography, you understand. Maybe that was true once, but now It's . . . inside. Somehow It's gotten inside. That's the only way I know to understand all of the terrible things that have happened here – the nominally explicable as well as the utterly inexplicable. There was a fire at a Negro nightclub called the Black Spot in 1930. A year before that, a bunch of half-bright Depression outlaws was gunned down on Canal Street in the middle of the afternoon.'

'The Bradley Gang,' Bill said. 'The FBI got them, right?'

'That's what the histories say, but that's not precisely true. So far as I've been able to find out – and I'd give a lot to believe that it wasn't so, because I love this town – the Bradley Gang, all seven of them, were actually gunned down by the good citizens of Derry. I'll tell you about it sometime.

'There was the explosion at the Kitchener Ironworks during an Easter-egg hunt in 1906. There was a horrible series of animal mutilations that same year that was finally traced to Andrew Rhulin, the grand-uncle of the man who now runs the Rhulin Farms. He was apparently bludgeoned to death by the three deputies who were supposed to bring him in. None of the deputies were ever brought to trial.'

Mike Hanlon produced a small notebook from an inner pocket and paged through it, talking without looking up. 'In 1877 there were four lynchings inside the incorporated town limits. One of those that climbed a rope was the lay preacher of the Methodist Church, who apparently drowned all four of his children in the bathtub as if they were kittens and then shot his wife in the head. He put the gun in her hand to make it look like suicide, but no one was fooled. A year before that four loggers were found dead in a cabin downstream on the Kenduskeag, literally torn apart. Disappearances of children, of whole families, are recorded in old diary extracts . . . but not in any public document. It goes on and on, but perhaps you get the idea.'

'I get the idea, all right,' Ben said. 'Something's going on here, but it's private.'

Mike closed his notebook, replaced it in his inner pocket, and looked at them soberly.

'If I were an insurance man instead of a librarian, I'd draw you a graph, maybe. It would show an unusually high rate of every violent crime we know of, not excluding rape, incest, breaking and entering, auto theft, child abuse, spouse abuse, assault.

'There's a medium-sized city in Texas where the violent-crime-rate is far below what you'd expect for a city of its size and mixed racial make-up. The extraordinary placidity of the people who live there has been traced to something in the water . . . a natural trank of some kind. The exact opposite holds true here. Derry is a violent place to live in an ordinary year. But every twenty-seven years – although the cycle has never been perfectly exact – that violence has escalated to a furious peak . . . and it has *never* been national news.'

'You're saying there's a cancer at work here,' Beverly said.

'Not at all. An untreated cancer invariably kills. Derry hasn't died; on the contrary, it has thrived . . . in an unspectacular, unnewsworthy way, of course. It is simply a fairly prosperous small city in a relatively unpopulous state where bad things happen too often . . . and where ferocious things happen every quarter of a century or so.'

'That holds true all down the line?' Ben asked.

Mike nodded. 'All down the line. 1715–16, 1740 until roughly 1743 – that must have been a bad one – 1769–70, and on and on. Right up to the present time. I have a feeling that it's been getting steadily worse, maybe because there have been more people in Derry at the end of each cycle, maybe for some other reason. And in 1958, the cycle appears to have come to a premature end. For which we were responsible.'

Bill Denbrough leaned forward, his eyes suddenly bright. 'You're sure of that? *Sure?*'

'Yes,' Mike said. 'All the other cycles reached their peak around September and then ended in a big way. Life usually took on its more or less normal tenor by Christmas . . . Easter at the latest. In other words, there were bad "years" of fourteen to twenty months every twenty-seven years. But the bad year that began when your brother was killed in October of 1957 ended quite abruptly in August of 1958.'

'Why?' Eddie asked urgently. His breath had thinned; Bill remembered that high whistle as Eddie inhaled breath, and knew that he would soon be tooting on the old lung-sucker. 'What did we *do*?'

The question hung there. Mike seemed to regard it . . . and at last he shook his head. 'You'll remember,' he said. 'In time you'll remember.'

'What if we don't?' Ben asked.

'Then God help us all.'

'Nine children dead this year,' Rich said. 'Christ.'

'Lisa Albrecht and Steven Johnson in late 1984,' Mike said. 'In February a boy named Dennis Torrio disappeared. A high-school boy. His body was found in mid-March, in the Barrens. Mutilated. This was nearby.'

He took a photograph from the same pocket into which he had replaced the notebook. It made its way around the table. Beverly and Eddie looked at it, puzzled, but Richie Tozier reacted violently. He dropped it as if it were hot. 'Jesus! Jesus, Mike!' He looked up, his eyes wide and shocked. A moment later he passed the picture to Bill.

Bill looked at it and felt the world swim into gray tones all around him. For a moment he was sure he would pass out. He heard a groan, and knew he had made the sound. He dropped the picture.

'What is it?' he heard Beverly saying. 'What does it mean, Bill?'

'It's my brother's school picture,' Bill said at last. 'It's Juh-Georgie. The picture from his album. The one that moved. The one that winked.'

They handed it around again then, while Bill sat as still as stone at the head of the table, looking out into space. It was a photograph of a photograph. The picture showed a tattered school photo propped up against a white background – smiling lips parted to exhibit two holes where new teeth had never grown (*unless they grow in your coffin*, Bill thought, and shuddered). On the margin below George's picture were the words SCHOOL FRIENDS 1957–58.

'It was found *this year*?' Beverly asked again. Mike nodded and she turned to Bill. 'When did you last see it, Bill?'

He wet his lips, tried to speak. Nothing came out. He tried again, hearing the words echo in his head, aware of the stutter coming back, fighting it, fighting the terror.

'I haven't seen that picture since 1958. That spring, the year after George died. When I tried to show it to Richie, it was g-gone.'

There was an explosive gasping sound that made them all look around. Eddie was setting his aspirator back on the table and looking slightly embarrassed.

'Eddie Kaspbrak blasts off!' Richie cried cheerfully, and then, suddenly and eerily, the Voice of the MovieTone Newsreel Narrator came from Rich's mouth: 'Today in Derry, a whole city turns out for Asthmatics on Parade, and the star of the show is Big Ed the Snothead, known all over New England as –'

He stopped abruptly, and one hand moved toward his face, as if to cover his eyes, and Bill suddenly thought: *No – no, that's not it. Not to cover his eyes but to push his glasses up on his nose. The glasses that aren't even there anymore. Oh dear Christ, what's going on here?*

'Eddie, I'm sorry,' Rich said. 'That was cruel. I don't know what the hell I was thinking about.' He looked around at the others, bewildered.

Mike Hanlon spoke into the silence.

'I'd promised myself after Steven Johnson's body was discovered that if anything else happened – if there was one more clear case – I would make the calls that I ended up not making for another two months. It was as if I was hypnotized by what was happening, by the *consciousness* of it – the *deliberateness* of it. George's picture was found by a fallen log less than ten feet from the Torrio boy's body. It wasn't hidden; quite the contrary. It was as if the killer wanted it to be found. As I'm sure the killer did.'

'How did you get the police photo, Mike?' Ben asked. 'That's what it is, isn't it?'

'Yes, that's what it is. There's a fellow in the Police Department who isn't averse to making a little extra money. I pay him twenty bucks a month – all that I can afford. He's a pipeline.

'The body of Dawn Roy was found four days after the Torrio boy. McCarron Park. Thirteen years old. Decapitated.

'April 23rd of this year. Adam Terrault. Sixteen. Reported missing when he didn't come home from band practice. Found the next day just off the path that runs through the greenbelt behind West Broadway. Also decapitated.

'May 6th. Frederick Cowan. Two and a half. Found in an upstairs bathroom, drowned in the toilet.'

'Oh, Mike!' Beverly cried.

'Yeah, it's bad,' he said, almost angrily. 'Don't you think I know that?'

'The police are convinced that it couldn't have been – well, some kind of accident?' Bev asked.

Mike shook his head. 'His mother was hanging clothes in the back yard. She heard sounds of a struggle – heard her son screaming. She ran as fast as she could. As she went up the stairs, she says she heard the sound of the toilet flushing repeatedly – that, and someone laughing. She said it didn't sound human.'

'And she saw nothing at all?' Eddie asked.

'Her son,' Mike said simply. 'His back had been broken, his skull fractured. The glass door of the shower-stall was broken. There was blood everywhere. The mother is in the Bangor Mental Health Institute, now. My . . . my Police Department source says she's quite lost her mind.'

'No fucking wonder,' Richie said hoarsely. 'Who's got a cigarette?'

Beverly gave him one. Rich lit it with hands that shook badly.

'The police line is that the killer came in through the front door while the Cowan boy's mother was hanging her clothes in the back yard. Then, when she ran up the back stairs, he supposedly jumped from the bathroom window into the yard she'd just left and got away clean. But the window is only one of those half-sized jobs; a kid of seven would have to wriggle to get through it. And the drop was twenty-five feet to a stone-flagged patio. Rademacher doesn't like to talk about those things, and no one in the press – certainly no one at the *News* – has pressed him about them.'

Mike took a drink of water and then passed another picture down the line. This was not a police photograph; it was another school picture. It showed a grinning boy who was maybe thirteen. He was dressed in his best for the school photo and his hands were clean and folded neatly in his lap . . . but there was a devilish little glint in his eyes. He was black.

'Jeffrey Holly,' Mike said. 'May 13th. A week after the Cowan boy was killed. Torn open. He was found in Bassey Park, by the Canal.

'Nine days after that, May 22nd, a fifth-grader named John Feury was found dead out on Neibolt Street –'

Eddie uttered a high, quavering scream. He groped for his aspirator and knocked it off the table. It rolled down to Bill, who picked it up. Eddie's face had gone a sickish yellow color. His breath whistled coldly in his throat.

'Get him something to drink!' Ben roared. 'Somebody get him –'

But Eddie was shaking his head. He triggered the aspirator down his throat. His chest heaved as he tore in a gulp of air. He triggered the aspirator again and then sat back, eyes half-closed, panting.

'I'll be all right,' he gasped. 'Gimme a minute, I'm with you.'

'Eddie, are you sure?' Beverly asked. 'Maybe you ought to lie down –'

'I'll be all right,' he repeated querulously. 'It was just . . . the shock. You know. The shock. I'd forgotten all about Neibolt Street.'

No one replied; no one had to. Bill thought: *You believe your capacity has been reached, and then Mike produces another name, and yet another, like a black magician with a hatful of malign tricks, and you're knocked on your ass again.*

It was too much to face all at once, this outpouring of inexplicable violence, somehow directly aimed at the six people here – or so George's photograph seemed to suggest.

'Both of John Feury's legs were gone,' Mike continued softly, 'but the medical examiner says that happened after he died. His heart gave out. He seems to have quite literally died of fear. He was found by the postman, who saw a hand sticking out from under the porch –'

'It was 29, wasn't it?' Rich said, and Bill looked at him quickly. Rich glanced back at him, nodded slightly, and then looked at Mike again. 'Twenty-nine Neibolt Street.'

'Oh yes,' Mike said in that same calm voice. 'It was number 29.' He drank more water. 'Are you really all right, Eddie?'

Eddie nodded. His breathing had eased.

'Rademacher made an arrest the day after Feury's body was discovered,' Mike said. 'There was a front-page editorial in the *News* that same day, calling for his resignation, incidentally.'

'After eight murders?' Ben said. 'Pretty radical of them, wouldn't you say?'

Beverly wanted to know who had been arrested.

'A guy who lives in a little shack way out on Route 7, almost over the town line and into Newport,' Mike said. 'Kind of a hermit. Burns scrapwood in his stove, roofed the place with scavenged shingles and hubcaps. Name of Harold Earl. Probably doesn't see two hundred dollars in cash money over the course of a year. Someone driving by saw him standing out in his dooryard, just looking up at the sky, on the day John Feury's body was discovered. His clothes were covered with blood.'

'Then maybe –' Rich began hopefully.

'He had three butchered deer in his shed,' Mike said. 'He'd been jacking over in Haven. The blood on his clothes was deer-blood.

Rademacher asked him if he killed John Feury, and Earl is supposed to have said, "Oh ayuh, I killed a lot of people. I shot most of them in the war." He also said he'd seen things in the woods at night. Blue lights sometimes, floating just a few inches off the ground. Corpse-lights, he called them. And Bigfoot.

'They sent him up to the Bangor Mental Health. According to the medical report, his liver's almost entirely gone. He's been drinking paint-thinner –'

'Oh my God,' Beverly said.

'– and is prone to hallucinations. They've been holding on to him, and until three days ago Rademacher was sticking to his idea that Earl was the most likely suspect. He had eight guys out there, digging around his shack and looking for the missing heads, lampshades made out of human skin, God knows what.'

Mike paused, head lowered, and then went on. His voice was slightly hoarse now. 'I'd held off and held off. But when I saw this last one, I made the calls. I wish to God I'd made them sooner.'

'Let's see,' Ben said abruptly.

'The victim was another fifth-grader,' Mike said. 'A classmate of the Feury boy. He was found just off Kansas Street, near where Bill used to hide his bike when we were in the Barrens. His name was Jerry Bellwood. He was torn apart. What . . . what was left of him was found at the foot of a cement retaining wall that was put in along most of Kansas Street about twenty years ago to stop the soil erosion. This police photograph of the section of that wall where Bellwood was found was taken less than half an hour after the body was removed. Here.'

He passed the picture to Rich Tozier, who looked and passed it on to Beverly. She glanced at it briefly, winced, and passed it on to Eddie, who gazed at it long and raptly before handing it on to Ben. Ben passed it to Bill with barely a glance.

Printing straggled its way across the concrete retaining wall. It said:

COME HOME COME HOME COME HOME

Bill looked up at Mike grimly. He had been bewildered and frightened; now he felt the first stirrings of anger. He was glad. Angry was not such a great way to feel, but it was better than the shock, better than the miserable fear. 'Is that written in what I think it's written in?'

'Yes,' Mike said. 'Jerry Bellwood's blood.'

5

Richie Gets Beeped

Mike had taken his photographs back. He had an idea that Bill might ask for the one of George's last school picture, but Bill did not. He put them in his inside jacket pocket, and when they were out of sight, all of them – Mike included – felt a sense of relief.

'Nine children,' Beverly was saying softly. 'I can't believe it. I mean . . . I can believe it, but I can't *believe* it. Nine kids and nothing? Nothing at *all*?'

'It's not quite like that,' Mike said. 'People are angry, people are scared . . . or so it seems. It's really impossible to tell which ones really feel that way and which ones are faking.'

'*Faking*?'

'Beverly, do you remember, when we were kids, the man who just folded his newspaper and went inside his house while you were screaming at him for help?'

For a moment something seemed to jump in her eyes and she looked both terrified and aware. Then she only looked puzzled. 'No . . . when was that, Mike?'

'Never mind. It will come to you in time. All I can say now is that everything looks the way it should in Derry. Faced with such a grisly string of murders, people are doing all the things you'd expect them to do, and most of them are the same things that went on while kids were disappearing and getting murdered back in '58. The Save Our Children Committee is meeting again, only this time at Derry Elementary School instead of Derry High. There are sixteen detectives from the State Attorney General's office in town, and a contingent of FBI agents as well – I don't know how many, and although Rademacher talks big, I don't think he does, either. The curfew's back in effect –'

'Oh yes. The curfew.' Ben was rubbing the side of his neck slowly and deliberately. 'That did wonders back in '58. I remember that much.'

'– and there are Mothers' Walker Groups to make sure that every child who goes to school, grades K through eight, is chaperoned home. The *News* has gotten over two thousand letters demanding a solution in the last three weeks alone. And, of course, the out-migration has begun again. I sometimes think that's the only way to *really* tell who's sincere about wanting it stopped and who isn't. The really sincere ones get scared and leave.'

'People really are leaving?' Richie asked.

'It happens each time the cycle cranks up again. It's impossible to tell just how many go, because the cycle hasn't fallen squarely in a census year since 1850 or so. But it's a fairish number. They run like kids who just found out the house was haunted for real after all.'

'Come home, come home, come home,' Beverly said softly. When she looked up from her hands it was Bill she looked at, not Mike. 'It *wanted* us to come back. Why?'

'It *may* want us all back,' Mike said a little cryptically. 'Sure. It *may*. It may want revenge. After all, we balked It once before.'

'Revenge . . . or just to set things back in order,' Bill said.

Mike nodded. 'Things are out of order with your own lives, too, you know. None of you left Derry untouched . . . without Its mark on you. All of you forgot what happened here, and your memories of that summer are still only fragmentary. And then there's the passingly curious fact that you're all rich.'

'Oh, come on now!' Richie said. 'That's hardly –'

'Be soft, be soft,' Mike said, holding his hand up and smiling faintly. 'I'm not accusing you of anything, just trying to get the facts out on the table. You are rich by the standards of a small-town librarian who makes just under eleven grand a year after taxes, okay?'

Rich shrugged the shoulders of his expensive suit uncomfortably. Ben appeared deeply absorbed in tearing small strips from the edge of his napkin. No one was looking directly at Mike except Bill.

'None of you are in the H. L. Hunt class, certainly,' Mike said, 'but you are all well-to-do even by the standards of the American upper-middle class. We're all friends here, so fess up: if there's one of you who declared less than ninety thousand dollars on his or her 1984 tax return, raise your hand.'

They glanced around at each other almost furtively, embarrassed, as Americans always seem to be, by the raw fact of their own success – as if cash were hardcooked eggs and affluence the farts that inevitably follow an overdose of same. Bill felt hot blood in his cheeks and was helpless to stop its rise. He had been paid ten thousand more than the sum Mike had mentioned just for doing the first draft of the *Attic Room* screenplay. He had been promised an additional twenty thousand dollars each for two rewrites, if needed. Then there were royalties . . . and the hefty advance on a two-book contract just signed . . . how much *had* he declared on his '84 tax return? Just about eight hundred thousand dollars, right? Enough, anyway, to seem almost monstrous in light of Mike Hanlon's stated income of just under eleven thousand a year.

So that's how much they pay you to keep the lighthouse, Mike old kid, Bill thought. *Jesus Christ, somewhere along the line you should have asked for a raise!*

Mike said: 'Bill Denbrough, a successful novelist in a society where there are only a few novelists and fewer still lucky enough to be making a living from the craft. Beverly Rogan, who's in the rag trade, a field to which more are called but even fewer chosen. She is, in fact, the most sought-after designer in the middle third of the country right now.'

'Oh, it's not *me*,' Beverly said. She uttered a nervous little laugh and lit a fresh cigarette from the smoldering stub of the old one. 'It's Tom. Tom's the one. Without him I'd still be relining skirts and sewing up hems. I don't have any business sense at all, even Tom says so. It's just . . . you know, Tom. And luck.' She took a single deep drag from her cigarette and then snuffed it.

'Methinks the lady doth protest too much,' Richie said slyly.

She turned quickly in her seat and gave him a hard look, her color high. 'Just what's that supposed to mean, Richie Tozier?'

'Doan hits me, Miz Scawlett!' Richie cried in a high, trembling Pickaninny Voice – and in that moment Bill could see with an eerie clarity the boy he had known; he was not just a superseded presence lurking under Rich Tozier's grownup exterior but a creature almost more real than the man himself. 'Doan hits me! Lemme bring you anothuh mint joolip, Miz Scawlett! Youse goan drink hit out on de po'ch where it's be a little bit cooluh! Doan whup disyere boy!'

'You're impossible, Richie,' Beverly said coldly. 'You ought to grow up.'

Richie looked at her, his grin fading slowly into uncertainty. 'Until I came back here,' he said, 'I thought I had.'

'Rich, you may just be the most successful disc jockey in the United States,' Mike said. 'You've certainly got LA in the palm of your hand. On top of that there are two syndicated programs, one of them a straight top-forty countdown show, the other one something called *The Freaky Forty* –'

'You better watch out, fool,' Richie said in a gruff Mr T Voice, but he was blushing. 'I'll make your front and back change places. I'll give you brain-surgery with my fist. I'll –'

'Eddie,' Mike went on, ignoring Richie, 'you've got a healthy limousine service in a city where you just about have to elbow long black cars out of your way when you cross the street. Two limo companies a week go smash in the Big Apple, but you're doing fine.

'Ben, you're probably the most successful young architect in the world.'

Ben opened his mouth, probably to protest, and then closed it again abruptly.

Mike smiled at them, spread his hands. 'I don't want to embarrass anyone, but I do want all the cards on the table. There are people who succeed young, and there are people who succeed in highly specialized jobs – if there weren't people who bucked the odds successfully, I guess everybody would give up. If it was just one or two of you, we could pass it off as coincidence. But it's not just one or two; it's *all* of you, and that includes Stan Uris, who was the most successful young accountant in Atlanta . . . which means in the whole South. My conclusion is that your success stems from what happened here twenty-seven years ago. If you had all been exposed to asbestos at that time and had all developed lung cancer by now, the correlative would be no less clear or persuasive. Do any of you want to dispute it?'

He looked at them. No one answered.

'All except you,' Bill said. 'What happened to you, Mikey?'

'Isn't it obvious?' He grinned. 'I stayed here.'

'You kept the lighthouse,' Ben said. Bill jerked around and looked at him, startled, but Ben was staring hard at Mike and didn't see. 'That doesn't make me feel so good, Mike. In fact, it makes me feel sort of like a bugturd.'

'Amen,' Beverly said.

Mike shook his head patiently. 'You have nothing to feel guilty about, any of you. Do you think it was my choice to stay here, any more than it was your choice – any of you – to leave? Hell, we were *kids*. For one reason or another your parents moved away, and you guys were part of the baggage they took along. My parents stayed. And was it really their decision – any of *them*? I don't think so. How was it decided who would go and who would stay? Was it luck? Fate? It? Some Other? I don't know. But it wasn't us guys. So quit it.'

'You're not . . . not bitter?' Eddie asked timidly.

'I've been too busy to be bitter,' Mike said. 'I've spent a long time watching and waiting . . . I was watching and waiting even before I knew it, I think, but for the last five years or so I've been on what you might call red alert. Since the turn of the year I've been

481

keeping a journal. And when a man writes, he thinks harder . . . or maybe just more specifically. And one of the things I've spent time writing and thinking about is the nature of It. It changes; we know that. I think It also manipulates, and leaves Its marks on people just by the nature of what It is – the way you can smell a skunk on you even after a long bath, if it lets go its bag of scent too near you. The way a grasshopper will spit bug juice into your palm if you catch it in your hand.'

Mike slowly unbuttoned his shirt and spread it wide. They could all see the pinkish scrawls of scar across the smooth brown skin of his chest between the nipples.

'The way claws leave scars,' he said.

'The werewolf,' Richie almost moaned. 'Oh Christ, Big Bill, the werewolf! When we went back to Neibolt Street!'

'What?' Bill asked. He sounded like a man called out of a dream. 'What, Richie?'

'Don't you *remember*?'

'No . . . do you?'

'I . . . I almost do . . .' Looking both confused and scared, Richie subsided.

'Are you saying this thing isn't evil?' Eddie asked Mike abruptly. He was staring at the scars as if hypnotized. 'That it's just some part of the . . . the natural order?'

'It's no part of a natural order we understand or condone,' Mike said, rebuttoning his shirt, 'and I see no reason to operate on any other basis than the one we *do* understand: that It kills, kills children, and that's wrong. Bill understood that before any of us. Do you remember, Bill?'

'I remember that I wanted to kill It,' Bill said, and for the first time (and ever after) he heard the pronoun gain proper-noun status in his own voice. 'But I didn't have much of a world-view on the subject, if you see what I mean – I just wanted to kill It because It killed George.'

'And do you still?'

Bill considered this carefully. He looked down at his spread hands on the table and remembered George in his yellow slicker, his hood up, the paper boat with its thin glaze of paraffin in one hand. He looked up at Mike.

'M-M-More than ever,' he said.

Mike nodded as if this were exactly what he had expected. 'It left Its mark on us. It worked Its will on us, just as It has worked Its will on this whole town, day in and day out, even during those long periods when It is asleep or hibernating or whatever It does between Its more . . . more lively periods.'

Mike raised one finger.

'But if It worked Its will on us, at some point, in some way, *we also worked our will on It.* We stopped It before It was done – I know we did. Did we weaken It? Hurt It? Did we, in fact, almost kill It? I think we did. I think we came so close to killing It that we went away thinking we had.'

'But you don't remember that part either, do you?' Ben asked.

'No. I can remember everything up until August 15th 1958 with almost perfect clarity. But from then until September 4th or so, when school was called in again, everything is a total blank. It isn't murky or hazy; it is just completely gone. With one exception: I seem to remember Bill screaming about something called the dead-lights.'

Bill's arm jerked convulsively. It struck one of his empty beer bottles, and the bottle shattered on the floor like a bomb.

'Did you cut yourself?' Beverly asked. She had half-risen.

'No,' he said. His voice was harsh and dry. His arms had broken out in gooseflesh. It seemed that his skull had somehow grown; he could feel

(*the deadlights*)

it pressing out against the stretched skin of his face in steady numbing throbs.

'I'll pick up the –'

'No, just sit down.' He wanted to look at her and couldn't. He couldn't take his eyes off Mike.

'Do you remember the deadlights, Bill?' Mike asked softly.

'No,' he said. His mouth felt the way it did when the dentist got a little too enthusiastic with the novocaine.

'You will.'

'I hope to God I don't.'

'You will anyway,' Mike said. 'But for now . . . no. Not me, either. Do any of you?'

One by one they shook their heads.

'But we did *something*,' Mike said quietly. 'At some point we were able to exercise some sort of group will. At some point we achieved some special understanding, whether conscious or unconscious.' He stirred restlessly. 'God, I wish Stan was here. I have a feeling that Stan, with his ordered mind, might have had some idea.'

'Maybe he did,' Beverly said. 'Maybe that's why he killed himself.

Maybe he understood that if there was magic, it wouldn't work for grownups.'

'I think it could, though,' Mike said. 'Because there's one other thing we six have in common. I wonder if any of you have realized what that is.'

It was Bill's turn to open his mouth and then shut it again.

'Go on,' Mike said. 'You know what it is. I can see it on your face.'

'I'm not *sure* I know,' Bill replied, 'but I *think* w-we're all childless. Is that ih–it?'

There was a moment of shocked silence.

'Yeah,' Mike said. 'That's it.'

'Jesus Christ Almighty!' Eddie spoke up indignantly. 'What in the world does *that* have to do with the price of beans in Peru? What gave you the idea that everyone in the world has to have kids? That's nuts!'

'Do you and your wife have children?' Mike asked.

'If you've been keeping track of us all the way you said, then you know goddam well we don't. But I still say it doesn't mean a damn thing.'

'Have you *tried* to have children?'

'We don't use birth control, if that's what you mean.' Eddie spoke with an oddly moving dignity, but his cheeks were flushed. 'It just so happens that my wife is a little . . . Oh hell. She's a *lot* overweight. We went to see a doctor and she told us my wife might never have kids if she didn't lose some weight. Does that make us criminals?'

'Take it easy, Eds,' Richie soothed, and leaned toward him.

'Don't call me Eds and don't you *dare* pinch my cheek!' he cried, rounding on Richie. 'You know I hate that! I *always* hated it!'

Richie recoiled, blinking.

'Beverly?' Mike asked. 'What about you and Tom?'

'No children,' she said. 'Also no birth control. Tom wants kids . . . and so do I, of course,' she added hastily, glancing around at them quickly. Bill thought her eyes seemed overbright, almost the eyes of an actress giving a good performance. 'It just hasn't happened yet.'

'Have you had those tests?' Ben asked her.

'Oh yes, of course,' she said, and uttered a light laugh that was almost a titter. And in one of those leaps of comprehension that sometimes come to people who are gifted with both curiosity and insight, Bill suddenly understood a great deal about Beverly and her husband Tom, alias the Greatest Man in the World. *Beverly* had gone to have fertility tests. His guess was that the Greatest Man in the World had refused to entertain even for a moment the notion that there might be something wrong with the sperm being manufactured in the Sacred Sacs.

'What about you and your wife, Big Bill?' Rich asked. 'Been trying?' They all looked at him curiously . . . because his wife was someone they knew. Audra was by no means the best-known or the best-loved actress in the world, but she was certainly part of the celebrity coinage that had somehow replaced talent as a medium of exchange in the latter half of the twentieth century; there had been a picture of her in *People* magazine when she cut her hair short, and during a particularly boring stretch in New York (the play she had been planning to do Off Broadway fell through) she had done a week-long stint on *Hollywood Squares*, over her agent's strenuous objections. She was a stranger whose lovely face was known to them. He thought Beverly looked particularly curious.

'We've been trying off and on for the last six years,' Bill said. 'For the last eight months or so it's been off, because of the movie we were doing – *Attic Room*, it's called.'

'You know, we run a little entertainment syndie every day from five-fifteen in the afternoon until five-thirty,' Richie said. '*Seein' Stars*, it's called. They had a feature on that damned movie just last week – Husband and Wife Working Happily Together kind of thing. They said both of your names and I never made the connection. Funny, isn't it?'

'Very,' Bill said. 'Anyway, Audra said it would be just our luck if she caught pregnant while we were in preproduction and she had to do ten weeks of strenuous acting and being morning-sick at the same time. But we want kids, yes. And we've tried quite hard.'

'Had fertility tests?' Ben asked.

'Uh-huh. Four years ago, in New York. The doctors discovered a very small benign tumor in Audra's womb, and they said it was a lucky thing because, although it wouldn't have prevented her from getting pregnant, it might have caused a tubal pregnancy. She and I are both fertile, though.'

Eddie repeated stubbornly, 'It doesn't *prove* a goddam thing.'

'Suggestive, though,' Ben murmured.

'No little accidents on your front, Ben?' Bill asked. He was shocked and amused to find that his mouth had very nearly called Ben Haystack instead.

'I've never been married, I've always been careful, and there have been no paternity suits,' Ben said. 'Beyond that I don't think there's any real way of telling.'

'You want to hear a funny story?' Richie asked. He was smiling, but there was no smile in his eyes.

'Sure,' Bill said. 'You were always good at the funny stuff, Richie.'

'Your face and me own buttocks, boyo,' Richie said in the Irish Cop's Voice. It was a *great* Irish Cop's Voice. *You've improved out of all measure, Richie*, Bill thought. *As a kid, you couldn't do an Irish Cop no matter how you busted your brains. Except once . . . or twice . . . when*

(*the deadlights*)

was that?

'Your face and me own buttocks; just keep rememb'rin that com-pay-ri-son, me foine bucko.'

Ben Hanscom suddenly held his nose and cried in a high quavering boyish voice: 'Beep-beep, Richie! Beep-beep! Beep-beep!'

After a moment, laughing, Eddie held his own nose and joined in. Beverly did the same.

'Awright! Awright!' Richie cried, laughing himself. 'Awright, I give up! Chrissake!'

'Oh man,' Eddie said. He collapsed back in his chair, laughing so hard he was almost crying. 'We gotcha that time, Trashmouth. Way to go, Ben.'

Ben was smiling but he looked a little bewildered.

'Beep-beep,' Bev said, and giggled. 'I forgot all *about* that. We always used to beep you, Richie.'

'You guys never appreciated true talent, that's all,' Richie said comfortably. As in the old days, you could knock him off-balance, but he was like one of those inflatable Joe Palooka dolls with sand in the base – he floated upright again almost at once. 'That was one of your little contributions to the Losers' Club, wasn't it, Haystack?'

'Yeah, I guess it was.'

'What a man!' Richie said in a trembling, awestruck voice and then began to salaam over the table, nearly sticking his nose in his tea-cup each time he went down. 'What a man! Oh chillun, what a man!'

'Beep-beep, Richie,' Ben said solemnly, and then exploded laughter in a hearty baritone utterly unlike his wavering childhood voice. 'You're the same old roadrunner.'

'You guys want to hear this story or not?' Richie asked. 'I mean, no big deal one way or the other. Beep away if you want to. I can take abuse. I mean, you're looking at a man who once did an interview with Ozzy Osbourne.'

'Tell it,' Bill said. He glanced over at Mike and saw that Mike looked happier – or more at rest – since the luncheon had begun. Was it because he saw the almost unconscious knitting-together that was happening, the sort of easy falling-back into old roles that almost never happened when old chums got together? Bill thought so. And he thought, *If there are certain preconditions for the belief in magic that makes it possible to use the magic, then maybe those preconditions will inevitably arrange themselves.* It was not a very comforting thought. It made him feel like a man strapped to the nosecone of a guided missile.

Beep-beep indeed.

'Well,' Richie was saying, 'I could make this long and sad or I could give you the Blondie and Dagwood comic-strip version, but I'll settle for something in the middle. The year after I moved out to California I met a girl, and we fell pretty hard for each other. Started living together. She was on the pill at first, but it made her feel sick almost all the time. She talked about getting an IUD, but I wasn't too crazy about that – the first stories about how they might not be completely safe were just starting to come out in the papers.

'We had talked a lot about kids, and had pretty well decided we didn't want them even if we decided to legalize the relationship. Irresponsible to bring kids into such a shitty, dangerous, overpopulated world . . . and blah-blah-blah, babble-babble-babble, let's go out and put a bomb in the men's room of the Bank of America and then come on back to the crashpad and smoke some dope and talk about the difference between Maoism and Trotskyism, if you see what I mean.

'Or maybe I'm being too hard on both of us. Shit, we were young and reasonably idealistic. The upshot was that I got my wires cut, as the Beverly Hills crowd puts it with their unfailing vulgar chic. The operation went with no problem and I had no adverse aftereffects. There can be, you know. I had a friend whose balls swelled up to roughly the size of the tires on a 1959 Cadillac. I was gonna give him a pair of suspenders and a couple of barrels for his birthday – sort of a designer truss – but they went down before then.'

'All put with your customary tact and dignity,' Bill remarked, and Beverly began to laugh again.

Richie offered a large, sincere smile. 'Thank you, Bill, for those words of support. The word "fuck" was used two hundred and six times in your last book. I counted.'

'Beep-beep, Trashmouth,' Bill said solemnly, and they all laughed. Bill found it nearly impossible to believe they had been talking about dead children less than ten minutes ago.

'Press onward, Richie,' Ben said. 'The hour groweth late.'

'Sandy and I lived together for two and a half years,' Richie went on. 'Came really close to getting married twice. As things turned out, I guess we saved ourselves a lot of heartache and all that community-property bullshit by keeping it simple. She got an offer to join a corporate law-firm in Washington around the same time I got an offer to come to KLAD as a weekend jock – not much, but a foot in the door. She told me it was her big chance and I had to be the most insensitive male chauvinist oinker in the United States to be dragging my feet, and furthermore she'd had it with California anyway. I told her I *also* had a chance. So we thrashed it out, and we trashed each other out, and at the end of all the thrashing and trashing Sandy went.

'About a year after that I decided to try and get the vasectomy reversed. No real reason for it, and I knew from the stuff I'd read that the chances were pretty spotty, but I thought what the hell.'

'You were seeing someone steadily then?' Bill asked.

'No – that's the funny part of it,' Richie said, frowning. 'I just woke up one day with this . . . I dunno, this hobbyhorse about getting it reversed.'

'You must have been nuts,' Eddie said. 'General anesthetic instead of a local? Surgery? Maybe a week in the hospital afterward?'

'Yeah, the doctor told me all of that stuff,' Richie replied. 'And I told him I wanted to go ahead anyway. I don't know why. The doc asked me if I understood the aftermath of the operation was sure to be painful while the result was only going to be a coin-toss at best. I said I did. He said okay, and I asked him when – my attitude being the sooner the better, you know. So he says hold your horses, son, hold your horses, the first step is to get a sperm sample just to make sure the reversal operation is necessary. I said, "Come on, I had the exam after the vasectomy. It worked." He told me that sometimes the vasa reconnected spontaneously. "Yo mamma!" I says. "Nobody ever told me that." He said the chances were very small – infinitesimal, really – but because the operation was so serious, we ought to check it out. So I popped into the men's room with a Frederick's of Hollywood catalogue and jerked off into a Dixie cup –'

'Beep-beep, Richie,' Beverly said.

'Yeah, you're right,' Richie said. 'The part about the Frederick's catalogue is a lie – you never find anything that good in a doctor's office. Anyway, the doc called me three days later and asked me which I wanted first, the good news or the bad news.

IT

'"Gimme the good news first," I said.

'"The good news is the operation won't be necessary," he said. "The bad news is that anybody you've been to bed with over the last two or three years could hit you with a paternity suit pretty much at will."

'"Are you saying what I think you're saying?" I asked him.

'"I'm telling you that you aren't shooting blanks and haven't been for quite awhile now," he said. "Millions of little wigglies in your sperm sample. Your days of going gaily in bareback with no questions asked have temporarily come to an end, Richard."

'I thanked him and hung up. Then I called Sandy in Washington.

'"Rich!" she says to me,' and Richie's voice suddenly *became* the voice of this girl Sandy whom none of them had ever met. It was not an imitation or even a likeness, exactly; it was more like an auditory painting. '"It's great to hear from you! I got married!"

'"Yeah, that's great," I said. "You should have let me know. I would have sent you a blender."

'She goes, "Same old Richie, always full of gags."

'So I said "Sure, same old Richie, always full of gags. By the way, Sandy, you didn't happen to have a kid or anything after you left LA, did you? Or maybe an unscheduled d and c, or something?"

'"That gag isn't so funny, Rich," she said, and I had a brainwave that she was getting ready to hang up on me, so I told her what happened. She started laughing, only this time it was real hard – she was laughing the way I always used to laugh with you guys, like somebody had told her the world's biggest bellybuster. So when she finally starts slowing down I ask her what in God's name is funny. "It's just so wonderful," she said. "This time the joke's on you. After all these years the joke is finally on Records Tozier. How many bastards have you sired since I came east, Rich?"

'"I take it that means you still haven't experienced the joys of motherhood?" I ask her.

'"I'm due in July," she says. "Were there any more questions?"

'"Yeah," I go. "When did you change your mind about the immorality of bringing children into such a shitty world?"

'"When I finally met a man who wasn't a shit," she answers, and hangs up.'

Bill began to laugh. He laughed until tears rolled down his cheeks. 'Yeah,' Richie said. 'I think she cut it off quick so she'd really get the last word, but she could have hung on the line all day. I know when I've been aced. I went back to the doctor a week later and asked him if he could be a little clearer on the odds against that sort of spontan-

489

eous regeneration. He said he'd talked with some of his colleagues about the matter. It turned out that in the three-year period 1980–82, the California branch of the AMA logged twenty-three reports of spontaneous regeneration. Six of those turned out to be simply botched operations. Six others were either hoaxes or cons – guys looking to take a bite out of some doctor's bank account. So . . . eleven real ones in three years.'

'Eleven out of how many?' Beverly asked.

'Twenty-eight thousand six hundred and eighteen,' Richie said calmly.

Silence around the table.

'So I went and beat Irish Sweepstakes odds,' Richie said, 'and still no kid to show for it. That give you any good chucks, Eds?'

Eddie began stubbornly: 'It still doesn't *prove* –'

'No,' Bill said, 'it doesn't prove a thing. But it certainly suggests a link. The question is, what do we do now? Have you thought about that, Mike?'

'I've thought about it, sure,' Mike said, 'but it was impossible to decide anything until you all got together again and talked, the way you've been doing. There was no way I could predict how this reunion would go until it actually happened.'

He paused for a long time, looking thoughtfully at them.

'I've got one idea,' he said, 'but before I tell you what it is, I think we have to agree on whether or not we have business to do here. Do we want to try again to do what we tried to do once before? Do we want to try to kill It again? Or do we just divide the check up six ways and go back to what we were doing?'

'It seems as if –' Beverly began, but Mike shook his head at her. He wasn't done.

'You have to understand that our chances of success are impossible to predict. I know they're not good, just as I know they would have been a little better if Stan was here, too. Still not real good, but better. With Stan gone, the circle we made that day is broken. I don't really think we can destroy It, or even send It away for a little while, as we did before, with a broken circle. I think It will kill us, one by one by one, and probably in some extremely horrible ways. As children we made a complete circle in some way I don't understand even now. I think that, if we agree to go ahead, we'll have to try to form a smaller circle. I don't know if that can be done. I believe it might be possible to *think* we'd done it, only to discover – when it was too late – well . . . that it was too late.'

Mike regarded them again, eyes sunken and tired in his brown face. 'So I think we need to take a vote. Stay and try it again, or go home. Those are the choices. I got you here on the strength of an old promise I wasn't even sure you'd remember, but I can't hold you here on the strength of that promise. The results of that would be worse and more of it.'

He looked at Bill, and in that moment Bill understood what was coming. He dreaded it, was helpless to stop it, and then, with the same feeling of relief he imagined must come to a suicide when he takes his hands off the wheel of the speeding car and simply uses them to cover his eyes, he accepted it. Mike had gotten them here, Mike had laid it all neatly out for them . . . and now he was relinquishing the mantle of leadership. He intended that mantle to go back to the person who had worn it in 1958.

'What do you say, Big Bill? Call the question.'

'Before I do,' Bill said, 'd-does everyone *understand* the question? You were going to say something, Bev.'

She shook her head.

'All right; I g-guess the question is, do we stay and fight or do we forget the whole thing? Those in favor of staying?'

No one at the table moved at all for perhaps five seconds, and Bill was reminded of auctions he had attended where the price on an item suddenly soared into the stratosphere and those who didn't want to bid anymore almost literally played statues; one was afraid to scratch an itch or wave a fly off the end of one's nose for fear the auctioneer would take it for another five grand or twenty-five.

Bill thought of Georgie, Georgie who had meant no one any harm, who had only wanted to get out of the house after being cooped up all week, Georgie with his color high, his newspaper boat in one hand, snapping the buckles of his yellow rainslicker with the other, Georgie thanking him . . . and then bending over and kissing Bill's fever-heated cheek: *Thanks, Bill. It's a neat boat.*

He felt the old rage rise in him, but he was older now and his perspective was wider. It wasn't just Georgie now. A horrid slew of names marched through his head: Betty Ripsom, found frozen into the ground, Cheryl Lamonica, fished out of the Kenduskeag, Matthew Clements, torn from his tricycle, Veronica Grogan, nine years old and found in a sewer, Steven Johnson, Lisa Albrecht, all the others, and God only knew how many of the missing.

He raised his hand slowly and said, 'Let's kill It. This time let's really kill It.'

For a moment his hand hung there alone, like the hand of the only kid in class who knows the right answer, the one all the other kids hate. Then Richie sighed, raised his own hand, and said: 'What the hell. It can't be any worse than interviewing Ozzy Osbourne.'

Beverly raised her hand. Her color was back now, but in hectic patches that flared along her cheekbones. She looked both tremendously excited and scared to death.

Mike raised his hand.

Ben raised his.

Eddie Kaspbrak sat back in his chair, looking as if he wished he could actually melt into it and thus disappear. His face, thin and delicate-looking, was miserably afraid as he looked first right and then left and then back to Bill. For a moment Bill felt sure Eddie was simply going to push back his chair, rise, and bolt from the room without looking back. Then he raised one hand in the air and grasped his aspirator tightly in the other.

'Way to go, Eds,' Richie said. 'We're really gonna have ourselves some chucks this time, I bet.'

'Beep-beep, Richie,' Eddie said in a wavering voice.

6

The Losers Get Dessert

'So what's your one idea, Mike?' Bill asked. The mood had been broken by Rose, the hostess, who had come in with a dish of fortune cookies. She looked around at the six people who had their hands in the air with a carefully polite lack of curiosity. They lowered them hastily, and no one said anything until Rose was gone again.

'It's simple enough,' Mike said, 'but it might be pretty damn dangerous, too.'

'Spill it,' Richie said.

'I think we ought to split up for the rest of the day. I think each of us ought to go back to the place in Derry he or she remembers best . . . outside the Barrens, that is. I don't think any of us should go there – not yet. Think of it as a series of walking-tours, if you like.'

'What's the purpose, Mike?' Ben asked.

'I'm not entirely sure. You have to understand that I'm going pretty much on intuition here –'

'But this has got a good beat and you can dance to it,' Richie said.

The others smiled. Mike did not; he nodded instead. 'That's as good a way of putting it as any. Going on intuition *is* like picking up a beat and dancing to it. Using intuition is a hard thing for grownups to do, and that's the main reason I think it might be the right thing for us to do. Kids, after all, operate on it about eighty percent of the time, at least until they're fourteen or so.'

'You're talking about plugging back into the situation,' Eddie said.

'I suppose so. Anyway, that's my idea. If no specific place to go comes to you, just follow your feet and see where they take you. Then we meet tonight, at the library, and talk over what happened.'

'If *anything* happens,' Ben said.

'Oh, I think things will.'

'What sort of things?' Bill asked.

Mike shook his head. 'I have no idea. I think whatever happens is apt to be unpleasant. I think it's even possible that one of us may not turn up at the library tonight. No reason for thinking that ... except that intuition thing again.'

Silence greeted this.

'Why alone?' Beverely asked finally. 'If we're supposed to do this as a group, why do you want us to start alone, Mike? Especially if the risk really turns out to be as high as you think it might be?'

'I think I can answer that,' Bill said.

'Go ahead, Bill,' Mike said.

'It *started* alone for each of us,' Bill said to Beverly. 'I don't remember everything – not yet – but I sure remember that much. The picture in George's room that moved. Ben's mummy. The leper that Eddie saw under the porch on Neibolt Street. Mike finding the blood on the grass near the Canal in Bassey Park. And the bird ... there was something about a bird, wasn't there, Mike?'

Mike nodded grimly.

'A big bird.'

'Yes, but not as friendly as the one on *Sesame Street*.'

Richie cackled wildly. 'Derry's answer to James Brown Gets Off A Good One! Oh chillun, is we blessed or is we blessed!'

'Beep-beep, Richie,' Mike said, and Richie subsided.

'For you it was the voice from the pipe and the blood that came out of the drain,' Bill said to Beverly. 'And for Richie ...' But here he paused, puzzled.

'I must be the exception that proves the rule, Big Bill,' Richie said. 'The first time I came in contact with anything that summer that was weird – I mean really big-league weird – was in George's room, with you. When you and I went back to your house that day and looked at his photo album. The picture of Center Street by the Canal started to move. Do you remember?'

'Yes,' Bill said. 'But are you sure there was nothing before that, Richie? Nothing at all?'

'I –' Something flickered in Richie's eyes. He said slowly, 'Well, there was the day Henry and his friends chased me – before the end of school, this was, and I got away from them in the toy department of Freese's. I went up by City Center and sat down on a park bench for awhile and I thought I saw . . . but that was just something I *dreamed*.'

'What was it?' Beverly asked.

'Nothing,' Richie said, almost brusquely. 'A dream. Really.' He looked at Mike. 'I don't mind taking a walk, though. It'll kill the afternoon. Views of the old homestead.'

'So we're agreed?' Bill asked.

They nodded.

'And we'll meet at the library tonight at . . . when do you suggest, Mike?'

'Seven o'clock. Ring the bell if you're late. The libe closes at seven on weekdays until summer vacation starts for the kids.'

'Seven it is,' Bill said, and let his eyes range soberly over them. 'And be careful. You want to remember that none of us really knows what we're d-d-doing. Think of this as reconnaissance. If you should see something, don't fight. Run.'

'I'm a lover, not a fighter,' Richie said in a dreamy Michael Jackson Voice.

'Well, if we're going to do it, we ought to get going,' Ben said. A small smile pulled up the left corner of his mouth. It was more bitter than amused. 'Although I'll be damned if I could tell you right this minute where I'm going to go, if the Barrens are out. That was the best of it for me – going down there with you guys.' His eyes moved to Beverly, held there for a moment, moved away. 'I can't think of anyplace else that means very much to me. Probably I'll just wander around for a couple of hours, looking at buildings and getting wet feet.'

'You'll find a place to go, Haystack,' Richie said. 'Visit some of your old food-stops and gas up.'

Ben laughed. 'My capacity's gone down a lot since I was eleven. I'm so full you guys may just have to roll me out of here.'

'Well, I'm all set,' Eddie said.

'Wait a sec!' Beverly cried as they began to push back from their chairs. 'The fortune cookies! Don't forget those!'

'Yeah,' Richie said. 'I can see mine now. YOU WILL SOON BE EATEN UP BY A LARGE MONSTER. HAVE A NICE DAY.'

They laughed and Mike passed the little bowl of fortune cookies to Richie, who took one and then sent it on around the table. Bill noticed that no one opened his or her cookie until each had one; they sat with the little hat-shaped cookies either in front of them or held in their hands, and even as Beverly, still smiling, picked hers up, Bill felt a cry rising in his throat: *No! No, don't do that, it's part of it, put it back, don't open it!*

But it was too late. Beverly had broken hers open, Ben was doing the same to his, Eddie was cutting into his with the edge of his fork, and just before Beverly's smile turned to a grimace of horror Bill had time to think: *We knew, somehow we knew, because no one simply bit into his or her fortune cookie. That would have been the normal thing to do, but no one did it. Somehow, some part of us still remembers . . . everything.*

And he found that insensate underknowledge somehow the most horrifying realization of all; it spoke more eloquently than Mike could have about how surely and deeply It had touched each one of them . . . and how Its touch was still upon them.

Blood spurted up from Beverly's fortune cookie as if from a slashed artery. It splashed across her hand and then gouted onto the white napery which covered the table, staining it a bright red that sank in and then spread out in grasping pink fingers.

Eddie Kaspbrak uttered a strangled cry and pushed himself away from the table with such a sudden revolted confusion of arms and legs that his chair nearly tipped over. A huge bug, its chitinous carapace an ugly yellow-brown, was pushing its way out of his fortune cookie as if from a cocoon. Its obsidian eyes stared blindly forward. As it lurched onto Eddie's bread-and-butter plate, cookie crumbs fell from its back in a little shower that Bill heard clearly and which came back to haunt his dreams when he slept for a while later that afternoon. As it freed itself entirely it rubbed its thin rear legs together, producing a dry reedy hum, and Bill realized it was some sort of terribly mutated cricket. It lumbered to the edge of the dish and tumbled onto the tablecloth on its back.

'Oh God!' Richie managed in a choked voice. 'Oh God Big Bill it's an eye dear God it's an eye a fucking *eye* –'

Bill's head snapped around and he saw Richie staring down at his fortune cookie, his lips drawn back from his teeth in a kind of sickened leer. A chunk of his cookie's glazed surface had fallen onto the tablecloth, revealing a hole from which a human eyeball stared with glazed intensity. Cookie crumbs were scattered across its blank brown iris and embedded in its sclera.

Ben Hanscom threw his – not a calculated throw but the startled reaction of a person who has been utterly surprised by some piece of nasty work. As his fortune cookie rolled across the table Bill saw two teeth inside its hollow, their roots dark with clotted blood. They rattled together like seeds in a hollow gourd.

He looked back at Beverly and saw she was hitching in breath to scream. Her eyes were fixed on the thing that had crawled out of Eddie's cookie, the thing that was now kicking its sluggish legs as it lay overturned on the tablecloth.

Bill got moving. He was not thinking, only reacting. *Intuition,* he thought crazily as he lunged out of his seat and clapped his hand over Beverly's mouth just before she could utter the scream. *Here I am, acting on intuition. Mike should be proud of me.*

What came out of Beverly's mouth was not a scream but a strangled '*Mmmmph!*'

Eddie was making those whistling sounds that Bill remembered so well. No problem there, a good honk on the old lung-sucker would set Eddie right. *Right as a trivet,* Freddie Firestone would have said, and Bill wondered – not for the first time – why a person had such weird thoughts at times like these.

He glanced around fiercely at the others, and what came out was something else from that summer, something that sounded both impossibly archaic and exactly right: 'Dummy up! All of you! Not one sound! Just *dummy up!*'

Rich wiped a hand across his mouth. Mike's complexion had gone a dirty gray, but he nodded at Bill. All of them moved away from the table. Bill had not opened his own fortune cookie, but now he could see its sides moving slowly in and out – bulge and relax, bulge and relax, bulge and relax – as his own party-favor tried to escape.

'*Mmmmmph!*' Beverly said against his hand again, her breath tickling his palm.

'Dummy up, Bev,' he said, and took his hand away.

Her face seemed to be all eyes. Her mouth twitched. 'Bill . . . Bill, did you see . . .' Her eyes strayed back to the cricket and then fixed there. The cricket appeared to be dying. Its rugose eyes stared back at her, and presently Beverly began to moan.

'Quh-Quh-Quit that,' he said grimly. 'Pull back to the table.'

'I can't, Billy, I can't get near that thi –'

'You can! You *h-have* to!' He heard footsteps, light and quick, coming up the short hall on the other side of the beaded curtain. He looked around at the others. 'All of you! Pull up to the table! Talk! Look natural!'

Beverly looked at him, eyes pleading, and Bill shook his head. He sat down and pulled his chair in, trying not to look at the fortune cookie on his plate. It had swelled like some unimaginable boil which was filling with pus. And still it pulsed slowly in and out. *I could have bitten into that*, he thought faintly.

Eddie triggered his aspirator down his throat again, gasping mist into his lungs in a long, thin screaming sound.

'So who do you think's going to win the pennant?' Bill asked Mike, smiling insanely. Rose came through the curtain just then, her face politely questioning. Out of the corner of his eye Bill saw that Bev had pulled up to the table again. *Good girl*, he thought.

'I think the Chicago Bears look good,' Mike said.

'Everything is all right?' Rose asked.

'F-Fine,' Bill said. He cocked a thumb in Eddie's direction. 'Our friend had an asthma attack. He took his medication. He's better now.'

Rose looked at Eddie, concerned.

'Better,' Eddie wheezed.

'You would like that I clear now?'

'Very shortly,' Mike said, and offered a large false smile.

'Was good?' Her eyes surveyed the table again, a bit of doubt overlaying a deep well of serenity. She did not see the cricket, the eye, the teeth, or the way Bill's fortune cookie appeared to be breathing. Her eye similarly passed over the bloodstain splotched on the tablecloth without trouble.

'Everything was *very* good,' Beverly said, and smiled – a more natural smile than either Bill's or Mike's. It seemed to set Rose's mind at rest, convinced her that if something had gone wrong in here, it had been the fault of neither Rose's service nor her kitchen. *Girl's got a lot of guts*, Bill thought.

'Fortunes were good?' Rose asked.

'Well,' Richie said, 'I don't know about the others, but I for one got a real eyeful.'

Bill heard a minute cracking sound. He looked down at his plate and saw a leg poking blindly out of his fortune cookie. It scraped at his plate.

I could have bitten into that, he thought again, but held onto his smile. 'Very fine,' he said.

Richie was looking at Bill's plate. A great grayish-black fly was slowing birthing itself from the collapsing remains of his cookie. It buzzed weakly. Yellowish goo flowed sluggishly out of the cookie and puddled on the tablecloth. There was a smell now, the bland thick smell of an infected wound.

'Well, if I can help you in no way at this moment . . .'

'Not right now,' Ben said. 'A wonderful meal. Most . . . most unusual.'

'I leave you then,' she said, and bowed out through the beaded curtain. The beads were still swaying and clacking together when all of them pushed away from the table again.

'What is it?' Ben asked huskily, looking at the thing on Bill's plate.

'A fly,' Bill said. 'A mutant fly. Courtesy of a writer named George Langlahan, I think. He wrote a story called "The Fly." A movie was made out of it – not a terribly good one. But the story scared the bejesus out of me. It's up to Its old tricks, all right. That fly business has been on my mind a lot lately, because I've sort of been planning this novel – *Roadbugs*, I've been thinking of calling it. I know the title sounds p-pretty stupid, but you see –'

'Excuse me,' Beverly said distantly. 'I have to vomit, I think.'

She was gone before any of the men could rise.

Bill shook out his napkin and threw it over the fly, which was the size of a baby sparrow. Nothing so large could have come from something as small as a Chinese fortune cookie . . . but it had. It buzzed twice under the napkin and then fell silent.

'Jesus,' Eddie said faintly.

'Let's get the righteous fuck out of here,' Mike said. 'We can meet Bev in the lobby.'

Beverly was just coming out of the women's room as they gathered by the cash register. She looked pale but composed. Mike paid the check, kissed Rose's cheek, and then they all went out into the rainy afternoon.

'Does this change anyone's mind?' Mike asked.

'I don't think it changes mine,' Ben said.

'No,' Eddie said.

'*What* mind?' Richie said.

Bill shook his head and then looked at Beverly.

'I'm staying,' she said. 'Bill, what did you mean when you said It's up to Its old tricks?'

'I've been thinking about writing a bug story,' he said. 'That Langlahan story had woven itself into my thinking. And so I saw a fly. Yours was blood, Beverly. Why was blood on your mind?'

'I guess because of the blood from the drain,' Beverly said at once. 'The blood that came out of the bathroom drain in the old place, when I was eleven.' But was that really it? She didn't really think so. Because what had flashed immediately to mind when the blood spurted across her fingers in a warm little jet had been the bloody footprint she had left behind her after stepping on the broken perfume bottle. Tom. And

(*Bevvie sometimes I worry* a lot)

her father.

'You got a bug, too,' Bill said to Eddie. 'Why?'

'Not just a bug,' Eddie said. 'A *cricket*. There are crickets in our basement. Two-hundred-thousand-dollar house and we can't get rid of the crickets. They drive us crazy at night. A couple of nights before Mike called, I had a really terrible nightmare. I dreamed I woke up and my bed was full of crickets. I was trying to shoot them with my aspirator, but all it would do when I squeezed it was make crackling noises, and just before I woke up I realized *it* was full of crickets, too.'

'The hostess didn't see any of it,' Ben said. He looked at Beverly. 'Like your folks never saw the blood that came out of the drain, even though it was everywhere.'

'Yes,' she said.

They stood looking at each other in the fine spring rain.

Mike looked at his watch. 'There'll be a bus in twenty minutes or so,' he said, 'or I can take four of you in my car, if we cram. Or I can call some cabs. Whatever way you want to do it.'

'I think I'm going to walk from here,' Bill said. 'I don't know where I'm going, but a little fresh air seems like a great idea along about now.'

'I'm going to call a cab,' Ben said.

'I'll share it with you, if you'll drop me off downtown,' Richie said.

'Okay. Where you going?'

Richie shrugged. 'Not really sure yet.'

The others elected to wait for the bus.

'Seven tonight,' Mike reminded. 'And be careful, all of you.'

They agreed to be careful, although Bill did not know how you could truthfully make a promise like that when dealing with such a formidable array of unknown factors.

He started to say so, then looked at their faces and saw that they knew it already.

He walked away instead, raising one hand briefly in farewell. The misty air felt good against his face. The walk back to town would be a long one, but that was all right. He had a lot to think about. He was glad that the reunion was over and the business had begun.

CHAPTER ELEVEN
WALKING TOURS

1

Ben Hanscom Makes a Withdrawal

Richie Tozier got out of the cab at the three-way intersection of Kansas Street, Center Street, and Main Street, and Ben dismissed it at the top of Up-Mile Hill. The driver was Bill's 'religious fella,' but neither Richie nor Ben knew it: Dave had lapsed into a morose silence. Ben could have gotten off with Richie, he supposed, but it seemed better somehow that they all start off alone.

He stood on the corner of Kansas Street and Daltrey Close, watching the cab pull back into traffic, hands stuffed deeply into his pockets, trying to get the lunch's hideous conclusion out of his mind. He couldn't do it; his thoughts kept returning to that black-gray fly crawling out of the fortune cookie on Bill's plate, its veined wings plastered to its back. He would try to divert his mind from this unhealthy image, think he had succeeded, only to discover five minutes later that his mind was back at it.

I'm trying to justify it somehow, he thought, meaning it not in the moral sense but rather in the mathematical one. Buildings are built by observing certain natural laws; natural laws may be expressed by equations; equations must be justified. Where was the justification in what had happened less than half an hour ago?

Let it alone, he told himself, not for the first time. *You can't justify it, so let it alone.*

Very good advice; the problem was that he couldn't take it. He remembered that the day after he had seen the mummy on the iced-up Canal, his life had gone on as usual. He had known that whatever it had been had come very close to getting him, but his life had gone on: he had attended school, taken an arithmetic test, visited the library when school was over, and eaten with his usual heartiness. He had simply incorporated the thing he had seen on the

501

Canal into his life, and if he had almost been killed by it . . . well, kids were always almost getting killed. They dashed across streets without looking, they got horsing around in the lake and suddenly realized they had floated far past their depth on their rubber rafts and had to paddle back, they fell off monkey-bars on their asses and out of trees on their heads.

Now, standing here in the fading drizzle in front of a Trustworthy Hardware Store that had been a pawnshop in 1958 (Frati Brothers, Ben recalled, the double windows always full of pistols and rifles and straight-razors and guitars hung up by their necks like exotic animals), it occurred to him that kids were better at almost dying, and they were also better at incorporating the inexplicable into their lives. They believed implicitly in the invisible world. Miracles both bright and dark were to be taken into consideration, oh yes, most certainly, but they by no means stopped the world. A sudden upheaval of beauty or terror at ten did not preclude an extra cheese-dog or two for lunch at noon.

But when you grew up, all that changed. You no longer lay awake in your bed, sure something was crouching in the closet or scratching at the window . . . but when something *did* happen, something beyond rational explanation, the circuits overloaded. The axons and dendrites got hot. You started to jitter and jive, you started to shake rattle and roll, your imagination started to hop and bop and do the funky chicken all over your nerves. You couldn't just incorporate what had happened into your life experience. It didn't digest. Your mind kept coming back to it, pawing it lightly like a kitten with a ball of string . . . until eventually, of course, you either went crazy or got to a place where it was impossible for you to function.

And if that happens, Ben thought, *It's got me. Us. Cold.*

He started to walk up Kansas Street, not conscious of heading anyplace in particular. And thought suddenly: *What did we do with the silver dollar?*

He still couldn't remember.

The silver dollar, Ben . . . Beverly saved your life with it. Yours . . . maybe all the others' . . . and especially Bill's. It almost ripped my guts out before Beverly did . . . what? What did she do? And how was it able to work? She backed it off, and we all helped her. But how?

A word came to him suddenly, a word that meant nothing at all but which tightened his flesh: *Chüd.*

He looked down at the sidewalk and for a moment saw the shape of a turtle chalked there, and the world seemed to swim before

502

his eyes. He shut them tightly and when he opened them saw it was not a turtle; only a hopscotch grid half-erased by the light rain.

Chüd.

What did that mean?

'I don't know,' he said aloud, and when he looked around quickly to see if anyone had heard him talking to himself, he saw that he had turned off Kansas Street and onto Costello Avenue. At lunch he had told the others that the Barrens were the only place in Derry where he had felt happy as a kid . . . but that wasn't quite true, was it? There had been another place. Either accidentally or unconsciously, he had come to that other place: the Derry Public Library.

He stood in front of it for a minute or two, hands still in his pockets. It hadn't changed; he admired its lines as much now as he had as a child. Like so many stone buildings that had been well-designed, it succeeded in confounding the closely observing eye with contradictions: its stone solidity was somehow balanced by the delicacy of its arches and slim columns; it looked both bank-safe squat and yet slim and clean (well, it *was* slim as city buildings went, especially those erected around the turn of the century, and the windows, crisscrossed with narrow strips of iron, were graceful and rounded). These contradictions saved it from ugliness, and he was not entirely surprised to feel a wave of love for the place.

Nothing much had changed on Costello Avenue. Glancing along it, he could see the Derry Community House, and he found himself wondering if the Costello Avenue Market was still there at the point where the avenue, which was semicircular, rejoined Kansas Street.

He walked across the library lawn, barely noticing that his dress boots were getting wet, to have a look at that glassed-in passageway between the grownups' library and the Children's Library. It was also unchanged, and from here, standing just outside the bowed branches of a weeping willow tree, he could see people passing back and forth. The old delight flooded him, and he really forgot what had happened at the end of the reunion lunch for the first time. He could remember walking around to this very same spot as a kid, only in the winter, plowing his way through snow that was almost hip-deep, and then standing for as long as fifteen minutes. He would come at dusk, he remembered, and again it was the contrasts that drew him and held him there with the tips of his fingers going numb and snow melting inside his green gumrubber boots. It would be drawing-down-dark out where he was, the world going purple with early winter shadows, the sky the color of ashes in the east and embers in the west. It would be cold where he was, ten degrees perhaps, and chillier than that if the wind was blowing across from the frozen Barrens, as it so often did.

But there, less than forty yards from where he stood, people walked back and forth in their shirtsleeves. There, less than forty yards from where he stood, was a tubeway of bright white light, thrown by the overhead fluorescents. Little kids giggled together, high-school sweethearts held hands (and if the librarian saw them, she would make them stop). It was somehow magical, magical in a good way that he had been too young to account for with such mundane things as electric power and oil heat. The magic was that glowing cylinder of light and life connecting those two dark buildings like a lifeline, the magic was in watching people walk through it across the dark snowfield, untouched by either the dark or the cold: It made them lovely and Godlike.

Eventually he would walk away (as he was doing now) and circle the building to the front door (as he was doing now), but he would always pause and look back once (as he was doing now) before the bulking stone shoulder of the adult library cut off the sight-line to that delicate umbilicus.

Ruefully amused at the ache of nostalgia around his heart, Ben went up the steps to the door of the adult library, paused for a moment on the narrow verandah just inside the pillars, always so high and cool no matter how hot the day. Then he pulled open the iron-bound door with the book-drop slot in it and went into the quiet.

The force of memory almost dizzied him for a moment as he stepped into the mild light of the hanging glass globes. The force was not physical – not like a shot to the jaw or a slap. It was more akin to that queer feeling of time doubling back on itself that people call, for want of a better term, *déjà-vu*. Ben had had the feeling before, but it had never struck him with such disorienting power; for the moment or two he stood inside the door, he felt literally lost in time, not really sure how old he was. Was he thirty-eight or eleven?

Here was the same murmuring quiet, broken only by an occasional whisper, the faint thud of a librarian stamping books or overdue notices, the hushed riffle of newspaper or magazine pages being turned. He loved the quality of the light as much now as then. It slanted through the high windows, gray as a pigeon's wing on this rainy afternoon, a light that was somehow somnolent and dozey.

He walked across the wide floor with its red-and-black linoleum pattern almost completely worn away, trying as he had always tried back then to hush the sound of his footfalls – the adult library rose up to a dome in the middle, and all sounds were magnified.

He saw that the circular iron staircases leading to the stacks were still there, one on either side of the horseshoe-shaped main desk, but he also saw that a tiny cagework elevator had been added at some point in the twenty-five years since he and his mamma had moved away. It was something of a relief – it drove a wedge into that suffocating feeling of *déjà-vu*.

He felt like an interloper crossing the wide floor, a spy from another country. He kept expecting the librarian at the desk to raise her head, look at him, and then challenge him in clear, ringing tones that would shatter the concentration of every reader here and focus every eye upon him: '*You! Yes, you! What are you doing here? You have no business here! You're from Outside! You're from Before! Go back where you came from! Go back right now, before I call the police!*'

She did look up, a young girl, pretty, and for one absurd moment it seemed to Ben that the fantasy was really going to come true, and his heart rose into his throat as her pale-blue eyes touched his. Then they passed on indifferently, and Ben found he could walk again. If he was a spy, he hadn't been found out.

He passed under the coil of one of the narrow and almost suicidally steep wrought-iron staircases on his way to the corridor leading to the Children's Library, and was amused to realize (only after he had done it) that he had run down another old track of his childhood behavior. He had looked up, hoping, as he had hoped as a kid, to see a girl in a skirt coming down those steps. He could remember (*now* he could remember) glancing up there for no reason at all one day when he was eight or nine and looking right up the chino skirt of a pretty high-school girl and seeing her clean pink underwear. As the sudden sunlit glint of Beverly Marsh's ankle-bracelet had shot an arrow of something more primitive than simple love or affection through his heart on the last day of school in 1958, so had the sight of the high-school girl's panties affected him; he could remember sitting at a table in the Children's Library and thinking of that unexpected view for perhaps as long as twenty minutes, his cheeks and forehead hot, a book about the history of trains open and unread before him, his penis a hard little branch in his pants, a branch that had sunk its roots all the way up into his belly. He had fantasized the two of them married, living in a small house on the outskirts of town, indulging in pleasures he did not in the least understand.

The feelings had passed off almost as suddenly as they had come, but he had never walked under the stairway again without glancing up. He hadn't ever seen anything else as interesting or affecting (once a fat lady working her way down with ponderous care, but he had looked away from *that* sight hastily, feeling ashamed, like a violator), but the habit persisted – he had done it again now, as a grown man.

He walked slowly down the glassed-in passageway, noticing other changes now: Yellow decals that said OPEC LOVES IT WHEN YOU WASTE ENERGY, SO SAVE A WATT! had been plastered over the switchplates. The framed pictures on the far wall when he entered this scaled-down world of blondewood tables and small blondewood chairs, this world where the drinking fountain was only four feet high, were not of Dwight Eisenhower and Richard Nixon but of Ronald Reagan and George Bush – Reagan, Ben recalled, had been host of *GE Theater* in the year that Ben had graduated from the fifth grade, and George Bush would not have seen thirty yet.

But –

That feeling of *déjà-vu* swept him again. He was helpless before it, and this time he felt the numb horror of a man who finally realizes, after half an hour of helpless splashing, that the shore is growing no closer and he is drowning.

It was story hour, and over in the corner a group of roughly a dozen little ones sat solemnly on their tiny chairs in a semicircle, listening. '*Who is that trip-trapping upon my bridge?*' the librarian said in the low, growling tones of the troll in the story, and Ben thought: *When she raises her head I'll see that it's Miss Davies; yes, it'll be Miss Davies and she won't look a day older –*

But when she did raise her head, he saw a much younger woman than Miss Davies had been even then.

Some of the children covered their mouths and giggled, but others only watched her, their eyes reflecting the eternal fascination of the fairy story: would the monster be bested . . . or would it feed?

'It is I, Billy Goat Gruff, trip-trapping on your bridge,' the librarian went on, and Ben, pale, walked past her.

How can it be the same story? The very same story? *Am I supposed to believe that's just coincidence? Because I don't . . . goddammit, I just don't!*

He bent to the drinking fountain, bending so far he felt like Richie doing one of his salami-salami-baloney routines.

I ought to talk to someone, he thought, panicked. *Mike . . . Bill . . . someone. Is something really stapling the past and present together here, or am I only imagining it? Because if I'm not, I'm not sure I bargained for this much. I –*

He looked at the checkout desk, and his heart seemed to stop in his chest for a moment before beginning to race doubletime. The poster was simple, stark . . . and familiar. It said simply:

REMEMBER THE CURFEW.
7 P.M.
DERRY POLICE DEPARTMENT

In that instant it all seemed to come clear to him – it came in a grisly flash of light, and he realized that the vote they had taken was a joke. There was no turning back, never had been. They were on a track as preordained as the memory-track which had caused him to look up when he passed under the stairway leading to the stacks. There was an echo here in Derry, a deadly echo, and all they could hope for was that the echo could be changed enough in their favor to allow them to escape with their lives.

'Christ,' he muttered, and scrubbed a palm up one cheek, hard.

'Can I help you, sir?' a voice at his elbow asked, and he jumped a little. It was a girl of perhaps seventeen, her dark-blonde hair held back from her pretty high-schooler's face with barrettes. A library assistant, of course; they'd had them in 1958 too, high-school girls and boys who shelved books, showed kids how to use the card catalogue, discussed book reports and school papers, helped bewildered scholars with their footnotes and bibliographies. The pay was a pittance, but there were always kids willing to do it. It was agreeable work.

On the heels of this, reading the girl's pleasant but questioning look a little more closely, he remembered that he no longer really belonged here – he was a giant in the land of little people. An intruder. In the adults' library he had felt uneasy about the possibility of being looked at or spoken to, but here it was something of a relief. For one thing, it proved he was still an adult, and the fact that the girl was clearly braless under her thin Western-style shirt was also more relief than turn-on: if proof that this was 1985 and not 1958 was needed, the clearly limned points of her nipples against the cotton of her shirt was it.

'No thank you,' he said, and then, for no reason at all that he could understand, he heard himself add: 'I was looking for my son.'

'Oh? What's his name? Maybe I've seen him.' She smiled. 'I know most of the kids.'

'His name is Ben Hanscom,' he said. 'But I don't see him here.'

'Tell me what he looks like and I'll give him a message, if there is one.'

'Well,' Ben said, uncomfortable now and beginning to wish he had never started this, 'he's on the stout side, and he looks a little bit like me. But it's no big deal, miss. If you see him, just tell him his dad popped by on his way home.'

'I will,' she said, and smiled, but the smile didn't reach her eyes, and Ben suddenly realized that she hadn't come over and spoken to him out of simple politeness and a wish to help. She happened to be a library assistant in the Children's Library in a town where nine children had been slain over a span of eight months. You see a strange man in this scaled-down world where adults rarely come except to drop their kids off or pick them up. You're suspicious . . . of course.

'Thank you,' he said, gave her a smile he hoped was reassuring, and then got the hell out.

He walked back through the corridor to the adults' library and went to the desk on an impulse he didn't understand . . . but of course they were supposed to follow their impulses this afternoon, weren't they? Follow their impulses and see where they led.

The name plate on the circulation desk identified the pretty young librarian as Carole Danner. Behind her, Ben could see a door with a frosted-glass panel; lettered on this was MICHAEL HANLON HEAD LIBRARIAN.

'May I help you?' Ms Danner asked.

'I think so,' Ben said. 'That is, I hope so. I'd like to get a library card.'

'Very good,' she said, and took out a form. 'Are you a resident of Derry?'

'Not presently.'

'Home address, then?'

'Rural Star Route 2, Hemingford Home, Nebraska.' He paused for a moment, a little amused by her stare, and then reeled off the Zip Code: '59341.'

'Is this a joke, Mr Hanscom?'

'Not at all.'

'Are you moving to Derry, then?'

'I have no plans to, no.'

'This is a long way to come to borrow books, isn't it? Don't they have libraries in Nebraska?'

'It's kind of a sentimental thing,' Ben said. He would have thought telling a stranger this would be embarrassing, but he found it wasn't. 'I grew up in Derry, you see. This is the first time I've been back since I was a kid. I've been walking around, seeing what's changed and what hasn't. And all at once it occurred to me that I spent about ten years of my life here between ages three and thirteen, and I don't have a single thing to remember those years by. Not so much as a postcard. I had some silver dollars, but I lost one of them and gave the rest to a friend. I guess what I want is a souvenir of my childhood. It's late, but don't they say better late than never?'

Carole Danner smiled, and the smile changed her pretty face into one that was beautiful. 'I think that's very sweet,' she said. 'If you'd like to browse for ten or fifteen minutes, I'll have the card made up for you when you come back to the desk.'

Ben grinned a little. 'I guess there'll be a fee,' he said. 'Out-of-towner and all.'

'Did you have a card when you were a boy?'

'I sure did.' Ben smiled. 'Except for my friends, I guess that library card was the most important −'

'Ben, would you come up here?' a voice called suddenly, cutting across the library hush like a scalpel.

He turned around, jumping guiltily the way people do when someone shouts in a library. He saw no one he knew . . . and realized a moment later that no one had looked up or shown any sign of surprise or annoyance. The old men still read their copies of the Derry News, the Boston Globe, National Geographic, Time, Newsweek, U.S. News & World Report. At the tables in the Reference Room, two high-school girls still had their heads together over a stack of papers and a pile of file-cards. Several browsers went on looking through the books on the shelves marked CURRENT FICTION − SEVEN−DAY−LOAN. An old man in a ridiculous driving-cap, a cold pipe clenched between his teeth, went on leafing through a folio of Luis de Vargas' sketches.

He turned back to the young woman, who was looking at him, puzzled.

'Is anything wrong?'

'No,' Ben said, smiling. 'I thought I heard something. I guess I'm more jet-lagged than I thought. What were you saying?'

'Well, actually you were saying. But I was about to add that if you had a card when you were a resident, your name will still be in the files,' she said. 'We keep everything on microfiche now. Some change from when you were a kid here, I guess.'

'Yes,' he said. 'A lot of things have changed in Derry . . . but a lot of things also seem to have remained the same.'

'Anyway, I can just look you up and give you a renewal card. No charge.'

'That's great,' Ben said, and before he could add thanks the voice cut through the library's sacramental silence again, louder now, ominously jolly: '*Come on up, Ben! Come on up, you fat little fuck! This Is Your Life, Ben Hanscom!*'

Ben cleared his throat. 'I appreciate it,' he said.

'Don't mention it.' She cocked her head at him. 'Has it gotten warm outside?'

'A little,' he said. 'Why?'

'You're –'

'*Ben Hanscom did it!*' the voice screamed. It was coming from above – coming from the stacks. '*Ben Hanscom killed the children! Get him! Grab him!*'

'– perspiring,' she finished.

'Am I?' he said idiotically.

'I'll have this made up right away,' she said.

'Thank you.'

She headed for the old Royal typewriter at the corner of her desk.

Ben walked slowly away, his heart a thudding drum in his chest. Yes, he was sweating; he could feel it trickling down from his forehead, his armpits, matting the hair on his chest. He looked up and saw Pennywise the Clown standing at the top of the lefthand staircase, looking down at him. His face was white with greasepaint. His mouth bled lipstick in a killer's grin. There were empty sockets where his eyes should have been. He held a bunch of balloons in one hand and a book in the other.

Not he, Ben thought. *It. I am standing here in the middle of the Derry Public Library's rotunda on a late-spring afternoon in 1985, I am a grown man, and I am face to face with my childhood's greatest nightmare. I am face to face with It.*

'Come on up, Ben,' Pennywise called down. 'I won't hurt you. I've got a book for you! A book . . . and a balloon! Come on up!'

Ben opened his mouth to call back, *You're insane if you think I'm going up there*, and suddenly realized that if he did that, everyone here would be looking at him, everyone here would be thinking, *Who is that crazyman?*

'Oh, I know you can't answer,' Pennywise called down, and giggled. 'Almost fooled you there for a minute, though, didn't I? "Pardon me, sir, do you have Prince Albert in a can? . . . You do? . . . Better let the poor guy out!" "Pardon me, ma'am, is your refrigerator running? . . . It is? . . . Then hadn't you better go catch it?"'

The clown on the landing threw its head back and shrieked laughter. It roared and echoed in the dome of the rotunda like a flight of black bats, and Ben was only able to keep from clapping his hands over his ears with a tremendous effort of will.

'Come on up, Ben,' Pennywise called down. 'We'll talk. Neutral ground. What do you say?'

I'm not coming up there, Ben thought. *When I finally come to you, you won't want to see me, I think. We're going to kill you.*

The clown shrieked laughter again. 'Kill me? *Kill* me?' And suddenly, horribly, the voice was Richie Tozier's voice, not *his* voice, precisely, but Richie Tozier doing his Pickaninny Voice: 'Doan kill me, massa, I be a good nigguh, doan kill thisyere black boy, Haystack!' Then that shrieking laughter again.

Trembling, white-faced, Ben walked across the echoing center of the adults' library. He felt that soon he would vomit. He stood in front of a shelf of books and took one down at random with a hand that trembled badly. His cold fingers flittered the pages.

'This is your one chance, Haystack!' the voice called from behind and above him. 'Get out of town. Get out before it gets dark tonight. I'll be after you tonight . . . you and the others. You're too old to stop me, Ben. You're *all* too old. Too old to do anything but get yourselves killed. Get out, Ben. Do you want to see this tonight?'

He turned slowly, still holding the book in his icy hands. He didn't want to look, but it were as if there were an invisible hand under his chin, tilting his head up and up and up.

The clown was gone. Dracula was standing at the top of the lefthand stairway, but it was no movie Dracula; it was not Bela Lugosi or Christopher Lee or Frank Langella or Francis Lederer or Reggie Nalder. An ancient man-thing with a face like a twisted root stood there. Its face was deadly pale, its eyes purplish-red, the color of blood-clots. Its mouth dropped open, revealing a mouthful of Gillette Blue-Blades that had been set in the gums at angles; it was like looking into a deadly mirror-maze where a single misstep could get you cut in half.

'KEEE-RUNCH!' it screamed, and its jaws snapped closed. Blood gouted from its mouth in a red-black flood. Chunks of its severed lips fell to the glowing white silk of its formal shirt and slid down its front, leaving snail-trails of blood behind.

'*What did Stan Uris see before he died?*' the vampire on the landing screamed down at him, laughing through the bloody hole of its mouth. '*Was it Prince Albert in a can? Was it Davy Crockett, King of the Wild Frontier? What did he see, Ben? Do you want to see it too? What did he see?*

511

What did he see?' Then that shrieking laughter again, and Ben knew that he would scream now himself, yes, there was no way to stop the scream, it was going to come. Blood was pattering down from the landing in a grisly shower. One drop had landed on the arthritis-bunched hand of an old man who was reading *The Wall Street Journal*. It was running down between his knuckles, unseen and unfelt.

Ben hitched in breath, sure the scream would follow, unthinkable in the quiet of this softly drizzling spring afternoon, as shocking as the slash of a knife . . . or a mouthful of razor-blades.

Instead, what came out in a shaky, uneven rush, spoken instead of screamed, spoken low like a prayer, were these words: 'We made slugs out of it, of course. We made the silver dollar into silver slugs.'

The gentleman in the driving-cap who had been perusing the de Vargas sketches looked up sharply. 'Nonsense,' he said. Now people *did* look up; someone hissed 'Shhh!' at the old man in an annoyed voice.

'I'm sorry,' Ben said in a low, trembling voice. He was faintly aware that his face was now running with sweat, and that his shirt was plastered to his body. 'I was thinking aloud —'

'Nonsense,' the old gentleman repeated, in a louder voice. 'Can't make silver bullets from silver dollars. Common misconception. Pulp fiction. Problem is with specific gravity —'

Suddenly the woman, Ms Danner, was there. 'Mr Brockhill, you'll have to be quiet,' she said kindly enough. 'People are reading —'

'Man's sick,' Brockhill said abruptly, and went back to his book. 'Give him an aspirin, Carole.'

Carole Danner looked at Ben and her face sharpened with concern. '*Are* you ill, Mr Hanscom? I know it's terribly impolite to say so, but you look terrible.'

Ben said, 'I . . . I had Chinese food for lunch. I don't think it's agreed with me.'

'If you want to lie down, there's a cot in Mr Hanlon's office. You could —'

'No. Thanks, but no.' What he wanted was not to lie down but to get the hell out of the Derry Public Library. He looked up at the landing. The clown was gone. The vampire was gone. But tied to the low wrought-iron railing which surrounded the landing was a balloon. Written on its bulging skin were the words: HAVE A GOOD DAY! TONIGHT YOU DIE!

512

'I've got your library card,' she said, putting a tentative hand on his arm. 'Do you still want it?'

'Yes, thanks,' Ben said. He drew a deep, shuddery breath. 'I'm very sorry about this.'

'I just hope it isn't food-poisoning,' she said.

'Wouldn't work,' Mr Brockhill said without looking up from de Vargas or removing his dead pipe from the corner of his mouth. 'Device of pulp fiction. Bullet would tumble.'

And speaking again with no foreknowledge that he was going to speak, Ben said: '*Slugs*, not bullets. We realized almost right away that we couldn't make bullets. I mean, we were just kids. It was my idea to –'

'*Shhhh!*' someone said again.

Brockhill gave Ben a slightly startled look, seemed about to speak, then went back to the sketches.

At the desk, Carole Danner handed him a small orange card with DERRY PUBLIC LIBRARY stamped across the top. Bemused, Ben realized it was the first adult library-card he had owned in his whole life. The one he'd had as a kid had been canary-yellow.

'Are you sure you don't want to lie down, Mr Hanscom?'

'I'm feeling a little better, thanks.'

'Sure?'

He managed a smile. 'I'm sure.'

'You do look a little better,' she said, but she said it doubtfully, as if understanding that this was the proper thing to say but not really believing it.

Then she was holding a book under the microfilm gadget they used these days to record book-loans, and Ben felt a touch of almost hysterical amusement. *It's the book I grabbed off the shelf when the clown started to do its Pickaninny Voice*, he thought. *She thought I wanted to borrow it. I've made my first withdrawal from the Derry Public Library in twenty-five years, and I don't even know what the book is. Furthermore, I don't care. Just let me out of here, okay? That'll be enough.*

'Thank you,' he said, putting the book under his arm.

'You're more than welcome, Mr Hanscom. Are you sure you wouldn't like an aspirin?'

'Quite sure,' he said – and then hesitated. 'You wouldn't by any chance know what happened to Mrs Starrett, would you? Barbara Starrett? She used to be the head of the Children's Library.'

'She died,' Carole Danner said. 'Three years ago. It was a stroke,

I understand. It was a great shame. She was relatively young . . . fifty-eight or -nine, I think. Mr Hanlon closed the library for the day.'

'Oh,' Ben said, and felt a hollow place open in his heart. That's what happened when you got back to your used-to-be, as the song put it. The frosting on the cake was sweet, but the stuff underneath was bitter. People forgot you, or died on you, or lost their hair and teeth. In some cases you found that they had lost their minds. Oh it was great to be alive. Boy howdy.

'I'm sorry,' she said. 'You liked her, didn't you?'

'All the kids liked Mrs Starrett,' Ben said, and was alarmed to realize that tears were now very close.

'Are you –'

If she asks me if I'm all right one more time, I really am going to cry, I think. Or scream. Or something.

He glanced at his watch and said, 'I really have to run. Thanks for being so nice.'

'Have a nice day, Mr Hanscom.'

Sure. Because tonight I die.

He tipped a finger her way and started back across the floor. Mr Brockhill glanced up at him once, sharply and suspiciously.

He looked up at the landing which topped the lefthand staircase. The balloon still floated there, tied by its string to lacy wrought-iron. But now the printing on its side read.

I KILLED BARBARA STARRETT!
– PENNYWISE THE CLOWN

He looked away, feeling the pulse in his throat starting to run again. He let himself out and was startled by sunlight – the clouds overhead were coming unravelled and a warm late-May sun was shafting down, making the grass look impossibly green and lush. Ben felt something start to lift from his heart. It seemed to him that he had left some insupportable burden behind in the library . . . and then he looked down at the book he had inadvertently withdrawn and his teeth clamped together with sudden, painful force. It was *Bulldozer*, by Stephen W. Meader, one of the books he had withdrawn from the library on the day he had dived into the Barrens to get away from Henry Bowers and his friends.

And speaking of Henry, the track of his engineer boot was still on the book's cover.

Shaking, fumbling at the pages, he turned to the back. The library had gone over to a microfilm checkout system; he had *seen* that. But there was still a pocket in the back of this book with a card tucked into it. There was a name written on each line of the card followed by the librarian's return-date stamp. Looking at the card, Ben saw this:

NAME OF BORROWER	RETURN BY STAMPED DATE
Charles N. Brown	MAY 14 58
David Hartwell	JUN 1 58
Joseph Brennan	JUN 17 58

And, on the last line of the card, his own childish signature, written in heavy pencil-strokes:

Benjamin Hanscom	JUL 9 58

Stamped across this card, stamped across the book's flyleaf, stamped across the thickness of the pages, stamped again and again in smeary red ink that looked like blood, was one word: CANCEL.

'Oh dear God,' Ben murmured. He did not know what else to say; that seemed to cover the entire situation. 'Oh dear God, dear God.'

He stood in the new sunlight, suddenly wondering what was happening to the others.

2

Eddie Kaspbrak Makes a Catch

Eddie got off the bus at the corner of Kansas Street and Kossuth Lane. Kossuth was a street that ran a quarter of a mile downhill before dead-ending abruptly where the crumbling earth sloped into the Barrens. He had absolutely no idea why he had chosen this place to leave the bus; Kossuth Lane meant nothing to him, and he had known no one on this particular section of Kansas Street. But it seemed like the right place. That was all he knew, but at this point it seemed to be enough. Beverly had climbed off the bus with a little wave at one of the Lower Main Street stops. Mike had taken his car back to the library.

Now, watching the small and somehow absurd Mercedes bus pull away, he wondered exactly what he was doing here, standing on an obscure street-corner in an obscure town nearly five hundred miles away from Myra, who was undoubtedly worried to tears about him. He felt an instant of almost painful vertigo, touched his jacket pocket, and remembered that he had left his Dramamine back at the Town House along with the rest of his pharmacopeia. He had aspirin, though. He would no more have gone out *sans* aspirin than he would have gone out *sans* pants. He chugged a couple dry and began to walk along Kansas Street thinking vaguely that he might go to the Public Library or perhaps cross over to Costello Avenue. It was beginning to clear now, and he supposed he could even walk across to West Broadway and admire the old Victorian houses that stood there along the only two really handsome residential blocks in Derry. He used to do that sometimes when he was a kid – just walk along West Broadway, sort of casual, like he was on his way to somewhere else. There was the Muellers', near the corner of Witcham and West Broadway, a red house with turrets on either side and hedges in front. The Muellers had a gardener who always looked at Eddie with suspicious eyes until he had passed on his way.

Then there was the Bowies' house, which was four down from the Muellers' on the same side – one of the reasons, he supposed, that Greta Bowie and Sally Mueller had been such great friends in grammar school. It was green-shingled and also had turrets . . . but while the turrets on the Muellers' house were squared off, those on the Bowies' house were capped with funny cone-shaped things that looked to Eddie like squatty duncecaps. In the summer there was always lawn-furniture on the side lawn – a table with a sporty yellow umbrella over it, wicker chairs, a rope hammock stretched between two trees. There was always a croquet game set up out back, too. Eddie knew this although he had never been invited over to Greta's house to play croquet. Walking by casually (like he was on his way to somewhere else) Eddie would sometimes hear the click of the balls, laughter, groans as someone's ball was 'sent away.' Once he had seen Greta herself, a lemonade in one hand and her croquet mallet in the other, looking slim and pretty beyond the words of all the poets (even her sunburned shoulders seemed wonderfully pretty to Eddie Kaspbrak, who had at that time been nine), going after her ball, which had been 'sent away'; it had ricocheted off a tree and had thus brought Greta into Eddie's view.

He fell in love with her a little that day – her shining blonde hair falling to the shoulders of her culotte dress, which was a cool blue. She glanced around and for a moment he thought she had seen him, but that proved not to be so, because when he raised his hand in a timid hello, she did not raise hers in return but only whacked her ball back onto the rear lawn and then ran after it. He had walked on with no resentment at the unreturned hello (he genuinely believed she must not have seen him) or at the fact that he had never been invited to attend one of the Saturday-afternoon croquet games: why would a beautiful girl like Greta Bowie want to invite a kid like him? He was thin-chested, asthmatic, and had the face of a drowned water-rat.

Yeah, he thought, walking aimlessly back down Kansas Street, *I should have gone over to West Broadway and looked at all those houses again . . . the Muellers', the Bowies', Dr Hale's place, the Trackers' –*

His thoughts broke off abruptly at that last name, because – speak of the devil! – here he was, standing in front of Tracker Brothers' Truck Depot.

'Still right here,' Eddie said aloud, and laughed. 'Son of a gun!'

The house on West Broadway which belonged to Phil and Tony Tracker, a pair of life-long bachelors, was probably the loveliest of the large houses on that street, a spotlessly white mid-Victorian with green lawns and great beds of flowers that rioted (in a neatly landscaped way, of course) all the spring and summer long. Their driveway was freshly sealed each fall so that it always remained as black as a dark mirror, the slate shingles on the many slants of the roof were always a perfect mint green that almost exactly matched the lawn, and people sometimes stopped to take pictures of the mullioned windows, which were very old and quite remarkable.

'Any two men who bother keeping a house so nice must be queers,' Eddie's mother had once said in a disgruntled sort of way, and Eddie hadn't dared ask for clarification.

The Truck Depot was the exact opposite of the Tracker house on West Broadway. It was a low brick structure; the bricks were old and crumbling in places, their dirty-orange hue shading to a sooty black at the building's footings. The windows were uniformly filthy except for a small circular place on one of the lower panes of the starter's office. This one pane had been kept spotlessly clean by kids before Eddie and those who came after, because the starter kept a *Playboy* calendar over his desk. No boy came to play scratch baseball in the back lot without first stopping to wipe at the glass with his ball-glove and examine that month's pinup.

The depot was surrounded by a waste of gravel on three sides. Long-distance haulers – Jimmy-Petes and Kenworths and Rios – all painted with the words TRACKER BROS. DERRY NEWTON PROVIDENCE HARTFORD NEW YORK, sometimes stood here in tangled disordered profusion. Sometimes they were put together and sometimes there were just cabs or body-boxes, standing silent on their rear wheels and support-struts.

The brothers kept their trucks out of the lot at the back of the building as much as they could, because they were both avid baseball fans and liked the kids to come and play. Phil Tracker drove freight himself so the boys rarely saw him, but Tony Tracker, a man with huge slab arms and a gut to match, kept the books and the accounts, and Eddie (who never played – his mother would have killed him if she had heard he was playing baseball, racing around and getting dust in his delicate lungs, risking broken legs, concussions, and God alone knew what else) got used to seeing him. He was a summer fixture, his voice as much a part of the game to Eddie then as Mel Allen's later became: Tony Tracker, large but somehow ghostlike, his white shirt glimmering as summer dusk drew down and fireflies began to loom the air with their lace of lights, yelling: *'You got to get under that bawl before you can catch it, Red! . . . You took your eye off 'n the bawl, Half-Pint! You can't hit the goddam thing if you ain't looking at it! . . . Slide, Horsefoot! You get the soles of them Keds in that second-baseman's face, he ain't never goan tag you out!'*

Never called any of them by name, Eddie remembered. It was always hey Red, hey Blondie, hey Four-Eyes, hey Half-Pint. It was never a ball, it was always a bawl. It was never a bat, it was always something Tony Tracker called an 'ash-handle,' as in 'You ain't never goan hit that bawl if you don't choke up on the ash-handle, Horsefoot.'

Grinning, Eddie walked a little closer . . . and then the grin faded. The long brick building where orders had been processed, trucks repaired, and goods stored on a short-term basis was now dark and silent. Weeds were growing up through the gravel, and there were no trucks in either side yard . . . only a single box, its sides rusty and dull.

Getting closer still, he saw that there was a realtor's FOR SALE sign in the window.

Tracker's out of business he thought, and was surprised at the sadness the thought carried with it . . . as if someone had died. He was glad now he hadn't walked over to West Broadway. If Tracker Brothers could have gone under – Tracker Brothers, which had seemed eternal – what might have happened on that street he had liked so much to walk down as a kid? He realized uneasily that he didn't want to know. He didn't want to see Greta Bowie with gray in her hair, her hips and legs thickened with much sitting and much eating and much drinking; it was better – safer – to just stay away.

That's what we all should have done, just stayed away. We've got no business here. Coming back to where you grew up is like doing some crazy yoga trick, putting your feet in your own mouth and somehow swallowing

518

yourself so there's nothing left; it can't be done, and any sane person ought to be fucking glad it can't . . . what do you suppose happened to Tony and Phil Tracker, anyway?

A heart attack for Tony, perhaps; he had been carrying maybe seventy-five extra pounds of meat on his bones. You had to watch out for what your heart might be up to. The poets might romance about broken hearts and Barry Manilow sing about them, and that was fine by Eddie (he and Myra had every album Barry Manilow had ever recorded), but he himself preferred a good solid EKG every year. Sure, Tony's heart had probably given it up as a bad job. And Phil? Bad luck on the highway maybe. Eddie, who made his living behind the wheel himself (or had; these days he only ·drove the celebs and spent the rest of his time driving a desk), knew about bad luck on the highway. Old Phil might have jack-knifed a rig somewhere in New Hampshire or in the Hainesville Woods up north in Maine when the going was icy or maybe he had lost his brakes on some long hill south of Derry, heading into Haven in a driving springtime rain. Those things or any of the others you heard in those shitkicking country songs about truck-drivers who wore Stetson hats and had cheating on their minds. Driving a desk was sometimes lonely, but Eddie had been in the driver's-seat himself more than once, his aspirator riding there with him on the dashboard, its trigger reflected ghostly in the windshield (and a bucket-load of pills in the glove compartment), and he knew that real loneliness was a smeary red: the color of the taillights of the car ahead of you reflected on wet hottop in a driving rain.

'Oh shit the time goes by,' Eddie Kaspbrak said in a sighing sort of whisper, and was not even aware that he had spoken aloud.

Feeling both mellow and unhappy – a state more common to him than he ever would have believed – Eddie skirted the building, Gucci loafers crunching in the gravel, to look at the lot where the baseball games had been played when he was a kid – when, it seemed, ninety percent of the world had been made up of kids.

The lot wasn't much changed, but a look was enough to convince him beyond doubt that the games had stopped – a tradition that had simply died out at some point in the years between, for reasons of its own.

In 1958 the diamond shape of the infield had been defined not by limed basepaths but in ruts made by running feet. They had no actual bases, those boys who had played baseball here (boys who were all older than the Losers, although Eddie remembered now that Stan Uris had sometimes played; his batting was only fair, but in the outfield he could run fast and he had the reflexes of an angel), but four pieces of dirty canvas were always kept under the loading-bay behind the long brick building, to be ceremonially taken out when enough kids had drifted into the back lot to play ball, and just as ceremonially returned when the shades of evening had fallen thickly enough to end further play.

Standing here now, Eddie could see no trace of those rutted basepaths. Weeds had grown up through the gravel in patchy profusion. Broken soda and beer bottles twinkled here and there; in the old days, such shards of broken glass had been religiously removed. The only thing that was the same was the chainlink fence at the back of the lot, twelve feet high and as rusty as dried blood. It framed the sky in droves of diamond shapes.

That was home-run territory, Eddie thought, standing bemused with his hands in his pockets at the place where home plate had been twenty-seven years ago. *Over the fence and down into the Barrens. They used to call it The Automatic.* He laughed out loud and then looked around nervously, as if it were a ghost who had laughed out loud instead of a guy in sixty-dollar slacks, a guy as solid as . . . well, as solid as . . . as . . .

Get off it, Eds, Richie's voice seemed to whisper. *You ain't solid at all, and in the last few years the chucks have been few and far between. Right?* 'Yeah, right,' Eddie said in a low voice, and kicked a few loose stones away in a rattle.

In truth, he had only seen two balls go over the fence at the back of the lot behind Tracker Brothers, both of them hit by the same kid: Belch Huggins. Belch had been almost comically big, already six feet tall at twelve, weighing maybe a hundred and seventy. He had gotten his nickname because he was able to articulate belches of amazing length and loudness – at his best, he sounded like a cross between a bullfrog and a cicada. Sometimes he would pat a hand rapidly across his open mouth while belching, emitting a sound like a hoarse Indian.

Belch had been big and not really fat, Eddie remembered now, but it was as if God had never really intended for a boy of twelve to attain such remarkable size; if he had not died that summer, he might have grown to six-six or better, and might have learned along the way how to maneuver his outsized body through a world of smaller denizens. He might even, Eddie thought, have learned gentleness. But at twelve he had been both clumsy and mean, not retarded but almost seeming so because all his body's actions seemed so amazingly graceless and lunging. He had none of Stanley's built-in rhythms;

520

it was as if Belch's body did not talk to his brain at all but existed in its own cosmos of slow thunder. Eddie could remember the evening a long, slow fly ball had been hit directly to Belch's position in the outfield – Belch didn't even have to move. He stood looking up, raised his glove in an almost aimless punching gesture, and instead of settling into his glove, the ball had struck him squarely on top of the head, producing a hollow *bonk!* sound. It was as if the ball had been dropped from three stories up onto the roof of a Ford sedan. It bounced up a good four feet and came down neatly into Belch's glove. An unfortunate kid named Owen Phillips had laughed at that bonking sound. Belch had walked over to him and had kicked his ass so hard that the Phillips kid had run screaming for home with a hole in the seat of his pants. No one else laughed . . . at least not on the outside. Eddie supposed that if Richie Tozier had been there, he wouldn't have been able to help it, and Belch probably would have put him in the hospital. Belch was similarly slow at the plate. He was easy to strike out, and if he hit a grounder even the most fumble-fingered infielders had no trouble throwing him out at first. But when he got all of one, it went a long, long way. The two balls Eddie had seen Belch hit over the fence had both been wonders. The first had never been recovered, although more than a dozen boys had tramped back and forth over the steeply slanting slope which plunged down into the Barrens, looking for it.

The second, however, *had* been recovered. The ball belonged to another sixth-grader (Eddie could not now remember what his real name had been, only that all the other kids called him Snuffy because he always had a cold) and had been in use for most of the late spring and early summer of '58. As a result, it was no longer the nearly perfect spherical creation of white horsehide and red stitching that it had been when it came out of the box; it was scuffed, grassstained, and cut in several places by its hundreds of bouncing trips over the gravel in the outfield. Its stitching was beginning to come unravelled in one place, and Eddie, who shagged foul balls when his asthma wasn't too bad (relishing every casual *Thanks, kid!* when he threw the ball back to the playing field), knew that soon someone would produce a roll of Black Cat friction tape and embalm it so they could get another week or so out of it.

But before that day came, a seventh-grader with the unlikely name of Stringer Dedham tossed what he fancied a 'change of speed' pitch to Belch Huggins. Belch timed the pitch perfectly (the slow ones were, you should pardon the pun, just his speed) and hit Snuffy's elderly

Spalding so hard that the cover came right off and fluttered down just a few feet shy of second base like a big white moth. The ball itself had continued up and up into a gorgeous twilit sky, unravelling and unravelling as it went, kids turning to follow its progress in dumb wonder; up and over the chainlink fence it went, still rising, and Eddie remembered Stringer Dedham had said 'Ho-ly shit!' in a soft and awestruck voice as it went, riding a track into the sky, and they had all seen the unwinding string, and maybe even before it hit, six boys had been monkeying up that fence, and Eddie could remember Tony Tracker laughing in an amazed loonlike way and crying: 'That one would have been out of Yankee Stadium! Do you hear me? That one would have been out of *fucking Yankee Stadium!*'

It had been Peter Gordon who found the ball, not far from the stream the Losers' Club would dam up less than three weeks later. What was left was not even three inches through the center; it was some kind of cockeyed miracle that the twine had never broken.

By unspoken consent, the boys had brought the remains of Snuffy's ball back to Tony Tracker, who examined it without saying a word, surrounded by boys who were likewise silent. Seen from a distance that circle of boys standing around the tall man with the big sloping belly might have seemed almost religious in its intent – the veneration of a holy object. Belch Huggins had not even run around the bases. He only stood among the others like a boy who had no precise idea of where he was. What Tony Tracker handed him that day was smaller than a tennis ball.

Eddie, lost in these memories, walked from the place where home had been, across the pitcher's mound (only it had never been a mound; it had been a depression from which the gravel had been scraped clean), and out into shortstop country. He paused briefly, struck by the silence, and then strolled on out to the chainlink fence. It was rustier than ever, and overgrown by some sort of ugly climbing vine, but still there. Looking through it, he could see how the ground sloped away, aggressively green.

The Barrens were more junglelike than ever, and for the first time he found himself wondering why a stretch of such tangled and virulent growth should have been called the Barrens at all: it was many things, but barren was not one of them. Why not the Wilderness? Or the Jungle?

Barrens.

It had an ominous, almost sinister sound, but what it conjured up in the mind were not tangles of shrubs and trees so thick they had to fight for sunspace; it called up pictures of sand dunes shifting away endlessly, or gray slate expanses of hardpan and desert. Barren. Mike had said earlier that they were all barren, and it seemed true enough. Seven of them, and not a kid among them. Even in these days of planned parenthood, that was bucking the odds.

He looked through the rusty diamond-shapes, hearing the faraway drone of cars on Kansas Street, the faraway trickle and rush of water down below. He could see glints of it in the spring sunshine, like flashes of glass. The bamboo stands were still down there, looking unhealthily white, like patches of fungus in all the green. Beyond them, in the marshy stretches of ground bordering the Kenduskeag, there was supposed to have been quickmud.

I spent the happiest times of my childhood down there in that mess, he thought, and shivered.

He was about to turn away when something else caught his eye: a cement cylinder with a heavy steel cap on the top. Morlock holes, Ben used to call them, laughing with his mouth but not quite laughing with his eyes. If you went over to one, it would stand maybe waist-high on you (if you were a kid) and you would see the words DERRY DEPARTMENT OF PUBLIC WORKS stamped in raised metal in a semicircle. And you could hear a humming noise from deep inside. Some sort of machinery.

Morlock holes.

That's where we went. In August. In the end. We went into one of Ben's Morlock holes, into the sewers, but after awhile they weren't sewers anymore. They were . . . were . . . what?

Patrick Hockstetter was down there. Before It took him Beverly saw him doing something bad. It made her laugh but she knew it was bad. Something to do with Henry Bowers, wasn't it? Yes, I think so. And —

He turned away suddenly and started back toward the abandoned depot, not wanting to look down into the Barrens anymore, not liking the thoughts they conjured up. He wanted to be home with Myra. He didn't want to be here. He . . .

'Catch, kid!'

He turned toward the sound of the voice and here came some sort of a ball, right over the fence and toward him. It struck the gravel and bounced. Eddie stuck out his hand and caught it. In his unthinking reflex the catch was so neat it was almost elegant.

He looked down at what was in his hand and everything inside him went cool and loose. Once it had been a baseball. Now it was only a string-wrapped sphere, because the cover had been knocked off. He could see the string trailing away. It went over the top of the fence like a strand of spiderweb and disappeared into the Barrens.

Oh Jesus, he thought. *Oh Jesus, It's here, It's here with me NOW* –

'Come on down and play, Eddie,' the voice on the other side of the fence said, and Eddie realized with a fainting sort of horror that it was the voice of Belch Huggins, who had been murdered in the tunnels under Derry in August of 1958. And now here was Belch himself, struggling up and over the bank on the other side of the fence.

He wore a pinstriped New York Yankees baseball uniform that was flecked with bits of autumn leaves and smeared with green. He was Belch but he was also the leper, a creature hideously arisen from long years in a wet grave. The flesh of his heavy face hung in putrescent strings and runners. One eyesocket was empty. Things squirmed in his hair. He wore a moss-slimed baseball-glove on one hand. He poked the rotting fingers of his right hand through the diamonds of the chainlink fence, and when he curled them, Eddie heard a dreadful *squirting* sound which he thought might drive him mad.

'That one would have been out of Yankee Stadium,' Belch said, and grinned. A toad, noxiously white and squirming, dropped from his mouth and tumbled to the ground. 'Do you hear me? That one would have been out of *fucking Yankee Stadium!* And by the way, Eddie, do you want a blow job? I'll do it for a dime. Hell, I'll do it for free.'

Belch's face changed. The jellylike bulb of nose fell in, revealing two raw red channels that Eddie had seen in his dreams. His hair coarsened and drew back from his temples, turned cobweb-white. The rotting skin on his forehead split open, revealing white bone covered with a mucusy substance, like the bleared lens of a searchlight. Belch was gone; the thing which had been under the porch at 29 Neibolt Street was here now.

'Bobby blows me for a dime,' it crooned, beginning to climb the fence. It left little pieces of its flesh in the diamond shapes the crisscrossing wires made. The fence jingled and rattled with its weight. When it touched the climbing, vinelike weeds, they turned black. 'He will do it anytime. Fifteen cents for overtime.'

Eddie tried to scream. Nothing but a dry senseless squeak came out of him. His lungs felt like the world's oldest ocarinas. He looked down at the ball in his hand and suddenly blood began to sweat up from between the wrapped strings. It pattered to the gravel and splashed on his loafers.

He threw it down and took two lurching stagger-steps backward, his eyes bulging from his face, rubbing his hands on the front of his shirt. The leper had reached the top of the fence. Its head swayed in silhouette against the sky, a nightmare shape like a bloated Halloween jackolantern. Its tongue lolled out, four feet long, perhaps six. It twined its way down the fence like a snake from the leper's grinning mouth.

There one second . . . gone the next.

It did not fade, like a ghost in a movie; it simply winked out of existence. But Eddie heard a sound which confirmed its essential solidity: a *pop*! sound, like a cork blowing out of a champagne bottle. It was the sound of air rushing in to fill the place where the leper had been.

He turned and began to run, but before he had gone ten feet, four stiff shapes flew out from the shadows under the loading-bay of the abandoned brick depot. He thought at first they were bats and he screamed and covered his head . . . Then he saw that they were squares of canvas – the squares of canvas that had been the bases when the big kids played here.

They whirled and twirled in the still air; he had to duck to avoid one of them. They settled in their accustomed places all at once, kicking up little puffs of grit: home, first, second, third.

Gasping, his breath short in his throat, Eddie ran past home plate, his lips drawn back, his face as white as cottage cheese.

WHACK! The sound of a bat hitting a phantom ball. And then –

Eddie stopped, the strength going out of his legs, a groan passing his lips. The ground was bulging in a straight line from home to first, as if a gigantic gopher was tunneling rapidly just below the surface of the ground. Gravel rolled off to either side. The shape under the earth reached the base and the canvas flipped up into the air. It went up so hard and fast it made a popping sound – the sound a shoeshine kid makes when he's feeling good and pops the rag. The ground began to ridge between first and second, racing and racing. Second base flew into the air with a similar popping sound and had barely settled back before the shape under the ground had reached third and was racing for home.

Home plate flew up as well, but before it could come down the thing had popped out of the ground like some grisly party-favor, and the thing was Tony Tracker, his face a skull to which a few blackened chunks of flesh still clung, his white shirt a mess of rotted linen strings. He poked out of the earth at home plate from the waist up, swaying back and forth like a grotesque worm.

'Don't matter how much you choke up on that ash-handle,' Tony Tracker said in a gritty, grinding voice. Exposed teeth grinned in lunatic chumminess. 'Don't matter, Wheezy. We'll get you. You and your friends. We'll have a *BAWL!*'

Eddie shrieked and staggered away. There was a hand on his shoulder. He shrank away from it. The hand tightened for a moment, then gave way. He turned. It was Greta Bowie. She was dead. Half of her face was gone; maggots crawled in the churned red meat that was left. She held a green balloon in one hand.

'Car crash,' the recognizable half of her mouth said, and grinned. The grin caused an unspeakable ripping sound, and Eddie could see raw tendons moving like terrible straps. 'I was eighteen, Eddie. Drunk and done up on reds. Your friends are here, Eddie.'

Eddie backed away from her, his hands held up in front of his face. She walked toward him. Blood had splashed, then dried on her legs in long splotches. She was wearing penny-loafers.

And now, beyond her, he saw the ultimate horror: Patrick Hockstetter was shambling toward him across the outfield. He too was wearing a New York Yankees uniform.

Eddie ran. Greta clutched at him again, tearing his shirt and spilling some terrible liquid down the back of his collar. Tony Tracker was pulling himself out of his man-sized gopher-run. Patrick Hockstetter stumbled and staggered. Eddie ran, not knowing where he was finding the breath to run, but running somehow anyway. And as he ran, he saw words floating in front of him, the words that had been printed on the side of the green balloon Greta Bowie had been holding:

ASTHMA MEDICINE CAUSES LUNG CANCER!
COMPLIMENTS OF CENTER STREET DRUG

Eddie ran. He ran and ran and at some point he collapsed in a dead faint near McCarron Park and some kids saw him and steered clear of him because he looked like a wino to them like he might have some kind of weird disease for all they knew he might even be the killer and they talked about reporting him to the police but in the end they didn't.

3

Bev Rogan Pays a Call

Beverly walked absently down Main Street from the Derry Town House, where she had gone to change into a pair of bluejeans and a bright yellow smock-blouse. She was not thinking about where she was going. Instead she thought this:

> *Your hair is winter fire,*
> *January embers.*
> *My heart burns there, too.*

She had hidden that in her bottom drawer, beneath her underwear. Her mother might have seen it, but that was all right. The important thing was, that was one drawer her father never looked in. If he had seen it, he might have looked at her with that bright, almost friendly, and utterly paralyzing stare of his and asked in his almost friendly way: 'You been doing something you shouldn't be doing, Bev? You been doing something with some boy?' And if she said yes or if she said no, there would be a quick wham-bam, so quick and so hard it didn't even hurt at first – it took a few seconds for the vacuum to dissipate and the pain to fill the place where the vacuum had been. Then his voice again, almost friendly: 'I worry a *lot* about you, Beverly. I worry an awful *lot*. You got to grow up, isn't that so?'

Her father might still be living here in Derry. He had been living here the last time she had heard from him, but that had been . . . how long ago? Ten years? Long before she had married Tom, anyway. She had gotten a postcard from him, not a plain postcard like the one the poem had been written on but one showing the hideous plastic statue of Paul Bunyan which stood in front of City Center. The statue had been erected sometime in the fifties, and it had been one of the landmarks of her childhood, but her father's card had called up no nostalgia or memories for her; it might as well have been a card showing Gateway Arch in Saint Louis or the Golden Gate Bridge in San Francisco.

'Hope you are doing well and being good,' the card read. 'Hope you will send me something if you can, as I don't have much. I love you Bevvie. Dad.'

He *had* loved her, and in some ways she supposed that had everything to do with why she had fallen so desperately in love with Bill Denbrough that long summer of 1958 – because of all the boys, Bill was the one who projected the sense of authority she associated with her father . . . but it was a different sort of authority, somehow – it was authority that listened. She saw no assumption in either his eyes or his actions that he believed her father's kind of *worrying* to be the only reason authority needed to exist . . . as if people were pets, to be both cosseted and disciplined.

Whatever the reasons, by the end of their first meeting as a complete group in July of that year, that meeting of which Bill had taken such complete and effortless charge, she had been madly, head-over-heels in love with him. Calling it a simple schoolgirl crush was like saying a Rolls-Royce was a vehicle with four wheels, something like a hay-wagon. She did not giggle wildly and blush when she saw him, nor did she chalk his name on trees or write it on the walls of the Kissing Bridge. She simply lived with his face in her heart all the time, a kind of sweet, hurtful ache. She would have died for him.

It was natural enough, she supposed, for her to want to believe it had been Bill who sent her the love-poem ... although she had never gotten so far gone as to actually convince herself it was so. No, she had known who wrote the poem. And later on – at some point – hadn't its author admitted this to her? Yes, Ben had told her so (although she could not now remember, not for the life of her, just when or under what circumstances he had actually said it out loud), and although his love for her had been almost as well hidden as the love she had felt for Bill

(*but you told him Bevvie you did you told him you loved*)

it was obvious to anyone who really looked (and who was kind) – it was in the way he was always careful to keep some space between them, in the draw of his breath when she touched his arm or his hand, in the way he dressed when he knew he was going to see her. Dear, sweet, fat Ben.

It had ended somehow, that difficult pre-adolescent triangle, but just *how* it had ended was one of the things she still couldn't remember. She thought that Ben had confessed authoring and sending the little love-poem. She thought she had told Bill she loved him, that she would love him forever. And somehow, those two tellings had helped save all of their lives ... or had they? She couldn't remember. These memories (or memories of memories: that was really closer to what they were) were like islands that were not really islands at all but only knobs of a single coral spine which happened to poke up above the waterline, not separate at all but one piece. Yet whenever she tried to dive deep and see the rest, a maddening image intervened: the grackles which came back each spring to New England, crowding the telephone lines, trees and rooftops, jostling for places and filling the thawing late-March air with their raucous gossip. This image came to her again and again, foreign and disturbing, like a heavy radio beam that blankets the signal you really want to pick up.

She realized with sudden shock that she was standing outside of the Kleen-Kloze Washateria, where she and Stan Uris and Ben and Eddie had taken the rags that day in late June – rags stained with blood which only they could see. The windows were now soaped opaque and there was a hand-lettered FOR SALE BY OWNER sign taped to the door. Peering between the swashes of soap, she could see an empty room with lighter squares on the dirty yellow walls where the washers had stood.

I'm going home, she thought dismally, but walked on anyway.

This neighborhood hadn't changed much. A few more of the trees were gone, probably elms felled by disease. The houses looked a little tackier; broken windows seemed slightly more common than they had been when she was a girl. Some of the broken panes had been replaced with cardboard. Some hadn't.

And here she stood in front of the apartment house, 127 Lower Main Street. Still here. The peeling white she remembered had become a peeling chocolate brown at some point during the years between, but it was still unmistakable. There was the window which looked in on what had been their kitchen; there was the window of her bedroom.

(*Jim Doyon, you come out of that road! Come out right now, you want to get run over and killed?*)

She shivered, hugging her arms across her breasts in an X, cupping her elbows in her palms.

Daddy could still be living here; oh yes he could. He wouldn't move unless he had to. Just walk on up there, Beverly. Look at the mailboxes. Three boxes for three apartments, just like in the old days. And if there's one which says MARSH, you can ring the bell and pretty soon there'll be the shuffle of slippers down the hall and the door will open and you can look at him, the man whose sperm made you redheaded and lefthanded and gave you the ability to draw . . . remember how he used to draw? He could draw anything he wanted. If he felt like it, that is. He didn't feel like it often. I guess he had too many things to worry about. But when he did, you used to sit for hours and watch while he drew cats and dogs and horses and cows with MOO coming out of their mouths in balloons. You'd laugh and he'd laugh and then he'd say Now you, Bevvie, and when you held the pen he'd guide your hand and you'd see the cow or the cat or the smiling man unspooling beneath your own fingers while you smelled his Mennen Skin Bracer and the warmth of his skin. Go on up, Beverly. Ring the bell. He'll come and he'll be old, the lines will be drawn deep in his face and his teeth – those that are left – will be yellow, and he'll look at you, and he'll say Why it's Bevvie, Bevvie's come home to see her old dad, come on in Bevvie, I'm so glad to see you, I'm glad because I worry about you Bevvie, I worry a LOT.

She walked slowly up the path, and the weeds growing up between the cracked concrete sections brushed at the legs of her jeans. She looked closely at the first-floor windows, but they were curtained off. She looked at the mailboxes. Third floor, STARK-WEATHER. Second floor, BURKE. First floor – her breath caught – MARSH.

But I won't ring. I don't want to see him. I won't ring the bell.

This was a firm decision, at last! The decision that opened the gate to a full and useful lifetime of firm decisions! She walked down the path! Back to downtown! Up to the Derry Town House! Packed! Cabbed! Flew! Told Tom to bug out! Lived successfully! Died happily!

Rang the bell.

She heard the familiar chimes from the living room – chimes that had always sounded to her like a Chinese name: *Ching-Chong!* Silence. No answer. She shifted on the porch from one foot to the other, suddenly needing to pee.

No one home, she thought, relieved. *I can go now.*

Instead she rang again: *Ching-Chong!* No answer. She thought of Ben's lovely little poem and tried to remember exactly when and how he had confessed its authorship, and why, for a brief second, it called up an association with having her first menstrual period. Had she begun menstruating at eleven? Surely not, although her breasts had begun their first achy growth around mid-winter. Why . . . ? Then, intervening, a mental picture of thousands of grackles on phone lines and rooftops, all babbling at a white spring sky.

I'll leave now. I've rung twice; that's enough.

But she rang again.

Ching-Chong!

Now she heard someone approaching, and the sound was just as she had imagined: the tired whisper of old slippers. She looked around wildly and came very, very close to just taking to her heels. Could she make it down the cement walk and around the corner, leaving her father to think it had been nothing but kids playing pranks? *Hey mister, you got Prince Albert in a can . . . ?*

She let out a sudden sharp breath and had to tighten her throat because what wanted to come out was a laugh of relief. It wasn't her father at all. Standing in the doorway and looking out at her was a tall woman in her late seventies. Her hair was long and gorgeous, mostly white but shot through with lodes of purest gold. Behind her rimless spectacles were eyes as blue as the water in the fjords her ancestors had perhaps hailed from. She wore a purple dress of watered silk. It was shabby but still dignified. Her wrinkled face was kind.

'Yes, miss?'

'I'm sorry,' Beverly said. The urge to laugh had passed as swiftly as it had come. She noticed that the old woman wore a cameo at her throat. It was almost certainly real ivory, surrounded by a band of gold so thin it was nearly invisible. 'I must have rung the wrong bell.' *Or rang the wrong bell on purpose*, her mind whispered. 'I meant to ring for Marsh.'

'Marsh?' Her forehead wrinkled delicately.

'Yes, you see –'

'There's no Marsh *here*,' the old woman said.

'But –'

'Unless . . . you don't mean *Alvin* Marsh, do you?'

'Yes!' Beverly said. 'My father!'

The old woman's hand rose to the cameo and touched it. She peered more closely at Beverly, making her feel ridiculously young, as if she should perhaps have a box of Girl Scout cookies in her hands, or maybe some tags – support the Derry High School Tigers. Then the old woman smiled . . . a kind smile that was nonetheless sad.

'Why you *have* fallen out of touch, miss. I don't want to be the one who tells you this, a stranger, but your father has been dead these last five years.'

'But . . . on the bell . . .' She looked again and uttered a small, bewildered sound that was not quite a laugh. In her agitation, in her subconscious but rock-solid certainty that her old man would still be here, she had read KERSH as MARSH.

'You're Mrs Kersh?' she asked. She was staggered by this news of her father, but she also felt stupid about the mistake – the lady would think her little more than illiterate.

'Mrs Kersh,' she agreed.

'You . . . did you know my dad?'

'Very little did I know him,' Mrs Kersh said. She sounded a little like Yoda in *The Empire Strikes Back*, and Beverly felt like laughing again. When had her emotions gone whipsawing so violently back and forth? The truth was she couldn't remember a time . . . but she was dismally afraid she would before much longer. 'He rented the ground-floor apartment before me. We saw each other, me coming and him going, over a space of a few days. He moved down to Roward Lane. Do you know it?'

'Yes,' Beverly said. Roward Lane branched off from Lower Main Street four blocks farther down, where the apartment buildings were smaller and even more desperately shabby.

'I used to see him at the Costello Avenue Market sometimes,' Mrs Kersh said, 'and at the Washateria before they closed it. We passed a word from time to time. We – girl, you're pale. I'm sorry. Come in and let me give you tea.'

'No, I couldn't,' Beverly said weakly, but in fact she actually *felt* pale, like clouded glass that you could nearly look through. She could use tea, and a chair in which to sit and drink it.

'You could and you will,' Mrs Kersh said warmly. 'It's the least I can do for having told you such unpleasant news.'

Before she could protest, Beverly found herself being led up the gloomy hall and into her old apartment, which now seemed much smaller but safe enough – safe, she supposed, because almost everything was different. Instead of the pink-topped Formica table with its three chairs, there was a small round table, really not much bigger than an endtable, with silk flowers in a pottery vase. Instead of the old Kelvinator refrigerator with the round drum on top (her father tinkered with it constantly to keep it going), there was a copper-colored Frigidaire. The stove was small but efficient-looking. There was an Amana Radar Range above it. Bright blue curtains hung in the windows, and she could see flowerboxes outside them. The floor, linoleum when she was a girl here, had been stripped to its original wood. Many applications of oil made it glow mellowly.

Mrs Kersh looked around from the stove, where she was placing a teapot. 'You grew up here?'

'Yes,' Beverly said. 'But it's very different now . . . so trim and tidy . . . wonderful!'

'How kind you are,' Mrs Kersh said, and her smile made her younger. It was radiant. 'I have a little money, you see. Not much, but with my Social Security I am comfortable. Once I was a girl in Sweden. I came to this country in 1920, a girl of fourteen with no money – which is the best way to learn the value of money, would you agree?'

'Yes,' Bev said.

'At the hospital I worked,' Mrs Kersh said. 'Many years – from 1925 I worked there. I rose to the position of head housekeeper. All the keys I had. My husband invested our money quite well. Now I have reached a little harbor. Look around, miss, while the water boils!'

'No, I couldn't –'

'Please . . . still I feel guilty. Look, if you like!'

And so she did look. Her parents' bedroom was now Mrs Kersh's bedroom, and the difference was profound. The room seemed brighter and airier now. A large cedar chest, the initials RG inlaid into it, breathed its gentle aroma into the air. A gigantic surprise-quilt lay on the bed. On it she could see women drawing water, boys driving cattle, men building haystacks. A wonderful quilt.

Her room had become a sewing room. A black Singer machine stood on a wrought-iron table under a pair of starkly efficient Tensor lamps. A picture of Jesus hung on one wall, a picture of John F. Kennedy on another. A beautiful breakfront stood below the picture of JFK – it was filled with books instead of china, but seemed none the worse for that.

She went into the bathroom last.

It had been redone in a rose color that was too low and pleasant to seem gaudy. All of the fixtures were new, and yet she approached the basin feeling that the old nightmare had gripped her again; she would peer down into that black and lidless eye, the whispering would begin, and then the blood –

She leaned over the sink, catching a glimpse of her pallid face and dark eyes in the mirror over the basin, and then she stared into that eye, waiting for the voices, the laughter, the groans, the blood.

How long might she have stood there, bent over the sink, waiting for the sights and sounds twenty-seven years gone, she didn't know; it was Mrs Kersh's voice that bid her return: 'Tea, miss!'

She jerked back, the semi-hypnosis broken, and left the bathroom. If there had been dark magic somewhere down in that drain, it was gone now . . . or was sleeping.

'Oh, you shouldn't have!'

Mrs Kersh looked up at her brightly, smiling a little. 'O miss, if you knew how seldom company calls these days, you'd not say so. Why, I put on more than this for the man from the Bangor Hydro who comes to read my meter! I'm making him fat!'

Delicate cups and saucers stood on the round kitchen table, a clean bone-white edged with blue. There was a plate of small cakes and cookies. Beside the sweets a pewter teapot chuffed mild steam and pleasant fragrance. Bemused, Bev thought that the only things missing were the tiny sandwiches with the crusts cut off: *auntsandwiches*, she'd thought them, always one word. Three main types of auntsandwiches – cream cheese and olive, watercress, and egg salad.

'Sit down,' said Mrs Kersh. 'Sit down, miss, and I'll pour out.'

'I'm not a miss,' Beverly said, and raised her left hand so that her ring would show.

Mrs Kersh smiled and pushed a hand through the air – *pshaw*!

the gesture said. 'I call all the pretty young girls miss,' she said. 'Just a habit. Don't take offense.'

'No,' Beverly said, 'not at all.' But for some reason she felt a feather-touch of unease: there was something in the old woman's smile that had seemed a little . . . what? Unpleasant? False? Knowing? But that was ridiculous, wasn't it?

'I love what you've done to the place.'

'Do you?' Mrs Kersh said, and poured out. The tea looked dark, muddy. Beverly wasn't sure she wanted to drink it . . . and suddenly she wasn't sure she wanted to be here at all.

It did say Marsh under the doorbell, her mind whispered suddenly, and she was frightened.

Mrs Kersh passed her tea.

'Thank you,' Beverly said. The look of it might have been muddy; the aroma, however, was wonderful. She tasted. It was fine. *Stop jumping at shadows,* she told herself. 'That cedar chest in particular is a wonderful piece.'

'An antique, that one!' Mrs Kersh said, and laughed. Beverly noticed that the old woman's beauty was flawed on only one score, and that was common enough here in the northlands. Her teeth were very bad – strong-looking, but bad all the same. They were yellow, and the front two had crossed each other. The canines seemed very long, almost like tusks.

They were white . . . when she came to the door she smiled and you thought to yourself how white they were.

Suddenly she was not just a *little* frightened. Suddenly she wanted – needed – to be away from here.

'Very old, oh yes!' Mrs Kersh exclaimed, and drank her cup of tea off at a single gulp, with a sudden, shocking slurping sound. She smiled at Beverly – *grinned* at her – and Beverly saw that the woman's eyes had changed, too. The corneas were now yellow, ancient, threaded with bleary stitches of red. Her hair was thinner; the braid looked malnourished, no longer silver shot with bright yellow but a dull gray.

'Very old,' Mrs Kersh reminisced over her empty cup, looking slyly at Beverly from her yellowed eyes. Her snaggle teeth showed in that repulsive, almost leering grin. 'From home with me it came. The RG carved into it? You noticed?'

'Yes.' Her voice came from far away, and a part of her brain yammered *If she doesn't know you've seen the change perhaps you're still all right, if she doesn't know, doesn't see –*

'My father,' she said, pronouncing it *fadder,* and Beverly saw that

534

her dress had also changed. It had become a scabrous, peeling black. The cameo was a skull, its jaw hung in a diseased gape. 'His name was Robert Gray, better known as Bob Gray, better known as Pennywise the Dancing Clown. Although that was not his name, either. But he did love his joke, my fadder.'

She laughed again. Some of her teeth had turned as black as her dress. The wrinkles in her skin now cut deep. Her milk-rose skin had gone a sickly yellow. Her fingers were claws. She grinned at Beverly. 'Have something to eat, dear.' Her voice had risen half an octave, but the octave was cracked in this register, and her voice was the sound of a crypt door swinging mindlessly on hinges clogged with black earth.

'No, thank you,' Beverly heard her mouth say in a child's high oh-I-must-be-going voice. The words did not seem to originate in her brain; rather they came out of her mouth and then had to travel around to her ears before she was aware of what she had said.

'No?' the witch asked, and grinned. Her claws scrabbled on the plate and she began to cram thin molasses cookies and delicate frosted slices of cake into her mouth with both hands. Her horrid teeth plunged and reared, plunged and reared; her fingernails, long and dirty, dug into the sweets; crumbs tumbled down the bony slab of her chin. Her breath was the smell of long-dead things burst wide open by the gases of their own decay. Her laugh was now a dead cackle. Her hair was thinner. Scaly scalp showed in patches.

'Oh, he loved his joke, my fadder! This is a joke, miss, if you enjoy them: my fadder bore me rather than my mutter. He shat me from his asshole! Hee! Hee! Hee!'

'I ought to go,' Beverly heard herself say in that same high wounded voice – the voice of a small girl who has been viciously embarrassed at her first party. There was no strength in her legs. She was dimly aware that it was not tea in her cup but shit, liquid shit, a little party-favor from the sewers under the city. She had *drunk* some of that, not much but a sip, *oh God, oh God, oh blessed Jesus, please, please* –

The woman was shrinking before her eyes, thinning; it was now a crone with an apple-doll's face who sat across from her, giggling in a high, squealing voice and rocking back and forth.

'Oh my fadder and I are one,' she said, 'just me, just him, and dear, if you are wise you will run, run back to where you came from, run quickly, because to stay will mean worse than your death. No one who dies in Derry really dies. You knew that before; believe it now.'

In slow motion Beverly gathered her legs under her. As if from outside she saw herself gaining her feet and backing away from the table and from the witch in an agony of horror and disbelief, disbelief because she realized for the first time that the neat little dining-room table was not dark oak but fudge. Even as she watched, the witch, still giggling, her ancient yellow eyes slanted slyly off into the corner of the room, broke a piece of it off and stuffed it avidly into the black-ringed trap that was her mouth.

The cups, she saw, were white bark that had been carefully looped with blue-dyed frosting. The pictures of Jesus and John Kennedy were creations of nearly transparent spun sugar, and as she looked at them, Jesus stuck out His tongue and Kennedy dropped a stinky wink.

'We're all waiting for you!' the witch screamed, and her finger-nails scrabbled over the surface of the fudge table, drawing deep scars in its shining surface. 'Oh yes! Oh yes!'

The overhead lights were globes of hard candy. The wainscotting was caramel taffy. She looked down and saw that her shoes were leaving prints on the floorboards, which were not boards at all but slices of chocolate. The smell of candy was cloying.

Oh God it's Hansel and Gretel it's the witch the one that always scared me the worst because she ate the children –

'*You and your friends!*' the witch screamed, laughing. '*You and your friends! In the cage! In the cage until the oven's hot!*' She screamed laughter, and Beverly ran for the door, but she ran as if in slow motion. The witch's laughter beat and swirled around her head, a cloud of bats. Beverly shrieked. The hall stank of sugar and nougat and toffee and sickening synthetic strawberries. The doorknob, mock crystal when she came in, was now a monstrous sugar diamond.

'*I worry about you, Bevvie . . . I worry a LOT!*'

She turned, swirls of red hair floating around her face, to see her father staggering toward her down the hallway, wearing the witch's black dress and skull cameo; her father's face hung with doughy, running flesh, his eyes as black as obsidian, his hands clenching and unclenching, his mouth grinning with soupy fervor.

'*I beat you because I wanted to FUCK you, Bevvie, that's all I wanted to do, I wanted to FUCK you, I wanted to EAT you, I wanted to eat your PUSSY, I wanted to SUCK your CLIT up between my teeth, YUM-YUM, Bevvie, oooohhhhh, YUMMY IN MY TUMMY, I wanted to put you in the cage . . . and get the oven hot . . . and feel your CUNT . . . your plump CUNT . . . and when it was plump enough to eat . . . to eat . . . EAT . . .*'

Screaming, she grasped the sticky doorknob and bolted out onto a porch that was decorated with praline doodads and floored with fudge. Far away, dim, seeming to swim in her vision, she saw cars passing back and forth, and a woman pushing a cartful of groceries back from Costello's.

I have to get out there, she thought, just barely coherent. *That's reality out there, if I can only get out to the sidewalk –*

'Won't do you any good to run, Bevvie,' her father

(*my fadder*)

told her, laughing. 'We've waited a long time for this. This is going to be *fun*. This is going to be *YUMMY* in our *TUMMIES*.'

She looked back again and now her dead father was not wearing the witch's black dress but the clown suit with the big orange buttons. There was a 1958-style coonskin cap, the kind popularized by Fess Parker in the Disney movie about Davy Crockett, perched on its head. In one hand it held a bunch of balloons. In the other it held the leg of a child like a chicken drumstick. Written on each balloon was the legend IT CAME FROM OUTER SPACE.

'Tell your friends I am the last of a dying race,' it said, grinning its sunken grin as it staggered and lurched down the porch steps after her. 'The only survivor of a dying planet. I have come to rob all the women . . . rape all the men . . . and learn to do the Peppermint Twist!'

It began to do a mad shuck-and-jive, balloons in one hand, severed, bleeding leg in the other. The clown costume writhed and flapped, but Beverly felt no wind. Her legs tangled in each other and she spilled to the pavement, throwing out her palms to take up the shock, which went all the way to her shoulders. The woman pushing the grocery cart paused and looked back doubtfully, then hurried on a little faster.

The clown came toward her again, casting the severed leg aside. It landed on the lawn with an indescribable thud. Beverly only lay sprawled on the pavement for a moment, sure somewhere inside that she must wake soon, this couldn't be real, had to be a dream –

She realized that wasn't true a moment before the clown's crooked, long-clawed fingers touched her. It was real; it could kill her. As it had killed the children.

'*The grackles know your real name!*' she screamed at it suddenly. It recoiled, and it seemed to her that for a moment the grin on the lips inside the great red grin that had been painted on and around them became a grimace of hate and pain . . . and perhaps of fear as well. It might only have been her imagination, and she certainly had no idea why she had said such a crazy thing, but it bought her an instant of time.

She was on her feet and running. Brakes squealed and a hoarse voice, both mad and scared, yelled: 'Why don't you look where you're going, you dumb quiff!' She had a blurred impression of the bakery truck that had almost hit her when she bolted into the street like a child after a rubber ball, and then she was standing on the opposite sidewalk, panting, a hot stitch in her left side. The bakery truck went on down Lower Main.

The clown was gone. The leg was gone. The house still stood there, but she saw now that it was crumbling and deserted, the windows boarded up, the steps leading up to the porch cracked and broken.

Was I really in there, or did I dream it all?

But her jeans were dirty, her yellow blouse smeared with dust. And there was chocolate on her fingers.

She rubbed them on the legs of her jeans and walked away fast, her face hot, her back cold as ice, her eyeballs seeming to pulse in and out with the rapid thud of her heart.

We can't beat It. Whatever It is, we can't beat It. It even wants us to try — It wants to settle the old score. Can't be happy with a draw, I guess. We ought to get out of here . . . just leave.

Something brushed against her calf, light as a cat's questing paw.

She jerked away from it with a little shriek. She looked down and cringed, one hand against her mouth.

It was a balloon, as yellow as her blouse. Written on the side of it in electric blue were the words THAT'S WIGHT, WABBIT.

As she watched, it went bouncing lightly up the street, urged by the pleasant late-spring breeze.

4

Richie Tozier Makes Tracks

Well, there was the day Henry and his friends chased me — before the end of school, this was . . .

Richie was walking along Outer Canal Street, past Bassey Park. Now he stopped, hands stuffed in his pockets, looking toward the Kissing Bridge but not really seeing it.

I got away from them in the toy department of Freese's . . .

Since the mad conclusion of the reunion lunch, he had been walking aimlessly, trying to make his peace with the awful things which had been in the fortune cookies ... or the things which had *seemed* to be in the cookies. He thought that most likely nothing at all had come out of them. It had been a group hallucination brought on by all the spooky shit they had been talking about. The best proof of the hypothesis was that Rose had seen nothing at all. Of course, Beverly's parents had never seen any of the blood that came out of the bathroom drain either, but this wasn't the same.

No? Why not?

'Because we're grownups now,' he muttered, and discovered the thought had absolutely no power or logic at all; it might as well have been a nonsense line from a kid's skip-rope chant.

He started to walk again.

I went up by City Center and sat down on a park bench for awhile and I thought I saw ...

He stopped again, frowning.

Saw what?

... but that was just something I dreamed.

Was it? Was it really?

He looked to the left and saw the big glass-brick-and-steel building that had looked so modern in the late fifties and now looked rather antique and tacky.

And here I am, he thought. *Right back to fucking City Center. Scene of that other hallucination. Or dream. Or whatever it was.*

The others saw him as the Klass Klown, the Krazy Kut-up, and he had fallen neatly and easily into that role again. *Ah, we all fell neatly and easily back into our old roles again, didn't you notice?* But was there anything very unusual about that? He thought you would probably see much the same thing at any tenth or twentieth high school reunion – the class comedian who had discovered a vocation for the priesthood in college would, after two drinks, revert almost automatically to the wise-acre he had been; the Great English Brain who had wound up with a GM truck dealership would suddenly begin spouting off about John Irving or John Cheever; the guy who had played with the Moondogs on Saturday nights and who had gone on to become a mathematics professor at Cornell would suddenly find himself on stage with the band, a Fender guitar strapped over his shoulder, whopping out 'Gloria' or 'Surfin' Bird' with gleeful drunken ferocity. What was it Springsteen said? No retreat, baby, no surrender ... but it was easier to believe in the oldies on the record-player after a couple of drinks or some pretty good Panama Red.

But, Richie believed, it was the reversion that was the hallucination, not the present life. Maybe the child was the father of the man, but fathers and sons often shared very different interests and only a passing resemblance. They –

But you say grownups and now it sounds like nonsense; it sounds like so much bibble-babble. Why is that, Richie? Why?

Because Derry is as weird as ever. Why don't we just leave it at that?

Because things weren't that simple, that was why.

As a kid he had been a goof-off, a sometimes vulgar, sometimes amusing comedian, because it was one way to get along without getting killed by kids like Henry Bowers or going absolutely loony-tunes with boredom and loneliness. He realized now that a lot of the problem had been his own mind, which was usually moving at a speed ten or twenty times that of his classmates. They had thought him strange, weird, or even suicidal, depending on the escapade in question, but maybe it had been a simple case of mental overdrive – if anything about being in constant mental overdrive was simple.

Anyway, it was the sort of thing you got under control after awhile – you got it under control or you found outlets for it, guys like Kinky Briefcase or Buford Kissdrivel, for instance. Richie had discovered that in the months after he had wandered into the college radio station, pretty much on a whim, and had discovered everything he had ever wanted during his first week behind the microphone. He hadn't been very good at first; he had been too *excited* to be good. But he had understood his potential not to be just good at the job but great at it, and just that knowledge had been enough to put him over the moon on a cloud of euphoria. At the same time he had begun to understand the great principle that moved the universe, at least that part of the universe which had to do with careers and success: you found the crazy guy who was running around inside of you, fucking up your life. You chased him into a corner and grabbed him. But you didn't kill him. Oh no. Killing was too good for the likes of *that* little bastard. You put a harness over his head and then started plowing. The crazy guy worked like a demon once you had him in the traces. And he supplied you with a few chucks from time to time. That was really all there was. And that was enough.

He had been funny, all right, a laugh a minute, but in the end he had outgrown the nightmares that were on the dark side of all those laughs. Or he thought he had. Until today, when the word *grownup* suddenly stopped making sense to his own ears. And now here was something else to cope with, or at least think about; here was the huge and totally idiotic statue of Paul Bunyan in front of City Center.

I must be the exception that proves the rule, Big Bill.

Are you sure there was nothing, Richie? Nothing at all?

Up by City Center . . . I thought I saw . . .

Sharp pain needled at his eyes for the second time that day and he clutched at them, a startled moan coming out of him. Then it was gone again, as quickly as it had come. But he had also smelled something, hadn't he? Something that wasn't really there, but something that *had* been there, something that made him think of

(*I'm right here with you Richie hold my hand can you catch hold*)

Mike Hanlon. It was *smoke* that had made his eyes sting and water. Twenty-seven years ago they had breathed that smoke; in the end there had just been Mike and himself left and they had seen –

But it was gone.

He took a step closer to the plastic Paul Bunyan statue, as amazed by its cheerful vulgarity now as he had been overwhelmed by its size as a child. The mythical Paul stood twenty feet high, and the base added another six feet. He stood smiling down at the car and pedestrian traffic on Outer Canal Street from the edge of the City Center lawn. City Center had been erected in the years 1954–55 for a minor-league basketball team that had never materialized. The Derry City Council had voted money for the statue a year later, in 1956. It had been hotly debated, both in the council's public meetings and in the letters-to-the-editor columns of the Derry *News*. Many thought it would be a perfectly lovely statue, certain to become a tourist attraction of note. There were others who found the idea of a plastic Paul Bunyan horrible, garish, and unbelievably gauche. The art teacher at Derry High School, Richie remembered, had written a letter to the *News* saying that if such a monstrosity were actually to be erected in Derry, she would blow it up. Grinning, Richie wondered if *that* babe's contract had been renewed.

The controversy – which Richie recognized now as an utterly typical big-town/small-city tempest in a teapot – had raged for six months, and of course it had been entirely meaningless; the statue had been purchased, and even if the City Council had done something as aberrant (especially for New England) as deciding not to use an item for which money had been paid, where in God's name could it have been *stored*? Then the statue, not really sculpted at all but simply cast in some Ohio plastics plant, had been set in place, still shrouded in a whack of canvas big enough to serve as a clippership sail. It had been unveiled on May 13th, 1957, which was the incorporated township's one-hundred-and-fiftieth birthday. One faction gave voice to predictable moans of outrage; the other to equally predictable moans of rapture.

When Paul was revealed that day he was wearing his bib overalls and a red-and-white-checked shirt. His beard was splendidly black, splendidly full, splendidly lumber jack-y. A plastic axe, surely the Godzilla of all plastic axes, was slung over one shoulder, and he grinned unceasingly at the northern skies, which on the day of the unveiling had been as blue as the skin of Paul's reputed companion (Babe was not present at the unveiling, however; the cost estimate of adding a blue ox to the tableau had been prohibitive).

The children who attended the ceremonies (there were hundreds of them, and ten-year-old Richie Tozier, in the company of his dad, had been among them) were totally and uncritically delighted by the plastic giant. Parents boosted toddlers up onto the square pedestal on which Paul stood, took photos, and then watched with mixed apprehension and amusement as the kids climbed and crawled, laughing, over Paul's huge black boots (correction: huge black *plastic* boots).

It had been March of the following year when Richie, exhausted and terrified, had finished up on one of the benches in front of the statue after eluding – by the barest of margins – Messrs. Bowers, Criss, and Huggins in a chase that had led from Derry Elementary School across most of the downtown area. He had finally ditched them in the toy department of Freese's Department Store.

The Derry branch of Freese's was a poor thing compared with the grand downtown department store in Bangor, but Richie had been far past caring about such things – by then it was a case of any port in a storm. Henry Bowers had been right behind him and by then Richie had been flagging badly. He had dodged into the mouth of the department store's revolving door as a last resort. Henry, who apparently didn't understand the physics of such devices, had nearly lost the tips of his fingers trying to grab Richie as Richie trundled around and into the store.

Pelting downstairs, shirttail flying out behind him, he had heard the revolving door give off a series of reports almost as loud as TV gunfire and understood that Larry, Moe, and Curly were still after him. He was laughing as he went down the stairs to the basement level but that was only a nervous tic; he was as full of terror as a rabbit caught in a wire snare. They really meant to beat him up good this time (he had no idea that in another ten weeks or so he would believe the three of them, Henry in particular, capable of anything short of murder, and he surely would have whitened with shock if he had known of the apocalyptic rockfight in July, when even that last qualification would disappear from his mind). And the whole thing had been so utterly, typically stupid.

Richie and the other boys in his fifth-grade class had been filing into the gym. A sixth-grade class, Henry hulking among them like an ox among cows, had been coming out. Although he was still in the fifth grade, Henry went to gym with the older boys. The overhead pipes had been dripping again and Mr Fazio hadn't yet gotten around to putting up his CAUTION! WET FLOOR! sign on its little easel. Henry had slipped in a puddle and had landed on his keister.

Before he could stop it Richie's traitor mouth had bugled: 'Way to go, banana-heels!'

There had been an explosion of laughter from both Henry's classmates and Richie's, but there had been no laughter on Henry's face as he picked himself up − only a dull flush the color of freshly fired brick.

'Later for you, four-eyes,' he said, and walked on.

The laughter died at once. The boys in the hall looked at Richie as one already dead. Henry did not pause to check reactions; he simply walked off, head down, elbows red from catching the fall, a large wet place on the seat of his pants. Looking at that wet spot, Richie felt his suicidally witty mouth drop open again . . . but this time he snapped it shut again, so fast he almost amputated the tip of his tongue with the falling gate of his teeth.

Well, but he'll forget, he told himself uneasily as he changed up for gym. *Sure he will. Ole Hank just hasn't got that many memory circuits working. Every time he takes a shit he probably has to look up the directions in the instruction booklet, ha-ha.*

Ha-ha.

'You're dead, Trashmouth,' Vince 'Boogers' Taliendo told him, pulling his jock up over a dork roughly the size and shape of an anemic peanut. He said it with a certain sad respect. 'Don't worry, though. I'll bring flowers.'

'Cut off your ears and bring cauliflowers,' Richie had come back smartly, and everyone laughed, even ole 'Boogers' Taliendo laughed, why not, they could all afford to laugh. What, me worry? They would all be home watching Jimmy Dodd and the Mouse-keteers on the *Mickey Mouse Club* or Frankie Lymon singing 'I'm Not a Juvenile Delinquent' on *American Bandstand* while Richie went shagging ass through ladies' lingerie and housewares on his way to the toy department with sweat pouring down his back into the crack of his ass and his terrified balls strung up so high they felt like they might be hung over his bellybutton. Sure, they could laugh. Har-de-har-har-har.

Henry hadn't forgotten. Richie had left by the door at the kindergarten end of the school building just in case, but Henry had stuck Belch Huggins there, *also* just in case. Har-de-har-har-har.

Richie saw Belch first or there would have been no contest at all. Belch was looking out toward Derry Park, holding an unlit cigarette in one hand and dreamily picking the seat of his chinos out of his ass with the other. Heart pounding hard, Richie had walked quietly across the playground and was most of the way down Charter Street before Belch turned his head and saw him. He yelled for Henry and Victor, and since then the chase had been on.

When Richie reached the toy department it had been utterly, horribly deserted. There wasn't even a sales clerk hanging out – a welcome adult to put a stop to things before they got entirely out of hand. He could hear the three dinosaurs of the apocalypse closing in now. And he simply couldn't run anymore. Each breath produced a deep hurting stitch in his left side.

His eye fixed on a door which read EMERGENCY EXIT *ONLY*! ALARM WILL SOUND! Hope kindled in his chest.

Richie ran down an aisle crammed with Donald Duck jack-in-the-boxes, United States Army tanks made in Japan, Lone Ranger cap pistols, wind-up robots. He reached the door and slammed the push-bar as hard as he could. The door opened, letting in cool mid-March air. The alarm went off with a strident bray. Richie immediately doubled back and dropped to his hands and knees in the next aisle over. He was down before the door could settle closed again.

Henry, Belch, and Victor thundered into the toy department just as the door clicked shut and the alarm cut off. They raced for it, Henry in the lead, his face set and intent.

A sales clerk finally appeared, coming on the run. He wore a blue nylon duster over a plaid sportcoat of excruciating ugliness. The rims of his spectacles were as pink as the eyes of a white rabbit. Richie thought he looked like Wally Cox in his Mr Peepers role, and he had to slam his traitor mouth into the fat part of his forearm to keep from screaming out gales of exhausted laughter.

'You boys!' Mr Peepers exclaimed. 'You boys can't go out there! That's an emergency exit! You! Hey! *You boys!*'

Victor glanced at him a little nervously, but Henry and Belch never turned from their course and Victor followed them. The alarm brayed again, longer this time as they charged into the alley. Before it stopped clanging Richie was on his feet and trotting back toward ladies' lingerie.

'You boys will be barred from the store!' the clerk yelled after him.

Looking back over his shoulder Richie squealed in his Granny Grunt Voice, 'Did anyone ever tell you you look *just* like Mr Peepers, young man?'

And so he had escaped. And so he had finished up almost a mile from Freese's, in front of City Center . . . and, he devoutly hoped, out of harm's way. At least for the time being. He was spent. He sat down on a bench just to the left of the Paul Bunyan statue, wanting only a little peace while he got himself back together. In a bit he would get up and head home, but for now it felt too good to just sit here in the afternoon sun. The day had opened in a cold drizzly gloom, but now you could believe spring might actually be on the way.

Farther up the lawn he could see the City Center marquee, which on that March day bore this message in large blue translucent letters:

HEY TEENS!
COMING MARCH 28TH
THE ARNIE 'WOO-WOO' GINSBERG ROCK AND ROLL SHOW!
JERRY LEE LEWIS
THE PENGUINS
FRANKIE LYMON AND THE TEENAGERS
GENE VINCENT AND THE BLUE CAPS
FREDDY 'BOOM-BOOM' CANNON
AN EVENING OF WHOLESOME ENTERTAINMENT!!

That was a show Richie really wanted to see, but he knew there wasn't a chance. His mother's idea of wholesome entertainment did not include Jerry Lee Lewis telling the young people of America we got chicken in the barn, whose barn, what barn, my barn. Nor, for that matter, did it include Freddy Cannon, whose Tallahassee lassie had a hi-fi chassis. She was willing to admit that she had done her share of screaming for Frank Sinatra (whom she now called Frankie the Snot) as a bobby-soxer, but, like Bill Denbrough's mother, she was death on rock and roll. Chuck Berry terrified her, and she declared that Richard Penniman, better known to his teen and subteen constituency as Little Richard, made her want to 'barf like a chicken.'

This was a phrase for which Richie had never asked a translation.

His dad was neutral on the subject of rock and roll and could perhaps have been swayed, but Richie knew in his heart that his mother's wishes would rule on this subject – until he was sixteen or seventeen, anyway – and by then, his mother was firmly convinced, the country's rock and roll mania would have passed.

Richie thought Danny and the Juniors were more right on that subject than his mom – rock and roll would never die. He himself loved it, although his sources were really only two – *American Bandstand* on Channel 7 in the afternoon and WMEX out of Boston at night, when the air had thinned and the hoarse enthusiastic voice of Arnie Ginsberg came wavering in and out like the voice of a ghost called up at a seance. The beat did more than make him happy. It made him feel bigger, stronger, more *there*. When Frankie Ford sang 'Sea Cruise' or Eddie Cochran sang 'Summertime Blues,' Richie was actually transported with joy. There was power in that music, a power which seemed to most rightfully belong to all the skinny kids, fat kids, ugly kids, shy kids – the world's losers, in short. In it he felt a mad hilarious voltage which had the power to both kill and exalt. He idolized Fats Domino (who made even Ben Hanscom look slim and trim) and Buddy Holly, who, like Richie, wore glasses, and Screaming Jay Hawkins, who popped out of a coffin at his concerts (or so Richie had been told), and the Dovells, who danced as good as black guys.

Well, *almost*.

He would have his rock and roll someday if he wanted it – he was confident it would still be there for him when his mother finally gave in and let him have it – but that would not be on March 28th, 1958 . . . or in 1959 . . . or . . .

His eyes had drifted away from the marquee and then . . . well . . . then he must have fallen asleep. It was the only explanation that made sense. What had happened next could only happen in dreams.

And now here he was again, a Richie Tozier who had finally gotten all the rock and roll he had ever wanted . . . and who had found, happily, that it still wasn't enough. His eyes went to the marquee in front of City Center and saw that, with a hideous kind of serendipity, those same blue letters spelled out:

JUNE 14TH
HEAVY METAL MANIA!!
JUDAS PRIEST
IRON MAIDEN
BUY YOUR TICKETS HERE OR AT ANY TICKETRON OUTLET

Somewhere along the way they dropped the wholesome entertainment line, thought Richie, *but as far as I can tell that's just about the only difference,*

And heard Danny and the Juniors, dim and distant, like voices heard down a long corridor coming out of a cheap radio: *Rock and roll will never die, I'll dig it to the end . . . It'll go down in history, just you watch my friend . . .*

Richie looked back at Paul Bunyan, patron saint of Derry – Derry, which had come into being, according to the stories, because this was where the logs fetched up when they came downriver. There had been a time when, in the spring, both the Penobscot and the Kenduskeag would have been solid logs from one side to the other, their black bark hides glistening in the spring sun. A fellow who was fast on his feet could walk from Wally's Spa in Hell's Half-Acre over to Ramper's in Brewster (Ramper's was a tavern of such horrible repute that it was commonly called the Bucket of Blood) without getting his boots wet over the third crossing of his rawhide laces. Or so it had been storied in Richie's youth, and he supposed there was a bit of Paul Bunyan in all such stories.

Old Paul, he thought, looking up at the plastic statue. *What you been doing since I've been gone? Made any new riverbeds coming home tired and dragging your axe behind you? Made any new lakes on account of wanting a bathtub big enough so you could sit in water up to your neck? Scared any more little kids the way you scared me that day?*

Ah, and suddenly he remembered it all, the way you will sometimes suddenly remember a word which has been dancing on the tip of your tongue.

There he had been, sitting in that mellow March sunshine, drowsing a little, thinking about going home and catching the last half hour of *Bandstand*, and suddenly there had been a warm swash of air into his face. It blew his hair back from his forehead. He looked up and Paul Bunyan's huge plastic face had been right in front of his, bigger than a face on a movie screen, filling everything. The rush of air had been caused by Paul bending down . . . although he did not precisely look like Paul anymore. The forehead was now low and beetling; tufts of wiry hair poked from a nose as red as the nose of a long-time drunkard; his eyes were bloodshot and one had a slight cast to it.

The axe was no longer on his shoulder. Paul was leaning on its haft, and the blunt end of its head had crushed a trench in the concrete of the sidewalk. He was still grinning, but there was nothing cheery about it now. From between gigantic yellow teeth there drifted a smell like small animals rotting in hot underbrush.

'I'm going to eat you up,' the giant had said in a low rumbling voice. It was the sound of boulders rocking against each other during an earthquake. 'Unless you give me back my hen and my harp and my bags of gold, I'm going to eat you right the fuck *up*!'

The breath of these words made Richie's shirt flutter and flap like a sail in a hurricane. He shrank back against the bench, eyes bugging, hair standing out to all sides like quills, wrapped in a pocket of carrion-stink.

The giant began to laugh. It settled its hands on the haft of its axe the way Ted Williams might have laid hold of his favorite baseball bat (or ash-handle, if you prefer), and pulled it out of the hole it had made in the sidewalk. The axe began to rise into the air. It made a low lethal rushing sound. Richie suddenly understood that the giant meant to split him right down the middle.

But he felt that he could not move; a logy sort of apathy had stolen over him. What did it matter? He was dozing, having a dream. Any moment now some driver would blow his horn at a kid running across the street and he would wake up.

'That's right,' the giant had rumbled, 'you'll wake up in *hell*!' And at the last instant, as the axe slowed to its apogee and balanced there, Richie understood that this wasn't a dream at all . . . and if it was, it was a dream that could kill.

Trying to scream but making no sound at all, he rolled off the bench and onto the raked gravel plot which surrounded what had been a statue and was now only a base with two huge steel bolts sticking out of it where the feet had been. The sound of the descending axe filled the world with its pressing insistent whisper; the giant's grin had become a murderer's grimace. Its lips had pulled back so far from its teeth that its plastic red gums, hideously red, gleamed.

The blade of the axe struck the bench where Richie had been only an instant before. The edge was so sharp that there was almost no sound at all, but the bench was sheared instantly in two. The halves sagged away from each other, the wood inside the green-painted skin a bright and somehow sickening white.

Richie was on his back. Still trying to scream, he pushed himself with his heels. Gravel went down the collar of his shirt, down the back of his pants. And there was Paul, towering above him, looking down at him with eyes the size of manhole covers; there was Paul, looking down at one small boy cowering on the gravel.

548

The giant took a step toward him. Richie felt the ground shudder when the black boot came down. Gravel spumed up in a cloud.

Richie rolled over onto his stomach and staggered to his feet. His legs were already trying to run before he was balanced, and as a result he fell flat on his belly again. He heard the wind whoof out of his lungs. His hair fell in his eyes. He could see the traffic going back and forth on Canal and Main Streets as it did every day, as if nothing was happening, as if no one in any of those cars could see or care that Paul Bunyan had come to life and stepped down from its pedestal in order to commit murder with an axe roughly the size of a deluxe motor home.

The sunshine was blotted out. Richie lay in a patch of shade that looked like a man.

He scrambled to his knees, almost fell over sideways, managed to get to his feet, and ran as fast as he could – he ran with his knees popping almost all the way up to his chest and his elbows pistoning. Behind him he could hear that awful persistent whisper building again, a sound that seemed to be not really sound at all but pressure on the skin and eardrums: *Swiiipppppp!* –

The earth shook. Richie's upper and lower teeth rattled against each other like china plates in an earthquake. He did not have to look to know that Paul's axe had buried itself haft-deep in the sidewalk inches behind his feet.

Madly, in his mind, he heard the Dovells: *Oh the kids in Bristol are sharp as a pistol When they do the Bristol Stomp . . .*

He passed out of the giant's shadow into sunlight again, and as he did he began to laugh – the same exhausted laughter that had come from him when he bolted downstairs in Freese's. Panting, that hot stitch in his side again, he had at last risked a glance back over his shoulder.

There was the statue of Paul Bunyan, standing on its pedestal where it always stood, axe on its shoulder, head cocked toward the sky, lips parted in the eternal optimistic grin of the myth-hero. The bench which had been sheared in two was whole and intact, thank you very much. The gravel where Tall Paul (*He's-a my all*, Annette Funicello sang maniacally in Richie's head) had planted his huge foot was raked and immaculate except for the scuffed spot where Richie had fallen off while he was

(*getting away from the giant*)

dreaming. There was no footprint, no axe-slash in the concrete. There was nothing here but a boy who had been chased by other boys, bigger boys, and so had had himself a very small (but very potent) dream about a homicidal Colossus . . . the Giant Economy-Size Henry Bowers, if you pleased.

'Shit,' Richie said in a tiny wavering voice, and then uttered an uncertain laugh.

He stood there awhile longer, waiting to see if the statue would move again – perhaps wink, perhaps shift its axe from one shoulder to the other, perhaps come down and have at him again. But of course none of those things happened.

Of course.

What, me worry? Har-de-har-har-har.

A doze. A dream. No more than that.

But, as Abraham Lincoln or Socrates or someone like that had once observed, enough was enough. It was time to go home and cool out; to make like Kookie on *77 Sunset Strip* and just lay chilly.

And although it would have been quicker to cut through the City Center grounds, he decided not to. He didn't want to get close to that statue again. So he had gone the long way around and by that evening he had nearly forgotten the incident.

Until now.

Here sits a man, he thought, *here sits a man dressed in a mossy-green sportcoat purchased at one of the best shops on Rodeo Drive; here sits a man with Bass Weejuns on his feet and Calvin Klein underwear to cover his ass; here sits a man with soft contact lenses resting easily on his eyes; here sits a man remembering the dream of a boy who thought an Ivy League shirt with a fruit-loop on the back and a pair of Snap Jack shoes was the height of fashion; here sits a grownup looking at the same old statue, and hey, Paul, Tall Paul, I'm here to say you're the same in every way, you ain't aged a motherfucking day.*

The old explanation still rang true in his mind: a dream.

He supposed he could believe in monsters if he had to; monsters were no big deal. Hadn't he sat in radio studios at one time or another reading news copy about such fellows as Idi Amin Dada and Jim Jones and that guy who had blown away all those folks in a McDonald's just down the road apiece? Shit fire and save matches, monsters were cheap! Who needed a five-buck movie ticket when you could read about them in the paper for thirty-five cents or hear about them on the radio for free? And he supposed if he could believe in the Jim Jones variety, he could believe in Mike Hanlon's version, at least for awhile; It even had Its own sorry charm, because It came from *Outside* and no one had to claim responsibility for It. He could believe in a monster that had as many faces as there are rubber masks in a novelty shop (if you're gonna have one, you might as well have a pack of em, he thought, cheaper by the dozen, right, gang?), at least for the sake of argument . . . but a thirty-foot-high plastic statue that stepped off its pedestal and then tried to carve you up with its plastic axe? That was just a little too ripe. As Abraham Lincoln or Socrates or someone had *also* said, I'll eat fish and I'll eat meat, but there is some shit I will not eat. It just wasn't –

That sharp needling pain struck his eyes again, without warning, jerking a dismayed cry from him. This was the worst yet, going deeper and lasting longer, scaring the bejesus out of him. He clapped his hands to his eyes and then groped instinctively for the bottom lids with his forefingers, meaning to pop his contacts out. *It's maybe some kind of infection, he thought dimly. But Jesus it hurts!*

He pulled the lids down and was ready to give the single practiced blink that would send them tumbling out (and he would spend the next fifteen minutes grovelling myopically for them in the gravel surrounding the bench but Jesus God who gave a shit, right now it felt like there were *nails* in his eyes), when the pain disappeared. It did not dwindle; it just went. One moment there, the next moment gone. His eyes teared briefly and then stopped.

He lowered his hands slowly, his heart running fast in his chest, ready to blink them out the instant the pain started again. It didn't. And suddenly he found himself thinking about the only horror movie that had ever really scared him as a kid, possibly because he had taken so much shit about his glasses and had spent so much time thinking about his eyes. That movie had been *The Crawling Eye*, with Forrest Tucker. Not very good. The other kids had laughed themselves into hysterics over it, but Richie had not laughed. Richie had been rendered cold and white and dumb, for once with not a single Voice to command, as that gelatinous tentacled eye came out of the manufactured fog of some English movie set, waving its fibrous tentacles in front of it. The sight of that eye had been very bad, the embodiment of a hundred not-quite-realized fears and disquiets. On some night not long after, he had dreamed of looking at himself in a mirror and bringing a large pin up and sticking it slowly into the black iris of his eye and feeling a numb, watery springiness as the bottom of his eye filled up with blood. He remembered – now he remembered – waking up and discovering that he had wet the bed. The best indicator of how gruesome that dream had been was that his primary feeling had been not shame at his nocturnal indiscretion but relief;

he had embraced the warm wet patch with his body and blessed the reality of his sight.

'Fuck this,' Richie Tozier said in a low voice that was not quite steady, and started to get up.

He would go back to the Derry Town House and take a nap. If this was Memory Lane, he preferred the LA. Freeway at rush-hour. The pain in his eyes was probably no more than a signal of exhaustion and jet-lag, plus the stress of meeting the past all at once, in one afternoon. Enough shocks; enough exploring. He didn't like the way his mind was skittering from one subject to the next. What was that Peter Gabriel tune? 'Shock the Monkey.' Well, this monkey had been shocked enough. It was time to catch some z's and maybe gain a little perspective.

As he rose his eyes went to the marquee in front of City Center again. All at once the strength ran out of his legs and he sat down again. Hard.

RICHIE TOZIER MAN OF 1000 VOICES
RETURNS TO DERRY LAND OF 1000 DANCES

IN HONOR OF TRASHMOUTH'S RETURN CITY CENTER PROUDLY PRESENTS
THE RICHIE TOZIER 'ALL-DEAD' ROCK SHOW

BUDDY HOLLY   RICHIE VALENS   THE BIG BOPPER
FRANKIE LYMON   GENE VINCENT   MARVIN GAYE
HOUSE BAND
JIMI HENDRIX   LEAD GUITAR
JOHN LENNON   RHYTHM GUITAR
PHIL LYNOTT   BASS GUITAR
KEITH MOON   DRUMS

SPECIAL GUEST VOCALIST JIM MORRISON

WELCOME HOME RICHIE!
YOU'RE DEAD TOO!

He felt as if someone had whopped all the breath out of him . . . and then he heard that sound again, that sound that was half pressure on the skin and eardrums, that keen homicidal whispering rush – *Swiipppp!* He rolled off the bench onto the gravel, thinking *So this is what they mean by* déjà-vu, *now you know, you'll never have to ask anybody again* –

He hit on his shoulder and rolled, looking up at the Paul Bunyan statue — only it was no longer Paul Bunyan. The clown stood there instead, resplendent and evident, fantastic in plastic, twenty feet of Day-Glo colors, its painted face surmounting a cosmic comic ruff. Orange pompom buttons cast in plastic, each as big as a volleyball, ran down the front of the silvery suit. Instead of an axe it held a huge bunch of plastic balloons. Engraved on each were two legends: IT's STILL ROCK AND ROLL TO ME and RICHIE TOZIER'S 'ALL-DEAD' ROCK SHOW.

He scrambled backward, using his heels and his palms. Gravel went down the back of his pants. He heard a seam tear loose in the underarm of his Rodeo Drive sportcoat. He rolled over, gained his feet, staggered, looked back. The clown looked down at him. Its eyes rolled wetly in their sockets.

'Did I give you a scare, m'man?' it rumbled.

And Richie heard his mouth say, quite independently of his frozen brain: 'Cheap thrills in the back of my car, Bozo. That's all.'

The clown grinned and nodded as if it had expected no more. Red paint-bleeding lips parted to show teeth like fangs, each one coming to a razor point. 'I could have you now if I wanted you now,' it said. 'But this is going to be too much fun.'

'Fun for me too,' Richie heard his mouth say. 'The most fun of all when we come to take your fucking head off, baby.'

The clown's grin spread wider and wider. It raised one hand, clad in a white glove, and Richie felt the wind of the movement blow the hair off his forehead as it had on that day twenty-seven years ago. The clown's index finger popped out at him. It was as big as a beam.

Big as a bea —, Richie thought, and then the pain struck again. It drove rusty spikes into the soft jelly of his eyes. He screamed and clutched at his face.

'Before removing the mote from thy neighbor's eye, attend the beam in thine own,' the clown intoned, its words rumbling and vibrating, and Richie was again enveloped in the sweet stink of its carrion breath.

He looked up, and took half a dozen hurried steps backward. The clown was bending down, its gloved hands on its gaily pantalooned knees.

'Want to play some more, Richie? How about if I point at your pecker and give you prostate cancer? Or I could point at your head and give you a good old brain tumor — although I'm sure some people would say that would only be adding to what was already there. I can

553

point at your mouth and your stupid flapping tongue will turn into so much running pus. I can do it, Richie. Want to see?'

Its eyes were widening, widening, and in those black pupils, each as big as a softball, Richie saw the mad darkness that must exist over the rim of the universe; he saw a shitty happiness that he felt would drive him insane. In that moment he understood It could do any of these things and more.

And yet again he heard his mouth, but this time it was not his voice, or any of his created Voices, past or present; it was a Voice he had never heard before. Later he would tell the others, hesitantly, that it was a kind of Mr Jiveass Nigger Voice, loud and proud, self-parodying and screechy. 'Git off mah case you big ole honky clown!' he shouted, and suddenly he was laughing again. 'No shit an no shine, muhfuh! I got d'walk, I got d'talk, and I got d'big boppin cock! I got d' *'time*, I got d' *'mine*, I'm a *man* wit' a *plan* an if you doan *shit*, you goan *git*! You hear me, you whiteface bunghole?'

Richie thought the clown recoiled, but he did not stick around to find out for sure. He ran, elbows pumping, sportcoat flying out in wings behind him, not caring that a father who had stopped so his toddler could admire Paul was now staring warily at him, as if he had gone crazy. *As a matter of fact, folks*, Richie thought, *I feel like I've gone crazy. Oh God do I ever. And that had to have been the shittiest Grandmaster Flash imitation in history but somehow it did the trick, somehow —*

And then the clown's voice thundered after him. The father of the little boy did not hear it, but the toddler's face suddenly pinched in upon itself and he began to wail. The dad picked his son up and hugged him, bewildered. Even through his own terror, Richie observed this little sideshow closely. The voice of the clown was perhaps angrily gleeful, perhaps just angry: *'We've got the eye down here, Richie . . . you hear me? The one that crawls. If you don't want to fly, don't wanna say goodbye, you come on down under this here town and give a great big hi to one great big eye! You come down and see it anytime. Just any old time you like. You hear me, Richie? Bring your yo-yo. Have Beverly wear a big full skirt with four or five petticoats underneath. Have her wear her husband's ring around her neck! Get Eddie to wear his saddle-shoes! We'll play some bop, Richie! We'll play AAALLLL THE HITS!'*

Reaching the sidewalk, Richie dared to look back over his shoulder, and what he saw was in no way comforting. Paul Bunyan was still gone, and now the clown was gone, too. Where they had stood there was now a twenty-foot-high plastic statue of Buddy Holly.

He was wearing a button on one of the narrow lapels of his plaid sportcoat. RICHIE TOZIER 'S 'ALL-DEAD' ROCK SHOW, the button read.

One bow of Buddy's glasses had been mended with adhesive tape.

The little boy was still crying hysterically; his father was walking rapidly back toward downtown with the weeping child in his arms. He gave Richie a wide berth.

Richie got walking

(*feets don't fail me now*)

trying not to think about

(*we'll play AAALLLL THE HITS!*)

what had just happened. All he wanted to think about was the monster jolt of Scotch he was going to have in the Derry Town House bar before he went up to take that nap.

The thought of a drink – just your ordinary garden-variety drink – made him feel a little better. He looked over his shoulder one more time and the fact that Paul Bunyan was back, grinning at the sky, plastic axe over his shoulder, made him feel better still. Richie began to walk faster, making tracks, putting distance between himself and that statue. He had even begun to think about the possibility of hallucinations when the pain struck his eyes again, deep and agonizing, causing him to cry out hoarsely. A pretty young girl who had been walking ahead of him, looking dreamily up at the breaking clouds, looked back at him, hesitated, then hurried over.

'Mister, are you all right?'

'It's my contacts,' he said in a strained voice. 'My damned contact le – *oh my God that hurts!*'

This time he got his forefingers up so quickly he almost jabbed them into his eyes. He pulled down the lower lids and thought, *I won't be able to blink them out, that's what's going to happen, I won't be able to blink them out and it's just going to go on hurting and hurting and hurting until I go blind go blind go bl –* But one blink did it as one blink always had. The sharp and defined world, where colors stayed inside the lines and where faces that you saw were clear and obvious, simply fell away. Wide bands of pastel fuzz took their place. And although he and the high-school girl, who was both helpful and concerned, searched the paving of the sidewalk for almost fifteen minutes, neither could find even a single lens.

In the back of his head Richie seemed to hear the clown laughing.

5

Bill Denbrough Sees a Ghost

Bill did not see Pennywise that afternoon – but he *did* see a ghost. A real ghost. So Bill believed then, and no subsequent event caused him to change his mind.

He had walked up Witcham Street and paused for some time by the drain where George met his end on that rainy October day in 1957. He squatted down and peered into the drain, which was cut into the stonework of the curbing. His heart was beating hard, but he looked anyway.

'Come out, why don't you,' he said in a low voice, and he had the not-quite-mad idea that his voice was floating along dark and dripping passageways, not dying out but continuing onward and onward, feeding on its own echoes, bouncing off moss-covered stone walls and long-dead machinery. He felt it float over still and sullen waters and perhaps issue softly from a hundred different drains in other parts of the city at the same time.

'Come out of there or we'll come in and g-get you.'

He waited nervily for a response, crouched down with his hands between his thighs like a catcher between pitches. There was no response.

He was about to stand up when a shadow fell over him.

Bill looked up sharply, eagerly, ready for anything . . . but it was only a little kid, maybe ten, maybe eleven. He was wearing faded Boy Scout shorts which displayed his scabby knees to good advantage. He had a Freeze-Pop in one hand and a Fiberglas skateboard which looked almost as battered as his knees in the other. The Freeze-Pop was a fluorescent orange. The skateboard was a fluorescent green.

'You always talk into the sewers, mister?' the boy asked.

'Only in Derry,' Bill said.

They looked at each other solemnly for a moment and then burst into laughter at the same time.

'I want to ask you a stupid queh-question,' Bill said.

'Okay,' the kid said.

'You ever h-hear anything down in one of these?'

The kid looked at Bill as though he had flipped out.

'O-Okay,' Bill said, 'forget I a-asked.'

He started to walk away and had gotten maybe twelve steps – he was headed up the hill, vaguely thinking he would take a look at the home place – when the kid called, 'Mister?'

Bill turned back. He had his sportcoat hooked on his finger and slung over his shoulder. His collar was unbuttoned, his tie loosened. The boy was watching him carefully, as if already regretting his decision to speak further. Then he shrugged, as if saying *Oh what the hell*.

'Yeah.'

'Yeah?'

'Yeah.'

'What did it say?'

'I don't know. It talked some foreign language. I heard it coming out of one of those pumpin stations down in the Barrens. One of those pumpin stations, they look like pipes coming out of the ground –'

'I know what you mean. Was it a kid you heard?'

'At first it was a kid, then it sounded like a man.' The boy paused. 'I was some scared. I ran home and told my father. He said maybe it was an echo or something, coming all the way down the pipes from someone's house.'

'Do you believe that?'

The boy smiled charmingly. 'I read in my *Ripley's Believe It or Not* book that there was this guy, he got music from his teeth. Radio music. His fillings were, like, little radios. I guess if I believed that, I could believe anything.'

'A-Ayuh,' Bill said. 'But did you *believe* it?'

The boy reluctantly shook his head.

'Did you ever hear those voices again?'

'Once when I was taking a bath,' the boy said. 'It was a girl's voice. Just crying. No words. I was ascared to pull the plug when I was done because I thought I might, you know, drownd her.'

Bill nodded again.

The kid was looking at Bill openly now, his eyes shining and fascinated. 'You know about those voices, mister?'

'I heard them,' Bill said. 'A long, long time ago. Did you know any of the k-kids that have been murdered here, son?'

The shine went out of the kid's eyes; it was replaced by caution and disquiet. 'My dad says I'm not supposed to talk to strangers. He says anybody could be that killer.' He took an additional step away from Bill, moving into the dappled shade of an elm tree that Bill had once driven his bike into twenty-seven years ago. He had taken a spill and bent his handlebars.

'Not me, kid,' he said. 'I've been in England for the last four months. I just got into Derry yesterday.'

'I still don't have to talk to you,' the kid replied.

'That's right,' Bill agreed. 'It's a f-f-free country.'

He paused and then said, 'I used to pal around with Johnny Feury some of the time. He was a good kid. I cried,' the boy finished matter-of-factly, and slurped down the rest of his Freeze-Pop. As an afterthought he ran out his tongue, which was temporarily bright orange, and lapped off his arm.

'Keep away from the sewers and drains,' Bill said quietly. 'Keep away from empty places and deserted places. Stay out of trainyards. But most of all, stay away from the sewers and the drains.'

The shine was back in the kid's eyes, and he said nothing for a very long time. Then: 'Mister? You want to hear something funny?'

'Sure.'

'You know that movie where the shark ate all the people up?'

'Everyone does. *J-J-Jaws.*'

'Well, I got this friend, you know? His name's Tommy Vicananza, and he's not that bright. Toys in the attic, you get what I mean?'

'Yeah.'

'He thinks he saw that shark in the Canal. He was up there by himself in Bassey Park a couple of weeks ago, and he said he seen this fin. He says it was eight or nine feet tall. Just the *fin* was that tall, you get me? He goes, "That's what killed Johnny and the other kids. It was Jaws, I know because I saw it." So I go, "That Canal's so polluted nothing could live in it, not even a minnow. And you think you saw Jaws in there. You got toys in the attic, Tommy." Tommy says it reared right out of the water like it did at the end of that movie and tried to bite him and he just got back in time. Pretty funny, huh, mister?'

'Pretty funny,' Bill agreed.

'Toys in the attic, right?'

Bill hesitated. 'Stay away from the Canal too, son. You follow?'

'You mean you *believe* it?'

Bill hesitated. He meant to shrug. Instead he nodded.

The kid let out his breath in a low, hissing rush. He hung his head as if ashamed. 'Yeah. Sometimes I think *I* must have toys in the attic.'

'I know what you mean.' Bill walked over to the kid, who glanced up at him solemnly but didn't shy away this time. 'You're killing your knees on that board, son.'

The kid glanced down at his scabby knees and grinned. 'Yeah, I guess so. I bail out sometimes.'

'Can I try it?' Bill asked suddenly.

The kid looked at him, gape-mouthed at first, then laughing. 'That'd be funny,' he said. 'I never saw a grownup on a skateboard.'

'I'll give you a quarter,' Bill said.

'My dad said −'

'Never take money or c-candy from strangers. Good advice. I'll still give you a q-quarter. What do you say? Just to the corner of Juh-Jackson Street.'

'Never mind the quarter,' the kid said. He burst into laughter again − a gay and uncomplicated sound. A fresh sound. 'I don't need your quarter. I got two bucks. I'm practically rich. I got to see this, though. Just don't blame me if you break something.'

'Don't worry,' Bill said. 'I'm insured.'

He turned one of the skateboard's scuffed wheels with his finger, liking the speedy ease with which it turned − it sounded like there was about a million ball-bearings in there. It was a good sound. It called up something very old in Bill's chest. Some desire as warm as want, as lovely as love. He smiled.

'What do you think?' the kid asked.

'I think I'm g-gonna kill myself,' Bill said, and the kid laughed.

Bill put the skateboard on the sidewalk and put one foot on it. He rolled it back and forth experimentally. The kid watched. In his mind Bill saw himself rolling down Witcham Street toward Jackson on the kid's avocado-green skateboard, the tails of his sportcoat ballooning out behind him, his bald head gleaming in the sun, his knees bent in that fragile way snowbunnies bend their knees their first day on the slopes. It was a posture that told you that in their heads they were already falling down. He bet the kid didn't ride the board like that. He bet the kid rode

(to beat the devil)

like there was no tomorrow.

That good feeling died out of his chest. He saw, all too clearly, the board going out from under his feet, shooting unencumbered down the street, an improbable fluorescent green, a color that only a child could love. He saw himself coming down on his ass, maybe on his back. Slow dissolve to a private room at the Derry Home Hospital, like the one they had visited Eddie in after his arm had been broken. Bill Denbrough in a full body-cast, one leg held up by pulleys and wires. A doctor comes in, looks at his chart, looks at him, and then says: 'You were guilty of two major lapses, Mr Denbrough. The first was mismanagement of a skateboard. The second was forgetting that you are now approaching forty years of age.'

He bent, picked the skateboard back up, and handed it back to the kid. 'I guess not,' he said.

'Chicken,' the kid said, not unkindly.

Bill hooked his thumbs into his armpits and flapped his elbows. 'Buck-buck-buck,' he said.

The kid laughed. 'Listen, I got to get home.'

'Be careful on that,' Bill said.

'You can't be careful on a skateboard,' the kid replied, looking at Bill as if he might be the one with toys in the attic.

'Right,' Bill said. 'Okay. As we say in the movie biz, I hear you. But stay away from drains and sewers. And stay with your friends.'

The kid nodded. 'I'm right near home.'

So was my brother, Bill thought.

'It'll be over soon, anyway,' Bill told the kid.

'Will it?' the kid asked.

'I think so,' Bill said.

'Okay. See you later . . . chicken!'

The kid put one foot on the board and pushed off with the other. Once he was rolling he put the other foot on the board as well and went thundering down the street at what seemed to Bill a suicidal pace. But he rode as Bill had suspected he would: with lazy hipshot grace. Bill felt love for the boy, and exhilaration, and a desire to *be* the boy, along with an almost suffocating fear. The boy rode as if there were no such things as death or getting older. The boy seemed somehow eternal and ineluctable in his khaki Boy Scout shorts and scuffed sneakers, his ankles sockless and quite dirty, his hair flying back behind him.

Watch out, kid, you're not going to make the corner! Bill thought, alarmed, but the kid shot his hips to the left like a break-dancer, his toes revolved on the green Fiberglas board, and he zoomed effortlessly around the corner and onto Jackson Street, simply assuming no one would be there to get in his way. *Kid*, Bill thought, *it won't always be that way*.

He walked up to his old house but did not stop; he only slowed his walk down to an idler's pace. There were people on the lawn – a mother in a lawn chair, a sleeping baby in her arms, watching two kids, maybe ten and eight, play badminton in grass that was still wet from the rain earlier. The younger of the two, a boy, managed to hit the bird back over the net and the woman called, 'Good one, Sean!'

The house was the same dark-green color and the fanlight was still over the door, but his mother's flower-beds were gone. So, from what he could see, was the jungle-gym his father had built from scavenged pipes in the back yard. He remembered the day Georgie had fallen off the top and chipped a tooth. How he had screamed!

He saw these things (the ones there and the ones gone), and thought of walking over to the woman with the sleeping baby in her arms. He thought of saying *Hello, my name is Bill Denbrough. I used to live here.* And the woman saying, *That's nice.* What else could there be? Could he ask her if the face he had carved carefully in one of the attic beams – the face he and Georgie sometimes used to throw darts at – was still there? Could he ask her if her kids sometimes slept on the screened-in back porch when the summer nights were especially hot, talking together in low tones as they watched heat-lightning dance on the horizon? He supposed he might be able to ask some of those things, but he felt he would stutter quite badly if he tried to be charming . . . and did he really want to know the answers to any of those questions? After Georgie died it had become a cold house, and whatever he had come back to Derry for was not here.

So he went on to the corner and turned right, not looking back.

Soon he was on Kansas Street, headed back downtown. He paused for awhile at the fence which bordered the sidewalk, looking down into the Barrens. The fence was the same, rickety wood covered with fading whitewash, and the Barrens looked the same . . . wilder, if anything. The only differences he could see were that the dirty smudge of smoke which had always marked the town dump was gone (the dump had been replaced with a modern waste-treatment plant), and a long overpass marched across the tangled greenery now – the turnpike extension. Everything else was so similar that he might last have seen it the previous summer: weeds and bushes sloping down to that flat marshy area on the left and to dense copses of junky-scrubby trees on the right. He could see the stands of what they had called bamboo, the silvery-white stalks twelve and fourteen feet high. He remembered that Richie had once tried to smoke some of it, claiming it was like the stuff jazz musicians smoked and could get you high. All Richie had gotten was sick.

Bill could hear the trickle of water running in many small streams, could see the sun heliographing off the broader expanse of the Kenduskeag. And the smell was the same, even with the dump gone.

The heavy perfume of growing things at the height of their spring strut did not quite mask the smell of waste and human offal. It was faint but unmistakable. A smell of corruption; a whiff of the underside.

That's where it ended before, and that's where it's going to end this time, Bill thought with a shiver. *In there . . . under the city.*

He stood awhile longer, convinced that he must see something – some manifestation – of the evil he had come back to Derry to fight. There was nothing. He heard water running, a springlike and vital sound that reminded him of the dam they had built down there. He could see trees and bushes ruffling in the faint breeze. There was nothing else. No sign. He walked on, dusting a faint whitewash stain from his hands as he went.

He kept heading downtown, half-remembering, half-dreaming, and here came another kid – this one a little girl of about ten in high-waisted corduroy pants and a faded red blouse. She was bouncing a ball with one hand and holding a babydoll by its blonde Arnel hair in the other.

'Hey!' Bill said.

She looked up. 'What!'

'What's the best store in Derry?'

She thought about it. 'For me or for anyone?'

'For you,' Bill said.

'Secondhand Rose, Secondhand Clothes,' she said with no hesitation whatsoever.

'I beg your pardon?' Bill asked.

'You beg *what*?'

'I mean, is that a store name?'

'Sure,' she said, looking at Bill as though he might well be enfeebled. 'Secondhand *Rose*, Secondhand *Clothes*. My mom says it's a junkshop, but I like it. They have old things. Like records you never heard of. Also postcards. It smells like a attic. I have to go home now. Bye.'

She walked on, not looking back, bouncing her ball and holding her dolly by the hair.

'Hey!' he shouted after her.

She looked back whimsically. 'I beg your whatchamacallit?'

'The store! Where is it?'

She looked back over her shoulder and said, 'Just the way you're going. It's at the bottom of Up-Mile Hill.'

Bill felt that sense of the past folding in on itself, folding in on him. He hadn't meant to ask that little girl anything; the question had popped out of his mouth like a cork flying from the neck of a champagne bottle.

He descended Up-Mile Hill toward downtown. The warehouses and packing plants he remembered from childhood – gloomy brick buildings with dirty windows from which titanic meaty smells issued – were mostly gone, although the Armour and the Star Beef meat-packing plants were still there. But Hemphill was gone and there was a drive-in bank and a bakery where Eagle Beef and Kosher Meats had been. And there, where the Tracker Brothers' Annex had stood, was a sign painted in oldfashioned letters which read, just as the girl with the doll had said, SECONDHAND ROSE, SECONDHAND CLOTHES. The red brick had been painted a yellow which had perhaps been jaunty ten or twelve years ago, but was now dingy – a color Audra called urine-yellow.

Bill walked slowly toward it, feeling that sense of *déjà-vu* settle over him again. Later he told the others he knew what ghost he was going to see before he actually saw it.

The show-window of Secondhand Rose, Secondhand Clothes was more than dingy; it was filthy. No Downeast antique shop this, with nifty little spool-beds and Hoosier cabinets and sets of Depression glassware highlighted by hidden spotlights; this was what his mother called with utter disdain 'a Yankee pawnshop.' The items were strewn in rickrack profusion, heaped aimlessly here, there, and everywhere. Dresses slumped off coathangers. Guitars hung from their necks like executed criminals. There was a box of 45 rpm records 10¢ APIECE, the sign read. TWELVE FOR A BUCK. ANDREWS SISTERS, PERRY COMO, JIMMY ROGERS, OTHERS. There were kids' outfits and dreadful–looking shoes with a card in front of them which read SECONDS, BUT NOT BAD! $1.00 A PAIR. There were two TVs that looked blind. A third was casting bleared images of *The Brady Bunch* out toward the street. A box of old paperbacks, most with stripped covers (2 FOR A QUARTER, 10 FOR A DOLLAR, MORE INSIDE, SOME 'HOT') sat atop a large radio with a filthy white plastic case and a tuning dial as big as an alarm clock. Bunches of plastic flowers sat in dirty vases on a chipped, gouged, dusty dining-room table.

All of these things Bill saw as a chaotic background to the thing his eyes had fixed upon immediately. He stood staring at it with wide unbelieving eyes. Gooseflesh ran madly up and down his body. His forehead was hot, his hands cold, and for a moment it seemed that all the doors inside would swing wide and he would remember everything.

Silver was in the righthand window.

His kickstand was still gone and rust had flowered on the front and back fenders, but the oogah-horn was still there on the handlebars, its rubber bulb now glazed with cracks and age. The horn itself, which Bill had always kept neatly polished, was dull and pitted. The flat package carrier where Richie had often ridden double was still on the back fender, but it was bent now, hanging by a single bolt. At some point someone had covered the seat with imitation tiger-skin which was now rubbed and frayed to a point where the stripes were almost indistinguishable.

Silver.

Bill raised an absent hand to wipe away the tears that were running slowly down his cheeks. After he had done a better job with his handkerchief, he went inside.

The atmosphere of Secondhand Rose, Secondhand Clothes was musty with age. It was, as the girl had said, an attic smell – but not a good smell, as some attic smells are. This was not the smell of linseed oil rubbed lovingly into the surface of old tables or of ancient plush and velvet. In here was a smell of rotting book-bindings, dirty vinyl cushions that had been half-cooked in the hot suns of summers past, dust, mouse-turds.

From the TV in the window the Brady Bunch cackled and whooped. Competing with them from somewhere in the back was the radio voice of a disc jockey identifying himself as 'your pal Bobby Russell' promising the new album by Prince to the caller who could give the name of the actor who had played Wally on *Leave It to Beaver*. Bill knew – it had been a kid named Tony Dow – but he didn't want the new Prince album. The radio was sitting on a high shelf amid a number of nineteenth-century portraits. Below it and them sat the proprietor, a man of perhaps forty who was wearing designer jeans and a fishnet tee-shirt. His hair was slicked back and he was thin to the point of emaciation. His feet were cocked up on his desk, which was piled high with ledgers and dominated by an old scrolled cash register. He was reading a paperback novel which Bill thought had never been nominated for the Pulitzer Prize. It was called *Construction Site Studs*. On the floor in front of the desk was a barber pole, its stripe revolving up and up into infinity. Its frayed cord wound across the floor to a baseboard plug like a tired snake. The sign in front of it read: A DYEING BREED! $250.

When the bell over the door jingled, the man behind the desk marked his place with a matchbook cover and looked up. 'Help you?'

'Yes,' Bill said, and opened his mouth to ask about the bike in the window. But before he could speak, his mind was suddenly filled with a single haunting sentence, words that drove away all other thought:

He thrusts his fists against the posts and still insists he sees the ghosts. What in the name of God?

(*thrusts*)

'Looking for anything in particular?' the proprietor asked. His voice was polite enough, but he was looking at Bill closely.

He's looking at me, Bill thought, amused in spite of his distress, *as if he's got an idea I've been smoking some of that stuff that gets the jazz musicians high.*

'Yes, I was ih-ih-interested ih-in –'

(*his fists against the posts*)

'– in that puh-puh-post –'

'The barber pole, you mean?' The proprietor's eyes now showed Bill something which, even in his present confused state, he remembered and hated from his childhood: the anxiety of a man or woman who must listen to a stutterer, the urge to jump in quickly and finish the thought, thus shutting the poor bastard up. *But I* don't *stutter! I beat it! I DON'T FUCKING STUTTER! I –*

(*and still insists*)

The words were so clear in his mind that it seemed someone else must be speaking in there, that he was like a man possessed by demons in Biblical times – a man invaded by some presence from Outside. And yet he recognized the voice and knew it was his own. He felt sweat pop out warmly on his face.

'I could give you

(*he sees the ghosts*)

a deal on that post,' the proprietor was saying. 'Tell you the truth, I can't move it at two-fifty. I'd give it to you for one-seventy-five, how's that? It's the only real antique in the place.'

(*post*)

'*POLE*,' Bill almost screamed, and the proprietor recoiled a little. 'Not the *pole* I'm interested in.'

'Are you okay, mister?' the proprietor asked. His solicitous tone belied the expression of hard wariness in his eyes, and Bill saw his left hand leave the desk. He knew, with a flash of something that was really more inductive reasoning than intuition, that there was an open drawer below Bill's own sight-line, and that the proprietor had almost surely put his hand on a pistol of some type. He was maybe worried about robbery; more likely he was just worried. He was, after all, clearly gay, and this was the town where the local juveniles had given Adrian Mellon a terminal bath.

(*he thrusts his fists against the posts and still insists he sees the ghosts*)

It drove out all thought; it was like being insane. Where had it come from?

(*he thrusts*)

Repeating and repeating.

With a sudden titanic effort, Bill attacked it. He did this by forcing his mind to translate the alien sentence into French. It was the same way he had beaten the stutter as a teenager. As the words marched across his field of thought, he changed them . . . and suddenly he felt the grip of the stutter loosen.

He realized that the proprietor had been saying something.

'P-P-Pardon me?'

'I said if you're going to have a fit, take it out on the street. I don't need shit like that in here.'

Bill drew in a deep breath.

'Let's start o-over,' he said. 'Pretend I just came i-in.'

'Okay,' the proprietor said, agreeably enough. 'You just came in. Now what?'

'The b-bike in the window,' Bill said. 'How much do you want for the bike?'

'Take twenty bucks.' He sounded easier now, but his left hand still hadn't come back into view. 'I think it was a Schwinn at one time, but it's a mongrel now.' His eye measured Bill. 'Big bike. You could ride it yourself.'

Thinking of the kid's green skateboard, Bill said, 'I think my bike-riding days are o-o-over.'

The proprietor shrugged. His left hand finally came up again. 'Got a boy?'

'Y-Yes.'

'How old is he?'

'Eh-Eh-Eleven.'

'Big bike for an eleven-year-old.'

'Will you take a traveller's check?'

'Long as it's no more than ten bucks over the amount of the purchase.'

'I can give you a twenty,' Bill said. 'Mind if I make a phone call?'

'Not if it's local.'

'It is.'

'Be my guest.'

Bill called the Derry Public Library. Mike was there. 'Where are you, Bill?' he asked, and then immediately: 'Are you all right?'

'I'm fine. Have you seen any of the others?'

'No. We'll see them tonight.' There was a brief pause. 'That is, I presume. What can I do you for, Big Bill?'

'I'm buying a bike,' Bill said calmly. 'I wondered if I could wheel it up to your house. Do you have a garage or something I could store it in?'

There was silence.

'Mike? Are you –'

'I'm here,' Mike said. 'Is it Silver?'

Bill looked at the proprietor. He was reading his book again . . . or maybe just looking at it and listening carefully.

'Yes,' he said.

'Where are you?'

'It's called Secondhand Rose, Secondhand Clothes.'

'All right,' Mike said. 'My place is 61 Palmer Lane. You'd want to go up Main Street –'

'I can find it.'

'All right, I'll meet you there. Want some supper?'

'That would be nice. Can you get off work?'

'No problem. Carole will cover for me.' Mike hesitated again. 'She said that a fellow was in about an hour before I got back here. Said he left looking like a ghost. I got her to describe him. It was Ben.'

'You sure?'

'Yeah. And the bike. That's part of it, too, isn't it?'

'Shouldn't wonder,' Bill said, keeping an eye on the proprietor, who still appeared to be absorbed in his book.

'I'll see you at my place,' Mike said. 'Number 61. Don't forget.'

'I won't. Thank you, Mike.'

'God bless, Big Bill.'

Bill hung up. The proprietor promptly closed his book again. 'Got you some storage space, my friend?'

'Yeah.' Bill took out his traveller's checks and signed his name to a twenty. The proprietor examined the two signatures with a care that, in less distracted mental circumstances, Bill would have found rather insulting.

At last the proprietor scribbled a bill of sale and popped the traveller's check into his old cash register. He got up, put his hands on the small of his back and stretched, then walked to the front of the store. He picked his way around the heaps of junk and almost-junk merchandise with an absent delicacy Bill found fascinating.

He lifted the bike, swung it around, and rolled it to the edge of the display space. Bill laid hold of the handlebars to help him, and as he did another shudder whipped through him. Silver. Again. It was Silver in his hands and

(*he thrusts his fists against the posts and still insists he sees the ghosts*)

he had to force the thought away because it made him feel faint and strange.

'That back tire's a little soft,' the proprietor said (it was, in fact, as flat as a pancake). The front tire was up, but so bald the cord was showing through in places.

'No problem,' Bill said.

'You can handle it from here?'

(*I used to be able to handle it just fine; now I don't know*)

'I guess so,' Bill said. 'Thanks.'

'Sure. And if you want to talk about that barber pole, come back.'

The proprietor held the door for him. Bill walked the bike out, turned left, and started toward Main Street. People glanced with amusement and curiosity at the man with the bald head pushing the huge bike with the flat rear tire and the oogah-horn protruding over the rusty bike-basket, but Bill hardly noticed them. He was marvelling at how well his grownup hands still fitted the rubber handgrips, was remembering how he had always meant to knot some thin strips of plastic, different colors, into the holes in each grip so they would flutter in the wind. He had never gotten around to that.

He stopped at the corner of Center and Main, outside of Mr Paperback. He leaned the bike against the building long enough to strip off his sportcoat. Pushing a bike with a flat tire was hard work, and the afternoon had come off hot. He tossed the coat into the basket and went on.

Chain's rusty, he thought. *Whoever had it didn't take very good care of*

(*him*)

it.

He stopped for a moment, frowning, trying to remember just what *had* happened to Silver. Had he sold it? Given it away? Lost it, perhaps? He couldn't remember. Instead, that idiotic sentence

(*his fists against the posts and still insists*)

resurfaced, as strange and out of place as an easy chair on a battlefield, a record-player in a fireplace, a row of pencils protruding from a cement sidewalk.

Bill shook his head. The sentence broke up and dispersed like smoke. He pushed Silver on to Mike's place.

6

Mike Hanlon Makes a Connection

But first he made supper – hamburgers with sautéed mushrooms and onions and a spinach salad. They had finished working on Silver by then and were more than ready to eat.

The house was a neat little Cape Cod, white with green trim. Mike had just been arriving when Bill pushed Silver up Palmer Lane. He was behind the wheel of an old Ford with rusty rocker panels and a cracked rear window, and Bill remembered the fact Mike had so quietly pointed out: the six members of the Losers' Club who left Derry had quit being losers. Mike had stayed behind and was still behind.

Bill rolled Silver into Mike's garage, which was floored with oiled dirt and was every bit as neat as the house proved to be. Tools hung from pegs, and the lights, shielded with tin cones, looked like the lights which hang over pool tables. Bill leaned the bike against the wall. The two of them looked at it without speaking for a bit, hands in pockets.

'It's Silver, all right,' Mike said at last. 'I thought you might have been wrong. But it's him. What are you going to do with him?'

'Fucked if I know. Have you got a bicycle pump?'

'Yeah. I think I've got a tire-patching kit, too. Are those tube-less tires?'

'They always were.' Bill bent down to look at the flat tire. 'Yeah. Tubeless.'

'Getting ready to ride it again?'

'Of c-course not,' Bill said sharply. 'I just don't like to see it si-hi-hitting there on a flat.'

'Whatever you say, Big Bill. You're the boss.'

Bill looked around sharply at that, but Mike had gone to the garage's back wall and was taking down a tire-pump. He got a tin tire-patching kit from one of the cabinets and handed it to Bill, who looked at it curiously. It was as he remembered such things from his

569

childhood: a small tin box of about the same size and shape as those kept by men who roll their own cigarettes, except the top was bright and pebbled – you used it for roughing the rubber around the hole before you put on the patch. The box looked brand-new, and there was a Woolco price sticker on it that said $7.23. It seemed to him that when he was a kid such a kit had gone for about a buck-twenty-five.

'You didn't just have this hanging around,' Bill said. It wasn't a question.

'No,' Mike agreed. 'I bought it last week. Out at the mall, as a matter of fact.'

'You've got a bike of your own?'

'No,' Mike said, meeting his eyes.

'You just happened to buy this kit.'

'Just got the urge,' Mike agreed, his eyes still on Bill's. 'Woke up thinking it might come in handy. The thought kept coming back all day. So . . . I got the kit. And here you are to use it.'

'Here I am to use it,' Bill agreed. 'But like they say on the soaps, what does it all mean, dear?'

'Ask the others,' Mike said. 'Tonight.'

'Will they all be there, do you think?'

'I don't know, Big Bill.' He paused and added: 'I think there's a chance that all of them won't be. One or two of them may decide to just creep out of town. Or . . .' He shrugged.

'What do we do if that happens?'

'I don't know.' Mike pointed to the tire-patching kit. 'I paid seven bucks for that thing. Are you going to do something with it or just look at it?'

Bill took his sportcoat out of the basket and hung it carefully on an unoccupied wallpeg. Then he turned Silver upside down so that he rested on his seat and began to carefully rotate the rear tire. He didn't like the rusty way the axle squeaked, and remembered the almost silent click of the ball-bearings in the kid's skateboard. *A little 3-in-1 oil would fix that right up*, he thought. *Wouldn't hurt to oil the chain, either. It's rusty as hell . . . And playing cards. It needs playing cards on the spokes. Mike would have cards, I bet. The good ones. Bikes, with the celluloid coating that made them so stiff and so slippery that the first time you tried to shuffle them they always sprayed all over the floor. Playing cards, sure, and clothespins to hold them –*

He stopped, suddenly cold.

What in the name of Jesus are you thinking of?

'Something wrong, Bill?' Mike asked softly.

'Nothing.' His fingers touched something small and round and hard. He got his nails under it and pulled. A small tack came out of the tire. 'Here's the cuh-cuh-culprit,' he said, and it rose in his mind again, strange, unbidden, and powerful: *He thrusts his fists against the posts and still insists he sees the ghosts.* But this time the voice, his voice, was followed by his mother's voice, saying: *Try again, Billy. You almost had it that time.* And Andy Devine as Guy Madison's sidekick Jingles yelling, *Hey, Wild Bill, wait for me!*

He shivered.

(*the posts*)

He shook his head. *I couldn't say that without stuttering even now,* he thought, and for just a moment he felt that he was on the edge of understanding it all. Then it was gone.

He opened the tire-patching kit and went to work. It took a long time to get it just right. Mike leaned against the wall in a bar of late-afternoon sun, the sleeves of his shirt rolled up and his tie yanked down, whistling a tune which Bill finally identified as 'She Blinded Me with Science.'

While he waited for the tire cement to set, Bill had – just for something to do, he told himself – oiled Silver's chain, sprocket, and axles. It didn't make the bike look any better, but when he spun the tires he found that the squeak was gone, and that was satisfying. Silver never would have won any beauty-contests anyway. His one virtue was that he could go like a blue streak.

By that time, five-thirty in the afternoon, he had nearly forgotten Mike was there; he had become completely absorbed in small yet utterly satisfying acts of maintenance. He screwed the nozzle of the pump onto the rear tire's valve and watched the tire fatten, shooting for the right pressure by guess and by gosh. He was pleased to see that the patch was holding nicely.

When he thought he had it right, he unscrewed the pump-nozzle and was about to turn Silver over when he heard the rapid snap-flutter of playing cards behind him. He whirled, almost knocking Silver over.

Mike was standing there with a deck of blue-backed Bicycle playing cards in one hand. 'Want these?'

Bill let out a long, shaky sigh. 'You've got clothespins, too, I suppose?'

Mike took four from the flap pocket of his shirt and held them out.

'Just happened to have them around, I suh-huppose?'

'Yeah, something like that,' Mike said.

571

Bill took the cards and tried to shuffle them. His hands shook and the cards sprayed out of his hands. They went everywhere . . . but only two landed face-up. Bill looked at them, then up at Mike. Mike's gaze was frozen on the littered playing cards. His lips had pulled back from his teeth.

The two up cards were both the ace of spades.

'That's impossible,' Mike said. 'I just opened that deck. Look.' He pointed at the swill-can just inside the garage door and Bill saw the cellophane wrapper. 'How can one deck of cards have two aces of spades?'

Bill bent down and picked them up. 'How can you spray a deck of cards all over the floor and have only two of them land face up?' he asked. 'That's an even better que –'

He turned the aces over, looked, and then showed them to Mike. One of them was a blueback, the other a redback.

'Holy Christ, Mikey, what have you got us into?'

'What are you going to do with those?' Mike asked in a numb voice.

'Why, put them on,' Bill said, and suddenly he began to laugh. 'That's what I'm supposed to do, isn't it? If there are certain preconditions for the use of magic, those preconditions will inevitably arrange themselves. Right?'

Mike didn't reply. He watched as Bill went to Silver's rear wheel and attached the playing cards. His hands were still shaking and it took awhile, but he finally got it done, drew in one tight breath, held it, and spun the rear wheel. The playing cards machine-gunned loudly against the spokes in the garage's silence.

'Come on,' Mike said softly. 'Come on in, Big Bill. I'll make us some chow.'

They had scoffed the burgers and now sat smoking, watching dark begin to unfold from dusk in Mike's back yard. Bill took out his wallet, found someone's business card, and wrote upon it the sentence that had plagued him ever since he had seen Silver in the window of Secondhand Rose, Secondhand Clothes. He showed it to Mike, who read it carefully, lips pursed.

'Does it mean anything to you?' Bill asked.

'"He thrusts his fists against the posts and still insists he sees the ghosts."' He nodded. 'Yes, I know what that is.'

'Well then, tell me. Or are you going to give me some more cuh-cuh-crap about figuring it out for myself?'

'No,' Mike said, 'in this case I think it's okay to tell you. The

572

phrase goes back to English times. It's a tongue-twister that became a speech exercise for lispers and stutterers. Your mother kept trying to get you to say it that summer. The summer of 1958. You used to go around mumbling it to yourself.'

'I did?' Bill said, and then, slowly, answering his own question: 'I did.'

'You must have wanted to please her very much.'

Bill, who suddenly felt he might cry, only nodded. He didn't trust himself to speak.

'You never made it,' Mike told him. 'I remember that. You tried like hell but your tang kept getting all tungled up.'

'But I *did* say it,' Bill replied. 'At least once.'

'When?'

Bill brought his fist down on the picnic table hard enough to hurt. '*I don't remember!*' he shouted. And then, dully, he said it again: 'I just don't remember.'

CHAPTER TWELVE
THREE UNINVITED
GUESTS

1

On the day after Mike Hanlon made his calls, Henry Bowers began to hear voices. Voices had been talking to him all day long. For awhile, Henry thought they were coming from the moon. In the late afternoon, looking up from where he was hoeing in the garden, he could see the moon in the blue daytime sky, pale and small. A ghost-moon.

That, in fact, was why he believed it was the moon that was talking to him. Only a ghost-moon would talk in ghost-voices – the voices of his old friends, and the voices of those little kids who had played down in the Barrens so long ago. Those, and another voice . . . one he did not dare name.

Victor Criss spoke from the moon first. *They comin back, Henry. All of em, man. They comin back to Derry.*

Then Belch Huggins spoke from the moon, perhaps from the dark side of the moon. *You're the only one, Henry. The only one of us left. You'll have to get em for me and Vic. Ain't no little kids can rank us out like that. Why, I hit a ball one time down to Tracker's, and Tony Tracker said that ball would have been out of Yankee Stadium.*

He hoed, looking up at the ghost-moon in the sky, and after awhile Fogarty came over and hit him in the back of the neck and knocked him flat on his face.

'You're hoein up the peas right along with the weeds, you ijit.'

Henry got up, brushing dirt off his face and out of his hair. There stood Fogarty, a big man in a white jacket and white pants, his belly swelled out in front of him. It was illegal for the guards (who were called 'counsellors' here at Juniper Hill) to carry billy-clubs, so a number of them – Fogarty, Adler, and Koontz were the worst – carried rolls of quarters in their pockets. They almost always hit you with them in the same place, right in the back of the neck. There was no rule against

574

quarters. Quarters were not considered a deadly weapon at Juniper Hill, an institution for the mentally insane which stood on the outskirts of Augusta near the Sidney town line.

'I'm sorry, Mr Fogarty,' Henry said, and offered a big grin which showed an irregular line of yellow teeth. They looked like the pickets in a fence outside a haunted house. Henry had begun to lose his teeth when he was fourteen or so.

'Yeah, you're sorry,' Fogarty said. 'You'll be a lot sorrier if I catch you doing it again, Henry.'

'Yes sir, Mr Fogarty.'

Fogarty walked away, his black shoes leaving big brown tracks in the dirt of West Garden. Because Fogarty's back was turned, Henry took a moment to look around surreptitiously. They had been shooed out to hoe as soon as the clouds cleared, everyone from the Blue Ward – which was where they put you if you had once been very dangerous but were now considered only moderately dangerous. Actually, all the patients at Juniper Hill were considered moderately dangerous; it was a facility for the criminally insane. Henry Bowers was here because he had been convicted of killing his father in the late fall of 1958 – it had been a famous year for murder trials, all right; when it came to murder trials, 1958 had been a pip.

Only of course it wasn't just his *father* they thought he had killed; if it had only been his *father*, Henry would not have spent twenty years in the Augusta State Mental Hospital, much of that time under physical and chemical restraint. No, not just his *father*; the authorities thought he had killed all of them, or at least most of them.

Following the verdict the *News* had published a front-page editorial titled 'The End of Derry's Long Night.' In it they had recapped the salient points: the belt in Henry's bureau that belonged to the missing Patrick Hockstetter; the jumble of schoolbooks, some signed out to the missing Belch Huggins and some to the missing Victor Criss, both known chums of the Bowers boy, in Henry's closet; most damning of all, the panties found tucked into a slit in Henry's mattress, panties which had been identified by laundry-mark as having belonged to Veronica Grogan, deceased.

Henry Bowers, the *News* declared, had been the monster haunting Derry in the spring and summer of 1958.

But then the *News* had proclaimed the end of Derry's long night on the front page of its December 6th edition, and even an ijit like Henry knew that in Derry night *never* ended.

They had bullied him with questions, had stood around him in a circle, had pointed fingers at him. Twice the Chief of Police had slapped him across the face and once a detective named Lottman had punched him in the gut, telling him to fess up, and be quick.

'There's people outside and they ain't happy, Henry,' this Lottman had said. 'There ain't been a lynching in Derry for a long time, but that don't mean there couldn't *be* one.'

He supposed they would have kept it up as long as necessary, not because any of them really believed the good Derryfolk were going to break into the police station, carry Henry out, and hang him from a sour-apple tree, but because they were desperate to close the books on that summer's blood and horror; they *would* have, but Henry didn't make them. They wanted him to confess to everything, he understood after awhile. Henry didn't mind. After the horror in the sewers, after what had happened to Belch and Victor, he didn't seem to mind about anything. Yes, he said, he had killed his father. This was true. Yes, he had killed Victor Criss and Belch Huggins. This was also true, at least in the sense that he had led them into the tunnels where they had been murdered. Yes, he had killed Patrick. Yes, Veronica. Yes one, yes all. Not true, but it didn't matter. Blame needed to be taken. Perhaps that was why he had been spared. And if he refused . . .

He understood about Patrick's belt. He had won it from Patrick playing scat one day in April, discovered it didn't fit, and tossed it in his bureau. He understood about the books, too – hell, the three of them chummed around together and they cared no more for their summer textbooks than they had for their regular ones, which is to say, they cared for them about as much as a woodchuck cares for tap-dancing. There were probably as many of his books in their closets, and the cops probably knew it, too.

The panties . . . no, he didn't know how Veronica Grogan's panties had come to be in his mattress.

But he thought he knew who – or *what* – had taken care of it.

Best not to talk about such things.

Best to just dummy up.

So they sent him to Augusta and finally, in 1979, they had transferred him to Juniper Hill, and he had only run into trouble once here and that was because at first no one understood. A guy had tried to turn off Henry's nightlight. The nightlight was Donald Duck doffing his little sailor hat. Donald was protection after the sun went down. With no light, *things* could come in. The locks on the door and the wire mesh did not stop them. They came like mist. *Things*. They talked and laughed . . . and sometimes they clutched. Hairy *things*, smooth *things, things* with eyes. The sort of *things* that had *really* killed Vic and Belch when the three of them had chased the kids into the tunnels under Derry in August of 1958.

Looking around now, he saw the others from the Blue Ward. There was George DeVille, who had murdered his wife and four children one winter night in 1962. George's head was studiously bent, his white hair blowing in the breeze, snot running gaily out of his nose, his huge wooden crucifix bobbing and dancing as he hoed. There was Jimmy Donlin, and all they said in the papers about Jimmy was that he had killed his mother in Portland during the summer of 1965, but what they hadn't said in the papers was that Jimmy had tried a novel experiment in body-disposal: by the time the cops came Jimmy had eaten more than half of her, including her brains. 'They made me twice as smart,' Jimmy had confided to Henry one night after lights-out.

In the row beyond Jimmy, hoeing fanatically and singing the same line over and over, as always, was the little Frenchman Benny Beaulieu. Benny had been a firebug – a pyromaniac. Now as he hoed he sang this line from the Doors over and over: 'Try to set the night on fire, try to set the night on fire, try to set the night on fire, try to –'

It got on your nerves after awhile.

Beyond Benny was Franklin D'Cruz, who had raped over fifty women before being caught with his pants down in Bangor's Terrace Park. The ages of his victims ranged from three to eighty-one. Not very particular was Frank D'Cruz. Beyond him but way back was Arlen Weston, who spent as much time looking dreamily at his hoe as he did using it. Fogarty, Adler, and John Koontz had all tried the roll-of-quarters-in-the-fist trick on Weston to try and convince him he could move a bit faster, and one day Koontz had hit him maybe a little too hard because blood came not only from Arlen Weston's nose but also from Arlen's ears and that night he had a convulsion. Not a big one; just a little one. But since then Arlen had drifted further and further into his own interior blackness and now he was a hopeless case, almost totally unplugged from the world. Beyond Arlen was –

'You want to pick it up or I'll give you some more help, Henry!' Fogarty bawled over, and Henry began to hoe again. He didn't want any convulsions. He didn't want to end up like Arlen Weston.

Soon the voices started in again. But this time they were the voices of the others, the voices of the kids that had gotten him into this in the first place, whispering down from the ghost-moon.

You couldn't even catch a fatboy, Bowers, one of them whispered.
Now I'm rich and you're hoeing peas. Ha-ha on you, asshole!

*B-B-Bowers, you c-c-couldn't c-catch a c-c-cold! Read a-any g-g-good
b-b-books since you've been in th-there? I ruh-ruh-wrote lots! I'm ruh-ruh-rich
and y-you're in Juh-Juh-hooniper Hill! Ha-ha on you, you stupid asshole!*

'Shut up,' Henry whispered to the ghost-voices, hoeing faster,
beginning to hoe up the new pea-plants along with the weeds. Sweat
rolled down his cheeks like tears. 'We could've taken you. We *could've.*'

We got you locked up, you asshole, another voice laughed. *You
chased me and couldn't catch me and I got rich, too! Way to go, banana-heels!*

'Shut up,' Henry muttered, hoeing faster. 'Just shut up!'

Did you want to get in my panties, Henry? another voice teased.
*Too bad! I let all of them do me, I was nothing but a slut, but now I'm rich
too and we're all together again, and we're doing it again but you couldn't do
it now even if I let you because you couldn't get it up, so ha-ha on you,
Henry, ha-ha all OVER you –*

He hoed madly, weeds and dirt and pea-plants flying; the ghost-
voices from the ghost-moon were very loud now, echoing and flying
in his head, and Fogarty was running toward him, bellowing, but Henry
could not hear. Because of the voices.

Couldn't even get hold of a nigger like me, could you? another jeering
ghost-voice chimed in. *We killed you guys in that rockfight! We fucking
killed you!! Ha-ha, asshole! Ha-ha all over you!*

Then they were all babbling together, laughing at him, calling
him banana-heels, asking him how he'd liked the shock-treatments
they'd given him when he came up here to the Red Ward, asking
him if he liked it here at Juh-Juh-hooniper Hill, asking and laughing,
laughing and asking, and Henry dropped his hoe and began to scream
up at the ghost-moon in the blue sky and at first he was screaming
in fury, and then *the moon itself* changed and became the face of the
clown, its face a rotted pocked cheesy white, its eyes black holes, its
red bloody grin turned up in a smile so obscenely ingenuous that it
was insupportable, and so then Henry began to scream not in fury
but in mortal terror and the voice of the clown spoke from the ghost-
moon now and what it said was *You have to go back, Henry. You have
to go back and finish the job. You have to go back to Derry and kill them
all. For Me. For –*

Then Fogarty, who had been standing nearby and yelling at
Henry for almost two minutes (while the other inmates stood in their
rows, hoes grasped in their hands like comic phalluses, their expressions
not exactly interested but almost, yes, almost *thoughtful,* as if they

understood that this was all a part of the mystery that had put them here, that Henry Bowers's sudden attack of the screaming meemies in West Garden was interesting in some more than technical way), got tired of shouting and gave Henry a real blast with his quarters, and Henry went down like a ton of bricks, the voice of the clown following him down into that terrible whirlpool of darkness, chanting over and over again: *Kill them all, Henry, kill them all, kill them all, kill them all.*

2

Henry Bowers lay awake.

The moon was down and he felt a sharp sense of gratitude for that. The moon was less ghostly at night, more real, and if he should see that dreadful clown-face in the sky, riding over the hills and fields and woods, he believed he would die of terror.

He lay on his side, staring at his nightlight intently. Donald Duck had burned out; he had been replaced by Mickey and Minnie Mouse dancing a polka; they had been replaced with the green-glowing face of Oscar the Grouch from *Sesame Street*, and late last year Oscar had been replaced by the face of Fozzie Bear. Henry had measured out the years of his incarceration with burned-out nightlights instead of coffee-spoons.

At exactly 2:04 A.M. on the morning of May 30th, his nightlight went out. A little moan escaped him – no more. Koontz was on the door of the Blue Ward tonight – Koontz who was the worst of the lot. Worse even than Fogarty, who had hit him so hard in the afternoon that Henry could barely turn his head.

Sleeping around him were the other Blue Ward inmates. Benny Beaulieu slept in elastic restraints. He had been allowed to watch an *Emergency* rerun on the wardroom TV when they came in from hoeing and around six o'clock had begun jerking off constantly and without let-up, screaming 'Try to set the night on *fire*! Try to set the night on *fire*! Try to set the night on *fire*!' He had been sedated, and that was good for about four hours, and then he had started in again around eleven when the Elavil wore off, whipping his old dingus so hard it had started to bleed through his fingers, shrieking 'Try to set the night on *fire*!' So they sedated him again and put him in restraints. Now he slept, his pinched little face as grave in the dim light as Aristotle's.

From around his bed Henry could hear low snores and loud ones, grunts, an occasional bedfart. He could hear Jimmy Donlin's breathing; it was unmistakable even though Jimmy slept five beds over. Rapid and faintly whistling, for some reason it always made Henry think of a sewing machine. From beyond the door giving on the hall he could hear the faint sound of Koontz's TV. He knew that Koontz would be watching the late movies on Channel 38, drinking Texas Driver and eating his lunch. Koontz favored sandwiches made out of chunky peanut-butter and Bermuda onions. When Henry heard this he had shuddered and thought: *And they say all the crazy people are locked up.*

This time the voice didn't come from the moon.

This time it came from under the bed.

Henry recognized the voice at once. It was Victor Criss, whose head had been torn off somewhere beneath Derry twenty-seven years ago. It had been torn off by the Frankenstein-monster. Henry had seen it happen, and afterward he had seen the monster's eyes shift and had felt its watery yellow gaze on him. Yes, the Frankenstein-monster had killed Victor and then it had killed Belch, but here was Vic again, like the almost ghostly rerun of a black-and-white program from the Nifty Fifties, when the President was bald and the Buicks had portholes.

And now that it had happened, now that the voice had come, Henry found that he was calm and unafraid. Relieved, even.

'Henry,' Victor said.

'Vic!' Henry cried. 'What you doing under there?'

Benny Beaulieu snorted and muttered in his sleep. Jimmy's neat nasal sewing-machine inhales and exhales paused for a moment. In the hall, the volume on Koontz's small Sony was turned down and Henry Bowers could sense him, head cocked to one side, one hand on the TV's volume knob, the fingers of the other hand touching the cylinder which bulged in the righthand pocket of his whites – the roll of quarters.

'You don't have to talk out loud, Henry,' Vic said. 'I can hear you if you just think. And they can't hear me at all.'

What do you want, Vic? Henry asked.

There was no reply for a long time. Henry thought that maybe Vic had gone away. Outside the door the volume of Koontz's TV went up again. Then there was a scratching noise from under the bed; the springs squealed slightly as a dark shadow pulled itself out from under. Vic looked up at him and grinned. Henry grinned back uneasily. Ole Vic was looking a little bit like the Frankenstein-monster himself these days. A scar like a hangrope tattoo circled his neck. Henry thought maybe that was where his head had been sewed back on. His eyes were a weird gray-green color, and the corneas seemed to float on a watery viscous substance.

Vic was still twelve.

'I want the same thing you want,' Vic said. 'I want to pay em back.'

Pay em back, Henry Bowers said dreamily.

'But you'll have to get out of here to do it,' Vic said. 'You'll have to go back to Derry. I need you, Henry. We all need you.'

They can't hurt You, Henry said, understanding he was talking to more than Vic.

'They can't hurt Me if they only half-believe,' Vic said. 'But there have been some distressing signs, Henry. We didn't think they could beat us back then, either. But the fatboy got away from you in the Barrens. The fatboy and the smartmouth and the quiff got away from us that day after the movies. And the rockfight, when they saved the nigger —'

Don't talk about that! Henry shouted at Vic, and for a moment all of the peremptory hardness that had made him their leader was in his voice. Then he cringed, thinking Vic would hurt him — surely Vic could do whatever he wanted, since he was a ghost — but Vic only grinned.

'I can take care of them if they only half-believe,' he said, 'but you're alive, Henry. You can get them no matter if they believe, half-believe, or don't believe at all. You can get them one by one or all at once. You can pay em back.'

Pay em back, Henry repeated. Then he looked at Vic doubtfully again. But I can't get out of here, Vic. There's wire on the windows and Koontz is on the door tonight. Koontz is the worst. Maybe tomorrow night . . .

'Don't worry about Koontz,' Vic said, standing up. Henry saw he was still wearing the jeans he had been wearing that day, and that they were still splattered with drying sewer-muck. 'I'll take care of Koontz.' Vic held out his hand.

After a moment Henry took it. He and Vic walked toward the Blue Ward door and the sound of the TV. They were almost there when Jimmy Donlin, who had eaten his mother's brains, woke up. His eyes widened as he saw Henry's late-night visitor. It was his mother. Her slip was showing just a quarter-inch or so, as it always had. The top of her head was gone. Her eyes, horribly red, rolled toward him, and when she grinned, Jimmy saw the lipstick smears on her yellow, horsy teeth as he always had. Jimmy began to shriek. '*No, Ma! No, Ma! No, Ma!*'

The TV went off at once, and even before the others could begin to stir, Koontz was jerking the door open and saying, 'Okay, asshole, get ready to catch your head on the rebound. I've *had* it.'

'*No, Ma! No, Ma! Please, Ma! No, Ma —*'

Koontz came rushing in. First he saw Bowers, standing tall and paunchy and nearly ridiculous in his johnny, his loose flesh doughy in the light spilling in from the corridor. Then he looked left and screamed out two lungfuls of silent spun glass. Standing by Bowers was a thing in a clown suit. It stood perhaps eight feet tall. Its suit was silvery. Orange pompoms ran down the front. There were oversized funny shoes on its feet. But its head was not that of a man or a clown; it was the head of a Doberman pinscher, the only animal on God's green earth of which John Koontz was frightened. Its eyes were red. Its silky muzzle wrinkled back to show huge white teeth.

A cylinder of quarters fell from Koontz's nerveless fingers and rolled across the floor and into the corner. Late the following day Benny Beaulieu, who slept through the whole thing, would find them and hide them in his footlocker. The quarters bought him cigarettes – tailor-mades – for a month.

Koontz hitched in breath to scream again as the clown lurched toward him.

'It's time for the circus!' the clown screamed in a growling voice, and its white-gloved hands fell on Koontz's shoulders.

Except that the hands inside those gloves felt like paws.

3

For the third time that day – that long, long day – Kay McCall went to the telephone.

She got further this time than she had on the first two occasions; this time she waited until the phone had been picked up on the other end and a hearty Irish cop's voice said 'Sixth Street Station, Sergeant O'Bannon, how may I help you?' before hanging up.

Oh, you're doing fine. Jesus, yes. By the eighth or ninth time you'll have mustered up guts enough to give him your name.

She went into the kitchen and fixed herself a weak Scotch-and-soda, although she knew it probably wasn't a good idea on top of the Darvon. She recalled a snatch of folk-song from the college coffee-houses of her youth – *Got a headful of whiskey and a bellyful of gin/*

Doctor say it kill me but he don't say when – and laughed jaggedly. There was a mirror running along the top of the bar. She saw her reflection in it and stopped laughing abruptly.

Who is that woman?

One eye swollen nearly shut.

Who is that battered woman?

Nose the color of a drunken knight's after thirty or so years of tilting at ginmills, and puffed to a grotesque size.

Who is that battered woman who looks like the ones who drag themselves to a women's shelter after they finally get frightened enough or brave enough or just plain mad enough to leave the man who is hurting them, who has systematically hurt them week in and week out, month in and month out, year in and year out?

Laddered scratch up one cheek.

Who is she, Kay-Bird?

One arm in a sling.

Who? Is it you? Can it be you?

'Here she is . . . Miss America,' she sang, wanting her voice to come out tough and cynical. It started out that way but warbled on the seventh syllable and cracked on the eighth. It was not a tough voice. It was a scared voice. She knew it; she had been scared before and had always gotten over it. She thought she would be a long time getting over this.

The doctor who had treated her in one of the little cubicles just off Emergency Admitting at Sisters of Mercy half a mile down the road had been young and not bad-looking. Under different circumstances she might have idly (or not so idly) considered trying to get him home and take him on a sexual tour of the world. But she hadn't felt in the least bit horny. Pain wasn't conducive to horniness. Neither was fear.

His name was Geffin, and she didn't care for the fixed way he was looking at her. He took a small white paper cup to the room's sink, half-filled it with water, produced a pack of cigarettes from the drawer of his desk, and offered them to her.

She took one and he lit it for her. He had to chase the tip for a second or two with the match because her hand was shaking. He tossed the match in a paper cup. *Fssss.*

'A wonderful habit,' he said. 'Right?'

'Oral fixation,' Kay replied.

He nodded and then there was silence. He kept looking at her. She got the feeling he was expecting her to cry, and it made her mad because she felt she might just do that. She hated to be emotionally preguessed, and most of all by a man.

'Boyfriend?' he asked at last.

'I'd rather not talk about it.'

'Uh-huh.' He smoked and looked at her.

'Didn't your mother ever tell you it was impolite to stare?'

She wanted it to come out hard-edged, but it sounded like a plea: *Stop looking at me, I know how I look, I saw.* This thought was followed by another, one she suspected her friend Beverly must have had more than once, that the worst of the beating took place inside, where you were apt to suffer something that might be called interspiritual bleeding. She knew what she looked like, yes. Worse still, she knew what she felt like. She felt yellow. It was a dismal feeling.

'I'll say this just once,' Geffin said. His voice was low and pleasant. 'When I work E.R. – my turn in the barrel, you might say – I see maybe two dozen battered women a week. The interns treat two dozen more. So look – there's a telephone right here on the desk. It's my dime. You call Sixth Street, give them your name and address, tell them what happened and who did it. Then you hang up and I'll take the bottle of bourbon I keep over there in the file cabinet – strictly for medicinal purposes, you understand – and we'll have a drink on it. Because I happen to think, this is just my personal opinion, that the only lower form of life than a man who would beat up a woman is a rat with syphilis.'

Kay smiled wanly. 'I appreciate the offer,' she said, 'but I'll pass. For the time being.'

'Uh-huh,' he said. 'But when you go home take a good look at yourself in the mirror, Ms McCall. Whoever it was, he jobbed you good.'

She did cry then. She couldn't help it.

Tom Rogan had called around noon of the day after she had seen Beverly safely off, wanting to know if Kay had been in touch with his wife. He sounded calm, reasonable, not the least upset. Kay told him she hadn't seen Beverly in almost two weeks. Tom thanked her and hung up.

Around one the doorbell rang while she was writing in her study. She went to the door.

'Who is it?'

'Cragin's Flowers, ma'am,' a high voice said, and how stupid she had been not to realize it had been Tom doing a bad falsetto, how stupid she had been to believe that Tom had given up so easily, how stupid she had been to take the chain off before opening the door.

In he had come, and she had gotten just this far: 'You get out of h –' before Tom's fist came flying out of nowhere, slamming into her right eye, closing it and sending a bolt of incredible agony through her head. She had gone reeling backward down the hallway, clutching at things to try and stay upright: a delicate one-rose vase that had gone smashing to the tiles, a coat-tree that had tumbled over. She fell over her own feet as Tom closed the front door behind him and walked toward her.

'Get out of here!' she had screamed at him.

'As soon as you tell me where she is,' Tom said, walking down the hall toward her. She was dimly aware that Tom didn't look very good – well, actually, *terrible* might have been a better word – and she felt a dim but ferocious gladness skyrocket through her. Whatever Tom had done to Bev, it looked as if Bev had given it back in spades. It had been enough to keep him off his feet for one whole day, anyhow – and he still didn't look as if he belonged anywhere but in a hospital.

But he also looked very mean, and very angry.

Kay scrambled to her feet and backed away, keeping her eyes on him as you might keep your eyes on a wild animal that had escaped its cage.

'I told you I haven't seen her and that was the truth,' she said. 'Now get out of here before I call the police.'

'You've seen her,' Tom said. His swollen lips were trying to grin. She saw that his teeth had a strange jagged look. Some of the front ones had been broken. 'I call up, tell you I don't know where Bev is. You say you haven't seen her in two weeks. Never a single question. Never a discouraging word, even though I know damn well that you hate my guts. So where is she, you numb cunt? Tell me.'

Kay turned then and ran for the end of the hall, wanting to get into the parlor, rake the sliding mahogany doors closed on their recessed tracks, and turn the thumb-bolt. She got there ahead of him – he was limping – but before she could slam the doors shut he had inserted his body between. He gave one convulsive lunge and pushed through. She turned to run again; he caught her by her dress and yanked her so hard he tore the entire back of it straight down to her waist. *Your wife made that dress, you shit*, she thought incoherently, and then she was twisted around.

'*Where is she?*'

Kay brought her hand up in a walloping slap that rocked his

head back and started the cut on the left side of his face bleeding again. He grabbed her hair and pulled her head forward into his fist. It felt to her for a moment as if her nose had exploded. She screamed, inhaled to scream again, and began to cough on her own blood. She was in utter terror now. She had not known there could be so much terror in all the wide world. The crazy son of a bitch was going to kill her.

She screamed, she screamed, and then his fist looped into her belly, driving the air out of her and she could only gasp. She began to cough and gasp at the same time and for one terrifying moment she thought she was going to choke.

'Where is she?'

Kay shook her head. 'Haven't . . . seen her,' she gasped. 'Police . . . you'll go to jail . . . asshole . . .'

He jerked her to her feet and she felt something give in her shoulder. More pain, so strong it was sickening. He whirled her around, still holding onto her arm, and now he twisted her arm up behind her and she bit down on her lower lip, promising herself that she would not scream again.

'Where is she?'

Kay shook her head.

He jerked her arm up again, jerked it so hard that she heard him grunt. His warm breath puffed against her ear. She felt her closed right fist strike her own left shoulderblade and she screamed again as that thing in her shoulder gave some more.

'Where is she?'

'. . . know . . .'

'What?'

'I don't KNOW!'

He let go of her and gave her a push. She collapsed to the floor, sobbing, snot and blood running out of her nose. There was an almost musical crash, and when she looked around, Tom was bending over her. He had broken the top off another vase, this one of Waterford crystal. He held the base. The jagged neck was only inches from her face. She stared at it, hypnotized.

'Let me tell you something,' he said, the words coming out in little pants and blows of warm air, 'you're going to tell me where she went or you're going to be picking your face up off the floor. You've got three seconds, maybe less. When I'm mad it seems like time goes a lot faster.'

My face, she thought, and that was what finally caused her to give in . . . or cave in, if you liked that better: the thought of this monster using the jagged neck of the Waterford vase to cut her face apart.

'She went home,' Kay sobbed. 'Her home town. Derry. It's a place called Derry, in Maine.'

'How did she go?'

'She took a b-b-bus to Milwaukee. She was going to fly from there.'

'That shitty little *cooze*!' Tom cried, straightening up. He walked around in a large, aimless semicircle, running his hands through his hair so that it stood up in crazy spikes and whorls. 'That *cunt*, that *cooze*, that nickelplated *crotch*!' He picked up a delicate wood sculpture of a man and woman making love – she'd had it since she was twenty-two – and threw in into the fireplace, where it shattered to splinters. He came face to face with himself for a moment in the mirror over the fireplace and stood wide-eyed, as if looking at a ghost. Then he whirled on her again. He had taken something from the pocket of the sportcoat he was wearing, and she saw with a stupid kind of wonder that it was a paperback novel. The cover was almost completely black, except for the red-foil letters which spelled out the title and a picture of several young people standing on a high bluff over a river. *The Black Rapids.*

'Who's this fuck?'

'Huh? What?'

'Denbrough. Denbrough.' He shook the book impatiently in front of her face, then suddenly slapped her with it. Her cheek flared with pain and then dull red heat, like stove-coals. 'Who is he?'

She began to understand.

'They were friends. When they were children. They both grew up in Derry.'

He whacked her with the book again, this time from the other side.

'Please,' she sobbed. 'Please, Tom.'

He pulled an Early American chair with spindly, graceful legs over to her, turned it around, and sat down on it. His jackolantern face looked down at her over the chairback.

'Listen to me,' he said. 'You listen to your old uncle Tommy. Can you do that, you bra-burning bitch?'

She nodded. She could taste blood, hot and coppery, in her throat. Her shoulder was on fire. She prayed it was only dislocated and not broken. But that was not the worst. *My face, he was going to cut up my* face –

'If you call the police and tell them I was here, I'll deny it. You can't prove a fucking thing. It's the maid's day off and we're all by our twosome. Of course, they might arrest me anyway, anything's possible, right?'

She found herself nodding again, as if her head was on a string.

'Sure it is. And what I'd do is post bail and come right back here. They'd find your tits on the kitchen table and your eyes in the fishbowl. Do you understand me? Are you getting your old uncle Tommy?'

Kay burst into tears again. That string attached to her head was still working; it bobbed up and down.

'Why?'

'What? I . . . I don't . . .'

'Wake up, for God's sake! Why did she go back?'

'I don't know!' Kay nearly screamed.

He wiggled the broken vase at her.

'I don't know,' she said in a lower voice. 'Please. She didn't tell me. Please don't hurt me.'

He tossed the vase in the wastebasket and stood up.

He left without looking back, head down, a big shambling bear of a man.

She rushed after him and locked the door. She rushed into the kitchen and locked that door. After a moment's pause she had limped upstairs (as fast as her aching belly would allow) and had locked the french doors which gave on the upstairs verandah – it was not beyond possibility that he might decide to shinny up one of the pillars and come in again that way. He was hurt, but he was also insane.

She went for the telephone for the first time and had no more than dropped her hand on it before remembering what he had said.

What I'd do is post bail and come right back here . . . your tits on the kitchen table and your eyes in the fishbowl.

She jerked her hand off the phone.

She went into the bathroom then and looked at her dripping tomato nose, her black eye. She didn't weep; the shame and horror she felt were too deep for tears. *Oh Bev, I did the best I could, dear*, she thought. *But my face . . . he said he would cut up my face . . .*

There was Darvon and Valium in the medicine cabinet. She debated between them and finally swallowed one of each. Then she went to Sisters of Mercy for treatment and met the famous Dr Geffin, who right now was the only man she could think of whom she would not be perfectly happy to see wiped off the face of the earth.

And from there home again, home again, jiggety-jog.

She went to her bedroom window and looked out. The sun was low on the horizon now. On the East Coast it would be late twilight – just going on seven o'clock in Maine.

You can decide what to do about the cops later. The important thing now is to warn Beverly.

It would be a hell of a lot easier, Kay thought, *if you had told me where you were staying, Beverly my love. I suppose you didn't know yourself.*

Although she had quit smoking two years before, she kept a pack of Pall Malls in the drawer of her desk for emergencies. She shot one out of the pack, lit up, grimaced. She had last smoked from this pack around December of 1982, and this baby was staler than the ERA in the Illinois state Senate. She smoked it anyway, one eye half-lidded against the smoke, the other just half-lidded, period. Thanks to Tom Rogan.

Using her left hand laboriously – the son of a bitch had dislocated her good arm – she dialed Maine information and asked for the name and number of every hotel and motel in Derry.

'Ma'am, that's going to take awhile,' the directory-assistance operator said dubiously.

'It's going to take even longer than that, sister,' Kay said. 'I'm going to have to write with my stupid hand. My good one's on vacation.'

'It is not customary for –'

'Listen to me,' Kay said, not unkindly. 'I'm calling you from Chicago, and I'm trying to reach a woman-friend of mine who has just left her husband and gone back to Derry, where she grew up. Her husband knows where she went. He got the information out of me by beating the living shit out of me. This man is a psycho. She needs to know he's coming.'

There was a long pause, and then the directory-assistance operator said in a decidedly more human voice, 'I think the number you really need is the Derry Police Department.'

'Fine. I'll take that, too. But she has to be warned,' Kay said. 'And . . .' She thought of Tom's cut cheeks, the knot on his forehead, the one on his temple, his limp, his hideously swelled lips. 'And if she knows he's coming, that may be enough.'

There was another long pause.

'You there, sis?' Kay asked.

'Arlington Motor Lodge,' the operator said, '643–8146. Bassey Park Inn, 648–4083. The Bunyan Motor Court –'

'Slow down a little, okay?' she asked, writing furiously. She looked for an ashtray, didn't see one, and mashed the Pall Mall out on the desk blotter. 'Okay, go on.'

'The Clarendon Inn —'

4

She got half-lucky on her fifth call. Beverly Rogan was registered at the Derry Town House. She was only half-lucky because Beverly was out. She left her name and number and a message that Beverly should call her the instant she came back, no matter how late it was.

The desk clerk repeated the message. Kay went upstairs and took another Valium. She lay down and waited for sleep. Sleep didn't come. *I'm sorry, Bev*, she thought, looking into the dark, floating on the dope. *What he said about my face . . . I just couldn't stand that. Call soon, Bev. Please call soon. And watch out for the crazy son of a bitch you married.*

5

The crazy son of a bitch Bev had married did better on connections than Beverly had the day before because he left from O'Hare, the hub of commercial aviation in the continental United States. During the flight he read and reread the brief note on the author at the end of *The Black Rapids*. It said that William Denbrough was a native of New England and the author of three other novels (which were also available, the note added helpfully, in Signet paperback editions). He and his wife, the actress Audra Phillips, lived in California. He was currently at work on a new novel. Noticing that the paperback of *The Black Rapids* had been issued in 1976, Tom supposed the guy had written some of the other novels since then.

Audra Phillips . . . he had seen her in the movies, hadn't he? He rarely noticed actresses — Tom's idea of a good flick was a crime story, a chase story, or a monster picture — but if this babe was the one he was thinking of, he had noticed her especially because she looked a lot like Beverly: long red hair, green eyes, tits that wouldn't quit.

He sat up a little straighter in his seat, tapping the paperback against his leg, trying to ignore the ache in his head and in his mouth. Yes, he was sure. Audra Phillips was the redhead with the good tits. He had seen her in a Clint Eastwood movie, and then about a year later in a horror flick called *Graveyard Moon*. Beverly had gone with him to see that one, and coming out of the theater, he had mentioned his idea that the actress looked a lot like her. 'I don't think so,' Bev had said. 'I'm taller and she's prettier. Her hair's a darker red, too.' That was all. He hadn't thought of it again until now.

He and his wife, the actress Audra Phillips . . .

Tom had some dim understanding of psychology; he had used it to manipulate his wife all the years of their marriage. And now a nagging unpleasantness began to nag at him, more feeling than thought. It centered on the fact that Bev and this Denbrough had played together as kids and that Denbrough had married a woman who, in spite of what Beverly said, looked amazingly like Tom Rogan's wife.

What sort of games had Denbrough and Beverly played when they were kids? Post-office? Spin-the-bottle?

Other games?

Tom sat in his seat and tapped the book against his leg and felt his temples begin to throb.

When he arrived at Bangor International Airport, and canvassed the rental-car booths, the girls – some dressed in yellow, some in red, some in Irish green – looked at his blasted dangerous face nervously and told him (more nervously still) that they had no cars to rent, so sorry.

Tom went to the newsstand and got a Bangor paper. He turned to the want-ads, oblivious to the looks he was getting from people passing by, and isolated three likelies. He hit paydirt on his second call.

'Paper says you've got a '76 LTD wagon. Fourteen hundred bucks.'

'Right, sure.'

'I tell you what,' Tom said, touching the wallet in his jacket pocket. It was fat with cash – six thousand dollars. 'You bring it out to the airport and we'll do the deal right here. You give me the car and a bill of sale and your pink-slip. I'll give you cash money.'

The fellow with the LTD for sale paused and then said, 'I'd have to take my plates off.'

'Sure, fine.'

'How will I know you, Mr – ?'

'Mr Barr,' Tom said. He was looking at a sign across the terminal lobby that said BAR HARBOR AIRLINES GIVES YOU NEW ENGLAND – AND THE WORLD! 'I'll be standing by the far door. You'll know me because my face doesn't look so hot. My wife and I went roller-skating yesterday and I took one hell of a fall. Things could be worse, I guess. I didn't break anything but my face.'

'Gee, I'm sorry to hear that, Mr Barr.'

'I'll mend. You just get the car out here, my good buddy.'

He hung up, walked across to the door, and stepped out into the warm fragrant May night.

The guy with the LTD showed up ten minutes later driving out of the late-spring dusk. He was only a kid. They did the deal; the kid scribbled him a bill of sale which Tom stuffed indifferently into his overcoat pocket. He stood there and watched the kid take off the LTD's Maine plates.

'Give you an extra three bucks for the screwdriver,' Tom said when he was done.

The kid looked at him thoughtfully for a moment, shrugged, handed the screwdriver over, and took the three ones Tom was holding out. *None of my business*, the shrug said, and Tom thought: *How right you are, my good little buddy.* Tom saw him into a cab, then got behind the wheel of the Ford.

It was a piece of shit: transmission whiny, universal groany, body rattly, brakes slushy. None of it mattered. He drove around to the long-term parking lot, took a ticket, and drove in. He parked next to a Subaru that looked as if it had been there for awhile. He used the kid's screwdriver to remove the Subaru's plates and put them on the LTD. He hummed as he worked.

By 10:00 P.M. he was driving east on Route 2, a Maine road map open on the seat beside him. He had discovered that the LTD's radio didn't work, so he drove in silence. That was all right. He had plenty to think about. All the wonderful things he was going to do to Beverly when he caught up with her, for instance.

He was sure in his heart, quite sure, that Beverly was close by. And smoking.

Oh my dear girl, you fucked with the wrong man when you fucked with Tom Rogan. And the question is this – what, exactly, are we to do with you?

The Ford bulled its way through the night, chasing its high beams, and by the time Tom got to Newport, he knew. He found a drugs-and-sundries shop on the main drag that was still open. He went inside and bought a carton of Camels. The proprietor wished him a good evening. Tom wished him the same.

He tossed the carton on the seat and got moving again. He drove slowly on up Route 7, hunting for his turnoff. Here it was – Route 3, with a sign which read HAVEN 21 DERRY 15.

He made the turn and got the Ford rolling faster. He glanced at the carton of cigarettes and smiled a little. In the green glow of the dashlights, his cut and lumpy face looked strange, ghoulish.

Got some cigarettes for you, Bevvie, Tom thought as the wagon ran between stands of pine and spruce, heading toward Derry at a little better than sixty. *Oh my yes. A whole carton. Just for you. And when I see you, dear, I'm going to make you eat every fucking one. And if this guy Denbrough needs some education, we can arrange that, too. No problem, Bevvie. No problem at all.*

For the first time since the dirty bitch had bushwhacked him and run out, Tom began to feel good.

6

Audra Denbrough flew first class to Maine in a British Airways DC-10. She had left Heathrow at ten minutes of six that afternoon and had been chasing the sun ever since. The sun was winning – had won, in fact – but that didn't really matter. By a stroke of providential luck she had discovered that British Airways flight 23, London to Los Angeles, made one refueling stop . . . at Bangor International Airport.

The day had been a crazy nightmare. Freddie Firestone, the producer of *Attic Room*, had of course wanted Bill first thing. There had been some kind of ballsup about the stuntwoman who was supposed to fall down a flight of stairs for Audra. It seemed that stuntpeople had a union too, and this woman had fulfilled her quota of stunts for the week, or some silly thing. The union was demanding that Freddie either sign an extension-of-salary waiver or hire another woman to do the stunt. The problem was there was no other woman close enough to Audra's body-type available. Freddie told the union boss that they would have to get a man to do the stunt, then, wouldn't they? It wasn't as if the fall had to be taken in bra and panties. They had the auburn-haired wig, and the wardrobe woman could fit the fellow up with falsies and hip-padding. Even some arse-pads, if that was necessary.

Can't be done, mate, the union boss said. Against the union charter to have a man step in for a woman. Sexual discrimination.

In the movie business Freddie's temper was fabled, and at that point he had lost it. He told the union boss, a fat man whose BO was almost paralyzing, to bugger himself. The union boss told Freddie he better watch his gob or there would be no more stunts on the set of *Attic Room* at all. Then he had rubbed his thumb and forefinger together in a *baksheesh* gesture that had driven Freddie crazy. The union boss was big but soft; Freddie, who still played football every chance he got and who had once scored a century at cricket, was big and hard. He threw the union boss out, went back into his office to meditate, and then came out again twenty minutes later hollering for Bill. He wanted the entire scene rewritten so that the fall could be scrubbed. Audra had to tell Freddie that Bill was no longer in England.

'*What*?' Freddie said. His mouth hung open. He was looking at Audra as if he believed she had gone mad. 'What are you telling me?'

'He's been called back to the States – that's what I'm telling you.'

Freddie made as if to grab her and Audra shrank back, a bit afraid. Freddie looked down at his hands, then put them in his pockets and only looked at her.

'I'm sorry, Freddie,' she said in a small voice. 'Really.'

She got up and poured herself a cup of coffee from the Silex on Freddie's hotplate, noticing that her hands were trembling slightly. As she sat down she heard Freddie's amplified voice over the studio loud-speakers, telling everyone to go home or to the pub; the day's shooting was off. Audra winced. There went a minimum of ten thousand pounds, right down the bog.

Freddie turned off the studio intercom, got up, poured his own cup of coffee. He sat down again and offered her his pack of Silk Cut cigarettes.

Audra shook her head.

Freddie took one, lit it, and squinted at her through the smoke. 'This is serious, isn't it?'

'Yes,' Audra said, keeping her composure as best she could.

'What's happened?'

And because she genuinely liked Freddie and genuinely trusted him, Audra told him everything she knew. Freddie listened intently, gravely. It didn't take long to tell; doors were still slamming and engines starting in the parking lot outside when she finished.

Freddie was silent for some time, looking out his window. Then he swung back to her. 'He's had a nervous breakdown of some sort.'

Audra shook her head. 'No. It wasn't like that. *He* wasn't like that.' She swallowed and added, 'Maybe you had to be there.'

Freddie smiled crookedly. 'You must realize that grown men rarely feel compelled to honor promises they made as little boys. And you've read Bill's work; you know how much of it is about childhood, and it's very good stuff indeed. Very much on the nail. The idea that he's forgotten everything that ever happened to him back then is absurd.'

'The scars on his hands,' Audra said. 'They were never there. Not until this morning.'

'Bollocks! You just didn't notice them until this morning.'

594

She shrugged helplessly. 'I'd've noticed.'

She could see he didn't believe that, either.

'What's to do, then?' Freddie asked her, and she could only shake her head. Freddie lit another cigarette from the smoldering end of the first. 'I can square it with the union boss,' he said. 'Not myself, maybe; right now he'd see me in hell before giving me another stunt. I'll send Teddy Rowland round to his office. Teddy's a pouf, but he could talk the birds down from the trees. But what happens after? We've got four weeks of shooting left, and here's your husband somewhere in Massachusetts —'

'Maine —'

He waved a hand. 'Wherever. And how much good are you going to be without him?'

'I —'

He leaned forward. 'I like you, Audra. I genuinely do. And I like Bill — even in spite of this mess. We can make do, I guess. If the script needs cobbling up, I can cobble it. I've done my share of that sort of shoemaking in my time, Christ knows ... If he doesn't like the way it turns out, he'll have no one but himself to blame. I can do without Bill, but I can't do without you. I can't have you running off to the States after your man, and I've got to have you putting out at full power. Can you do that?'

'I don't know.'

'Nor do I. But I want you to think about something. We can keep things quiet for awhile, maybe for the rest of the shoot, if you'll stand up like a trouper and do your job. But if you take off, it can't be kept quiet. I can be pissy, but I'm not vindictive by nature and I'm not going to tell you that if you take off I'll see that you never work in the business again. But you should know that if you get a reputation for temperament, you might end up stuck with just that. I'm talking to you like a Dutch uncle, I know. Do you resent it?'

'No,' she said listlessly. In truth, she didn't care much one way or the other. Bill was all she could think of. Freddie was a nice enough man, but Freddie didn't understand; in the last analysis, nice man or not, all *he* could think of was what this was going to do to his picture. He had not seen the look in Bill's eyes ... or heard him stutter.

'Good.' He stood up. 'Come on over to the Hare and Hounds with me. We can both use a drink.'

She shook her head. 'A drink's the last thing I need. I'm going home and think this out.'

'I'll call for the car,' he said.

'No. I'll take the train.'

He looked at her fixedly, one hand on the telephone. 'I believe you mean to go after him,' Freddie said, 'and I'm telling you that it's a serious mistake, dear girl. He's got a bee in his bonnet, but at bottom he's steady enough. He'll shake it, and when he does he'll come back. If he'd wanted you along, he would have said so.'

'I haven't decided anything,' she said, knowing that she had in fact decided everything; had decided even before the car picked her up that morning.

'Have a care, love,' Freddie said. 'Don't do something you'll regret later.'

She felt the force of his personality beating on her, demanding that she give in, make the promise, do her job, wait passively for Bill to come back . . . or to disappear again into that hole of the past from which he had come.

She went to him and kissed him lightly on the cheek. 'I'll see you, Freddie.'

She went home and called British Airways. She told the clerk she might be interested in reaching a small Maine city called Derry if it was at all possible. There had been silence while the woman consulted her computer terminal . . . and then the news, like a sign from heaven, that BA #23 made a stop in Bangor, which was less than fifty miles away.

'Shall I book the flight for you, ma'am?'

Audra closed her eyes and saw Freddie's craggy, mostly kind, very earnest face, heard him saying: *Have a care, love. Don't do something you'll regret later.*

Freddie didn't want her to go; Bill didn't want her to go; so why was her heart screaming at her that she *had* to go? She closed her eyes. *Jesus, I feel so fucked up—*

'Ma'am? Are you still holding the wire?'

'Book it,' Audra said, then hesitated. *Have a care, love . . .* Maybe she should sleep on it; get some distance between herself and the craziness. She began to rummage in her purse for her American Express card. 'For tomorrow. First class if you have it, but I'll take anything.' *And if I change my mind I can cancel. Probably will. I'll wake up sane and everything will be clear.*

But nothing had been clear this morning, and her heart clamored just as loudly for her to go. Her sleep had been a crazy tapestry of nightmares. So she had called Freddie, not because she wanted to but because she felt she owed him that. She had not gotten far – she was trying, in some stumbling way, to tell him how much she felt Bill might need her – when there was a soft click at Freddie's end. He had hung up without saying a word after his initial hello.

But in a way, Audra thought, that soft click said everything that needed to be said.

7

The plane landed at Bangor at 7:09, EDT. Audra was the only passenger to deplane, and the others looked at her with a kind of thoughtful curiosity, probably wondering why anyone would choose to get off here, in this godforsaken little place. Audra thought of telling them *I'm looking for my husband, that's why. He came back to a little town near here because one of his boyhood chums called him and reminded him of a promise he couldn't quite remember. The call also reminded him that he hadn't thought of his dead brother in over twenty years. Oh yes: it also brought back his stutter . . . and some funny white scars on the palms of his hands.*

And then, she thought, the customs agent standing by in the jetway would whistle up the men in the white coats.

She collected her single piece of luggage – it looked very lonely riding the carousel all by itself – and approached the rental-car booths as Tom Rogan would about an hour later. Her luck was better than his would be; National Car Rental had a Datsun.

The girl filled out the form and Audra signed it.

'I thought it was you,' the girl said, and then, timidly: 'Might I please have your autograph?'

Audra gave it, writing her name on the back of a rental form, and thought: *Enjoy it while you can, girl. If Freddie Firestone is right, it won't be worth doodley-squat five years from now.*

With some amusement she realized that, after only fifteen minutes back in the States, she had begun to think like an American again.

She got a roadmap, and the girl, so star-struck she could barely talk, managed to trace out her best route to Derry.

Ten minutes later Audra was on the road, reminding herself at every intersection that if she forgot and began driving on the left, they would be scrubbing her off the asphalt.

And as she drove, she realized that she was more frightened than she had ever been in her life.

8

By one of those odd quirks of fate or coincidence which sometimes obtain (and which, in truth, obtained more frequently in Derry), Tom had taken a room at the Koala Inn on Outer Jackson Street and Audra had taken a room at the Holiday Inn; the two motels were side by side, their parking lots divided only by a raised concrete sidewalk. And as it so happened, Audra's rented Datsun and Tom's purchased LTD wagon were parked nose-to-nose, separated only by that walkway. Both slept now, Audra quietly on her side, Tom Rogan on his back, snoring so heavily that his swollen lips flapped.

9

Henry spent that day hiding – hiding in the puckies beside Route 9. Sometimes he slept. Sometimes he lay watching police cruisers slide by like hunting dogs. While the Losers ate lunch, Henry listened to voices from the moon.

And when dark fell, he went out to the verge of the road and stuck out his thumb.

After awhile, some fool came along and picked him up.

DERRY:

THE THIRD
INTERLUDE

'A bird came down the Walk –
He did not know I saw –
He bit an Angleworm in halves
And ate the fellow, raw'
                    – Emily Dickinson,
'A Bird Came Down the Walk'

The fire at the Black Spot happened in the late fall of 1930. So far as I am able to determine, that fire – the one my father barely escaped – ended the cycle of murder and disappearance which happened in the years 1929–30, just as the explosion at the Ironworks ended a cycle some twenty-five years before. It is as if a monstrous sacrifice is needed at the end of the cycle to quiet whatever terrible force it is which works here . . . to send It to sleep for another quarter-century or so.

But if such a sacrifice is needed to end each cycle, it seems that some similar event is needed to set each cycle in motion.

Which brings me to the Bradley Gang.

Their execution took place at the three-way intersection of Canal, Main, and Kansas – not far, in fact, from the place shown in the picture which began to move for Bill and Richie one day in June of 1958 – some thirteen months before the fire at the Black Spot, in October of 1929 . . . not long before the stock-market crash.

As with the fire at the Black Spot, many Derry residents affect not to remember what happened that day. Or they were out of town, visiting relatives. Or they were napping that afternoon and never found out what had happened until they heard it on the radio news that night. Or they will simply look you full in the face and lie to you.

The police logs for that day indicate that Chief Sullivan was not even in town (*Sure I remember*, Aloysius Nell told me from a chair on the sun-terrace of the Paulson Nursing Home in Bangor. *That was my first year on the force, and I ought to remember. He was off in western Maine, bird-hunting. They'd been sheeted and carried off by the time he got back. Madder than a wet hen was Jim Sullivan*), but a picture in a reference book on gangsters called *Bloodletters and Badmen* shows a grinning man standing beside the bullet-riddled corpse of Al Bradley in the morgue, and if that man is not Chief Sullivan, it is surely his twin brother.

It was from Mr Keene that I finally got what I believe to be the true version of the story – Norbert Keene, who was the proprietor of the Center Street Drug Store from 1925 until 1975. He talked to me willingly enough, but, like Betty Ripsom's father, he made me turn off my tape-recorder before he would really unwind the tale – not that it mattered; I can hear his papery voice yet – another *a capella* singer in the damned choir that is this town.

'No reason not to tell you,' he said. 'No one will print it, and no one would believe it even if they did.' He offered me an old-fashioned apothecary jar. 'Licorice whip? As I remember, you were always partial to the red ones, Mikey.'

I took one. '*Was* Chief Sullivan there that day?'

Mr Keene laughed and took a licorice whip for himself. 'You wondered about that, did you?'

'I wondered,' I agreed, chewing a piece of the red licorice. I hadn't had one since I was a kid, shoving my pennies across the counter to a much younger and sprier Mr Keene. It tasted just as fine as it had back then.

'You're too young to remember when Bobby Thomson hit his home run for the Giants in the play-off game in 1951,' Mr Keene said. 'You wouldn't have been but four years old. Well! They ran an article about that game in the newspaper a few years after, and it seemed like just about a million folks from New York claimed they were there in the ballpark that day.' Mr Keene gummed his licorice whip and a little dark drool ran down from the corner of his mouth. He wiped it off fastidiously with his handkerchief. We were sitting in the office behind the drugstore, because although Norbert Keene was eighty-five and retired ten years, he still did the books for his grandson.

'Just the opposite when it comes to the Bradley Gang!' Keene exclaimed. He was smiling, but it was not a pleasant smile – it was cynical, coldly reminiscent. 'There was maybe twenty thousand people who lived in downtown Derry back then. Main Street and Canal Street had both been paved for four years, but Kansas Street was still dirt. Raised dust in the summer and turned into a boghole every March and November. They used to oil Up-Mile Hill every June and every Fourth of July the Mayor would talk about how they were going to pave Kansas Street, but it never happened until 1942. It . . . but what was I saying?'

'Twenty thousand people who lived right downtown,' I prompted.

'Ayuh. Well, of those twenty thousand, there's probably half that have passed away since, maybe even more – fifty years is a long time. And people have a funny way of dying young in Derry. Perhaps it is the air. But of those left, I don't think you'd find more than a dozen who'd say they were in town the day the Bradley Gang went to Tophet. Butch Rowden over at the meat market would fess up to it, I guess – he keeps a picture of one of the cars they had up on the wall where he cuts meat. Looking at that picture you'd hardly know it was a car. Charlotte Littlefield would tell you a thing or two, if you could get on her good side; she teaches over to the high school, and although I reckon she must not have been more than ten or twelve at the time I bet she remembers plenty. Carl Snow . . . Aubrey Stacey . . . Eben Stampnell . . . and that old geezer who paints those funny pictures and drinks all night at Wally's – Pickman, I think his name is – they'd remember. They were all there . . .'

He trailed off vaguely, looking at the licorice whip in his hand. I thought of prodding him and decided not to.

At last he said, 'Most of the others would lie about it, the way people lied and said they were there when Bobby Thomson hit his homer, that's all I mean. But people lied about being at that ballgame because they wished they had been there. People would lie to you about being in Derry that day because they wish they *hadn't* been. Do you understand me, sonny?'

I nodded.

'You sure you want to hear the rest of this?' Mr Keene asked me. 'You're looking a bit peaked, Mr Mikey.'

'I don't,' I said, 'but I think I better, all the same.'

'Okay,' Mr Keene said mildly. It was my day for memories; as he offered me the apothecary jar with the licorice whips in it, I suddenly remembered a radio program my mother and dad used to listen to when I was just a little kid: *Mr Keene, Tracer of Lost Persons*.

'Sheriff was there that day, all right. He was s'posed to go bird-hunting, but he changed his mind damn quick when Lal Machen came in and told him that he was expecting Al Bradley that very afternoon.'

'How did Machen know that?' I asked.

'Well, that's an instructive tale in itself,' Mr Keene said, and the cynical smile creased his face again. 'Bradley wasn't never Public Enemy Number One on the FBI's hit parade, but they had wanted him – since 1928 or so. To show they could cut the mustard, I guess. Al Bradley and his brother George hit six or seven banks across the Midwest and then kidnapped a banker for ransom. The ransom was paid – thirty thousand dollars, a big sum for those days – but they killed the banker anyway.

'By then the Midwest had gotten a little toasty for the gangs that ran there, so Al and George and their litter of ratlings run northeast, up this way. They rented themselves a big farmhouse just over the town line in Newport, not far from where the Rhulin Farms are today.

'That was in the dog-days of '29, maybe July, maybe August, maybe even early September . . . I don't know for sure just when. There were eight of em – Al Bradley, George Bradley, Joe Conklin and *his* brother Cal, an Irishman named Arthur Malloy who was called "Creeping Jesus Malloy" because he was nearsighted but wouldn't put on his specs unless he absolutely had to, and Patrick Caudy, a young fellow from Chicago who was said to be kill-crazy but as handsome as Adonis. There were also two women with them: Kitty Donahue, George Bradley's common-law wife, and Marie Hauser, who belonged to Caudy but sometimes got passed around, according to the stories we all heard later.

'They made one bad assumption when they got up here, sonny – they got the idea they were so far away from Indiana that they were safe.

'They laid low for awhile, and then got bored and decided they wanted to go hunting. They had plenty of firepower but they were a bit low on ammunition. So they all came into Derry on the seventh of October in two cars. Patrick Caudy took the women around shopping while the other men went into Machen's Sporting Goods. Kitty Donahue bought a dress in Freese's, and she died in it two days later.

'Lal Machen waited on the men himself. He died in 1959. Too fat, he was. Always too fat. But there wasn't nothing wrong with his eyes, and he knew it was Al Bradley the minute he walked in, he said. He thought he recognized some of the others, but he wasn't sure of Malloy until he put on his specs to look at a display of knives in a glass case.

'Al Bradley walked up to him and said, "We'd like to buy some ammunition."

'"Well," Lal Machen says, "you come to the right place."

'Bradley handed him a paper and Lal read it over. The paper has been lost, at least so far as I know, but Lal said it would have turned your blood cold. They wanted five hundred rounds of .38-caliber ammunition, eight hundred rounds of .45-caliber, sixty rounds of .50-caliber, which they don't even make anymore, shotgun shells loaded both with buck and bird, and a thousand rounds each of .22 short- and long-rifle. Plus – get this – sixteen thousand rounds of .45 machine-gun bullets.'

'Holy *shit*!' I said.

Mr Keene smiled that cynical smile again and offered me the apothecary jar. At first I shook my head and then I took another whip.

'"This here is quite a shopping-list, boys," Lal says.

'"Come on, Al," Creeping Jesus Malloy says. "I told you we wasn't going to get it in a hick town like this. Let's go on up to Bangor. They won't have nothing there either, but I can use a ride."

'"Now hold your horses," Lal says, just as cool as a cucumber. "This here is one hell of a good order and I wouldn't want to lose it to that Jew up Bangor. I can give you the .22s right now, also the bird and half the buck. I can give you a hundred rounds each of the .38- and .45-caliber, too. I could have the rest for you . . ." And here Lal sort of half-closed his eyes and tapped his chin, as if calculating it out. ". . . by day after tomorrow. How'd that be?"

'Bradley grinned like he'd split his head around the back and said it sounded just as fine as paint. Cal Conklin said he'd still like to go on up to Bangor, but he was outvoted. "Now, if you're not sure you can make good on this order, you ought to say so right now," Al Bradley says to Lal, "because I'm a pretty fine fellow but when I get mad you don't want to get into a pissing contest with me. You follow?"

'"I do," Lal says, "and I'll have all the ammo you could want, Mr –?"

'"Rader," Brady says. "Richard D. Rader, at your service."

'He stuck out his hand and Lal pumped it, grinning all the while. "Real pleased, Mr Rader."

'So then Bradley asked him what would be a good time for him and his friends to drop by and pick up the goods, and Lal Machen asked them right back how two in the afternoon sounded to them. They agreed that would be fine. Out they went. Lal watched them go. They met the two women and Caudy on the sidewalk outside. Lal recognized Caudy, too.

'So,' Mr Keene said, looking at me bright-eyed, 'what do you think Lal done then? Called the cops?'

'I guess he didn't,' I said, 'based on what happened. Me, I would have broken my leg getting to the telephone.'

'Well, maybe you would and maybe you wouldn't,' Mr Keene said with that same cynical, bright-eyed smile, and I shivered because I knew what he meant . . . and he knew I knew. Once something heavy begins to roll, it can't be stopped; it's simply going to roll until it finds a flat place long enough to wear away all of its forward motion.

You can stand in front of that thing and get flattened . . . but that won't stop it, either.

'Maybe you would have and maybe you wouldn't,' Mr Keene repeated. 'But I can tell you what Lal Machen did. The rest of that day and all of the next, when someone he knew came in – some man – why, he would tell them that he knew who had been out in the woods around the Newport-Derry line shooting at deer and grouse and God knows what else with Kansas City typewriters. It was the Bradley Gang. He knew for a fact because he had recognized em. He'd tell em that Bradley and his men were coming back the next day around two to pick up the rest of their order. He'd tell them he'd promised Bradley all the ammunition he could want, and that was a promise he intended to keep.'

'How many?' I asked. I felt hypnotized by his glittering eye. Suddenly the dry smell of this back room – the smell of prescription drugs and powders, of Musterole and Vicks VapoRub and Robitussin cough syrup – suddenly all those smells seemed suffocating . . . but I could no more have left than I could kill myself by holding my breath.

'How many men did Lal pass the word to?' Mr Keene asked.

I nodded.

'Don't know for sure,' Mr Keene said. 'Didn't stand right there and take up sentry duty. All those he felt he could trust, I suppose.'

'Those he could trust,' I mused. My voice was a little hoarse.

'Ayuh,' Mr Keene said. 'Derrymen, you know. Not that many of em raised cows.' He laughed at this old joke before going on. 'I came in around ten the day after the Bradleys first dropped in on Lal. He told me the story, then asked how he could help me. I'd only come in to see if my last roll of pictures had been developed – in those days Machen's handled all the Kodak films and cameras – but after I got my photos I also said I could use some ammo for my Winchester.

'"You gonna shoot some game, Norb?" Lal asks me, passing over the shells.

'"Might plug some varmints," I said, and we had us a chuckle over that.' Mr Keene laughed and slapped his skinny leg as if this was still the best joke he had ever heard. He leaned forward and tapped my knee. 'All I mean, son, is that the story got around all it needed to. Small towns, you know. If you tell the right people, what you need to pass along will *get* along . . . see what I mean? Like another licorice whip?'

I took one with numb fingers.

'Make you fat,' Mr Keene said, and cackled. He looked old then
. . . infinitely old, with his bifocals slipping down the gaunt blade of
his nose and the skin stretched too tight and thin across his cheeks to
wrinkle.

'The next day I brought my rifle into the store with me and
Bob Tanner, who worked harder than any assistant I ever had after
him, brought in his pop's shotgun. Around eleven that day Gregory
Cole came in for a bicarb of soda and damned if he didn't have a Colt
.45 jammed right in his belt.

'"Don't blow your balls off with that, Greg," I said.

'"I come out of the woods all the way from Milford for this and
I got one *fuck* of a hangover," Greg says. "I guess I'll blow *someone's*
balls off before the sun goes down."

'Around one-thirty, I put the little sign I had, BE BACK SOON,
PLEASE BE PATIENT, in the door and took my rifle and walked out the
back into Richard's Alley. I asked Bob Tanner if he wanted to come
along and he said he'd better finish filling Mrs Emerson's prescription
and he'd see me later. "Leave me a live one, Mr Keene," he said, but
I allowed as how I couldn't promise nothing.

'There was hardly any traffic on Canal Street at all, either on
foot or by car. Every now and then a delivery truck would pass, but
that was about all. I saw Jake Pinnette cross over and he had a rifle in
each hand. He met Andy Criss, and they walked over to one of the
benches that used to stand where the War Memorial was – you know,
where the Canal goes underground.

'Petie Vanness and Al Nell and Jimmy Gordon were all sitting
on the courthouse steps, eating sandwiches and fruit out of their
dinnerbuckets, trading with each other for stuff that looked better to
them, the way kids do on the schoolyard. They was all armed. Jimmy
Gordon had himself a World War I Springfield that looked bigger than
he did.

'I see a kid go walking toward Up-Mile Hill – I think maybe it
was Zack Denbrough, the father of your old buddy, the one who
turned out to be a writer – and Kenny Borton says from the window
of the Christian Science Reading Room, "You want to get out of
here, kid; there's going to be shooting." Zack took one look at his
face and ran like hell.

'There were men everywhere, men with guns, standing in doorways and sitting on steps and looking out of windows. Greg Cole was
sitting in a doorway down the street with his .45 in his lap and about
two dozen shells lined up beside him like toy sojers. Bruce Jagermeyer

and that Swede, Olaf Theramenius, were standing underneath the marquee of the Bijou in the shade.'

Mr Keene looked at me, through me. His eyes were not sharp now; they were hazy with memory, soft as the eyes of a man only become when he is remembering one of the best times of his life – the first home run he ever hit, maybe, or the first trout he ever landed that was big enough to keep, or the first time he ever lay with a willing woman.

'I remember I heard the wind, sonny,' he said dreamily. 'I remember hearing the wind, hearing the courthouse clock toll two. Bob Tanner came up behind me and I was so tight-wired I almost blew his head off.

'He only nodded at me and crossed over to Vannock's Dry Goods, trailing his shadow out behind him.

'You would have thought that when it got to be two-ten and nothing happened, then two-fifteen, then two-twenty, folks would have just up and left, wouldn't you? But it didn't happen that way at all. People just kept their place. Because –'

'Because you knew they were going to come, didn't you?' I asked. 'There was never any question at all.'

He beamed at me like a teacher pleased with a student's recital. 'That's right!' he said. 'We knew. No one had to talk about it, no one had to say, "Wellnow, let's wait until twenty past and if they don't show I've got to get back to work." Things just stayed quiet, and around two-twenty-five that afternoon these two cars, one red and one dark blue, started down Up-Mile Hill and came into the intersection. One of them was a Chevrolet and the other was a La Salle. The Conklin brothers, Patrick Caudy, and Marie Hauser were in the Chevrolet. The Bradleys, Malloy, and Kitty Donahue were in the La Salle.

'They started through the intersection okay, and then Al Bradley slammed on the brakes of that La Salle so sudden that Caudy damn near ran into him. The street was too quiet and Bradley knew it. He wasn't nothing but an animal, but it doesn't take much to put up an animal's wind when it's been chased like a weasel in the corn for four years.

'He opened the door of the La Salle and stood up on the running board for a moment. He looked around, then he made a "go-back" gesture to Caudy with his hand. Caudy said "What, boss?" I heard that plain as day, the only thing I heard any of them say that day. There was a wink of sun, too, I remember that. It came off a compact mirror. The Hauser woman was powdering her nose.

'That was when Lal Machen and *his* helper, Biff Marlow, came running out of Machen's store. "Put em up, Bradley, you're surrounded!" Lal shouts, and before Bradley could do more than turn his head, Lal started blasting. He was wild at first, but then he put one into Bradley's shoulder. The claret started to pour out of that hole right away. Bradley caught hold of the La Salle's doorpost and swung himself back into the car. He threw it into gear, and that's when everyone started to shoot.

'It was all over in four, maybe five minutes, but it seemed a whole hell of a lot longer while it was happening. Petie and Al and Jimmy Gordon just sat there on the courthouse steps and poured bullets into the back end of the Chevrolet. I saw Bob Tanner down on one knee, firing and working the bolt on that old rifle of his like a madman. Jagermeyer and Theramenius were shooting into the right side of the La Salle from under the theater marquee and Greg Cole stood in the gutter, holding that .45 automatic out in both hands, pulling the trigger just as fast as he could work it.

'There must have been fifty, sixty men firing all at once. After it was all over Lal Machen dug thirty-six slugs out of the brick sides of his store. And that was three days later, after just about every-damn-body in town who wanted one for a souvenir had come down and dug one out with his penknife. When it was at its worst, it sounded like the Battle of the Marne. Windows were blown in by rifle-fire all around Machen's.

'Bradley got the La Salle around in a half-circle and he wasn't slow but by the time he'd done he was running on four flats. Both the headlights were blowed out, and the windscreen was gone. Creeping Jesus Malloy and George Bradley were each at a backseat window, firing pistols. I seen one bullet take Malloy high up in the neck and tear it wide open. He shot twice more and then collapsed out the window with his arms hanging down.

'Caudy tried to turn the Chevrolet and only ran into the back end of Bradley's La Salle. That was really the end of em right there, son. The Chevrolet's front bumper locked with the La Salle's back one and there went any chance they might have had to make a run for it.

'Joe Conklin got out of the back seat and just stood there in the middle of the intersection, a pistol in each hand, and started to pour it on. He was shooting at Jake Pinnette and Andy Criss. The two of them fell off the bench they'd been sitting on and landed in the grass, Andy Criss shouting "I'm killed! I'm killed!" over and over again, although he was never so much as touched; neither of them were.

'Joe Conklin, he had time to fire both his guns empty before anything so much as touched him. His coat flew back and his pants twitched like some woman you couldn't see was stitching on them. He was wearing a straw hat, and it flew off his head so you could see how he'd center-parted his hair. He had one of his guns under his arm and was trying to reload the other when someone cut the legs out from under him and he went down. Kenny Borton claimed him later, but there was really no way to tell. Could have been anybody.

'Conklin's brother Cal came out after him soon's Joe fell and down he went like a ton of bricks with a hole in his head.

'Marie Hauser came out. Maybe she was trying to surrender, I dunno. She still had the compact she'd been using to powder her nose in her right hand. She was screaming, I believe, but by then it was hard to hear. Bullets was flying all around them. That compact mirror was blown right out of her hand. She started back to the car then but she took one in the hip. She made it somehow and managed to crawl inside again.

'Al Bradley revved the La Salle up just as high as it would go, and managed to get it moving again. He dragged the Chevrolet maybe ten feet before the bumper tore right off 'n it.

'The boys poured lead into it. All the windows was busted. One of the mudguards was laying in the street. Malloy was dead hanging out the window, but both of the Bradley brothers were still alive. George was firing from the back seat. His woman was dead beside him with one of her eyes shot out.

'Al Bradley got to the big intersection, then his auto mounted the curb and stopped there. He got out from behind the wheel and started running up Canal Street. He was riddled.

'Patrick Caudy got out of the Chevrolet, looked as if he was going to surrender for a minute, then he grabbed a .38 from a cheater-holster under his armpit. He triggered it off maybe three times, just firing wild, and then his shirt blew back from his chest in flames. He slid down the side of the Chevy until he was sitting on the running board. He shot one more time, and so far as I know that was the only bullet that hit anyone; it ricocheted off something and then grazed across the back of Greg Cole's hand. Left a scar he used to show off when he was drunk until someone – Al Nell, maybe – took him aside and told him it might be a good idea to shut up about what happened to the Bradley Gang.

'The Hauser woman came out and that time wasn't any doubt

she was trying to surrender – she had her hands up. Maybe no one really meant to kill her, but by then there was a crossfire and she walked right into it.

'George Bradley run as far as that bench by the War Memorial, then someone pulped the back of his head with a shotgun blast. He fell down dead with his pants full of piss . . .'

Hardly aware I was doing it, I took a licorice whip from the jar.

'They went on pouring rounds into those cars for another minute or so before it began to taper off,' Mr Keene said. 'When men get their blood up, it doesn't go down easy. That was when I looked around and saw Sheriff Sullivan behind Nell and the others on the courthouse steps, putting rounds through that dead Chevy with a Remington pump. Don't let anyone tell you he wasn't there; Norbert Keene is sitting in front of you and telling you he was.

'By the time the firing stopped, those cars didn't look like cars at all anymore, just hunks of junk with glass around them. Men started to walk over to them. No one talked. All you could hear was the wind and feet gritting over broken glass. That's when the picture-taking started. And you ought to know this, sonny: when the picture-taking starts, the story is over.'

Mr Keene rocked in his chair, his slippers bumping placidly on the floor, looking at me.

'There's nothing like that in the Derry *News*,' was all I could think of to say. The headline for that day had read STATE POLICE, FBI GUN DOWN BRADLEY GANG IN PITCHED BATTLE. With the subhead 'Local Police Lend Support.'

'Course not,' Mr Keene said, laughing delightedly. 'I seen the publisher, Mack Laughlin, put two rounds into Joe Conklin himself.'

'Christ,' I muttered.

'Get enough licorice, sonny?'

'I got enough,' I said. I licked my lips. 'Mr Keene, how could a thing of that . . . that magnitude . . . be covered up?'

'Wasn't no cover-up,' he said, looking honestly surprised. 'It was just that no one talked about it much. And really, who cared? It wasn't President and Mrs Hoover that went down that day. It was no worse than shooting mad dogs that would kill you with a bite if you give them half a chance.'

'But the women?'

'Couple of whores,' he said indifferently. 'Besides, it happened in Derry, not in New York or Chicago. The *place* makes it news as much as what *happened* in the place, sonny. That's why there are bigger headlines when an earthquake kills twelve people in Los Angeles than there are when one kills three thousand in some heathen country in the Mideast.'

Besides, it happened in Derry.

I've heard it before, and I suppose if I continue to pursue this I'll hear it again . . . and again . . . and again. They say it as if speaking patiently to a mental defective. They say it the way they would say *Because of gravity* if you asked them how come you stick to the ground when you walk. They say it as if it were a natural law any natural man should understand. And, of course, the worst of that is I *do* understand.

I had one more question for Norbert Keene.

'Did you see anyone at all that day that you didn't recognize once the shooting started?'

Mr Keene's answer was quick enough to drop my blood temperature ten degrees – or so it felt. 'The clown, you mean? How did you find out about him, sonny?'

'Oh, I heard it somewhere,' I said.

'I only caught a glimpse of him. Once things got hot, I tended pretty much to my own knittin. I glanced around just once and saw him upstreet beyond them Swedes under the Bijou's marquee,' Mr Keene said. 'He wasn't wearing a clown suit or nothing like that. He was dressed in a pair of farmer's biballs and a cotton shirt underneath. But his face was covered with that white grease-paint they use, and he had a big red clown smile painted on. Also had these tufts of fake hair, you know. Orange. Sorta comical.

'Lal Machen never saw that fellow, but Biff did. Only Biff must have been confused, because he thought he saw him in one of the windows of an apartment over somewhere to the left, and once when I asked Jimmy Gordon – he was killed in Pearl Harbor, you know, went down with his ship, the *California*, I think it was – he said he saw the guy behind the War Memorial.'

Mr Keene shook his head, smiling a little.

'It's funny how people get during a thing like that, and even funnier what they remember after it's all over. You can listen to sixteen different tales and no two of them will jibe together. Take the gun that clown fellow had, for instance –'

'Gun?' I asked. 'He was shooting, too?'

'Ayuh,' Mr Keene said. 'The one glimpse I caught of him, it looked like he had a Winchester bolt-action, and it wasn't until later that I figured out I must have thought that because that's what *I* had. Biff Marlow thought he had a Remington, because that was what *he* had. And when I asked Jimmy about it, he said that guy was shooting an old Springfield, just like his. Funny, huh?'

'Funny,' I managed. 'Mr Keene . . . didn't any of you wonder what in hell a clown, especially one in farmer's biballs, was doing there just then?'

'Sure,' Mr Keene said. 'It wasn't no big deal, you understand, but sure we wondered. Most of us figured it was somebody who wanted to attend the party but didn't want to be recognized. A Town Council member, maybe. Horst Mueller, maybe, or even Trace Naugler, who was mayor back then. Or it could just have been a professional man who didn't want to be recognized. A doctor or a lawyer. I wouldn't 've recognized my own father in a get-up like that.'

He laughed a little and I asked him what was funny.

'There's also a possibility that it was a real clown,' he said. 'Back in the twenties and thirties the county fair in Esty came a lot earlier than it does now, and it was set up and going full blast the week that the Bradley Gang met their end. There were clowns at the county fair. Maybe one of them heard we were going to have our own little carnival and rode down because he wanted to be in on it.'

He smiled at me, dryly.

'I'm about talked out,' he said, 'but I'll tell you one more thing, since you 'pear to be so interested and you listen so close. It was something Biff Marlow said about sixteen years later, when we were having a few beers up to Pilot's in Bangor. Right out of a clear blue sky he said it. Said that clown was leanin out of the window so far that Biff couldn't believe he wasn't *fallin* out. It wasn't just his head and shoulders and arms that was out; Biff said he was right out to the knees, hanging there in midair, shooting down at the cars the Bradleys had come in, with that big red grin on his face. "He was tricked out like a jackolantern that had got a bad scare," was how Biff put it.'

'Like he was floating,' I said.

'Ayuh,' Mr Keene agreed. 'And Biff said there was something else, something that bothered him for weeks afterward. One of those things you get right on the tip of your tongue but won't quite come off, or something that lights on your skin like a mosquito or a noseeum. He said he finally figured out what it was one night when he had to get up and tap a kidney. He stood there whizzing into the bowl, thinking of nothing in particular, when it come to him all at once that it was two-twenty-five in the afternoon when the shooting started and the sun was out but that clown didn't cast any shadow. No shadow at all.'

PART 4

JULY OF 1958

'You lethargic, waiting upon me, waiting for the fire and I
attendant upon you, shaken by your beauty

Shaken by your beauty
Shaken.'

> – William Carlos Williams,
> *Paterson*

> 'Well I was born in my birthday suit
> The doctor slapped my behind
> He said "You gonna be special
> You sweet little toot toot."'
> – Sidney Simien,
> 'My Toot Toot'

CHAPTER THIRTEEN
THE APOCALYPTIC ROCKFIGHT

1

Bill's there first. He sits in one of the wing-back chairs just inside the Reading Room door watching as Mike deals with the library's last few customers of the night – an old lady with a clutch of paperback gothics, a man with a huge historical tome on the Civil War, and a skinny kid waiting to check out a novel with a seven-day-rental sticker in an upper corner of its plastic cover. Bill sees with no sense of surprise or serendipity at all that it is his own latest novel. He feels that surprise is beyond him, serendipity a believed-in reality that has turned out to be only a dream after all.

A pretty girl, her tartan skirt held together with a big gold safety pin (Christ, I haven't seen one of those in years, *Bill thinks*, are they coming back?), *is feeding quarters into the Xerox machine and copying an off print with one eye on the big pendulum clock behind the checkout desk. The sounds are library-soft and library-comforting: the hush-squeak of soles and heels on the red-and-black linoleum of the floor; the steady tock and tick of the clock dropping off dry seconds; the catlike purr of the copying machine.*

The boy takes his William Denbrough novel and goes to the girl at the copier just as she finishes and begins to square up her pages.

'You can just leave that off print on the desk, Mary,' Mike says. 'I'll put it away.'

She flashes a grateful smile. 'Thanks, Mr Hanlon.'

'Goodnight. Goodnight, Billy. The two of you go right home.'

'The boogeyman will get you if you don't . . . watch . . . out!' *Billy, the skinny kid, chants, and slips a proprietary arm around the girl's slim waist.*

'Well, I don't think he'd want a pair as ugly as you two,' Mike says, 'but be careful, all the same.'

'We will, Mr Hanlon,' Mary replies, seriously enough, and punches the boy lightly on the shoulder. 'Come on, ugly,' she says, and giggles. When she does this she is transformed from a pretty mildly desirable high-school junior

617

*into the coltish not-quite-gawky eleven-year-old that Beverly Marsh had been
. . . and as they pass him Bill is shaken by her beauty . . . and he feels fear;
he wants to go to the boy and tell him earnestly that he must go home by
well-lighted streets and not look around if someone speaks.*

You can't be careful on a skateboard, mister, *a phantom voice says
inside his head, and Bill smiles a rueful grownup's smile.*

*He watches the boy open the door for his girl. They go into the vestibule,
moving closer together, and Bill would have bet the royalties of the book the
boy named Billy is holding under his arm that he has stolen a kiss before
opening the outer door for the girl.* More fool you if you didn't, Billy my
man, *he thinks.* Now see her home safe. For Christ's sake see her home
safe!

Mike calls, 'Be right with you, Big Bill. Just let me file this.'

*Bill nods and crosses his legs. The paper bag on his lap crackles a little.
There's a pint of bourbon inside and he reckons he has never wanted a drink
so badly in his life as he does right now. Mike will be able to supply water,
if not ice – and the way he feels right now, a very little water will be enough.*

*He thinks of Silver, leaning against the wall of Mike's garage on Palmer
Lane. And from that his thoughts progress naturally to the day they had met
in the Barrens – all except Mike – and each had told his tale again: lepers
under porches; mummies who walked on the ice; blood from drains and dead
boys in the Standpipe and pictures that moved and werewolves that chased
small boys down deserted streets.*

*They had gone deeper into the Barrens that day before the Fourth of
July, he remembers now. It had been hot in town but cool in the tangled shade
on the eastern bank of the Kenduskeag. He remembers one of those concrete
cylinders not far away, humming to itself the way the Xerox machine had
hummed for the pretty high-school girl just now. Bill remembers that, and how,
when all the stories were done, the others had looked at him.*

*They had wanted him to tell them what they should do next, how they
should proceed, and he simply didn't know. The not knowing had filled him
with a kind of desperation.*

*Looking at Mike's shadow now, looming large on the darkly paneled
wall in the reference room, a sudden sureness comes to him: he hadn't known
then because they hadn't been complete when they met that July 3rd afternoon.
The completion had come later, at the abandoned gravel-pit beyond the dump,
where you could climb out of the Barrens easily on either side – Kansas Street
or Merit Street. Right around, in fact, where the Interstate overpass was now.
The gravel-pit had no name; it was old, its crumbly sides crabby with weeds
and bushes. There had still been plenty of ammunition there – more than
enough for an apocalyptic rockfight.*

But before that, on the bank of the Kenduskeag, he hadn't been sure what to say – what did they want him to say? What did he want to say? He remembers looking from one face to the next – Ben's; Bev's; Eddie's; Stan's; Richie's. And he remembers music. Little Richard. 'Whomp-bomp-a-lomp-bomp . . .'

Music. Low. And darts of light in his eyes. He remembers the darts of light because

2

Richie had hung his transistor radio over the lowermost branch of the tree he was leaning against. Although they were in the shade, the sun bounced off the surface of the Kenduskeag, onto the radio's chrome facing, and from there into Bill's eyes.

'T-Take that th-hing d-d-d-own, Ruh-Ruh-Richie,' Bill said. 'It's gonna buh-blind m-m-me.'

'Sure, Big Bill,' Richie said at once, with no smartmouth at all, and removed the radio from the branch. He also turned it off, and Bill wished he hadn't done that; it made the silence, broken only by the rippling water and the vague hum of the sewage-pumping machinery, seem very loud. Their eyes watched him and he wanted to tell them to look somewhere else, what did they think he was, a *freak*?

But of course he couldn't do that, because all they were doing was waiting for him to tell them what to do now. They had come by dreadful knowledge, and they needed him to tell them what to do with it. *Why me?* he wanted to shout at them, but of course he knew that, too. It was because, like it or not, he had been tapped for the position. Because he was the idea-man, because he had lost a brother to whatever it was, but most of all because he had become, in some obscure way he would never completely understand, Big Bill.

He glanced at Beverly and looked away quickly from the calm trust in her eyes. Looking at Beverly made him feel funny in the pit of his stomach. Fluttery.

'We cuh-can't go to the p-p-police,' he said at last. His voice sounded harsh to his own ears, too loud. 'We c-ca-han't g-go to our puh-huh-harents, either. Unless . . .' He looked hopefully at Richie. 'What a-a-about your m-mom and d-dad, four-eyes? They suh-heem p-pretty reh-reh-regular.'

'My good man,' Richie said in his Toodles the Butler Voice, 'you obviously have no understahnding whatsoevah of my mater and pater. They –'

'Talk American, Richie,' Eddie said from his spot by Ben. He was sitting by Ben for the simple reason that Ben provided enough shade for Eddie to sit in. His face looked small and pinched and worried – an old man's face. His aspirator was in his right hand.

'They'd think I was ready for Juniper Hill,' Richie said. He was wearing an old pair of glasses today. The day before a friend of Henry Bowers's named Gard Jagermeyer had come up behind Richie as Richie left the Derry Ice Cream Bar with a pistachio cone. 'Tag, you're it!' this Jagermeyer, who outweighed Richie by forty pounds or so, screamed, and slammed Richie full in the back with both hands laced together. Richie flew into the gutter, losing his glasses and his ice-cream cone. The left lens of his glasses had shattered, and his mother was furious with him about it, lending very little credence to Richie's explanations.

'All I know is that it was a lot of fooling around,' she had said. 'Honestly, Richie, do you think there's a glasses-tree somewhere and we can just pull off a new pair of spectacles for you whenever you break the old pair?'

'But Mom, this kid pushed me, he came up behind me, this big kid, and pushed me –' Richie was by then near tears. This failure to make his mother understand hurt much worse than being slammed into the gutter by Gard Jagermeyer, who was so stupid they hadn't even bothered to send him to summer-school.

'I don't want to hear any more about it,' Maggie Tozier said flatly. 'But the next time you see your father come in looking whipped after working late three nights in a row, you think a little bit, Richie. You think about it.'

'But Mom –'

'No more, I said.' Her voice was curt and final – worse, it was near tears. She left the room then and the TV went on much too loud. Richie had been left alone sitting miserably at the kitchen table.

It was this memory that caused Richie to shake his head again. 'My folks are okay, but they'd never believe something like this.'

'W-What a-a-about other kih-kids?'

And they looked around, Bill would remember years later, as if for someone who wasn't there.

'Who?' Stan asked doubtfully. 'I can't think of anyone else I trust.'

'Just the suh-suh-same . . .' Bill said in a troubled voice, and a little silence fell among them while Bill thought about what to say next.

620

3

If asked, Ben Hanscom would have told you that Henry Bowers hated him more than any of the others in the Losers' Club, because of what had happened that day when he and Henry had shot the chutes down into the Barrens from Kansas Street, because of what had happened the day he and Richie and Beverly escaped from the Aladdin, but most of all because, by not allowing Henry to copy during examinations, he had caused Henry to be sent to summer-school and incur the wrath of his father, the reputedly insane Butch Bowers.

If asked, Richie Tozier would have told you Henry hated *him* more than any of the others, because of the day he had fooled Henry and his two other musketeers in Freese's.

Stan Uris would have told you that Henry hated *him* most of all because he was a Jew (when Stan had been in the third grade and Henry the fifth, Henry had once washed Stan's face with snow until it bled and he was screaming hysterically with pain and fear).

Bill Denbrough believed that Henry hated him the most because he was skinny, because he stuttered, and because he liked to dress well ('L-L-Look at the f-f-f-fucking puh-puh-*PANSY!*' Henry had cried when the Derry School had had Careers Day in April and Bill had come wearing a tie; before the day was over, the tie had been ripped off and flung into a tree halfway down Charter Street).

He *did* hate all four of them, but the boy in Derry who was number one on Henry's personal Hate Parade was not in the Losers' Club at all on that July 3rd; he was a black boy named Michael Hanlon, who lived a quarter of a mile down the road from the shirttail Bowers farm.

Henry's father, who was every bit as crazy as he was reputed to be, was Oscar 'Butch' Bowers. Butch Bowers associated his financial, physical, and mental decline with the Hanlon family in general and with Mike's father in particular. Will Hanlon, he was fond of telling his few friends and his son, had had him thrown in the county jail when all of his, Hanlon's, chickens died. 'So's he could get the insurance money, don't you know,' Butch would say, eying his audience with all the baleful interrupt-if-you-dare pugnacity of Captain Billy Bones in the Admiral Benbow. 'He got some of his friends to lie him up, and that's why I had to sell my Merc'ry.'

'Who lied him up, Daddy?' Henry had asked when he was eight, burning at the injustice that had been done to his father. He thought to himself that when he was a grownup he would find liar-uppers and coat them with honey and stake them out over anthills, like in some of those Western movies they showed at the Bijou Theater on Saturday afternoons.

And because his son was a tireless listener (although, if asked, Butch would have maintained that was only as it should be), Bowers Senior filled his son's ears with a litany of hate and hard luck. He explained to his son that while all niggers were stupid, some were cunning as well – and down deep they all hated white men and wanted to plow a white woman's furrow. Maybe it wasn't just the insurance money after all, Butch said; maybe Hanlon had decided to lay the blame for the dead chickens at his door because Butch had the next produce stand down the road. He done it, anyway, and that was just as sure as shit sticks to a blanket. He done it and then got a bunch of white nigger bleeding hearts from town to lie him up and threaten Butch with state prison if he didn't pay that nigger off. 'And why not?' Butch would ask his round-eyed dirty-necked silent son. 'Why not? *I* was just a man who fought the Japs for his country. There was lots of guys like us, but *he* was the only nigger in the county.'

The chicken business had been followed by one unlucky incident after another – his Deere tractor had blown a rod; his good harrow got busted in the north field; he got a boil on his neck which became infected, had to be lanced, then became infected again and had to be removed surgically; the nigger started using his foully gotten money to undercut Butch's prices so they lost custom.

In Henry's ears, it was a constant litany: the nigger, the nigger, the nigger. Everything was the nigger's fault. The nigger had a nice white house with an upstairs and an oil furnace while Butch and his wife and his son lived in what was not much better than a tarpaper shack. When Butch couldn't make enough money farming and had to go to work in the woods for awhile, it was the nigger's fault. When their well went dry in 1956, it was the nigger's fault.

Later that same year Henry, who was then ten years old, started to feed Mike's dog Mr Chips old stewbones and bags of potato-chips. It got so Mr Chips would wag his tail and come running when Henry called. When the dog was well used to Henry and Henry's treats, Henry one day fed him a pound of hamburger laced with insect poison. The bug-killer he found in the back shed; he had saved three weeks to buy the meat at Costello's.

Mr Chips ate half the poisoned meat and then stopped. 'Go on, finish your treat, Niggerdog,' Henry had said. Mr Chips wagged his tail. Since Henry had called him this from the beginning, he believed it was his other name. When the pains started, Henry produced a piece of clothesline and tied Mr Chips to a birch so he couldn't get away and run home. He then sat on a flat sun-warmed rock, put his chin in his palms, and watched the dog die. It took a good long time, but Henry considered it time well spent. At the end Mr Chips began to convulse and a thin green foam ran from between his jaws.

'How do you like that, Niggerdog?' Henry asked it, and it rolled its dying eyes up at the sound of Henry's voice and tried to wag its tail. 'Did you like your lunch, you shitty mutt?'

When the dog was dead, Henry removed the clothesline, went home, and told his father what he had done. Oscar Bowers was *extremely* crazy by that time; a year later his wife would leave him after he beat her nearly to death. Henry was likewise frightened of his father and felt a terrible hate for him sometimes, but he also loved him. And that afternoon, after he had told, he felt he had finally found the key to his father's affections, because his father had clapped him on the back (so hard that Henry almost fell over), taken him in the living room, and given him a beer. It was the first beer Henry had ever had, and for all the rest of his years he would associate that taste with positive emotions: victory and love.

'Here's to a good job well done,' Henry's crazy father had said. They clicked their brown bottles together and drank them down. So far as Henry knew, the niggers had never found out who killed their dog, but he supposed they had their suspicions. He hoped they did.

The others in the Losers' Club knew Mike by sight – in a town where he was the only Negro child, it would have been strange it they had not – but that was all, because Mike didn't go to Derry Elementary School. His mother was a devout Baptist and Mike was therefore sent to the Neibolt Street Church School. In between geography, reading, and arithmetic there were Bible drills, lessons on such subjects as The Meaning of the Ten Commandments in a Godless World, and discussion-groups on how to handle everyday moral problems (if you saw a buddy shoplifting, for instance, or heard a teacher taking the name of God in vain).

Mike thought the Church School was okay. There were times when he suspected, in a vague way, that he was missing some things – a wider communication with kids his own age perhaps – but he was willing to wait until high school for these things to happen. The prospect made him a little nervous because his skin was brown, but both his mother and father had been well treated in town as far as Mike could see, and Mike believed he would be treated well if he treated others the same way.

The exception to this rule, of course, was Henry Bowers.

Although he tried to show it as little as possible, Mike went in constant terror of Henry. In 1958 Mike was slim and well built, taller than Stan Uris but not quite as tall as Bill Denbrough. He was fast and agile, and that had saved him from several beatings at Henry's hands. And, of course, he went to a different school. Because of that and the age difference, their paths rarely coincided. Mike took pains to keep things that way. So the irony was this: although Henry hated Mike Hanlon more than any other kid in Derry, Mike had been the least hurt of any of them.

Oh, he had taken his lumps. The spring after he had killed Mike's dog, Henry sprang out of the bushes one day while Mike was walking toward town to go to the library. It was late March, warm enough for bike-riding, but in those days Witcham Road turned to dirt just beyond the Bowers place, which meant that it was a quagmire of mud – no good for bikes.

'Hello, nigger,' Henry had said, emerging from the bushes, grinning.

Mike backed off, eyes flicking warily right and left, watching for a chance to get away. He knew that if he could buttonhook around Henry, he could outdistance him. Henry was big and Henry was strong, but Henry was also slow.

'Gonna make me a tarbaby,' Henry said, advancing on the smaller boy. 'You're not black enough, but I'll fix that.'

Mike cut his eyes to the left and twitched his body in that direction. Henry took the bait and broke that way – too fast and too far to pull himself back. Reversing with a sweet and natural speed, Mike took off to the right (in high school he would make the varsity football team as a tailback his sophomore year, and was only kept from breaking the school's all-time scoring record by a broken leg halfway through his senior season). He would have made it easily past Henry but for the mud. It was greasy, and Mike slipped to his knees. Before he could get up, Henry was upon him.

'*Niggerniggernigger!*' Henry cried in a kind of religious ecstasy as he rolled Mike over. Mud went up the back of Mike's shirt and down the back of his pants. He could feel it squoozing into his shoes. But he did not begin to cry until Henry slathered mud across his face, plugging up both of his nostrils.

'*Now* you're black!' Henry had screamed gleefully, rubbing mud in Mike's hair. 'Now you're *REEEELY* black!' He ripped up Mike's poplin jacket and the tee-shirt beneath and slammed a poultice of mud down over the boy's bellybutton. 'Now you're as black as *midnight* in a *MINESHAFT*!' Henry screamed triumphantly, and slammed mudplugs into both of Mike's ears. Then he stood back, muddy hands hooked into his belt, and yelled: '*I killed your dog, black boy!*' But Mike did not hear this because of the mud in his ears and his own terrified sobs.

Henry kicked a final sticky clot of mud onto Mike and then turned and walked home, not looking back. A few moments later, Mike got up and did the same, still weeping.

His mother was of course furious; she wanted Will Hanlon to call Chief Borton and have him out to the Bowers house before the sun went down. 'He's been after Mikey before,' Mike heard her say. He was sitting in the bathtub and his parents were in the kitchen. This was his second tub of water; the first had turned black almost the moment he had stepped into it and sat down. In her fury, his mother had lapsed into a thick Texas *patois* Mike could barely understand. 'You put the law on him, Will Hanlon! Both the dog and the pup! You *law* em, hear me?'

Will heard, but did not do as his wife asked. Eventually, when she cooled down (by then it was that night and Mike two hours asleep), he refreshed her on the facts of life. Chief Borton was not Sheriff Sullivan. If Borton had been sheriff when the incident of the poisoned chickens occurred, Will would never have gotten his two hundred dollars and would have had to be content with that state of affairs. Some men would stand behind you and some men wouldn't; Borton was of the latter type. He was, in fact, a jellyfish.

'Mike has had trouble with that kid before, yes,' he told Jessica. 'But he hasn't had much because he's careful around Henry Bowers. This will serve to make him more careful.'

'You mean you're just going to let it go?'

'Bowers has told his son stories about his dealings with me, I guess,' Will said, 'and his son hates the three of us because of them, and because his father has also told him that hating niggers is what men are supposed to do. It all comes back to that. I can't change the fact that our son is a Negro any more than I can sit here and tell you that Henry Bowers is going to be the last one to take after him because his skin's brown. He's going to have to deal with it all the rest of his life, as I have dealt with it, and you have dealt with it. Why, right there in that Christian school you were bound he was going to go to the teacher told them blacks weren't as good as whites because Noah's son Ham looked at his father while he was drunk and naked and Noah's other two boys cast their eyes aside. That's why the sons of Ham were condemned to always be hewers of wood and drawers of water, she said. And Mikey said she was lookin right at him while she told that story to them.'

Jessica looked at her husband, mute and miserable. Two tears fell, one from each eye, and tracked slowly down her face. 'Isn't there ever any getting away from it?'

His reply was kind but implacable; it was a time when wives believed their husbands, and Jessica had no reason to doubt her Will.

'No. There is no getting away from the word nigger, not now, not in the world we've been given to live in, you and me. Country niggers from Maine are still niggers. I have thought, times, that the reason I came back to Derry was that there is no better place to remember that. But I'll have a talk with the boy.'

The next day he called Mike out of the barn. Will sat on the yoke of his harrow and patted a place next to him for Mike.

'You want to stay out of that Henry Bowers's way,' he said.

Mike nodded.

'His father is crazy.'

Mike nodded again. He had heard as much around town. His few glimpses of Mr Bowers had reinforced the notion.

'I don't mean just a little crazy,' Will said, lighting a home-rolled Bugler cigarette and looking at his son. 'He's about three steps away from the boobyhatch. He came back from the war that way.'

'I think Henry's crazy too,' Mike said. His voice was low but firm, and that strengthened Will's heart . . . although he was, even after a checkered life whose incidents had included almost being burned alive in a juryrigged speakeasy called the Black Spot, unable to believe a kid like Henry could be crazy.

'Well, he's listened to his father too much, but that is only natural,' Will said. Yet on this his son was closer to the truth. Henry Bowers, either because of his constant association with his father or because of something else – some interior thing – was indeed slowly but surely going crazy.

'I don't want you to make a career out of running away,' his father said, 'but because you're a Negro, you're apt to be put upon a good deal. Do you know what I mean?'

'Yes, Daddy,' Mike said, thinking of Bob Gautier at school, who had tried to explain to Mike that nigger could not be a bad word, because his father used it all the time. In fact, Bob told Mike earnestly, it was a good word. When a fighter on the *Friday Night Fights* took a bad beating

626

and managed to stay on his feet, his daddy said, 'His head is as hard as a nigger's,' and when someone was really putting out at his work (which, for Mr Gautier, was Star Beef in town), his daddy said, 'That man works like a nigger.' 'And my daddy is just as much a Christian as your daddy,' Bob had finished. Mike remembered that, looking at Bob Gautier's white earnest pinched face, surrounded by the mangy fur of his hand-me-down snowsuit-hood, he had felt not anger but a terrible sadness that made him feel like crying. He had seen honesty and good intent in Bob's face, but what he had *felt* was loneliness, distance, a great whistling emptiness between himself and the other boy.

'I see that you do know what I mean,' Will said, and ruffled his son's hair. 'And what it all comes down to is that you have to be careful where you take your stand. You have to ask yourself if Henry Bowers is worth the trouble. Is he?'

'No,' Mike said. 'No, I don't think so.' It would be yet awhile before he changed his mind; July 3rd, 1958, in fact.

4

While Henry Bowers, Victor Criss, Belch Huggins, Peter Gordon, and a half-retarded high-school boy named Steve Sadler (known as Moose, after the character in the Archie comics) were chasing a winded Mike Hanlon through the trainyard and toward the Barrens about half a mile away, Bill and the rest of the Losers' Club were still sitting on the bank of the Kenduskeag, pondering their nightmare problem.

'I nuh-know w-where ih-ih-it is, I think,' Bill said, finally breaking the silence.

'The sewers,' Stan said, and they all jumped at a sudden, harsh rattling noise. Eddie smiled guiltily as he lowered his aspirator back into his lap.

Bill nodded. 'I wuh-wuh-was a-asking my fuh-father about the suh-sewers a f-few nuh-hi-hights a-a-ago.'

'All of this area was originally marsh,' Zack told his son, 'and the town fathers managed to put what's downtown these days in the very worst part of it. The section of the Canal that runs under Center and Main and comes out in Bassey Park is really nothing but a drain that happens to hold the Kenduskeag. Most of the year those drains are almost empty, but they're important when the spring runoff comes or when there are floods . . .' He paused here, perhaps thinking that it had been during the flood of the previous autumn that he had lost his younger son. '. . . because of the pumps,' he finished.

'Puh-puh-pumps?' Bill asked, turning his head a little without even thinking about it. When he stuttered over the plosive sounds, spittle flew from his lips.

'The drainage pumps,' his father said. 'They're in the Barrens. Concrete sleeves that stick about three feet out of the ground –'

'Buh-Buh-Ben H-H-H-Hanscom calls them Muh-Morlock h-holes,' Bill said, grinning.

Zack grinned back . . . but it was a shadow of his old grin. They were in Zack's workshop, where he was turning chair-dowels without much interest. 'Sump-pumps is all they really are, kiddo,' he said. 'They sit in cylinders about ten feet deep, and they pump the sewage and the runoff along when the slope of the land levels out or angles up a little. It's old machinery, and the city should have some new pumps, but the Council always pleads poverty when the item comes up on the agenda at budget meetings. If I had a quarter for every time I've been down there, up to my knees in crap, rewiring one of those motors . . . but you don't want to hear all this, Bill. Why don't you go watch TV? I think *Sugarfoot*'s on tonight.'

'I *d-d-do* wuh-want to h-hear it,' Bill said, and not only because he had come to the conclusion that there was something terrible under Derry someplace.

'Why do you want to hear about a bunch of sewer-pumps?' Zack asked.

'Skuh-skuh-hool ruh-report,' Bill said wildly.

'School's out.'

'N-N-Next year.'

'Well, it's a pretty dull subject,' Zack said. 'Teacher'll probably give you an F for putting him to sleep. Look, here's the Kenduskeag' – he drew a straight line in the light fall of sawdust on the table in which his bandsaw was embedded – 'and here's the Barrens. Now, because downtown's lower than the residential areas – Kansas Street, say, or the Old Cape, or West Broadway – most of the downtown waste has to be pumped into the river. The waste from the houses flows down to the Barrens pretty much on its own. You see?'

'Y-Y-Yes,' Bill said, drawing a little closer to his father to look at the lines, close enough so that his shoulder was against his father's arm.

'Someday they'll put a stop to pumping raw sewage into the river and that'll be an end to the whole business. But for now, we've got those pumps in the . . . what did your buddy call em?'

'Morlock holes,' Bill said, with not a trace of a stutter; neither he nor his father noticed.

'Yeah. That's what the pumps in the Morlock holes are for, anyway, and they work pretty well except when there's too much rain and the streams overflow. Because, although the gravity drains and the sewers with the pumps were meant to be separate systems, they actually crisscross all over the place. See?' He drew a series of 'X's radiating out from the line which represented the Kenduskeag, and Bill nodded. 'Well, the only thing you need to know about water draining is that it will go wherever it can. When it gets high, it starts to fill up the drains as well as the sewers. When the water in the drains gets high enough to reach those pumps, it shorts them out. Makes trouble for me, because I have to fix them.'

'Dad, h-how big are the suh-sewers and drains?'

'You mean, what's the bore on them?'

Bill nodded.

'The main sewers are maybe six feet in diameter. The secondaries, from the residential areas, are three or four, I guess. Some of them might be a little bigger. And believe me when I tell you this, Billy, and you can tell your friends: you never want to go into one of those pipes, not in a game, not on a dare, not for any reason.'

'Why?'

'A dozen different town governments have built on them since 1885 or so. During the Depression the WPA put in a whole secondary drain system and a tertiary sewer system; there was lots of money for public works back then. But the fellow who bossed those projects got killed in World War II, and about five years later the Water Department found out that the system blueprints were mostly gone. That's about nine pounds of blues that just disappeared sometime between 1937 and 1950. My point is that nobody knows where all the damned sewers and drains go, or why.

'When they work, nobody cares. When they don't, there's three or four sad sacks from Derry Water who have to try and find out which pump went flooey or where the plug-up is. And when they go down there, they damn well pack a lunch. It's dark and it's smelly and there are rats. Those are all good reasons to stay out, but the best reason is that you could get lost. It's happened before.'

Lost under Derry. Lost in the sewers. Lost in the dark. There was something so dismal and chilling about the idea that Bill was momentarily silenced. Then he said, 'But haven't they ever suh-suh-hent people down to map –'

'I ought to finish these dowels,' Zack said abruptly, turning his back and pulling away. 'Go on in and see what's on TV'

'B-B-But Dah-Dah-Dad —'

'Go on, Bill,' Zack said, and Bill could feel the coldness again. That coldness made suppers a kind of torture as his father leafed through electrical journals (he hoped for a promotion the following year), as his mother read one of her endless British mysteries: Marsh, Sayers, Innes, Allingham. Eating in that coldness robbed food of its taste; it was like eating frozen dinners that had never seen the inside of an oven. Sometimes, after, he would go up to his room and lie on his bed, holding his griping stomach, and think: *He thrusts his fists against the posts and still insists he sees the ghosts.* He thought of that more and more since Georgie had died, although his mother had taught him the phrase two years before. It had taken on a talismanic cast in his mind: the day he could walk up to his mother and simply speak that phrase without tripping or stuttering, looking her right in the eye as he spoke it, the coldness would break apart; her eyes would light up and she would hug him and say, 'Wonderful, Billy! What a good boy! What a good boy!'

He had, of course, told this to no one. Wild horses would not have dragged it from him; neither the rack nor the boot would have induced him to give up this secret fantasy, which lay at the very center of his heart. If he could say this phrase which she had taught him casually one Saturday morning as he and Georgie sat watching Guy Madison and Andy Devine in *The Adventures of Wild Bill Hickok*, it would be like the kiss that awakened Sleeping Beauty from her cold dreams to the warmer world of the fairytale prince's love.

He thrusts his fists against the posts and still insists he sees the ghosts.

Nor did he tell it to his friends on that July 3rd — but he told them what his father had told him about the Derry sewer and drain systems. He was a boy to whom invention came easily and naturally (sometimes more easily than telling the truth), and the scene he painted was quite different from the scene in which the conversation had actually taken place: he and his old man had been watching the tube together, he said, having cups of coffee.

'Your dad lets you have coffee?' Eddie asked.

'Sh-sh-sure,' Bill said.

'Wow,' Eddie said. 'My mother would never let me have a coffee. She says the caffeine in it is dangerous.' He paused. 'She drinks quite a bit of it herself, though.'

'My dad lets me have coffee if I want it,' Beverly said, 'but he'd kill me if he knew I smoked.'

'What makes you so sure it's in the sewers?' Richie asked, looking from Bill to Stan Uris and then back to Bill again.

'E-E-Everything g-goes back t-to th-th-that,' Bill said. 'The v-voices Beh-he-heverly heard c-came from the d-d-drain. And the bluh-blood. When the c-c-clown ch-chased us, those o-orange buh-buh-buttons were by a suh-sewer. And Juh juh-George –'

'It wasn't a clown, Big Bill,' Richie said. 'I *told* you that. I know it's crazy, but it was a werewolf.' He looked at the others defensively. 'Honest to God. I *saw* it.'

Bill said: 'It was a werewolf for y-y-you.'

'Huh?'

Bill said, 'D-Don't you s-s-see? It was a wuh-wuh-werewolf for y-you because y-you saw that duh-humb movie at the A-A-A-Aladdin.'

'I don't get it.'

'I think I do,' Ben said quietly.

'I went to the l-l-library and l-looked it uh-uh-up,' Bill said. 'I think It's a gluh-gluh' – he paused, throat straining, and spat it out – 'a *glamour*.'

'Glammer?' Eddie asked doubtfully.

'G-G-Glamour,' Bill said, and spelled it. He told them about an encyclopedia entry on the subject and a chapter he had read in a book called *Night's Truth*. Glamour, he said, was the Gaelic name for the creature which was haunting Derry; other races and other cultures at other times had different words for it, but they all meant the same thing. The Plains Indians called it a manitou, which sometimes took the shape of a mountain-lion or an elk or an eagle. These same Indians believed that the spirit of a manitou could sometimes enter them, and at these times it was possible for them to shape the clouds themselves into representations of those animals for which their houses had been named. The Himalayans called it a *tallus* or *taelus*, which meant an evil magic being that could read your mind and then assume the shape of the thing you were most afraid of. In Central Europe it had been called *eylak*, brother of the *vurderlak*, or vampire. In France it was *le loup-garou*, or skin-changer, a concept that had been crudely translated as the werewolf, but, Bill told them, *le loup-garou* (which he pronounced 'le loop-garoo') could be anything, anything at all: a wolf, a hawk, a sheep, even a bug.

'Did any of those articles tell you how to beat a glamour?' Beverly asked.

Bill nodded, but he didn't look hopeful. 'The H-H-Himalayans had a rih-hi-hitual to g-get rih-rid of i-i-it, but ih-it's pretty gruh-gruh-gruesome.'

They looked at him, not wanting to hear but needing to.

'I-I-It was cuh-called the R-R-Ritual of *Chüd-Chüd*,' Bill said, and went on to explain what that was. If you were a Himalayan holy-man, you tracked the *taelus*. The *taelus* stuck its tongue out. You stuck *yours* out. You and it overlapped tongues and then you both bit in all the way so you were sort of stapled together, eye to eye.

'Oh, I think I'm gonna puke,' Beverly said, rolling over on the dirt. Ben patted her back tentatively, then looked around to see if he had been observed. He hadn't been; the others were looking at Bill, mesmerized.

'What then?' Eddie asked.

'W-W-Well,' Bill said, 'this sounds cuh-cuh-crazy, b-but the book s-said that th-then y-you started telling juh-jokes and rih-riddles.'

'*What*?' Stan asked.

Bill nodded, his face that of a correspondent who wants you to know – without coming right out and saying it – that he doesn't make the news but only reports it. 'R-Right. F-First the *t-taelus* monster would tell o-o-one, then *y-y-you* got to t-t-tell o-one, and y-you w-w-went o-on like thuh-that, t-tay-takin t-turns –'

Beverly sat up again, knees against her chest, hands linked around her shins. 'I don't see how people could talk with their tongues, you know, nailed together.'

Richie immediately ran out his tongue, gripped it with his fingers, and intoned: 'My father works in a shit-yard!' That broke them all up for awhile even though it *was* a baby joke.

'M-Maybe it was suh-suh-suhpposed to be tuh-telepathy,' Bill said. 'A-Anyway, i-if the *h-h-human* laughed f-f-first in spi-hite of the p-p-p-p –'

'Pain?' Stan asked.

Bill nodded. '– then the *taelus* g-got to k-k-kill h-him and e-e-e-eat him. His soul, I think. B-But i-if the muh-man c-c-ould make the *t-taelus* l-laugh f-f-first, it had to go away for a huh-huh-hundred y-years.'

'Did the book say where a thing like that would come from?' Ben asked.

Bill shook his head.

'Do you believe any of it?' Stan asked, sounding as if he wanted to scoff but could not quite find the moral or mental force to do so.

Bill shrugged and said, 'I a-a-almost d-do.' He seemed about to say more, then shook his head and remained silent.

'It explains a lot,' Eddie said slowly. 'The clown, the leper, the werewolf . . .' He looked over at Stan. 'The dead boys, too, I guess.'

'This sounds like a job for Richard Tozier,' Richie said, in the MovieTone Newsreel Announcer's Voice. 'Man of a thousand jokes and six thousand riddles.'

'If we sent you to do it, we'd all get killed,' Ben said. 'Slowly. In great pain.' At this they all laughed again.

'So what do we do about it?' Stan demanded, and once again Bill could only shake his head ... and feel he almost knew. Stan stood up. 'Let's go somewhere else,' he said. 'I'm getting fanny fatigue.'

'I like it here,' Beverly said. 'It's shady and nice.' She glanced at Stan. 'I suppose you want to do something *babyish* like going down to the dump and breaking bottles with rocks.'

'I *like* breaking bottles with rocks,' Richie said, standing up beside Stan. 'It's the j.d. in me, baby.' He flipped up his collar and began to stalk around like James Dean in *Rebel Without a Cause*. 'They *hurt* me,' he said, looking moody and scratching his chest. 'You know, like wow. My parents. School. So-SY-ety. Everyone. It's pressure, baby. It's –'

'It's shit,' Beverly said, and sighed.

'I've got some firecrackers,' Stan said, and they forgot all about glamours, manitous, and Richie's bad James Dean imitation as Stan produced a package of Black Cats from his hip pocket. Even Bill was impressed.

'J-Jesus Christ, Stuh-Stuh-han, w-where did you g-g-get thuh-hose?'

'From this fat kid that I go to synagogue with sometimes,' Stan said. 'I traded a bunch of Superman and Little Lulu funnybooks for em.'

'Let's shoot em off!' Richie cried, nearly apoplectic in his joy. 'Let's go shoot em off, Stanny, I won't tell any more guys you and your dad killed Christ, I promise, what do you say? I'll tell em your nose is *small*, Stanny! I'll tell em you're not circumcised!'

At this Beverly began to shriek with laughter and actually appeared to be approaching apoplexy before covering her face with her hands. Bill began to laugh, Eddie began to laugh, and after a moment even Stan joined in. The sound of it drifted across the broad shallow expanse of the Kenduskeag on that day before July 4th, a summer-sound, as bright as the sunrays darting off the water, and none of them saw the orange eyes staring at them from a tangle of brambles and sterile black-berry bushes to their left. This brambly patch scrubbed the entire bank for thirty feet, and in the center of it was one of Ben's Morlock holes. It was from this raised concrete pipe that the eyes, each more than two feet across, stared.

5

The reason Mike ran afoul of Henry Bowers and his not-so-merry band on that same day was because the next day was the Glorious Fourth. The Church School had a band in which Mike played the trombone. On the Fourth, the band would march in the annual holiday parade, playing 'The Battle Hymn of the Republic,' 'Onward Christian Soldiers,' and 'America the Beautiful.' This was an occasion that Mike had been looking forward to for over a month. He walked to the final rehearsal because his bike had a busted chain. The rehearsal was not scheduled until two-thirty, but he left at one because he wanted to polish his trombone, which was stored in the school's music room, until it glowed. Although his trombone-playing was really not much better than Richie's Voices, he was fond of the instrument, and whenever he felt blue a half an hour of foghorning Sousa marches, hymns, or patriotic airs cheered him right up again. There was a can of Saddler's brass polish in one of the flap pockets of his khaki shirt and two or three clean rags were dangling from the hip pocket of his jeans. The thought of Henry Bowers was the furthest thing from his mind.

A glance behind as he approached Neibolt Street and the Church School would have changed his mind in a hurry, because Henry, Victor, Belch, Peter Gordon, and Moose Sadler were spread across the road behind him. If they had left the Bowers house five minutes later, Mike would have been out of sight over the crest of the next hill; the apocalyptic rockfight and everything that followed it might have happened differently, or not at all.

But it was Mike himself, years later, who advanced the idea that perhaps none of them were entirely their own masters in the events of that summer; that if luck and free will had played parts, then their roles had been narrow ones. He would point out a number of these suspicious coincidences to the others at their reunion lunch, but there was at least one of which he was unaware. The meeting in the Barrens that day broke up when Stan Uris produced the Black Cats and the Losers' Club headed toward the dump to shoot them off. And Victor, Belch, and the others had come out to the Bowers farm because Henry had firecrackers, cherry-bombs, and M–80s (the possession of these last would a few years hence become a felony). The big boys were planning to go down beyond the trainyard coalpit and explode Henry's treasures.

None of them, not even Belch, went out to the Bowers farm under ordinary circumstances – primarily because of Henry's crazy father but also because they always ended up helping Henry do his chores: the weeding, the endless rock-picking, the lugging of wood, the toting of water, the pitching of hay, the picking of whatever happened to be ripe at the time of the season – peas, cukes, tomatoes, potatoes. These boys were not exactly allergic to work, but they had plenty to do at their own places without sweating for Henry's kooky father, who didn't much care who he hit (he had once taken a length of stovewood to Victor Criss when the boy dropped a basket of tomatoes he was lugging out to the roadside stand). Getting whopped with a chunk of birch was bad enough; what made it worse was that Butch Bowers had chanted 'I'm gonna kill *all* the Nips! I'm gonna kill *all* the fuckin Nips!' when he did it.

Dumb as he was, Belch Huggins had expressed it best: 'I don't fuck with crazy people,' he told Victor one day two years before. Victor had laughed and agreed.

But the siren-song of all those firecrackers had been too great to be withstood.

'Tell you what, Henry,' Victor said when Henry called him up that morning at nine and invited him out. 'I'll meet you at the coalpit around one o'clock, what do you say?'

'You show up at the coalpit around one and I'm not gonna be there,' Henry replied. 'I got too many chores. If you show up at the coalpit around three, I *will* be there. And the first M-80 is going to go right up your old tan track, Vic.'

Vic hesitated, then agreed to come over and help with the chores.

The others came as well, and with the five of them, all big boys, working like fiends around the Bowers place, they got all the chores finished by early afternoon. When Henry asked his father if he could go, Bowers the elder simply waved a languid hand at his son. Butch was settled in for the afternoon on the back porch, a quart milk-bottle filled with exquisitely hard cider by his rocker, his Philco portable radio on the porch rail (later that afternoon the Red Sox would be playing the Washington Senators, a prospect that would have given a man who was *not* crazy a bad case of cold chills). An unsheathed Japanese sword lay across Butch's lap, a war souvenir which, Butch said, he had taken off the body of a dying Nip on the island of Tarawa (he had actually traded six bottles of Budweiser and three joysticks for the sword in Honolulu). Lately Butch almost always got out his sword when he drank. And since all of the boys, including Henry himself, were secretly convinced that sooner or later he would use it on someone, it was best to be far away when it made its appearance on Butch's lap.

The boys had no more than stepped out into the road when Henry spied Mike Hanlon up ahead. 'It's the nigger!' he said, his eyes lighting up like the eyes of a small child contemplating Santa Claus's imminent arrival on Christmas Eve.

'The nigger?' Belch Huggins looked puzzled – he had seen the Hanlons only rarely – and then his dim eyes lit up. 'Oh yeah! The nigger! Let's get him, Henry!'

Belch broke into a thunderous trot. The others were following suit when Henry grabbed Belch and hauled him back. Henry had more experience than the others chasing Mike Hanlon, and he knew that catching him was easier said than done. That black boy could *move*.

'He don't see us. Let's just walk fast till he does. Cut the distance.'

They did so. An observer might have been amused: the five of them looked as if they were trying out for that peculiar Olympic walking competition. Moose Sadler's considerable belly joggled up and down inside his Derry High School tee-shirt. Sweat rolled down Belch's face, which soon grew red. But the distance between them and Mike closed – two hundred yards, a hundred and fifty yards, a hundred – and so far Little Black Sambo hadn't looked back. They could hear him whistling.

'What you gonna do to him, Henry?' Victor Criss asked in a low voice. He sounded merely interested, but in truth he was worried. Just lately Henry had begun to worry him more and more. He wouldn't care if Henry wanted them to beat the Hanlon kid up, maybe even rip his shirt off or throw his pants and underwear up in a tree, but he was not sure that was all Henry had in mind. This year there had been several unpleasant encounters with the children from Derry Elementary Henry referred to as 'the little shits.' Henry was used to dominating and terrorizing the little shits, but since March he had been balked by them time and time again. Henry and his friends had chased one of them, the four-eyes Tozier kid, into Freese's, and had lost him somehow just when it seemed his ass was surely theirs. Then, on the last day of school, the Hanscom kid –

But Victor didn't like to think of that.

What worried him, simply, was this: Henry might go TOO FAR. Just what TOO FAR might be was something Victor didn't like to think of . . . but his uneasy heart had prompted the question just the same.

'We're gonna catch him and take him down to that coalpit,' Henry said. 'I thought we'd put a couple of firecrackers in his shoes and see if he dances.'

'But not the M-80s, Henry, right?'

If Henry intended something like that Victor was going to take a powder. An M-80 in each shoe would blow that nigger's feet off, and that was *much* TOO FAR.

'I've got only four of those,' Henry said, not taking his eyes off Mike Hanlon's back. They had closed the distance to seventy-five yards now and he also spoke in a low voice. 'You think I'd waste two of em on a fuckin nightfighter?'

'No, Henry. Course not.'

'We'll just put a couple of Black Cats in his loafers,' Henry said, 'then strip him bareass and throw his clothes down into the Barrens. Maybe he'll catch poison ivy going after them.'

'We gotta roll im in the coal, too,' Belch said, his formerly dim eyes now glowing brightly. 'Okay, Henry? Is that cool?'

'Cool as a moose,' Henry said in a casual way Victor didn't quite like. 'We'll roll im in the coal, just like I rolled im in the mud that other time. And . . .' Henry grinned, showing teeth that were already beginning to rot at the age of twelve. 'And I got something to tell him. I don't think he heard when I told im before.'

'What's that, Henry?' Peter asked. Peter Gordon was merely interested and excited. He came from one of Derry's 'good families'; he lived on West Broadway and in two years he would be sent to prep school in Groton – or so he believed on that July 3rd. He was brighter than Vic Criss, but had not hung around long enough to understand how Henry was eroding.

'You'll find out,' Henry said. 'Now shut up. We're gettin close.'

They were twenty-five yards behind Mike and Henry was just opening his mouth to give the order to charge when Moose Sadler set off the first firecracker of the day. Moose had eaten three plates of baked beans the night before, and the fart was almost as loud as a shotgun blast.

Mike looked around. Henry saw his eyes widen.

'Get him!' Henry howled.

Mike froze for a moment; then he took off, running for his life.

6

The Losers wound their way through the bamboo in the Barrens in this order: Bill; Richie; Beverly behind Richie, walking slim and pretty in bluejeans and a white sleeveless blouse, zoris on her feet; then Ben, trying not to puff too loudly (although it was eighty-one that day, he was wearing one of his baggy sweatshirts); Stan; Eddie bringing up the rear, the snout of his aspirator poking out of his right front pants pocket.

Bill had fallen into a 'jungle-safari' fantasy, as he often did when walking through this part of the Barrens. The bamboo was high and white, limiting visibility to the path they had made through here. The earth was black and squelchy, with sodden patches that had to be avoided or jumped over if you didn't want to get mud in your shoes. The puddles of standing water had oddly flat rainbow colors. The air had a reeky smell that was half the dump and half rotting vegetation.

Bill halted one turn away from the Kenduskeag and turned back to Richie. 'T–T–Tiger up ahead, T–T–Tozier.'

Richie nodded and turned back to Beverly. 'Tiger,' he breathed.

'Tiger,' she told Ben.

'Man-eater?' Ben asked, holding his breath to keep from panting.

'There's blood all over him,' Beverly said.

'Man-eating tiger,' Ben muttered to Stan, and he passed the news back to Eddie, whose thin face was hectic with excitement.

They faded into the bamboo, leaving the path of black earth that looped through it magically bare. The tiger passed in front of them and all of them nearly saw it: heavy, perhaps four hundred pounds, its muscles moving with grace and power beneath the silk of its striped pelt. They nearly saw its green eyes, and the flecks of blood around its snout from the last batch of pygmy warriors it had eaten alive.

The bamboo rattled faintly, a noise both musical and eerie, and then was still again. It might have been a breath of summer breeze . . . or it might have been the passage of an African tiger on its way toward the Old Cape side of the Barrens.

'Gone,' Bill said. He let out a pent-up breath and stepped out onto the path again. The others followed suit.

Richie was the only one who had come armed: he produced a cap-pistol with a friction-taped handgrip. 'I could have had a clear shot at him if you'd moved, Big Bill,' he said grimly. He pushed the bridge of his old glasses up on his nose with the muzzle of the gun.

'There's Wuh–Wuh–Watusis around h–h–here,' Bill said. 'C–C–Can't rih-risk a shot. Y–You w–want them down on t–t–top of us?'

'Oh,' Richie said, convinced.

Bill made a come-on gesture with his arm and they were back on the path again, which narrowed into a neck at the end of the bamboo patch. They stepped out onto the bank of the Kenduskeag, where a series of stepping-stones led across the river. Ben had shown them how to place them. You got a big rock and plopped it in the water, then you got a second and plopped it in the water while you were stepping on the first, then you got a third and plopped it in the water while you were stepping on the second, and so on until you were all the way across the river (which here, and at this time of year, was less than a foot deep and shaled with tawny sandbars) with your feet still dry. The trick was so simple it was damn near babyish, but none of them had seen it until Ben pointed it out. He was good at stuff like that, but when he showed you he never made you feel like a dummy.

They went down the bank in single file and started across the dry backs of the rocks they had planted.

'Bill!' Beverly called urgently.

He froze at once, not looking back, arms held out. The water chuckled and rilled around him. 'What?'

'There's piranha fish in here! I saw them eat a whole cow two days ago. A minute after it fell in, there was nothing but bones. Don't fall off!'

'Right,' Bill said. 'Be careful, men.'

They teetered their way across the rocks. A freight-train charged by on the railway embankment as Eddie Kaspbrak neared the halfway point, and the sudden blast of its airhorn caused him to jiggle on the edge of balance. He looked into the bright water and for one moment, between the sunflashes that darted arrows of light into his eyes, he actually *saw* the cruising piranhas. They were not part of the make-believe that went with Bill's jungle safari fantasy; he was quite sure of that. The fish he saw looked like oversized goldfish with the great ugly jaws of catfish or groupers. Sawteeth protruded between their thick lips and, like goldfish, they were orange. As orange as the fluffy pompoms you sometimes saw on the suits the clowns wore at the circus.

They circled in the shallow water, gnashing.

Eddie pinwheeled his arms. *I'm going in*, he thought. *I'm going in and they'll eat me alive –*

Then Stanley Uris gripped his wrist firmly and brought him back to dead center.

'Close call,' Stan said. 'If you fell in, your mother'd give you heck.'

Thoughts of his mother were, for once, the furthest things from Eddie's mind. The others had gained the far bank now and were counting cars on the freight. Eddie stared wildly into Stan's eyes, then looked into the water again. He saw a potato-chip bag go dancing by, but that was all. He looked up at Stan again.

'Stan, I saw –'

'What?'

Eddie shook his head. 'Nothing, I guess,' he said. 'I'm just a little

(*but they were there yes they were and they would have eaten me alive*)

jumpy. The tiger, I guess. Keep going.'

This western bank of the Kenduskeag – the Old Cape bank – was a quagmire of mud during rainy weather and the spring runoff, but there had been no heavy rain in Derry for two weeks or more and the bank had dried to an alien crack-glaze from which several of those cement cylinders poked, casting grim little shadows. About twenty yards farther down, a cement pipe jutted out over the Kenduskeag and spilled a steady thin stream of foul-looking brown water into the river.

Ben said quietly, 'It's creepy here,' and the others nodded.

Bill led them up the dry bank and back into the heavy shrubbery, where bugs whirred and chiggers chigged. Every now and then there would be a heavy ruffle of wings as a bird took off. Once a squirrel ran across their path, and about five minutes later, as they approached the low wrinkle of ridge that guarded the town dump's blind side, a large rat with a bit of cellophane caught in its whiskers trundled in front of Bill, passing along its own secret run through its own microcosmic wilderness.

The smell of the dump was now clear and pungent; a black column of smoke rose in the sky. The ground, while still heavily overgrown except for their own narrow path, began to be strewn with litter. Bill had dubbed this 'dump-dandruff,' and Richie had been delighted; he had laughed almost until he cried. 'You ought to write that down, Big Bill,' he said. 'That's really good.'

Papers caught on branches wavered and flapped like cut-rate pennants; here was a silver gleam of summer sun reflected from a clutch of tin cans lying at the bottom of a green and tangled hollow; there the hotter reflection of sunrays bouncing off a broken beer bottle. Beverly spied a babydoll, its plastic skin so brightly pink it looked almost boiled. She picked it up, then dropped it with a little cry as she saw the whitish-gray beetles squirming from beneath its moldy skirt and down its rotting legs. She rubbed her fingers on her jeans.

They climbed to the top of the ridge and looked down into the dump.

'Oh shit,' Bill said, and jammed his hands into his pockets as the others gathered around him.

They were burning the northern end today, but here, at their end, the dumpkeeper (he was, in fact, Armando Fazio, Mandy to his friends, and the bachelor brother of the Derry Elementary School janitor) was tinkering on the World War II D-9 'dozer he used to push the crap into piles for burning. His shirt was off, and the big portable radio sitting under the canvas parasol on the 'dozer's seat was putting out the Red Sox–Senators pregame festivities.

'Can't go down there,' Ben agreed. Mandy Fazio was not a bad guy, but when he saw kids in the dump he ran them off at once – because of the rats, because of the poison he regularly sowed to keep the rat population down, because of the potential for cuts, falls, and burns ... but mostly because he believed a dump was no place for children to be. 'Ain't you nice?' he would yell at the kids he spied who had been drawn to the dump with their .22s to plink away at bottles (or rats, or seagulls) or by the exotic fascination of 'dump-picking': you might find a toy that still worked, a chair that could be mended for a clubhouse, or a junked TV with the picture-tube still intact – if you threw a rock through one of these there was a very satisfying explosion. 'Ain't you kids *nice*?' Mandy would bellow (he bellowed not because he was angry but because he was deaf and wore no hearing-aid). 'Dintchore folks teach you to be nice? Nice boys and girls don't play in the dump! Go to the park! Go to the liberry! Go down to Community House and play box-hockey! Be *nice*!'

'Nope,' Richie said. 'Guess the dump's out.'

They all sat down for a few moments to watch Mandy work on his 'dozer, hoping he would give up and go away but not really believing he would: the presence of the radio suggested Mandy intended to stay all afternoon. It was enough to piss off the Pope, Bill thought. There was really no better place to come with firecrackers than the dump. You could put them under tin cans and then watch the cans fly into the air when the firecrackers went off, or you could light the fuses and drop them into bottles and then run like hell. The bottles didn't always break, but usually they did.

'Wish we had some M-80s,' Richie sighed, unaware of how soon one would be chucked at his head.

'My mother says people ought to be happy with what they have,' Eddie said so solemnly that they all laughed.

When the laughter died away, they all looked toward Bill again.

Bill thought about it and then said, 'I nuh-know a p-place. There's an old gruh-gruh-gravel-pit at the end of the Buh-Barrens by the t-t-trainyards –'

'Yeah!' Stan said, getting to his feet. 'I know that place! You're a genius, Bill!'

'They'll really echo there,' Beverly agreed.

'Well, let's go,' Richie said.

The six of them, one shy of the magic number, walked along the brow of the hill which circled the dump. Mandy Fazio glanced up once and saw them silhouetted against the blue sky like Indians out on a raiding party. He thought about hollering at them – the Barrens was no place for kids – and then he turned back to his work instead. At least they weren't in his dump.

7

Mike Hanlon ran past the Church School without pausing and pelted straight up Neibolt Street toward the Derry trainyards. There was a janitor at NCS, but Mr Gendron was very old and even deafer than Mandy Fazio. Also, he liked to spend most of his summer days asleep in the basement by the summer-silent boiler, stretched out in a battered old reclining chair with the Derry *News* in his lap. Mike would still be pounding on the door and shouting for the old man to let him in when Henry Bowers came up behind him and tore his freaking head off.

So Mike just ran.

But not blindly; he was trying to pace himself, trying to control his breathing, not yet going all out. Henry, Belch, and Moose Sadler presented no problems; even relatively fresh they ran like wounded buffalo. Victor Criss and Peter Gordon, however, were much faster. As Mike passed the house where Bill and Richie had seen the clown – or the werewolf – he snapped a glance back and was alarmed to see that Peter Gordon had almost closed the distance. Peter was grinning cheerfully – a steeplechase grin, a full-out polo grin, a pip-pip-jolly-good-show grin, and Mike thought: *I wonder if he'd grin that way if he knew what's going to happen if they catch me . . . Does he think they're just going to say 'Tag, you're it,' and run away?*

As the trainyard gate with its sign – PRIVATE PROPERTY KEEP OUT VIOLATORS WILL BE PROSECUTED – loomed up, Mike was forced to let himself out to the limit. There was no pain – his breathing was rapid yet still controlled – but he knew everything was going to start hurting if he had to keep this pace up for long.

The gate was standing halfway open. He snapped a second look back and saw that he'd pulled away from Peter again. Victor was perhaps ten paces behind Peter, the others now forty or fifty yards back. Even in that quick glance Mike could see the black anger on Henry's face.

He skittered through the opening, whirled, and slammed the gate closed. He heard the click as it latched. A moment later Peter Gordon slammed into the chainlink, and a moment after that, Victor Criss ran up beside him. Peter's smile was gone; a sulky, balked look had replaced it. He grabbed for the latch, but of course there was none: the latch was on the inside.

Incredibly, he said: 'Come on, kid, open the gate. That's not fair.'

'What's your idea of fair?' Mike asked, panting. 'Five against one?'

'Fair-up,' Peter repeated, as if he had not heard Mike at all.

Mike looked at Victor, saw the troubled look in Victor's eyes. He started to speak, but that was when the others pulled up to the gate.

'Open up, nigger!' Henry bawled. He began to shake the chainlink with such ferocity that Peter looked at him, startled. 'Open up! Open up *right now*!'

'I won't,' Mike said quietly.

'Open up!' Belch shouted. 'Open up, ya fuckin jigaboo!'

Mike backed away from the gate, his heart beating heavily in his chest. He couldn't remember ever being quite this scared, quite this *upset*. They lined their side of the gate, shouting at him, calling him names for nigger he had never dreamed existed – nightfighter, Ubangi, spade, blackberry, junglebunny, others. He was barely aware that Henry was taking something from his pocket, that he had popped a wooden match alight with his thumbnail – and then a round red something came over the fence and he flinched instinctively away as the cherry-bomb exploded to his left, kicking up dust.

The bang silenced them all for a moment – Mike stared unbelievingly at them through the fence, and they stared back. Peter Gordon looked utterly shocked, and even Belch looked stunned.

They're ascared of him now, Mike thought suddenly, and a new voice spoke inside of him, perhaps for the first time, a voice that was disturbingly adult. *They're ascared, but that won't stop them. You got to get away, Mikey, or something's going to happen. Not all of them will want it to happen, maybe – not Victor and maybe not Peter Gordon – but it will happen anyway because Henry will make it happen. So get away. Get away fast.*

He backed up another two or three steps and then Henry Bowers said: 'I was the one killed your dog, nigger.'

Mike froze, feeling as if he had been hit in the belly with a bowling ball. He stared into Henry Bowers's eyes and understood that Henry was telling the simple truth: he had killed Mr Chips.

That moment of understanding seemed nearly eternal to Mike – looking into Henry's crazed sweat-ringed eyes and his rage-blackened face, it seemed to him that he understood a great many things for the first time, and the fact that Henry was far crazier than Mike had ever dreamed was only the least of them. He realized above all that the world was not kind, and it was more this than the news itself that forced the cry from him: 'You honky chickenshit *bastard*!'

Henry uttered a shriek of rage and attacked the fence, monkeying his way toward the top with a brute strength that was terrifying. Mike paused a moment longer, wanting to see if that adult voice that had spoken inside had been a true voice, and yes, it had been true: after the slightest hesitation, the others spread out and also began to climb.

Mike turned and ran again, sprinting across the trainyards, his shadow trailing squat at his feet. The freight which the Losers had seen crossing the Barrens was long gone now, and there was no sound but Mike's own breathing in his ears and the musical jingle of chainlink as Henry and the others climbed the fence.

Mike ran across one triple set of tracks, his sneakers kicking back cinders as he ran across the space between. He stumbled crossing the second set of tracks, and felt pain flare briefly in his ankle. He got up and ran on again. He heard a thud as Henry jumped down from the top of the fence behind him. '*Here I come for your ass, nigger!*' Henry bawled.

Mike's reasoning self had decided that the Barrens were his only chance now. If he could get down there he could hide in the tangles of underbrush, in the bamboo . . . or, if things became really desperate, he could climb into one of the drainpipes and wait it out.

He could do those things, maybe . . . but there was a hot spark of fury in his chest that had nothing to do with his reasoning self. He could understand Henry chasing after him when he got the chance, but Mr Chips? . . . killing Mr Chips? *My DOG wasn't a nigger, you cheapshit bastard*, Mike thought as he ran, and the bewildered anger grew.

Now he heard another voice, this one his father's. *I don't want you to make a career out of running away . . . and what it all comes down to is that you have to be careful where you take your stand. You have to ask yourself if Henry Bowers is worth the trouble . . .*

Mike had been running a straight line across the trainyards toward the storage quonsets. Beyond them another chainlink fence divided the trainyards from the Barrens. He had been planning to scale that fence and jump over to the other side. Instead he veered hard right, toward the gravel-pit.

This gravel-pit had been used as a coalpit until 1935 or so – it had been a stoking-point for the trains which ran through the Derry yards. Then the diesels came, and the electrics. For a number of years after the coal was gone (much of the remainder stolen by people with coal-fired furnaces) a local contractor had dug gravel there, but he went bust in 1955 and since then the pit had been deserted. A spur railroad line still ran in a loop up to the pit and then back toward the switching-yards, but the tracks were dull with rust, and ragweed grew up between the rotting ties. These same weeds grew in the pit itself, vying for space with goldenrod and nodding sunflowers. Amid the vegetation there was still plenty of slag coal – the stuff people had once called 'clinkers.'

As Mike ran toward this place, he took his shirt off. He reached the rim of the pit and looked back. Henry was coming across the tracks, his buddies spread out around him. That was okay, maybe.

Moving as quickly as he could, using his shirt for a bindle, Mike picked up half a dozen handfuls of hard clinkers. Then he ran back toward the fence, swinging his shirt by the arms. Instead of climbing the fence when he reached it, he turned so his back was against it. He dumped the coal out of his shirt, stooped, and picked up a couple of chunks.

Henry didn't see the coal; he only saw that he had the nigger trapped against the fence. He sprinted toward him, yelling.

'*This is for my dog, you bastard!*' Mike cried, unaware that he had begun to cry. He threw one of the chunks of coal overhand. It flew in a hard direct line. It struck Henry's forehead with a loud *bonk*! and then rebounded into the air. Henry stumbled to his knees. His hands went to his head. Blood seeped through his fingers at once, like a magician's surprise.

The others skidded to a stop, their faces stamped with identical expressions of disbelief. Henry uttered a high scream of pain and got to his feet again, still holding his head. Mike threw another chunk of coal. Henry ducked. He began to walk toward Mike, and when Mike threw a third chunk of coal, Henry removed one hand from his gashed forehead and batted the chunk of coal almost casually aside. He was grinning.

'Oh, you're gonna get such a surprise,' he said. 'Such a – *OH*

MY GAWD! Henry tried to say more, but only inarticulate gargling noises emerged from his mouth.

Mike had pegged another chunk of coal and this one had struck Henry square in the throat. Henry buckled to his knees again. Peter Gordon gaped. Moose Sadler's brow was furrowed, as if he were trying to figure out a difficult math problem.

'*What are you guys waiting for?*' Henry managed. Blood seeped between his fingers. His voice sounded rusty and foreign. '*Get* him! *Get* the little cocksucker!'

Mike didn't wait to see if they would obey or not. He dropped his shirt and leaped at the fence. He began to pull himself up toward the top and then he felt rough hands grab his foot. He looked down and saw Henry Bowers's contorted face, smeared by blood and coal. Mike yanked his foot up. His sneaker came off in Henry's hand. He pistoned his bare foot down into Henry's face and heard something crunch. Henry screamed again and staggered backward, now holding his spouting nose.

Another hand – Belch Huggins's – snagged briefly in the cuff of Mike's jeans, but he was able to pull free. He threw one leg over the top of the fence, and then something struck him with blinding force on the side of his face. Warmth trickled down his cheek. Something else struck his hip, his forearm, his upper thigh. They were throwing his own ammunition at him.

He hung briefly by his hands and then dropped, rolling over twice. The scrubby ground sloped downward here, and perhaps that saved Mike Hanlon's eyesight or even his life; Henry had approached the fence again and now looped one of his four M–80s over the top of the fence. It went off with a terrific *CRRRACK!* that echoed and blew a wide bare patch in the grass.

Mike, his ears ringing, went head-over-heels and staggered to his feet. He was now in high grass, on the edge of the Barrens. He wiped a hand down his right cheek and it came away bloody. The blood did not particularly worry him; he had not expected to come out of this unscathed.

Henry tossed a cherry-bomb, but Mike saw this one coming and moved away easily.

'Let's get him!' Henry roared, and began to climb the fence.

'Jeez, Henry, I don't know –' This had gone too far for Peter Gordon, who had never encountered a situation that had turned so suddenly savage. Things were not supposed to get bloody – at least not for your team – when the odds were comfortably slugged in your favor.

'You *better* know,' Henry said, looking back at Peter from halfway up the fence. He hung there like a bloated poisonous spider in human shape. His baleful eyes stared at Peter; blood rimmed them on either side. Mike's downward kick had broken his nose, although Henry would not be aware of the fact for some time yet. 'You *better* know, or I'll come after *you*, you fucking jerk.'

The others began to climb the fence, Peter and Victor with some reluctance, Belch and Moose as vacantly eager as before.

Mike waited to see no more. He turned and ran into the scrub. Henry bellowed after him: '*I'll find you, nigger! I'll find you!*'

8

The Losers had reached the far side of the gravel-pit, which was little more than a huge weedy pockmark in the earth now, three years after the last load of gravel had been taken out of it. They were all gathered around Stan, looking appreciatively at his package of Black Cats, when the first explosion came. Eddie jumped – he was still goofed up over the piranha fish he thought he had seen (he wasn't sure what *real* piranha fish looked like, but he was pretty sure they didn't look like oversized goldfish with teeth).

'Merrow down easy, Eddie-san,' Richie said, doing his Chinese Coolie Voice. 'Iss just other kids shooting off fireclackers.'

'That s-s-sucks the r-r-root, Rih-Rih-Richie,' Bill remarked. The others laughed.

'I keep trying, Big Bill,' Richie said. 'I feel like, if I get good enough, someday I'll earn your love.' He made dainty kissing gestures at the air. Bill shot him the finger. Ben and Eddie stood side by side, grinning.

'Oh I'm so young and you're so old,' Stan Uris piped up suddenly, doing an eerily accurate Paul Anka imitation, 'this my darling I've been told –'

'He can *sayng*!' Richie screeched in his Pickaninny Voice. 'Lawks-a-mussy, thisyere boy can *sayng*!' And then, in the Movie-Tone Announcer's Voice: 'Want you to sign right here, boy, on this dotted line.' Richie slung an arm around Stan's shoulders and favored him with a gigantic gleaming smile. 'We're going to grow your hair out, boy. Going to give you a *git*-tar. Going to –'

Bill popped Richie twice on the arm, quickly and lightly. They were all excited at the prospect of shooting off firecrackers.

'Open them up, Stan,' Beverly said. 'I've got some matches.'

They gathered around again as Stan carefully opened the package of firecrackers. There were exotic Chinese letters on the black label and a sober caution in English that got Richie giggling again. 'Do not hold in hand after fuse is lit,' this warning read.

'Good thing they told me,' Richie said. 'I always used to hold them after I lit them. I thought that's how you got rid of your frockin hangnails.'

Working slowly, almost reverently, Stan removed the red cellophane and laid the block of cardboard tubes, blue and red and green, on the palm of his hand. Their fuses had been braided together in a Chinese pigtail.

'I'll unwind the –' Stan began, and then there was a much louder explosion. The echo rolled slowly across the Barrens. A cloud of gulls rose from the eastern side of the dump, squalling and crying. They all jumped this time. Stan dropped the firecrackers and had to pick them up.

'Was that dynamite?' Beverly asked nervously. She was looking at Bill, whose head was up, his eyes wide. She thought he had never looked so handsome – but there was something too alert, too strung-up, in the attitude of his head. He was like a deer scenting fire in the air.

'That was an M-80, I think,' Ben said quietly. 'Last Fourth of July I was in the park and there were these high-school kids that had a couple. They put one of them in a steel trash-can. It made a noise like that.'

'Did it blow a hole in the can, Haystack?' Richie asked.

'No, but it bulged out the side. Looked like there was some little guy inside who just stroked it one. They ran away.'

'The big one was closer,' Eddie said. He also glanced at Bill.

'Do you guys want to shoot these off or not?' Stan asked. He had unbraided about a dozen of the firecrackers and had put the rest neatly back in the waxed paper for later.

'Sure,' Richie said.

'P-P-Put them a-a-away.'

They looked at Bill questioningly, a little scared – it was his abrupt tone more than what he had said.

'P-P-Puh-hut them *a-a-a-away*,' Bill repeated, his face contorting with the effort he was making to get the words out. Spit flew from his lips. 'S-S-Suh-homething's g-g-gonna h-h-happen.'

Eddie licked his lips, Richie shoved his glasses up the sweaty slope of his nose with his thumb, and Ben moved closer to Beverly without even thinking about it.

Stan opened his mouth to say something and then there was another, smaller explosion – another cherry-bomb.

'Ruh-Rocks,' Bill said.

'What, Bill?' Stan asked.

'Ruh-Ruh-*Rocks*. *A-A-Ammo*.' Bill began to pick up stones, stuffing them into his pockets until they bulged. The others stared at him as though he had gone crazy . . . and then Eddie felt sweat break on his forehead. All of a sudden he knew what a malaria attack felt like. He had sensed something like this on the day he and Bill had met Ben (except Eddie, like the others, was already coming to think of Ben as Haystack), the day Henry Bowers had casually bloodied his nose – but this felt worse. This felt like maybe it was going to be Hiroshima time in the Barrens.

Ben started to get rocks, then Richie, moving quickly, not talking now. His glasses slipped all the way off and clicked to the gravelly surface of the ground. He folded them up absently and put them inside his shirt.

'Why did you do that, Richie?' Beverly asked. Her voice sounded thin, too taut.

'Don't know, keed,' Richie said, and went on picking up rocks.

'Beverly, maybe you better, uh, go back toward the dump for awhile,' Ben said. His hands were full of rocks.

'*Shit* on that,' she said. 'Shit all *over* that, Ben Hanscom.' She bent and began to gather rocks herself.

Stan looked at them thoughtfully as they grubbed for rocks like lunatic farmers. Then he began to gather them himself, his lips pressed into a thin and prissy line.

Eddie felt the familiar tightening sensation as his throat began to close up to a pinhole.

Not this time, dammit, he thought suddenly. *Not if my friends need me. Like Bev said, shit all* over *that*.

He also began to gather rocks.

9

Henry Bowers had gotten too big too fast to be either quick or agile under ordinary circumstances, but these circumstances were not ordinary. He was in a frenzy of pain and rage, and these lent him an ephemeral unthinking physical genius. Conscious thought was gone; his mind felt the way a late-summer grassfire looks as dusk comes on, all rose-red and smoke-gray. He took after Mike Hanlon like a bull after a red flag. Mike was following a rudimentary path along the side of the big pit, a path which would eventually lead to the dump, but Henry was too far gone to bother with such niceties as paths; he slammed through the bushes and the brambles on a straight line, feeling neither the tiny cuts inflicted by the thorns nor the slaps of limber bushes striking his face, neck, and arms. The only thing that mattered was the nigger's kinky head, drawing closer. Henry had one of the M–80s in his right hand and a wooden match in his left. When he caught the nigger he was going to strike the match, light the fuse, and stuff that ashcan right down the front of his pants.

Mike knew that Henry was gaining and the others were close on his heels. He tried to push himself faster. He was badly scared now, keeping panic at bay only by a grim effort of will. He had turned his ankle more seriously crossing the tracks than he had thought at first, and now he was limp-skipping along. The crackle and crash of Henry's go-for-broke progress behind him called up unpleasant images of being chased by a killer dog or a rogue bear.

The path opened out just ahead, and Mike more fell than ran into the gravel-pit. He rolled to the bottom, got to his feet, and was halfway across before he realized that there were kids there, six of them. They were spread out in a straight line and there was a funny look on their faces. It wasn't until later, when he'd had a chance to sort out his thoughts, that he realized what was so odd about that look: it was as if they had been expecting him.

'Help,' Mike managed as he limped toward them. He spoke instinctively to the tall boy with the red hair. 'Kids . . . big kids –'

That was when Henry burst into the gravel-pit. He saw the six of them and came to a skidding halt. For a moment his face was marked with uncertainty and he looked back over his shoulder. He saw his troops, and when Henry looked back at the Losers (Mike was now standing beside and slightly behind Bill Denbrough, panting rapidly), he was grinning.

'I know you, kid,' he said, speaking to Bill. He glanced at Richie. 'I know you, too. Where's your glasses, four-eyes?' And before Richie could reply, Henry saw Ben. 'Well, son of a bitch! The Jew and the fatboy are here too! That your girlfriend, fatboy?'

Ben jumped a little, as if goosed.

Just then Peter Gordon pulled up beside Henry. Victor arrived and stood on Henry's other side; Belch and Moose Sadler arrived last. They flanked Peter and Victor, and now the two opposing groups stood facing each other in neat, almost formal lines.

Panting heavily as he spoke and still sounding more than a little like a human bull, Henry said, 'I got bones to pick with a lot of you, but I can let that go for today. I want that nigger. So you little shits buzz off.'

'Right!' Belch said smartly.

'He killed my dog!' Mike cried out, his voice shrill and breaking. 'He said so!'

'You come on over here right now,' Henry said, 'and maybe I won't kill you.'

Mike trembled but did not move.

Speaking softly and clearly, Bill said: 'The B-Barrens are ours. You k-k-kids get out of h-here.'

Henry's eyes widened. It was as if he'd been slapped unexpectedly. 'Who's gonna make me?' he asked. 'You, horsefoot?'

'Uh-Uh-Us,' Bill said. 'We're through t-t-taking your shit, B-B-Bowers. Get ow-ow-out.'

'You stuttering *freak*,' Henry said. He lowered his head and charged.

Bill had a handful of rocks; all of them had a handful except Mike and Beverly, who was only holding one. Bill began to throw at Henry, not hurrying his throws, but chucking hard and with fair accuracy. The first rock missed; the second struck Henry on the shoulder. If the third had missed, Henry might have closed with Bill and wrestled him to the ground, but it didn't miss; it struck Henry's lowered head.

Henry cried out in surprised pain, looked up . . . and was hit four more times: a little *billet-doux* from Richie Tozier on the chest, one from Eddie that ricocheted off his shoulder-blade, one from Stan Uris that struck his shin, and Beverly's one rock, which hit him in the belly.

He looked at them unbelievingly, and suddenly the air was full of whizzing missiles. Henry fell back, that same bewildered, pained expression on his face. '*Come on, you guys!*' he shouted. '*Help me!*'

'Ch-ch-charge them,' Bill said in a low voice, and not waiting to see if they would or not, he ran forward.

They came with him, firing rocks not only at Henry now but at all the others. The big boys were grubbing on the ground for ammunition of their own, but before they could gather much, they had been peppered. Peter Gordon screamed as a rock thrown by Ben glanced off his cheekbone and drew blood. He backed up a few steps, paused, threw a hesitant rock or two back . . . and then fled. He had had enough; things were not done this way on West Broadway.

Henry grabbed up a handful of rocks in a savage sweeping gesture. Most of them, fortunately for the Losers, were pebbles. He threw one of the larger ones at Beverly and it cut her arm. She cried out.

Bellowing, Ben ran for Henry Bowers, who looked around in time to see him coming but not in time to sidestep. Henry was off-balance; Ben was one hundred and fifty trying for one-sixty; the result was no contest. Henry did not go sprawling but flying. He landed on his back and skidded. Ben ran toward him again and was only vaguely aware of a warm, blooming pain in his ear as Belch Huggins nailed him with a rock roughly the size of a golf ball.

Henry was getting groggily to his knees as Ben reached him and kicked him hard, his sneakered foot connecting solidly with Henry's left hip. Henry rolled over heavily on his back. His eyes blazed up at Ben.

'You ain't supposed to throw rocks at girls!' Ben shouted. He could not remember ever in his life feeling so outraged. 'You ain't –'

Then he saw a flame in Henry's hand as Henry popped the wooden match alight. He touched it to the thick fuse of the M–80, which he then threw at Ben's face. Acting with no thought at all, Ben struck the ashcan with the palm of his hand, swinging at it as one would swing a racket at a badminton birdie. The M–80 went back down. Henry saw it coming. His eyes widened and then he rolled away, screaming. The ashcan exploded a split-second later, blackening the back of Henry's shirt and tearing some of it away.

A moment later Ben was hit by Moose Sadler and driven to his knees. His teeth clicked together over his tongue, drawing blood. He blinked around, dazed. Moose was coming toward him, but before he could reach the place where Ben was kneeling, Bill came up behind him and began pelting the big kid with rocks. Moose wheeled around, bellowing.

'You hit me from behind, yellowbelly!' Moose screamed. 'You fuckin dirtyfighter!'

He gathered himself to charge, but Richie joined Bill and also began to fire rocks at Moose. Richie was unimpressed with Moose's rhetoric on the subject of what might or might not constitute yellow-belly behavior; he had seen the five of them chasing one scared kid, and he didn't think that exactly put them up there with King Arthur and the Knights of the Round Table. One of Richie's missiles split the skin above Moose's left eyebrow. Moose howled.

Eddie and Stan Uris moved up to join Bill and Richie. Beverly moved in with them, her arm bleeding but her eyes wildly alight.

Rocks flew. Belch Huggins screamed as one of them clipped his crazy-bone. He began to dance lumbersomely, rubbing his elbow. Henry got to his feet, the back of his shirt hanging in rags, the skin beneath almost miraculously unmarked. Before he could turn around, Ben Hanscom bounced a rock off the back of his head and drove him to his knees again.

It was Victor Criss who did the most damage to the Losers that day, partly because he was a pretty fair fastball pitcher, but mostly – paradoxically – because he was the least emotionally involved. More and more he didn't want to be here. People could get seriously hurt in rockfights; a kid could get his skull split, a mouthful of broken teeth, could even lose an eye. But since he was in it, he was *in* it. He intended to dish out some trouble.

That coolness had allowed him to take an extra thirty seconds and pick up a handful of good-sized rocks. He threw one at Eddie as the Losers re-formed their rough skirmish line, and it struck Eddie on the chin. He fell down, crying, the blood already starting to flow. Ben turned toward him but Eddie was already getting up again, the blood gruesomely bright against his pallid skin, his eyes slitted.

Victor threw at Richie and the rock thudded off Richie's chest. Richie threw back but Vic ducked it easily and threw one sidearm at Bill Denbrough. Bill snapped his head back, but not quite quickly enough; the rock cut his cheek wide open.

Bill turned toward Victor. Their eyes locked, and Victor saw something in the stuttering kid's gaze that scared the hell out of him. Absurdly, the words *I take it back!* trembled behind his lips . . . except that was nothing you said to a little kid. Not if you didn't want your buddies to start ranking you to the dogs and back.

Bill started to walk toward Victor now, and Victor began to walk toward Bill. At the same moment, as if by some telepathic signal, they began to throw rocks at each other, still closing the distance. The fighting flagged around them as the others turned to watch; even Henry turned his head.

Victor ducked and bobbed, but Bill made no such effort. Victor's rocks slammed him in the chest, the shoulder, the stomach. One clipped by his ear. Apparently unshaken by any of this, Bill threw one rock after another, pegging them with murderous force. The third one struck Victor's knee with a brittle chipping sound and Victor uttered a stifled groan. He was out of ammunition. Bill had one rock left. It was smooth and white, shot with quartz, roughly the size and shape of a duck's egg. To Victor Criss it looked very hard.

Bill was less than five feet away from him.

'Y-Y-You g-get ow-out of h-h-here now,' he said, 'or I'm g-going to spuh-puh-lit your h-head o-o-open. I m-mean ih-ih-it.'

Looking into his eyes, Victor saw that he really did. Without another word, he turned and headed back the way Peter Gordon had gone.

Belch and Moose Sadler were looking around uncertainly. Blood trickled from the corner of the Sadler boy's mouth, and blood from a scalp-wound was sheeting down the side of Belch's face.

Henry's mouth worked but no sound came out.

Bill turned toward Henry. 'G-G-Get out,' he said.

'What if I won't?' Henry was trying to sound tough, but Bill could now see a different thing in Henry's eyes. He was scared, and he would go. It should have made Bill feel good – triumphant, even – but he only felt tired.

'I-If you w-won't,' Bill said, 'w-w-we're g-going to muh-move i-in on y-you. I think the s-s-six of u-us can p-put you in the huh-huh-hospital.'

'Seven,' Mike Hanlon said, and joined them. He had a softball-sized rock in each hand. 'Just try me, Bowers. I'd love to.'

'*You fucking NIGGER!*' Henry's voice broke and wavered on the edge of tears. That voice took the last of the fight out of Belch and Moose; they backed away, their remaining rocks dropping from relaxing hands. Belch looked around as if wondering exactly where he might be.

'Get out of our place,' Beverly said.

'Shut up, you cunt,' Henry said. 'You –' Four rocks flew at once, hitting Henry in four different places. He screamed and scrambled backward over the weed-raddled ground, the tatters of his shirt flapping around him. He looked from the grim, old-young faces of the little kids to the frantic ones of Belch and Moose. There was no help there; no help at all. Moose turned away, embarrassed.

Henry got to his feet, sobbing and snuffling through his broken nose. 'I'll kill you all,' he said, and suddenly ran for the path. A moment later he was gone.

'G-G-Go on,' Bill said, speaking to Belch. 'Get ow-out. And d-don't c-c-come down h-here anymore. The B-B-Barrens are ow-ow-ours.'

'You're gonna wish you didn't cross Henry, kid,' Belch said. 'Come on, Moose.'

They started away, heads down, not looking back.

The seven of them stood in a loose semicircle, all of them bleeding somewhere. The apocalyptic rockfight had lasted less than four minutes, but Bill felt as if he had fought his way through all of World War II, both theaters, without so much as a single time-out.

The silence was broken by Eddie Kaspbrak's whooping, whining struggle for air. Ben went toward him, felt the three Twinkies and four Ding-Dongs he had eaten on his way down to the Barrens begin to struggle and churn in his stomach, and ran past Eddie and into the bushes, where he was sick as privately and quietly as he could be.

It was Richie and Bev who went to Eddie. Beverly put an arm around the thin boy's waist while Richie dug his aspirator out of his pocket. 'Bite on this, Eddie,' he said, and Eddie took a hitching, gasping breath as Richie pulled the trigger.

'Thanks,' Eddie managed at last.

Ben came back out of the bushes, blushing, wiping a hand over his mouth. Beverly went over to him and took both of his hands in hers.

'Thanks for sticking up for me,' she said.

Ben nodded, looking at his dirty sneakers. 'Any time, keed,' he said.

One by one they turned to look at Mike, Mike with his dark skin. They looked at him carefully, cautiously, thoughtfully. Mike had felt such curiosity before – there had not been a time in his life when he had not felt it – and he looked back candidly enough.

Bill looked from Mike to Richie. Richie met his eyes. And Bill seemed almost to hear the click – some final part fitting neatly into a machine of unknown intent. He felt ice-chips scatter up his back. *We're all together now*, he thought, and the idea was so strong, so *right*, that for a moment he thought he might have spoken it aloud. But of course there was no need to speak it aloud; he could see it in Richie's eyes, in Ben's, in Eddie's, in Beverly's, in Stan's.

We're all together now, he thought again. *Oh God help us. Now it really starts. Please God, help us.*

'What's your name, kid?' Beverly asked.

'Mike Hanlon.'

'You want to shoot off some firecrackers?' Stan asked, and Mike's grin was answer enough.

CHAPTER FOURTEEN
THE ALBUM

1

As it turns out, Bill isn't the only one; they all bring booze.

Bill has bourbon, Beverly has vodka and a carton of orange juice, Richie a sixpack, Ben Hanscom a bottle of Wild Turkey. Mike has a sixpack in the little refrigerator in the staff lounge.

Eddie Kaspbrak comes in last, holding a small brown bag.

'What you got there, Eddie?' Richie asks. 'Za-Rex or Kool-Aid?'

Smiling nervously, Eddie removes first a bottle of gin and then a bottle of prune juice.

In the thunderstruck silence which follows, Richie says quietly: 'Somebody call for the men in the white coats. Eddie Kaspbrak's finally gone over the top.'

'Gin-and-prune juice happens to be very healthy,' Eddie replies defensively . . . and then they're all laughing wildly, the sound of their mirth echoing and re-echoing in the silent library, rolling up and down the glassed-in hall between the adult library and the Children's Library.

'You go head-on,' Ben says, wiping his streaming eyes. 'You go head-on, Eddie. I bet it really moves the mail, too.'

Smiling, Eddie fills a paper cup three-quarters full of prune juice and then soberly adds two capfuls of gin.

'Oh Eddie, I do love you,' Beverly says, and Eddie looks up, startled but smiling. She gazes up and down the table. 'I love all of you.'

Bill says, 'W-We love you too, B-Bev.'

'Yes,' Ben says. 'We love you.' His eyes widen a little, and he laughs. 'I think we still all love each other . . . Do you know how rare that must be?'

There's a moment of silence, and Mike is really not surprised to see that Richie is wearing his glasses.

'My contacts started to burn and I had to take them out,' Richie says briefly when Mike asks. 'Maybe we should get down to business?'

They all look at Bill then, as they had in the gravel-pit, and Mike thinks: They look at Bill when they need a leader, at Eddie when they need a navigator. Get down to business, what a hell of a phrase that is. Do I tell them that the bodies of the children that were found back then and now weren't sexually molested, not even precisely mutilated, but partially eaten? Do I tell them I've got seven miner's helmets, the kind with strong electric lights set into the front, stored back at my house, one of them for a guy named Stan Uris who couldn't make the scene, as we used to say? Or is it maybe enough just to tell them to go home and get a good night's sleep, because it ends tomorrow or tomorrow night for good – either for It or us?

None of those things have to be said, perhaps, and the reason why they don't has already been stated: they still love one another. Things have changed over the last twenty-seven years, but that, miraculously, hasn't. It is, Mike thinks, our only real hope.

The only thing that really remains is to finish going through it, to complete the job of catching up, of stapling past to present so that the strip of experience forms some half-assed kind of wheel. Yes, Mike thinks, that's it. Tonight the job is to make the wheel; tomorrow we can see if it still turns . . . the way it did when we drove the big kids out of the gravel-pit and out of the Barrens.

'Have you remembered the rest?' *Mike asks Richie.*

Richie swallows some beer and shakes his head. 'I remember you telling us about the bird . . . and about the smoke-hole.' *A grin breaks over Richie's face.* 'I remembered about that walking over here tonight with Bevvie and Ben. What a fucking horror-show that was –'

'Beep-beep, Richie,' *Beverly says, smiling.*

'Well, you know,' *he says, still smiling himself and punching his glasses up on his nose in a gesture that is eerily reminiscent of the old Richie. He winks at Mike.* 'You and me, right, Mikey?'

Mike snorts laughter and nods.

'Miss Scawlett! Miss Scawlett!' *Richie shrieks in his Pickaninny Voice.* 'It's gettin a little wa'am in de smokehouse, Miss Scawlett!'

Laughing, Bill says, 'Another engineering and architectural triumph by Ben Hanscom.'

Beverly nods. 'We were digging out the clubhouse when you brought your father's photograph album to the Barrens, Mike.'

'Oh, Christ!' *Bill says, sitting suddenly bolt-upright.* 'And the pictures –'

Richie nods grimly. 'The same trick as in Georgie's room. Only that time we all saw it.'

Ben says, 'I remembered what happened to the extra silver dollar.'

They all turn to look at him.

'I gave the other three to a friend of mine before I came out here,' Ben says quietly. 'For his kids. I remembered there had been a fourth, but I couldn't remember what happened to it. Now I do.' He looks at Bill. 'We made a silver slug out of it, didn't we? You, me, and Richie. At first we were going to make a silver bullet —'

'You were pretty sure you could do it,' Richie agrees. 'But in the end —'

'We got c-cold fuh-feet.' Bill nods slowly. The memory has fallen naturally into its place, and he hears that same low but distinct *click!* when it happens. *We're getting closer,* he thinks.

'We went back to Neibolt Street,' Richie says. 'All of us.'

'You saved my life, Big Bill,' Ben says suddenly and Bill shakes his head. 'You did, though,' Ben persists, and this time Bill doesn't shake his head. He suspects that maybe he had done just that, although he does not yet remember how . . . and was it him? He thinks maybe Beverly . . . but that is not there. Not yet, anyway.

'Excuse me for a second,' Mike says. 'I've got a sixpack in the back fridge.'

'Have one of mine,' Richie says.

'Hanlon no drinkum white man's beer,' Mike replies. 'Especially not yours, Trashmouth.'

'Beep-beep, Mikey,' Richie says solemnly, and Mike goes to get his beer on a warm wave of their laughter.

He snaps on the light in the lounge; a tacky little room with seedy chairs, a Silex badly in need of scrubbing, and a bulletin board covered with old notices, wage and hour information, and a few New Yorker cartoons now turning yellow and curling up at the edges. He opens the little refrigerator and feels the shock sink into him, bone-deep and icewhite, the way February cold sank into you when February was here and it seemed that April never would be. Blue and orange balloons drift out in a flood, dozens of them, a New Year's Eve bouquet of party-balloons, and he thinks incoherently in the midst of his fear, *All we need is Guy Lombardo tootling away on 'Auld Lang Syne.'* They waft past his face and rise toward the lounge ceiling. He's trying to scream, unable to scream, seeing what had been behind the balloons, what It had popped into the refrigerator beside his beer, as if for a late-night snack after his worthless friends have all told their worthless stories and gone back to their rented beds in this home town that is no longer home.

Mike takes a step backward, his hands going to his face, shutting the vision out. He stumbles over one of the chairs, almost falls, and takes his hands away. It is still there; Stan Uris's severed head beside Mike's sixpack of Bud Light, the head not of a man but of an eleven-year-old boy. The mouth is open in a soundless scream but Mike can see neither teeth nor tongue because the mouth has been stuffed full of feathers. The feathers are a light brown and unspeakably huge. He knows well enough what bird those feathers came from. Oh yes. Oh yes indeed. He had seen the bird in May of 1958 and they had all seen it in early August of 1958 and then, years later, while visiting his dying father, he had found out that Will Hanlon had seen it once, too, after his escape from the fire at the Black Spot. The blood from Stan's tattered neck has dripped down and formed a coagulated pool on the fridge's bottom shelf. It glitters dark ruby-red in the uncompromising glow shed by the fridge bulb.

'Uh . . . uh . . . uh . . .' Mike manages, but no more sound than that can he make. Then the head opens its eyes, and they are the silver-bright eyes of Pennywise the Clown. Those eyes roll in his direction and the head's lips begin to squirm around the mouthful of feathers. It is trying to speak, perhaps trying to deliver prophecy like the oracle in a Greek play.

Just thought I'd join you, Mike, because you can't win without me. You can't win without me and you know it, don't you? You might have had a chance if all of me had shown up, but I just couldn't stand the strain on my all-American brain, if you see what I mean, jellybean. All the six of you can do on your own is hash over some old times and then get yourselves killed. So I thought I'd head you off at the pass. Head you off, get it, Mikey? Get it, old pal? Get it, you fucking scumbag nigger?

You're not real! he screams, but no sound comes out; he is like a TV with the volume control turned all the way down.

Incredibly, grotesquely, the head winks at him.

I'm real, all right. Real as raindrops. And you know what I'm talking about, Mikey. What the six of you are planning to try is like taking off in a jet plane with no landing gear. There's no sense in going up if you can't get back down, is there? No sense in going down if you can't get back up, either. You'll never think of the right riddles and jokes. You'll never make me laugh, Mikey. You've all forgotten how to turn your screams upside-down. Beep-beep, Mikey, what do you say? Remember the bird? Nothing but a sparrow, but say-hey! it was a lulu, wasn't it? Big as a barn, big as one of those silly Japanese movie monsters that used to scare you when you were a little kid. The days when you knew how to turn that bird from your door are gone forever. Believe it, Mikey. If you know how to use *your* head, you'll get out of here, out of Derry, right now. If you don't know how to use it, it'll end up just like this one here. Today's guidepost along the great road of life is use it before you lose it, my good man.

The head rolls over on its face (the feathers in its mouth make a horrid *crumpling sound) and falls out of the refrigerator. It thuks to the floor and rolls toward him like a hideous bowling ball, its blood-matted hair changing places with its grinning face; it rolls toward him leaving a gluey trail of blood and dismembered bits of feather behind, its mouth working around its clot of feathers.*

Beep-beep, Mikey! *it screams as Mike backs madly away from it, hands held out in a warding-off gesture.* Beep-beep, beep-beep, beep-fucking-beep!

*Then there is a sudden loud pop – the sound of a plastic cork thumbed out of a bottle of cheap champagne. The head disappears (*Real, *Mike thinks sickly;* there was nothing supernatural about that pop, anyway; that was the sound of air rushing back into a suddenly vacated space . . . real, oh God, real). *A thin net of blood droplets floats up and then patters back down. No need to clean the lounge, though; Carole will see nothing when she comes in tomorrow, not even if she has to plow her way through the balloons to get to the hotplate and make her first cup of coffee. How handy. He giggles shrilly.*

He looks up and yes, the balloons are still there. The blue ones say: DERRY NIGGERS GET THE BIRD. *The orange ones say:* THE LOSERS ARE STILL LOSING, BUT STANLEY URIS IS FINALLY AHEAD

No sense going up if you can't get back down, *the speaking head had assured him,* no sense going down if you can't get back up. *This latter makes him think again of the stored miner's helmets. And was it true? Suddenly he's thinking about the first day he went down to the Barrens after the rockfight. July 6th, that had been, two days after he had marched in the Fourth of July parade . . . two days after he had seen Pennywise the Clown in person for the first time. It had been after that day in the Barrens, after listening to their stories and then, hesitantly, telling his own, that he had gone home and asked his father if he could look at his photograph album.*

Why exactly had he gone down to the Barrens that July 6th? Had he known he would find them there? It seemed that he had – and not just that they would be there, but where *they would be. They had been talking about a clubhouse of some sort, he remembers, but it had seemed to him that they had been talking about that because there was something else that they didn't know how to talk about.*

Mike looks up at the balloons, not really seeing them now, trying to remember exactly how it had been that day, that hot hot day. Suddenly it seems very important to remember just what had happened, what every nuance had been, what his state of mind had been.

Because that was when everything began to happen. Before that the others had talked about killing It, but there had been no forward motion, no plan. When Mike had come the circle closed, the wheel began to roll. It had

been later that same day that Bill and Richie and Ben went down to the library and began to do serious research on an idea that Bill had had a day or a week or a month before. It had all begun to –

'Mike?' Richie calls from the Reference Room where the others are gathered. 'Did you die in there?'

Almost, *Mike thinks, looking at the balloons, the blood, the feathers inside the fridge.*

He calls back: 'I think you guys better come in here.'

He hears the scrape of their chairs, the mutter of their voices; he hears Richie saying 'Oh Jesus, what's up now?' and another ear, this one in his memory, hears Richie saying something else, and suddenly he remembers what it is he has been searching for; even more, he understands why it has seemed so elusive. The reaction of the others when he stepped into the clearing in the darkest, deepest, and most overgrown part of the Barrens that day had been . . . nothing. No surprise, no questions about how he had found them, no big deal. Ben had been eating a Twinkie, he remembers, Beverly and Richie had been smoking cigarettes, Bill had been lying on his back with his hands behind his head, looking at the sky, Eddie and Stan were looking doubtfully at a series of strings which had been pegged into the ground to form a square of about five feet on a side.

No surprise, no questions, no big deal. He had simply shown up and been accepted. It was as if, without even knowing it, they had been waiting for him. And in that third ear, memory's ear, he hears Richie's Pickaninny Voice raised as it was earlier tonight: 'Lawdy, Miss Clawdy, here come

2

that black chile again! Lawks-a-mussy, I doan know what thisyere Barrens is comin to! Look at that there nappy haid, Big Bill!' Bill didn't even look around; he just went on staring dreamily at the fat summer clouds marching across the sky. He was giving an important question his most careful consideration. Richie was not offended by the lack of attention, however. He pushed onward. 'Jest lookin at that nappy haid makes me b'leeve I needs me another mint joolip! I'se gwinter have it out on the verandah, where it's be a little bit coolah –'

'Beep-beep, Richie,' Ben said from around a mouthful of Twinkie, and Beverly laughed.

'Hi,' Mike said uncertainly. His heart was beating a little too hard, but he was determined to go on with this. He owed his thanks, and his father had told him that you always paid what you owed – and as quick as you could, before the interest mounted up.

Stan looked around. 'Hi,' he said, and then looked back at the square of strings pegged into the center of the clearing. 'Ben, are you sure this is going to work?'

'It'll work,' Ben said. 'Hi, Mike.'

'Want a cigarette?' Beverly asked. 'I got two left.'

'No thank you.' Mike took a deep breath and said, 'I wanted to thank you all again for helping me the other day. Those guys meant to hurt me bad. I'm sorry some of you guys got banged up.'

Bill waved his hand, dismissing it. 'D-D-Don't wuh-wuh-horry a-a-bout it. Th-they've h-had it i-i-in f-for us all y-y-year.' He sat up and looked at Mike with sudden starry interest. 'C-Can I a-ask you s-s-something?'

'I guess so,' Mike said. He sat down gingerly. He had heard such prefaces before. The Denbrough kid was going to ask him what it was like to be a Negro.

But instead Bill said: 'When L-L-Larsen pitched the n-no-h-hitter in the World S-Series two years ago, d-do you think that was just luh-luck?'

Richie dragged deep on his cigarette and started to cough. Beverly pounded him good-naturedly on the back. 'You're just a beginner, Richie, you'll learn.'

'I think it's gonna fall in, Ben,' Eddie said worriedly, looking at the pegged square. 'I don't know how cool I am on the idea of getting buried alive.'

'You're not gonna get buried alive,' Ben said. 'And if you are, just suck your damn old aspirator until someone pulls you out.'

This struck Stanley Uris as deliciously funny. He leaned back on his elbow, his head turned up to the sky, and laughed until Eddie kicked his shin and told him to shut up.

'Luck,' Mike said finally. 'I think any no-hitter's more luck than skill.'

'M-M-Me t-too,' Bill said. Mike waited to see if there was more, but Bill seemed satisfied. He lay down again, laced his hands behind his head again, and went back to studying the clouds as they floated by.

'What are you guys up to?' Mike asked, looking at the square of strings pegged just above the ground.

'Oh, this is Haystack's big idea of the week,' Richie said. 'Last time he flooded out the Barrens and that was pretty good, but this one's a real dinner-winner. This is Dig Your Own Clubhouse Month. Next month –'

'Y-You don't nuh-nuh-need to put B-B-B-Ben d-duh-hown,' Bill said, still looking at the sky. 'It's going to be guh-guh-good.'

'God's sake, Bill, I was just kidding.'

'Suh-Sometimes you k-k-kid too much, Rih-Richie.'

Richie accepted the rebuke silently.

'I still don't get it,' Mike said.

'Well, it's pretty simple,' Ben said. 'They wanted a treehouse, and we could do that, but people have a bad habit of breaking their bones when they fall out of treehouses —'

'Kookie . . . Kookie . . . lend me your bones,' Stan said, and laughed again while the others looked at him, puzzled. Stan did not have much sense of humor, and the bit he did have was sort of peculiar.

'You ees goin loco, senhorr,' Richie said. 'Eees the heat an the *cucarachas*, I theenk.'

'Anyway,' Ben said, 'what we'll do is dig down about five feet in the square I pegged out there. We can't go much deeper than that or we'll hit groundwater, I guess. It's pretty close to the surface down here. Then we'll shore up the sides just to make sure they don't cave in.' He looked significantly at Eddie here, but Eddie was worried.

'Then what?' Mike asked, interested.

'We'll cap off the top.'

'Huh?'

'Put boards over the top of the hole. We can put in a trapdoor or something so we can get in and out, even windows if we want —'

'We'll need some hih-hih-hinges,' Bill said, still looking at the clouds.

'We can get those at Reynolds Hardware,' Ben said.

'Y-You guh-guh-guys have your a-a-allowances,' Bill said.

'I've got five dollars,' Beverly said. 'I saved it up from babysitting.'

Richie immediately began to crawl toward her on his hands and knees. 'I love you, Bevvie,' he said, making dog's eyes at her. 'Will you marry me? We'll live in a pine-studded bungalow —'

'A *what?*' Beverly asked, while Ben watched them with an odd mixture of anxiety, amusement, and concentration.

'A bung-studded pinealow,' Richie said. 'Five bucks is enough, sweetie, you and me and baby makes three —'

Beverly laughed and blushed and moved away from him.

'We sh-share the e-expenses,' Bill said. 'That's why we got a club.'

'So after we cap the hole with boards,' Ben went on, 'we put down this heavy-duty glue – Tangle-Track, they call it – and put the sods back on. Maybe sprinkle it with pine needles. We could be down there and people – people like Henry Bowers – could walk right over us and not even know we were there.'

'You thought of that?' Mike said. 'Jeez, that's great!'

Ben smiled. It was his turn to blush.

Bill sat up suddenly and looked at Mike. 'You w-w-want to heh-help?'

'Well . . . sure,' Mike said. 'That'd be fun.'

A look passed among the others – Mike felt it as well as saw it. *There are seven of us here*, Mike thought, and for no reason at all he shivered.

'When are you going to break ground?'

'P-P-hretty s-soon,' Bill said, and Mike knew – knew – that it wasn't just Ben's underground clubhouse Bill was talking about. Ben knew it, too. So did Richie, Beverly, and Eddie. Stan Uris had stopped smiling. 'W-We're g-gonna start this pruh-huh-hoject pretty suh-suh-soon.'

There was a pause then, and Mike was suddenly aware of two things: they wanted to say something, tell him something . . . and he was not entirely sure he wanted to hear it. Ben had picked up a stick and was doodling aimlessly in the dirt, his hair hiding his face. Richie was gnawing at his already ragged fingernails. Only Bill was looking directly at Mike.

'Is something wrong?' Mike asked uneasily.

Speaking very slowly, Bill said: 'W-W-We're a cluh-club. Y-You can be in the club if you w-w-want, but y-y-you have to kee-keep our see-see-secrets.'

'You mean, like the clubhouse?' Mike asked, now more uneasy than ever. 'Well, sure –'

'We've got another secret, kid,' Richie said, still not looking at Mike. 'And Big Bill says we've got something more important to do this summer than digging underground clubhouses.'

'He's right, too,' Ben added.

There was a sudden, whistling gasp. Mike jumped. It was only Eddie, blasting off. Eddie looked at Mike apologetically, shrugged, and then nodded.

'Well,' Mike said finally, 'don't keep me in suspense. Tell me.'

Bill was looking at the others. 'I-Is there a-a-anyone who d-doesn't want him in the cluh-club?'

No one spoke or raised a hand.

'W-Who wants to t-tell?' Bill asked.

There was another long pause, and this time Bill didn't break it. At last Beverly sighed and looked up at Mike.

'The kids who have been killed,' she said. 'We know who's been doing it, and it's not human.'

3

They told him, one by one: the clown on the ice, the leper under the porch, the blood and voices from the drain, the dead boys in the Standpipe. Richie told about what had happened when he and Bill went back to Neibolt Street, and Bill spoke last, telling about the school photo that had moved, and the picture he had stuck his hand into. He finished by explaining that it had killed his brother Georgie, and that the Losers' Club was dedicated to killing the monster . . . whatever the monster really was.

Mike thought later, going home that night, that he should have listened with disbelief mounting into horror and finally run away as fast as he could, not looking back, convinced either that he was being put on by a bunch of white kids who didn't like black folks or that he was in the presence of six authentic lunatics who had in some way caught their lunacy from each other, the way everyone in the same class could catch a particularly virulent cold.

But he didn't run, because in spite of the horror, he felt a strange sense of comfort. Comfort and something else, something more elemental: a feeling of coming home. *There are seven of us here*, he thought again as Bill finally finished speaking.

He opened his mouth, not sure of what he was going to say.

'I've seen the clown,' he said.

'What?' Richie and Stan asked together, and Beverly turned her head so quickly that her pony-tail flipped from her left shoulder to her right.

'I saw him on the Fourth,' Mike said slowly, speaking to Bill mostly. Bill's eyes, sharp and utterly concentrated, were on his, demanding that he go on. 'Yes, on the Fourth of July . . .' He trailed off momentarily, thinking: *But I knew him. I knew him because that wasn't the first time I saw him. And it wasn't the first time I saw something . . . something wrong.*

He thought of the bird then, the first time he'd really allowed himself to think of it – except in nightmares – since May. He had

thought he was going crazy. It was a relief to find out he wasn't crazy
. . . but it was still a scary relief. He wet his lips.

'Go on,' Bev said impatiently. 'Hurry up.'

'Well, the thing is, I was in the parade. I —'

'I saw you,' Eddie said. 'You were playing the saxophone.'

'Well, it's actually a trombone,' Mike said. 'I play with the
Neibolt Church School Band. Anyway, I saw the clown. He was
handing out balloons to kids on the three-way corner downtown. He
was just like Ben and Bill said. Silver suit, orange buttons, white
make-up on his face, big red smile. I don't know if it was lipstick or
make-up, but it looked like blood.'

The others were nodding, excited now, but Bill only went on
looking at Mike closely. 'O-O-Orange tufts of h-h-hair?' he asked
Mike, making them unconsciously over his own head with his fingers.

Mike nodded.

'Seeing him like that . . . it scared me. And while I was looking
at him, he turned around and waved at me, like he'd read my mind,
or my feelings, or whatever you call it. And that . . . like, scared me
worse. I didn't know why then, but he scared me so bad for a couple
of seconds I couldn't play my 'bone anymore. All the spit in my mouth
dried up and I felt . . .' He glanced briefly at Beverly. He remembered
it all so clearly now, how the sun had suddenly seemed intolerably
dazzling on the brass of his horn and the chrome of the cars, the music
too loud, the sky too blue. The clown had raised one white-gloved
hand (the other was full of balloon strings) and had waved slowly back
and forth, his bloody grin too red and too wide, a scream turned
upside-down. He remembered how the flesh of his testicles had begun
to crawl, how his bowels had suddenly felt all loose and hot, as if he
might suddenly drop a casual load of shit into his pants. But he couldn't
say any of that in front of Beverly. You didn't say stuff like that in
front of girls, even if they were the sort of girls you could say things
like 'bitch' and 'bastard' in front of. '. . . I felt scared,' he finished,
feeling that was too weak, but not knowing how to say the rest. But
they were nodding as if they understood, and he felt an indescribable
relief wash through him. Somehow that clown looking at him, smiling
his red smile, his white-gloved hand penduluming slowly back and
forth . . . that had been worse than having Henry Bowers and the rest
after him. Ever so much worse.

'Then we were past,' Mike went on. 'We marched up Main
Street Hill. And I saw him *again*, handing out balloons to kids. Except
a lot of them didn't want to take them. Some of the little ones were

crying. I couldn't figure out how he could have gotten up there so fast. I thought to myself that there must be two of them, you know, both of them dressed the same way. A team. But then he turned around and waved to me again and I knew it was him. It was the same man.'

'He's not a man,' Richie said, and Beverly shuddered. Bill put his arm around her for a moment and she looked at him gratefully.

'He waved to me . . . and then he winked. Like we had a secret. Or like . . . like maybe he knew I'd recognized him.'

Bill dropped his arm from Beverly's shoulders. 'You *reh-reh-rehrecognized* him?'

'I think so,' Mike said. 'I have to check something before I say it's for sure. My father's got some pictures . . . He collects them . . . Listen, you guys play down here a lot, don't you?'

'Sure,' Ben said. 'That's why we're building a clubhouse.'

Mike nodded. 'I'll check and see if I'm right. If I am, I can bring the pictures.'

'O-O-Old pic-pictures?' Bill asked.

'Yes.'

'W-W-What else?' Bill asked.

Mike opened his mouth and then closed it again. He looked around at them uncertainly and then said, 'You'd think I was crazy. Crazy or lying.'

'D-Do y-y-you th-think we're cruh-cruh-crazy?'

Mike shook his head.

'You bet we're not,' Eddie said. 'I got a lot wrong with me, but I'm not bughouse. I don't think.'

'No,' Mike said. 'I don't think you're crazy.'

'Well, we-we won't th-think you're cruh-cruh . . . nuts, e-e-either,' Bill said.

Mike looked them all over, cleared his throat, and said: 'I saw a bird. Couple, three months ago. I saw a bird.'

Stan Uris looked at Mike. 'What kind of a bird?'

Speaking more reluctantly than ever Mike said: 'It looked like a sparrow, sort of, but it also looked like a robin. It had an orange chest.'

'Well, what's so special about a bird?' Ben asked. 'There are lots of birds in Derry.' But he felt uneasy, and looking at Stan, he felt sure that Stan was remembering what had happened in the Standpipe, and how he had somehow stopped it from happening by shouting out the names of birds. But he forgot all about that and everything else when Mike spoke again.

'This bird was bigger than a housetrailer,' he said.

He looked at their shocked, amazed faces. He waited for their laughter, but none came. Stan looked as if someone had clipped him with a brick. His face had gone so pale it was the color of muted November sunlight.

'I swear it's true,' Mike said. 'It was a giant bird, like one of those birds in the monster-movies that are supposed to be prehistoric.'

'Yeah, like in *The Giant Claw*,' Richie said. He thought the bird in that had been sort of fake-looking, but by the time it got to New York he had still been excited enough to spill his popcorn over the balcony railing at the Aladdin. Foxy Foxworth would have kicked him out, but the movie was over by then anyway. Sometimes you got the shit kicked out of you, but as Big Bill said, sometimes you won one, too.

'But it didn't look prehistoric,' Mike said. 'And it didn't look like one of those whatdoyoucallums the Greeks and Romans made up stories about —'

'Ruh-Ruh-Rocs?' Bill suggested.

'Right, I guess so. It wasn't like those, either. It was just like a combination robin and sparrow. The two most common birds you see.' He laughed a little wildly.

'W-W-Where —' Bill began.

'Tell us,' Beverly said simply, and after a moment to collect his thoughts, Mike did. And telling it, watching their faces grow concerned and scared but not disbelieving or derisive, he felt an incredible weight lift from his chest. Like Ben with his mummy or Eddie with his leper and Stan with the drowned boys, he had seen a thing that would have driven an adult insane, not just with terror but with the walloping force of an unreality too great to be explained away or, lacking any rational explanation, simply ignored. Elijah's face had been burned black by the light of God's love, or so Mike had read; but Elijah had been an old man when it happened, and maybe that made a difference. Hadn't one of those other Bible fellows, this one little more than a kid, actually wrestled an angel to a draw?

He had seen it and he had gone on with his life; he had integrated the memory into his view of the world. He was still young enough so that view was tremendously wide. But what had happened that day had nonetheless haunted his mind's darker corners, and sometimes in his dreams he ran from that grotesque bird as it printed its shadow on him from above. Some of these dreams he remembered and some he did not, but they were there, shadows which moved by themselves.

How little of it he had forgotten and how greatly it had troubled him (as he went about his daily round: helping his father, going to school, riding his bike, doing errands for his mother, waiting for the black groups to come on *American Bandstand* after school) was perhaps measurable in only one way – the relief he felt in sharing it with the others. As he did, he realized it was the first time he had even allowed himself to think of it fully since that early morning by the Canal, when he had seen those odd grooves . . . and the blood.

4

Mike told the story of the bird at the old Ironworks and how he had run into the pipe to escape it. Later on that afternoon, three of the Losers – Ben, Richie, Bill – walked toward the Derry Public Library. Ben and Richie were keeping a close watch for Bowers and Company, but Bill only looked at the sidewalk, frowning, lost in thought. About an hour after telling them his story Mike had left them, saying his father wanted him home by four to pick peas. Beverly had to do some marketing and fix dinner for her father, she said. Both Eddie and Stan had their own things to do. But before they broke up for the day they began digging what was to become – if Ben was right – their underground clubhouse. To Bill (and to all of them, he suspected), the groundbreaking had seemed an almost symbolic act. They had begun. Whatever it was they were supposed to do as a group, as a *unit*, they had begun.

Ben asked Bill if he believed Mike Hanlon's story. They were passing Derry Community House and the library was just ahead, a stone oblong comfortably shaded by elms a century old and as yet untouched by the Dutch Elm disease that would later plague and thin them.

'Yeah,' Bill said. 'I th-think it was the truh-hooth. C-C-Crazy, but true. What about you, Ruh-Ruh-Richie?'

Richie nodded. 'Yeah. I hate to believe it, if you know what I mean, but I guess I do. You remember what he said about the bird's tongue?'

Bill and Ben nodded. Orange fluffs on it.

'That's the kicker,' Richie said. 'It's like some comic-book villain. Lex Luthor or the Joker or someone like that. It always leaves a trademark.'

Bill nodded thoughtfully. It *was* like some comic-book villain. Because they saw it that way? Thought of it that way? Yes, perhaps so. It was kid's stuff, but it seemed that was what this thing thrived on – kid's stuff.

They crossed the street to the library side.

'I a-a-asked Stuh-Stuh-Stan i-if he e-ever h-h-heard of a buh-bird l-like that,' Bill said. 'Nuh-nuh-not n-necessarily a b-b-big wuh-wuh-one, but j-just a-a-a –'

'A *real* one?' Richie suggested.

Bill nodded. 'H-He suh-said there m-m-might be a buh-bird like that in Suh-houth America or A-A-A-Africa, but nuh-nuh-not a-around h-h-here.'

'He didn't believe it, then?' Ben asked.

'H-H-He buh-believed i-i-it,' Bill said. And then he told them something else Stan had suggested when Bill walked with him back to where Stan had left his bike. Stan's idea was that nobody else could have seen that bird before Mike told them that story. Something else, maybe, but not that bird, because the bird was Mike Hanlon's personal monster. But now . . . why, now that bird was the property of the whole Losers' Club, wasn't it? *Any* of them might see it. It might not look exactly the same; Bill might see it as a crow, Richie as a hawk, Beverly as a golden eagle, for all Stan knew – but It could be a bird to all of them now. Bill told Stan that if that was true, then any of them might see the leper, the mummy, or possibly the dead boys.

'Which means we ought to do something pretty soon if we're going to do anything at all,' Stan had replied. 'It knows . . .'

'Wuh-What?' Bill had asked sharply. 'Eh-Everything we nuh-know?'

'Man, if It knows that, we're sunk,' Stan had answered. 'But you can bet It knows *we* know about *It*. I think It'll try to get us. Are you still thinking about what we talked about yesterday?'

'Yes.'

'I wish I could go with you.'

'Buh-Buh-Ben and Rih-Richie w-w-will. Ben's really s-s-smart, and Rih-Rih-Richie is, too, when he ih-isn't fucking o-off.'

Now, standing outside the library, Richie asked Bill exactly what it was he had in mind. Bill told them, speaking slowly so he wouldn't stutter too badly. The idea had been circling in his mind for the last two weeks, but it had taken Mike's story of the bird to crystallize it.

What did you do if you wanted to get rid of a bird?

Well, shooting it was pretty goddam final.

What did you do if you wanted to get rid of a monster? Well, the movies suggested that shooting it with a silver bullet was pretty goddam final.

Ben and Richie listened to this respectfully enough. Then Richie asked, 'How do you get a silver bullet, Big Bill? Send away for it?'

'Very fuh-fuh-funny. We'll have to m-m-make it.'

'How?'

'I guess that's what we're at the library to find out,' Ben said. Richie nodded and pushed his glasses up on his nose. Behind them, his eyes were sharp and thoughtful . . . but doubtful, Bill thought. He felt doubtful himself. At least there was no foolishness in Richie's eyes, and that was a step in the right direction.

'You thinking about your dad's Walther?' Richie asked. 'The one we took to Neibolt Street?'

'Yes,' Bill said.

'Even if we could really make silver bullets,' Richie said, 'where would we get the silver?'

'Let me worry about that,' Ben said quietly.

'Well . . . okay,' Richie said. 'We'll let Haystack worry about that. Then what? Neibolt Street again?'

Bill nodded. 'Nee-Nee-Neibolt Street a-a-again. And then we buh-blow its fucking h-h-head o-off.'

The three of them stood there a moment longer, looking at each other solemnly, and then they went into the library.

5

'Sure an begorrah, it's that black feller again!' Richie cried in his Irish Cop Voice.

A week had passed; it was nearly mid July and the underground clubhouse was almost finished.

'Top o the mornin to ye, Mr O'Hanlon, sor! And a foine, foine day it promises to be, foine as pertaters a-growin, as me old mither used to –'

'So far as I know, noon is the top of the morning, Richie,' Ben said, popping up in the hole, 'and noon was two hours ago.' He and Richie had been putting in shoring around the sides of the hole. Ben had taken off his sweatshirt because the day was hot and the work was hard. His tee-shirt was gray with sweat and stuck to his chest and pouch of a stomach. He seemed remarkably unselfconscious of the way he looked, but Mike guessed that if Ben heard Beverly coming, he would be inside that baggy sweatshirt again before you could say puppy love.

'Don't be so picky – you sound like Stan the Man,' Richie said. He had gotten out of the hole five minutes before because, he told Ben, it was time for a cigarette break.

'I thought you said you didn't have any cigarettes,' Ben had said.

'I don't,' Richie had replied, 'but the principle remains the same.'

Mike had his father's photograph album under his arm. 'Where is everybody?' he asked. He knew Bill had to be somewhere around, because he had left his own bike parked under the bridge near Silver.

'Bill and Eddie went down to the dump about half an hour ago to liberate some more boards,' Richie said. 'Stanny and Bev went down to Reynolds Hardware to get hinges. I don't know what the frock Haystack's up to down there – up to down there, ha-ha, you get it? – but it's probably no good. Boy needs someone to keep an eye on him, you know. By the way, you owe us twenty-three cents if you still want to be in this club. Your share of the hinges.'

Mike switched the album from his right arm to his left and dug into his pocket. He counted out twenty-three cents (leaving a grand total of one dime in his own personal treasury) and handed it over to Richie. Then he walked over to the hole and looked in.

Except it really wasn't a hole anymore. The sides had been neatly squared off. Each side had been shored up. The boards were all mongrels, but Ben, Bill, and Stan had done a good job of sizing them with tools from Zack Denbrough's shop (and Bill had been at great pains to make sure every tool was returned every night, and in the same condition as when it was taken). Ben and Beverly had nailed cross-pieces between the supports. The hole still made Eddie a little nervous, but that was Eddie's nature. Piled carefully to one side were squares of sod which would later be glued to the top.

'I think you guys know what you're doing,' Mike said.

'Sure,' Ben said, and pointed to the album. 'What you got?'

'My father's Derry album,' Mike said. 'He collects old pictures and clippings about the town. It's his hobby. I was looking through it a couple of days ago – I told you I thought I'd seen that clown before. And I did. In here. So I brought it down.' He was too ashamed to add that he had not dared to ask his father's permission to do this. Afraid of the questions to which such a request might lead, he had taken it from the house like a thief while his father planted potatoes in the west field and his mother hung clothes in the back yard. 'I thought you guys ought to take a look, too.'

'Well, let's see,' Richie said.

'I'd like to wait until everybody's here. It might be better.'

'Okay.' Richie was, in truth, not that anxious to look at more pictures of Derry, in this or any other album. Not after what had happened in Georgie's room. 'You want to help me and Ben with the rest of the shoring?'

'You bet.' Mike put his father's album down carefully, far enough from the hole so it wouldn't be pelted with flying dirt, and took Ben's shovel.

'Dig right here,' Ben said, showing Mike the spot. 'Go down about a foot. Then I'll set a board in and hold it flush against the side while you shovel the dirt back in.'

'Good plan, man,' Richie said sagely from where he sat on the edge of the excavation with his sneakers dangling down.

'What's wrong with *you?*' Mike asked.

'Got a bone in my leg,' Richie said comfortably.

'How's your project with Bill going?' Mike stopped long enough to strip off his shirt and then began to dig. It was hot down here, even in the Barrens. Crickets hummed sleepily like summer clocks in the brush.

'Well . . . not too bad,' Richie said, and Mike thought he flashed Ben a mildly warning look. 'I guess.'

'Why don't you play your radio, Richie?' Ben asked. He slipped a board into the hole Mike had dug and held it there. Richie's transistor was hung by the strap in its accustomed place, on the thick branch of a nearby shrub.

'Batteries are worn out,' Richie said. 'You had to have my last twenty-five cents for hinges, remember? Cruel, Haystack, very cruel. After all the things I've done for you. Besides, all I can only get down here is WABI and they only play pansy rock.'

'Huh?' Mike asked.

'Haystack thinks Tommy Sands and Pat Boone sing rock and roll,' Richie said, 'but that's because he's ill. *Elvis* sings rock and roll. *Ernie K. Doe* sings rock and roll. *Carl Perkins* sings rock and roll. Bobby Darin. Buddy Holly. "Ah-ow Peggy . . . my Peggy Suh-uh-oo . . ."'

'*Please*, Richie,' Ben said.

'Also,' Mike said, leaning on his shovel, 'there's Fats Domino, Chuck Berry, Little Richard, Shep and the Limelights, LaVerne Baker, Frankie Lymon and the Teenagers, Hank Ballard and the Midnighters, the Coasters, the Isley Brothers, the Crests, the Chords, Stick McGhee –'

They were looking at him with such amazement that Mike laughed.

'You lost me after Little Richard,' Richie said. He liked Little Richard, but if he had a secret rock-and-roll hero that summer it was Jerry Lee Lewis. His mom had happened to come into the living room while Jerry Lee was performing on *American Bandstand*. This was at the point in his act where Jerry Lee actually climbed onto his piano and played it upside down with his hair hanging in his face. He had been singing 'High School Confidential.' For a moment Richie believed his mom was going to faint. She didn't, but she was so traumatized by what she had seen that she talked at dinner that night about sending Richie to one of those military-type camps for the rest of the summer. Now Richie shook his hair down over his eyes and began to sing: 'Come on over baby all the cats are at the high school rockin –'

Ben began to stagger around the hole, grasping his large belly and pretending to puke. Mike held his nose, but he was laughing so hard tears squirted out of his eyes.

'What's wrong?' Richie demanded. 'I mean, what *ails* you guys? That was *good*! I mean, that was really *good*!'

'Oh man,' Mike said, and now he was laughing so hard he could barely talk. 'That was priceless. I mean, that was really priceless.'

'Negroes have no taste,' Richie said. 'I think it even says so in the Bible.'

'Yo mamma,' Mike said, laughing harder than ever. When Richie asked, with honest bewilderment, what *that* meant, Mike sat down with a thump and rocked back and forth, howling and holding his stomach.

'You probably think I'm jealous,' Richie said. 'You probably think I *want* to be a Negro.'

Now Ben also fell down, laughing wildly. His whole body rippled and quaked alarmingly. His eyes bulged. 'No more, Richie,' he managed. 'I'm gonna shit my pants. I'm gonna d-d-die if you don't stuh-stop –'

'I *don't* want to be a Negro,' Richie said. 'Who wants to wear pink pants and live in Boston and buy pizza by the slice? I want to be Jewish like Stan. I want to own a pawnshop and sell people switchblades and plastic dog-puke and used guitars.'

Ben and Mike were now actually screaming with laughter. Their laughter echoed through the green and jungly ravine that was the misnamed Barrens, causing birds to take wing and squirrels to freeze momentarily on limbs. It was a young sound, penetrating, lively, vital, unsophisticated, free. Almost every living thing within range of that sound reacted to it in some way, but the thing which had tumbled out of a wide concrete drain and into the upper Kenduskeag was not living. The previous afternoon there had been a sudden driving thunderstorm (the clubhouse-to-be had not been much affected – since digging operations had begun, Ben had covered the hole carefully each evening with a ragged piece of tarpaulin Eddie had scrounged from behind Wally's Spa; it smelled painty but it did the job), and the stormdrains under Derry had run with violent water for two or three hours. It was that spate of water that had pushed this unpleasant baggage into the sun for the flies to find.

It was the body of a nine-year-old named Jimmy Cullum. Except for the nose, his face was gone. There was a churned and featureless mess where it had been. This raw meat was dotted with deep black marks that perhaps only Stan Uris would have recognized for what they were: pecks. Pecks made by a very large beak.

Water rilled over Jimmy Cullum's muddy chino pants. His white hands floated like dead fish. They had also been pecked, although not as badly. His paisley shirt ballooned out and collapsed back, ballooned out and collapsed back, like a bladder.

Bill and Eddie, loaded down with boards scrounged from the dump, crossed the Kenduskeag by stepping-stones less than forty yards from the body. They heard Richie, Ben, and Mike laughing, smiled a little themselves, and hurried past the unseen ruin of Jimmy Cullum to see what was so funny.

6

They were *still* laughing as Bill and Eddie came into the clearing, sweating under their load of lumber. Even Eddie, usually as pale as cheese, had some color in his face. They dropped the new boards on the almost depleted supply-pile. Ben climbed out of the hole to inspect them.

'Good deal!' he said. 'Wow! Great!'

Bill collapsed to the ground. 'Can I h-have my heart a-a-attack now or do I h-have to wuh-wait until luh-hater?'

'Have it later,' Ben said absently. He had brought a few tools of his own down to the Barrens and was now going over the new boards carefully, pounding out nails and removing screws. He tossed one aside because it was splintered. Rapping on another returned a dull punky sound in at least three places, and he also tossed that one aside. Eddie sat on a pile of dirt, watching him. He took a honk on his aspirator as Ben pulled a rusty nail from a board with the claw end of his hammer. The nail squealed like some small unpleasant animal that had been stepped on and didn't like it.

'You can get tetanus if you cut yourself on a rusty nail,' Eddie informed Ben.

'Yeah?' Richie said. 'What's titnuss? Sounds like a woman's disease.'

'You're a bird,' Eddie said. 'It's *tetanus*, not *titnuss*, and it means lock jaw. There's these special microbes that grow in rust, see, and if you cut yourself they can get inside your body and, um, fuck up your nerves.' Eddie went an even darker red and took another fast honk on his aspirator.

'Lock jaw, Jesus,' Richie said, impressed. 'That sounds mean.'

'You bet. First your jaw locks up so tight you can't open your mouth, not even to eat. They have to cut a hole in your cheek and feed you liquids through a tube.'

'Oh man,' Mike said, standing up in the hole. His eyes were wide, the corneas very white in his brown face. 'For sure?'

'My mom told me,' Eddie said. 'Then your throat locks up and you can't eat anymore and you starve to death.'

They contemplated this horror in silence.

'There's no cure,' Eddie amplified.

More silence.

'So,' Eddie said briskly, 'I always watch out for rusty nails and shit like that. I had to have a tetanus shot once and it really hurt.'

'So why'd you go to the dump with Bill and bring all this crap back?' Richie asked.

Eddie glanced briefly at Bill, who was looking into the clubhouse, and there was all the love and hero-worship in that gaze needed to answer such a question but Eddie said softly, 'Some stuff has to be done even if there *is* a risk. That's the first important thing I ever found out I didn't find out from my mother.'

A further silence, not quite uncomfortable, followed. Then Ben went back to pounding out rusty nails, and after awhile Mike Hanlon joined him.

Richie's transistor, robbed of its voice (at least until Richie's allowance came in or he found a lawn to mow), swung from its low branch in a mild breeze. Bill had time to reflect upon how odd all this was, how odd and how perfect, that they should all be here this summer. There were kids he knew visiting relatives. Kids he knew who were off on vacations at Disneyland in California or on Cape Cod or, in the case of one chum, an unimaginably distant-sounding place with the queer but somehow evocative name of Gstaad. There were kids at church camp, kids at Scout camp, kids at rich-kid camps where you could learn to swim and play golf, camps where you learned to say 'Hey, good one!' instead of 'Fuck you!' when your opponent got a killer serve past you at tennis; kids whose parents had simply taken them AWAY. Bill could understand that. He knew some kids who wanted to go AWAY, frightened by the boogeyman stalking Derry this summer, but suspected there were more parents frightened by that boogeyman. People who had planned to take their vacations at home suddenly decided to go AWAY

(*Gstaad? was that in Sweden? Argentina? Spain?*)

instead. It was a little like the polio scare of 1956, when four kids who went swimming in the O'Brian Memorial Pool had gotten the disease. Grownups – a word absolutely synonymous in Bill's mind with mothers and fathers – had decided then, as now, that AWAY was better. Safer. Anyone able to clear out had cleared. Bill understood AWAY, and he could muse over a word of such fabulous wonder as Gstaad, but wonder was cold comfort compared with desire; Gstaad was AWAY; Derry was desire.

And none of us have gone AWAY, he thought, watching as Ben and Mike pounded used nails out of used boards, as Eddie strolled off into the bushes to take a whiz (you had to go as soon as you could, in order to avoid seriously straining your bladder, he told Bill once, but you also had to watch out for poison ivy, because who needed a case of *that* on your pecker). *We're all here in Derry. No camp, no relatives, no vacations, no AWAY. All right here. Present and accounted for.*

'There's a door down there,' Eddie said, zipping his fly as he came back.

'Hope you shook off, Eds,' Richie said. 'If you don't shake off each time, you can get cancer. My mom told me so.'

Eddie looked startled, thinly worried, and then saw Richie's grin. He withered him (or tried to) with a babies-must-play look and then said, 'It was too big for us to carry. But Bill said if all of us went down we could get it up here.'

'Of course, you can never shake off *completely*,' Richie went on. 'You want to know what a wise man once told me, Eds?'

'No,' Eddie said, 'and I don't want you to call me Eds anymore, Richie. I mean, I'm sincere. I don't call you Dick, as in "You got any gum on ya, Dick?", so I don't see why –'

'This wise man,' Richie said, 'told me this: "No matter how

much you squirm and dance, the last two drops go in your pants."
And that's why there's so much cancer in the world, Eddie my love.'

'The reason there's so much cancer in the world is because nerds
like you and Beverly Marsh smoke cigarettes,' Eddie said.

'Beverly is not a nerd,' Ben said in a forbidding voice. 'You just
watch what you say, Trashmouth.'

'Beep-beep, you g-guys,' Bill said absently. 'And speaking of
B-B-Beverly, she's pretty struh-struh-strong. She could h-h-help get
that duh-door.'

Ben asked what kind of door it was.

'Muh-Muh-hogany, I th-think.'

'Somebody threw out a *mahogany door*?' Ben asked, surprised but
not unbelieving.

'People throw out *everything*,' Mike said. 'That dump? It kills me
to go down there. I mean it *kills* me.'

'Yeah,' Ben agreed. 'A lot of that stuff could be fixed up easy.
And there are people in China and South America with nothing. That's
what *my* mother says.'

'There's people with nothing right here in Maine, Sunny Jim,'
Richie said grimly.

'W-W-What's th-this?' Bill asked, noticing the album Mike had
brought. Mike told him, saying he would show them the picture of
the clown when Stan and Beverly got back with the hinges.

Bill and Richie exchanged a look.

'What's wrong?' Mike asked. 'Is it what happened in your brother's room, Bill?'

'Y-Yeah,' Bill said, and would say no more.

They took turns working on the hole until Stan and Beverly
came back, each with a brown paper bag containing hinges. As Mike
talked, Ben sat crosslegged, tailor-fashion, and made glassless windows
that would swing open and shut in two of the long boards. Perhaps
only Bill noticed how quickly and easily his fingers moved; how adept
and knowing they were, like surgeon's fingers. Bill admired that.

'Some of these pictures go back a hundred years, my dad said,'
Mike told them, holding the album on his lap. 'He gets them at those
sales people have in their yards, and at secondhand shops. Sometimes
he buys them or trades other collectors for them. Some of them are
stereoscopes – there's two of them just the same on a long card, and
when you look at them through this thing like binoculars, it looks like
one picture, only in 3-D. Like *House of Wax* or *The Creature from the
Black Lagoon*.'

'Why does he like all that stuff?' Beverly asked. She was wearing ordinary Levi's but she had done something amusing to the cuffs, blousing them out with a bright paisley material for the final four inches so that they looked like pants out of some sailor's whimsy.

'Yeah,' Eddie said. 'Most of the time, Derry's pretty boring.'

'Well, I don't know for sure, but I think it's because he wasn't born here,' Mike said diffidently. 'It's like – I don't know – like it's all new to him, or like, you know, if you came in during the middle of a movie –'

'Sh-sh-sure, you'd want to see the s-start,' Bill said.

'Yeah,' Mike said. 'There's a lot of history lying around in Derry. I kind of like it. And I think some of it has to do with this thing – this It, if you want to call it that.'

He looked at Bill and Bill nodded, his eyes thoughtful.

'So I was looking through it after the Fourth of July parade because I *knew* I'd seen that clown before. I knew it. And look.'

He opened the book, thumbed through it, then handed it to Ben, who was sitting on his right.

'D-D-Don't t-t-touch the puh-puh-pages!' Bill said, and there was such urgency in his voice that they all jumped. He had fisted the hand he had cut reaching into Georgie's album, Richie saw. Fisted it into a tight, protective knot.

'Bill's right,' Richie said, and that subdued, totally un-Richielike voice was a powerful convincer. 'Be careful. It's like Stan said. If we saw it happen, you guys could see it happen, too.'

'*Feel* it,' Bill added grimly.

The album went from hand to hand, each of them holding the book gingerly, by the edges, as if it were old dynamite sweating big beads of nitro.

It came back to Mike. He opened it to one of the first pages.

'Daddy says there's no way to date that one, but it's probably from the early or mid-seventeen-hundreds,' Mike said. 'He repaired a guy's bandsaw for a box of old books and pictures. That was one of them. He says it might be worth forty bucks or even more.'

The picture was a woodcut, the size of a large postcard. When Bill's turn came to look at it, he was relieved to see that Mike's father had the kind of album where the pictures were under a protective plastic sheet. He looked, fascinated, and he thought: *There. I'm seeing him – or It. Really seeing. That's the face of the enemy.*

The picture showed a funny fellow juggling oversized bowling pins in the middle of a muddy street. There were a few houses on either side of the street, and a few huts that Bill guessed were stores, or trading posts, or whatever they called them back then. It didn't look like Derry at all, except for the Canal. *It* was there, neatly cobbled on both sides. In the upper background, Bill could see a team of mules on a towpath, dragging a barge.

There was a group of maybe half a dozen kids gathered around the funny fellow. One of them was wearing a pastoral straw hat. Another had a hoop and a stick to roll it with. Not the sort of stick that would come with a hoop that you bought today in a Woolworth's; it was a branch from a tree. Bill could see the bare knobs on it where smaller branches had been lopped off with a knife or a hatchet. *That baby wasn't made in Taiwan or Korea*, he thought, fascinated by this boy who could have been him if he'd been born four or five generations before.

The funny fellow had a huge grin on his face. He wore no make-up (except to Bill his whole *face* looked like make-up), but he was bald except for two tufts of hair that stuck up like horns over his ears, and Bill had no trouble recognizing their clown. *Two hundred years ago or more*, he thought, and felt a crazy surge of terror, anger, and excitement rush through him. Twenty-seven years later, sitting in the Derry Public Library and remembering his first look into Mike's father's album, he realized he had felt the way a hunter might feel, coming upon the first fresh spoor of an old killer tiger. *Two hundred years ago ... that long, and only God knows how much longer*. This led him to wonder just how long the spirit of Pennywise *had* been here in Derry – but he found that was a thought he did not really want to pursue.

'Gimme, Bill!' Richie was saying, but Bill held the album a moment longer, staring fixedly at the woodcut, sure it would begin to move: the bowling pins (if that's what they were) which the funny fellow was juggling would rise and fall, rise and fall, the kids would laugh and applaud (except maybe they wouldn't *all* laugh and applaud; some of them might scream and run instead), the mule-team pulling the barge would move beyond the borders of the picture.

It didn't happen, and he passed the book on to Richie.

When the album came back to Mike he turned some more pages, hunting. 'Here,' he said. 'This one is from 1856, four years before Lincoln was elected President.'

The book went around again. This was a color picture – a sort of cartoon – which showed a bunch of drunks standing in front of a saloon while a fat politician with muttonchop whiskers declaimed from a board that had been set between two hogsheads. He held a foamy pitcher of beer in one hand. The board upon which he stood was considerably bowed with his weight. Some distance off, a group of bonneted women were looking at this show of mingled buffoonery and intemperance with disgust. The caption below the picture read: POLITICS IN DERRY IS THIRSTY WORK, SEZ SENATOR GARNER!

'Daddy says pictures like this were really popular for about twenty years before the Civil War,' Mike said. 'They called them "foolcards," and people used to send them to each other. They were like some of the jokes in *Mad*, I guess.'

'Suh-suh-satire,' Bill said.

'Yeah,' Mike said. 'But now look down in the corner of this one.'

The picture was like *Mad* in another way – it had as many details and little side-jokes as a big Mort Drucker panel in a *Mad* magazine movie take-off. There was a grinning fat man pouring a glass of beer down a spotted dog's throat. There was a woman who had fallen on her prat in a mudpuddle. There were two street urchins slyly sticking sulphur-headed matches into the soles of a prosperous-looking business-man's shoes, and a girl swinging from her heels in an elm tree so that her underpants showed. But despite this bewildering intaglio of detail, none of them really needed Mike to point the clown out. Dressed in a loud checked vest-busting drummer's suit, he was playing the shell-game with a bunch of drunken loggers. He was winking at a lumber jack who had, to judge by the gape-mouthed look of surprise on his face, just picked the wrong nutshell. The drummer/clown was taking a coin from him.

'Him again,' Ben said. 'What . . . a hundred years later?'

'Just about,' Mike said. 'And here's one from 1891.'

It was a clipping from the front page of the Derry *News*. HUZZAH! the headline proclaimed exuberantly. IRONWORKS OPENS! Just below this: '*Town Turns Out for Gala Picnic.*' The picture showed a woodcut of the ribbon-cutting ceremony at the Kitchener Ironworks; its style reminded Bill of the Currier and Ives prints his mother had in the dining room, although this was nowhere near as polished. A fellow tricked out in a morning coat and tophat was holding a large pair of open-jawed scissors above the Ironworks ribbon while a crowd of perhaps five hundred watched. Off to the left was a clown – their clown – turning a hand-spring for a group of children. The artist had caught him upside down, turning his smile into a scream.

He passed the book on quickly to Richie.

The next picture was a photograph under which Will Hanlon had written: *1933: Repeal in Derry*. Although none of the boys knew much about either the Volstead Act or its repeal, the picture made the salient facts clear. The photo was of Wally's Spa down in Hell's Half-Acre. The place was almost literally filled to the rafters with men wearing open-collared white shirts, straw boaters, lumbermen's shirts, tee-shirts, banker's suits. All of them were holding glasses and bottles victoriously aloft. There were two big signs in the window. WELCOME BACK, JOHN BARLEYCORN! one read. The other said: FREE BEER TONIGHT. The clown, dressed like the biggest dandy you ever saw (white shoes, spats, gangster pants), had his foot on the running board of a Reo auto and was drinking champagne from a lady's high-heeled shoe.

'1945,' Mike said.

The Derry *News* again. The headline: JAPAN SURRENDERS – IT'S OVER! THANK GOD IT'S OVER! A parade was snake-dancing its way along Main Street toward Up-Mile Hill. And there was the clown in the background, wearing his silver suit with the orange buttons, frozen in the matrix of dots that made up the grainy newsprint photo, seeming to suggest (at least to Bill) that nothing was over, no one had surrendered, nothing was won, nil was still the rule, zilch still the custom; seeming to suggest above all that all was still lost.

Bill felt cold and dry and scared.

Suddenly the dots in the picture disappeared and it began to move.

'That's what –' Mike began.

'L-L-Look,' Bill said. The word dropped out of his mouth like a partially melted ice-cube. '*A-A-All of you luh-look at th-this!*'

They crowded around.

'Oh my *God*,' Beverly whispered, awed.

'*That's IT!*' Richie nearly screamed, pounding Bill on the back in his excitement. He looked around at Eddie's white, drawn face and Stan Uris's frozen one. 'That's what we saw in George's room! *That's exactly what we –*'

'Shhh,' Ben said. 'Listen.' And, almost sobbing: 'You can hear them – Christ, you can hear them in there.'

And in the silence that was only broken by the mild stir of the summer breeze, they all realized they could. The band was playing a martial marching tune, made faint and tinny by distance . . . or the passage of time . . . or whatever it was. The cheering of the crowd was like sounds that might come through on a badly tuned radio station. There were popping noises, also faint, like the muffled sound of snapping fingers.

'Firecrackers,' Beverly whispered, and rubbed at her eyes with hands that shook. 'Those are firecrackers, aren't they?'

No one answered. They watched the picture, their eyes eating up their faces.

The parade wiggled its way toward them, but just before the marchers reached the extreme foreground – at the point where it seemed they must march right out of the picture and into a world thirteen years later – they dropped from sight, as if on some kind of unknowable curve. The World War I soldiers first, their faces strangely old under their pie-plate helmets, with their sign which read THE DERRY VFW WELCOMES HOME OUR BRAVE BOYS, then the Boy Scouts, the Kiwanians, the Home Nursing Corps, the Derry Christian Marching Band, then the Derry World War II vets themselves, with the high-school band behind them. The crowd moved and shifted. Tickertape and confetti fluttered down from the second- and third-floor windows of the business buildings that lined the streets. The clown pranced along the sidelines, doing splits and cartwheels, miming a sniper, miming a salute. And Bill noticed for the first time that people were turning from him – but not as if they *saw* him, exactly; it was more as if they felt a draft or smelled something bad.

Only the children really saw him, and they shrank away.

Ben stretched his hand out to the picture, as Bill had done in George's room.

'Nuh-Nuh-Nuh-NO!' Bill cried.

'I think it's all right, Bill,' Ben said. 'Look.' And he laid his hand on the protective plastic over the picture for a moment and then took it back. 'But if you stripped off that cover –'

Beverly screamed. The clown had left off its antics when Ben withdrew his hand. It rushed toward them, its paint-bloody mouth gibbering and laughing. Bill winced back but held onto the book all the same, thinking it would drop out of sight as the parade had done, and the marching band, and the Boy Scouts, and the Cadillac convertible carrying Miss Derry of 1945.

But the clown did not disappear along that curve that seemed to define the edge of that old existence. Instead, it leaped with a scary, nimble grace onto a lamppost that stood in the extreme left foreground of the picture. It shinnied up like a monkey on a stick – and suddenly its face was pressed against the tough plastic sheet Will Hanlon had put over each of the pages in his book. Beverly screamed again and this time Eddie joined her, although his scream was faint and blue-breathless. The plastic bulged out – later they would all agree they saw it. Bill saw the bulb of the clown's red nose flatten, the way your nose will flatten when you press it against a windowpane.

'*Kill you all!*' The clown was laughing and screaming. '*Try to stop me and I'll kill you all! Drive you crazy and then kill you all! You can't stop me! I'm the Gingerbread Man! I'm the Teenage Werewolf!*'

And for a moment It *was* the Teenage Werewolf, the moon-silvered face of the lycanthrope peering out at them from over the collar of the silver suit, white teeth bared.

'*Can't stop me, I'm the leper!*'

Now the leper's face, haunted and peeling, rotting with sores, stared at them with the eyes of the living dead.

'*Can't stop me, I'm the mummy!*'

The leper's face aged and ran with sterile cracks. Ancient bandages swam halfway out of its skin and solidified there. Ben turned away, his face as white as curds, one hand plastered over his neck and ear.

'*Can't stop me, I'm the dead boys!*'

'*No!*' Stan Uris screamed. His eyes bulged above bruised-looking crescents of skin – *shockflesh*, Bill thought randomly, and it was a word he would use in a novel twelve years later, with no idea where it had come from, simply taking it, as writers take the right word at the right time, as a simple gift from that outer space

(*otherspace*)

where the good words come from sometimes.

Stan snatched the album from his hands and slammed it shut. He held it closed with both hands, the tendons standing out along the inner surfaces of his wrists and forearms. He looked around at the others with eyes that were nearly insane. 'No,' he said rapidly. 'No, no, no.'

And suddenly Bill found he was more concerned with Stan's repeated denials than with the clown, and he understood that this was exactly the sort of reaction the clown had hoped to provoke, because . . .

Because maybe It's scared of us . . . really scared for the first time in Its long, long life.

He grabbed Stan and shook him twice, hard, holding onto his shoulders. Stan's teeth clicked together and he dropped the album. Mike picked it up and put it aside in a hurry, not liking to touch it after what he had seen. But it was still his father's, and he understood intuitively that his father would never see in it what he had just seen.

'No,' Stan said softly.

'Yes,' Bill said.

'No,' Stan said again.

'*Yes*. We a-a-all –'

'No.'

'– a-a-all suh-haw it, Stan,' Bill said. He looked at the others.

'Yes,' Ben said.

'Yes,' Richie said.

'Yes,' Mike said. 'Oh my God, yes.'

'Yes,' Bev said.

'Yes,' Eddie managed, gasping it out of his rapidly closing throat.

Bill looked at Stan, demanding with his eyes that Stan look back at him. 'Duh-don't let it g-g-get y-you, man,' Bill said. 'Yuh-you suh-saw it, t-t-too.'

'*I didn't want to!*' Stan wailed. Sweat stood out on his brow in an oily sheen.

'But y-y-you *duh-duh-did*.'

Stan looked at the others, one by one. He ran his hands through his short hair and fetched up a great, shuddering sigh. His eyes seemed to clear of that lowering madness that had so disturbed Bill.

'Yes,' he said. 'Yes. Okay. Yes. That what you want? Yes.'

Bill thought: *We're still all together. It didn't stop us. We can still kill It. We can still kill It . . . if we're brave.*

Bill looked around at the others and saw in each pair of eyes some measure of Stan's hysteria. Not quite as bad, but there.

'Y-Y-Yeah,' he said, and smiled at Stan. After a moment Stan smiled back and some of that horrible shocked look left his face. 'That's what I wuh-wuh-wanted, you weh-weh-wet end.'

'Beep-beep, Dumbo,' Stan said, and they all laughed. It was hysterical screaming laughter, but better than no laughter at all, Bill reckoned.

'C-C-Come on,' he said, because someone had to say something. 'Let's f-f-finish the clubhouse. What do you s-s-say?'

He saw the gratitude in their eyes and felt a measure of gladness for them . . . but their gratitude did little to heal his own horror. In fact, there was something in their gratitude which made him want to hate them. Would he never be able to express his own terror, lest the fragile welds that made them into one thing should let go? And even to think such a thing wasn't really fair, was it? Because in some measure at least he was using them – using his friends, risking their lives – to settle the score for his dead brother. And was even that the bottom? No, because George was dead, and if revenge could be exacted at all, Bill suspected it could only be exacted on behalf of the living. And what did that make him? A selfish little shit waving a tin sword and trying to make himself look like King Arthur?

Oh Christ, he groaned to himself, *if this is the stuff adults have to think about I never want to grow up.*

His resolve was still strong, but it was a bitter resolve.

Bitter.

CHAPTER FIFTEEN
THE SMOKE-HOLE

1

Richie Tozier pushes his glasses up on his nose (already the gesture feels perfectly familiar, although he has worn contact lenses for twenty years) and thinks with some amazement that the atmosphere has changed in the room while Mike recalled the incident with the bird out at the Ironworks and reminded them about his father's photograph album and the picture that had moved.

Richie had felt a mad, exhilarating kind of energy growing in the room. He had done cocaine nine or ten times over the last couple of years – at parties, mostly; coke wasn't something you wanted just lying around your house if you were a bigga-time disc jackey – and the feel was something like that, but not exactly. This feeling was purer, more of a mainline high. He thought he recognized the feeling from his childhood, when he had felt it every day and had come to take it merely as a matter of course. He supposed that, if he had ever thought about that deep-running aquifer of energy as a kid (he could not recall that he ever had), he would have simply dismissed it as a fact of life, something that would always be there, like the color of his eyes or his disgusting hammertoes.

Well, that hadn't turned out to be true. The energy you drew on so extravagantly when you were a kid, the energy you thought would never exhaust itself – that slipped away somewhere between eighteen and twenty-four, to be replaced by something much duller, something as bogus as a coke high: purpose, maybe, or goals, or whatever rah-rah Junior Chamber of Commerce word you wanted to use. It was no big deal; it didn't go all at once, with a bang. And maybe, Richie thought, that's the scary part. How you don't stop being a kid all at once, with a big explosive bang, like one of that clown's trick balloons with the Burma-Shave slogans on the sides. The kid in you just leaked out, like the air out of a tire. And one day you looked in the mirror and there was a grownup looking back at you. You could go on wearing blue-jeans, you could keep going to Springsteen and Seger concerts, you could dye your hair, but that was a grownup's face in the mirror just the same. It all happened while you were asleep, maybe, like a visit from the Tooth Fairy.

No, *he thinks*. Not the Tooth Fairy. The *Age* Fairy.

He laughs aloud at the stupid extravagance of this image, and when Beverly looks at him questioningly, he waves a hand at her. 'Nothing, babe,' he says. 'Just thinkin me thinks.'

But now that energy is back. No, not all the way back — not yet, anyway — but coming back. And it's not just him; he can feel it filling the room. Mike looks okay to Richie for the first time since they all got together for that hideous lunch out by the mall. When Richie walked into the lobby and saw Mike sitting there with Ben and Eddie, he thought, shocked: There's a man who's going crazy, getting ready to commit suicide, maybe. But *that look is gone now. Not just sublimated; gone. Richie has sat right here and watched the last of it slip out of Mike's face while he relived the experience of the bird and the album. He's been energized. And it is the same with all of them. It's in their faces, their voices, their gestures.*

Eddie pours himself another gin-and-prune juice. Bill knocks back some bourbon, and Mike cracks another beer. Beverly glances up at the balloons Bill has tethered to the microfilm recorder at the main desk and finishes her third screwdriver in a hurry. They have all been drinking pretty enthusiastically, but none of them are drunk. Richie doesn't know where that energy he feels is coming from, but it's not out of a liquor bottle.

DERRY NIGGERS GET THE BIRD: Blue.

THE LOSERS ARE STILL LOSING, BUT STANLEY URIS IS FINALLY AHEAD: Orange.

Christ, *Richie thinks, opening a fresh beer for himself,* it isn't bad enough It can be any damn monster It wants to be, and it isn't bad enough that It can feed off our fears. It also turns out to be Rodney Dangerfield in drag.

It's Eddie who breaks the silence. 'How much do you think It knows about what we're doing now?' he asks.

'It was here, wasn't It?' Ben says.

'I'm not sure that means much,' Eddie replies.

Bill nods. 'Those are just images,' he says. 'I'm not sure that means It can see us, or know what we're up to. You can see a news commentator on TV, but he can't see you.'

'Those balloons aren't just images,' Beverly says, and jerks a thumb over her shoulder at them. 'They're real.'

'That's not true, though,' Richie says, and they all look at him. 'Images are real. *Sure they are. They —'*

And suddenly something else clicks into place, something new: it clicks into place with such firm force that he actually puts his hands to his ears. His eyes widen behind his glasses.

'Oh my God!' he cries suddenly. He gropes for the table, half-stands, then falls back into his chair with a boneless thud. He knocks his can of beer over reaching for it, picks it up, and drinks what's left. He looks at Mike while the others look at him, startled and concerned.

'The burning!' he almost shouts. 'The burning in my eyes! Mike! The burning in my eyes –'

Mike is nodding, smiling a little.

'R-Richie?' Bill asks. 'What i-is it?'

But Richie barely hears him. The force of the memory sweeps through him like a tide, turning him alternately hot and cold, and he suddenly understands why these memories have come back one at a time. If he had remembered everything at once, the force would have been like a psychological shotgun blast let off an inch from his temple. It would have torn off the whole top of his head.

'We saw It come!' he says to Mike. 'We saw It come, didn't we? You and me . . . or was it just me?' He grabs Mike's hand, which lies on the table. 'Did you see it too, Mikey, or was it just me? Did you see it? The forest fire? The crater?'

'I saw it,' Mike says quietly, and squeezes Richie's hand. Richie closes his eyes for a moment, thinking he has never felt such a warm and powerful wave of relief in his life, not even when the PSA jet he had taken from LA to San Francisco skidded off the runway and just stopped there – nobody killed, nobody even hurt. Some luggage had fallen out of the overhead bins and that was all. He had jumped onto the yellow emergency slide and helped a woman away from the plane. The woman had turned her ankle on a hummock concealed in the high grass. She was laughing and saying, 'I can't believe I'm not dead, I can't believe it, I just can't believe it.' So Richie, who was half-carrying the woman with one arm and waving with the other to the firemen who were making frantic come-on gestures to the deplaning passengers, said: 'Okay, you're dead, you're dead, you feel better now?' and they both laughed crazily. That had been relief-laughter . . . but this relief is greater.

'What are you guys talking about?' Eddie asks, looking from one to the other.

Richie looks at Mike, but Mike shakes his head. 'You go ahead, Richie. I've had my say for the evening.'

'The rest of you don't know or maybe don't remember, because you left,' Richie tells them. 'Me and Mikey, we were the last two Injuns in the smoke-hole.'

'The smoke-hole,' Bill muses. His eyes are far and blue.

'The burning sensation in my eyes,' Richie says, 'under my contact lenses. I felt it for the first time right after Mike called me in California. I

689

didn't know what it was then, but I do now. It was smoke. Smoke that was twenty-seven years old.' He looks at Mike. 'Psychological, would you say? Psychosomatic? Something from the subconscious?'

'I would say not,' Mike answers quietly. 'I would say that what you felt was as real as those balloons, or the head I saw in the icebox, or the corpse of Tony Tracker that Eddie saw. Tell them, Richie.'

Richie says: 'It was four or five days after Mike brought his dad's album down to the Barrens. Sometime just after the middle of July, I guess. The clubhouse was done. But . . . the smoke-hole thing, that was your idea, Haystack. You got it out of one of your books.'

Smiling a little, Ben nods.

Richie thinks: It was overcast that day. No breeze. Thunder in the air. Like the day a month or so later when we stood in the stream and made a circle and Stan cut our hands with that chunk of Coke bottle. The air was just sitting there, waiting for something to happen, and later Bill said that was why it got so bad in there so quick, because there was no draft.

July 17th. Yes, that was it, that had been the day of the smoke-hole. *July 17th, 1958, almost a month after summer vacation began and the nucleus of the Losers — Bill, Eddie, and Ben — had formed down in the Barrens.* Let me look up the weather forecast for that day almost twenty-seven years ago, *Richie thinks*, and I'll tell you what it said before I even read it: Richard Tozier, aka the Great Mentalizer. 'Hot, humid, chance of thundershowers. And watch out for the visions that may come while you're down in the smoke-hole . . .'

It had been two days after the body of Jimmy Cullum was discovered, the day after Mr Nell had come down to the Barrens again and sat right on the clubhouse without knowing it was there, because by then they had capped it off and Ben himself had carefully overseen the replacement of the sods. Unless you got right down on your hands and knees and crawled around, you'd have no idea anything was there. Like the dam, Ben's clubhouse had been a roaring success, but this time Mr Nell didn't know anything about it.

He had questioned them carefully, officially, taking down their answers in his black notebook, but there had been little they could tell him — at least about Jimmy Cullum — and Mr Nell had gone away again, after reminding them once more that they were not to play in the Barrens alone . . . ever. Richie guessed that Mr Nell would have told them simply to get out if anyone in the Derry Police Department had really believed that the Cullum boy (or any of the others) had actually been killed in the Barrens. But they knew better; because of the sewer and stormdrain system, that was simply where the remains tended to finish up.

Mr Nell had come on the 16th, yes, a hot and humid day also, but sunny. The 17th had been overcast.

'Are you going to talk to us or not, Richie?' Bev asks. She is smiling a little, her lips full and a pale rose-red, her eyes alight.

'I'm just thinking about where to start,' Richie says. He takes his glasses off, wipes them on his shirt, and suddenly he knows where: with the ground opening up at his and Bill's feet. Of course he knew about the clubhouse — so did Bill and the rest of them, but it still freaked him out, seeing the ground suddenly open on a slit of darkness like that.

He remembers Bill riding him double on the back of Silver to the usual place on Kansas Street and then stowing his bike under the little bridge. He remembers the two of them walking along the path toward the clearing, sometimes having to turn sideways because the brush was so thick — it was midsummer now, and the Barrens was at that year's apogee of lushness. He remembers swatting at the mosquitoes that hummed maddeningly close to their ears; he even remembers Bill saying (oh how clearly it all comes back, not as if it happened yesterday, but as if it is happening now), 'H-H-Hold it a s-s-s

2

-econd, Ruh-Richie. There's a damn guh-guh-hood one on the b-back of your neh-neck.'

'Oh Christ,' Richie said. He hated mosquitoes. Little flying vampires, that's all they were when you got right down to the facts. 'Kill it, Big Bill.'

Bill swatted the back of Richie's neck.

'Ouch!'

'Suh-suh-see?'

Bill held his hand in front of Richie's face. There was a broken mosquito body in the center of an irregular patch of blood. *My blood*, Richie thought, *which was shed for you and for many*. 'Yeeick,' he said.

'D-Don't w-worry,' Bill said. 'Li'l fucker'll neh-never dance the tuh-tuh-tango again.'

They walked on, slapping at mosquitoes, waving at the clouds of noseeums attracted by something in the smell of their sweat — something which would years later be identified as 'pheromones.' Whatever *they* were.

'Bill, when you gonna tell the rest of em about the silver bullets?' Richie asked as they approached the clearing. In this case 'the rest of them' meant Bev, Eddie, Mike, and Stan — although Richie guessed Stan already had a good idea of what they were studying up on down at the Public Library. Stan was sharp – too sharp for his own good, Richie sometimes thought. The day Mike brought his father's album down to the Barrens Stan had almost flipped out. Richie had, in fact, been nearly convinced that they wouldn't see Stan again and the Losers' Club would become a sextet (a word Richie liked a lot, always with the emphasis on the first syllable). But Stan had been back the next day, and Richie had respected him all the more for that. 'You going to tell them today?'

'Nuh–not t-today,' Bill said.

'You don't think they'll work, do you?'

Bill shrugged, and Richie, who maybe understood Bill Denbrough better than anyone ever would until Audra Phillips, suspected all the things Bill might have said if not for the roadblock of his speech impediment: that kids making silver bullets was boys' book stuff, comic-book stuff . . . In a word, it was crap. Dangerous crap. They could try it, yeah. Ben Hanscom might even be able to bring it off, yeah. In a movie it *would* work, yeah. But . . .

'So?'

'I got an i-i-i-idea,' Bill said. 'Simpler. But only if Beh-Beh-Beverly –'

'If Beverly what?'

'Neh–hever mind.'

And Bill would say no more on the subject.

They came into the clearing. If you looked closely, you might have thought that the grass there had a slightly matted look – a slightly *used* look. You might even have thought that there was something a bit artificial – almost arranged – about the scatter of leaves and pine needles on top of the sods. Bill picked up a Ring-Ding wrapper – Ben's, almost certainly – and put it absently in his pocket.

The boys crossed to the center of the clearing . . . and a piece of ground about ten inches long by three inches wide swung up with a dirty squall of hinges, revealing a black eyelid. Eyes looked out of that blackness, giving Richie a momentary chill. But they were only Eddie Kaspbrak's eyes, and it was Eddie, whom he would visit in the hospital a week later, who intoned hollowly: 'Who's that trip-trapping on my bridge?'

Giggles from below, and a flashlight flicker.

'Thees ees the *rurales*, senhorr,' Richie said, squatting down, twirling an invisible mustache, and speaking in his Pancho Vanilla Voice.

'Yeah?' Beverly asked from below. 'Let's see your badges.'

'*Batches?*' Richie cried, delighted. 'We doan need no stinkin *batches!*'

'Go to hell, Pancho,' Eddie replied, and slammed the big eyelid closed. There were more muffled giggles from below.

'*Come out with your hands up!*' Bill cried in a low, commanding adult voice. He began to tramp back and forth across the sod-covered cap of the clubhouse. He could see the ground springing up and down with his back-and-forth passage, but just barely; they had built well. '*You haven't got a chance!*' he bellowed, seeing himself as fearless Joe Friday of the LAPD in his mind's eye. '*Come on out of there, punks! Or we'll come in SHOOTIN!*'

He jumped up and down once to emphasize his point. Screams and giggles from below. Bill was smiling, unaware that Richie was looking at him wisely – looking at him not as one child looks at another but, in that brief moment, as an adult looks at a child.

He doesn't know that he doesn't always, Richie thought.

'Let them in, Ben, before they crash the roof in,' Bev said. A moment later a trapdoor flopped open like the hatch of a submarine. Ben looked out. He was flushed. Richie knew at once that Ben had been sitting next to Beverly.

Bill and Richie dropped down through the hatch and Ben closed it again. Then there they all were, sitting snug against board walls with their legs drawn up, their faces dimly revealed in the beam of Ben's flashlight.

'S-S-So wh-what's g-g-going o-on?' Bill asked.

'Not too much,' Ben said. He was indeed sitting next to Beverly, and his face looked happy as well as flushed. 'We were just –'

'Tell em, Ben,' Eddie interrupted. 'Tell em the story! See what they think.'

'Wouldn't do much for your asthma,' Stan told Eddie in his best someone-has-to-be-practical-here tone of voice.

Richie sat between Mike and Ben, holding his knees in his linked hands. It was delightfully cool down here, delightfully *secret*. Following the gleam of the flashlight as it moved from face to face, he temporarily forgot what had so astounded him outside only a minute ago. 'What are you talkin about?'

'Oh, Ben was telling us a story about this Indian ceremony,' Bev said. 'But Stan's right, it wouldn't be very good for your asthma, Eddie.'

'It might not bother it,' Eddie said, sounding – to his credit, Richie thought – only a little uneasy. 'Usually it's only when I get upset. Anyway, I'd like to try it.'

'Try w-w-what?' Bill asked him.

'The Smoke-Hole Ceremony,' Eddie said.

'W-W-What's th-that?'

The beam of Ben's flashlight drifted upward and Richie followed it with his eyes. It tracked aimlessly across the wooden roof of their clubhouse as Ben explained. It crossed the gouged and splintered panels of the mahogany door the seven of them had carried back here from the dump three days ago – the day before the body of Jimmy Cullum was discovered. The thing Richie remembered about Jimmy Cullum, a quiet little boy who also wore spectacles, was that he liked to play Scrabble on rainy days. *Not going to be playing Scrabble anymore*, Richie thought, and shivered a little. In the dimness no one saw the shiver, but Mike Hanlon, sitting shoulder to shoulder with him, glanced at him curiously.

'Well, I got this book out of the library last week,' Ben was saying. '*Ghosts of the Great Plains*, it's called, and it's all about the Indian tribes that lived out west a hundred and fifty years ago. The Paiutes and the Pawnees and the Kiowas and the Otoes and the Comanches. It was really a good book. I'd love to go out there sometime to where they lived. Iowa, Nebraska, Colorado, Utah . . .'

'Shut up and tell about the Smoke-Hole Ceremony,' Beverly said, elbowing him.

'Sure,' he said. 'Right.' And Richie believed his response would have been the same if Beverly had given him the elbow and said, 'Drink the poison now, Ben, okay?'

'See, almost all those Indians had a special ceremony, and our clubhouse made me think of it. Whenever they had to make a big decision – whether to move on after the buffalo herds, or to find fresh water, or whether or not to fight their enemies – they'd dig a big hole in the ground and cover it up with branches, except for a little vent in the top.'

'The smuh-smuh-smoke-hole,' Bill said.

'Your quick mind never ceases to amaze me, Big Bill,' Richie said gravely. 'You ought to go on *Twenty-One*. I'll bet you could even beat ole Charlie Van Doren.'

Bill made as if to hit him and Richie recoiled, bumping his head a pretty good one on a piece of shoring.

'*Ouch!*'

'You d-deserved it,' Bill said.

'I keel you, rotten gringo sumbeesh,' Richie said. 'We doan need no stinkin –'

'Will you guys stop it?' Beverly asked. 'This is *interesting*.' And she favored Ben with such a warm look that Richie believed steam would start curling out of Haystack's ears in a couple of minutes.

'Okay, B–B–Ben,' Bill said. 'Go o-o-on.'

'Sure,' Ben said. The word came out in a croak. He had to clear his throat and start again. 'When the smoke-hole was finished, they'd start a fire down there. They'd use green wood so it would be a really *smoky* fire. Then all the braves would go down there and sit around the fire. The place would fill up with smoke. The book said this was a religious ceremony, but it was also kind of a contest, you know? After half a day or so most of the braves would bug out because they couldn't stand the smoke anymore, and only two or three would be left. And they were supposed to have visions.'

'Yeah, if I breathed smoke for five or six hours, I'd probably have some visions, all right,' Mike said, and they all laughed.

'The visions were supposed to tell the tribe what to do,' Ben said. 'And I don't know if this part is true or not, but the book said that most times the visions were right.'

A silence fell and Richie looked at Bill. He was aware that they were *all* looking at Bill, and he had the feeling – again – that Ben's story of the smoke-hole was more than a thing you read about in a book and then had to try for yourself, like a chemistry experiment or a magic trick. He knew it, they all knew it. Perhaps Ben knew it most of all. This was something they were *supposed* to do.

They were supposed to have visions . . . Most times the visions were right.

Richie thought: *I'll bet if we asked him, Haystack would tell us that book practically jumped into his hand. Like something wanted him to read that one particular book and then tell us about the smoke-hole ceremony. Because there's a tribe right here, isn't there? Yeah. Us. And, yeah, I guess we do need to know what happens next.*

This thought led to another: *Was this supposed to happen? From the time Ben got the idea for an underground clubhouse instead of a treehouse, was this supposed to happen? How much of this are we thinking up ourselves, and how much is being thought up for us?*

In a way, he supposed such an idea should have been almost comforting. It was nice to imagine that something bigger than you, *smarter* than you, was doing your thinking for you, like the adults that planned your meals, bought your clothes, and managed your time – and Richie was convinced that the force that had brought them together, the force that had used Ben as its messenger to bring them the idea of the smoke-hole – that force wasn't the same as the one killing the children. This was some kind of counterforce to that other . . . to

(*oh well you might as well say it*)

It. But all the same, he didn't like this feeling of not being in control of his own actions, of being managed, of being *run*.

They all looked at Bill; they all waited to see what Bill would say.

'Y-You nuh-nuh-know,' he said, 'that sounds rih-really n-neat.'

Beverly sighed and Stan stirred uncomfortably . . . that was all.

'Rih-rih-really nuh-neat,' Bill repeated, looking down at his hands, and perhaps it was only the uneasy flashlight beam in Ben's hands or his own imagination, but Richie thought Bill looked a little pale and a lot scared, although he was smiling. 'Maybe we could u-use a vih-hision to tell us what to d-d-do about o-our pruh-pruh-hob-lem.'

And if anyone has a vision, Richie thought, *it will be Bill*. But about that he was wrong.

'Well,' Ben said, 'it probably only works for Indians, but it might be flippy to try it.'

'Yeah, we'll probably all pass out from the smoke and die in here,' Stan said gloomily. 'That'd be really flippy, all right.'

'You don't want to, Stan?' Eddie asked.

'Well, I sort of do,' Stan said. He sighed. 'I think you guys are making me crazy, you know it?' He looked at Bill. 'When?'

Bill said, 'W-Well, nuh-no t-time like the puh-puh-puh-hresent, i-is there?'

There was a startled, thoughtful silence. Then Richie got to his feet, straight-arming the trapdoor open and letting in the muted light of that still summer day.

'I got my hatchet,' Ben said, following him out. 'Who·wants to help me cut some green wood?'

In the end they all helped.

3

It took them about an hour to get ready. They cut four or five armloads of small green branches, from which Ben had stripped the twigs and leaves. 'They'll smoke, all right,' he said. 'I don't even know if we'll be able to get them going.'

Beverly and Richie went down to the bank of the Kenduskeag and brought back a collection of good-sized stones, using Eddie's jacket (his mother always made him take a jacket, even if it *was* eighty degrees

– it might rain, Mrs Kaspbrak said, and if you have a jacket to put on, your skin won't get soaked if it does) as a makeshift sling. Carrying the rocks back to the clubhouse, Richie said: 'You can't do this, Bev. You're a girl. Ben said it was just the braves that went down in the smoke-hole, not the squaws.'

Beverly paused, looking at Richie with mixed amusement and irritation. A lock of hair had escaped from her pony-tail; she pushed out her lower lip and blew it off her forehead.

'I could wrestle you to a fall any day, Richie. And you know it.'

'*Dat* doan mattuh, Miss Scawlett!' Richie said, popping his eyes at her. 'You is still a girl and you is always *goan* be a girl! You sho ain't no Injun brave!'

'I'll be a bravette, then,' Beverly said. 'Now are we going to take these rocks back to the clubhouse or am I going to bounce a few of them off your asshole skull?'

'Lawks-a-mussy, Miss Scawlett, I ain't got no asshole in mah *skull*!' Richie screeched, and Beverly laughed so hard she dropped her end of Eddie's jacket and all the stones fell out. She scolded Richie all the time they were picking them up again, and Richie joked and screeched in many Voices, and thought to himself how beautiful she was.

Although Richie had not been serious when he spoke of excluding her from the smoke-hole on the basis of her sex, Bill Denbrough apparently was.

She stood facing him, her hands on her hips, her cheeks flushed with anger. 'You can just take that and stuff it with a long pole, Stuttering Bill! I'm in on this too, or aren't I a member of your lousy club anymore?'

Patiently, Bill said: 'I-It's not l-like that, B-B-Bev, and y-you nuh-know i-it. Somebody *has* to stay u-uh-up here.'

'Why?'

Bill tried, but the roadblock was in again. He looked at Eddie for help.

'It's what Stan said,' Eddie told her quietly. 'About the smoke. Bill says that might really happen – we could pass out down there. Then we'd die. Bill says that's what happens to most people in housefires. They don't burn up. They choke to death on the smoke. They –'

Now she turned to Eddie. 'Well, okay. He wants somebody to stay up on top in case there's trouble?'

Miserably, Eddie nodded.

'Well, what about *you*? You're the one with the asthma.'

Eddie said nothing. She turned back to Bill. The others stood around, hands in their pockets, looking at their sneakers.

'It's because I'm a girl, isn't it? That's really it, isn't it?'

'Beh-Beh-Beh-Beh —'

'You don't have to talk,' she snapped. 'Just nod your head or shake it. Your *head* doesn't stutter, does it? Is it because I'm a girl?'

Reluctantly, Bill nodded his head.

She looked at him for a moment, her lips trembling, and Richie thought she would cry. Instead, she exploded.

'Well, *fuck you*!' She whirled around to look at the others, and they flinched from her gaze, so hot it was nearly radioactive. 'Fuck *all* of you if you think the same thing!' She turned back to Bill and began to talk fast, rapping him with words. 'This is something more than some diddlyshit kid's game like tag or guns or hide-and-go-seek, and *you know it*, Bill. We're *supposed* to do this. That's *part* of it. And you're not going to cut me out just because I'm a girl. Do you understand? You better, or I'm leaving right now. And if I go, I'm *gone*. For good. You understand?'

She stopped. Bill looked at her. He seemed to have regained his calm, but Richie felt afraid. He felt that any chance they had of winning, of finding a way to get to the thing that had killed Georgie Denbrough and the other kids, getting to It and killing It, was now in jeopardy. *Seven*, Richie thought. *That's the magic number. There has to be seven of us. That's the way it's supposed to be.*

A bird sang somewhere; stopped; sang again.

'A-All r-right,' Bill said, and Richie let his breath out. 'But suh-suh-somebody has to s-stay tuh-hopside. Who w-w-wants to d-do it?'

Richie thought Eddie or Stan would surely volunteer for this duty, but Eddie said nothing. Stan stood pale and thoughtful and silent. Mike had his thumbs hooked into his belt like Steve McQueen in *Wanted: Dead or Alive*, nothing moving but his eyes.

'Cuh-cuh-come o-on,' Bill said, and Richie realized that all pretense had gone out of the thing now; Bev's impassioned speech and Bill's grave, too-old face had seen to that. This was a part of it, perhaps as dangerous as the expedition he and Bill had made to the house at 29 Neibolt Street. They knew it . . . and no one was backing down. Suddenly he was very proud of them, very proud to be with them. After all the years of being counted out, he was counted in. Finally counted in. He didn't know if they were still losers or not, but he knew they were together. They were friends. Damn good friends. Richie took his glasses off and rubbed them vigorously with the tail of his shirt.

'I know how to do it,' Bev said, and took a book of matches from her pocket. On the front, so tiny you'd need a magnifying glass to get a really good look at them, were pictures of that year's candidates for the title of Miss Rheingold. Beverly lit a match and then blew it out. She tore out six more and added the burned match. She turned away from them, and when she turned back the white ends of the seven matches poked out of her closed fist. 'Pick,' she said, holding the matches out to Bill. 'The one who picks the match with the burned head stays up here and pulls the rest out if they go flippy.'

Bill looked at her levelly. 'Th-This is h-h-how you w-want i-it?'

She smiled at him then, and her smile made her face radiant. 'Yeah, you big dummy, this is how I want it. What about you?'

'I luh-luh-love you, B-B-Bev,' he said, and color rose in her cheeks like hasty flames.

Bill did not appear to notice. He studied the match-tails sticking out of her fist, and at length he picked one. Its head was blue and unburned. She turned to Ben and offered the remaining six.

'I love you too,' Ben said hoarsely. His face was plum-colored; he looked like he was on the verge of a stroke. But no one laughed. Somewhere deeper in the Barrens, the bird sang again. *Stan would know what it was*, Richie thought randomly.

'Thank you,' she said, smiling, and Ben picked a match. Its head was unburned.

She offered them to Eddie next. Eddie smiled, a shy smile that was incredibly sweet and almost heartbreakingly vulnerable. 'I guess I love you, too, Bev,' he said, and then picked a match blindly. Its head was blue.

Beverly now offered the four match-tails in her hand to Richie.

'Ah *loves* yuh, Miss Scawlett!' Richie screamed at the top of his voice, and made exaggerated kissing gestures with his lips. Beverly only looked at him, smiling a little, and Richie suddenly felt ashamed. 'I do love you, Bev,' he said, and touched her hair. 'You're cool.'

'Thank you,' she said.

He picked a match and looked at it, positive he'd picked the burned one. But he hadn't.

She offered them to Stan.

'I love you,' Stan said, and plucked one of the matches from her fist. Unburned.

'You and me, Mike,' she said, and offered him his pick of the two left.

He stepped forward. 'I don't know you well enough to love you,' he said, 'but I love you anyway. You could give my mother shoutin lessons, I guess.'

They all laughed, and Mike took a match. Its head was also unburned.

'I guess it's y-y-you a-after all, Bev,' Bill said.

Looking disgusted – all that flash and fire for nothing – Beverly opened her hand.

The head of the remaining match was also blue and unburned.

'Y-Y-You jih-jig-jiggered them,' Bill accused.

'No. I didn't.' Her tone was not one of angry protest – which would have been suspect – but flabbergasted surprise. 'Honest to God I didn't.'

Then she showed them her palm. They all saw the faint mark of soot from the burned match-head there.

'Bill, I swear on my mother's name!'

Bill looked at her for a moment and then nodded. By common unspoken consent, they all handed the matches back to Bill. Seven of them, their heads intact. Stan and Eddie began to crawl around on the ground, but there was no burned match there.

'I *didn't*,' Beverly said again, to no one in particular.

'So what do we do now?' Richie asked.

'We a-a-all go down,' Bill said. 'Because that's w-what w-w-we're *suh-supposed* to do.'

'And if we all pass out?' Eddie asked.

Bill looked at Beverly again. 'I-If B-Bev's t-telling the truh-truth, and s-she i-i-is, w-we won't.'

'How do you *know*?' Stan asked.

'I-I j-just d-d-do.'

The bird sang again.

4

Ben and Richie went down first and the others handed the rocks down one by one. Richie passed them on to Ben, who made a small stone circle in the middle of the dirt clubhouse floor. 'Okay,' he said. 'That's enough.'

The others came down, each with a handful of the green twigs they'd cut with Ben's hatchet. Bill came last. He closed the trapdoor and opened the narrow hinged window. 'Th-Th-There,' he said. 'Th-there's our smuh-smoke-hole. Do we h-have any kih-kih-kindling?'

'You can use this, if you want,' Mike said, and took a battered Archie funnybook out of his hip pocket. 'I read it already.'

Bill tore the pages out of the funnybook one by one, working slowly and gravely. The others sat around the walls, knee to knee and shoulder to shoulder, watching, not speaking. The tension was thick and still.

Bill laid small twigs and branches over the paper and then looked at Beverly. 'Y-Y-You g-got the muh-matches,' he said.

She lit one, a tiny yellow flare in the gloom. 'Darn thing probably won't catch anyway,' she said in a slightly uneven voice, and touched a light to the paper in several places. When the matchflame got close to her fingers, she tossed it into the center.

The flames blazed up yellow, crackling, throwing their faces into sharp relief, and in that moment Richie had no trouble believing Ben's Indian story, and he thought it must have been like this back in those old days when the idea of white men was still no more than a rumor or a tall tale to those Indians who followed buffalo herds so big they could cover the earth from horizon to horizon, herds so big that their passing shook the ground like an earthquake. In that moment Richie could picture those Indians, Kiowas or Pawnees or whatever they were, down in their smoke-hole, knee to knee and shoulder to shoulder, watching as the flames guttered and sank into the green wood like hot sores, listening to the faint and steady *sssssss* of sap oozing out of the damp wood, waiting for the vision to descend.

Yeah. Sitting here now he could believe it all . . . and looking at their somber faces as they studied the flames and the charring pages of Mike's Archie funnybook, he could see that they believed it, too.

The branches were catching. The clubhouse began to fill up with smoke. Some of it, white as cotton smoke-signals in a Saturday-matinee movie starring Randolph Scott or Audie Murphy, escaped from the smoke-hole. But with no moving air outside to create a draft, most of it stayed below. It had an acrid bite that made eyes sting and throats throb. Richie heard Eddie cough twice – a flat sound like dry boards being whacked together – and then fall silent again. *He shouldn't be down here*, he thought . . . but something else apparently felt otherwise.

Bill tossed another handful of green twigs on the smoldering fire and asked in a thin voice that was not much like his usual speaking voice: 'Anyone having a-any vih-vih-visions?'

'Visions of getting out of here,' Stan Uris said. Beverly laughed at this, but her laughter turned into a fit of coughing and choking.

Richie leaned his head back against the wall and looked up at the smoke-hole – a thin rectangle of mellow white light. He thought about the Paul Bunyan statue that day in March . . . but that had only been a mirage, a hallucination, a

(*vision*)

'Smoke's *killin* me,' Ben said. 'Whoo!'

'So leave,' Richie murmured, not taking his eyes off the smoke-hole. He felt as if he was getting a handle on this. He felt as if he had lost ten pounds. And he sure as shit felt as if the clubhouse had gotten bigger. Damn straight on that last. He had been sitting with Ben Hanscom's fat right leg squashed against his left one and Bill Denbrough's bony left shoulder socked into his right arm. Now he was touching neither of them. He glanced lazily to his right and left to verify that his perception was true, and it was. Ben was a foot or so to his left. On his right, Bill was even farther away.

'Place is bigger, friends and neighbors,' he said. He took a deeper breath and coughed hard. It hurt, hurt deep in his chest, the way a cough hurt when you had the flu or the grippe or something. For awhile he thought it would never pass; that he would just go on coughing until they had to pull him out. *If they still can*, he thought, but the thought was really too dim to be frightening.

Then Bill was pounding him on the back, and the coughing fit passed.

'You don't know you don't always,' Richie said. He was looking at the smoke-hole again instead of at Bill. How bright it seemed! When he closed his eyes he could still see the rectangle, floating there in the dark, but bright green instead of bright white.

'Whuh-whuh-what do you m-mean?' Bill asked.

'Stutter.' He paused, aware that someone else was coughing but not sure who it was. 'You ought to do the Voices, not me, Big Bill. You –'

The coughing got louder. Suddenly the clubhouse was flooded with daylight, so sudden and so bright Richie had to squint against it. He could just make out Stan Uris, climbing and clawing his way out.

'Sorry,' Stan managed, through his spasmodic coughing. 'Sorry, can't –'

'It's all right,' Richie heard himself say. 'You doan need no stinkin' batches.' His voice sounded as if it were coming from a different body.

The trapdoor slammed shut a moment later, but enough fresh

air had come in to clear his head a little. Before Ben moved over a little to fill the space Stan had vacated, Richie became aware of Ben's leg again, pressing his. How had he gotten the idea that the clubhouse had gotten bigger?

Mike Hanlon threw more sticks on the smoky fire. Richie resumed taking shallow breaths and looking up at the smoke-hole. He had no sense of real time passing, but he was vaguely aware that, in addition to the smoke, the clubhouse was getting good and hot.

He looked around, looked at his friends. They were hard to see, half-swallowed in shadowsmoke and still white summerlight. Bev's head was tilted back against a piece of shoring, her hands on her knees, her eyes closed, tears trickling down her cheeks toward her earlobes. Bill was sitting cross-legged, his chin on his chest. Ben was –

But suddenly Ben was getting to his feet, pushing the trapdoor open again.

'There goes Ben,' Mike said. He was sitting Indian-fashion directly across from Richie, his eyes as red as a weasel's.

Comparative coolness struck them again. The air freshened as smoke swirled up through the trap. Ben was coughing and dry-retching. He pulled himself out with Stan's help, and before either of them could close the trapdoor, Eddie was staggering to his feet, his face a deadly pale except for the bruised-looking patches under his eyes and traced just below his cheekbones. His thin chest was hitching up and down in quick, shallow spasms. He groped weakly for the edge of the escape hatch and would have fallen if Ben had not grabbed one hand and Stan the other.

'Sorry,' Eddie managed in a squeaky little whisper, and then they hauled him up. The trapdoor banged down again.

There was a long, quiet period. The smoke built up until it was a thick still fog in the clubhouse. *Looks like a pea-souper to me, Watson*, Richie thought, and for a moment he imagined himself as Sherlock Holmes (a Holmes who looked a great deal like Basil Rathbone and who was totally black and white), moving purposefully along Baker Street; Moriarty was somewhere near, a hansom cab awaited, and the game was afoot.

The thought was amazingly clear, amazingly *solid*. It seemed almost to have weight, as if it were not a little pocket-daydream of the sort he had all the time (batting cleanup for the Bosox, bottom of the ninth, bases loaded, *and there it goes, it's up . . . IT'S GONE! Home run, Tozier . . . and that breaks the Babe's record!*), but something that was almost *real*.

There was still enough of the wiseacre in him to think that if all he was getting out of this was a vision of Basil Rathbone as Sherlock Holmes, then the whole idea of vision was pretty overrated.

Except of course it isn't Moriarty that's out there. It's out there – some It – and It's real. It –

Then the trapdoor opened again and Beverly was struggling her way out, coughing dryly, one hand cupped over her mouth. Ben got one hand and Stan grabbed her under the other arm. Half-pulled, half-scrambling under her own power, she was up and gone.

'Ih-Ih-It *i-is* bi-higger,' Bill said.

Richie looked around. He saw the circle of stones with the fire smoldering within, fuming out clouds of smoke. Across the way he saw Mike sitting cross-legged like a totem carved from mahogany, staring at him through the fire with his smoke-reddened eyes. Except Mike was better than twenty yards away, and Bill was even farther away, on Richie's right. The underground clubhouse was now at least the size of a ballroom.

'Doesn't matter,' Mike said. 'It's gonna come pretty quick. *Somethin* is.'

'Y-Y-Yeah,' Bill said. 'But I . . . I . . . I –'

He began to cough. He tried to control it, but the cough worsened, a dry rattling. Dimly Richie saw Bill stumble to his feet, lunge for the trapdoor, and shove it open.

'Guh-Guh-Good luh-luh-luh –'

And then he was gone, dragged up by the others.

'Looks like it's you and me, ole Mikey,' Richie said, and then he began to cough himself. 'I thought for sure that it would be Bill –'

The cough worsened. He doubled over, hacking dryly, unable to get his breath. His head was thudding – whacking – like a turnip filled with blood. His eyes teared behind his glasses.

From far away, he heard Mike saying: 'Go on up if you have to, Richie. Don't go flippy. Don't kill yourself.'

He raised a hand toward Mike and flapped it at him

(*no stinkin batches*)

in a negative gesture. Little by little he began to get the coughing under control again. Mike was right; something was going to happen, and soon. He wanted to still be here when it did.

He tilted his head back and looked up at the smoke-hole again. The coughing fit had left him feeling light-headed, and now he seemed to be floating on a cushion of air. It was a pleasant feeling.

He took shallow breaths and thought: *Someday I'm going to be a rock-and-roll star. That's it, yes. I'll be famous. I'll make records and albums and movies. I'll have a black sportcoat and white shoes and a yellow Cadillac. And when I come back to Derry, they'll all eat their hearts out, even Bowers. I wear glasses, but what the fuck? Buddy Holly wears glasses. I'll bop till I'm blue and dance till I'm black. I'll be the first rock-and-roll star to ever come from Maine. I'll –*

The thought drifted away. It didn't matter. He found that now he didn't need to take shallow breaths. His lungs had adapted. He could breathe as much smoke as he wanted. Maybe he was from Venus.

Mike threw more sticks on the fire. Not to be outdone, Richie tossed on another handful himself.

'How you feeling, Rich?' Mike asked.

Richie smiled. 'Better. Good, almost. You?'

Mike nodded and smiled back. 'I feel okay. Have you been having some funny thoughts?'

'Yeah. Thought I was Sherlock Holmes for a minute there. Then I thought I could dance like the Dovells. Your eyes are so red you wouldn't believe it, you know it?'

'Yours too. Just a coupla weasels in the pen, that's what we are.'

'Yeah?'

'Yeah.'

'You wanna say all right?'

'All right. You wanna say you got the word?'

'I got it, Mikey.'

'Yeah, okay.'

They grinned at each other and then Richie let his head tilt back against the wall again and looked up at the smoke-hole. Shortly he began to drift away. No . . . not away. *Up.* He was drifting up. Like

(*float down here we all*)

a balloon.

'Yuh-yuh-you g-g-guys all ri-right?'

Bill's voice, coming down through the smoke-hole. Coming from Venus. Worried. Richie felt himself thud back down inside himself.

'All right,' he heard his voice, distant, irritated. 'All right, we *said* all right, be quiet, Bill, let us get the word, we wanna say we got the

(*world*)

word.'

The clubhouse was bigger than ever, floored now in some polished

705

wood. The smoke was fog-thick and it was hard to see the fire. That floor! Jesus-come-please-us! It was as big as a ballroom floor in an MGM musical extravaganza. Mike looked at him from the other side, a shape almost lost in the fog.

You coming, ole Mikey?
Right here with you, Richie.
You still want to say all right?
Yeah . . . but hold my hand . . . can you catch hold?
I think so.

Richie held his hand out, and although Mike was on the far side of this enormous room he felt those strong brown fingers close over his wrist. Oh and that was good, that was a good touch – good to find desire in comfort, to find comfort in desire, to find substance in smoke and smoke in substance –

He tilted his head back and looked at the smoke-hole, so white and wee. It was farther up now. *Miles* up. Venusian skylight.

It was happening. He began to float. *Come on then*, he thought, and began to rise faster through the smoke, the fog, the mist, whatever it was.

5

They weren't inside anymore.

The two of them were standing together in the middle of the Barrens, and it was nearly dusk.

It was the Barrens, he knew that, but everything was different. The foliage was lusher, deeper, savagely fragrant. There were plants he had never seen before, and Richie realized some of the things he had first taken for trees were really giant ferns. There was the sound of running water, but it was much louder than it should have been – this water sounded not like the leisurely flow of the Kenduskeag Stream but more the way he imagined the Colorado River would sound as it cut its way through the Grand Canyon.

It was hot, too. Not that it didn't get hot in Maine during the summer, and humid enough so that sometimes you felt sticky just lying in your bed at night, but this was more heat and more humidity than he had ever felt in his whole life. A low mist, smoky and thick, lay in the hollows of the land and crept around the boys' legs. It had a thin acrid smell like burning green wood.

He and Mike began to move toward the sound of the running water without speaking, pushing their way through the strange foliage.

Thick ropy lianas lay between some of the trees like spidery hammocks, and once Richie heard something go crashing off through the under-brush. It sounded bigger than a deer.

He stopped long enough to look around, turning in a circle, studying the horizon. He knew where the Standpipe's thick white cylinder should have been, but it wasn't there. Neither was the railroad trestle going over to the trainyards at the end of Neibolt Street or the Old Cape housing development – low bluffs and red sandstone outcrop-pings of rock bulged out of thick stands of giant fern and pine trees where the Old Cape should have been.

There was a flapping noise overhead. The boys ducked as a squadron of bats flapped by. They were the biggest bats Richie had ever seen, and for a moment he was more terrified than he had been even when Bill was trying to get Silver rolling and he had heard the werewolf closing in on them from behind. The stillness and the alien-ness of this land were both terrible, but its awful *familiarity* was somehow worse.

No need to be scared, he told himself. *Remember that this is just a dream, or a vision, or whatever you want to call it. Me and ole Mikey are really back in the clubhouse, goofed up on smoke. Pretty soon Big Bill is gonna get noivous from the soivice because we're not answering anymore, and he and Ben will come down and haul us out. It's just like Conway Twitty says – only make-believe.*

But he could see how one of the bats' wings was so ragged the hazy sun shone through it, and when they passed beneath one of the giant ferns he could see a fat yellow caterpillar trundling across a wide green frond, leaving its shadow behind it. There were tiny black mites jumping and sizzling on the caterpillar's body. If this was a dream, it was the clearest one he had ever had.

They went on toward the sound of the water, and in the thick knee-high groundmist, Richie was unable to tell if his feet were touching the ground or not. They came to a place where both the mist and the ground stopped. Richie looked, unbelieving. This was not the Kenduskeag – and yet it was. The stream boiled and roiled through a narrow watercourse cut through that same crumbly rock – looking across to the far side, he could see ages cut into those stacked layers of stone, red and then orange and then red again. You couldn't walk across this stream on stepping-stones; you'd need a rope bridge, and if you fell in you would be swept away at once. The sound of the water was the sound of bitter foolish anger, and as Richie watched, slack-jawed, he saw a pinkish-silver fish jump in an impossibly high arc, snapping at the bugs that made shifting clouds just above the surface of the water. It splashed down again, giving Richie just time enough to register its presence, and to realize he had never seen a fish exactly like that in his whole life, not even in a book.

Birds flocked across the sky, squalling harshly. Not a dozen or two dozen; for a moment the sky was so dark with birds that they blotted out the sun. Something else crashed through the bushes, and then more things. Richie wheeled, his heart thudding painfully in his chest, and saw something that looked like an antelope flash by, heading southeast.

Something's going to happen. And they know it.

The birds passed, presumably alighting somewhere *en masse* farther south. Another animal crashed by them . . . and another. Then there was silence except for the steady rumble of the Kenduskeag. The silence had a waiting quality about it, a pregnant quality Richie didn't like. He felt the hairs shifting and trying to stand up on the back of his neck and he groped for Mike's hand again.

Do you know where we are? he shouted at Mike. *You got the word? Jesus, yes!* Mike shouted back. *I got it! This is* ago, *Richie!* Ago!

Richie nodded. Ago, as in once upon a time, long long ago, when we all lived in the forest and nobody lived anywhere else. They were in the Barrens as they had been God knew how many thousands of years ago. They were in some unimaginable past before the ice age, when New England had been as tropical as South America was today . . . if there still *was* a today. He looked around again, nervously, almost expecting to see a brontosaurus raise its cranelike neck against the sky and stare down at them, its mouth full of mud and dripping uprooted plants, or a saber-toothed tiger come stalking out of the undergrowth.

But there was only that silence, as in the five or ten minutes before a vicious thundersquall strikes, when the purple heads stack up and up in the sky overhead and the light turns a queer, bruised purple-yellow and the wind dies completely and you can smell a thick aroma like overcharged car batteries in the air.

We're in the ago, a million years back, maybe, or ten million, or eighty million, but here we are and something's going to happen, I don't know what but something and I'm scared I want it to end I want to be back and Bill please Bill please pull us out it's like we fell into the picture some picture please please help –

Mike's hand tightened on his and he realized that now the silence had been broken. There was a steady low vibration – he could feel it more than hear it, working against the tight flesh of his eardrums, buzzing the tiny bones that conducted the sound. It grew steadily. It had no tone; it simply *was*:

(*the word in the beginning was the word the world the*)

a tuneless, soulless sound. He groped for the tree they stood near and as his hand touched it, cupped the curve of the bole, he could feel the vibration caught inside. At the same moment he realized he could feel it in his feet, a steady tingling that went up his ankles and calves to his knees, turning his tendons into tuning forks.

It grew. And grew.

It was coming out of the sky. Not wanting to but unable to help himself, Richie turned his face up. The sun was a molten coin burning a circle in the low-hanging overcast, surrounded by a fairy-ring of moisture. Below it, the verdant green slash that was the Barrens lay utterly still. Richie thought he understood what this vision was: they were about to see the coming of It.

The vibration took on a voice – a rumbling roar that built to a shattering crescendo of sound. He clapped his hands to his ears and screamed and could not hear himself scream. Beside him, Mike Hanlon was doing the same, and Richie saw that Mike's nose was bleeding a little.

The clouds in the west lit with a bloom of red fire. It traced its way toward them, widening from an artery to a stream to a river of ominous color; and then, as a burning, falling object broke through the cloud cover, the wind came. It was hot and searing, smoky and suffocating. The thing in the sky was gigantic, a flaming match-head that was nearly too bright to look at. Arcs of electricity bolted from it, blue bullwhips that flashed out from it and left thunder in their wake.

A spaceship! Richie screamed, falling to his knees and covering his eyes. *Oh my God it's a spaceship!* But he believed – and would tell the others later, as best he could – that it was *not* a spaceship, although it might have come *through* space to get here. Whatever came down on that long-ago day had come from a place much farther away than another star or another galaxy, and if *spaceship* was the first word to come into his mind, perhaps that was only because his mind had no other way of grasping what his eyes were seeing.

There was an explosion then – a roar of sound followed by a rolling concussion that knocked them both down. This time it was Mike who groped for Richie's hand. There was another explosion. Richie opened his eyes and saw a glare of fire and a pillar of smoke rising into the sky.

It! he screamed at Mike, in an ecstasy of terror now – never in his life, before or after, would he feel any emotion so deeply, be so overwhelmed by feeling. *It! It! It!*

Mike dragged him to his feet and they ran along the high bank of the young Kenduskeag, never noticing how close they were to the drop. Once Mike stumbled and went skidding to his knees. Then it was Richie's turn to go down, barking his shin and tearing his pants. The wind had come up and it was pushing the smell of the burning forest toward them. The smoke grew thicker, and Richie became dimly aware that he and Mike were not running alone. The animals were on the move again, fleeing from the smoke, the fire, the death in the fire. Running from It, perhaps. The new arrival in their world.

Richie began to cough. He could hear Mike beside him, also coughing. The smoke was thicker, washing out the greens and grays and reds of the day. Mike fell again and Richie lost his hand. He groped for it and could not find it.

Mike! He screamed, panicked, coughing. *Mike, where are you? Mike! MIKE!*

But Mike was gone; Mike was nowhere.

richie! richie! richie!

(!!WHACKO!!)

'richie! richie! richie, are you

6

all right?'

His eyes fluttered open and he saw Beverly kneeling beside him, wiping his mouth with a handkerchief. The others – Bill, Eddie, Stan, and Ben – stood behind her, their faces solemn and scared. The side of Richie's face hurt like hell. He tried to speak to Beverly and could only croak. He tried to clear his throat and almost vomited. His throat and lungs felt as if they had somehow been lined with smoke.

At last he managed, 'Did you slap me, Beverly?'

'It was all I could think of to do,' she said.

'Whacko,' Richie muttered.

'I didn't think you were going to be all right, is all,' Bev said, and suddenly burst into tears.

Richie patted her clumsily on the shoulder and Bill put a hand on the back of her neck. She reached around at once, took it, squeezed it.

Richie managed to sit up. The world began to swim in waves. When it steadied down he saw Mike leaning against a tree nearby, his face dazed and ashy-pale.

'Did I puke?' Richie asked Bev.

She nodded, still crying.

In a croaking, stumbling Irish Cop's Voice, he asked, 'Get any on ye, darlin?'

Bev laughed through her tears and shook her head. 'I turned you on your side. I was afraid . . . a-a-afraid you'd ch-ch-choke on it.' She began to cry hard again.

'Nuh-Nuh-No f-fair,' Bill said, still holding her hand. 'I-I-I'm the one who stuh-huh-hutters a-around h-here.'

'Not bad, Big Bill,' Richie said. He tried to get to his feet and sat down again heavily. The world was still swimming. He began to cough and turned his head away, aware that he was going to retch again only a moment before it happened. He threw up a mess of green foam and thick saliva that mostly came out in ropes. He closed his eyes tight and croaked, 'Anyone want a snack?'

'Oh *shit*!' Ben cried, disgusted and laughing at the same time.

'Looks more like puke to me,' Richie said, although, in truth, his eyes were still tightly shut. 'The shit usually comes out the other end, at least for me. I dunno about you, Haystack.' When he opened his eyes at last, he saw the clubhouse about twenty yards away. Both the window and the big trapdoor were thrown open. Smoke, thinning now, puffed from both.

This time Richie was able to get to his feet. For a moment he was quite sure he was going to retch again, or faint, or both. 'Whacko,' he murmured, watching the world waver and warp in front of his eyes. When the feeling passed, he made his way over to where Mike was. Mike's eyes were still weasel-red, and from the dampness on his pants cuffs, Richie thought that maybe ole Mikey had taken a ride on the stomach-elevator, too.

'For a white boy you did pretty good,' Mike croaked, and punched Richie weakly on the shoulder.

Richie was at a loss for words — a condition of exquisite rarity.

Bill came over. The others came with him.

'You pulled us out?' Richie asked.

'M-Me and Buh-Ben. Y-You were scuh-scuh-rheaming. B-Both of y-y-you. B-B-But —' He looked over at Ben.

Ben said, 'It must have been the smoke, Bill.' But there was no conviction in the big boy's voice at all.

Flatly, Richie said: 'You mean what I think you mean?'

Bill shrugged. 'W-W-What's th-that, Rih-Richie?'

Mike answered. 'We weren't there at first, were we? You went down because you heard us screaming, but at first we weren't there.'

'It was really smoky,' Ben said. 'Hearing you both screaming that way, that was scary enough. But the screaming . . . it sounded . . . well . . .'

'It s-s-sounded very f-f-f-far a-away,' Bill said. Stuttering badly, he told them that when he and Ben had gone down, they hadn't been able to see either Richie or Mike. They had gone plunging around in the smoky clubhouse, panicked, scared that if they didn't act quickly the two boys might die of smoke poisoning. At last Bill had gripped a hand – Richie's. He had given 'a *huh-huh-hell* of a yuh-yank' and Richie had come flying out of the gloom, only about one-quarter conscious. When Bill turned around he had seen Ben with Mike in a bear-hug, both of them coughing. Ben had thrown Mike up and out through the trapdoor.

Ben listened to all this, nodding.

'I kept grabbing, you know? Really not doing anything except jabbing my hand out like I wanted to shake hands. You grabbed it, Mike. Damn good thing you grabbed it when you did. I think you were just about gone.'

'You guys make the clubhouse sound a lot bigger than it is,' Richie said. 'Talking about stumbling around in it and all. It's only five feet on every side.'

There was a moment's silence while they all looked at Bill, who stood in frowning concentration.

'It *w-w-was* b-bigger,' he said at last. 'W-W-Wasn't it, Ben?'

Ben shrugged. 'It sure seemed like it. Unless it was the smoke.'

'It wasn't the smoke,' Richie said. 'Just before it happened – before we went out – I remember thinking it was at least as big as a ballroom in a movie. Like one of those musicals. *Seven Brides for Seven Brothers*, something like that. I could barely see Mike against the other wall.'

'Before you went *out*?' Beverly asked.

'Well . . . what I mean . . . like . . .'

She grabbed Richie's arm. 'It happened, didn't it? It really happened! You had a vision, just like in Ben's book!' Her face was glowing. 'It really *happened*!'

Richie looked down at himself, and then at Mike. One of the knees of Mike's corduroy pants was out, and both the knees of his own jeans were torn. He could look through the holes and see bleeding scrapes on both his knees.

'If it was a vision, I never want to have another one,' he said. 'I don't know about de Kingfish over there, but when I went down there, I didn't have any holes in my pants. They're practically new, for gosh sakes. My mom's gonna give me hell.'

'What happened?' Ben and Eddie asked together.

Richie and Mike exchanged a glance and then Richie said, 'Bevvie, you got a smoke?'

She had two, wrapped in a piece of tissue. Richie put one of them in his mouth and when she lit it the first drag made him cough so badly that he handed it back to her. 'Can't,' he said. 'Sorry.'

'It was the past,' Mike said.

'Shit on that,' Richie said. 'It wasn't just the past. It was *ago*.'

'Yeah, right. We were in the Barrens, but the Kenduskeag was going a mile a minute. It was deep. It was fuckin *wild*. Sorry, Bevvie, but it *was*. And there were fish in it. Salmon, I think.'

'M–My d–d–dad s–says th–there haven't been a–a–any fuh–fish in the K–Kendusk–k–keag for a l–l–long tuh–hime. B–Because of the suh–sewage.'

'This was a long time, all right,' Richie said. He looked around at them uncertainly. 'I think it was a million years ago, at least.'

A thunderstruck silence greeted this. Beverly broke it at last. 'But what *happened*?'

Richie felt the words in his throat, but he had to struggle to bring them out. It felt almost like vomiting again. 'We saw It come,' he said at last. 'I *think* that was it.'

'Christ,' Stan muttered. 'Oh Christ.'

There was a sharp hiss–gasp as Eddie used his aspirator.

'It came out of the sky,' Mike said. 'I never want to see anything like that again in my whole life. It was burning so hot you couldn't really look at it. And it was thowin off electricity and makin thunder. The noise . . .' He shook his head and looked at Richie. 'It sounded like the end of the world. And when it hit, it started a forest fire. That was at the end of it.'

'Was it a spaceship?' Ben asked.

'Yes,' Richie said. 'No,' Mike said.

They looked at each other.

'Well, I guess it was,' Mike said, and at the same time Richie said: 'No, it really wasn't a *spaceship*, you know, but –'

They paused again while the others looked at them, perplexed.

'You tell,' Richie said to Mike. 'We mean the same thing, I think, but they're not getting it.'

Mike coughed into his fist and then looked up at the others, almost apologetically. 'I don't know just how to tell you,' he said.

'*T-T-Try*,' Bill said urgently.

'It came out of the sky,' Mike repeated, 'but it wasn't a *spaceship*, exactly. It wasn't a meteor, either. It was more like . . . well . . . like the Ark of the Covenant, in the Bible, that was supposed to have the Spirit of God inside of it . . . except this wasn't God. Just feeling It, watching It come, you knew It meant bad, that It *was* bad.'

He looked at them.

Richie nodded. 'It came from . . . *outside*. I got that feeling. From *outside*.'

'Outside where, Richie?' Eddie asked.

'Outside everything,' Richie said. 'And when It came down . . . It made the biggest damn hole you ever saw in your life. It turned this big hill into a doughnut, just about. It landed right where the downtown part of Derry is now.'

He looked at them. 'Do you get it?'

Beverly dropped the cigarette half-smoked and crushed it out under one shoe.

Mike said, 'It's *always* been here, since the beginning of time . . . since before there were men *anywhere*, unless maybe there were just a few of them in Africa somewhere, swinging through the trees or living in caves. The crater's gone now, and the ice age probably scraped the valley deeper and changed some stuff around and filled the crater in . . . but It was here then, sleeping, maybe, waiting for the ice to melt, waiting for the people to come.'

'That's why It uses the sewers and the drains,' Richie put in. 'They must be regular freeways for It.'

'You didn't see what It looked like?' Stan Uris asked abruptly and a little hoarsely.

They shook their heads.

'Can we beat It?' Eddie said in the silence. 'A thing like that?'
No one answered.

CHAPTER SIXTEEN
EDDIE'S BAD BREAK

1

By the time Richie finishes, they're all nodding. Eddie is nodding along with them, remembering *along with them, when the pain suddenly races up his left arm. Races up? No. Rips through: it feels as if someone is trying to sharpen a rusty saw on the bone in there. He grimaces and reaches into the pocket of his sport jacket, sorts through a number of bottles by feel, and takes out the Excedrin. He swallows two with a gulp of gin-and-prune juice. The arm has been paining him off and on all day. At first he dismissed it as the twinges of bursitis he sometimes gets when the weather is damp. But halfway through Richie's story, a new memory clicks into place for him and he understands the pain.* This isn't Memory Lane we're wandering down anymore, *he thinks;* it's getting more and more like the Long Island Expressway.

Five years ago, during a routine check-up (Eddie has a routine check-up every six weeks), the doctor said matter-of-factly: 'There's an old break here, Ed . . . Did you fall out of a tree when you were a kid?'

'Something like that,' Eddie agreed, not bothering to tell Dr Robbins that his mother undoubtedly would have fallen down dead of a brain hemorrhage if she had seen or heard of her Eddie climbing trees. The truth was, he hadn't been able to remember exactly how he broke the arm. It didn't seem important (although, Eddie thinks now, that lack of interest was in itself very odd – he is, after all, a man who attaches importance to a sneeze or a slight change in the color of his stools). But it was an old break, a minor irritation, something that happened a long time ago in a boyhood he could barely remember and didn't care to recall. It pained him a little when he had to drive long hours on rainy days. A couple of aspirin took care of it nicely. No big deal.

But now it is not just a minor irritation; it is some madman sharpening that rusty saw, playing bone-tunes, and he remembers that was how it felt in the hospital, especially late at night, in the first three or four days after it happened. Lying there in bed, sweating in the summer heat, waiting for the nurse to bring him a pill, tears running silently down his cheeks into the bowls of his ears, thinking It's like some kook's sharpening a saw in there.

715

If this is Memory Lane, Eddie thinks, I'd trade it for one great big brain enema: a mental high colonic.

Unaware he is going to speak, he says: 'It was Henry Bowers who broke my arm. Do you remember that?'

Mike nods. 'That was just before Patrick Hockstetter disappeared. I don't remember the date.'

'I do,' Eddie says flatly. 'It was the 20th of July. The Hockstetter kid was reported missing on . . . what? . . . the 23rd?'

'Twenty-second,' Beverly Rogan says, although she doesn't tell them why she is so sure of the date: it is because she saw It take Hockstetter. Nor does she tell them that she believed then and believes now that Patrick Hockstetter was crazy, perhaps even crazier than Henry Bowers. She will tell them, but this is Eddie's turn. She will speak next, and then she supposes that Ben will narrate the climax of that July's events . . . the silver bullet they had never quite dared to make. A nightmare agenda if ever there was one, she thinks – but that crazy exhilaration persists. When did she last feel this young? She can hardly sit still.

'The 20th of July,' Eddie muses, rolling his aspirator along the table from one hand to the other. 'Three or four days after the smoke-hole thing. I spent the rest of the summer in a cast, remember?'

Richie slaps his forehead in a gesture they all remember from the old days and Bill thinks, with a mixture of amusement and unease, that for a moment there Richie looked just like Beaver Cleaver. 'Sure, of course! You were in a cast when we went to the house on Neibolt Street, weren't you? And later . . . in the dark . . .' But now Richie shakes his head a little, puzzled.

'What, R-Richie?' Bill asks.

'Can't remember that part yet,' Richie admits. 'Can you?' Bill shakes his head slowly.

'Hockstetter was with them that day,' Eddie says. 'It was the last time I ever saw him alive. Maybe he was a replacement for Peter Gordon. I guess Bowers didn't want Peter around anymore after he ran the day of the rockfight.'

'They all died, didn't they?' Beverly asks quietly. 'After Jimmy Cullum, the only ones who died were Henry Bowers's friends . . . or his ex-friends.'

'All but Bowers,' Mike agrees, glancing toward the balloons tethered to the microfilm recorder. 'And he's in Juniper Hill. A private insane asylum in Augusta.'

Bill says, 'W-W-What about when they broke your arm, E-E-Eddie?'

'Your stutter's getting worse, Big Bill,' Eddie says solemnly, and finishes his drink in one gulp.

'Never mind that,' Bill says. 'T-Tell us.'

'Tell us,' Beverly repeats, and puts her hand lightly on his arm. The pain flares there again.

'All right,' Eddie says. He pours himself a fresh drink, studies it, and says, 'It was a couple of days after I came home from the hospital that you guys came over to the house and showed me those silver ball-bearings. You remember, Bill?'

Bill nods.

Eddie looks at Beverly. 'Bill asked you if you'd shoot them, if it came to that . . . because you had the best eye. I think you said you wouldn't . . . that you'd be too afraid. And you told us something else, but I just can't remember what it was. It's like –' Eddie sticks his tongue out and plucks the end of it, as if something were stuck there. Richie and Ben both grin. 'Was it something about Hockstetter?'

'Yes,' Beverly says. 'I'll tell when you're done. Go ahead.'

'It was after that, after all you guys left, that my mother came in and we had a big fight. She didn't want me to hang around with any of you guys again. And she might have gotten me to agree – she had a way, a way of working on a guy, you know . . .'

Bill nods again. He remembers Mrs Kaspbrak, a huge woman with a strange schizophrenic face, a face capable of looking stony and furious and miserable and frightened all at the same time.

'Yeah, she might have gotten me to agree,' Eddie says. 'But something else happened the same day Bowers broke my arm. Something that really shook me up.'

He utters a little laugh, thinking: It shook me up, all right . . . Is that all you can say? What good's talking when you can never tell people how you really feel? In a book or a movie what I found out that day before Bowers broke my arm would have changed my life forever and nothing would have happened the way it did . . . in a book or a movie it would have set me free. In a book or a movie I wouldn't have a whole suitcase full of pills back in my room at the Town House, I wouldn't be married to Myra, I wouldn't have this stupid fucking aspirator here right now. In a book or a movie. Because –

Suddenly, as they all watch, Eddie's aspirator rolls across the table by itself. As it rolls it makes a dry rattling sound, a little like maracas, a little like bones . . . a little like laughter. As it reaches the far side, between Richie and Ben, it flips itself up into the air and falls on the floor. Richie makes a startled half-grab and Bill cries sharply, 'Don't t-t-touch it!'

'The balloons!' Ben yells, and they all turn.

Both balloons tethered to the microfilm recorder now read ASTHMA MEDICINE GIVES YOU CANCER! Below the slogan are grinning skulls.

They explode with twin bangs.

Eddie looks at this, mouth dry, the familiar sensation of suffocation starting to tighten down in his chest like locking bolts.

Bill looks back at him. 'Who t-told you and w-w-what did they tell you?'

Eddie licks his lips, wanting to go after his aspirator, not quite daring to. Who knew what might be in it now?

He thinks about that day, the 20th, about how it was hot, about how his mother gave him a check, all filled out except for the amount, and a dollar in cash for himself – his allowance.

'Mr Keene,' he says, and his voice sounds distant to his own ears, without power. 'It was Mr Keene.'

'Not exactly the nicest man in Derry,' Mike says, but Eddie, lost in his thoughts, barely hears him.

Yes, it was hot that day, but cool inside the Center Street Drug, the wooden fans turning leisurely below the pressed-tin ceiling, and there was that comforting smell of mixed powders and nostrums. This was the place where they sold health – that was his mother's unstated but clearly communicated conviction, and with his body-clock set at half-past eleven, Eddie had no suspicion that his mother might be wrong about that, or anything else.

Well, Mr Keene sure put an end to that, he thinks now with a kind of sweet anger.

He remembers standing at the comic rack for awhile, spinning it idly to see if there were any new Batmans or Superboys, or his own favorite, Plastic Man. He had given his mother's list (she sent him to the drugstore as other boys' mothers might send them to the corner grocery) and his mother's check to Mr Keene; he would fill the order and then write in the amount on the check, giving Eddie the receipt so she could deduct the amount from her checking balance. This was all SOP for Eddie. Three different kinds of prescription for his mother, plus a bottle of Geritol because, she told him mysteriously, 'It's full of iron, Eddie, and women need more iron than men.' Also, there would be his vitamins, a bottle of Dr Swett's Elixir for Children . . . and, of course, his asthma medicine.

It was always the same. Later he would stop in the Costello Avenue Market with his dollar and get two candy-bars and a Pepsi. He would eat the candy, drink the soda, and jingle his pocket-change all the way home. But this day was different; it would end with him in the hospital and that was certainly different, but it started being different when Mr Keene called him. Because instead of handing him the big white bag full of cures and the receipt, admonishing him to put the receipt in his pocket so he wouldn't lose it, Mr Keene looked at him thoughtfully and said 'Come

2

back into the office for a minute, Eddie. I want to talk to you.'

Eddie only looked at him for a moment, blinking, a little scared. The idea that maybe Mr Keene thought he had been shoplifting flashed briefly through his mind. There was that sign by the door that he always read when he came into the Center Street Drug. It was written in accusing black letters so large that he bet even Richie Tozier could read it without his glasses: SHOPLIFTING IS NOT A 'KICK' OR A 'GROOVE' OR A 'GASSER'! SHOPLIFTING IS A *CRIME*, AND *WE WILL PROSECUTE*!

Eddie had never shoplifted anything in his life, but that sign always made him feel guilty – made him feel as if Mr Keene knew something about him that he didn't know about himself.

Then Mr Keene confused him even further by saying, 'How about an ice-cream soda?'

'Well –'

'Oh, it's on the house. I always have one in the office around this time of day. Good energy, unless you need to watch your weight, and I'd say neither of us do. My wife says I look like stuffed string. Your friend there, the Hanscom boy, he's the one who needs to have a care about his weight. What flavor, Eddie?'

'Well, my mother said to get home as soon as I –'

'You look like a chocolate man to me. Chocolate okay for you?' Mr Keene's eyes twinkled, but it was a dry twinkle, like the sun shining on mica in the desert. Or so Eddie, a fan of such Western writers as Max Brand and Archie Jocelyn, thought.

'Sure,' Eddie gave in. Something about the way Mr Keene pushed his gold-rimmed glasses up on his blade of a nose made him edgy. Something about the way Mr Keene seemed both nervous and secretly pleased. He didn't want to go into the office with Mr Keene. This wasn't about a soda. Nope. And whatever it *was* about, Eddie had an idea it wasn't such great news.

Maybe he's going to tell me I got cancer or something, Eddie thought wildly. That kid-cancer. Leukemia. Jesus!

Oh, don't be so stupid, he answered himself back, trying to sound, in his own mind, like Stuttering Bill. Stuttering Bill had replaced Jock Mahoney, who played the Range Rider on TV Saturday mornings, as the great hero of Eddie's life. In spite of the fact that he couldn't talk right, Big Bill always seemed to be on top of things. *This guy's a pharmacist, not a doctor, for cripe's sake.* But Eddie was still nervous.

719

Mr Keene had raised the counter-gate and was beckoning to Eddie with one bony finger. Eddie went, but reluctantly.

Ruby, the counter-girl, was sitting by the cash register and reading a *Silver Screen*. 'Would you make two ice-cream sodas, Ruby?' Mr Keene called to her. 'One chocolate, one coffee?'

'Sure,' Ruby said, marking her place in the magazine with a tinfoil gum wrapper and getting up.

'Bring them into the office.'

'Sure.'

'Come on, son. I'm not going to bite you.' And Mr Keene actually winked, astounding Eddie completely.

He had never been in back of the counter before, and he gazed at all the bottles and pills and jars with interest. He would have lingered if he had been on his own, examining Mr Keene's mortar and pestle, his scales and weights, the fishbowls full of capsules. But Mr Keene propelled him forward into the office and closed the door firmly behind him. When it clicked shut Eddie felt a warning tightness in his chest and fought it. There would be a fresh aspirator in with his mother's things, and he could have a long satisfying honk on it as soon as he was out of here.

A bottle of licorice whips stood on the corner of Mr Keene's desk. He offered it to Eddie.

'No thank you,' Eddie said politely.

Mr Keene sat down in the swivel chair behind his desk and took one. Then he opened his drawer and took something out. He put it down next to the tall bottle of licorice whips and Eddie felt real alarm course through him. It was an aspirator. Mr Keene tilted back in his swivel chair until his head was almost touching the calendar on the wall behind him. The picture on the calendar showed more pills. It said SQUIBB. And –

– and for one nightmare moment, when Mr Keene opened his mouth to speak, Eddie remembered what had happened in the shoe store when he was just a little kid, when his mother had screamed at him for putting his foot in the X-ray machine. For that one nightmare moment Eddie thought Mr Keene would say: 'Eddie, nine out of ten doctors agree that asthma medicine gives you cancer, just like the X-ray machines they used to have in the shoe stores. You've probably got it already. Just thought you ought to know.'

But what Mr Keene *did* say was so peculiar that Eddie could think of no response at all; he could only sit in the straight wooden chair on the other side of Mr Keene's desk like a nit.

'This has gone on long enough.'

Eddie opened his mouth and then closed it again.

'How old are you, Eddie? Eleven, isn't it?'

'Yes, sir,' Eddie said faintly. His breathing was indeed shallowing up. He wasn't yet whistling like a tea-kettle (which was how Richie put it: *Somebody turn Eddie off! He's reached the boil!*), but that might happen at any time. He looked longingly at the aspirator on Mr Keene's desk, and because something else seemed required, he said: 'I'll be twelve in November.'

Mr Keene nodded, then leaned forward like a TV pharmacist in a commercial and clasped his hands together. His eyeglasses gleamed in the strong light thrown by the overhead fluorescent bars. 'Do you know what a placebo is, Eddie?'

Nervously, taking his best guess, Eddie said: 'Those are the things on cows that the milk comes out of, aren't they?'

Mr Keene laughed and rocked back in his chair. 'No,' he said, and Eddie blushed to the roots of his flattop haircut. Now he could hear the whistle creeping into his breathing. 'A placebo —'

He was interrupted by a brisk double tap at the door. Without waiting for a come-in call, Ruby entered with an oldfashioned ice-cream-soda glass in each hand. 'Yours must be the chocolate,' she said to Eddie, and gave him a grin. He returned it as best he could, but his interest in ice-cream sodas was at its lowest ebb in his entire personal history. He felt scared in a way that was both vague and specific; it was the way he felt scared when he was sitting on Dr Handor's examination table in his underpants, waiting for the doctor to come in and knowing his mother was out in the waiting room, taking up most of one sofa, a book (most likely Norman Vincent Peale's *The Power of Positive Thinking* or *Dr Jarvis's Vermont Folk Medicine*) held firmly up to her eyes like a hymnal. Stripped of his clothes and defenseless, he felt caught between the two of them.

He sipped some of his soda as Ruby went out, hardly tasting it.

Mr Keene waited until the door was shut and then smiled his dry sun-on-mica smile again. 'Loosen up, Eddie. I'm not going to bite you, or hurt you.'

Eddie nodded, because Mr Keene was a grownup and you were supposed to agree with grownups at all costs (his mother had taught him that), but inside he was thinking: *Oh, I've heard that bullshit before.* It was about what the doctor said when he opened his sterilizer and the sharp frightening smell of alcohol drifted out, stinging his nostrils. That was the smell of shots and this was the smell of bullshit and both came down to the same thing: when they said it was just going to be a little prick, something you hardly felt at all, that meant it was going to hurt *plenty*.

He tried another half-hearted suck on his soda straw, but it was no good; he needed all the space in his narrowing throat just to suck in air. He looked at the aspirator sitting in the middle of Mr Keene's blotter, wanted to ask for it, didn't quite dare. A weird thought occurred to him: maybe Mr Keene *knew* he wanted it but didn't dare ask for it, that maybe Mr Keene was

(*torturing*)

teasing him. Except that was a really stupid idea, wasn't it? A grownup – particularly a *health-dispensing* grownup – wouldn't tease a little kid that way, would he? Surely not. It wasn't even to be considered, because consideration of such an idea might necessitate a terrifying reappraisal of the world as Eddie understood it.

But there it was, there it was, so near and yet so far, like water just beyond the reach of a man who was dying of thirst in the desert. There it was, standing on the desk below Mr Keene's smiling mica eyes.

Eddie wished, more than anything else, that he was down in the Barrens with his friends around him. The thought of a monster, some great monster, lurking under the city where he had been born and where he had grown up, using the sewers and drains to creep from place to place – that was a frightening thought, and the thought of actually *fighting* that creature, of *taking it on*, was even more frightening . . . but somehow this was worse. How could you fight a grownup who said it wasn't going to hurt when you knew it was? How could you fight a grownup who asked you funny questions and said obscurely ominous things like *This has gone on long enough?* And almost idly, in a kind of side-thought, Eddie discovered one of his childhood's great truths. *Grownups are the real monsters*, he thought. It was no big deal, not a thought that came in a revelatory flash or announced itself with trumpets and bells. It just came and was gone, almost buried under the stronger, overriding thought: *I want my aspirator and I want to be out of here.*

'Loosen up,' Mr Keene said again. 'Most of your trouble, Eddie, comes from being so tight and stiff all the time. Take your asthma, for instance. Look here.'

Mr Keene opened his desk drawer, fumbled around inside, and then brought out a balloon. Expanding his narrow chest as much as possible (his tie bobbed like a narrow boat riding a mild wave), he huffed into it and blew it up. CENTER STREET DRUG, the balloon said.

PRESCRIPTIONS, SUNDRIES, OSTOMY SUPPLIES. Mr Keene pinched the balloon's rubber neck and held the balloon out in front of him. 'Now pretend for just a moment that this is a lung,' he said. '*Your* lung. I should really blow up two, of course, but since I only had one left from the sale we had just after Christmas −'

'Mr Keene, could I have my aspirator now?' Eddie's head was starting to pound. He could feel his windpipe sealing itself up. His heartrate was up, and sweat stood out on his forehead. His chocolate ice-cream soda stood on the corner of Mr Keene's desk, the cherry on top sinking slowly into a goo of whipped cream.

'In a minute,' Mr Keene said. 'Pay attention, Eddie. I want to help you. It's time somebody did. If Russ Handor isn't man enough to do it, I'll have to. Your lung is like this balloon, except it's surrounded by a blanket of muscle; these muscles are like the arms of a man operating a bellows, you understand? In a healthy person, those muscles help the lungs to expand and contract easily. But if the owner of those healthy lungs is always getting stiff and tight, the muscles begin to work *against* the lungs rather than with them. Look!'

Mr Keene wrapped a bunched, bony, liverspotted hand around the balloon and squeezed. The balloon bulged over and under his fist and Eddie winced, trying to get ready for the pop. Simultaneously he felt his breathing stop altogether. He leaned over the desk and grabbed for the aspirator on the blotter. His shoulder struck the heavy ice-cream-soda glass. It toppled off the desk and shattered on the floor like a bomb.

Eddie heard that only dimly. He was clawing the top off the aspirator, slamming the nozzle into his mouth, triggering it off. He took a tearing heaving breath, his thoughts a ratrun of panic as they always were at moments like this: *Please Mommy I'm suffocating I can't BREATHE oh my dear God oh dear Jesus meekandmild I can't BREATHE please I don't want to die don't want to die oh please −*

Then the fog from the aspirator condensed on the swollen walls of his throat and he could breathe again.

'I'm sorry,' he said, nearly crying. 'I'm sorry about the glass . . . I'll clean it up and pay for it . . . just please don't tell my mother, okay? I'm sorry, Mr Keene, but I couldn't *breathe* −'

There was that double tap at the door again and Ruby poked her head in. 'Is everything −'

'Everything's fine,' Mr Keene said sharply. 'Leave us.'

'Well I'm *saw*-ry!' Ruby said. She rolled her eyes and closed the door.

Eddie's breath was starting to whistle in his throat again. He took another pull at the aspirator and then began his fumbling apology once more. He ceased only when he saw that Mr Keene was smiling at him – that peculiar dry smile. Mr Keene's hands were laced over his middle. The balloon lay on his desk. A thought came to Eddie; he tried to hold it back and couldn't. Mr Keene looked as if Eddie's asthma attack had tasted better to him than his half-finished coffee soda.

'Don't be concerned,' he said. 'Ruby will clean up the mess later, and if you want to know the truth, I'm rather glad you broke the glass. Because I promise not to tell your mother that you broke it if *you* promise not to tell her we had this little talk.'

'Oh, I promise that,' Eddie said eagerly.

'Good,' Mr Keene said. 'We have an understanding. And you feel much better now, don't you?'

Eddie nodded.

'Why?'

'Why? Well . . . because I had my medicine.' He looked at Mr Keene the way he looked at Mrs Casey in school when he had given an answer he wasn't quite sure of.

'But you *didn't* have any medicine,' Mr Keene said. 'You had a *placebo*. A placebo, Eddie, is something that *looks* like medicine and *tastes* like medicine but *isn't* medicine. A placebo isn't medicine because it has no active ingredients. Or, if it *is* medicine, it's medicine of a very special sort. Head-medicine.' Mr Keene smiled. 'Do you under-stand that, Eddie? *Head-medicine.*'

Eddie understood, all right; Mr Keene was telling him he was crazy. But through numb lips he said, 'No, I don't get you.'

'Let me tell you a little story,' Mr Keene said. 'In 1954, a series of medical tests on ulcer patients was run at DePaul University. One hundred ulcer patients were given pills. They were all told the pills would help their ulcers, but fifty of the patients really got placebos . . . They were, in fact, M&M's given a uniform pink coating.' Mr Keene uttered a strange shrill giggle – that of a man describing a prank rather than an experiment. 'Of those one hundred patients, ninety-three said they felt a definite improvement, and eighty-one *showed* an improve-ment. So what do you think? What conclusion do you draw from such an experiment, Eddie?'

'I don't know,' Eddie said faintly.

Mr Keene tapped his head solemnly. 'Most sickness starts in here, that's what *I* think. I've been in this business a long, long time, and I knew about placebos a mighty stretch of years before those doctors at

DePaul University did their study. Usually it's old folks who end up getting the placebos. The old fellow or the old girl will go to the doctor, convinced that they've got heart disease or cancer or diabetes or some damn thing. But in a good many cases it's nothing like that at all. They don't feel good because they're old, that's all. But what's a doctor to do? Tell them they're like watches with wornout mainsprings? Huh! Not likely. Doctors like their fees too much.' And now Mr Keene's face wore an expression somewhere between a smile and a sneer.

Eddie just sat there waiting for it to be over, to be over, to be over. *You didn't have any medicine*: those words clanged in his mind.

'The doctors don't tell them that, and I don't tell them that, either. Why bother? Sometimes an old party will come in with a prescription blank that will say it right out: *Placebo*, or *25 grains Blue Skies*, which was how old Doc Pearson used to put it.'

Mr Keene cackled briefly and then sucked on his coffee soda.

'Well, what's wrong with it?' he asked Eddie, and when Eddie only sat there, Mr Keene answered his own question. 'Why, nothing! Nothing at all!

'At least . . . usually.

'Placebos are a blessing for old people. And then there are other cases – folks with cancer, folks with degenerative heart disease, folks with terrible things that we don't understand yet, some of them children just like you, Eddie! In cases like that, if a placebo makes the patient feel better, where is the harm? Do you see the harm, Eddie?'

'No sir,' Eddie said, and looked down at the splatter of chocolate ice cream, soda-water, whipped cream, and broken glass on the floor. In the middle of all this was the maraschino cherry, as accusing as a blood-clot at a crime scene. Looking at this mess made his chest feel tight again.

'Then we're like Ike and Mike! We think alike! Five years ago, when Vernon Maitland had cancer of the esophagus – a painful, painful sort of cancer – and the doctors had run out of anything effective they could give him for his pain, I came by his hospital room with a bottle of sugar-pills. He was a special friend, you see. And I said, "Vern, these are special experimental pain-pills. The doctor doesn't know I'm giving them to you, so for God's sake be careful and don't tattle on me. They might not work, but I think they will. Take no more than one a day, and only if the pain is especially bad." He thanked me with tears in his eyes. *Tears*, Eddie! And they worked for him! *Yes*! They were only sugar-pills, but they killed most of his pain . . . because pain is here.'

Solemnly, Mr Keene tapped his head again.

725

Eddie said: 'My medicine does so work.'

'I know it does,' Mr Keene replied, and smiled a maddening complacent grownup's smile. 'It works on your chest because it works on your head. HydrOx, Eddie, is water with a dash of camphor thrown on to give it a medicine taste.'

'No,' Eddie said. His breath had begun to whistle again.

Mr Keene drank some of his soda, spooned some of the melting ice cream, and fastidiously wiped his chin with his handkerchief while Eddie used his aspirator again.

'I want to go now,' Eddie said.

'Let me finish, please.'

'No! I want to go, you've got your money and I want to go!'

'Let me finish,' Mr Keene said, so forbiddingly that Eddie sat back in his chair. Grownups could be so hateful in their power sometimes. So hateful.

'Part of the problem here is that your doctor, Russ Handor, is weak. And part of the problem is that your mother is determined you are ill. You, Eddie, have been caught in the middle.'

'I'm not crazy,' Eddie whispered, the words coming out in a bare husk.

Mr Keene's chair creaked like a monstrous cricket. 'What?'

'I said I'm not crazy!' Eddie shouted. Then, immediately, a miserable blush rose into his face.

Mr Keene smiled. Think what you like, that smile said. Think what *you* like, and I'll think what *I* like.

'All I'm telling you, Eddie, is that you're not physically ill. Your *lungs* don't have asthma; your *mind* does.'

'You mean I'm crazy.'

Mr Keene leaned forward, looking at him intently over his folded hands.

'I don't know,' he said softly. 'Are you?'

'It's all a lie!' Eddie cried, surprised the words came out so strongly from his tight chest. He was thinking of Bill, how Bill would react to such amazing charges. Bill would know what to say, stutter or not. Bill would know how to be brave. 'All a great big lie! I *do* have asthma, I *do*!'

'Yes,' Mr Keene said, and now the dry smile had become a weird skeletal grin. 'But who gave it to you, Eddie?'

Eddie's brain thudded and whirled. Oh, he felt sick, he felt very sick.

'Four years ago, in 1954 – the same year as the DePaul tests, oddly enough – Dr Handor began prescribing this HydrOx for you. That stands for hydrogen and oxygen, the two components of water. I have condoned this deception since then, but I will not condone it anymore. Your asthma medicine works on your mind rather than your body. Your asthma is the result of a nervous tightening of the diaphragm that is ordered by your mind . . . or your mother.

'You are not sick.'

A terrible silence descended.

Eddie sat in his chair, his mind whirling. For a moment he considered the possibility that Mr Keene might be telling the truth, but there were ramifications in such an idea that he could not face. Yet why would Mr Keene lie, especially about something so serious?

Mr Keene sat and smiled his bright dry heartless desert smile.

I do *have asthma, I* do. *The day that Henry Bowers punched me in the nose, the day Bill and I were trying to make a dam in the Barrens, I almost* died. *Am I supposed to think that my mind was just . . . just making all of that up?*

But why would he lie? (It was only years later, in the library, that Eddie asked himself the more terrible question: *Why would he tell me the truth?*)

Dimly he heard Mr Keene saying: 'I've kept my eye on you, Eddie. I told you all this because you're old enough to understand, but also because I've noticed you've finally made some friends. They are good friends, aren't they?'

'Yes,' Eddie said.

Mr Keene tilted his chair back (it made that cricketlike noise again), and closed one eye in what might or might not have been a wink. 'And I'll bet your mother doesn't like them much, does she?'

'She likes them fine,' Eddie said, thinking of the cutting things his mother had said about Richie Tozier (*He has a foul mouth . . . and I've smelled his breath, Eddie . . . I think he smokes*), her sniffing remark not to loan any money to Stan Uris because he was a Jew, her outright dislike of Bill Denbrough and 'that fatboy.'

He repeated to Mr Keene: 'She likes them a lot.'

'Does she?' Mr Keene said, still smiling. 'Well, maybe she's right and maybe she's wrong, but at least you *have* friends. Maybe you ought to talk to them about this problem of yours. This . . . this mental weakness. See what they have to say.'

Eddie didn't reply. He was through talking to Mr Keene; that seemed safer. And he was afraid that if he didn't get out of here soon, he really would cry.

727

'Well!' Mr Keene said, standing up. 'I think that just about finishes us up, Eddie. If I've upset you, I'm sorry. I was only doing my duty as I saw it. I —'

But before he could say any more, Eddie had snatched up his aspirator and the white bag of pills and nostrums and had fled. One of his feet skidded in the ice-creamy mess on the floor and he almost fell. Then he was running, bolting from the Center Street Drug Store in spite of his whistling breath. Ruby stared after him over her movie magazine, her mouth open.

Behind him he seemed to sense Mr Keene standing in the doorway of his office and watching his graceless retreat over the prescription counter, gaunt and neat and thoughtful and smiling. Smiling that dry desert smile.

He paused outside on the three-way corner of Kansas, Main, and Center. He took another deep pull from his aspirator while sitting on the low stone wall by the bus-stop — his throat was now positively slimy with that medicinal taste

(*nothing but water with some camphor thrown in*) and he thought that if he had to use the aspirator again today he would probably puke his guts.

He slipped it into his pocket and watched the traffic pass back and forth, headed up Main Street and down Up-Mile Hill. He tried not to think. The sun beat down on his head, blaringly hot. Each passing car threw bright darts of reflection into his eyes, and a headache was starting in his temples. He couldn't find a way to stay angry at Mr Keene, but he had no trouble at all feeling bad for Eddie Kaspbrak. He felt *real* bad for Eddie Kaspbrak. He supposed that Bill Denbrough never wasted time feeling sorry for himself, but Eddie just couldn't seem to help it.

More than anything else he wanted to do exactly what Mr Keene had suggested: go down to the Barrens and tell his friends everything, see what they would say, find out what answers they had. But he couldn't do that now. His mother would expect him home with her medicines soon

(*your mind . . . or your mother*)

and if he wasn't there

(*your mother is determined you are ill*)

trouble would follow. She would assume he had been with Bill or Richie or 'the Jewboy,' as she called Stan (insisting that she meant no prejudice by so calling him, but was simply 'slapping down the cards' — her phrase for truth-telling in difficult situations). And standing here on this corner, trying hopelessly to sort out his flying thoughts, Eddie knew what she would say if she knew one of his other friends was a Negro and another was a girl – a girl old enough to be getting bosoms.

He started slowly toward Up-Mile Hill, dreading the stiff climb in this heat. It felt almost hot enough to fry an egg on the sidewalk. For the first time he found himself wishing for school to be in again, for a new grade and a new teacher's peculiarities to contend with. For this dreadful summer to be over.

He stopped halfway up the hill, not far from where Bill Denbrough would rediscover his bike Silver twenty-seven years later, and pulled his aspirator from his pocket. *HydrOx Mist*, the label said. *Administer as needed*.

Something else clicked home. *Administer as needed*. He was only a kid, still wet behind the ears (as his mother sometimes told him when she was 'slapping down the cards'), but even a kid of eleven knew that you didn't give someone real medicine and then write on the label *Administer as needed*. If it was real medicine, it would be too easy to kill yourself as you went happy-assholing around and administering as needed. He supposed you could kill yourself with plain old aspirin doing that.

He looked fixedly at the aspirator, unaware of the old lady who glanced curiously at him as she passed on down the hill toward Main Street with her shopping basket over her arm. He felt betrayed. And for one moment he almost cast the plastic squeeze-bottle into the gutter – better yet, he thought, throw it down that sewer-grating. Sure! Why not? Let It have it down there in Its tunnels and dripping sewer-pipes. Have a pla-cee-bo, you hundred-faced creep! He uttered a wild laugh and came within an ace of doing it. But in the end, habit was simply too strong. He replaced the aspirator in his right front pants pocket and walked on, hardly hearing the occasional blare of a horn or the diesel drone of the Bassey Park bus as it passed him. He was likewise unaware of how close he was to discovering what being hurt – really hurt – was all about.

3

When he came out of the Costello Avenue Market twenty-five minutes later with a Pepsi in one hand and two Payday candybars in the other, Eddie was unpleasantly surprised to see Henry Bowers, Victor Criss, Moose Sadler, and Patrick Hockstetter kneeling on the crushed gravel to the left of the little store. For a moment Eddie thought they were shooting craps; then he saw they were pooling their money on Victor's baseball shirt. Their summer-school text-books lay off to one side in an untidy heap.

On an ordinary day Eddie might have simply faded quietly back into the store and asked Mr Gedreau if he could leave by the back door but this had been no ordinary day. Eddie froze right where he was instead, one hand still holding the screen door with its tin cigarette signs (WINSTON TASTES GOOD, LIKE A CIGARETTE SHOULD, TWENTY-ONE GREAT TOBACCOS MAKE TWENTY WONDERFUL SMOKES, the bellboy who was shouting CALL FOR PHILIP MORRIS), the other clutching the brown grocery bag and the white drugstore bag.

Victor Criss saw him and elbowed Henry. Henry looked up; so did Patrick Hockstetter. Moose, whose relays worked more slowly, went on counting out pennies for five seconds or so before the sudden silence sank into him and he also looked up.

Henry stood, brushing loose pieces of gravel from the knees of the biballs he was wearing. There were splints on the sides of his bandaged nose, and his voice had a nasal foghorning quality. 'Well I be go to hell,' he said. 'One of the rock-throwers. Where's your friends, asshole? They inside?'

Eddie was shaking his head numbly before he realized this was another mistake.

Henry's smile broadened. 'Well, that's okay,' he said. 'I don't mind taking you one by one. Come on down here, asshole.'

Victor stood beside Henry; Patrick Hockstetter trailed behind them, smiling in a porky vacant way Eddie was familiar with from school. Moose was still getting up.

'Come on, asshole,' Henry said. 'Let's talk about throwing rocks. Let's talk about that, you wanna?'

Now that it was too late Eddie decided it would be wise to go back into the store. Back in the store where there was a grownup. But as he retreated Henry darted forward and grabbed him. He pulled Eddie's arm, pulled hard, his smile turning into a snarl. Eddie's hand was ripped free of the screen door. He was pulled off the steps and would have crashed headlong into the gravel if Victor hadn't caught him roughly under the arms. Victor threw him. Eddie managed to keep on his feet, but only by whirling around twice. The four boys faced him now over a distance of about ten feet, Henry slightly ahead of the others, smiling. His hair stood up at the back in a cowlick.

Behind Henry and on his left was Patrick Hockstetter, a genuinely spooky kid. Eddie hadn't ever seen him with anyone else until today. He was just enough overweight so that his belly always hung slightly over his belt, which had a Red Ryder buckle. His face was perfectly round, and usually as pale as cream. Now he had a slight sunburn. It was heaviest on his nose, which was peeling, but it spread out toward either cheek like wings. In school, Patrick liked to kill flies with his green plastic SkoolTime ruler and put them in his pencil-box. Sometimes he would show his fly collection to some new kid in the playyard at recess, his heavy lips smiling, his gray-green eyes sober and thoughtful. He never spoke when he exhibited his dead flies, no matter what the new kid might say to him. That expression was on his face now.

'How ya doin, Rock Man?' Henry asked, advancing across the distance between them. 'Got any rocks on you?'

'Leave me alone,' Eddie said in a trembling voice.

'"Leave me alone,"' Henry mimicked, waving his hands in mock terror. Victor laughed. 'What are you going to do if I don't, Rock Man? Huh?' His hand flashed out, incredibly fast, and exploded against Eddie's cheek with a gunshot sound. Eddie's head rocked back. Tears began to pour from his left eye.

'My friends are inside,' Eddie said.

'"My friends are inside,"' Patrick Hockstetter squealed. 'Ooooh! Ooooh! *Ooooh!*' He began to circle to Eddie's right.

Eddie started to turn in that direction, Henry's hand flashed out again, and this time his other cheek flamed.

Don't cry, he thought, *that's what they want, but don't you do it Eddie, Bill wouldn't do it, Bill wouldn't cry, and don't you cry, eith –*

Victor stepped forward and gave Eddie a hard open-handed push in the middle of his chest. Eddie stumbled half a step backward and then fell sprawling over Patrick, who had crouched directly behind his feet. He thudded to the gravel, scraping his arms. There was a *whoof!* as the wind rushed out of him.

A moment later Henry Bowers was on top of him, his knees pinning Eddie's arms, his butt on Eddie's stomach.

'Got any rocks, Rock Man?' Henry raved down at him, and Eddie was more frightened by the mad light in Henry's eyes than he was by the pain in his arms or by his inability to get his breath back. Henry was nuts. Somewhere close by, Patrick tittered.

'You wanna throw rocks? Huh? I'll give you rocks! Here! Here's some rocks!'

Henry swept up a handful of gravel and slammed it down into

Eddie's face. He rubbed the gravel into Eddie's skin, cutting his cheeks, his eyelids, his lips. Eddie opened his mouth and screamed.

'Want rocks? I'll give you rocks! Here's some rocks, Rock Man! You want rocks? Okay! Okay! Okay!'

Gravel slammed into his open mouth, lacerating his gums, grinding against his teeth. He felt sparks fly against his fillings. He screamed again and spat gravel out.

'Want some more rocks? Okay? How about a few more? How about –'

'Stop that! Here, here! Stop that! You, boy! Quit on him! Right now! You hear me? Quit on him!'

Through half–lidded, tear–blurred eyes, Eddie saw a big hand come down and grab Henry by the collar of his shirt and the right strap of his biballs. The hand gave a yank and Henry was pulled off. He landed in the gravel and got up. Eddie rose more slowly. He was trying to scramble to his feet, but his scrambler seemed temporarily broken. He gasped and spat chunks of bloody gravel out of his mouth.

It was Mr Gedreau, dressed in his long white apron, and he looked furious. There was no fear in his face, although Henry stood about three inches taller and probably outweighed him by fifty pounds. There was no fear in his face because he was the grownup and Henry was the kid. Except this time, Eddie thought, that might not mean anything. Mr Gedreau didn't understand. He didn't understand that Henry was nuts.

'You get out of here,' Mr Gedreau said, advancing on Henry until he stood toe to toe with the hulking sullen–faced boy. 'You get out and you don't want to come back, either. I don't hold with bullying. I don't hold with four against one. What would your mothers think?'

He swept the others with his hot, angry eyes. Moose and Victor dropped their gazes and examined their sneakers. Patrick only stared at and through Mr Gedreau with that vacant gray–green look. Mr Gedreau looked back at Henry and got just as far as 'You get on your bikes and –' when Henry gave him a good hard push.

An expression of surprise that would have been comical in other circumstances spread across Mr Gedreau's face as he flew backward, loose gravel spurting out from under his heels. He struck the steps leading up to the screen door and sat down hard.

'Why you –' he began.

Henry's shadow fell on him. 'Get inside,' he said.

'You –' Mr Gedreau said, and this time he stopped on his own.

Mr Gedreau had finally seen it, Eddie realized – the light in Henry's eyes. He got up quickly, apron flapping. He went up the stairs as fast as he could, stumbling on the second one from the top and going briefly to one knee. He was up again at once, but that stumble, as brief as it had been, seemed to rob him of the rest of his grownup authority.

He spun around at the top and yelled: 'I'm calling the cops!'

Henry made as if to lunge for him, and Mr Gedreau flinched back. That was the end, Eddie realized. As incredible, as unthinkable as it seemed, there was no protection for him here. It was time to go.

While Henry was standing at the bottom of the steps and glaring up at Mr Gedreau and while the others were staring, transfixed (and, except for Patrick Hockstetter, not a little horrified) by this sudden successful defiance of adult authority, Eddie saw his chance. He whirled, took to his heels, and ran.

He was halfway up the block before Henry turned, his eyes blazing. '*Get him!*' he bellowed.

Asthma or no asthma, Eddie ran them a good race that day. There were spaces, some of them as long as fifty feet, when he couldn't remember if the soles of his P.F. Flyers had touched the sidewalk or not. For a few moments he even entertained the giddy notion that he might be able to outrun them.

Then, just before he reached Kansas Street and what might have been safety, a little kid on a trike suddenly pedaled out of a driveway and right into Eddie's path. Eddie tried to swerve, but running full-out as he had been, he might have done better to jump over the kid (the kid's name, in fact, was Richard Cowan, and he would grow up, marry, and father a son named Frederick Cowan, who would be drowned in a toilet and then be partially eaten by a thing that rose up from the toilet like black smoke and then took an unthinkable shape), or at least to try.

One of Eddie's feet caught on the trike's back deck, where an adventurous little shit might stand and push the trike along like a scooter. Richard Cowan, whose unborn son would be murdered by It twenty-seven years later, barely rocked on his trike. Eddie, however, went flying. He struck the sidewalk on his shoulder, rebounded, came down again, and skidded ten feet, erasing the skin from his elbows and knees. He was trying to get up when Henry Bowers hit him like a shell from a bazooka and knocked him flat. Eddie's nose connected briskly with the concrete. Blood flew.

Henry did a quick side-roll like a paratrooper and was up again.

He grabbed Eddie by the nape of the neck and by his right wrist. His breath, snorting through his swelled and splinted nose, was warm and moist.

'Want rocks, Rock Man? Sure! Shit!' He jerked Eddie's wrist halfway up his back. Eddie yelled. 'Rocks for the Rock Man, right, Rock Man?' He jerked Eddie's wrist up even higher. Eddie screamed. Behind him, dimly, he could hear the others approaching, and the little kid on the trike starting to bawl. *Join the club, kid,* he thought, and in spite of the pain, in spite of the tears and the fear, he brayed a huge donkeylike hee-haw of laughter.

'You think this is *funny*?' Henry asked, sounding suddenly astounded rather than furious. 'You think this is funny?' And did Henry also sound *scared*? Years later Eddie would think *Yes, scared, he sounded scared*.

Eddie twisted his wrist in Henry's grip. He was slick with sweat and he almost got away. Perhaps that was why Henry shoved Eddie's wrist up harder this time than before. Eddie heard a crack in his arm like the sound of winterwood giving under an accumulated plate of ice. The pain that rolled out of his fractured arm was gray and huge. He shrieked, but the sound seemed distant. The color was washing out of the world, and when Henry let go of him and pushed, he seemed to float toward the sidewalk. It took a long time to get down to that old sidewalk. He had a good look at every single crack in it as he glided down. He had a chance to admire the way the July sun glinted off the flecks of mica in that old sidewalk. He had a chance to note the remains of a very old hopscotch grid that had been done in pink chalk on that old sidewalk. Then, for just a moment, it swam and looked like something else. It looked like a turtle.

He might have fainted then, but he struck on his newly broken arm, and this fresh pain was sharp, bright, hot, terrible. He felt the splintered ends of the greenstick fracture grind together. He bit his tongue, bringing fresh blood. He rolled over on his back and saw Henry, Victor, Moose, and Patrick standing over him. They looked impossibly tall, impossibly high up, like pallbearers peering into a grave.

'You like that, Rock Man?' Henry asked, his voice drifting down over a distance, floating through clouds of pain. 'You like that action, Rock Man? You like that jobba-nobba?'

Patrick Hockstetter giggled.

'Your father's crazy,' Eddie heard himself say, 'and so are you.'

Henry's grin faded so fast it might have been slapped off his face.

He drew his foot back to kick ... and then a siren rose in the still hot afternoon. Henry paused. Victor and Moose looked around uneasily.

'Henry, I think we better get out of here,' Moose said.

'I know damn well *I'm* getting out of here,' Victor said. How far away their voices seemed! Like the clown's balloons, they seemed to float. Victor took off toward the library, cutting into McCarron Park to get off the street.

Henry hesitated a moment longer, perhaps hoping the cop-car was on some other business and he could continue with his own. But the siren rose again, closer. 'You got lucky, fuckface,' he said. He and Moose took off after Victor.

Patrick Hockstetter waited for a moment. 'Here's a little something extra for you,' he whispered in his low, husky voice. He inhaled and spat a large green lunger into Eddie's upturned, sweating, bloody face. *Splat.* 'Don't eat it all at once if you don't want,' Patrick said, smiling his liverish unsettling smile. 'Save some for later, if you want.'

Then he turned slowly and was also gone.

Eddie tried to wipe the lunger off with his good arm, but even that little movement made the pain flare again.

Now when you started off for the drugstore, you never thought you'd end up on the Costello Avenue sidewalk with a busted arm and Patrick Hockstetter's snot running down your face, did you? You never even got to drink your Pepsi. Life's full of surprises, isn't it?

Incredibly, he laughed again. It was a weak sound, and it hurt his broken arm to laugh, but it felt good. And there was something else: no asthma. His breathing was okay, at least for now. A good thing, too. He never would have been able to get to his aspirator. Never in a thousand years.

The siren was very close now, whooping and whooping. Eddie closed his eyes and saw red under his eyelids. Then the red turned black as a shadow fell over him. It was the little kid with the trike.

'You okay?' the little kid asked.

'Do I look okay?' Eddie asked.

'No, you look *terrible*,' the little kid said, and pedaled off, singing 'The Farmer in the Dell.'

Eddie began to giggle. Here was the cop-car; he could hear the squeal of its brakes. He found himself hoping vaguely that Mr Nell would be in it, even though he knew Mr Nell was a foot patrolman.

Why in the name of God are you giggling?

He didn't know, any more than he knew why he should feel, in spite of the pain, such intense relief. Was it maybe just because he was still alive, that the worst he had suffered was a broken arm, and there were still some pieces to pick up? He settled for that, but years later, sitting in the Derry Library with a glass of gin and prune juice in front of him and his aspirator near at hand, he told the others he thought it was something more than that; he had been old enough to feel that something more, but not to understand or define it.

I think it was the first real pain I ever felt in my life, he would tell the others. *It wasn't what I thought it would be at all. It didn't put an end to me as a person. I think . . . it gave me a basis for comparison, finding out you could still exist inside the pain*, in spite *of the pain.*

Eddie turned his head weakly to the right and saw large black Firestone tires, blinding chrome hubcaps, and pulsing blue lights. He heard Mr Nell's voice then, thickly Irish, impossibly Irish, more like Richie's Irish Cop Voice than Mr Nell's real voice . . . but perhaps that was the distance:

'Holy Jaysus, it's the Kaspbrak bye!'

At this point Eddie floated away.

4

And, with one exception, stayed away for quite awhile.

There was a brief period of consciousness in the ambulance. He saw Mr Nell sitting across from him, tipping a drink from his little brown bottle and reading a paperback called *I the Jury*. The girl on the cover had the biggest bosoms Eddie had ever seen. His eyes shifted past Mr Nell to the driver up front. The driver peered around at Eddie with a big leering grin, his skin livid with greasepaint and talcum powder, his eyes shiny as new quarters. It was Pennywise.

'Mr Nell,' Eddie husked.

Mr Nell looked up and smiled. 'How are you feelin, me bye?'

'. . . driver . . . the driver . . .'

'Yes, we'll be there in a jig,' Mr Nell said, and handed him the little brown bottle. 'Suck some of this. It'll make ye feel better.'

Eddie drank what tasted like liquid fire. He coughed, hurting his arm. He looked toward the front and saw the driver again. Just some guy with a crewcut. No clown.

He drifted off again.

Much later there was the Emergency Room and a nurse wiping blood and dirt and snot and gravel off his face with a cold cloth. It stung, but it felt wonderful at the same time. He heard his mother bugling and clarioning outside, and he tried to tell the nurse not to let her in, but no words would come out, no matter how hard he tried.

'. . . if he's dying, I want to know!' his mother was bellowing. 'You hear me? It's my right to know, and it's my right to see him! I can sue you, you know! I know lawyers, plenty of lawyers! Some of my best friends are lawyers!'

'Don't try to talk,' the nurse said to Eddie. She was young, and he could feel her bosoms pressing against his arm. For a moment he had this crazy idea that the nurse was Beverly Marsh, and then he drifted away again.

When he came back his mother *was* in the room, talking to Dr Handor at a mile-a-minute clip. Sonia Kaspbrak was a huge woman. Her legs, encased in support hose, were trunklike but weirdly smooth. Her face was pale now except for hectic flaring blots of rouge.

'Ma,' Eddie managed, '. . . all right . . . I'm all right . . .'

'You're *not*, you're *not*,' Mrs Kaspbrak moaned. She wrung her hands. Eddie heard her knuckles crack and grind. He began to feel his breath shorten up as he looked at her, seeing what a state she was in, how this latest escapade of his had hurt her. He wanted to tell her to take it easy or she'd have a heart attack, but he couldn't. His throat was too dry. 'You're *not* all right, you've had a serious accident, a *very serious* accident, but you *will* be all right, I promise you that, Eddie, you *will* be all right, even if we need to bring in every specialist in the book, oh Eddie . . . Eddie . . . your poor *arm* . . .'

She burst into honking sobs. Eddie saw that the nurse who had washed his face was looking at her without much sympathy.

All through this aria, Dr Handor had been stuttering, 'Sonia . . . please, Sonia . . . Sonia . . . ?' He was a skinny, limp-looking man with a little mustache that hadn't grown very well and which, in addition, had been clipped unevenly, so it was longer on the left side than on the right. He looked nervous. Eddie remembered what Mr Keene had told him that morning and felt a certain sorrow for Dr Handor.

At last, gathering himself, Russ Handor managed to say: 'If you can't control yourself, you'll have to leave, Sonia.'

She whirled on him and he drew back. 'I'll do no such thing! Don't you even suggest it! This is my *son* lying here in agony! *My son lying here on his bed of pain!*'

Eddie astounded them all by finding his voice. 'I want you to leave, Ma. If they're going to do something that'll make me yell, and I think they are, you'll feel better if you go.'

She turned to him, astonished . . . and hurt. At the sight of the hurt on her face, he felt his chest begin to tighten down inexorably. 'I certainly will *not!*' she cried. 'What an awful thing to *say*, Eddie! You're delirious! You don't *understand* what you're saying, that's the *only* explanation!'

'I don't know what the explanation is, and I don't care,' the nurse said. 'All I know is that we're standing here doing nothing while we should be setting your son's arm.'

'Are you suggesting –' Sonia began, her voice rising toward the high, bugling note it took on when she was most upset.

'Please, Sonia,' Dr Handor said. 'Let's not have an argument here. Let's help Eddie.'

Sonia stood back, but her glowering eyes – the eyes of a mother bear whose cub has been threatened – promised the nurse that there would be trouble later. Possibly even a suit. Then her eyes misted, extinguishing the glower or at least hiding it. She took Eddie's good hand and squeezed it so painfully that he winced.

'It's bad, but you'll be well again *soon*,' she said. 'Well again *soon*, I promise you *that*.'

'Sure, Ma,' Eddie wheezed. 'Could I have my aspirator?'

'Of course,' she said. Sonia Kaspbrak looked at the nurse triumphantly, as if vindicated of some ridiculous criminal charge. 'My son has asthma,' she said. 'It's quite serious, but he copes with it *beautifully*.'

'Good,' the nurse said flatly.

His ma held the aspirator for him so he could inhale. A moment later Dr Handor was feeling Eddie's broken arm. He was as gentle as possible but the pain was still enormous. Eddie felt like screaming and gritted his teeth against it. He was afraid if he screamed his mother would scream, too. Sweat stood out on his forehead in large clear drops.

'You're hurting him,' Mrs Kaspbrak said. 'I *know* you are! There's no need of that! Stop it! There's no need for you to hurt him! He's very delicate, he can't stand that sort of pain!'

Eddie saw the nurse lock her furious eyes with Dr Handor's tired, worried ones. He saw the wordless conversation that passed between them: *Send that woman out of here, doctor.* And in the drop of his eyes: *I can't. I don't dare.*

There was great clarity inside the pain (although, in truth, this was not a clarity that Eddie would want to experience often: the price was too high), and in that unspoken conversation, Eddie accepted everything Mr Keene had told him. His HydrOx aspirator was filled

738

with nothing more than flavored water. The asthma wasn't in his throat or his chest or his lungs but in his head. Somehow or other he was going to have to deal with that truth.

He looked at his mother, seeing her clear in his pain: each flower on her Lane Bryant dress, the sweat-stains under her arms where the pads she wore had soaked through, the scuff-marks on her shoes. He saw how small her eyes were in their pockets of flesh, and now a terrible thought came to him: those eyes were almost predatory, like the eyes of the leper that had crawled out of the basement at 29 Neibolt Street. *Here I come, that's all right . . . it won't do you any good to run, Eddie . . .*

Dr Handor put his hands gently around Eddie's broken arm and squeezed. The pain exploded.

Eddie drifted away.

5

They gave him some liquid to drink and Dr Handor set the fracture. He heard Dr Handor telling his ma that it was a greenstick fracture, no more serious than any childhood break: 'It's the sort of break kids get falling out of trees,' he said, and Eddie heard his ma respond furiously: 'Eddie doesn't *climb* trees! Now I want the truth! How bad is he?'

Then the nurse was giving him a pill. He felt her bosoms against his shoulder again and was grateful for their comforting pressure. Even through the haze he could see that the nurse was angry and he thought he said, *She's not the leper, please don't think that, she's only eating me because she loves me*, but perhaps nothing came out because the nurse's angry face didn't change.

He had a faint recollection of being pushed up a corridor in a wheelchair and his mother's voice somewhere behind, fading: 'What do you mean, *visiting hours*? Don't talk to me about *visiting hours*, that's my *son!*'

Fading. He was glad she was fading, glad he was fading. The pain was gone and the clarity was gone with it. He didn't want to think. He wanted to drift. He was aware that his right arm felt very heavy. He wondered if they had put it in a cast yet. He couldn't seem to see if they had or not. He was vaguely aware of radios playing from rooms, of patients who looked like ghosts in their hospital johnnies walking up and down the wide halls, and that it was hot . . . so very hot. When he was wheeled into his room, he could see the sun going down in an angry orange boil of blood and thought incoherently: *Like a great big clown-button.*

'Come on, Eddie, you can walk,' a voice was saying, and he found that he could. He was slid between crisp cool sheets. The voice told him that he would have some pain in the night, but not to ring for a pain-killer unless it got very bad. Eddie asked if he could have a drink of water. The water came with a straw that had an accordion middle so you could bend it. It was cool and good. He drank it all.

There was pain in the night, a good deal of it. He lay awake in bed, holding the call-button in his left hand but not pressing it. A thunderstorm was going on outside, and when the lightning flashed blue-white, he turned his head away from the windows, afraid he might see a monstrous, grinning face etched across the sky in that electric fire.

At last he slept again, and in his sleep he had a dream. In it he saw Bill, Ben, Richie, Stan, Mike, and Bev – his friends – arriving at the hospital on their bikes (Bill was riding Richie double on Silver). He was surprised to see that Beverly was wearing a dress – it was a lovely green, the color of the Caribbean in a *National Geographic* plate. He couldn't remember if he had ever seen her in a dress before; all he remembered were jeans and pedal-pushers and what the girls called 'school-sets': skirts and blouses, the blouses usually white with round collars, the skirts usually brown and pleated and hemmed at mid-shin, so that the scabs on their knees didn't show.

In the dream he saw them coming in for the 2:00 P.M. visiting hours and his mother, who had been waiting patiently since eleven, shouting so loudly at them that everyone turned to look at her.

If you think you're going to go in there, you've got another think coming! Eddie's mother shouted, and now the clown, who had been sitting here in the waiting room all along (but way back in one corner, with a copy of *Look* magazine held up in front of his face until now), jumped up and mimed applause, patting his white-gloved hands together rapidly. He capered and danced, now turning a cartwheel, now executing a neat back-over flip, as Mrs Kaspbrak ranted at Eddie's fellow Losers and as they shrank, one by one, behind Bill, who only stood there, pale but outwardly calm, his hands stuffed deep into the pockets of his jeans (maybe so no one, including Bill himself, would be able to see if they were shaking or not). No one saw the clown except Eddie . . . although a baby who had been sleeping peacefully in his mother's arms awoke and began to cry lustily.

You've done enough damage! Eddie's ma shouted. *I know who those boys were! They've been in trouble at school, they've even been in trouble with the* police! *And just because those boys have something against you is no reason for them to have something against him. I told him so, and he agrees with me. He wants me to tell you to go away, he's done with you, he never wants to see any of you again. He doesn't want your so-called friendship anymore! Any of you! I knew it would lead to trouble, and look at this! My Eddie in the hospital! A boy as delicate as he is . . .*

The clown capered and jumped and did splits and stood on one hand. Its smile was real enough now, and in his dream Eddie realized that this was of course what the clown wanted, a nice big wedge to drive among them, splitting them apart and destroying any chance of concerted action. In a kind of filthy ecstasy, the clown did a double barrel-roll and burlesqued kissing his mother's cheek.

Th-Th-Those b-b-b-hoys who dih-did it – Bill began.

Don't you speak back to me! Mrs Kaspbrak shrieked. *Don't you dare speak back to me! He's done with you, I say!* Done.

Then an intern came running into the waiting room and told Eddie's ma she would have to be quiet or leave the hospital. The clown started to fade, started to wash out, and as it did it began to change. Eddie saw the leper, the mummy, the bird; he saw the werewolf, and a vampire whose teeth were Gillette Blue-Blades set at crazy angles like mirrors in a carnival mirror-maze; he saw Frankenstein, the creature, and something fleshy and shell-like that opened and closed like a mouth; he saw a dozen other terrible things, a hundred. But just before the clown washed out completely, he saw the most terrible thing of all: his ma's face.

No! he tried to scream. *No! No! Not her! Not my ma!*

But no one looked around; no one heard. And in the dream's fading moments, he realized with a cold and wormy horror that they couldn't hear him. He was dead. It had killed him and he was dead. He was a ghost.

6

Sonia Kaspbrak's sour-sweet triumph at sending Eddie's so-called friends away evaporated almost as soon as she stepped into Eddie's private room the next afternoon, on the 21st of July. She could not tell exactly why the feeling of triumph should fade like that, or why it should be displaced by an unfocused fear; it was something in her son's pale face, which was not blurred with pain or anxiety but instead bore an expression she could not remember ever having seen there before. It was sharp, somehow. Sharp and alert and set.

The confrontation between Eddie's friends and Eddie's ma had not occurred in the waiting room, as in Eddie's dream; she had known they would be coming – Eddie's 'friends,' who were probably teaching him to smoke cigarettes in spite of his asthma, his 'friends' who had such an unhealthy hold over him that they were all he talked about when he came home for the evening, his 'friends' who got his arm broken. She had told all of this to Mrs Van Prett next door. 'The time has come,' Mrs Kaspbrak had said grimly, 'to slap a few cards down on the table.' Mrs Van Prett, who had horrible skin-problems and who could almost always be counted upon to agree eagerly, almost pathetically, with everything Sonia Kaspbrak said, in this case had the temerity to disagree.

I should think you'd be glad he's made some friends, Mrs Van Prett said as they hung out their washes in the early-morning cool before work – this had been during the first week of July. *And he's safer if he's with other children, Mrs Kaspbrak, don't you think so? With all that's going on in this town, and all the poor children that have been murdered?*

Mrs Kaspbrak's only reply had been an angry sniff (in fact, she couldn't just then think of an adequate verbal response, although she thought of dozens – some of them extremely cutting – later on), and when Mrs Van Prett called her that evening, sounding rather anxious, to ask if Mrs Kaspbrak would be going to the Beano down at Saint Mary's with her like usual, Mrs Kaspbrak had replied coldly that she believed she would just stay home that evening and put her feet up instead.

Well, she hoped Mrs Van Prett was satisfied now. She hoped Mrs Van Prett saw now that the only danger abroad in Derry this summer wasn't the sex-maniac killing children and babies. Here was her son, lying on his bed of pain in Derry Home Hospital, he might never be able to use his good right arm again, she had heard of such things, or, God forbid, loose splinters from the break might work through his bloodstream to his heart and puncture it and kill him, oh of course God would never allow that to happen, but she had *heard* of it happening, so that meant God *could* allow such a thing to happen. In certain cases.

So she lingered on the Home Hospital's long and shady front porch, knowing they would show up, coldly determined to put paid to this so-called 'friendship,' this camaraderie that ended in broken arms and beds of pain, once and for all.

Eventually they came, as she had known they would, and to her horror she saw that one of them was a nigger. Not that she had anything against niggers; she thought they had every right to ride where they wanted to on the buses down south, and eat at white lunch-counters, and should not be made to sit in nigger heaven at the movies unless they bothered white

(*women*)

people, but she also believed firmly in what she called the Bird Theory: Blackbirds flew with other blackbirds, not with the robins. Grackles roosted with grackles; they did not mix in with the bluebirds or the nightingales. To each his own was her motto, and seeing Mike Hanlon pedal up with the others just as if he belonged there caused her resolution, like her anger and her dismay, to grow apace. She thought reproachfully, as if Eddie were here and could listen to her: *You never told me that one of your 'friends' was a nigger.*

Well, she thought, twenty minutes later, stepping into the hospital room where her son lay with his arm in a huge cast that was strapped to his chest (it hurt her heart just to look at it), she had sent them packing in jig time . . . no pun intended. None of them except for the Denbrough boy, the one who had such a *horrible* stutter, had had the nerve to so much as speak back to her. The girl, whoever she was, had flashed a pair of decidedly slutty jade's eyes at Sonia – *from Lower Main Street or someplace even worse*, had been Sonia Kaspbrak's opinion – but she had wisely kept her mouth shut. If she had dared so much as to let out a peep, Sonia would have given her a piece of her mind; would have told her what sort of girls ran with the boys. There were names for girls like that, and she would not have her son associated, now or ever, with the girls who bore them.

The others had done no more than look down at their shuffling feet. That was about what she had expected. When she was done saying what she had to say, they had gotten on their bikes and ridden away. The Denbrough boy had the Tozier boy riding double behind him on a huge, unsafe-looking bike, and with an interior shudder Mrs Kaspbrak had wondered how many times her Eddie had ridden on that dangerous bike, risking his arms and his legs and his neck and his life.

I did this for you, Eddie, she thought as she walked into the hospital with her head firmly up. *I know you may feel a bit disappointed at first; that's natural enough. But parents know better than their children; the reason God made parents in the first place was to guide, instruct . . . and protect.* After his initial disappointment, he would understand. And if she felt a certain relief now, it was of course on Eddie's behalf and not on her own. Relief was only to be expected when you had saved your son from bad companions.

Except that her sense of relief was marred by fresh unease now, looking into Eddie's face. He was not asleep, as she had thought he would be. Instead of a drugged doze from which he would wake disoriented, dimwitted, and psychologically vulnerable, there was this sharp, watchful look, so different from Eddie's usual soft tentative glance. Like Ben Hanscom (although Sonia did not know this), Eddie was the sort of boy who would look quickly into a face, as if to test the emotional weather brewing there, and glance just as quickly away. But he was looking at her steadily now (*perhaps it's the medication*, she thought, *of course that's it; I'll have to consult with Dr Handor about his medication*), and she was the one who felt a need to glance aside. *He looks like he's been waiting for me*, she thought, and it was a thought that should have made her happy – a boy waiting for his mother must surely be one of God's most favored creations –

'You sent my friends away.' The words came out flatly, with no doubt or question in them.

She flinched almost guiltily, and certainly the first thought to flash through her mind *was* a guilty one – *How does he know that? He can't know that!* – and she was immediately furious with herself (and him) for feeling that way. So she smiled at him.

'How are we feeling today, Eddie?'

That was the right response. Someone – some foolish candy-striper, or perhaps even that incompetent and antagonistic nurse from the day before – had been carrying tales. Someone.

'How are we feeling?' she asked again when he didn't respond. She thought he hadn't heard her. She'd never read in any of her medical literature of a broken bone affecting the sense of hearing, but she supposed it was possible, anything was possible.

Eddie still didn't respond.

She came farther into the room, hating the tentative, almost timid feeling inside her, distrusting it because she had never felt tentative or timid around Eddie before. She felt anger as well, although that was still nascent. What right did he have to make her feel that way, after all she had done for him, after all she had sacrificed for him?

'I've talked to Dr Handor, and he assures me that you're going to be perfectly all right,' Sonia said briskly, sitting down in the straight-backed wooden chair by the bed. 'Of course if there's the slightest problem, we'll go to see a specialist in Portland. In *Boston*, if that's what it takes.' She smiled, as if conferring a great favor. Eddie did not smile back. And still he did not reply.

'Eddie, are you hearing me?'

'You sent my friends away,' he repeated.

'Yes,' she said, dropping the pretense, and said no more. Two could play at that game. She simply looked back at him.

But a strange thing happened; a terrible thing, really. Eddie's eyes seemed to . . . to grow, somehow. The flecks of gray in them seemed actually to be moving, like racing stormclouds. She became aware suddenly that he was not 'in a snit,' or 'having a poopie,' or any of those things. He was furious with her . . . and Sonia was suddenly scared, because something more than her son seemed to be in this room. She dropped her eyes and fumbled her purse open. She began searching for a Kleenex.

'Yes, I sent them away,' she said, and found that her voice was strong enough and steady enough . . . as long as she wasn't looking at him. 'You've been seriously injured, Eddie. You don't need any visitors right now except for your own ma, and you don't need visitors like that, ever. If it hadn't been for *them*, you'd be home watching the TV right now, or building on your soapbox racer in the garage.'

It was Eddie's dream to build a soapbox racer and take it to Bangor. If he won there, he would be awarded an all-expenses-paid trip to Akron, Ohio, for the National Soapbox Derby. Sonia was perfectly willing to allow him this dream as long as it seemed to her that completion of the racer, which was made out of orange crates and the wheels from a Choo-Choo Flyer wagon, was just that – a dream. She certainly had no intention of letting Eddie risk his life in such a dangerous contraption, not in Derry, not in Bangor, and certainly not in Akron, which (Eddie had informed her) would mean riding in an airplane as well as making a suicidal run down a steep hill in a wheeled orange crate with no brakes. But, as her own mother had often said, what a person didn't know couldn't hurt him (her mother had also been fond of saying 'Tell the truth and shame the devil,' but when it came to the recollection of aphorisms Sonia, like most people, could be remarkably selective).

'My friends didn't break my arm,' Eddie said in that same flat voice. 'I told Dr Handor last night and I told Mr Nell when he came in this morning. Henry Bowers broke my arm. Some other kids were with him, but Henry did it. If I'd been with my friends, it never would have happened. It happened because I was alone.'

This made Sonia think of Mrs Van Prett's comment about how it was safer to have friends, and that brought the rage back like a tiger. She snapped her head up. 'That doesn't matter and you know it! What do you think, Eddie? That your ma fell off a haytruck yesterday? Is that what you think? I know well enough why the Bowers boy broke your arm. That Paddy cop was at our house, too. That big boy broke your arm because you and your "friends" crossed him somehow. Now do you think that would have happened if you'd listened to me and stayed away from them in the first place?'

'No – I think that something even worse might have happened,' Eddie said.

'Eddie, you don't mean that.'

'I mean it,' he said, and she felt that power coming off him, coming *out* of him, in waves. 'Bill and the rest of my friends will be back, Ma. That's something *I* know. And when they come, you're not going to stop them. You're not going to say a word to them. They're my friends, and you're not going to steal my friends just because you're scared of being alone.'

She stared at him, flabbergasted and terrified. Tears filled her eyes and spilled down her cheeks, wetting the powder there. 'This is how you talk to your mother now, I guess,' she said through her sobs. 'Maybe this is the way your "friends" talk to *their* folks. I guess you learned it from them.'

She felt safer in her tears. Usually when she cried Eddie cried, too. A low weapon, some might say, but were there really any low weapons when it came to protecting her son? She thought not.

She looked up, the tears streaming from her eyes, feeling both unutterably sad, bereft, betrayed . . . and sure. Eddie would not be able to stand against such a flood of tears and sorrow. That cold sharp look would leave his face. Perhaps he would begin to gasp and wheeze a little bit, and that would be a sign, as it was always a sign, that the fight was over and that she had won another victory . . . for him, of course. Always for him.

She was so shocked to see that same expression on his face – it had, if anything, deepened – that her voice caught in mid-sob. There was sorrow under his expression, but even that was frightening: it struck her in some way as an *adult* sorrow, and thinking of Eddie as adult in any way always caused a panicky little bird to flutter inside her mind. This was how she felt on the infrequent occasions when she wondered what would happen to her if Eddie didn't want to go to Derry Business College or the University of Maine in Orono or Husson in Bangor so he could come home every day after his classes were done, what would happen if he met a girl, fell in love, wanted to get married. *Where's the place for me in any of that?* the panicky bird-voice would cry when these strange, almost nightmarish thoughts came. *Where would* my *place be in a life like that? I* love *you, Eddie! I* love *you! I take*

care of you and I love you! You don't know how to cook, or change your
sheets, or wash your underwear! Why should you? I know those things for
you! I know because I love you!

He said it himself now: 'I love you, Ma. But I love my friends,
too. I think . . . I think you're making yourself cry.'

'Eddie, you hurt me so much,' she whispered, and fresh tears
doubled his pale face, trebled it. If her tears a few moments ago had
been calculated, these were not. In her own peculiar way she was tough
– she had seen her husband into his grave without cracking up, she had
gotten a job in a depressed job-market where it wasn't easy to get a job,
she had raised her son, and when it had been necessary, she had fought
for him. These were the first totally unaffected and uncalculated tears
she had wept in years, perhaps since Eddie had gotten the bronchitis
when he was five and she had been so sure he would die as he lay there
in his bed of pain, glowing bright with fever, whooping and coughing
and gasping for breath. She wept now because of that terribly adult,
somehow *alien* expression on his face. She was afraid *for* him, but she
was also, in some way, afraid *of* him, afraid of that aura that seemed to
surround him . . . which seemed to demand something of her.

'Don't make me have to choose between you and my friends,
Ma,' Eddie said. His voice was uneven, strained, but still under control.
'Because that's not fair.'

'They're *bad* friends, Eddie!' she cried in a near-frenzy. 'I know
that, I feel that with all my heart, they'll bring you nothing but pain
and grief!' And the most horrible thing of all was that she *did* sense
that; some part of her had intuited it in the eyes of the Denbrough
boy, who had stood before her with his hands in his pockets, his red
hair flaming in the summer sun. His eyes had been so grave, so strange
and distant . . . like Eddie's eyes now.

And hadn't that same aura been around him as was around Eddie
now? The same, but even stronger? She thought yes.

'Ma –'

She stood up so suddenly she almost knocked the straight-backed
chair over. 'I'll come back this evening,' she said. 'It's the shock, the
accident, the pain, those things, that make you talk this way. I know
it. You . . . you . . .' She groped, and found her original text in the
flying confusion of her mind. 'You've had a bad accident, but you're
going to be *just fine*. And you'll see I'm right, Eddie. They're *bad*
friends. Not our sort. Not for you. You think it over and ask yourself
if your ma ever told you wrong before. You think about it and . . .
and . . .'

I'm running! she thought with a sick and hurtful dismay. *I'm running away from my own son! Oh God, please don't let this be!*

'Ma.'

For a moment she almost fled anyway, scared of him now, oh yes, he was more than Eddie; she sensed the others in him, his 'friends' and something else, something that was beyond even them, and she was afraid it might flash out at her. It was as if he were in the grip of something, some dreadful fever, as he had been in the grip of the bronchitis that time when he was five, when he had almost died.

She paused, her hand on the doorknob, not wanting to hear what he might say . . . and when he said it, it was so unexpected that for a moment she didn't really understand it. When comprehension crashed down, it came like a loose load of cement, and for a moment she thought she would faint.

Eddie said: 'Mr Keene said my asthma medicine is just water.'

'What? What?' She turned blazing eyes on him.

'Just water. With some stuff added to make it taste like medicine. He said it was a pla-cee-bo.'

'That's a lie! That is nothing but a solid lie! Why would Mr Keene want to tell you a lie like that? Well, there are other drug-stores in Derry, I guess. I guess –'

'I've had time to think about it,' Eddie said, softly and implacably, his eyes never leaving hers, 'and *I* think he's telling the truth.'

'Eddie, I tell you he's *not!*' The panic was back, fluttering.

'What I think,' Eddie said, 'is that it must be the truth or there would be some kind of warning on the bottle, like if you take too much it will kill you or at least make you sick. Even –'

'Eddie, I don't want to *hear* this!' she cried, and clapped her hands to her ears. 'You're . . . you're . . . *you're just not yourself and that's all that it is!*'

'Even if it's something you can just go in and buy without a prescription, they put special instructions on it,' he went on, not raising his voice. His gray eyes lay on hers, and she couldn't seem to drop her gaze, or even move it. 'Even if it's just Vicks cough syrup . . . or your Geritol.'

He paused for a moment. Her hands dropped from her ears; it seemed too much work to hold them up. They seemed very heavy.

'And it's like . . . you must have known that, too, Ma.'

'Eddie!' She nearly wailed it.

'Because,' he went on, as if she had not spoken at all – he was frowning now, concentrating on the problem, 'because your folks are

748

supposed to know about medicines. Why, I use that aspirator five, sometimes six times a day. And you wouldn't let me do that if you thought it could, like, hurt me. Because it's your job to protect me. I know it is, because that's what you always say. So . . . did you know, Ma? Did you know it was just water?'

She said nothing. Her lips were trembling. It felt as if her whole face was trembling. She was no longer crying. She felt too scared to cry.

'Because if you *did*,' Eddie said, still frowning, 'if you *did* know, I'*d* want to know why. I can figure some things out, but not why my ma would want me to think water was medicine . . . or that I had asthma *here*' – he pointed to his chest – 'when Mr Keene says I only have it up *here*' – and he pointed to his head.

She thought she would explain everything then. She would explain it quietly and logically. How she had thought he was going to die when he was five, and how that would have driven her crazy after losing Frank only two years before. How she came to understand that you could only protect your child through watchfulness and love, that you must tend a child as you tended a garden, fertilizing, weeding, and yes, occasionally pruning and thinning, as much as that hurt. She would tell him that sometimes it was better for a child – particularly a delicate child like Eddie – to *think* he was sick than to really *get* sick. And she would finish by talking to him about the deadly foolishness of doctors and the wonderful power of love; she would tell him that she *knew* he had asthma, and it didn't matter what the doctors thought or what they gave him for it. She would tell him you could make medicine with more than a malicious meddling druggist's mortar and pestle. *Eddie*, she would say, *it's medicine because your mother's love* makes *it medicine, and in just that way, for as long as you want me and let me, I can do that. This is a power that God gives to loving caring mothers. Please, Eddie, please, my heart's own love, you must believe me.*

But in the end she said nothing. Her fright was too great.

'But maybe we don't even have to talk about it,' Eddie went on. 'Mr Keene might have been joking with me. Sometimes grownups . . . you know, they like to play jokes on kids. Because kids believe almost anything. It's mean to do that to kids, but sometimes grownups do it.'

'Yes,' Sonia Kaspbrak said eagerly. 'They like to joke and sometimes they're stupid . . . mean . . . and . . . and . . .'

'So I'll kind of keep an eye out for Bill and the rest of my friends,' Eddie said, 'and keep right on using my asthma medicine. That's probably best, don't you think?'

She realized only now, when it was too late, how neatly – how cruelly – she had been trapped. What he was doing was almost black-mail, but what choice did she have? She wanted to ask him how he could be so calculating, so manipulative. She opened her mouth to ask . . . and then closed it again. It was too likely that, in his present mood, he might answer.

But she knew one thing. Yes. One thing for sure: she would never never *never* set foot into Mr Nosy-Parker Keene's drugstore again in her life.

His voice, oddly shy now, interrupted her thoughts. 'Ma?'

She looked up and saw it was Eddie again, *just* Eddie, and she went to him gladly.

'Can I have a hug, Ma?'

She hugged him, but carefully, so as not to hurt his broken arm (or dislodge any loose bone-fragments so they could run an evil race around his bloodstream and then lodge in his heart – what mother would kill her son with love?), and Eddie hugged her back.

7

As far as Eddie was concerned, his ma left just in time. During the horrible confrontation with her he had felt his breath piling up and up and up in his lungs and throat, still and tideless, stale and brackish, threatening to poison him.

He held on until the door had snicked shut behind her and then he began to gasp and wheeze. The sour air working in his tight throat jabbed up and down like a warm poker. He grabbed for his aspirator, hurting his arm but not caring. He triggered a long blast down his throat. He breathed deep of the camphor taste, thinking: *It doesn't matter if it's a pla-cee-bo, words don't matter if a thing works.*

He lay back against his pillows, eyes closed, breathing freely for the first time since she had come in. He was scared, plenty scared. The things he had said to her, the way he had acted – it had been him and yet it hadn't been him at all. There had been something working in him, working *through* him, some force . . . and his mother had felt it, too. He had seen it in her eyes and in her trembling lips. He had no sense that this power was an evil one, but its enormous strength was frightening. It was like getting on an amusement-park ride that was really dangerous and realizing you couldn't get off until it was over, come what might.

No turning around, Eddie thought, feeling the hot, itchy weight of the cast that encased his broken arm. *No one goes home until we get to the end. But God I'm so scared, so scared.* And he knew that the truest reason for demanding she not cut him off from his friends was something he could never have told her: *I can't face this alone.*

He cried a little then, and then drifted off into a restless sleep. He dreamed of a darkness in which machinery – pumping machinery – ran on and on.

8

It was threatening showers again that evening when Bill and the rest of the Losers returned to the hospital. Eddie was not surprised to see them come filing in. He had known they would be back.

It had been hot all day – it was generally agreed later that that third week of July was the hottest of an exceptionally hot summer – and the thunderheads began to build up around four in the afternoon, purple-black and colossal, pregnant with rain, loaded with lightnings. People went about their errands quickly and a little uneasily, with one eye always cocked at the sky. Most agreed it would rain good and hard by dinnertime, washing some of the thick humidity out of the air. Derry's parks and playgrounds, underpopulated all summer, were totally deserted that evening by six. The rain had still not fallen, and the swings hung moveless and shadeless in a light that was a queer flat yellow. Thunder rumbled thickly – that, a barking dog, and the low mutter of traffic on Outer Main Street were the only sounds that drifted in through Eddie's window until the Losers came.

Bill was first, followed by Richie. Beverly and Stan followed them, then Mike. Ben came last. He looked excruciatingly uncomfortable in a white turtleneck sweater.

They came to his bed, solemn. Not even Richie was smiling.

Their faces, Eddie thought, fascinated. *Jeezum-crow, their faces!*

He was seeing in them what his mother had seen in him that afternoon: that odd combination of power and helplessness. The yellow stormlight lay on their skins, making their faces seem ghost-like, distant, shadowy.

We're passing over, Eddie thought. *Passing over into something new – we're on the border. But what's on the other side? Where are we going? Where?*

'H-h-Hello, Eh-Eh-Eddie,' Bill said. 'How you d-d-doin?'

'Okay, Big Bill,' Eddie said, and tried to smile.

'Had a day yesterday, I guess,' Mike said. Thunder rumbled

751

behind his voice. Neither the overhead light nor the bedside lamp was on in Eddie's room, and all of them seemed to fade in and out of the bruised light. Eddie thought of that light all over Derry right now, lying long and still across McCarron Park, falling through the holes in the roof of the Kissing Bridge in smudged lackadaisical rays, making the Kenduskeag look like smoky glass as it cut its broad shallow path through the Barrens; he thought of seesaws standing at dead angles behind Derry Elementary as the thunderheads piled up and up; he thought of this thundery yellow light, and the stillness, as if the whole town had fallen asleep . . . or died.

'Yes,' he said. 'It was a big day.'

'My f-folks are g-going out to a muh-muh-movie the night a-a-after n-next,' Bill said. 'When the p-pic-hictures change. We're g-going to m-make them then. The suh-suh-suh —'

'Silver balls,' Richie said.

'I thought —'

'It's better this way,' Ben said quietly. 'I still think we could have made the bullets, but thinking isn't good enough. If we were grownups —'

'Oh yeah, the world would be peachy if we were grownups,' Beverly said. 'Grownups can make anything they want, can't they? Grownups can *do* anything they want, and it always comes out right.' She laughed, a jagged nervous sound. 'Bill wants *me* to shoot It. Can you feature that, Eddie? Just call me Beverly Oakley.'

'I don't know what you're talking about,' Eddie said, but he thought he did — he was getting some kind of picture, anyway.

Ben explained. They would melt down one of his silver dollars and make two silver balls a little smaller than ball-bearings. And then, if there really was a werewolf residing at 29 Neibolt Street, Beverly would put a silver ball into Its head with Bill's Bullseye slingshot. Goodbye werewolf. And if they were right about one creature who wore many faces, goodbye It.

There must have been some sort of expression on Eddie's face, because Richie laughed and nodded.

'I know how you feel, man. I thought Bill must have lost his few remaining marbles when he started talking about using his slingshot instead of his dad's gun. But this afternoon —' He stopped and cleared his throat. *This afternoon after your ma blew us out of the water* was how he had been about to start, and that obviously wouldn't do. 'This afternoon we went down to the dump. Bill brought his Bullseye. Look.' From his back pocket Richie took a flattened can which had once held Del Monte pineapple chunks. There was a ragged hole about two inches in diameter through the middle of it. 'Beverly did that with a rock, from twenty feet away. Looks like a .38 to me. De Trashmouth was convinced. And when de Trashmouth is convinced, de Trashmouth is *convinced*.'

'Killing cans is one thing,' Beverly said. 'If it was something else . . . something alive . . . Bill, you should be the one. Really.'

'N-no,' Bill said. 'We a-a-all t-took turns. You suh-suh-saw how it w-w-went.'

'How *did* it go?' Eddie asked.

Bill explained, slowly and haltingly, while Beverly looked out the window with her lips pressed so tightly together they were white. She was, for reasons she could not explain even to herself, more than afraid: she was deeply embarrassed by what had happened today. On the way over here tonight she had argued again, passionately, that they try to make the bullets after all . . . not because she was any more sure than Bill or Richie that they would actually work when the time came, but because – if something did happen out at that house – the weapon would be in

(*Bill's*)

someone else's hands.

But facts were facts. They had each taken ten rocks each and shot the Bullseye at ten cans set up twenty feet away. Richie had gotten one out of ten (and his one hit was really only a nick), Ben had gotten two, Bill four, Mike five.

Beverly, shooting almost casually and appearing to aim not at all, had banged nine of the ten cans dead center. The tenth fell over when the rock she fired bounced off the rim.

'But first w-w-w-we g-gotta make the uh-uh-ammo.'

'Night after next? I should be out by then,' Eddie said. His mother would protest that . . . but he didn't think she would protest too much. Not after this afternoon.

'Does your arm hurt?' Beverly asked. She was wearing a pink dress (not the dress he had seen in his dream; perhaps she had worn that this afternoon, when Ma sent them away) on which she had appliquéd small flowers. And silk or nylon hose; she looked very adult but also somehow very childlike, like a girl playing dress-up. Her expression was dreamy and distant. Eddie thought: *I bet that's how she looks when she's sleeping*.

'Not too much,' he said.

They talked for awhile, their voices punctuated by thunder. Eddie did not ask them about what had happened when they came to the hospital earlier that day, and none of them mentioned it. Richie took out his yo-yo, made it sleep once or twice, then put it back.

Conversation lagged, and in one of the pauses there was a brief click that made Eddie look around. Bill had something in his hand, and for a moment Eddie felt his heart speed up in alarm. For that brief moment he thought it was a knife. But then Stan turned on the room's overhead, dispelling the gloom, and he saw it was only a ballpoint pen. In the light they all looked natural again, *real*, only his friends.

'I thought we ought to sign your cast,' Bill said. His eyes met Eddie's squarely.

But that's not it, Eddie thought with sudden and alarming clarity. *It's a contract. It's a contract, Big Bill, isn't it, or the closest we'll ever get to one.* He was frightened . . . and then ashamed and angry at himself. If he had broken his arm before this summer, who would have signed the cast? Anyone besides his mother, and perhaps Dr Handor? His aunts in Haven?

These were his *friends*, and his mother was wrong: they weren't bad friends. *Maybe*, he thought, *there aren't any such things as good friends or bad friends — maybe there are just friends, people who stand by you when you're hurt and who help you feel not so lonely. Maybe they're always worth being scared for, and hoping for, and living for. Maybe worth dying for, too, if that's what has to be. No good friends. No bad friends. Only people you want, need to be with; people who build their houses in your heart.*

'Okay,' Eddie said, a little hoarsely. 'Okay, that'd be real good, Big Bill.'

So Bill leaned solemnly over his bed and wrote his name on the hillocky plaster of Paris that encased Eddie's mending arm, the letters large and looping. Richie signed with a flourish. Ben's handwriting was as narrow as he was wide, the letters slanting backward. They looked ready to fall over at the slightest push. Mike Hanlon's writing was large and awkward because he was lefthanded and the angle was bad for him. He signed above Eddie's elbow and circled his name. When Beverly bent over him, he could smell some light flowery perfume on her. She signed in a round Palmer-method script. Stan came last, and wrote his name in tight-packed little letters by Eddie's wrist.

They all stepped back then, as if aware of what they had done. Outside, thunder muttered heavily again. Lightning washed the hospital's wooden exterior in brief stuttering light.

'That's it?' Eddie asked.

Bill nodded. 'C-C-Come oh-oh-over to my h-house a-after suh-hupper day a-a-after t-tomorrow if you c-c-can, o-okay?'

Eddie nodded, and the subject was closed.

There was another period of desultory, almost aimless conversation. Some of it was about the dominant topic in Derry that July – the trial of Richard Macklin for the bludgeon-murder of his stepson Dorsey, and the disappearance of Dorsey's older brother, Eddie Corcoran. Macklin would not break down and confess, weeping, on the witness stand for another two days, but the Losers were in agreement that Macklin probably had nothing to do with Eddie's disappearance. The boy had either run away . . . or It had gotten him.

They left around quarter of seven, and the rain still had not fallen. It continued to threaten until long after Eddie's ma had come, made her visit, and gone home again (she had been horrified at the signatures on Eddie's cast, and even more horrified at his determination to leave the hospital the following day – she had been envisioning a stay of a week or more in absolute quiet, so that the ends of the break could 'set together,' as she said).

Eventually the stormclouds broke apart and drifted away. Not so much as a drop of rain had fallen in Derry. The humidity remained, and people slept on porches and on lawns and in sleeping bags in back fields that night.

The rain came the next day, not long after Beverly saw something terrible happen to Patrick Hockstetter.

CHAPTER SEVENTEEN
ANOTHER ONE OF THE MISSING: THE DEATH OF PATRICK HOCKSTETTER

1

When he finishes, Eddie pours himself another drink with a hand not completely steady. He looks at Beverly and says, 'You saw It, didn't you? You saw It take Patrick Hockstetter the day after you all signed my cast.'

The others lean forward.

Beverly pushes her hair back in a reddish cloud. Beneath it her face looks extraordinarily pale. She fumbles a fresh cigarette out of her pack – the last one – and flicks her Bic. She can't seem to guide the flame to the tip of her cigarette. After a moment Bill holds her wrist lightly but firmly and puts the flame where it's supposed to go. Beverly looks at him gratefully and exhales a cloud of bluish-gray smoke.

'Yeah,' she says. 'I saw that happen.'

She shivers.

'He was cruh-cruh-crazy,' Bill says, and thinks: Just the fact that Henry let a flako like Patrick Hockstetter hang around as that summer wore on ... that says something, doesn't it? Either that Henry was losing some of his charm, some of his attraction, or that Henry's own craziness had progressed far enough so that the Hockstetter kid seemed okay to him. Both came to the same thing – Henry's increasing ... what? degeneration? Is that the word? Yes, in light of what happened to him, where he ended up, I think it is.

There's something else to support the idea, too, *Bill thinks, but as yet he can only remember it vaguely. He and Richie and Beverly had been down at Tracker Brothers – early August by then, and the summer-school that had kept Henry out of their hair for most of the summer was just about to end – and hadn't Victor Criss approached them? A very frightened Victor Criss? Yes, that had happened. Things had been rapidly approaching the end by then, and Bill thinks now that every kid in Derry had sensed it – the Losers and Henry's group most of all. But that had been later.*

'Oh yeah you got that right,' Beverly says flatly. 'Patrick Hockstetter was crazy. None of the girls would sit in front of him in school. You'd be sitting there, doing your arithmetic or writing a story or a composition, and all at once you'd feel this hand . . . almost as light as a feather, but warm and sweaty. Meaty.' *She swallows, and there is a small click in her throat. The others watch her solemnly from around the table.* 'You'd feel it on your side, or maybe on your breast. Not that any of us had much in the way of breasts back then. But Patrick didn't seem to care about that.

'You'd feel that . . . that touch, and you'd jerk away from it, and turn around, and there Patrick would be, grinning with those big rubbery lips. He had a pencil-box –'

'Full of flies,' Richie says suddenly. 'Sure. He'd kill em with this green ruler he had and then put em in his pencil-box. I even remember what it looked like – red, with a wavy white plastic cover that slid open and closed.'

Eddie is nodding.

'You'd jerk away and he'd grin and then maybe he'd open his pencil-box so you could see the dead flies inside,' Beverly says. 'And the worst thing – the horrible thing – was the way he'd smile and never say anything. Mrs Douglas knew. Greta Bowie told on him, and I think Sally Mueller said something once, too. But . . . I think Mrs Douglas was scared of him, too.'

Ben has rocked back on the rear legs of his chair, and his hands are laced behind his neck. She still cannot believe how lean he is. 'I'm pretty sure you're right,' *he says.*

'Wh-What h-happened to h-h-him, Beverly?' *Bill asks.*

She swallows again, trying to fight off the nightmarish power of what she saw that day in the Barrens, her roller skates tied together and hung over her shoulder, one knee a stinging net of pain from a fall she had taken on Saint Crispin's Lane, another of the short tree-lined streets that dead-ended where the land fell (and still falls) sharply into the Barrens. She remembers (oh these memories, when they come, are so clear and so powerful) that she was wearing a pair of denim shorts – really too short, they came only to just below the hem of her panties. She had become more conscious of her body over the last year – over the last six months, actually, as it began to curve and become more womanly. The mirror was one reason for this heightened consciousness, of course, but not the main one; the main one was that her father seemed even sharper just lately, more apt to use his slapping hand or even his fists. He seemed restless, almost caged, and she was more and more nervous when she was around him, more and more on her mark. It was as if there was a smell they made between them, a smell that wasn't there when she was in the apartment alone, one that had never been there when they were in it together – not until this summer. And when Mom was gone it was worse. If there was a smell, some smell, then he knew it too, maybe, because Bev saw less and less of him as the hot weather wore on, partly because of his summer bowling league, partly because he was helping his friend Joe Tammerly fix cars . . . but she suspects it was partly that smell, the one they made between them, neither of them meaning to but making it just the same, as helpless to stop it as either was helpless to stop sweating in July.

The vision of the birds, hundreds and thousands of them, descending on the roofpeaks of houses, on telephone wires, on TV aerials, intervenes again.

'And poison ivy,' she says aloud.

'W-W-What?' Bill asks.

'Something about poison ivy,' she says slowly, looking at him. 'But it wasn't. It just felt *like poison ivy. Mike –?'*

'Never mind,' Mike says. 'It will come. Tell us what you do remember, Bev.'

I remember the blue shorts, *she would tell them,* and how faded they were getting; how tight around my hips and butt. I had half a pack of Lucky Strikes in one pocket and the Bullseye in the other –

'Do you remember the Bullseye?' she asks Richie, but they all nod.

'Bill gave it to me,' she says. 'I didn't want it, but it . . . he . . .' She smiles at Bill, a little wanly. *'You couldn't say no to Big Bill, that was all. So I had it and that's why I was out by myself that day. To practice. I still didn't think I'd have the guts to use it when the time came. Except . . . I used it that day. I had to. I killed one of them . . . one of the parts of It. It was terrible. Even now it's hard for me to think of. And one of the others got me. Look.'*

She raises her arm and turns it over so they can all see a puckery scar on the roundest part of her upper forearm. It looks as if a hot circular object about the size of a Havana cigar had been pressed against her skin. It is slightly sunken, and looking at it gives Mike Hanlon a chill. This is one of the parts of the story which, like Eddie's unwilling heart-to-heart with Keene, he has suspected but never actually heard.

'You were right about one thing, Richie,' she says. 'That Bullseye was a killer. I was scared of it, but I sorta loved it, too.'

Richie laughs and claps her on the back. 'Shit, I knew that back then, you stupid skirt.'

'You did? Really?'

'Yeah, really,' he says. 'It was something in your eyes, Bevvie.'

'I mean, it looked like a toy, but it was real. You could blow holes in things.'

'And you blew a hole in something with it that day,' Ben muses.

She nods.

'Was it Patrick you —'

'No, God no!' Beverly says. 'It was the other . . . wait.' She crushes out her cigarette, sips her drink, and gets herself under control again. Finally she is: Well . . . no. But she has a feeling it's the closest she's going to get tonight. 'I was roller-skating, you see, and I fell down and gave myself a good scrape. Then I decided I'd go down to the Barrens and practice. I went by the clubhouse first to see if you guys were there. You weren't. Just that smoky smell. You guys remember how long that place went on smelling of smoke?'

They all nod, smiling.

'We never really did get the smell out, did we?' Ben says.

'So then I headed down to the dump,' she says, 'because that's where we had the . . . the tryouts, I guess you'd call them, and I knew there'd be lots of things to shoot at. Maybe even, you know, rats.' She pauses. There's a fine misty sweat on her forehead now. 'That's what I really wanted to shoot at,' she says finally. 'Something that was alive. Not a seagull — I knew I couldn't shoot a gull — but a rat . . . I wanted to see if I could.

'I'm glad I came from the Kansas Street side instead of the Old Cape side, though, because there wasn't much cover over there by the railroad embankment. They would have seen me and God knows what would have happened then.'

'Who would have suh-suh-seen y-you?'

'Them,' Beverly says. 'Henry Bowers, Victor Criss, Belch Huggins, and Patrick Hockstetter. They were down in the dump and —'

Suddenly, amazing all of them, she begins to giggle like a child, her cheeks turning rose-red. She giggles until tears stand in her eyes.

'What the hell, Bev,' Richie says. 'Let us in on the joke.'

'Oh it was a joke, all right,' she says. 'It was a joke, but I think they might have killed me if they knew I'd seen.'

'I remember now!' Ben cries, and he begins to laugh, too. 'I remember you telling us!'

Giggling wildly, Beverly says, 'They had their pants down and they were lighting farts.'

There is an instant of thunderstruck silence and then they all begin to laugh — the sound echoes through the library.

Thinking of exactly how to tell them of Patrick Hockstetter's death, the thing she fixes on first is how approaching the town dump from the Kansas

759

Street side was like entering some weird asteroid belt. There was a rutted dirt track (a town road, actually; it even had a name, Old Lyme Street) that ran from Kansas Street to the dump, the only actual road into the Barrens – the city's dump trucks used it. Beverly walked near Old Lyme Street but didn't take it – she had grown more cautious – she supposed all of them had – since Eddie's arm had been broken. Especially when she was alone.

She wove her way through the heavy undergrowth, skirting a patch of poison ivy with its reddish oily leaves, smelling the dump's smoky rot, hearing the seagulls. On her left, through occasional breaks in the foliage, she could see Old Lyme Street.

The others are looking at her, waiting. She checks her cigarette pack and finds it empty. Wordlessly, Richie tosses her one of his.

She lights up, looks around at them, and says: 'Heading toward the dump from the Kansas Street side was a little like

2

entering some weird asteroid belt. The dumpoid belt. At first there was nothing but the underbrush growing from the spongy ground underfoot, and then you would see your first dumpoid: a rusty can that had once contained Prince Spaghetti Sauce, maybe, or an S 'OK sodabottle crawling with bugs attracted by the sweet-sticky remains of cream soda or birch beer. Then there would be a bright wink of sun kicking off a scrap of tinfoil caught in a tree. You might see a bedspring (or trip over it, if you weren't watching where you were going) or a bone some dog had carried away, gnawed, dropped.

The dump itself wasn't so bad – was, in fact, sort of interesting, Beverly thought. What was nasty (and sort of creepy) was the way it had of spreading. Of creating this dumpoid belt.

She was getting closer now; the trees were bigger, mostly firs, and the bushes were thinning out. The gulls cheeped and cried in their shrill querulous voices, and the air was smudgy with the smell of burning.

Now, on Beverly's right, leaning at an angle against the base of a spruce tree, was a rusty Amana refrigerator. Beverly glanced at it, thinking vaguely of the state policeman who had visited her class when she had been in the third grade. He had told them that such things as discarded refrigerators were dangerous – a kid could climb into one while playing hide-and-go-seek, for instance, and smother to death inside. Although why anyone would want to get in a scroungy old –

She heard a shout, so close it made her jump, followed by laughter. Beverly grinned. So they *were* here. They had left the club-house because of the smoky smell and had come down here. They were maybe breaking bottles with rocks, maybe just dump-picking.

She began to walk a little faster, the nasty scrape she had gotten earlier now forgotten in her eagerness to see them . . . to see *him*, with his red hair so much like hers, to see if he would smile at her in that oddly endearing one-sided way of his. She knew she was too young to love a boy, too young to have anything but 'crushes,' but she loved Bill just the same. And she walked a little faster, her skates swinging heavily from her shoulder, the sling of his Bullseye beating soft time against her left buttock.

She almost walked into them before realizing it wasn't her gang at all, but Bowers's.

She walked out of the screening bushes and the dump's steepest side lay about seventy yards ahead, a twinkling avalanche of junk lying along the high angle of the gravel-pit. Mandy Fazio's bulldozer was off to the left. Much closer in front of her was a wilderness of junked cars. At the end of each month these were crushed and hauled off to Portland for scrap, but now there were a dozen or more, some sitting on bare wheel-rims, some on their sides, one or two lying on their roofs like dead dogs. They were arranged in two rows and Beverly walked down the rough trash-littered aisle between them like some punk bride of the future, wondering idly if she could break a windshield with the Bullseye. One of the pockets of her blue shorts bulged with the small ball-bearings that were her practice ammo.

The voices and laughter were coming from beyond the junked-out cars and to the left, at the edge of the dump proper. Beverly rounded the last one, a Studebaker with its entire front end missing. Her hail of greeting died on her lips. The hand she had put up to wave did not exactly fall back to her side; it seemed to wilt.

Her first furiously embarrassed thought was: *Oh dear God, why are they all naked?*

This was followed by the scary realization of who they were. She froze there in front of the half-Studebaker with her shadow stapled to the heels of her low-topped sneakers. For that one moment she was totally visible to them; if any of the four had looked up from the circle they were squatting in, he could not have missed her, a girl of slightly more than medium height, a pair of skates over one shoulder, the knee of one long coltish leg still oozing blood, her mouth slack-jawed, her cheeks scarlet.

Before darting back behind the Studebaker she saw that they weren't entirely naked after all; they had their shirts on, and their pants and underpants were simply pulled down to their shoetops, as if they had to Go Number Two (in her shock, Beverly's mind had automatically reverted to the euphemism she had been taught as a toddler) – except whoever heard of four boys Going Number Two at the same time?

Once out of sight again, her first thought was to get away – get away fast. Her heart was pumping hard, her muscles heavy with adrenaline. She looked around, seeing what she hadn't bothered to notice walking up here, when she had thought the voices she heard belonged to her friends. The row of junked cars on her left was really pretty thin – they were by no means packed in door to door as they would be in the week or so before the crusher came to turn them into rough blocks of twinkling metal. She had been exposed to the boys several times walking up to where she was now; if she retreated, she would be exposed again, and this time she might be seen.

Also, she felt a certain shameful curiosity: what in the *world* could they be doing?

Carefully, she peeked around the Studebaker.

Henry and Victor Criss were more or less facing in her direction. Patrick Hockstetter was on Henry's left. Belch Huggins had his back to her. She observed the fact that Belch had an extremely large, extremely *hairy* ass, and half-hysterical giggles suddenly bubbled up her throat like the head on a glass of ginger ale. She had to clap both hands over her mouth and withdraw behind the Studebaker again, struggling to hold the giggles in.

You've got to get out of here, Beverly. If they catch you –

She looked back down between the junked cars, still holding her hands over her mouth. The aisle was maybe ten feet wide, littered with cans, twinkling with little jigsaw pieces of Saf-T-Glas, scruffy with weeds. If she so much as made a sound, they might hear her ... particularly if their absorption in whatever strange thing they were doing flagged. When she thought of how casually she had walked up here, her blood ran cold. Also ...

What in the world can they be doing?

She peeked again, seeing more of the details this time. There was a careless scatter of books and papers nearby – schoolbooks. They had just come from their summer classes, then, what most of the kids called Dummy School or Make-up School. And, because Henry and Victor were facing her way, she could see their *things*. They were the first *things* she had ever seen in her life, other than pictures in a smudgy little book that Brenda Arrowsmith had showed her the year before, and in those pictures you really couldn't see very much. Bev observed now that their things were little tubes that hung down between their legs. Henry's was small and hairless, but Victor's was quite big, and there was a cloudy fuzz of fine black hair just over it.

Bill has one of those, she thought, and suddenly her whole body seemed to flush at once – heat rushed through her in a wave that made her feel giddy and faint and almost sick to her stomach. In that moment she felt much the way Ben Hanscom had felt on the last day of school, looking down at her ankle bracelet and observing the way it flashed in the sun . . . but he had not felt the intermixed sense of terror she felt now.

She looked behind her once more. Now the pathway between the cars leading to the shelter of the Barrens seemed much longer. She was scared to move. If they knew she had seen their *things*, they *would* probably hurt her. And not just a little, they would hurt her badly.

Belch Huggins bellowed suddenly, making her jump, and Henry yelled: 'Three feet! No shit, Belch! It was three *feet*! Wasn't it, Vic?'

Vic agreed it was, and they all roared with troll-like laughter.

Beverly tried another look around the junked Studebaker.

Patrick Hockstetter had turned and half-risen so that his butt was nearly in Henry's face. In Henry's hand was a silvery, glinting object. After a moment's study she made it out as a lighter.

'I thought you said you felt one coming on,' Henry said.

'I do,' Patrick said. 'I'll tell you when. Get ready! . . . Get ready, it's coming! Get . . . *now*!'

Henry flicked the lighter. At the same moment there was the unmistakable ripping sound of a really good fart. There was no mistaking that sound; Beverly had heard it enough in her own house, usually on Saturday night, after the beans and franks. A regular bear for his beans was her father. As Patrick blew off and Henry flicked the lighter, she saw something that made her jaw drop. A bright blue jet of flame appeared to roar directly out of Patrick's bum. To Bev it looked like the pilot-light on a gasburner.

The boys roared their troll-like laughter and Beverly withdrew behind the sheltering car, stifling mad giggles again. She was laughing, but not because she was amused. In some very weird way it was funny, yes, but mostly she was laughing because she felt a deep revulsion accompanied by a sort of horror. She was laughing because she knew of no other way to cope with what she had seen. It had something to

do with seeing the boys' *things*, but that was by no means all or even
the great part of what she felt. She had known, after all, that boys had
things, the same way she knew that girls had different *things*; this was
only what you might call a confirmed sighting. But the rest of what they
were doing seemed so strange, so ludicrous and yet at the same time so
deadly-primitive that she found herself, in spite of the giggling fit, groping
for the core of herself with some desperation.

Stop, she thought, as if this were the answer, *stop, they'll hear you,
so just you stop it, Bevvie!*

But that was impossible. The best she could do was to laugh
without engaging her vocal cords, so that the sounds came out of her
in a series of almost inaudible chuffs, her hands pasted over her mouth,
her cheeks as red as Mac apples, her eyes swimming with tears.

'Holy *shit*, that *hurts!*' Victor roared.

'Twelve *feet!*' Henry bellowed. 'I swear to God, Vic, *twelve fuckin
feet!* I swear it on my mother's *name!*'

'I don't care if it was *twenty* fuckin feet, you burned my ass off!'
Victor howled, and there was more bellowing laughter; still trying to
giggle silently from behind the sheltering car, Beverly thought of a
movie she had seen on TV. Jon Hall had been in it. It was about this
jungle tribe, they had a secret rite, and if you saw it, you got sacrificed
to their god, which was this big stone idol. This did not stop her
giggles, but infused them with a nearly frantic quality. They were
becoming more and more like silent screams. Her belly hurt. Tears
streamed down her face.

3

Henry, Victor, Belch, and Patrick Hockstetter ended up in the dump
lighting each others' farts on that hot July afternoon because of Rena
Davenport.

Henry knew what resulted from consuming large amounts of
baked beans. This result was perhaps best expressed in a little ditty he
had learned at his father's knee when he was still in short pants: *Beans,
beans, the musical fruit! The more you eat, the more you toot! The more you
toot, the better you feel! Then you're ready for another meal!*

Rena Davenport and his father had been courting for nearly eight
years. She was fat, forty, and usually filthy. Henry supposed that Rena
and his father sometimes fucked, although he could not imagine anyone
squashing his body down on Rena Davenport's.

Rena's beans were her pride. She soaked them Saturday nights and baked them over a slow fire all day Sunday. Henry supposed they were okay – they were something to shovel into your mouth and chew up, anyway – but after eight years *anything* lost its charm.

Nor was Rena content to make just a few beans; she cooked them in job lots. When she turned up Sunday evenings in her old green De Soto (a naked rubber babydoll hung from the rearview mirror, looking like the world's youngest lynch-mob victim), she usually had the Bowerses' beans steaming on the seat beside her in a twelve-gallon galvanized-steel pail. The three of them would eat the beans that night (Rena raving about her own cooking all the while, crazy Butch Bowers grunting and mopping up bean juice with a piece of Sonny Boy bread or simply telling her to shut up if there was a ballgame on the radio, Henry just eating, staring out the window, thinking his own thoughts – it was over a plate of Sunday-night beans that he had conceived the idea of poisoning Mike Hanlon's dog Mr Chips), and Butch would reheat a mess of them the next night. On Tuesdays and Wednesdays Henry would take a Tupperware box full of them to school. By Thursday or Friday, neither Henry nor his father could eat any more. The house's two bedrooms would smell of stale farts in spite of the open windows. Butch would take the remains and mix them into the other slops and feed them to Bip and Bop, the Bowerses' two pigs. Rena would like as not show up the following Sunday with another steaming pail, and the cycle would start all over again.

That morning Henry had put up an enormous quantity of leftover beans, and the four of them had eaten the whole lot at noon, sitting out on the playground in the shade of a big old elm. They had eaten until they were nearly bursting.

It had been Patrick who suggested they go down to the dump, which would be fairly quiet in the middle of a working-day summer afternoon. By the time they arrived, the beans were doing their work quite nicely.

4

Little by little, Beverly got herself under control again. She knew she had to get out; beating a retreat was ultimately less dangerous than hanging around. They were absorbed in what they were doing, and even if worse came to worst, she could get a head-start (and in the back of her mind she had also decided that, if worst came to terrible, a few shots from the Bullseye might discourage them).

She was about to begin creeping away when Victor said, 'I gotta go, Henry. My dad wants me to help him pick corn this afternoon.'

'Oh shit,' Henry said. 'He'll live.'

'No, he's mad at me. Because of what happened the other day.'

'Fuck him if he can't take a joke.'

Beverly listened more closely now, suspecting it might be the scuffle which had ended with Eddie's broken arm that they were talking about.

'No, I gotta go.'

'I think his ass hurts,' Patrick said.

'Watch your mouth, fuckface,' Victor said. 'It might grow on you.'

'I got to go too,' Belch said.

'Your father want you to pick corn?' Henry asked angrily. This was what might have passed for a jest in Henry's mind; Belch's father was dead.

'No. But I got a job delivering the *Weekly Shopper*. I gotta do that tonight.'

'What's this *Weekly Shopper* crap?' Henry asked, now sounding upset as well as angry.

'It's a *job*,' Belch said with ponderous patience. 'I make *money*.'

Henry made a disgusted sound, and Beverly risked another peek around the car. Victor and Belch were standing, buckling their belts. Henry and Patrick were still squatting with their pants down. The lighter glinted in Henry's hand.

'*You're* not chickening out, are you?' Henry asked Patrick.

'Nope,' Patrick said.

'You don't have to pick corn or go do some pussy job?'

'Nope,' Patrick said again.

'Well,' Belch said uncertainly, 'see you around, Henry.'

'Sure,' Henry said, and spat near one of Belch's clodhopping workshoes.

Vic and Belch started off together toward the two rows of wrecked cars . . . toward the Studebaker behind which Beverly was crouching. At first she could only cringe, frozen with fear like a rabbit. Then she slid around the left side of the Studebaker and backed down the gap between it and the battered, doorless Ford next to it. For a moment she paused, looking from side to side, hearing them approach. She hesitated, her mouth cottony-dry, her back itchy with sweat; a part of her mind was numbly wondering how she'd look in a cast like Eddie's, with the Losers' names signed on it. Then she dived into the Ford on the passenger side. She curled up on the filthy floormat, making herself as small as possible. It was boiling hot inside the junked-out Ford, and it smelled so thickly of dust, rotting upholstery, and elderly rat-crap that she had to struggle grimly to keep from sneezing or coughing. She heard Belch and Victor pass close by, talking in low voices. Then they were gone.

She sneezed three times, quickly and quietly, into her cupped hands.

She supposed she could go now, if she was careful. The best way to do it would be to shift over to the driver's side of the Ford, sneak back to the aisle, and then just do a fade. She believed she could manage it, but the shock of almost being discovered had robbed her of her courage, at least for the time being. She felt safer here in the Ford. And maybe, now that Victor and Belch had gone, the other two would also go soon. Then she could go back to the clubhouse. She had lost all interest in target-shooting.

Also, she had to pee.

Come on, she thought. *Come on, hurry up and go, hurry up and go, puh-LEEZE!*

A moment later she heard Patrick roar with mixed laughter and pain.

'Six feet!' Henry bellowed. 'Just like a fuckin blowtorch! Swear to God!'

Silence then for awhile. Sweat trickling down her back. The sun beating through the Ford's cracked windshield on the nape of her neck. Heaviness in her bladder.

Henry bellowed so loud that Beverly, who had been close to dozing in spite of her discomfort, almost cried out herself. '*Damn* it, Hockstetter! You burned my frigging ass! What are you doing with that lighter?'

'Ten feet,' Patrick giggled (just the sound of it made Bev feel cold and revolted, as if she had seen a worm squirm its way out of her salad). 'Ten feet if it was an inch, Henry. Bright blue. Ten feet if it was an inch. Swear to God!'

'Gimme that,' Henry grunted.

Come on, come on, you stupidniks, go, get out!

When Patrick spoke again his voice was so low Bev could barely hear it. If there had been the slightest breath of wind on the air that baking afternoon, she would not have done.

'Let me show you something,' Patrick said.

'What?' Henry asked.

'Just something.' Patrick paused. 'It feels good.'

'What?' Henry asked again.

Then there was silence.

I don't want to look, I don't want to see what they're doing now, and besides, they might see me, in fact they probably will because you've used up all your luck today, girly-o. So just stay right here. No peeking . . .

But her curiosity had overcome her good sense. There was something strange in that silence, something a little bit scary. She raised her head inch by inch until she could look through the Ford's cracked cloudy windshield. She needn't have worried about being seen; both of the boys were concentrating on what Patrick was doing. She didn't understand what she was seeing, but she knew it was nasty . . . not that she would have expected anything else from Patrick, who was just so *weird*.

He had one hand between Henry's thighs and one hand between his own. One hand was flogging Henry's *thing* gently; with his other hand Patrick was rubbing his own. Except he wasn't exactly rubbing it – he was kind of . . . *squoozing* it, pulling it, letting it flop back down.

What is he doing? Beverly wondered, dismayed.

She didn't know, not for sure, but it scared her. She didn't think she had been this scared since the blood had vomited out of the bathroom drain and splattered all over everything. Some deep part of her cried out that if they discovered she had seen this, whatever it was, they might do more than hurt her; they might actually kill her.

Still, she couldn't look away.

She saw that Patrick's *thing* had gotten a little longer, but not much; it still dangled between his legs like a snake with no backbone. Henry's, however, had grown amazingly. It stood up stiff and hard, almost poking his bellybutton. Patrick's hand went up and down, up and down, sometimes pausing to squeeze, sometimes tickling that odd, heavy sac under Henry's *thing*.

Those are his balls, Beverly thought. *Do boys have to go around with those all the time? God, I'd go* crazy! Another part of her mind then whispered: *Bill has those.* On its own, her mind visualized her holding them, cupping them in her hand, testing their texture . . . and that hot feeling raced through her again, sparking off a furious blush.

Henry stared at Patrick's hand as if hypnotized. His lighter lay on the rocky scree beside him, reflecting hot afternoon sun.

'Want me to put it in my mouth?' Patrick asked. His big, livery lips smiled complacently.

'Huh?' Henry asked, as if startled from some deep dream.

'I'll put it in my mouth if you want. I don't m –'

Henry's hand flashed out, half-curled, not quite a fist. Patrick was knocked sprawling. His head thudded on the gravel. Beverly dived down again, her heart crashing in her chest, her teeth locked against a little whimpering moan. After knocking Patrick down, Henry had turned and for a moment, just before she dropped back into her little huddled ball on the passenger side of the driveshaft hump, it seemed that her eyes and Henry's had locked.

Please God the sun was in his eyes, she prayed. *Please God I'm sorry I peeked. Please God.*

There was an agonizing pause then. Her white blouse was plastered to her body with sweat. Droplets like seed pearls gleamed on her tanned arms. Her bladder throbbed painfully. She felt that very soon she would wet her pants. She waited for Henry's furious crazy face to appear in the opening where the Ford's passenger door had been, sure it was going to happen – how could he have missed seeing her? He would drag her out and hurt her. He would –

A new and even more terrible thought now occurred to her, and once again she had to engage in a painful, crampy struggle to keep from wetting her pants. Suppose he did something to her with his *thing*? Suppose he wanted her to put it in her somewhere? She knew where it was *supposed* to go, all right; it seemed that knowledge had suddenly sprung into her mind full-blown. She thought that if Henry tried to put his *thing* in her she would go crazy.

Please no, please God don't let him have seen me, please, okay?

Then Henry spoke, and to her growing horror his voice was coming from someplace much closer. 'I don't go for that queer stuff.'

From farther off, Patrick's voice: 'You liked it.'

'I didn't *like* it!' Henry shouted. 'And if you tell anyone I did, I'll *kill* you, you fucking little pansy!'

'You got a boner,' Patrick said. He sounded like he was smiling. As much as she feared Henry Bowers, the smile would not have surprised Beverly. Patrick was crazy, crazier than Henry, maybe, and people *that* crazy weren't afraid of anything. 'I saw it.'

Footsteps crunched over the gravel – closer and closer. Beverly looked up, her eyes bulging. Through the Ford's old windshield she could now see the back of Henry's head. He was looking toward Patrick now, but if he turned around –

'If you tell anyone, I'll say you're a cocksucker,' Henry said. 'Then I'll kill you.'

'You don't scare me, Henry,' Patrick said, and giggled. 'But I might not tell if you gave me a dollar.'

Henry shifted restlessly. He turned slightly; Beverly could now see one-quarter of his profile instead of just the back of his head. *Please God please God*, she begged incoherently, and her bladder throbbed more strongly.

'If you tell,' Henry said, his voice low and deliberate, 'I'll tell what you've been doing with the cats. With the dogs, too. I'll tell them about your refrigerator. You know what'll happen, Hockstetter? They'll come and take you away and put you into the fucking-A loonybin.'

Silence from Patrick.

Henry drummed his fingers on the hood of the Ford Beverly was hiding in. 'Do you hear me?'

'I hear you.' Patrick sounded sullen now. Sullen and a little scared. He burst out: 'You liked it! You got a boner! Biggest boner I ever saw!'

'Yeah, I bet you seen a lot of em, you fuckin little homo faggot. You just remember what I said about the refrigerator. *Your* refrigerator. And if I see you around again, I'll knock your block off.'

More silence from Patrick.

Henry moved away. Beverly turned her head and saw him pass by the driver's side of the Ford. If he had looked to his left even a little bit, he would have seen her. But he didn't look. A moment later she heard him heading off the way Victor and Belch had gone.

Now there was just Patrick.

Beverly waited, but nothing happened. Five minutes dragged by. Her need to urinate was now desperate. She might be able to hold out for another two or three minutes, but no more. And it made her uneasy not to know for sure where Patrick was.

She peeked through the windshield again and saw him just sitting there. Henry had forgotten his lighter. Patrick had put his schoolbooks back into a small canvas carrier sack and had slung it around his neck like a newsboy's, but his pants and underpants were still down around his ankles. He was playing with the lighter. He would spin the wheel, produce a flame that was almost invisible in the bright day, snap the lighter closed, and then start all over again. He seemed hypnotized. A line of blood ran from the corner of his mouth to his chin, and his lips were swelling up on the right side. He seemed not to notice, and once again Beverly felt a squirmy sort of revulsion. Patrick was crazy, all right; she had never in her life wanted so badly to get away from someone.

Moving very carefully, she crawled backward over the Ford's driveshaft hump and squeezed under the steering wheel. She put her feet out on the ground and crept to the back of the Ford. Then she ran quickly back the way she had come. When she had entered the pines beyond the junked cars, she looked back over her shoulder. No one was there. The dump dozed in the sun. She felt the bands of tension around her chest and stomach loosen with relief, and all that was left was the need to urinate, so great that she now felt sick with it.

She hurried down the path a short way and then ducked off to the right. She had her shorts unsnapped almost before the underbrush had closed behind her again. She took a quick look around to make sure there was no poison ivy at hand; then she squatted, holding the tough trunk of a bush for balance.

She was pulling her shorts up again when she heard approaching footsteps from the dump. All she could see through the bushes were flashes of blue denim and the faded plaid of a school-shirt. It was Patrick. She ducked down, waiting for him to pass by toward Kansas Street. She was more sanguine about her position here. The cover was good, she no longer had to pee, and Patrick was off in his own cuckoo world. When he was gone she would double back and head for the clubhouse.

But Patrick didn't pass by. He stopped on the path almost directly opposite her and stood looking at the rusting Amana refrigerator.

Beverly could observe Patrick along a natural sight-line in the bushes without too much chance of being seen. Now that she was relieved, she found she was curious again – and if Patrick did happen to see her, she felt certain she could outrun him. He wasn't as fat as Ben, but he was podgy. She pulled the Bullseye out of her back pocket, however, and put half a dozen steel pellets in the breast pocket of her old Ship 'n Shore. Crazy or not, a good one to the knee might discourage the likes of Patrick Hockstetter in a hurry.

She remembered the refrigerator well enough now. There were lots of discarded fridges at the dump, but it suddenly occurred to her that this was the only one she'd seen which Mandy Fazio hadn't disarmed by either tearing out the latching mechanism with pliers or simply removing the door altogether.

Patrick began to hum and sway back and forth in front of the rusty old refrigerator, and Beverly felt a fresh chill course through her. He was like a guy in a horror movie trying to summon a dead body out of a crypt.

What's he up to?

But if she had known that, or what was going to happen when Patrick finished his private ritual and opened the dead Amana's rusty door, she would have run away as fast as she could.

5

No one – not even Mike Hanlon – had the slightest idea of how crazy Patrick Hockstetter really was. He was twelve, the son of a paint salesman. His mother was a devout Catholic who would die of breast cancer in 1962, four years after Patrick was consumed by the dark entity which existed in and below Derry. Although his IQ tested out as low normal, Patrick had already repeated two grades, the first and third. He was taking summer classes this year so he would not have to repeat the fifth as well. His teachers found him an apathetic student (this several of them noted on the bare six lines of the Derry Elementary School's report cards reserved for TEACHER'S COMMENTS) and a rather disturbing one as well (which none noted – their feelings were too vague, too diffuse, to be expressed in sixty lines, let alone six). If he had been born ten years later, a guidance counsellor might have steered him toward a child psychologist who might (or might not; Patrick was far more clever than his lackluster IQ results indicated) have realized the frightening depths behind that slack and pallid moonface.

He was a sociopath, and perhaps, by that hot July in 1958, he had become a full-fledged psychopath. He could not remember a time when he had believed that other people – any other living creatures, for that matter – were 'real.' He believed himself to be an actual creature, probably the only one in the universe, but was by no means convinced that his actuality made him 'real.' He had no sense of hurting, exactly, and no real sense of being hurt (his indifference to being struck in the mouth by Henry in the dump was a case in point). But while he found reality a totally meaningless concept, he understood the concept of 'rules' perfectly. And while all of his teachers had found him odd (both Mrs Douglas, his fifth-grade teacher, and Mrs Weems, who had had Patrick in the third grade, knew about the pencil-box full of flies, and while neither of them totally ignored the implications, each had between twenty and twenty-eight other students, each with problems of his or her own), none of them had serious disciplinary problems with him. He might turn in test papers that were utterly blank – or blank except for a large, decorative question-mark – and Mrs Douglas had discovered it was best to keep him away from the girls because of his Roman hands and Russian fingers, but he was quiet, so quiet that there were times when he might have been taken for a big lump of clay that had been crudely fashioned to look like a boy. It was easy to ignore a Patrick, who failed quietly, when you had to cope with boys like Henry Bowers and Victor Criss, who were actively disruptive and insolent, boys who would steal milk-money or happily deface school property if given a chance, and girls like the unfortunately named Elizabeth Taylor, who was epileptic and whose few poor brain-cells worked only sporadically and who had to be discouraged from pulling her dresses up in the playyard to show off a new pair of panties. In other words, Derry Elementary School was the typical confused educational carnival, a circus with so many rings that Pennywise himself might have gone unnoticed. Certainly none of Patrick's teachers (or his parents, for that matter) suspected that, when he was five, Patrick had murdered his baby brother Avery.

Patrick had not liked it when his mother brought Avery home from the hospital. He didn't care (or so he at first told himself) if his parents had two kids, five kids, or five dozen kids, as long as the kid or kids didn't alter his own schedule. But he found that Avery did. Meals came late. The baby cried in the night and woke him up. It seemed that his parents were always hanging over its crib, and often when he tried to get their attention he found that he could not. For one of the few times in his life, Patrick became frightened. It occurred to him that if his parents had brought *him*, Patrick, home from the hospital, and if he *was* 'real,' then Avery might be 'real,' too. It might even be that, when Avery got big enough to walk and talk, to bring in his father's copy of the Derry *News* from the front step and to hand his mother the bowls when she baked bread, they might decide to get rid of Patrick altogether. It was not that he feared they loved Avery more (although it was obvious to Patrick that they *did* love him more, and in this case his judgment was probably correct). What he cared about was (1) the rules that were being broken or had changed since Avery's arrival, (2) Avery's possible reality, and (3) the possibility that they might throw *him* out in favor of Avery.

Patrick went into Avery's room one afternoon around two-thirty, shortly after the school-bus had dropped him off from his afternoon kindergarten session. It was January. Outside, snow was beginning to fall. A powerful wind boomed across McCarron Park and rattled the frosty upstairs storm windows. His mother was napping in her bedroom; Avery had been fussy all the previous night. His father was at work. Avery was sleeping on his stomach, his head turned to one side.

Patrick, his moonface expressionless, turned Avery's head so his face was pressed directly into the pillow. Avery made a snuffling noise and turned his head back to the side. Patrick observed this, and stood thinking about it while the snow melted off his yellow boots and puddled on the floor. Perhaps five minutes passed (quick thinking was not Patrick's specialty), and then he turned Avery's face into the pillow again and held it there for a moment. Avery stirred under his hand, struggling. But his struggles were weak. Patrick let go. Avery turned his head to the side again, made one snorting little cry, and then went on sleeping. The wind gusted, rattling the windows. Patrick waited to see if the one little cry would awaken his mother. It didn't.

Now he felt swept by a great excitement. The world seemed to stand out in front of him clearly for the first time. His emotional equipment was severely defective, and in those few moments he felt as a totally color-blind person might feel if given a shot which enabled him to perceive colors for a short time . . . or as a junkie who has just fixed feels as the smack rockets his brain into orbit. This was a new thing. He had not suspected it existed.

Very gently, he turned Avery's face into the pillow again. This time when Avery struggled, Patrick did not let go. He pressed the baby's face more firmly into the pillow. The baby was making steady muffled cries now, and Patrick knew it was awake. He had a vague idea that it might tell on him to his mother if he stopped. He held it down. The baby struggled. Patrick held it down. The baby farted. Its struggles weakened. Patrick still held it down. It eventually became totally still. Patrick held it down for another five minutes, feeling that excitement crest and then begin to ebb: the shot wearing off, turning the world gray again, the fix mellowing into an accustomed low doze.

Patrick went downstairs and got himself a plate of cookies and poured himself a glass of milk. His mother came down half an hour later and said she hadn't even heard him come in, she had been *that* tired (*you won't be anymore, Mom*, Patrick thought, *don't worry, I fixed it*). She sat down with him, ate one of his cookies, and asked him how school had been. Patrick said it was all right and showed her his drawing of a house and a tree. His paper was covered with looping meaningless scribbles made with black and brown crayon. His mother said it was very nice. Patrick brought home the same looping scrawls of black and brown every day. Sometimes he said it was a turkey, sometimes a

Christmas tree, sometimes a boy. His mother always told him it was very nice . . . although sometimes, in a part of her so deep she hardly knew it was there, she worried. There was something a little disquieting about the dark sameness of those big scribbled loops of black and brown.

She didn't discover Avery's death until nearly five o'clock; until then she had simply assumed he was taking a very long nap. By then Patrick was watching *Crusader Rabbit* on their seven-inch TV, and he went on watching TV through all the uproar that followed. *Whirlybirds* was on when Mrs Henley arrived from next door (his screaming mother had been holding the baby's corpse in the open kitchen door, believing in some blind way that the cold air might revive it; Patrick was cold and got a sweater out of the downstairs closet). *Highway Patrol*, Ben Hanscom's favorite, was on when Mr Hockstetter arrived home from work. By the time the doctor arrived, *Science Fiction Theater*, with Your Host Truman Bradley, was just coming on. 'Who knows what strange things the universe may hold?' Truman Bradley speculated while Patrick's mother shrieked and struggled in her husband's arms in the kitchen. The doctor observed Patrick's deep calm and unquestioning stare and assumed the boy was in shock. He wanted Patrick to take a pill. Patrick didn't mind.

It was diagnosed as crib-death. Years later there might have been questions about such a fatality, deviations from the usual infant-death syndrome observed. But when it happened, the death was simply noted and the baby buried. Patrick was gratified that once things finally settled down his meals began to come on time again.

In the madness of that afternoon and evening – people banging in and out of the house, the red lights of the Home Hospital ambulance pulsing on the walls, Mrs Hockstetter screaming and wailing and refusing to be comforted – only Patrick's father came within brushing distance of the truth. He was standing numbly by Avery's empty crib some twenty minutes after the body had been removed, simply standing there, unable to believe any of this had happened. He looked down and saw a pair of tracks on the hardwood floor. They had been made by the snow melting off Patrick's yellow rubber boots. He looked at them, and a dreadful thought rose briefly in his mind like bad gas from a deep mineshaft. His hand went slowly to his mouth and his eyes widened. A picture began to form in his mind. Before it could come clear he left the room, slamming the door behind him so hard that the top of the frame splintered.

He never asked Patrick any questions.

Patrick had never done anything like that again, although he might have done so if the chance had presented itself. He felt no guilt, had no bad dreams. As time passed, however, he became more aware of what would have happened to him if he had been caught. There were rules. Unpleasant things happened to you if you didn't follow them . . . or if you were caught breaking them. You could be locked up or stuck in the electrocution chair.

But that remembered feeling of excitement – that feeling of color and sensation – was simply too powerful and too wonderful to give over entirely. Patrick killed flies. At first he only smacked them with his mother's flyswatter; later he discovered he could kill them quite efficiently with a plastic ruler. He also discovered the joys of flypaper. A long sticky runner of it could be purchased for two cents at the Costello Avenue Market and Patrick sometimes stood for as long as two hours in the garage, watching the flies land and then struggle to get free, his mouth ajar, his dusty eyes alight with that rare excitement, sweat running down his round face and his thick body. Patrick killed beetles, but if possible he captured them first. Sometimes he would steal a long needle from his mother's pincushion, impale a Japanese beetle on it, and sit cross-legged in the garden watching it die. His expression at these times was the expression of a boy who is reading a very good book. Once he had discovered a run-over cat that was dying in the gutter on Lower Main Street and sat watching it until an old woman saw him pushing the squashed and mewing thing around with his foot. She whacked him with the broom she had been using to sweep her walk. *Go on home!* she had shouted at him. *What are you, crazy?* Patrick had gone on home. He wasn't mad at the old woman. He had been caught breaking the rules, that was all.

Then, last year (it would not have surprised Mike Hanlon or any of the others at that point to have known that it was, in fact, on the same day that George Denbrough had been murdered), Patrick had discovered the rusty Amana refrigerator – one of the larger dumpoids in the belt surrounding the dump itself.

Like Bev, he had heard the cautionary warnings about such abandoned appliances, about how thirty-squirty million kids got their stupid selves smoked in them each year. Patrick had stood looking at the refrigerator for a long time, idly playing pocket-pool with himself. That excitement was back, stronger than it had ever been, except for the time he had fixed Avery. The excitement was back because, in the chilly yet fuming wastes that passed for his mind, Patrick Hockstetter had had an idea.

The Luces, who lived three houses down from the Hockstetters, missed their cat, Bobby, a week later. The Luce kids, who couldn't remember a time when Bobby hadn't been there, spent hours combing the neighborhood for him. They even pooled their money and put an ad in the Derry *News* Lost and Found column. Nothing came of it. And if any of them had seen Patrick that day, bulkier than ever in his mothball-smelling winter parka (after the flood-waters receded in that fall of '57, it had come off bitterly cold almost at once), carrying a cardboard carton, they would have thought nothing of it.

The Engstroms, a block over and almost directly behind the Hockstetter home, lost their cocker pup about ten days before Thanksgiving. Other families lost dogs and cats over the next six or eight months, and Patrick of course had taken them all, not to mention a dozen unremarked strays from the Hell's Half-Acre area of Derry.

He put them into the rusty Amana near the dump, one by one. Each time he brought another animal down, his heart thundering in his chest, his eyes hot and watery with excitement, he would expect to find that Mandy Fazio had pulled the Amana's latch or popped the hinges with his sledgehammer. But Mandy never touched that particular refrigerator. Perhaps he didn't realize it was there, perhaps the force of Patrick's will kept him away . . . or perhaps some other force did that.

The Engstroms' cocker lasted the longest. In spite of the single-number cold, it was still alive when Patrick came back for the third time in as many days, although it had lost all of its original friskiness (it had been wagging its tail and lapping his hands frantically when he originally hauled it out of the box and stuffed it into the refrigerator). When he came back a day after putting it in, the puppy had damn near gotten away. Patrick had to chase it almost all the way to the dump before he was able to jump it and get hold of one rear leg. The puppy had nipped Patrick with its sharp little teeth. Patrick didn't mind. In spite of the nips, he had taken the cocker back to the refrigerator and bundled it back in. He had a hard-on when he did it. This was not uncommon.

On the second day the puppy had tried to get out again, but it moved much too slowly. Patrick shoved it back in, slammed the Amana's rusty door, and leaned against it. He could hear the puppy scratching against the door. He could hear its muffled whines. 'Good dog,' said Patrick Hockstetter. His eyes were closed and he was breathing fast. 'That's a good dog.' On the third day the puppy could only roll its eyes toward Patrick's face when the door opened. Its sides were heaving rapidly and shallowly. When Patrick returned the next day, the cocker was dead with a cake of foam frozen around its mouth and muzzle. This made Patrick think of coconut Popsicles, and he laughed quite hard as he hauled the frozen corpse from his killing-bottle and threw it in the bushes.

The supply of victims (which Patrick thought of, when he thought of them at all, as 'test animals') had been thin this summer. Questions of reality aside, his sense of self-preservation was well developed, his intuition exquisite. He suspected he was suspected. By whom he was not sure: Mr Engstrom? Perhaps. Mr Engstrom had turned around and given Patrick a long speculative look in the A&P one day this spring. Mr Engstrom had been buying cigarettes and Patrick had been sent for bread. Mrs Josephs? Maybe. She sat in her parlor window with a telescope sometimes and was, according to Mrs Hockstetter, a 'nosy parker.' Mr Jacubois, who had an ASPCA sticker on the back bumper of his car? Mr Nell? Someone else? Patrick didn't know for sure, but his intuition told him he was suspected, and he never argued with his intuition. He had taken a few wandering animals from among the rotted tenements in the Half-Acre, picking only those that looked thin or diseased, but that was all.

He discovered, however, that the refrigerator near the dump had gotten an oddly powerful hold over him. He began to draw pictures of it in school when he was bored. He sometimes dreamed of it at night, and in his dreams the Amana was perhaps seventy feet tall, a whited sepulchre, a ponderous crypt iced in chilly moonlight. In these dreams the giant door would swing open and he would see huge eyes staring out at him. He would awake in a cold sweat, but he found he could not give up the joys of the refrigerator entirely.

Today he had finally found out who had suspected. Bowers. Knowing that Henry Bowers held the secret of his killing-bottle in his hands left Patrick as close to panic as he was ever apt to get. This was not very close at all, in truth, but he still found this – not fear exactly, but mental unrest – oppressive and unpleasant. Henry knew. Knew that Patrick sometimes broke the rules.

His latest victim had been a pigeon he discovered on Jackson Street two days ago. The pigeon had been struck by a car and couldn't fly. Patrick went home, got his box out of the garage, and put the pigeon inside. The pigeon pecked the back of Patrick's hand several times, leaving shallow, bloody digs. Patrick didn't mind. When he checked the refrigerator the next day, the pigeon had been quite dead, but Patrick hadn't removed the corpse then. Now, following Henry's threat to tell, Patrick decided he better get rid of the pigeon's body right away. Perhaps he would even get a bucket of water and some rags and scrub out the interior of the refrigerator. It didn't smell very good. If Henry told and Mr Nell came down to check, he might be able to tell that something – several somethings, in fact – had died in there.

If he tells, Patrick thought, standing in the grove of pines and looking at the rusty Amana, *I'll tell that he broke Eddie Kaspbrak's arm*. Of course they probably knew that already, but they couldn't prove anything because all of *them* said they had been playing out at Henry's house that day and Henry's crazy father had backed them up. *But if he tells, I'll tell. Tit for tat.*

Never mind that now. What he had to do now was get rid of the bird. He would leave the refrigerator door open and then come back with the rags and the water and clean it up. Good.

Patrick opened the refrigerator door on his own death.

At first he was simply puzzled, unable to cope in any way with what he was seeing. It meant nothing to him at all. It had no context. Patrick merely stared, his head cocked to one side, his eyes wide.

The pigeon was nothing but a skeleton surrounded by a ragged fall of feathers. There was no flesh left on its body at all. And around it, stuck on the refrigerator's inner walls, hanging from the underside of the freezer compartment, dangling from the wire shelves, were dozens of flesh-colored objects that looked like big macaroni shells. Patrick saw that they were moving slightly, fluttering, as if in a breeze. Except there was no breeze. He frowned.

Suddenly one of the shell-like things unfurled insectile wings. Before Patrick could do more than register the fact, it had flown across the space between the refrigerator and Patrick's left arm. It struck with a smacking sound. There was an instant of heat. It faded and Patrick's arm felt just like always again ... but the shell-like creature's pale flesh turned first pink, and then, with shocking suddenness, rose-red.

Although Patrick was afraid of almost nothing in the commonly understood sense of the word (it's hard to be afraid of things that aren't 'real'), there was at least one thing that filled him with wretched loathing. He had come out of Brewster Lake one warm August day when he was seven to discover four or five leeches clinging to his stomach and legs. He had screamed himself hoarse until his father had pulled them off.

Now, in a deadly burst of inspiration, he realized that this was some weird kind of flying leech. They had infested his refrigerator.

Patrick began to scream and beat at the thing on his arm. It had swelled to nearly the size of a tennis ball. At the third blow it broke open with a sickening *squtt* sound. Blood – his blood – sprayed his arm from elbow to wrist, but the thing's jellylike eyeless head held on. In a way, it was like a bird's narrow head, ending in a beaklike structure, but this beak was not flat or pointed; it was tubular and blunt, like the proboscis of a mosquito. This proboscis was buried in Patrick's arm.

Still screaming, he pinched the splattered creature between his fingers and pulled it off. The proboscis came out cleanly, followed by a watery flow of blood mixed with some yellowish-white liquid like pus. It had made a painless dime-sized hole in his arm.

And the creature, although exploded, was still twisting and moving and seeking in his fingers.

Patrick threw it away, turned . . . and more of them flew out of the refrigerator, lighting on him even as he groped for the Amana's handle. They landed on his hands, his arms, his neck. One touched down on his forehead. When Patrick raised his hand to pick it off, he saw four others on his hand, trembling minutely, turning first pink and then red.

There was no pain . . . but there *was* a hideous *draining* sensation. Screaming, whirling, beating at his head and neck with his leech-encrusted hands, Patrick Hockstetter's mind yammered: *It isn't real, it's just a bad dream, don't worry, it's not real, nothing is real –*

But the blood pouring from the smashed leeches seemed real enough, the sound of their buzzing wings seemed real enough . . . and his own terror seemed real enough.

One of them fell down inside his shirt and settled on his chest. While he was beating frantically at it and watching the bloodstain spread above the place where it had taken its hold, another settled on his right eye. Patrick closed it, but that did no good; he felt a brief hot flare as the thing's sucker poked through his eyelid and began to suck the fluid out of his eyeball. Patrick felt his eye collapse in its socket and he screamed again. A leech flew into his mouth when he did and roosted on his tongue.

It was all almost painless.

Patrick went staggering and flapping up the path toward the junked cars. Parasites hung all over him. Some of them drank to capacity and then burst like balloons; when this happened to the bigger ones, they drenched Patrick with almost half a pint of his own hot blood. He could feel the leech inside his mouth swelling up and he opened his jaws because the only coherent thought he had left was that it must not burst in there; it must not, must not.

But it did. Patrick ejected a huge spray of blood and parasite-flesh like vomit. He fell down in the gravelly dirt and began to roll over and over, still screaming. Little by little the sound of his own screams began to seem faint, faraway.

Just before he passed out, he saw a figure step from behind the last of the junked cars. At first Patrick thought he was a guy, Mandy Fazio perhaps, and he would be saved. But as the figure drew closer, he saw its face was running like wax. Sometimes it began to harden and look like something – or someone – and then it would start to run again, as if it couldn't make up its mind who or what it wanted to be.

'Hello and goodbye,' a bubbling voice said from inside the running tallow of its features, and Patrick tried to scream again. He didn't want to die; as the only 'real' person, he wasn't *supposed* to die. If he did, everyone else in the world would die with him.

The manshape laid hold of his leech-encrusted arms and began to drag him away toward the Barrens. His bloodstained book-carrier bumped and thumped along beside him, its strap still twisted about his neck. Patrick, still trying to scream, lost consciousness.

He awoke only once: when, in some dark, smelly, drippy hell where no light shone, no light at all, It began to feed.

6

At first Beverly was not entirely sure what she was seeing or what was happening . . . only that Patrick Hockstetter had begun to thrash and dance and scream. She got up warily, holding the slingshot in one hand and two of the ball-bearings in the other. She could hear Patrick blundering off down the path, still yelling his head off. In that moment, Beverly looked every inch the lovely woman she was going to become, and if Ben Hanscom had been around to see her just then, his heart might not have been able to stand it.

She was standing fully upright, her head cocked to the left, her eyes wide, her hair done in braids that had been tied off with two small red velvet bows which she had bought in Dahlie's for a dime. Her posture was one of total attention and concentration; it was feline, lynxlike. She had shifted forward on her left foot, her body half-turned as if to go after Patrick, and the legs of her faded shorts had pulled up enough to show the edging on her yellow cotton panties. Below them, her legs were already smoothly muscled, beautiful in spite of the scabs, bruises, and smutches of dirt.

It's a trick. He saw you and he knows he probably can't catch you in a fair chase, so he's trying to get you to come out. Don't go, Bevvie!

But another part of her thought there was too much pain and fear in those screams. She wished she had seen whatever had happened to Patrick – if anything had – more clearly. She wished more than anything else that she had come into the Barrens a different way and missed the whole crazy shenanigans.

Patrick's screams stopped. A moment later Beverly heard someone speak – but she knew *that* had to be her imagination. She heard her father say, 'Hello and goodbye.' Her father wasn't even *in* Derry that day: he had set off for Brunswick at eight o'clock. He and Joe Tammerly were going to pick up a Chevy truck in Brunswick. She shook her head as if to clear it. The voice didn't speak again. Her imagination, obviously.

She walked out of the bushes to the path, ready to run the instant she saw Patrick charging at her, her reactions on triggers as delicate as a cat's whiskers. She looked down at the path and her eyes widened. There was blood here. Quite a lot of it.

Fake blood, her mind insisted. *You can buy a bottle of it at Dahlie's for forty-nine cents. Be careful, Bevvie!*

She knelt and quickly touched the blood with her fingers. She looked at them closely. It wasn't fake blood.

There was a flash of heat in her left arm, just below the elbow. She looked down and saw something that she first thought was some kind of burr. No – not a burr. Burrs didn't twitch and flutter. This thing was alive. A moment after that she realized it was *biting* her. She struck it hard with the back of her right hand and it spattered, spraying blood. She backed up a step, getting ready to scream now that it was over . . . and then she saw that it wasn't over at all. The thing's featureless head was still on her arm, its snout buried in her flesh.

With a shrill cry of disgust and fear, she picked it off and saw its proboscis come out of her arm like a small dagger, dripping with blood. She understood the blood on the path now, oh yes, and her eyes went to the refrigerator.

The door had swung closed and latched again, but a number of the parasites had been left outside and were crawling sluggishly over the rusty-white porcelain. As Beverly looked, one of them unfurled its membranous fly-like wings and buzzed toward her.

She acted without thinking, loading one of the steel ball-bearings into the cup of the Bullseye and pulling the sling back. As the muscles of her left arm flexed smoothly, she saw loose blood squirt from the hole the thing had made in her arm. She let fly anyway, unconsciously leading the flying thing.

Shit! Missed! she thought as the Bullseye snapped and the ball-bearing flew, a glittering chunk of light in the hazy sun. And she would later tell the other Losers that she *knew* she had missed it, the same way a bowler knows he has missed the strike as soon as a bad ball leaves his hand. But then she saw the ball-bearing *curve*. It happened in a split-second, but the impression was very clear: it had *curved*. It struck the flying thing and splattered it to mush. There was a shower of yellowish droplets which pattered on the path.

Beverly backed up slowly at first, her eyes huge, her lips trembling, her face a shocked grayish-white. Her gaze was pinned to the front of the discarded refrigerator, waiting to see if any of the other things would smell or sense her. But the parasites only crawled slowly back and forth, like autumn flies drugged with the cold.

At last she turned and ran.

Panic beat darkly against her thoughts, but she would not give in to it entirely. She held the Bullseye in her left hand and looked back over her shoulder from time to time. There was still blood dappled brightly on the path and on the leaves of some of the bushes bordering it, as if Patrick had woven from side to side as he ran.

Beverly burst out into the area of the junked cars again. Ahead of her there was a bigger splash of blood, just beginning to soak into the gravelly earth. The ground looked disturbed, darker streaks of earth lined into the powdery-white surface. As if there had been a struggle there. Two grooves, about two and a half feet apart, led away from this spot.

Beverly halted, panting. She looked at her arm and was relieved to see that the flow of blood was finally slowing, although her lower forearm and the palm of her hand were streaked and tacky with it. The pain had begun now, a low steady throb. It felt the way her mouth felt about an hour after the dentist's, when the novocaine began to wear off.

She looked behind again, saw nothing, then looked back at those grooves leading away from the junked cars, away from the dump, and into the Barrens.

Those things were in the refrigerator. They got all over him – sure they did, look at all the blood. He got this far, and then

(*hello and goodbye*)

something else happened. What?

She was terribly afraid she knew. The leeches were a part of It, and they had driven Patrick into another part of It much as a panic-maddened steer is driven down the chute and into the slaughtering-pen.

Get out of here! Get out, Bevvie!

Instead she followed the grooves in the earth, holding the Bullseye tightly in her sweating hand.

At least get the others!

I will . . . in a little while.

She walked on, following the grooves as the ground sloped down and became softer. She followed them into heavy foliage again. Somewhere a cicada burred loudly and then unwound into silence. Mosquitoes lighted on her blood-streaked arm. She waved them away. Her teeth were clenched on her lower lip.

There was something lying on the ground ahead. She picked it up and looked at it. It was a handmade wallet, the sort of thing a kid might make as a crafts project at Community House. Except it was obvious to Bev that the kid who made this hadn't been much of a craftsman; the wide plastic stitching was already coming unravelled and the bill compartment flapped like a loose mouth. She found a quarter in the change compartment. The only other thing in the wallet was a library card, made out in the name of Patrick Hockstetter. She tossed the wallet aside, library card and all. She wiped her fingers on her shorts.

Fifty feet farther on she found a sneaker. The underbrush was now too dense for her to be able to follow the grooves in the earth, but you didn't have to be the Pathfinder to follow the splashes and drips of blood on the bushes.

The trail wound down through a steep brake. Bev lost her footing once, slid, and was raked by thorns. Fresh lines of blood appeared on her upper thigh. She was breathing fast now, her hair sweaty and matted to her skull. The spots of blood led out onto one of the faint paths through the Barrens. The Kenduskeag was nearby.

Patrick's other sneaker, its laces bloody, lay marooned on the path.

She approached the river with the Bullseye's sling half-drawn. The grooves in the earth had reappeared. They were shallower now – *that's because he lost his sneakers*, she thought.

She came around a final bend and faced the river. The grooves went down the bank and led ultimately to one of those concrete cylinders – one of the pumping-stations. There they stopped. The iron cover capping the top of this cylinder was a little ajar.

As she stood above it, looking down, a thick and monstrous chuckle suddenly issued from beneath.

It was too much. The panic which had threatened now descended. Beverly turned and fled toward the clearing and clubhouse, her bloody left arm up to shield her face from the branches which whipped and slapped her.

Sometimes I worry too, Daddy, she thought wildly. *Sometimes I worry a LOT.*

7

Four hours later all of the Losers except Eddie crouched in the bushes near the spot where Beverly had hidden and watched Patrick Hockstetter go to the refrigerator and open it. The sky overhead had darkened with thunderheads, and the smell of rain was in the air again. Bill was holding the end of a long length of clothesline in his hands. The six of them had pooled their available cash and bought the line and a Johnson's first-aid kit for Beverly. Bill had carefully affixed a gauze pad over the bloody hole in her arm.

'T-Tell your puh-puh-harents you g-got a scruh-hape when you were skuh-skuh-skating,' Bill said.

'My skates!' Beverly cried, dismayed. She had forgotten all about them.

'There,' Ben said, and pointed. They were lying in a heap not far away, and she went to retrieve them before Ben or Bill or any of the others could offer. She remembered now that she had put them aside before urinating. She didn't want any of the others over there.

Bill himself had tied one end of the clothesline to the handle of the Amana refrigerator, although they had all cautiously approached it together, ready to bolt at the first sign of movement. Bev had offered to give the Bullseye back to Bill; he had insisted she keep it. As it turned out, nothing had moved. Although the area on the path in front of the refrigerator was splattered with blood, the parasites were gone. Perhaps they had flown away.

'You could bring Chief Borton and Mr Nell and a hundred other cops down here and it still wouldn't matter,' Stan Uris said bitterly.

'Nope. They wouldn't see a frockin thing,' Richie agreed. 'How's your arm, Bev?'

'Hurts.' She paused, looking from Bill to Richie and back to

Bill again. 'Would my mom and dad see the hole that thing made in my arm?'

'I d-d-don't th-think s-s-so,' Bill said. 'Get reh-ready to ruh-ruh-run. I'm gonna t-t-t-tie it uh-uh-on.'

He looped the end of the clothesline around the refrigerator's rust-flecked chrome handle, working with the care of a man defusing a live bomb. He tied a granny-knot and then stepped back, paying out the clothesline.

He grinned a small shaky grin at the others when they had made some distance. 'Whooo,' he said. 'G-Glad that's oh-over.'

Now, a safe (they hoped) distance from the refrigerator, Bill told them again to get ready to run. Thunder boomed directly overhead and they all jumped. The first scattered drops began to fall.

Bill jerked the clothesline as hard as he could. His granny-knot popped off the handle, but not before it had pulled the refrigerator door open again. An avalanche of orange pompoms fell out, and Stan Uris uttered a painful groan. The others only stared, open-mouthed.

The rain began to come harder. Thunder whipcracked above them, making them cringe, and purplish-blue lightning flared as the refrigerator door swung all the way open. Richie saw it first and screamed, a high, hurt sound. Bill uttered some sort of angry, frightened cry. The others were silent.

Written on the inside of the door, written in drying blood, were these words:

STOP NOW BEFORE I KILL YOU ALL
A WORD TO THE WISE FROM YOUR FRIEND
PENNYWISE

Hail mixed with the driving rain. The refrigerator door shuddered back and forth in the rising wind, the letters painted there beginning to drip and run now, taking on the draggling ominous look of a horror-movie poster.

Bev was not aware that Bill had gotten up until she saw him advancing across the path toward the refrigerator. He was shaking both fists. Water streamed down his face and plastered his shirt to his back.

'W-We're going to k-k-kill you!' Bill screamed. Thunder whacked and cracked. Lightning flashed so brightly that she could smell it, and not far away there was a splintering, rending sound as a tree fell.

'Bill, come back!' Richie was yelling. 'Come back, man!' He started to get up and Ben hauled him back down again.

'You killed my brother George! You son of a bitch! You bastard! You whoremaster! Let's see you now! Let's see you now!'

Hail came in a spate, stinging them even through the screening bushes. Beverly held her arm up to protect her face. She could see red welts on Ben's streaming cheeks.

'Bill, come back!' she screamed despairingly, and another thundercrack drowned her out; it rolled across the Barrens below the low black clouds.

'Let's see you come out now, you fucker!'

Bill kicked wildly at the heap of pompoms that had spilled out of the refrigerator. He turned away and began to walk back toward them, his head down. He seemed not to feel the hail, although it now covered the ground like snow.

He blundered into the bushes, and Stan had to grab his arm to keep him from going into the prickerbushes. He was crying.

'That's okay, Bill,' Ben said, putting a clumsy arm around him.

'Yeah,' Richie said. 'Don't worry. We're not gonna chicken out.' He stared around at them, his eyes looking wildly out of his wet face. 'Is there anyone here who's gonna chicken out?'

They shook their heads.

Bill looked up, wiping his eyes. They were all soaked to the skin and looked like a litter of pups that had just forded a river. 'Ih-It's scuh-scuh-hared of u-u-us, you know,' he said. 'I can fuh-feel th-that. I swear to Guh-God I c-c-can.'

Bev nodded soberly. 'I think you're right.'

'H-H-Help m-m-me,' Bill said. 'P-P-Pl-Please. H-H-Help m-m-me.'

'We will,' Beverly said. She took Bill in her arms. She had not realized how easily her arms would go around him, how thin he was. She could feel his heart racing under his shirt; she could feel it next to hers. She thought that no touch had ever seemed so sweet and strong.

Richie put his arms around both of them and laid his head on Beverly's shoulder. Ben did the same from the other side. Stan Uris put his arms around Richie and Ben. Mike hesitated, and then slipped one arm around Beverly's waist and the other over Bill's shivering shoulders. They stood that way, hugging, and the sleet turned back to driving pouring rain, rain so heavy it seemed almost like a new atmosphere. The lightning walked and the thunder talked. No one spoke. Beverly's eyes were tightly shut. They stood in the rain in a huddled group, hugging each other, listening to it hiss down on the bushes. That was what she remembered best: the sound of the rain and their own shared silence and a vague sorrow that Eddie was not there with them. She remembered those things.

She remembered feeling very young and very strong.

CHAPTER EIGHTEEN
THE BULLSEYE

1

'Okay, Haystack,' Richie says. *'Your turn. The redhead's smoked all of her cigarettes and most of mine. The hour groweth late.'*

Ben glances up at the clock. Yes, it's late: nearly midnight. Just time for one more story, *he thinks.* One more story before twelve. Just to keep us warm. What should it be? *But that, of course, is only a joke, and not a very good one; there is only one story left, at least only one he remembers, and that is the story of the silver slugs — how they were made in Zack Denbrough's workshop on the night of July 23rd and how they were used on the 25th.*

'I've got my own scars,' he says. *'Do you remember?'*

Beverly and Eddie shake their heads; Bill and Richie nod. Mike sits silent, his eyes watchful in his tired face.

Ben stands up and unbuttons the work-shirt he is wearing, spreading it open. An old scar in the shape of the letter H shows there. Its lines are broken — the belly was much bigger when that scar was put there — but its shape still identifiable.

The heavy scar depending downward from the cross-bar of the H is much clearer. It looks like a twisted white hangrope from which the noose has been cut.

Beverly's hand goes to her mouth. 'The werewolf! In that house! Oh Jesus Christ!' *And she turns to the windows, as if to see it lurking outside in the darkness.*

'That's right,' Ben said. *'And you want to know something funny? That scar wasn't there two days ago. Henry's old calling-card was; I know, because I showed it to a friend of mine, a bar-tender named Ricky Lee back in Hemingford Home. But this one —'* He laughs without much humor and begins buttoning his shirt again. *'This one just came back.*

'Like the ones on our hands.'

'Yeah,' Mike says as Ben buttons his shirt up again. *'The werewolf. We all saw It as the werewolf that time.'*

789

'Because that's how R-R-Richie saw Ih-It before,' Bill murmurs. 'That's it, isn't it?'

'Yes,' Mike says.

'We were close, weren't we?' Beverly says. Her voice is softly marvelling. 'Close enough to read each other's minds.'

'Ole Big Hairy damn near had your guts for garters, Ben,' Richie says, and he is not smiling as he says it. He pushes his mended glasses up on his nose and behind them his face looks white and haggard and ghostly.

'Bill saved your bacon,' Eddie says abruptly. 'I mean, Bev saved us all, but if it hadn't been for you, Bill —'

'Yes,' Ben agrees. 'You did, Big Bill. I was, like, lost in the funhouse.'

Bill points briefly at the empty chair. 'I had some help from Stan Uris. And he paid for it. Maybe died for it.'

Ben Hanscom is shaking his head. 'Don't say that, Bill.'

'But it's t-true. And if it's yuh-your f-fault, it's my fault, too, and e-e-everyone else's here, because we went on. Even after Patrick, and what was written on that r-re-frigerator, we went on. It would be my fault m-most of all, I guess, because I wuh-wuh-wanted us to go on. Because of Juh-George. Maybe even because I thought that if I killed whatever k-killed George, my puh-harents would have to luh-luh-luh —'

'Love you again?' Beverly asks gently.

'Yes. Of course. But I d-d-don't think it was a-a-anyone's fuh-hault, Ben. It was just the w-w-way Stan was built.'

'He couldn't face it,' Eddie says. He is thinking of Mr Keene's revelation about his asthma medicine, and how he could still not give it up. He is thinking that he might have been able to give up the habit of being sick; it was the habit of believing he had been unable to kick. As things had turned out, maybe that habit had saved his life.

'He was great that day,' Ben says. 'Stan and his birds.'

A chuckle stirs through them, and they look at the chair where Stan would have been in a rightful sane world where all the good guys won all of the time. I miss him, Ben thinks. God, how I miss him! He says, 'You remember that day, Richie, when you told him you heard somewhere he killed Christ, and Stan says totally deadpan, "I think that was my father"?'

'I remember,' Richie says in a voice almost too low to hear. He takes his handkerchief out of his back pocket, removes his glasses, wipes his eyes, then puts his glasses back on. He puts away the handkerchief and without looking up from his hands he says, 'Why don't you just tell it, Ben?'

'It hurts, doesn't it?'

'Yeah,' Richie says, his voice so thick it is hard to understand him. 'Why, sure. It hurts.'

Ben looks around at them, then nods. 'All right, then. One more story before twelve. Just to keep us warm. Bill and Richie had the idea of the bullets –'

'No,' Richie demurs. 'Bill thought of it first, and he got nervous first.'

'I just started to wuh-wuh-worry –'

'Doesn't really matter, I guess,' Ben says. 'The three of us spent some heavy library time that July. We were trying to find out how to make silver bullets. I had the silver; four silver dollars that were my father's. Then Bill got nervous, thinking about what kind of shape we'd be in if we had a misfire with some kind of monster coming down our throats. And when we saw how good Beverly was with that slingshot of his, we ended up using one of my silver dollars to make slugs instead. We got the stuff together and all of us we went down to Bill's place. Eddie, you were there –'

'I told my mother we were going to play Monopoly,' Eddie says. 'My arm was really hurting, but I had to walk. That's how pissed she was at me. And every time I heard someone behind me on the sidewalk I'd whip around, thinking it was Bowers. It didn't help the pain.'

Bill grins. 'And what we did was stand around and watch Ben make the ammo. I think Ben r-really could have made sih-silver bullets.'

'Oh, I'm not so sure of that,' Ben says, although he still is. He remembers how the dusk was drawing down outside (Mr Denbrough had promised them all rides home), the sound of the crickets in the grass, the first lightningbugs blinking outside the windows. Bill had carefully set up the Monopoly board in the dining room, making it look as if the game had been going on for an hour or more.

He remembers that, and the clean pool of yellow light falling on Zack's worktable. He remembers Bill saying, 'We gotta be c-c-

2

careful. I don't want to leave a muh-muh-mess. My dad'll be –'

He spat out a number of 'p's, and finally managed to say 'pissed off.'

Richie made a burlesque of wiping his cheek. 'Do you serve towels with your showers, Stuttering Bill?'

Bill made as if to hit him. Richie cowered, shrieking in his Pickaninny Voice.

Ben took very little notice of them. He watched Bill lay out the implements and tools one by one in the light. Part of his mind was wishing that someday he might have such a nice worktable as this himself. Most of it was centered directly on the job ahead. Not as difficult as making silver bullets would have been, but he would still be careful. There was no excuse for sloppy workmanship. This was not something he had been taught or told, just something he knew.

Bill had insisted that Ben make the slugs, just as he continued to insist that Beverly would be the one carrying the Bullseye. These things could have and had been discussed, but it was only twenty-seven years later, telling the story, that Ben realized no one had even suggested that a silver bullet or slug might not stop a monster – they had the weight of what seemed like a thousand horror movies on their side.

'Okay,' Ben said. He cracked his knuckles and then looked at Bill. 'You got the molds?'

'Oh!' Bill jumped a little. 'H-H-Here.' He reached into his pants pocket and brought out his handkerchief. He put it on the workbench and unfolded it. There were two dull steel balls inside, each with a small hole in it. They were bearing molds.

After deciding on slugs instead of bullets, Bill and Richie had gone back to the library and had researched how bearings were made. 'You boys are *so* busy,' Mrs Starrett had said. 'Bullets one week and bearings the next! And it's summer vacation, too!'

'We like to stay sharp,' Richie said. 'Right, Bill?'

'Ruh–Ruh–Right.'

It turned out that making bearings was a cinch, once you had the molds. The only real question was where to get them. A couple of discreet questions to Zack Denbrough had taken care of that . . . and none of the Losers were too surprised to find that the only machine-shop in Derry where such molds might be obtained was Kitchener Precision Tool & Die. The Kitchener who owned and ran it was a great-great-grandnephew of the brothers who had owned the Kitchener Ironworks.

Bill and Richie had gone over together with all the cash the Losers had been able to raise on short notice – ten dollars and fifty-nine cents – in Bill's pocket. When Bill asked how much a couple of two-inch bearing molds might cost, Carl Kitchener – who looked like a veteran boozehound and smelled like an old horse-blanket – asked what a couple of kids wanted with bearing molds. Richie let Bill speak, knowing things would probably go easier that way – children made fun of Bill's stutter; adults were embarrassed by it. Sometimes this was surprisingly helpful.

Bill got halfway through the explanation he and Richie had worked out on the way over – something about a model windmill for next year's science project – when Kitchener waved for him to shut up and quoted them the unbelievable price of fifty cents per mold.

Hardly able to believe their good fortune, Bill forked over a single dollar bill.

'Don't expect me to give you a bag,' Carl Kitchener said, eying them with the bloodshot contempt of a man who believes he has seen everything the world holds, most of it twice. 'You don't get no bag unless you spend at least five bucks.'

'That's o-o-okay, suh-sir,' Bill said.

'And don't hang around out front,' Kitchener said. 'You both need haircuts.'

Outside Bill said: 'Y-Y-You ever nuh-hotice, Ruh-Richie, how guh-guh-grownups w-w-won't sell you a-a-anything except c-candy or cuh-cuh-homic books or m-maybe movie t-t-tickets without first they w-want to know what y-you want it f-for?'

'Sure,' Richie said.

'W-Why? Why ih-is that?'

'Because they think we're dangerous.'

'Y-Yeah? You thuh-thuh-think s-so?'

'Yeah,' Richie said, and then giggled. 'Let's hang around out front, want to? We'll put up our collars and sneer at people and let our hair grow.'

'Fuck y-you,' Bill said.

3

'Okay,' Ben said, looking at the molds carefully and then putting them down. 'Good. Now –'

They gave him a little more room, looking at him hopefully, the way a man with engine trouble who knows nothing about cars will look at a mechanic. Ben didn't notice their expressions. He was concentrating on the job.

'Gimme that shell,' he said, 'and the blowtorch.'

Bill handed a cut-down mortar shell to him. It was a war souvenir. Zack had picked it up five days after he and the rest of General Patton's army had crossed the river into Germany. There had been a time, when Bill was very young and George was still in diapers, that his father had used it as an ashtray. Later he had quit smoking, and the mortar shell had disappeared. Bill had found it in the back of the garage just a week ago.

Ben put the mortar shell into Zack's vise, tightened it, and then took the blowtorch from Beverly. He reached into his pocket, brought out a silver dollar, and dropped it into the makeshift crucible. It made a hollow sound.

'Your father gave you that, didn't he?' Beverly asked.

'Yes,' Ben said, 'but I don't remember him very well.'

'Are you sure you want to do this?'

He looked at her and smiled. 'Yes,' he said.

She smiled back. It was enough for Ben. If she had smiled at him twice, he would gladly have made enough silver bearings to shoot a platoon of werewolves. He looked hastily away. 'Okay. Here we go. No problem. Easy as pie, right?'

They nodded hesitantly.

Years later, recounting all of this, Ben would think: *These days a kid could just run out and buy a propane torch . . . or his dad would have one in the workshop.*

There had been no such things in 1958, however; Zack Denbrough had a tank-job, and it made Beverly nervous. Ben could tell she was nervous, wanted to tell her not to worry, but was afraid his voice would tremble.

'Don't worry,' he said to Stan, who was standing next to her.

'Huh?' Stan said, looking at him and blinking.

'Don't *worry.*'

'I'm *not.*'

'Oh. I thought you were. And I just wanted you to know this is perfectly safe. *If* you were. Worrying, I mean.'

'Are you okay, Ben?'

'Fine,' Ben muttered. 'Gimme the matches, Richie.'

Richie gave him a book of matches. Ben twisted the valve on the tank and lit a match under the nozzle of the torch. There was a *flump*! and a bright blue-orange glare. Ben tuned the flame to a blue edge and began to heat the base of the mortar shell.

'You got the funnel?' he asked Bill.

'R-R-Right here.' Bill handed over a homemade funnel that Ben had made earlier. The tiny hole at its base fit the hole in the bearing molds almost exactly. Ben had done this without taking a single measurement. Bill had been amazed – almost flabbergasted – but did not know how to say so without embarrassing Ben.

Absorbed in what he was doing, Ben could talk to Beverly – he spoke with the dry precision of a surgeon addressing a nurse.

'Bev, you got the steadiest hands. Stick the funnel in the hole. Use one of those gloves so you don't get burned.'

Bill handed her one of his father's work gloves. Beverly put the tin funnel in the mold. No one spoke. The hissing of the blowtorch flame seemed very loud. They watched it, eyes squinted almost shut.

'Wuh-wuh-wait,' Bill said suddenly, and dashed into the house. He came back a minute later with a pair of cheap Turtle wraparound sunglasses that had been languishing in a kitchen drawer for a year or more. 'Better p-put these uh-on, H-H-Haystack.'

Ben took them, grinned, and slipped them on.

'Shit, it's Fabian!' Richie said. 'Or Frankie Avalon, or one of those *Bandstand* wops.'

'Fuck you, Trashmouth,' Ben said, but he started giggling in spite of himself. The idea of him being Fabian or someone like that was just too weird. The flame wavered and he stopped laughing; his concentration narrowed to a point again.

Two minutes later he handed the torch to Eddie, who held it gingerly in his good hand. 'It's ready,' he said to Bill. 'Gimme that other glove. Fast! Fast!'

Bill gave it to him. Ben put it on and held the mortar shell with the gloved hand while he turned the vise lever with the other.

'Hold it steady, Bev.'

'I'm ready, don't wait for me,' she rapped back at him.

Ben tilted the shell over the funnel. The others watched as a rivulet of molten silver flowed between the two receptacles. Ben poured precisely; not a drop was spilled. And for a moment, he felt galvanized. He seemed to see everything magnified through a strong white glow. For that one moment he did not feel like plain fat old Ben Hanscom, who wore sweatshirts to disguise his gut and his tits; he felt like Thor, working thunder and lightning at the smithy of the gods.

Then the feeling was gone.

'Okay,' he said. 'I'm gonna have to reheat the silver. Someone shove a nail or something up the spout of the funnel before the goop hardens in there.'

Stan did it.

Ben clamped the mortar shell in the vise again and took the torch from Eddie.

'Okay,' he said, 'number two.'

And went back to work.

4

Ten minutes later it was done.

'Now what?' Mike asked.

'Now we play Monopoly for an hour,' Ben said, 'while they harden in the molds. Then I clip em open with a chisel along the cut-lines and we're done.'

Richie looked uneasily at the cracked face of his Timex, which had taken a great many lickings and kept on ticking. 'When will your folks be back, Bill?'

'N-N-Not until tuh-ten or ten-thuh-thuh-hirty,' Bill said. 'It's a double f-f-f-feature at the Uh-Uh-Uh –'

'Aladdin,' Stan said.

'Yeah. And they'll stop in for a slice of p-p-pizza after. They a-almost always d-do.'

'So we have plenty of time,' Ben said.

Bill nodded.

'Then let's go in,' Bev said. 'I want to call home. I promised I would. And don't any of you talk. He thinks I'm at Community House and that I'm getting a ride home from there.'

'What if he wants to come down and pick you up early?' Mike asked.

'Then,' Beverly said, 'I'm going to be in a lot of trouble.'

Ben thought: *I'd protect you, Beverly.* In his mind's eye, an instant daydream unfolded, one with an ending so sweet he shivered. Bev's father started to give her a hard time; to bawl her out and all that (even in his daydream he did not imagine how bad all that could get with Al Marsh). Ben threw himself in front of her and told Marsh to lay off.

If you want trouble, fatboy, you just keep protecting my daughter.

Hanscom, usually a quiet bookish type, can be a ravening tiger when you get him mad. He speaks to Al Marsh with great sincerity. *If you want to get to her, you'll have to come through me first.*

Marsh starts forward . . . and then the steely glint in Hanscom's eyes stops him.

You'll be sorry, he mumbles, but it's clear all the fight has gone out of him. He's just a paper tiger after all.

Somehow I doubt that, Hanscom says with a tight Gary Cooper smile, and Beverly's father slinks away.

What's happened to you, Ben? Bev cries, but her eyes are shining and full of stars. *You looked ready to kill him!*

Kill him? Hanscom says, the Gary Cooper smile still lingering on his lips. *No way, baby. He may be a creep, but he's still your father. I might have roughed him up a little, but that's only because when someone talks wrong to you I get a little hot under the collar. You know?*

She throws her arms around him and kisses him (on the *lips!* on the *LIPS!*). *I love you, Ben!* she sobs. He can feel her small breasts pressing firmly against his chest and –

He shivered a little, throwing this bright, terribly clear picture off with an effort. Richie stood in the doorway, asking him if he was coming, and Ben realized he was all alone in the workroom.

'Yeah,' he said, starting a little. 'Sure I am.'

'You're goin senile, Haystack,' Richie said as Ben went though the door, but he clapped Ben on the shoulder. Ben grinned and hooked an elbow briefly around Richie's neck.

5

There was no problem with Beverly's dad. He had come home late from work, Bev's mother told her over the phone, fallen asleep in front of the TV, and waked up just long enough to get himself into bed.

'You got a ride home, Bevvie?'

'Yes. Bill Denbrough's dad is going to take a whole bunch of us home.'

Mrs Marsh sounded suddenly alarmed. 'You're not on a *date*, are you, Bevvie?'

'No, of course not,' Bev said, looking through the arched doorway between the darkened hall where she was and the dining room, where the others were sitting down around the Monopoly board. *But I sure wish I was.* 'Boys, uck. But they have a sign-up sheet down here, and every night a different dad or mom takes kids home.' That much, at least, was true. The rest was a lie so outrageous that she could feel herself blushing hotly in the dark.

'All right,' her mom said. 'I just wanted to be sure. Because if your dad caught you going on dates at your age, he'd be mad.' Almost as an afterthought she added: 'I would be, too.'

'Yeah, I know,' Bev said, still looking into the dining room. She *did* know; yet here she was, not with one boy but six of them, in a house where the parents were gone. She saw Ben looking at her anxiously, and she sketched a smiling little salute at him. He blushed but gave her the little salute right back.

'Are any of your girlfriends there?'

What *girlfriends, Mamma*?

'Um, Patty O'Hara's here. And Ellie Geiger, I think. She's playing shuffleboard downstairs.' The facility with which the lies came from her lips made her ashamed. She wished she were talking to her father; she would have been more scared but less ashamed. She supposed she really wasn't a very good girl.

'I love you, Mamma,' she said.

'Same goes back to you, Bev.' Her mother paused briefly and added: 'Be careful. The paper says there may be another one. A boy named Patrick Hockstetter. He's missing. Did you know him, Bevvie?'

She closed her eyes briefly. 'No, Mom.'

'Well . . . goodbye, then.'

'Bye.'

She joined the others at the table and for an hour they played Monopoly. Stan was the big winner.

'Jews are very good at making money,' Stan said, putting a hotel on Atlantic Avenue and two more green houses on Ventnor Avenue. 'Everybody knows that.'

'Jesus, make me Jewish,' Ben said promptly, and everyone laughed. Ben was almost broke.

Beverly glanced across the table from time to time at Bill, noting his clean hands, his blue eyes, the fine red hair. As he moved the little silver shoe he was using as a marker around the board, she thought, *If he held my hand, I think I'd be so glad I'd probably die.* A warm light seemed to glow briefly in her chest and she smiled secretly down at her hands.

6

The evening's finale was almost anticlimactic. Ben took one of Zack's chisels from the shelf and used a hammer to strike the molds on the cut-lines. They opened easily. Two small silver balls fell out. In one they could faintly see part of a date: 925. In the other, wavery lines Beverly thought were the remnants of Lady Liberty's hair. They looked at them without speaking for a moment, and then Stan picked one up.

'Pretty small,' he said.

'So was the rock in David's sling when he went up against Goliath,' Mike said. 'They look powerful to me.'

Ben found himself nodding. They did to him, as well.

'We're all d-d-done?' Bill asked.

'All done,' Ben said. 'Here.' He tossed the second slug to Bill, who was so surprised he almost fumbled it.

The slugs went around the circle. Each of them looked closely at both, marvelling at their roundness, weight, actuality. When they came back to Ben, he held them in his hand and then looked at Bill. 'What do we do with them now?'

'G-G-Give them to B-Beverly.'

'No!'

He looked at her. His face was kind enough, but stern. 'B-B-Bev, we've been thruh-through this a-a-already, and –'

'I'll do it,' she said. 'I'll shoot the goddamned things when the time comes. *If* it comes. I'll probably get us all killed, but I'll do it. I don't want to take them home, though. One of my

(*father*)

parents might find them. Then I'd be in dutch.'

'Don't you have a secret hiding place?' Richie asked. 'Criminy, I got four or five.'

'I've got a place,' Beverly said. There was a small slit in the bottom of her box-spring where she sometimes stashed cigarettes, comic books, and, just lately, film and fashion magazines. 'But nothing I'd trust for something like this. You keep them, Bill. Until it's time, anyway, you keep them.'

'Okay,' Bill said mildly, and just then lights splashed into the driveway. 'Holy cruh-crow, they're e-e-early. L-Let's get out of h-here.'

They were just sitting down around the Monopoly board again when Sharon Denbrough opened the kitchen door.

Richie rolled his eyes and mimed wiping sweat from his forehead; the others laughed heartily. Richie had Gotten Off A Good One.

A moment later she came in. 'Your dad's waiting for your friends in the car, Bill.'

'O-O-Okay, M-Mom,' Bill said. 'W-We were juh-just f-f-finishing, a-anyway.'

'Who won?' Sharon asked, smiling bright-eyed at Bill's little friends. The girl was going to be very pretty, she thought. She supposed in another year or two the children would have to be chaperoned if there were going to be girls instead of just the regular gang of boys. But surely it was still too soon to worry about sex rearing its ugly head.

'St-Stan wuh-wuh-won,' Bill said. 'Juh-Juh-Jews are very g-g-good at m-making money.'

'*Bill!*' she cried, horrified and blushing . . . and then she looked around at them, amazed, as they roared with laughter, Stan included. Amazement turned to something like fear (although she said nothing of this to her husband later, in bed). There was a feeling in the air, like static electricity, only somehow much more powerful, much more scary. She felt that if she touched any of them, she would receive a walloping shock. *What's happened to them?* she thought, dismayed, and perhaps she even opened her mouth to say something like that. Then Bill was saying he was sorry (but still with that devilish glint in his eye), and Stan was saying that was all right, it was just a joke they laid on him from time to time, and she found herself too confused to say anything at all.

But she felt relieved when the children were gone and her own puzzling, stuttering son had gone to his room and turned off the light.

7

The day that the Losers' Club finally met It in face-to-face combat, the day It almost had Ben Hanscom's guts for garters, was July 25th, 1958. It was hot and muggy and still. Ben remembered the weather clearly enough; it had been the last day of the hot weather. After that day, a long spell of cool and cloudy had come in.

They arrived at 29 Neibolt Street around ten that morning, Bill riding Richie double on Silver, Ben with his ample buttocks spilling over either side of the sagging seat on his Raleigh. Beverly came down Neibolt Street on her girl's Schwinn, her red hair held back from her forehead by a green band. It streamed out behind her. Mike came by himself, and about five minutes later Stan and Eddie walked up together.

'H-H-How's your a-a-arm, Eh-Eh-Eddie?'

'Aw, not too bad. Hurts if I roll over on that side while I'm sleeping. Did you bring the stuff?'

There was a canvas-wrapped bundle in Silver's bike-basket. Bill took it out and unwrapped it. He handed the slingshot to Beverly, who took it with a little grimace but said nothing. There was also a tin Sucrets box in the bundle. Bill opened it and showed them the two silver balls. They looked at them silently, gathered close together on the balding lawn on 29 Neibolt Street – a lawn where only weeds seemed to grow. Bill, Richie, and Eddie had seen the house before; the others hadn't, and they looked at it curiously.

The windows look like eyes, Stan thought, and his hand went to the paperback book in his back pocket. He touched it for luck. He carried the book with him almost everywhere – it was M. K. Handey's *Guide to North American Birds*. *They look like dirty blind eyes.*

It stinks, Beverly thought. *I can smell it – but not with my nose, not exactly.*

Mike thought, *It's like that time out where the Ironworks used to be. It has the same feel . . . as if it's telling us to step on in.*

This is one of Its places, all right, Ben thought. *One of the places like the Morlock holes, where It goes out and comes back in. And It knows we're out here. It's waiting for us to come in.*

'Yuh-yuh-you all still want to?' Bill asked.

They looked back at him, pale and solemn. No one said no. Eddie fumbled his aspirator out of his pocket and took a long whooping gasp at it.

'Gimme some of that,' Richie said.

Eddie looked at him, surprised, waiting for the punchline.

Richie held out his hand. 'No fake, Jake. Can I have some?'

Eddie shrugged with his good shoulder – an oddly disjointed movement – and handed it over. Richie triggered the aspirator and breathed deep. 'Needed that,' he said, and handed it back. He was coughing a little, but his eyes were sober.

'Me too,' Stan said. 'Okay?'

So one after another they used Eddie's aspirator. When it came back to him, Eddie jammed it in his back pocket, where the nozzle stuck out. They turned to look at the house again.

'Does *anybody* live on this street?' Beverly asked in a low voice.

'Not this end of it,' Mike said. 'Not anymore. I guess there are still bums sometimes. Guys that come through on the freights.'

'They wouldn't see anything,' Stan said. 'They'd be safe. Most of them, anyway.' He looked at Bill. 'Can any grownups at all see It, do you think, Bill?'

'I don't nuh-know,' Bill said. 'There must be *suh-suh-some*.'

'I wish we could meet one,' Richie said glumly. 'This really isn't a job for kids, you know what I mean?'

Bill knew. Whenever the Hardy Boys got into trouble, Fenton Hardy was around to bail them out. Same with Rick Brant's dad in the Rick Brant Science Adventures. Shit, even Nancy Drew had a father who would show up in the nick of time if the bad guys tied her up and threw her into an abandoned mine or something.

'Ought to be a grownup along,' Richie said, looking at the closed house with its peeling paint, its dirty windows, its shadowy porch. He sighed tiredly. For a moment, Ben felt their resolution falter.

Then Bill said, 'Cuh-cuh-home a-a-a-around h-here. Look at th-this.'

They walked around to the left side of the porch, where the skirting was torn off. The brambly, run-to-the-wild roses were still there . . . and those It had touched when It climbed out were still black and dead.

'It just touched them and it did *that*?' Beverly asked, horrified.

Bill nodded. 'Are you guh-huys *s-s-sure*?'

For a moment nobody replied. They *weren't* sure; even though all of them knew by Bill's face that he would go on without them, they weren't sure. There was also a species of shame on Bill's face. As he had told them before, George hadn't been their brother.

But all the other kids, Ben thought. *Betty Ripsom, Cheryl Lamonica, that Clements kid, Eddie Corcoran (maybe), Ronnie Grogan . . . even Patrick Hockstetter. It kills kids, goddamit, kids!*

'I'll go, Big Bill,' he said.

'Shit, yeah,' Beverly said.

'Sure,' Richie said. 'You think we're gonna let you have all the fun, mushmouth?'

Bill looked at them, his throat working, and then he nodded. He handed the tin box to Beverly.

'Are you *sure*, Bill?'

'Sh-Sh-Sure.'

She nodded, at once horrified by the responsibility and bewitched by his trust. She opened the box, took out the slugs, and slipped one into the right front pocket of her jeans. The other she socketed in the Bullseye's rubber cup, and it was by the cup that she carried the slingshot. She could feel the ball tightly enclosed in her fist, cold at first and then warming.

'Let's go,' she said, her voice not quite steady. 'Let's go before I chicken out.'

Bill nodded, then looked sharply at Eddie. 'Cuh-Can you d-d-do this, Eh-Eh-Eddie?'

Eddie nodded. 'Sure I can. I was alone last time. This time I'm with my friends. Right?' He looked at them and grinned a little. His expression was shy, fragile, and quite beautiful.

Richie clapped him on the back. 'Thass right, senhorr. Anywhunn tries to steal your assipirator, we keel heem. But we keel heem *slow*.'

'That's terrible, Richie,' Bev said, giggling.

'Uh-Uh-under the p-porch,' Bill said. 'A-All of you b-b-behind me. Then into the suh-suh-cellar.'

'If you go first and that thing jumps you, what do I do?' Beverly asked. 'Shoot through you?'

'If y-you have to,' Bill said. 'But I suh-suh-suggest y-y-you try guh-hoing a-around, first.'

Richie laughed wildly at this.

'We'll g-g-go through the whole puh-puh-place, if we have t-to.' He shrugged. 'Maybe we won't find a-a-anything.'

'Do you believe that?' Mike asked.

'No,' Bill said briefly. 'It's h-h-here.'

Ben believed he was right. The house at 29 Neibolt Street seemed to be encased in a poisonous envelope. It could not be seen . . . but it could be felt. He licked his lips.

'You ruh-ruh-ready?' Bill asked them.

They all looked back at him. 'Ready, Bill,' Richie said.

'Cuh-come on, th-then,' Bill said. 'Stay cluh-close behind me, B-Beverly.' He dropped to his knees, crawled through the blighted rosebushes and under the porch.

8

They went this way: Bill, Beverly, Ben, Eddie, Richie, Stan, Mike. The leaves under the porch crackled and puffed up a sour old smell. Ben wrinkled his nose. Had he ever smelled fallen leaves like these? He thought not. And then an unpleasant idea struck him. They smelled the way he imagined a mummy would smell, just after its discoverer had levered open its coffin: all dust and bitter ancient tannic acid.

Bill had reached the broken cellar window and was looking into the cellar. Beverly crawled up beside him. 'You see anything?'

Bill shook his head. 'But that d-doesn't m-m-mean nuh-huthin's there. L-Look; there's the c-coal-pile me and R-R-Richie used to get ow-out.'

Ben, who was looking between them, saw it. He was becoming excited as well as afraid now, and he welcomed the excitement, instinctively recognizing the fact that it could be a tool. Seeing the coal-pile was a little like seeing a great landmark about which you had only read or heard from others.

Bill turned around and slipped lithely through the window. Beverly gave Ben the Bullseye, folding his hand over the cup and ball nestled in it. 'Give it to me the second I'm down,' she said. 'The *second*.'

'Got you.'

She slipped down as easily and lithely as Bill had before her. There was – for Ben, at least – one heart-stopping instant when her blouse pulled out of her jeans and he saw her flat white belly. Then there was the thrill of her hands over his as he handed the slingshot down.

'Okay, I've got it. Come on.'

Ben turned around himself and began to wriggle through the window. He should have foreseen what happened next; it was really inevitable. He got stuck. His fanny bound up against the rectangular cellar window and he couldn't go in any further. He started to pull himself out and realized, horrified, that he could do it, but was very apt to yank his pants – and perhaps his underpants as well – down to his knees when he did. And there he would be, with his extremely large ass practically in his beloved's face.

'Hurry up!' Eddie said.

Ben pushed grimly with both hands. For a moment he still couldn't move, and then his butt popped through the window-hole. His bluejeans dragged painfully up into his crotch, squashing his balls. The top of the window rucked his shirt all the way up to his shoulderblades. Now his gut was stuck.

'Suck in, Haystack,' Richie said, giggling hysterically. 'You better suck in or we'll have to send Mike after his dad's chainfall to pull you out again.'

'Beep-beep, Richie,' Ben said through gritted teeth. He sucked his belly in as much as he could. He had never really realized just how big his stupid stomach was until this supremely embarrassing moment. He moved a little further, then stopped again.

He turned his head as far as he could, fighting panic and claustrophobia. His face had gone a bright sweaty red. The sour smell of the leaves was heavy in his nostrils, cloying. 'Bill! Can you guys pull me?'

He felt Bill grasp one of his ankles, Beverly the other. He sucked his belly in as far as he could. A moment later he came tumbling through the window. Bill grabbed him. Both of them almost fell over. Ben couldn't look at Bev. He had never in his life been as embarrassed as he was at that moment.

'Y-Y-You okay, m-m-man?'

'Yeah.'

Bill laughed shakily. Beverly joined him, and then Ben was able to laugh a little too, although it would be years before he could see anything remotely funny in what had happened.

'Hey!' Richie called down. 'Eddie needs help, okay?'

'O-O-Okay.' Bill and Ben took up positions below the window. Eddie came through on his back. Bill got his legs just above the knees.

'Watch what you're doing,' Eddie said in a querulous, nervous voice. 'I'm ticklish.'

'Ramon ees *plenny* teekeleesh, senhorr,' Richie's voice called down.

Ben got Eddie around the waist, trying to keep his hand away from the cast and the sling. The two of them manhandled Eddie through the cellar window like a corpse. Eddie cried out once, but that was all.

'Eh-Eh-Eddie?'

'Yeah,' Eddie said, 'okay. No big deal.' But large drops of sweat stood out on his forehead and he was breathing in quick rasps. His eyes darted around the cellar.

Bill stepped back again. Beverly stood near him, now holding the Bullseye by the shaft and the cup, ready to fire if necessary. Her eyes swept the cellar constantly. Richie came through next, followed by Stan and Mike. Both of the latter moved with a smooth grace that Ben deeply envied. Then they were all down, down in the cellar where Bill and Richie had seen It only a month before.

The room was dim, but not dark. Dusky light shafted in through the windows and pooled on the dirt floor. The cellar seemed very big to Ben, almost *too* big, as if he were witnessing an optical illusion of some sort. Dusty rafters crisscrossed overhead. The furnace-pipes were rusty. Some sort of dirty white cloth hung from the water-pipes in dirty strings and strands. The smell was down here too. A dirty yellow smell. Ben thought: *It's here, all right. Oh yeah.*

Bill started toward the stairs. The others fell in behind him. He halted at their foot and glanced underneath. He reached under with one foot and kick-pawed something out. They looked at it wordlessly. It was a white clown-glove, now streaked with dirt and dust.

'Uh-uh-upstairs,' he said.

They went up and emerged into a dirty kitchen. One plain straight-backed chair stood marooned in the center of the humped hillocky linoleum. That was it for furniture. There were empty liquor bottles in one corner. Ben could see others in the pantry. He could smell booze – wine, mostly – and old stale cigarettes. Those smells were dominant, but that other smell was there, too. It was getting stronger all the time.

Beverly went to the cupboards and opened one of them. She

screamed piercingly as a blackish-brown Norway rat tumbled out almost into her face. It struck the counter with a plop and glared around at them with its black eyes. Still screaming, Beverly raised the Bullseye and pulled the sling back.

'*NO!*' Bill roared.

She turned her pale terrified face toward him. Then she nodded and relaxed her arm, the silver ball unfired – but Ben thought she had been very, very close. She backed up slowly, ran into Ben, jumped. He put an arm around her, tight.

The rat scurried down the length of the counter, jumped to the floor, ran into the pantry, and was gone.

'It wanted me to shoot at it,' Beverly said in a faint voice. 'Use up half of our ammunition on it.'

'Yes,' Bill said. 'It's l-l-like the FBI training r-range at Quh–Quh-Quantico, in a w-w-way. They seh-send y-you down this f-f-hake street and p-pop up tuh-hargets. If you shuh-shoot any honest citizens ih-instead of just cruh-crooks, you l-lose puh-hoints.'

'I can't do this, Bill,' she said. 'I'll mess it up. Here. You.' She held the Bullseye out, but Bill shook his head.

'You *h-h-have* to, B-Beverly.'

There was a mewling from another cupboard.

Richie walked toward it.

'Don't get too close!' Stan barked. 'It might –'

Richie looked inside and an expression of sick disgust crossed his face. He slammed the cupboard shut with a bang that produced a dead echo in the empty house.

'A litter.' Richie sounded ill. 'Biggest litter I ever saw . . . *anyone* ever saw, probably.' He rubbed the back of his hand across his mouth. 'There's *hundreds* of them in there.' He looked at them, his mouth twitching a little on one side. 'Their *tails* . . . they were all tangled up, Bill. Knotted together.' He grimaced. 'Like snakes.'

They looked at the cupboard door. The mewling was muffled but still audible. *Rats*, Ben thought, looking at Bill's white face and, over Bill's shoulder, Mike's ashy-gray one. *Everyone's ascared of rats. It knows it, too.*

'C-C-Come on,' Bill said. 'H-Here on Nuh-Nuh-Neibolt Street, the f-f-fun just neh-hever stops.'

They went down the front hall. Here the unlovely smells of rotting plaster and old urine were intermixed. They were able to look out at the street through dirty panes of glass and see their bikes. Bev's and Ben's were heeled over on their kickstands. Bill's leaned against a stunted maple tree. To Ben the bikes looked a thousand miles away, like things seen through the wrong end of a telescope. The deserted street with its casual patchings of asphalt, the faded humid sky, the steady *ding-ding-ding* of a locomotive running on a siding ... these things seemed like dreams to him, hallucinations. What was real was this squalid hallway with its stinks and shadows.

There was a shatter of broken brown glass in one corner – Rheingold bottles.

In the other corner, wet and swelled, was a digest-sized girly-book. The woman on the cover was bent over a chair, her skirt up in the back to show the tops of her fishnet hose and her black panties. The picture did not look particularly sexy to Ben, nor did it embarrass him that Beverly had also glanced at it. Moisture had yellowed the woman's skin and moisture had humped the cover in ripples that became wrinkles on her face. Her salacious wink had become the leer of a dead whore.

(Years later, as Ben recounted this, Bev suddenly cried out, startling all of them – they were not so much listening to the story as reliving it. 'It was her!' Bev yelled. 'Mrs Kersh! It was her!')

As Ben looked, the young/old crone on the girlybook cover winked at him. She wiggled her fanny in an obscene come-on.

Cold all over, yet sweating, Ben looked away.

Bill pushed open a door on the left and they followed him into a vaultlike room that might once have been a parlor. A crumpled pair of green pants was hung over the light-fixture which depended from the ceiling. Like the cellar, this room seemed much too big to Ben, almost as long as a freight-car. Much too long for a house as small as this one had appeared from the outside –

Oh, but that was outside, a new voice spoke inside his mind. It was a jocular, squealing voice, and Ben realized with sudden numbing certainty that he was hearing Pennywise Itself; Pennywise was speaking to him on some crazy mental radio. *Outside, things always look smaller than they really are, don't they, Ben?*

'Go away,' he whispered.

Richie turned to look at him, his face still strained and pale. 'You say something?'

Ben shook his head. The voice was gone. That was an important thing, a good thing. Yet

(*outside*)

he had understood. This house was a special place, a kind of station, one of the places in Derry, one of the many, perhaps, from which It was able to find its way into the overworld. This stinking rotted house where everything was somehow *wrong*. It wasn't just that it seemed too big; the *angles* were wrong, the perspective crazy. Ben was standing just inside the door between the parlor and the hallway and the others were moving away from him across a space that now looked almost as big as Bassey Park . . . but as they moved away, they seemed to grow *larger* instead of smaller. The floor seemed to slope, and –

Mike turned. 'Ben!' he called, and Ben saw alarm on his face. 'Catch up! We're losing you!' He could barely hear the last word. It trailed away as if the others were being swept off on a fast train.

Suddenly terrified, he began to run. The door behind him swept shut with a muffled bang. He screamed . . . and something seemed to sweep through the air just behind him, ruffling his shirt. He looked back but there was nothing there. That did not change his belief, however, that something had been.

He caught up with the others. He was panting, out of breath, and would have sworn he had run half a mile at least . . . but when he looked back, the parlor's far wall was not ten feet away.

Mike grasped his shoulder hard enough to hurt.

'You scared me, man,' he said. Richie, Stan, and Eddie were looking at Mike questioningly. 'He looked *small*,' Mike said. 'Like he was a mile away.'

'Bill!'

Bill looked back.

'We gotta make sure everybody stays close,' Ben panted. 'This place . . . it's like the funhouse in a carnival, or something. We'll get lost. I think It *wants* us to get lost. To get separated.'

Bill looked at him for a moment, lips thin. 'All right,' he said. 'We a-all stay cluh-cluh-hose. No s-s-stragglers.'

They nodded back, frightened, clustered outside the hall door. Stan's hand groped at the bird-book in his back pocket. Eddie was holding his aspirator in one hand, crunching it, loosening up, then crunching it again, like a ninety-eight-pound weakling trying to build up his muscles with a tennis ball.

Bill opened the door and here was another, narrower hall. The wallpaper, which showed runners of roses and elves wearing green caps, was falling away from the spongy plaster in draggling leaves. Yellow waterstains spread in senile rings on the ceiling overhead. A scummy wash of light fell through a dirty window at the end of the hall.

Abruptly the corridor seemed to elongate. The ceiling rose and then began to diminish above them like some weird rocket. The doors grew with the ceiling, pulled up like taffy. The faces of the elves grew long and became alien, their eyes bleeding black holes.

Stan shrieked and clapped his hands to his eyes.

'*Ih-Ih-hit's not ruh-ruh-ruh-REAL!*' Bill screamed.

'It *is!*' Stan screamed back, his small closed fists plugging his eyes. 'It's *real*, you *know* it is, God, I'm going crazy, this is *crazy, this is crazy –*'

'*Wuh-wuh-WATCH!*' Bill bellowed at Stan, at all of them, and Ben, his head reeling, watched at Bill bent down, coiled, and suddenly flung himself upward. His closed left fist struck nothing, nothing at all, but there was a heavy *crr-rack*! sound. Plaster dust puffed from a place where there was no longer any ceiling . . . and then there was. The hallway was just a hallway again, narrow, low-ceilinged, dirty. But the walls no longer stretched up into forever. There was only Bill, looking at them and nursing his bleeding hand, which was floury with plaster-dust. Overhead was the clear mark his fist had made in the soft plaster of the ceiling.

'N-N-Not ruh-ruh-real,' he said to Stan, to all of them. 'Just a f-f-false f-fuh-face. Like a Huh-Huh-Huh-Halloween muh-muh-mask.'

'To *you*, maybe,' Stan said dully. His face was shocked and horrified. He looked around as if no longer sure where he was. Looking at him, smelling the sour reek coming out of his pores, Ben, who had been overjoyed at Bill's victory, got scared all over again. Stan was close to cracking up. Soon he would go into hysterics, begin to scream, perhaps, and what would happen then?

'To *you*,' Stan said again. 'But if I'd tried that, nothing would have happened. Because . . . you've got your brother, Bill, but I don't have anything.' He looked around – first back toward the parlor, which had taken on a somber brown atmosphere, so thick and smoggy they could barely see the door through which they had entered it, to this hall, which was bright but somehow dark, somehow filthy, somehow utterly mad. Elves capered on the decaying wallpaper under runners of roses. Sun glared on the panes of the window at the end of the hall, and Ben knew that if they went down there they would see dead flies . . . more broken glass . . . and then what? The floorboards spreading apart, spilling them into a dead darkness where grasping fingers waited to catch them? Stan was right, God, why had they come into Its lair with nothing but their two stupid silver slugs and a fucking slingshot?

He saw Stan's panic leap from one of them to the next to the next – like a grassfire driven by a hot wind, it widened in Eddie's eyes, dropped Bev's mouth into a wounded gasp, made Richie push his glasses up with both hands and stare around as if followed from close behind by a fiend.

They trembled on the brink of flight, Bill's warning to stay together almost forgotten. They were listening to gale-force panicwinds blowing between their ears. As if in a dream Ben heard Miss Davies, the assistant librarian, reading to the little ones: *Who is that trip-trapping on my bridge?* And he saw them, the little ones, the babies, leaning forward, their faces still and solemn, their eyes reflecting the eternal fascination of the fairy-story: would the monster be bested . . . or would It feed?

'I don't have anything!' Stan Uris wailed, and he seemed very small, almost small enough to slip through one of the cracks in the hallway's plank flooring like a human letter. 'You got your brother, man, but I don't have *anything!*'

'You *duh-duh-duh-do!*' Bill yelled back. He grabbed Stan and Ben felt sure he was going to bust him one and his thoughts moaned, *No, Bill, please, that's Henry's way, if you do that It'll kill us all right now!*

But Bill didn't hit Stan. He whirled him around with rough hands and tore the paperback from the back pocket of Stan's jeans.

'Gimme it!' Stan screamed, beginning to cry. The others stood stunned, shrinking away from Bill, whose eyes now seemed to actually burn. His forehead glowed like a lamp, and he held the book out to Stan like a priest holding out a cross to ward off a vampire.

'*You guh-guh-got your b-b-bi-bir-bir –*'

He turned his head up, the cords in his neck standing out like cables, his adam's apple like an arrowhead buried in his throat. Ben was filled with both fear and pity for his friend Bill Denbrough; but there was also a strong sense of wonderful relief. Had he doubted Bill? Had any of them? *Oh Bill, say it, please, can't you say it?*

And somehow, Bill did. '*You got your BUH-BUH-BUH-BIRDS! Your BUH-BUH-BIRDS!*'

He thrust the book at Stan. Stan took it, and looked at Bill dumbly. Tears glimmered on his cheeks. He held the book so tightly that his fingers were white. Bill looked at him, then at the others.

'Cuh-cuh-home on,' he said again.

'Will the birds work?' Stan asked. His voice was low, husky.

'They worked in the Standpipe, didn't they?' Bev asked him.

Stan looked at her uncertainly.

Richie clapped him on the shoulder. 'Come on, Stan-kid,' he said. 'Is you a man or is you a mouse?'

'I must be a man,' Stan said shakily, and wiped tears from his face with the heel of his left hand. 'So far as I know, mice don't shit their pants.'

They laughed and Ben could have sworn he felt the house pulling away from them, from that sound. Mike turned. 'That big room. The one we just came through. Look!'

They looked. The parlor was now almost black. It was not smoke, nor any kind of gas; it was just blackness, a nearly solid blackness. The air had been robbed of its light. The blackness seemed to roll and flex as they stared into it, to almost coalesce into faces.

'Come oh-oh-on.'

They turned away from the black and walked down the hall. Three doors opened off it, two with dirty white porcelain door-knobs, the third with only a hole where the knob's shaft had been. Bill grabbed the first knob, turned it, and pushed the door open. Bev crowded up next to him, raising the Bullseye.

Ben drew back, aware that the others were doing the same, crowding behind Bill like frightened quail. It was a bedroom, empty save for one stained mattress. The rusty ghosts of the coils in a box-spring long departed were tattooed into the mattress's yellow hide. Outside the room's one window, sunflowers dipped and nodded.

'There's nothing –' Bill began, and then the mattress began to bulge in and out rhythmically. It suddenly ripped straight down the middle. A black sticky fluid began to spill out, staining the mattress and then running over the floor toward the doorway. It came in long ropy tendrils.

'Shut it, Bill!' Richie shouted. 'Shut the fuckin door!'

Bill slammed it shut, looked around at them, and nodded. 'Come on.' He had barely touched the knob of the second door – this one on the other side of the narrow hall – when the buzzing scream began behind the cheap wood.

9

Even Bill drew back from that rising, inhuman cry. Ben felt the sound might drive him mad; his mind visualized a giant cricket behind the door, like something from a movie where radiation made all the bugs get big – *The Beginning of the End*, maybe, or *The Black Scorpion*, or that one about the ants in the Los Angeles stormdrains. He could not have run even if that buzzing rugose horror had splintered the panels of the door and begun caressing him with its great hairy legs. Beside him, he was dimly aware that Eddie was breathing in hacking gasps.

The scream rose in pitch, never losing that buzzing, insectile quality. Bill fell back another step, no blood in his face now, his eyes bulging, his lips only a purple scar below his nose.

'Shoot it, Beverly!' Ben heard himself cry. 'Shoot it through the door, shoot it before it can get us!' And the sun fell through the dirty window at the end of the hall, a heavy feverish weight.

Beverly raised the Bullseye like a girl in a dream as the buzzing scream rose louder, louder, louder –

But before she could pull the sling back, Mike was shouting: 'No! No! Don't, Bev! Oh gosh! I'll be dipped!' And incredibly, Mike was laughing. He pushed forward, grabbed the knob, turned it, and shoved the door open. It came free of the swollen jamb with a brief grinding noise. 'It's a mooseblower! Just a mooseblower, that's all, something to scare the crows!'

The room was an empty box. Lying on the floor was a Sterno can with both ends cut off. In the middle, strung tight and knotted outside holes punched in the can's sides, was a waxed length of string. Although there was no breeze in the room – the one window was shut and indifferently boarded over, letting light pass only in chinks and rays – there could be no doubt that the buzzing was coming from the can.

Mike walked to it and fetched it a solid kick. The buzzing stopped as the can tumbled into a far corner.

'Just a mooseblower,' he said to the others, as if apologizing. 'We put em on the scarecrows. It's nothing. Only a cheap trick. But *I* ain't a crow.' He looked at Bill, not laughing anymore but smiling still. 'I'm still scared of It – I guess we all are – but It's scared of us, too. Tell you the truth, I think It's scared pretty bad.'

Bill nodded. 'I-I do, too,' he said.

They went down to the door at the end of the hall, and as Ben watched Bill hook his finger into the hole where the doorknob's shaft had been, he understood that this was where it was going to end; there would be no trick behind this door. The smell was worse now, and that thundery feeling of two opposing powers swirling around them was much stronger. He glanced at Eddie, one arm in a sling, his good hand clutching his aspirator. He looked at Bev on his other side, white-faced, holding the slingshot up like a wishbone. He thought: *If we have to run, I'll try to protect you, Beverly. I swear I'll try.*

She might have heard his thought, because she turned toward him and offered him a strained smile. Ben smiled back.

Bill pulled the door open. Its hinges uttered a dull scream and then were silent. It was a bathroom . . . but something was wrong with it. *Someone broke something in here* was all that Ben could make out at first. *Not a booze bottle . . . what?*

White chips and shards, glimmering wickedly, lay strewn everywhere. Then he understood. It was the crowning insanity. He laughed. Richie joined him.

'Somebody must have let the granddaddy of all farts,' Eddie said, and Mike began to giggle and nod his head. Stan was smiling a little. Only Bill and Beverly remained grim.

The white pieces littered across the floor were shards of porcelain. The toilet-bowl had exploded. The tank stood drunkenly at an angle in a puddle of water, saved from falling over by the fact that the toilet had been placed in one corner of the room and the tank had landed kitty-corner.

They crowded in behind Bill and Beverly, their feet gritting on bits of porcelain. *Whatever it was*, Ben thought, *it blew that poor toilet right to hell.* He had a vision of Henry Bowers dropping two or three of his M–80s into it, slamming the lid down, then bugging out in a hurry. He couldn't think of anything else short of dynamite that would have done such a cataclysmic job. There were a few chunks, but damned few; most of what was left were wicked-looking slivers like blowgun darts. The wallpaper (rose-runners and capering elves, as in the hall) was peppered with holes all the way around the room. It looked like shotgun blasts but Ben knew it was more porcelain, driven into the walls by the force of the explosion.

There was a bathtub standing on claw feet with generations of grimy toe-jam between each blunt talon. Ben peeked into it and saw a tidal-flat of silt and grit on the bottom. A rusty showerhead glared down from above. There was a basin and a medicine cabinet standing ajar above it, disclosing empty shelves. There were small rust-rings on these shelves, where bottles had once stood.

'I wouldn't get too close to that, Big Bill!' Richie said sharply, and Ben looked around.

Bill was approaching the mouth of the drainhole in the floor, over which the toilet had once sat. He leaned toward it . . . and then turned back to the others.

'I can h-h-hear the puh-pumping muh-muh-machinery . . . just like in the Buh-Buh-harrens!'

Bev drew closer to Bill. Ben followed her, and yes, he could hear it; that steady thrumming noise. Except, echoing up through the pipes, it didn't sound like machinery at all. It sounded like something alive.

'Th-Th-This is w-w-where It cuh-cuh-hame fr-from,' Bill said. His face was still deadly pale, but his eyes were alight with excitement. 'This is w-where it cuh-hame from that d-d-day, and th-hat's w-w-where it a-a-always comes fr-rom! The druh-druh-drains!'

Richie was nodding. 'We were in the cellar, but that isn't where It was – It came down the stairs. Because this is where It could get out.'

'And It did *this*?' Beverly asked.

'Ih-It was in a h-h-hurry, I th-think,' Bill said gravely.

Ben looked into the pipe. It was about three feet in diameter and dark as a mineshaft. The inner ceramic surface of the pipe was crusted with stuff he didn't want to know about. That thrumming sound floated up hypnotically . . . and suddenly he saw something. He did not see it with his physical eyes, not at first, but with one buried deep in his mind.

It was rushing toward them, moving at express-train speed, filling the throat of this dark pipe from side to side; It was in Its own form now, whatever that might be; It would take some shape from their minds when It got here. It was coming, coming up from Its own foul runs and black catacombs under the earth, Its eyes glowing a feral yellowish green, coming, coming; It was coming.

And then, at first like sparks, he saw Its eyes down in that darkness. They took shape – flaring and malignant. Over the thrumming sound of the machinery, Ben could now hear a new noise – *Whooooooooo* . . . A fetid smell belched from the ragged mouth of the drainpipe and he fell back, coughing and gagging.

'It's coming!' he screamed. 'Bill, I saw It, It's coming!'

Beverly raised the Bullseye. 'Good,' she said.

Something exploded out of the drainpipe. Ben, trying to recall that first confrontation later, could only remember a silvery-orange shifting shape. It was not ghostly; it was solid, and he sensed some other shape, some real and ultimate shape, behind it . . . but his eyes could not grasp what he was seeing, not precisely.

Then Richie was stumbling backward, his face a scrawl of terror, screaming over and over again: 'The Werewolf! Bill! It's the Werewolf! The Teenage Werewolf!' And suddenly the shape locked into reality, for Ben, for all of them. Richie's It became their It.

The Werewolf stood poised over the drainpipe, one hairy foot on either side of where the toilet had once been. Its green eyes glared at them from Its feral face. Its muzzle wrinkled back and yellowish-white foam seeped through Its teeth. It uttered a shattering growl. Its arms pistoned out toward Beverly, the cuffs of Its high-school letter jacket pulling back from Its fur-covered arms. Its smell was hot and raw and murderous.

Beverly screamed. Ben grabbed the back of her blouse and yanked so hard that the seams under the arms tore. One clawed hand swept through the air where she had been only a moment before. Beverly went stumbling backwards against the wall. The silver ball popped out of the cup of the Bullseye. For a moment it glimmered in the air. Mike, quicker than quick, snatched it and gave it back to her.

'Shoot it, baby,' he said. His voice was perfectly calm; almost serene. 'You shoot it right now.'

The Werewolf uttered a shattering roar that became a flesh-freezing howl, Its snout turned up toward the ceiling.

The howl became a laugh. It lunged at Bill as Bill turned to look at Beverly. Ben shoved him aside and Bill went sprawling.

'*Shoot It, Bev!*' Richie screamed. '*For God's sake, shoot It!*'

The Werewolf sprang forward, and there was no question in Ben's mind, then or later, that It knew exactly who was in charge here. Bill was the one It was after. Beverly drew and fired. The ball flew and again it was off the mark but this time there was no saving curve. It missed by more than a foot, punching a hole in the wallpaper above the tub. Bill, his arms peppered with bits of porcelain and bleeding in a dozen pieces, uttered a screaming curse.

The Werewolf's head snapped around; its gleaming green eyes considered Beverly. Not thinking, Ben stepped in front of her as she groped in her pocket for the other silver slug. The jeans she wore were too tight. She had donned them with no thought of provocation; it was just that, like the shorts she had worn on the day of Patrick Hockstetter and the refrigerator, she was still wearing last year's model. Her fingers closed on the ball but it squirted away. She groped again and got it. She pulled it, turning her pocket inside out and spilling fourteen cents, the stubs of two Aladdin tickets, and a quantity of pocket-lint onto the floor.

The Werewolf lunged at Ben, who was standing protectively in front of her . . . and blocking her field of fire. Its head was cocked at the predator's deadly questing angle, Its jaws snapping. Ben reached blindly for It. There seemed to be no room in his reactions now for terror – he felt a clear-headed sort of anger instead, mixed with bewilderment and a sense that somehow time had come to a sudden unexpected screech-halt. He snagged his hands in tough matted hair – *the pelt*, he thought, *I've got Its pelt* – and he could feel the heavy bone of Its skull beneath. He thrust at that wolvish head with all of his force, but although he was a big boy, it did no good at all. If he had not stumbled back and struck the wall, the thing would have torn his throat open with Its teeth.

It came after him, Its greenish-yellow eyes flaring. It growled with each breath. It smelled of the sewer and something else, some wild yet unpleasant odor like rotten hazelnuts. One of Its heavy paws rose and Ben skittered aside as best he could. The paw, tipped with heavy claws, ripped bloodless wounds through the wallpaper and into the cheesy plaster beneath. He could dimly hear Richie bellowing something, Eddie howling at Beverly to shoot It, shoot It. But Beverly did not. This was her only other chance. It didn't matter; she intended that it be the only one she *would* need. A clear coldness she never saw again in her life fell over her sight. In it everything stood out and forward; never again would she see the three dimensions of reality so clearly defined. She possessed every color, every angle, every distance. Fear departed. She felt the hunter's simple lust of certainty and oncoming consummation. Her pulse slowed. The hysterical trembling grip in which she had been holding the Bullseye loosened, then firmed and became natural. She drew in a deep breath. It seemed to her that her lungs would never fill completely. Dimly, faintly, she heard popping sounds. Didn't matter, whatever they were. She tracked left, waiting for the Werewolf's improbable head to fall with cool perfection into the wishbone beyond the extended V of the drawn-back sling.

The Werewolf's claws descended again. Ben tried to duck under them . . . but suddenly he was in Its grip. It jerked him forward as if he had been no more than a ragdoll. Its jaws snapped open.

'Bastard –'

He thrust a thumb into one of Its eyes. It bellowed with pain, and one of those claw-tipped paws ripped through his shirt. Ben sucked his stomach in, but one of the claws pulled a sizzling line of pain down his chest and stomach. Blood gushed out of him and splattered on his pants, his sneakers, the floor. The Werewolf threw him into the bathtub. He thumped his head, saw stars, struggled into a sitting position, and saw his lap was full of blood.

The Werewolf whirled around. Ben observed with that same lunatic clarity that It was wearing faded Levi Strauss bluejeans. The seams had split open. A snot-caked red bandanna, the sort a train-man might carry, hung from one back pocket. Written on the back of Its silver and orange high school jacket were the words DERRY HIGH SCHOOL KILLING TEAM. Below this, the name PENNYWISE. And in the center, a number: 13.

It went for Bill again. He had gotten to his feet and now stood with his back to the wall, looking at It steadily.

'*Shoot It, Beverly!*' Richie screamed again.

'Beep-beep, Richie,' she heard herself reply from roughly a thousand miles away. The Werewolf's head was suddenly there, in the wishbone. She covered one of its green eyes with the cup and released. There was no shake in either of her hands; she fired as smoothly and naturally as she had fired at the cans in the dump on the day they had all taken turns to see who was the best.

There was time for Ben to think *Oh Beverly if you miss this time we're all dead and I don't want to die in this dirty bathtub but I can't get out.* There was no miss. A round eye – not green but dead black – suddenly appeared high up in the center of Its snout: she had aimed for the right eye and missed by less than half an inch.

Its scream – an almost human scream of surprise, pain, fear and rage – was deafening. Ben's ears rang with it. Then the perfect round hole in Its snout was gone, obscured by freshets of blood. It was not flowing; it gouted from the wound in a high-pressure torrent. The freshet drenched Bill's face and hair. *Doesn't matter*, Ben thought hysterically. *Don't worry, Bill. Nobody will be able to see it anyway when we get out of here. If we ever do.*

Bill and Beverly advanced on the Werewolf, and behind them, Richie cried out hysterically: 'Shoot It again, Beverly! Kill It!'

'Kill It!' Mike screamed.

'That's right, kill It!' Eddie chimed in.

'*Kill It!*' Bill cried, his mouth drawn down in a quivering bow. There was a whitish-yellow streak of plaster dust in his hair. '*Kill It, Beverly, don't let It get away!*'

No ammo left, Ben thought incoherently, *we're slugged out. What are you talking about, kill It?* But he looked at Beverly and understood. If his heart had never been hers before that moment, it would have flown to her then. She had pulled the sling back again. Her fingers were closed over the cup, hiding its emptiness.

'Kill It!' Ben screamed, and flopped clumsily over the edge of the tub. His jeans and underwear were soaked against his skin with blood. He had no idea if he was hurt badly or not. Following the original hot sizzle there hadn't been much pain, but there sure was an awful lot of blood.

The Werewolf's greenish eyes flickered among them, now filled with uncertainty as well as pain. Blood poured down the front of Its jacket in freshets.

Bill Denbrough smiled. It was a gentle, rather lovely smile . . . but it did not touch his eyes. 'You shouldn't have started with my brother,' he said. 'Send the fucker to hell, Beverly.'

The uncertainty left the creature's eyes − It believed. With lithe smooth grace, It turned and dove into the drain. As It went, It changed. The Derry High jacket melted into Its pelt and the color ran out of both. The shape of Its skull elongated, as if it had been made of wax which was now softening and beginning to run. Its shape changed. For one instant Ben believed he had nearly seen what shape It really was, and his heart froze inside his chest, leaving him gasping.

'*I'll kill you all!*' a voice roared from inside the drainpipe. It was thick, savage, not in the least human. '*Kill you all . . . kill you all . . . kill you all . . .*' The words faded back and back, diminishing, washing out, growing distant . . . at last joining the low throbbing hum of the pumping machinery floating through the pipes.

The house seemed to settle with a heavy sub-audible thud. But it wasn't settling, Ben realized; in some strange way it was *shrinking*, coming back to its normal size. Whatever magic It had used to make the house at 29 Neibolt Street seem bigger was now withdrawn. The house snapped back like an elastic. It was only a house now, smelling damp and a little rotten, an unfurnished house where winos and hobos sometimes came to drink and talk and sleep out of the rain.

It was gone.

In Its wake the silence seemed very loud.

10

'W-W-We guh-got to g-g-get ow-ow-out of this p-place,' Bill said. He walked over to where Ben was trying to get up and grabbed one of his outstretched hands. Beverly was standing near the drain. She looked down at herself and that coldness disappeared in a flush that seemed to turn all her skin into one warm stocking. It must have been a deep breath indeed. The dim popping sounds had been the buttons on her blouse. They were gone, every single one of them. The blouse hung open and her small breasts were clearly revealed. She snatched the blouse closed.

'Ruh-Ruh-Richie,' Bill said. 'Help me with B-B-Ben. He's h-h-h –'

Richie joined him, then Stan and Mike. The four of them got Ben to his feet. Eddie had gone to Beverly and put his good arm awkwardly around her shoulders. 'You did great,' he said, and Beverly burst into tears.

Ben took two big staggering steps to the wall and leaned against it before he could fall over again. His head felt light. Color kept washing in and out of the world. He felt decidedly pukey.

Then Bill's arm was around him, strong and comforting.

'How b-b-bad ih-ih-is it, H-H-Haystack?'

Ben forced himself to look down at his stomach. He found performing two simple actions – bending his neck and spreading apart the slit in his shirt – took more courage than he had needed to enter the house in the first place. He expected to see half his insides hanging down in front of him like grotesque udders. Instead he saw that the flow of blood had slowed to a sluggish trickle. The Werewolf had slashed him long and deep, but apparently not mortally.

Richie joined them. He looked at the cut which ran a twisting course down Ben's chest and petered out on the upper bulge of his stomach, then soberly into Ben's face. 'It just about had your guts for suspenders, Haystack. You know it?'

'No fake, Jake,' Ben said.

He and Richie stared at each other for a long, considering moment, and then they broke into hysterical giggles at the same instant, spraying each other with spittle. Richie took Ben into his arms and pounded his back. 'We beat It, Haystack! We beat It!'

'W-W-We dih-dih-dih-didn't beat It,' Bill said grimly. 'We got l-l-lucky. Let's g-get out b-b-before Ih-Ih-It d-d-decides to come buh-back.'

'Where?' Mike asked.

'The Buh-Buh-Barrens,' Bill said.

Beverly made her way over to them, still holding her blouse closed. Her cheeks were bright red. 'The clubhouse?'

Bill nodded.

'Can I have someone's shirt?' Beverly asked, blushing more furiously than ever. Bill glanced down at her, and the blood came into his own face, all in a rush. He turned his eyes away hastily, but in that instant Ben felt a rush of knowledge and dismal momentary jealousy. In that instant, that one bare second, Bill had become aware of her in a way that only Ben had himself been before.

The others had also looked and then looked away. Richie coughed against the back of his hand. Stan turned red. And Mike Hanlon dropped back a step or two as if actually frightened by the sideswell of that one small white breast, visible below her hand.

Beverly threw her head up, shaking her tangled hair back behind her. She was still blushing, but her face was lovely.

'I can't help it that I'm a girl,' she said, 'or that I'm starting to get big on top . . . now can't I please have someone's shirt?'

'Sh-sh-sure,' Bill said. He pulled his white t-shirt over his head, baring his narrow chest, the visible rack of his ribs, his sunburned, freckled shoulders. 'H-H-Here.'

'Thank you, Bill,' she said, and for one hot, smoking moment their eyes locked directly. Bill did not look away this time. His gaze was firm, adult.

'W-W-W-Welcome,' he said.

Good luck, Big Bill, Ben thought, and he turned away from that gaze. It was hurting him, hurting him in a deeper place than any Vampire or Werewolf would ever be able to reach. But all the same, there was such a thing as propriety. The word he didn't know; on the concept he was very clear. Looking at them when they were looking at each other that way would be as wrong as looking at her breasts when she let go of the front of her blouse to pull Bill's t-shirt over her head. *If that's the way it is. But you'll never love her the way I do. Never.*

Bill's t-shirt came down almost to her knees. If not for the jeans poking out from beneath its hem, she would have looked as if she was wearing a slip.

'L-L-Let's guh-guh-go,' Bill repeated. 'I duh-don't nuh-know about you g-guys, but I've h-h-had ee-ee-enough for wuh-wuh-one d-day.'

Turned out they all had.

11

The passage of an hour found them in the clubhouse, both the window and the trapdoor open. It was cool inside, and the Barrens were blessedly silent that day. They sat without talking much, each lost in his or her own thoughts. Richie and Bev passed a Marlboro back and forth. Eddie took a brief snort from his aspirator. Mike sneezed several times and apologized. He said he was catching a cold.

'Thass the oney theeng you *could* catch, senhorr,' Richie said, companionably enough, and that was all.

Ben kept expecting the mad interlude in the house on Neibolt Street to take on the hues of a dream. *It'll recede and fall apart,* he thought, *the way that bad dreams do. You wake up gasping and sweating all over, but fifteen minutes later you can't remember what the dream was even about.*

But that didn't happen. Everything that had happened, from the time he had forced his way in through the cellar window to the moment Bill had used the chair in the kitchen to break a window so they could get out, remained bright and clearly fixed in his memory. It had not been a dream. The clotted wound on his chest and belly was not a dream, and it didn't matter if his mom could see it or not.

At last Beverly stood up. 'I have to go home,' she said. 'I want to change before my mom gets home. If she sees me wearing a boy's shirt, she'll kill me.'

'Keel you, senhorrita,' Richie agreed, 'but she will keel you *slow.*'

'Beep-beep, Richie.'

Bill was looking at her gravely.

'I'll return your shirt, Bill.'

He nodded and waved a hand to show that this wasn't important.

'Will you get in trouble? Coming home without it?'

'N-No. They h-h-hardly nuh-hotice when I'm a-a-around, anyway.'

She nodded, bit her full underlip, a girl of eleven who was tall for her age and simply beautiful.

'What happens next, Bill?'

'I d-d-don't nuh-nuh-know.'

'It's not over, is it?'

Bill shook his head.

Ben said, 'It'll want us more than ever now.'

'More silver slugs?' she asked him. He found he could barely stand to meet her glance. *I love you, Beverly . . . just let me have that. You can have Bill, or the world, or whatever you need. Just let me have that, let me go on loving you, and I guess it'll be enough.*

'I don't know,' Ben said. 'We could, but . . .' He trailed off vaguely, shrugged. He could not say what he felt, was somehow not able to bring it out – that this was like being in a monster movie, but it wasn't. The Mummy had looked different in some ways . . . ways that confirmed its essential reality. The same was true of the Werewolf – he could testify to that because he had seen It in a paralyzing close-up no film, not even one in 3-D, allowed, he had had his hands in the wiry underbrush of Its tangled pelt, he had seen a small, baleful-orange firespot (like a pompom!)

in one of Its green eyes. These things were ... well ... they were dreams-made-real. And once dreams became real, they escaped the power of the dreamer and became their own deadly things, capable of independent action. The silver slugs had worked because the seven of them had been unified in their belief that they would. But they hadn't killed It. And next time It would approach them in a new shape, one over which silver wielded no power.

Power, power, Ben thought, looking at Beverly. It was okay now; her eyes had met Bill's again and they were looking at each other as if lost. It was only for a moment, but to Ben it seemed very long.

It always comes back to power. I love Beverly Marsh and she has power over me. She loves Bill Denbrough and so he has power over her. But – I think – he is coming to love her. Maybe it was her face, how it looked when she said she couldn't help being a girl. Maybe it was seeing one breast for just a second. Maybe just the way she looks sometimes when the light is right, or her eyes. Doesn't matter. But if he's starting to love her, she's starting to have power over him. Superman has power, except when there's Kryptonite around. Batman has power, even though he can't fly or see through walls. My mom has power over me, and her boss down in the mill has power over her. Everyone has some ... except maybe for little kids and babies.

Then he thought that even little kids and babies had power; they could cry until you had to do something to shut them up.

'Ben?' Beverly asked, looking back at him. 'Cat got your tongue?'

'Huh? No. I was thinking about power. The power of the slugs.'

Bill was looking at him closely.

'I was wondering where that power came from,' Ben said.

'Ih-Ih-It –' Bill began, and then shut his mouth. A thoughtful, vague expression drifted over his face.

'I really have to go,' Beverly said. 'I'll see you all, huh?'

'Sure, come on down tomorrow,' Stan said. 'We're going to break Eddie's other arm.'

They all laughed. Eddie pretended to throw his aspirator at Stan.

'Bye, then,' Beverly said, and boosted herself up and out.

Ben looked at Bill and saw that he hadn't joined in the laughter. That thoughtful expression was still on his face, and Ben knew you would have to call his name two or three times before he would answer. He knew what Bill was thinking about; he would be thinking about it himself in the days ahead. Not all the time, no. There would be clothes to hang out and take in for his mother, games of tag and guns in the Barrens, and, during a rainy spell the first four days of August, the seven of them would go on a mad Parcheesi jag at Richie

Tozier's house, making blockades, sending each other back with great abandon, deliberating exactly how to split the roll of the dice while rain dripped and ran outside. His mother would announce to him that she believed Pat Nixon was the prettiest woman in America, and be horror-struck when Ben opted for Marilyn Monroe (except for the color of her hair, he thought that Bev looked like Marilyn Monroe). There would be time to eat as many Twinkies and Ring-Dings and Devil Dogs as he could get his hands on, and time to sit on the back porch reading *Lucky Starr and the Moons of Mercury*. There would be time for all of those things while the wound on his chest and belly healed to a scab and began to itch, because life went on and at eleven, although bright and apt, he held no real sense of perspective. He could live with what had happened in the house on Neibolt Street. The world was, after all, full of wonders.

But there would be odd moments of time when he pulled the questions out again and examined them: *The power of the silver, the power of the slugs — where does power like that come from? Where does any power come from? How do you get it? How do you use it?*

It seemed to him that their lives might depend on those questions. One night as he was falling asleep, the rain a steady lulling patter on the roof and against the windows, it occurred to him that there was another question, perhaps the *only* question. *It* had some real shape; he had nearly seen it. To see the shape was to see the secret. Was that also true of power? Perhaps it was. For wasn't it true that power, like It, was a shape-changer? It was a baby crying in the middle of the night, it was an atomic bomb, it was a silver slug, it was the way Beverly looked at Bill and the way Bill looked back.

What, exactly what, *was* power, anyway?

12

Nothing much happened for the next two weeks.

DERRY:

THE FOURTH INTERLUDE

'You got to lose
You can't win all the time.
You got to lose
You can't win all the time, what'd I say?
I know, pretty baby,
I see trouble comin down the line.'
        – John Lee Hooker,
            'You Got to Lose'

Tell you what, friends and neighbors – I'm drunk tonight. Fuck-drunk. Rye whiskey. Went down to Wally's and got started, went to the greenfront down on Center Street half an hour before they closed, and bought a fifth of rye. I know what I'm up to. Drink cheap tonight, pay dear tomorrow. So here he sits, one drunk nigger in a public library after closing, with this book open in front of me and the bottle of Old Kentucky on my left. 'Tell the truth and shame the devil,' my mom used to say, but she forgot to tell me that sometimes you can't shame Mr Splitfoot sober. The Irish know, but of course they're God's white niggers and who knows, maybe they're a step ahead.

Want to write about drink and the devil. Remember *Treasure Island*? The old seadog at The Admiral Benbow. 'We'll do 'em yet, Jacky!' I bet the bitter old fuck even believed it. Full of rum – or rye – you can believe anything.

Drink and the devil. Okay.

Amuses me sometimes to think how long I'd last if I actually published some of this stuff I write in the dead of night. If I flashed some of the skeletons in Derry's closet. There is a library Board of Directors. Eleven of them. One is a seventy-year-old writer who suffered a stroke two years ago and who now often needs help to find his place on each meeting's printed agenda (and who has sometimes been observed picking large dry boogers out of his hairy nostrils and placing them carefully in his ear, as if for safe-keeping). Another is a pushy woman who came here from New York with her doctor husband and who talks in a constant, whiny monologue about how provincial Derry is, how no one here understands THE JEWISH EXPERIENCE and how one has to go to Boston to buy a skirt one would care to be seen in. Last time this anorexic babe spoke to me without the services of an intermediary was during the Board's Christmas party about a year and a half ago. She had consumed a pretty large amount of gin, and asked me if anyone in Derry understood THE BLACK

827

EXPERIENCE. I had also consumed a pretty large amount of gin, and answered: 'Mrs Gladry, Jews may be a great mystery, but niggers are understood the whole world round.' She choked on her drink, whirled around so sharply that her panties were momentarily visible under her flaring skirt (not a very interesting view; would that it had been Carol Danner!), and so ended my last informal conversation with Mrs Ruth Gladry. No great loss.

The other members of the Board are the descendants of the lumber barons. Their support of the library is an act of inherited expiation; they raped the woods and now care for these books the way a libertine might decide, in his middle age, to provide for the gaily gotten bastards of his youth. It was their grandfathers and great-grand-fathers who actually spread the legs of the forests north of Derry and Bangor and raped those green-gowned virgins with their axes and peaveys. They cut and slashed and strip-timbered and never looked back. They tore the hymen of those great forests open when Grover Cleveland was President and had pretty well finished the job by the time Woodrow Wilson had his stroke. These lace-ruffled ruffians raped the great woods, impregnated them with a litter of slash and junk spruce, and changed Derry from a sleepy little ship-building town into a booming honky-tonk where the ginmills never closed and the whores turned tricks all night long. One old campaigner, Egbert Thoroughgood, now ninety-three, told me of taking a slat-thin prostitute in a crib on Baker Street (a street which no longer exists; middle-class apartment housing stands quietly where Baker Street once boiled and brawled).

'I only realized after I spent m'spunk in her that she was laying in a pool of jizzum maybe an inch deep. Stuff had just about gone to jelly. "Girl," I says, "ain't you never cared for y'self?" She looks down and says, "I'll put on a new sheet if you want to go again. There's two in the cu'bud down the hall, I think. I knows pretty much what I'm layin in until nine or ten, but by midnight my cunt's so numb it might's well be in Ellsworth."'

So that was Derry right through the first twenty or so years of the twentieth century: all boom and booze and balling. The Penobscot and the Kenduskeag were full of floating logs from ice-out in April to ice-in in November. The business began to slacken off in the twenties without the Great War or the hardwoods to feed it, and it staggered to a stop during the Depression. The lumber barons put their money in those New York or Boston banks that had survived the Crash and left Derry's economy to live – or die – on its own. They retreated to their gracious houses on West Broadway and sent their children to private schools in New Hampshire, Massachusetts, and New York. And lived on their interest and political connections.

What's left of their supremacy seventy-some years after Egbert Thoroughgood spent his love with a dollar whore in a spermy Baker Street bed are empty wildwoods in Penobscot and Aroostook Counties and the great Victorian houses which stand for two blocks along West Broadway . . . and my library, of course. Except those good folks from West Broadway would take 'my library' away from me in jig time (pun *definitely* intended) if I published anything about the Legion of Decency, the fire at the Black Spot, the execution of the Bradley Gang . . . or the affair of Claude Heroux and the Silver Dollar.

The Silver Dollar was a beerjoint, and what may have been the queerest mass murder in the entire history of America took place there in September of 1905. There are still a few oldtimers in Derry who claim to remember it, but the only account that I really trust is Thoroughgood's. He was eighteen when it happened.

Thoroughgood now lives in the Paulson Nursing Home. He's toothless, and his St John's Valley Franco/Downeast accent is so thick that probably only another old Mainer could understand what he was saying if his talk were written down phonetically. Sandy Ives, the folklorist from the University of Maine whom I have mentioned previously in these wild pages, helped me to translate my audio tapes.

Claude Heroux was, according to Thoroughgood, 'Un bat Canuck sonofawhore widdin eye that'd roll adju like a mart's in dem oonlight.'

(Translation: 'One bad Canuck son of a whore with an eye that would roll at you like a mare's in the moonlight.')

Thoroughgood said that he – and everyone else who had worked with Heroux – believed the man was as sly as a chicken-stealing dog . . . which made his hatchet-wielding foray into the Silver Dollar all the more startling. It was not in character. Up until then, lumbermen in Derry had believed Heroux's talents ran more to lighting fires in the woods.

The summer of '05 was long and hot and there had been many fires in the woods. The biggest of them, which Heroux later admitted he set by simply putting a lighted candle in the middle of a pile of woodchips and kindling, happened in Haven's Big Injun Woods. It burned twenty thousand acres of prime hardwood, and you could smell the smoke of it thirty-five miles away as the horse-drawn trollies breasted Up-Mile Hill in Derry.

In the spring of that year there had been some brief talk about unionizing. There were four lumbermen involved in organizing (not that there was much to organize; Maine workingmen were anti-union then and are, for the large part, anti-union now), and one of the four was Claude Heroux, who probably saw his union activities mostly as a chance to talk big and spend a lot of time drinking down on Baker and Exchange Streets. Heroux and the other three called themselves 'organizers'; the lumber barons called them 'ringleaders.' A proclamation nailed to the cooksheds in lumber camps from Monroe to Haven Village to Sumner Plantation to Millinocket informed lumbermen that any man overheard talking union would be fired off the job immediately.

In May of that year there was a brief strike up near Trapham Notch, and although the strike was broken in short order, both by scabs and by 'town constables' (and that was rather peculiar, you understand, since there were nearly thirty 'town constables' swinging axe-handles and creasing skulls, but before that day in May, there hadn't been so much as a single constable in Trapham Notch – which had a population of 79 in the census of 1900 – so far as anyone knew), Heroux and his organizing friends considered it a great victory for their cause. Accordingly, they came down to Derry to get drunk and to do some more 'organizing' . . . or 'ringleading,' depending on whose side you favored. Whichever, it must have been dry work. They hit most of the bars in Hell's Half-Acre, finishing up in The Sleepy Silver Dollar, arms around each other's shoulders, pissing-down-your-leg drunk, alternating union songs with bathetic tunes like 'My Mother's Eyes Are Looking Down from Heaven', although I myself think any mother looking down from there and seeing her son in such a state might well have been excused for turning away.

According to Egbert Thoroughgood, the only reason anyone could figure for Heroux being in the movement at all was Davey Hartwell. Hartwell was the chief 'organizer' or 'ringleader,' and Heroux was in love with him. Nor was he the only one; most of the men in the movement loved Hartwell deeply and passionately, with that proud love men save for those of their own sex who possess a magnetism that seems to approach divinity. 'Davvey Ardwell wadda main who walk lak e ohn heffa de worl an haddim a daylah on de resp,' Thoroughgood said.

(Translation: 'Davey Hartwell was a man who walked like he owned half of the world and had him a deadlock on the rest.')

'He wadda great main inniz way; no use sayn he woint. He haddim *foce*, he haddim some big dinnity iniz walk anniz talk. Ainno use sayin he wadda *good* main. Just trine dellya he wadda *great* un.'

Heroux followed Hartwell into the organizing business the way he would have followed him if he had decided to go for a shipbuilder up in Brewer or down in Bath, or building the Seven Trestles over in Vermont, or trying to bring back the Pony Express out west, for that matter. Heroux was sly and he was mean, and I suppose that in a novel that would preclude any good qualities at all. But sometimes, when a man has spent a life being distrusted and distrustful, being a loner (or a Loser) both by choice and by reason of society's opinions of him, he can find a friend or a lover and simply live for that person, the way a dog lives for its master. That's the way it appeared to have been between Heroux and Hartwell.

Anyway, there were four of them who spent that night in the Brentwood Arms Hotel, which was then called the Floating Dog by the lumbermen (the reason why is lost in obscurity – not even Egbert Thoroughgood remembers). Four checked in; none checked out. One of them, Andy DeLesseps, was never seen again; for all history tells he might have spent the rest of his life living in pleasant ease in Portsmouth. But somehow I doubt it. Two of the other 'ringleaders,' Amsel Bickford and Davey Hartwell himself, were found floating face-down in the Kenduskeag. Bickford was missing his head; someone had taken it off with the swipe of a woodsman's two-hander. Both of Hartwell's legs were gone, and those who found him swore that they had never seen such an expression of pain and horror on a human face. Something had distended his mouth, stuffing out his cheeks, and when his discoverers turned him over and spread his lips, seven of his toes fell out onto the mud. Some thought he might have lost the other three during his years working in the woods; others held the opinion that he might have swallowed them before he died.

Pinned to the back of each man's shirt was a paper with the word UNION on it.

Claude Heroux was never brought to trial for what happened in the Silver Dollar on the night of September 9th, 1905, so there's no way of knowing exactly how he escaped the fate of the others that night in May. We could make assumptions; he had been on his own a long time, had learned how to jump fast, had perhaps developed the knack some cur-dogs have of getting out just before real trouble develops. But why didn't he take Hartwell with him? Or was he perhaps taken into the woods with the rest of the 'agitators'? Maybe they were saving him for last, and he was able to get away even while Hartwell's screams (which would have grown muffled as they jammed his toes into his mouth) were echoing in the dark and scaring birds off their roosts. There's no way of knowing, not for sure, but that last feels right to my heart.

Claude Heroux became a ghost-man. He would come strolling into a camp in the St John's Valley, line up at the cook-shed with the rest of the loggers, get a bowl of stew, eat it, and be gone before anyone realized he wasn't one of the topping gang. Weeks after that he'd show up in a Winterport beerjoint, talking union and swearing he'd have his revenge on the men that had murdered his friends – Hamilton Tracker, William Mueller, and Richard Bowie were the names he mentioned the most frequently. All of them lived in Derry, and their gabled gambrelled cupola-ed houses stand on West Broadway to this day. Years later, they and their descendants would fire the Black Spot.

That there were people who would have liked Claude Heroux put out of the way cannot be doubted, particularly after the fires started in June of that year. But although Heroux was seen frequently, he was quick and had an animal's awareness of danger. So far as I have been able to find out, no official warrant was ever sworn out against him, and the police never took a hand. Maybe there were fears about what Heroux might say if he was brought to trial for arson.

Whatever the reasons, the woods around Derry and Haven burned all that hot summer. Children disappeared, there were more fights and murders than usual, and a pall of fear as real as the smoke you could smell from the top of Up-Mile Hill lay over the town.

The rains finally came on September first, and it rained for a solid week. Downtown Derry was flooded out, which was not unusual, but the big houses on West Broadway were high above downtown, and in some of those big houses there must have been sighs of relief. Let the crazy Canuck hide out in the woods all winter, if that's what he wants, they might have said. His work's done for this summer, and we'll get him before the roots dry next June.

Then came September 9th. I cannot explain what happened; Thoroughgood cannot explain it; so far as I know, no one can. I can only relate the events which occurred.

The Sleepy Silver Dollar was full of loggers drinking beer. Outside, it was drawing down toward misty dark. The Kenduskeag was high and silver-sullen, filling its channel from bank to bank, and according to Egbert Thoroughgood, 'a fallish wind was blowin – the kine dat allus fine de hole in y'paints and blow strayduppa cracka yo ais.' The streets were quagmires. There was a card game going on at one of the tables in the back of the room. They were William Mueller's men.

Mueller was part owner of the GS&WM rail line as well as a lumber potentate who owned millions of acres of prime timber, and the men who were playing poker around an oilcloth-covered table in the Dollar that night were part-time lumbermen, part-time railroad bulls, and full time trouble. Two of them, Tinker McCutcheon and Floyd Calderwood, had done jail-time. With them were Lathrop Rounds (his nickname, as obscure as The Floating Dog Hotel, was El Katook), David 'Stugley' Grenier, and Eddie King — a bearded man whose spectacles were almost as fat as his gut. It seems very likely that they were at least some of the men who had spent the last two and a half months keeping an eye out for Claude Heroux. It seems just as likely — although there is not a shred of proof — that they were in on the little cutting party in May when Hartwell and Bickford were laid low.

The bar was crowded, Thoroughgood said; dozens of men were bellied up there, drinking beer and eating bar lunches and dripping onto the sawdust-covered dirt floor.

The door opened and in came Claude Heroux. He had a woods-man's double-bitted axe in his hand. He stepped up to the bar and elbowed himself a place. Egbert Thoroughgood was standing on his left; he said that Heroux smelled like a polecat stew. The barman brought Heroux a schooner of beer, two hard-cooked eggs in a bowl, and a shaker of salt. Heroux paid him with a two-dollar bill and put his change — a dollar-eighty-five — into one of the flap pockets of his lumberman's jacket. He salted his eggs and ate them. He salted his beer, drank it off, and uttered a belch.

'More room out than there is in, Claude,' Thoroughgood said, just as if half the enforcers in northern Maine hadn't been on the prod for Heroux all that summer.

'You know *that's* the truth,' Heroux said, except, being a Canuck, what he probably said came out sounding more like 'You know *dat* da troot.'

He ordered himself another schooner, drank up, and belched again. Talk at the bar went on; there was no silence like the ones in the western movies when the good guy or the bad guy pushes his way through the batwings and makes his ominous way to the bar. Several people called to him. Claude nodded and waved, but he didn't smile. Thoroughgood said he looked like a man who was half in a dream. At the table in back, the poker game went on. El Katook was dealing. No one bothered to tell any of the players that Claude Heroux was in the bar . . . although, since their table was no more than twenty feet away, and since Claude's name was hollered more than once by people who knew him, it is hard to know how they could have gone on playing, unaware of his potentially murderous presence. But that is what occurred.

After he finished his second schooner of beer, Heroux excused himself to Thoroughgood, picked up his two-hander, and went back to the table where Mueller's men were playing five-card stud. Then he started cutting.

Floyd Calderwood had just poured himself a glass of rye whiskey and was setting the bottle back down when Heroux arrived and chopped Calderwood's hand off at the wrist. Calderwood looked at his hand and screamed; it was still holding the bottle but all of a sudden wasn't attached to anything but wet gristle and trailing veins. For a moment the severed hand clutched the bottle even tighter, and then it fell off and lay on the table like a dead spider. Blood spouted from his wrist.

At the bar, somebody called for more beer and someone else asked the bartender, whose name was Jonesy, if he was still dyeing his hair. 'Never dyed it,' Jonesy said in an ill-tempered way; he was vain of his hair.

'Met a whore down at Ma Courtney's who said what grows around your pecker is just as white as snow,' the fellow said.

'She was a liar,' Jonesy replied.

'Drop your pants and let's us see,' said a lumberman named Falkland, with whom Egbert Thoroughgood had been matching for drinks before Heroux came in. This provoked general laughter.

Behind them, Floyd Calderwood was shrieking. A few of the men leaning against the bar took a casual look around in time to see Claude Heroux bury his woodsman's axe in Tinker McCutcheon's head. Tinker was a big man with a black beard going gray. He got halfway up, blood pouring down his face in freshets, then sat down again. Heroux pulled the axe out of his head. Tinker started to get up again, and Heroux slung the axe sideways, burying it in his back. It made a sound, Thoroughgood said, like a load of laundry being dropped on a rug. Tinker flopped over the table, his cards spraying out of his hand.

The others players were hollering and bellowing. Calderwood, still shrieking, was trying to pick up his right hand with his left as his life's blood ran out of his stump of a wrist in a steady stream. Stugley Grenier had what Thoroughgood called a 'clutch-pistol' (meaning a gun in a shoulder-holster) and he was grabbing for it with no success whatsoever. Eddie King tried to get up and fell right out of his chair on his back. Before he could get up, Heroux was standing astride him, the axe slung up over his head. King screamed and held up both hands in a warding-off gesture.

'*Please, Claude, I just got married last month!*' King screamed.

The axe came down, its head almost disappearing in King's ample gut. Blood sprayed all the way up to the Dollar's beamed roof. Eddie began to crawfish on the floor. Claude pulled the axe out of him the way a good woodsman will pull his axe out of a softwood tree, kind of rocking it back and forth to loosen the clinging grip of the sappy wood. When it was free he slung it up over his head. He brought it down again and Eddie King stopped screaming. Claude Heroux wasn't done with him, however; he began to chop King up like kindling-wood.

At the bar, conversation had turned to what sort of winter lay ahead. Vernon Stanchfield, a farmer from Palmyra, claimed it would be a mild one – fall rain uses up winter snow was his scripture. Alfie Naugler, who had a farm out on the Naugler Road in Derry (it is gone now; where Alfie Naugler once grew his peas and beans and beets, the Interstate extension now runs its 8.8 mile, six-lane course), begged to disagree. Alfie claimed the coming winter was going to be a jeezer. He had seen as many as eight rings on some of the mohair caterpillars, he said, an unheard-of number. Another man held out for ice; another for mud. The Blizzard of '01 was duly recalled. Jonesy sent schooners of beer and bowls of hardcooked eggs skidding down the bar. Behind them the screaming went on and the blood flowed in rivers.

At this point in my questioning of Egbert Thoroughgood, I turned off my cassette recorder and asked him: 'How did it happen? Are you saying you didn't know it was going on, or that you knew but you let it go on, or just what?'

Thoroughgood's chin sank down to the top button of his food-spotted vest. His eyebrows drew together. He said nothing for a long, long time. Outside it was winter, and I could hear – very faintly – the yells and laughter of the children sliding down the big hill in McCarron Park. The silence in Thoroughgood's room, small, cramped, and medi-cinal-smelling, spun out so long that I was about to repeat my question, when he replied: 'We knew. But it didn't seem to matter. It was like politics, in a way. Ayuh, like that. Like town business. Best let people who understand politics take care of that and people who understand town business take care of *that*. Such things be best done if working men don't mix in.'

'Are you really talking about fate and just afraid to come out and say so?' I asked suddenly. The question was simply jerked out of me, and I certainly did not expect Thoroughgood, who was old and slow and unlettered, to answer it . . . but he did, with no surprise at all.

'Ayuh,' he said. 'Mayhap I am.'

While the men at the bar went on talking about the weather, Claude Heroux went on cutting. Stugley Grenier had finally managed to clear his clutch-pisrol. The axe was descending for another chop at Eddie King, who was by then in pieces. The bullet Grenier fired struck the head of the axe and richocheted off with a spark and a whine.

El Katook got to his feet and started backing away. He was still holding the deck he had been dealing from; cards were fluttering off the bottom and onto the floor. Claude came after him. El Katook held out his hands. Stugley Grenier got off another round, which didn't come within ten feet of Heroux.

'Stop, Claude,' El Katook said. Thoroughgood said it appeared like Katook was trying to smile. 'I wasn't with them. I didn't mix in at all.'

Heroux only growled.

'I was in Millinocket,' El Katook said, his voice starting to rise toward a scream. '*I was in Millinocket, I swear it on my mother's name! Ask anybody if you don't believe meeeee . . .*'

Claude raised the dripping axe, and El Katook sprayed the rest of the cards into his face. The axe came down, whistling. El Katook ducked. The axe-head buried itself in the planking that formed the Silver Dollar's back wall. El Katook tried to run. Claude hauled the axe out of the wall and poked it between his ankles. El Katook went sprawling. Stugley Grenier shot at Heroux again, this time having a bit more luck. He had been aiming at the crazed lumberman's head; the bullet struck home in the fleshy part of Heroux's thigh.

Meantime, El Katook was crawling busily toward the door with his hair hanging in his face. Heroux swung the axe again, snarling and gibbering, and a moment later Katook's severed head was rolling across the sawdust-strewn floor, the tongue popped bizarrely out between the teeth. It rolled to a stop by the booted foot of a lumberman named Varney, who had spent most of the day in the Dollar and who, by then, was so exquisitely slopped that he didn't know if he was on land or at sea. He kicked the head away without looking down to see what it was, and hollered for Jonesy to run him down another beer.

El Katook crawled another three feet, blood spraying from his neck in a high-tension jet, before he realized he was dead and collapsed.

That left Stugley. Heroux turned on him, but Stugley had run into the outhouse and locked the door.

Heroux chopped his way in, hollering and blabbering and raving, slobber falling from his jaws. When he got in Stugley was gone, although the cold, leaky little room was windowless. Heroux stood there for a moment, head lowered, powerful arms slimed and splattered with blood, and then, with a roar, he flipped up the lid of the three-holer. He was just in time to see Stugley's boots disappearing under the ragged board skirting of the outhouse wall. Stugley Grenier ran screaming down Exchange Street in the rain, beshitted from top to toe, crying that he was being murdered. He survived the cutting party in the Silver Dollar – he was the only one who did – but after three months of listening to jokes about his method of escape, be quitted the Derry area forever.

Heroux stepped out of the toilet and stood in front of it like a bull after a charge, head down, his axe held in front of him. He was puffing and blowing and covered with gore from head to foot.

'Shut the door, Claude, that shitpot stinks to high heaven,' Thoroughgood said. Claude dropped his axe on the floor and did as he had been asked. He walked over to the card-strewn table where his victims had been sitting, kicking one of Eddie King's severed legs out of his way. Then he simply sat down and put his head in his arms. The drinking and conversation at the bar went on. Five minutes later more men began to pile in, three or four sheriff's deputies among them (the one in charge was Lal Machen's father, and when he saw the mess he had a heart attack and had to be taken away to Dr Shratt's office). Claude Heroux was led away. He was docile when they took him, more asleep than awake.

That night the bars all up and down Exchange and Baker Streets boomed and hollered with news of the slaughter. A righteous drunken sort of fury began to build up, and when the bars closed better than seventy men headed downtown toward the jail and the court-house. They had torches and lanterns. Some were carrying guns, some had axes, some had peaveys.

The County Sheriff wasn't due from Bangor until the noon stage the next day, so *he* wasn't there, and Goose Machen was laid up in Dr Shratt's infirmary with his heart attack. The two deputies who were sitting in the office playing cribbage heard the mob coming and got out of there fast. The drunks broke in and dragged Claude Heroux out of his cell. He didn't protest much; he seemed dazed, vacant.

They carried him on their shoulders like a football hero; down to Canal Street they carried him, and there they lynched him from an old elm that overhung the Canal. 'He was so far gone that he didn't kick but twice,' Egbert Thoroughgood said. It was, so far as the town records show, the only lynching to ever take place in this part of Maine. And almost needless to say, it was not reported in the Derry *News*. Many of those who had gone on drinking unconcernedly while Heroux went about his business in the Silver Dollar were in the necktie party that strung him up. By midnight their mood had changed.

I asked Thoroughgood my final question: had he seen anyone he didn't know during that day's violent activities? Someone who struck him as strange, out of place, funny, even clownish? Someone who would have been drinking at the bar that afternoon, someone who had maybe turned into one of the rabble-rousers that night as the drinking went on and the talk turned to lynching?

'Mayhap there was,' Thoroughgood replied. He was tired by then, drooping, ready for his afternoon nap. 'It were a long time ago, mister. Long and long.'

'But you remember something,' I said.

'I remember thinkin that there must be a county fair up Bangor way,' Thoroughgood said. 'I was having a beer in the Bloody Bucket that night. The Bucket was about six doors from the Silver Dollar. There was a fella in there . . . comical sort of fella . . . doing flips and rollovers . . . jugglin glasses . . . tricks . . . put four dimes on his forrid and they'd stay right there . . . comical, you know . . .'

His bony chin had sunk to his chest again. He was going to sleep right in front of me. Spittle began to bubble at the corners of his mouth, which had as many tucks and wrinkles as a lady's change-purse.

'Seen him a few now 'n thens since,' Thoroughgood said. 'Figure maybe he had such a good time that night . . . that he decided to stick around.'

'Yeah. He's been around a long time,' I said.

His only response was a weak snore. Thoroughgood had gone to sleep in his chair by the window, with his medicines and nostrums lined up beside him on the sill, soldiers of old age at muster. I turned off my tape-recorder and just sat looking at him for a moment, this strange time-traveller from the year 1890 or so, who remembered when there were no cars, no electric lights, no airplanes, no state of Arizona. Pennywise had been there, guiding them down the path toward another gaudy sacrifice – just one more in Derry's long history of gaudy sacrifices. That one, in September of 1905, ushered in a heightened period of terror that would include the Easter-tide explosion of the Kitchener Ironworks the following year.

This raises some interesting (and, for all I know, vitally important) questions. What does It *really* eat, for instance? I know that some of the children have been partially eaten – they show bite-marks, at least – but perhaps it is *we* who drive It to do that. Certainly we have all been taught since earliest childhood that what the monster does when it catches you in the deep wood is eat you. That is perhaps the worst thing we can conceive. But it's really faith that monsters live on, isn't it? I am led irresistibly in to this conclusion: Food may be life, but the source of power is not food but faith. And who is more capable of a total act of faith than a child?

But there's a problem: kids grow up. In the church, power is perpetuated and renewed by periodic ritualistic acts. In Derry, power seems to be perpetuated and renewed by periodic ritualistic acts, too. Can it be that It protects Itself by the simple fact that, as the children grow into the adults, they become either incapable of faith or crippled by a sort of spiritual and imaginative arthritis?

Yes. I think that's the secret here. And if I make the calls, how much will they remember? How much will they believe? Enough to end this horror once and for all, or only enough to get them killed? They *are* being called – I know that much. Each murder in this new cycle has been a call. We almost killed It twice, and in the end we drove It deep in Its warren of tunnels and stinking rooms under the city. But I think It knows another secret: although *It* may be immortal (or almost so), we are not. It had only to wait until the act of faith, which made us potential monster-killers as well as sources of power, had become impossible. Twenty-seven years. Perhaps a period of sleep for It, as short and refreshing as an afternoon nap would be for us. And when It awakes, It is the same, but a third of our lives has gone by. Our perspectives have narrowed; our faith in the magic that makes magic possible has worn off like the shine on a new pair of shoes after a hard day's walking.

Why call us back? Why not just let us die? Because we nearly killed It, because we frightened It, I think. Because It wants revenge.

And now, now that we no longer believe in Santa Claus, the Tooth Fairy, Hansel and Gretel, or the troll under the bridge, It is ready for us. *Come on back,* It says. *Come on back, let's finish our business in Derry. Bring your jacks and your marbles and your yo-yos! We'll play. Come on back and we'll see if you remember the simplest thing of all: how it is to be children, secure in belief and thus afraid of the dark.*

On that one, at least, I score a thousand per cent: I am frightened. So goddam frightened.

PART 5

THE RITUAL OF CHÜD

'It is not to be done. The seepage has
rotted out the curtain. The mesh
is decayed. Loosen the flesh
from the machine, build no more
bridges. Through what air will you
fly to span the continents? Let the words
fall any way at all – that they may
hit love aslant. It will be a rare
visitation. They want to rescue too much,
the flood has done its work'
                          – William Carlos Williams,
                                        Paterson

'Look and remember. Look upon this land,
Far, far across the factories and the grass.
Surely, there, surely they will let you pass.
Speak then and ask the forest and the loam.
What do you hear? What does the land command?
The earth is taken: this is not your home.'
                          – Karl Shapiro,
                              'Travelogue for Exiles'

CHAPTER NINETEEN
IN THE WATCHES
OF THE NIGHT

1

The Derry Public Library/1:15 A.M.

When Ben Hanscom finished the story of the silver slugs, they wanted to talk, but Mike told them he wanted them all to get some sleep. 'You've had enough for now,' he said, but Mike was the one who looked as if he had had enough; his face was tired and drawn, and Beverly thought he looked physically ill.

'But we're not done,' Eddie said. 'What about the rest of it? I still don't remember –'

'Mike's r-r-right,' Bill said. 'Either we'll remember or we w-won't. I think we w-will. We've remembered all that we nuh-need to.'

'Maybe all that's good for us?' Richie suggested.

Mike nodded. 'We'll meet tomorrow.' Then he glanced at the clock. 'Later today, I mean.'

'Here?' Beverly asked.

Mike shook his head slowly. 'I suggest we meet on Kansas Street. Where Bill used to hide his bike.'

'We're going down into the Barrens,' Eddie said, and suddenly shivered.

Mike nodded again.

There was a moment of quiet while they looked around at each other. Then Bill got to his feet, and the others rose with him.

'I want you all to be careful for the rest of the night,' Mike said. 'It's been here; It can be wherever you are. But this meeting has made me feel better.' He looked at Bill. 'I'd say it still can be done, wouldn't you, Bill?'

Bill nodded slowly. 'Yes. I think it still can be done.'

'It will know that, too,' Mike said, 'and It will do whatever It can to slug the odds in Its favor.'

'What do we do if It shows up?' Richie asked. 'Hold our noses, shut our eyes, turn around three times, and think good thoughts? Puff some magic dust in Its face? Sing old Elvis Presley songs? What?'

Mike shook his head. 'If I could tell you that, there would be no problem, would there? All I know is that there's another force – at least there was when we were kids – that wanted us to stay alive and to do the job. Maybe it's still there.' He shrugged. It was a weary gesture. 'I thought two, maybe as many as three of you would be gone by the time we started our meeting tonight. Missing or dead. Just seeing you turn up gave me reason to hope.'

Richie looked at his watch. 'Quarter past one. How the time flies when you're having fun, right, Haystack?'

'Beep-beep, Richie,' Ben said, and smiled wanly.

'You want to walk back to the Tuh-Tuh-Townhouse with me, Beverly?' Bill asked.

'All right.' She was putting on her coat. The library seemed very silent now, shadowy, frightening. Bill felt the last two days catching up with him all at once, piling up on his back. If it had just been weariness, that would have been okay, but it was more: a feeling that he was cracking up, dreaming, having delusions of paranoia. A sensation of being watched. *Maybe I'm really not here at all*, he thought. *Maybe I'm in Dr Seward's lunatic asylum, with the Count's crumbling townhouse next door and Renfield just across the hall, him with his flies and me with my monsters, both of us sure the party is really going on and dressed to the nines for it, not in tuxedos but in straitwaistcoats.*

'What about you, R-Richie?'

Richie shook his head. 'I'm going to let Haystack and Kaspbrak lead me home,' he said. 'Right, fellers?'

'Sure,' Ben said. He looked briefly at Beverly, who was standing close to Bill, and felt a pain he had almost forgotten. A new memory trembled, almost within his grasp, then floated away.

'What about you, M-M-Mike?' Bill asked. 'Want to walk with Bev and m-me?'

Mike shook his head. 'I've got to –'

That was when Beverly screamed, a high-pitched hurt sound in the stillness. The vaulted dome overhead picked it up, and the echoes were like the laughter of banshees, flying and flapping around them.

Bill turned toward her; Richie dropped his sportcoat as he was taking it off the back of his chair; there was a crash of glass as Eddie's arm swept an empty gin bottle onto the floor.

Beverly was backing away from them, her hands held out, her

face as white as good bond paper. Her eyes, deep in dusky-purple sockets, bulged. '*My hands!*' she screamed. '*My hands!*'

'What –' Bill began, and then he saw the blood dripping slowly between her shaking fingers. He started forward and felt sudden lines of painful warmth cross his own hands. The pain was not sharp; it was more like the pain one sometimes feels in an old healed wound.

The old scars on his palms, the ones which had reappeared in England, had broken open and were bleeding. He looked sideways and saw Eddie Kaspbrak peering stupidly down at his own hands. They were also bleeding. So were Mike's. And Richie's. And Ben's.

'We're in it to the end, aren't we?' Beverly asked. She had begun to cry. This sound was also magnified in the library's still emptiness; the building itself seemed to be weeping with her. Bill thought that if he had to listen to that sound for long, he would go mad. 'God help us, we're in it to the end.' She sobbed, and a runner of snot depended from one of her nostrils. She wiped it off with the back of one shaking hand, and more blood dripped on the floor.

'Quh-Quh-hick!' Bill said, and seized Eddie's hand.

'What –'

'*Quick!*'

He held out his other hand, and after a moment Beverly took it. She was still crying.

'Yes,' Mike said. He looked dazed – almost drugged. 'Yes, that's right, isn't it? It's starting again, isn't it, Bill? It's all starting to happen again.'

'Y-Y-Yes, I th-think –'

Mike took Eddie's hand and Richie took Beverly's other hand. For a moment Ben only looked at them, and then, like a man in a dream, he raised his bloody hands to either side and stepped between Mike and Richie. He grasped their hands. The circle closed.

(*Ah Chüd this is the Ritual of Chüd and the Turtle cannot help us*)

Bill tried to scream but no sound came out. He saw Eddie's head tilt back, the cords on his neck standing out. Bev's hips bucked twice, fiercely, as if in an orgasm as short and sharp as the crack of a .22 pistol. Mike's mouth moved strangely, seeming to laugh and grimace at the same time. In the silence of the library doors banged open and shut, the sound rolling like bowling balls. In the Periodicals Room, magazines flew in a windless hurricane. In Carole Danner's office, the library's IBM typewriter whirred into life and typed:
hethrusts
hisfistsagainst

thepostsandstillinsistshesees
theghostshethrustshisfistsagainstthe

The type-ball jammed. The typewriter sizzled and uttered a thick electronic belch as everything inside overloaded. In Stack Two, the shelf of occult books suddenly tipped over, spilling Edgar Cayce, Nostradamus, Charles Fort, and the Apocrypha everywhere.

Bill felt an exalting sense of power. He was dimly aware that he had an erection, and that every hair on his head was standing up straight. The sense of force in the completed circle was incredible.

All the doors in the library slammed shut in unison.

The grandfather clock behind the checkout desk chimed once.

Then it was gone, as if someone had flicked off a switch.

They dropped their hands, looking at each other, dazed. No one said anything. As the sense of power ebbed, Bill felt a terrible sense of doom creep over him. He looked at their white, strained faces, and then down at his hands. Blood was smeared there, but the wounds which Stan Uris had made with a jagged piece of Coke bottle in August 1958 had closed up again, leaving only crooked white lines like knotted twine. He thought: *That was the last time the seven of us were together . . . the day Stan made those cuts in the Barrens. Stan's not here; he's dead. And this is the last time the six of us are going to be together. I know it, I feel it.*

Beverly was pressed against him, trembling. Bill put an arm around her. They all looked at him, their eyes huge and bright in the dimness, the long table where they had sat, littered with empty bottles, glasses, and overflowing ashtrays, a little island of light.

'That's enough,' Bill said huskily. 'Enough entertainment for one evening. We'll save the ballroom dancing for another time.'

'I remembered,' Beverly said. She looked up at Bill, her eyes huge, her pale cheeks wet. 'I remembered *everything*. My father finding out about you guys. Running. Bowers and Criss and Huggins. How I ran. The tunnel . . . the birds . . . It . . . *I remember everything.*'

'Yeah,' Richie said. 'I do, too.'

Eddie nodded. 'The pumping-station –'

Bill said, 'And now Eddie –'

'Go back now,' Mike said. 'Get some rest. It's late.'

'Walk with us, Mike,' Beverly said.

'No. I have to lock up. And I have to write a few things down . . . the minutes of the meeting, if you like. I won't be long. Go ahead.'

They moved toward the door, not talking much. Bill and Beverly were together, Eddie, Richie, and Ben behind them. Bill held the door for her and she murmured thanks. As she went out onto the wide granite steps, Bill thought how young she looked, how vulnerable . . . He was dismally aware that he might be falling in love with her again. He tried to think of Audra but Audra seemed far away. She would be sleeping in their house in Fleet now as the sun came up and the milkman began his rounds.

Derry's sky had clouded over again, and a low groundfog lay across the empty street in thick runners. Further up the street, the Derry Community House, narrow, tall, Victorian, brooded in blackness. Bill thought *And whatever walked in Community House, walked alone.* He had to stifle a wild cackle. Their footfalls seemed very loud. Beverly's hand touched his and Bill took it gratefully.

'It started before we were ready,' she said.

'Would we eh-eh-ever have been r-ready?'

'*You* would have been, Big Bill.'

The touch of her hand was suddenly both wonderful and necessary. He wondered what it would be like to touch her breasts for the second time in his life, and suspected that before this long night was over he would know. Fuller now, mature . . . and his hand would find hair when he cupped the swelling of her *mons veneris*. He thought: *I loved you, Beverly . . . I love you. Ben loved you . . . he loves you. We loved you then . . . we love you now. We better, because it's starting. No way out now.*

He glanced behind and saw the library half a block away. Richie and Eddie were on the top step; Ben was standing at the bottom, looking after them. His hands were stuffed in his pockets, his shoulders were slumped, and seen through the drifting lens of the low fog, he might almost have been eleven again. If he had been able to send Ben a thought, Bill would have sent this one: *It doesn't matter, Ben. The love is what matters, the caring . . . it's always the desire, never the time. Maybe that's all we get to take with us when we go out of the blue and into the black. Cold comfort, maybe, but better than no comfort at all.*

'My father knew,' Beverly said suddenly. 'I came home one day from the Barrens and he just knew. Did I ever tell you what he used to say to me when he was mad?'

'What?'

'"I worry about you, Bevvie." That's what he used to say. "I worry a *lot*."' She laughed and shivered at the same time. 'I think he meant to hurt me, Bill. I mean . . . he'd hurt me before, but that last time was different. He was . . . well, in many ways he was a strange man. I loved him. I loved him very much, but –'

She looked at him, perhaps wanting him to say it for her. He wouldn't; it was something she was going to have to say for herself, sooner or later. Lies and self-deceptions had become a ballast they could not afford.

'I hated him, too,' she said, and her hand bore down convulsively upon Bill's for a long second. 'I never told that to anyone in my life before. I thought God would strike me dead if I ever said it out loud.'

'Say it again, then.'

'No, I –'

'Go on. It'll hurt, but maybe it's festered in there long enough. Say it.'

'I hated my dad,' she said, and began to sob helplessly. 'I hated him, I was scared of him, I hated him, I could never be a good enough girl to suit him and I hated him, I did, but I loved him, too.'

He stopped and held her tight. Her arms went around him in a panicky grip. Her tears wet the side of his neck. He was very conscious of her body, ripe and firm. He moved his torso away from hers slightly, not wanting her to feel the erection he was getting . . . but she moved against him again.

'We'd spent the morning down there,' she said, 'playing tag or something like that. Something *harmless*. We hadn't even talked about It that day, at least not then . . . we usually talked about It every day, at some point, though. Remember?'

'Yes,' he said. 'At some p-p-point. I remember.'

'It was overcast . . . hot. We played most of the morning. I went home around eleven-thirty. I thought I'd have a sandwich and a bowl of soup after I took a shower. And then I'd go back and play some more. My parents were both working. But he was there. He was home. He

2

Lower Main Street / 11:30 A.M.

threw her across the room before she had even gotten all the way through the door. A startled scream was jerked out of her and then cut off as she hit the wall with shoulder-numbing force. She collapsed onto their sagging sofa, looking around wildly. The door to the front hall banged shut. Her father had been standing behind it.

'I worry about you, Bevvie,' he said. 'Sometimes I worry a *lot*. You know that. I tell you that, don't I? You bet I do.'

848

'Daddy what —'

He was walking slowly toward her across the living room, his face thoughtful, sad, deadly. She didn't want to see that last, but it was there, like the blind shine of dirt on still water. He was nibbling reflectively on a knuckle of his right hand. He was dressed in his khakis, and when she glanced down she saw that his high-topped shoes were leaving tracks on her mother's carpet. *I'll have to get the vacuum out*, she thought incoherently. *Vacuum that up. If he leaves me able to vacuum. If he —*

It was mud. Black mud. Her mind sideslipped alarmingly. She was back in the Barrens with Bill, Richie, Eddie, and the others. There was black, viscous mud like the kind on Daddy's shoes down there in the Barrens, in the swampy place where the stuff Richie called bamboo stood in a skeletal white grove. When the wind blew the stalks rattled together hollowly, producing a sound like voodoo drums, and had her father been down in the Barrens? Had her father —

WHAP!

His hand rocketed down in a wide sweeping orbit and struck her face. Her head thudded back against the wall. He hooked his thumbs in his belt and looked at her with that expression of deadly disconnected curiosity. She felt a trickle of blood running warmly from the left corner of her lower lip.

'I have seen you getting big,' he said, and she thought he would say something more, but for the time being that seemed to be all.

'Daddy, what are you talking about?' she asked in a low trembling voice.

'If you lie to me, I'll beat you within an inch of your life, Bevvie,' he said, and she realized with horror that he wasn't looking at her; he was looking at the Currier and Ives picture over her head, on the wall above the sofa. Her mind sideslipped crazily again and she was four, sitting in the bathtub with her blue plastic boat and her Popeye soap; her father, so big and so well-loved, was kneeling beside her, dressed in gray twill pants and a strappy tee-shirt, a washcloth in one hand and a glass of orange soda in the other, soaping her back and saying, *Lemme see those ears, Bevvie; your ma needs taters for supper.* And she could hear her small self giggling, looking up at his slightly grizzled face, which she had then believed must be eternal.

'I . . . I won't lie, Daddy,' she said. 'What's wrong?' Her view of him was gradually shivering apart as the tears came.

'You been down there in the Bar'ns with a gang of boys?'

Her heart leaped; her eyes dropped to his mud-caked shoes again.

That black, clingy mud. If you stepped into it too deep it would suck your sneaker or your loafer right off . . . and both Richie and Bill believed that, if you went in all the way, it turned to quickmud.

'I play down there somet –'

Whap! the hand, covered with hard calluses, rocketing down again. She cried out, hurt, afraid. That look on his face scared her, and the way he wouldn't look at her scared her, too. There was something wrong with him. He had been getting worse . . . What if he meant to kill her? What if

(*oh stop it Beverly he's your FATHER and FATHERS don't kill DAUGHTERS*)

he lost control, then? What if –

'What have you let them do to you?'

'Do? What –' She had no idea what he meant.

'Take your pants off.'

Her confusion increased. Nothing he said seemed connected to anything else. Trying to follow him made her feel . . . seasick, almost.

'What . . . why . . . ?'

His hand rose; she flinched back. 'Take them off, Bevvie. I want to see if you are intact.'

Now there was a new image, crazier than the rest: she saw herself pulling her jeans off, and one of her legs coming off with them. Her father belting her around the room as she tried to hop away from him on her one good leg, Daddy shouting: *I knew you wasn't intact! I knew it! I knew it!*

'Daddy, I don't know what –'

His hand came down, not slapping this time but clutching. It bit into her shoulder with furious strength. She screamed. He pulled her up, and for the first time looked directly into her eyes. She screamed again at what she saw there. It was . . . *nothing*. Her father was gone. And Beverly suddenly understood that she was alone in the apartment with It, alone with It on this dozey August morning. There was not the thick sense of power and untinctured evil she had felt in the house on Neibolt Street a week and a half ago – It had been diluted somehow by her father's essential humanity – but It was here, working through him.

He threw her aside. She struck the coffee table, tripped over it, and went sprawling on the floor with a cry. *This is how it happens*, she thought. *I'll tell Bill so he understands. It's everywhere in Derry. It just . . . It just fills the hollow places, that's all.*

She rolled over. Her father was walking toward her. She skidded away from him on the seat of her jeans, her hair in her eyes.

'I know you been down there,' he said. 'I was told. I didn't believe it. I didn't believe my Bevvie would be hanging around with a gang of boys. Then I seen you myself this morning. My Bevvie with a bunch of boys. Not even twelve and hanging around with a bunch of boys!' This latter thought seemed to send him into a fresh rage; it trembled through his scrawny frame like volts. '*Not even twelve years old!*' he shouted, and fetched a kick at her thigh that made her scream. His jaws snapped over this fact or concept or whatever it was to him like the jaws of a hungry dog worrying a piece of meat. '*Not even twelve! Not even twelve! Not even TWELVE!*'

He kicked. Beverly scrambled away. They had worked their way into the kitchen area of the apartment now. His workboot struck the drawer under the stove, making the pots and pans inside jangle.

'Don't you run from me, Bevvie,' he said. 'You don't want to do that or it'll be the worse for you. Believe me, now. Believe your dad. This is serious. Hanging around with the boys, letting them do God knows what to you – not even *twelve* – that's serious, Christ knows.' He grabbed her and jerked her to her feet by her shoulder.

'You're a pretty girl,' he said. 'There's plenty of people happy to roon a pretty girl. Plenty of pretty girls willing to be roont. You been a slutchild to them boys, Bevvie?'

At last she understood what It had put in his head . . . except part of her knew the thought might almost have been there all along; that It might only have used the tools that had been there just lying around, waiting to be picked up.

'No Daddy. No Daddy –'

'*I seen you smoking!*' he bellowed. This time he struck her with the palm of his hand, hard enough to send her reeling back in drunken strides to the kitchen table where she sprawled, a flare of agony in the small of her back. The salt and pepper shakers fell to the floor. The pepper shaker broke. Black flowers bloomed and disappeared before her eyes. Sounds seemed too deep. She saw his face. Something in his face. He was looking at her chest. She was suddenly aware that her blouse had come untucked, that some of the buttons had popped off, and that she wasn't wearing a bra . . . as of yet, she owned only one, a training bra. Her mind sideslipped back to the house at Neibolt Street, when Bill had given her his shirt. She had been aware of the way her breasts poked at the thin cotton material, but their occasional, skittering glances had not bothered her; these had seemed perfectly natural. And *Bill's* look had seemed more than natural – it had seemed warm and wanted, if deeply dangerous.

Now she felt guilt mix with her terror. Was her father so wrong? Hadn't she had

(*you been a slutchild to them*)

thoughts? Bad thoughts? Thoughts of whatever it was that he was talking about?

It's not the same thing! It's not the same thing as the way

(*you been a slutchild*)

he's looking at me now! Not the same!

She tucked her blouse back in.

'Bevvie?'

'Daddy, we just *play*, that's all. We play ... We ... we don't do anything like ... anything *bad*. We –'

'I seen you smoking,' he said again, walking toward her. His eyes moved across her chest and her narrow uncurved hips. He chanted suddenly, in a high schoolboy's voice that frightened her even more: '*A girl who will chew gum will smoke! A girl who will smoke will drink! And a girl who will drink, everyone knows what a girl like that will do!*'

'*I DIDN'T DO ANYTHING!*' she screamed at him as his hands descended on her shoulders. He was not pinching or hurting now. His hands were gentle. And that was somehow scariest of all.

'Beverly,' he said with the inarguable, mad logic of the totally obsessed, 'I seen you with boys. Now you want to tell me what a girl does with boys down in all that trashwood if it ain't what a girl does on her back?'

'*Let me alone!*' she cried at him. The anger flashed up from a deep well she had never suspected. The anger made a bluish-yellow flame in her head. It threatened her thoughts. All the times he had scared her; all the times he had shamed her; all the times he had hurt her. '*You just let me alone!*'

'Don't talk to your daddy like that,' he said, sounding startled.

'*I didn't do what you're saying! I never did!*'

'Maybe. Maybe not. I'm going to check and make sure. I know how. Take your pants off.'

'*No.*'

His eyes widened, showing yellowed cornea all the way around the deep blue irises. '*What* did you say?'

'I said *no*.' His eyes were fixed on hers and perhaps he saw the blazing anger there, the bright upsurge of rebellion. 'Who told you?'

'Bevvie –'

'Who told you we play down there? Was it a stranger? Was it a man dressed in orange and silver? Did he wear gloves? Did he look like a clown even if he wasn't a clown? What was his name?'

'Bevvie, you want to stop –'

'No: *you* want to stop,' she told him.

He swung his hand again, not open but this time closed in a fist meant to break something. Beverly ducked. His fist whistled over her head and crashed into the wall. He howled and let go of her, putting the fist to his mouth. She backed away from him in quick mincing steps.

'You come back here!'

'No,' she said. 'You want to hurt me. I love you, Daddy, but I hate you when you're like this. You can't do it anymore. *It's* making you do it, but *you* let It in.'

'I don't know what you're talking about,' he said, 'but you better get over here to me. I am not going to ask you no more.'

'No,' she said, beginning to cry again.

'Don't make me come over there and collect you, Bevvie. You're going to be one sorry little girl if I have to do that. Come to me.'

'Tell me who told you,' she said, 'and I will.'

He leaped at her with such scrawny, catlike agility that, although she suspected such a leap was coming, she was almost caught. She fumbled for the kitchen doorknob, pulled the door open just wide enough so she could slip though, and then she was running down the hall toward the front door, running in a dream of panic, as she would run from Mrs Kersh twenty-seven years later. Behind her, Al Marsh crashed against the door, slamming it shut again, cracking it down the center.

'*YOU GET BACK HERE RIGHT NOW BEVVIE!*' he howled, yanking it open and coming after her.

The front door was on the latch; she had come home the back way. One of her trembling hands worked at the lock while the other yanked fruitlessly at the knob. Behind, her father howled again; the sound of an

(*take those pants off slutchild*)

animal. She turned the lock-knob and the front door finally swept open. Hot breath plunged up and down in her throat. She looked over her shoulder and saw him right behind her, reaching for her, grinning and grimacing, his horsey yellow teeth a beartrap in his mouth.

Beverly bolted out through the screen door and felt his fingers skid down the back of her blouse without catching hold. She flew

853

down the steps, overbalanced, and went sprawling on the concrete walkway, erasing the skin from both knees.

'*YOU GET BACK HERE NOW BEVVIE OR BEFORE GOD I'LL WHIP THE SKIN OFF YOU!*'

He came down the steps and she scrambled to her feet, holes in the legs of her jeans,

(*your pants off*)

her kneecaps sizzling blood, exposed nerve-endings singing 'Onward Christian Soldiers.' She looked back and here he came again, Al Marsh, janitor and custodian, a gray man dressed in khaki pants and a khaki shirt with two flap pockets, a keyring attached to his belt by a chain, his hair flying. But he wasn't in his eyes – the essential he who had washed her back and punched her in the gut and had done both because he worried about her, worried a *lot*, the he who had once tried to braid her hair when she was seven, made a botch of it, and then got giggling with her about the way it stuck out everyway, the he who knew how to make cinnamon eggnogs on Sunday that tasted better than anything you could buy for a quarter at the Derry Ice Cream Bar, the father-he, maleman of her life, delivering a mixed post from that other sexual state. None of that was in his eyes now. She saw blank murder there. She saw It there.

She ran. She ran from It.

Mr Pasquale looked up, startled, from where he was watering his crab-grassy lawn and listening to the Red Sox game on a portable radio sitting on his porch rail. The Zinnerman kids stood back from the old Hudson Hornet which they had bought for twenty-five dollars and washed almost every day. One of them was holding a hose, the other a bucket of soapsuds. Both were slack-jawed. Mrs Denton looked out of her second-floor apartment, one of her six daughters' dresses in her lap, more mending in a basket on the floor, her mouth full of pins. Little Lars Theramenius pulled his Red Ball Flyer wagon quickly off the cracked sidewalk and stood on Bucky Pasquale's dying lawn. He burst into tears as Bevvie, who had spent a patient morning that spring showing him how to tie his sneakers so they would stay tied, flashed by him, screaming, her eyes wide. A moment later her father passed, hollering at her, and Lars, who was then three and who would die twelve years later in a motorcycle accident, saw something terrible and inhuman in Mr Marsh's face. He had nightmares for three weeks after. In them he saw Mr Marsh turning into a spider inside his clothes.

Beverly ran. She was perfectly aware that she might be running for her life. If her father caught her now, it wouldn't matter that they were on the street. People did crazy things in Derry sometimes; she didn't have to read the newspapers or know the town's peculiar history to understand that. If he caught her he would choke her, or beat her, or kick her. And when it was over, someone would come and collect him and he would sit in a cell the way Eddie Cochran's stepfather was sitting in a cell, dazed and uncomprehending.

She ran toward downtown, passing more and more people as she went. They stared – first at her, then at her pursuing father – and they looked surprised, some of them even amazed. But what was on their faces went no further. They looked and then they went on toward wherever they had been going. The air circulating in her lungs was growing heavier now.

She crossed the Canal, feet pounding on cement while cars rumbled over the heavy wooden slats of the bridge to her right. To her left she could see the stone semicircle where the Canal went under the downtown area. She cut suddenly across Main Street, oblivious of the honking horns and squealing brakes. She went right because the Barrens lay in that direction. It was still almost a mile away, and if she was to get there she would somehow have to outdistance her father on the gruelling slope of Up-Mile Hill (or one of the even steeper side-streets). But that was all there was.

'COME BACK YOU LITTLE BITCH I'M WARNING YOU!'

As she gained the sidewalk on the far side of the street she snatched another glance behind her, the heavy weight of her red hair shifting over her shoulder as she did. Her father was crossing the street, as heedless of the traffic as she had been, his face a bright sweaty red.

She ducked down an alley that ran behind Warehouse Row. This was the rear of the buildings which fronted on Up-Mile Hill: Star Beef, Armour Meatpacking, Hemphill Storage & Warehousing, Eagle Beef & Kosher Meats. The alley was narrow and cobbled, made narrower still by the bunches of fuming garbage cans and bins set out here. The cobbles were slimy with God knew what offal and ordure. There was a mixture of smells, some bland, some sharp, some simply titanic . . . but all spoke of meat and slaughter. Flies buzzed in clouds. From inside some of the buildings she could hear the blood-curdling whine of bone-saws. Her feet stuttered unevenly on the slick cobbles. One hip struck a galvanized garbage can and packages of tripe wrapped in newspaper fell out like great meaty jungle blossoms.

'YOU GET RIGHT THE HELL BACK HERE BEVVIE! I MEAN IT NOW! DON'T MAKE IT ANY WORSE THAN IT ALREADY IS, GIRL!'

Two men lounged in the loading doorway of the Kirshner Packing Works, munching thick sandwiches. 'You in a woeful place, girl,' one of them said mildly. 'Looks like you're goin to the woodshed with your pa.' The other laughed.

He was gaining. She could hear his thundering footfalls and heavy respiration almost behind her now; looking to her right she could see the black wing of his shadow flying along the high board fence there.

Then he yelled in surprise and fury as his feet slipped out from under him and he thumped to the cobblestones. He was up a moment later, no longer bellowing words but only shrieking out his incoherent fury while the men in the doorway laughed and slapped each other on the back.

The alley zigged to the left . . . and Beverly came to a skittering halt, her mouth opening in dismay. A city dumpster was parked across the alley's mouth. There was not even nine inches of clearance on either side. Its motor was idling. Under that sound, barely audible, she could hear the murmur of conversation from the dumpster's cab. More men on lunch-break. It lacked no more than three or four minutes of noon; soon the courthouse clock would begin to chime the hour.

She could hear him coming again, closing in. She threw herself down and hooked her way under the dumpster, using her elbows and wounded knees. The stink of exhaust and diesel fuel mixed with the smell of ripe meat and made her feel a kind of giddy nausea. In a way, the ease of her progress was worse; she was skidding greasily over a coating of slime and garbagey crud. She kept moving, once rising too high off the cobbles so that her back came in contact with the dumpster's hot exhaust-pipe. She had to bite back a scream.

'Beverly? You under there?' Each word separated from the last by an out-of-breath gasp for air. She looked back and met his eyes as he bent and peered under the truck.

'Leave . . . me alone!' she managed.

'You *bitch*,' he replied in a thick, spit-choked voice. He threw himself flat, keys jingling, and began to crawl after her, using a grotesque swimming stroke to pull himself along.

Beverly clawed her way from under the truck's cab, grabbed one of the huge tires – her fingers hooked their way into a tread up to the second knuckle – and yanked herself up. She banged her tail-bone on the dumpster's front bumper and then she was running again, heading up Up-Mile Hill now, her blouse and jeans smeared with goop and stinking to high heaven. She looked back and saw her father's hands and freckled arms shoot out from under the dumpster's cab like the claws of some imagined childhood monster from under the bed.

Quickly, hardly thinking at all, she darted between Feldman's Storage and the Tracker Brothers' Annex. This covert, too narrow to even be called an alley, was filled with broken crates, weeds, sunflowers, and, of course, more garbage. Beverly dived behind a pile of crates and crouched there. A few moments later she saw her father pound by the mouth of the covert and on up the hill.

Beverly got up and hurried to the far end of the covert. There was a chainlink fence here. She monkeyed her way to the top, got over, and worked her way down the far side. She was now on Derry Theological Seminary property. She ran up the manicured back lawn and around the side of the building. She could hear someone inside playing something classical on an organ. The notes seemed to engrave their pleasant, calm selves on the still air.

There was a tall hedge between the Seminary and Kansas Street. She peered through it and saw her father on the far side of the street, breathing hard, patches of sweat darkening his gray work-shirt under the arms. He was peering around, hands on hips. His keyring twinkled brightly in the sun.

Beverly watched him, also breathing hard, her heart beating rabbit-fast in her throat. She was very thirsty, and her simmering smell disgusted her. *If I was drawn in a comicstrip*, she thought distractedly, *there'd be all those wavy stink-lines coming up from me.*

Her father crossed slowly to the Seminary side.

Beverly's breath stopped.

Please God, I can't run anymore. Help me, God. Don't let him find me.

Al Marsh walked slowly down the sidewalk, directly past where his daughter crouched on the far side of the hedge.

Dear God, don't let him smell me!

He didn't – perhaps because, after a tumble in the alleyway and crawling under the dumpster himself, Al smelled as bad as she did. He walked on. She watched him go back down Up-Mile Hill until he was out of sight.

Beverly picked herself up slowly. Her clothes were covered with garbage, her face was dirty, her back hurt where she had burnt it on the exhaust-pipe of the dumpster. These physical things paled before the confused swirl of her thoughts – she felt that she had sailed off the edge of the world, and none of the normal patterns of behavior seemed to apply. She could not imagine going home; but she could not imagine *not* going home. She had defied her father, *defied* him —

She had to push that thought away because it made her feel weak and trembly, sick to her stomach. She loved her father. Wasn't one of the Ten Commandments 'Honor thy mother and father that thy days may be long upon the earth'? Yes. But he hadn't been himself. Hadn't been her father. Had, in fact, been someone completely different. An imposter. It —

Suddenly she went cold as a terrible question occurred to her. Was this happening to the others? Or something like it? She ought to warn them. They had hurt It, and perhaps now It was taking steps to assure Itself they would never hurt It again. And, really, where else was there to go? They were the only friends she had. Bill. Bill would know what to do. Bill would tell her what to do, Bill would supply the *what next*.

She stopped where the Seminary walk joined the Kansas Street sidewalk and peered around the hedge. Her father was truly gone. She turned right and began to walk along Kansas Street toward the Barrens. Probably none of them would be there right now; they would be at home, eating their lunches. But they would be back. Meantime, she could go down into the cool clubhouse and try to get herself under some kind of control. She would leave the little window wide open so she could have some sunshine, and perhaps she would even be able to sleep. Her tired body and overstrained mind grasped eagerly at the thought. Sleep, yes, that would be good.

Her head drooped as she plodded past the last bunch of houses before the land grew too steep for houses and plunged down into the Barrens — the Barrens where, as incredible as it seemed to her, her father had been lurking and spying.

She certainly did not hear footfalls behind her. The boys there were at great pains to be quiet. They had been outrun before; they did not intend to be outrun again. They drew closer and closer to her, walking cat-soft. Belch and Victor were grinning, but Henry's face was both vacant and serious. His hair was uncombed and snarly. His eyes were as unfocused as Al Marsh's had been in the apartment. He held one dirty finger pressed over his lips in a *shhh* gesture as they closed the distance from seventy feet to fifty to thirty.

Through that summer Henry had been edging steadily out over some mental abyss, walking on a bridge that had grown relentlessly more and more narrow. On the day when he had allowed Patrick Hockstetter to caress him, that bridge had narrowed to a tightrope. The tightrope had snapped this morning. He had gone out into the yard, naked except for his ragged, yellowing undershorts, and looked up into the sky. The ghost of last night's moon still lingered there, and as he looked at it the moon had suddenly changed into a skeletal grinning face. Henry had fallen on his knees before this face, exalted with terror and joy. Ghost-voices came from the moon. The voices changed, sometimes seemed to merge together in a soft babble that was barely understandable . . . but he sensed the truth, which was simply that all these voices were one voice, one intelligence. The voice told him to hunt up Belch and Victor and be at the corner of Kansas Street and Costello Avenue around noon. The voice told him he would know what to do then. Sure enough, the cunt had come bopping along. He waited to hear what the voice would tell him to do next. The answer came as they continued to close the distance. The voice came not from the moon, but from the sewer-grating they were passing. The voice was low but clear. Belch and Victor glanced toward the grating in a dazed, almost hypnotized way, then back at Beverly.

Kill her, the voice from the sewer said.

Henry Bowers reached into the pocket of his jeans and brought out a slim nine-inch-long instrument with imitation-ivory inlays along its sides. A small chromium button glittered at one end of this dubious *objet d'art*. Henry pushed it. A six-inch blade popped out of the slit at the end of the handle. He bounced the switchblade on his palm. He began to walk a little faster. Victor and Belch, still looking dazed, increased their own walking speed to keep up with him.

Beverly did not *hear* them, precisely; that was not what made her turn her head as Henry Bowers closed the distance. Bent-kneed, shuffling, a frozen grin on his face, Henry was as silent as an Indian. No; it was simply a feeling, too clear and direct and powerful to be denied, of

3

The Derry Public Library/1:55 A. M. May 31st, 1983

being watched.

Mike Hanlon laid his pen aside and looked across the shadowy inverted bowl of the library's main room. He saw islands of light thrown by the hanging globes; he saw books fading up into dimness; he saw the iron staircases making their graceful trellised spirals up to the stacks. He saw nothing out of place.

All the same, he did not believe he was alone in here. Not anymore.

After the others were gone, Mike had cleaned up with a care that was only habit. He was on autopilot, his mind a million miles – and twenty-seven years – away. He dumped ashtrays, threw away the empty liquor bottles (putting a layer of waste over them so that Carole wouldn't be shocked), and the returnable cans in a box behind his desk. Then he got the broom and swept up the remains of the gin bottle Eddie had broken.

When the table was clean, he had gone into the Periodicals Room and picked up the scattered magazines. As he did these simple chores, his mind sifted the stories they had told – concentrating the most, perhaps, on what they had left out. They believed they remembered everything; he thought that Bill and Beverly almost did. But there was more. It would come to them . . . if It allowed them the time. In 1958, there had been no chance for preparation. They had talked endlessly – their talk interrupted only by the rockfight and that one act of group heroism at 29 Neibolt Street – and might, in the end, have done no more than talk. Then August 14th had come, and Henry and his friends had simply chased them into the sewers.

Maybe I should have told them, part of it, and perhaps that sense of circularity was part of it, too. Maybe that last act was going to repeat itself, in some updated fashion, as well. He had put flashlights and miner's helmets carefully by against tomorrow; he had the blueprints of the Derry sewer and drain systems neatly rolled up and held with rubber bands in that same closet. But, when they were kids, all their talk and all their plans, half-baked or otherwise, had come to nothing in the end; in the end they had simply been chased into the drains, hurled into the confrontation which had followed. Was that going to happen again? Faith and power, he had come to believe, were interchangeable. Was the final truth even simpler? That no act of faith was possible until you were rudely pushed out into the screaming middle of things like a newborn child skydiving chutelessly out of his mother's womb? Once you were falling, you were forced to believe in the chute, into existence, weren't you? Pulling the ring as you fell became your final statement on the subject, one way or the other.

Jesus Christ, it's Fulton Sheen in blackface, Mike thought, and laughed a little.

Mike cleaned, neatened, thought his thoughts, while another part of his brain expected that he would finish and finally find himself tired enough to go home and sleep for a few hours. But when he finally did finish, he found himself as wide awake as ever. So he had gone to the single closed stack behind his office, unlocking the wire gate with a key from his ring and letting himself in. This stack, supposedly fire-proof when the vault-type door was closed and locked, contained the library's valuable first editions, books signed by writers long since dead (among the signed editions were *Moby Dick* and Whitman's *Leaves of Grass*), historical matter relating to the town, and the personal papers of the few writers who had lived and worked in Derry. Mike hoped, if all of this ended well, to persuade Bill to leave his manuscripts to the Derry Public Library. Walking down the third aisle of the stack beneath tin-shaded light-bulbs, smelling the familiar library scents of must and dust and cinnamony, ageing paper, he thought: *When I die, I guess I'll go with a library card in one hand and an* OVERDUE *stamp in the other. Well, maybe that's better than dying with a gun in your hand, nigger.*

He stopped halfway down this third aisle. His dog-eared steno notebook, which contained the jotted tales of Derry and his own troubled wanderings, was tucked between Fricke's *Old Derry-Town* and Michaud's *History of Derry*. He had pushed the notebook so far back it was nearly invisible. No one would stumble across it unless they were looking for it.

Mike took it and went back to the table where they had held their meeting, pausing to turn off the lights in the closed stack and to re-lock the wire mesh. He sat down and flipped through the pages he had written, thinking what a strange, crippled affidavit he had created: half-history, half-scandal, part diary, part confessional. He had not entered since April 6th. *Have to get a new book soon*, he thought, thumbing the few blank pages that were left. He thought bemusedly for a moment of Margaret Mitchell's first draft of *Gone with the Wind*, written in longhand in stacks and stacks and stacks of school composition books. Then he uncapped his pen and wrote *May 31st* two lines below the end of his last entry. He paused, looking vaguely across the empty library, and then began to write about everything that had happened during the last three days, beginning with his telephone call to Stanley Uris.

He wrote carefully for fifteen minutes, and then his concentration began to come unravelled. He paused more and more frequently. The image of Stan Uris's severed head in the refrigerator tried to intrude, Stan's bloody head, the mouth open and full of feathers, falling out of the refrigerator and rolling across the floor toward him. He banished it with an effort and went on writing. Five minutes later he jerked upright and whirled around, convinced he would see that head rolling across the old black and red tiles of the main floor, eyes as glassy and avid as the eyes in the mounted head of a deer.

There was nothing. No head, no sound except the muffled drum of his own heart.

Got to get ahold of yourself, Mikey. It's the jim-jams, that's all. Nothing else to it.

But it was no use. The words began to get away from him, the thoughts seemed to dangle just out of reach. There was a pressure on the back of his neck, and it seemed to grow heavier.

Being watched.

He put his pen down and got up from the table. 'Is anyone here?' he called, and his voice echoed back from the rotunda, giving him a jolt. He licked his lips and tried again. 'Bill? . . . Ben?'

Bill-ill-ill . . . Ben-en-en . . .

Suddenly Mike decided he wanted to be home. He would simply take the notebook with him. He reached for it . . . and heard a faint sliding footstep.

He looked up again. Pools of light surrounded by deepening lagoons of shadow. Nothing else . . . at least nothing he could see. He waited, heart beating hard.

The footstep came again, and this time he pinpointed the location. The glassed-in passageway that connected the adult library to the Children's Library. In there. Someone. Something.

Moving quietly, Mike walked across to the checkout desk. The double doors leading into the passageway were held open by wooden chocks, and he could see a little way in. He could see what looked like feet, and with sudden swooning horror he wondered if maybe Stan had come after all, if maybe Stan was going to step out of the shadows with his bird encyclopedia in one hand, his face white, his lips purple, his wrists and forearms cut open. *I finally came*, Stan would say. *It took me awhile because I had to pull myself out of a hole in the ground, but I finally came . . .*

There was another footstep and now Mike could see shoes for sure – shoes and ragged pantslegs – denim, with strings hanging down against sockless ankles. And, in the darkness almost six feet above those ankles, he could see glittering eyes.

He groped over the surface of the semicircular checkout desk and felt along the other side without taking his gaze from those moveless, glittering eyes. His fingers felt one wooden corner of a small box – the overdue cards. A paper box – paper clips and rubber bands. They happened on something that was metal and seized it. It was a letter-opener with the words JESUS SAVES stamped on the handle. A flimsy thing that had come in the mail from the Grace Baptist Church as part of a fund-raising drive. Mike had not attended services in fifteen years, but Grace Baptist had been his mother's church and he had sent them five dollars he could not really afford. He had meant to throw the letter-opener out but it had stayed here, amid the clutter on his side of the desk (Carole's side was always spotlessly clean) until now.

He clutched it with feverish strength and stared into the shadowy hallway.

There was another step . . . another. Now the ragged denim pants were visible up to the knees. He could see the shape these lower legs belonged to: It was big, hulking. The shoulders were rounded. There was a suggestion of ragged hair. The figure was ape-like.

'Who are you?'

There was no answer. The shape merely stood there, contemplating him.

Although still afraid, Mike had gotten over the debilitating idea that it might be Stan Uris, returned from the grave, called back by the scars on his palms, some eldritch magnetism which had brought him back like a zombie in a Hammer horror film. Whoever this was, it wasn't Stan Uris, who had finished at five-seven when he had his full growth.

The shape took another step, and now the light from the globe closest to the passageway fell across the beltless loops of the jeans around the shape's waist.

Suddenly Mike knew. Even before the shape spoke, he knew.

'Why, it's the nigger,' the shape said. 'Been throwing rocks at anyone, nigger? Want to know who poisoned your fucking dog?'

The shape stepped forward. The light fell on the face of Henry Bowers. It had grown fat, the skin had an unhealthy tallowy hue; sagging; the cheeks had become hanging jowls that were specked with stubble, almost as much white in that stubble as black. Wavy lines – three of them – were engraved in the shelf of the forehead above the bushy brows. Other lines formed parentheses at the corners of the full-lipped mouth. The eyes were small and mean inside discolored pouches of flesh – bloodshot and thoughtless. It was the face of a man being pushed into a premature age, a man who was thirty-nine going on seventy-three. But it was also the face of a twelve-year-old boy. Henry's clothes were still green with whatever bushes he had spent the day hiding in.

'Ain't you ganna say howdy, nigger?' Henry asked.

'Hello, Henry.' It occurred to him dimly that he had not listened to the radio for the last two days, and he had not even read the paper, which was a ritual with him. Too much going on. Too busy.

Too bad.

Henry emerged from the corridor between the Children's Library and the adult library and stood there, peering at Mike with his piggy little eyes. His lips parted in an unspeakable grin, revealing rotted back-Maine teeth.

'Voices,' he said. 'You hear voices, nigger?'

'Which voices are those, Henry?' He put both hands behind his back, like a schoolboy called upon to recite, and transferred the letter-opener from his left hand to his right. The grandfather clock, given by Horst Mueller in 1923, ticked solemn seconds into the smooth pond of library silence.

'From the moon,' Henry said. He put a hand in his pocket. 'Came from the moon. Lots of voices.' He paused, frowned slightly, then shook his head. 'Lots but really only one. *It's* voice.'

'Did you see it, Henry?'

'Yep,' Henry said. 'Frankenstein. Tore off Victor's head. You should have heard it. Made a sound like a great big zipper going down. Then It went after Belch. Belch fought It.'

'Did he?'

'Yep. That's how I got away.'

'You left him to die.'

'*Don't you say that!*' Henry's cheeks flushed a dull red. He took two steps forward. The farther he walked from the umbilicus connecting the Children's Library to the adult library, the younger he looked to Mike. He saw the same old meanness in Henry's face, but he saw something else as well: the child who had been brought up by crazy Butch Bowers on a good farm that had gone to shitshack shambles over the years. '*Don't you say that! It would have killed me, too.*'

'It didn't kill us.'

Henry's eyes gleamed with rancid humor. 'Not yet. But It will. 'Less I don't leave any of you for It to get.' He pulled his hand out of his pocket. In it was a slim nine-inch-long instrument with imitation-ivory inlays along its sides. A six-inch steel blade popped out of the slit at the end of the handle. He bounced the switchblade on his palm and began to walk toward the checkout desk a little faster.

'Look what I found,' he said. 'I knew where to look.' Obscenely, one red-rimmed eyelid drooped in a wink. 'The man in the moon told me.' Henry revealed his teeth again. 'Hid today. Yesterday, too.

Hitchhiked a ride tonight. Old man. Hit him. Killed him, I think. Ditched the car over in Newport. Just over the Derry town line, I heard that voice. I looked in a drain. There was these clothes. And the knife. My old knife.'

'You're forgetting something, Henry.'

Henry, grinning, only shook his head.

'We got away and you got away. If It wants us, It wants you too.'

'No.'

'I think yes. Maybe you yo-yos did Its work, but It didn't exactly play favorites, did It? It got both of your friends, and while Belch was fighting It, you got away. But now you're back. I think you're part of Its unfinished business, Henry. I really do.'

'No!'

'Maybe Frankenstein's what you'll see. Or the Werewolf? A Vampire. The Clown. Or Henry! *Maybe you'll really see what It looks like*, Henry. We did. Want me to tell you? Want me to –'

'You shut up!' Henry screamed, and launched himself at Mike.

Mike stepped aside and stuck out one foot. Henry tripped over it and went skidding over the footworn tiles like a shuffleboard weight. His head struck a leg of the table where the Losers had sat earlier that night, telling their tales. For a moment he was stunned; the knife hung loose in his hand.

Mike went after him, went after the knife. In that moment he could have finished Henry; it would have been possible to have planted the JESUS SAVES letter-opener which had come in the mail from his mother's old church in the back of Henry's neck and then called the police. There would have been a certain amount of official nonsense, but not too much of it – not in Derry, where such weird and violent events were not entirely exceptional.

What stopped him was a realization, almost too lightninglike to be conscious, that if he killed Henry, he would be doing Its work as surely as Henry would be doing Its work by killing Mike. And something else; that other look he had seen on Henry's face, the tired, bewildered look of the badly used child who has been set on a poisonous path for some unknown purpose. Henry had grown up within the contaminated radius of Butch Bowers's mind; surely he had belonged to It even before he suspected It existed.

So instead of planting the letter-opener in Henry's vulnerable neck, he dropped to his knees and snatched at the knife. It twisted in his hand – seemingly of its own volition – and his fingers closed on the blade. There was no immediate pain; only red blood flowing down the first three fingers of his right hand and into his scarred palm.

He pulled back. Henry rolled away and grabbed the knife again. Mike got to his knees and the two of them faced each other that way, each bleeding: Mike's fingers, Henry's nose. Henry shook his head and droplets flew away into the darkness.

'Thought you were so smart!' he cried hoarsely. 'Fucking sissies is all you were! We could have beat you in a fair fight!'

'Put the knife down, Henry,' Mike said quietly. 'I'll call the police. They'll come and get you and take you back to Juniper Hill. You'll be out of Derry. You'll be safe.'

Henry tried to talk and couldn't. He couldn't tell this hateful jig that he *wouldn't* be safe in Juniper Hill, or Los Angeles, or the rain-forests of Timbuktu. Sooner or later the moon would rise, bone-white and snow-cold, and the ghost-voices would start, and the face of the moon would change into Its face, babbling and laughing and ordering. He swallowed slick-slimy blood.

'You never fought fair!'

'Did you?' Mike asked.

'You nigger boogie night-fighter jungle-bunny apeman *coon*!' Henry screamed, and leaped at Mike again.

Mike leaned back to avoid his blundering, awkward rush, over-balanced, and went sprawling on his back. Henry struck the table again, rebounded, turned, and clutched Mike's arm. Mike swept the letter-opener around and felt it go deep into Henry's forearm. Henry screamed, but instead of letting go, he tightened his grip. He pulled himself toward Mike, his hair in his eyes, blood flowing from his ruptured nose over his thick lips.

Mike tried to get a foot in Henry's side and push him away. Henry swung the switchblade in a glittering arc, and all six inches of it went into Mike's thigh. It went in effortlessly, as if into a warm cake of butter. Henry pulled it out, dripping, and with a scream of combined pain and effort, Mike shoved him away.

He struggled to his feet but Henry was up more quickly, and Mike was barely able to avoid Henry's next blundering rush. He could feel blood pouring down his leg in an alarming flood, filling his loafer. *He got my femoral artery, I think. Jesus, he got me bad. Blood everywhere. Blood on the floor. Shoes won't be any good, shit, just bought them two months ago –*

Henry came again, panting and puffing like a bull in heat. Mike staggered aside and swept the letter-opener at him again. It tore through Henry's ragged shirt and pulled a deep cut across his ribs. Henry grunted as Mike shoved him away again.

'*You dirty-fighting nigger!*' he wailed. '*Look what you done!*'

'Drop the knife, Henry,' Mike said.

There was a titter from behind them. Henry looked . . . and then screamed in utter horror, clapping his hands to his cheeks like an offended old maid. Mike's gaze jerked toward the circulation desk. There was a loud, vibrating ka-spanggg! sound, and Stan Uris's head popped up from behind the desk. A spring corkscrewed up and into his severed, dripping neck. His face was livid with greasepaint. There was a fever spot of rouge on each cheek. Great orange pompoms flowered where the eyes had been. This grotesque Stan-in-the-box head nodded back and forth at the end of its spring like one of the giant sunflowers beside the house on Neibolt Street. Its mouth opened and a squealing, laughing voice began to chant: '*Kill him, Henry! Kill the nigger, kill the coon, kill him, kill him, KILL HIM!*'

Mike wheeled back toward Henry, dismally aware that he had been tricked, wondering faintly whose face Henry had seen at the end of that spring. Stan's? Victor Criss's? His father's, perhaps?

Henry shrieked and rushed at Mike, the switchblade plunging up and down like the needle of a sewing machine. '*Gaaaah, nigger!*' Henry was screaming. '*Gaaaah, nigger! Gaaaah, nigger!*'

Mike back-pedaled, and the leg Henry had stabbled buckled under him almost at once, spilling him to the floor. There was hardly any feeling at all left in that leg. It felt cold and distant. Looking down, he saw that his cream-colored slacks were now bright red.

Henry's blade flashed by in front of his nose.

Mike stabbed out with the JESUS SAVES letter-opener as Henry turned back for another go. Henry ran into it like a bug onto a pin. Warm blood doused Mike's hand. There was a snap, and when he drew his hand back, he only had the haft of the letter-opener. The blade was in Henry's stomach.

'*Gaaah! Nigger!*' Henry screamed, clapping a hand over the protruding jag of blade. Blood poured through his fingers. He looked at it with bulging, unbelieving eyes. The head of the end of the creaking, dipping jack-in-the-box squealed and laughed. Mike, feeling sick and dizzy now, looked back at it and saw Belch Huggin's head, a human champagne cork wearing a New York Yankees baseball cap turned backward. He groaned aloud, and the sound was far away, echoey, in his own ears. He was aware that he was sitting in a pool of warm blood . . . his own. *If I don't get a tourniquet on my leg, I'm going to die.*

'*Gaaaaaaaaaah! Neeeeeeegaaaa!*' Henry screamed. Still holding his bleeding belly with one hand and the switchblade with the other, he staggered away from Mike and toward the library doors. He wove drunkenly from side to side, progressing across the echoing main room like a pinball in an electronic game. He struck one of the easy-chairs and knocked it over. His groping hand spilled a rack of newspapers onto the floor. He reached the doors, straight-armed one of them; and plunged out into the night.

Mike's consciousness was fading now. He worked at the buckle of his belt with fingers he could barely feel. At last he got it unhooked and managed to pull it free of its loops. He put it around his bleeding leg just below the groin and cinched it tight. Holding it with one hand, he began to crawl toward the circulation desk. The phone was there. He wasn't sure how he was going to reach it, but for now that didn't matter. The trick was just to get there. The world wavered, blurred, grew faint behind waves of gray. He stuck his tongue out and bit down on it savagely. The pain was immediate and exquisite. The world swam back into focus. He became aware that he was still holding the ragged haft of the letter-opener, and he tossed it away. Here, at last, was the circulation desk, looking as tall as Everest.

Mike got his good leg under him and pushed himself up, clutching at the edge of the desk with the hand that wasn't holding the belt tight. His mouth was drawn down in a trembling grimace, his eyes slitted. At last he managed to get all the way up. He stood there, storklike, and groped the telephone over to him. Taped to the side were three numbers: fire, police, and hospital. With one shaking finger that looked at least ten miles away, Mike dialed the hospital: 555-3711. He closed his eyes as the phone began to ring . . . and then they opened wide as the voice of Pennywise the Clown answered.

'Howdy nigger!' Pennywise cried, and then screamed laughter as sharp as broken glass into Mike's ear. 'What do you say? How you doon? I think you're dead, what do you think? I think Henry did the job on you! Want a balloon, Mikey? Want a balloon? How you doon? Hello there!'

Mike's eyes turned up to the face of the grandfather clock, the Mueller Clock, it was called, and saw with no surprise at all that the clockface had been replaced with his father's face, gray and raddled with cancer. The eyes were turned up to show only bulging whites.

Suddenly his father popped his tongue out and the clock began to strike.

Mike lost his grip on the circulation desk. He swayed for a moment on his good leg and then he fell down again. The phone swung before him at the end of its cord like a mesmerist's amulet. It was becoming very hard to hold onto the belt now.

'Hello dere Amos!' Pennywise cried brightly from the swinging telephone handset. 'Dis here's de Kingfish! I is de Kingfish in Derry anyhow, and *dat's* de troof. Wouldn't you say so, boy?'

'If there's anyone there,' Mike croaked, 'a real voice behind the one I am hearing, please help me. My name is Michael Hanlon and I'm at the Derry Public Library. I am bleeding to death. If you're there, I can't hear you. I'm not being allowed to hear you. If you're there, please hurry.'

He lay on his side, drawing his legs up until he was in a fetal position. He took two turns around his right hand with the belt and concentrated on holding it as the world drifted away in those cottony, balloon-like clouds of gray.

'Hello dere, howyadoon?' Pennywise screamed from the dangling, swinging phone. 'Howyadoon, you dirty coon? Hello

4

Kansas Street/12:20 P.M.

... there,' Henry Bowers said. 'Howyadoon, you little cunt?'

Beverly reacted instantly, turning to run. It was a quicker reaction than any of them had expected, and she might actually have gotten a running start ... but for her hair. Henry snatched at it, caught part of its long flow, and pulled her back. He grinned into her face. His breath was thick and warm and stinking.

'Howyadoon?' Henry Bowers asked her. 'Where ya goin? Back to play with your asshole friends some more? I think I'll cut off your nose and make you eat it. You like that?'

She struggled to get free. Henry laughed and shook her head back and forth by the hair. The knife flashed dangerously in the hazy August sunshine.

Abruptly a car-horn honked – a long blast.

'Here! Here! What are you boys doing? Let that girl go!'

It was an old lady behind the wheel of a well-preserved 1950

Ford. She had pulled up to the curb and was leaning across the blanket-covered seat to peer out the passenger-side window. At the sight of her angry, honest face, the blank, dazed look left Victor Criss's eyes for the first time and he looked nervously at Henry. 'What –'

'Please!' Bev cried shrilly. 'He's got a knife! A *knife!*'

The old lady's anger now became concern, surprise, and fear as well. 'What are you boys doing? Let her *alone!*'

Across the street – Bev saw this quite clearly – Herbert Ross got out of the lawn-chair on his porch, approached the porch rail, and looked over. His face was as blank as Belch Huggins's. He folded his paper, turned, and went quietly into the house.

'Let her *be!*' the old lady cried shrilly.

Henry bared his teeth and suddenly ran at her car, dragging Beverly after him by the hair. She stumbled, went to one knee, was dragged. The pain in her scalp was excruciating, monstrous. She felt some of her hair rip out.

The old lady screamed and cranked the passenger side window frantically. Henry, still roaring, stabbed down, and the switchblade skated across glass. The woman's foot came off the old Ford's clutch-pedal and it went down Kansas Street in three big jerks, bouncing up over the curb, where it stalled. Henry went after it, still pulling Beverly along. Victor licked his lips and looked around. Belch pushed the New York Yankees baseball cap he was wearing up on his forehead and then dug at his ear in a puzzled gesture.

Bev saw the old woman's white, frightened face for one moment, and then saw her pawing at the door-locks, first on the passenger side, then on her own. The Ford's engine ground and caught. Henry lifted one booted foot and kicked out a taillight.

'Get outta here, you dried-up old bitch!'

The tires screamed as the old lady pulled back out in the street. An oncoming pickup truck swerved to avoid her; its horn blasted. Henry turned back toward Bev, beginning to smile again, and she hiked one sneakered foot directly into his balls.

The smile on Henry's face turned into a grimace of agony. The switchknife dropped from his hand and clattered onto the sidewalk. His other hand left its nesting-place in the tangle of her hair (pulling once more, terribly, as it went) and then he sank to his knees, trying to scream, holding his crotch. She could see strands of her own coppery hair on one hand, and in that instant all of her terror turned to bright hate. She drew in a great, hitching breath and hocked a remarkably large looey onto the top of his head.

Then she turned and ran.

Belch lumbered three steps after her and then stopped. He and Victor went to Henry, who threw them aside and then staggered to his feet, both hands still cupping his balls; it was not the first time that summer that he had been kicked there.

He leaned over and picked up the switchblade. '. . . on,' he wheezed.

'What, Henry?' Belch said anxiously.

Henry turned a face toward him that was so full of sweating pain and sick, blazing hate that Belch fell back a step. 'I said . . . come . . . on!' he managed, and began to stagger and lurch up the street after Beverly, holding his crotch.

'We can't catch her now, Henry,' Victor said uneasily. 'Hell, you can hardly walk.'

'We'll catch her,' Henry panted. His upper lip was rising and falling in an unconscious dog-like sneer. Beads of sweat stood out on his forehead and ran down his hectic cheeks. 'We'll catch her, all right. Because I know where she's going. She's going down into the Barrens to be with her asshole

5

The Derry Town House/2:00 A.M.

friends,' Beverly said.

'Hmmm?' Bill looked at her. His thoughts had been far away. They had been walking hand-in-hand, the silence between them companionable, slightly charged with mutual attraction. He had caught only the last word of what she had said. A block ahead, the lights of the Town House shone through the low ground-fog.

'I said, you were my best friends. The only friends I ever had back then.' She smiled. 'Making friends has never been my strong suit, I guess, although I've got a good one back in Chicago. A woman named Kay McCall. I think you'd like her, Bill.'

'Probably would. I've never been real fast to make friends myself.' He smiled. 'Back then, we were all we nuh-nuh-needed.' He saw beads of moisture in her hair, appreciated the way the lights made a nimbus about her head. Her eyes were turned gravely up to his.

'I need something now,' she said.

'W-What's that?'

'I need you to kiss me,' she said.

871

He thought of Audra, and for the first time it occurred to him that she *looked* like Beverly. He wondered if maybe that had been the attraction all along, the reason he had been able to find guts enough to ask Audra out near the end of the Hollywood party where they had been introduced. He felt a pang of unhappy guilt . . . and then he took Beverly, his childhood friend, in his arms.

Her kiss was firm and warm and sweet. Her breasts pushed against his open coat and her hips moved against him . . . away . . . and then against him again. When her hips moved away a second time, he plunged both of his hands into her hair and moved against her. When she felt him growing hard, she uttered a little gasp and put her face against the side of his neck. He felt her tears on his skin, warm and secret.

'Come on,' she said. 'Quick.'

He took her hand and they walked the rest of the way to the Town House. The lobby was old, festooned with plants, and still possessed of a certain fading charm. The decor was very much Nineteenth Century Lumberman. It was deserted at this hour except for the desk clerk, who could be dimly seen in the inner office, his feet cocked up on the desk, watching TV. Bill pushed the third-floor button with a finger that trembled just slightly – excitement? nervousness? guilt? all of the above? Oh yeah sure, and a kind of almost insane joy and fear as well. These feelings did not mix pleasantly, but they seemed necessary. He led her down the hallway toward his room, deciding in some confused way that if he were to be unfaithful, it should be a complete act of infidelity, consummated in his place, not hers. He found himself thinking of Susan Browne, his first book-agent and, at the age of not quite twenty, his first lover.

Cheating. Cheating on my wife. He tried to get this through his head, but it seemed both real and unreal at the same time. What seemed strongest was an unhappy sense of homesickness: an oldfashioned feeling of falling away. Audra would be up by now, making coffee, sitting at the kitchen table in her robe, perhaps studying lines, perhaps reading a Dick Francis novel.

His key rattled in the lock of room 311. If they had gone to Beverly's room on the fifth floor, they would have seen the message-light on her phone blinking; the TV-watching desk clerk would have given her a message to call her friend Kay in Chicago (after Kay's third frantic call, he had finally remembered to post the message), things might have taken a different course: the five of them might not have been fugitives from the Derry police when that day's light finally broke. But they went to his – as things had, perhaps, been arranged.

The door opened. They were inside. She looked at him, eyes bright, cheeks flushed, her breast rising and falling rapidly. He took her in his arms and was overwhelmed by the feeling of *rightness* – the feeling of the circle between past and present closing with a triumphant seamlessness. He kicked the door shut clumsily with one foot and she laughed her warm breath into his mouth.

'My heart –' she said, and put his hand on her left breast. He could feel it below that firm, almost .maddening softness, racing like an engine.

'Your h-h-heart –'

'My heart.'

They were on the bed, still dressed, kissing. Her hand slipped inside his shirt, then out again. She traced a finger down the row of buttons, paused at his waist . . . and then that same finger slipped lower, tracing down the stony thickness of his cock. Muscles he hadn't been aware of jumped and fluttered in his groin. He broke the kiss and moved his body away from hers on the bed.

'Bill?'

'Got to stuh-stuh-stop for a m-m-minute,' he said. 'Or else I'm going to shoot in my p-p-pants like a k-kid.'

She laughed again, softly, and looked at him. 'Is it that? Or are you having second thoughts?'

'Second thoughts,' Bill said. 'I a-a-always have those.'

'I don't. I hate him,' she said.

He looked at her, the smile fading.

'I didn't know it all the way to the top of my mind until tonight,' she said. 'Oh, I knew it – somewhere – all along, I guess. He hits and he hurts. I married him because . . . because my father always worried about me, I guess. No matter how hard I tried, he worried. And I guess I knew he'd approve of Tom. Because Tom would worry, too. He worried a lot. And as long as someone was worrying about me, I'd be safe. More than safe. *Real*.' She looked at him solemnly. Her blouse had pulled out of the waistband of her slacks, revealing a white stripe of stomach. He wanted to kiss it. 'But it wasn't real. It was a nightmare. Being married to Tom was like going back into the nightmare. Why would a person do that, Bill? Why would a person go back into the nightmare of her own accord?'

Bill said, 'The o-o-only reason I can f-figure is that p-people go back to f-f-find thems-s-selves.'

'The nightmare's here,' Bev said. 'The nightmare is Derry. Tom looks small compared to that. I can see him better now. I loathe myself for the years I spent with him . . . You don't know . . . the things he made me do, and oh, I was happy enough to do them, you know, because he worried about me. I'd cry . . . but sometimes there's too much shame. You know?'

'Don't,' he said quietly, and put his hand over hers. She held it tightly. Her eyes were overbright, but the tears didn't fall. 'Everybody g-g-goofs it. But it's not an eh-eh-exam. You just go through it the b-b-best you can.'

'What I mean,' she said, 'is that I'm not cheating on Tom, or trying to use you to get my own back on him, or anything like that. For me, it would be like something . . . sane and normal and sweet. But I don't want to hurt you, Bill. Or trick you into something you'll be sorry for later.'

He thought about this, thought about it with a real and deep seriousness. But the odd little mnemonic – *he thrusts his fists*, and so on – had begun to circle back, breaking into his thoughts. It had been a long day. Mike's call and the invitation to lunch at Jade of the Orient seemed a hundred years ago. So many stories since then. So many memories, like photographs from George's album.

'Friends don't t-t-trick each o-other,' he said, and leaned toward her on the bed. Their lips touched and he began to unbutton her blouse. One of her hands went to the back of his neck and held him closer while the other first unzipped her slacks and then pushed them down. For a moment his hand was on her stomach, warm; then her panties were gone in a whisper; then he nudged and she guided.

As he entered her, she arched her back gently toward the thrust of his sex and muttered, 'Be my friend . . . I love you, Bill.'

'I love you too,' he said, smiling against her bare shoulder. They began slowly and he felt sweat begin to flow out of his skin as she quickened beneath him. His consciousness began to drain downward, becoming focused more and more strongly on their connection. Her pores had opened, releasing a lovely musky odor.

Beverly felt her climax coming. She moved toward it, working for it, never doubting that it would come. Her body suddenly stuttered and seemed to leap upward, not orgasming but reaching a plateau far above any she had reached with Tom or the other two lovers she had had before Tom. She became aware that this wasn't going to be just a come; it was going to be a tactical nuke. She became a little afraid . . . but her body picked up the rhythm again. She felt Bill's long length stiffen against her, his whole body suddenly becoming as hard as the part of him inside herself, and at that same moment she climaxed – *began* to climax pleasure so great it was nearly agony spilled out of unsuspected floodgates, and she bit down on his shoulder to stifle her cries.

'Oh my God,' Bill gasped, and although she was never sure later, she believed he was crying. He pulled back and she thought he was going to withdraw from her – she tried to prepare for that moment, which always brought a fleeting, inexplicable sense of loss and emptiness, something like a footprint – and then he thrust forward strongly again. Right away she had a second orgasm, something she hadn't known was possible for her, and the window of memory opened again and she saw birds, thousands of birds, descending onto every roofpeak and telephone line and RFD mailbox in Derry, spring birds against a white April sky, and there was pain mixed with pleasure – but mostly it was low, as a white spring sky seems low. Low physical pain mixed with low physical pleasure and sense of affirmation. She had bled . . . she had . . . had . . .

'*All* of you?' she cried suddenly, her eyes widening, stunned.

He did pull back and out of her this time, but in the sudden shock of the revelation, she barely felt him go.

'What? Beverly? A-Are you all r –'

'*All of you? I made love to all of you?*'

She saw shocked surprise on Bill's face, the drop of his jaw . . . and sudden understanding. But it was not her revelation; even in her own shock she saw that. It was his own.

'We –'

'Bill? What is it?'

'That was y-y-your way to get us out,' he said, and now his eyes blazed so brightly they frightened her. 'Beverly, duh-duh-don't you *uh-understand*? That was *y-y-your way to get us out!* We all . . . but we were . . .' Suddenly he looked frightened, unsure.

'Do you remember the rest now?' she asked.

He shook his head slowly. 'Not the spuh-spuh-specifics. But . . .' He looked at her, and she saw he was badly frightened. 'What it really c-c-came down to was we *wuh-wuh-wished* our way out. And I'm not s-sure . . . Beverly, I'm not sure that grownups can do that.'

She looked at him without speaking for a long moment, and sat on the edge of the bed and took her clothes off with no particular self-consciousness. Her body was smooth and lovely, the line of her backbone barely discernible in the dimness as she bent to take off the knee-high nylon stockings she had been wearing. Her hair was a sheaf coiled over one shoulder. He thought he would want her again before morning, and that feeling of guilt came again, tempered only by the guilty comfort of knowing that Audra was an ocean away. *Put another nickel in the juke-box*, he thought. *This tune is called 'What She Don't Know Won't Hurt Her.' But it hurts somewhere. In the spaces between people, maybe.*

Beverly got up and turned the bed down. 'Come to bed. We need sleep. Both of us.'

'A-A-All right.' Because that was right, that was a big ten-four. More than anything else he wanted to sleep . . . but not alone, not tonight. The latest shock was wearing off – too quickly, perhaps, but he felt so tired now, so used-up. Second-to-second reality had the quality of a dream, and in spite of the guilt he felt, he also felt that this was a safe place. It would be possible to lie here for a little while, to sleep in her arms. He wanted her warmth and her friendliness. Both were sexually charged, but that could hurt neither of them now.

He stripped off his socks and shirt and got in next to her. She pressed against him, her breasts warm, her long legs cool. Bill held her, aware of the differences – her body was longer than Audra's, and fuller at the breast and the hip. But it was a welcome body.

It should have been Ben with you, dear, he thought drowsily. *I think that was the way it was really supposed to be. Why wasn't it Ben?*

Because it was you then and it's you now, that's all. Because what goes around always comes around. I think Bob Dylan said that . . . or maybe it was Ronald Reagan. And maybe it's me now because Ben's the one who's supposed to see the lady home.

Beverly wriggled against him, not in a sexual way (although, even as he fled toward sleep, she felt him stir again against her leg and was glad), but only wanting his warmth. She was already half asleep herself. Her happiness here with him, after all these years, was real. She knew that because of its bitter undertaste. There was tonight, and perhaps there would be another time for them tomorrow morning. Then they would go down in the sewers as they had before, and they would find their It. The circle would close even tighter and their present lives would merge smoothly with their own childhoods; they would become like creatures on some crazy Moebius strip.

Either that, or they would die down there.

She turned over. He slipped an arm between her side and her arm and cupped one breast gently. She did not have to lie awake, wondering if the hand might suddenly clamp down in a hard pinch.

Her thoughts began to break up as sleep slid into her. As always, she saw brilliant wildflower patterns as she crossed over — masses and masses of them nodding brightly under a blue sky. These faded and there was a falling sensation — the sort of sensation that had sometimes snapped her awake and sweating as a child, a scream on the other side of her face. Childhood dreams of falling, she had read in her college psychology text, were common.

But she didn't snap back this time; she could feel the warm and comforting weight of Bill's arm, his hand cradling her breast. She thought that if she was falling, at least she wasn't falling alone.

Then she touched down and was running: this dream, whatever it was, moved fast. She ran after it, pursuing sleep, silence, maybe just time. The years moved fast. The years ran. If you turned around and ran after your own childhood, you'd have to really let out your stride and bust your buns. Twenty-nine, the year she had streaked her hair (*faster*). Twenty-two, the year she had fallen in love with a football player named Greg Mallory who had damn near raped her after a fraternity party (*faster, faster*). Sixteen, getting drunk with two of her girlfriends on the Bluebird Hill Overlook in Portland. Fourteen . . .
. . . twelve . . .

faster, faster, faster . . .

She ran into sleep, chasing twelve, catching it, running through the barrier of memory that It had cast over all of them (it tasted like cold fog in her laboring dreamlungs), running back into her eleventh year, running, running like hell, running to beat the devil, looking back now, looking back

6

The Barrens/12:40 P.M.

over her shoulder for any sign of them as she slipped and scrambled her way down the embankment. No sign, at least not yet. She had 'really fetched it to him,' as her father sometimes said . . . and just thinking of her father brought another wave of guilt and despondency washing over her.

She looked under the rickety bridge, hoping to see Silver heeled over on his side, but Silver was gone. There was a cache of toy guns which they no longer bothered to take home, and that was all. She started down the path, looked back . . . and there they were, Belch and Victor supporting Henry between them, standing on the edge of the embankment like Indian sentries in a Randolph Scott movie. Henry was horribly pale. He pointed at her. Victor and Belch began to help him down the slope. Dirt and gravel spilled from beneath their heels.

Beverly looked at them for a long moment, almost hypnotized. Then she turned and sprinted through the trickle of brook-water that ran out from under the bridge, ignoring Ben's stepping-stones, her sneakers spraying out flat sheets of water. She ran down the path, the breath hot in her throat. She could feel the muscles in her legs trembling. She didn't have much left now. The clubhouse. If she could get there, she might still be safe.

She ran along the path, branches whipping even more color into her cheeks, one striking her eye and making it water. She cut to the right, blundered through tangles of underbrush, and came out into the clearing. Both the camouflaged trapdoor and the slit window stood open; rock n roll drifted up. At the sound of her approach, Ben Hanscom popped up. He had a box of Junior Mints in one hand and an Archie comic book in the other.

He got a good look at Bev and his mouth fell open. Under other circumstances it would have been almost funny. 'Bev, what the *hell* –'

She didn't bother replying. Behind her, and not too far behind, either, she could hear branches snapping and whipping; there was a muffled shouted curse. It sounded as if Henry was getting livelier. So she just ran at the square trapdoor opening, her hair, tangled now with green leaves and twigs as well as the crud from her scramble under the garbage truck, streaming out behind her.

Ben saw she was coming in like the 101st Airborne and disappeared as quickly as he had come out. Beverly jumped and he caught her clumsily.

'Shut everything,' she panted. 'Hurry up, Ben, for heaven's sake! They're coming!'

'Who?'

'Henry and his friends! Henry's gone crazy, he's got a knife –'

That was enough for Ben. He dropped his Junior Mints and his funnybook. He pulled the trapdoor shut with a grunt. The top was covered with sods; Tangle-Track was still holding them remarkably well. A few blocks of sod had gotten a little loose, but that was all. Beverly stood on tiptoe and closed the window. They were in darkness.

She groped for Ben, found him, and hugged him with panicky tightness. After a moment he hugged her back. They were both on their knees. With sudden horror Beverly realized that Richie's transistor radio was still playing somewhere in the blackness: Little Richard singing 'The Girl Can't Help It.'

'Ben . . . the radio . . . they'll hear . . .'

'Oh God!'

He bunted her with one meaty hip and almost knocked her sprawling in the dark. She heard the radio fall to the floor. 'The girl can't help it if the menfolks stop and stare,' Little Richard informed them with his customary hoarse enthusiasm. 'Can't help it!' the back-up group testified, 'the girl can't help it!' Ben was panting now, too. They sounded like a couple of steam-engines. Suddenly there was a crunch . . . and silence.

'Oh shit,' Ben said. 'I just squashed it. Richie's gonna have a bird.' He reached for her in the dark. She felt his hand touch one of her breasts, then jerk away, as if burned. She groped for him, got hold of his shirt, and drew him close.

'Beverly, what –'

'Shhh!'

He quieted. They sat together, arms around each other, looking up. The darkness was not quite perfect; there was a narrow line of light down one side of the trapdoor, and three others outlined the slit window. One of these three was wide enough to let a slanted ray of sunlight fall into the clubhouse. She could only pray *they* wouldn't see it.

She could hear them approaching. At first she couldn't make out the words . . . and then she could. Her grip on Ben tightened.

'If she went into the bamboo, we can pick up her trail easy,' Victor was saying.

'They play around here,' Henry replied. His voice was strained, his words emerging in little puffs, as if with great effort. 'Boogers Taliendo said so. And the day we had that rockfight, they were coming from here.'

'Yeah, they play guns and stuff,' Belch said.

Suddenly there were thudding footfalls right above them; the sod-covered cap vibrated up and down. Dirt sifted onto Beverly's upturned face. One, two, maybe even all three of them were standing on top of the clubhouse. A cramp laced her belly; she had to bite down against a cry. Ben put one big hand on the side of her face and pressed it against his arm as he looked up, waiting to see if they would guess . . . or if they knew already and were just playing games.

'They got a place,' Henry was saying. 'That's what Boogers told me. Some kind of a treehouse or something. They call it their club.'

'I'll club em, if they want a club,' Victor said. Belch uttered a thunderous heehawing of laughter at this.

Thump, thump, thump, overhead. The cap moved up and down a little more this time. Surely they would notice it; ordinary ground just didn't have that kind of give.

'Let's look down by the river,' Henry said. 'I bet she's down there.'

'Okay,' Victor said.

Thump, thump. They were moving off. Bev let a little sigh of relief trickle through her clamped teeth . . . and then Henry said: 'You stay here and guard the path, Belch.'

'Okay,' Belch said, and he began to march back and forth, sometimes leaving the cap, sometimes coming back across it. More dirt sifted down. Ben and Beverly looked at each other with strained, dirty faces. Bev became aware that there was more than the smell of smoke in the clubhouse – a sweaty, garbagey stink was rising as well. *That's me*, she thought dismally. In spite of the smell, she hugged Ben even tighter. His bulk seemed suddenly very welcome, very comforting, and she was glad there was a lot of him to hug. He might have been nothing but a frightened fat-boy when school let out for the summer, but he was more than that now; like all of them, he had changed. If Belch discovered them down here, Ben just might give him a surprise.

'I'll club em if they want a club,' Belch said, and chuckled. A Belch Huggins chuckle was a low, troll-like sound. 'Club em if they want a club. That's good. That's pretty much okey-dokey.'

She became aware that Ben's upper body was heaving up and down in short, sharp movements; he was pulling air into his lungs and letting it out in sharp little bursts. For one alarmed moment she thought he was starting to cry, and then she got a closer look at his face and realized he was struggling against laughter. His eyes, leaking tears, caught hers, rolled madly, and looked away. In the faint light which leaked in through the cracks around the closed trapdoor and the window, she could see his face was nearly purple with the strain of holding it in.

'Club em if they want an ole clubby-dubby,' Belch said, and sat down heavily right in the center of the cap. This time the roof trembled more alarmingly, and Bev heard a low but ominous *crrrack* from one of the supports. The cap had been meant to support the chunks of camouflaging sod laid on top of it . . . but not the added one hundred and sixty pounds of Belch Huggins's weight.

If he doesn't get up he's going to land in our laps, Bev thought, and she began to catch Ben's hysteria. It was trying to boil out of her in rancid whoops and brays. In her mind's eye she suddenly saw herself pushing the window up enough on its hinges for her hand to creep out and administer a really good goose to Belch Huggins's backside as he sat there in the hazy afternoon sunshine, muttering and giggling. She buried her face against Ben's chest in a last-ditch effort to keep it inside.

'Shhh,' Ben whispered. 'For Christ's sake, Bev –'

Crrrrackk. Louder this time.

'Will it hold?' she whispered back.

'It might, if he doesn't fart,' Ben said, and a moment later Belch *did* cut one – a loud and fruity trumpet-blast that seemed to go on for at least three seconds. They held each other even tighter, muffling each other's frantic giggles. Beverly's head hurt so badly that she thought she might soon have a stroke.

Then, faintly, she heard Henry yelling Belch's name.

'*What?*' Belch bellowed, getting up with a thump and a thud that sifted more dirt down on Ben and Beverly. '*What, Henry?*'

Henry yelled something back; Beverly could only make out the words *bank* and *bushes.*

'*Okay!*' Belch bawled, and his feet crossed the cap for the last time. There was a final cracking noise, this one much louder, and a splinter of wood landed in Bev's lap. She picked it up wonderingly.

'Five more minutes,' Ben said in a low whisper. 'That's all it would have taken.'

'Did you hear him when he let go?' Beverly asked, beginning to giggle again.

'Sounded like World War III,' Ben said, also beginning to laugh.

It was a relief to be able to let it out, and they laughed wildly, trying to do it in whispers.

Finally, unaware she was going to say it at all (and certainly not because it had any discernible bearing on this situation), Beverly said: 'Thank you for the poem, Ben.'

Ben stopped laughing all at once and regarded her gravely, cautiously. He took a dirty handkerchief from his back pocket and wiped his face with it slowly. 'Poem?'

'The haiku. The haiku on the postcard. You sent it, didn't you?'

'No,' Ben said. 'I didn't send you any haiku. Cause if a kid like me – a fat kid like me – did something like that, the girl would probably laugh at him.'

'I didn't laugh. I thought it was beautiful.'

'I could never write anything beautiful. Bill, maybe. Not me.'

'Bill will write,' she agreed. 'But he'll never write anything as nice as that. May I use your handkerchief?'

He gave it to her and she began to clean her face as best she could.

'How did you know it was me?' he asked finally.

'I don't know,' she said. 'I just did.'

Ben's throat worked convulsively. He looked down at his hands. 'I didn't mean anything by it.'

She looked at him gravely. 'You better not mean that,' she said. 'If you do, it's really going to spoil my day, and I'll tell you, it's going downhill already.'

He continued to look down at his hands and spoke at last in a voice she could barely hear. 'Well, I mean I love you, Beverly, but I don't want that to spoil anything.'

'It won't,' she said, and hugged him. 'I need all the love I can get right now.'

'But you specially like Bill.'

'Maybe I do,' she said, 'but that doesn't matter. If we were grown-ups, maybe it would, a little. But I like you all specially. You're the only friends I have. I love you too, Ben.'

'Thank you,' he said. He paused, trying, and brought it out. He was even able to look at her as he said it. 'I wrote the poem.'

They sat without saying anything for a little while. Beverly felt safe. Protected. The images of her father's face and Henry's knife seemed less vivid and threatening when they sat close like this. That sense of protection was hard to define and she didn't try, although much later she would recognize the source of its strength: she was in the arms of a male who would die for her with no hesitation at all. It was a fact that she simply knew: it was in the scent that came from his pores, something utterly primitive that her own glands could respond to.

'The others were coming back,' Ben said suddenly. 'What if they get caught out?'

She straightened up, aware that she had almost been dozing. Bill, she remembered, had invited Mike Hanlon home to lunch with him. Richie was going to go home with Stan and have sandwiches. And Eddie had promised to bring back his Parcheesi board. They would be arriving soon, totally unaware that Henry and his friends were in the Barrens.

'We've got to get to them,' Beverly said. 'Henry's not just after me.'

'If we come out and they come back –'

'Yes, but at least we *know* they're here. Bill and the other guys don't. Eddie can't even run, they already broke his arm.'

'Jeezum-crow,' Ben said. 'I guess we'll have to chance it.'

'Yeah,' She swallowed and looked at her Timex. It was hard to read in the dimness, but she thought it was a little past one. 'Ben . . .'

'What?'

'Henry's *really* gone crazy. He's like that kid in *The Blackboard Jungle*. He was going to kill me and the other two were going to help him.'

'Aw, no,' Ben said. 'Henry's crazy, but not *that* crazy. He's just . . .'

'Just what?' Beverly said. She thought of Henry and Patrick in the automobile graveyard in the thick sunshine. Henry's blank eyes.

Ben didn't answer. He was thinking. Things had changed, hadn't they? When you were inside the changes, they were harder to see. You had to step back to see them . . . you had to try, anyway. When school let out he'd been afraid of Henry, but only because Henry was bigger, and because he was a bully – the kind of kid who would grab a first-grader, Indian-rub his arm and send him away crying. That was about all. Then he had engraved Ben's belly. *Then* there had been the rockfight, and Henry had been chucking M-80s at people's heads. You could kill somebody with one of those things. You could kill somebody easy. He had started to look different . . . haunted, almost. It seemed that you always had to be on the watch for him, the way you'd always have to be on the watch for tigers or poisonous snakes if you were in the jungle. But you got used to it; so used to it that it didn't even seem unusual, just the way things were. But Henry *was* crazy, wasn't he? Yes. Ben had known that on the day school ended, and had willfully refused to believe it, or remember it. It wasn't the kind of thing you wanted to believe or remember. And suddenly a thought – a thought so strong it was almost a certainty – crept into his mind fullblown, as cold as October mud. *It's using Henry. Maybe the others too, but It's using them through Henry. And if that's the truth, then she's probably right. It's not just Indian rubs or rabbit-punches in the back of the neck during study-time near the end of the schoolday while Mrs Douglas reads her book at her desk, not just a push on the playground so that you fall down and skin your knee. If It's using him, then Henry will use the knife.*

'An old lady saw them trying to beat me up,' Beverly was saying. 'Henry went after *her*. He kicked her taillight out.'

This alarmed Ben more than anything else. He understood instinct-ively, as most kids did, that they lived below the sight-lines, and hence the thought-lines, of most adults. When a grownup was ditty-bopping down the street, thinking his grownup thoughts about work and appointments and buying cars and whatever else grownups thought about, he never noticed kids playing hopscotch or guns or kick-the-can or ring-a-levio or hide-and-go-seek. Bullies like Henry could get away with hurting other kids quite a lot if they were careful to stay below that sight-line. At the very most, a passing adult was apt to say something like, 'Why don't you quit that?' and then just continue ditty-bopping along without waiting to see if the bully stopped or not. So the bully would wait until the grownup had turned the corner . . . and then go back to business as usual. It was like adults thought that real life only started when a person was five feet tall.

If Henry had gone after some old lady, he had gone above that sight-line. And that more than anything else suggested to Ben that he really *was* crazy.

Beverly saw the belief in Ben's face and felt relief sweep over her. She would not have to tell him about how Mr Ross had simply folded his paper and walked into his house. She didn't want to tell him about that. It was too scary.

'Let's go up to Kansas Street,' Ben said, and abruptly pushed open the trapdoor. 'Get ready to run.'

He stood up in the opening and looked around. The clearing was silent. He could hear the chuckling voice of the Kenduskeag close by, birdsong, the thum-thud-thum-thud of a diesel engine snorting its way into the trainyards. He heard nothing else and that made him uneasy. He would have felt much better if he'd heard Henry, Victor, and Belch cursing their way through the heavy undergrowth down by the stream. But he couldn't hear them at all.

'Come on,' he said, and helped Beverly up. She also looked around uneasily, brushing her hair back with her hands and grimacing at its greasy feel.

He took her hand and they pushed through a screen of bushes toward Kansas Street. 'We'd better stay off the path.'

'No,' she said, 'we've got to hurry.'

He nodded. 'All right.'

They got to the path and started toward Kansas Street. Once she stumbled over a rock in the path and

7

fell heavily on the moon-silvered sidewalk. A grunt was forced out of him, and a runner of blood came with the grunt, splatting on the cracked concrete. In the moonlight it looked as black as beetle-blood. Henry looked at it for a long dazed moment, then raised his head to look around.

Kansas Street was early-morning silent, the houses shut up and dark except for a scatter of nightlights.

Ah. Here was a sewer-grate.

A balloon with a smiley-smile face was tied to one of its iron bars. It bobbed and dipped in the faint breeze.

Henry got to his feet again, one sticky hand pressed to his belly. The nigger had stuck him pretty good, but Henry had gone him one better. Yessir. As far as the nigger was concerned, Henry felt like he was pretty much okey-dokey.

'Kid's a gone goose,' Henry muttered, and made his shaky staggering way past the floating balloon. Fresh blood glimmered on his hand as it continued to flow from his stomach. 'Kid's all done. Greased the sucker. Gonna grease them all. Teach them to throw rocks.'

The world was coming in slow-rolling waves, big combers like the ones they used to show at the beginning of every *Hawaii Five-O* episode on the ward TV

(*book em Danno, ha-ha Jack Fuckin Lord okay. Jack Fuckin Lord was pretty much okey-dokey*)

and Henry could Henry could Henry could almost

(*hear the sound those Oahu big boys make as they rise curl and shake

(*shakeshakeshake

(*the reality of the world. 'Pipeline'. Chantays. Remember 'Pipeline'? 'Pipeline' was pretty much okey-dokey. 'Wipe-Out'. Crazy laugh there at the start. Sounded like Patrick Hockstetter. Fucking queerboy. Got greased himself and as far as I*)

he was concerned that was a

(*fuck of a lot better than okey-dokey, that was just FINE, that was JUST AS FINE AS PAINT*

(*okay* Pipeline *shoot the line don't back down not my boys catch a wave and

(*shoot

(*shootshootshoot

885

(a wave and go sidewalk surfin with me shoot
(the line shoot the world but keep)

an ear inside his head: it kept hearing that *ka-spanggg* sound; an eye inside his head: it kept seeing Victor's head rising on the end of that spring, eyelids and cheeks and forehead tattooed with rosettes of blood.

Henry looked blearily to his left and saw that the houses had been replaced with a tall, black stand of hedge. Looming above it was the narrow, gloomily Victorian pile of the Theological Seminary. Not a window shone light. The Seminary had graduated its last class in June of 1974. It had closed its doors that summer, and whatever walked there now walked alone . . . and only by permission of the chattering women's club that called itself the Derry Historical Society.

He came to the walk which led up to the front door. It was barred by a heavy chain from which a metal sign hung: NO TRESPASSIN THIS ORDER ENFORCED BY DERRY POLICE DEPT.

Henry's feet tangled on this track and he fell heavily again – *whap*! – to the sidewalk. Up ahead, a car turned onto Kansas Street from Hawthorne. Its headlights washed down the street. Henry fought the dazzle long enough to see the lights on top: it was a fuzzmobile.

He crawled under the chain and crabbed his way to the left so he was behind the hedge. The night-dew on his hot face was wonderful. He lay face down, turning his head from side to side, wetting his cheeks, drinking what he could drink.

The police car floated by without slowing.

Then, suddenly, its bubble-lights came on, washing the darkness with erratic blue pulses of light. There was no need for the siren on the deserted streets, but Henry heard its mill suddenly crank up to full revs. Rubber blistered a startled scream from the pavement.

Caught, I'm caught, his mind gibbered . . . and then he realized that the police-car was heading away from him, up Kansas Street. A moment later a hellish warbling sound filled the night, heading toward him from the south. He imagined some huge silky black cat loping through the dark, all green eyes and silky flexing pelt, It in a new shape, coming for him, coming to gobble him up.

Little by little (and only as the warbling began to veer away) he realized it was an ambulance, heading in the direction the fuzz-mobile had gone. He lay shuddering on the wet grass, too cold now, struggling

(fuzzit cousin buzzit cousin rock it roll it we got chicken in the barn what barn whose barn my)

not to vomit. He was afraid that if he vomited, all of his guts would come up . . . and there were five of them still to get.

Ambulance and police car. Where are they heading? The library, of course. The nigger. But they're too late. I greased him. Might as well turn off your sireen, boys. He ain't gonna hear it. He's just as dead as a fencepost. He —

But was he?

Henry licked his peeling lips with his arid tongue. If he was dead, there would be no warbling siren in the night like the cry of a wounded panther. Not unless the nigger had called them. So maybe — just *maybe* — the nigger wasn't dead.

'No,' Henry breathed. He rolled over on his back and stared up at the sky, at the billions of stars up there. It had come from there, he knew. From somewhere up in that sky . . . It

(came from outer space with a lust for Earthwomen came to rob all the women and rape all the men say Frank don't you mean rob all the men and rape all the women whoth running this show, thilly man, you or Jesse? Victor used to tell that one and that was pretty much)

came from the spaces between the stars. Looking up at that starry sky gave him the creeps: it was too big, too black. It was all too possible to imagine it turning blood-red, all too possible to imagine a Face forming in lines of fire . . .

He closed his eyes, shivering and holding his arms crossed on his belly, and he thought: *The nigger is dead. Someone heard us fighting and sent the cops to investigate, that's all.*

Then why the ambulance?

'Shut up, shut up,' Henry groaned. He felt the old baffled rage again; he remembered how they had beaten him again and again in the old days — old days that seemed so close and so vital now — how, every time, when he believed he had them, they had somehow slipped through his fingers. It had been like that on the last day, after Belch saw the bitch running down Kansas Street toward the Barrens. He remembered that, oh yes, he remembered that clearly enough. When you got kicked in the balls, you remembered it. IT happened to him again and again that summer.

Henry struggled to a sitting position, wincing at the deep dagger of pain in his guts.

Victor and Belch had helped him down into the Barrens. He had walked as fast as he could in spite of the agony that griped and pulled at his groin and the root of his belly. The time had come to finish it. They had followed the path to a clearing from which five or six paths radiated like strands of a spider-web. Yes, there had been kids playing around there; you didn't have to be Tonto to see that. There were scraps of candy-wrapper, the curled tail of a shot-off roll of Bang caps, red and black. A few boards and a fluffy scatter of sawdust, as if something had been built there.

He remembered standing in the center of the clearing and scanning the trees, looking for their baby treehouse. He would spot it and then he would climb up and the girl would be cowering there, and he would use the knife to cut her throat and feel her titties nice and easy until they stopped moving.

But he hadn't been able to see any treehouse; neither had Belch or Victor. The old familiar frustration rose in his throat. He and Victor left Belch to guard the clearing while they went down the river. But there had been no sign of her there, either. He remembered bending over and picking up a rock and

8

The Barrens/12:55 P.M.

heaving it far down the stream, furious and bewildered. 'Where the fuck did she go?' he demanded, wheeling toward Victor.

Victor shook his head slowly. 'Don't know,' he said. 'You're bleeding.'

Henry looked down and saw a dark spot, the size of a quarter, on the crotch of his jeans. The pain had withdrawn to a low, throbbing ache, but his underpants felt too small and too tight. His balls were swelling. He felt that anger inside him again, something like a knotted rope around his heart. *She* had done this.

'Where *is* she?' he hissed at Victor.

'Don't know,' Victor said again in that same dull voice. He seemed hypnotized, sunstruck, not really there at all. 'Ran away, I guess. She could be all the way over to the Old Cape by now.'

'She's not,' Henry said. 'She's hiding. They've got a place and she's hiding there. Maybe it's not a treehouse. Maybe it's something else.'

'What?'

'*I . . . don't . . . know!*' Henry shouted, and Victor flinched back.

Henry stood in the Kenduskeag, the cold water boiling over the tops of his sneakers, looking around. His eyes fixed on a cylinder poking out of the embankment about twenty feet downstream – a pumping-station. He climbed out of the water and walked down to it, feeling a sort of necessary dread settle into him. His skin seemed to be tightening, his eyes widening so that they were able to see more and more; it seemed he could feel the tiny hairs in his ears stirring and moving like kelp in an underwater tidal flow.

Low humming came from the pumping-station, and beyond it he could see a pipe jutting out of the embankment over the Kenduskeag. A steady flow of sludge pulsed out of the pipe and ran into the water.

He leaned over the cylinder's round iron top.

'Henry?' Victor called nervously. 'Henry? What you doing?'

Henry paid no attention. He put his eye to one of the round holes in the iron and saw nothing but blackness. He exchanged eye for ear.

'*Wait . . .*'

The voice drifted up to him from the blackness inside, and Henry felt his interior temperature plummet to zero, his veins and arteries freezing into crystal tubes of ice. But with these sensations came an almost unknown feeling: love. His eyes widened. A clownish smile spread his lips in a large nerveless arc. It was the voice from the moon. Now It was down in the pumping-station . . . down in the drains.

'*Wait . . . watch . . .*'

He waited, but there was no more: only the steady soporific drone of the pumping machinery. He walked back down to where Victor stood on the bank, watching him cautiously. Henry ignored him and hollered for Belch. In a little while Belch came.

'Come on,' he said.

'What are we gonna do, Henry?' Belch asked.

'Wait. Watch.'

They crept back toward the clearing and sat down. Henry tried to pull his underpants away from his aching balls, but it hurt too much.

'Henry, what –' Belch began.

'Shhh!'

Belch fell obligingly silent. Henry had Camels but he didn't share them out. He didn't want the bitch to smell cigarette smoke if she was around. He could have explained, but there was no need. The voice had only spoken two words to him, but they seemed to explain everything. They played down here. Soon the others would come back. Why settle for just the bitch when they could have all seven of the little shitepokes?

They waited and watched. Victor and Belch seemed to have gone to sleep with their eyes open. It was not a long wait, but there was time for Henry to think of a good many things. How he had found the switchblade this morning, for instance. It wasn't the same one he'd had on the last day of school; he'd lost that one somewhere. This one looked a lot cooler.

It came in the mail.

Sort of.

He had stood on the porch, looking at their battered leaning RFD box, trying to grasp what he was seeing. The box was decked with balloons. Two were tied to the metal hook where the postman sometimes hung packages; others were tied to the flag. Red, yellow, blue, green. It was as if some weird circus had crept by on Witcham Road in the dead of night, leaving this sign.

As he approached the mailbox, he saw there were faces on the balloons – the faces of the kids who had deviled him all this summer, the kids who seemed to mock him at every turn.

He had stared at these apparitions, gape-mouthed, and then the balloons popped, one by one. That had been good; it was as if he were making them pop just by thinking about it, killing them with his mind.

The front of the mailbox suddenly swung down. Henry walked toward it and peered in. Although the mailman didn't get this far out until the middle of the afternoon, he felt no surprise when he saw a flat rectangular package inside. He pulled it out. MR HENRY BOWERS, RFD #2, DERRY, MAINE, the address read. There was even a return-address of sorts: MR ROBERT GRAY, DERRY, MAINE.

He opened the package, letting the brown paper drift down heedlessly by his feet. There was a white box inside. He opened it. Lying on a bed of white cotton had been the switchknife. He took it into the house.

His father was lying on his pallet in the bedroom they shared, surrounded by empty beer cans, his belly bulging over the top of his yellow underpants. Henry knelt beside him, listening to the snort and flutter of his father's breathing, watching his father's horsy lips purse and pucker with each breath.

Henry placed the business-end of the switchknife against his father's scrawny neck. His father moved a little and then settled back into beery sleep again. Henry kept the knife like that for almost five minutes, his eyes distant and thoughtful, the ball of his left thumb caressing the silver button set into the switchblade's neck. The voice from the moon spoke to him – it whispered like the spring wind which is warm with a cold blade buried somewhere in its middle, it buzzed like a paper nest full of roused hornets, it huckstered like a hoarse politician.

Everything the voice said seemed pretty much okey-dokey to Henry and so he pushed the silver button. There was a *click* inside the knife as the suicide-spring let go, and six inches of steel drove through Butch Bowers's neck. It went in as easily as the tines of a meat-fork into the breast of a well-roasted chicken. The tip of the blade popped out on the other side, dripping.

Butch's eyes flew open. He stared at the ceiling. His mouth dropped open. Blood ran from the corners of it and down his cheeks toward the lobes of his ears. He began to gurgle. A large blood-bubble formed between his slack lips and popped. One of his hands crept to Henry's knee and squeezed convulsively. Henry didn't mind. Presently the hand fell away. The gurgling noises stopped a moment later. Butch Bowers was dead.

Henry pulled the knife out, wiped it on the dirty sheet that covered his father's pallet, and pushed the blade back in until the spring clicked again. He looked at his father without much interest. The voice had told him about the day's work while he knelt beside Butch with the knife against Butch's neck. The voice had explained everything. So he went into the other room to call Belch and Victor.

Now here they were, all three, and although his balls still ached horribly, the knife made a comforting bulge in his left front pants pocket. He felt that the cutting would begin soon. The others would come back down to resume whatever baby game they had been playing, and then the cutting would begin. The voice from the moon had laid it out for him as he knelt by his father, and on his way into town he had been unable to take his eyes from that pale ghost-disc in the sky. He saw that there was indeed a man in the moon – a grisly glimmering ghost-face with cratered holes for eyes and a glabrous grin that seemed to reach halfway up Its cheekbones. It talked

(*we float down here Henry we all float you'll float too*)

all the way to town. *Kill them all, Henry*, the ghost-voice from the moon said, and Henry could dig it; Henry felt he could second that emotion. He would kill them all, his tormentors, and then those feelings – that he was losing his grip, that he was coming inexorably to a larger world he would not be able to dominate as he had dominated the playyard at Derry Elementary, that in the wider world the fat-boy and the nigger and the stuttering freak might somehow grow larger while he somehow only grew older – would be gone.

He would kill them all, and the voices – those inside and the one which spoke to him from the moon – would leave him alone. He would kill them and then go back to the house and sit on the back porch with his father's souvenir Jap sword across his lap. He would drink one of his father's Rheingolds. He would listen to the radio, too, but no baseball. Baseball was strictly Squaresville. He would listen to rock and roll instead. Although Henry didn't know it (and wouldn't have cared if he did), on this one subject he and the Losers agreed: rock and roll was pretty much okey-dokey. *We got chicken in the barn, whose barn, what barn, my barn.* Everything would be good then; everything would be the ginchiest then; everything would be okeyfine then and anything which might come next would not matter. The voice would take care of him – he sensed that. If you took care of It, It would take care of you. That was how things had always been in Derry.

But the kids had to be stopped, stopped soon, stopped today. The voice had told him so.

Henry took his new knife out of his pocket, looked at it, turned it this way and that, admiring the way the sun winked and slid off the chrome facing. Then Belch was grabbing his arm and hissing: 'Look that, Henry! Jeezly-old-crow! Look that!'

Henry looked and felt the clear light of understanding burst over him. A square section of the clearing was rising as if by magic, revealing a growing slice of darkness beneath. For just a moment he felt a jolt of terror as it occurred to him that this might be the owner of the voice . . . for surely It lived somewhere under the city. Then he heard the gritty squall of dirt in the hinges and understood. They hadn't been able to see the treehouse because there was none.

'By God, we was standin right on top of em,' Victor grunted, and as Ben's head and shoulders appeared in the square hatchway in the center of the clearing, he made as if to charge forward. Henry grabbed him and held him back.

'Ain't we gonna get em, Henry?' Victor asked as Ben boosted himself up. Both of them were puffing and blowing.

'We'll get em,' Henry said, never taking his eyes from the hated fat-boy. Another ball-kicker. *I'll kick your balls so high up you can wear them for earrings, you fat fuck. Wait and see if I don't.* 'Don't worry.'

The fat-boy was helping the bitch out of the hole. She looked around doubtfully, and for a moment Henry believed she looked right at him. Then her eyes passed on. The two of them murmured together and then they pushed their way into the thick undergrowth and were gone.

'Come on,' Henry said, when the sound of snapping branches and rustling leaves had faded almost to inaudibility. 'We'll follow em. But keep back and keep quiet. I want em all together.'

The three of them crossed the clearing like soldiers on patrol, bent low, their eyes wide and moving. Belch paused to look down into the clubhouse and shook his head in admiring wonder. 'Sittin right over their heads, I was,' he said.

Henry motioned him forward impatiently.

They took the path, because it was quieter. They were halfway back to Kansas Street when the bitch and the fat-boy, holding hands (*isn't that cute?* Henry thought in a kind of ecstasy), emerged almost directly in front of them.

Luckily, their backs were to Henry's group, and neither of them looked around. Henry, Victor, and Belch froze, then drew into the shadows at the side of the path. Soon Ben and Beverly were just two shirts seen through a tangle of shrubs and bushes. The three of them began to pursue again . . . cautiously. Henry took the knife out again and

9

Henry Gets a Lift/2:30 A.M.

pressed the chrome button in the handle. The blade popped out. He looked at it dreamily in the moonlight. He liked the way the starlight ran along the blade. He had no idea exactly what time it was. He was drifting in and out of reality now.

A sound impinged on his consciousness and began to grow. It was a car engine. It drew closer. Henry's eyes widened in the dark. He held the knife more tightly, waiting for the car to pass by.

It didn't. It drew up at the curb beyond the seminary hedge and simply stopped there, engine idling. Grimacing (his belly was stiffening now; it had gone board-hard, and the blood seeping sluggishly between his fingers had the consistency of sap just before you took the taps out of the maples in late March or early April), he got on his knees and pushed aside the stiff hedge-branches. He could see headlights and the shape of a car. Cops? His hand squeezed the knife and relaxed, squeezed and relaxed, squeezed and relaxed.

I sent you a ride, Henry, the voice whispered. *Sort of a taxi, if you can dig that. After all, we have to get you over there to the Town House pretty soon. The night's getting old.*

The voice uttered one thin bonelike chuckle and fell silent. Now the only sounds were the crickets and the steady rumble of the idling car. *Sounds like cherry-bomb mufflers*, Henry thought distractedly.

He got awkwardly to his feet and worked his way back to the seminary walk. He peeked around at the car. Not a fuzzmobile: no bubbles on the roof, and the shape was all wrong. The shape was . . . *old*.

Henry heard that giggle again . . . or perhaps it was only the wind.

He emerged from the shadow of the hedge, crawled under the chain, got to his feet again, and began to walk toward the idling car, which existed in a black-and-white Polaroid-snapshot world of bright moonlight and impenetrable shadow. Henry was a mess: his shirt was black with blood, and it had soaked through his jeans almost to the knees. His face was a white blotch under an institutional crewcut.

He reached the intersection of the seminary path and the sidewalk and peered at the car, trying to make sense out of the hulk behind the wheel. But it was the car he recognized first – it was the one his father always swore he would own someday, a 1958 Plymouth Fury. It was red and white and Henry knew (hadn't his father told him often enough?) that the engine rumbling under the hood was a V-8 327. Available horsepower of 255, able to hit seventy from the git-go in just about nine seconds, gobbling hi-test through its four-barrel carb. *I'm gonna get that car and then when I die they can bury me in it*, Butch had been fond of saying . . . except, of course, he had never gotten the car and the state had buried him after Henry had been taken away, raving and screaming of monsters, to the funny farm.

If that's him inside I don't think I can take it, Henry thought, squeezing down on the knife, swaying drunkenly back and forth, looking at the shape behind the wheel.

Then the passenger door of the Fury swung open, the dome-light came on, and the driver turned to look at him. It was Belch Huggins. His face was a hanging ruin. One of his eyes was gone, and a rotted hole in one parchment cheek revealed blackened teeth. Perched on Belch's head was the New York Yankees baseball cap he had been wearing the day he died. It was turned around backward. Gray-green mold oozed along the bill.

'Belch!' Henry cried, and agony ripped its way up from his belly, making him cry out again, wordlessly.

Belch's dead lips stretched in a grin, splitting open in whitish-gray bloodless folds. He held one twisted hand out toward the open door in invitation.

Henry hesitated, then shuffled around the Fury's grille, allowing one hand to touch the V-shaped emblem there, just as he had always

894

touched it when his father took him into the Bangor showroom when he was a kid to look at this same car. As he reached the passenger side, grayness overwhelmed him in a soft wave and he had to grab the open door to keep his feet. He stood there, head down, breathing in snuffling gasps. At last the world came back – partway, anyhow – and he was able to work his way around the door and fall into the seat. Pain skewered his guts again, and fresh blood squirted out into his hand. It felt like warm jelly. He put his head back and gritted his teeth, the cords on his neck standing out. At last the pain began to subside a little.

The door swung shut by itself. The domelight went out. Henry saw one of Belch's rotted hands close over the transmission lever and drop it into drive. The bunched white knots of Belch's knuckles glimmered through the decaying flesh of his fingers.

The Fury began to move down Kansas Street toward Up-Mile Hill.

'How you doin, Belch?' Henry heard himself say. It was stupid, of course – Belch couldn't be here, dead people couldn't drive cars – but it was all he could think of.

Belch didn't reply. His one sunken eye stared at the road. His teeth glared sickly at Henry through the hole in his cheek. Henry became vaguely aware that ole Belch smelled pretty ripe. Ole Belch smelled, in fact, like a bushel-basket of tomatoes that had gone bad and watery.

The glove compartment flopped open, banging Henry's knees, and in the light of the small bulb inside he saw a bottle of Texas Driver, half-full. He took it out, opened it, and had himself a good shot. It went down like cool silk and hit his stomach like an explosion of lava. He shuddered all over, moaning . . . and then began to feel a little better, a little more connected to the world.

'Thanks,' he said.

Belch's head turned toward him. Henry could hear the tendons in Belch's neck; the sound was like the scream of rusty screen-door hinges. Belch regarded him for a moment with a dead one-eyed stare, and Henry realized for the first time that most of Belch's nose was gone. It looked like something had been at the ole Belcher's nose. Dog, maybe. Or maybe rats. Rats seemed more likely. The tunnels they had chased the little kids into that day had been full of rats.

Moving just as slowly, Belch's head turned toward the road again. Henry was glad. Ole Belch staring at him that way, well, Henry hadn't

895

been able to dig it too much. There had been something in Belch's single sunken eye. Reproach? Anger? What?

There is a dead boy behind the wheel of this car.

Henry looked down at his arm and saw that huge goosebumps had formed there. He quickly had another snort from the bottle. This one hit a little easier and spread its warmth farther.

The Plymouth rolled down Up-Mile Hill and made its way around the counter-clockwise traffic circle . . . except at this time of night there was no traffic; all the traffic-lights had changed to yellow blinkers splashing the empty streets and closed buildings with steady pulses of light. It was so quiet that Henry could hear the relays clicking inside each light . . . or was that his imagination?

'Never meant to leave you behind that day, Belcher,' Henry said. 'I mean, if that was, you know, on your mind.'

That scream of dried tendons again. Belch looking at him again with his one sunken eye. And his lips stretched in a terrible grin that revealed gray-black gums which were growing their own garden of mold. *What sort of a grin is that?* Henry asked himself as the car purred silkily up Main Street, past Freese's on the one side, Nan's Luncheonette and the Aladdin Theater on the other. *Is it a forgiving grin? An old-pals grin? Or is it the kind of grin that says I'm going to get you, Henry, I'm going to get you for running out on me and Vic? What kind of grin?*

'You have to understand how it was,' Henry said, and then stopped. How *had* it been? It was all confused in his mind, the pieces jumbled up like the pieces of a jigsaw puzzle that had just been dumped out on one of the shitty cardtables in the rec room at Juniper Hill. How *had* it been, exactly? They had followed the fatboy and the bitch back to Kansas Street and had waited back in the bushes, watching them climb up the embankment to the top. If they had disappeared from view, he and Victor and Belch would have dropped the stalking game and simply gone after them; two of them were better than none at all, and the rest would be along in time.

But they hadn't disappeared. They had simply leaned against the fence, talking and watching the street. Every now and then they would check down the slope into the Barrens, but Henry kept his two troops well out of sight.

The sky, Henry remembered, had become overcast, clouds moving in from the east, the air thickening. There would be rain that afternoon.

What had happened next? What –

A bony, leathery hand closed over his forearm and Henry

screamed. He had been drifting away again into that cottony grayness, but Belch's dreadful touch and the dagger of pain in his stomach from the scream brought him back. He looked around and Belch's face was less than two inches from Henry's; he gasped in breath and wished he hadn't. The ole Belcher really had gone to seed. Henry was again reminded of tomatoes going quietly putrescent in some shadowy shed corner. His stomach roiled.

He remembered the end suddenly – the end for Belch and Vic, anyway. How something had come out of the darkness as they stood in a shaft with a sewer-grating at the top, wondering which way to go next. *Something* . . . Henry hadn't been able to tell what. Until Victor shrieked, '*Frankenstein! It's Frankenstein!*' And so it was, it was the Frankenstein monster, with bolts coming out of its neck and a deep stitched scar across its forehead, lurching along in shoes like a child's blocks.

'*Frankenstein!*' Vic had screamed, '*Fr –*' And then Vic's head was gone, Vic's head was flying across the shaftway to strike the stonework of the far side with a sour sticky thud. The monster's watery yellow eyes had fallen on Henry, and Henry had frozen. His bladder let go and he felt warmth flood down his legs.

The creature lurched toward him, and Belch . . . Belch had . . .

'Listen, I know I ran,' Henry said. 'I shouldn't have done that. But . . . but . . .'

Belch only stared.

'I got lost,' Henry whispered, as if to tell the ole Belcher that he had paid, too. It sounded weak, like saying *Yeah, I know you got killed, Belch, but I got one* fuck *of a splinter under my thumbnail.* But it *had* been bad . . . really bad. He had wandered around in a world of stinking darkness for hours, and finally, he remembered, he had started to scream. At some point he had fallen – a long, dizzying fall, in which he had time to think *Oh good in a minute I'll be dead, I'll be out of this* – and then he had been in fast-running water. Under the Canal, he supposed. He had come out into fading sunlight, had flailed his way toward the bank, and had finally climbed out of the Kenduskeag less than fifty yards from the place where Adrian Mellon would drown twenty-six years later. He slipped, fell, bashed his head, blacked out. When he woke up it was after dark. He had somehow found his way out to Route 2 and had hooked a ride to the home place. And there the cops had been waiting for him.

But that was then and this was now. Belch had stepped in front of Frankenstein's monster and it had peeled the left side of his face down to the skull – so much Henry had seen before fleeing. But now Belch was back, and Belch was pointing at something.

Henry saw that they had pulled up in front of the Derry Town House, and suddenly he understood perfectly. The Town House was the only real hotel left in Derry. Back in '58 there had also been the Eastern Star at the end of Exchange Street, and the Traveller's Rest on Torrault Street. Both had disappeared during urban renewal (Henry knew all about this; he had read the Derry *News* faithfully every day in Juniper Hill). Only the Town House was left, and a bunch of ticky-tacky little motels out by the Interstate.

That's where they'll be, he thought. *Right in there. All of them that are left. Asleep in their beds, with visions of sugarplums – or sewers, maybe – dancing in their heads. And I'll get them. One by one, I'll get them.*

He took the bottle of Texas Driver out again and bit off a snort. He could feel fresh blood trickling into his lap, and the seat was tacky beneath him, but the wine made it better; the wine seemed to make it not matter. He could have done with some good bourbon, but the Driver was better than nothing.

'Look,' he said to Belch, 'I'm sorry I ran. I don't know why I ran. Please . . . don't be mad.'

Belch spoke for the first and only time, but the voice wasn't his voice. The voice that came from Belch's rotting mouth was deep and powerful, terrifying. Henry whimpered at the sound of it. It was the voice from the moon, the voice of the clown, the voice he had heard in his dreams of drains and sewers where water rushed on and on.

'Just shut up and get them,' the voice said.

'Sure,' Henry whined. 'Sure, okay, I *want* to, no problem –'

He put the bottle back in the glove compartment. Its neck chattered briefly like teeth. And he saw a paper where the bottle had been. He took it out and unfolded it, leaving bloody fingerprints on the corners. Embossed across the top was this logo, in bright scarlet:

A MEMO FROM PENNYWISE!

Below this, carefully printed in capital letters:

BILL DENBROUGH	311
BEN HANSCOM	404
EDDIE KASPBRAK	609
BEVERLY MARSH	518
RICHIE TOZIER	217

Their room numbers. That was good. That saved time. 'Thanks, Be –'

But Belch was gone. The driver's seat was empty. There was only the New York Yankees baseball cap lying there, mold crusted on its bill. And some slimy stuff on the knob of the gearshift.

Henry stared, his heart beating painfully in his throat . . . and then he seemed to hear something move and shift in the back seat. He got out quickly, opening the door and almost falling to the pavement in his haste. He gave the Fury, which still burbled softly through its dual cherry-bomb mufflers (cherry-bombs had been outlawed in the State of Maine in 1962), a wide berth.

It was hard to walk; each step pulled and tore at his belly. But he gained the sidewalk and stood there, looking at the eight-floor brick building which, along with the library and the Aladdin Theater and the seminary, was one of the few he remembered clearly from the old days. Most of the lights on the upper floors were out now, but the frosted-glass globes which flanked the main doorway blazed softly in the darkness, haloed with moisture from the lingering groundfog.

Henry made his laborious way toward and between them, shouldering open one of the doors.

The lobby was wee-hours silent. There was a faded Turkish rug on the floor. The ceiling was a huge mural, executed in rectangular panels, which showed scenes from Derry's logging days. There were overstuffed sofas and wing chairs and a great fireplace which was now dead and silent, a birch log thrown across the andirons – a real log, no gas; the fireplace in the Town House was not just a piece of lobby stage dressing. Plants spilled out of low pots. The glass double doors leading to the bar and the restaurant were closed. From some inner office, Henry could hear the gabble of a TV, turned low.

He lurched across the lobby, his pants and shirt streaked with blood. Blood was grimed into the folds of his hands; it ran down his cheeks and slashed his forehead like warpaint. His eyes bulged from their sockets. Anyone in the lobby who had seen him would have run, screaming, in terror. But there was no one.

The elevator doors opened as soon as he pushed the UP button. He looked at the paper in his hand, then at the floor buttons. After a moment of deliberation, he pushed 6 and the doors closed. There was a faint hum of machinery as the elevator began to rise.

Might as well start at the top and work my way down.

He slumped against the rear wall of the car, eyes half-closed. The hum of the elevator was soothing. Like the hum of the machinery in the pumping-stations of the drainage system. That day: it kept coming back to him. How everything seemed almost prearranged, as if all of them were just playing parts. How Vic and the ole Belcher had seemed . . . well, almost drugged. He remembered –

The car came to a stop, jolting him and sending another wave of griping pain into his stomach. The doors slid open. Henry stepped out into the silent hallway (more plants here, hanging ones, spiderplants, he didn't want to touch any of them, not those oozy green runners, they reminded him too much of the things that had been hanging down there in the dark). He rechecked the paper. Kaspbrak was in 609. Henry started down that way, running one hand along the wall for support, leaving a faint bloody track on the wallpaper as he went (ah, but he stepped away whenever he came close to one of the hanging spiderplants; he wanted no truck with those). His breathing was harsh and dry.

Here it was. Henry pulled the switchblade from his pocket, swashed his dry lips with his tongue, and knocked on the door. Nothing. He knocked again, louder this time.

'Whozit?' Sleepy. Good. He'd be in his 'jammies, only half-awake. And when he opened the door, Henry would drive the switchblade directly into the hollow at the base of his neck, the vulnerable hollow just below the adam's apple.

'Bellboy, sir,' Henry said. 'Message from your wife.' Did Kaspbrak have a wife? Maybe that had been a stupid thing to say. He waited, coldly alert. He heard footsteps – the shuffle of slippers.

'From Myra?' He sounded alarmed. Good. He would be more alarmed in a few seconds. A pulse beat steadily in Henry's right temple.

'I guess so, sir. There's no name. It just says your wife.'

There was a pause, then a metallic rattle as Kaspbrak fumbled with the chain. Grinning, Henry pushed the button on the switchblade's handle. *Click.* He held the blade up by his cheek, ready. He heard the thumb-bolt turn. In just a moment he would plunge the blade into the skinny little creep's throat. He waited. The door opened and Eddie

10

The Losers All Together/1:20 P.M.

saw Stan and Richie just coming out of the Costello Avenue Market, each of them eating a Rocket on a push-up stick. 'Hey!' he shouted. 'Hey, wait up!'

They turned around and Stan waved. Eddie ran to join them as quickly as he could, which was not, in truth, very quickly. One arm was immured in a plaster-of-Paris cast and he had his Parcheesi board under the other.

'Whatchoo say, Eddie? Whatchoo say, boy?' Richie asked in his grandly rolling Southern Gentleman Voice (the one that sounded more like Foghorn Leghorn in the Warner Brothers cartoons than anything else). 'Ah say . . . Ah say . . . the boy's got a broken ahm! Lookit that, Stan, the boy's got a broken ahm! Ah say . . . be a good spote and carreh the boy's Pawcheeseh bo-wud for him!'

'I can carry it,' Eddie said, a little out of breath. 'How about a lick on your Rocket?'

'Your mom wouldn't approve, Eddie,' Richie said sadly. He began to eat faster. He had just gotten to the chocolate stuff in the middle, his favorite part. '*Germs*, boy! Ah say . . . Ah say you kin get germs eatin after someone else!'

'I'll chance it,' Eddie said.

Reluctantly, Richie held his Rocket up to Eddie's mouth . . . and snatched it away quickly as soon as Eddie had gotten in a couple of moderately serious licks.

'You can have the rest of mine, if you want,' Stan said. 'I'm still full from lunch.'

'Jews don't eat much,' Richie instructed. 'It's part of their religion.' The three of them were walking along companionably enough now, headed up toward Kansas Street and the Barrens. Derry seemed lost in a deep hazy afternoon doze. The blinds of most of the houses they passed were pulled down. Toys stood abandoned on lawns, as if their owners had been hastily called in from play or put down for naps. Thunder rumbled thickly in the west.

'Is it?' Eddie asked Stan.

'No, Richie's just pulling your leg,' Stan said. 'Jews eat as much as normal people.' He pointed at Richie. 'Like him.'

'You know, you're pretty fucking mean to Stan,' Eddie told Richie. 'How would you like somebody to say all that made-up shit about you, just because you're a Catholic?'

'Oh, Catholics do plenty,' Richie said. 'My dad told me once that Hitler was a Catholic, and Hitler killed billions of Jews. Right, Stan?'

'Yeah, I guess so,' Stan said. He looked embarrassed.

'My mom was *furious* when my dad told me that,' Richie went on. A little reminiscent grin had surfaced on his face. 'Absolutely fyoo-rious.

Us Catholics also had the Inquisition, that was the little dealie with the rack and the thumbscrews and all that stuff. I figure all religions are pretty weird.'

'Me too,' Stan said quietly. 'We're not Orthodox, or anything like that. I mean, we eat ham and bacon. I hardly even know what being a Jew is. I was born in Derry, and sometimes we go up to synagogue in Bangor for stuff like Yom Kippur, but –' He shrugged.

'Ham? Bacon?' Eddie was mystified. He and his mom were Methodists.

'Orthodox Jews don't eat stuff like that,' Stan said. 'It says something in the Torah about not eating anything that creeps through the mud or walks on the bottom of the ocean. I don't know exactly how it goes. But pigs are supposed to be out, also lobster. But my folks eat them. I do too.'

'That's weird,' Eddie said, and burst out laughing. 'I never heard of a religion that told you what you could *eat*. Next thing, they'll be telling you what kind of gas you can buy.'

'Kosher gas,' Stan said, and laughed by himself. Neither Richie nor Eddie understood what he was laughing about.

'You gotta admit, Stanny, it *is* pretty weird,' Richie said. 'I mean, not being able to eat a sausage just because you happen to be Jewish.'

'Yeah?' Stan said. 'You eat meat on Fridays?'

'Jeez, no!' Richie said, shocked. 'You can't eat meat on Friday, because –' He began to grin a little. 'Oh, okay, I see what you mean.'

'Do Catholics really go to hell if they eat meat on Fridays?' Eddie asked, fascinated, totally unaware that, until two generations before, his own people had been devout Polish Catholics who would no more have eaten meat on Friday than they would have gone outside with no clothes on.

'Well, I'll tell you what, Eddie,' Richie said. 'I don't really think God would send me down to the Hot Place just for forgetting and having a baloney sandwich for lunch on a Friday, but why take a chance? Right?'

'I guess not,' Eddie said. 'But it seems so –' *So stupid*, he was going to say, and then he remembered a story Mrs Portleigh had told the Sunday-school class when he was just a little kid – a first-grader in Little Worshippers. According to Mrs Portleigh, a bad boy had once stolen some of the communion bread when the tray was passed and put it in his pocket. He took it home and threw it into the toilet bowl just to see what would happen. At once – or so Mrs Portleigh reported to her rapt Little Worshippers – the water in the toilet bowl had turned a bright red. It was the Blood of Christ, she said, and it had appeared to that little boy because he had done a very bad act called a BLASPHEMY. It had appeared to warn him that, by throwing the flesh of Jesus into the toilet, he had put his immortal soul in danger of Hell.

Up until then, Eddie had rather enjoyed the act of communion, which he had only been allowed to take since the previous year. The Methodists used Welch's grape juice instead of wine, and the Body of Christ was represented by cut-up cubes of fresh, springy Wonder Bread. He liked the idea of taking in food and drink as a religious rite. But following Mrs Portleigh's story, his awe of the ritual darkened into something more potent, something rather dreadful. Simply reaching for the cubes of bread became an act which required courage, and he always feared an electrical shock . . . or worse, that the bread would suddenly change color in his hand, become a blood-clot, and a disem-bodied Voice would begin to thunder in the church: *Not worthy! Not worthy! Damned to Hell! Damned to Hell!* Often, after he had taken communion, his throat would close up, his breath would begin to wheeze in and out, and he would wait with panicky impatience for the benediction to be over so he could hurry into the vestibule and use his aspirator.

You don't want to be so silly, he told himself as he grew older. *That was nothing but a story, and Mrs Portleigh sure wasn't any saint — Mamma said she was divorced down in Kittery and that she plays Bingo at Saint Mary's in Bangor, and that* real *Christians don't gamble, real Christians leave gambling for pagans and Catholics.*

All that made perfect sense, but it didn't relieve his mind. The story of the communion bread that turned the water in the toilet bowl to blood worried at him, gnawed at him, even caused him to lose sleep. It came to him one night that the way to get this behind him once and for all would be to take a piece of the bread himself, toss it in the toilet, and see what happened.

But such an experiment was far beyond his courage; his rational mind could not stand against that sinister image of the blood spreading its cloud of accusation and potential damnation in the water. It could not stand against that talismanic magical incantation: *This is my body, take, eat; this is my blood, shed for you and for many.*

No, he had never made the experiment.

'I guess all religions are weird,' Eddie said now. But *powerful*, his mind added, almost *magical* . . . or was that BLASPHEMY? He began to think about the thing they had seen on Neibolt Street, and for the first time he saw a crazy parallel – the Werewolf had, after all, come out of the toilet.

'Boy, I guess everybody's asleep,' Richie said, tossing his empty Rocket-tube nonchalantly into the gutter. 'You ever see it so quiet? What, did everybody go to Bar Harbor for the day?'

'H-H-H-Hey you guh-guh-guys!' Bill Denbrough shouted from behind them. 'Wuh-Wuh-hait up!'

Eddie turned, delighted as always to hear Big Bill's voice. He was wheeling Silver around the corner of Costello Avenue, outdistancing Mike, although Mike's Schwinn was almost brand-new.

'*Hi-yo Silver, AWAYYYY!*' Bill yelled. He rolled up to them doing perhaps twenty miles an hour, the playing cards clothes-pinned to the fender-struts roaring. Then he back-pedalled, locked the brakes, and produced an admirably long skid-mark.

'Stuttering Bill!' Richie said. 'Howaya, boy? Ah say . . . Ah say . . . how *aw* you, boy?'

'I'm o-o-okay,' Bill said. 'Seen Ben or Buh-Buh-heverly?'

Mike rode up and joined them. Sweat stood out on his face in little drops. 'How fast does that bike go, anyway?'

Bill laughed. 'I d-d-don't nuh-know, e-exactly. Pretty f-f-fast.'

'I haven't seen them,' Richie said. 'They're probably down there, hanging out. Singing two-part harmony. "Sh-boom, sh-boom . . . yada-da-da-da-da-da . . . you look like a dream, shweetheart."'

Stan Uris made throwing-up noises.

'He's just jealous,' Richie said to Mike. 'Jews can't sing.'

'Buh-buh-buh –'

'"Beep-beep, Richie,"' Richie said for him, and they all laughed.

They started toward the Barrens again, Mike and Bill pushing their bikes. Conversation was brisk at first, but then it lagged. Looking at Bill, Eddie saw an uneasy look on his face, and he thought that maybe the quiet was getting to him, too. He knew Richie had meant it as a joke, but it really *did* seem that everyone in Derry had gone to Bar Harbor for the day . . . to *somewhere*. Not a car moved on the street; there wasn't a single old lady pushing a carrier full of groceries back to her house or apartment.

'Sure is quiet, isn't it?' Eddie ventured, but Bill only nodded.

They crossed to the Barrens side of Kansas Street, and then they saw Ben and Beverly, running toward them, shouting. Eddie was shocked by Beverly's appearance; she was usually so neat and clean, her hair always washed and tied back in a pony-tail. Now she was streaked with what looked like every kind of gluck in the universe.

Her eyes were wide and wild. There was a scratch on one cheek. Her jeans were caked with crap and her blouse was torn.

Ben fell behind her, puffing, his stomach wobbling.

'Can't go down in the Barrens,' Beverly was panting. 'The boys . . . Henry . . . Victor . . . they're down there somewhere . . . the knife . . . he has a knife . . .'

'Sluh-slow down,' Bill said, taking charge at once in that effortless, almost unconscious way of his. He glanced at Ben as he ran up, his cheeks flushed bright, his considerable chest heaving.

'She says Henry's gone crazy, Big Bill,' Ben said.

'Shit, you mean he used to be *sane?*' Richie asked, and spat between his teeth.

'Sh-Shut uh-up, Ruh-Richie,' Bill said, and then looked back at Beverly. 'Teh-Tell,' he said. Eddie's hand crept into his pocket and touched his aspirator. He didn't know what all this was, but he already knew it wasn't good.

Forcing herself to speak as calmly as possible, Beverly managed to get out an edited version of the story – a version that began with Henry, Victor, and Belch catching up to her on the street. She didn't tell them about her father – she was desperately ashamed of that.

When she was finished Bill stood silent for a moment, hands in his pockets, chin down, Silver's handlebars leaning against his chest. The others waited, throwing frequent glances at the railing that ran along the edge of the dropoff. Bill thought for a long time, and no one interrupted him. Eddie became aware, suddenly and effortlessly, that this might be the final act. That was how the day's silence felt, wasn't it? The feeling that the whole town had up and left, leaving only the deserted husks of buildings behind.

Richie was thinking about the picture in George's album that had suddenly come to life.

Beverly was thinking about her father, how pale his eyes had been.

Mike was thinking about the bird.

Ben was thinking about the mummy, and a smell like dead cinnamon.

Stan Uris was thinking of bluejeans, black and dripping, and hands as white as wrinkled paper, also dripping.

'Cuh-Cuh-Come oh-oh-on,' Bill said at last. 'W-We're going d-d-down.'

'Bill –' Ben said. His face was troubled. 'Beverly said Henry was really *crazy*. That he meant to kill –'

905

'Ih-It's nuh-not *theirs*,' Bill said, gesturing at the green dagger-shaped slash of the Barrens to their right and below them – the underbrush, the choked groves of trees, the bamboo, the glint of water. 'Ih-Ih-It's not their *pruh-pruh-hopperty*.' He looked around at them, his face grim. 'I'm t-t-tired of b-being scuh-schuh-hared by them. We b-b-beat them in the ruh-rockfight, and if we h-h-have to beat them a-a-again, we'll duh-duh-do it.'

'But Bill,' Eddie said, 'what if it's not just *them*?'

Bill turned to Eddie, and with real shock Eddie saw how tired and drawn Bill's face was – there was something frightening about that face, but it wasn't until much, much later, as an adult drifting toward sleep after the meeting at the library, that he understood what that frightening thing was: it was the face of a boy driven close to the brink of madness, a boy who was perhaps ultimately no more sane or in control of his own decisions than Henry was. Yet the essential Bill was still there, looking out of those haunted scarified eyes . . . an angry, determined Bill.

'Well,' he said, 'whuh-whuh-what if it's *nuh-nuh-not*?'

No one answered him. Thunder boomed, closer now. Eddie looked at the sky and saw the stormclouds moving in from the west in black thunderheads. It was going to rain a bitch, as his mother sometimes said.

'Nuh-nuh-how I'll t-t-tell you what,' Bill said, looking at them. 'None of you have to guh-guh-go w-with me if you d-don't want to. That's uh-uh-up to you.'

'I'll go along, Big Bill,' Richie said quietly.

'Me too,' Ben said.

'Sure,' Mike said with a shrug.

Beverly and Stan agreed, and Eddie last.

'I don't think so, Eddie,' Richie said. 'Your arm's not, you know, looking too cool.'

Eddie looked at Bill.

'I w-w-want h-him,' Bill said. 'You w-w-walk with muh-muh-me, Eh-Eh-Eddie. I'll keep an eye on yuh-you.'

'Thanks, Bill,' Eddie said. Bill's tired, half-crazy face seemed suddenly lovely to him – lovely and well loved. He felt a dim sense of amazement. *I'd die for him, I guess, if he told me to. What kind of power is that? If it makes you look like Bill looks now, it's maybe not such a good power to have.*

'Yeah, Bill's got the ultimate weapon,' Richie said. 'BO bombs.' He raised his left arm and fluttered his right hand under the exposed armpit. Ben and Mike laughed a little, and Eddie smiled.

Thunder boomed again, close and loud enough this time to make them jump and huddle closer together. The wind was picking up, rattling trash around in the gutter. The first of the dark clouds sailed over the hazy ringed disc of the sun, and their shadows melted away. The wind was cold, chilling the sweat on Eddie's uncovered arm. He shivered.

Bill looked at Stan and said a peculiar thing then.

'You got your b-b-bird-book, Stan?'

Stan tapped his hip pocket.

Bill looked at them again. 'Let's g-g-go down,' he said.

They went down the embankment single-file except for Bill, who stayed with Eddie as he had promised. He allowed Richie to push Silver down, and when they had reached the bottom, Bill put his bike in its accustomed place under the bridge. Then they stood together, looking around.

The coming storm did not produce a darkness; not even, precisely, a dimness. But the quality of the light had changed, and things stood out in a kind of dreamlike steely relief: shadowless, clear, chiselled. Eddie felt a sinking of horror and apprehension in his guts as he realized why the quality of this light seemed so familiar – it was the same sort of light he remembered from the house at 29 Neibolt Street.

A streak of lightning tattooed the clouds, bright enough to make him wince. He put a hand up to his face and found himself counting: *One . . . two . . . three . . .* And then the thunder came in a single coughing bark, an explosive sound, a sound like an M-80 firecracker, and they drew even closer together.

'Wasn't any rain forecast this morning,' Ben said uneasily. 'The paper said hot and hazy.'

Mike was scanning the sky. The clouds up there were black-bottomed keelboats, high and heavy, swiftly overrunning the blue haze that had covered the sky from horizon to horizon when he and Bill came out of the Denbrough house after lunch. 'It's comin fast,' he said. 'Never saw a storm come so fast.' And as if in confirmation, thunder whacked again.

'C-C-Come on,' Bill said. 'L-Let's put Eh-Eh-Eddie's Parchee-hee-si board in the cluh-cluh-clubhouse.'

They started along the path they had beaten in the weeks since the incident of the dam. Bill and Eddie were at the head of the line, their shoulders brushing the broad green leaves of the shrubs, the others behind them. The wind gusted again, making the leaves on the trees and bushes whisper together. Farther ahead, the bamboo rattled eerily, like drums in a jungle tale.

'Bill?' Eddie said in a low voice.

'What?'

'I thought this was just in the movies, but . . .' Eddie laughed a little. 'I feel like somebody's watching me.'

'Oh, they're th-th-there, all r-r-right,' Bill said.

Eddie looked around nervously and held his Parcheesi board a little tighter. He

11

Eddie's Room/3:05 A.M.

opened the door on a monster from a horror comic.

A gore-streaked apparition stood there and it could only be Henry Bowers. Henry looked like a corpse which has returned from the grave. Henry's face was a frozen witch-doctor's mask of hate and murder. His right hand was cocked at cheek-level, and even as Eddie's eyes widened and he began to draw in his first shocked breath, the hand pistoned forward, the switchblade glittering like silk.

With no thought – there was no time; if he had stopped to think he would have died – Eddie slammed the door closed. It struck Henry's forearm, deflecting the knife's course so that it swung in a savage side-to-side arc less than an inch from Eddie's neck.

There was a crunch as the door pinched Henry's arm against the jamb. Henry uttered a muffled cry. His hand opened. The knife clattered to the floor. Eddie kicked it. It skittered under the TV.

Henry threw his weight against the door. He outweighed Eddie by over a hundred pounds and Eddie was driven back like a doll; his knees struck the bed and he fell on it. Henry came into the room and swept the door shut behind him. He twisted the thumb-bolt as Eddie sat up, wide-eyed, his throat already starting to whistle.

'Okay, fag,' Henry said. His eyes dropped momentarily to the floor, hunting for the knife. He didn't see it. Eddie groped on the night-table and found one of the two bottles of Perrier water he had ordered earlier that day. This was the full one; he had drunk the other before going to the library because his nerves were shot and he had a bad case of acid-burn. Perrier was very good for the digestion.

As Henry dismissed the knife and started toward him, Eddie gripped the green pear-shaped bottle by the neck and smashed it on the edge of the nighttable. Perrier foamed and fizzed across it, flooding out most of the pill-bottles that stood there.

Henry's shirt and pants were heavy with blood, both fresh and semi-dried. His right hand now hung at a strange angle.

'Babyfag,' Henry said, 'teach you to throw rocks.'

He made it to the bed and reached for Eddie, who still hardly realized what was happening. No more than forty seconds had elapsed since he had opened the door. Henry grabbed for him. Eddie thrust the ragged base of the Perrier bottle at him. It ripped into Henry's face, pulling open his right cheek in a twisted flap and puncturing Henry's right eye.

Henry uttered a breathless scream and staggered backward. His slit eye, leaking whitish-yellow fluid, hung loosely from its socket. His cheek sprayed blood in a gaudy fountain. Eddie's own cry was louder. He got off the bed and went toward Henry – to help him, perhaps, he wasn't really sure – and Henry lurched at him again. Eddie thrust with the Perrier bottle as if with a fencing sword, and this time the jagged points of green glass punched deep into Henry's left hand and sawed at his fingers. Fresh blood flowed. Henry made a thick grunting noise, the sound, almost, of a man clearing his throat, and shoved Eddie with his right hand.

Eddie flew back and struck the writing-desk. His left arm twisted behind him somehow and he fell on it heavily. The pain was a sudden sickening flare. He felt the bone go along the fault-line of that old break, and he had to clench his teeth against a scream of agony.

A shadow blotted out the light.

Henry Bowers was standing over him, swaying back and forth. His knees buckled. His left hand was dripping blood on the front of Eddie's robe.

Eddie had held onto the stump of the Perrier bottle and now, as Henry's knees came completely unhinged, he got it in front of him, jagged base pointing upward, the cap braced against his sternum. Henry came down like a tree, impaling himself on the bottle. Eddie felt it shatter in his hand and a fresh bolt of grinding agony shuddered through his left arm, which was still trapped under his body. Fresh warmth cascaded over him. He wasn't sure if this batch was Henry's blood or his.

Henry twitched like a landed trout. His shoes rattled an almost syncopated beat on the carpet. Eddie could smell his rotten breath. Then Henry stiffened and rolled over. The bottle protruded grotesquely from his midsection, capped end pointing toward the ceiling, as if it had grown there.

'*Gug*,' Henry said, and said no more. He looked up at the ceiling. Eddie thought he might be dead.

Eddie fought off the waves of faintness that wanted to cover him over and drag him down. He got to his knees, and finally to his feet. There was fresh pain as his broken arm swung out in front of him and that cleared his head a little. Wheezing, fighting for breath, he made it to the nighttable. He picked his aspirator out of a puddle of carbonated water, stuck it in his mouth, and triggered it off. He shuddered at the taste, then gave himself another blast. He looked around at the body on the carpet – could that be Henry? could it possibly be? It was. Grown old, his crewcut more gray than black, his body now fat and white and sluglike, it was still Henry. And Henry was dead. At long last, Henry was –

'*Gug*,' Henry said, and sat up. His hands clawed at the air, as if for holds which only Henry could see. His gouged eye leaked and dribbled; its bottom arc now bulged pregnantly down onto his cheek. He looked around, saw Eddie shrinking back against the wall, and tried to get up.

He opened his mouth and a stream of blood gushed out. Henry collapsed again.

Heart racing, Eddie fumbled for the telephone and succeeded only in knocking it off the table and onto the bed. He snatched it up and dialed 0. The phone rang again and again and again.

Come on, Eddie thought, *what are you doing down there, jacking off? Come on, please, answer the frigging phone!*

It rang again and again. Eddie kept his eyes on Henry, expecting him to start trying to gain his feet again at any moment. Blood. Dear God, so much blood.

'Desk,' a fuzzy, resentful voice said at last.

'Ring Mr Denbrough's room,' Eddie said. 'Quick as you can.' With his other ear he was now listening to the rooms around him. How loud had they been? Was someone going to pound on the door and ask if everything was all right in there?

'You sure you want me to ring?' the clerk asked. 'It's ten after three.'

'Yes, *do* it!' Eddie nearly screamed. The hand holding the phone was trembling in convulsive little bursts. There was a nest of waspy, rotten-ugly singing in his other arm. Had Henry moved again? No; surely not.

'Okay, okay,' the clerk said. 'Cool your jets, my friend.'

There was a click, and then the hoarse burr of a room-phone ringing. *Come on, Bill, come on, c –*

A sudden thought, gruesomely plausible, occurred to him. Suppose Henry had visited Bill's room first? Or Richie's? Ben's? Bev's? Or had Henry perhaps paid a visit to the library? Surely he had been *somewhere* else first; if someone hadn't softened Henry up, it would have been Eddie lying dead on the floor, with a switchblade growing out of his chest the way the neck of the Perrier bottle was growing out of Henry's gut. Or suppose Henry had visited *all* the others first, catching them bleary and half-asleep, as Henry had caught him? Suppose they were all dead? And that thought was so awful Eddie believed he would soon begin screaming if someone didn't answer the phone in Bill's room.

'Please, Big Bill,' Eddie whispered. 'Please be there, man.'

The phone was picked up and Bill's voice, uncharacteristically cautious, said: 'H-H-Hello?'

'Bill,' Eddie said . . . almost babbled. 'Bill, thank God.'

'Eddie?' Bill's voice grew momentarily fainter, speaking to someone else, telling the someone who it was. Then he was back strong. 'W-What's the muh-hatter, Eddie?'

'It's Henry Bowers,' Eddie said. He looked at the body on the floor again. Had it changed position? This time it was not so easy to persuade himself it hadn't. 'Bill, he came here . . . and I killed him. He had a knife. I think . . .' He lowered his voice. 'I think it was the same knife he had that day. When we went into the sewers. Do you remember?'

'I r-r-remember,' Bill said grimly. 'Eddie, listen to me. I want you to

12

The Barrens / 1:55 P.M.

g-g-go back and tell B-B-Ben to c-come up h-h-here.'

'Okay,' Eddie said, and dropped back at once. They were approaching the clearing now. Thunder rumbled in the overcast sky, and the bushes sighed in the rising breeze.

Ben joined him as they came into the clearing. The trapdoor to the clubhouse stood open, an improbable square of blackness in the green. The sound of the river was very clear, and Bill was suddenly struck by a crazy certainty: that he was experiencing that sound, and this place, for the last time in his childhood. He drew a deep breath, smelling earth and air and the distant sooty dump, fuming like a sullen volcano that cannot quite make up its mind to erupt. He saw a flock of birds fly off the railroad trestle and toward the Old Cape. He looked up at the boiling clouds.

'What is it?' Ben asked.

'Why h-h-haven't they tried to guh-guh-het u-us?' Bill asked. 'They're th-there. Eh-Eh-Eddie was ruh-hight about that. I can *fuh-fuh-heel* them.'

'Yeah,' Ben said. 'I guess they might be stupid enough to think we're going back into the clubhouse. Then they'd have us trapped.'

'Muh-muh-maybe,' Bill said, and he felt a sudden helpless fury at his stutter, which made it impossible for him to talk fast. Perhaps they were things he would have found impossible to say anyway – how he felt he could almost see through Henry Bowers's eyes, how he felt that, although on opposite sides, pawns controlled by opposing forces, he and Henry had grown very close.

Henry expected them to stand and fight.

It expected them to stand and fight.

And be killed.

A chilly explosion of white light seemed to fill his head. They would be victims of the killer that had been stalking Derry ever since George's death – all seven of them. Perhaps their bodies would be found, perhaps not. It all depended on whether or not It could or would protect Henry – and, to a lesser degree, Belch and Victor. *Yes. To the outside, to the rest of this town, we'll have been victims of the killer. And that's right, in a funny sort of way that really is right. It wants us dead. Henry's the tool to get it done so It doesn't have to come out. Me first, I think – Beverly and Richie might be able to hold the others, or Mike, but Stan's scared, and so's Ben, although I think he's stronger than Stan. And Eddie's got a broken arm. Why did I lead them down here? Christ! Why did I?*

'Bill?' Ben said anxiously. The others joined them beside the clubhouse. Thunder whacked again, and the bushes began to rustle more urgently. The bamboo rattled on in the fading stormy light.

'Bill –' It was Richie now.

'Shhh!' The others fell uneasily silent under his blazing haunted eyes.

He stared at the underbrush, at the path twisting away through it and back toward Kansas Street, and felt his mind suddenly go up another notch, as if to a higher plane. There was no stuttering in his mind; he felt as if his thoughts had been borne away on a mad flow of intuition – as if everything were coming to him.

George at one end, me and my friends at the other. And then it will stop

(*again*)

again, yes, again, because this has happened before and there always has to be some sacrifice at the end, some terrible thing to stop it, I don't know how I can know that but I do . . . and they . . . they . . .

'They luh-luh-let it happen,' Bill muttered, staring wide-eyed at the ratty pigtail of path. 'Shuh-Shuh-Sure they d-d-do.'

'Bill?' Bev asked, pleading. Stan stood on one side of her, small and neat in a blue polo shirt and chinos. Mike stood on the other, looking at Bill intensely, as if reading his thoughts.

They let it happen, they always do, and things quiet down, things go on, It . . . It . . .

(*sleeps*)

sleeps . . . or hibernates like a bear . . . and then it starts again, and they know . . . people know . . . they know it has to be so *It* can be.

'I luh-luh-luh-l-l-l –'

Oh please God oh please God he thrusts his fists please God against the posts let me get this out the posts and still insists oh God oh Christ OH PLEASE LET ME BE ABLE TO TALK!

'I l-l-led you d-down huh-here b-b-b-b-because nuh-nuh-noplace is s-s-safe,' Bill said. Spittle blabbered from his lips; he wiped them with the back of one hand. '*Duh-Duh-Derry* is It. D-D-Do you uh-uh-understand m-m-me?' He glared at them; they drew away a little, their eyes shiny, almost thanotropic with fright. '*Duh-herry is Ih-Ih-It!* Eh-Eh-hennyp-p-place we g-g-go . . . when Ih-Ih-It g-g-gets uh-us, they w-w-wuh-hon't *suh-suh-see*, they w-w-won't *huh-huh-hear*, they w-w-won't *nuh-nuh-know*.' He looked at them, pleading. 'Duh-don't y-y-you suh-see h-how it ih-ih-is? A-A-All we c-c-can duh-duh-do is to t-t-try and fuh-hinish w-what w-w-w-we stuh-harted.'

Beverly saw Mr Ross getting up, looking at her, folding his paper, and simply going into his house. *They won't see, they won't hear, they won't know. And my father*

(*take those pants off slutchild*)

had meant to kill her.

Mike thought of lunch with Bill. Bill's mother had been off in her own dreamy world, seeming not to see either of them, reading a

Henry James novel while the boys made sandwiches and gobbled them standing at the counter. Richie thought of Stan's neat but utterly empty house. Stan had been a little surprised; his mother was almost always home at lunchtime. On the few occasions when she wasn't, she left a note saying where she could be reached. But there had been no note today. The car was gone, and that was all. 'Probably went shopping with her friend Debbie,' Stan said, frowning a little, and had set to work making egg-salad sandwiches. Richie had forgotten about it. Until now. Eddie thought of his mother. When he had gone out with his Parcheesi board there had been none of the usual cautions: *Be careful, Eddie, get under cover if it rains, Eddie, don't you dare play any rough games, Eddie.* She hadn't asked if he had his aspirator, hadn't told him what time to be home, hadn't warned him against 'those rough boys you play with.' She had simply gone on watching her soap-opera story on TV, as if he didn't exist.

As if he didn't exist.

A version of the same thought went through all of the boys' minds: they had, at some point between getting up this morning and lunch-time, simply become ghosts.

Ghosts.

'Bill,' Stan said harshly, 'if we cut across? Through the Old Cape?'

Bill shook his head. 'I don't thuh-thuh-hink s-s-so. We'd g-g-get c-c-caught in the buh-buh-bam-b-b-boo . . . the quh-quh-quick-m-mud . . . or there'd b-b-be ruh-ruh-real p-p-p-pirahna fuh-fuh-fish in the K-K-Kenduskeag . . . o-o-or suh-suh -homething e-e-else.'

Each had his or her own different vision of the same end. Ben saw bushes which suddenly became man-eating plants. Beverly saw flying leeches like the ones that had come out of that old refrigerator. Stan saw the mucky ground in the bamboo vomiting up the living corpses of children caught in there by the fabled quickmud. Mike Hanlon imagined small Jurassic reptiles with horrid sawteeth suddenly boiling out of the cleft of a rotten tree, attacking them, biting them to pieces. Richie saw the Crawling Eye oozing down on top of them as they ran under the railroad trestle. And Eddie saw them climbing the Old Cape embankment only to look up and see the leper standing at the top, his sagging flesh acrawl with beetles and maggots, waiting for them.

'If we could get out of town somehow . . .' Richie muttered, then winced as thunder shouted a furious negative from the sky. More rain fell — it was still only squalling, but soon it would begin to come down seriously, in sheets and torrents. The day's hazy peace was now utterly gone, as if it had never been at all. 'We'd be safe if we could just get out of this fucking town.'

Beverly began: 'Beep-b –' And then a rock came flying out of the shaggy bushes and struck Mike on the side of the head. He staggered backward, blood flowing through the tight cap of his hair, and would have fallen if Bill hadn't caught him.

'Teach you to throw rocks!' Henry's voice floated mockingly to them.

Bill could see the others looking around, wild-eyed, ready to bolt in six different directions. And if they did that, it really would be over.

'B–B–Ben!' he said sharply.

Ben looked at him. 'Bill, we gotta run. They –'

Two more rocks flew out of the bushes. One struck Stan on the upper thigh. He yelled, more surprised than hurt. Beverly sidestepped the second. It struck the ground and rolled through the clubhouse trapdoor.

'D–D–Do you r-r-ruh-remember the f-f-first duh-day you c-c-came d-down here?' Bill shouted over the thunder. 'The d-d-d-day schuh-hool l-let ow-out?'

'Bill –' Richie shouted.

Bill thrust a shushing hand at him; his eyes remained fixed on Ben, pinning him to the spot.

'Sure,' Ben said, miserably trying to look in all directions at once. The bushes were now wavering and dancing wildly, their motion nearly tidal.

'The druh-druh-drain,' Bill said. 'The p-p-pumping-stuh-hation. Thah-that's where we're suh-suh-hupposed to g-g-go. Take us there!'

'But –'

'Tuh-tuh-take us th-there!'

A fusillade of rocks whizzed out of the bushes and for a moment Bill saw Victor Criss's face, somehow frightened, drugged, and avid all at the same time. Then a rock smashed into his cheekbone and it was Mike's turn to keep Bill from falling down. For a moment he couldn't see straight. His cheek felt numb. Then sensation returned in painful throbs and he felt blood running down his face. He swiped at his cheek, wincing at the painful knob that was rising there, looked at the blood, wiped it on his jeans. His hair whipped wildly in the freshening wind.

'Teach you to throw rocks, you stuttering asshole!' Henry half-laughed, half-screamed.

'Tuh-Tuh-Take us!' Bill yelled. He understood now why he had

sent Eddie back to get Ben; it was that pumping-station they were supposed to go to, *that very one*, and only Ben knew exactly which one it was – they ran along both banks of the Kenduskeag at irregular intervals. 'Ih-ih-hit's the pluh-pluh-hace! The w-w-way ih-in! The wuh-wuh-wuh-way to It!'

'Bill, you can't *know* that!' Beverly cried.

He shouted furiously at her – at all of them: 'I *know*!'

Ben stood there for a moment, wetting his lips, looking at Bill. Then he struck off across the clearing, heading toward the river. A brilliant bolt of lightning streaked across the sky, purplish-white, followed by a rip of thunder that made Bill reel on his feet. A fist-sized chunk of rock sailed past his nose and struck Ben's buttocks. He yipped with pain and his hand went to the spot.

'*Yaah, fatboy!*' Henry cried in that same half-laughing, half-screaming voice. The bushes rustled and crashed and Henry appeared as the rain stopped fooling around and came in a downpour. Water ran in Henry's crewcut, in his eyebrows, down his cheeks. His grin showed all his teeth. 'Teach you to throw r –'

Mike had found one of the pieces of scrapwood left over from building the clubhouse roof and now he threw it. It flipped over twice and struck Henry's forehead. He screamed, clapped one hand to the spot like a man who's just had one hell of a good idea, and sat down hard.

'*Ruh-ruh-run!*' Bill hollered. 'A-After Buh-Buh-Ben!'

More crashings and stumblings in the bushes, and as the rest of the Losers ran after Ben Hanscom, Victor and Belch appeared, Henry stood up, and the three of them gave chase.

Even later, when the rest of that day had come back to Ben, he recalled only jumbled images of their run through the bushes. He remembered branches overloaded with dripping leaves slapping against his face, dousing him with cold water; he remembered that the thunder and lightning seemed to have become almost constant, and he remembered that Henry's screams for them to come back and fight seemed to merge with the sound of the Kenduskeag as they drew closer to it. Every time he slowed, Bill would whack him on the back to make him hurry up.

What if I can't find it? What if I can't find that particular pumping-station?

The breath tore in and out of his lungs, hot and bloody-tasting in the back of his throat. A stitch was sinking into his side. His buttocks sang where the rock had hit him. Beverly had said Henry and his friends meant to kill them, and Ben believed it now, yes he did.

He came to the Kenduskeag's bank so suddenly that he nearly plunged over the edge. He managed to get his balance, and then the embankment, undercut by the spring runoff, collapsed and he went tumbling over anyway, skidding all the way to the edge of the fast-running water, his shirt rucking up in the back, clayey mud streaking and sticking to his skin.

Bill piled into him and yanked him to his feet.

The others burst out of the bushes which overhung the bank one after the other. Richie and Eddie were last, Richie with one arm slung around Eddie's waist, his dripping specs clinging precariously to the end of his nose.

'*Wuh-Wuh-Where?*' Bill shouted.

Ben looked first left and then right, aware that the time was suicidally short. The river seemed higher already, and the rain-dark sky had given it a dangerous slate-gray color as it boiled its way along. Its banks were choked with underbrush and stunted trees, all of them now dancing to the wind's tune. He could hear Eddie sobbing for breath.

'*Wuh-wuh-where?*'

'I don't kn –' he began, and then he saw the leaning tree and the eroded cave beneath it. That was where he had hidden that first day. He had dozed off, and when he woke up he had heard Bill and Eddie goofing around. Then the big boys had come ... seen ... conquered. *Ta-ta, boys, it was a real baby dam, believe me.*

'There!' he shouted. 'That way!'

Lightning flashed again and this time Ben could *hear* it, a buzzing noise like an overloaded Lionel train-transformer. It struck the tree and blue-white electric fire sizzled its gnarly base into splinters and toothpicks sized for a fairytale giant. It fell toward the river with a rending crash, driving spray high into the air. Ben drew in a dismayed gasp and smelled something hot and punky and wild. A fireball rolled up the bole of the downed tree, seemed to flash brighter, and went out. Thunder exploded, not above them but *around* them, as if they stood in the center of the thunderclap. The rain sheeted down.

Bill thumped him on the back, awaking him from his dazed contemplation of these things. '*Guh-guh-GO!*'

Ben went, splashing and stumbling along the verge of the river, his hair hanging in his eyes. He reached the tree – the little root-cave beneath it had been obliterated – and climbed over it, digging his toes into its wet hide, scraping his hands and forearms.

Bill and Richie manhandled Eddie over, and as he stumbled off

917

the tree-trunk, Ben caught him. They both went tumbling to the ground. Eddie cried out.

'You all right?' Ben shouted.

'I guess so,' Eddie shouted back, getting to his feet. He fumbled for his aspirator and almost dropped it. Ben grabbed it for him and Eddie gave him a grateful look as he stuffed it into his mouth and triggered it.

Richie came over, then Stan and Mike. Bill boosted Beverly up onto the tree and Ben and Richie caught her coming down on the far side, her hair plastered to her head, her blue jeans now black.

Bill came last, pulling himself onto the trunk and swinging his legs around. He saw Henry and the other two splashing down the river toward them, and as he slid off the fallen tree he shouted: 'Ruh-ruh-rocks! Throw rocks!'

There were plenty of them here on the bank, and the lightning-struck tree made a perfect barricade. In a moment or two all seven of them were chucking rocks at Henry and his pals. They had nearly reached the tree; the range was point-blank. They were driven back, yelling with pain and fury, as rocks struck their faces, their chests, their arms and legs.

'Teach us to throw rocks!' Richie shouted, and chucked one the size of a hen's egg at Victor. It struck his shoulder and bounced almost straight up into the air. Victor howled. 'Ah say . . . Ah say . . . go on an teach us, boy! We learn *good*!'

'*Yeeeeh-aaaah!*' Mike screamed. 'How do you like it? How do you *like* it?'

The answer was not much. They retreated until they were out of range and huddled together. A moment later they climbed the bank, slipping and stumbling on the slick wet earth, which was already honeycombed with little running streamlets, holding onto branches to stay upright.

They disappeared into the underbrush.

'They're gonna go around us, Big Bill,' Richie said, pushing his glasses up on his nose.

'That's oh-oh-okay,' Bill said. 'G-Go on, B-B-Ben. We'll fuh-fuh-follow y-you.'

Ben trotted along the embankment, paused (expecting that Henry and the others would burst out into his face at any moment), and saw the pumping-station twenty yards farther down the streambed. The others followed him to it. They could see other cylinders on the opposite bank, one fairly close, the other forty yards upstream. Those two were both shooting torrents of muddy water into the Kenduskeag, but only a trickle was coming from the pipe sticking out of the embankment below this one. It wasn't humming, either, Ben noticed. The pumping machinery had broken down.

He looked at Bill thoughtfully . . . and with some fright.

Bill was looking at Richie, Stan, and Mike. 'W-W-We g-guh-hotta get the l-l-lid oh-oh-off,' he said. 'H-H-Help m-m-me.'

There were handholds in the iron, but the rain had made them slippery and the lid itself was incredibly heavy. Ben moved in next to Bill, and Bill shifted his hands a little to make room. Ben could hear water dripping inside – an echoey, unpleasant sound, like water dripping into a well.

'*Nuh-nuh-NOW!*' Bill shouted, and the five of them heaved in unison. The lid moved with an ugly grating sound.

Beverly grabbed on beside Richie and Eddie pushed with his good arm.

'One, two, three, *push!*' Richie chanted. The lid grated a little farther off the top of the cylinder. Now a crescent of darkness showed.

'One, two, three, *push!*'

The crescent fattened.

'One, two, three, *push!*'

Ben shoved until red spots danced in front of his eyes.

'Stand back!' Mike shouted. 'There it goes, there it goes!'

They stood away and watched as the big circular cap overbalanced, then fell. It dug a slash in the wet earth and landed upside down, like an oversized checker. Beetles scurried off its surface and into the matted grass.

'Uck,' Eddie said.

Bill peered inside. Iron rungs descended to a circular pool of black water, its surface now pocked with raindrops. The silent pump brooded in the middle of this, half-submerged. He could see water flowing into the pumping-station from the mouth of its inflow pipe, and with a sinking in his guts he thought: *That's where we have to go. In there.*

'Eh-Eh-Eh-Eddie. G-Grab on to m-m-me.'

Eddie looked at him, uncomprehending.

'Like a puh-puh-pigger-back. Hold on with y-your g-g-good ah-ah-arm.' He demonstrated.

Eddie understood but was reluctant.

'Quick!' Bill snapped. 'Th-Th-They'll *b-b-be* here!'

Eddie grabbed on around Bill's neck; Stan and Mike boosted him up so he could hook his legs around Bill's midsection. As Bill

919

swung clumsily over the lip of the cylinder, Ben saw that Eddie's eyes were tightly shut.

Over the rain, he could hear another sound: whipping branches, snapping twigs, voices. Henry, Victor, and Belch. The world's ugliest cavalry charge.

Bill gripped the rough concrete lip of the cylinder and felt his way down, step by careful step. The iron rungs were slippery. Eddie had him in what was almost a deathgrip, and Bill supposed he was getting a pretty graphic demonstration of what Eddie's asthma was really all about.

'I'm scared, Bill,' Eddie whispered.

'I-I-I am, too.'

He let go of the concrete rim and grabbed the topmost rung. Although Eddie was nearly choking him and felt as if he had already gained forty pounds, Bill paused a moment, looking at the Barrens, the Kenduskeag, the racing clouds. A voice inside – not a frightened voice, just a firm one – had told him to take a good look, in case he never saw the upper world again.

So he looked, then began to descend with Eddie clinging to his back.

'I can't hold on much longer,' Eddie managed.

'You w-w-won't have to,' Bill said. 'We're almost duh-hown.'

One of his feet went into chilly water. He felt for the next rung and found it. There was another below that and then the ladder ended. He was standing in knee-deep water beside the pump.

He squatted, wincing as the cold water soaked his pants, and let Eddie off. He drew a deep breath. The smell wasn't so hot, but it was great not to have Eddie's arm wrapped around his throat.

He looked up at the cylinder's mouth. It was about ten feet over his head. The others were grouped around the rim, looking down. 'C-C-Come on!' he shouted. 'Wuh-one at a t-t-time! Be quick!'

Beverly came first, swinging easily over the rim and grabbing the ladder, and Stan next. The others followed. Richie came last, pausing to listen to the progress of Henry and friends. He thought, from the sound of their blundering progress, that they would probably pass a little to the left of this pumping-station, but almost certainly not by enough to make a difference.

At that moment Victor bellowed: 'Henry! There! Tozier!'

Richie looked around and saw them rushing toward him. Victor was in the lead . . . and then Henry pushed him aside so savagely that

Victor skidded to his knees. Henry had a knife, all right, a regular pigsticker. Drops of water were falling from the blade.

Richie glanced into the cylinder, saw Ben and Stan helping Mike off the ladder, and swung over himself. Henry understood what he was doing and screamed at him. Richie, laughing crazily, slammed his left hand in the crook of his right elbow and stuck his forearm skyward, his hand fisted in what may be the world's oldest gesture. To be sure Henry got the point, he popped his middle finger up.

'*You'll die down there!*' Henry shouted.

'*Prove it!*' Richie shouted, laughing. He was terrified of going into this concrete throat, but he still couldn't stop laughing. And in his Irish Cop's Voice he bugled: 'Sure an begorrah, the luck of the Irish *nivver* runs out, me foine lad!'

Henry slipped on the wet grass and went sprawling on his butt less than twenty feet from where Richie stood, his feet on the top rung of the ladder bolted to the inner curve of the pumping-station, his head and chest out.

'*Hey, banana-heels!*' Richie shouted, delirious with triumph, and then scooted down the ladder. The iron rungs were slick and once he almost fell. Then Bill and Mike grabbed him and he was standing up to his knees in water with the rest of them in a loose circle around the pump. He was trembling all over, he felt hot and cold chills chasing each other up his back, and still he couldn't stop laughing.

'You should have seen him, Big Bill, clumsy as ever, still can't get out of his own frockin way –'

Henry's head appeared in the circular opening at the top. Scratches from branches and brambles crisscrossed his cheeks. His mouth was working, and his eyes blazed.

'Okay,' he shouted down at them. His words had a flat resonance inside the concrete cylinder, not quite an echo. 'Here I come. Got you now.'

He swung one leg over, felt for the topmost rung with his foot, found it, swung the other one over.

Speaking loud, Bill said: 'W-When h-h-he guh-gets d-d-down cluh-hose e-e-enough, w-w-we all gruh-grub-grab h-him. P-P-Pull h-him d-d-down. Duh-Duh-Duck him uh-under. G-G-Got i-it?'

'Right-o, guv'nor,' Richie said, and snapped a salute with one trembling hand.

'Got you,' Ben said.

Stan tipped a wink at Eddie, who didn't understand what was going on – except it seemed to him that Richie had gone crazy. He was laughing like a loon while Henry Bowers – the *dreaded* Henry Bowers – prepared to come down and kill them all like rats in a rain-barrel.

'All ready for him, Bill!' Stan cried.

Henry froze three rungs down. He looked down at the Losers over his shoulder. His face seemed, for the first time, doubtful.

Eddie suddenly got it. If they came down, they would have to come one at a time. It was too high to jump, especially with the pumping machinery to land on, and here they were, the seven of them, waiting in a tight little circle.

'Cuh-cuh-home oh-on, H-Henry,' Bill said pleasantly. 'Wuh-wuh-what are you w-w-waiting for?'

'That's right,' Richie chimed in. 'You like to beat up little kids, right? Come on, Henry.'

'We're waiting, Henry,' Bev said sweetly. 'I don't think you'll like it when you get down here, but come on if you want to.'

'Unless you're chicken,' Ben added. He began to make chicken sounds. Richie joined him at once and soon all of them were doing it. The derisive clucking rebounded between the damp, trickling walls. Henry looked down at them, the knife clutched in his left hand, his face the color of old bricks. He put up with perhaps thirty seconds of it and then climbed out again. The Losers sent up catcalls and insults.

'O-O-Okay,' Bill said. He spoke in a lower voice. 'W-We guh-got to get ih-ih-into that druh-hain. Quh-quh-quick.'

'Why?' Beverly asked, but Bill was spared the effort of an answer. Henry reappeared at the rim of the pumping-station and dropped a rock the size of a soccer ball into the pipe. Beverly screamed and Stan pulled Eddie against the circular wall with a hoarse yell. The rock struck the pumping machinery's rusty housing and produced a musical *bonggg*! It ricocheted left and struck the concrete wall, missing Eddie by less than half a foot. A chip of concrete flicked painfully against his cheek. The rock fell into the water with a splash.

'*Quh-quh-quick!*' Bill shouted again, and they crowded around the pumping-station's inflow pipe. Its bore was about five feet in diameter. Bill sent them in one after another (a vague circus image – all the big clowns coming out of the little car – passed across his consciousness in a meteoric flash; years later he would use the same image in a book called *The Black Rapids*), and climbed in last, after ducking another rock. As they watched, more rocks flew down, most striking the pump housing and rebounding at crazy angles.

When they stopped falling, Bill looked out and saw Henry coming down the ladder again, as quick as he could. '*G-G-Get h-h-him!*' he shouted to the others. Richie, Ben, and Mike floundered out behind Bill. Richie leaped high and grabbed Henry's ankle. Henry cursed and shook his leg as if trying to kick away a small dog with big teeth – a terrier, perhaps, or a Pekinese. Richie grabbed a rung, scrabbled up even higher, and actually did manage to sink his teeth into Henry's ankle. Henry screamed and pulled himself up quickly. One of his loafers came off and splashed into the water, where it sank with no ado at all.

'Bit me!' Henry was screaming. 'Bit me! Cocksucker bit me!'

'Yeah, good thing I had a tetanus shot this spring!' Richie flung at him.

'Bash them!' Henry was raving. 'Bash them, bomb them back to the stone age, bash their brains in!'

More rocks flew. The boys backed into the drain again quickly. Mike was struck on the arm by a small rock and he held it tight, wincing, until the pain began to abate.

'It's a standoff,' Ben said. 'They can't get down and we can't get up.'

'We're not s-supposed to get up,' Bill said quietly, 'and y-y-you all know it. W-We're nuh-hot e-ever supposed to g-g-get up a-again.'

They looked at him, their eyes hurt and afraid. No one said anything.

Henry's voice, fury masquerading as mockery, floated down: 'We can wait up here all day, you guys!'

Beverly had turned away and was looking back along the bore of the inflow pipe. The light grew diffuse quickly, and she could not see much. What she could see was a concrete tunnel, its lower third filled with rushing water. It was higher on her now than it had been when they first squeezed in here, she realized; that would be because this pump wasn't working and only some of the water was exiting on the Kenduskeag side. She felt claustrophobia touch her throat, turning the skin there to something that felt like flannel. If the water rose enough, they would drown.

'Bill, do we have to?'

He shrugged. It said everything. Yeah, they had to; what else was there? Be killed by Henry, Victor, and Belch in the Barrens? Or by something else – maybe something worse – in town? She understood his thought well enough now; there was no stutter in his shrug. Better for them to go to It. Have it out, like the showdown in a Western movie. Cleaner. Braver.

Richie said: 'What was that ritual you told us about, Big Bill? The one in the library book?'

'*Ch-Ch-Chüd*,' Bill said, smiling a little.

'*Chüd*.' Richie nodded. 'You bite Its tongue and It bites yours, right?'

'Ruh-ruh-right.'

'Then you tell jokes.'

Bill nodded.

'Funny,' Richie said, looking into the dark pipe, 'I can't think of a single one.'

'Me either,' Ben said. The fear was heavy in his chest, almost suffocating. He felt that the only thing keeping him from just sitting down in the water and blubbering like a baby – or just going crazy – was Bill's calm, sure presence . . . and Beverly. He felt he would rather die than show Beverly how afraid he was.

'Do you know where this pipe goes?' Stan asked Bill.

Bill shook his head.

'Do you know how to find It?'

Bill shook his head again.

'We'll know when we're getting close,' Richie said suddenly. He drew a deep, trembling breath. 'If we have to do it, then let's go.'

Bill nodded. 'I'll be f-f-first. Then Eh-Eddie. B-B-Ben. Bev. Stuh-han the M-M-Man. M-M-Mike. You luh-last, Rih-Richie. E-Everyone k-k-keep one h-h-hand on the shuh-houlder of the p-p-person in fruh-fruh-front of y-y-you. It's gonna be d-dark.'

'You coming out?' Henry Bowers shrieked down at them.

'We're gonna come out somewhere,' Richie muttered. 'I guess.'

They formed up like a procession of blindmen. Bill looked back once, confirming that each had a hand on the shoulder of the person ahead. Then, bending forward slightly against the rush of the current, Bill Denbrough led his friends into the dark where the boat he had made for his brother had gone almost a year before.

CHAPTER TWENTY
THE CIRCLE CLOSES

1

Tom

Tom Rogan was having one fuck of a crazy dream. In it he was killing his father.

Part of his mind understood how crazy this was; his father had died when Tom was only in the third grade. Well . . . maybe 'died' wasn't such a good word. Maybe 'committed suicide' was actually the truth. Ralph Rogan had made himself a gin-and-lye cocktail. One for the road, you might say. Tom had been put in nominal charge of his brother and sisters, and then he began to receive 'whuppins' if anything went wrong with them.

So he couldn't have killed his father . . . except there he was, in this frightening dream, holding what looked like a harmless handle of some sort to his father's neck . . . only it wasn't really harmless, was it? There was a button in the end of the handle, and if he pushed it a blade would pop out and go right through his father's neck. *I'm not going to do anything like that, Daddy, don't worry*, his dreaming mind thought just before his finger jammed down on the button and the blade popped out. His father's sleeping eyes opened and stared up at the ceiling; his father's mouth opened and a bloody gargling sound came out. *Daddy, I didn't do it!* his mind screamed. *Someone else –*

He struggled to wake up and couldn't. The best he could do (and it turned out to be not very good at all) was to fade into a new dream. In this one he was splashing and slogging his way down a long dark tunnel. His balls hurt and his face stung because it was crisscrossed with scratches. There were others with him, but he could only make out vague shapes. It didn't matter, anyway. What mattered were the kids somewhere up ahead. They needed to pay. They needed

(*a whuppin*)

to be punished.

Whatever purgatory this was, it was a smelly one. Water dripped and echoed. His shoes and pants were soaked. The little shitpots were somewhere up ahead in this maze of tunnels, and perhaps they thought

(*Henry*)

Tom and his friends would get lost, but the joke was on them

(*ha-ha all* over *you!*)

because he had another friend, oh yes, a special friend, and this friend had marked the path they were to take with . . . with . . .

(*Moon-Balloons*)

thingamajigs that were big and round and somehow lighted from within so that they shed a glow like that which falls mysteriously from oldfashioned streetlamps. One of these balloons floated and drifted at each intersection, and on the side of each was an arrow, pointing the way into the tunnel-branch he and

(*Belch and Victor*)

his unseen friends were to take. And it was the *right* path, oh yes: he could hear the others ahead, their splashing progress echoing back, the distorted murmurs of their voices. They were getting closer, catching up. And when they did . . . Tom looked down and saw that he still had the switchknife in his hand.

For a moment he was frightened – this was like one of those crazy astral experiences he sometimes read about in the weekly tabloids, when your spirit left your body and entered someone else's. The shape of his body felt different to him, as if he were not Tom but

(*Henry*)

someone else, someone younger. He began to fight his way out of the dream, panicked, and then a voice was talking to him, a soothing voice, whispering in his ear: *It doesn't matter* when *this is, and it doesn't matter who* you *are. What matters is that Beverly is up there, she's with them, my good friend, and do you know what? She's been doing something one hell of a lot worse than sneaking smokes. You know what? She's been fucking her old friend Bill Denbrough! Yes indeed! She and that stuttering freak, going right at it! They –*

That's a lie! he tried to scream. *She wouldn't dare!*

But he knew it was no lie. She had used a belt on his

(*kicked me in the*)

balls and run off and she now had cheated on him, the slutty

(*child*)

little roundheels bitch had actually *cheated* on him, and oh dear friends, oh good neighbors, she was going to get the whuppin of all whuppins – first her and then Denbrough, her novel-writing *friend*.

And anyone who tried to get in his way, you could count them in for a piece of the action, too.

He stepped up his pace, although the breath was already whistling in and out of his throat. Up ahead he could see another luminous circle bobbing in the darkness – another Moon-Balloon. He could hear the voices of the people ahead of him, and the fact that they were childish voices no longer bothered him. It was as the voice said: it didn't matter *where, when* or *who. Beverly* was up there, and oh dear friends, oh good neighbors –

'Come on, you guys, move your asses,' he said, and it didn't even matter that his voice wasn't his own but the voice of a boy.

Then, as they approached the Moon-Balloon, he looked around and saw his companions for the first time. Both of them were dead. One was headless. The face of the other had been split open, as if by a great talon.

'We're moving as fast as we can, Henry,' the boy with the split face said, and his lips moved in two pieces, grotesquely out of sync with each other, and that was when Tom shrieked the dream to pieces and came back to himself, tottering on the brink of what felt like some great empty space.

He struggled to keep his balance, lost it, and tumbled to the floor. The floor was carpeted but the fall still sent a sickening burst of pain through his hurt knee and he stifled another cry against his forearm.

Where am I? Where the fuck am I?

He became aware of a faint but clear white light, and for a frightening moment he thought he was back in the dream again, that it was light cast by one of those crazy balloons. Then he remembered leaving the bathroom door partially open and the fluorescent light in there on. He always left the light on when staying in a strange place; it saved you barking your shins if you had to get up in the night to pee.

That clicked reality into place. It had been a dream, all some crazy dream. He was in a Holiday Inn. This was Derry, Maine. He had chased his wife here, and, in the middle of a crazy nightmare, he had fallen out of bed. That was all; that was the long and the short of it.

That wasn't just a nightmare.

He jumped as if the words had been spoken beside his ear instead of inside his own mind. It didn't seem like his own interior voice at all – it was cold, alien . . . but somehow hypnotic and believable.

He got up slowly, fumbled a glass of water off the table beside the bed, and drank it down. He ran shaky hands through his hair. The clock on the table said ten past three.

Go back to sleep. Wait until morning.

That alien voice answered: *But there will be people around in the morning — too many people. And besides, you can* beat *them down there this time. This time you can be* first.

Down there? He thought of his dream: the water, the dripping dark.

The light suddenly seemed brighter. He turned his head, not wanting to but helpless to stop. A groan slipped out of his mouth. A balloon was tied to the knob of the bathroom door. It floated at the end of a string about three feet long. The balloon glowed, full of a ghostly white light; it looked like a will-o-the-wisp glimpsed in a swamp, floating dreamily between trees overhung with gray ropes of moss. An arrow was printed on the balloon's gently bulging skin, an arrow that was blood-scarlet.

It was pointing at the door leading out into the hall.

It doesn't really matter who I am, the voice said soothingly, and Tom realized now that it wasn't coming from either his own head or from beside his ear; it was coming from the balloon, from the center of that strange lovely white light. *All that matters is that I am going to see that everything turns out to your satisfaction, Tom. I want to see her take a whuppin; I want to see them all take a whuppin. They've crossed my path once too often . . . and much too late in the day for them. So listen, Tom. Listen very carefully. All together now . . . follow the bouncing ball . . .*

Tom listened. The voice from the balloon explained.

It explained everything.

When it was done, it popped in one final flash of light and Tom began to dress.

2

Audra

Audra also had nightmares.

She awoke with a start, sitting bolt-upright in bed, the sheet pulled around her waist, her small breasts moving with her quick, agitated breathing.

Like Tom's, her dreaming had been a jumbled, distressful experience. Like Tom, she had had the sensation of being someone else — or rather, of having her own consciousness deposited (and partially submerged) in another body and another mind. She had been in a dark place with a number of others around her, and she had been aware of an oppressive sensation of danger – they were going into the danger deliberately and she wanted to scream at them to stop, to explain to her what was happening . . . but the person with whom she had merged seemed to know, and to believe it was necessary.

She was also aware that they were being chased, and that their pursuers were catching up, little by little.

Bill had been in the dream, but his story about how he had forgotten his childhood must have been on her mind, because in her dream Bill was only a boy, ten or twelve years old – he still had all his hair! She was holding his hand, and was dimly aware that she loved him very much, and that her willingness to go on was based on the rock-solid belief that Bill would protect her and all of them, that Bill, Big Bill, would somehow bring them through this and back into the daylight again.

Oh but she was so terrified.

They came to a branching of many tunnels and Bill stood there, looking from one to the next, and one of the others – a boy with his arm in a cast which glimmered a ghostly-white in the darkness – spoke up: 'That one, Bill. The bottom one.'

'Y-Y-You're s-s-sure?'

'Yes.'

And so they had gone that way and then there had been a door, a wee wooden door no more than three feet high, the sort of door you might see in a fairytale book, and there had been a mark on the door. She could not remember what that mark had been, what strange rune or symbol. But it had brought all her terror to a focusing-point and she had yanked herself out of that other body, that girl's body, whoever

(*Beverly – Beverly*)

she might have been. She awoke bolt-upright in a strange bed, sweaty, wide-eyed, gasping as if she had just run a race. Her hands flew to her legs, half-expecting to find them wet and cold with the water she had been walking through in her head. But she was dry.

Disorientation followed – this was not their home in Topanga Canyon or the rented house in Fleet. It was noplace – limbo furnished with a bed, a dresser, two chairs, and a TV.

'Oh God, come on, Audra –'

She scrubbed her hands viciously across her face and that sickening feeling of mental vertigo receded. She was in Derry. Derry, Maine, where her husband had grown through a childhood he claimed no longer to remember. Not a familiar place to her, or a particularly good place by its feel, but at least a known place. She was here because Bill was here, and she would see him tomorrow, at the Derry Town House. Whatever terrible thing was wrong here, whatever those new scars on his hands meant, they would face it together. She would call him, tell him she was here, then join him. After that . . . well . . .

Actually, she had no idea what came after that. The vertigo, that sense of being in a place that was really noplace, was threatening again. When she was nineteen she had done a whistle-stop tour with a scraggy little production company, forty not-so-wonderful performances of *Arsenic and Old Lace* in forty not-so-wonderful towns and small cities. All of this in forty-seven not-so-wonderful days. They began at the Peabody Dinner Theater in Massachusetts and ended at Play It Again Sam in Sausalito. And somewhere in between, in some Midwestern town like Ames Iowa or Grand Isle Nebraska or maybe Jubilee North Dakota, she had awakened like this in the middle of the night, panicked by disorientation, unsure what town she was in, what day it was, or why she was wherever she was. Even her name seemed unreal to her.

That feeling was back now. Her bad dreams had carried over into her waking and she felt a nightmarish free-floating terror. The town seemed to have wrapped itself around her like a python. She could sense it, and the feelings it produced were not good. She found herself wishing that she had heeded Freddie's advice and stayed away.

Her mind fixed on Bill, grasping at the thought of him the way a drowning woman would grip at a spar, a life-preserver, anything that

(*we all float down here, Audra*)

floats.

A chill raced through her and she crisscrossed her arms across her naked breasts. She shivered and saw goosebumps ripple their way up her flesh. For a moment it seemed to her that a voice had spoken aloud, but inside her head. As if there was an alien presence in there.

Am I going crazy? God, is that it?

No, her mind responded. *It's just disorientation . . . jet-lag . . . worry over your man. Nobody's talking inside your head. Nobody –*

'We all float down here, Audra,' a voice said from the bathroom. It was a real voice, real as houses. And sly. Sly and dirty and evil. 'You'll float, too.' The voice uttered a fruity little giggle that dropped in pitch until it sounded like a clogged drain bubbling thickly. Audra cried out . . . then pressed her hands against her mouth.

I didn't hear that.

930

She said it out loud, daring the voice to contradict her. It didn't. The room was silent. Somewhere, far away, a train whistled in the night.

Suddenly she needed Bill so badly that waiting until daylight seemed impossible. She was in a standardized motel room exactly like the other thirty-nine units in the place, but suddenly it was too much. Everything. When you started hearing voices, it was just too much. Too creepy. She seemed to be slipping back into the nightmare she'd so lately escaped. She felt scared and terribly alone. *It's worse than that*, she thought. *I feel dead.* Her heart suddenly skipped two beats in her chest, making her gasp and utter a startled cough. She felt an instant of prison-panic, claustrophobia inside her own body, and wondered if all this terror didn't have a stupidly ordinary physical root after all: maybe she was going to have a heart attack. Or was already having one.

Her heart settled, but uneasily.

Audra turned on the light by the bed-table and looked at her watch. Twelve past three. He would be sleeping, but that didn't matter to her now – nothing mattered except hearing his voice. She wanted to finish the night with him. If Bill was beside her, her clockwork would fall in sync with his and settle down. The nightmares would stay away. He sold nightmares to others – that was his trade – but to her he had never given anything but peace. Outside that odd cold nut imbedded in his imagination, peace seemed to be all he was made for or meant for. She got the Yellow Pages, found the number for the Derry Town House, and dialed it.

'Derry Town House.'

'Would you please ring Mr Denbrough's room? Mr William Denbrough?'

'Does that guy ever get any calls in the daytime?' the clerk said, and before she could think to ask what *that* was supposed to mean, he had plugged her call through. The phone burred once, twice, three times. She could imagine him, sleeping with everything under the covers except the top of his head; she could imagine one hand coming out, feeling for the phone. She had seen him do it before, and a fond little smile touched her lips. It faded as the phone rang a fourth time . . . and a fifth, and a sixth. Halfway through the seventh ring, the connection was broken.

'That room does not answer.'

'No shit, Sherlock,' Audra said, more upset and frightened than ever. 'Are you sure you rang the right room?'

'Ayup,' the clerk said. 'Mr Denbrough had an inter-room call not five minutes ago. I know he answered that one, because the light stayed on the switchboard a minute or two. He must have gone to the person's room.'

'Well, which room was it?'

'I don't remember. Sixth floor, I think. But –'

She dropped the phone back into its cradle. A queer disheartening certainty came to her. It was a woman. Some woman had called him . . . and he had gone to her. Well, what now, Audra? How do we handle this?

She felt tears threaten. They stung her eyes and her nose; she could feel the lump of a sob in the back of her throat. No anger, at least not yet . . . only a sick sense of loss and abandonment.

Audra, get hold of yourself. You're jumping to conclusions. It's the middle of the night and you had a bad dream and now you've got Bill with some other woman. But it ain't necessarily so. What you're going to do is sit up – you'll never get back to sleep now anyway. Turn on some lights and finish the novel you brought to read on the plane. Remember what Bill says? Finest kind of dope. Book-Valium. No more heebie-jeebies. No more whim-whams and hearing voices. Dorothy Sayers and Lord Peter, that's the ticket. The Nine Tailors. That'll take you through to dawn. That'll –

The bathroom light suddenly went on; she could see it under the door. Then the latch clicked and the door juddered open. She stared at this, eyes widening, arms instinctively crossing over her breasts again. Her heart began to slam against her ribcage and the sour taste of adrenaline flooded her mouth.

That voice, low and dragging, said: 'We all float down here, Audra.' The last word became a long, low, fading scream – *Audraaaaa* – that ended once again in that sick, clogged, bubbly sound that was so much like laughter.

'Who's there?' she cried, backing away. That *wasn't my imagination, no way, you're not going to tell me that –*

The TV clicked on. She whirled around and saw a clown in a silvery suit with big orange buttons capering around on the screen. There were black sockets where its eyes should have been, and when its madeup lips stretched even wider in a grin, she saw teeth like razors. It held up a dripping, severed head. Its eyes were turned up to the whites and the mouth sagged open, but she could see well enough that it was Freddie Firestone's head. The clown laughed and danced. It swung the head around and drops of blood splashed against the inside of the TV screen. She could hear them sizzling in there.

Audra tried to scream and nothing came out but a little whine. She grabbed blindly for the dress lying over the back of the chair, and for her purse. She bolted into the hall and slammed the door behind her, gasping, her face paper-white. She dropped the purse between her feet and slipped the dress over her head.

'Float,' a low, chuckling voice said from behind her, and she felt a cold finger caress her bare heel.

She uttered another high out-of-breath scream and danced away from the door. White corpse-fingers were seeking back and forth under it, the nails peeled away to show purplish-white bloodless quicks. They made hoarse whispering noises on the rough nap of the hall carpet.

Audra snagged the strap of her purse and ran barefooted for the door at the end of the corridor. She was in a blind panic now, her only thought that she had to find the Derry Town House, and Bill. It didn't matter if he was in bed with enough other women to make up a harem. She would find him and get him to take her away from whatever unspeakable thing there was in this town.

She fled down the walkway and into the parking-lot, looking around wildly for her car. For a moment her mind froze and she couldn't even remember what she had been driving. Then it came: Datsun, tobacco-brown. She spotted it standing hubcap-deep in the still, curdled groundmist, and hurried over to it. She couldn't find the keys in her purse. She swept through it with steadily increasing panic, shuffling Kleenex, cosmetics, change, sun-glasses, and sticks of gum into a meaningless jumble. She didn't notice the battered LTD wagon parked nose-to-nose with her rented car, or the man sitting behind the wheel. She didn't notice when the LTD's door opened and the man got out; she was trying to cope with the growing certainty that she had left the Datsun's keys in the room. She couldn't go back in there; she *couldn't*.

Her fingers touched hard serrated metal under a box of Altoid mints and she seized at it with a little cry of triumph. For a terrible moment she thought it might be the key to their Rover, now sitting in the Fleet railway station's car-park three thousand miles away, and then she felt the lucite rental-car tab. She fumbled the key into the door-lock, breathing in harsh little gasps, and turned it. That was when a hand fell on her shoulder, and she screamed . . . screamed loudly this time. Somewhere a dog barked in answer, but that was all.

The hand, as hard as steel, bit cruelly in and forced her around. The face she saw looming over hers was puffed and lumpy. The eyes glittered. When the swelled lips spread in a grotesque smile, she saw

933

that some of the man's front teeth had been broken. The stumps looked jagged and savage.

She tried to speak and could not. The hand squeezed tighter, digging in.

'Haven't I seen you in the movies?' Tom Rogan whispered.

3

Eddie's Room

Beverly and Bill dressed quickly, without speaking, and went up to Eddie's room. On their way to the elevator they heard a phone-bell begin somewhere behind them. It was muffled, a somewhere-else sound.

'Bill, was that yours?'

'C-Could have b-b-been,' he said. 'One of the uh-others c-calling, muh-haybe.' He punched the UP button.

Eddie opened the door for them, his face white and strained. His left arm was at an angle both peculiar and weirdly evocative of old times.

'I'm okay,' he said. 'I took two Darvon. Pain's not bad right now.' But it was clearly not good, either. His lips, pressed so tightly together they had almost disappeared, were purple with shock.

Bill looked past him and saw the body on the floor. One look was enough to satisfy him of two things – it was Henry Bowers, and he was dead. He moved past Eddie and knelt by the body. The neck of a Perrier bottle had been driven into Henry's midsection, pulling the tatters of his shirt in after it. Henry's eyes were half-open, glazed. His mouth, filled with coagulating blood, snarled. His hands were claws.

A shadow fell over him and Bill looked up. It was Beverly. She looked down at Henry with no expression at all.

'All the times he ch-ch-chased us,' Bill said.

She nodded. 'He doesn't look old. You know that, Bill? He doesn't look old at all.' Abruptly she looked back at Eddie, who was sitting on the bed. *Eddie* looked old; old and haggard. His arm lay in his lap, useless. 'We've got to call the doctor for Eddie.'

'No,' Bill and Eddie said in unison.

'But he's hurt! His arm –'

'It's the same as luh-luh-last t-t-time,' Bill said. He got to his feet and held her by the arms, looking into her face. 'Once we g-go outside . . . once w-w-we ih-inv-v-holve the t-t-town –'

'They'll arrest me for murder,' Eddie said dully. 'Or they'll arrest all of us. Or they'll detain us. Or something. Then there'll be an accident. One of the special accidents that only happen in Derry. Maybe they'll stick us in jail and a deputy sheriff will go berserk and shoot us all. Maybe we'll all die of ptomaine, or decide to hang ourselves in our cells.'

'Eddie, that's crazy! That's –'

'Is it?' he asked. 'Remember, this is Derry.'

'But we're grownups now! Surely you don't think . . . I mean, he came here in the middle of the night . . . attacked you . . .'

'W-With what?' Bill said. 'Where's the nuh-nuh-knife?'

She looked around, didn't see it, and dropped on her knees to look under the bed.

'Don't bother,' Eddie said in that same faint, whistly voice. 'I slammed the door on his arm when he tried to stick me with it. He dropped it and I kicked it under the TV. It's gone now. I already looked.'

'B-B-Beheverly, c-call the others,' Bill said. 'I can spuh-splint E-E-Eddie's arm, I th-think.'

She looked at him for a long moment, then she looked down at the body on the floor again. She thought that the picture this room presented should tell a perfectly clear story to any policeman with half a brain. The place was a mess. Eddie's arm was broken. This man was dead. It was a clear case of self-defense against a night-prowler. And then she remembered Mr Ross. Mr Ross getting up and looking and then simply folding his newspaper and going back into the house.

Once we go outside . . . once we involve the town . . .

That made her remember Bill as a kid, his face white and tired and half-crazy. Bill saying *Derry is It. Do you understand me? . . . Any place we go . . . when It gets us, they won't see, they won't hear, they won't know. Don't you see how it is? All we can do is to try and finish what we started.*

Standing here now, looking down at Henry's corpse, Beverly thought: *They're both saying we've all become ghosts again. That it's started to repeat. All of it. As a kid I could accept that, because kids almost are ghosts. But –*

'Are you sure?' she asked desperately. 'Bill, are you *sure*?'

He was sitting on the bed with Eddie, gently touching his arm. 'A-A-Aren't y-you?' he asked. 'After a-a-all that's huh-happened t-today?'

Yes. All that had happened. The gruesome mess at the end of

their reunion. The beautiful old woman who had turned into a crone before her eyes,

(*my fadder was also my mudder*)

the round of stories at the library tonight with the accompanying phenomena. All of those things. And still . . . her mind shouted at her desperately to stop this now, to spike it with sanity, because if she did not they were surely going to finish up this night by going down to the Barrens and finding a certain pumping-station and –

'I don't know,' she said. 'I just . . . I don't know. Even after everything that's happened, Bill, it seems to me that we could call the police. Maybe.'

'C-C-Call the uh-others,' he said again. 'We'll s-s-see what they th-think.'

'All right.'

She called Richie first, then Ben. Both agreed to come right away. Neither asked what had happened. She found Mike's telephone number in the book and dialed it. There was no answer; after a dozen rings she hung up.

'T-T-Try the luh-luh-hibrary,' Bill said. He had taken the short curtain rods down from the smaller of the two windows in Eddie's room and was binding them firmly to Eddie's arm with the belt of his bathrobe and the drawstring from his pyjamas.

Before she could find the number there was a knock at the door. Ben and Richie had arrived together, Ben in jeans and an untucked shirt, Richie in a pair of smart gray cotton trousers and his pyjama top. His eyes looked warily around the room from behind his glasses.

'Christ, Eddie, what happened to –'

'Oh my God!' Ben cried. He had seen Henry on the floor.

'B-B-Be quh-hiet!' Bill said sharply. 'And close th-the d-door!'

Richie did it, his eyes fixed on the body. 'Henry?'

Ben took three steps toward the corpse and then stopped, as if afraid it might bite him. He looked helplessly at Bill.

'Y-Y-You t-tell,' he said to Eddie. 'G-G-Goddam stuh-huh-hutter is g-getting wuh-wuh-worse all the t-t-time.'

Eddie sketched in what had happened while Beverly hunted up the number for the Derry Public Library and called it. She expected that perhaps Mike had fallen asleep there – he might even have a bunk in his office. What she did not expect was what happened: the phone was picked up on the second ring and a voice she had never heard before said hello.

936

'Hello,' she answered, looking toward the others and making a shushing gesture with one hand. 'Is Mr Hanlon there?'

'Who's this?' the voice asked.

She wet her lips with her tongue. Bill was looking at her piercingly. Ben and Richie had looked around. The beginnings of real alarm stirred inside her.

'Who are *you*?' she countered. 'You're not Mr Hanlon.'

'I'm Derry Chief of Police Andrew Rademacher,' the voice said. 'Mr Hanlon is at the Derry Home Hospital right now. He was assaulted and badly wounded a short time ago. Now who are you, please? I want your name.'

But she barely heard this last. Waves of shock rode through her, lifting her dizzily up and up, outside of herself. The muscles in her stomach and legs and crotch all went loose and numb, and she thought in a detached way: *This must be how it happens, when people get so scared they wet their pants. Sure. You just lose control of those muscles –*

'How badly has he been hurt?' she heard herself asking in a papery voice, and then Bill was beside her, his hand on her shoulder, and Ben was there, and Richie, and she felt such a rush of gratitude for them. She held her free hand out and Bill took it. Richie placed his hand over Bill's and Ben put his over Richie's. Eddie had come over, and now he put his good hand on top.

'I want your name, please,' Rademacher said briskly, and for a moment the skittering little craven inside of her, the one that had been bred by her father and cared for by her husband, almost answered: *I'm Beverly Marsh and I'm at the Derry Town House. Please send Mr Nell over. There's a dead man here who's still half a boy and we're all very frightened.*

She said: 'I . . . I'm afraid I can't tell you. Not just yet.'

'What do you know about this?'

'Nothing,' she said, shocked. 'What makes you think I do? Jesus Christ!'

'You just make a habit of calling the library every morning about three-thirty,' Rademacher said, 'is that it? Can the bullshit, young lady. This is assault, and the way the guy looks, it could be murder by the time the sun comes up. I'll ask you again: who are you and how much do you know about this?'

Closing her eyes, gripping Bill's hand with all her strength, she asked again: 'He might die? You're not just saying that to scare me? He really might die? Please tell me.'

'He's very badly hurt. And if that doesn't scare you, miss, it ought to. Now I want to know who you are and why –'

As if in a dream she watched her hand float through space and drop the phone back into the cradle. She looked over at Henry and felt shock as keen as a slap from a cold hand. One of Henry's eyes had closed. The other one, the shattered one, oozed as nakedly as before.

Henry seemed to be winking at her.

4

Richie called the hospital. Bill led Beverly over to the bed, where she sat with Eddie, looking off into space. She thought she would cry, but no tears came. The only feeling she was strongly and immediately aware of was a wish that someone would cover Henry Bowers. That winky look was really not cool at all.

In one giddy instant Richie became a reporter from the Derry *News*. He understood that Mr Michael Hanlon, the town's head librarian, had been assaulted while working late. Did the hospital have any word on Mr Hanlon's condition?

Richie listened, nodding.

'I understand, Mr Kerpaskian – do you spell that with two k's? You do. Okay. And you are –'

He listened, now enough into his own fiction to make doodling motions with one finger, as if writing on a pad.

'Uh-huh . . . uh-huh . . . yes. Yes, I understand. Well, what we usually do in cases like this is to quote you as "a source." Then, later on, we can . . . uh-huh . . . right! Just right!' Richie laughed heartily and armed a film of sweat from his forehead. He listened again. 'Okay, Mr Kerpaskian. Yes. I'll . . . yes, I got it, K-E-R-P-A-S-K-I-A-N, right! Czech-Jewish, is it? Really! That's . . . that's most unusual. Yes, I will. Goodnight. Thank you.'

He hung up and closed his eyes. 'Jesus!' he cried in a thick, low voice. 'Jesus! Jesus! Jesus!' He made as if to shove the phone off the table and then simply let his hand fall. He took his glasses off and wiped them on his pyjama top.

'He's alive, but in grave condition,' he told the others. 'Henry sliced him up like a Christmas turkey. One of the cuts chopped into his femoral artery and he's lost all the blood a man can and still stay alive. Mike managed to get some kind of tourniquet on it, or he would have been dead when they found him.'

Beverly began to cry. She did it like a child, with both hands plastered to her face. For a little while her hitching sobs and the rapid whistle of Eddie's breathing were the only sounds in the room.

'Mike wasn't the only one who got sliced up like a Christmas turkey,' Eddie said at last. 'Henry looked like he just went twelve rounds with Rocky Balboa in a Cuisinart.'

'D-Do you still w-w-want to g-g-go to the p-p-police, Bev?'

There were Kleenex on the nighttable but they were a caked and sodden mass in the middle of a puddle of Perrier. She went into the bathroom, making a wide circle around Henry, got a wash-cloth, and ran cool water on it. It felt delicious against her hot puffy face. She felt that she could think clearly again – not rationally but clearly. She was suddenly sure that rationality would kill them if they tried to use it now. That cop. Rademacher. He had been suspicious. Why not? People didn't call the library at three-thirty in the morning. He had assumed some guilty knowledge. What would he assume if he found out that she had called him from a room where there was a dead man on the floor with a jagged bottle-neck planted in his guts? That she and four other strangers had just come into town the day before for a little reunion and this guy just happened to drop by? Would she buy the tale if the shoe were on the other foot? Would anyone? Of course, they could buttress their tale by adding that they had come back to finish the monster that lived in the drains under the city. *That* would certainly add a convincing note of gritty realism.

She came out of the bathroom and looked at Bill. 'No,' she said. 'I don't want to go to the police. I think Eddie's right – something might happen to us. Something final. But that isn't the real reason.' She looked at the four of them. 'We swore it,' she said. 'We swore. Bill's brother . . . Stan . . . all the others . . . and now Mike. I'm ready, Bill.'

Bill looked at the others.

Richie nodded. 'Okay, Big Bill. Let's try.'

Ben said, 'The odds look worse than ever. We're two short now.'

Bill said nothing.

'Okay.' Ben nodded. 'She's right. We swore.'

'E-E-Eddie?'

Eddie smiled wanly. 'I guess I get another pigger-back down that ladder, huh? If the ladder's still there.'

'No one throwing rocks this time, though,' Beverly said. 'They're dead. All three of them.'

'Do we do it now, Bill?' Richie asked.

'Y-Y-Yes,' Bill said. 'I th-think this is the t-t-time.'

'Can I say something?' Ben asked abruptly.

Bill looked at him and grinned a little. 'A-A-Any time.'

'You guys are still the best friends I ever had,' Ben said. 'No matter how this turns out. I just ... you know, wanted to tell you that.'

He looked around at them, and they looked solemnly back at him.

'I'm glad I remembered you,' he added. Richie snorted. Beverly giggled. Then they were all laughing, looking at each other in the old way, in spite of the fact that Mike was in the hospital, perhaps dying or already dead, in spite of the fact that Eddie's arm was broken (again), in spite of the fact that it was the deepest ditch of the morning.

'Haystack, you have *such* a way with words,' Richie said, laughing and wiping his eyes. '*He* should have been the writer, Big Bill.'

Still smiling a little, Bill said: 'And on that nuh-nuh-note –'

5

They took Eddie's borrowed limo. Richie drove. The groundfog was thicker now, drifting through the streets like cigarette smoke, not quite reaching the hooded streetlamps. The stars overhead were bright chips of ice, spring stars ... but by cocking his head to the half-open window on the passenger side, Bill thought he could hear summer thunder in the distance. Rain was being ordered up somewhere over the horizon.

Richie turned on the radio and there was Gene Vincent singing 'Be-Bop-A-Lula.' He hit one of the other buttons and got Buddy Holly. A third punch brought Eddie Cochran singing 'Summertime Blues.'

'I'd like to help you, son, but you're too young to vote,' a deep voice said.

'Turn it off, Richie,' Beverly said softly.

He reached for it, and then his hand froze. 'Stay tuned for more of the Richie Tozier All-Dead Rock Show!' the clown's laughing, screaming voice cried over the finger-pops and guitar-chops of the Eddie Cochran tune. 'Don't touch that dial, keep it tuned to the rockpile, they're gone from the charts but not from our hearts and you keep coming, come right along, come on everybody! We play *aaaalll* the hits down here! *Aaalllll* the hits! And if you don't believe me, just listen to this morning's graveyard-shift guest deejay, Georgie Dcnbrough! Tell em, Georgie!'

And suddenly Bill's brother was wailing out of the radio.

'You sent me out and It killed me! I thought It was in the cellar, Big

Bill, I thought It was in the cellar but It was in the drain, It was in the drain and It killed me, you let It kill me, Big Bill, you let It –'

Richie snapped the radio off so hard the knob spun away and hit the floormat.

'Rock and roll in the sticks really sucks,' he said. His voice was not quite steady. 'Bev's right, we'll leave it off, what do you say?'

No one replied. Bill's face was pale and still and thoughtful under the glow of the passing streetlamps, and when the thunder muttered again in the west they all heard it.

6

In the Barrens

Same old bridge.

Richie parked beside it and they got out and moved to the railing – same old railing – and looked down.

Same old Barrens.

It seemed untouched by the last twenty-seven years; to Bill the turnpike overpass, which was the only new feature, looked unreal, something as ephemeral as a matte painting or a rear-screen projection effect in a movie. Cruddy little trees and scrub bushes glimmered in the twining fog and Bill thought: *I guess this is what we mean when we talk about the persistence of memory, this or something like this, something you see at the right time and from the right angle, image that kicks off emotion like a jet engine. You see it so clear that all the things which happened in between are gone. If desire is what closes the circle between world and want, then the circle has closed.*

'Cuh-Cuh-Come on,' he said, and climbed over the railing. They followed him down the embankment in a scatter of scree and pebbles. When they reached the bottom Bill checked automatically for Silver and then laughed at himself. Silver was leaning against the wall of Mike's garage. It seemed Silver had no part to play in this at all, although that was strange, after the way it had turned up.

'Tuh-Take us there,' Bill told Ben.

Ben looked at him and Bill read the thought in his eyes – *It's been twenty-seven years, Bill, dream on* – and then he nodded and headed into the undergrowth.

The path – *their* path – had long since grown over, and they had to force themselves through tangles of thornbushes, prickers, and wild hydrangea so fragrant it was cloying. Crickets sang somnolently all around them, and a few lightning-bugs, early arrivals at summer's luscious party, poked at the dark. Bill supposed kids still played down here, but they had made their own runs and secret ways.

They came to the clearing where the clubhouse had been, but now there was no clearing here at all. Bushes and lackluster scrub pines had reclaimed it all.

'Look,' Ben whispered, and crossed the clearing (in their memories it was still here, simply overlaid with another of those matte paintings). He yanked at something. It was the mahogany door they had found on the edge of the dump, the one they had used to finish off the clubhouse roof. It had been cast aside here and looked as if it hadn't been touched in a dozen years or more. Creepers were firmly entrenched across its dirty surface.

'Leave it alone, Haystack,' Richie murmured. 'It's old.'

'Tuh-Tuh-Take us th-there, B-Ben,' Bill repeated from behind them.

So they went down to the Kenduskeag following him, bearing left away from the clearing that didn't exist anymore. The sound of running water grew steadily louder, but they still almost fell into the Kenduskeag before any of them saw it: the foliage had grown up in a tangled wall on the edge of the embankment. The edge broke off under the heels of Ben's cowboy boots and Bill yanked him back by the scruff of the neck.

'Thanks,' Ben said.

'*De nada.* In the o-old d-days, you wuh-hould have puh-pulled me ih-in a-a-after you. D-Down this wuh-way?'

Ben nodded and led them along the overgrown bank, fighting through the tangles of bushes and brambles, thinking how much easier this was when you were only four feet five and able to go under most tangles (those in your mind as well as those in your path, he supposed) in one nonchalant duck. Well, everything changed. *Our lesson for today, boys and girls, is the more things change, the more things change. Whoever said the more things change the more things stay the same was obviously suffering severe mental retardation. Because –*

His foot hooked under something and he fell over with a thud, nearly striking his head on the pumping-station's concrete cylinder. It was almost completely buried in a wallow of blackberry bushes. As he got to his feet again he realized that his face and arms and hands had been striped by blackberry thorns in two dozen places.

'Make that three dozen,' he said, feeling thin blood running down his cheeks.

'What?' Eddie asked.

'Nothing.' He bent down to see what he had tripped over. A root, probably.

But it wasn't a root. It was the iron manhole cover. Someone had pushed it off.

Of course, Ben thought. We *did*. *Twenty-seven years ago*.

But he realized that was crazy even before he saw fresh metal twinkling through the rust in parallel scrape-marks. The pump hadn't been working that day. Sooner or later someone would have come down to fix it, and would have replaced the cover in the bargain.

He stood up and the five of them gathered around the cylinder and looked in. They could hear the faint sound of dripping water. That was all. Richie had brought all the matches from Eddie's room. Now he lit an entire book of them and tossed it in. For a moment they could see the cylinder's damp inner sleeve and the silent bulk of the pumping machinery. That was all.

'Could have been off for a long time,' Richie said uneasily. 'Didn't necessarily have to happen t −'

'It's happened fairly recently,' Ben said. 'Since the last rain, anyway.' He took another book of matches from Richie, lit one, and pointed out the fresh scratches.

'There's suh-suh-something uh-under it,' Bill said as Ben shook out the match.

'What?' Ben asked.

'C–C–Couldn't tuh-tuh-tell. Looked like a struh-struh-strap. You and Rih–Richie help me t-t-turn it o-over.'

They grabbed the cover and flipped it like a giant coin. This time Beverly lit the match and Ben cautiously picked up the purse which had been under the manhole cover. He held it up by the strap. Beverly started to shake out the match and then looked at Bill's face. She froze until the flame touched the ends of her fingers and then dropped it with a little gasp. 'Bill? What is it? What's wrong?'

Bill's eyes felt too heavy. They couldn't leave that scuffed leather bag with its long leather strap. Suddenly he could remember the name of the song which had been playing on the radio in the back room of the leather-goods shop when he had bought it for her. 'Sausalito Summer Nights.' It was the surpassing weirdism. All the spit was gone out of his mouth, leaving his tongue and inner cheeks as smooth and dry as chrome. He could hear the crickets and see the lightning-bugs and smell big green growing dark out of control all around him and he thought *It's another trick another illusion she's in England and this is*

943

just a cheap shot because It's scared, oh yes, It's maybe not as sure as It was when It called us all back, and really, Bill, get serious — how many scuffed leather purses with long straps do you think there are in the world? A million? Ten million?

Probably more. But only one like this. He had bought it for Audra in a Burbank leather-goods store while 'Sausalito Summer Nights' played on the radio in the back room.

'*Bill?*' Beverly's hand on his shoulder, shaking him. Far away. Twenty-seven leagues under the sea. What was the name of the group that sang 'Sausalito Summer Nights'? Richie would know.

'*I* know,' Bill said calmly into Richie's scared, wide-eyed face, and smiled. 'It was Diesel. How's that for total recall?'

'Bill, what's wrong?' Richie whispered.

Bill screamed. He snatched the matches out of Beverly's hand, lit one, and then yanked the purse away from Ben.

'Bill, Jesus, what —'

He unzipped the purse and turned it over. What fell out was so much Audra that for a moment he was too unmanned to scream again. Amid the Kleenex, sticks of chewing gum, and items of make-up, he saw a tin of Altoid mints . . . and the jewelled compact Freddie Firestone had given her when she signed for *Attic Room*.

'My wuh-wuh-wife's down there,' he said, and fell on his knees and began pushing her things back into the purse. He brushed hair that no longer existed out of his eyes without even thinking about it.

'Your wife? *Audra?*' Beverly's face was shocked, her eyes huge.

'Her p-p-purse. Her th-things.'

'Jesus, Bill,' Richie muttered. 'That can't be, you know th —'

He had found her alligator wallet. He opened it and held it up. Richie lit another match and was looking at a face he had seen in half a dozen movies. The picture on Audra's California driver's license was less glamorous but completely conclusive.

'But Huh-Huh-Henry's dead, and Victor, and B-B-Belch . . . so who's got her?' He stood up, staring around at them with febrile intensity. '*Who's got her?*'

Ben put a hand on Bill's shoulder. 'I guess we better go down and find out, huh?'

Bill looked around at him, as if unsure of who Ben might be, and then his eyes cleared. 'Y-Yeah,' he said. 'Eh-Eh-Eddie?'

'Bill, I'm sorry.'

'Can you cluh-climb on?'

'I did once.'

Bill bent over and Eddie hooked his right arm around Bill's neck. Ben and Richie boosted him up until he could hook his legs around Bill's midsection. As Bill swung one leg clumsily over the lip of the cylinder, Ben saw that Eddie's eyes were tightly shut . . . and for a moment he thought he heard the world's ugliest cavalry charge bashing its way through the bushes. He turned, expecting to see the three of them come out of the fog and the brambles, but all he had heard was the rising breeze rattling the bamboo a quarter of a mile or so from here. Their old enemies were all gone now.

Bill gripped the rough concrete lip of the cylinder and felt his way down, step by step and rung by rung. Eddie had him in a death-grip and Bill could barely breathe. *Her purse, dear God, how did her purse get here? Doesn't matter. But if You're there, God, and if You're taking requests, let her be all right, don't let her suffer for what Bev and I did tonight or for what I did one summer when I was a boy . . . and was it the clown? Was it Bob Gray who got her? If it was, I don't know if even God can help her.*

'I'm scared, Bill,' Eddie said in a thin voice.

Bill's foot touched cold standing water. He lowered himself into it, remembering the feel and the dank smell, remembering the claus-trophobic way this place had made him feel . . . and, just by the way, what had happened to them? How had they fared down in these drains and tunnels? Where exactly had they gone, and how exactly had they gotten out again? He still couldn't remember any of that; all he could think of was Audra.

'I am t-t-too.' He half-squatted, wincing as the cold water ran into his pants and over his balls, and let Eddie off. They stood shindeep in the water and watched the others descend the ladder.

CHAPTER TWENTY-ONE
UNDER THE CITY

1

It/August 1958

Something new had happened.

For the first time in forever, something new.

Before the universe there had been only two things. One was Itself and the other was the Turtle. The Turtle was a stupid old thing that never came out of its shell. It thought that maybe the Turtle was dead, had been dead for the last billion years or so. Even if it wasn't, it was still a stupid old thing, and even if the Turtle had vomited the universe out whole, that didn't change the fact of its stupidity.

It had come here long after the Turtle withdrew into its shell, here to Earth, and It had discovered a depth of imagination here that was almost new, almost of concern. This quality of imagination made the food very rich. Its teeth rent flesh gone stiff with exotic terrors and voluptuous fears: they dreamed of nightbeasts and moving muds; against their will they contemplated endless gulphs.

Upon this rich food It existed in a simple cycle of waking to eat and sleeping to dream. It had created a place in Its own image, and It looked upon this place with favor from the deadlights which were Its eyes. Derry was Its killing-pen, the people of Derry Its sheep. Things had gone on.

Then . . . these children.

Something new.

For the first time in forever.

When It had burst up into the house on Neibolt Street, meaning to kill them all, vaguely uneasy that It had not been able to do so already (and surely that unease had been the first new thing), something had happened which was totally unexpected, utterly unthought of, and there had been pain, pain, great roaring pain all through the shape It had taken, and for one moment there had also been fear, because the only thing It had in common with the stupid old Turtle and the cosmology of the macroverse outside the puny egg of this universe was just this: all living things must abide by the laws of the shape they inhabit. For the first time It realized that perhaps Its ability to change Its shapes might work against It as well as for It. There had never been pain before, there had never been fear before, and for a moment It had thought It might die — oh Its head had been filled with a great white silver pain, and it had roared and mewled and bellowed and somehow the children had escaped.

But now they were coming. They had entered Its domain under the city, seven foolish children blundering through the darkness without lights or weapons. It would kill them now, surely.

It had made a great self-discovery: It did not want change or surprise. It did not want new things, ever. It wanted only to eat and sleep and dream and eat again.

Following the pain and that brief bright fear, another new emotion had arisen (as all genuine emotions were new to It, although It was a great mocker of emotions): anger. It would kill the children because they had, by some amazing accident, hurt It. But It would make them suffer first because for one brief moment they had made It fear them.

Come to me then, It thought, listening to their approach. Come to me, children, and see how we float down here . . . how we all float.

And yet there was a thought that insinuated itself no matter how strongly It tried to push the thought away. It was simply this: if all things flowed from It (as they surely had done since the Turtle sicked up the universe and then fainted inside its shell), how could any creature of this or any other world fool It or hurt It, no matter how briefly or triflingly? How was that possible?

And so a last new thing had come to It, this not an emotion but a cold speculation: suppose It had not been alone, as It had always believed?

Suppose there was Another?

And suppose further that these children were agents of that Other?

Suppose . . . suppose . . .

It began to tremble.

Hate was new. Hurt was new. Being crossed in Its purpose was new. But the most terrible new thing was this fear. Not fear of the children, that had passed, but the fear of not being alone.

No. There was no other. Surely there was not. Perhaps because they were children their imaginations had a certain raw power It had briefly underestimated. But now that they were coming, It would let them come. They would come and It would cast them one by one into the macroverse . . . into the deadlights of Its eyes.

Yes.

When they got here It would cast them, shrieking and insane, into the deadlights.

2

In the Tunnels/2:15 P.M.

Bev and Richie had maybe ten matches between them, but Bill wouldn't let them use them. For the time being, at least, there was still dim light in the drain. Not much, but he could make out the next four feet in front of him, and as long as he could keep doing that, they would save the matches.

He supposed the little light they were getting must be coming from vents in curbings over their heads, maybe even from the circular vents in manhole covers. It seemed surpassingly strange to think they were under the city, but of course by now they must be.

The water was deeper now. Three times dead animals had floated past: a rat, a kitten, a bloated shiny thing that might have been a woodchuck. He heard one of the others mutter disgustedly as that baby cruised by.

The water they were crawling through was relatively placid, but all that was going to come to an end fairly soon: there was a steady hollow roaring not too far up ahead. It grew louder, rising to a one-note roar. The drain elbowed to the right. They made the turn and here were three pipes spewing water into their pipe. They were lined up vertically like the lenses on a traffic light. The drain deadended here. The light was marginally brighter. Bill looked up and saw they were in a square stone-faced shaft about fifteen feet high. There was a sewer-grating up there and water was sloshing down on them in buckets. It was like being in a primitive shower.

Bill surveyed the three pipes helplessly. The top one was venting water which was almost clear, although there were leaves and sticks and bits of trash in it – cigarette butts, chewing-gum wrappers, things like that. The middle pipe was venting gray water. And from the lowest one came a grayish-brown flood of lumpy sewage.

'Eh-Eh-Eddie!'

Eddie floundered up beside him. His hair was plastered to his head. His cast was a soaking, drippy mess.

'Wh-Wh-Which wuh-wuh-one?' If you wanted to know how to build something, you asked Ben; if you wanted to know which way to go, you asked Eddie. They didn't talk about this, but they all knew it. If you were in a strange neighborhood and wanted to get back to a place you knew, Eddie could get you there, making lefts and rights with undiminished confidence until you were reduced simply to following him and hoping that things would turn out right . . . which they always seemed to do. Bill told Richie once that when he and Eddie first began to play in the Barrens, he, Bill, was constantly afraid of getting lost. Eddie had no such fears, and he always brought the two of them out right where he said he was going to. 'If I g-g-got luh-lost in the Hainesville Woods and Eh-Eddie was with me, I wouldn't wuh-hurry a b-bit,' Bill told Richie. 'He just *nuh-nuh-knows*. My d-d-dad says some people, ih-hit's l-like they got a cuh-huh-hompass in their heads. Eddie's l-l-like that.'

'*I can't hear you!*' Eddie shouted.

'I said wh-which *one*?'

'Which one *what*?' Eddie had his aspirator clutched in his good hand, and Bill thought he actually looked more like a drowned muskrat than a kid.

'Which one do we *tuh-tuh-take*?'

'Well, that all depends on where we want to go,' Eddie said, and Bill could have cheerfully throttled him even though the question made perfect sense. Eddie was looking dubiously at the three pipes. They could fit into all of them, but the bottom one looked pretty snug.

Bill motioned the others to move up into a circle. 'Where the fuck *is* Ih-Ih-It?' he asked them.

'Middle of town,' Richie said promptly. 'Right under the middle of town. Near the Canal.'

Beverly was nodding. So was Ben. So was Stan.

'Muh-Muh-Mike?'

'Yes,' he said. 'That's where It is. Near the Canal. Or under it.'

Bill looked back at Eddie. 'W-W-Which one?'

Eddie pointed reluctantly at the lower pipe . . . and although Bill's heart sank, he wasn't at all surprised. 'That one.'

'Oh, gross,' Stan said unhappily. 'That's a shit-pipe.'

'We don't –' Mike began, and then broke off. He cocked his head in a listening gesture. His eyes were alarmed.

'What –' Bill began, and Mike put a finger across his lips in a *Shhhh*! gesture. Now Bill could hear it too: splashing sounds. Approaching. Grunts and muffled words. Henry still hadn't given up.

'Quick,' Ben said. 'Let's go.'

Stan looked back the way they had come, then he looked at the lowest of the three pipes. He pressed his lips tightly together and nodded. 'Let's go,' he said. 'Shit washes off.'

'Stan the Man Gets Off A Good One!' Richie cried. 'Wacka-wacka-wa –'

'Richie, will you shut *up*?' Beverly hissed at him.

Bill led them to the pipe, grimacing at the smell, and crawled in. The smell: it was sewage, it was shit, but there was another smell here, too, wasn't there? A lower, more vital smell. If an animal's grunt could have a smell (and, Bill supposed, if the animal in question had been eating the right things, it could), it would be like this undersmell. *We're headed in the right direction, all right. It's been here . . . and It's been here a lot.*

By the time they had gone twenty feet, the air had grown rancid and poisonous. He squished slowly along, moving through stuff that wasn't mud. He looked back over his shoulder and said, 'You fuh-fuh-follow right behind m-me, Eh-Eh-Eddie. I'll nuh-need y-you.'

The light faded to the faintest gray, held that way briefly, and then it was gone and they were

(*out of the blue and*)

into the black. Bill shuffled forward through the stink, feeling that he was almost cutting through it physically, one hand held out before him, part of him expecting that at any moment it would encounter rough hair and green lamplike eyes would open in the darkness. The end would come in one hot flare of pain as It walloped his head off his shoulders.

The dark was stuffed with sounds, all of them magnified and echoing. He could hear his friends shuffling along behind him, sometimes muttering something. There were gurglings and strange clanking groans. Once a flood of sickeningly warm water washed past and between his legs, wetting him to the thighs and rocking him back on his heels. He felt Eddie clutch frantically at the back of his shirt, and then the small flood slackened. From the end of the line Richie bellowed with sorry good humor: 'I think we just been pissed on by the Jolly Green Giant, Bill.'

Bill could hear water or sewage running in controlled bursts through the network of smaller pipes which now must be over their heads. He remembered the conversation about Derry's sewers with his father and thought he knew what this pipe must be – it was to handle the overflow that only occurred during heavy rains and during the flood season. The stuff up there would be leaving Derry to be dumped in Torrault Stream and the Penobscot River. The city didn't like to pump its shit into the Kenduskeag because it made the Canal stink. But all the so-called gray water went into the Kenduskeag, and if there was too much for the regular sewer-pipes to handle, there would be a dump-off . . . like the one that had just happened. If there had been one, there could be another. He glanced up uneasily, not able to see anything but knowing that there must be grates in the top arch of the pipe, possibly in the sides as well, and that any moment there might be –

He wasn't aware he'd reached the end of the pipe until he fell out of it and staggered forward, pinwheeling his arms in a helpless effort to keep his balance. He fell on his belly into a semi-solid mass about two feet below the mouth of the pipe he'd just tumbled out of. Something ran squeaking over his hand. He screamed and sat up, clutching his tingling hand to his chest, aware that a rat had just run over it; he had felt the loathsome, plated drag of the thing's hairless tail.

He tried to stand up and rapped his head on the new pipe's low ceiling. It was a hard hit, and Bill was driven back to his knees with large red flowers exploding in the darkness before his eyes.

'Be c-c-careful!' he heard himself shouting. His words echoed flatly. 'It drops off here! Eh-Eddie! Where a-a-are yuh-you?'

'Here!' One of Eddie's waving hands brushed Bill's nose. 'Help me out, Bill, I can't see! It's –'

There was a huge watery *ker-whasssh*! Beverly, Mike, and Richie all screamed in unison. In the daylight, the almost perfect harmony the three of them made would have been funny; down here in the dark, in the sewers, it was terrifying. Suddenly all of them were tumbling out. Bill clutched Eddie in a bear-hug, trying to save his arm.

'Oh Christ, I thought I was gonna drown,' Richie moaned. 'We got doused – oh boy, a shit-shower, oh great, they ought to have a class trip down here sometime, Bill, we could get Mr Carson to lead it –'

'And Miss Jimmison could give a health lecture afterward,' Ben said in a trembling voice, and they all laughed shrilly. As the laughter was tapering off, Stan suddenly burst into miserable tears.

'Don't, man,' Richie said, putting a fumbling arm around Stan's sticky shoulders. 'You'll get us all cryin, man.'

'I'm all right!' Stan said loudly, still crying. 'I can stand to be scared, but I *hate* being dirty like this, I hate not knowing where I am –'

'D-Do y-y-you th-think a-a-any of the muh-matches are still a-a-any guh-good?' Bill asked Richie.

'I gave mine to Bev.'

Bill felt a hand touch his in the darkness and press a folder of matches into it. They felt dry.

951

'I kept them in my armpit,' she said. 'They might work. You can try them, anyway.'

Bill tore a match out of the folder and struck it. It popped alight and he held it up. His friends were huddled together, wincing at the brief bright flare of light. They were splashed and daubed with ordure and they all looked very young and very afraid. Behind them he could see the sewer-pipe they had come out of. The pipe they were in now was smaller still. It ran straight in both directions, its floor caked with layers of filthy sediment. And —

He drew in a quick hiss and shook the match out as it burned his fingers. He listened and heard the sounds of fast-running water, dripping water, the occasional gushing roar as the overflow valves worked, sending more sewage into the Kenduskeag, which was now God only knew how far behind them. He didn't hear Henry and the others — yet.

He said quietly, 'There's a d-d-dead boh-body on my r-r-right. About t-t-ten fuh-feet a-a-away from uh-us. I think it m-might be Puh-Puh-Puh —'

'Patrick?' Beverly asked, her voice trembling on the edge of hysteria. 'Is it Patrick Hockstetter?'

'Y-Y-Yes. Do you want me to luh-light a-a-another m-match?'

Eddie said, 'You got to, Bill. If I don't see how the pipe runs, I won't know which way to go.'

Bill lit the match. In its glow they all saw the green, swelled thing that had been Patrick Hockstetter. The corpse grinned at them in the dark with horrid chumminess, but with only half a face; sewer rats had taken the rest. Patrick's summer-school books were scattered around him, bloated to the size of dictionaries in the damp.

'Christ,' Mike said hoarsely, his eyes wide.

'I hear them again,' Beverly said. 'Henry and the others.'

The acoustics must have carried her voice to them as well; Henry bellowed down the sewer-pipe and for a moment it was as if he was standing right there.

'We'll get youuuuuu —'

'You come on right ahead!' Richie shouted. His eyes were bright, dancing, febrile. 'Keep coming, banana-heels! This is just like the YMCA swimming pool down here! Keep —'

Then a shriek of such mad fear and pain came through the pipe that the guttering match fell from Bill's fingers and went out. Eddie's arm had curled around him and Bill hugged Eddie back, feeling his body trembling like a wire as Stan Uris packed close to him on the other side. That shriek rose and rose . . . and then there was an obscene, thick flapping noise, and the shriek was cut off.

'Something got one of them,' Mike choked, horrified, in the darkness. 'Something . . . some monster . . . Bill, we got to get out of here . . . please . . .'

Bill could hear whoever was left – one or two, with the acoustics it was impossible to tell – stumbling and scrabbling through the sewer-pipe toward them. 'Wuh-Which w-w-way, Eh-Eddie?' he asked urgently. 'D-Do you nuh-know?'

'Toward the Canal?' Eddie asked, shaking in Bill's arms.

'Yes!'

'To the right. Past Patrick . . . or over him.' Eddie's voice suddenly hardened. 'I don't care that much. He was one of the ones that broke my arm. Spit in my face, too.'

'Let's guh-go,' Bill said, looking back at the sewer-pipe they had just quitted. 'S-Single luh-line! Keep a t-t-touch on e-each uh-uh-other, like b-b-before!'

He groped forward, dragging his right shoulder along the slimy porcelain surface of the pipe, gritting his teeth, not wanting to step on Patrick . . . or into him.

So they crawled farther into the darkness while waters rushed around them and while, outside, the storm walked and talked and brought an early darkness to Derry – a darkness that screamed with wind and stuttered with electric fire and racketed with falling trees that sounded like the death-cries of huge prehistoric creatures.

3

It/May 1985

Now they were coming again, and while everything had gone much as It had foreseen, something It had not foreseen had returned: that maddening, galling fear . . . that sense of Another. It hated the fear, would have turned on it and eaten it if It could have . . . but the fear danced mockingly out of reach, and It could only kill the fear by killing them.

Surely there was no need for such fear; they were older now, and their number had been reduced from seven to five. Five was a number of power, but it did not have the mystical talismanic quality of seven. It was true that Its dogsbody hadn't been able to kill the librarian, but the librarian would die in the hospital. Later, just before dawn touched the sky, It would send a male nurse with a bad pill habit to finish the librarian once and for all.

The writer's woman was now with It, alive yet not alive — her mind had been utterly destroyed by her first sight of It as It really was, with all of Its little masks and glamours thrown aside — and all of the glamours were only mirrors, of course, throwing back at the terrified viewer the worst thing in his or her own mind, heliographing images as a mirror may bounce a reflection of the sun into a wide unsuspecting eye and stun it to blindness.

Now the mind of the writer's wife was with It, in It, beyond the end of the macroverse; in the darkness beyond the Turtle; in the outlands beyond all lands.

She was in Its eye; she was in Its mind.

She was in the deadlights.

Oh but the glamours were amusing. Hanlon, for instance. He would not remember, not consciously, but his mother could have told him where the bird he had seen at the Ironworks came from. When he was a baby only six months old, his mother had left him sleeping in his cradle in the side yard while she went around back to hang sheets and diapers on the line. His screams had brought her on the run. A large crow had lighted on the edge of the carriage and was pecking at baby Mikey like an evil creature in a nursery tale. He had been screaming in pain and terror, unable to drive away the crow, which had sensed weak prey. She had struck the bird with her fist and driven it off, seen that it had brought blood in two or three places on baby Mikey's arms, and taken him to Dr Stillwagon for a tetanus shot. A part of Mike had remembered that always — tiny baby, giant bird — and when It came to Mike, Mike had seen the giant bird again.

. But when the dogsbody husband of the girl from before brought the writer's woman, It had put on no face — It did not dress when It was at home. The dogsbody husband had looked once and had dropped dead of shock, his face gray, his eyes filling with the blood that had squirted out of his brain in a dozen places. The writer's woman had put out one powerful, horrified thought — OH DEAR JESUS IT IS FEMALE — and then all thoughts ceased. She swam in the deadlights. It came down from Its place and took care of her physical remains; prepared them for later feeding. Now Audra Denbrough hung high up in the middle of things, crisscrossed in silk, her head lolling against the socket of her shoulder, her eyes wide and glazed, her toes pointing down.

But there was still power in them. Diminished but still there. They had come here as children and somehow, against all the odds, against all that was supposed to be, all that could be, they had hurt It badly, had almost killed It, had forced It to flee deep into the earth, where it huddled, hurt and hating and trembling in a spreading pool of Its own strange blood.

So another new thing, if you please: for the first time in Its neverending history, It needed to make a plan; for the first time It found Itself afraid simply to take what It wanted from Derry, Its private game-preserve.

It had always fed well on children. Many adults could be used without knowing they had been used, and It had even fed on a few of the older ones over the years – adults had their own terrors, and their glands could be tapped, opened so that all the chemicals of fear flooded the body and salted the meat. But their fears were mostly too complex. The fears of children were simpler and usually more powerful. The fears of children could often be summoned up in a single face ... and if bait were needed, why, what child did not love a clown?

It understood vaguely that these children had somehow turned Its own tools against It – that, by coincidence (surely not on purpose, surely not guided by the hand of any Other), by the bonding of seven extraordinarily imaginative minds, It had been brought into a zone of great danger. Any of these seven alone would have been Its meat and drink, and if they had not happened to come together, It surely would have picked them off one by one, drawn by the quality of their minds just as a lion might be drawn to one particular waterhole by the scent of zebra. But together they had discovered an alarming secret that even It had not been aware of: that belief has a second edge. If there are ten thousand medieval peasants who create vampires by believing them real, there may be one – probably a child – who will imagine the stake necessary to kill it. But a stake is only stupid wood; the mind is the mallet which drives it home.

Yet in the end It had escaped; had gone deep, and the exhausted, terrified children had elected not to follow It when It was at Its most vulnerable. They had elected to believe It dead or dying, and had retreated.

It was aware of their oath, and had known they would come back just as a lion knows the zebra will eventually return to the waterhole. It had begun to plan even as It began to drowse. When It woke It would be healed, renewed – but their childhoods would be burned away like seven fatty candles. The former power of their imaginations would be muted and weak. They would no longer imagine that there were piranha in the Kenduskeag or that if you stepped on a crack you might really break your mother's back or that if you killed a ladybug which lit on your shirt your house would catch fire that night. Instead, they would believe in insurance. Instead, they would believe in wine with dinner – something nice but not too pretentious, like a Pouilly-Fuissé '83, and let that breathe, waiter, would you? Instead, they would believe that Rolaids consume forty-seven times their own weight in excess stomach acid. Instead, they would believe in public television, Gary Hart, running to prevent heart attacks, giving up red meat to prevent colon cancer. They would believe in Dr Ruth when it came to getting well fucked and Jerry Falwell when it came to *getting well saved. As each year passed their dreams would grow smaller. And when It woke It would call them back, yes, back, because fear was fertile, its child was rage, and rage cried for revenge.*

It would call them and then kill them.

Only now that they were coming, the fear had returned. They had grown up, and their imaginations had weakened – but not as much as It had believed. It had felt an ominous, upsetting growth in their power when they joined together, and It had wondered for the first time if It had perhaps made a mistake.

But why be gloomy? The die was cast and not all the omens were bad. The writer was half-mad for his wife, and that was good. The writer was the strongest, the one who had somehow trained his mind for this confrontation over all the years, and when the writer was dead with his guts falling out of his body, when their precious 'Big Bill' was dead, the others would be Its quickly.

It would feed well . . . and then perhaps It would go deep again. And doze. For awhile.

4

In the Tunnels / 4:30 A.M.

'Bill!' Richie shouted into the echoing pipe. He was moving as fast as he could, but that wasn't very fast. He remembered that as kids they had walked bent over in this pipe, which led away from the pumping-station in the Barrens. He was crawling now, and the pipe seemed impossibly tight. His glasses kept wanting to slide off the end of his nose and he kept pushing them up again. He could hear Bev and Ben behind him.

'Bill!' he bawled again. 'Eddie!'

'I'm here!' Eddie's voice floated back.

'Where's Bill?' Richie shouted.

'Up ahead!' Eddie called. He was very close now, and Richie sensed rather than saw him just ahead. 'He wouldn't wait!'

Richie's head butted Eddie's leg. A moment later Bev's head butted Richie's ass.

'*Bill!*' Richie screamed at the top of his voice. The pipe channelled his shout and sent it back at him, hurting his own ears. '*Bill, wait for us! We have to go together, don't you know that?*'

Faintly, echoing, Bill: '*Audra! Audra! Where are you?*'

'Goddam you, Big Bill!' Richie cried softly. His glasses fell off.

He cursed, groped for them, and set them, dripping, back on his nose. He pulled in breath and shouted again: '*You'll get lost without Eddie, you fucking asshole! Wait up! Wait up for us! You hear me, Bill? WAIT UP FOR US, DAMMIT!*'

There was an agonizing moment of silence. It seemed that no one breathed. All Richie could hear was distant dripping water; the drain was dry this time, except for the occasional stagnant puddle.

'*Bill!*' He ran a trembling hand through his hair and fought the tears. '*COME ON . . . PLEASE, MAN! WAIT UP! PLEASE!*'

And, fainter still, Bill's voice came back: 'I'm waiting.'

'Thank God for small favors,' Richie muttered. He slapped Eddie's can. 'Go.'

'I don't know how long I can with just one arm,' Eddie said apologetically.

'Go anyway,' Richie said, and Eddie began crawling again.

Bill, looking haggard and almost used-up, was waiting for them in the sewer-shaft where the three pipes were lined up like lenses on a dead traffic light. There was room enough here for them to stand up.

'Over there,' Bill said. 'Cuh-Criss. And B-B-Belch.'

They looked. Beverly moaned and Ben put an arm around her. The skeleton of Belch Huggins, clad in moldering rags, seemed more or less intact. What remained of Victor was headless. Bill looked across the shaftway and saw a grinning skull.

There it was; there was the rest of him. *Should have left it alone, guys*, Bill thought, and shivered.

This section of the sewer system had fallen into disuse; Richie thought the reason why was pretty clear. The waste-treatment plant had taken over. Sometime during the years when they were all busy learning to shave, to drive, to smoke, to fuck around a little, all that good shit, the Environmental Protection Agency had come into being, and the EPA had decided dumping raw sewage – and even gray water – into rivers and streams was a no-no. So this part of the sewer system had simply moldered, and the bodies of Victor Criss and Belch Huggins had moldered along with it. Like Peter Pan's Wild Boys, Victor and Belch had never grown up. Here were the skeletons of two boys in the shredded remains of tee-shirts and jeans that had rotted away to rags. Moss had grown over the warped xylophone of Victor's ribcage, and over the eagle on the buckle of his garrison-belt.

'Monster got em,' Ben said softly. 'Do you remember? We heard it happen.'

'Audra's d-dead.' Bill voice was mechanical. 'I know it.'

'You don't know *any such thing!*' Beverly said with such fury that Bill stirred and looked at her. 'All you know for sure is that a lot of *other* people have died, most of them children.' She walked across to him and stood before him with her hands on her hips. Her face and hands were streaked with grime, her hair matted with dirt. Richie thought she looked absolutely magnificent. 'And you know what did it.'

'I nuh-never should have t-t-told her where I was guh-going,' Bill said. 'Why did I do that? Why did I −'

Her hands pistoned out and seized him by the shirt. Amazed, Richie watched as she shook him.

'No more! You know what we came for! We swore, *and we're going to do it!* Do you understand me, Bill? If she's dead, she's dead . . . *but It's not!* Now, we need you. Do you get it? We *need* you!' She was crying now. 'So you stand up for us! You stand up for us like before or none of us are going to get out of here!'

He looked at her for a long time without speaking, and Richie found himself thinking, *Come on, Big Bill. Come on, come on −*

Bill looked around at the rest of them and nodded. 'Eh-Eddie.'

'I'm here, Bill.'

'D-Do y-you still ruh-remember which p-p-pipe?'

Eddie pointed past Victor and said: 'That one. Looks pretty small, doesn't it?'

Bill nodded again. 'Can you do it? With your a-a-arm broken?'

'I can for you, Bill.'

Bill smiled: the weariest, most terrible smile Richie had ever seen. 'Tuh-hake us there, Eh-Eddie. Let's g-get it done.'

5

In the Tunnels/4:55 A.M.

As he crawled, Bill reminded himself of the dropoff at the end of this pipe, but it still surprised him. At one moment his hands were shuffling along the crusted surface of the old pipe; at the next they were skating on air. He pitched forward and rolled instinctively, landing on his shoulder with a painful crunch.

'Be c-c-careful!' he heard himself shouting. 'Here's the druh-hopoff! Eh-Eh-Eddie?'

'Here!' One of Eddie's waving hands brushed across Bill's forehead. 'Can you help me out?'

He got his arms around Eddie and lifted him out, trying to be careful of the bad arm. Ben came next, then Bev, then Richie.

'You got any muh-muh-matches, Ruh-Richie?'

'I do,' Beverly said. Bill felt a hand touch his in the darkness and press a folder of matches into it. 'There's only eight or ten, but Ben's got more. From the room.'

Bill said, 'Did you keep them in your a-a-armpit, B-Bev?'

'Not this time,' she said, and put her arms around him in the dark. He hugged her tight, eyes closed, trying to take the comfort that she wanted so badly to give.

He released her gently and struck a match. The power of memory was great – they all looked at once to their right. What remained of Patrick Hockstetter's body was still there, amid a few lumpy, overgrown things that might have been books. The only really recognizable thing was a jutting semicircle of teeth, two or three of them with fillings.

And something nearby. A gleaming circle barely seen in the match's guttering light.

Bill shook the match out and lit another. He picked it up. 'Audra's wedding ring,' he said. His voice was hollow, expressionless.

The match went out in his fingers.

In the darkness he put the ring on.

'Bill?' Richie said hesitantly. 'Do you have any idea

6

In the Tunnels/2:20 P.M.

how long they had been wandering through the tunnels under Derry since they had left the place where Patrick Hockstetter's body was, but Bill was sure he could never find his way back. He kept thinking about what his father had said: *You could wander for weeks.* If Eddie's sense of direction failed them now, they wouldn't need It to kill them; they would wander until they died . . . or, if they got into the wrong set of pipes, until they were drowned like rats in a rain-barrel.

But Eddie didn't seem a bit worried. Every now and then he would ask Bill to light one of their diminishing store of matches, look around thoughtfully, and then set off again. He made rights and lefts seemingly at random. Sometimes the pipes were so big Bill could not reach their tops even by stretching his hand up all the way. Sometimes they had to crawl, and once, for five horrible minutes (which felt more like five hours), they wormed their way along on their bellies, Eddie now leading, the others following with their noses to the heels of the person ahead.

The only thing Bill was completely sure of was that they had somehow gotten into a disused section of the Derry sewer system. They had left all the active pipes either far behind or far above. The roar of running water had dimmed to a far-off thunder. These pipes were older, not kiln-fired ceramic but a crumbly claylike stuff that sometimes oozed springs of unpleasant-smelling fluid. The smells of human waste – those ripe gassy smells that had threatened to suffocate them all – had faded, but they had been replaced by another smell, yellow and ancient, that was worse.

Ben thought it was the smell of the mummy. To Eddie it smelled like the leper. Richie thought it smelled like the world's oldest flannel jacket, now moldering and rotting – a lumberman's jacket, a very big one, big enough for a character like Paul Bunyan, perhaps. To Beverly it smelled like her father's sock-drawer. In Stan Uris it woke a dreadful memory from his earliest childhood – an oddly Jewish memory in a boy who had only the haziest understanding of his own Jewishness. It smelled like clay mixed with oil and made him think of an eyeless, mouthless demon called the Golem, a clay man that renegade Jews were supposed to have raised in the Middle Ages to save them from the *goyim* who robbed them and raped their women and then sent them packing. Mike thought of the dry smell of feathers in a dead nest.

When they finally reached the end of the narrow pipe, they slithered like eels down the curved surface of another which ran at an oblique angle to the one they had been in, and found they could stand up again. Bill felt the heads of the matches left in the book. Four. His mouth tightened and he resolved not to tell the others how close they were to the end of their light . . . not unless he absolutely had to.

'Huh-Huh-How you g-g-guys d-doin?'

They murmured replies, and he nodded in the dark. No panic, and no tears since Stan's. That was good. He felt for their hands and they stood together in the dark that way for awhile, both taking and giving from the touch. Bill felt clear exultation in this, a sure sense that they were somehow producing more than the sum of their seven selves; they had been re-added into a more potent whole.

He lit one of the remaining matches and they saw a narrow tunnel stretching ahead on a downward slant. The top of this pipe was festooned with sagging cobwebs, some water-broken and hanging in shrouds. Looking at them gave Bill an atavistic chill. The floor here was dry but thick with ancient mold and what might have been leaves, fungus . . . or some unimaginable droppings. Farther up he saw a pile of bones and a drift of green rags. They might once have been that stuff they called 'polished cotton,' workman's clothes. Bill imagined some Sewer Department or Water Department worker who had gotten lost, wandered down here, and been discovered . . .

The match guttered. He tipped its head downward, wanting the light to last a little longer.

'Do y-y-you nuh-know where w-w-we are?' he asked Eddie.

Eddie pointed down the slightly crooked bore of the tunnel. 'Canal's that way,' he said. 'Less'n half a mile, unless this thing turns in a different direction. We're under Up-Mile Hill right now, I think. But Bill –'

The match burned Bill's fingers and he let it drop. They were in darkness again. Someone – Bill thought it was Beverly – sighed. But before the match had gone out, he had seen the worry on Eddie's face.

'W-W-What? What ih-is it?'

'When I say we're under Up-Mile Hill, I mean we're *really* under it. We been going down for a long time now. Nobody'd *ever* put sewer-pipe in this deep. When you put a tunnel this deep you call it a mine-shaft.'

'How deep do you figure we are, Eddie?' Richie asked.

'Quarter of a mile,' Eddie said. 'Maybe more.'

'Jesus-please-us,' Beverly said.

'These aren't sewer-pipes, anyway,' Stan said from behind them. 'You can tell by that smell. It's bad, but it's not a *sewery* smell.'

'I think I'd rather smell the sewer,' Ben said. 'It smells like –'

A scream floated down to them, issuing from the mouth of the pipe they had just left, lifting the hair on the nape of Bill's neck. The seven of them drew together, clutching each other.

'– *gonna get you sons of bitches. We're gonna get youuuuuuuu* –'

'Henry,' Eddie breathed. 'Oh my God, he's still coming.'

'I'm not surprised,' Richie said. 'Some people are too stupid to quit.'

They could hear faint panting, the scrape of shoes, the whisper of cloth.

'– *youuuuuuuuuu* –'

'Cuh-Cuh-Come on,' Bill said.

They started down the pipe, now walking double except for

961

Mike, who was at the back of the line: Bill and Eddie, Richie and Bev, Ben and Stan.

'H-H-How fuh-far b-b-back do y-you think H-H-Henry ih-his?'

'I couldn't tell, Big Bill,' Eddie said. 'The echoes are bad.' He dropped his voice. 'Did you see that pile of bones?'

'Y-Y-Yes,' Bill said, dropping his own voice.

'There was a tool-belt with the clothes. I think it was a Water Department guy.'

'I guh-guess s-s-so.'

'How long you think –?'

'I d-d-don't nuh-nuh-know.'

Eddie closed his good hand over Bill's arm in the darkness.

It was perhaps fifteen minutes later when they heard something coming toward them in the dark.

Richie stopped, frozen cold all the way through. Suddenly he was three years old again. He listened to that squelching, shifting move-ment – closing in on them, closing – and to the whispering branchlike sounds that accompanied it, and even before Bill struck a match he knew what it would be.

'*The Eye!*' he screamed. '*Christ, it's the Crawling Eye!*'

For a moment the others were not sure what they were seeing (Beverly had an impression that her father had found her, even down here, and Eddie had a fleeting vision of Patrick Hockstetter come back to life, somehow Patrick had flanked them and gotten in front of them), but Richie's cry, Richie's *certainty*, froze the shape for all of them. They saw what Richie saw.

A gigantic Eye filled the tunnel, the glassy black pupil two feet across, the iris a muddy russet color. The white was bulgy, membranous, laced with red veins that pulsed steadily. It was a lidless lashless gelat-inous horror that moved on a bed of raw-looking tentacles. These fumbled over the tunnel's crumbly surface and sank in like fingers, so that the impression given in the glow of Bill's guttering match was of an Eye that had somehow grown nightmare fingers which were pulling It along.

It stared at them with blank, feverish avarice. The match went out.

In the darkness, Bill felt those branchlike tentacles caress his ankles, his shins . . . but he could not move. His body was frozen solid. He sensed It approaching, he could feel the heat radiating out from It, and could hear the wet pulse of blood wetting Its membranes. He imagined the stickiness he would feel when It touched him and still he could not scream. Even when fresh tentacles slipped around his waist and hooked themselves into the loops of his jeans and began to drag him forward, he could not scream or struggle. A deadly sleepiness seemed to have suffused his whole body.

Beverly felt one of the tentacles slip around the cup of her ear and suddenly draw noose-tight. Pain flared and she was dragged forward, twisting and moaning, as if an old-lady schoolteacher were giving her an out-of-patience come-along to the back of the room, where she would be forced to sit on a stool and wear a duncecap. Stan and Richie tried to back away, but a forest of unseen tentacles now wavered and whispered about them. Ben put an arm around Beverly and tried to tug her back. She clasped his hands with panicky tightness.

'Ben . . . Ben, It's got me . . .'

'No It don't . . . Wait . . . I'll pull . . .'

He pulled with all his might, and Beverly screamed as pain tore through her ear and blood began to flow. A tentacle, dry and hard, scraped over Ben's shirt, paused, then twisted in a painful knot around his shoulder.

Bill put out a hand, and it slapped into a gluey yielding wetness. *The Eye!* his mind screamed. *Oh God I got my hand in the Eye! Oh God! Oh dear sweet God! The Eye! My hand in the Eye!*

He began to fight now, but the tentacles drew him forward inexorably. His hand disappeared into that wet avid heat. His forearm. Now his arm was plunged into the Eye up to the elbow. At any moment the rest of his body would come against that sticky surface and he felt that he would go mad in that instant. He fought frantically, chopping at the tentacles with his other hand.

Eddie stood like a boy in a dream, hearing the muffled screams and sounds of struggle as his friends were being pulled in. He sensed the tentacles around him but none had as yet actually landed on him.

Run home! his mind commanded him quite loudly. *Run home to your mamma, Eddie! You can find the way!*

Bill screamed in the dark – a high, despairing sound that was followed by hideous squishings and slobberings.

Eddie's paralysis broke wide open – It was trying to take Big Bill!

'*No!*' Eddie bellowed – it was a full-blown roar. One might never have guessed such a Norse-warrior sound could issue from such a thin chest, Eddie Kaspbrak's chest, Eddie Kaspbrak's *lungs*, which were of course afflicted with the most terrible case of asthma in Derry. He bolted forward, jumping over questing tentacles without seeing them, his broken arm thumping his own chest as it swung back and forth in its soggy cast. He fumbled in his pocket and brought out his aspirator.

(*acid that's what it tastes like acid acid battery acid*)

He collided with Bill Denbrough's back and slammed him aside. There was a watery ripping sound, followed by a low eager mewling that Eddie did not so much hear with his ears as feel with his mind. He raised the aspirator

(*acid it's acid if I want it to be so eat it eat it eat*)

'*BATTERY ACID, FUCKNUTS!*' Eddie screamed, and triggered off a blast. At the same time he kicked at the Eye. His foot went deep into the jelly of Its cornea. There was a gush of hot fluid over his leg. He pulled his foot back, only dimly aware that he had lost his shoe.

'*FUCK OFF! CRAM IT, SAM! GO AWAY, JOSÉ! GET LOST! FUCK OFF!*'

He felt tentacles touch him, but tentatively. He triggered the aspirator again, coating the Eye, and felt/heard that mewling again . . . now a hurt, surprised sound.

'*Fight It!*' Eddie raved at the others. '*It's just a fucking Eye! Fight It! You hear me? Fight It, Bill! Kick the shit out of the sucker! Jesus Christ you fucking pussies I'm doing the Mashed Potatoes all over It AND I GOT A BROKEN ARM!*'

Bill felt his strength return. He ripped his dripping arm out of the Eye . . . and then slammed it, fist-first, back in. A moment later Ben was beside him. He ran into the Eye, grunted with surprise and disgust, and then began to rain punches onto its jellied quivering surface. '*Let her go!*' he yelled. '*You hear me? Let her go! Get outta here! Get outta here!*'

'*Just an Eye! Just a fucking Eye!*' Eddie was screaming deliriously. He triggered his aspirator again and felt It draw back. The tentacles which had settled on him now dropped away. '*Richie! Richie! Get it! It's just an Eye!*'

Richie stumbled forward, unable to believe he was doing this, actually approaching the worst, most terrible monster in the world. But he was.

He only threw a single weak punch, and the feel of his fist sinking into the Eye – it was thick and wet and somehow gristly – made him throw his guts up in one big tasteless convulsion. A sound came out of him – *glurt!* – and the thought that he'd actually puked *on* the Eye caused him to do it again. It was only a single punch, but since he had created this particular monster, perhaps that was all that was necessary. Suddenly the tentacles were gone. They could hear It withdrawing . . . and then the only sounds were Eddie panting and Beverly crying softly, one hand to her bleeding ear.

Bill struck one of their three remaining matches and they stared at each other with dazed, shocked faces. Bill's left arm was running with a thick, cloudy goo that looked like a mixture of partially congealed eggwhite and snot. Blood was trickling slowly down the side of Beverly's neck, and there was a fresh cut on Ben's cheek. Richie slowly pushed his glasses up on his nose.

'A-A-Are we all ruh-ruh-right?' Bill asked hoarsely.

'Are *you*, Bill?' Richie asked.

'Y-Y-Yeah.' He turned to Eddie and hugged the smaller boy with fierce intensity. 'You suh-suh-saved my luh-life, man.'

'It ate your *shoe*,' Beverly said, and uttered a wild laugh. 'Isn't that too *bad*.'

'I'll buy you a new pair of Keds when we get out of here,' Richie said. He clapped Eddie on the back in the dark. 'How did you do it, Eddie?'

'Shot it with my aspirator. Pretended it was acid. That's how it tastes after awhile if I'm having, you know, a bad day. Worked great.'

' "I'm doing the Mashed Potatoes all over It and I GOT A BROKEN ARM," ' Richie said, and giggled madly. 'Not too shabby, Eds. Actually pretty chuckalicious, tell you what.'

'I hate it when you call me Eds.'

'I know,' Richie said, hugging him tightly, 'but somebody has to toughen you up, Eds. When you stop leading the sheltered igszistence of a child and grow up, you gonna, Ah say, Ah say you gonna find out life ain't always this easy, boy!'

Eddie began to shriek with laughter. 'That's the shittiest Voice I ever heard, Richie.'

'Well, keep that aspirator thing handy,' Beverly said. 'We might need it again.'

'You didn't see It anywhere?' Mike asked. 'When you lit the match?'

'Ih-Ih-It's g-g-gone,' Bill said, and then added grimly: 'But we're getting close to It. To the pluh-hace where Ih-It stuh-stuh-stays. And I th-think we h-h-hurt Ih-hit th-that time.'

'Henry's still coming,' Stan said. His voice was low and hoarse. 'I can hear him back there.'

'Then let's move out,' Ben said.

They did. The tunnel progressed steadily downward, and that

smell — that low, wild stench — grew steadily stronger. At times they could hear Henry behind them, but now his cries seemed far away and not at all important. There was a feeling in all of them — similar to that feeling of skew and disconnection they had felt in the house on Neibolt Street — that they had progressed over the edge of the world and into some queer nothingness. Bill felt (although he did not have the vocabulary to express what he knew) that they were approaching Derry's dark and ruined heart.

It seemed to Mike Hanlon that he could almost feel that heart's diseased, arrhythmic beat. Beverly felt a sense of evil power growing around her, seeming to enfold her, certainly trying to split her off from the others and make her alone. Nervously, she reached out on either side of herself and clasped Bill's hand and Ben's. It seemed to her that she had to reach too far, and she called out nervously: 'Hang onto hands! It's like we're moving away from each other!'

It was Stan who first realized he could see again. There was a low, strange radiance in the air. At first he could only see hands — his, clasping Ben's on one side and Mike's on the other. Then he realized he could see the buttons on Richie's muddy shirt and the Captain Midnight ring — just some junky cereal-box prize — that Eddie liked to wear on his little finger.

'Can you guys see?' Stan asked, coming to a stop. The others stopped, too. Bill looked around, first aware that he *could* see — a little, anyway — and then that the tunnel had widened out amazingly. They were now in a curved chamber easily as big as the Sumner Tunnel in Boston. Bigger, he amended as he looked around with a growing sense of awe.

They craned their necks back to see the ceiling, which was now fifty feet or more above them, and held up by outcurving buttresses of stone like ribs. Nets of dirty cobweb hung between them. The floor was now stone-flagged, but overlaid with such a drift of ancient dirt that the quality of their footfalls had never changed. The up-curving walls were easily fifty feet away on either side.

'Waterworks must have really gone crazy down here,' Richie said, and laughed uneasily.

'Looks like a cathedral,' Beverly said softly.

'Where's the light coming from?' Ben wanted to know.

'Coming r-right out of the w-w-walls, looks l-like,' Bill said.

'I don't like it,' Stan said.

'Let's guh-go. H-H-Henry'll be breathing d-d-down our nuh-necks —'

A loud, braying cry split the gloom, and then the ruffling, heavy thunder of wings. A shape came cruising out of the dark, one eye glaring – the other was a dark lamp.

'The bird!' Stan screamed. 'Look out, it's the bird!'

It dived at them like an obscene fighter-plane, Its plated orange beak opening and closing to reveal the pink inner lining of Its mouth, plush as a satin pillow in a coffin.

It went straight for Eddie.

Its beak raked his shoulder and he felt pain sink into his flesh like acid. Blood flowed down his chest. He cried out as the backwash of Its beating wings blew noxious tunnel air in his face. It wheeled back, Its eye glaring malevolently, rolling in Its socket, blurring only as Its nictitating eyelid jittered down momentarily to cover the eye with tissue-thin film. Its claws sought Eddie, who ducked, screaming. They razored through the back of his shirt, cutting it open, drawing shallow scarlet lines along his shoulder-blades. Eddie yelled and tried to crawl away but the bird wheeled back again.

Mike broke forward, digging in his pocket. He came out with a one-blade Buck knife. As the bird dived on Eddie again, he swept it in a quick, tight arc across one of the bird's talons. It cut deep, and blood poured out. The bird banked away and then came back, folding Its wings, diving in like a bullet. Mike fell to one side at the last moment, slashing upward with the Buck knife. He missed, and the bird's claw hit his wrist with such force that his hand went numb and tingly – the bruise that later bloomed there went most of the way to his elbow. The Buck flew into the dark.

The bird came back, screeching triumphantly, and Mike rolled his body over Eddie's and waited for the worst.

Stan walked forward toward the two boys huddled on the floor as the bird returned. He stood, small and somehow trim in spite of the dirt grimed into his hands and arms and pants and shirt, and suddenly held his hands out in a curious gesture – palms up, fingers down. The bird uttered another squawk and sheared off, bulleting by Stan, missing him by inches, lifting his hair and then dropping it in the buffeting wake of Its passage. He turned in a tight circle to face Its return.

'I believe in scarlet tanagers even though I never saw one,' he said in a high clear voice. The bird screamed and banked away as if he'd shot at it. 'Same with vultures, and the New Guinea mudlark and the flamingos of Brazil.' The bird screamed, circled, and suddenly flew on up the tunnel, squawking. '*I believe in the golden bald eagle!*' Stan screamed after it. '*And I think there really might be a phoenix somewhere!*

But I don't believe in you, so get the fuck out of here! Get out! Hit the road, Jack!'

He stopped then, and the silence seemed very large.

Bill, Ben, and Beverly went to Mike and Eddie; they helped Eddie to his feet and Bill looked at the cuts. 'Nuh-not d-d-deep,' he said. 'But I b-bet they h-hurt like h-h-hell.'

'It tore my shirt to pieces, Big Bill.' Eddie's cheeks glistened with tears, and he was wheezing again. The bellowing barbarian's voice was gone; it was hard to believe it had ever been there. 'What am I going to tell my mom?'

Bill smiled a little. 'Why d-d-don't we wuh-worry about that when we g-g-g-get out of here? Give yourself a bluh-hast, E-Eddie.'

Eddie did, inhaling deeply and then wheezing.

'That was great, man,' Richie told Stan. 'That was just frockin *great!*'

Stan was shivering all over. 'There's no bird like that, that's all. There never has been and there never will be.'

'*We're coming!*' Henry screamed from behind them. His voice was utterly demented. He was laughing and howling now. He sounded like something that has crawled out of a crack in the roof of hell. '*Me'n Belch! We're coming and we'll get you little punks! You can't get away!*'

Bill shouted: '*G-G-Get out, H-H Henry! W-W-While there's still tuh-tuh-time!*'

Henry's response was a hollow, inarticulate scream. They heard a hustle of footsteps and in a burst of comprehension Bill understood Henry's whole purpose: he was real, he was mortal, he could not be stopped by an aspirator or a bird-book. Magic would not work on Henry. He was too stupid.

'C-C-Come oh-on. We guh-gotta stay a-a-ahead of h-h-him.'

They went on again, holding hands, Eddie's tattered shirt flapping behind him. The light grew brighter, the tunnel ever huger. As it canted downward, the ceiling flew away above until they could barely see it. It now seemed to them that they were not walking in a tunnel at all but making their way through a titanic underground courtyard, the approach to some cyclopean castle. The light from the walls had become a running green-yellow fire. The smell was stronger, and they began to pick up a vibration that might have been real or might have been only in their minds. It was steady and rhythmic.

It was a heartbeat.

'It ends up ahead!' Beverly cried. 'Look! It's a blank wall!'

But as they drew closer, antlike now on this great floor of dirty stone blocks, each block bigger than Bassey Park, it seemed, they saw that the wall was not entirely blank after all. It was broken by a single door. And although the wall itself towered hundreds of feet above them, the door was very small. It was no more than three feet high, a door of the sort you might see in a fairytale book, made of stout oaken boards bound with iron strips in an X-pattern. It was, they all realized at once, a door made only for children.

Ghostly, in his mind, Ben heard the librarian reading to the little ones: *Who is that trip-trapping upon my bridge?* The children lean forward, all the old fascination glistening in their eyes: will the monster be bested . . . or will It feed?

There was a mark on the door, and heaped at its foot was a pile of bones. Small bones. The bones of God alone knew how many children.

They had come to the place of It.

The mark on the door, then: what was that?

Bill marked it as a paper boat.

Stan saw it as a bird rising toward the sky – a phoenix, perhaps.

Michael saw a hooded face – that of crazy Butch Bowers, perhaps, if it could only be seen.

Richie saw two eyes behind a pair of spectacles.

Beverly saw a hand doubled up into a fist.

Eddie believed it to be the face of the leper, all sunken eyes and wrinkled snarling mouth – all disease, all sickness, was stamped into that face.

Ben Hanscom saw a tattered pile of wrappings and seemed to smell old sour spices.

Later, arriving at that same door with Belch's screams still echoing in his ears, alone at the end of it, Henry Bowers would see it as the moon, full, ripe . . . and black.

'I'm scared, Bill,' Ben said in a wavering voice. 'Do we have to?'

Bill toed the bones, and suddenly scattered them in a powdery, rattling drift with one foot. He was scared, too . . . but there was George to consider. It had ripped off George's arm. Were those small and fragile bones among these? Yes, of course they were.

They were here for the owners of the bones, George and all the others – those who had been brought here, those who might be brought here, those who had been left in other places simply to rot.

'We have to,' Bill said.

'What if it's locked?' Beverly asked in a small voice.

'Ih-It's not l-locked,' Bill said, and then told her what he knew from deeper inside: 'Pluh-haces like this are n-never luh-luh-locked.'

He placed the tented fingers of his right hand on the door and pushed. It swung open on a flood of sick yellow-green light. That zoo smell wafted out at them, incredibly strong, incredibly potent now.

One by one they passed through the fairytale door, and into the lair of It. Bill

7

In the Tunnels/4:59 A.M.

stopped so suddenly that the others piled up like freight-cars when the engine suddenly comes to a panic-stop. 'What is it?' Ben called.

'Ih-Ih-It was h-h-here. The Eh-Eh-Eye. D-Do you r-r-remember?'

'I remember,' Richie said. 'Eddie stopped it with his aspirator. By pretending it was acid. He said something about some dance. Pretty chuckalicious, but I can't remember exactly what it was.'

'It d-d-doesn't m-m-matter. We won't suh-see anything we saw b-b-before,' Bill said. He struck a light and looked around at the others. Their faces were luminous in the glow of the match, luminous and mystic. And they seemed very young. 'H-H-How you guys d-doin?'

'We're okay, Big Bill,' Eddie said, but his face was drawn with pain. Bill's makeshift splint was coming apart. 'How bout you?'

'Oh-Oh-kay,' Bill said, and shook out the match before his face could tell them any different story.

'How did it happen?' Beverly asked him, touching his arm in the dark. 'Bill, how could she–?'

'B-B-Because I muh-hentioned the n-name of the town. Sh-She c-c-came ah-hafter m-m-me. Even wh-when I was d-d-doing it, suh-suh-homething ih-hinside was t-t-telling me to sh-sh-shut uh-up. B-But I d-d-didn't luh-luh-histen.' He shook his head helplessly in the dark.

'But even if sh-she came to Duh-Duh-Derry, I d-d-don't uh-hunder-stand h-h-how she c-could have guh-hotten d-d-down *h-here*. If H-H-Henry dih-didn't b-b-bring her, then who d-did?'

'It,' Ben said. 'It doesn't have to look bad, we know that. It could have shown up and said you were in trouble. Taken her here in order to . . . to fuck you up, I suppose. To kill our guts. Cause that's what you always were, Big Bill. Our guts.'

'Tom?' Beverly said in a low, almost musing voice.

'*W-W-Who?*' Bill struck another match.

She was looking at him with a kind of desperate honesty. 'Tom. My husband. He knew, too. At least, I think I mentioned the name of the town to him, the way you mentioned it to Audra. I . . . I don't know if it took or not. He was pretty angry with me at the time.'

'Jesus, what is this, some kind of soap opera where everybody turns up sooner or later?' Richie said.

'Not a soap opera,' Bill said, sounding sick, 'a show. Like the circus. Bev here went and married Henry Bowers. When she left, why wouldn't he come here? After all, the real Henry did.'

'No,' Beverly said. 'I didn't marry Henry. I married my father.'

'If he beat on you, what's the difference?' Eddie asked.

'C-C-Come around me,' Bill said. 'Muh-muh-move in.'

They did. Bill reached out to either side and found Eddie's good hand and one of Richie's hands. Soon they stood in a circle, as they had done once before when their number was greater. Eddie felt someone put an arm around his shoulders. The feeling was warm and comforting and deeply familiar.

Bill felt the sense of power that he remembered from before, but understood with some desperation that things really *had* changed. The power was nowhere near as strong – it struggled and flickered like a candle-flame in foul air. The darkness seemed thicker and closer to them, more triumphant. And he could smell It. *Down this passageway*, he thought, *and not so terribly far, is a door with a mark on it. What was behind that door? It's the one thing I still can't remember. I can remember making my fingers stiff, because they wanted to tremble, and I can remember pushing the door open. I can even remember the flood of light that streamed out and how it seemed almost alive, as if it wasn't just light but fluorescent snakes. I remember the smell, like the monkey-house in a big zoo, but even worse. And then . . . nothing.*

'Do a-a-any of y-y-y-you rem-m-member what It really w-w-was?'

'No,' Eddie said.

'I think . . .' Richie began, and then Bill could almost feel him shake his head in the dark. 'No.'

'No,' Beverly said.

'Huh-uh.' That was Ben. 'That's the one thing I still can't remember. What It was . . . or how we fought It.'

'Chüd,' Beverly said. 'That's how we fought it. But I don't remember what that means.'

'Stand by m-me,' Bill said, 'and I-I'll stuh-stuh-hand by y-y-you guys.'

'Bill,' Ben said. His voice was very calm. 'Something is coming.'

Bill listened. He heard dragging, shambling footsteps approaching them in the dark . . . and he was afraid.

'A-A-Audra?' he called . . . and knew already that it was not her. Whatever was shambling toward them drew closer.

Bill struck a light.

8

Derry/5:00 A.M.

The first wrong thing happened on that late-spring day in 1985 two minutes before official sunrise. To understand how wrong it was one would have to have known two facts that were known to Mike Hanlon (who lay unconscious in the Derry Home Hospital as the sun came up), both concerning the Grace Baptist Church, which had stood on the corner of Witcham and Jackson since 1897. The church was topped with a slender white spire which was the apotheosis of every Protestant church-steeple in New England. There were clock-faces on all four sides of the steeple-base, and the clock itself had been constructed and shipped from Switzerland in the year 1898. The only one like it stood in the town square of Haven Village, forty miles away.

Stephen Bowie, a timber baron who lived on West Broadway, donated the clock to the town at a cost of some $17,000. Bowie could afford it. He was a devout churchgoer and deacon for forty years (during several of those later years he was also president of Derry's Legion of White Decency chapter). In addition, he was known for his devout layman sermons on Mother's Day, which he always referred to reverently as Mother's Sunday.

From the time of its installation until May 31st, 1985, that clock had faithfully chimed each hour and each half – with one notable exception. On the day of the explosion at the Kitchener Ironworks it had not chimed the noon-hour. Residents believed that the Reverend Jollyn had silenced the clock to show that the church was in mourning for the dead children, and Jollyn never disabused them of this notion, although it was not true. The clock had simply not chimed.

Nor did it chime the hour of five on the morning of May 31st, 1985.

At that moment, all over Derry, old-timers opened their eyes and sat up, disturbed for no reason they could put their fingers on. Medicines were gulped, false teeth put in, pipes and cigars lit.

The old folks stood a watch.

One of them was Norbert Keene, now in his nineties. He hobbled to the window and looked out at a darkening sky. The weather report the night before had called for clear skies, but his bones told him it was going to rain, and hard. He felt scared, deep inside him; in some obscure way he felt threatened, as if a poison were working its way relentlessly toward his heart. He thought randomly of the day the Bradley Gang had ridden heedlessly into Derry, into the sights of seventy-five pistols and rifles. That kind of work left a man feeling kind of warm and lazy inside, like everything was . . . was somehow *confirmed*. He couldn't put it any better than that, even to himself. Work like that left a man feeling like he maybe might live forever, and Norbert Keene damn near had. Ninety-six years old come June 24th, and he still walked three miles every day. But now he felt scared.

'Those kids,' he said, looking out his window, unaware he had spoken. 'What is it with them damn kids? What they monkeying around with this time?'

Egbert Thoroughgood, ninety-nine, who had been in the Silver Dollar when Claude Heroux tuned up his axe and played 'The Dead March' for four men on it, awoke at the same moment, sat up, and let out a rusty scream that no one heard. He had dreamed of Claude, only Claude had been coming after *him*, and the axe had come down, and a moment after it did Thoroughgood had seen his own severed hand twitching and curling on the counter.

Something wrong, he thought in his muddy way, frightened and shaking all over in his pee-stained longjohns. *Something dreadful wrong*.

Dave Gardener, who had discovered George Denbrough's mutilated body in October of 1957 and whose son had discovered the first victim of this new cycle earlier in the spring, opened his eyes on the stroke of five and thought, even before looking at the clock on the bureau: *Grace Church clock didn't chime the hour . . . What's wrong?* He felt a large ill-defined fright. Dave had prospered over the years; in 1965 he had purchased The Shoeboat, and now there was a second Shoeboat at the Derry Mall and a third up in Bangor. Suddenly all of those things – things he had spent his life working for – seemed in jeopardy. *From what?* he cried to himself, looking at his sleeping wife. *From* what, *why you so goddam antsy just because that clock didn't chime?* But there was no answer.

He got up and went to the window, hitching at the waistband of his pyjamas. The sky was restless with clouds racing in from the west, and Dave's disquiet grew. For the first time in a very long while he found himself thinking of the screams that had brought him to his porch twenty-seven years ago, to see that writhing figure in the yellow rainslicker. He looked at the approaching clouds and thought: *We're in danger. All of us. Derry.*

Chief Andrew Rademacher, who really believed he had tried his best to solve the new string of child-murders that had plagued Derry, stood on the porch of his house, thumbs in his Sam Browne belt, looking up at the clouds, and felt the same disquiet. *Something getting ready to happen. Looks like it's going to pour buckets, for one thing. But that's not all.* He shuddered . . . and as he stood there on his porch, the smell of the bacon his wife was cooking wafting out through the screen door, the first dime-sized drops of rain darkened the sidewalk in front of his pleasant Reynolds Street home and, somewhere just over the horizon from Bassey Park, thunder rumbled.

Rademacher shivered again.

9

George/5:01 A.M.

Bill held the match up . . . and uttered a long trembling despairing screech.

It was George wavering up the tunnel toward him, George, still dressed in his blood-spattered yellow rainslicker. One sleeve dangled limp and useless. George's face was white as cheese and his eyes were shiny silver. They fixed on Bill's own.

'*My boat!*' Georgie's lost voice rose, wavering, in the tunnel. '*I can't find it, Bill, I've looked everywhere and I can't find it and now I'm dead and it's your fault your fault YOUR FAULT –*'

'Juh-Juh-Georgie!' Bill shrieked. He felt his mind tottering, ripping free of its moorings.

George stumble-staggered toward him and now his one remaining arm rose toward Bill, the white hand at the end of it hooked into a claw. The nails were dirty and grasping.

'*Your fault,*' George whispered, and grinned. His teeth were fangs; they opened and closed slowly, like the teeth in a beartrap. '*You sent me out and it's all . . . your . . . fault.*'

'Nuh-Nuh-No, Juh Juh-Georgie!' Bill cried. 'I dih-dih-didn't nuh-hun-nuh-know –'

'*Kill you!*' George cried, and a mixture of doglike sounds came out of that fanged mouth: yips, yelps, howls. A kind of laughter. Bill could smell him now, could smell George rotting. It was a cellar-smell, squirmy, the smell of some final monster standing slumped and yellow-eyed in the corner, waiting to unzip some small boy's guts.

George's teeth gnashed together. The sound was like billiard balls clicking off one another. Yellow pus began to leak from his eyes and dribble down his face . . . and the match went out.

Bill felt his friends disappear – they were running, of course they were, they were leaving him alone. They were cutting him off, as his parents had cut him off, because George was right: it was all his fault. Soon he would feel that single hand seize his throat, soon he would feel those fangs pulling him open, and that would be right. That would be only just. He had sent George out to die, and he had spent his whole adult life writing about the horror of that betrayal – oh, he had put many faces on it, almost as many faces as It had put on for their benefit, but the monster at the bottom of everything was only George, running out into the receding flood with his paraffin-coated paper boat. Now would come the atonement.

'You deserve to die for killing me,' George whispered. He was very close now. Bill closed his eyes.

Then yellow light splashed the tunnel and he opened them. Richie was holding up a match. 'Fight It, Bill!' Richie shouted. 'God's sake! Fight It!'

What are you doing here? He looked at them, bewildered. They hadn't run after all. How could that be? How could that be after they had seen how foully he had murdered his own brother?

'Fight It!' Beverly was screaming. 'Oh Bill, fight It! Only you can do this one! Please –'

George was less than five feet away now. He suddenly stuck his tongue out at Bill. It was crawling with white fungoid growths. Bill screamed again.

'Kill It, Bill!' Eddie shouted. 'That's not your brother! Kill It while It's small! *Kill It NOW!*'

George glanced at Eddie, cutting his shiny-silver eyes that way for just a moment, and Eddie reeled back and struck the wall as if he had been pushed. Bill stood mesmerized, watching his brother come toward him, George again after all these years, it was George at the end as it had been George at the beginning, oh yes, and he could hear the creak of George's yellow slicker as George closed the distance, he could hear the jingle of the buckles on his overshoes and he could smell something like wet leaves, as if underneath the slicker George's body was made of them, as if the feet inside George's galoshes were leaf-feet, yes, a leaf-man, that was it, that was George, he was a rotted balloon face and a body made of dead leaves, the kind that sometimes choke the sewers after a flood.

Dimly he heard Beverly shriek.

(*he thrusts his fists*)

'Bill, please Bill —'

(*against the posts and still insists*)

'We'll look for my boat together,' George said. Thick yellow pus, mock tears, rolled down his cheeks. He reached for Bill and his head cocked sideward, his teeth peeling back from those fangs.

(*he sees the ghosts he sees the ghosts HE SEES*)

'We'll find it,' George said and Bill could smell Its breath and it was a smell like exploded animals lying on the highway at midnight. As George's mouth yawned, he could see things squirming around inside there. 'It's still down here, everything floats down here, we'll float, Bill, we'll all float —'

George's fishbelly hand closed on Bill's neck.

(*HE SEES THE GHOSTS WE SEE THE GHOSTS THEY WE YOU SEE THE GHOSTS —*)

George's contorted face drifted toward Bill's neck.

'— *float* —'

'*He thrusts his fists against the posts!*' Bill cried. His voice was deeper, hardly his own at all, and in a searing flash of memory Richie remembered that Bill only stuttered in his own voice: when he pretended to be someone else, he *never* did.

The George-thing recoiled, hissing, Its hand going to Its face in a warding-off gesture.

'That's it!' Richie screamed deliriously. 'You got It, Bill! Get It! Get It! Get It!'

'*He thrusts his fists against the posts and still insists he sees the ghosts!*' Bill thundered. He advanced on the George-thing. '*You're* no ghost! *George* knows I didn't mean for him to die! My folks were wrong! They took it out on me *and that was wrong! Do you hear me?*'

The George-thing abruptly turned, squealing like a rat. It began to run and ripple under the yellow slicker. The slicker itself seemed to be dripping, running in bright blots of yellow. It was losing Its shape, becoming amorphous.

'*He thrusts his fists against the posts, you son of a bitch!*' Bill Denbrough screamed, '*and still insists he sees the ghosts!*' He leaped at It and his fingers snagged in the yellow rainslicker that was no longer a rainslicker. What he grabbed felt like some strange warm taffy that melted under his fingers as soon as he had closed his fist around it. He fell to his knees. Then Richie yelled as the guttering match burned his fingers and they were plunged into darkness again.

Bill felt something begin to grow in his chest, something hot and choking and as painful as fiery nettles. He gripped his knees and drew them up to his chin, hoping it would stop the pain, or perhaps ease it; he was dimly thankful for the dark, glad that the others couldn't see this agony.

He heard a sound escape him – a wavering moan. There was a second; a third. '*George!*' he cried. '*George, I'm sorry! I never meant for anything b-b-b-bad to huh-huh-happen!*'

Perhaps there was something else to say, but he could not say it. He was sobbing then, lying on his back with one arm over his eyes, remembering the boat, remembering the steady beat of the rain against his bedroom windows, remembering the medicines and the tissues on the nighttable, the faint ache of fever in his head and in his body, remembering George, most of all that: remembering George, George in his yellow hooded slicker.

'*George, I'm sorry!*' he cried through his tears. '*I'm sorry, I'm sorry, please, I'm suh-suh-SORRY –*'

And then they were around him, his friends, and no one lit a match, and someone held him, he didn't know who, Beverly maybe, or maybe Ben, or Richie. They were with him, and for that little while the darkness was kind.

10

Derry/5:30 A.M.

By 5:30 it was raining hard. The weather forecasters on the Bangor radio stations expressed mild surprise and tendered mild apologies to all the people who had made plans for picnics and outings on the basis of yesterday's forecasts. Tough break, folks; just one of those odd weather patterns that sometimes developed in the Penobscot Valley with startling suddenness.

On WZON, meteorologist Jim Witt described what he called an 'extraordinarily disciplined' low-pressure system. That was putting it mildly. Conditions went from cloudy in Bangor to showery in Hampden to drizzly in Haven to moderate rain in Newport. But in Derry, only thirty miles from downtown Bangor, it was pouring. Travellers on Route 7 found themselves moving through water that was eight inches deep in places, and beyond the Rhulin Farms a plugged culvert in a dip had covered the highway with so much water that the highway was actually impassable. By six that morning the Derry Highway Patrol had orange DETOUR signs on both sides of the dip.

Those who waited under the shelter on Main Street for the first bus of the day to take them to work stood looking over the railing at the Canal, where the water was ominously high in its concrete channel. There would be no flood, of course; all agreed on *that*. The water was still four feet below the high-water mark of 1977, and there had been no flood that year. But the rain came down with steady pounding persistence, and thunder grumbled in the low clouds. Water ran down Up-Mile Hill in streams and roared in the stormdrains and sewers.

No flood, they agreed, but there was a patina of unease on every face.

At 5:45 a power-transformer on a pole beside the abandoned Tracker Brothers' Truck Depot exploded in a flash of purple light, spraying twisted chunks of metal onto the shingled roof. One of the flying chunks of metal severed a high-tension wire, which also fell on the roof, spluttering and twisting like a snake, shooting an almost liquid stream of sparks. The roof caught fire in spite of the downpour, and soon the depot was blazing. The power-cable tumbled from the roof to the weedy verge that led around to the lot where small boys had once played baseball. The Derry Fire Department rolled for the first time that day at 6:02 A.M. and arrived at Tracker Brothers' at 6:09. One of the first firemen off the truck was Calvin Clark, one of the Clark twins with whom Ben, Beverly, Richie, and Bill had gone to school. His third step away from the truck brought the sole of his leather boot down on the live line. Calvin was electrocuted almost instantly. His tongue popped out of his mouth and his rubber fireman's coat began to smolder. He smelled like burning tires at the town dump.

At 6:05 A.M., residents of Merit Street in the Old Cape felt something that might have been an underground explosion. Plates fell from shelves and pictures from walls. At 6:06, every toilet on Merit

Street suddenly exploded in a geyser of shit and raw sewage as some unimaginable reversal took place in the pipes which fed the holding tanks of the new waste-treatment plant in the Barrens. In some cases these explosions were strong enough to tear holes in bathroom ceilings. A woman named Anne Stuart was killed when an ancient gear-wheel catapulted from her toilet along with a gout of sewage. The gear-wheel went through the frosted glass of the shower door and passed through her throat like a terrible bullet as she washed her hair. She was nearly decapitated. The gear-wheel was a relic of the Kitchener Ironworks, and had found its way into the sewers almost three-quarters of a century before. Another woman was killed when the sudden violent reversal of sewage, driven by expanding methane gases, caused her toilet to explode like a bomb. The unfortunate woman, who was sitting on the john at the time and reading the current Banana Republic catalogue, was torn to pieces.

At 6:19 A.M., a bolt of lightning struck the so-called Kissing Bridge, which spanned the Canal between Bassey Park and Derry High School. The splintered pieces were thrown high into the air and then rained down into the swiftly moving Canal to be carried away.

The wind was rising. At 6:30 A.M., the gauge in the lobby of the courthouse building registered it at just over fifteen miles an hour. By 6:45, it had risen to twenty-four miles an hour.

At 6:46 A.M., Mike Hanlon awoke in his room at the Derry Home Hospital. His return to consciousness was a kind of slow dissolve – for a long time he thought he was dreaming. If so, it was an odd sort of dream – an anxiety dream, his old psych prof Doc Abelson might have called it. There seemed to be no overt reason for the anxiety, but it was there all the same; the plain white room seemed to shriek menace.

He gradually realized that he was awake. The plain white room was a hospital room. Bottles hung over his head, one full of clear liquid, the other a deep dark red one. Whole blood. He saw a blank TV set bolted to the wall and became aware of the steady sound of rain beating against the window.

Mike tried to move his legs. One moved freely but the other, his right leg, wouldn't move at all. The feeling in that leg was very faint, and he realized it was tightly bandaged.

Little by little it came back. He had settled down to write in his notebook and Henry Bowers had turned up. A real blast from the past, a golden gasser. There had been a fight, and –

Henry! Where had Henry gone? After the others?

Mike groped for the call-bell. It was draped over the head of the bed, and he had it in his hands when the door opened. A nurse stood there. Two buttons of his white tunic were unbuttoned and his dark hair was mussed, giving him a rumpled Ben Casey look. He wore a Saint Christopher medal around his neck. Even in his soupy, only-three-quarters-awake state, Mike placed him immediately. In 1958, a sixteen-year-old girl named Cheryl Lamonica had been killed in Derry, killed by It. The girl had had a fourteen-year-old brother named Mark, and this was him.

'Mark?' he said weakly. 'I have to talk to you.'

'Shhh,' Mark said. His hand was in his pocket. 'No talk.'

He walked into the room, and as he stood at the foot of the bed, Mike saw with a hopeless chill how blank Mark Lamonica's eyes were. His head was slightly cocked, as if hearing distant music. He took his hand out of his pocket. There was a syringe in it.

'This will put you to sleep,' Mark said, and began to walk toward the bed.

11

Under the City/6:49 A.M.

'*Shhhhh!*' Bill cried suddenly, although there had been no sound except their own faint footsteps.

Richie struck a light. The walls of the tunnel had moved away, and the five of them seemed very small in this space under the city. They huddled together and Beverly felt a dreamy sense of *déjà-vu* as she observed the gigantic flagstones on the floor and the hanging nets of cobweb. They were close now. Close.

'What do you hear?' she asked Bill, trying to look everywhere as the match in Richie's hand burned down, expecting to see some new surprise come lurching or flying out of the darkness. Rodan, anyone? The alien from that gruesome movie with Sigourney Weaver? A great scuttering rat with orange eyes and silver teeth? But there was nothing – only the dusty smell of the dark, and, far away, the thunder of running water, as if the drains were filling up.

'S-S-Something ruh-ruh-wrong,' Bill said. 'Mike –'

'Mike?' Eddie asked. 'What about Mike?'

'I felt it, too,' Ben said. 'Is it . . . Bill, did he die?'

'No,' Bill said. His eyes were hazy and distant, unemotional – all of his alarm was in his tone and the defensive posture of his body. 'He

... H-H-He ...' He swallowed. There was a click in his throat. His eyes widened 'Oh Oh *no* −!'

'Bill?' Beverly cried, alarmed. 'Bill, what is it? What −'

'Gruh-gruh-grab my huh-hands!' Bill screamed. '*Kwuh-kwuh-quick!*'

Richie dropped the match and seized one of Bill's hands. Beverly grabbed the other. She groped with her free hand, and Eddie grasped it feebly with the hand at the end of his broken arm. Ben grasped his other hand and completed the circle by holding Richie's hand.

'*Send him our power!*' Bill cried in that same strange, deep voice. '*Send him our power, whatever You are, send him our power! Now! Now! Now!*'

Beverly felt something go out from them and toward Mike. Her head rolled on her shoulders in a kind of ecstasy, and the harsh whistle of Eddie's breathing merged with the headlong thunder of water in the drains.

12

'Now,' Mark Lamonica said in a low voice. He sighed − the sigh of a man who feels orgasm approaching.

Mike pushed the call-button in his hands again and again. He could hear it ringing at the nurses' station down the hall, but no one came. With a kind of hellish second sight he understood that the nurses were sitting around down there, reading the morning paper, drinking coffee, hearing his call-bell but not hearing it, hearing but not responding, they would respond only later when it was all over, because that was how things worked in Derry. In Derry some things were better not seen or heard ... until they were over.

Mike let the call-button fall from his hands.

Mark bent toward him, the tip of the syringe glittering. His Saint Christopher medal swung hypnotically back and forth as he drew the sheet down.

'Right there,' he whispered. 'The sternum.' And sighed again.

Mike suddenly felt power wash into him − some primitive power that crammed his body like volts. He stiffened, fingers splaying out as if in a convulsion. His eyes widened. A grunt jerked out of him, and that sense of dreadful paralysis was driven from him as if by a round-house slap.

His right hand pistoned out toward the nighttable. There was a plastic pitcher there and a heavy cafeteria-style water-glass beside it.

His hand closed around the glass. Lamonica sensed the change; that dreamy, pleased light disappeared from his eyes and was replaced by wary confusion. He drew back a bit, and then Mike brought the glass up and smashed it into his face.

Lamonica screamed and staggered backward, dropping the syringe. His hands went to his spouting face; blood ran down his wrists and splashed on his white tunic.

The power left as suddenly as it had come. Mike looked dully at the shards of broken glass on the bed and his hospital johnny and his own bleeding hand. He heard the quick, light sound of crepe-soled shoes in the hall, approaching.

Now they come, he thought, *Oh yes, now. And after they're gone, who'll show up? Who'll show up next?*

As they burst into his room, the nurses who had sat calmly on station as his call-bell rang frantically, Mike closed his eyes and prayed for it to be over. He prayed his friends were somewhere under the city, he prayed they were all right, he prayed they would end it.

He didn't know exactly Who he prayed to . . . but he prayed nonetheless.

13

Under the City/6:54 A.M.

'He's a-a-all ruh-right,' Bill said presently.

Ben didn't know how long they had stood in the darkness, holding hands. It seemed to him that he had felt something – something from them, from their circle – go out and then come back. But he did not know where that thing – if it existed at all – had gone, or done.

'Are you sure, Big Bill?' Richie asked.

'Y-Y-Yes.' Bill released Richie's hand and Beverly's. 'But we h-have to finish this as kwuh-quick as we c-can. C-Come oh-oh-on.'

They went on, Richie or Bill periodically lighting matches. *We don't have so much as a pea-shooter among us,* Ben thought. *But that's part of it, too, isn't it? Chüd. What does that mean? What was It, exactly? What was Its final face? And even if we didn't kill It, we hurt It. How did we do that?*

The chamber they walked through – it could no longer be called a tunnel – grew larger and larger. Their footfalls echoed. Ben remembered the smell, that thick zoo smell. He became aware that the matches were no longer necessary – there was light now, light of a sort: a ghastly effulgence that was growing steadily stronger. In that marshy light, his friends all looked like walking corpses.

'Wall up ahead, Bill,' Eddie said.

'I nuh-nuh-know.'

Ben felt his heart begin to pick up speed. There was a sour taste in his mouth and his head had begun to ache. He felt slow and frightened. He felt fat.

'The door,' Beverly whispered.

Yes, here it was. Once, twenty-seven years before, they had been able to pass through that door by doing no more than ducking their heads. Now they would have to duck-walk their way through, or crawl on hands and knees. They had grown; here was final proof, if final proof were needed.

The pulse-points in Ben's neck and wrists felt hot and bloody; his heart had picked up a light and rapid flutter that was close to arrhythmia. *Pigeon-pulse*, he thought randomly, and licked his lips.

Bright greenish-yellow light flooded out from under the door; it shot through the ornate keyhole in a twisting shaft that looked almost thick enough to cut.

The mark was on the door, and again they all saw something different in that strange device. Beverly saw Tom's face. Bill saw Audra's severed head with blank eyes that stared at him in dreadful accusation. Eddie saw a grinning skull poised over two crossed bones, the symbol for poison. Richie saw the bearded face of a degenerate Paul Bunyan, eyes narrowed to killer's slits. And Ben saw Henry Bowers.

'Bill, are we strong enough?' he asked. 'Can we do this?'

'I duh-hon't nuh-nuh-know,' Bill said.

'What if it's locked?' Beverly asked in a small voice. Tom's face mocked her.

'Ih-It's not,' Bill said. 'Pluh-haces like this are n-never luh-luh-locked.' He placed the tented fingers of his right hand on the door – he had to bend over to do it – and pushed. It swung open on a flood of sick yellow-green light. That zoo smell wafted out at them, the smell of the past become the present, horribly alive, obscenely vital.

Roll, wheel, Bill thought randomly, and looked around at them. Then he dropped to his hands and knees. Beverly followed, then Richie, then Eddie. Ben came last, his flesh crawling at the feel of the ancient grit on the floor. He passed through the portal, and as he straightened up in the weird glow of fire crawling up and down the dripping stone walls in snakes of light, the last memory socked home with the force of a psychic battering ram.

He cried out, staggering back, one hand going to his head, and his first incoherent thought was *No wonder Stan committed suicide! Oh God, I wish I had!* He saw the same expressions of stunned horror and dawning realization on the faces of the others as the last key turned in the last lock.

Then Beverly was shrieking, clinging to Bill, as It raced down the gossamer curtain of Its webbing, a nightmare Spider from beyond time and space, a Spider from beyond the fevered imaginings of whatever inmates may live in the deepest depths of hell.

No, Bill thought coldly, *not a Spider either, not really, but this shape isn't one It picked out of our minds; it's just the closest our minds can come to*
(*the deadlights*)
whatever It really is.

It was perhaps fifteen feet high and as black as a moonless night. Each of Its legs was as thick as a muscle-builder's thigh. Its eyes were bright malevolent rubies, bulging from sockets filled with some dripping chromium-colored fluid. Its jagged mandibles opened and closed, opened and closed, dripping ribbons of foam. Frozen in an ecstasy of horror, tottering on the brink of utter lunacy, Ben observed with an eye-of-the-storm calm that this foam was alive; it struck the stinking stone-flagged floor and then began to writhe away into the cracks like protozoa.

But It's something else, there's some final shape, one that I can almost see the way you might see the shape of a man moving behind a movie screen while the show is on, some other shape, but I don't want to see It, please God, don't let me see It . . .

And it didn't matter, did it? They were seeing what they were seeing, and Ben understood somehow that It was imprisoned in this final shape, the shape of the Spider, by their common unsought and unfathered vision. It was against this It that they would live or die.

The creature was squealing and mewling, and Ben became quite sure he was hearing sounds It made twice – in his head, and then, a split second later, in his ears. *Telepathic,* he thought, *I'm reading Its mind.* Its shadow was a squat egg that raced along the ancient wall of this keep that was Its lair. Its body was covered by coarse hair, and Ben saw that It was possessed of a stinger long enough to impale a man. A clear fluid dripped from its tip, and Ben saw that this was also alive; like the saliva, the poison writhed away into the cracks of the floor. Its stinger, yes . . . but below that, Its belly bulged grotesquely, almost dragging on the floor as It moved, now changing direction slightly, heading unerringly toward their leader, toward Big Bill.

That's Its egg-sac, Ben thought, and his mind seemed to shriek at the implication. *Whatever It is beyond what we see, this representation is at least symbolically correct: It's female, and It's pregnant . . . It was pregnant then and none of us knew except Stan, oh Jesus Christ YES, it was Stan, Stan, not Mike, Stan who understood, Stan who told us . . . That's why we had to come back, no matter what, because It is female, It's pregnant with some unimaginable spawn . . . and Its time has drawn close.*

Incredibly, Bill Denbrough was stepping forward to meet It.

'*Bill, no!*' Beverly screamed.

'Stuh-Stuh-Stay b-b-back!' Bill shouted without looking around. And then Richie was running toward him, shouting his name, and Ben found his own legs in motion. He seemed to feel a phantom stomach swaying in front of him, and he welcomed the sensation. *Got to become a child again*, he thought incoherently. *That's the only way I can keep It from driving me crazy. Got to become a kid again . . . got to accept it. Somehow.*

Running. Shouting Bill's name. Vaguely aware that Eddie was running beside him, his broken arm flopping, the belt of the bathrobe Bill had cinched around it now trailing on the floor. Eddie had drawn his aspirator. He looked like a crazed malnourished gunslinger with some weird pistol.

Ben heard Bill bellow: '*You k-k-killed my brother, you fuh-fuh-fucking BITCH!*'

Then It was rearing up over Bill, burying Bill in Its shadow. Its legs pawing the air. Ben heard Its eager mewling, looked into Its timeless, evil red eyes . . . and for an instant *did* see the shape behind the shape: saw lights, saw an endless crawling hairy thing which was made of light and nothing else, orange light, dead light that mocked life.

The ritual began for the second time.

CHAPTER TWENTY-TWO
THE RITUAL OF CHÜD

1

In the Lair of It/1958

It was Bill who held them together as that great black Spider raced down Its web, creating a noxious breeze that tousled their hair. Stan shrieked like a baby, his brown eyes bulging from their sockets, his fingers harrowing his cheeks. Ben backed slowly away until his ample ass struck the wall to the left of the door. He felt cold fire burn through his pants and stepped away again, but dreamily. Surely none of this could be happening; it was simply the world's worst nightmare. He found he could not lift his hands. They seemed to have big weights tied to them.

Richie found his eyes drawn to that web. Hanging here and there, partially wrapped in silken strands that seemed to move as if alive, were a number of rotted half-eaten bodies. He thought he recognized Eddie Corcoran near the ceiling, although both of Eddie's legs and one of his arms were gone.

Beverly and Mike clung to each other like Hansel and Gretel in the woods, watching, paralyzed, as the Spider reached the floor and scrabbled toward them, Its distorted shadow racing along beside It on the wall.

Bill looked around at them, a tall, skinny boy in a mud-and-sewage-splattered tee-shirt that had once been white, jeans with cuffs, mud-caked Keds. His hair lay across his forehead, and his eyes were blazing. He surveyed them, seemed to dismiss them, and turned back toward the Spider. And, incredibly, he began to cross the room toward It, not running but walking fast, his elbows cocked, his forearms corded, his hands fisted.

'Yuh-Yuh-You k-k-killed my bruh-hother!'

'No, Bill!' Beverly shrieked, struggling free of Mike's embrace and running toward Bill, her red hair flying out behind her. '*Leave him alone!*' she screamed at the Spider. '*Don't you touch him!*'

Shit! Beverly! Ben thought, and then he was running too, stomach swaying back and forth in front of him, legs pumping. He was vaguely aware that Eddie Kaspbrak was running on his left, holding his aspirator in his good hand like a pistol.

And then It was rearing up over Bill, who was unarmed; It buried Bill in Its shadow, Its legs pawing at the air. Ben grabbed for Beverly's shoulder. His hand slapped it, then slipped off. She turned toward him, her eyes wild, her lips drawn back from her teeth.

'*Help him!*' she screamed.

'*How?*' Ben screamed back. He wheeled toward the Spider, heard Its eager mewling, looked into Its timeless, evil eyes, and saw something behind the shape; something much worse than a spider. Something that was all insane light. His courage faltered . . . but it was Bev who had asked him. Bev, and he loved her.

'*Goddam you, leave Bill alone!*' he shrieked.

A moment later a hand swatted his back so hard he almost fell over. It was Richie, and although tears were running down his cheeks, Richie was grinning madly. The corners of his mouth seemed to reach almost to the lobes of his ears. Spit leaked out between his teeth. '*Let's get her, Haystack!*' Richie screamed. '*Chüd! Chüd!*'

Her? Ben thought stupidly. Her, *did he say?*

Aloud: '*Okay, but what is it? What's Chüd?*'

'*Frocked if I know!*' Richie yelled, then ran toward Bill and into the shadow of It.

It had somehow squatted on Its rear legs. Its front legs pawed the air just over Bill's head. And Stan Uris, forced to approach, compelled to approach in spite of every instinct in his mind and body, saw that Bill was staring up at It, his blue eyes fixed on Its inhuman orange ones, eyes from which that awful corpse-light spilled. Stan stopped, understanding that the Ritual of Chüd – whatever that was – had begun.

2

Bill in the Void/Early

– *who are you and why do you come to Me?*

I'm Bill Denbrough. You know who I am and why I'm here. You killed my brother and I'm here to kill You. You picked the wrong kid, bitch.

– *I am eternal. I am the Eater of Worlds.*

Yeah? That so? Well, you've had your last meal, sister.

— you have no power; here is the power; feel the power, brat, and then speak again of how you come to kill the Eternal. You think you see Me? You see only what your mind will allow. Would you see Me? Come, then! Come, brat! Come!

Thrown —

(he)

No, not thrown, *fired*, fired like a living bullet, like the Human Cannonball at the Shrine Circus that came to Derry each May. He was picked up and *heaved* across the Spider's chamber. *It's only in my mind!* he screamed at himself. *My body's still standing right there, eye to eye with It, be brave, it's only a mind-trick, be brave, be true, stand, stand —*

(thrusts)

Roaring forward, slamming into a black and dripping tunnel lined with decaying, crumbling tiles that were fifty years old, a hundred, a thousand, a million-billion, who knew, rushing in deadly silence past intersections, some lit by that twisting green-yellow fire, some by glowing balloons full of a ghastly white skull-light, others dead black; he was thrown at a speed of a thousand miles an hour past piles of bones, some human, some not, speeding like a rocket-powered dart in a wind-tunnel, now angling upward, but not toward light but toward dark, some titanic dark

(his fists)

and exploding outward into utter blackness, the blackness was everything, the blackness was the cosmos and the universe, and the floor of the blackness was *hard, hard*, it was like polished ebonite and he was skidding along on his chest and belly and thighs like a weight on a shuffleboard. He was on the ballroom floor of eternity, and eternity was *black*.

(against the posts)

— stop that why do you say that? that won't help you, stupid boy and still insists he sees the ghosts!

— stop it!

he thrusts his fists against the posts and still insists he sees the ghosts!

— stop it! stop it! I demand, I command, that you stop it!

Don't like that, do you?

And thinking: *If I could only say it out loud, say it without stuttering, I could break this illusion —*

— this is no illusion, you foolish little boy — this is eternity, My eternity, and you are lost in it, lost forever, never to find your way back; you are eternal now, and condemned to wander in the black . . . after you meet Me face to face, that is

But there was something else here. Bill sensed it, felt it, in a crazy way smelled it: some large presence ahead in the dark. A Shape. He felt not fear but a sense of overmastering awe; here was a power which dwarfed Its power, and Bill had only time to think incoherently: *Please, please, whatever You are, remember that I am very small —*

He rushed toward it and saw it was a great Turtle, its shell plated with many blazing colors. Its ancient reptilian head slowly poked out of its shell, and Bill thought he felt a vague contemptuous surprise from the thing that had cast him out here. The eyes of the Turtle were kind. Bill thought it must be the oldest thing anyone could imagine, older by far than It, which had claimed to be eternal.

What are you? —

I'm the Turtle, son. I made the universe, but please don't blame me for it; I had a bellyache.

Help me! Please help me!

— I take no stand in these matters.

My brother —

— has his own place in the macroverse; energy is eternal, as even a child such as yourself must understand

He was flying past the Turtle now, and even at his tremendous skidding speed, the Turtle's plated side seemed to go on and on to his right. He thought dimly of riding in a train and passing one going in the other direction, a train that was so long it seemed eventually to stand still or even move backward. He could still hear It, yammering and buzzing, Its voice high and angry, not human, full of mad hate. But when the Turtle spoke, Its voice was blanked out utterly. The Turtle spoke in Bill's head, and Bill understood somehow that there was yet Another, and that Final Other dwelt in a void beyond this one. This Final Other was, perhaps, the creator of the Turtle, which only watched, and It, which only ate. This Other was a force beyond the universe, a power beyond all other power, the author of all there was.

Suddenly he thought he understood: It meant to thrust him through some wall at the end of the universe and into some other place

(*what that old Turtle called the macroverse*)

where It really lived; where It existed as a titanic, glowing core which might be no more than the smallest mote in that Other's mind; he would see It naked, a thing of unshaped destroying light, and there he would either be mercifully annihilated or live forever, insane and yet conscious inside Its homicidal endless formless hungry being.

Please help me! For the others –

– you must help yourself, son

But how? Please tell me! How? How? HOW?

He had reached the Turtle's heavily scaled back legs now; there was time enough to observe its titanic yet ancient flesh, time to be struck with the wonder of its heavy toenails – they were an odd bluish-yellow color, and he could see galaxies swimming in each one.

Please, you are good, I sense and believe that you are good, and I am begging you . . . won't you please help me?

– you already know. there is only Chüd. and your friends.

Please oh please –

son, you've got to thrust your fists against the posts and still insist you see the ghosts . . . that's all I can tell you. once you get into cosmological shit like this, you got to throw away the instruction manual

He realized the voice of the Turtle was fading. He was beyond it now, bulleting into a darkness that was deeper than deep. The Turtle's voice was being overcome, overmastered, by the gleeful, gibbering voice of the Thing that had thrust him out and into this black void – the voice of the Spider, of It.

– how do you like it out here, Little Friend? do you like it? do you love it? do you give it ninety-eight points because it has a good beat and you can dance to it? can you catch it on your tonsils and heave it left and right? did you enjoy meeting my friend the Turtle? I thought that stupid old fuck died years ago, and for all the good he could do you, he might as well have, did you think he could help you?

no no no no he thrusts no he thuh-thuh-huh-huh-rusts no

– stop babbling! the time is short; let us talk while we still can. tell me about yourself, Little Friend . . . tell me, do you love all the cold dark out here? are you enjoying your grand tour of the nothingness that lies Outside? wait until you break through, Little Friend! wait until you break through to where I am! wait for that! wait for the deadlights! you'll look and you'll go mad . . . but you'll live . . . and live . . . and live . . . inside them . . . inside Me . . .

It screamed noxious laughter, and Bill became aware that Its voice was beginning both to fade and to swell, as if he was simultaneously drawing out of Its range . . . and hurtling into it. And wasn't that just what was happening? Yes. He thought it was. Because while the voices were in perfect sync, the one he was now rushing toward was totally alien, speaking syllables no human tongue or throat could reproduce. *That's the voice of the deadlights,* he thought.

– the time is short; let us talk while we still can

Its human voice fading the way the Bangor radio stations faded when you were in the car and travelling south. Bright, flaring terror filled him. He would shortly be beyond sane communication with It . . . and some part of him understood that, for all Its laughter, for all Its alien glee, that was what It wanted. Not just to send him out to whatever It really was, but to break their mental communication. If that ceased, he would be utterly destroyed. To pass beyond communication was to pass beyond salvation; he understood that much from the way his parents had behaved toward him after George had died. It was the only lesson their refrigerator coldness had had to teach him.

Leaving It . . . and approaching It. But the leaving was somehow more important. If It wanted to eat little kids out here, or suck them in, or whatever It did, why hadn't It sent them *all* out here? Why just him?

Because It had to rid Its Spider-self of him, that was why. Somehow the Spider-It and the It which It called the deadlights were linked. Whatever lived out here in the black might be invulnerable when It was here and nowhere else . . . but It was also on earth, under Derry, in a form that was physical. However repulsive It might be, in Derry it was *physical* . . . and what was physical could be killed.

Bill skidded through the dark, his speed still increasing. *Why do I sense so much of Its talk is nothing but a bluff, a big shuck-and jive? Why should that be? How can that be?*

He understood how, maybe . . . just maybe.

There is only Chüd, the Turtle had said. And suppose this was it? Suppose they had bitten deep into each other's tongues, not physically but mentally, spiritually? And suppose that if It could throw Bill far enough into the void, far enough toward Its eternal discorporate self, the ritual would be over? It would have ripped him free, killed him, and won everything all at the same time.

– you're doing good, son, but very shortly it's going to be too late It's scared! Scared of me! Scared of all of us!

– skidding, he was skidding, and there was a wall up ahead, he sensed it, sensed it in the dark, the wall at the edge of the continuum, and beyond it the other shape, the deadlights *–*

– don't talk to me, son, and don't talk to yourself – it's tearing you loose. bite in if you care, if you dare, if you can be brave, if you can stand . . . bite in, son!

Bill bit in – not with his teeth, but with teeth in his mind.

Dropping his voice a full register, making it not his own (making it, in fact, his father's voice, although Bill would go to his grave not knowing this; some secrets are never known, and it's probably better so), drawing in a great breath, he cried: '*HE THRUSTS HIS FISTS AGAINST THE POSTS AND STILL INSISTS HE SEES THE GHOSTS NOW LET ME GO!*'

He felt It scream in his mind, a scream of frustrated petulant rage . . . but it was also a scream of fear and pain. It was not used to not having Its own way; such a thing had never happened to It, and until the most recent moments of Its existence It had not suspected such a thing could.

Bill felt It writhing at him, not pulling but *pushing* – trying to get him *away*.

'*THRUSTS HIS FISTS AGAINST THE POSTS, I SAID!*

'*STOP IT!*

'*BRING ME BACK! YOU MUST! I COMMAND IT! I DEMAND IT!*'

It screamed again, Its pain more intense now – perhaps partly because, while It had spent Its long, long existence inflicting pain, feeding on it, It had never experienced it as a part of Itself.

Still It tried to push him, to get rid of him, blindly and stubbornly insisting on winning, as It had always won before. It pushed . . . but Bill sensed that his outward speed had slowed, and a grotesque image came into his mind: Its tongue, covered with that living spittle, extended like a thick rubber band, cracking, bleeding. He saw himself clinging to the tip of that tongue by his teeth, ripping through it a little at a time, his face bathed in the convulsive ichor that was Its blood, drowning in Its dead stench, yet still holding on, holding on somehow, while It struggled in Its blind pain and towering rage not to let Its tongue snap back –

(*Chüd, this Chüd, stand, be brave, be true, stand for your brother, your friends; believe, believe in all the things you have believed in, believe that if you tell the policeman you're lost he'll see that you get home safely, that there is a Tooth Fairy who lives in a huge enamel castle, and Santa Claus below the North Pole, making toys with his trove of elves, and that Captain Midnight could be real, yes, he* could *be in spite of Calvin and Cissy Clark's big brother Carlton saying that was all a lot of baby stuff, believe that your mother and father will love you again, that courage is possible and words will come smoothly every time; no more Losers, no more cowering in a hole in the ground and calling it a clubhouse, no more crying in Georgie's room because you couldn't save him and didn't know, believe in yourself, believe in the heat of that desire*)

He suddenly began to laugh in the darkness, not in hysteria but in utter delighted amazement.

'*OH SHIT, I BELIEVE IN ALL OF THOSE THINGS!*' he shouted, and it was true: even at eleven he had observed that things turned out right a ridiculous amount of the time. Light flared around him. He raised his arms out and above his head. He turned his face up, and suddenly he felt power rush through him.

He heard It scream again . . . and suddenly he was being drawn back the way he had come, still holding that image of his teeth planted deep in the strange meat of Its tongue, his teeth locked together like grim old death. He flew through the dark, legs trailing behind him, the tips of his mud-crusted sneaker laces flying like pennants, the wind of this empty place blowing in his ears.

He was pulled past the Turtle and saw that its head had withdrawn into its shell; its voice emerged hollow and distorted, as if even the shell it lived in were a well eternities deep:

– not bad, son, but I'd finish it now; don't let It get away. energy has a way of dissipating, you know; what can be done when you're eleven can often never be done again

The voice of the Turtle faded, faded, faded. There was only the rushing dark . . . and then the mouth of a cyclopean tunnel . . . smells of age and decay . . . cobwebs brushing at his face like rotted skeins of silk in a haunted house . . . moldering tiles blurring by . . . intersections, all dark now, the moon-balloons all gone, and It was screaming, screaming:

– let me go let me go I'll leave never come back let me GO IT HURTS IT HURTS IT HURRRRRRRRRR

'*Thrusts his fists!*' Bill screamed, nearly delirious now. He could see light ahead but it was fading, guttering like great candles which had at last burned low . . . and for a moment he saw himself and the others holding hands in a line, Eddie on one side of him and Richie on the other. He saw his own body, sagging, his head rolled back on his neck, staring up at the Spider, which twisted and whirled like a dervish, Its coarse, spiny legs beating at the floor, poison dripping from Its stinger.

It was screaming in Its death-agony.

So Bill honestly believed.

Then he was slamming back into his body with all the impact of a line drive slamming into a baseball glove, the force of it tearing his hands loose from Richie's and Eddie's, driving him to his knees and skidding him across the floor to the edge of the web. He reached out for one of the strands without thinking, and his hand immediately went numb, as if it had been injected with a hypo full of novocaine. The strand itself was as thick as a telephone-pole guy-wire.

'Don't touch that, Bill!' Ben yelled, and Bill yanked his hand away in one quick jerk, leaving a raw place across his palm just below the fingers. It filled with blood and he staggered to his feet, eyes on the Spider.

It was scrabbling away from them, making Its way into the growing dimness at the back of the chamber as the light failed. It left puddles and pools of black blood behind as It went; somehow their confrontation had ruptured Its insides in a dozen, maybe a hundred places.

'Bill, the web!' Mike screamed. 'Look out!'

He stepped backward, craning his neck up, as strands of Its web came floating down, striking the stone-flagged floor on either side of him like the bodies of meaty white snakes. They immediately began to lose shape, to flow into the cracks between the stones. The web was falling apart, coming loose from its many moorings. One of the bodies, wrapped up like a fly, came plunging down to strike the floor with a sickening rotted-gourd sound.

'The Spider!' Bill yelled. 'Where is It?'

He could still hear It in his head, mewling and crying out in Its pain, and understood dimly that It had gone into the same tunnel It had thrown Bill into . . . but had It gone in there to flee back to the place where It had meant to send Bill . . . or to hide until they were gone? To die? Or escape?

'Christ, the lights!' Richie shouted. 'The *lights*'re going out! What happened, Bill? Where did you go? We thought you were dead!'

In some confused part of his mind Bill knew that wasn't true: if they had really thought him dead, they would have run, scattered, and It would have picked them off easily, one by one. Or perhaps it would be truer to say that they had *thought* him dead, but *believed* him alive.

We have to make sure! If It's dying or gone back to where It came from, where the rest of It is, that's fine. But what if It's just hurt? What if It can get better? What —

Stan's shriek cut across his thoughts like broken glass. In the fading light Bill saw that one of the strands of webbing had come down on Stan's shoulder. Before Bill could reach him, Mike had thrown himself at the smaller boy in a flying tackle. He drove Stan away and the piece of webbing snapped back, taking a piece of Stan's polo shirt with it.

'Get back!' Ben yelled at them. '*Get away from it, it's all coming down!*' He seized Beverly's hand and pulled her back toward the child-sized door while Stan struggled to his feet, looked dazedly around, and then grabbed Eddie. The two of them started toward Ben and Beverly, helping each other, looking like phantoms in the fading light.

Overhead, the spiderweb was drooping, collapsing on itself, losing its fearful symmetry. Bodies twirled lazily in the air like nightmarish plumb-bobs. Cross-strands fell in like the rotted rungs of some strange complex of ladders. Severed strands hit the stone flagging, hissed like cats, lost their shape, began to run.

Mike Hanlon wove his way through them as he would later weave his way through the opposing lines of nearly a dozen high-school football teams, head down, ducking and dodging. Richie joined him. Incredibly, Richie was laughing, although his hair was standing straight up on his head like the quills of a porcupine. The light grew dimmer, the phosphorescence that had coiled on the walls now dying away.

'Bill!' Mike shouted. 'Come on! Get the frock out of there!'

'*What if It's not dead?*' Bill screamed back. '*We got to go after It, Mike! We got to make sure!*'

A snarl of webbing sagged outward like a parachute and then fell with a nasty ripping sound that was like skin being pulled apart. Mike grabbed Bill's arm and pulled him, stumbling, out of the way.

'It's dead!' Eddie cried, joining them. His eyes were febrile lamps, his breathing a chilly winter-whistle in his throat. Fallen strands of webbing had sizzled complex scars into the plaster of Paris of his cast. 'I heard It, It was dying, you don't sound like that if you're on your way to a sock hop, It was dying, I'm sure of it!'

Richie's hands groped out of the darkness, seized Bill, and pulled him into a rough embrace. He began to pound Bill's back ecstatically. 'I heard It, too − It was dying, Big Bill! It was dying . . . *and you're not stuttering! Not at all!* Howdja do it? How in the hell −?'

Bill's brain was whirling. Exhaustion tugged at him with thick and clumsy hands. He could not remember ever feeling this tired . . . but in his mind he heard the drawling, almost weary voice of the Turtle: *I'd finish it now; don't let It get away . . . what can be done when you're eleven can often never be done again.*

'But we have to be sure −'

The shadows were joining hands and now the darkness was almost complete. But before the light failed utterly, he thought he saw the same hellish doubt on Beverly's face ... and in Stan's eyes. And still, as the last of the light gave way, they could hear the tenebrous whisper-shudder-thump of Its unspeakable web falling to pieces.

3

Bill in the Void/Late

— well here you are again, Little Buddy! but what's happened to your hair? you're just as bald as a cueball! sad! what sad, short lives humans live! each life a short pamphlet written by an idiot! tut-tut, and all that

I'm still Bill Denbrough. You killed my brother and you killed Stan the Man you tried to kill Mike. And I'm going to tell you something: this time I'm not going to stop until the job's done

— the Turtle was stupid, too stupid to lie. he told you the truth, Little Buddy ... the time only comes around once. you hurt me ... you surprised me. never again. I am the one who called you back. I.

You called, all right, but You weren't the only one

— your friend the Turtle ... he died a few years ago. the old idiot puked inside his shell and choked to death on a galaxy or two. very sad, don't you think? but also quite bizarre. deserves a place in Ripley's Believe It or Not, *that's what I think. happened right around the same time you had that writer's block. you must have felt him go, Little Buddy*

I don't believe that, either

— oh you'll believe ... you'll see. this time, Little Buddy, I intend you to see everything. including the deadlights

He sensed Its voice rising, buzzing and racketing — at last he sensed the full extent of Its fury, and he was terrified. He reached for the tongue of Its mind, concentrating, trying desperately to recapture the full extent of that childish belief, understanding at the same time that there was a deadly truth in what It had said: last time It had been unprepared. This time ... well, even if It had not been the only one to call them, It sure had been waiting.

But still —

He felt his own fury, clean and singing, as his eyes fixed on Its eyes. He sensed Its old scars, sensed that It had truly been hurt, and that It was still hurt.

And as It threw him, as he felt his mind swatted out of his body, he concentrated all of his being on seizing Its tongue ... *and missed his grip.*

4

The other four watched, paralyzed. It was an exact replay of what had happened before – at first. The Spider, which seemed about to seize Bill and gobble him up, grew suddenly still. Bill's eyes locked with Its ruby ones. There was a sense of contact . . . a contact just beyond their ability to divine. But they felt the struggle, the clash of wills.

Then Richie glanced up into the new web, and saw the first difference.

There were bodies there, some half-eaten and half-rotted, and that was the same . . . but high up, in one corner, was another body, and Richie was sure this one was still fresh, possibly even still alive. Beverly had not looked up – her eyes were fixed on Bill and the Spider – but even in his terror, Richie saw the resemblance between Beverly and the woman in the web. Her hair was long and red. Her eyes were open but glassy and unmoving. A line of spittle had run from the left corner of her mouth down to her chin. She had been attached to one of the web's main cables by a gossamer harness that went around her waist and under both arms so that she lolled forward in a half-bow, arms and legs dangling limply. Her feet were bare.

Richie saw another body crumpled at the foot of her web, a man he had never seen before . . . and yet his mind registered an almost subconscious resemblance to the late unlamented Henry Bowers. Blood had run from both of the stranger's eyes and caked in a foam around his mouth and on his chin. He –

Then Beverly was screaming. '*Something's wrong! Something's gone wrong, do something, for Christ's sake won't somebody DO something –*'

Richie's gaze snapped back to Bill and the Spider . . . and he sensed/heard monstrous laughter. Bill's face was stretching in some subtle way. His skin had gone parchment-sallow, as shiny as the skin of a very old person. His eyes were rolled up to the whites.

Oh Bill, where are you?

As Richie watched, blood suddenly burst from Bill's nose in a foam. His mouth was writhing, trying to scream . . . and now the Spider was advancing on him again. It was turning, presenting Its stinger.

It means to kill him . . . kill his body, anyway . . . while his mind is somewhere else. It means to shut him out forever. It's winning . . . Bill, where are you? For Christ's sake, where are you?

And somewhere, faintly, from some unimaginable distance, he heard Bill scream . . . and the words, although meaningless, were crystal-clear and full of sickening

(*the Turtle is dead oh God the Turtle really is dead*)

despair.

Bev shrieked again and put her hands to her ears as if to shut out that fading voice. The Spider's stinger rose and Richie bolted at It, a grin spreading up toward his ears, and he called out in his best Irish Cop's Voice:

'*Here, here, me foine girl! Just what in the hell do ye think ye're doin? Belay that guff before I snatch yer pettiskirts and snap yer smithy- riddles!*'

The Spider stopped laughing, and Richie felt a rising howl of anger and pain inside Its head. *Hurt It!* he thought triumphantly. *Hurt It, how about that, hurt It, and guess what? I'VE GOT ITS TONGUE! I THINK BILL MISSED IT SOMEHOW BUT WHILE IT WAS DISTRACTED I GOT –*

Then, screaming at him, Its cries a hive of furious bees in his head, Richie was whacked out of himself and into darkness, dimly aware that It was trying to shake him loose. It was doing a pretty good job, too. Terror washed through him, and then was replaced by a sense of cosmic absurdity. He remembered Beverly with his Duncan yo-yo, showing him how to make it sleep, walk the dog, go around the world. And now here he was, Richie the Human Yo-Yo, and Its tongue was the string. Here he was, and this wasn't called walking the dog but maybe walking the Spider, and if that wasn't funny, what was?

Richie laughed. It wasn't polite to laugh with your mouth full, of course, but he doubted if anybody out here read Miss Manners.

That got him laughing again, and he bit in harder.

The Spider screamed and shook him furiously, howling Its anger at being surprised again – It had believed only the writer would challenge It, and now this man who was laughing like a crazy boy had seized It when It was least prepared.

Richie felt himself slipping.

– *hold eet a secon, senhorrita, we ees goin out here together or I ain gonna sell you no tickets in* la lotería *after all, and every one is a big winner, I swear on my mamma's name*

He felt his teeth catch again, more firmly this time. And there was a fainting sort of pain as It drove Its fangs into his own tongue. Boy, it was still pretty funny, though. Even in the dark, being hurled after Bill with only the tongue of this unspeakable monster left to connect him to his own world, even with the pain of Its poisonous fangs suffusing his mind like a red fog, it was pretty goddamned funny. *Check it out, folks. You'll believe a disc jockey can fly.*

He was flying, all right.

Richie was in greater darkness than he had ever known, than he had ever suspected might exist, travelling at what felt like the speed of light, and being shaken as a terrier shakes a rat. He sensed that there was something up ahead, some titanic corpse. The Turtle he had heard Bill lamenting in his fading voice? Must be. It was only a shell, a dead husk. Then he was past, rushing on into the darkness.

Really steaming now, he thought, and felt that wild urge to cackle again.

bill! bill, can you hear me?

– he's gone, he's in the deadlights, let me go! LET ME GO!

(richie?)

Incredibly distant; incredibly far out in the black.

bill! bill! here I am! catch hold! for God's sake catch hold

– he's dead, you're all dead, you're too old, don't you understand that? now let me GO!

hey bitch, you're never too old to rock and roll

– LET ME GO!

take me to him and maybe I will

Richie

– closer, he was closer now, thank God –

here I come, Big Bill! Richie to the rescue! Gonna save your old cracked ass! Owe you one from that day on Neibolt Street, remember?

– let me GOOOO!

It was hurting badly now, and Richie understood how completely he had caught It by surprise – It had believed It had only Bill to deal with. Well, good. Good 'nuff. Richie didn't care about killing It right now; he was no longer sure It *could* be killed. But *Bill* could be killed, and Richie sensed that Bill's time was now very, very short. Bill was closing in on some large nasty surprise out here, something best not thought about.

Richie, no! Go back! It's the edge of everything up here! The deadlights!

souns like what you turn on when you drivinn you hearse at midnie, senhorr . . . and where is you, honeychile? smile, so I can see where you is!

And suddenly Bill was there, skidding along on

(the left? right? there was no direction here)

one side or the other. And beyond him, coming up fast, Richie could see/sense something that finally dried up his laughter. It was a barrier, something of a strange, non-geometrical shape that his mind could not grasp. Instead his mind translated it as best it could, as it had translated the shape of It into a Spider, allowing Richie to think of it as a colossal gray wall made of fossilized wooden stakes. These stakes went forever up and forever down, like the bars of a cage. And from between them shone a great blind light. It glared and moved, smiled and snarled. The light was alive.

(*deadlights*)

More than alive: it was full of a force – magnetism, gravity, perhaps something else. Richie felt himself lifted and dropped, swirled and pulled, as if he were shooting a fast throat of rapids in an innertube. He could feel the light moving eagerly over his face . . . and the light was *thinking*.

This is It, this is It, the rest of It.

– let me go, you promised to let me GO

I know but sometimes, honeychile, I lie – my mamma she beat me fo it but my daddy, he done just about give up

He sensed Bill tumbling and flailing toward one of the gaps in the wall, sensed evil fingers of light reaching for him, and with a final despairing effort, he reached for his friend.

Bill! Your hand! Give me your hand! YOUR HAND, GODDAMMIT! YOUR HAND!

Bill's hand shot out, the fingers opening and closing, that living fire crawling and twisting over Audra's wedding ring in runic, Moorish patterns – wheels, crescents, stars, swastikas, linked circles that grew into rolling chains. Bill's face was overlaid with the same light, making him look tattooed. Richie stretched out as far as he could, hearing It scream and yammer.

(*I missed him, oh dear God I missed he's going to shoot through*)

Then Bill's fingers closed over Richie's, and Richie clenched his hand into a fist. Bill's legs flew through one of the gaps in the frozen wood, and for one mad moment Richie realized he could see all the bones and veins and capillaries inside them, as if Bill had shot halfway into the maw of the world's strongest X-ray machine. Richie felt the muscles in his arm stretch like taffy, felt the ball-and-socket joint in his shoulder creak and groan in protest as the foot-pounds of pressure built up.

He summoned all of his force and shouted: '*Pull us back! Pull us back or I'll kill you! I . . . I'll Voice you to death!*'

The Spider screeched again, and Richie suddenly felt a great, snapping whiplash curl through his body. His arm was a white-hot bar of agony. His grip on Bill's hand began to slip.

'Hold on, Big Bill!'

'I got you! Richie, I got you!'

You better, Richie thought grimly, *because I think you could walk ten billion miles out here and never find a fucking pay toilet.*

They whistled back, that crazy light fading, becoming a series of brilliant pinpoints that finally winked out. They drove through the darkness like torpedoes, Richie gripping Its tongue with his teeth and Bill's wrist with one aching hand. There was the Turtle; there and gone in a single eyeblink.

Richie sensed them drawing closer to whatever passed for the real world (although he believed he would never think of it as exactly 'real' again; he would see it as a clever canvas scene underlaid with a crisscrossing of support-cables . . . cables like the strands of a spiderweb). *But we're going to be all right*, he thought. *We're going to get back. We —*

The buffeting began then — the whipping, slamming, side-to-side flailing as It tried one final time to shake them off and leave them Outside. And Richie felt his grip slipping. He heard Its guttural roar of triumph and concentrated his being on holding . . . but he continued to slip. He bit down frantically, but Its tongue seemed to be losing substance and reality; it seemed to be becoming gossamer.

'*Help!*' Richie screamed. '*I'm losing it! Help! Somebody help us!*'

5

Eddie

Eddie was half-aware of what was happening; he felt it somehow, saw it somehow, but as if through a gauzy curtain. Somewhere, Bill and Richie were struggling to come back. Their bodies were here, but the rest of them — the *real* of them — was far away.

He had seen the Spider turn to impale Bill with Its stinger, and then Richie had run forward, yelling at It in that ridiculous Irish Cop's Voice he used to use . . . only Richie must have improved his act a hell of a lot over the years, because this Voice sounded eerily like Mr Nell from the old days.

The Spider had turned toward Richie, and Eddie had seen Its unspeakable red eyes bulge in their sockets. Richie yelled again, this time in his Pancho Vanilla Voice, and Eddie had *felt* the Spider scream in pain. Ben yelled hoarsely as a split appeared in Its hide along the line of one of Its scars from the last time. A stream of ichor, black as crude oil, sprayed out. Richie had started to say something else . . . and his voice had begun to *diminish*, like the fade at the end of a pop song. His head had rolled back on his neck, his eyes fixed on Its eyes. The Spider grew quiet again.

Time passed – Eddie had no idea just how much. Richie and the Spider stared at each other; Eddie sensed the connection between them, felt a swirl of talk and emotion somewhere far away. He could make out nothing exactly, but sensed the tones of things in colors and hues.

Bill lay slumped on the floor, nose and ears bleeding, fingers twitching slightly, his long face pale, his eyes closed.

The Spider was now bleeding in four or five places, badly hurt again, badly hurt but still dangerously vital, and Eddie thought: *Why are we just standing around here? We could hurt It while It's occupied with Richie! Why doesn't somebody move, for Christ's sake?*

He sensed a wild triumph – and that feeling was clearer, sharper. Closer. *They're coming back!* he wanted to shout, but his mouth was too dry, his throat too tight. *They're coming back!*

Then Richie's head began to turn slowly from side to side. His body seemed to *ripple* inside his clothes. His glasses hung on the end of his nose for a moment . . . then fell off and shattered on the stone floor.

The Spider stirred, its spiny legs making a dry clittering on the floor. Eddie heard It cry out in terrible triumph, and a moment later, Richie's voice burst clearly into his head:

(*help! I'm losing it! somebody help me!*)

Eddie ran forward then, yanking his aspirator from his pocket with his good hand, his lips drawn back in a grimace, his breath whistling painfully in and out of a throat that now felt the size of a pinhole. Crazily, his mother's face danced before him and she was crying: *Don't go near that Thing, Eddie! Don't go near It! Things like that give you cancer!*

'Shut up, Ma!' Eddie screamed in a high, shrieky voice – all the voice he had left. The Spider's head turned toward the sound, Its eyes momentarily leaving Richie's.

'Here!' Eddie howled in his fading voice. 'Here, have some of this!'

He leaped at It, triggering the aspirator at the same time, and for an instant all his childhood belief in the medicine came back to him, the childhood medicine that could solve everything, that could make him feel better when the bigger boys roughed him up or when he was knocked over in the rush to get through the doors when school let out or when he had to sit on the edge of the Tracker

Brothers' vacant lot, out of the game because his mother wouldn't allow him to play baseball. It was good medicine, *strong* medicine, and as he leaped into the Spider's face, smelling Its foul yellow stench, feeling himself overwhelmed by Its single-minded fury and determination to wipe them all out, he triggered the aspirator into one of Its ruby eyes.

He felt-heard Its scream – no rage this time, only pain, a horrid screaming agony. He saw the mist of droplets settle on that blood-red bulge, saw the droplets turn white where they landed, saw them sink in as a splash of carbolic acid would sink in; he saw Its huge eye begin to flatten out like a bloody egg-yolk and run in a ghastly stream of living blood and ichor and maggoty pus.

'*Come home now, Bill!*' he screamed with the last of his voice, and then he struck It, he felt Its noisome heat baking into him; he felt a terrible wet warmth and realized that his good arm had slipped into the Spider's mouth.

He triggered the aspirator again, shooting the stuff right down Its throat this time, right down Its rotten evil stinking gullet, and there was sudden, flashing pain, as clean as the drop of a heavy knife, as Its jaws closed and ripped his arm off at the shoulder.

Eddie fell to the floor, the ragged stump of his arm spraying blood, faintly aware that Bill was getting shakiiy to his feet, that Richie was weaving and stumbling toward him like a drunk at the end of a long hard night.

'– eds –'

Far away. Unimportant. He could feel everything running out of him along with his life's blood . . . all the rage, all the pain, all the fear, all the confusion and hurt. He supposed he was dying but he felt . . . ah, God, he felt so *lucid*, so *clear*, like a window-pane which has been washed clean and now lets in all the gloriously frightening light of some unsuspected dawning; the *light*, oh God, that perfect rational light that clears the horizon somewhere in the world every second.

'– eds oh my god bill ben someone he's lost his arm, his –'

He looked up at Beverly and saw she was crying, the tears coursing down her dirty cheeks as she got an arm under him; he became aware that she had taken off her blouse and was trying to staunch the flow of blood, and that she was screaming for help. Then he looked at Richie and licked his lips. Fading, fading back. Becoming clearer and clearer, emptying out, all of the impurities flowing out of him so he could become clear, so that the light could flow through, and if he had had time enough he could have preached on this, he could have sermonized: *Not bad*, he would begin. *This is not bad at all.* But there was something else he had to say first.

'Richie,' he whispered.

'What?' Richie was down on his hands and knees, staring at him desperately.

'Don't call me Eds,' he said, and smiled. He raised his left hand slowly and touched Richie's cheek. Richie was crying. 'You know I . . . I . . .' Eddie closed his eyes, thinking how to finish, and while he was still thinking it over he died.

6

Derry / 7:00–9:00 A.M.

By 7:00 A.M., the wind-speed in Derry had picked up to about thirty-seven miles an hour, with gusts up to forty-five. Harry Brooks, a National Weather Service forecaster based at Bangor International Airport, made an alarmed call to NWS headquarters in Augusta. The winds, he said, were coming out of the west and blowing in a queer semicircular pattern he had never seen before . . . but it looked to him more and more like some weird species of pocket hurricane, one that was limited almost exclusively to Derry Township. At 7:10, the major Bangor radio stations broadcast the first severe-weather warnings. The explosion of the power-transformer at Tracker Brothers' had killed the power all over Derry on the Kansas Street side of the Barrens. At 7:17, a hoary old maple on the Old Cape side of the Barrens fell with a terrific rending crash, flattening a Nite-Owl store on the corner of Merit Street and Cape Avenue. An elderly patron named Raymond Fogarty was killed by a toppling beer cooler. This was the same Raymond Fogarty who, as the minister of the First Methodist Church of Derry, had presided over the burial rites of George Denbrough in October of 1957. The maple also pulled down enough power lines to knock out the power in both the Old Cape and the somewhat more fashionable Sherburn Woods development beyond it. The clock in the steeple of the Grace Baptist Church had chimed neither six nor seven. At 7:20, three minutes after the maple fell in the Old Cape and about an hour and fifteen minutes after every toilet and domestic drain over there had suddenly reversed itself, the clock in the tower chimed thirteen times. A minute later, a blue-white stroke of lightning struck the steeple. Heather Libby, the minister's wife, happened to be looking out the window of the parsonage's kitchen at the time, and she said that the steeple 'exploded like someone loaded it up with dynamite.' Whitewashed boards, chunks of beams, and clockwork from Switzerland showered down on the street. The ragged remains of the steeple burned briefly and then guttered out in the rain, which was now a tropical downpour. The streets leading downhill into the downtown shopping area foamed and ran. The progress of the Canal under Main Street had become a steady shaking thunder that made people look at each other uneasily. At 7:25, with the titanic crash of the Grace Baptist steeple still reverberating all over Derry, the janitor who came into Wally's Spa every morning except Sunday to swamp the place out saw something which sent him screaming into the street. This fellow, who had been an alcoholic ever since his first semester at the University of Maine lo these eleven years ago, was paid a pittance for his services – his real pay, it was understood, was his absolute freedom to finish up anything left in the beer kegs under the bar from the night before. Richie Tozier might or might not have remembered him; he was Vincent Caruso Taliendo, better known to his fifth-grade contemporaries as 'Boogers' Taliendo. As he was mopping up on that apocalyptic morning in Derry, working his way gradually closer and closer to the serving area, he saw all seven of the beer taps – three Bud, two Narragansett, one Schlitz (known more familiarly to the bleary patrons of Wally's as Slits), and one Miller Lite – nod forward, as if pulled by seven invisible hands. Beer ran from them in streams of gold-white foam. Vince started forward, thinking not of ghosts or phantoms but of his morning's dividend going down the drain. Then he skidded to a stop, eyes widening, and a wailing, horrified scream rose in the empty, beer-smelling cave that was Wally's Spa. Beer had given way to arterial streams of blood. It swirled in the chromium drains, overflowed, and ran down the side of the bar in little streamlets. Now hair and chunks of flesh began to splurt out of the beer-taps. 'Boogers' Taliendo watched this, transfixed, not even able to summon enough strength to scream again. Then there was a thudding, toneless blast as one of the beer kegs under the counter exploded. All of the cupboard doors under the bar swung wide. Greenish smoke, like the aftermath of a magician's trick, began to drift out of them. 'Boogers' had seen enough. Screaming, he fled into the street, which was now a shallow canal. He fell on his butt, got up, and threw a terrified glance back over his shoulder. One of the bar windows blew out with a loud shooting-gallery sound. Whickers of broken glass whistled all around Vince's head. A moment later the other window exploded. Once again he was miraculously untouched . . . but he decided on the spur of the moment that the time had come to see his sister up Eastport. He started off at once, and his journey to the Derry town limits and beyond would make a saga in itself . . . but suffice it to say that he did eventually get out of town. Others were not so lucky. Aloysius Nell, who had turned seventy-seven not long since, was sitting with his wife in the parlor of their home on Strapham Street, watching the storm pound Derry. At 7:32, he suffered a fatal stroke. His wife told her brother a week later that Aloysius dropped his coffee cup on the rug, sat bolt-upright, his eyes wide and staring, and screamed: '*Here, here, me foine girl! Just what in the hell do ye think ye're doin? Belay that guff before I snatch yer pettiskirrrr –*' Then he fell out of his chair, smashing his coffee cup under him. Maureen Nell, who knew well how bad his ticker had been for the last three years, understood immediately that all was over with him, and after loosening his collar she had run for the telephone to call Father McDowell. But the phone was out of order. A funny noise like a police siren was all it would make. And so, although she knew it was probably a blasphemy she would have to answer for to Saint Peter, she had attempted to give him the last rites herself. She felt confident, she told her brother, that God would understand even if Saint Peter didn't. Aloysius had been a good husband and a good man, and if he drank too much, that was only the Irish in him coming out. At 7:49 a series of explosions shook the Derry Mall, which stood on the site of the defunct Kitchener Ironworks. No one was killed; the mall didn't open until 10:00, and the five-man janitorial squad hadn't been due to arrive until 8:00 (and on such a morning as this, very few of them would have shown up anyway). A team of investigators later dismissed the idea of sabotage. They suggested – rather vaguely – that the explosions had probably been caused by water which had seeped into the mall's electrical system. Whatever the reason, no one was going to go shopping at the Derry Mall for a long time. One explosion totally wiped out Zale's Jewelry Store. Diamond rings, ID bracelets, strings of pearls, trays of wedding rings, and Seiko digital watches flew everywhere in a hail of bright, sparkly trinkets. A music-box flew the length of the east corridor and landed in the fountain outside of the J. C. Penney's, where it briefly played a bubbly rendition of the theme from *Love Story* before shutting down. The same blast tore a hole through the Baskin-Robbins next door, turning the thirty-one flavors into ice-cream soup that ran away along the floor in cloudy runnels. The blast which tore through Sears lifted off a chunk of the roof and the rising wind sailed it away like a kite; it came down a thousand yards away, slicing cleanly through the silo of a farmer named Brent Kilgallon.

Kilgallon's sixteen-year-old son rushed out with his mother's Kodak and took a picture. The *National Enquirer* bought it for sixty dollars, which the boy used to buy two new tires for his Yamaha motorcycle. A third explosion ripped through Hit or Miss, sending flaming skirts, jeans, and underwear out into the flooded parking-lot. And a final explosion tore open the mall branch of the Derry Farmer's Trust like a rotted box of crackers. A chunk of the bank's roof was also torn off. Burglar alarms went off with a bray that would not be silenced until the security system's independent wiring hookup was shorted out four hours later. Loan contracts, banking instruments, deposit slips, cash-drawer chits, and Money-Manager forms were lifted into the sky and blown away by the rising wind. And money: tens and twenties mostly, with a generous helping of fives and a soupçon of fifties and hundreds. Better than $75,000 blew away, according to the bank's officers . . . Later, after a mass shakeup in the bank's executive structure (and an FSLIC bail-out), some would admit – strictly off the record, of course – that it had been more like $200,000. A woman in Haven Village named Rebecca Paulson found a fifty-dollar bill fluttering from her back-door welcome mat, two twenties in her bird-house, and a hundred plastered against an oak tree in her back yard. She and her husband used the money to make an extra two payments on their Bombardier Skidoo. Dr Hale, a retired doctor who had lived on West Broadway for nearly fifty years, was killed at 8:00 A.M. Dr Hale liked to boast that he had taken the same two-mile walk from his West Broadway home and around Derry Park and the Elementary School for the last twenty-five of those fifty years. Nothing stopped him; not rain, sleet, hail, howling nor'easters, or subzero cold. He set out on the morning of May 31st in spite of his housekeeper's worried fussings. His exit-line from the world, spoken back over his shoulder as he went through the front door, pulling his hat firmly down to his ears, was: 'Don't be so goddamned silly, Hilda. This is nothing but a capful of rain. You should have seen it in '57! *That* was a storm!' As Dr Hale turned back onto West Broadway, a manhole cover in front of the Mueller place suddenly lifted off like the payload of a Redstone rocket. It decapitated the good doctor so quickly and neatly that he walked on another three steps before collapsing, dead, on the sidewalk.

And the wind continued to rise.

7

Eddie led them through the darkened tunnels for an hour, perhaps an hour and a half, before admitting, in a tone that was more bewildered than frightened, that for the first time in his life he was lost.

They could still hear the dim thunder of water in the drains, but the acoustics of all of these tunnels was so crazed that it was impossible to tell if the water-sounds were coming from ahead or behind, left or right, above or below. Their matches were gone. They were lost in the dark.

Bill was scared . . . plenty scared. The conversation he'd had with his father in his father's shop kept coming back to him. *There's nine pounds of blueprints that just disappeared somewhere along the line . . . My point is that nobody knows where all the damned sewers and drains go, or why. When they work, nobody cares. When they don't, there's three or four sad sacks from Derry Water who have to try and find out which pump went flooey or where the plug-up is . . . It's dark and smelly and there are rats. Those are all good reasons to stay out, but the best reason is that you could get lost. It's happened before.*

Happened before. Happened before. It's happened –

Sure it had. There was that bundle of bones and polished cotton they had passed on the way to Its lair, for instance.

Bill felt panic trying to rise and pushed it back. It went, but not easily. He could feel it back there, a live thing, struggling and twisting, trying to get out. Adding to it was the nagging unanswerable question of whether they had killed It or not. Richie said yes, Mike said yes, so did Eddie. But he hadn't liked the frightened doubtful look on Bev's face, or on Stan's, as the light died and they crawled back through the small door, away from the susurrating collapsing web.

'So what do we do now?' Stan asked. Bill heard the frightened, little-boy tremble in Stan's voice and knew the question was aimed directly at him.

'Yeah,' Ben said. 'What? Damn, I wish we had a flashlight . . . or even a can . . . candle.' Bill thought he heard a stifled sob in the second ellipsis. It frightened him more than anything else. Ben would have been astounded to know it, but Bill thought the fat boy tough and resourceful, steadier than Richie and less apt to cave in suddenly than Stan. If Ben was getting ready to crack, they were on the edge of very bad trouble. It was not the skeleton of the Water Department guy to which Bill's own mind kept returning but to Tom Sawyer and Becky Thatcher, lost in McDougal's Cave. He would push the thought away and then it would come stealing back.

Something else was troubling him, but the concept was too large and too vague for his tired boy's mind to grasp. Perhaps it was the very simplicity of the idea that made it elusive: they were falling away from each other. The bond that had held them all this long summer was dissolving. It had been faced and vanquished. It might be dead, as Richie and Eddie thought, or It might be wounded so badly It would sleep for a hundred years, or a thousand, or ten thousand. They had faced It, seen It with Its final mask laid aside, and It had been horrible enough – oh, for sure! – but once seen, Its physical form was not so bad and Its most potent weapon was taken away from It. They all had, after all, seen spiders before. They were alien and somehow crawlingly dreadful, and he supposed that none of them would ever be able to see another one

(*if we ever get out of this*)

without feeling a shudder of revulsion. But a spider was, after all, only a spider. Perhaps at the end, when the masks of horror were laid aside, there was nothing with which the human mind could not cope. That was a heartening thought. Anything except

(*the deadlights*)

whatever had been out there, but perhaps even that unspeakable living light which crouched at the doorway to the macroverse was dead or dying. The deadlights, and the trip into the black to the place where they had been, was already growing hazy and hard to recall in his mind. And that wasn't really the point. The point, felt but not grasped, was simply that the fellowship was ending . . . it was ending and they were still in the dark. That Other had, through their friendship, perhaps been able to make them something more than children. But they were becoming children again. Bill felt it as much as the others.

'What now, Bill?' Richie asked, finally saying it right out.

'I d-d-don't nuh-nuh-know,' Bill said. His stutter was back, alive and well. He heard it, they heard it, and he stood in the dark, smelling the sodden aroma of their growing panic, wondering how long it would be before somebody – Stan, most likely it would be Stan – tore things wide open by saying: *Well, why don't you know? You got us into this!*

'And what about Henry?' Mike asked uneasily. 'Is he still out there, or what?'

'Oh, Jeez,' Eddie said . . . almost moaned. 'I forgot about *him*. Sure he is, *sure* he is, he's probably as lost as we are and we could run into him any time . . . Jeez, Bill, don't you have *any* ideas? Your dad works down here! Don't you have any ideas at *all*?'

Bill listened to the distant mocking thunder of the water and tried to have the idea that Eddie — all of them — had a right to demand. Because yes, correct, he had gotten them into this and it was his responsibility to get them back out again. Nothing came. Nothing.

'I have an idea,' Beverly said quietly.

In the dark, Bill heard a sound he could not immediately place. A whispery little sound, but not scary. Then there was a more easily placed sound . . . a zipper. *What* — ? he thought, and then he realized what. She was undressing. For some reason, Beverly was undressing.

'What are you *doing*?' Richie asked, and his shocked voice cracked on the last word.

'I know something,' Beverly said in the dark, and to Bill her voice sounded older. 'I know because my father told me. I know how to bring us back together. And if we're not together we'll never get out.'

'What?' Ben asked, sounding bewildered and terrified. 'What are you talking about?'

'Something that will bring us together forever. Something that will show —'

'Nuh-Nuh-No, B-B-Beverly!' Bill said, suddenly understanding, understanding everything.

'— that will show that I love you all,' Beverly said, 'that you're all my friends.'

'What's she t —' Mike began.

Calmly, Beverly cut across his words. 'Who's first?' she asked. 'I think

8

In the Lair of It / 1985

he's dying,' Beverly wept. 'His arm, It ate his *arm* —' She reached for Bill, clung to him, and Bill shook her off.

'*It's getting away again!*' he roared at her. Blood caked his lips and chin. '*Cuh-Cuh-Come on! Richie! B-B-Ben! This tuh-time we're g-g-going to fuh-hinish her!*'

Richie turned Bill toward him, looked at him as you would look at a man who is hopelessly raving. 'Bill, we have to take care of Eddie. We have to get a tourniquet on him, get him out of here.'

But Beverly was now sitting with Eddie's head in her lap, cradling him. She had closed his eyes. 'Go with Bill,' she said. 'If you let him die for nothing . . . if It comes back in another twenty-five years, or fifty, or even two thousand, I swear I'll . . . I'll haunt your ghosts. *Go!*'

Richie looked at her for a moment, indecisive. Then he became aware that her face was losing definition, becoming not a face but a pale shape in the growing shadows. The light was fading. It decided him. 'All right,' he said to Bill. 'This time we chase.'

Ben was standing in back of the spiderweb, which had begun to decay again. He had also seen the shape swaying high up in it, and he prayed that Bill would not look up.

But as the web began to fall in drifts and strands and skeins, Bill did.

He saw Audra, sagging as if in a very old and creaky elevator. She dropped ten feet, stopped, swaying from side to side, and then abruptly dropped another fifteen. Her face never changed. Her eyes, china-blue, were wide open. Her bare feet swung back and forth like pendulums. Her hair hung lankly over her shoulders. Her mouth was ajar.

'*AUDRA!*' he screamed.

'Bill, come on!' Ben shouted.

The web was falling all around them now, thudding to the floor and beginning to run. Richie suddenly grabbed Bill around the waist and propelled him forward, shooting for a ten-foot-high gap between the floor and the bottommost cross-strand of the sagging web. 'Go, Bill! Go! Go!'

'*That's Audra!*' Bill shouted desperately. '*Thuh-That's* AUDRA!'

'I don't give a shit if it's the Pope,' Richie said grimly. 'Eddie's dead and we're going to kill It, if It's still alive. We're going to finish the job this time, Big Bill. Either she's alive or she's not. Now *come on!*'

Bill hung back a moment longer, and then snapshots of the children, all the dead children, seemed to flutter through his mind like lost photographs from George's album. SCHOOL FRIENDS.

'A-All ruh-right. Let's g-go. Guh-Guh-God forgive m-me.'

He and Richie ran under the strand of cross-webbing seconds before it collapsed, and joined Ben on the other side. They ran after It as Audra swung and dangled fifty feet above the stone floor, wrapped in a numbing cocoon that was attached to the decaying web.

9

Ben

They followed the trail of Its black blood – oily pools of ichor that ran and dripped into the cracks between the flagstones. But as the floor began to rise toward a semicircular black opening at the far side of the chamber, Ben saw something new: a trail of eggs. Each was black and rough-shelled, perhaps as big as an ostrich-egg. A waxy light shone from within them. Ben realized they were semi-transparent; he could see black shapes moving inside.

Its children, he thought, and felt his gorge rise. *Its miscarried children. God! God!*

Richie and Bill had stopped and were staring at the eggs with stupid, dazed wonder.

'Go on! Go on!' Ben shouted. 'I'll take care of them! Get It!'

'Here!' Richie shouted, and threw Ben a pack of Derry Town House matches.

Ben caught them. Bill and Richie ran on. Ben watched them in the rapidly dimming light for a moment. They ran into the darkness of Its escape-passage and were lost from sight. Then he looked down at the first of the thin-shelled eggs, at the black, mantalike shadow inside, and felt his determination waver. This . . . hey guys, this was too much. This was simply too awful. And surely they would die without his help; they had not been so much laid as dropped.

But Its time was close . . . and if one of them is capable of surviving . . . even one . . .

Summoning all of his courage, summoning up Eddie's pale, dying face, Ben brought one Desert Driver boot down on the first egg. It broke with a sodden squelch as some stinking placenta ran out around his boot. Then a spider the size of a rat was scrabbling weakly across the floor, trying to get away, and Ben could hear it in his head, its high mewling cries like the sound of a handsaw being bent rapidly back and forth so that it makes ghost-music.

Ben lurched after it on legs that felt like stilts and brought his foot down again. He felt the spider's body crunch and splatter under the heel of his boot. His gorge clenched and this time there was no way he could hold back. He vomited, then twisted his heel, grinding the thing into the stones, listening to the cries in his head fade to nothing.

How many? How many eggs? Didn't I read somewhere that spiders can lay thousands . . . or millions? I can't keep doing this, I'll go mad –

You have to. You have to. Come on, Ben . . . get it together!

He went to the next egg and repeated the process in the last of the dying light. Everything was repeated: the brittle snap, the squelch of liquid, the final *coup de grâce*. The next. The next. The next. Making his way slowly toward the black arch into which his friends had gone. The darkness was complete now, Beverly and the decaying web somewhere behind him. He could still hear the whisper of its collapse. The eggs were pallied stones in the dark. As he reached each one he struck a light from the matchbook and broke it open. In each case he was able to follow the course of the dazed spiderling and crush it before the light flickered out. He had no idea how he was going to proceed if his matches gave out before he had crushed the last of the eggs and killed each one's unspeakable cargo.

10

It/1985

Still coming.

It sensed them still coming, gaining, and Its fear grew. Perhaps It was not eternal after all – the unthinkable must finally be thought. Worse, It sensed the death of Its young. A third of these hated hateful men-boys was walking steadily up Its trail of birth, almost insane with revulsion but continuing nonetheless, methodically stamping the life from each of Its eggs.

No! It wailed, lurching from side to side, feeling Its life-force running from a hundred wounds, none of them mortal in itself, but each a song of pain, each slowing It. One of Its legs hung by a single living twist of meat. One of Its eyes was blind. It sensed a terrible rupture inside, the result of whatever poison one of the hated men-boys had managed to shoot down Its throat.

And still they came on, closing the distance, and how could this happen? It whined and mewled, and when It sensed them almost directly behind, It did the only thing It could do now: It turned to fight.

11

Beverly

Before the last of the light faded and utter dark closed down, she saw Bill's wife plunge another twenty feet and then fetch up again. She had begun to spin, her long red hair fanning out. *His wife*, she thought. *But I was his first love, and if he thought some other woman was his first, it was only because he forgot . . . forgot Derry.*

Then she was in darkness, alone with the sound of the falling web and Eddie's simple moveless weight. She didn't want to let him go, didn't want to let his face lie on the foul floor of this place. So she held his head in the crook of an arm that had gone mostly numb and brushed his hair away from his damp forehead. She thought of the birds . . . that was something she supposed she had gotten from Stan. Poor Stan, who hadn't been able to face this.

All of them . . . I was their first love.

She tried to remember it – it was something good to think about in all this darkness, where you couldn't place the sounds. It made her feel less alone. At first it wouldn't come; the image of the birds intervened – crows and grackles and starlings, spring birds that came back from somewhere while the streets were still running with meltwater and the last patches of crusted dirty snow clung grimly to their shady places.

It seemed to her that it was always on a cloudy day that you first heard and saw those spring birds and wondered where they came from. Suddenly they were just back in Derry, filling the white air with their raucous chatter. They lined the telephone wires and roofpeaks of the Victorian houses on West Broadway; they jostled for places on the aluminum branches of the elaborate TV antenna on top of Wally's Spa; they loaded the wet black branches of the elms on Lower Main Street. They settled, they talked to each other in the screamy babbling voices of old countrywomen at the weekly Grange Bingo games, and then, at some signal which humans could not discern, they all took wing at once, turning the sky black with their numbers . . . and came down somewhere else.

Yes, the birds, I was thinking of them because I was ashamed. It was my father who made me ashamed, I guess, and maybe that was It's doing, too. Maybe.

The memory came – the memory behind the birds – but it was vague and disconnected. Perhaps this one always would be. She had –

Her thoughts broke off as she realized that Eddie

12

Love and Desire/August 10th, 1958

comes to her first, because he is the most frightened. He comes to her not as her friend of that summer, or as her brief lover now, but the way he would have come to his mother only three or four years ago, to be comforted; he doesn't draw back from her smooth nakedness and at first she doubts

if he even feels it. He is trembling, and although she holds him the dark-
ness is so perfect that even this close she cannot see him; except for the
rough cast he might as well be a phantom.

'What do you want?' he asks her.

'You have to put your thing in me,' she says.

He tries to pull back but she holds him and he subsides against her.
She has heard someone – Ben, she thinks – draw in his breath.

'Bevvie, I can't do that. I don't know how –'

'I think it's easy. But you'll have to get undressed.' She thinks about
the intricacies of managing cast and shirt, first somehow separating and then
rejoining them, and amends, 'Your pants, anyway.'

'No, I can't!' But she thinks part of him can, and wants to, because
his trembling has stopped and she feels something small and hard which presses
against the right side of her belly.

'You can,' she says, and pulls him down. The surface beneath her bare
back and legs is firm, clayey, dry. The distant thunder of the water is drowsy,
soothing. She reaches for him. There's a moment when her father's face inter-
venes, harsh and forbidding

(I want to see if you're intact)

and then she closes her arms around Eddie's neck, her smooth cheek
against his smooth cheek, and as he tentatively touches her small breasts she
sighs and thinks for the first time This is Eddie *and she remembers a day in*
July – could it only have been last month? – when no one else turned up in
the Barrens but Eddie, and he had a whole bunch of Little Lulu comic books
and they read together for most of the afternoon, Little Lulu looking for beeble-
berries and getting in all sorts of crazy situations, Witch Hazel, all of those
guys. It had been fun.

She thinks of birds; in particular of the grackles and starlings and crows
that come back in the spring, and her hands go to his belt and loosen it, and
he says again that he can't do that; she tells him that he can, she knows *he*
can, and what she feels is not shame or fear now but a kind of triumph.

'Where?' he says, and that hard thing pushes urgently against her inner
thigh.

'Here,' she says.

'Bevvie, I'll fall on you!' he says, and she hears his breath start to
whistle painfully.

'I think that's sort of the idea,' she tells him and holds him gently and
guides him. He pushes forward too fast and there is pain.

Sssss! *– she draws her breath in, her teeth biting at her lower lip and*
thinks of the birds again, the spring birds, lining the roofpeaks of houses, taking
wing all at once under low March clouds.

'Beverly?' he says uncertainly. *'Are you okay?'*

'Go slower,' she says. *'It'll be easier for you to breathe.'* He does move more slowly, and after awhile his breathing speeds up but she understands this is not because there is anything wrong with him.

The pain fades. Suddenly he moves more quickly, then stops, stiffens, and makes a sound — some sound. She senses that this is something for him, something extraordinarily special, something like . . . like flying. She feels powerful: she feels a sense of triumph rise up strongly within her. Is this what her father was afraid of? Well he might be! There was power in this act, all right, a chain-breaking power that was blood-deep. She feels no physical pleasure, but there is a kind of mental ecstasy in it for her. She senses the closeness. He puts his face against her neck and she holds him. He's crying. She holds him. And feels the part of him that made a connection between them begin to fade. It is not leaving her, exactly; it is simply fading, becoming less.

When his weight shifts away she sits up and touches his face in the darkness.

'Did you?'

'Did I what?'

'Whatever it is. I don't know, exactly.'

He shakes his head — she feels it with her hand against his cheek.

'I don't think it was exactly like . . . you know, like the big boys say. But it was . . . it was really something.' He speaks low so the others can't hear. *'I love you, Bevvie.'*

Her consciousness breaks down a little there. She's quite sure there's more talk, some whispered, some loud, and can't remember what is said. It doesn't matter. Does she have to talk each of them into it all over again? Yes, probably. But it doesn't matter. They have to be talked into it, this essential human link between the world and the infinite, the only place where the bloodstream touches eternity. It doesn't matter. What matters is love and desire. Here in this dark is as good a place as any. Better than some, maybe.

Mike comes to her, then Richie, and the act is repeated. Now she feels some pleasure, dim heat in her childish unmatured sex, and she closes her eyes as Stan comes to her and she thinks of the birds, spring and the birds, and she sees them, again and again, all lighting at once, filling up the winter-naked trees, shockwave riders on the moving edge of nature's most violent season, she sees them take wing again and again, the flutter of their wings like the snap of many sheets on the line, and she thinks: A month from now every kid in Derry Park will have a kite, they'll run to keep the strings from getting tangled with each other. *She thinks again:* This is what flying is like.

With Stan as with the others, there is that rueful sense of fading, of *leaving, with whatever they truly need from this act — some ultimate — close but as yet unfound.*

'Did you?' she asks again, and although she doesn't know exactly what 'it' is, she knows that he hasn't.

There is a long wait, and then Ben comes to her.

He is trembling all over, but it is not the fearful trembling she felt in Stan.

'Beverly, I can't,' he says in a tone which purports to be reasonable and is anything but.

'You can too. I can feel it.'

She sure can. There's more of this hardness; more of *him*. She can feel it below the gentle push of his belly. Its size raises a certain curiosity and she touches the bulge lightly. He groans against her neck, and the blow of his breath causes her bare body to dimple with goosebumps. She feels the first twist of real heat race through her — suddenly the feeling in her is very large; she recognizes that it is too big

(*and is he too big, can she take that into herself?*)

and too old for her, something, some feeling that walks in boots. This is like Henry's M-80s, something not meant for kids, something that could explode and blow you up. But this was not the place or time for worry; here there was love, desire, and the dark. If they didn't try for the first two they would surely be left with the last.

'Beverly, don't —'

'Yes.'

'I . . .'

'Show me how to fly,' she says with a calmness she doesn't feel, aware by the fresh wet warmth on her cheek and neck that he has begun to cry. 'Show me, Ben.'

'No . . .'

'If you wrote the poem, show me. Feel my hair if you want to, Ben. It's all right.'

'Beverly . . . I . . . I . . .'

He's not just trembling now; he's shaking all over. But she senses again that this ague is not all fear — part of it is the precursor of the throe this act is all about. She thinks of

(*the birds*)

his face, his dear sweet earnest face, and knows it is not fear; it is wanting he feels, a deep passionate wanting now barely held in check, and she feels that sense of power again, something like flying, something like looking down from above and seeing all the birds on the roofpeaks, on the TV antenna atop Wally's, seeing streets spread out maplike, oh desire, right, this was something, it was love and desire that taught you to fly.

'Ben! Yes!' she cries suddenly, and the leash breaks.

She feels pain again, and for a moment there is the frightening sensation of being crushed. Then he props himself up on the palms of his hands and that feeling is gone.

He's big, oh yes – the pain is back, and it's much deeper than when Eddie first entered her. She has to bite her lip again and think of the birds until the burning is gone. But it does go, and she is able to reach up and touch his lips with one finger, and he moans.

The heat is back, and she feels her power suddenly shift to him; she gives it gladly and goes with it. There is a sensation first of being rocked, of a delicious spiralling sweetness which makes her begin to turn her head helplessly from side to side, and a tuneless humming comes from between her closed lips, this is flying, this, oh love, oh desire, oh this is something impossible to deny, binding, giving, making a strong circle: binding, giving . . . flying.

'Oh Ben, oh my dear, yes,' she whispers, feeling the sweat stand out on her face, feeling their connection, something firmly in place, something like eternity, the number 8 rocked over on its side. 'I love you so much, dear.'

And she feels the thing begin to happen – something of which the girls who whisper and giggle about sex in the girls' room have no idea, at least as far as she knows; they only marvel at how gooshy sex must be, and now she realizes that for many of them sex must be some unrealized undefined monster; they refer to the act as It. Would you do It, do your sister and her boyfriend do It, do your mom and dad still do It, and how they never intend to do It; oh yes, you would think that the whole girls' side of the fifth-grade class was made up of spinsters-to-be, and it is obvious to Beverly that none of them can suspect this . . . this conclusion, and she is only kept from screaming by her knowledge that the others will hear and think her badly hurt. She puts the side of her hand in her mouth and bites down hard. She understands the screamy laughter of Greta Bowie and Sally Mueller and all the others better now: hadn't they, the seven of them, spent most of this, the longest, scariest summer of their lives, laughing like loons? You laugh because what's fearful and unknown is also what's funny, you laugh the way a small child will sometimes laugh and cry at the same time when a capering circus clown approaches, knowing it is supposed to be funny . . . but it is also unknown, full of the unknown's eternal power.

Biting her hand will not stay the cry, and she can only reassure them – and Ben – by crying out her affirmative in the darkness.

'Yes! Yes! Yes!' Glorious images of flight fill her head, mixing with the harsh calling of the grackles and starlings; these sounds become the world's sweetest music.

So she flies, she flies up, and now the power is not with her or with *him but somewhere between them, and he cries out, and she can feel his arms trembling, and she arches up and into him, feeling his spasm, his touch, his total fleeting intimacy with her in the dark. They break through into the life-light together.*

Then it is over and they are in each other's arms and when he tries to say something – perhaps some stupid apology that would hurt what she remembers, some stupid apology like a handcuff, she stops his words with a kiss and sends him away.

Bill comes to her.

He tries to say something, but his stutter is almost total now.

'You be quiet,' she says, secure in her new knowledge, but aware that she is tired now. Tired and damned sore. The insides and backs of her thighs feel sticky, and she thinks it's maybe because Ben actually finished, or maybe because she is bleeding. 'Everything is going to be totally okay.'

'A-A-Are you shuh-shuh-shuh-hure?'

'Yes,' she says, and links her hands behind his neck, feeling the sweaty mat of his hair. 'You just bet.'

'Duh-duh-does ih-ih . . . does ih-ih-ih –'

'Shhh . . .'

It is not as it was with Ben; there is passion, but not the same kind. Being with Bill now is the best conclusion to this that there could be. He is kind; tender; just short of calm. She senses his eagerness, but it is tempered and held back by his anxiety for her, perhaps because only Bill and she herself realize what an enormous act this is, and how it must never be spoken of, not to anyone else, not even to each other.

At the end, she is surprised by that sudden upsurge and she has time to think: Oh! It's going to happen again, I don't know if I can stand it –

But her thoughts are swept away by the utter sweetness of it, and she barely hears him whispering, 'I love you, Bev, I love you, I'll always love you' saying it over and over and not stuttering at all.

She hugs him to her and for a moment they stay that way, his smooth cheek against hers.

He withdraws from her without saying anything and for a little while she's alone, pulling her clothes back together, slowly putting them on, aware of a dull throbbing pain of which they, being male, will never know, aware also of a certain exhausted pleasure and the relief of having it over. There is an emptiness down there now, and although she is glad that her sex is her own again, the emptiness imparts a strange melancholy which she could never express . . . except to think of bare trees under a white winter sky, empty trees, trees waiting for blackbirds to come like ministers at the end of March to preside over the death of snow.

She finds them by groping for their hands.

For a moment no one speaks and when someone does, it does not surprise her much that it's Eddie. 'I think when we went right two turns back, we shoulda gone left. Jeez, I knew *that, but I was so sweaty and frigged up –'*

'Been frigged up your whole life, Eds,' Richie says. His voice is pleasant. The raw edge of panic is completely gone.

'We went wrong some other places too,' Eddie says, ignoring him, 'but that's the worst one. If we can find our way back there, we just might be okay.'

They form up in a clumsy line, Eddie first, Beverly second now, her hand on Eddie's shoulder as Mike's is on hers. They begin to move again, faster this time. Eddie displays none of his former nervous care.

We're going home, *she thinks,* and shivers with relief and joy. Home, yes. And that will be good. We've done our job, what we came for, now we can go back to just being kids again. And that will be good, too.

As they move through the dark she realizes the sound of running water is closer.

CHAPTER TWENTY-THREE

OUT

1

Derry/9:00–10:00 A.M.

By ten past nine, Derry windspeeds were being clocked at an average of fifty-five miles an hour, with gusts up to seventy. The anemometer in the courthouse registered one gust of eighty-one, and then the needle dropped all the way back to zero. The wind had ripped the whirling cuplike device on the courthouse roof off its moorings and it flew away into the rainswept dimness of the day. Like George Denbrough's boat, it was never seen again. By nine-thirty, the thing the Derry Water Department had sworn was now impossible seemed not only possible but imminent: that downtown Derry might be flooded for the first time since August of 1958, when many of the old drains had clogged up or caved in during a freak rainstorm. By quarter of ten, men with grim faces were arriving in cars and pick-up trucks along both sides of the Canal, their foul-weather gear rippling crazily in the freight-train wind. For the first time since October of 1957, sandbags began to go up along the Canal's cement sides. The arch where the Canal went under the three-way intersection at the heart of Derry's downtown area was full almost to the top; Main Street, Canal Street, and the foot of Up-Mile Hill were impassable except by foot, and those who splashed and hurried their way toward the sandbagging operation felt the very streets beneath their feet trembling with the frenzied flow of the water, the way a turnpike overpass will tremble when big trucks pass each other. But this was a steady vibration, and the men were glad to be on the north side of downtown, away from that steady rumbling that was felt rather than heard. Harold Gardener shouted at Alfred Zitner, who ran Zitner's Realty on the west side of town, asked him if the streets were going to collapse. Zitner said hell would freeze over before something like that happened. Harold had a brief image of Adolf Hitler and Judas Iscariot handing out ice-skates and went on heaving sandbags.

1021

The water was now less than three inches below the top of the Canal's cement walls. In the Barrens the Kenduskeag was already out of its banks, and by noon the luxuriant undergrowth and scrub trees would be poking out of a vast shallow, stinking lake. The men continued to work, pausing only when the supply of sandbags ran out . . . and then, at ten of ten, they were frozen by a great rending ripping sound. Harold Gardener later told his wife he thought maybe the end of the world had come. It wasn't downtown falling into the earth – not then – it was the Standpipe. Only Andrew Keene, Norbert Keene's grandson, actually saw it happen, and he had smoked so much Colombian Red that morning that at first he thought it had to be a hallucination. He had been wandering Derry's stormswept streets since about eight o'clock, roughly the same time that Dr Hale was ascending to that great family medical practice in the sky. He was drenched to the skin (except for the two-ounce baggie of pot tucked up into his armpit, that was) but totally unaware of it. His eyes widened in disbelief. He had reached Memorial Park, which stood on the flank of Standpipe Hill. And unless he was wrong, the Standpipe now had a pronounced *lean*, like that fucked-up tower in Pisa that was on all the macaroni boxes. 'Oh, *wow!*' Andrew Keene cried, his eyes widening even more – they looked as if they might be on small tough springs now – as the splintering sounds began. The Standpipe's lean was becoming more and more acute as he stood there with his jeans plastered to his skinny shanks and his drenched paisley headband dripping water into his eyes. White shingles were popping off the downtown side of the great round water-tower . . . no, not exactly popping off; it was more like they were *squirting* off. And a definite crinkle had appeared about twenty feet above the Standpipe's stone foundation. Water suddenly began to spray out through this crinkle, and now the shingles weren't squirting off the Standpipe's downtown side; they were spewing into the windstream. A rending sound began to come from the Standpipe, and Andrew could *see* it moving, like the hand of a great clock inclining from noon to one to two. The baggie of pot fell out of his armpit and fetched up inside his shirt somewhere near his belt. He didn't notice. He was utterly fetched. Large twanging sounds came from inside the Standpipe, as if the strings of the world's biggest guitar were being broken one by one. These were the cables inside the cylinder, which had provided the proper balance of stress against the water-pressure. The Standpipe began to heel over faster and faster, boards and beams ripping apart, splinters jumping and whirling into the air. '*FAAAR FUCKING OWWWWT!*' Andrew Keene shrieked, but it was lost in the Standpipe's final crashing fall, and by the rising sound of one and three-quarters million gallons of water, seven thousand tons of water, pouring out of the building's ruptured spouting side. It went in a gray tidal wave, and of course if Andrew Keene had been on the downhill side of the Standpipe, he would have exited the world in no time. But God favors drunks, small children, and the cataclysmically stoned; Andrew was standing in a place where he could see it all and not be touched by a single drop. '*GREAT FUCKING SPECIAL EFFECTS!*' Andrew screamed as the water rolled over Memorial Park like a solid thing, sweeping away the sundial beside which a small boy named Stan Uris had often stood watching birds with his father's field glasses. '*STEVEN SPIELBERG EAT YOUR HEART OUT!*' The stone birdbath also went. Andrew saw it for a moment, turning over and over, pedestal for dish and dish for pedestal, and then it was gone. A line of maples and birches separating Memorial Park from Kansas Street were knocked down like so many pins in a bowling alley. They took wild spiky snarls of power lines with them. The water rolled across the street, beginning to spread now, beginning to look more like water than that mind-boggling solid wall that had taken sundial, birdbath, and trees, but it still had power enough to sweep almost a dozen houses on the far side of Kansas Street off their foundations and into the Barrens. They went with sickening ease, most of them still whole. Andrew Keene recognized one of them as belonging to the Karl Massensik family. Mr Massensik had been his sixth-grade teacher, a real pooch. As the house went over the edge and down the slope, Andrew realized he could still see a candle burning brightly in one window, and he wondered briefly if he might be mentally highsiding it, if you could dig the concept. There was an explosion from the Barrens and a brief gout of yellow flame as someone's Coleman gas lantern ignited oil pouring out of a ruptured fuel-tank. Andrew stared at the far side of Kansas Street, where until just forty seconds ago there had been a neat line of middle-class houses. They were Gone City now, and you better believe it, sweet thing. In their places were ten cellar-holes that looked like swimming-pools. Andrew wanted to advance the opinion that this was far fucking out, but he couldn't yell anymore. Seemed like his yeller was busted. His diaphragm felt weak and useless. He heard a series of crunching thuds, the sound of a giant with his shoes full of Ritz crackers marching down a flight of stairs. It was the Standpipe rolling down the hill, a huge white cylinder still spouting the last of its water supply, the thick cables that had helped to hold it together flying into the air and then cracking down again like steel bullwhips, digging runnels in the soft earth that immediately filled up with rushing rainwater. As Andrew watched, with his chin resting somewhere between his collarbones, the Standpipe, horizontal now, better than a hundred and twenty-five feet long, flew out into the air. For a moment it seemed frozen there, a surreal image straight out of rubber-walled strait-jacketed toodle-oo land, rainwater sparkling on its shattered sides, its windows broken, casements hanging, the flashing light on top, meant as a warning for low-flying light planes, still flashing, and then it fell into the street with a final rending crash. Kansas Street had channelled a lot of the water, and now it began to rush toward downtown by way of Up-Mile Hill. *There used to be houses over there*, Andrew Keene thought, and suddenly all the strength ran out of his legs. He sat down heavily – kersplash. He stared at the broken stone foundation on which the Standpipe had stood for his whole life. He wondered if anyone would ever believe him.

He wondered if he believed it himself.

2

The Kill/10:02 A.M. May 31, 1985

Bill and Richie saw It turn toward them, Its mandibles opening and closing, Its one good eye glaring down at them, and Bill realized It gave off Its own source of illumination, like some grisly lightning-bug. But the light was flickering and uncertain; It was badly hurt. Its thoughts buzzed and racketed

(*let me go! let me go and you can have everything you've ever wanted – money, fame, fortune, power – I can give you these things*)

in his head.

Bill moved forward empty-handed, his eyes fixed on Its single red one. He felt the power growing inside him, investing him, knotting his arms into cords, filling each clenched fist with its own force. Richie walked beside him, his lips pulled back over his teeth.

(*I can give you your wife back – I can do it, only I – she'll remember nothing as the seven of you remembered nothing*)

They were close, very close now. Bill could smell Its stinking aroma and realized with sudden horror that it was the smell of the Barrens, the smell they had taken for the smell of sewers and polluted streams and the burning dump ... but had they ever really believed those were all it had been? It was the smell of It, and perhaps it had been strongest in the Barrens but it had hung over all Derry like a cloud and people just didn't smell it, the way zoo-keepers don't smell their charges after awhile, or even wonder why the visitors wrinkle their noses when they come in.

'Us two,' he muttered to Richie, and Richie nodded without taking his eyes off the Spider, which now shrank back from them, Its abominable spiny legs clittering, brought to bay at last.

(*I can't give you eternal life but I can touch you and you will live long long lives – two hundred years, three hundred, perhaps five hundred – I can make you gods of the Earth – if you let me go if you let me go if you let me –*)

'Bill?' Richie asked hoarsely.

With a scream building in him, building up and up and up, Bill charged. Richie ran with him stride for stride. They struck together with their right fists, but Bill understood it was not really their fists they were striking with at all; it was their combined force, augmented by the force of that Other; it was the force of memory and desire; above all else, it was the force of love and unforgotten childhood like one big wheel.

The Spider's shriek filled Bill's head, seeming to splinter his brains. He felt his fist plunge deep into writhing wetness. His arm followed it in up to the shoulder. He pulled it back, dripping with the Spider's black blood. Ichor poured from the hole he had made.

He saw Richie standing almost beneath Its bloated body, covered with Its darkly sparkling blood, standing in the classic boxer's stance, his dripping fists pumping.

The Spider lashed at them with Its legs. Bill felt one of them rip down his side, parting his shirt, parting skin. Its stinger pumped uselessly against the floor. Its screams were clarion-bells in his head. It lunged clumsily forward, trying to bite him, and instead of retreating Bill drove forward, using not just his fist now but his whole body, making himself into a torpedo. He ran into Its gut like a sprinting fullback who lowers his shoulders and simply drives straight ahead.

For a moment he felt Its stinking flesh simply give, as if it would rebound and send him flying. With an inarticulate scream he drove harder, pushing forward and upward with his legs, digging at It with his hands. And he broke through; was inundated with Its hot fluids. They ran across his face, in his ears. He snuffled them up his nose in thin squirming streams.

He was in the black again, up to his shoulders inside Its convulsing body. And in his clogged ears he could hear a sound like the steady *whack-WHACK-whack-WHACK* of a big bass drum, the one that leads the parade when the circus comes to town with its complement of freaks and strutting capering clowns.

The sound of Its heart.

He heard Richie scream in sudden pain, a sound that rose into a quick, gasping moan and was cut off. Bill suddenly thrust both fisted hands forward. He was choking, strangling in Its pulsing bag of guts and waters.

Whack-WHACK-whack-WHACK –

He plunged his hands into It, ripping, tearing, parting, seeking the source of the sound; rupturing organs, his slimed fingers opening and closing, his locked chest seeming to swell from lack of air.

Whack-WHACK-whack-WHACK –

And suddenly it was in his hands, a great living thing that pumped and pulsed against his palms, pushing them back and forth.

(*NONONONONONONO*)

Yes! Bill cried, choking, drowning. *Yes! Try this, you bitch! TRY THIS ONE OUT! DO YOU LIKE IT? DO YOU LOVE IT? DO YOU?*

He laced his fingers together over the pulsing narthex of Its heart, palms spread apart in an inverted V – and brought them together with all the force he could muster.

There was one final shriek of pain and fear as Its heart exploded between his hands, running out between his fingers in jittering strings.

Whack-WHACK-whack-WHA

The scream, fading, dwindling. Bill felt Its body clench around him suddenly, like a fist in a slick glove. Then everything loosened. He became aware that Its body was tilting, slipping slowly off to one side. At the same time he began pulling back, his consciousness leaving him.

The Spider collapsed on Its side, a huge bundle of steaming alien meat, Its legs still quivering and jerking, caressing the sides of the tunnel and scraping across the floor in random scrawls.

Bill staggered away, breathing in whooping gasps, spitting in an effort to clear his mouth of Its horrible taste. He tripped over his own feet and fell to his knees.

And clearly, he heard the Voice of the Other; the Turtle might be dead, but whatever had invested it was not.

'Son, you did real good.'

Then it was gone. The power went with it. He felt weak, revulsed, half-insane. He looked over his shoulder and saw the dying black nightmare of the Spider, still jerking and quivering.

'Richie!' he cried out in a hoarse, breaking voice. *'Richie, where are you man?'*

No answer.

The light was gone now. It had died with the Spider. He fumbled in the pocket of his matted shirt for the last book of matches. They were there, but they wouldn't light; the heads were soaked with blood.

'*Richie!*' he screamed again, beginning to weep now. He began to crawl forward, first one hand and then the other groping in the dark. At last one of them struck something which yielded limply to his touch. His hands flew over it . . . and stopped as they touched Richie's face.

'*Richie! Richie!*'

Still no answer. Struggling in the dark, Bill got one arm under Richie's back and the other under his knees. He wobbled to his feet and began to stumble back the way they had come with Richie in his arms.

3

Derry / 10:00–10:15 A.M.

At 10:00 the steady vibration which had been running through Derry's downtown streets increased to a rumbling roar. The Derry *News* would later write that the supports of the Canal's underground portion, weakened by the savage assault of what amounted to a flash flood, simply collapsed. There were, however, people who disagreed with that view. 'I was there, I know,' Harold Gardener later told his wife. 'It wasn't just that the Canal's supports collapsed. It was an *earthquake*, that's what it was. It was a fucking *earthquake*.'

Either way, the results were the same. As the rumbling built steadily up and up, windows began to shatter, plaster ceilings began to fall, and the inhuman cry of twisting beams and foundations swelled into a frightening chorus. Cracks raced up the bullet-pocked brick façade of Machen's like grasping hands. The cables holding the marquee of the Aladdin Theater out over the street snapped and the marquee came crashing down. Richard's Alley, which ran behind the Center Street Drug, suddenly filled up with an avalanche of yellow brick as the Brian X Dowd Professional Building, erected in 1952, came crashing down. A huge screen of jaundice-colored dust rose in the air and was snatched away like a veil.

At the same time the statue of Paul Bunyan in front of the City Center exploded. It was as if that long-ago art teacher's threat to blow it up had finally proved to be dead serious after all. The bearded grinning head rose straight up in the air. One leg kicked forward, the other back, as if Paul had attempted some sort of a split so enthusiastic it had resulted in dismemberment. The statue's midsection blew out in a cloud of shrapnel and the head of the plastic axe rose into the rainy sky, disappeared, and then came down again, twirling end over end. It sheared through the roof of the Kissing Bridge, and then its floor.

And then, at 10:02 A.M., downtown Derry simply collapsed.

Most of the water from the ruptured Standpipe had crossed Kansas Street and ended up in the Barrens, but tons of it rushed down into the business district by way of Up-Mile Hill. Perhaps that was the straw that broke the camel's back . . . or perhaps, as Harold Gardener told his wife, there really *was* an earthquake. Cracks raced across the surface of Main Street. They were narrow at first . . . and then they began to gape like hungry mouths and the sound of the Canal floated up, not muffled now but frighteningly loud. Everything began to shake. The neon sign proclaiming OUT-LET MOCCASINS in front of Shorty Squires's souvenir shop hit the street and shorted out in three feet of water. A moment or two later, Shorty's building, which stood next to Mr Paperback, began to *descend*. Buddy Angstrom was the first to see this phenomenon. He elbowed Alfred Zitner, who looked, gaped, and then elbowed Harold Gardener. Within a space of seconds the sandbagging operation stopped. The men lining both sides of the Canal only stood and stared toward downtown in the pouring rain, their faces stamped with identical expressions of horrified wonder. Squires's Souvenirs and Sundries appeared to have been built on some huge elevator which was now on the way down. It sank into the apparently solid concrete with ponderous stately dignity. When it came to a stop, you could have dropped to your hands and knees on the flooded sidewalk and entered through one of the third-floor windows. Water sprayed up all around the building, and a moment later Shorty himself appeared on the roof, waving his arms madly for rescue. Then he was obliterated as the office-building next door, the one which housed Mr Paperback at ground level, also sank into the ground. Unfortunately, this one did not go straight down as Shorty's building had done; the Mr Paperback building developed a marked lean (for a moment, in fact, it bore a strong resemblance to that fucked-up tower in Pisa, the one on the macaroni boxes). As it tilted, bricks began to shower from its top and sides. Shorty was struck by several. Harold Gardener saw him reel backward, hands to his head . . . and then the top three floors of the Mr Paperback building slid off as neatly as pancakes from the top of a stack. Shorty disappeared. Someone on the sandbag line screamed, and then everything was lost in the grinding roar of destruction. Men were knocked off their feet or sent wobbling and staggering back from the Canal. Harold Gardener saw the buildings which faced each other across Main Street lean forward, like ladies kibbitzing over a card-game, their heads almost touching. The street itself was sinking, cracking, breaking up. Water splashed and sprayed. And then, one after another, buildings on both sides of the street simply swayed past their centers of gravity and crashed into the street – the Northeast Bank, The Shoeboat, Alvey's Smokes 'n Jokes, Bailley's Lunch, Bandler's Record and Music Barn. Except that by then there was really no street for them to crash into. The street had fallen into the Canal, stretching like taffy at first and then breaking up into bobbing chunks of asphalt. Harold saw the traffic-island at the three-street intersection suddenly drop out of sight, and as water geysered up, he suddenly understood what was going to happen.

'*Gotta get out of here!*' he screamed at Al Zitner. '*It's gonna backwater! Al! It's gonna backwater!*'

Al Zitner gave no sign that he had heard. His was the face of a sleepwalker, or perhaps of a man who has been deeply hypnotized. He stood in his soaked red-and-blue-checked sportcoat, in his open-collared Lacoste shirt with the little alligator on the left boob, in his blue socks with the crossed white golf-clubs knitted into their sides, in his brown L. L. Bean's boat shoes with the rubber soles. He was watching perhaps a million dollars of his own personal investments sinking into the street, three or four millions of his friends' investments – the guys he played poker with, the guys he golfed with, the guys he skied with at his time-sharing condo in Rangely. Suddenly his home town, Derry, *Maine*, for Christ's sake, looked bizarrely like that fucked-up city where the wogs pushed people around in those long skinny canoes. Water roiled and boiled between the buildings that were still standing. Canal Street ended in a jagged black diving board over the edge of a churning lake. It was really no wonder Zitner hadn't heard Harold. Others, however, had come to the same conclusion Gardener had come to – you couldn't drop that much shit into a raging body of water without causing a lot of trouble. Some dropped the sandbags they had been holding and took to their heels. Harold Gardener was one of these, and so he lived. Others were not so lucky and were still somewhere in the general area as the Canal, its throat now choked with tons of asphalt, concrete, brick, plaster, glass, and about four million dollars' worth of assorted merchandise, backsurged and poured over its concrete sleeve, carrying away men and sandbags impartially. Harold kept thinking it meant to have him; no matter how fast he ran the water kept gaining. He finally escaped by clawing his way up a steep embankment covered with shrubbery. He looked back once and saw a man he believed to be Roger Lernerd, the head loan officer at Harold's credit union, trying to start his car in the parking-lot of the Canal Mini-Mall. Even over the roar of the water and the bellowing wind, Harold could hear the K-car's little sewing-machine engine cranking and cranking and cranking as smooth black water ran rocker-panel high on both sides of it. Then, with a deep thundering cry, the Kenduskeag poured out of its banks and swept both the Canal Mini-Mall and Roger Lernerd's bright red K-car away. Harold began climbing again, grabbing onto branches, roots, anything that looked solid enough to take his weight. Higher ground, that was the ticket. As Andrew Keene might have said, Harold Gardener was really into the concept of higher ground that morning. Behind him he could hear downtown Derry continuing to collapse. The sound was like artillery fire.

4

Bill

'*Beverly!*' he shouted. His back and arms were one solid throbbing ache. Richie now seemed to weigh at least five hundred pounds. *Put him down, then*, his mind whispered. *He's dead, you know damn well he is, so why don't you just put him down?*

But he wouldn't, couldn't, do that.

'*Beverly!*' he shouted again. '*Ben! Anyone!*'

He thought: *This is where It threw me – and Richie – except It threw us farther – so much farther. What was that like? I'm losing it, forgetting . . .*

'Bill?' It was Ben's voice, shaky and exhausted, somewhere fairly close. 'Where are you?'

'Over here, man. I've got Richie. He got . . . he's hurt.'

'Keep talking.' Ben was closer now. 'Keep talking, Bill.'

'We killed It,' Bill said, walking toward where Ben's voice had come from. 'We killed the bitch. And if Richie's dead –'

'*Dead?*' Ben called, alarmed. He was very close now . . . and then his hand groped out of the dark and pawed lightly at Bill's nose. 'What do you mean, dead?'

'I . . . he . . .' They were supporting Richie together now. 'I can't see him,' Bill said. 'That's the thing. I cuh-cuh-han't *suh-suh-see* him!'

'*Richie!*' Ben shouted, and shook him. '*Richie, come on! Come on, goddammit!*' Ben's voice was blurring now, becoming shaky. '*RICHIE WILL YOU WAKE THE FUCK UP?*'

And in the dark, Richie said in a sleepy, irritable, just-coming-out-of-it voice: 'All rye, Haystack. All rye. We doan need no stinkin batches . . .'

'*Richie!*' Bill screamed. '*Richie, are you all right?*'

'Bitch threw me,' Richie muttered in that same tired, just-coming-out-of-sleep voice. 'I hit something hard. That's all . . . all I remember. Where's Bevvie?'

'Back this way,' Ben said. Quickly, he told them about the eggs. 'I stamped over a hundred. I think I got all of them.'

'I pray to God you did,' Richie said. He was starting to sound better. 'Put me down, Big Bill. I can walk . . . Is the water louder?'

'Yes,' Bill said. The three of them were holding hands in the dark. 'How's your head?'

'Hurts like hell. What happened after I got knocked out?'

Bill told them as much as he could bring himself to tell.

'And It's dead,' Richie marvelled. 'Are you sure, Bill?'

'Yes,' Bill said. 'This time I'm really shuh-hure.'

'Thank God,' Richie said. 'Hold onto me, Bill, I gotta barf.'

Bill did, and when Richie was done they walked on. Every now and then his foot struck something brittle that rolled off into the darkness. Parts of the Spider's eggs that Ben had tromped to pieces, he supposed, and shivered. It was good to know they were going in the right direction, but he was still glad he couldn't see the remains.

'*Beverly!*' Ben shouted. '*Beverly!*'

'*Here —*'

Her cry was faint, almost lost in the steady rumble of the water. They moved forward in the dark, calling to her steadily, zeroing in.

When they finally reached her, Bill asked if she had any matches left. She put half a pack in his hand. He lit one and saw their faces spring into ghostly being — Ben with his arm around Richie, who was standing slumped, blood running from his right temple, Beverly with Eddie's head in her lap. Then he turned the other way. Audra was lying crumpled on the flagstones, her legs asprawl, her head turned away. The webbing had mostly melted off her.

The match burned his fingers and he let it drop. In the darkness he mis-judged the distance, tripped over her, and nearly went sprawling.

'Audra! Audra, can you h-h-hear m-me?'

He got an arm under her back and sat her up. He slipped a hand under the sheaf of her hair and pressed his fingers against the side of her neck. Her pulse was there: a slow, steady beat.

He lit another match, and as it flared he saw her pupils contract. But that was an involuntary function; the fix of her gaze did not change, even when he brought the match close enough to her face to redden her skin. She was alive, but unresponsive. Hell, it was worse than that and he knew it. She was catatonic.

The second match burned his fingers. He shook it out.

'Bill, I don't like the sound of that water,' Ben said. 'I think we ought to get out of here.'

'How will we do it without Eddie?' Richie murmured.

'We can do it,' Bev said. 'Bill, Ben's right. We have to get out.'

'I'm taking her.'

'Of course. But we ought to go now.'

'Which way?'

'You'll know,' Beverly said softly. 'You killed It. You'll know, Bill.'

He picked Audra up as he had picked Richie up and went back to the others. The feel of her in his arms was disquieting, creepy; she was like a breathing waxwork.

'Which way, Bill?' Ben asked.

'I d-d-don't –'

(*you'll know, you killed It and you'll know*)

'Well, c-come on,' Bill said. 'Let's see if we can't find out. Beverly, gruh–gruh–hab these.' He handed her the matches.

'What about Eddie?' she asked. 'We have to take him out.'

'How c-can w-we?' Bill asked. 'It's . . . B–Beverly, the pluh–hace is f-falling apart.'

'We *gotta* get him out of here, man,' Richie said. 'Come on, Ben.'

Between them they managed to hoist up Eddie's body. Beverly lit them back to the fairytale door. Bill took Audra through it, holding her up from the floor as best he could. Richie and Ben carried Eddie through.

'Put him down,' Beverly said. 'He can stay here.'

'It's too dark,' Richie sobbed. 'You know . . . it's too dark. Eds . . . he . . .'

'No, it's okay,' Ben said. 'Maybe this is where he's supposed to be. I think maybe it is.'

They put him down, and Richie kissed Eddie's cheek. Then he looked blindly up at Ben. 'You sure?'

'Yeah. Come on, Richie.'

Richie got up and turned toward the door. '*Fuck you, Bitch!*' he cried suddenly, and kicked the door shut with his foot. It made a solid *chukking* sound as it closed and latched.

'Why'd you do that?' Beverly asked.

'I don't know,' Richie said, but he knew well enough. He looked back over his shoulder just as the match Beverly was holding went out.

'Bill – the mark on the door?'

'What about it?' Bill panted.

Richie said: 'It's gone.'

5

Derry/10:30 A.M.

The glass corridor connecting the adult library to the Children's Library suddenly exploded in a single brilliant flare of light. Glass flew out in an umbrella shape, whickering through the straining whipping trees which dotted the library grounds. Someone could have been severely hurt or even killed by such a deadly fusillade, but there was no one there, either inside or out. The library had not been opened that day at all. The tunnel which had so fascinated Ben Hanscom as a boy would never be replaced; there had been so much costly destruction in Derry that it seemed simpler to leave the two libraries as separate unconnected buildings. In time, no one on the Derry City Council could even remember what that glass umbilicus had been for. Perhaps only Ben himself could really have told them how it was to stand outside in the still cold of a January night, your nose running, the tips of your fingers numb inside your mittens, watching the people pass back and forth inside, walking through winter with their coats off and surrounded by light. He could have told them . . . but maybe it wasn't the sort of thing you could have gotten up and testified about at a City Council meeting – how you stood out in the cold dark and learned to love the light. All of that's as may be; the facts were just these: the glass corridor blew up for no apparent reason, no one was hurt (which was a blessing, since the final toll taken by that morning's storm – in human terms, at least – was sixty-seven killed and better than three hundred and twenty injured), and it was never rebuilt. After May 31st of 1985, if you wanted to get from the Children's Library to the adult library, you had to walk outside to do it. And if it was cold, or raining, or snowing, you had to put on your coat.

6

Out/10:54 A.M., May 31st, 1985

'Wait,' Bill gasped. 'Give me a chance . . . rest.'

'Let me help you with her,' Richie said again. They had left Eddie back in the Spider's lair, and that was something none of them wanted to talk about. But Eddie was dead and Audra was still alive – at least, technically.

'I'll do it,' Bill said between choked gasps for air.

'Bullshit. You'll give yourself a fucking heart attack. Let me help you, Big Bill.'

'How's your h-h-head?'

'Hurts,' Richie said. 'Don't change the subject.'

Reluctantly, Bill let Richie take her. It could have been worse; Audra was a tall girl whose normal weight was one hundred and forty pounds. But the part she'd been scheduled to play in *Attic Room* was that of a young woman being held hostage by a borderline psychotic who fancied himself a political terrorist. Because Freddie Firestone had wanted to shoot all of the attic sequences first, Audra had gone on a strict poultry – cottage-cheese – tuna-fish diet and lost twenty pounds. Still, after stumble-staggering along with her in the dark for a quarter of a mile (or a half, or three-quarters of a mile, or who knew), that one hundred and twenty felt more like two hundred.

'Th-Thanks, m-m-man,' he said.

'Don't mention it. Your turn next, Haystack.'

'Beep-beep, Richie,' Ben said, and Bill grinned in spite of himself. It was a tired grin, and it didn't last long, but a little was better than none.

'Which way, Bill?' Beverly asked. 'That water sounds louder than ever. I don't really fancy drowning down here.'

'Straight ahead, then left,' Bill said. 'Maybe we better try to go a little faster.'

They went on for half an hour, Bill calling the lefts and rights. The sound of the water continued to swell until it seemed to surround them, a scary Dolby stereo effect in the dark. Bill felt his way around a corner, one hand trailing over damp brick, and suddenly water was running over his shoes. The current was shallow and fast.

'Give me Audra,' he said to Ben, who was panting loudly. 'Upstream now.' Ben passed her carefully back to Bill, who managed to sling her over his shoulder in a fireman's carry. If she'd only protest . . . move . . . *do* something. 'How's matches, Bev?'

'Not many. Half a dozen, maybe. Bill . . . *do* you know where you're going?'

'I think I d-d-do,' he said. 'Come on.'

They followed him around the corner. The water foamed about Bill's ankles, then it was up to his shins, and then it was thigh-deep. The thunder of the water had deepened to a steady bass roar. The tunnel they were in was shaking steadily. For awhile Bill thought the current was going to become too strong to walk against, but then they passed a feeder-pipe that was pouring a huge jet of water into their tunnel – he marvelled at the white-water force of it – and the current slacked off somewhat, although the water continued to deepen. It –

I saw the water coming out of that feeder-pipe! Saw it!

'*H-H-Hey!*' he shouted. '*Can y-y-you guys see a-anything?*'

'It's been getting lighter for the last fifteen minutes or so!' Beverly shouted back. '*Where are we, Bill? Do you know?*'

I thought I did, Bill almost said. '*No! Come on!*'

He had believed they must be approaching the concrete-channelled section of the Kenduskeag that was called the Canal . . . the part that went under downtown and came out in Bassey Park. But there was light down here, *light*, and surely there could be no light in the Canal under the city. But it brightened steadily just the same.

Bill was beginning to have serious problems with Audra. It wasn't the current – that had slackened – it was the depth. *Pretty soon I'll be floating her*, he thought. He could see Ben on his left and Beverly on his right; by turning his head slightly, he could see Richie behind Ben. The footing was getting decidedly odd. The bottom of the tunnel was now heaped and mounded with detritus – bricks, it felt like. And up ahead, something was sticking out of the water like the prow of a ship that is in the process of sinking.

Ben floundered toward it, shivering in the cold water. A soggy cigar box floated into his face. He pushed it aside and grabbed at the thing sticking out of the water. His eyes widened. It appeared to be a large sign. He was able to read the letters AL, and below that, FUT. And suddenly he knew.

'Bill! Richie! Bev!' He was laughing with astonishment.

'What is it, Ben?' Beverly shouted.

Grabbing it with both hands, Ben rocked it back. There was a grating sound as one side of the sign scraped along the wall of the tunnel. Now they could read: ALADDI, and, below that, BACK TO THE FUTURE.

'It's the marquee for the Aladdin,' Richie said. 'How –'

'The street caved in,' Bill whispered. His eyes were widening. He stared up the tunnel. The light was brighter still up ahead.

'*What*, Bill?'

'What the fuck *happened*?'

'Bill? *Bill*? What –'

'All these drains!' Bill said wildly. 'All these old drains! There's been another flood! And I think this time –'

He began to flounder ahead again, holding Audra up. Ben, Bev, and Richie fell in behind him. Five minutes later Bill looked up and saw blue sky. He was looking through a crack in the ceiling of the tunnel, a crack that widened to better than seventy feet across as it ran away from where he stood. The water was broken by many islands and archipelagos up ahead – piles of bricks, the back deck of a Plymouth sedan with its trunk sprung open and pouring water, a parking-meter leaning against the tunnel wall at a drunken slant, its red VIOLATION flag up.

The footing had become almost impossible now – mini-mountains that rose and fell with no rhyme or reason, inviting a broken ankle. The water ran mildly around their armpits.

Mild now, Bill thought. *But if we'd been here two hours ago, even one, I think we might have gotten the ride of our lives.*

'What the fuck is this, Big Bill?' Richie asked. He was standing at Bill's left elbow, his face soft with wonder as he looked up at the rip in the roof of the tunnel – *except it's not the roof of any tunnel* Bill thought. *It's Main Street. At least it used to be.*

'I think most of downtown Derry is now in the Canal and being carried down the Kenduskeag River. Pretty soon it'll be in the Penobscot and then it will be in the Atlantic Ocean and good fucking riddance. Can you help me with Audra, Richie? I don't think I can –'

'Sure,' Richie said. 'Sure, Bill. No sweat.'

He took Audra from Bill. In this light, Bill could see her better than he perhaps wanted to – her pallor masked but not hidden by the dirt and ordure that smeared her forehead and caked her cheeks. Her eyes were still wide open . . . wide open and innocent of all sense. Her hair hung lank and wet. She might as well have been one of those inflatable dollies they sold at the Pleasure Chest in New York or along the Reeperbahn in Hamburg. The only difference was her slow, steady respiration . . . and that might have been a clockwork trick, no more than that.

'How are we going to get up from here?' he asked Richie.

'Get Ben to give you ten fingers,' Richie said. 'You can yank Bev up, and the two of you can get your wife. Ben can boost me and we'll get Ben. And after that I'll show you how to set up a volleyball tournament for a thousand sorority girls.'

'Beep-beep, Richie.'

'Beep-beep your ass, Big Bill.'

The tiredness was going through him in steady waves. He caught Beverly's level gaze and held it for a moment. She nodded to him slightly, and he made a smile for her.

'Give me ten fingers, B-B-Ben?'

Ben, who also looked unutterably weary, nodded. A deep scratch ran down one cheek. 'I think I can handle that.'

He stooped slightly and laced his hands together. Bill hiked one foot, stepped into Ben's hand, and jumped up. It wasn't quite enough. Ben lifted the step he had made with his hands and Bill grabbed the edge of the broken-in tunnel roof. He yanked himself up. The first thing he saw was a white-and-orange crash barrier. The second thing was a crowd of milling men and women beyond the barrier. The third was Freese's Department Store – only it had an oddly bulged-out, foreshortened look. It took him a moment to realize that almost half of Freese's had sunk into the street and the Canal beneath. The top half had slued out over the street and seemed in danger of toppling over like a pile of badly stacked books.

'Look! Look! There's someone in the street!'

A woman was pointing toward the place where Bill's head had poked out of the crevasse in the shattered pavement.

'Praise God, there's someone else!'

She started forward, an elderly woman with a kerchief tied over her head peasant-style. A cop held her back. 'Not safe out there, Mrs Nelson. You know it. Rest of the street might go any time.'

Mrs Nelson, Bill thought. *I remember you. Your sister used to sit George and me sometimes.* He raised his hand to show her he was all right, and when she raised her own hand in return, he felt a sudden surge of good feelings – and hope.

He turned around and lay flat on the sagging pavement, trying to distribute his weight as evenly as possible, the way you were supposed to do on thin ice. He reached down for Bev. She grasped his wrists and, with what seemed to be the last of his strength, he pulled her up. The sun, which had disappeared again, now ran out from behind a brace of mackerel-scale clouds and gave them their shadows back. Beverly looked up, startled, caught Bill's eyes, and smiled.

'I love you, Bill,' she said. 'And I pray she'll be all right.'

'Thuh-hank you, Bevvie,' he said, and his kind smile made her start to cry a little. He hugged her and the small crowd gathered behind the crash barrier applauded. A photographer from the Derry *News* snapped a picture. It appeared in the June 1st edition of the paper, which was printed in Bangor because of water damage to the *News*'s presses. The caption was simple enough, and true enough for Bill to cut the picture out and keep it tucked away in his wallet for years to come: SURVIVORS, the caption read. That was all, but that was enough.

It was six minutes of eleven in Derry, Maine.

7

Derry/Later the Same Day

The glass corridor between the Children's Library and the adult library had exploded at 10:30 A.M. At 10:33, the rain stopped. It didn't taper off; it stopped all at once, as if Someone Up There had flicked a toggle switch. The wind had already begun to fall, and it fell so rapidly that people stared at each other with uneasy, superstitious faces. The sound was like the wind-down of a 747's engines after it has been safely parked at the gate. The sun peeked out for the first time at 10:47. By midafternoon the clouds had burned away entirely, and the day had come off fair and hot. By 3:30 P.M. the mercury in the Orange Crush thermometer outside the door of Secondhand Rose, Secondhand Clothes read eighty-three – the highest reading of the young season. People walked through the streets like zombies, not talking much. Their expressions were remarkably similar: a kind of stupid wonder that would have been funny if it was not also so frankly pitiable. By evening reporters from ABC, CBS, NBC, and CNN had arrived in Derry, and the network news reporters would bring some version of the truth home to most people; they would make it real . . . although there were those who might have suggested that reality is a highly untrustworthy concept, something perhaps no more solid than a piece of canvas stretched over an interlacing of cables like the strands of a spiderweb. The following morning Bryant Gumble and Willard Scott of the *Today* show would be in Derry. During the course of the program, Gumble would interview Andrew Keene. 'Whole Standpipe just crashed over and rolled down the hill,' Andrew said. 'It was like wow. You know what I mean? Like Steven Spielberg eat your heart out, you know? Hey, I always got the idea looking at you on TV that you were, you know, a lot bigger.' Seeing themselves and their neighbors on TV – that would make it real. It would give them a place from which to grasp this terrible, ungraspable thing. It had been a FREAK STORM. In the days following, THE DEATH-COUNT would rise in THE WAKE OF THE KILLER STORM. It was, in fact, THE WORST SPRING STORM IN MAINE HISTORY. All of these headlines, as terrible as they were, were useful – they helped to blunt the essential strangeness of what had happened . . . or perhaps *strangeness* was too mild a word. *Insanity* might have been better. Seeing themselves on TV would help make it concrete, less insane. But in the hours before the news crews arrived, there were only the people from Derry, walking through their rubble-strewn, mud-slicked streets with expressions of stunned unbelief on their faces. Only the people from Derry, not talking much, looking at things, occasionally picking things up and then tossing them down again, trying to figure out what had happened during the last seven or eight hours. Men stood on Kansas Street, smoking, looking at houses lying upside down in the Barrens. Other men and women stood beyond the white-and-orange crash barriers, looking into the black hole that had been downtown until ten that morning. The headline of that Sunday's paper read: WE WILL REBUILD, VOWS DERRY MAYOR, and perhaps they would. But in the weeks that followed, while the City Council wrangled over how the rebuilding should begin, the huge crater that had been downtown continued to grow in an unspectacular but steady way. Four days after the storm, the office building of the Bangor Hydroelectric Company collapsed into the hole. Three days after that, the Flying Doghouse, which sold the best kraut- and chili-dogs in eastern Maine, fell in. Drains backed up periodically in houses, apartment buildings, and businesses. It got so bad in the Old Cape that people began to leave. June 10th was the first evening of horse-racing at Bassey Park; the first race was scheduled for 8:00 P.M. and that seemed to cheer everyone up. But a section of bleachers collapsed as the trotters in the first race turned into the home stretch, and half a dozen people were hurt. One of them was Foxy Foxworth, who had managed the Aladdin Theater until 1973. Foxy spent two weeks in the hospital, suffering from a broken leg and a punctured testicle. When he was released, he decided to go to his sister's in Somersworth, New Hampshire.

He wasn't the only one. Derry was falling apart.

8

They watched the orderly slam the back doors of the ambulance and go around to the passenger seat. The ambulance started up the hill toward the Derry Home Hospital. Richie had flagged it down at severe risk of life and limb, and had argued the irate driver to a draw when the driver insisted he just didn't have any more room. He had ended up stretching Audra out on the floor.

'Now what?' Ben asked. There were huge brown circles under his eyes and a grimy ring of dirt around his neck.

'I'm g-going back to the Town House,' Bill said. 'G-Gonna sleep for about suh-hixteen hours.'

'I second that,' Richie said. He looked hopefully at Bev. 'Got any cigarettes, purty lady?'

'No,' Beverly said. 'I think I'm going to quit again.'

'Sensible enough idea.'

They began to walk slowly up the hill, the four of them side by side.

'It's o-o-over,' Bill said.

Ben nodded. 'We did it. *You* did it, Big Bill.'

'We all did it,' Beverly said. 'I wish we could have brought Eddie up. I wish that more than anything.'

They reached the corner of Upper Main and Point Street. A kid in a red rainslicker and green rubber boots was sailing a paper boat along the brisk run of water in the gutter. He looked up, saw them looking at him, and waved tentatively. Bill thought it was the boy with the skateboard – the one whose friend had seen Jaws in the Canal. He smiled and stepped toward the boy.

'It's all right n-n-now,' he said.

The boy studied him gravely, and then grinned. The smile was sunny and hopeful. 'Yeah,' he said. 'I think it is.'

'Bet your a-a-ass.'

The kid laughed.

'You g-gonna be careful on thuh-hat skateboard?'

'Not really,' the kid said, and this time Bill laughed. He restrained an urge to ruffle the kid's hair – that probably would have been resented – and returned to the others.

'Who was that?' Richie asked.

'A friend,' Bill said. He stuffed his hands in his pockets. 'Do you remember it? When we came out before?'

Beverly nodded. 'Eddie got us back to the Barrens. Only we ended up on the other side of the Kenduskeag somehow. The Old Cape side.'

'You and Haystack pushed the lid off one of those pumping-stations,' Richie said to Bill, 'because you had the most weight.'

'Yeah,' Ben said. 'We did. The sun was out, but it was almost down.'

'Yeah,' Bill said. 'And we were all there.'

'But nothing lasts forever,' Richie said. He looked back down the hill they had just climbed and sighed. 'Look at this, for instance.'

He held his hands out. The tiny scars in the palms were gone. Beverly put her hands out; Ben did the same; Bill added his. All were dirty but unmarked.

'Nothing lasts forever,' Richie repeated. He looked up at Bill, and Bill saw tears cut slowly through the dirt on Richie's cheeks.

'Except maybe for love,' Ben said.

'And desire,' Beverly said.

'How about friends?' Bill asked, and smiled. 'What do you think, Trashmouth?'

'Well,' Richie said, smiling and rubbing his eyes, 'Ah got to thank about it, boy; Ah say, Ah say Ah got to *thank* about it.'

Bill put his hands out and they joined theirs with his and stood there for a moment, seven who had been reduced to four but who could still make a circle. They looked at each other. Ben was crying now too, the tears spilling from his eyes. But he was smiling.

'I love you guys so much,' he said. He squeezed Bev's and Richie's hands tight-tight-tight for a moment, and then dropped them. 'Now could we see if they've got such a thing as breakfast in this place? And we ought to call Mike. Tell him we're okay.'

'Good thinnin, senhorr,' Richie said. 'Every now an then I theenk you might turn out okay. Watchoo theenk, Beeg Beel?'

'I theenk you ought to go fuck yourself,' Bill said.

They walked into the Town House on a wave of laughter, and as Bill pushed through the glass door, Beverly caught sight of something which she never spoke of but never forgot. For just a moment she saw their reflections in the glass – only there were six, not four, because Eddie was behind Richie and Stan was behind Bill, that little half-smile on his face.

9

Out/Dusk, August 10th, 1958

The sun sits neatly on the horizon, a slightly oblate red ball that throws a flat feverish light over the Barrens. The iron cover on top of one of the pumping-stations rises a little, settles, rises again, and begins to slide.

'P-P-Push it, Buh-Ben, it's bruh-breaking my shoulder —'

The cover slides farther, tilts, and falls into the shrubbery that has grown up around the concrete cylinder. Seven children come out one by one and look around, blinking owlishly in silent wonder. They are like children who have never seen daylight before.

'It's so quiet,' Beverly says softly.

The only sounds are the loud rush of water and the somnolent hum of insects. The storm is over but the Kenduskeag is still very high. Closer to town, not far from the place where the river is corseted in concrete and called a canal, it has overflowed its banks, although the flooding is by no means serious — a few wet cellars is the worst of it. This time.

Stan moves away from them, his face blank and thoughtful. Bill looks around and at first he thinks Stan has seen a small fire on the riverbank — fire is his first impression: a red glow almost too bright to look at. But when Stan picks the fire up in his right hand the angle of the light changes, and Bill sees it's nothing but a Coke bottle, one of the new clear ones, which someone has dropped by the river. He watches as Stan reverses it, holds it by the neck, and brings it down on a shelf of rock jutting out of the bank. The bottle breaks, and Bill is aware they are all watching Stan now as he pokes through the shattered remains of the bottle, his face sober and studious and absorbed. At last he picks up a narrow wedge of glass. The westering sun throws red glints from it, and Bill thinks again: Like a fire.

Stan looks up at him and Bill suddenly understands: it is perfectly clear to him, and perfectly right. He steps forward toward Stan with his hands held out, palms up. Stan backs away, into the water. Small black bugs stitch along just above the surface, and Bill can see an iridescent dragonfly go buzzing off into the reeds along the far bank like a small flying rainbow. A frog begins a steady bass thud, and as Stan takes his left hand and draws the edge of glass down his palm, peeling skin and bringing thin blood, Bill thinks in a kind of ecstasy: There's so much life down here!

'Bill?'

'Sure. Both.'

Stan cuts his other hand. There is pain, but not much. A whippoorwill has begun to call somewhere, a cool sound, peaceful. Bill thinks: That whippoorwill is raising the moon.

He looks at his hands, both of them bleeding now, and then around him. The others are there — Eddie with his aspirator clutched tightly in one hand; Ben with his big belly pushing palely out through the tattered remains of his shirt; Richie, his face oddly naked without his glasses; Mike, silent and solemn, his normally full lips compressed to a thin line. And Beverly, her head up, her eyes wide and clear, her hair still somehow lovely in spite of the dirt that mats it.

All of us. All of us are here.

And he sees them, really sees them, for the last time, because in some way he understands that they will never all be together again, the seven of them − not this way. No one talks. Beverly holds out her hands, and after a moment Richie and Ben hold out theirs. Mike and Eddie do the same. Stan cuts them one by one as the sun begins to slip behind the horizon, cooling that red furnace-glow to a dusky rose-pink. The whippoorwill cries again, Bill can see the first faint swirls of mist on the water, and he feels as if he has become a part of everything − this is a brief ecstasy which he will no more talk about than Beverly will later talk about the brief reflection she sees of two dead men who were, as boys, her friends.

A breeze touches the trees and bushes, making them sigh, and he thinks: This is a lovely place, and I'll never forget it. It's lovely, and *they* are lovely; each one of them is gorgeous. *The whippoorwill cries again, sweet and liquid, and for a moment Bill feels at one with it, as if he could sing and then be gone into the dusk − as if he could fly away, brave in the air.*

He looks at Beverly and she is smiling at him. She closes her eyes and holds her hands out to either side. Bill takes her left; Ben her right. Bill can feel the warmth of her blood mixing with his own. The others join in and they stand in a circle, all of their hands now sealed in that peculiarly intimate way.

Stan is looking at Bill with a kind of urgency; a kind of fear.

'Swuh-Swear to muh-me that you'll c-c-come buh-back,' Bill says. 'Swear to me that if Ih-Ih-It isn't d-d-dead, you'll cuh-home back.'

'Swear,' Ben said.

'Swear.' Richie.

'Yes − I swear.' Bev.

'Swear it,' Mike Hanlon mutters.

'Yeah. Swear.' Eddie, his voice a thin and reedy whisper.

'I swear too,' Stan whispers, but his voice falters and he looks down as he speaks.

'I-I swuh-swuh-swear.'

That was it; that was all. But they stand there for awhile longer, feeling the power that is in their circle, the closed body that they make. The light paints their faces in pale fading colors; the sun is now gone and sunset is dying. They stand together in a circle as the darkness creeps down into the Barrens, filling up the paths they have walked this summer, the clearings where they have played tag and guns, the secret places along the river banks where they have sat and discussed childhood's long questions or smoked Beverly's cigarettes or where they have merely been silent, watching the passage of the clouds reflected in the water. The eye of the day is closing.

At last Ben drops his hands. He starts to say something, shakes his head, and walks away. Richie follows him, then Beverly and Mike, walking together. No one talks; they climb the embankment to Kansas Street and simply take leave of one another. And when Bill thinks it over twenty-seven years later, he realizes that they really never did all get together again. Four of them quite often, sometimes five, and maybe six once or twice. But never all seven.

He's the last to go. He stands for a long time with his hands on the rickety white fence, looking down into the Barrens as, overhead, the first stars seed the summer sky. He stands under the blue and over the black and watches the Barrens fill up with darkness.

I never want to play down there again, *he thinks suddenly and is amazed to find the thought is not terrible or distressing but tremendously liberating.*

He stands there a moment longer and then turns away from the Barrens and starts home, walking along the dark sidewalk with his hands in his pockets, glancing from time to time at the houses of Derry, warmly lit against the night.

After a block or two he begins to walk faster, thinking of supper . . . and a block or two after that, he begins to whistle.

DERRY:

THE LAST INTERLUDE

'"The ocean, in these times, is a perfect fleet of ships, and we can hardly fail to encounter many, in running over. It is merely crossing," said Mr Micawber, trifling with his eyeglass, "merely crossing. The distance is quite imaginary."'
—Charles Dickens,
David Copperfield

Bill came in about twenty minutes ago and brought me this book – Carole found it on one of the tables in the library and gave it to him when he asked for it. I thought Chief Rademacher might have taken it, but apparently he didn't want anything to do with it.

Bill's stutter is disappearing again, but the poor man has aged four years in the last four days. He told me he expects Audra to be discharged from Derry Home Hospital (where I myself yet tarry) tomorrow, only to take a private ambulance north to the Bangor Mental Health Institute. Physically she's fine – minor cuts and bruises that are already healing. Mentally . . .

'You raise her hand and it stays up,' Bill said. He was sitting by the window, twiddling a can of diet soda between his hands. 'It just floats there until someone puts it down again. Her reflexes are there, but very slow. The EEG they did shows a severely repressed alpha wave. She's c-c-catatonic, Mike.'

I said, 'I've got an idea. Maybe not such a good one. If you don't like it, just say so.'

'What?'

'I'm going to be in here another week,' I said. 'Instead of sending Audra up to Bangor, why don't you take her to my place, Bill? Spend the week with her. Talk to her, even if she doesn't talk back. Is she . . . is she continent?'

'No,' Bill said bleakly.

'Can you – I mean, would you –'

'Would I change her?' He smiled, and it was such a painful smile that I had to look away for a moment. It was the way my father smiled the time he told me about Butch Bowers and the chickens. 'Yes. I think I could do that much.'

'I won't tell you to take it easy on yourself when you're obviously not prepared to do that,' I said, 'but please remember that you yourself agreed that much or all of what's happened was almost certainly ordained. That may include Audra's part in this.'

'I sh-should have kept my mouth shut about where I was g-going.'

Sometimes it's better to say nothing – so that's what I did.

'All right,' he said at last. 'If you really mean it –'

'I mean it. They've got my housekeys down at the Patient Services Desk. There's a couple of Delmonico steaks in the freezer. Maybe that was ordained, too.'

'She's eating mostly soft foods and, uh, luh-liquids.'

'Well,' I said, holding onto my smile, 'maybe there'll be cause for a celebration. There's a pretty good bottle of wine on the top shelf in the pantry, too. Mondavi. Domestic, but good.'

He came over and gripped my hand. 'Thank you, Mike.'

'Any time, Big Bill.'

He let go of my hand. 'Richie flew back to California this morning.'

I nodded. 'Think you'll stay in touch?'

'M-Maybe,' he said. 'For awhile, anyway. But . . .' He looked at me levelly. 'It's going to happen again, I think.'

'The forgetting?'

'Yes. In fact, I think it's already started. Just little things so far. Details. But I think it's going to spread.'

'Maybe that's best.'

'Maybe.' He looked out the window, still twiddling his can of diet soda, almost surely thinking about his wife, so wide-eyed and silent and beautiful and plastic. *Catatonic.* The sound of a door slamming shut and locked. He sighed. 'Maybe it is.'

'Ben? Beverly?'

He looked back at me and smiled a little. 'Ben's invited her to come back to Nebraska with him, and she's agreed to go, at least for awhile. You know about her friend in Chicago?'

I nodded. Beverly told Ben and Ben told me yesterday. If I may understate the case (*grotesquely* understate the case), Beverly's later description of her wonderful fantastic husband, Tom, was much truer than her original one. Wonderful fantastic Tom kept Bev in emotional, spiritual, and sometimes physical bondage for the last four years or so. Wonderful fantastic Tom got here by beating the information out of Bev's only close woman friend.

'She told me she's going to fly back to Chicago the week after next and file a missing-persons report on him. Tom, I mean.'

'Smart enough,' I said. 'No one's ever going to find him down *there.*' *Or Eddie either*, I thought but did not say.

'No, I suppose not,' Bill said. 'And when she goes back, I'm betting Ben will go with her. And you know something else? Something really crazy?'

'What?'

'I don't think she really remembers *what* happened to Tom.'

I just stared at him.

'She's forgotten or forgetting,' Bill said. 'And I can't remember what the *doorway* looked like anymore. The d-doorway into Its place. I try to think of it and the craziest thing happens – I get this ih-image of g-g-goats walking over a bridge. From that story "The Three Billy Goats Gruff." Crazy, huh?'

'They'll trace Tom Rogan to Derry eventually,' I said. 'He'll have left a paper trail a mile wide. Rent-a-car, plane tickets.'

'I'm not so sure of that,' Bill said, lighting a cigarette. 'I think he might have paid cash for his plane ticket and given a phony name. Maybe bought a cheap car here or stole one.'

'Why?'

'Oh, come on,' Bill said. 'Do you think he came all this way to give her a spanking?'

Our eyes met for a long moment and then he stood up. 'Listen, Mike . . .'

'Too hip, gotta split,' I said. 'I can dig it.'

He laughed at that, laughed hard, and when he had sobered he said: 'Thanks for the use of your place, Mikey.'

'I'm not going to swear to you it'll make any difference. It has no therapeutic qualities that I'm aware of.'

'Well . . . I'll see you.' He did an odd thing then, odd but rather lovely. He kissed my cheek. 'God bless, Mike. I'll be around.'

'Things may be okay, Bill,' I said. 'Don't give up hope. They may be okay.'

He smiled and nodded, but I think the same word was in both of our minds: *Catatonic.*

June 5th, 1985

Ben and Beverly came in today to say goodbye. They're not flying – Ben's rented a great big Cadillac from the Hertz people and they're going to drive, not hurrying. There's something in their eyes when they look at each other, and I'd bet my pension-plan that if they're not making it now, they will be by the time they get to Nebraska.

Beverly hugged me, told me to get well quickly, and then cried.

Ben also hugged me, and asked for the third or fourth time if I would write. I told him I would indeed write, and so I will . . . for awhile, at least. Because this time it's happening to me, as well.

I'm forgetting things.

As Bill said, right now it's only small things, details. But it feels like the sort of thing that's going to spread. It could be that in a month or a year, this notebook will be all I'll have to remind me of what happened here in Derry. I suppose the words themselves might begin to fade, eventually leaving this book as blank as when I first picked it up in the school-supplies department at Freese's. That's an awful thought and in the daytime it seems wildly paranoid . . . but, do you know, in the watches of the night it seems perfectly logical.

This forgetting . . . the prospect fills me with panic, but it also offers a sneaking sort of relief. It suggests to me more than anything else that this time they really *did* kill It; that there is no need of a watchman to stand and wait for the cycle to begin again.

Dull panic, sneaking relief. It's the relief I'll embrace, I think, sneaking or not.

Bill called to say he and Audra had moved in. There is no change in her.

'I'll always remember you.' That's what Beverly told me just before she and Ben left.

I think I saw a different truth in her eyes.

June 6th, 1985

Interesting piece in the Derry *News* today, on page one. The story was headed: STORM CAUSES HENLEY TO GIVE UP AUDITORIUM EXPANSION PLANS. The Henley in question is Tim Henley, a multi-millionaire developer who came into Derry like a whirlwind in the late sixties – it was Henley and Zitner who organized the consortium responsible for building the Derry Mall (which, according to another piece on page one, is probably going to be declared a total loss). Tim Henley was determined to see Derry grow. There was a profit-motive, yes indeed, but there was more to it than that: Henley genuinely wanted to see it happen. His sudden abandonment of the auditorium expansion suggests several things to me. That Henley may have soured on Derry is only the most obvious. I think it's also possible that he's in the process of losing his shirt because of the destruction of the mall.

But the article also suggests that Henley is not alone; that other investors and potential investors in Derry's future may be rethinking their options. Of course, Al Zitner won't have to bother; God retired him when downtown collapsed. Of the others, those who thought like Henley are now facing a rather difficult problem – how do you rebuild an urban area which is now at least fifty percent underwater?

I think that, after a long and ghoulishly vital existence, Derry may be dying . . . like a nightshade whose time to bloom has come and gone.

Called Bill Denbrough late this afternoon. No change in Audra.

An hour ago I put through another call, this one to Richie Tozier in California. His answering machine fielded the call, with Creedence Clearwater Revival music playing in the background. Those machines always fuck up my timing somehow. I left my name and number, hesitated, and added that I hoped he was able to wear his contact lenses again. I was about to hang up when Richie himself picked up the phone and said, 'Mikey! How you be?' His voice was pleased and warm . . . but there was an obvious bewilderment there as well. He was wearing the verbal expression of a man who has been caught utterly flat-footed.

'Hello, Richie,' I said. 'I'm doing pretty well.'

'Good. How much pain you having?'

'Some. It's going away. The itch is worse. I'll be damn glad when they finally decide to unstrap my ribs. By the way, I liked the Creedence.'

Richie laughed. 'Shit, that ain't Creedence, that's "Rock and Roll Girls," from Fogarty's new album. *Centerfield*, it's called. You haven't heard any of it?'

'Huh-uh.'

'You got to get it, it's great. It's just like . . .' He trailed off for a moment and then said, 'It's just like the old days.'

'I'll pick it up,' I said, and I probably will. I always liked John Fogarty. 'Green River' was my all-time Creedence favorite, I guess. Get back home, he says. Just before the fade he says it.

'What about Bill?'

'He and Audra are keeping house for me while I'm in here.'

'Good. That's good.' He paused for a moment. 'You want to hear something fucking bizarre, ole Mikey?'

'Sure,' I said. I had a pretty good idea what he was going to say.

'Well . . . I was sitting here in my study, listening to some of the new *Cashbox* hot prospects, going over some ad copy, reading memos . . . there's about two mountains of stuff backed up, and I'm looking at roughly a month of twenty-five-hour days. So I had the answering machine turned on, but with the volume turned up so I could intercept the calls I wanted and just let the dimwits talk to the tape. And the reason I let you talk to the tape as long as I did –'

'– was because at first you didn't have the slightest idea who I was.'

'Jesus, that's right! How did you know that?'

'Because we're forgetting again. All of us this time.'

'Mikey, are you *sure*?'

'What was Stan's last name?' I asked him.

There was silence on the other end of the line – a long silence. In it, faintly, I could hear a woman talking in Omaha . . . or maybe she was in Ruthven, Arizona, or Flint, Michigan. I heard her, as faint as a space-traveller leaving the solar system in the nosecone of a burned-out rocket, thank someone for the cookies.

Then Richie said, uncertainly: 'I think it was Underwood, but that isn't Jewish, it it?'

'It was Uris.'

'Uris!' Richie cried, sounding both relieved and shaken. 'Jesus, I *hate* it when I get something right on the tip of my tongue and can't quite pick it off. Someone brings out a Trivial Pursuit game, I say "Excuse me but I think the diarrhea's coming back so maybe I'll just go home, okay?" But you remember, anyhow, Mikey. Like before.'

'No. I looked it up in my address book.'

Another long silence. Then: 'You didn't remember?'

'Nope.'

'No shit?'

'No shit.'

'Then this time it's really over,' he said, and the relief in his voice was unmistakable.

'Yes, I think so.'

That long-distance silence fell again – all the miles between Maine and California. I believe we were both thinking the same thing: it was over, yes, and in six weeks or six months, we will have forgotten all about each other. It's over, and all it's cost us is our friendship and Stan and Eddie's lives. I've almost forgotten them, you know it? Horrible as it may sound, I have almost forgotten Stan and Eddie. Was it asthma

Eddie had, or chronic migraine? I'll be damned if I can remember for sure, although I think it was migraine. I'll ask Bill. He'll know.

'Well, you say hi to Bill and that pretty wife of his,' Richie said with a cheeriness that sounded canned.

'I will, Richie,' I said, closing my eyes and rubbing my forehead. He remembered Bill's wife was in Derry . . . but not her name, or what had happened to her.

'And if you're ever in LA, you got the number. We'll get together and mouth some chow.'

'Sure.' I felt hot tears behind my eyes. 'And if you get back this way, the same thing goes.'

'Mikey?'

'Right here.'

'I love you, man.'

'Same here.'

'Okay. Keep your thumb on it.'

'Beep-beep, Richie.'

He laughed. 'Yeah, yeah, yeah. Stick it in your ear, Mike. Ah say, in yo *ear*, boy.'

He hung up and so did I. Then I lay back on my pillows with my eyes shut and didn't open them for a long time.

June 7th, 1985

Police Chief Andrew Rademacher, who took over from Chief Borton in the late sixties, is dead. It was a bizarre accident, one I can't help associating with what has been happening in Derry . . . what has just ended in Derry.

The combination police-station–courthouse stands on the edge of the area that fell into the Canal, and while it didn't go, the upheaval – or the flood – must have caused structural damage of which no one was aware.

Rademacher was working late in his office last night, the story in the paper says, as he has every night since the storm and the flood. The Police Chief's office has moved from the third to the fifth floor since the old days, to just below an attic where all sorts of records and useless city artifacts are stored. One of those artifacts was the tramp-chair I have described earlier in these pages. It was made of iron and weighed better than four hundred pounds. The building shipped a quantity of water during the downpour of May 31st, and that must have weakened the attic floor (or so the paper says). Whatever the

1053

reason, the tramp-chair fell from the attic directly onto Chief Rademacher as he sat at his desk, reading accident reports. He was killed instantly. Officer Bruce Andeen rushed in and found him lying on the ruins of his shattered desk, his pen still in one hand.

Talked to Bill on the phone again. Audra is taking some solid food, he says, but otherwise there is no change. I asked him if Eddie's big problem had been asthma or migraine.

'Asthma,' he said promptly. 'Don't you remember his aspirator?'

'Sure,' I said, and did. But only when Bill mentioned it.

'Mike?'

'Yeah?'

'What was his last name?'

I looked at my address book lying on the nighttable, but didn't pick it up. 'I don't quite remember.'

'It was like Kerkorian,' Bill said, sounding distressed, 'but that wasn't quite it. You've got everything written down, though. Right?'

'Right,' I said.

'Thank God for that.'

'Have you had any ideas about Audra?'

'One,' he said, 'but it's so crazy I don't want to talk about it.'

'You sure?'

'Yeah.'

'All right.'

'Mike, it's scary, isn't it? Forgetting like this?'

'Yes,' I said. And it is.

June 8th, 1985

Raytheon, which had been scheduled to break ground on its Derry plant in July, has decided at the last minute to build in Waterville instead. The editorial on page one of the *News* expresses dismay ... and, if I read correctly between the lines, a little fright.

I think I know what Bill's idea is. He'll have to act quickly, before the last of the magic departs this place. If it hasn't already.

I guess what I thought before wasn't so paranoid after all. The names and addresses of the others in my little book are fading. The color and quality of the ink combine to make those entries look as if they were written fifty or seventy-five years before the others I've jotted in there. This has happened in the last four or five days. I'm convinced that by September their names will be utterly gone.

I suppose I could preserve them; I could just keep copying them.

But I'm also convinced that each would fade in its turn, and that very soon it would become an exercise in futility – like writing *I will not throw spit-balls in class* five hundred times. I would be writing names that meant nothing for a reason I didn't remember.

Let it go, let it go.

Bill, act quickly . . . but be careful!

June 9th, 1985

Woke up in the middle of the night from a terrible nightmare I couldn't remember, got panicky, couldn't breathe. Reached for the call-button and then couldn't use it. Had a terrible vision of Mark Lamonica answering the bell with a hypo . . . or Henry Bowers with his switch-blade.

I grabbed my address book and called Ben Hanscom in Nebraska . . . the address and number have faded still more, but they are still legible. No go, Joe. Got a recorded phone-company voice telling me service to that number has been cancelled.

Was Ben fat, or did he have something like a club foot?

Lay awake until dawn.

June 10th, 1985

They tell me I can go home tomorrow.

I called Bill and told him that – I suppose I wanted to warn him that his time is getting shorter all the time. Bill is the only one I remember clearly and I'm convinced that I'm the only one *he* remembers clearly. Because we are both still here in Derry, I suppose.

'All right,' he said. 'By tomorrow we'll be out of your hair.'

'You still got your idea?'

'Yeah. Looks like it's time to try it.'

'Be careful.'

He laughed and said something I both do and don't understand: 'You can't be c-c-careful on a skuh-hateboard, man.'

'How will I know how it turned out, Bill?'

'You'll know,' he said, and hung up.

My heart's with you, Bill, no matter how it turns out. My heart is with all of them, and I think that, even if we forget each other, we'll remember in our dreams.

I'm almost done with this diary now – and I suppose a diary is all that it will ever be, and that the story of Derry's old scandals and eccentricities has no place outside these pages. That's fine with me; I think that, when they let me out of here tomorrow, it might finally be time to start thinking about some sort of new life . . . although just what that might be is unclear to me.

I loved you guys, you know.

I loved you so much.

EPILOGUE
BILL DENBROUGH BEATS THE DEVIL – II

1

'I knew the bride when she used to do the Pony,
I knew the bride when she used to do the Stroll.
I knew the bride when she used to wanna party,
I knew the bride when she used to rock and roll.'

– Nick Lowe

'You can't be careful on a skateboard, man'

– some kid

1

Noon of a summer day.

Bill stood naked in Mike Hanlon's bedroom, looking at his lean body in the mirror on the door. His bald head gleamed in the light which fell through the window and cast his shadow along the floor and up the wall. His chest was hairless, his thighs and shanks skinny but overlaid with ropes of muscle. *Still*, he thought, *it's an adult's body we got here, no question about that. There's the pot belly that comes with a few too many good steaks, a few too many bottles of Kirin beer, a few too many poolside lunches where you had the Reuben or the French dip instead of the diet plate. Your seat's dropped, too, Bill old buddy. You can still serve an ace if you're not too hung over and if your eye's in, but you can't hustle after the old Dunlop the way you could when you were seventeen. You got lovehandles and your balls are starting to get that middle-aged dangly look. There's lines on your face that weren't there when you were seventeen . . . Hell, they weren't there on your first author photo, the one where you tried so hard to look as if you knew something . . . anything. You're too old for what you've got in mind, Billy-boy. You'll kill both of you.*

He put on his underpants.

If we'd believed that, we never could have . . . have done whatever it was we did.

Because he didn't really remember what it was they had done, or what had happened to turn Audra into a catatonic wreck. He only knew what he was supposed to do now, and he knew that if he didn't do it *now*, he would forget that, too. Audra was sitting downstairs in Mike's easy chair, her hair hanging lankly to her shoulders, staring with rapt attention at the TV, which was currently showing *Dialing for Dollars*. She didn't speak and would only move if you led her.

This is different. You're just too old, man. Believe it.

I won't.

Then die here in Derry. Big fucking deal.

He put on athletic socks, the one pair of jeans he had brought, the tank top he'd bought at the Shirt Shack in Bangor the day before. The tank was bright orange. Across the front it said WHERE THE HELL IS DERRY, MAINE? He sat down on Mike's bed – the one he had shared for the last week of nights with his warm but corpse-like wife – and put on his sneakers . . . a pair of Keds, which he had also bought yesterday in Bangor.

He stood up and looked at himself in the mirror again. He saw a man pressing middle age dressed up in a kid's clothes.

You look ludicrous.

What kid doesn't?

You're no kid. Give this up!

'Fuck, let's rock and roll a little,' Bill said softly, and left the room.

2

In the dreams he will have in later years, he is always leaving Derry alone, at sunset. The town is deserted; everyone has left. The Theological Seminary and the Victorian houses on West Broadway brood black against a lurid sky, every summer sunset you ever saw rolled up into one.

He can hear his footfalls echoing back as they rap along the concrete. The only other sound is water rushing hollowly through the stormdrains

3

He rolled Silver out into the driveway, put him on the kickstand, and checked the tires again. The front one was okay but the back one felt a little mushy. He got the bike pump that Mike had bought and firmed it up. When he put the pump back, he checked the playing cards and the clothespins. The bike's wheels still made those exciting machine-gun sounds Bill remembered from his boyhood. Good deal.

You've gone crazy.

Maybe. We'll see.

He went back into Mike's garage again, got the 3-in-1, and oiled the chain and sprocket. Then he stood up, looked at Silver, and gave the bulb of the oogah-horn a light, experimental squeeze. It sounded good. He nodded and went into the house.

4

and he sees all those places again, intact, as they were then: the hulking brick fort of Derry Elementary, the Kissing Bridge with its complex intaglio of initials, high-school sweethearts ready to crack the world open with their passion who had grown up to become insurance agents and car salesmen and waitresses and beauticians; he sees the statue of Paul Bunyan against that bleeding sunset sky and the leaning white fence which ran along the Kansas Street sidewalk at the edge of the Barrens. He sees them as they were, as they always will be in some part of his mind . . . and his heart breaks with love and horror.

Leaving, leaving Derry, *he thinks.* We are leaving Derry, and if this was a story it would be the last half-dozen pages or so; get ready to put this one up on the shelf and forget it. The sun's going down and there's no sound but my footfalls and the water in the drains. This is the time of

5

Dialing for Dollars had given way to *Wheel of Fortune.* Audra sat passively in front of it, her eyes never leaving the set. Her demeanor did not change when Bill snapped the TV off.

'Audra,' he said, going to her and taking her hand. 'Come on.'

She didn't move. Her hand lay in his, warm wax. Bill took her other hand from the arm of Mike's chair and pulled her to her feet. He had dressed her that morning much as he had dressed himself – she was wearing Levis and a blue shell top. She would have looked quite lovely if not for her wide-eyed vacant stare.

'Cuh-come on,' he said again, and led her through the door, into Mike's kitchen and, eventually, outside. She came willingly enough . . . although she would have plunged off the back porch stoop and gone sprawling in the dirt if Bill had not put an arm around her waist and guided her down the steps.

He led her over to where Silver stood heeled over on his kick-stand in the bright summer noonlight. Audra stood beside the bike, looking serenely at the side of Mike's garage.

'Get on, Audra.'

She didn't move. Patiently, Bill worked at getting her to swing one of her long legs over the carrier mounted on Silver's back fender. At last she stood there with the package carrier between her legs, not quite touching her crotch. Bill pressed his hand lightly to the top of her head and Audra sat down.

He swung onto Silver's saddle and put up the kickstand with his heel. He prepared to reach behind him for Audra's hands and draw them around his middle, but before he could do it they crept around him of their own accord, like small dazed mice.

He looked down at them, his heart beating faster, seeming to pump in his throat as much as in his chest. It was the first independent action Audra had taken all week, so far as he knew . . . the first independent action she had taken since *It* happened . . . whatever *It* had been.

'Audra?'

There was no answer. He tried to crane his neck around and see her but couldn't quite make it. There were only her hands around his waist, the nails showing the last chips of a red polish that had been put on by a bright, lively, talented young woman in a small English town.

'We're going for a ride,' Bill said, and he began to roll Silver forward toward Palmer Lane, listening to the gravel crunch under the tires. 'I want you to hold on, Audra. I think . . . I think I may go sort of f-f-fast.'

If I don't lose my guts.

He thought of the kid he had met earlier during his stay in Derry, when *It* had still been happening. *You can't be careful on a skateboard*, the kid had said.

Truer words were never spoken, kid.

'Audra? You ready?'

No answer. Had her hands tightened the tiniest bit across his middle? Probably just wishful thinking.

He reached the end of the driveway and looked right. Palmer Lane ran straight to Upper Main Street, where a left turn would take him onto the hill running downtown. Downhill. Picking up speed. He felt a tremor of fear at the image, and a disquieting thought

(*old bones break easy, Billy-boy*)

ran through his mind almost too quickly to read and was gone. But . . .

But it wasn't all disquiet, was it? No. It was desire as well . . . the feeling he'd had when he saw the kid walking along with the skateboard under his arm. The desire to go fast, to feel the wind race past you without knowing if you were racing toward or running away from, to just go. To fly.

Disquiet and desire. All the difference between world and want – the difference between being an adult who counted the cost and a child who just got on it and went, for instance. All the world between. Yet not that much difference at all. Bedfellows, really. The way you felt when the roller-coaster car approached the top of the first steep grade, where the ride *really* begins.

Disquiet and desire. What you want and what you're scared to try for. Where you've been and where you want to go. Something in a rock-and-roll song about wanting the girl, the car, the place to stand and be. Oh please God can you dig it.

Bill closed his eyes for a moment, feeling the soft dead weight of his wife behind him, feeling the hill somewhere ahead of him, feeling his own heart inside him.

Be brave, be true, stand.

He began to push Silver forward again. 'You want to rock and roll a little, Audra?'

No answer. But that was all right. He was ready.

'Hold on, then.'

He began to pedal. It was hard going at first. Silver wobbled alarmingly back and forth, Audra's weight adding to the imbalance . . . yet she *must* be doing some balancing, even unconsciously, or they would have crashed right away. Bill stood on the pedals, hands squeezing the handlegrips with maniacal tightness, his head turned skyward, his eyes slits, the cords on his neck standing out.

Gonna fall splat right here in the street, split her skull and mine —
(*no you ain't go for it Bill go for it go for the son of a bitch*)

He stood on the pedals, revolving them, feeling every cigarette he'd smoked over the last twenty years in his elevated blood-pressure and the race of his heart. *Fuck that, too!* he thought, and the rush of crazy exhilaration made him grin.

The playing cards, which had been firing isolated shots, now began to click-clock faster. They were new, nice new Bikes, and they made a good loud sound. Bill felt the first touch of breeze on his bald pate, and his grin widened. I *made that breeze*, he thought. *I made it by pumping these damn pedals.*

The STOP sign at the end of the lane was coming up. Bill began to brake . . . and then (his grin still widening, showing more and more of his teeth) he began to pump again.

Ignoring the STOP sign, Bill Denbrough swept to the left, onto Upper Main Street above Bassey Park. Again Audra's weight fooled him and they almost overbalanced and crashed. The bike wavered, wobbled, then righted itself. That breeze was stronger now, cooling the sweat on his forehead, evaporating it, rushing past his ears with a low intoxicating sound that was a little like the sound of the ocean in a conch shell but was really like nothing else on earth. Bill supposed it was a sound the kid with the skateboard was familiar with. *But it's a sound you'll fall out of touch with, kid*, he thought. *Things have a way of changing. It's a dirty trick, so be prepared for it.*

Pedaling faster now, finding a surer balance in speed. The ruins of Paul Bunyan on the left, like a fallen colossus. Bill shouted: '*Hi-yo Silver, AWAYYYYY!*'

Audra's hands tightened around his middle; he felt her stir against his back. But there was no urge to turn and try to see her now . . . no urge, no need. He pedaled faster, laughing out loud, a tall skinny bald man on a bike crouched over the handlebars to lessen the wind-resistance. People turned to look as he raced alongside Bassey Park.

Now Upper Main Street began to incline toward the caved-in center of town at a steeper angle, and a voice inside whispered to him that if he didn't brake soon he would find himself unable; he would simply go sweeping into the sunken remains of the three-way intersection like a bat out of hell and kill both of them.

Instead of braking he began to pedal again, urging the bike to go even faster. Now he was flying down Main Street Hill and he could see the white-and-orange crash barriers, the smudgepots with their smoky Halloween flames marking the edge of the cave-in, he could see the tops of buildings which jutted out of the streets like the figments of a madman's imagination.

'*Hi-yo Silver, AWAYYYYYYY!*' Bill Denbrough cried deliriously, and rushed down the hill toward whatever there would be, aware for one last time of Derry as his place, aware most of all that *he was alive under a real sky*, and that all was desire, desire, desire.

He raced down the hill on Silver: he raced to beat the devil.

6

leaving.

So you leave, and there is an urge to look back, to look back just once as the sunset fades, to see that severe New England skyline one final time – the spires, the Standpipe, Paul with his axe slung over his shoulder. But it is perhaps not such a good idea to look back – all the stories say so. Look what happened to Lot's wife. Best not to look back. Best to believe there will be happily ever afters all the way around – and so there may be; who is to say there will not be such endings? Not all boats which sail away into darkness never find the sun again, or the hand of another child; if life teaches anything at all, it teaches that there are so many happy endings that the man who believes there is no God needs his rationality called into serious question.

You leave and you leave quick when the sun starts to go down, he thinks in this dream. That's what you do. And if you spare a last thought, maybe it's ghosts you wonder about . . . the ghosts of children standing in the water at sunset, standing in a circle, standing with their hands joined together, their faces young, sure, but tough . . . tough enough, anyway, to give birth to the people they will become, tough enough to understand, maybe, that the people they will become must necessarily birth the people they were before they can get on with trying to understand simple mortality. The circle closes, the wheel rolls, and that's all there is.

You don't have to look back to see those children; part of your mind will see them forever, live with them forever, love with them forever. They are not necessarily the best part of you, but they were once the repository of all you could become.

Children I love you. I love you so much.

So drive away quick, drive away while the last of the light slips away, drive away from Derry, from memory . . . but not from desire. That stays, the bright cameo of all we were and all we believed as children, all that shone in our eyes even when we were lost and the wind blew in the night.

Drive away and try to keep smiling. Get a little rock and roll on the radio and go toward all the life there is with all the courage you can find and all the belief you can muster. Be true, be brave, stand.

All the rest is darkness.

7

'Hey!'

'Hey mister, you –'

'– look out!'

'Damn fool's gonna –'

Words whipped by in the slipstream, as meaningless as pennants in a breeze or untethered balloons. Here came the crash barriers; he could smell the sooty aroma of kerosene from the smudgepots. He saw the yawning darkness where the street had been, heard sullen water rushing down there in the tangled darkness, and laughed at the sound.

He dragged Silver hard left, so close to the crash barriers now that the leg of his jeans actually whispered along one of them. Silver's wheels were less than three inches from the place where the tar ended in empty space, and he was running out of maneuvering room. Up ahead the water had eroded all of the street and half the sidewalk in front of Cash's Jewelry Store. Barriers closed off what was left of the sidewalk; it had been severely undercut.

'Bill?' It was Audra's voice, dazed and a little thick. She sounded as if she had just awakened from a deep sleep. 'Bill, where are we? What are we *doing*?'

'*Hi yo, Silver!*' Bill shouted, pointing the rushing gantry that was Silver directly at the crash barrier jutting out at right angles to the empty Cash shop window. '*HI YO SILVER AWAYYYYY!*'

Silver struck the barrier at better than forty miles an hour and it went flying, the centerboard in one direction, the A-shaped supports in two others. Audra cried out and squeezed Bill so tightly that he lost his breath. Up and down Main Street, Canal Street, and Kansas Street, people stood in doorways and on sidewalks, watching.

Silver shot out onto the bridge of undercut sidewalk. Bill felt his left hip and knee chip the side of the jewelry store. He felt Silver's rear wheel sag suddenly and understood that the sidewalk was falling in behind them –

– and then Silver's forward motion carried them back onto solid roadway. Bill swerved to avoid an overturned trashcan and barrelled out into the street again. Brakes squealed. He saw the grille of a big truck approaching and still couldn't seem to stop laughing. He ran through the space the heavy truck wound up occupying a full second before it got there. Shit, time to spare!

Yelling, tears squirting from his eyes, Bill blew Silver's oogah-horn, listening to each hoarse bray embed itself in the day's bright light.

'Bill, you're going to kill us both!' Audra cried out, and although there was terror in her voice, she was also laughing.

Bill heeled Silver over, and this time he felt Audra leaning with him, making the bike easier to control, helping to make the two of them exist with it, at least for this small compact moment of time, as three living things.

'Do you think so?' he shouted back.

'I *know* so!' she cried, and then grabbed his crotch, where there was a huge and cheerful erection. 'But don't stop!'

He had nothing to say about it, however. Silver's speed was bleeding away on Up-Mile Hill, the heavy roar of the playing cards becoming single gunshots again. Bill stopped and turned to her. She was pale, wide-eyed, obviously scared and confused . . . but awake, aware, and *laughing*.

'Audra,' he said, laughing with her. He helped her off Silver, leaned the bike against a handy brick wall, and embraced her. He kissed her forehead, her eyes, her cheeks, her mouth, her neck, her breasts.

She hugged him while he did it.

'Bill, what's been happening? I remember getting off the plane at Bangor, and I can't remember a *thing* after that. Are you all right?'

'Yes.'

'Am I?'

'Yes. Now.'

She pushed him away so she could look at him. 'Bill, are you still stuttering?'

'No,' Bill said, and kissed her. 'My stutter is gone.'

'For good?'

'Yes,' he said. 'I think this time it's gone for good.'

'Did you say something about rock and roll?'

'I don't know. Did I?'

'I love you,' she said.

He nodded and smiled. When he smiled he looked very young, bald head or not. 'I love you too,' he said. 'And what else counts?'

8

He awakens from this dream unable to remember exactly what it was, or much at all beyond the simple fact that he has dreamed about being a child again. He touches his wife's smooth back as she sleeps her warm sleep and dreams her own dreams; he thinks that it is good to be a child, but it is also good to be grownup and able to consider the mystery of childhood . . . its beliefs and desires. I will write about all of this one day, he thinks, and knows it's just a dawn thought, an after-dreaming thought. But it's nice to think so for awhile in the morning's clean silence, to think that childhood has its own sweet secrets and confirms mortality, and that mortality defines all courage and love. To think that what has looked forward must also look back, and that each life makes its own imitation of immortality: a wheel.

Or so Bill Denbrough sometimes thinks on those early mornings after dreaming, when he almost remembers his childhood, and the friends with whom he shared it.

The book was begun in Bangor, Maine,
on September 9th, 1981,
and completed in Bangor, Maine,
on December 28th, 1985.

Coming from Hodder in Autumn 2019

STEPHEN KING
THE INSTITUTE

Deep in the woods of Maine, there is a dark state facility where kids, abducted from across the United States, are incarcerated. In the Institute they are subjected to a series of tests and procedures meant to combine their exceptional gifts – telepathy, telekinesis - for concentrated effect.

Luke Ellis is the latest recruit. He's just a regular twelve-year-old, except he's not just smart, he's super-smart. And he has another gift which the Institute wants to use...

Far away in a small town in South Carolina, former cop Tim Jamieson has taken a job working for the local sheriff. He's basically just walking the beat. But he's about to take on the biggest case of his career.

Back in the Institute's downtrodden playground and corridors where posters advertise 'just another day in paradise', Luke, his friend Kalisha and the other kids are in no doubt that they are prisoners, not guests. And there is no hope of escape.

But great events can turn on small hinges and Luke is about to team up with a new, even younger recruit, Avery Dixon, whose ability to read minds is off the scale. While the Institute may want to harness their powers for covert ends, the combined intelligence of Luke and Avery is beyond anything that even those who run the experiments – even the infamous Mrs Sigsby – suspect.

Thrilling, suspenseful, heartbreaking, THE INSTITUTE is a stunning novel of childhood betrayed and hope regained.

HODDER &
STOUGHTON

STEPHEN KING
DOCTOR SLEEP

Soon to be a major motion picture

Following a childhood haunted by the terrifying events at the Overlook Hotel, Danny Torrance has been drifting for decades.

Finally, he settles into a job where he draws on his remnant 'shining' power to help people pass on.

Then he meets Abra Stone, a young girl with the brightest 'shining' ever seen. But her gift is attracting a tribe of paranormals. They may look harmless, old and devoted to their Recreational Vehicles, but the True Knot live off the 'steam' that children like Abra produce.

Now Dan must confront his old demons as he battles for Abra's soul and survival…

'A powerful sequel to *The Shining*' – *Observer*

'Sheer page-turning suspense…addictive…a triumph from the world's finest horror novelist' – *Sunday Express*

HODDER

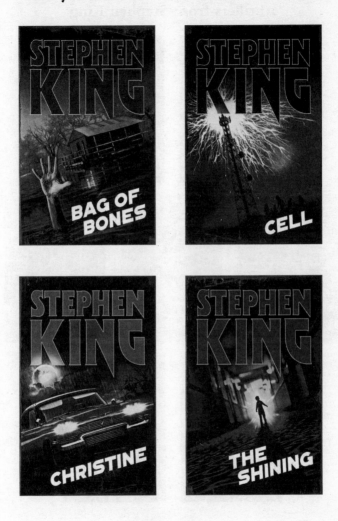

Don't miss the following epic thrillers from Stephen King